THE MAN IN THE MOSS

&

CRYBBE

Phil Rickman was born in Lancashire. He has won awards
for his TV and radio journalism, and his highly acclaimed
ealier novels *Candlelight*, *Crybbe*, *The Man in the Moss*,
December, *The Chalice*, and *The Wine of Angels* are also
available from Pan Books in paperback, as is *Midwinter of
the Spirit*, which charts Merrily Watkin's eventful debut as
diocesan exorcist. He is married and lives on the Welsh
Border.

Phil Rickman

THE MAN IN THE MOSS

&

CRYBBE

PAN BOOKS

The Man in the Moss first published 1994 by Macmillan.
First published in paperback 1994 by Pan Books.
Crybbe first published 1993 by Macmillan.
First published in paperback 1993 by Pan Books.

This omnibus first published 2005 by Pan Books
an imprint of Pan Macmillan Ltd
Pan Macmillan, 20 New Wharf Road, London N1 9RR
Basingstoke and Oxford
Associated companies throughout the world
www.panmacmillan.com

ISBN 0 330 44375 5

Copyright © Phil Rickman 1993, 1994

The right of Phil Rickman to be identified as the
author of this work has been asserted by him in accordance
with the Copyright, Designs and Patents Act 1988.

1 3 5 7 9 8 6 4 2

A CIP catalogue record for this book is available from
the British Library.

Printed and bound in Great Britain by
Mackays of Chatham plc, Chatham, Kent

THE MAN IN
THE MOSS

The author is indebted to the Dawber family and South Pennine Press for permission to reproduce sections of the text of *Dawber's Book of Bridelow*, a short guide to the village and its environs first published in 1896 and still updated every four or five years.

PROLOGUE

then . . .

I

A cold midwinter fogbank lay on the Moss.

It lay like a quilt on the black mattress of the peat, and nothing moved.

Not even the village schoolteacher standing on the promontory at the end of a ragged alley of graves where the churchyard seemed to overhang the bog's edge.

Damp January was clamped across the teacher's mouth and nose like a chloroform pad. He'd only been an hour out of bed, but the cold made him tired and the sight of the Moss only made him feel colder.

It was, as he'd explained to countless generations of pupils, the biggest surviving peatbog in the North of England, a gross product of violent death and centuries of decay . . . vast forests burned and torn down by the barbarian invaders . . . soaring greenery slashed and flattened and transformed by time into flat, black acres bounded by the hills and the moors.

The peat was dead. But, because of its acids, the peat had the power to preserve. Sometimes fragments of the ancient dead were found in there, from iron-hard limbs of trees to the arms and legs of corpses (which were taken away by the villagers and quietly buried).

Inside his long, deeply unfashionable overcoat, the teacher suddenly shivered.

Not at the thought of the corpses, but because he was waiting for the piper.

The piper on the Moss.

The sad, swollen drone, the bleak keening of a lost soul, had reached him on a sudden, spiked breeze during his habitual morning walk before school.

And he'd stopped, disquieted. The air had been still, weighted by the fog; no breeze at all except for this single, quick breath. As if it had been awoken only to carry the message that the piper was on the Moss.

This worried him, for the piping was never heard in winter.

3

As a rule, it came on summer evenings, when the Moss was firm and springy and the sound would be serene, rippling along the air currents, mingling with bird cries . . . plaintive enough to soften the clouds.

But the piper did not come in winter.

Seeking reassurance, the teacher turned around, looking for the soft blue eye of the Beacon over the village. But the fog had closed the eye; he could not even make out the outline of the Norman church tower.

And while his back was turned, it began. A distant, drifting miasma of music. Notes which sounded ragged at first but seemed to reassemble somehow in the air and harmonize eerily with the atmosphere.

Cold music, then, with a razor-edge of bitterness.

And more. An anger and a seeping menace . . . a violence, unsuppressed, which thrust and jabbed at the fog, made it swirl and squirm.

Trembling suddenly, the schoolteacher backed away from it; it was as if the fog and the frozen stillness of winter had combined to amplify the sound. And the sound made vibrant, pulsing images in his head.

It was as though the sky had been slashed and the rain bled from the clouds.

As though the cry had been physically torn from the ruptured breast of a bird in flight.

Or the morning itself had been ripped open, exposing the black entrails of another kind of night.

And then the piper himself came out of the fog with the black bladder like a throbbing tumour under one arm, and the sound exploded around him, a sound as dark as the peat under his plodding boots.

A black noise. The piper in a black mood.

'Why can't you keep away?' the teacher whispered. 'Why do you have to haunt us?'

He pulled his hat over his ears to muffle the piping and hurried away from it, back towards the church until the Beacon's ghostly disc emerged from the fog and he could see the vacant smile on the face of Our Sheila who fingered and flaunted her sex on the church porch.

He rushed past her and into the church, shutting the great oak door behind him, removing his hat and clamping it to his breast, staring up at the Winter Cross, all jagged branches, blunted thorns, holly and mistletoe.

He couldn't hear the pipes any more but felt he could *taste* the noise – that the oozing sound had entered his ears and been filtered down to the back of his throat where it came out tasting sourly of peat.

'Doesn't mean owt, does it?' he called out to the Winter Cross. 'We'll be all right, won't we? Nowt'll change?'

And nothing *would* change for more than fifteen winters of fog and damp. But fifteen years in the life of a Moss was barely a blink of the eye of God, and when the Moss revealed what it had preserved . . . *then* the changes would come, too many, too quickly and too horribly.

And the teacher, in retirement, feeling the kiss of the eternal night, would remember the first time the piper had appeared on the Moss in winter.

Meanwhile, later that week, the fog would lift and there would be snow.

then . . .

II

They were all around her at the stage door, like muggers in the night. She could smell the sweat and the beer . . . and a sour scent, like someone's rancid breath, squirting out of the darkness and straight to the back of her throat.

Coughing. Coughing at nothing. For as long as she could remember, hostility had occasionally come to her like this . . . like a single, piercing puff from a poisoned perfume spray.

But nothing there, really.

There were maybe twenty of them, but it was mostly OK,

wasn't it, mostly warm wishes and appreciation? Just never happened to her before. One of them had his jacket off, eyeing her. He was grinning and mumbling.

'Sign your *what*?' she said.

'Get used to it, lass.' Matt Castle grinning too. 'This is only the start of it. For you.'

Now the guy was rolling up a chequered shirt-sleeve in the sub-zero night, handing her this thick black felt-tip pen.

'Oh, your *arm*.' She tried to smile, printing her name all the way up the soft, hairless underside of his forearm.

M o i r a   C a i r n s.

Usually it would be just a handful of enthusiasts, harmless as train-spotters, chattering learnedly about the music and mainly to Matt. Dropping away as they headed for the car park. Shouting, See you again . . . stuff like that, mostly to Matt.

You should be loving this, hen, she told herself. Real fans. Can you believe that? You're a star.

Willie and Eric were loading the gear into Matt's old minibus, wanting to be away – more snow on the way, apparently. Two girls in leather jackets held open the back doors for the tea chest Willie kept his hand-drums in.

She felt it again, back of her throat. Nearly choked on it.

'Ta,' Eric said. Moira saw Little Willie sizing up the girls for future reference. Tonight, she knew, he was worried he wouldn't get home Across the Moss, if the snow came down.

Matt got into the driving seat, Eric slammed the back doors and climbed in on the passenger side. One of the girls in leather – buxom piece – opened a rear side door for Willie. Willie rolled his eyes at her, gave her his most seductively innocent grin. 'See you sometime, eh?'

Moira's throat was burning up.

The girl said, 'Yeah, I'll be around.' She held on to the open door. 'Gina,' she said. The wire-caged light over the back-stage exit threw a grille of shadows on to her pale, puffy cheeks.

Willie, five and a bit feet tall, liked his women big. 'Gina. Right,' he said, 'I'll remember.'

The first sparse snowflakes hit the wet black asphalt and dissolved. Moira, tucking her long hair down her coat collar, smiled at the girl, put out a foot to climb into the van next to Willie.

And then the moment froze, like life's big projector had jammed.

Moira turned in time to see the girl's eyes harden, glazing over like a doll's eyes as she whirled – a big, clumsy dancer – and flung the door. Like the door was a wrecking hammer and Moira was the side of a condemned building.

Snarling, *'Traitor!'* Discoloured, jagged teeth exposed. 'Fucking bitch!'

Willie had seen it. With both hands, he had pushed her back. She stumbled, fell over the kerb, the door connecting with a shuddering crunch and this girl Gina snarling, *'Bitch . . .'*, voice as deadly cold as the grinding metal.

And then the door reopened and Willie was hauling her in and snatching it shut behind her, the girl screaming, 'Go on . . . feather your own nest, fucking cow!' And beating on the panel into Moira's ear as Matt started the engine and pulled urgently away into the unheeding, desultory night traffic.

'Jesus,' Willie Wagstaff said. 'Could've had your fingers off.'

'Screw up ma glittering career, huh?' White face in the streetlight and a rasp of Glasgow giving it away that Moira was pretty damn shocked. 'Couldny play too well wi' a hook.'

Matt said mildly, 'Don't let it bother you. Always one or two. Just jealous.' The snow heavy enough now for him to get the wipers going.

'Wasny about envy.' Moira had her guitar in her arms. 'I'm no' exactly popular with your fans any more is the problem.'

'You're in good company,' Matt said. 'Look how the purists shunned Dylan when he went over to rock and roll.'

'Called me a traitorous cow.'

'Yeah, well,' Matt said. 'We've been over this.' So damned *nonchalant* about it. He seemed so determined she shouldn't feel bad that she felt a sight worse.

Eric, the mournful one who played fiddle and twelve-string, Eric, the mediator, the peacemaker, said, 'Weren't a bad gig though, were it?'

'Was a grand gig,' Moira said. Good enough, she thought, heartsick, to be the start of something, not the end.

Least her throat wasn't hurting so bad. The guitar case was warm in her arms. The snowflakes began to stick and cluster on the side windows as Matt drove first to Eric's house at Ashton Under Lyne, where Willie had left his Mini van. They switched the drum chest to the back of the little grey van, and Willie said, 'I won't mess about. If it's snowing like this down here it'll be thick as buggery over t'top.' He hung his arms around Moira's neck and gave her a big kiss just wide of the lips. 'Ta-ra, lass. Don't lose touch, eh?'

Then Eric kissed her too, mournfully, and by the time she got into the front seat next to Matt she was in tears, both arms wrapped around the guitar case for comfort.

'This is the worst thing I ever did, you know that, Matt?'

There was silence. Just the two of them now, for the last time. Time for some plain talking.

'Don't be so bloody daft.' Still his tone was curiously mild.

'She was right, that slag, I should have ma fingers chopped off.'

'Listen, kid.' He tapped at the steering-wheel. 'You made one sacrifice for this band when you threw up your degree course. That's it. No more. Don't owe us nowt. It's been nice – cracking couple of years, wouldn't've missed it. But you're not even twenty-one. We're owd men, us.'

'Aw, Matt . . .' Could anybody be this selfless?

'Gone as far as we're going. Think I want to be trailing me gear around the country when I'm sixty? No way. It's a good get-out, this, straight up. For all of us. Eric's got his kids, Willie's got his . . .'

Matt didn't finish the sentence, covering up the break by changing down to third, swinging sharp right and taking them through Manchester's Piccadilly: bright lights, couples scurrying through the snow. Snow was nice in the city, Moira thought. For a while. When it came by night.

Think about the snow. Because Matt's got to be lying through his teeth.

But the silence got too heavy. 'OK,' she said, to change the subject. 'What *do* you want to be doing?'

'Eh?'

'You said you didny wanna be trailing your gear around when you were sixty. What would you like to be doing?'

Matt didn't answer for a long time, not until they were out of the city centre.

'I'm not sure,' he said eventually. 'We're all right for money, me and Lottie. Thanks to you.'

'Matt . . .' *I can't stand this.*

'All right. I don't know. I don't know what I want to do. But I'll tell you this much . . . I know where I want to *be*.'

Moira waited. The snow was heavy now, but they were not too far from Whalley Range, where she lived, and it wouldn't take Matt long to get to his bit of Cheshire and Lottie.

'What I want,' he said, 'is to be out of these sodding suburbs. Want to go home.'

'Across the Moss?' The words feeling strange in Moira's mouth.

'Yeah,' Matt said.

Across the Moss. Willie and Matt would often slip the phrase to each other, surreptitiously, like a joint. Across the Moss was Over the Rainbow. Utopia. The Elysian Fields.

'Lottie likes it fine where we are. All the shops and the galleries and that. But it's not me, never was. Don't belong. No . . . echoes. So. Yeah. I'm going home. Might take a year, might take ten. But that's where I'm ending up.'

Which didn't make her feel any better. Twenty years older than her and here he was, talking about ending up. Did this happen to everybody when they turned forty?

'This is Willie's village, up in the moors?'

'Yeah. And Willie stayed. Willie's got family there. My lot moved to town when I was a lad. You never get rich up there, not even the farmers. But we were happy. We were *part of it*. Willie's still part of it. Drops down to town to play a gig or two, get his leg . . . go out with a woman.'

Moira smiled. Matt tended to be kind of proper, like a father, when they were alone.

'But he keeps going back. And his mother . . . she's never spent a night away, his ma, the whole of her life.'

'Some place, huh?'

9

'Special place.' He was staring unblinking through the windscreen and the snow. 'It's quite lonely and primitive in its way. And the Moss – biggest peatbog in the North.'

'Really?'

'Vast. And when you get across it – it's weird – but there's a different attitude. Different values.'

'Isn't that what everybody says about the place they were brought up?'

'Do you?'

She thought about this.

'No,' she said. 'Maybe not.'

The world outside was a finite place in the thickening snow. Matt was somewhere far inside himself. Across the Moss.

She glanced at him quickly. Thickset guy, coarse-skinned. Nobody's idea of a musician. Brooding eyes the colour of brown ale. Most times you thought you knew him; sometimes you weren't so sure. Occasionally you were damn sure you *didn't* know him, and couldn't.

After a while she said, 'What's it called? I forget.'

'Bridelow,' Matt said in a deliberate way, rounding out all the consonants. 'Bridelow Across the Moss.'

'Right,' she said vaguely.

'Dramatic place. To look at. Never saw that till I started going back. I take the little lad up there sometimes, of a weekend. When he's older we're going to go hiking on Sundays. Over the moors.'

'Sounds idyllic. Like to see it sometime.'

'But mostly I go alone.' Matt pulled up under the streetlamp in front of the Victorian villa where Moira had her apartment. 'Me and the pipes.'

'You take the *pipes*?'

Bagpipes. The Northumbrian pipes, played sitting down, had been Matt's instrument. Then he'd started experimenting with different kinds of bag, made of skins and things. He called them the Pennine Pipes, claiming they'd been played in these parts since before the Romans came to Britain.

The Pennine Pipes made this eerie, haunting sound, full of a kind of repressed longing.

'Releases me,' Matt said.

10

She didn't want to ask him what it released him from.

'Takes it away,' Matt said.

She didn't want to ask him what it was that piping took away.

'On the Moss,' Matt said. 'Only on the Moss.'

The tips of her fingers started to feel cold.

'The Moss takes it away,' Matt said. 'The Moss absorbs it.'

He switched off the engine. Snow was settling on the bonnet.

'But the Moss also preserves it,' Matt said. 'That's the only drawback. Peat preserves. You give it to the peat, and you've got rid of it, but the peat preserves it for ever.'

He turned and looked at her; she saw something swirling in his eyes and the truth exploded in her mind. *Oh, Christ, don't let me taste it. God almighty, don't let it come. Was the girl, what's her name, Gina . . . it was the girl, it wasny you, Matt, wasny you . . . please, don't let it be you . . .*

In the silence, the kind which only new snow seemed to make, they looked at each other in the streetlight made brighter by the snow.

'This is it then,' Matt said flatly.

'Think I might cry again.' But *she* was lying now. There was the residue of something unpleasant here, something more than sadness swirling in Matt's eyes.

Matt had his door open. 'Pass us your guitar.'

'Huh? Oh. Right. Sorry.'

The street was silent, snow starting to make the three- and four-storey houses look like soft furnishings. Lights shone pastel green, pink and cream behind drawn curtains. Matt took the guitar case, snowflakes making a nest in his denim cap. He pushed it back. He said, just as relaxed, just as mild and just as offhand as he'd been earlier, 'One thing I've always meant to ask. Why do you always take this thing on stage with you?'

'The guitar?'

'No, lass. The case. This old and cracked and not very valuable guitar case. You never let the bloody thing out of your sight.'

'Oh.' How long had he been noticing this? She looked at

him. His eyes were hard. He'd never asked her questions, everything he knew about her was stuff she'd volunteered. Matt was incurious.

And because of that she told him.

'There's . . . kind of a wee pocket inside the case, and inside of that there's, like, something my mother gave me when I was young.'

He didn't stop looking at her.

'It's only a comb. Kind of an antique, you know? Very old. Too heavy to carry around in your pocket. It means a lot to me, I suppose.'

'That's your mother, the . . . ?'

'The gypsy woman. Aye. Ma mother, the gypsy woman.' She shook snow off her hair. 'They're big on good luck tokens, the gypsies. Throw'm around like beads.'

Matt said roughly, 'Don't go making light of it.'

'Huh?'

'You're trying to make it seem of no account. Traditions are important. Sometimes I think they're all we have that's worthwhile.' He propped the instrument in its stiff black case against the wide concrete base of the streetlamp.

Moira said, 'Look, you're gonny get soaked.'

He laughed scornfully, like the noise a crow makes.

'Matt,' she said, 'I'll see you again, yeh?' And she did want to, she really did. Sure she did.

He smiled. 'We'll be on different circuits now, lass. You in a suite at the Holiday Inn, me over the kitchen at the Dog and Duck. Tell you what, I'll buy all your records. Even if it is rock and roll. How's that?'

She took a step towards him, hesitant. He was only a wee bit taller than she was.

This was it. The final seconds of the last reel.

Two years in the band, building up her reputation on the back of his. Matt watching her with some pride. A touch supervisory at first, then graciously taking half a pace back until even the wee folk clubs were announcing 'The Matt Castle Band with Moira Cairns'. And a couple of times, to her embarrassment, Moira Cairns in bigger letters.

And now she was leaving. Off to London for the big money.

Traitorous bitch.

'Matt . . .' It was the worst moment. She should kiss him too, but that would seem perfunctory, demeaning and pretty damn cheap.

Also, for the first time, she didn't want to go that close to him.

He'd pulled down his cap; she tried to peer under the peak, to find out what his eyes were saying.

Nothing. His eyes would show no resentment, no disappointment. She was leaving the band which had changed her life, made her name. Leaving the band just when she was starting to put something back, and Matt felt . . .

He felt nothing.

Because . . . Jesus . . .

'Did you go on the peat today?' she asked him in a very small voice, the snow falling between them. 'Did you go on the peat with the pipes? Did you let the damn peat absorb it?'

And then the projector stuttered and stalled again, images shivering on the screen of the night, and she saw him suddenly all in white. Maybe just an illusion of the snow. He was very still and framed in white. It wasn't nice. The white was frilled around him, like the musty lace handkerchiefs in the top dresser drawer at her gran's house.

And a whiff of soiled perfume.

Death?

For the first time, there was a real menace to him. Too transient to tell whether it was around him or *from* him. Her throat swelled. She coughed and the tears came, the wrong kind of tears. She felt the snow forming on the top of her own head; it was almost warm. Maybe she looked like that too, shrouded in white.

Matt held out his right hand and she gripped it like a lifeline, but the hand was deathly cold. She told herself, Cold hands, warm heart, yeah? And tried to pull him closer – but all the time wanting to keep him away and hating herself for that.

He dropped her hand and then put both of his on her shoulders. His arms were rigid, like girders, but she felt they were trembling, his whole body quivering with some titanic tension, something strong holding out against something potentially stronger, like a steel suspension bridge in a hurricane.

Then he said, 'Going to show me?' Voice colder than the snow.

She wanted to squirm away; she made herself remain still, trying to find his eyes. No. Please. Don't spoil this. I'll buy it. You're a selfless, self-sacrificing guy. I don't want to know any more.

'This famous comb,' he said with a smile that was faintly unpleasant.

'It's no' famous,' she said quickly, almost snapping.

His brown eyes were steady. Hey come *on* . . . this is Matt Castle. What's he gonna do, steal it off you, snatch it out your hand and drive away?

Keep it safe. Never take it out for show . . . Never treat it as a trinket or a wee souvenir. You understand, child?

No, see, all it is, right, he's decided in his own mind that we aren't going to meet again. He wants there to be no space for future recriminations. But he needs something to hold on to, right? A link.

That's all it is. He wants a link. A special moment, something between us and no one else.

You owe him. You owe him that.

You owe him nothing.

She stopped searching for his eyes, didn't want to know what they might have to tell her about Matt Castle, the kindly father figure, that Matt Castle who'd said, Take your chance, grab it while you can, lass. Never mind us. We're owd men.

Dumbly, Moira laid the guitar case on the pavement in the snow, and – hands shaking with the cold and the nerves – flipped up the chromium catch.

It was like opening someone's coffin.

Only the guitar lay in state. In a panic, she felt beneath the machine-heads for the velvet pouch which held the ancient metal comb.

I have to. I owe him, Mammy. I'm sorry, but I owe him.

PART ONE

THE SPRING CROSS

From *Dawber's Book of Bridelow*:

INTRODUCTION

THIS LITTLE BOOK bids you, the visitor, a cordial welcome to Bridelow Across the Moss, a site of habitation for over two thousand years and the home of the famous Bridelow Black Beer.

Bridelow folk would never be so immodest as to describe their tiny, lonely village as unique. But unique it is, both in situation and character.

Although little more than half an hour's drive from the cities of Manchester and Sheffield, the village is huddled in isolation between the South Pennine moors and the vast peatbog known as Bridelow Moss. So tucked away, as the local saying goes, 'It's a wonder the sun knows where to come of a morning . . .'

A spring morning. A hesitant sun edging over the moor out of a mist pale as milk. Only when it clears the church tower does the sun find a few patches of blue to set it off, give it a bit of confidence.

The sun hovers a while, blinking in and out of the sparse shreds of cloud before making its way down the village street, past the cottage where Ma Wagstaff lives, bluetits breakfasting from the peanuts in two mesh bags dangling from the rowan trees in the little front garden.

The cats, Bob and Jim, sitting together on Ma's front step – donkeystoned to a full-moon whiteness – observe the bluetits through narrowed green eyes but resist their instincts because Ma will be about soon.

And while Ma understands their instincts all too well, she does not appreciate blood on her step.

Milly Gill, shedding her cardigan at the Post Office door, thought the mist this morning was almost like a summer heat-haze, which wasn't bad for the second week in March.

It made Milly feel excited, somewhere deep inside her majestic bosom. It made her feel so energetic that she wanted to wander off for long walks, to fill up her reservoirs after the winter. And to go and see the Little Man. See what he had in *his* reservoir.

And of course it made her feel creative, too. Tonight she'd be pulling out that big sketch pad and the coloured pencils and getting to work on this year's design to be done in flowers for the dressing of the Holy Well. It was, she decided, going to reflect everything she could sense about her this morning.

Milly Gill thought, I'm forty-nine and I feel like a little girl.

This was what the promise of spring was *supposed* to do.

'Thank you, Mother,' Milly said aloud, with a big, innocent grin. 'And you too, sir!'

★

The Moss, a vast bed, hangs on to its damp duvet as usual until the sun is almost overhead. Behind temporary traffic-lights, about half a mile from the village, a Highways Authority crew is at work, widening the road which crosses the peat, a long-overdue improvement, although not everybody is in favour of improving access to the village.

It's close to midday before the foreman decides it's warm enough to strip to the waist.

This is the man who finds the chocolate corpse.

The splendour of the morning dimmed a little for the Rector when, on getting out of bed, he felt a twinge.

It was, as more often than not, in the area of his left knee. 'We really must get you a plastic one,' the doctor had said last time. 'I should think the pain's pretty awful, isn't it?'

'Oh.' The Rector flexing his creased-up Walter Matthau semi-smile. 'Could be worse.' Then the doctor ruefully shaking his head, making a joke about the Rector being determined to join the league of Holy Martyrs.

'I was thinking of joining the squash club, actually,' the Rector had said, and they'd both laughed and wondered how he was managing to keep this up.

The answer to this was Ma Wagstaff's mixture.

Standing by the window of his study, with sunshine strewn all over the carpet, pleasant around his bare feet, the Rector balanced a brimming teaspoonful of Ma's mixture, and his eyes glazed briefly at the horror of the stuff.

It looked like green frogspawn. He knew it was going to make his throat feel nostalgic for castor oil.

The bottle, as usual, was brown and semi-opaque so he wouldn't have to see the sinister strands and tendrils waving about in there like weed on the bottom of an aquarium.

But still, it worked.

Not a 'miracle' cure, of course. Ma Wagstaff, who promised nothing, would have been shocked at any such suggestion. 'Might just ease it a bit,' she'd say gruffly, leaving the bottle on his hall table, by the phone.

Through the study window the Rector saw sun-dappled gravestones and the great Norman tower of St Bride's.

He rubbed his feet into the sunshiny carpet, raised his eyes to heaven, the spoon to his lips, and swallowed.

Out on the Moss, the foreman stands in the middle of the trench, in front of the JCB, waving his arms until the driver halts the big digger and sticks his head inquiringly round the side of the cab.

''Owd on a bit, Jason. I've found summat.'

The trench, at this point, is about five feet deep.

'If it's money,' says the JCB driver, 'just pass it up 'ere and I'll hide it under t'seat.'

'Well,' said Mr Dawber, 'as it's such a lovely day, we'd best be thinking about the spring. Now – think back to last year – what does *that* mean?'

Some of them had the good manners to put their hands up, but two little lads at the back just shouted it out.

'THE SPRING CROSS!'

Mr Dawber didn't make an issue of it. 'Aye,' he said. 'The Spring Cross.' And the two troublemakers at the back cheered at that because it would get them out of the classroom, into the wood and on to the moors.

'So,' said Mr Dawber. 'Who can tell me what we'll be looking for to put in the Spring Cross?'

The hands went up as fast and rigid as old-fashioned railway signals. Ernie Dawber looked around, singled out a little girl. 'Yes . . . Meryl.'

'Catkins!'

'Aye, that's right, catkins. What else? Sebastian.'

'Pussy willows!'

'Ye-es. What else? Benjamin.'

'Acorns?'

They all had a good cackle at this. Benjamin was the smallest child in the class and had the air of one who found life

20

endlessly confusing. Ernie Dawber sympathized. He'd always reckoned that the day he retired he'd be able to sit back, job well enough done, and start to understand a few basics. But everything had just got hazier.

With them all looking at him, giggling and nudging each other, Benjamin seemed to get even smaller. Mr Dawber had a little deliberation about this while the class was settling down.

'Now then . . .' he said thoughtfully. 'Who can tell me when we find acorns?'

'AUTUMN!' four or five of the cleverer ones chorused scornfully.

'That's right. So, what I'm going to do – and don't forget to remind me when the times comes, lad – I'm going to put Benjamin, because he knows all about acorns . . . in charge of making the *Autumn* Cross.'

The clever ones looked aghast, unable to find any justice in this, and Ernie Dawber smiled to see it. Coming in just a few hours a week, to teach the children about nature, at least gave him more time to consider the psychology of the job.

'Now then.' He clapped his hands to change the mood. 'What else do we need for the Spring Cross? Tom.'

'Birds' eggs.'

Mr Dawber's voice dropped an octave.

'We most certainly do *not* take birds' eggs to put into the Spring Cross, or for any other reason, Thomas Garside. And if it comes to my notice that any of you have disturbed any nests there's going to be TROUBLE.'

There was silence.

'And don't anybody think I won't find out about it,' said Mr Dawber.

And they knew he would, because, one way or another, Mr Dawber found out about *everything*. And if it was important enough he put it in *The Book of Bridelow*.

The foreman tells the JCB driver to switch his engine off. His voice is shaking.

'Come down a minute, Jason. Come and take a look at this.'

The driver, a younger man, swings, loose-limbed, to the ground. His boots shudder on the surface of the Moss. 'What you got?'

'I'm not sure.' The foreman seems reluctant to go back in the trench.

The driver grinning, shambling over to the pit and balancing expertly on the rim. Can't make it out at first. Looks like a giant bar of dark chocolate.

Then, while the foreman is attempting to light a cigarette and nervously scattering matches over the peat, the driver suddenly realizes what he's staring at, and, when the thought lurches into his head, it's eerily echoed by the foreman's fractured croak.

'Looks like a dead 'un to me, Jason.'

The driver falls over backwards trying not to topple into the trench.

Just Eliza Horridge and Shaw now, and the drawing room at The Hall was too big.

He was taller but slighter than his father, who used to stand, legs apart, in front of the fireplace, lighting his pipe, belching dragon's breath and making it seem as if the room had been built around him. When Arthur Horridge spoke, the walls had closed in, as if the very fabric of the building was paying attention.

'The w-w-w-worst thing about all this . . .' Shaw's thin voice no more emphatic than the tinkling of the chandelier when a window was open, '. . . is that when der-der-Dad wanted to expand ter-ten years ago, the bank wouldn't back him, and now . . .'

'We'll ride it,' Liz Horridge told him firmly. 'We always have. We've got twenty-three people depending on us for an income.'

'Ter-ter-too many,' said Shaw. 'Fer-far . . .'

'No!' The first time ever that she hadn't waited politely for him to finish a sentence. 'That's *not* something your father would have said.'

She turned away from him, glaring out of the deep Georgian-style window at the brewery's grey tower through the bare brown treetrunks. Its stonework badly needed repointing, one more job they couldn't afford.

'When sales were sagging,' Liz said, as she'd said to him several times before, 'Arthur always blamed himself, and it was our belt – the family's – that was tightened. I remember when he sold the Jag to—'

'It was der-different then!' Shaw almost shrieked, making her look at him. 'There was no competition to ser-speak of. Wh-what did they need to know about mer-mer-market forces in those days?'

'And it's all changed so quickly, has it, in the six months since your father's death?'

'It was cher-changing . . . yer-years before. He just couldn't see it. He didn't w-want to ser-see it.'

'He knew what his duty was,' Liz snapped, and her son began to wring his hands in frustration.

The sun shone through the long window, a cruel light on Shaw, the top of his forehead winking like a feeble flashlight. If baldness was hereditary, people doubtless asked, why had Arthur managed to keep most of his hair until the end, while Shaw's had begun to fall out before he turned twenty?

Behind the anger, Liz felt the usual sadness for him, while acknowledging that sympathy was a poor substitute for maternal pride.

'Mother,' Shaw said determinedly, 'listen to me. We've ger-got to do it. Ser-soon. We've got to trim the workforce. Ser-ser-some of them have ger-got to go. Or else . . .'

'Never,' said Liz Horridge. But she knew that such certainty was not her prerogative. Shaw was the owner of the Bridelow Brewery now. He glared mutinously at her, thin lips pressed tight together, only too aware of how much authority he lost whenever he opened them.

'Or else what?' Liz demanded. 'What happens if we *don't* trim the workforce?'

She looked down at herself, at the baggy jeans she wore, for which she was rather too old and a little too shapeless these days. Realizing why she was wearing the jeans. Spring cleaning. An operation which she would, for the first time, be undertaking alone, because, when Josie had gone into hospital, she hadn't taken on another cleaner for economic reasons. Thus trimming her own workforce of one.

'The ber-ber-brewery's not a charity, Mother,' Shaw said pleadingly. 'Jim Ford says we could be out of ber-business inside a year.'

'Or else what?' Liz persisted.

'Or else we sell it,' Shaw said simply.

Liz laughed. 'To whom?'

'Ter-ter-to an outside . . . one of the big firms.'

'That's not an option,' Liz said flatly. 'You know that. Beer's been brewed in Bridelow since time immemorial. It's part of the local heritage.'

'And still cer-could be! Sell it as a going concern. Why not?'

'And you could live with that, could you?'

He didn't answer. Liz Horridge was shaking with astonishment. She faced him like an angry mother cat, narrowing her eyes, penetrating. 'Who's responsible for this? Who's been putting these thoughts in your head?'

'Ner-nobody.' But he couldn't hold her gaze. He was wearing a well-cut beige suit over a button-down shirt and a strange leather tie. He was going out again. He'd been going out a lot lately. He had no interest in the brewery, and he wasn't even trying to hide this any longer.

'And what about the pub? Is this fancy buyer going to take that on as well?'

'Ser-somebody will.' Shaw shrugged uselessly, backing towards the door. 'Anyway, we'll talk about it later, I've got to . . .'

'Where are you going?'

'I . . . I'm . . .' He went red and began to splutter. Pulled out a handkerchief and blew his nose, wiped his lips. For years she'd worried because he didn't go out enough, because he hadn't got a girlfriend (although this had hardly been surprising). Now at last, at the age of thirty-one, he was feebly groping for control of his own destiny . . . and floundering about, unbalancing *everything*.

Liz Horridge turned away from him and walked to the

other window, the one with the view of Bridelow, which summer would soon obscure. She could see the humped but still sprightly figure of Mrs Wagstaff in the distance, lugging a shopping basket across the cobbles to Gus Bibby's General Stores.

Her breast heaved and she felt tears pumping behind her eyes.

Arthur . . . it's not my fault.

Mrs Wagstaff stopped in the middle of the street and – although it was too far away for Liz to be certain – seemed to stare up through the trees at the Hall . . . at this very window.

As though the old girl had overheard Liz's thoughts. As though she could feel the agony.

When Liz turned around, wet-eyed, she found she was alone; Shaw had quietly left the room.

Although he'll be cool enough when the Press and the radio and TV reporters interview him in a few hours' time, the County Highways foreman is so shaken up right now that he has to be revived with whisky from the JCB driver's secret flask.

What he's discovered will come to be known as the Bridelow Bogman. Or the Man in the Moss. Important people are going to travel hundreds of miles to gaze with reverence upon its ancient face.

'And what was your reaction when you found it?' asks one of the reporters. 'What did you think it *was?*'

'Thought it were a sack o' spuds or summat,' the foreman says, quotably. His moment of glory. But out of his hands soon enough – so old and so exciting to the experts, like one of them Egyptian mummies, that nobody else seems to find it upsetting or horrifying, not like a *real* body.

But, though he'll never admit it, the foreman reckons he's never going to forget that first moment.

'And what did you think when you realized what it was?'

'Dunno, really . . . thought it were maybe an owd tramp or summat.'

'Were you shocked?'

'Nah. You find all sorts in this job.'

But that night the foreman will dream about it and awake with a whimper, reaching for his warm missus. And then fall asleep and wake again, his sweat all over both of them and his mind bulging with the moment he bent down and found his hand was gripping its cold and twisted face, his thumb between what might have been its teeth.

PART TWO

BLACK GLOW

From *Dawber's Book of Bridelow*:

THE FIRST-TIME VISITOR to Bridelow is strongly urged to approach it from the west, from which direction a most dramatic view of the village is attained.

From a distance of a mile or two, Bridelow appears almost as a craggy island when viewed from the narrow road which is virtually a causeway across Bridelow Moss.

A number of legends are attached to the Moss, some of which will be discussed later in this book.

CHAPTER I

In early summer, Bridelow hopefully dolls herself up, puts on a bit of make-up and an obliging smile for the sun. But the sun doesn't linger. On warm, cloudless evenings like this it saves its final pyrotechnics for the moor.

Sunset lures hues from the moor that you see at no other time – sensual pinks and melodramatic mauves which turn its stiff and spiky surface into velvet.

. . . a delusion, thought Joel Beard, soon to leave theological college. A red light tenderizing the face of an old whore.

He had his back to the sinking sun. To him, it seemed agitated tonight, throwing out its farewell flames in a long, dying scream. As well it might.

Most of the lonely village was below the moor, and the sun's flailing rays were missing it. The stone houses hanging from the hill were in shadow and so was the body of the church on its summit. Only the spikes of the church tower were dusted with red and gold.

Joel dismounted from his motorbike.

In the centre of the tower was a palely shining disc. Like a rising full moon, it sent sneering signals to the sun: as you fade, it promised gleefully, I'll grow ever brighter.

Joel glared at the village across the sullen, scabby surface of the Moss. He imagined Bridelow under moonlight, stark and white as crow-picked bones.

Its true self.

The disc at the centre of the tower was actually an illuminated clockface, from which the hands had long ago fallen. Often said to be a friendly face which turned the church into a lighthouse at night, across the black ocean of the Moss.

. . . you see, at one time, Mr Beard, very few people dared cross the Moss . . . except those for whom the Devil lit the way – have you heard that legend?

It was no legend. On a dark night, all you would see of the village would be this silver disc, Bridelow's own, permanent full moon.

Was this how the Devil lit the path? Was this the Devil's light, shining from the top of the stairs in God's house, a false beacon for the weak, the uncertain and the disturbed?

Joel's black leathers straightened him, like armour, and the hard white collar lifted his eyes above the village to the luminous moor. Its lurid colours too would soon grow dull under the night, like a harlot's cheap dress.

From the village, across the barren Moss, he heard voices raised, a shriek of laughter.

The village would be alive tonight. A new landlord had installed himself at the decrepit local inn, The Man I'th Moss, thus saving it from closure, a side-effect of the widely condemned sale of the Bridelow brewery.

Joel waited, astride his motorbike, his charger, until the moor no longer glowed and the illusion of beauty was gone.

Everyone saw shadows in the blackened cities, those obvious pits of filth and fornication, where EVIL was scrawled in neon and the homeless slept with the rats. And yet the source of it was up here, where city-dwellers surged at weekends to stroll through the springy heather, picnic among the gorse . . . young couples, families, children queuing at the roadside ice-cream vans, pensioners in small cars with their flasks of tea.

It's all around you, Mr Beard . . . once you know what you're looking for. Look at the church, look at the pub, look at the people . . . you'll see the signs everywhere.

Beneath him, the bike lurched into life, his strong, gauntleted hands making the engine roar and crackle, spitting holy fire.

He rode away from the village, back into the hills.

'Shades,' Ma Wagstaff would say later that night. 'Them's what's kept this place the way it is. Shades of things.'

Of all Ma's famous sayings, these were the words that would keep coming back at Ernie Dawber during the short, anxious days and the long, chill nights of the declining year.

And when, as local historian, he tried to find the beginning (as in, What exactly started the First World War? What caused the first spark that set off the Great Fire of London?), he'd keep coming back to this particular evening. A vivid evening at the end of May. The evening he'd blithely and thoughtlessly told Ma Wagstaff what he'd learned about the death of the bogman . . . and Ma had made a fateful prediction.

But it started well enough, with a big turn-out for the official reopening of The Man, under its new proprietor. The two bars couldn't hold all those come to welcome him home. So several dozen folk, including Ernie Dawber – best suit, waistcoat, watch-chain – were out on the cobbled forecourt, having a pint or two and watching the sun go down over the big hills beyond the Moss.

A vivid evening at the end of May. Laughter in the streets. Hope for the future. Most enmities sheathed and worries left at home under the settee cushions.

A real old Bridelow night. That was how it ought to have been enshrined in his memory. All those familiar faces.

A schoolteacher all his working life, Ernie Dawber had known at least three-quarters of this lot since they were five-year-olds at the front of the school hall: eager little faces, timid little faces . . . and a few belligerent ones too – always reckoned he could spot a future troublemaker in its pram.

He remembered Young Frank Manifold in the pram, throttling his panda.

'Well, well . . .' Twenty-odd years on, Young Frank strolling up to his boss, all jutting chin and pint mug clenched like a big glass knuckle-duster. 'It's *Mr Horridge.*'

Shaw said nothing.

'What's that you're drinking, *Mr Horridge?*' Sneering down at Shaw's slim glass.

Shaw's smile faltered. But he won't reply, Ernie thought, because if he does he'll start stuttering and he knows it.

There'd been a half-smile on Shaw's face as he stood alone on the cobbles. A nervous, forced-looking smile but a smile none the less. Ernie had to admire the lad, summoning the nerve to show himself tonight, not a month since Andy Hodgson died.

Especially with more than a few resentful brewery employees about.

'Looks like vodka,' Frank observed. 'That what it is, *Mr Horridge?* Vodka?' A few people starting to look warily at Frank and Shaw, a couple of men guiding their wives away.

''Course . . . I forgot. Bloody Gannons make vodka on t'side. Gannons'll make owt as'll sell. That *Gannons* vodka? That what it is . . . *Mr Horridge?*'

Shaw sipped his drink, not looking at Frank. This could be nerves. Or it could be an insult, Shaw pointedly pretending Young Frank was not there.

Whichever, Ernie decided he ought to break this up before it started to spoil the atmosphere. But somebody better equipped than him got there first.

'Where's your dad, Frank?' Milly Gill demanded, putting herself firmly between him and Shaw, like a thick, flowery bush sprouting between two trees.

'Be around somewhere.' Frank staring over the postmistress's head at Shaw, who was staring back now. Frank's knuckles whitening around the handle of his beermug.

'I think you'd better find him, Frank,' Milly said briskly. 'See he doesn't drink too much with that diabetes.'

Frank ignored her, too tanked-up to know his place. 'Fancy new car, I see . . . *Mr Horridge*. Porsche, int it? Andy Hodgson'd just got 'isself a new car, day before he fell. Well, I'm saying "new" – Austin Maestro, don't even make um no more. He were chuffed wi' it. Easily pleased, Andy, weren't he, Milly?'

'It was an accident,' Milly said tightly. 'As you well know.'

'Aye, sure it were, I'm not accusing Mr Horridge of *murder*. Only, why don't you ask him why Andy were suddenly ordered to reconnect a bloody old clapped-out pulley system for winching malt-sacks up to a storeroom right at top of t'building as isn't even *used* no more except by owls. You ask this bastard that, Milly.'

'We've had the inquest,' Milly said. 'Go and see to your dad.'

'Inquest? Fucking whitewash. I'll *tell* you why Andy were sent up. On account of place were being tarted up to look all *quaint* and *old-fashioned* for a visit from t'Gannons directors. Right, *Mr Horridge*?'

'Wasn't c . . . Not quite like that,' said Shaw quietly.

'Oh aye. How were it different? Lad dies for a bit of fucking *cosmetic*. You're all shit, you. Shit.'

The air between them fizzed. Shaw was silent. He'd been an expert at being silent during the three years Ernie had taught him before the lad was sent to prep school. And still an expert when he came back from University, poor bugger.

'And this Porsche.' Young Frank popped out the word with a few beery bubbles. 'How many jobs Gannons gonna axe to buy you that, eh?'

'Frank,' Milly Gill told him very firmly, big floral bosom swelling, 'I'll not tell you again!'

Careful, lass, Ernie thought. Don't do owt.

'You're a jammy little twat,' Frank spat. 'Don't give a shit. You never was a proper Horridge.'

A widening circle around them, conversations trailing off. 'Right.' Milly's eyes went still. 'That's enough. I'll not have this occasion spoiled. Am I getting through?'

'Now, Millicent,' Ernie said, knowing from experience

what might happen if she got riled. But Shaw Horridge startled them all. 'It's quite all right, Miss Gill.'

He smiled icily at Young Frank. 'Yes, it is a per-Porsche.' Held up his glass. 'Yes, it is vodka. Yes, it's mer-made in Sheffield by a s-subsidiary of Gannons Ales.'

He straightened up, taller than Frank now, his voice gaining strength. 'Gannons Ales. Without whom, yes, I wouldn't have a Porsche.'

And, stepping around Millie, he poked Young Frank in the chest with a thin but rigid forefinger. 'And without whom *you* wouldn't have a job . . . *Mr Manifold*.'

Ernie saw several men tense, ready to hold Young Frank back, but Frank didn't move. His eyes widened and his grip on the tankard slackened. Lad's as astonished as me, Ernie thought, at Shaw Horridge coming out with half a dozen almost fully coherent sentences one after the other.

The red sun shone into Shaw's eyes; he didn't blink.

The selling of the brewery was probably the worst thing that had happened to Bridelow this century. But not, apparently, the worst thing that had happened to Shaw Horridge.

He lowered his forefinger. 'Just remember that, please,' he said.

Looking rather commanding, where he used to look shyly hunched. And this remarkable confidence, as though somebody had turned his lights on. Letting them all see him – smiling and relaxed – after perpetrating the sale of the brewery, Bridelow's crime of the century. And indirectly causing a death.

Took some nerve, this did, from stuttering Shaw.

Arthur's lad at last. Maybe.

'Excuse me,' Shaw said dismissively. 'I have to meet someone.'

He turned his back on Young Frank Manifold and walked away, no quicker than he needed to, the sun turning the bald spot on the crown of his head into a bright golden coin.

'By 'eck,' Ernie Dawber said, but he noticed that Milly Gill was looking worried.

And she wasn't alone.

*

'Now then, Ernest. What's tha make of that, then?'

He hadn't noticed her edging up behind him, although he'd known she must be here somewhere. She was a Presence.

Just a little old woman in a pale blue woollen beret, an old grey cardigan and a lumpy brown woollen skirt.

'Well,' Ernie Dawber said, 'Arthur might have been mortified at what he's done with the brewery, but I think he'd be quite gratified at the way he stood up for himself there. Don't you?'

'Aye,' said Ma Wagstaff grimly. 'I'm sure his father'd be right pleased.'

Ernie looked curiously into the rubbery old features. Anybody who thought this was just a little old woman hadn't been long in Bridelow. He took a modest swallow from his half of Black. 'What's wrong then, Ma?'

'Everything.' Ma sighed. 'All coming apart.'

'Oh?' said Ernie. 'Nice night, though. Look at that sun.'

'Aye,' said Ma Wagstaff pessimistically. 'Going down, int it?'

'Well, yes.' Ernie straightened his glasses. 'It usually does this time of night.'

Ma Wagstaff nodded at his glass. 'What's that ale like now it's Gannons?'

'Nowt wrong with it as I can taste.' This wasn't true; it didn't seem to have quite the same brackish bite – or was that his imagination?

Ma looked up and speared him with her fierce little eyes. 'Got summat to tell me, Ernest Dawber?'

Ernie coughed. 'Not as I can think of.' She was making him uneasy.

'Anythin' in the post today?'

'This and that, Ma, this and that.'

'Like one of them big squashy envelopes, for instance?'

'A jiffy-bag, you mean?'

'Aye,' said Ma Wagstaff. 'Wi' *British Museum* stamped on it.'

Ernie fumed. You couldn't keep anything bloody private in this place. 'Time that Millicent kept her damn nose out!'

'Never mind that, lad, what's it say?'

'Now, look . . .' Ernie backed away, pulling at his waist-coat. 'In my capacity as local historian, I was able to provide Dr Hall and the British Museum with a considerable amount of information relating to the Moss, and as a result, following their examination of the body, they've kindly given me a preview of their findings, which . . .'

'Thought that'd be it.' Ma Wagstaff nodded, satisfied.

'. . . which will be published in due course. Until which time, I am not allowed . . .'

'If *you* know, why shouldn't *we* know?'

'I'm not *allowed*, Ma. It's what's called an embargo.'

'Oh.' Ma's eyes narrowed. 'That's what it's called, is it?' Means educated fellers like you get to know what's what and us common folk . . .'

Common folk? Ma Wagstaff? Ernie kept backing off, looking around for friendly faces. 'Please, Ma . . . don't push me on this. You'll find out soon enough.'

But the nearest person was a good ten yards away, and when his back hit the wall of the pub's outside lavatory block, he realized she'd got him into a corner in more ways than one.

'Now then,' Ma said kindly. 'How's that prostate of yours these days?'

'Nowt wrong with my prostate,' Ernie replied huffily.

Ma Wagstaff's eyes glinted. 'Not yet there int.'

CHAPTER II

'This is mer-madness,' Shaw said.

'No,' said Therese, 'it's exciting.'

'You're exciting,' he mumbled. 'That's all.' He pushed a hand through her sleek hair, and she smiled at him, tongue gliding out between her small, ice-white teeth. He was almost crying; she had him on the edge again. He pushed his back into the car's unfamiliar upholstery and clenched both hands on the wheel.

'Shall we go, then?'

'I can't.'

'I promise you,' Therese said, 'you'll feel so much better afterwards.'

And he would, he knew this from experience. Once, not long after they'd met, she'd made him go into a chemist and steal a bottle of Chanel perfume for her. *I'll buy it for you*, he'd almost shrieked. But that wasn't good enough. He was rich . . . buying her perfume – what would that demonstrate?

So he'd done it. Stolen it. Slipped it into the pocket of his sheepskin jacket and then bought himself two bottles of the shop's most expensive aftershave as an awkward sort of atonement.

But the awkwardness had just been a phase. He remembered lying awake all that night, convinced someone had seen him and the police would be at the door. *Don't worry*, she'd said, *it'll get easier*.

Jewellery next. Antique jewellery from a showcase, while Therese had distracted the manager.

You'll feel better, she'd say.

She was right. For the first time ever he was getting whole sentences out without stammering. Although his mother hadn't said anything, it was obvious she'd noticed. And been impressed. He'd felt quite wonderful, couldn't wait to see Therese again to tell her.

His confidence had increased daily. Soon he'd found he could speak openly to groups of men in the brewery like his father used to do, instead of slinking into his office and only communicating with the workers through the manager.

And when Gannons had made their approach, he'd found it surprisingly easy to make his decision – with a little help from Therese.

'Do you want really to stay in Bridelow all your life? Couldn't bear it, myself. Couldn't live here for a *week*.'

And he knew it was true. She wouldn't spend any time here. If they went for a walk, it had to be up on the moors. If they went for a drink, it had to be at some pub or club in Manchester or somewhere.

He wanted desperately to show her off, to show that stuttering Shaw Horridge could get himself a really beautiful girlfriend. But she seemed to find Bridelow beneath her.

'Dismal little place,' she said. 'Don't you think? I like lights and noise and people.'

So it hadn't been difficult, the decision to let Gannons have the brewery. Biggest thing he'd ever done and all over in a couple of weeks. All over before anyone in the village knew about it. *Fait accompli*.

'You'll feel better,' she said. And he had. He always did.

Sometimes the terror of what was happening would still flare and, for a moment, it would blind him. He'd freeze, become quite rigid. Like tonight, facing the oaf Manifold, who'd wanted to fight, wanted to take on stuttering Shaw, beat him publicly to the ground. Make a point in front of all his mates.

And Shaw had thought of Therese and felt his eyes grow hard, watched the effect of this on the thug Manifold.

'Start the car, Shaw,' Therese said softly.

Shaw laughed nervously, started the engine.

'Good,' she said. 'Now pull away gently. We don't want any screeching of tyres.'

It was a Saab Turbo. A black one. She'd blown the horn once and he'd known it was her.

It was a different car, but he wasn't unduly surprised; she'd often turn up in quite expensive ones. Her brother's, she'd say. Or her father's. Tonight she'd stopped the Saab in a lay-by the other side of the Moss, saying, 'I feel tired; you drive.'

'Would I be insured?'

Therese laughed a lot at that.

'Who owns it exactly?'

'How should I know? I stole it.'

'Interferin' devils.' Be unfair, perhaps, to say the old girl was xenophobic about Southerners, but ... No, on second thoughts, it wouldn't be unfair; Ma was suspicious of everybody south of Matlock.

'Aye,' Ernie said, 'I know you don't think he should have been taken to London, but this was a find of enormous national, nay, international significance, and they *are* the experts after all.'

He chuckled. 'By 'eck, they've had him – or bits of him, anyroad – all over the place for examination . . . Wembley, Harwell. And this report . . . well, it really is rather sensational, if you ask me. Going to cause quite a stir. You see, what they did . . .'

Putting on his precise, headmasterly tone, Ernie explained how the boffins had conducted a complete post-mortem examination, submitting the corpse to the kind of specialized forensic tests normally carried out only in cases of suspicious death.

'So they now know, for example, what he had for dinner on the day he died. Some sort of black bread, as it happened.'

Ma Wagstaff sniffed, obviously disapproving of this invasion of the bogman's intestinal privacy.

'Fascinating, though, isn't it,' Ernie said, 'that they've managed to conduct a proper autopsy on a chap who probably was killed back when Christ was a lad . . . ?'

He stopped. 'What's up, owd lass?'

Ma Wagstaff had gone stiff as a pillar-box.

'Killed,' she said starkly.

'Aye. Ritual sacrifice, Ma. So they reckon. But it was all a long time ago.'

Ma Wagstaff came quite dramatically to life. Eyes urgently flicking from side to side, she grabbed hold of the bottom of Ernie's tweed jacket and dragged him well out of everybody's earshot, into a deserted corner of the forecourt. Into the deepest shadows.

'Tell us,' she urged.

The weakening sun had become snagged in tendrils of low cloud and looked for a minute as if it might not make it into the hills but plummet to the Moss. From where, Ernie thought, in sudden irrational panic, it might never rise again.

He took a few breaths, pulling himself together, straightening his jacket.

'This is not idle curiosity, Ernest.'

'I could tell that, Ma, when you were threatening to bugger up my prostate.' How much of a coincidence had it been that he'd shortly afterwards felt an urgent need to relieve himself which seemed to dissipate as soon as he stood at the urinal?

'Eh, that were just a joke, Ernest. Can't you take a joke any more?'

'From you, Ma . . .'

'But this is deadly serious,' Ma said soberly.

The sun had vanished. Ridiculously, Ernie thought he heard the Moss burp. 'All right,' he said. From the inside pocket of his jacket he brought out some papers bound with a rubber band and swapped his regular specs for his reading glasses. Be public knowledge soon enough, anyroad.

Ernie cleared his throat.

'Seems our lad,' he said, 'was somewhere around his late twenties. Quite tall too, for the time, 'bout five-five or six. Peat preserves a body like vinegar preserves onions. The bones had gone soft, but the skin was tanned to perfection. Even the hair, as we know, remained. Anyroad, medical tests indicate no reason to think he wasn't in good shape. Generally speaking.'

'Get to t'point,' Ma said irritably.

'Well, he was killed. In no uncertain manner. That's to say, they made sure of the job. Blunt instrument, first of all. Back of the head. Then, er . . . strangulation. Garotte.'

'Eh?'

'Garotte? Well . . .' He wondered if she ever had nightmares. Probably wouldn't be the usual kind if she did.

Little Benjie, Ma's grandson, had wandered across the forecourt with that big dog of his. 'Hey.' Ernie scooped a hand at him. 'Go away.'

He lowered his voice. 'They probably put a cord – leather string, sinew – around his neck and . . . inserted a stick in the back of the cord and, as it were . . . twisted it, the stick. Thus tightening the sinew around his . . . that is, fragments of the cord have been found actually embedded. In his neck.'

Ma Wagstaff didn't react like a normal old woman. Didn't recoil or even wince. 'Well?' she said.

'Well what?' said Ernie.

'Anythin' else?'

Ernie went cold. How could she know there was more to

it? He looked over her head at the bloodied sky. 'Well, seems they . . . they'd have pulled his head back . . .'

His throat was suddenly dry. He'd read this report four times, quite dispassionately at first and then with a growing excitement. But an *academic* excitement. Which was all right. Emotionally he'd remained unmoved. It had, after all, happened a good two thousand years ago – almost in prehistory.

'So the head'd be sort of pulled back . . . with the . . . the garotte.'

When they'd brought the bogman out, a little crowd had assembled on the edge of the Moss. Ernie had decided it would be all right to take a few of the older children to witness this historic event. There'd been no big ceremony about it; the archaeologists had simply cut out a big chunk of peat with the body in the middle, quite small, half his legs missing and his face all scrunched up like a big rubber doll that'd been run over. Not very distressing; more like a fossil than a corpse. They'd wrapped him in clingfilm and put him in a wooden box.

Ernie was staring into Ma Wagstaff's eyes, those large brown orbs glowing amber out of that prune of a face, and he was seeing it for the first time, the real horror of it, the death of a young man two thousand years ago.

'He'd be helpless,' Ernie said. 'Semi-concussed by the blow, and he couldn't move, couldn't draw breath because of the garotte . . .'

Ma nodded.

'That was when they cut his throat,' Ernie said hoarsely.

Ma nodded again. Behind her, out on the pub forecourt, a huge cheer suddenly went up. The new landlord must have appeared.

'You knew,' Ernie said. He could feel the blood draining out of his face. 'You *knew* . . .'

'It were the custom,' Ma Wagstaff said, voice very drab. 'Three times dead. See, Ernest, I were holding out the hope as this'd be just a body . . . some poor devil as lost his way and died out on t'Moss.' She sighed, looking very old. 'I knew really. I knew it was goin' t'be what it is.'

41

'A sacrifice?' It was growing dark.

'Not just any sacrifice. We're in trouble, Ernest.'

Sometimes Shaw wanted to say, I feel like just *being* with you is illegal.

Some mornings he'd be thinking, I've got to get out of this. I'll be arrested, I'll be ruined.

But then, all through the day, the longing would be growing. And as he changed to go out, as he looked in the mirror at his thin, pale face, his receding hairline and his equally receding jawline, he saw why he could never get out . . . not as long as there was anything she wanted from him. Not as long as he continued to change.

They drove to a country pub and parked the Saab very noticeably under a lighted window at the front, being careful to lock it and check the doors. He wondered how exactly she'd stolen it and how she'd obtained the keys, but he knew that if he asked her she would simply laugh at him.

In the pub, as usual, he couldn't prise his hungry eyes from her. She sat opposite him, wearing an old fox fur coat, demurely fastened to the neck. Shaw wondered if, underneath the coat, above (and inside) her black tights, she was naked.

With that thought, he felt his desire could lift their heavy, glass-topped, cast-iron table a good two inches from the floor.

'You could arouse the dead,' he said, almost without breath.

'Would you like to?' Therese's lips smiled around her glass of port.

'Pardon?'

'Arouse the dead?'

He laughed uncomfortably. Quite often she would say things, the meaning of which, in due course, would become devastatingly apparent.

Later, two miles out of Macclesfield town, Shaw driving again, she said, 'All right, let's get deal with this, shall we?'

'What?'

But she was already unzipping his trousers, nuzzling her

head into his lap. He braked hard, in shock, panic and uncontainable excitement. 'Yes, Shaw,' she said, voice muffled, 'you *can* stop the car.'

'Somebody . . . somebody might see us . . . you know, somebody walking past.'

'Well,' Therese said, burrowing, 'I suppose somebody might see *you* . . .'

Five minutes later, while he was still shivering, she said, 'Now let's get rid of the car.' She had the interior light on, re-applying lipstick, using the vanity mirror. Her fur coat was still fastened. He would never know if she was naked underneath it.

'How are we going to get home?'

'Taxi. There's a phone box across the road. I'll ring up for one while you're dispensing with the car.'

A shaft of fear punctured his moment of relief. 'Disp . . . ? How?'

'I seem to remember there's a bus shelter along here. What . . . about a quarter of a mile . . . ? Just take it and ram it into that.'

He just stared at her. Through the windscreen he could see high, evergreen, suburban hedges, sitting-room lights glimmering here and there through the foliage.

Shaw said weakly, 'Why don't we just leave it somewhere? Parked, you know . . .'

'Discreetly,' Therese said. 'Under a tree. With the keys in.'

'Yes,' he said inadequately.

She opened her door to the pavement, looked scornfully back at him. 'Because it wouldn't do anything for you. Your whole life's been tidy and discreet. I'm trying to help you, Shaw.'

His fingers felt numb as he turned the key in the ignition. A car slowed behind them.

'What if there's somebody in the bus shelter?'

Therese shrugged, got out, slammed the car door. Shaw dug into his jacket pocket, pulled out a handful of tissues and began feverishly to scrub at the steering-wheel and the gear-lever and the door-handle and anything else he might have touched.

He'd been doing this for a couple of minutes when a wetness oozing between his fingers told him he was now using the tissue he'd employed to clean himself up after Therese had finished with him. And they could trace you through your semen now, couldn't they, DNA tests . . . genetic fingerprinting . . . oh, no . . . Banging his forehead against the steering-wheel . . . no . . . no . . . *no* . . .

The passenger door clicked gently open.

The police. The police had been surreptitiously following them for miles. That car going slowly, creeping up . . . He'd be destroyed.

Shaw reacted instinctively. He flung open his door, threw his weight against it, hurling himself out into the middle of the road, a heavy lorry grinding past less than a couple of feet away.

Across the roof of the Saab he looked not into a police uniform but into Therese's dark, calm eyes.

'I'll be listening out,' she whispered, 'for the sound of breaking glass.'

CHAPTER III

Matt Castle was standing on the pub steps with an arm around the shoulders of Lottie, his wife. Looked a bit awkward, Ernie noticed, on account of Lottie was very nearly as tall as Matt.

Lottie Castle. Long time since he'd seen her. By 'eck, still a stunner, hair strikingly red, although some of that probably came out of a bottle nowadays. Aye, that's it, lad, Ernie encouraged himself. Think about sex, what you can remember. Nowt like it for refocusing the mind after a shock.

How had she known? Was the bogman part of the Bridelow Tradition? Was that it? By 'eck, it needed some thinking about, did this.

But not now.

'I'll stand here.' Matt Castle was smiling so hard he could

hardly get the words between his teeth. 'So's you can all hear me, inside and out. *Can* you hear me?'

'What's he say?' somebody bleated, to merry laughter, from about three yards in front of Matt. Ernie noted, rather disapprovingly, that some of this lot were half-pissed already.

'Yes, we can,' Ernie called helpfully from the edge of the forecourt.

'Thank you, Mr Dawber.'

Ernie smiled. All his ex-pupils, from no matter how far back, insisted on calling him Mr Dawber. When they'd first met, he was a baby-faced twenty-one and Matt Castle was eleven, in the top class. So he'd be fifty-six or seven now. Talk about time flying . . .

'I just want to say,' said the new licensee, shock-haired and stocky, 'that . . . well . . . it's bloody great to be back!'

And of course a huge cheer went up on both sides of the door. Matt Castle, Bridelow-born, had returned in triumph, like the home team bringing back the cup.

Except this was more important to the community than a bit of local glory. 'Looks well, doesn't he?' Ernie whispered to Ma Wagstaff, who didn't reply.

'Always wanted a pub of me own,' Matt told everybody. 'Never dared to dream it'd be *this* pub.'

The Man I'th Moss hung around him like a great black overcoat many sizes too big. Ernie hoped to God it was all going to work out. Draughty old pile, too many rooms . . . cellars, attics . . . take a bit of upkeep, absorb all the contents of your bank account by osmosis.

'To me, like to everybody else, I suppose, this was always Bridelow Brewery's pub.' Matt was dressed up tonight, suit and tie. 'We thought it always would be.'

At which point, quite a few people turned to look for Shaw Horridge, who'd long gone.

'But everything changes,' Matt said. 'Fortunes rise and fall, and this village owes the Horridge family too much not to make the effort to understand why, in the end, they were forced to part with the pub . . . and, of course, the brewery.'

We've all made the effort, Ernie thought, as others murmured. And we still don't understand why.

'Eeeh,' Matt said, his accent getting broader the more he spoke. 'Eeeh, I wish I were rich. Rich enough to buy the bloody lot. But at least I could put together enough for this place. Couldn't stand seeing it turned into a Berni Inn or summat.'

No, lad, Ernie thought. Left to rot.

'But . . . we got ourselves a bit of a bank loan. And we managed it.' Lottie Castle's fixed smile never wavering, Ernie noted, when Matt switched from 'I' to 'we' covering the money aspect.

Matt went on about how he didn't know much about running a pub but what he did know was music. They could expect plenty of that at The Man I'th Moss.

Matt grinned. 'I know there's a few of you out there can sing a bit. And I remember, when I was a lad, there used to be a troupe of morris dancers. Where'd they go to?'

'Orthopaedic hospital,' somebody said.

'Bugger off,' said Matt. 'There's to be no more cynicism in this pub, all right? Anyroad, this is open house from now on for dancers and singers and instrumentalists. If there aren't enough in Bridelow we'll ship 'em in from outside . . . big names, too. And we'll build up a following, a regular audience from the towns . . . and, brewery or no brewery, we'll make The Man I'th Moss into a going concern again.'

At which point, somebody asked, as somebody was bound to, whether Matt and his old band would get together in Bridelow.

'Good point,' Matt accepted. 'Well, me old mucker Willie's here, Eric's not far off. And I'm working on a bit of a project which might just interest . . . well, somebody we used to work with . . . eeeh, must be fifteen years ago. Late 'seventies.'

Everybody listening now, not a chink of bottle on glass or the striking of a match. Outside, the sun was just a rosy memory.

Matt broke off. 'Hey up. For them as can't see, Lottie's giving me a warning look, she thinks I should shut up about this until we know one way or t'other . . .'

Lottie smiled wryly. Ernie Dawber was thinking, What the 'eck was her name, the girl who used to sing with Matt's band

and then went off on her own? *Very* popular she used to be, or so he'd heard.

'But, what the hell,' Matt said. 'If I'm going to do this right, I'll need your help. Fact is . . . it was this business of the bogman got me going. Lottie reckons I've become a bit obsessed.' He laughed self-consciously. 'But the thing is . . . here we are, literally face to face with one of our forefathers. And it's my belief there's a lot he can teach us . . .'

Ernie Dawber felt Ma Wagstaff go still and watchful by his side.

'I mean about ourselves. About this village. How we relate to it and each other, and how we've progressed. There's summat special about this place, I've always known that.'

Moira Cairns, Ernie remembered. That was her name. Scottish. Very beautiful. Long, black hair.

'Right.' Matt bawled back over his shoulder, into the bar, 'Let's have a few lights on. Like a flamin' mausoleum in there.'

Ma Wagstaff stiffened and plucked at Ernie's jacket.

The sun wasn't ever going to get out of that low cloud, he thought. Won't know till tomorrow if it's made it to the hills or if the Moss has got it.

'By 'eck,' he said ruefully, as if his fanciful thoughts were printed on the misting, mackerel sky where Ma Wagstaff could read them, 'I'm . . .'

'Getting a bit whimsy?'

Ernie laughed through his discomfort. She made it sound like a digestive problem.

'Not before time,' Ma said. 'Never any talking to you when you was headmaster. Jumped-up little devil. Knew it all – what teacher ever don't? Still . . . better late than not. Now then, Ernest Dawber, I'll try and teach thee summat.'

He let Ma Wagstaff lead him away to the edge of the forecourt, from where terraced stone cottages plodded up to the high-towered church, a noble sentinel over the Moss.

'What do you see?'

'This a trick question, Ma?'

Now, with the sun gone, all the houses had merged. You couldn't tell any more which ones had fresh paintwork, which had climbing roses or new porches. Only a few front steps stood out, the ones which had been recently donkey-stoned so they shone bright as morning.

'To be honest, Ma, I can't see that much. Can't even see colours.'

'What *can* you see, then?'

'It's not light,' Ernie said, half-closing his eyes, 'and it's not dark. Everything's melting together.'

'Go on.'

'I can't see the individual houses. I suppose I can only see the people who live in them. Young Frank and Susan and the little lad. Alf Beckett. Millicent Gill at the Post Office . . . Gus Bibby, Maurice and Dee at the chip shop. And I suppose . . . if I look a bit harder . . .'

'Aye, you do that.'

'If I look harder I can see the people who lived in the houses before . . . The Swains – Arthur Swain and his pigeons. Alf Beckett's mother, forty-odd years a widow. I can bring them all back when I've a mind. Specially at this time of day. But that's the danger, as you get older, seeing things as they were, not as they are.'

'The trick,' said Ma, 'is to see it all at same time. As it was and as it is. And when I says "as it was" I don't just mean in your lifetime or even in my lifetime. I mean as far back as yon bogman's time.'

Ernie felt himself shiver. He pushed the British Museum papers deeper into his inside pocket. Whatever secret knowledge of the bogman Ma possessed, he didn't want to know any more.

Ma said, 'You stand here long enough, you can see it all the way back, and you won't see no colours, you won't see no hard edges. Now when you're out on t'Moss, Brid'lo don't look that welcoming, does it? All cold stone. You know that, you've written about it enough. But it's not cold to us, is it? Not when we're inside. No hard edges, no bright colours, never owt like that.'

'No.'

'Only shades,' Ma said, almost dreamily. 'Them's what's kept this place the way it is. Shades of things.'

'Shades?'

'Old colours all run together. No clashes. Know what I'm telling you, Ernest?'

'Harmony?' Ernie said. 'Is that it? Which is not to say there's no bickering, or bits of bad feeling. But, fundamentally, I s'pose, Bridelow's one of those places where most of us are happy to be. Home. And there's no defining that. Not everybody's found it. We're lucky. We've *been* lucky.'

'Luck?' Something was kindling behind Ma's eyes. Eighty-five if she was a day and still didn't need glasses. '*Luck?* You don't see owt, do you?' Ernie'd had glasses full-time since he was thirty-five. 'What's it got to do wi' luck?'

'Just a figure of speech, Ma.'

'Balls,' said Ma. 'Luck! What this is, it's a balancing act. Very *complicated* for t'likes of us. Comes natural to nature.'

Ernie smiled. 'As it would.'

'Don't you mock me, Ernest Dawber.'

'I'm sorry, Ma.' She was just a shade herself now, even her blue beret faded to grey.

'Beware of bright, glaring colours,' she said. 'But most of all, beware of black. And beware of white.'

'I don't know what you mean.'

'You will,' said the little old woman. 'You're a teacher.' She put a hand on his arm. 'Ernest, I'm giving you a task.'

'Oh, 'eck.'

'You've to think of it as the most important task you've ever had in your life. You're a man of learning, Ernest. Man wi' authority.'

'Used to be, Ma. I'm just a pensioner now . . .' Like you, he was going to say, then he noticed how sad and serious she was looking.

'Get that man back.'

'Who?' But he knew. 'How?' he said, aghast.

'Like I said, Ernest. Tha's got authority.'

'Not that kind of authority, for God's sake.'

★

Nobody there. He swallowed. Nobody. Not in or near the bus shelter.

It was on his nearside, which was no good, he might get hurt, so he drove further along the road, reversing into someone's drive, heading back slowly until he could see the glass-sided shelter, an advertisement for Martini on the end panel, lit up like a cinema screen in the headlights: a handsome man with wavy hair leaning over a girl on a sofa, topping up her glass.

He was mentally measuring the distance.

What am I *doing*? *What am I bloody doing?*

I could park it just here. Leave it. Walk away. Too far, anyway, for her to hear the impact.

In his mind he saw Therese standing by the telephone kiosk, about to phone for a taxi. In his mind she stopped. She was frowning. She'd be thinking what a miserable, frightened little sod he was.

He *could* say there *had* been somebody in the bus shelter, two people. Get angry. Was he supposed to kill them? Was he supposed to do that?

But she would know.

He stopped the car, the engine idling. The bus shelter had five glass panels in a concrete frame. The glass would be fortified. He would have to take a run at it, from about sixty yards.

If he didn't she would know.

He remembered the occasions she'd lost her temper with him. He shivered, stabbed at the accelerator with the car in neutral, making it roar, clutching the handbrake, a slippery grip. Too much to lose. Gritting his teeth until his gums hurt. *Too much to lose.*

And you'll feel better afterwards.

Took his foot off. Closed his eyes, breathed rapidly, in and out. The road was quiet now, the hedges high on either side, high as a railway embankment.

Shaw backed up twenty or thirty yards, pulled into the middle of the road. Felt his jaw trembling and, to stiffen it, retracted his lips into a vicious snarl.

He threw the Saab into first gear. Realized, as the stolen car spurted under him, that he was screaming aloud.

On the side of the bus shelter, the handsome man leaned over the smiling girl on the sofa, topping up her glass from the bottle. In the instant before the crash, the dark, beautiful girl held out the glass in a toast to Shaw before bringing it to her lips and biting deeply into it, and when she smiled again, her smile was full of blood.

You'll feel . . . *better*.

The big lights came on in the bar and were sluiced into the forecourt through the open door where Matt Castle stood grinning broadly, with his tall red-haired wife. Behind them was the boy – big lad now, early twenties, must be. Not one of Ernie's old pupils, however; Dic had been educated in and around Manchester while his dad's band was manhandling its gear around the pubs and clubs.

'Happen he *will* bring a bit of new life,' Ernie said. 'He's a good man.'

'Goodness in most of us,' Ma Wagstaff said, 'is a fragile thing, as you'll have learned, Ernest.'

Ernie Dawber adjusted his glasses, looked down curiously at Ma. As the mother of Little Willie Wagstaff, long-time percussionist in Matt Castle's Band, the old girl could be expected to be at least a bit enthusiastic about Matt's plans.

Ma said, 'Look at him. See owt about him, Ernest?'

Matt Castle had wandered down the steps and was still shaking hands with people and laughing a lot. He looked, to Ernie, like a very happy man indeed, a man putting substance into a dream.

Lottie Castle had remained on the step, half inside the doorway, half her face in shadow.

'*She* knows,' Ma Wagstaff said.

'Eh?'

'I doubt as she can see it, but she knows, anyroad.'

'Ma . . . ?'

'Look at him. Look hard. Look like you looked up t'street.'

Matt Castle grinning, accepting a pint. Local hero.

'I don't understand,' said Ernie Dawber. He was beginning to think he'd become incapable of understanding. Forty-odd years a teacher and he'd been reduced to little-lad level by an old woman who'd most likely left school at fourteen.

Ma Wagstaff said, 'He's got the black glow, Ernest.'

'*What?*'

On top of everything else she'd come out with tonight, this jolted Ernie Dawber so hard he feared for his heart. It was just the way she said it, like picking out a bad apple at the greengrocer's. A little old woman in a lumpy woollen skirt and a shapeless old cardigan.

'What *are* you on about?' Ernie forcing joviality. Bloody hell, he thought, and it had all started so well. A real old Bridelow night.

'Moira?' Matt Castle was saying. 'Aye, I *do* think she'll come. If only for old times' sake.' People patting him on the shoulder. He looked fit and he looked happy. He looked like a man who could *achieve*.

'The black glow?' Ernie whispered. 'The *black glow*?'

What had been banished from his mind started to flicker back: images of the piper on the Moss over a period of fifteen, twenty years. Echoes of the pipes: gentle and plaintive on good days, but sometimes sour and sometimes savage.

'Black glow?' his voice sounding miles away.

Ma Wagstaff looked up at him. 'I'm buggered if I'm spelling it out for thee.'

PART THREE

BOG OAK

From *Dawber's Book of Bridelow*:

BRIDELOW MOSS IS A two-miles-wide blanket of black peat. Much of its native vegetation has been eroded and the surface peat made blacker by industrial deposits – although the nearest smut-exuding industries are more than fifteen miles away.

Bisected by two small rivers, The Moss slopes down, more steeply than is apparent, from the foothills of the northern Peak District almost to the edge of the village of Bridelow.

In places, the peat reaches a depth of three metres, and although there are several drainage gullies, conditions can be treacherous, and walkers unfamiliar with the Moss are not recommended to venture upon it in severe weather.

But then, on dull wet days in Autumn and Winter, the gloomy and desolate appearance of the Moss would deter all but the hardiest rambler . . .

CHAPTER I

OCTOBER

With the rain hissing venomously in their faces, they pushed the wheelchair across the cindered track to the peat's edge, and then Dic lost his nerve and stopped.

'Further,' Matt insisted.

'It'll sink, Dad. Look.'

Matt laughed, a cawing.

Dic looked at his mother for back-up. Lottie looked away, through her dripping hair and the swirling grey morning, to where the houses of Bridelow clung to the shivering horizon like bedraggled birds to a telephone wire.

'Mum . . . ?'

In the pockets of her sodden raincoat, Lottie made claws out of her fingers. She wouldn't look at Matt, even though she was sure – the reason she'd left her head bare – that you couldn't distinguish tears from rain.

'Right.' Abruptly, Matt pushed the tartan rug aside. 'Looks like I'll have to walk, then.'

'Oh, Christ, Dad . . .'

Still Lottie didn't look at the lad or the withered man in the wheelchair. Just went on glaring at the village, at the fuzzy outline of the church, coming to a decision. Then she said tonelessly, 'Do as he says, Dic.'

'Mum . . .'

Lottie whirled at him, water spinning from her hair. 'Will you just bloody well *do it*!'

She stood panting for a moment, then her lips set hard. She thought she heard Dic sob as he heaved the chair into the mire and the dark water bubbled up around the wheels.

The chair didn't sink. It wouldn't sink. It wouldn't be easy to get out, even with only poor, wasted Matt in there, but it wouldn't sink.

56

Maybe Matt was hoping they wouldn't *have* to get it out. That he'd be carried away, leaving the chair behind, suspended skeletally in the Moss, slowly corroding into the peat or maybe preserved there for thousands of years, like the Bogman.

'Fine,' Matt said. 'That's . . . fine. Thanks.'

The chair was only a foot or so from the path, embedded up to its footplate in Bridelow Moss. Dic stood there, tense, arms spread, ready to snatch at the chair if it moved.

'Go away, lad,' Matt said quietly. He always spoke quietly now. So *calm*. Never lost his temper, never – as Lottie would have done – railed at the heavens, screaming at the blinding injustice of it.

Stoical Matt. Dying so well.

Sometimes she wished she could hate him.

It was Sunday morning.

As they'd lifted Matt's chair from the van, a scrap of a hymn from the church had been washed up by the wind-powered rain, tossed at them like an empty crisp-packet then blown away again.

They'd moved well out of earshot, Lottie looking around. Thinking that on a Sunday there were always ramblers, up from Macclesfield and Glossop, Manchester and Sheffield, relishing the dirty weather, the way ramblers did. If it belonged to anybody, Bridelow Moss belonged to the ramblers, and they made sure everybody knew it.

But this morning there were none.

The bog, treacle-black under surface rust, fading to a mouldering green where it joined the mist. And not a glimmer of anorak-orange.

As if, somehow, they knew. As if word had been passed round, silently, like chocolate, before the ramble: avoid the bog, avoid Bridelow Moss.

So it was just the three of them, shadows in the filth of the morning.

'Go on, then,' Matt was saying, trying to pump humour into his voice. 'Bugger off, the pair of you.'

Lottie put out a hand to squeeze his shoulder, then drew

back because it would hurt him. Even a peck on the cheek hurt him these days.

It had all happened too quickly, a series of savage punches coming one after the other, faster and faster, until your body was numbed and your mind was concussed.

I don't think I need to tell you, do I, Mrs Castle.

That he's going to die? No. There were signs . . . Oh, small signs, but . . . I wanted him to come and see you weeks . . . months ago. He wouldn't. He has this . . . what can I call it . . . ? Fanatical exuberance? If he felt anything himself, he just overrode it. If there's something he wants to do, get out of his system, everything else becomes irrelevant. I did try, doctor, but he wouldn't come.

Please – don't blame yourself. I doubt if we'd have been able to do much, even if we'd found out two or three months before we did. However, this business of refusing medication . . .

Drugs.

It's not a dirty word, Mrs Castle. If you could persuade him, I think . . .

He's angry, doctor. He won't take anything that he thinks will dull his perceptions. He's . . . this is not anything you'd understand . . . he's reaching out for something.

'Go on,' Matt said. 'Get in the van, in the dry. You'll know when to come back.'

And what did he mean by *that*?

As they walked away, the son and the widow-in-waiting, she saw him pull something from under the rug and tumble it out into his lap. It looked, in this light, like a big dead crow, enfurled in its own limp wings.

The rain plummeted into Matt's blue denim cap, the one he wore on stage.

Dic said, 'He'll catch his dea—'

Stared, suddenly stricken, into his mother's eyes.

'I don't understand any more,' he said, panicked. 'Where he is . . . I've lost him. Is that . . . I mean, is it any place to be? In his state?'

'Move.' Lottie speaking in harsh monosyllables. 'Go.' The

only way she could speak at all. Turning him round and prodding him towards the van.

'Is it the drugs? Mum, is it the drugs responsible for this?'

Lottie climbed into the van, behind the wheel. Slammed the door with both hands. Wound the window down, keeping the rain on her face. She said nothing.

Dic clambered in the other side. He looked more like her than Matt, the way his dark red hair curled, defying the flattening rain. Matt didn't have hair any more, under his blue denim cap.

'Mum?'

'No,' Lottie said. 'There's no drugs. Listen.'

It was beginning.

Faint and fractured, remote and eerie as the call of a marsh bird, familiar but alien – alien, now, to *her*.

But not, she was sure, to the Moss.

She saw that Dic was crying, helpless, shoulders quaking. An aggressive thing, like little kids put on: I can't cope with this, I *refuse* to cope . . . take it away, take it *off* me.

She couldn't. She turned away, stared hard at the scratched metal dashboard, blobbed with rain from the open window.

Because she didn't understand it either. Nor, she was sure, was she meant to. Which hurt. The sound which still pierced her heart, which had been filtered through her husband, like the blood in his veins, for as long as she'd known him and some years before that.

It had begun. For the last time?

Please, God.

She looked out of the window-space, unblinking, cheeks awash.

Fifty yards away, hunched in the peat, bound in cold winding-sheets of rain, the black bag under his arm like a third lung . . .

. . . Matt Castle playing on his pipes.

Eerie as a marsh bird, and all the birds were silent in the rain.

The tune forming on the wind and falling with the water, the notes pure as tears and thin with illness.

Dic rubbed his eyes with his fingers. 'I don't know it,' he

said. 'I don't know this tune.' Petulant. As if this was some sort of betrayal.

'He only wrote it . . . a week or so ago,' Lottie said. 'When you were away. He said . . .' Trying to smile. 'Said it just came to him. Actually, it came hard. He'd been working at it for weeks.'

Lament for the Man, he'd called it. She'd thought at first that this was partly a reference simply to their pub, The Man I'th Moss, adrift on the edge of the village, cut off after all these years from the brewery.

But no. It was another call to *him*, wherever he was. As if Matt was summoning his spirit home.

Or pleading for the Man to summon him, Matt.

'I can't stand this,' Dic said suddenly. Dic, who could play the pipes too, and lots of other instruments. Who was a natural – in his blood too, his dad more proud than he'd ever admit, but not so proud that he'd encouraged the lad to make a profession of it.

'Christ,' said Dic, 'is this bloody suicide? Is it his way of . . . ?'

'You know him better than that.' Figuring he just wanted a row, another way of coping with it.

'It's not as if he's got an audience. Only us.'

'Only us,' Lottie said, although she knew that was wrong. Matt believed – why else would he be putting himself through all this? – that there had to be an audience. But, it was true, they were not it.

'All right, what if he dies?' Dic said sullenly, brutally. 'What if he dies out there now?'

Lottie sighed. What a mercy that would be.

'What I mean is . . . how would we even start to explain . . . ?'

She looked at him coldly until he subsided into the passenger seat.

'Sorry,' he said.

The piping was high on the wind, so high it no longer seemed to be coming from the sunken shape in the wheelchair, from the black lung. She wondered if any people could hear it back in Bridelow. Certainly the ones who mattered wouldn't be able to, the old ones, Ma Wagstaff, Ernie Dawber. They'd be in church. Perhaps Matt had chosen his time well, so they wouldn't hear it, the ones who might understand.

Dic said, 'How long . . . ?'

'Until he stops. You think this is easy for me, Dic? You think I believe in any of this flaming stupid . . . Oh, my God!'

The piping had suddenly sunk an octave, meeting the drone, the marsh bird diving, or falling, shot out of the sky. Lottie stopped breathing.

And then, with a subtle flourish of Matt's old panache, the tune was caught in mid-air, picked up and sent soaring towards the horizon. She wanted to scream, either with relief and admiration . . . or with the most awful, inexcusable kind of disappointment.

Instead she said, briskly, 'I'm going to call Moira tonight. I've been remiss. I should have told her the situation. He wouldn't.'

Dic said, 'Bitch.'

'That's not fair.' He was twenty, he was impulsive, things were black and white. She leaned her head back over the seat. 'I can understand why she didn't want to get involved. OK, if she'd known about his illness she'd have been down here right away, but at the end of the day I don't think that would have helped. Do you?'

The end of the day. Funny how circumstances could throw such a sad and sinister backlight on an old cliché.

Dic said, 'It would have taken his mind off his condition, maybe.'

Lottie shook her head. 'It's an unhealthy obsession, this whole bogman business.' They'd never really spoken of this. 'She'd have made things worse. She probably knew that.'

He said sourly, 'Why? You mean . . . because of his other unhealthy . . .'

Lottie suddenly sat up in the driving seat and slapped his face, hard. '*Stop it*. Stop it *now*.'

She closed her eyes on him. 'I'm tired.'

The pipes spun a pale filigree behind her sad, quivering eyelids, across the black moss where the rain blew in grey-brown gusts.

Take him, she prayed. To God. To the Man. Away.

Was this so wrong? Was it wrong, was it sinful, to pray to the Man?

God? The Man? The Fairies? Santa Claus? What did it matter?

A thrust of wind rattled the wound-down window, pulling behind it an organ trail from St Bride's, the final fragment of a hymn. It lay for a moment in strange harmony upon the eddy of the pipes.

No, Lottie decided. It's not wrong.

Take him. Please.

Anybody.

CHAPTER II

Three hours.

Three hours and he hadn't touched her. Chrissie had heard of men who paid prostitutes just to sit on the edge of the bed for half the night and listen to them rambling on about their domestic problems.

Maybe she should demand overtime.

'The other one,' Roger said, 'the one they found in Lindow, I mean, they christened him Pete Marsh. They had this instant kind of affection for the thing.'

Chrissie had been Dr Roger Hall's temporary admin assistant for nearly a fortnight and was a lot more interested in *him* than bog people. She poured coffee, watching him through the motel mirror. Unfortunately, he looked even more handsome when he was worried.

'Well, I mean, there's no way,' Roger went on, 'that I feel any kind of *affection* for *this* one. It's about knowledge.'

'So why not just let him go? After all, he must be pretty bloody creepy to have around,' said Chrissie, who shared an office at the Field Centre with a woman called Alice. She tried to imagine the situation if Alice was a corpse.

'It's not *creepy*, exactly.' Roger sat up in bed, carefully arranging the sheet over his small paunch.

'Spooks *me*,' Chrissie said, 'to be honest. And I never have to see him, thank God.'

'No, it's just . . . it's as if he knows how badly I need him. How much I need to *know* him, where he's coming from.'

'You're getting weird. You tell your wife stuff like this?'

'You're kidding. My wife's a doctor.'

That was a novel twist, Chrissie thought. My wife doesn't understand me – she's too intelligent. Chrissie didn't care for the underlying message Roger was sending out here. OK, he was tall, he had nice crinkles around his eyes, everybody said how dishy he looked on the telly. And OK, *she* was seducing *him* (with a bit of luck). But, in the end, one-to-one was the only kind of relationship Chrissie was basically interested in.

'No need to pout,' he said. 'I wasn't suggesting you were a bimbo. Just that a corpse is a corpse to Janet, regardless of its history.'

She brought him coffee. Outside, coming up to 7 p.m. on an autumn Sunday evening, traffic was still whizzing up the M6. Roger said he felt safe here: the one place he could count on people he knew not showing up was the local motor lodge. Chrissie had booked in; he'd arrived later, leaving his car on the main service area, away from any lights.

He was a very cautious man. He was supposed to be in London until tomorrow evening, on Bogman business. They were re-examining the stomach-lining or something equally yucky.

'Roger, look . . .' Chrissie lit a cigarette. 'I know how important he's been to you – for your career and everything. And I take your point about him giving the Field Centre a new lease of life – obvious we *were* being wound up, the amount of work we were actually *doing* . . . I mean, I've been wound up before.'

'I bet you have,' Roger said, looking at her tits, putting down his coffee cup. But he still didn't reach out for her.

Chrissie tried to find a smile but she'd run out of them. 'Sunday,' she said sadly.

'Didn't know you were religious.'

'I'm not.' She'd just suddenly thought, What a way to spend a Sunday evening, in a motel no more than two miles from where you live. With a bogman's minder. 'Do you touch him much?'

'You make it sound indecent. Of course I touch him. He feels a bit like a big leather cricket bag. You should pop in sometime, be an experience for you.'

Chrissie shuddered.

He grinned. 'Not that you'd get much out of it. He hasn't got one any more.'

'What, no . . . ?'

'Penis.'

Chrissie wrinkled her nose. 'Dissolved or something?'

'No, they must have chopped it off. And his balls. Part of the ritual.'

'Oh, yucky.' Chrissie wrapped her arms around her breasts and eased back into bed, bottom first.

'What I like best about your body,' Roger said, not moving, 'is that it's so nice and pale. All over.'

'Actually, I had quite a deep tan in the summer. Still there, in places.'

'Not as deep as *his* tan, I'll bet. That's what you *call* being tanned. Literally. Tanned and pickled. It's what it does to them. The acids. I like you. You're pale.'

It's not healthy, Chrissie thought, the way he brings everything back to that ancient thing. It's like 'Love me, love my bogman'. Oh, well . . . 'Roger,' she said hesitantly, looking at the gap between them, probably just about the size of the bloody bogman. 'Can I ask you something . . . ?'

'Sure,' he said tiredly, 'but if you want me to do anything complicated, you'll have to . . .'

'Don't worry. I just want to know something about you and . . . *him* . . . Just to clear the air. Then maybe we can relax. Thing is, there've not been all that many bogmen found, have there? All right, that Pete Marsh, and before him a bunch of them in Denmark. But when one's discovered in this country, it's still a major find, isn't it?'

'In archaeological terms, he's worth more than the average Spanish galleon, yes.'

'Hot property.'

'Very.'

'So what,' said Chrissie very slowly, 'is he *really* doing in a little-known university field centre behind a school playing-field in the North of England? Why did the British Museum experts and all these London people . . . why did they let you bring him back?'

Roger's eyes closed in on one another. This is where he starts lying, Chrissie deduced. The more university degrees a man had, she'd discovered, the more hopeless he was at concealing untruths.

'What I mean *is*,' she said, airing the bits of knowledge she'd rapidly absorbed from the Press cuttings file, 'they like to keep these things, don't they? They go to Harwell and Oxford for this radiocarbon dating, and then . . .'

'Well, he's been to Harwell. He's been to Oxford. And he's been to the British Museum.'

'And he's come back,' said Chrissie. 'Why's that?'

The Archdeacon poured himself a cognac, offered the bottle to the Rev. Joel Beard but wasn't entirely surprised when Joel declined.

Only we poor mortals have need of this stuff, the Archdeacon thought. He's above all such vices.

Sadly, he thought.

Between them on the leather three-seater Chesterfield sat a shining white dome, like a strange religious artefact.

It was Joel's crash-helmet.

He's deliberately placed it between us, the Archdeacon thought. He's heard about me. 'And so you know the place quite well, I gather,' he said hoarsely. 'You know Hans. And his family.'

'Well, I remember his daughter, Catherine,' Joel said. 'A wilful girl.'

All right, thought the Archdeacon. So you're one hundred per cent hetero. I can take a hint, damn you.

He edged back into his corner of the Chesterfield and looked into his drink, at the pictures on the wall, out of the window at the bare front garden, sepia under a Victorian streetlamp. Anywhere but at Golden Joel, the diocesan Adonis.

65

'Of course,' Joel said, 'he's been in better health.'

'Erm . . . quite. And it isn't, you know, that we think he's *failing* in some way. He's been an excellent man. In his time. He's a very . . . *tolerant* man. Perhaps that's part of the problem. Ah . . . not that I'm *decrying* his tolerance . . .'

The Archdeacon snatched a sip of his brandy. Oh dear. Why did he let Joel Beard do this to him?

Joel smiled. Or at least he exposed both rows of teeth. 'Look, perhaps I can clarify some of this, Simon. I don't think tolerance *is* such a fundamental virtue any more. I think we've been tolerant for so long that it looks as if . . . I mean, what, increasingly, is the public's idea of a typical Anglican clergyman?'

You dare, you brute, the Archdeacon thought. You *dare* . . .

'A ditherer,' said Joel. 'An ineffectual ditherer.'

'Oh.' The Archdeacon relaxed. 'Quite.'

'There's a big game going on, you know, Simon. We – the Church – ought to be out there. But where are we?'

'Ah . . . where indeed?'

'We aren't on the pitch. We aren't even on the touchline.'

'Perhaps not.'

'We're in the clubhouse making the bloody tea,' said Joel Beard.

'Well, I . . .'

'There's real evil about, you know. It's all around us and it's insidious. A burglary somewhere in Britain every thirty seconds or so. An assault. A rape. A husband beating his wife, sexually abusing his small children. We talk of social problems. Or if we use the word evil, it's *social* evil . . . We're making excuses for them and we're excusing ourselves. When I was a gym teacher . . .'

Oh, please . . . The Archdeacon saw beneath the cassock to the tensed stomach and the awesome golden chest.

'. . . before every rugby lesson, there'd be the same pathetic collection of little notes. "Dear Sir, Please excuse my son from games, he has a minor chest infection." This sort of nonsense. Same ones every other week. The wimps. Well, I'm afraid that's what *we* look like sometimes. "Dear People, Please excuse me from confronting Satan this week, but my steeple's developed stone-fatigue and I have to organize a garden party." This is what we've come to. We've reached the point where we're ashamed to wield the weapons forged for us by God.'

The Archdeacon refused to allow himself to contemplate the weapon God had forged for Joel Beard. He took a mouthful of cognac and held it there while Joel talked of the Church's manifest obligation to confront the Ancient Enemy again. Lord, but he was a magnificent sight when fired-up – that profile, hard as bronze, those rigid golden curls . . .

Upstairs, in his 'files', the Archdeacon kept seven photocopies of the famous picture of Joel in the *Sheffield Star* – the one of him brandishing his outsize pectoral cross. At the time this dramatic pose had only reinforced the Diocesan consternation expressed when Joel, still at college, had been on local radio threatening physical disruption of certain Hallowe'en festivities planned by the university students' union.

The Archdeacon had managed to placate the Bishop, who'd been suggesting immediate efforts ought to be made to interest this turbulent mature student in a period of foreign missionary work – the Colombian jungles or somewhere equally dangerous. Known his type before, the Bishop fumed. More trouble than they're worth, these self-publicists. Nonsense, said the Archdeacon. With respect, men like Beard must be considered the Church's Future . . . if the Church is to have one.

During these discussions about his future, Joel had apparently received a series of telephone calls alerting him to inbred evil in a small village in the Southern Pennines.

Anonymous, of course. But weren't they always? And wasn't the Archdeacon himself becoming just a little tired of Hans Gruber, the old-fashioned rural priest treading his own sheep-tracks, totally immersed in his parish, oblivious to the Diocese?

'. . . mustn't be afraid to get *physical*.' Joel thumped the back of the Chesterfield, and the Archdeacon almost fainted. 'Or, indeed, *meta*physical . . .'

'Well, then . . .' The Archdeacon's hand was shaking so much he had to put down his glass. 'If you're determined to face this thing head-on, we'll delay no longer. There's just this question of accommodation in Bridelow. Not had a curate for so long we let the house go.'

'I understand,' said Joel, 'that there's accommodation in the church itself.'

'In the ch . . . ? You don't mean this . . . priest's hole sort of place under the floor? You're not serious.'

'Well,' said Joel. 'Short-term, I see no reason why not. It was originally intended as emergency accommodation for visiting clergy, I gather. And how often does a priest get the opportunity to experience a night in the House of God?'

'Quite,' said the Archdeacon. 'Quite.' He was remembering the old story about an itinerant Bishop of Sheffield a century or so ago, who'd spent a night under the church at Bridelow and was supposed to have gone potty. Silly story. But still, was it wise for Joel to sleep down there? Alone?

The Archdeacon tingled.

Finally Chrissie said, 'Admit it, you're getting a bit obsessed.'

'That's ridiculous.' Not much conviction *there*. 'I'm just . . . stressed, that's all. I'm not good at deception.'

'No, you're not.'

'I meant with Janet. Look, would you mind putting that thing out.' He reached over her, took the cigarette from between her fingers and dropped it in an ashtray on the bedside ledge.

Well!

'Honestly, it's not an obsession,' he said. 'Not the way you think. Look, I'll tell you, OK. But you've got to keep it to yourself. Not a word, OK? Thing is, I've . . . I've had approaches.'

'Lucky you.' When, a few minutes ago, he'd put a hand experimentally on her thigh, it had felt like a lukewarm, wet sponge.

He said, 'When you were young . . .'

'Thank you very much, Roger.'

'No, no . . . I mean, when you were a child . . . Did you ever read Stanage's books?'

'Sta . . . Oh, *John Peveril* Stanage.' She felt a mild stirring of interest; not his usual type of stultifying archaeological tome. 'Well, who didn't?'

'He wanted to see me,' Roger said. 'Or rather he wanted me to go and see him.'

'Good God, is he still alive?'

'Very much so. Not yet sixty, I'd guess. 'Course, he's been a published writer since his early twenties, which makes him . . .'

'Very rich, I suppose,' Chrissie said.

'You wouldn't know it to see where he lives – end of one of those run-down Georgian terraces in Buxton. Sort of seedy – palatial inside, but I'm assured he's loaded. You remember much about his stuff?'

'I wasn't much of a reader,' Chrissie admitted. 'But you didn't need to be much of a reader to get into his books. Really exciting . . . and *interesting*, you know? Because they were usually about places we knew. King Arthur in Manchester, I remember that one – *Castle Fields*, it was called. I think. That right?'

'That's right.'

'And *The Bridestones*!' Chrissie sat up in bed. 'Gosh, yes. And *Blue John* . . . *Blue John's Way*? God, I remember when I was . . .'

'Yes, thank you, Chrissie. Anyway, turns out Stanage is quite a serious antiquarian, in an *amateur* sort of way. Obsessed for a long time with the Celtic history of the North-West – albeit in a fanciful, *mystical* fashion.' Roger sniffed. 'So naturally he's quite excited about our friend from the peat.'

God, Chrissie thought. Another one. What is it with this corpse?

'. . . and he's talking about establishing some sort of foundation . . . through the University . . . to set up an official Celtic museum . . . Keep this under your hat, won't you, Chrissie?'

I'm not wearing a bloody hat, she thought. I'm not wearing anything, in case you haven't noticed.

'. . . with the bog body as a centrepiece.'

'Oh.' She was starting to see. 'Money?'

'*Big* money,' said Roger. 'And Stanage's foundation would also support continued research, which would . . .'

'Keep us all in work.'

'To say the least. So, naturally, I'm keeping him to myself. We're going to work out the logistics of it between us and then present a complete package, an arrangement nobody – not the University, nor the British Museum – can afford to turn down.'

'And what does *he* get out of it? Stanage? I mean, what does the great man get out of dealing exclusively with you and keeping it all under wraps until you're ready to turn it to your advantage?'

'Er . . . He just likes being in on it, I think,' Roger said, trying to look as if this aspect hadn't occurred to him before. 'He gets access to the bogman pretty much whenever he wants.'

Which explained why Roger had been so keen to bring the body back to the Field Centre. Chrissie gave him a wry look he didn't appear to notice.

'So I'm having to keep all these balls in the air . . . juggle Stanage, the University, the British Museum . . . and now those sodding Bridelow people, who want the bloody thing *put back*!'

'Sorry?' Chrissie had been thinking ruefully about balls in the air. 'Who wants it back?'

Roger snorted. 'They're superstitious. We know that our friend . . . *him* . . . that he was sacrificed for some reason. Maybe to persuade the gods to keep the Romans at bay, after the Celts were driven out of the fertile lowlands of Cheshire and Clwyd and into the hills.'

'Barbaric times,' Chrissie said, thinking of Arnold Schwarzenegger in skins and a headband.

'So – incredible as it may seem that serious archaeological research in this day and age should still be complicated by this kind of crap – it appears some people in Bridelow feel that by taking the thing away we'll bring bad luck down on the village. As simple and as primitive as that.'

'Sort of like Tutankhamun's tomb?'

'If you like.'

Chrissie wanted to laugh. It was *pre*-Schwarzenegger. More

70

like one of those old Hammer films, Peter Cushing as Roger Hall.

'Keep getting pestered by this man Dawber. Who, admittedly, was quite useful at first. Used to be head teacher at the local school. Sort of . . . amateur historian.'

Roger said the words 'amateur historian' like other people would say 'dog turd'.

'Oh, of course, I know him,' Chrissie said. 'Mr Dawber. Tubby little chap. Rather cute. I suppose you think he's an eccentric, whereas Stanage . . .'

'Stanage *knows*,' Roger said strangely. He seemed to remember his coffee. It was cold. He put the cup down. Looked uncomfortable. 'Dawber's trouble. He says we should – get this – now we've done all our tests and found out everything we can, we should put the thing back in Bridelow Moss, in a secret location of *their* choosing – this is the bloody villagers – on the scientific basis that if the peat has preserved him for two thousand years it's probably the best way of keeping him in good nick for another two thousand . . .'

He laughed bitterly. 'The crackpot elements you have to deal with when you unearth something that catches the public imagination.'

Oh, you'll deal with crackpots, Roger, Chrissie thought. You'll deal with crackpots if there's something in it for you.

After about half an hour, Roger tried again.

Disastrously.

Stress, he explained. The stress of keeping your balls in the air.

They lay in the dark and talked some more. Talked about her ex-husband, who drank. Talked about his wife, who was brilliant and capable and seemed to power an entire hospital on an average of twenty-eight hours' sleep per week.

Talked about him, Roger . . . and him, *him*.

'Look . . . what I said about Stanage . . . forget it, will you? Forget I even mentioned Stanage.'

'All right,' Chrissie said.

A few minutes later, with a stagnant kind of sweat on his

forehead, Roger said to the ceiling, 'Sometimes . . . when Janet's on nights at the General . . . I wake up in the early hours, feeling really sort of cold and clammy.'

Which didn't exactly augur well, Chrissie thought, for the next few hours.

'And you know . . . I can almost feel it in the bed with me. Lumps of it.'

Jesus. She said, 'Lumps?'

'Peat. Lumps of peat.' Roger slid a damp and hopeless hand along her left thigh. 'That's stress for you.'

CHAPTER III

CENTRAL SCOTLAND

The Earl's place was nineteenth-century Gothic, a phoney Dracula's Castle with a lofty Great Hall that stank, the American thought, of aristocratic bullshit, domination and death.

He could tell the woman hated it too. Especially the skulls. Or maybe she had something else on her mind. She was worried; he could tell that much. Still, he wasn't about to miss this opportunity.

He'd kept glancing at her over dinner at the long baronial table, a couple of hours ago. All that wonderful long black hair with the single streak of grey. He'd never seen her before, not in concert, not even on TV, but he knew the face from the album covers, and he'd know the voice.

She was standing alone over by the doorway, frowning at the gruesome trophies on the walls. Not talking to anyone, although there were people all around her, expensively dressed people, crystal glasses hanging from their fingers like extra jewellery.

He supposed she'd be a couple years older than he was, which only added to that mysterious, lustrous glamour. Pretty soon she'd pick up her guitar, take her place on the central dais to sing for them all. Which didn't leave him much time.

What he needed was a neat, elegant opening line. Kind of imagining – her general aura being so magical – that one would come naturally.

He carried his glass across, stood alongside her, following her gaze around the overloaded walls.

He said, 'Uh . . .'

And followed up with something so dumb he could only hope to attribute it to the impact of fifteen-year-old malt on an uncultured brain.

'Impressive, huh?' he said.

She looked at him. Coldly. Looked at him like she was thinking, Yeah, well you *would* have to be impressed by this kind of Victorian shit. Where you come from, pal, this most likely is what passes for ancient, right?

'After its fashion,' she said mildly.

From the middle of a cluster of people, the Earl was watching them. Or rather, watching *him*, because he was American and therefore could maybe buy this place and everything else of its kind between here and Pitlochry many times over.

The Earl was a sleek man, English all the way down to the tip of his sporran. But the Earl wanted to be a real Celt and no doubt was counting on the American wanting that too, all the way down to the deepest part of his wallet.

A discreet buff-coloured card, handed to him several weeks ago by his mother – who also, unfortunately, was his boss – had said:

THE CELTIC BOND: A major conference of politicians and poets, writers, broadcasters and business people, to establish an international support-mechanism for the regeneration of a submerged European culture. Hosted, at his Scottish family seat, by . . . .

'Shit,' he'd said in some dismay. 'You're kidding, aren't you?'

She wasn't. Since she lost the use of her legs, the single most important element in his mother's life had become her Scottish ancestry. 'We are Celts, Mungo,' she'd say. 'Above all, never forget *that*.' By which she meant *her* side of the family; hence he bore *her* family name rather than that of his long-gone, long-forgotten father.

'If I can say this,' he said now, politely, trying to recover some credibility, 'you don't seem too relaxed.'

'No?' She wore a long, black dress, very plain. He could sense no perfume.

'I mean I can't imagine you'd be nervous about performing.'

She wasn't looking at him. She was still looking at the heads. Huge sets of antlers protruding from bleached fragments of skull, all over three walls, from just above head-height to within a couple of feet of the lavishly moulded ceiling.

'And I guess you aren't the nervous kind, anyway,' he said. 'So . . .'

Wherever you sat, the remains of three or four dozen butchered stags were always in view. On the central wooden dais, where she'd sit to sing, she'd probably feel herself constricted by some kind of grisly necklace of bone.

Gross.

'I was just wondering,' she said at last, when it must have been clear he wasn't about to go away, 'why people should think this is really such an essential part of being a Celt. Killing things for fun and showing off about it.'

A good word popped up in the American's head, like somebody had flashed him a prompt-card.

'Pantheistic,' he said. 'The old Celts were highly pantheistic. So I'm told.'

'That means they had *respect* for animals,' she said scornfully. She had a soft Scottish voice but not too much of an accent. 'A bit like your Red Indians.'

'Native Americans.' He smiled. 'To be politically and ethnically correct.' The smile was supposed to say, I may be devilishly attractive, with my untamed curly black hair, this cool white tuxedo, thistle in the buttonhole. But you can trust me. I'm a sincere guy. 'Can I get you another drink?'

'No,' she said. 'No, thank you.'

'I . . . ah . . .' He hesitated. 'I have a couple of your albums.'

'Oh?' She didn't seem too interested. 'Which ones?'

'Well, uh, my favourite, I guess, is still the one you did with The Philosopher's Stone. That'd be quite some years ago.'

'Oh.' She glanced away, as if looking for someplace else to put herself.

'Uh, I also have your first solo album,' he said quickly. 'How I recognized you. From the sleeve. You haven't changed.'

'Oh, I've changed, believe me. Look, I . . .'

'You never did cut your hair, though,' he said, urbanely displaying his knowledge of the album's prime cut.

'What?'

'"Never let them cut your hair,"' he quoted, '"or tell you where . . ." Listen, I . . . I just wanted to say it's real good to meet you . . . Moira. No one said you'd be here. Makes me glad I came after all.'

She said, 'I'm a last-minute replacement. For Rory McBain. He's sick. We have the same agent.'

A flunkey needed to come past with a tray of drinks, and he took the opportunity to manoeuvre her into a corner, unfortunately under two pairs of huge yellowing antlers. He said, 'Listen, that album – with the Stone – it had some magic.'

'He has bronchitis,' Moira said.

'Huh?'

'Rory McBain.'

He smiled. 'See, when I hear you sing, it always sounds to me like . . .'

'That album,' she said with an air of finality, 'was a mistake. I was too young, too stupid, and I never should have left Matt Castle's band.'

'Huh?'

She shook her head, wide-eyed, like she was waking up.

'Matt Castle?' He had his elbow resting on a wooden ledge below another damned antlered skull.

'He was . . . He was just the guy who taught me about traditional music when I was a wee girl. Look, I don't know why I said that, I . . .'

Her poise wavered. She looked suddenly confused and vulnerable. Something inside of him melted with pure longing while something else – something less admirable but more

75

instinctive – tensed like a big cat ready to spring. The album cover hadn't lied. Even after all these years, she was sensational.

'Traditional music,' he said, looking into her brown eyes. 'That's interesting, because that's all you do these days, right? You used to write all your own songs, and now you're just performing these traditional folksongs, like you're feeling there's something that old stuff can teach you. Is that this, uh, Matt Castle? His influence?'

'I . . . no . . . No, Matt was a long time ago, when I was in Manchester. He . . . Look, if you don't mind . . .'

He was losing her. He couldn't bear it. He tried to hold her eyes, babbling. 'Manchester? That's the North of England? See, why I find that interesting, this guy was telling us, at the conference this afternoon, how the English are the least significant people – culturally, that is – in these islands. Unlike the Scottish, the Welsh, the Irish, the English are mongrels with no basic ethnic tradition . . .'

She smiled faintly. 'Look, I'm sorry, I—'

'See, this guy, this Irish professor – McGann, McGuane? – he said there was nothing the English could give us. Best they could do is return what they took, but it's soiled goods. At which point this other guy, this writer . . . No, first off it was this Cornish bard, but he didn't make much sense . . . *then*, this writer – Stanton? Stanhope? – he's on his feet, and is he *mad* . . . This guy's face is *white*. I thought he was gonna charge across the room and bust the first guy, the professor, right in the mouth. He's going, Listen, where I come from we got a more pure, undiluted strain of, uh, heritage, tradition . . . than you'll find anywhere in Western Europe. And this guy, this Stanfield, he's from the North . . .'

Moira Cairns said, 'I'm sorry, I really do have to make a phone call.'

And she turned and glided out of the doorway, like the girl in the Irish folksong who went away from this guy and mov'd through the fair.

'. . . the North of England,' the American said to the stag's head.

This wasn't a *new* experience, a woman walking away from

76

him, but it was certainly rare. You blew it, he told himself, surprised.

She could feel him watching her through the doorway, all the way down the passage.

Was he the one?

She took a breath of cool air. The man was a fanatic. Probably one of those rich New Yorkers bankrolling the IRA. Surely there was some other unattached female he could find to sleep with tonight. Why were fanatics always promiscuous?

And was he the one whose examination she could feel all over her skin, like she was being touched up by hands in clinical rubber gloves?

'Phone?' she said to a butler-type person in the marble-tiled hallway.

'Next to the drawing room, madam, I'll take you.'

'Don't bother yourself, I'll find it.'

Dong.

She'd found herself, for no obvious reason, while this smoothie American was trying to come on to her, hearing the name Matt Castle, then saying it out aloud apropos of nothing . . . and then . . .

Dong.

This was the *dong.* The hollow chime. Not the *tink*, not the *ping.*

Aw, hey, no, please . . .

The phone turned out to be in the room where she'd left her guitar, where it would be safe – the black case lying in state, like a coffin, across two Jacobean chairs. Safe here, she'd thought, surely. This is a *castle.* But she'd take it with her when she'd made her call.

She stood in front of the phone, picked it up and put it back a couple of times. She didn't know who to ring.

Malcolm. If in doubt, call Malcolm. She was planning, anyway, to strangle the bastard for tonight. 'You'll enjoy it,' he'd insisted. 'You'll find it absolutely fascinating. Rory's mortified.'

She rang him at home in Dumbarton. 'Malcolm,' she said,

'I may never convince myself to forgive you for this. I may even cast about in the shark-infested waters you inhabit for a new agent.'

He didn't say a word. Had he heard all this before from her? More than once? Was she becoming querulous? Creeping middle age? She felt tired, woozy. She shook herself, straightened her back, raised her voice.

'Listen, there are so-called Celts here not only from Ireland and Wales and Brittany, but from Switzerland and Italy – with Mafia connections, no doubt – and America and some wee place nudging up to Turkey. And they are – to a man, Malcolm – they are a bunch of pretentious, elitist, possibly racist wankers.'

'Racism?' Malcolm said. 'I thought it was about money. EC grants. Minority languages. EC grants. Cultural exchanges. More EC grants . . .'

'Aye, well . . .'

'Is it not a good fee for you?'

'Is it the same fee as Rory's fee would've been?'

'Oh, Moira, come now . . .'

'Forget it. Listen, the real reason I disturbed you on the sabbath . . .'

'Not my sabbath, as it happens.'

'. . . is my answering-machine is on the blink and I suspect someone's trying to get hold of me, and it's no' my daddy because I called him.'

'Nothing urgent I'm aware of, Moira, don't you worry your head.'

'No messages?'

'None at all.' He paused. 'You aren't feeling unwell again, are you?'

'I'm fine.' Her left hand found the guitar case, clutched at it. She had that feeling again, of being touched. She shivered. She felt cold and isolated but also crowded in, under detailed examination. Too many impressions: the hollow chime, the eyes, the touch – impersonal, like a doctor's. Too much, too close. She had to get out of here.

'It's none of my business, of course,' said Malcolm, who

believed in the Agent's Right to Know, 'but what was it exactly that made you think someone wanted to contact you?'

'Just a feeling.'

'Just a *feeling*?'

'Aye,' she said wearily. There was nothing touching her now. The room was static and heavy, no atmosphere. The furniture lumpen, without style. A museum. Nothing here. *Nothing . . .* right?

He said, 'You are a strange, witchy woman, Moira.'

'Malcolm,' Moira said. 'Go fuck yourself, huh?'

From *Dawber's Book of Bridelow*:

RELIGION (i)

BRIDELOW IS DOMINATED by the ancient church dedicated to St Bride and built upon a small rise, thought to be the remains of the 'low' or burial mound from which the village gets the other half of its name.

The tower is largely Norman, with later medieval embellishments, although there was considerable reconstruction work to this and to the main body of the church in the eighteenth and nineteenth centuries. The clock was added to the tower following a donation by the Bridelow Brewery in 1889 and was subsequently illuminated, enhancing the role of the tower as a 'beacon' for travellers lost on Bridelow Moss. The churchyard offers a spectacular view over the Moss and the surrounding countryside, which, to the rear, gives way to a large tract of moorland, uninhabited since prehistoric days.

CHAPTER IV

During evensong, though he still didn't know quite what had happened with Matt, the Rector said a short prayer for the dying landlord of The Man I'th Moss.

Holding on to the lectern, eyes raised to the bent and woven branches of the Autumn Cross, he said carefully, 'Grant him strength, O Lord, and . . . and a peaceful heart.'

Not sure quite what he meant, but he felt it was the right thing to say; you learned to trust your instincts in Bridelow. Sure enough, several members of the congregation looked up at him, conveying tacit approval. Briefly, he felt the warmth of the place again, the warmth he'd always remember, a quite unexpected warmth the first time he'd experienced it.

Unexpected because, from the outside, the church had such a forbidding, fortress-like appearance, especially from a distance, viewed from the road which traversed the Moss. He remembered his first sight of the building, close on thirty years ago. Not inspiring, in those days, for a novice minister: hard and grey-black with too many spiky bits and growling gargoyles. And Our Sheila perpetually playing with herself over the porch.

This was the 1960s, when what a young clergyman dreamed of was a bright, modern church with a flat roof and abstract stained-glass (after ten years, it would look like a lavatory block, but in the sixties one imagined things could only get better and better).

'Amen,' the congregation said as one. The old schoolmaster, Ernest Dawber, glanced up at the Rector and gave him a quick, sad smile.

The warmth.

Sometimes it had seemed as if the church walls themselves were heating up under the pale amber of the lights – they were old gas-mantles converted to electricity, like the scattered streetlamps outside. And at Christmas and other festivals, it felt as though the great squat pillars either side of the nave had become giant radiator pipes.

But the warmth was rarely as apparent now. The Rector wondered if it would even be noticeable any more to a newcomer. Perhaps not. He'd gone to the expense of ordering more oil for the boiler and increasing the heat level. Knowing, all the same, as he went through the motions, that it couldn't be that simple.

There'd been a draught in the pulpit today; he certainly hadn't known that here before. The draught was needle-thin but it wasn't his imagination because, every so often, the Autumn Cross would sway a little over his head, rustling.

It rustled now, as he read out the parish notices, and something touched his hair, startling him. When he reached up, his fingers found a dead leaf. It crackled slightly, reminding him of the furious flurry of leaves blasted against his study window at dusk, like an admonishment: *you must not watch us . . . you must turn your face away*.

A strikingly cold autumn. October frost, nearly all the trees gone bare. His arthritis playing up.

Giving him a hard time tonight. Difficult keeping his mind on the job, wanting only to get it over and limp back to his study – even though, since Judy's death, this had become the loneliest place of all.

'. . . and on Wednesday evening, there'll be a meeting of the morrismen in the Function Room at The Man, that's 7.30 . . .'

The congregation numbered close on seventy tonight, not a bad turnout. A few regular faces missing, including several members of the committee of the Mothers' Union, but that wasn't too surprising, they'd been here this morning. Couldn't expect anyone to attend twice, even the Mothers.

He rounded off the service with a final hymn, accompanied as usual by Alfred Beckett on the harmonium – a primitive, reedy sound, but homely; there'd never been an organ in Bridelow Church, despite its size.

'Well done, lad,' Ernie Dawber said at the church door, patting his shoulder. 'Keep thi chin up.' Fifteen years his senior, Bridelow born and bred, Ernie Dawber had always called him 'lad'. When the Rector had first arrived, he'd expected a few problems over his name. It had still seemed too close to the War for the locals not to be dubious about a new minister called . . .

'. . . Hans Gruber,' the schoolmaster had repeated slowly, rolling it round his mouth like a boiled sweet.

'Yes.'

'That's German, isn't it?'

Hans had nodded. 'But I was actually born near Leighton Buzzard.'

Ernie Dawber had narrowed his eyes, giving the new minister a *very* hard look. 'Word of advice, lad. Keep quiet about that, I should. Thing is . . .' Glancing from side to side. '. . . there's a few folks round here who're not that keen on . . .' dropping his voice, '. . . southerners.'

The Rector said now, thinking of his lonely study, 'Come back for a glass, Ernie?'

'I don't think so, lad.' Ernie Dawber pulled on his hat. 'Not tonight.'

'I'll never forgive you for this.'

He was gripping the stiffened edge of the sheet like a prisoner clutching at the bars of his cell, his final appeal turned down.

'We should never have let you go home, Mr Castle,' the nursing sister said.

'Matt, please . . .' Lottie put her cool hand over his yellowed claw. 'Don't say that . . .'

'You never listen.' Feebly shaking his head, inconsolable.

All the way here in the ambulance, Lottie holding his hand, he'd been silent, away somewhere, still on the Moss perhaps.

His eyes shone with the tears that wouldn't come, no moisture left in his body.

The nurse said, 'I think he should have some sleep, don't you, Mrs Castle?'

'Sleep?' Matt was bleakly contemptuous. 'No real sleep in here. Comes out of the bloody . . . drug cabinet . . . only sort of sleep you can get in here.' He looked past the nurse. 'Where's Dic?'

'I told you, Matt,' Lottie said gently. 'He wouldn't come in. He's too confused. He's probably walking round the grounds, walking it off. He'll come in tomorrow, when he's . . .'

'Might be too late, tomorrow.'

Lottie smiled at him. 'Don't be soft.' There was a small commotion behind her, a nurse and a young porter putting screens around a bed opposite Matt's.

'Another one gone,' Matt grunted.

'Bath-time, that's all,' the nurse said unconvincingly.

'Give you any old crap in here. Look, tell Dic . . .' His faltering voice forming words as dry and frail as an ancient cobweb. '. . . Tell him, he can be in the band. If he wants to. When . . . when Moira comes, he can play. But you won't, will you? You never do owt I say.'

'You tell him,' Lottie said. 'Tell him when you see him in the morning.'

Matt Castle made no reply. He seemed too dehydrated to sweat or to weep. It was as though somebody had talcumed his face, like a . . .

Lottie swallowed hard.

'Useless . . . bitch.'

Matt fell asleep.

Shrivelled leaves, unseen, chattered on the window-pane.

The dead leaves said, *Go away, draw the curtains, put on the light.*

It's not your affair, the dead leaves said.

The Rector didn't move, just as he hadn't moved in the late afternoon, at dusk, when the warning flurry had hit the pane, as if flung.

At the top end, the vicarage garden almost vanished into the moor. When the light faded, the low stone wall between them dissolved into shadow and the garden and the moor became one. On the other side of the wall was a public footpath; it was along this they came, and sometimes, over the years, around dusk, the Rector had seen them, had made himself watch them.

Tonight, resting up before evening service, sitting in the window of the darkening study, wedged into a hard chair, his swollen foot on the piano stool, he'd watched three of them enter the churchyard from the footpath, passing through the wooden wicket gate. They were black, shapeless, hooded and silent. A crescent moon had wavered behind smoky cloud.

It was all over, though, as was usual, when he walked out across his garden, through the gate and into the churchyard half an hour before the evening service.

Now he was back in his study, listening to the leaves with the lights out. All he could see through the window was the reflection of two bars of the ineffectual electric fire. When Judy, his wife, was alive there'd been a coal fire in the study every night from the end of September until the end of April.

The Rector was cold. Eleven years now since Judy's death.

Where had all the warmth gone, the warmth which before had only increased with the drawing-in of the days? Where had the smiles gone, the smiles which lit the eyes while the mouths stayed firm?

And why, for that matter, had Ma Wagstaff's herbal preparation had so little effect this time on his arthritis?

He stood up, hobbled close to the window, cupped his hands to the pane and peered through.

At the garden's edge, a few graves lurched giddily on the slope, and then the church loomed like an enormous black beast. Lately, Hans Gruber had been wondering if life would not have been a good deal simpler in one of those modern churches, where one's main headache was glue-sniffing behind the vestry. Us and Them. Good and evil. God and Satan.

Hans thought, Wouldn't that be wonderful?

After his wife had left, they'd wheeled Mr Castle's bed into a side ward where, unless anyone was brought in suddenly, he'd be alone, until . . .

'Until morning,' the young nurse whispered, reassuring herself.

Mr Castle was sleeping. She was glad; she was still afraid of people who were dying, who were in the actual process of it. She wasn't yet sure how to talk to them, how to *look* at them. And the awful suspense – what it would be like, the atmosphere in this small, comparatively quiet space, in the moment, the very second when *it* happened.

She was never going to get used to this. She was supposed to comfort the dying, but more often than not it was the dying who comforted her – old ladies, all skin and bone and no hair, patting her hand, one actually saying, *Don't worry, luv, I won't keep you long*.

Less bothered, it often seemed, than she was. Sometimes it was like they were just waiting for a bus.

She sat at the desk by the door, under the angled, metal-shaded lamp, the only light in the room. There were four beds on the side ward, three of them empty. It was the only part of this hospital where you could usually count on finding a couple of spare beds, it being the place where terminal patients were often brought in the final stages so they wouldn't distress other patients who were not quite so terminal.

Tamsin, the other nurse, a year or two older, was out on the main ward. Sister Murtry would pop in occasionally, see they were all right.

Sister Murtry had been very firm with Mrs Castle, who was a tall, strong-looking woman – only Sister Murtry would have dared. 'Come on now, he needs his sleep and you need yours.' . . . Mr Castle waking up suddenly and chuckling in a ghastly, strangled way when she said *he* needed sleep.

(She looked across now at his face on the pillow; his skin

was like cold, lumpy, wrinkled custard. He wasn't so very old: fifty-seven, it said on his chart, not even elderly.)

'Will you be sure to . . .' Mrs Castle had been in the doorway. Sister Murtry's hands on her shoulders, pushing her out.

'Yes, I'll ring you myself if there's any change. But there probably won't be, you know . . . Just go and get your sleep, or we'll be seeing you in here too . . .'

She imagined Mrs Castle lying wide awake in a cold double bed, waiting for the phone to ring. The wind howling outside – they lived up by Bridelow Moor, didn't they? The wind always howled up there.

He was quite a famous man, Mr Castle. There'd been dozens of Get Well cards when he was in last year for tests and things. Dr Smethwick, the registrar, who was a folk music fan, had been thrilled to bits to have him in. 'Pioneer of the Pennine Pipes,' she remembered him saying, and Dr Burt had said, dry as a stick, 'Oh, he works for the Water Authority, does he?' And she'd rushed out, scared to giggle because she was still a student then, and Dr Smethwick was senior to Dr Burt.

Dr Smethwick had moved on, to a better job in Liverpool. Now there was nobody left who knew anything about Mr Castle or the Pennine Pipes. All he had tonight was her, and she was afraid of him because he was dying.

She wondered how many folk had died here, in this small space, over the years. Passed away, they still preferred you to say that to the relatives. She said it to herself.

Passssed . . . awayyyy. Soft, like a breath of air.

She jumped. Mr Castle had released a breath of air, but it wasn't soft. It was . . . *phtttt* . . . like a cork popping out of a bottle or like a quiet fart (one of the regular noises of the night here).

'Mr Castle . . . ?' Whispering, rising rapidly to her feet with a rustle of the uniform, bumping her head on the edge of the metal lampshade.

'All right, Mr Castle . . . Matt.' A hairgrip, dislodged by the lamp, fell to the desk, she felt her hair coming loose at the back. 'I'm here.'

But when she reached the bedside he was breathing normally again – well, not *normal* normal, but normal for a man who . . . for a man in his condition.

Holding her hair in place with one hand, the grip in her teeth, she went into the main ward to collect her mirror from her bag.

Plenty breathing out here, and snoring, and a few small moans, everything hospital-normal. Up the far end of the ward, Tamsin was bending over Miss Wately's bed, Miss Wately the retired headmistress who wouldn't be called by her first name, which was Eunice. Tamsin straightened up, saw her and raised a hand to her lips, tilting her head back as if the hand held a cup.

She nodded and smiled and pointed over her shoulder to the side ward, and Tamsin nodded and held up five fingers.

'Ger . . . yer owd bugger . . .' an old man rasped in his sleep. It was supposed to be a mixed ward but because of the attitude of patients like Miss Wately, the men tended to be at one end and the women at the other. Best, really, at their age. No kimono-style dressing-gowns and baby-doll nighties on this ward.

She found the mirror, slipped it into her pocket, went back into the side ward and sat down, her eyes moving instinctively from bed to bed, four beds, all empty.

'Moira?'

All *empty*.

'Oh!' She spun round, her hair unravelling down below her shoulders.

He said, 'You've come then, eh?'

God help us, he was hanging over her . . . like bones in pyjamas.

'Mr Ca—'

What was holding him up? She'd seen his legs, his muscles all wasted, gone to jelly. Been in a wheelchair weeks and weeks, they'd said to watch him, he might even die in the night, and here he was *standing up*, oh God, his lips all pulled back and frozen into a ric-rictus?

'Tam . . .' trying to shout for the other nurse, but her voice was so dry the name just dropped out of her mouth like a piece of chewing gum '. . . sin.' Hardly heard herself.

His eyes were far back in his head, black marbles, like the eyes had already died.

Then one of his hands reached out, it was all shrivelled and rigid, like a chicken's foot, and he started . . . he started playing with her hair, pulling it down and fingering it, looking down at it in his fingers, mumbling, *Moira . . . Moira.*

Eventually she managed to say, 'I'm not your wife, Mr . . . Mr Castle . . .'

But remembered Sister Murtry saying, 'Her name's Charlotte, I think.' And then, later, 'Come on, Charlotte, let's be having you, can't stay here all night. Not good for either of you.'

She couldn't move. The metal bars on the bedheads made hard shadows on the walls, the little ward was like a cage. If only Sister Murtry would come now, bustling in, short and dynamic. Nobody Sister Murtry couldn't handle.

Oh, God, this was the wrong job, she hated dying people, their stretched skin, their awful smell, especially this one – the damp stench of ripe, putrid earth (the grave?). She began to shiver and tried to stand up, drawing back, away from him, but there was nowhere to go, her bottom was pressed into the edge of the desk, and Mr Castle was still hanging over her like a skeleton in a rotting sack and smelling of wet earth.

How could he smell of earth, of *outside*?

'Tam . . . sin . . .' Her scream was a whisper, but her mouth was stretched wide as his greenish chickenfoot hand whipped out and seized her throat.

CHAPTER V

CENTRAL SCOTLAND

The scuffed sixteen-year-old Ovation guitar, with its fibreglass curves, was a comfort. Its face reflected the great fire blazing on the baronial hearth.

'Ladies of noble birth . . .' Adjusting the microphone. 'In those days, they didn't have too much of a say in it, when it came to husbands. This is . . .' thumbing an A-minor, tweaking the top string up a fraction, '. . . this is the story of a woman who's found herself betrothed to a titled guy much younger than she is. However . . .' gliding over a C, 'I doubt if we're talking toy-boys, as we know them. This is like . . . nine or ten, right?'

Tuning OK. 'I mean, you know, there's a limit to the things you can get from a boy of nine or ten.'

No reaction. You bastard, Malcolm. And you, Rory McBain – one day you really will be sick.

'Anyway, she's stuck with this kid. And she's standing on the castle walls, watching him playing down below, working out the dispiriting mathematics of the situation and wondering if . . .'

Shuffling on the stool, tossing back the black wings of her hair, the weight of it down her back pulling her upright so that she could see the audience and the gleaming stag skulls all around. The walls of neatly dressed stone, with spotlit banners and tapestries. The black eye-holes in the skulls, and the eyes of the conference delegates looking, from five or so yards away, just as opaque and unmoving.

'Anyway, don't expect a happy ending, OK? This is a traditional song. You don't get many happy endings in traditional songs. It's called . . . "Lang a-growin'".'

The bastard McBain would have handled this better. For the sake of ethnic credibility, he'd do a couple of songs in the Gaelic, of which he understood scarcely a word. What *she* had these days was a different kind of credibility: sophistication, fancy nightclub ethnic, low and sultry vocals, folk tunes with a touch of jazz guitar, strictly rationed to what she could handle without fracturing a fingernail.

'He's young . . .' Hearing her own voice drifting vacuously in the air, the words like cigarette smoke. '. . . but he's daily . . . growin' . . .'

Over an hour ago, she'd called Lottie's number. A guy answered, obviously not the boy, Dic. The guy'd said Lottie was at the hospital in Manchester. Muffled voices in the background – this was a pub, right? She'd asked no more questions. She'd call back.

The hospital. In Manchester. Oh, hell.

The Great Hall was huge, the acoustics lousy. When the song was over, applause went pop-pop-pop like a battery of distant shotguns. The stags' heads gathered grimly below the ceiling, so many that the antlers looked to be tangled up. 'Splendid,' she heard the Earl call out magnanimously. How many wee staggies did you pop yourself, my lord, your grace, whatever? Maybe you invited members of the Royal Family to assist. Traditional, right?

Moira did a bit of fine tuning on the guitar. She was wearing the black dress and the cameo brooch containing the stained plaid fragment that was reputed to have been recovered from a corpse at Culloden. Credibility.

'This song . . . You may not know the title, most of you, but the tune could be slightly familiar. It's . . . the lament of a girl whose man's gone missing at sea and she waits on the shore accosting all the homecoming fishermen as they reach land. The song's called "Cam Ye O'er Frae Campbelltoon". It's, er . . . it's traditional.'

Traditional my arse. Me and Kenny Savage wrote it, still half-pissed, at a party in Kenny's flat in 1982 – like, Hey, I know . . . how about we invent a totally traditional Celtic lament . . .

She told them, the assembled Celts, 'The chorus is very simple . . . so feel free to join in . . .'

And, by Christ, they *did* join in. Probably with tears in their eyes. All these Scots and Irish and Welsh and Bretons and the folk from the wee place up against Turkey . . . writers and poets and politicians united in harmony with a phoney chorus composed amidst empty Yugoslav Riesling bottles at the fag end of Kenny Savage's Decree Absolute party in dawn-streaked Stranraer.

What a sham, eh? I mean, what am I *doing* here?

And Matt Castle dying.

Tears in her own eyes now. Last year he'd told her on the phone that he'd be OK, the tests had shown it wasn't malignant. And she'd believed him; so much for intuition.

The damn tears would be glinting in the soft spotlight they'd put on her, and the Celtic horde out there, maudlin with malt, would think she was weeping for the girl on the shore at Stranraer – and weeping also, naturally, for the plight of Scotland and for the oldest race in Europe trampled into the mud of ages.

'Thank you,' she said graciously, as they applauded not so much her as themselves, a confusion of racial pride with communal self-pity.

And that makes it nine songs, over an hour gone, coming up to 10.30. Time to wind this thing up, yeh? Lifting the guitar strap out of her hair. Let's get the hell out of here.

At which point someone called out smoothly, 'Would it be in order to request an encore?'

She tried to smile.

'Maybe you could play "The Comb Song"?'

It was him. It would have to be. The New York supplier of Semtex money to the IRA.

'Aw, that's just a kiddies' song.' Standing up, the guitar-strap half-off.

'Well, I don't know about the other people here,' the voice said – and it was *not* the American, 'but it's the song I most associate with you, and I was rather disappointed not to hear it.'

'Oh, hell, it's a good long time ago, I don't think I even remember the words . . .' Who the fuck was this?

'If you go wrong, I'm sure we could help you out.' She couldn't make out his face behind the spotlight. She looked up, in search of inspiration, but her gaze got entangled in antlers.

'Also,' she said miserably, 'it isn't exactly traditional. And it's awful long. See, I don't want to bore your friends here . . .'

'Miss Cairns . . .' The Earl himself took a step towards the dais, into the spotlight, the light making tiny dollar-signs in his eyes. 'I doubt if any of us could *possibly* be bored by any of your songs.' A touch of threat under the mellifluousness? Some flunkey had replaced the empty Guinness glass by her stool with a full one. She picked it up, put it down again without drinking. There were murmurings.

What the hell am I going to do now? She felt their stares, the more charitable ones maybe wondering if she was ill. Aw, *shit . . .*

What she didn't feel any more were the eyes of the Watcher. This had maybe been a mistake. Sometimes you made mistakes. It probably had been the American and it probably was no heavier than lust.

'I warn you,' Moira said, as the Ovation's strap sank back into her shoulder, 'this is the longest song I ever wrote.'

And to the accompaniment of a thin cheer from the floor her fingers found the chord, and she sang the rather clumsy opening lines. Trying not to think about it, trying to board up her mind against all those heavyweight memories tramping up the stairs.

> *Her father works with papers and with plans,*
> *Her mother sees the world from caravans . . .*

The song telling the story of this shy, drab child growing up in the suburbs of a staid Clydeside town with the ever-present feeling that she's in the wrong place, that she really ought to be some other person. Bad times at school, no friends. Brought up at home by the grandmother, restrictive, old-fashioned Presbyterian.

> *I wish to God you hadna been born,*
> *Your hair's a mess, get it shorn,*
> *Get it shorn . . .*

Then the song becoming a touch obscure – one night, around the time of her adolescence, the child seems to be in this dark wood, when the moon breaks through the clouds and the trees, and she finds she's holding . . . this curious, ancient comb. It's a wonderful magic comb and apparently is the key to the alternative reality which for all these years has been denied to her. She runs it through her hair and becomes electrified, metamorphoses into some kind of beautiful princess. Fairytale stuff.

> *. . . She sees herself in colours and*
> *She weighs her powers in her hand . . .*

Dead silence out there. She had them. Oh, it had its magic, this bloody song which intelligent people were supposed to think was all allegorical and the comb a metaphor for the great Celtic heritage. Most likely this was how the American saw it, and the other guy who'd demanded the song.

A bastard to write, the words wouldn't hang together – sign of a song that didn't want to be written.

The song knew from the start: some things are too personal. Chorus:

> *Never let them cut your hair*
> *Or tell you where*
> *You've been,*
> *Or where you're going to*
> *From here . . .*

Couple of twiddly bits which, after all these years, she fluffed. Then dropping down to minor key for the main reason she hadn't wanted to perform this number, the creepy stuff, the heavy stuff.

> *And in the chamber of the dead*
> *Forgotten voices fill your head . . .*

Sure, there they are . . . tinny little voices, high-pitched, fragmented chattering, like a cheap transistor radio with its battery dying. Tune it in, tune it in.

Who is this? Who is it?

No.

No, no, NO!!!!!!!!!!!!!!!!!!

Oh, shit, please, don't die, Matt, don't die on me now . . . you have no *right* . . .

Singing on, through her wild tears, an awed silence in the room like a giant cavern, hall of ages, caged in bones. You think you know this song, these words, Mr New York Irishman . . . ?

> *. . . for the night is growing colder*
> *and you feel it at your shoulder . . .*

Icy-bright singing now, purged of that phoney, Guinnessy growl. One or two women out there shivering and reaching for their cardigans. The song rippling across the night sky, down the dark years, and you're watching its wavering passage from a different level, like an air traffic controller in a tower late at night. Something flying out to meet it, on a collision course.

> *Give up, you fool, there is no heat.*
> *The Abyss opens up beneath your feet . . .*

Here he is again, uncertainly into the spotlight, looking around. Hello again, Earl, something wrong is there, my lord, your grace . . . ? Is it cold for you in here? Will you get some servant to turn up the heating, throw more peat on the fire? And all the while, will you listen to these wee voices, chattering, chattering, chattering . . .

> *The comb is ice, it's brittle, oh,*
> *You cannot hold it, must let go . . .*

Yes, let it go. It's a trinket, it's worthless, it takes your energy. Let it drift. Let the night have it. Let . . .

These – Christ – these are not my words. These are somebody else's words.

I'm singing somebody else's goddamn words!

And the comb is being pulled away now in a deceptively soft silver haze, gently at first, just a tug. Then insistent, irritable – *let it come, you bitch* – and slender hands, slender like wires, scalpelling into her breast. Feeling delicately – but brutally and coldly, like a pathologist at an autopsy – for her emotional core, for the centre of her.

somebody . . .

In a frenzy, she's letting go of the song, she's groping wildly at the air, feeling her spirit straining in her body as the big lights come on, huge shimmering chandeliers.

Moira has fallen down from the stool.

She's lying twisted and squirming on the carpeted dais, both arms wrapped around the guitar. From miles away, people are screaming, or is it *her* screaming at *them* . . . Stop it! Catch it! Don't let it go from here! Help me! Help me!

She can hear them coming to help her, the army of her fellow-Celts. But they can't get through.

They can't get through the walls of bone.

The walls of jiggling, swelling bone. Not just the skulls any more; the plaster's fallen from the walls and the walls are walls of bone, whole skeletons interlocking, creaking and twisting and the jaws of the skulls opening and closing, grisly grins and a clacking laughter of teeth, right up against her face. She's trapped, like a beating, bloody heart inside a rib-cage.

She sees the comb and all it represents spinning away until it's nothing but a hairline crack of silver-blue. She watches it go like a mother who sees her baby toddling out of the garden gate into the dust spurting from the wheels of an oncoming articulated lorry.

Mammy!

But you can't hear me, can you, mammy? The connection's broken.

I'm on my own.

But no.

There is a man.

A tall, thin man, with a face so white it might be the face of some supernatural being.

No, this is a real man. He's wearing an evening suit, a bow-tie. He has a small voluptuous mouth and an expanse of white forehead marked with greyish freckles, and the white hair ripples back from the forehead; not receding, it has always been that way. She ought to know him; he knows *her*.

And where she keeps the comb.

This person, unnoticed in the hubbub by everyone but her, is lifting the black guitar case from the steps of the dais and examining it to see how it opens. He looks at her, furiously impatient, and the air between them splinters like ice and when she tries to see into his eyes, and they are not there, only the black sockets in a face as white as any of the skulls.

Their eyes meet at last. His have projected into the sockets from somewhere. They are light grey eyes. And there's a whiteness around him, growing into arms like tree-branches above his head. No, not arms, not branches.

Antlers.

*

95

Moira shrieked, flinging the guitar away from her. It made a mangled minor chord as it rolled down the steps of the dais. She threw herself after it, headlong into the glass-spattered Guinness-sodden tartan carpet, clawing at the pair of shiny, elegant evening shoes, the air at first full of swirling, unfocused energy.

And then, for a moment, everything was still.

Most of those in the room were still seated at their tables, with drinks in front of them, the men and women in their evening wear, white shirts and black bow-ties, jewellery and silk and satin. The American half out of his seat, dark Irish hair tumbling on to his forehead. The Earl on his feet; his expression . . . dismay turning to disgust: was this woman having a *fit*? In his castle?

Everybody shimmering with movement, but nobody going anywhere.

Projector-jam.

Until the first skull fell.

It was possibly the smallest of them, so comparatively insignificant that Moira wondered briefly why anyone would have admitted to having shot it, let alone wanted to display it. She watched it happen, saw the antlers just lean forward, as if it was bowing its head, and then the wooden shield it was mounted on splintered and the poor bleached exhibit crashed seven or eight feet on to a table, crystal glasses flying into the air around it.

'God almighty!' a man blurted.

The white, eyeless head toppled neatly from the table into the lap of a woman in a wine-coloured evening dress, the antlers suddenly seeming to be sprouting from her ample Celtic cleavage.

For a whole second, the woman just looked at it, as though it was some kind of novelty, like a big, fluffy bunny popped on her knees by an admirer at a party. Her glossy red lips split apart into what appeared for an instant to be an expression of pure delight.

It was this older woman next to her, whose ornate, red-brown coiffure had been speared by an antler, she was the one who screamed first.

More of an escalating gurgle actually. Both women jerking to their feet in quaking revulsion, clutching at one another, chairs flying . . .

. . . as, with a series of sickening ripping sounds, several other skulls cracked themselves from the walls, all at once . . .

('*Look!*' Some guy grabbing the Earl by the shoulders, shaking him.)

. . . and began to descend in, like, slow motion, some so old they fell apart in the air and came down in pieces.

Moira's audience in cowering disarray. 'Stop this!' the Earl commanding irrationally, limbs jerking in spasms, semaphoring incomprehensible fear, like a spider caught in its own web. 'Stop it! Stop it *at once!*'

This tumultuous rending and creaking from all the walls. Even the great fire looking cowed, burning back, low and smoky as though someone had thrown muffling peat at it.

Next to the fireplace, this severe and heavy lady – a matriarch of Welsh-language television, it was said – just sitting there blinking, confused because her spectacles had been torn off and then trodden on by a flailing bearded man, some distinguished professor of Celtic Studies, eyes full of broken glass, one cheek gashed by a blade of bone.

And, pulling her gaze away from this carnage, in the choking maw of the great fireplace Moira thought she saw a face . . . so grey it could only have been formed from smoke. The face swirled; two thrashing arms of smoke came out into the room, as if reaching for her.

Moira whispered faintly, 'Matt?' But it was smoke, only smoke.

The butler guy weaving about helplessly in the great doorway as the stag skulls fell and fell, this roaring, spitting avalanche of white bone and splattering glass, battered heads and scored skin, people yelping, moaning, hurling themselves under collapsing tables, craving shelter from the bone-storm.

She caught the black guitar case as it fell towards her. Caught it in her arms.

Come to mammy.

She sat bewildered on the bottom step of the dais, in the refrigerated air, in the absurdly shocking mess of glass and antlers.

I have to be leaving, she thought.

Hands on her shoulders. 'You OK? Moira, for Chrissake . . . ?'

'Get the fuck off me!'

But it was only the American, Mr Semtex.

'Please . . . You OK? Here, let me take that . . .'

'No! Let it alone, will you?'

She saw the white-faced man on his knees, not six feet away. He was holding one of the skulls, a big skull, one antler snapped off halfway, ending in a savage point, a dagger of bone. There was blood on the point.

And blood welling slowly out of his left eye, blood and mucus, a black pool around the eye.

The other eye was very pale, grey going on pink. He was staring at her out of it.

Moira clutched the guitar case defiantly to her throbbing breast.

'Just hang on in there, pal,' the American said to the white-faced man. 'We're gonna get you a doctor.'

Ignoring the American, the man with the injured eye said (and later the American would swear to her that he hadn't heard this, that the guy was too messed up to speak at all) . . .

The man said, very calm, very urbane, 'Don't think, Miss Cairns, that this is anything but the beginning.'

CHAPTER VI

In Matt Castle's band, Willie Wagstaff had played various hand-drums – bongo-type things and what the Irish called the *bodhran*, although Matt would never call it that; to him it was all *Pennine* percussion.

This morning, without some kind of drum under his hands, Willie looked vaguely disabled, both sets of fingers tapping nervously at his knees, creating complex, silent rhythms.

Lottie smiled wanly down at him. They were sitting on wooden stools at either end of the kitchen stove, for warmth.

'Can you finish it, Willie? Can it be done?'

Willie looked up at her through his lank, brown fringe, like a mouse emerging from a hole in the wall. Lukewarm autumn sunbeams danced with the dust in the big kitchen behind the public bar. Such a lot of dust. She'd been neglecting the cleaning, like everything else, since Matt had been bad. Now it was over. Dust to dust.

Willie said, 'We got two or three instrumental tracks down, y'know. The lament. It all got a bit, like . . . half-hearted, as you can imagine. Me and Eric, we could see it weren't going to get finished. Not wi' Matt, anyroad.'

'I want it finished,' Lottie said crisply. 'It was his last . . . I'm not going to use the word obsession, I've said it too much.' She hesitated. '. . . I'm not religious, Willie, you know that, not in any . . . any respect.'

Willie gave three or four nods, his chin keeping time with the fingers on his knees.

'But I just feel that he won't be at peace . . . that it won't be over . . . until that music's finished.'

'Aye.' Willie's fingers didn't stop. Nerves.

'So what about Dic?' Lottie said.

'Will Dic want to do it?'

Lottie said grimly, 'He'll do it. Is he good enough?'

'Oh, aye,' Willie said without much difficulty. 'I reckon he is. With a bit of practice, like. But really, like, what we could do with is . . .' He beat his knees harder to help him get it out. '. . . Moira.'

'She rang me,' Lottie said. 'Last night.'

Willie's eyes lit up, expectant. Dear God, Lottie thought, they're all in love with her.

'Actually, it was early this morning. I mean very early. Gone midnight. The kind of time people don't ring up unless it's an emergency.'

'Oh,' Willie said, and his hands were suddenly still.

'She asked me about Matt. She said, was he ill? I told her, yes, he was very ill. I told her it was close to the end. I told her . . .' Lottie stood up and put her hands on the warm metal covers over the hot-plates of the kitchen stove, pressing down with both hands, hard. 'I didn't *need* to tell her.'

Willie was quiet.

'We didn't say much. She started to explain why she'd put him off when he wrote to her. I stopped her. I said we'd discuss it some other time.'

There was a new kind of silence in the room.

'I put the phone down,' Lottie said. 'It was about twenty-five past twelve. I waited for a minute or two, in case Dic had heard the phone, but he was fast asleep. I thought, I'll make some cocoa, take it up with me. But I didn't move. I knew. I mean, why should she suddenly ring after all these years at that time of night? And sure enough, not five minutes had passed and the phone rang again, and it was Sister Murtry at the hospital. And I just said, He's gone, hasn't he?'

There was more silence, then Lottie said, 'I've not slept since. I've just sent Dic to bed for a few hours. I'm not tired, Willie. I'm not using up any energy – not thinking, you know?'

Lottie sat down again. 'I shan't be staying here. Only until it's done. His *bloody* project. I think coming back here, buying the pub, the whole bit, that was all part of it. The project. All I want is to draw a line under it, do you see? I mean, I hope somebody'll buy the pub, somebody sympathetic, but if not . . .' She shrugged. 'Well, I've got to get away, regardless.'

Willie nodded. Fingers starting up very slowly. 'Um . . . what about Moira?'

'I'm not inviting her to the funeral, that's for sure.' Lottie folded her arms, making a barrier. 'If she wants to help complete these songs, that'd be . . . I'll not be *begging*. No more of that. And another thing, Willie – tell whoever needs to be told, tell them I'm not having anything to do with these stupid . . . traditions. You know what I'm saying? Matt might've accepted it, I don't. All right?'

'Aye, all right,' Willie said, not sounding too happy. But that was *his* problem, Lottie thought. 'Yeh,' he said. 'I'll tell her.'

When Willie had gone, Lottie pushed her hands on to the hot-plate covers again, seeking an intensity of heat, needing to feel something. Something beyond this anaesthetized numbness.

Wanting pain – simple pain. Loss. Sorrow.

Not any of this confusion over the gratitude that he was gone and the wanting him back . . . but back as he used to be, before all this. Before his *project*.

A blinding sun through leafless trees ricocheted from the windscreens of cars on the forecourt. A perky breeze ruffled the flags projecting from the motel's awning and lifted tufts of Chrissie's auburn hair. She thought she probably looked quite good, all things considered.

That, she told herself, was what a good night's sleep could do for you.

Ha!

Roger Hall paused, gripping the door-handle of his Volvo Estate. Don't say it, Chrissie thought. Just don't give me that, *I still can't understand it, this has never happened to me before* . . .

He didn't. He merely put on an upside-down, pathetic grin. 'Can we try again sometime?' Eyes crinkled appealingly, full of silly morning optimism, and she felt herself falling for it – even if she knew he still wasn't telling the half of it.

'Why not,' she said, daft bitch. She squeezed his arm. 'How long will you be gone?'

'Oh, only until Tuesday. That is, I'll be back late tonight so I'll see you tomorrow morning. Have lunch together, shall we? Would that be . . . ?'

'Of course,' she said. She would have wangled the day off and gone to London with him. They'd been too close to the Field Centre last night, that was probably the problem. Too close to *him*.

'I'm really only going down there,' Roger said, 'to make sure we get all the stomach returned. Don't want them trying to pinch him back, bit by bit.'

Shut up! Just shut up about that fucking thing!

'Don't worry about it, Roger. Just drive carefully.'

As the Volvo slid away past the Exit Southbound sign, two commercial traveller types came out to their twin Cavaliers and gave her the once-over. Chrissie found herself smiling almost warmly at the younger one. It would be two years in January since her divorce.

She got into her Golf. She looked at her face in the driving-mirror and decided it could probably take a couple more years of this sort of thing before she ought to start looking for something . . . well, perhaps *semi*-permanent.

Sadly, Roger's marriage was now in no danger whatsoever. Not from her, anyway.

All the trouble he'd gone to to deceive his wife. Was that for her? Was that really all for her? And then he couldn't do it. Because of 'tension'.

She imagined him driving like the clappers to London, where he was supposed to have spent the night, and then driving determinedly back with the bogman's peaty giblets in a metal samples case.

There was his real love. And there was more to it.

After the way he'd been talking last night, she'd half-expected to wake up in the early hours to find him all wet and clammy and moaning in his sleep about lumps of the stuff in the bed.

But that hadn't happened either. Indeed, the only thing to remind her of soft, clammy peat was the consistency of Roger's dick.

Chrissie got out of the motel compound by the service entrance and drove to work.

Not to worry.

Later that morning, little Willie Wagstaff went to see his mother in her end-of-terrace cottage across from the post office.

'Need to find a job now, then,' the old girl said sternly before he'd even managed to clear himself a space on the settee. Ma was practical; no time for sentiment. Dead was dead. Matt Castle was dead; no living for Willie playing the drums on his own.

'Can't do owt yet,' Willie said. ''Sides, there's no work about.'

'Always work,' said Ma, 'for them as has a mind to find it.'

Willie grinned. Rather than see him relax for a while, Ma would have him commuting to Huddersfield or Chorlton-cum-Hardy to clean lavatories or sweep the streets.

'Devil makes work for idle hands,' she said. Her as ought to know – half the village reckoned she'd been in league with the bugger for years.

'Aye, well, I've been over to see Lottie this morning.'

'Oh aye? Relieved, was she? Looking better?'

'Ma!'

'Grief's one thing, our Willie, hypocrisy's summat else. She's done her grieving, that one.'

'I've to tell you . . .' Willie's fingers were off . . . dum, dum de-dum, side of his knees.

Ma's eyes narrowed. Her hair was tied up in a bun with half a knitting-needle shoved up it.

'Er . . .' Dum, dum, dum-di-di, dum-di-di . . .

'Gerrit out!' Ma squawked.

'No messing about,' Willie mumbled quickly. 'Lottie says, none of that.'

'What's that mean?' Making him say it.

'Well, like . . . well, naturally he'll be buried in t'church-yard. First one. First one since . . .' His fingers finding a different, more complicated rhythm. 'What I'm saying, Ma, is, do we *have* to . . . ? Does it have to be Matt?'

Ma scowled. She had a face like an over-ripe quince. She wore an old brown knee-length cardigan over a blue boiler-suit, her working clothes. The two cats, one black, one white, sat side-by-side on the hearth, still as china. Bob and Jim. Willie reckoned they must be the fourth or fifth generation of Ma's cats called Bob and Jim, and all females.

Willie liked his mother's cottage. Nothing changed. Bottles of stuff everywhere. On the table an evil-looking root was rotting inside a glass jar, producing a fluid as thick as Castrol. Comfrey – known as knitbone. And if it didn't knit your bones at least it'd stop your back gate from squeaking.

'Rector come round,' Ma told him. 'Said was I sure I'd given him right stuff for his arthritis.'

'Bloody hell,' said Willie. 'Chancing his arm there.'

'No, he were right,' said Ma surprisingly. 'It's not working. Never happened before, that hasn't. Never not worked, that arthritis mixture. Leastways, it's always done *summat*.'

She reached down to the hearth, picked up an old brown medicine bottle with a cork in it; Ma didn't believe in screw-tops. 'Full-strength too. Last summer's.'

Willy smiled slyly. 'Losing thi touch, Ma?'

'Now, don't you say that!' His mother pointing a forefinger stiff as a clothes-peg. 'Think what you want, but don't you go saying it. It's not lucky.'

'Aye. I'm sorry.'

'Still . . .' She squinted into the bottle then put it back on the hearth behind Bob or Jim. 'You're not altogether wrong, for once.'

'Nay.' Willie shook his head. 'Shouldn't've said it. Just come out, like.'

'I'm not what I was.'

'Well, what d'you expect? You're eighty . . . three? Six?'

'*That's* not what I'm saying, son.'

Ma's brown eyes were calm. She still didn't need glasses, and her eyes did wonderful things. In Manchester, of a Saturday, all dolled up, she could still summon a waitress in the café with them eyes, even when the waitress had her back turned. And Willie had once seen this right vicious-looking street-gang part clean down the middle to let her through; Ma had sent the eyes in first.

But now the eyes were oddly calm. Accepting. Worrying, that. Never been what you might call an accepter, hadn't Ma.

'*None* of us is what we was this time last year,' Ma said. 'Ever since yon bogman were took . . .'

'Oh, no,' Willie stood up. 'Not again. You start on about that bogman and I'm off.'

'Don't be so daft. You know I'm right, our Willie. Look at yer fingers, drummin' away, plonk, plonk. Always was a giveaway, yer fingers.'

'Nay,' Willie said uncomfortably, wishing he hadn't come.

'I'm telling you, we're not protected same as we was.' Ma Wagstaff stopped rocking. 'Sit down. Get your bum back on that couch a minute.'

Willie sat. He was suddenly aware of how dim it was in the parlour, despite all the sunlight, and how small it was. And how little and wizened Ma appeared. It was like looking at an old sepia photo from Victorian times. Hard to imagine this was the fiery-eyed old woman who'd blowtorched a path through a bunch of Moss Side yobboes.

'We've bin protected in this village,' Ma said. 'You know that.'

'I suppose so.'

'We're very old-established, y'see. Very old-established indeed.'

Well, this was true. And the family itself was old-established in Bridelow, at least on Ma's side. Dad had come from Oldham to work at the brewery, but Ma and her ma and her ma's ma . . . well, that was how it seemed to go back, through the women.

'But we've let it go,' Ma said.

Willy remembered how upset she'd been when her granddaughter, his sister's lass, had gone to college in London. Manchester or Sheffield would've been acceptable, but London . . . *It's too far . . . ties'll be broken. She'll not come back, that one . . .*

He said, 'Let it go?'

Ma Wagstaff leaned back in the rocking-chair, closing her eyes. 'Aye,' she said sadly. 'You say as you don't want to hear this, Willie, but you're goin t'ave to, sooner or later. You're like all the rest of um. If it's up on t'moor, or out on t'Moss, it's nowt to do wi' us. Can't do us no harm. Well, it *can* now, see, I'm telling thee.'

All eight of Willie's fingers started working on his knees.

Ma said, 'They're looking for openings. Looking for cracks in t'wall. Been gathering out there for years, hundreds of years.'

'What you on about, Ma?'

'Different uns, like,' Ma said. 'Not *same* uns, obviously.'

'Yobboes,' Willie said dismissively, realizing what she meant. 'Bloody hooligans. Always been yobboes and hooligans out there maulin' wi' them owd circles. Means nowt. Except to farmers, like. Bit of a bugger for farmers.'

'Eh . . .' Ma was scornful. 'Farmers loses more sheep to foxes. That's not what I'm saying.'

Her eyes popped open, giving him a shock because there was no peace in them now, no acceptance. All of a sudden they looked just like the little white marbles Willie had collected as a lad, shot through with the same veins of pure, bright red.

She stabbed a finger at him again. 'I can tell um, y'know. Couldn't always . . . Aye. Less said about *that* . . .'

Willie's own fingers stumbled out of rhythm, the tips gone numb. 'Now, don't upset yourself.'

'But there's one now,' Ma said, one hand clutching an arm of the rocking-chair like a parrot's claw on a perch. 'Comes and goes, like an infection. Looking for an opening . . .'

'Shurrup, Ma, will you. Whatever it is, Lottie doesn't want . . .'

'Listen,' Ma said without hesitation. 'You tell that Lottie to come and see me. Tell her to come tomorrow, I'm a bit busy now. Tell her I'll talk to her about it. Just like we talked to Matt. Matt knew what had to happen. Matt were chuffed as a butty.'

'Aye.' Matt and his mate, the bogman. Together at last.

'Only we've got to protect the lad,' Ma said.

'I don't like any of this, Ma. Lottie'll go spare.'

'Well, look.' Ma was on her feet, sprightly as a ten-year-old, moving bottles on the shelf. 'Give her this.'

'What is it?'

Daft question.

'Aye.' Accepting the little brown bottle. 'All right, then, I'll give it her. Tell her it'll calm her down. Make her feel better. But I'll not tell you're going ahead with . . .' Willie gave his knee a couple of climactic thumps. 'No way.'

He didn't tell Ma what Lottie had said about them finishing Matt's bogman song-cycle.

Because, when it came down to it, he didn't like the thought of that himself. And he had a pretty good idea how Ma would react.

I warned him not to meddle with stuff he knows nowt about, she'd say. And I don't expect to have to warn me own son.

So, in a way, Willie was hoping Lottie would have forgotten about the whole thing by the time the funeral was over.

A funeral which, if she'd any sense, she'd be attending with a very thick veil over her eyes.

CHAPTER VII

The man with two Dobermanns prowling the inside of the wiremesh perimeter fence was clearly too old to be a security guard. His appallingly stained trousers were held up by a dressing-gown cord with dirty gold tassels; a thinner golden cord was draped around the crown of his tattered trilby.

However, the dogs looked menacing enough, and when the man flung open the metal gate, they sprang.

For just a few seconds, the dun-coloured sky disappeared as the Dobermanns rose massively and simultaneously into the air. And then they were on her, both heads into her exposed face, hot breath pumping and the great, savage teeth.

'Oh, my God!' Moira shrieked as the rough tongues sliced through her make-up. 'Do you guys know what this bloody stuff *costs*?'

She threw an arm around each of the dogs, trapping the four big front paws to her tweed jacket, and they all staggered together through the gate and on to the site, knocking over an empty grey plastic dustbin.

The elderly man in the black trilby caught the bin as it fell. 'Moira!' he yelled. 'Hey!'

'Donald,' Moira said, arms full of black and gold paws. 'You all right?'

'Well, damn.' He pulled his hat off. 'We wisny expecting ye today, hen, the Duchess didny say . . .'

'That's because she didn't know,' Moira said. 'I hope she's not away from her van . . . Down, now . . .'

The dogs obediently sat at her feet. 'Ye've still got the way, all right,' Donald said admiringly.

'They've grown. Again. I swear I've never seen Dobermanns this big. What d'you feed them on?'

Donald didn't smile. 'Public health officials.'

'My daddy,' she reminded him gently, 'was a public health official.'

'Aye, I know. But yer daddy wisny like the hard-faced bastards they send round these days.' Donald turned his head and shouted at a woman pegging baby-clothes to a washing line outside a lilac-coloured caravan. 'Hey, Siobhan, the Duchess, she in now?'

'Oh, sure . . .' The woman stumbled and dropped a nappy in a puddle. She picked it up, wrung out the brown water and hung it on the line. 'Leastways, I haven't seen no red carpet goin' down today.'

'Tinkers,' Donald said disparagingly. 'They're all bloody tinkers here now, 'cept for the few of us.'

Moira followed him and the dogs through the site, with its forty-odd vans on concrete hard-standings and its unexpectedly spectacular views of the Ayrshire coast. It might have been a holiday caravan site but for the washing-lines full of fluttering clothes and the piles of scrap and all the kids and dogs.

They passed just one perfect old Romany caravan, bright

red and silver, originally designed for horses but with a tow-bar now. A man with a beard and an earring sat out on the step whittling chunks out of a hunk of dark wood. He wore a moleskin waistcoat trimmed with silver. Moira stared at him, amazed. 'Who the hell's that?'

Donald turned his head and spat. One of the Dobermanns growled. 'Oh,' Moira said. 'I see.'

'Bloody hippies. Call 'emselves *New Age* gypsies. Wis a time this wis a *select* site. All kindsa garbage we're gettin' now, hen.'

He stopped at the bottom of six concrete steps leading to the apex of the site, a flat-topped artificial mound with the sides banked into flowerbeds.

Nothing changes, Moira thought. Wherever she's living it's always the same.

Evergreen shrubs, mainly laurel, sprouted around the base of the shining silver metal palace which crowned the mound like the Mother Ship from *Close Encounters*. The old man mounted the bottom step. 'Hey, Duchess!'

It wasn't what you'd call a traditional Romany caravan. Few like it had been seen before on a statutory local authority gypsy site. Only movie stars on location lived quite like this.

Donald stayed on the bottom step, the Dobermanns silent either side of him. There were antique carriage lamps each side of the door, a heavy door of stained and polished Douglas fir, which slid open with barely a sigh.

She came out and stood fraily in the doorway, a soft woollen evening stole about her bony shoulders. The day was calm for the time of year, no breeze from the sea.

Donald said, 'Will you look who's here, Duchess.'

From the edges of the stole, the Duchess's hair tumbled like a cataract of white water almost to her waist. She looked down at Moira and her face was grave.

Moira said, 'Hullo, Mammy.'

'You OK?'

He'd looked anxious, his tuxedo creased, the thistle lolling from his buttonhole.

Well, actually, it was more than anxious; the guy had been as scared as any of them in the room full of splintered bone – twisted antlers across the tables on beds of broken glass, and one pair still hanging menacingly among the glittering shards of a chandelier.

Moira had said, 'You ever see bomb damage in Belfast?'

'Huh?'

She was up on her knees now, examining the guitar for fractures.

'Bomb damage,' she said, not looking at him.

He was silent. He crouched down next to her, the two of them by the dais, all the others, the multi-national Celts, brushing each other down, sheltering in groups in the corners of the Great Hall.

The pale man had been helped away by the Earl and some servants. He'd looked just once at Moira with his damaged eye.

There were no cracks in the body of the guitar, although its face was scratched and it looked to be very deeply offended.

'What's your name?' Moira turned to the American.

'Huh?'

'What are you called?'

'I, uh . . .' He grimaced, the suaveness gone, black curls sweated to his forehead. He looked as limp as the thistle he wore. 'I don't believe this has happened. Some kind of earthquake? Or what? Uh . . . Macbeth.'

'That's your name? My God. Here, hold this a second.' She passed him the guitar while she untangled her hair.

He held the instrument up by the neck, gripping it hard. 'You *have* earthquakes in these parts?'

'What?' She'd started to laugh.

'Earthquakes. Tremors.'

She said, 'Macbeth. I thought you were going to be Irish, despite the thistle. New York Irish.'

'Just New York. Born and raised. Mungo Macbeth. Of the Manhattan Macbeths. My mother said I should wear the kilt.' He straightened the thistle. 'We compromised.'

'That's a compromise?'

He said, 'You really are OK now?'

'Oh, I'm fine. Just fine.' Feeling like she'd come through a war – a whole war in just a few minutes.

Mungo Macbeth had been looking around at all the wreckage, where the stags' heads had fallen. Then up at the ceiling.

'There isn't one of them left hanging,' he'd said, awed. 'Not a goddamn one.'

He was right.

What have I done?

'I mean, is that weird?' Mungo Macbeth said. 'Or is that weird?'

'And what was it that made you think,' the Duchess said contemptuously, 'that it was you?'

She didn't sound at all like Moira. Her voice was like the refined *tink* you made when you tapped with your fingernail on crystal glass of the very highest quality. A most cultured lady who had never been to school.

'Not me on my own,' Moira said. 'Someone . . . something was . . . you know, like an invasion? I felt threatened. This guy . . . Also, I didn't like the setup anyway, generations of stalkers' trophies, and all these elitist folk, like "we are the Celtic aristocracy, we're the chosen ones . . ."'

The Duchess lifted her chin imperiously. 'What nonsense you talk. Do you seriously think that if you began to suddenly resent me or something, you could come in here and break everything on my walls?'

Virtually all the wallspace in the luxurious caravan had been decorated with fine china.

'Your walls, no,' Moira said.

'I should think not indeed.'

'But this place, I felt very threatened.'

She kept seeing, like on some kind of videotape loop, the man unfastening her guitar case. But it was all so dreamlike, part of the hallucination summoned by the song and the strangeness of the night. She couldn't talk about it.

'I'm mixed up, Mammy.'

'Don't whine,' the Duchess said mildly.

'I'm sorry.' And the smoky form in the fireplace? The sensation of Matt – and yet *not* Matt?

And the *knowing*. Confirmed by the call.

Lottie? Lottie, listen, I know it's late, I'm sorry . . . Only it's Matt. I've been thinking about Matt all night . . .

The Duchess said, 'Have you the comb with you?'

'Surely.' Moira pulled her bag on to her knee.

'Show me.'

The Earl had said he couldn't explain it; the heads had been accumulating on the walls for four or more generations, none had ever been dislodged before. Some sort of chain-reaction, perhaps, the domino effect. He had suggested everyone go through to the larger drawing room, and the servants had been dispatched for extra chairs and doctors to tend the injuries, none of them apparently major.

Uninjured, Moira and the American called Macbeth had gone outside into the grounds.

'Clear my head,' he said.

The house behind them was floodlit, looked like a wedding cake. A narrow terrace followed the perimeter of the house, and they walked along it, Moira carrying the guitar in its case. 'Why are you here?' she said, drifting. 'What do you do? Or are you just rich?'

'TV,' Macbeth said. 'I make lousy TV shows. But, yeah, also we're rich, the Macbeths. Which is why they let me make my lousy TV shows, and also why I'm here. That is, my mother . . . she was invited. She owns the company.'

'Uh huh.' Moira nodded, as if she was interested. White flakes of bone were still silently spattering her vision, like TV static.

'They sent me,' Macbeth said, 'on account of, A – I'm just about the most expendable member of the family, and B – she figured it was time I reconnected with my, uh, roots.'

'Roots sometimes need to stay buried,' Moira said. 'You dig up the roots, you kill the tree.'

'I never thought about it like that.'

'It's probably just a clever thing to say. You *found* your

roots? Have you been to where Birnam Wood came to Dunsinane?'

'No,' he said. 'But I think I just found one of the three witches.'

'Really?' Moira said coldly.

'Only these days they come more beautiful.' Macbeth stopped suddenly and threw up both hands. 'Ah, shit, I apologize. I don't mean to be patronizing, or sexist or anything. It was, uh . . . The hair . . . your wonderful, long, black hair . . .'

Oh, *please* . . .

'With that lonely grey strand,' Macbeth said. 'Like a vein in onyx. Or something. I recognized it soon as you came into the room tonight. See, I don't know much about Celtic history, but rock music and folk . . . I mean, I really do have those albums.'

'Would that you didn't,' Moira said quietly. Then she shook her hair. 'Sorry. Stupid. Forget it.'

Standing on the edge of the terrace overlooking a floodlit lawn, he cupped both palms around his face. 'I am such an asshole.'

No way she could disagree.

Macbeth hung his head. 'See, I . . . Aw, Jesus, I'm in this party of seriously intellectual Celtic people, and, like . . . what do I know? What's my contribution gonna be? What do I *know*? – I know a song. So I go – showing off my atom of knowledge – I go, how about you play The Comb Song? Just came out. Dumb, huh?'

She looked hard into his dark blue eyes. 'So it *was* you asked for the song.'

'Yeah, it just came to me to ask for that song. Then someone else took it up. It was confusing. I coulda bit off my tongue when it came clear you didn't want to do that number. I'm sorry.' He sat down on the paved area, legs hanging over the side of the terrace. He rubbed his eyes. 'All those stag heads. Like it was orchestrated.'

'You think it was somehow down to the song? Hence I'm a witch? You connect that with *me*?'

'Uh . . .' Macbeth looked *very* confused. 'I'm sorry. Whole thing scared the shit out of me. You feel the atmosphere in there? *Before* it happened?'

Headlight beams sliced through the trees along the drive. The ambulance probably. Maybe two. Maybe a whole fleet, seeing this was the Earl's place.

'Cold,' Macbeth said. 'Bone-freezing cold. I mean . . . shit . . . it isn't even cold *out here* . . . *now*.'

Moira had said, 'Can you excuse me? I need to make a phone call.'

She didn't know how old the comb was. Maybe a few hundred years old, maybe over a thousand. She'd never wanted to take it to an expert, a valuer; its value was not that kind.

The comb was of some heavy, greyish metal. It was not so very ornate and half its teeth were missing, but when she ran it through her hair it was like something was excavating deep furrows in her soul.

The Duchess weighed the comb in fingers that sprayed red and green and blue fire from the stones in her rings, eleven of them.

'My,' the Duchess said, 'you really are in a quandary, aren't you?'

'Else why would I have come.'

'And someone . . . You've not told me everything . . . I can sense a death.'

'Yes,' Moira whispered. Feeling, as usual, not so much like an acolyte at the feet of a guru, more like a sin-soaked Catholic at confession.

'Whose?'

'Matt Castle.'

'Who is he?'

'You know . . . He was the guy whose band I joined when I left the university in Manchester. Must be . . . a long time . . . seventeen years ago.'

'This was before . . . ?'

'Yes.'

The Duchess passed the comb from one hand to the other and back again. 'There's guilt here. Remorse.'

114

'Well, I . . . I've always felt bad about leaving the band when I did. And also . . . three, four months ago, he wrote to me. He wanted me to do some songs with him. He was back living in his old village, which is that same place they found the ancient body in the peat. Maybe you heard about that.'

'A little.' The Duchess's forefinger stroking the rim of the comb.

'Matt was seriously hung up on this thing,' Moira said, 'the whole idea of it. This was the first time . . . I mean, when we split, his attitude was, like, OK, that's it, nice while it lasted but it's the end of an era. So, although we've spoken several times on the phone, it's fifteen years last January since I saw him. Um . . . last year it came out he'd been to the hospital, for tests, but when I called him a week or so later he said it was OK, all negative, no problem. So . . . Goes quiet, we exchange Christmas cards and things, as usual. Then, suddenly – this'd be three, four, months ago – he writes, wanting to get me involved in this song-cycle he's working on, maybe an album. To be called *The Man in the Moss*.'

'And you would have nothing to do with it?'

'I . . . Yeh, I don't like to bugger about with this stuff any more. I get scared . . . scared what effect I'm gonna have, you know? I'm pretty timid these days.'

'So you told him no.'

'So I . . . No, I couldn't turn it down flat. This is the guy got me started. I owe him. So I just wrote back, said I was really sorry but I was tied up, had commitments till the autumn. Said I was honoured, all this crap, and I'd be in touch. Hoping, obviously, that he'd find somebody else.'

She paused. Her voice dropped. 'He died last night. About the same time all this . . .'

The Duchess passed the comb back to Moira. 'I don't like the feel of it. It's cold.'

The comb is icy, brittle, oh . . .

Her mother was glaring at her, making her wish she hadn't come. There was always a period of this before the tea and the biscuits and the Duchess saying, How is your father? Does he ever speak of me? And she'd smile and shake her head, for her daddy still didn't know, after all these years, that she'd even met this woman.

The Duchess said, 'That trouble you got into, with the rock and roll group. You dabbled. I said to you never to dabble. I said when you were ready to follow a spiritual path you should come to me. It was why I gave you the comb.'

'Yes, Mammy, I know that.' She'd always call her Mammy deliberately, in a vain effort to demystify the woman. 'I'm doing my best to avoid it. That's why . . .'

'The comb has not forgiven you,' the Duchess said severely. 'You have some damage to repair.'

'Aye, I know,' Moira said. 'I know that too.'

She'd returned from the phone floating like a ghost through a battlefield, blood and bandages everywhere – well, maybe not so much blood, maybe not any. Maybe the blood was in her head.

'You all right, Miss Cairns? You weren't hit?'

'I'm fine, Your . . . I'm fine.'

'You're very pale. Have a brandy.'

'No. No, thank you.'

All this solicitousness. Scared stiff some of his Celtic brethren would sue the piss out of him. She was impatient with him. Him and his precious guests and his precious trophies and his reputation. What did it matter? Nobody was dying.

Yes, Moira. Yes, he is. I'm sorry . . . No, not long. I'll know more in the morning. Perhaps you could call back then.

She had to get out of this house, didn't want to see wounds bathed and glass and antlers swept away. Didn't want to know what had happened to the pale man.

Outside, Mungo Macbeth, of the Manhattan Macbeths, still sat with his legs dangling over the edge of the terrace.

Moira joined him, feeling chilly now in her black dress, stiff down by the waist where it had soaked up spilled Guinness from the carpet.

And because he was there and because he was no threat any more, she began to talk to Macbeth. Talked about many things – *not* including Matt Castle.

116

In fact she was so determined not to talk about Matt – and, therefore, not to break down – that she blocked him out, and his dying, with something as powerful and as pertinent to the night: she found she was telling Mungo Macbeth about the Comb Song.

'Everybody thinks it's metaphor, you know?'

'It exists?'

'Aye. Sure.'

Then she thought, *Only person I ever told before was M . . .*

She said quickly, 'Your family make regular donations to the IRA?'

'. . . *what*?'

His eyebrows went up like they'd been pulled on wires and she stared good and hard into his eyes. They were candid and they were innocent.

'Sorry,' she said. 'I forgot. You aren't even Irish.'

'Moira, let's be factual here. I'm not even Scottish.'

She found herself smiling. Then she stopped. She said, 'Every year these gypsies would camp on the edge of the town, derelict land since before the War. Only this year it was to be redeveloped, and so the gypsies had to go. My daddy was the young guy the council sent to get rid of them. He was scared half to death of what they might do to him, the gypsy men, who would naturally all be carrying knives.'

Some night creature ran across the tiered lawn below them, edge to edge.

'My gran told me this. My daddy never speaks of it. Not *ever*. But it wasn't the gypsy men he had cause to fear, so much as the women. They had the poor wee man seduced.'

Macbeth raised an eyebrow, but not much.

'Like, how could he resist her? This quiet Presbyterian boy with the horn-rimmed spectacles and his first briefcase. How could he resist this, this . . .' Moira swung her legs and clicked her heels on the terrace wall.

'I can sympathize,' Macbeth said.

'She was a vision,' Moira said. 'Still is. He'd have laid down his beloved council job for her after the first week, but that wasn't what they wanted – they wanted the camp site until the autumn, for reasons of their own, whatever that was all about.

And they got it. My daddy managed to keep stalling the council, his employers, for reasons of *his* own. And then it all got complicated because she wasn't supposed to get herself pregnant. Certainly not by *him*.'

She'd glossed over the rest, her daddy's ludicrous threats to join the gypsies, her gran's battle for custody of the child, the decision by the gypsy hierarchy that, under the circumstances, it might be politic to let the baby go rather than be saddled with its father and pursued by *his* mother.

And then her own genteel, suburban, Presbyterian upbringing.

'And the rest is the song. Which you know.'

The American, sitting on the wall, shook his head, incredulous. 'This is prime-time TV, you know that? This is a goddamn *mini-series*.'

'Don't you even think about it, Mr Macbeth,' Moira said, 'or Birnam Wood'll be coming to Dunsinane faster than you can blink.'

'Yeah, uh, the wood. I was gonna ask you. The scene in the wood where you get the comb . . . ?'

'Poetic licence. What happened was, the gypsies were in town, right, just passing through. Two of them – I was twelve – these two gypsies were waiting for me outside the school. I'm thinking, you know . . . run like hell. But, aw . . . it was . . . intriguing. And they seemed OK, you know? And the camp was very public. So I went with them. Well . . . she'd be about thirty then and already very revered, you could tell. Even I could see she was my mother.'

'Holy shit,' said Macbeth.

'We didn't talk much. Nobody was gonna try and kidnap me or anything. Nobody offered me anything. Except the comb. She gave me that.'

'And is it a magic comb?'

'It's just a comb,' Moira said, more sharply than she intended.

'He's close to you,' the Duchess said.

'Who?'

'The departed one.'

'Still?'

'We'll have some tea,' the Duchess said in a slightly raised voice, and a young woman at once emerged from the kitchen with a large silver tray full of glistening white china. 'One of my nieces,' the Duchess said, 'Zelda.' There would always be nieces and nephews to fetch and carry for the Duchess.

She lifted the lid of the pot and sniffed. 'Earl Grey. Never mind. You should take a rest, Moira. Unravel yourself.'

'Maybe I'd rather not see what's inside of me.'

The Duchess stirred the tea in the pot, making it stronger, making the Earl Grey's rich perfume waft out. 'Maybe you should get away, and when you get back your problems will be in perspective. Go somewhere bland. St Moritz, Barbados . . .'

'Jesus, Mammy, how much money you think I'm making?'

'Well, England then. Tunbridge Wells or somewhere.'

'Tunbridge *Wells*?'

'You know what I mean.'

'Yeah. You're telling me it's something I'm not gonna get away from no matter where I go.'

'Am I?'

'You said there was damage to repair. You think I *damaged* Matt Castle?'

'Do *you*?'

'I don't kn . . . No! No, I don't see how I could have.'

'That's all right, then,' said the Duchess. She smiled.

Moira felt profoundly uneasy. 'Mammy, how was he when he died? Can you tell me that?'

'Moira, you're a grown woman. You *know* this man's essence has not returned to the source. I can say no more than that.'

Moira felt the weight of her bag on her knees, the bag with the comb in it. The bag felt twice as heavy as before, like a sack of stolen bullion.

She said in a rush, 'Mammy, somebody was after the comb. I had to fight for it.'

'Yes. That happens. The comb represents a commitment. Sometimes you have to decide whether or not you want to renew it.'

'So it was this struggle which caused . . . See, I'm confused. I feel exhausted, but I feel I made it through to a new level, a new plateau. But that usually means something heavy's on the way. Well, doesn't it?'

The Duchess blinked. 'How is your father?' she said brightly. 'Does he speak of me often?'

She said goodbye to Donald at the gate and patted the Dobermanns. Her old BMW was parked about fifty yards away near a derelict petrol station. Parked behind it was a car which had not been there before, a grey Metro with a hire-firm sticker on the rear window.

Leaning against the Metro was a man wearing a dinner jacket over a black T-shirt. On the T-shirt it said in red, I ♥ Govan. The remains of a thistle hung out of one lapel of the jacket.

His face fumbled a grin.

'Uh, hi,' he said.

Moira was furious.

'You followed me! You fucking *followed* me!'

'Listen . . . Moira . . . See, this has been . . . Like, this was the most bizarre, dramatic, *momentous* night of my life, you know?'

'So? You've had a sheltered life. Is that supposed . . . ?'

'I can't walk away from this. Am I supposed to like, push it aside, maybe introduce it as an anecdote over dinner with my associates?'

Moira stood with her key in the door of the BMW. She wanted to say, OK, while you're here maybe you can tell me something about a tall, pale man with white hair.

Instead, she said, 'Macbeth, you shouldn't believe everything a woman tells you when she's in shock.'

'I . . . Goddamnit, I *saw*. And I tried to sleep on it and I couldn't, so this morning . . .' Mungo Macbeth looked sheepish and spread his hands . . .

She gave him a cursory glance intended to wither, fade him out.

'I figured maybe you could use some help,' he said.

'OK,' she said. 'You see those gates? Behind those gates is a guy with two huge and ferocious dogs. The dogs'll do anything the guy says. And the guy – he'll do anything I say. You got the message?'

'Couldn't we go someplace? Get a bite to eat?'

'No, we could not.' Moira opened the driver's door of the BMW and got in, wound down the window. 'You think I need a strong male shoulder to lean on, that it? Or maybe a bedpost?'

Macbeth said helplessly, 'I just think . . . I just think you're an amazing person.'

'Macbeth . . .' She sighed. 'Just go away, huh?'

He nodded, expressionless, turned back to his hire car. He looked like he might cry.

This was *ridiculous*.

'Hey, Macbeth . . .' Moira leaned back out of the window, nodded at his T-shirt. 'You ever actually *been* to Govan?'

'Aw, hell . . .' Macbeth shrugged. 'I cruised most of those Western Isles. Just don't recall which is which.'

Moira found a grin, or the grin found her. Hurriedly, she put the car into gear, drove away, and when she looked back there was only a bus, a long way behind.

From *Dawber's Book of Bridelow*:

THE BREWERY

FINE BEERS HAVE BEEN brewed in the Bridelow area since time immemorial, the most famous being the almost-black Bridelow Bitter.

This, or something similar, was first produced commercially, on an extremely small scale, by Elsie Berry and her sons in the late seventeenth century, using a species of aromatic bog-myrtle as a preservative. The Berry family began by providing ale for the Bridelow pub, The Man I'th Moss, but demand grew swiftly in communities up to fifteen miles away.

The Bridelow Brewery as we know it today was founded in the early nineteenth century by Thomas Horridge, a businessman from Chesterfield who bought out the Berry Family and whose enterprise was to provide employment for many generations of Bridelow folk. He at once began work on the construction of the first proper road across the Moss to facilitate the movement of his brewery wagons.

Descendants of Thomas Horridge continued to develop the industry, and the family became Bridelow's greatest benefactors, building the village hall, enabling major repairs to be carried out to the ancient church and continuing to facilitate new housing as recently as the 1950s.

However . . .

CHAPTER VIII

In the bar at The Man I'th Moss, lunchtime, Young Frank Manifold said, in disgust, 'Bloody gnat's piss!'

And angrily pushed his glass away.

'I'll have draught Bass next time,' Young Frank said. 'Never thought I'd be saying that in this pub. *Never.*'

'Eh, tha's just bitter, lad,' said Frank Manifold Snr, who preferred Scotch anyway. 'Tha's a right to feel bitter, mind, I'm not saying tha's not . . . Know what they've done, now, Ernie? Only paid off our drivers and replaced um wi' their own blokes.'

'Ken and Peter?'

'Gone! Paid off! Cut down lorries from five to two – bigger uns, like. Needed experienced HGV drivers, *they* reckoned. Makes you spit.'

Ernie, who also was on whisky, had a sip out of Young Frank's beer glass. 'Lad's right, I'm afraid,' he said. 'It's gone off.'

'Well, thank you!' Young Frank said devoutly. 'Thank you very much, Mr Dawber.'

'Only just don't go shouting it around the place,' Ernie muttered. 'Lottie's got to sell the stuff and she's enough problems.'

'No, she doesn't,' said Young Frank, back-row smart-arse in Ernie's top class fourteen years ago. 'Doesn't have to sell it at all no more. Free house, int it?'

Lottie wasn't here this lunchtime. Stan Burrows, who'd also been made redundant from the brewery, was minding the bar. Stan said, 'I heard as how Gannons was kicking up, claiming they'd been sabotaged, not given proper recipe, like. Threatening legal action, what I heard.'

'Balls,' said Young Frank, glaring at his discarded glass. 'They don't give a shit.'

Ernie Dawber, on his usual stool at the end of the bar, by the telephone, pondered this. The way he saw it, there was no way the Horridge family could have got away with not providing Gannons with the correct recipe. And why should they want to, with Shaw Horridge on the Board?

Yet it was a fact. Since the brewery had been taken over, the stuff had been slowly shedding its distinctive flavour. Surprising, because it was well known that Gannons, whose bestselling product was a fizzy lager with a German name produced down Matlock way, had been anxious for some time to acquire their own genuine, old-established Real Ale – and would therefore be expected to treat Bridelow beer with more than a modicum of respect.

Ernie decided he'd better go up to the Hall one night and have a bit of a chat with Shaw Horridge or his mother. Bridelow Black Bitter had a reputation. Even if the brewery was in new hands, even if there'd been this swingeing 'rationalization', which meant firing half the lads, it was still *Bridelow* beer.

Gnat's piss! By 'eck, he'd never thought to hear that.

When his daughter rang from Oxford, in the early afternoon, the Rector barely made it to the phone in time.

'Were you in the garden?' Catherine asked him suspiciously, and Hans didn't deny it. It had taken him almost a minute to hobble from the kitchen to the study.

Pointless, however, trying to conceal anything from Cathy. 'How's the knee?' she demanded at once and with a certain menace.

'Oh,' Hans said, as airily as he could manage with clenched teeth. 'Could be worse, you know.'

'I've no doubt that it could, Pop. But worse than *what* is what I'd like to know.'

Hans tried to keep from screaming out loud as he fell into the window chair, pulling the phone on to his knees.

Cathy said, 'I don't suppose you'd even tell me if you'd had to have a Zimmer frame screwed into the back of the pulpit.'

The still-aggressive sun, having gouged chunks out of the church wall, began to attack the study window, and when the Rector twisted away from it, his left knee felt like a slab of volcanic rock with a core of molten lava.

'Well, actually,' he said, abandoning pretence with a sigh, 'it couldn't be a *lot* worse.'

'Right,' his daughter said. 'I'm on my way, Pop. Expect me for supper.'

'No, no, no. Your studies . . . whatever they are.'

Cathy said crisply, 'In a post-graduate situation, as I keep explaining, you get a fair bit of leeway. I'm coming up.'

'No. Listen. You don't understand.' Raising his voice, trying to shout down the pain as much as her. 'I'm getting a lot of help. The Mothers' Union . . . terribly kind, and . . . Look, when I need you, I promise I'll be in touch. You know I will.'

He swallowed a great slab of breath and bit his tongue, jamming his palm over the mouthpiece just in time. Change the subject. Talk about something else. 'Erm, Matt Castle . . . Poor Matt died on Sunday night.'

'Oh, no.'

'It was a mercy, Catherine.'

'Yes, I suppose it would be. Did . . . ?'

'Oh, very quick. In the end, he spent no more than a few hours in hospital. Kept signing himself out, you see. Determined to die in Bridelow. He was even out on the Moss yesterday morning, I'm told, with Lottie and the boy. Brave man. Poor Matt.'

'What's going to happen to the pub?'

'She'll stay on, I imagine. For a while. You know what she's like. Terribly independent. Old Mrs Wagstaff sent one of her special potions across, to help her sleep. Lottie bunged it back at once, with Willie. She's very resistant to all that.'

'When's the funeral?'

'Friday afternoon.'

'You're going to have difficulty, aren't you? Especially if it gets colder.'

Putting her finger on it, as usual. So Hans had to come out with what, apart from the pain, was on his mind. 'Cathy, they've given me a curate.'

'Oh,' she said, surprised. 'Well, you certainly could do with the help. But it, er . . . that could be a headache, couldn't it?'

'It was only a matter of time,' Hans said, 'parish this size. Suppose I've been holding out. Putting it off. That is, I realize this sort of thing – new chaps – has always taken care of itself in the past. I mean, I myself was not . . . well, not, perhaps, the man they would have chosen at the time. But one gets acclimatized. Headache? Hmm . . . let's hope not.'

'Anybody I know?'

'Oh, a young fellow, few months out of college. Simon's very keen . . . Well, actually not *that* young. Late twenties, I suppose. Used to be a teacher. Joel Beard, his name. Pleasant enough lad. Slightly earnest, but so many of them are, aren't they?'

Cathy said, 'Jesus Christ.'

Hans didn't say anything. His daughter never blasphemed for effect.

'I was at the high school with him.' Hans could hear her frowning. 'For a year or two. That is, he was four or five years in front of me. He was Head Boy. One of those who takes it seriously. Very authoritative, very *proper*. Seemed more of a grown-up than some of the teachers, do you know what I mean? Most of the girls were crazy about him. But I was never into Greek gods.'

She stopped. 'Pop, listen, you *do* know he was at St Oswald's, don't you?'

Yes, he did. He was surprised, though, that *she* knew the significance of this. 'It's not necessarily a drawback, you know, Cathy.'

He tried to straighten his right leg and, although there was no great pain in this one, the right knee fought him all the way. Both knees now. God save us. Wheelchair job soon. Or one could go into hospital and leave Joel Beard in charge.

'Simon thinks he's a star,' he said. 'Which means, I suppose, that the silly sod's fallen in love with him. He used, apparently . . . Joel, this is . . . he used to be some sort of

126

Born Again Christian. Before he decided to go straight, as it were.'

'You call two years at St Oswald's going *straight*? The most notoriously fundamentalist theological college in the country?'

'I like to think I'm broadminded,' Hans said.

'Sure, but how broadminded is Ma Wagstaff?'

'Look,' Hans said, 'people adjust. *Bridelow* adjusts people. I'd rather have a fundamentalist or a charismatic than some clerical bureaucrat with a briefcase and a mobile phone. Anyway, the Diocese likes him. "He's tough, he's athletic" – this is Simon talking – "and he's bringing God back into the arena." Bit of muscle. They're into that these days. The anti-pansy lobby. Even Simon, ironically. I mean, all right, I could refuse him, I could tell them to take him back, say he doesn't fit it . . . but somebody's going to ask, *why* doesn't he fit? And anyway, who's to say . . . ? They might not be . . . orthodox here, but they have a strong faith and strong, simple principles. Ma Wagstaff? *Very* broadminded in some ways.'

'Hmmm,' said Cathy, unconvinced.

'However, rest assured, I won't let him take Matt's funeral. I suspect the ladies have plans.'

'God, no, you mustn't let him do that.'

'So if I have to go out there on a pair of crutches . . . or a Zimmer frame.'

'Don't you go talking about Zimmer frames, Pop.'

'*You* did.'

'That's when I'll come,' Catherine decided. 'I'll come on Wednesday night. I'll get you through the funeral. I won't have you talking about Zimmer frames.'

'Now, look . . .'

'I'm not going to argue, my phone bill's getting ridiculous. I'll see you Wednesday night.'

And she hung up on him.

'Thank you,' the Rector said with resignation into the dead phone. 'I suppose.'

The Hall had once been surrounded by parkland, although now it just looked like ordinary fields with a well-ordered assembly of mature trees – beech and sycamore and horse-chestnut.

The trees were higher now, but not yet high enough to obscure the soaring stone walls of the brewery, four storeys high, an early Victorian industrial castle, as proud and firm in its setting as St Bride's Church.

She hated it now.

You could not see the brewery from the drawing room. But with all the trees nearly bare again, Eliza Horridge, from her window seat, could see the village in detail. She supposed she'd always preferred autumn and winter for this very reason: it brought her closer to Bridelow.

The sad irony of this made her ache. On the night the redundancies had been announced, she'd gone – rather bravely, she thought – down to the post office to buy some stamps which she didn't need. She'd just had to get it over, face the hostility.

Except there hadn't been any. Nobody had screamed Judas at her, nobody had ignored her or been short with her.

But nobody had said a word about the jobs either. They didn't blame her personally. But Liz Horridge blamed herself and since that night had never been back into Bridelow.

Self-imposed exile in this warm and shabby-luxurious house with its pictures and memories of Arthur Horridge. *Self*-imposed; could go out whenever she wanted. Couldn't she?

She snatched up the phone on its second ring to wrench her mind from what it couldn't cope with.

'Yes?' The number was ex-directory. There were too many people down there with whom she could no longer bear to speak.

'Yes? Hello? Is that you, Shaw?'

Something told her she was in for a shock, and her eyes clutched at the view of the village for support, following the steep cobbled street past the pub, past the post office, past a line of tiny stone cottages to the churchyard.

'Liiiiiz . . .' Mellifluously stretching the word, as he used to, into an embrace. 'Super!' Shattering her.

128

'Thought I saw you last week, m'girl, in Buxton. Was in a wine bar. Thought you came up the street. No?'

'Couldn't have been,' she scraped out. 'Never go . . .'

'Thought you *sensed* me . . . turned your head so *sharply*.'

'. . . to Buxton.' Her voice faded.

'And looked at the window of the wine bar, with a sort of yearning in your eyes. Couldn't see me, of course.'

She stared down at the village, but it was like watching a documentary on the television. Or a soap opera, because she could identify most of the people and could map out the paths of their lives from their movements, between the post office and the pub and the church.

'But perhaps it wasn't you, after all,' he said.

She could even hear their voices when the wind was in the right direction. And yes, it was a lot like the television – a thick glass screen between them, and she was very much alone, and the screen was growing darker.

'Or perhaps it was you as you *used* to be. Those chestnut curls of yore.'

Her hand went automatically to her hair, as coarse and dry now as the moorland grasses. She grabbed a handful of it to stop the hand shaking.

'One wonders,' he mused. 'Your hair grey now, Liz? Put on weight? Or angular and gaunt? I'd so much like to see.'

'What do you want?' Liz croaked.

'If you were with me, I suppose you'd keep in trim, dye your hair, have your skin surgically stretched. Probably wouldn't work, but you'd try. If you were with me.'

'How dare you?' Stung at last into anger. 'Where did you get this number?'

He laughed.

She felt alone and cold, terribly exposed, almost ill with it. 'What are you trying to do?'

He said, 'How's dear old Ma these days? Is she well?'

She said nothing.

'Perhaps you don't see her. Or any of them. The word is you've become something of a *recluse*. All alone in your rotting mansion.'

'What nonsense,' she said breathlessly.

'Also, one hears the Mothers' Union isn't as well supported as it was. Sad, secular times, Liz. What's it all coming to? Silly old bats, eh?'

'They had *your* measure,' Liz said, with a spurt of spirit. 'They saw you off.'

'Oh, *long* time ago. Things change. Barriers weaken. Look, old sweetheart, I've been thinking, why don't we meet up?'

'*Certainly not!*'

'Love to be able to come to Buxton, wouldn't you? Love to be smart and sprightly and well-dressed. Give anything to have those chestnut curls back. Perhaps it was you after all, sitting in your emotional prison and *day-dreaming* of Buxton. Perhaps *that's* what I saw. Perhaps you *projected* yourself. Ever tried that, Liz? Should do. Could be a way out – send the spirit, give the body the bottle to go for it. Perhaps I'll drop in on you. Like that, would you?'

'You can't! They won't let you!'

'Times change, m'girl, times change.'

'What do you mean?'

'Will you tell dearest Ma I called?'

She said nothing.

'Of course you won't. Don't see her any more, do you? You don't see any of them. Do you . . . *Liiiiiz?*'

'Leave me . . . !'

She crashed the phone down, and she and the phone sat and trembled.

'Alone,' she said, and began to weep.

'I thought perhaps I might leave early,' Alice said. 'I've got a check-up at the dentist's in Buxton at six and I've got some stuff to pick up at Boots, and I don't like the look of the weather. Is that all right?'

'Suppose so,' Chrissie said, bending over the filing cabinet. Roger had arrived mid-morning, seeming preoccupied, and had not even mentioned their lunch-date, just sloped off to some appointment. Now Chrissie would have to check every-thing, switch off the lights and lock up.

'You don't mind being alone with . . .' Alice giggled. '. . . *him?*'

'Couldn't be safer,' Chrissie said. 'Rog . . . Dr Hall was telling me he hasn't got one.'

'Hasn't he?' Alice was putting her stuff away in her calfskin handbag. She flicked a card across the desk at Chrissie. 'See, there's my appointment.'

'What for?'

'The dentist's. Just to show you I'm not making it up.'

'I never thought you were making it up, Alice, OK?'

'Why hasn't he got one?' asked Alice without much interest. She was a good ten years older than Chrissie, had grown-up kids and a big house. Didn't need the job but Chrissie supposed that in Alice's circle it was nice to say you worked for the University, even if it was only as a number two secretary in an overgrown Portacabin outside Congleton.

Chrissie said, 'Part of the ritual, apparently, when he was sacrificed.'

'I suppose that would be *quite* a sacrifice for a man,' said Alice, pretending to shudder.

'Actually, it's possible they just cut it off after he was dead.'

'I see.' Alice shrugged into her sheepskin coat. Hard luck, Chrissie thought. Now you'll never know how big they were in pre-Christian times.

Alice took her car keys out of her bag, stuck the bag under an arm. 'So it's all right then, if I leave now?'

'Yes,' Chrissie said. Yes, yes, *yes*! she screamed to herself.

But when Alice had gone, she decided it *wasn't* all right. Bloody fat-arsed cow got away with too much. Spends most of the day experimenting with this disgusting sea-green nail varnish, then pisses off to sprawl on the sofa and moan to her husband about how overworked she is.

Chrissie picked up the dentist's appointment card which Alice had left behind. It looked authentic enough, if you didn't happen to know Alice's eldest daughter was a dental receptionist.

It was 4.30. A dim grey afternoon, with all the lights on. She couldn't herself go in case somebody (Roger) rang, or one of the research students came in to raid the files.

She stared across the office at a double-locked metal door.

131

'Just me and you, chum, and you've got no dick.' Chrissie laughed.

Under the laughter, there was a soft noise from behind the metal door.

Chrissie breathed in hard. 'Who's that?'

There was silence.

Yes, that was it – just a *soft noise*. Not a thump, not a clang. She looked around and over her shoulder. The room had three desks, seven filing cabinets and two big metal-framed book cases. It was garishly lit by fluorescent tubes and the windows had Venetian blinds. Between the blinds she could see the deserted college playing-fields and, beyond, the tops of con tainer-lorries on the motorway.

She was alone in the Field Centre and there was nobody apparent outside. 'Now, look,' Chrissie said, 'this is not on. This is not bloody *on*.'

It was going dark out there.

The soft noise came again, like a heavy cushion – an old fashioned one, with brocade – being tossed on to a sofa.

Bravely, Chrissie slipped off her shoes and moved quietly to the metal door.

Should she check this out? *Dare* she?

Although she'd never been in there alone, she knew where there was a key.

She put her ear to the door.

There was silence.

Shaw's Porsche was coming up the drive, black as a funeral car – did it *have* to be a black one? She could tell by the speed that it wouldn't be stopping at the house but continuing up to the brewery. There was a new link road for the brewery lorries, so they never grumbled past the Hall these days, and no local vehicles, except for Shaw's Mercedes and his Porsche, ever laboured up from Bridelow any more.

So the Hall, sealed off from both the brewery and village, irrelevant now to both, might as well not exist.

'Nor me,' Liz Horridge whispered into the empty, high-ceilinged room with its bland Regency-striped wallpaper and its cold, crystal chandelier. 'I've become irrelevant to everybody.'

Even Shaw – famous mother's boy – had quite casually replaced her in his life. Always away at meetings, in Matlock, Buxton, Sheffield, London even. Or with his girlfriend, the mysterious Therese.

With whom Shaw appeared obsessed. As well he might. The girl was far too beautiful for him – at thirty-one, he was at least ten years older, losing his hair, conspicuously lacking in style despite his costly education. But being seen with Therese (Therese *Beaufort*, no less) had done wonders for his confidence, and his lifelong stutter had virtually disappeared.

Her delight had turned to a damp dismay. Years of speech therapy, of love and patient coaxing at the fireside. And what was it that finally killed Shaw's stutter?

Sex.

She could weep. *Had* wept.

And wept and wept.

Last week he'd made her position quite appallingly clear. 'If I were you, Mother,' he'd said in passing – everything Shaw said to her these days appeared to be in passing – 'If I were you I'd be off. Out of here. Somewhere warm. The Channel Islands. Malta.'

She clung to the sofa. 'But I don't *want* a holiday, Shaw.'

'No, not a holiday. I mean, for good. To live. Why not? It's warm, it's civilized. And absolutely everyone would want to come and stay with you.'

'What are you *saying*?'

Shaw had smiled affably and dashed off to his 'meeting'.

Every day since, she'd sat here, by this bay window, and listened to his voice in her head saying so smoothly, without a hint of impediment, *Somewhere warm. The Channel Islands. Malta* . . .

And envisaged Therese Beaufort, in some slinky designer costume, drink in hand, languid in this window, gazing out on *her* property.

Liz Horridge thought she could see old Mrs Wagstaff waddling up the main street of Bridelow towards the church. Or maybe it wasn't. Maybe she just needed to see the old girl.

How's dear old Ma these days? Is she well?

Three decades ago, in the crowded parlour full of bottles, two cats on the hearth, Ma Wagstaff cradling Liz's head. Sleeping in the little bedroom. *If he comes to you . . . scream. Don't matter what time.*

And now, *Perhaps I'll drop in. Wouldn't you like that?*

You can't. She'll stop you.

Things change. Barriers weaken.

She looked out at the village, willing it closer. She'd give anything to be able to shatter that damned glass screen before it all went black.

Well, look at it this way – there was no way anyone could have got in there without her or Alice knowing about it. Therefore there was no one in there, except for . . . well, yes.

The spare key was filed in the third filing cabinet. Under K, for key.

The problem was, suppose something was amiss in there? Suppose a rat or something had got in? Suppose something electrical had malfunctioned, threatening the bogman's welfare? And therefore Roger's. And hers.

Tentatively, she unlocked the third filing cabinet and located the key. It was smoky-coloured steel, about four inches long.

Who would Roger blame if something had gone wrong with the bogman, his future? Who was in charge of the office in Roger's absence?

Filed under B was a second and longer key for the double lock to the inner room, the specimen room, the bogman's bedroom.

She just rather wished, as she pushed in the first key, that she hadn't acquiesced so readily to Alice's 'request' to leave early.

Chrissie slipped on her cardigan. It would be cold in there, wouldn't it? Mustn't get the shivers, that would never do.

The metal door opened with a soft vacuum belch.

'Sorry to intrude,' Chrissie said softly.

Behind the door was a small hallway where two new

Portacabins had been pushed together. This was where the white coats were kept, and there were a couple of lavatory cubicles and a washbasin. Then there was another, unlocked door leading to an anteroom with a desk. And then the innermost metal door, with a double lock through which minions like her and Alice were not supposed to venture.

So there couldn't possibly be anybody in there.

Anybody *else*.

She'd been in there a couple of times, but only with Roger and not for very long. So she knew what *he* looked like, no problem about that.

The second key turned easily, twice, and Chrissie walked into an almost complete but alarmingly pleasant darkness which hummed faintly.

She didn't move. Apart from the hum, it was very, very quiet. Nothing scurried away. She'd left the door open behind her to allow a little light in there, but the velvety darkness absorbed it all within a yard or two of the opening and she had to fumble about for switches.

It was not cold. This was it. Well, of course, this was why it seemed so pleasant. The temperature was controlled to body heat. *Bog* body heat. He'd apparently been freeze-dried and then maintained in a controlled environment. She rather hoped he was packed away or at least covered up with something.

. . . do you touch him much?

Chrissie's hand found a switch, and the lights came on, flickering blue laboratory light, white on white tiles.

Mortuary light. Chrissie tensed, breathed in sharply.

But, of course, she was right. There was absolutely nobody here.

Nobody *else*.

. . . of course I touch him. He feels like a big leather cricket bag. You should pop in sometime, be an experience for you.

Actually he was rather smaller than the cricket bags Chrissie had seen when her ex-husband used to play.

He was lying on his table in his heat-regulated bubble, looking like somebody who'd spent far too long in a solarium.

Yes, he had a lovely tan.

Still hard to think of him as an actual corpse. He was too

old. But still, ancient as he was, when you thought about it, he was probably in a better state of preservation than Chrissie's late grandad was by now.

Chrissie laughed at her stupid self.

She leaned over the bogman, curled up under his plastic bubble.

'All right then, chuck?'

She wondered what he'd sound like if he could reply, what language he spoke. Welsh, probably.

She looked around. There were a couple of wires, naked rubber, emerging from the bottom of the container. Pretty primitive. The British Museum boffins would probably have a fit.

But nothing seemed amiss.

'I'll leave you, then,' Chrissie said. She tried to see his face. His nose was squashed, like a boxer's. There were whiskers around his contorted lips, which were half open, revealing the brown stumps of his teeth.

There was a fold in the side of his neck, a flap, like another lip. She thought, God, that's where they cut his throat, poor little devil.

Beaten over the head, garrotted, throat cut and then they chopped his dick off.

Oh, yuck.

Automatically, she glanced down to where his groin ought to be, where the body was bent.

And then Chrissie made a little involuntary noise at the back of her throat.

She glanced back at his face.

His twisted lips . . . leering at her now.

Her eyes flicked rapidly back to his groin, back to his face, back to his groin. She felt her own lips contorting, and she made the little noise again, a high-pitched strangled yelp, and she began to back off towards the door.

But she couldn't stop looking at him.

. . . *what, no* . . .

. . . *penis* . . . *must have chopped it off. Part of the ritual.*

Chrissie's hands began to tingle as they scrabbled frantically behind her back for the door-handle.

Get me *out* of here.

Far from being emasculated, the bogman, under his bubble, had the most enormous erection she had ever seen.

From *Dawber's Book of Bridelow*:

NATURAL HISTORY

BRIDELOW MOSS IS believed to be over four thousand years old, but there has been considerable erosion over the past two centuries and the bog appears to have been affected by pollution from industry twenty or more miles away, with much of the vegetation being destroyed and the surface becoming even darker due to soot-deposits.

Erosion is gradually exposing the hills and valleys submerged under the blanket bog, and many fragments of long-dead trees, commonly known as 'bog oak', have been discovered. Because of the preservative qualities of peat, wood recovered from the Moss is usually immensely strong and was once considered virtually indestructible . . .

CHAPTER IX

There was frost on the morning of the day Matt Castle was to be buried, and the heaped soil beside the prepared grave looked like rock.

The grave was in the highest corner of the churchyard, and the Rector could see it from the window of his study. A shovel was set in the soil, a stiff, scarecrow shape against the white morning.

Hans turned back to the room and to the kind of problem he didn't need, today of all days.

'I didn't know who else to come to,' the young farmer said, the empty teacup like a thimble in his massive hands. 'I've got kids.'

137

'Have you told the police?'

'What's the point?' The farmer wore black jeans and a torn leather jacket. He wasn't a churchgoer but Hans had christened his second child.

'If you've been losing stock . . .'

'Aye, one ram. But that were months ago. I told t'coppers about that. What could they do? Couldn't stake out whole moor, could they? Anyway, like they said, it's not a crime no more, witchcraft.'

'Devil worship,' Hans said gently. 'There's a difference. Usually.'

'All bloody same to me. With respect. Like I say, it's not summat they warn you about at agricultural college, Vicar. Sheep scab's one thing, Satanism's summat else.'

'Yes.' Hans didn't know what to do about this. The man wasn't interested in counselling, sympathy, platitudes; he wanted practical help.

'So I've come to you, like.' His name was Sam Davis. This was his first farm. A challenge – seventy acres, and more than half of it basically unfarmable moorland, with marsh and heather, great stone outcrops . . . and the remains of two prehistoric stone circles half a mile apart.

''Cause it's your job, really, int it?' said Sam Davis, thrusting out his ample jaw. A lad with responsibilities. Two kids, a nervy wife and no neighbours. 'T'Devil. An' all his works, like.'

And there he really had put his finger on it, this lad. If this was not a minister's job, what was? Hans tried to straighten his leg. Some minister *he* was, took him half an hour to climb into the pulpit.

'Tell me again,' he said. 'There was the remains of a fire. In the centre of the circle. Now . . . on the previous occasion, you actually found blood. And, er, the ram's head, of course. On the stone.'

'Just like they wanted me to find it,' Sam Davis said. 'Only it weren't me as found it, it were t'little girl.' He set his cup down in the hearth, as if afraid he was going to crush it in his anger.

'Yes. Obviously very distressing. For all of you. But you

138

know . . . It's easy for me to say this, obviously, I'm not living in quite such an exposed . . .'

'Hang on now, Vicar, I'm not . . .'

'I know . . . you're a big lad and well capable of taking care of your family. The actual point I was trying to make is that it's easy to get this kind of thing out of proportion. Quite often it's youngsters. They read books and see films about Satanism, they hear of these ritual places, the stone circles . . . not in Transylvania or somewhere but right here within twenty miles of Manchester and Sheffield . . .'

'So you think it's youngsters, then.'

'I don't know. All I'm saying is it's *often* kids. The kind, if you saw them, you could probably tuck a couple under each arm.'

'Aye, well, like I say, it's not me . . . so much as the wife. I wanted to wait up there, maybe surprise 'em, like, give 'em a bloody good hiding, but . . .'

'I think your wife was right,' Hans said. 'Don't get into a vendetta situation if you can help it. It's probably a phase, a fad. They'll go off and find another circle in a week or two, or perhaps they'll simply grow out of it. You've told the police, and apart from the, er, the ram . . .'

'I've not told coppers about last night. Only you. There's nowt to see. Only ashes. No blood. No bits.'

'How far is the nearest circle from where you live?'

'Half a mile . . . three-quarters. But it's a tricky climb at night, can't do it wi'out a light, and wi' a light they'd see me comin'. Jeep's no bloody use either, on that ground.'

'So you saw the fire . . .'

'Bit of a red glow, that were all.'

'And your wife heard . . .'

'She *thought* she heard. Like I say, could've bin a sheep . . . fox . . . owl . . . rabbit.'

'But she thought it was . . .'

'Aye,' said Sam Davis. 'A babby.'

'There's a dragon,' the boy said, and his bottom lip was trembling. 'There *is* . . .'

'Gerroff,' said Willie Wagstaff.

He'd been for his morning paper and didn't plan to bugger about on a day as cold as this, wanted to get home and put a match to his fire.

'You go an' look, Uncle Willie.'

This was Benjie, nearly eight, Willie's youngest sister Sally's lad. Tough little bugger as a rule. He had The Chief with him, an Alsatian, Benjie's minder.

Willie folded up his paper, stuck it under his arm. 'What you on about at all?'

'. . .'s a dragon, Uncle Willie . . .'s 'orrible . . .'

He was about to cry. Pale too. Cheeks ought to be glowing, morning like this. Especially with having the day off school, to go to Matt's funeral.

Then again, could be that was at the bottom of this. Death, funerals, everybody talking hushed, a big hole being dug in the churchyard for the feller he called Uncle Matt. And Benjie trying to understand it all, seeing this great big dragon.

'All right,' Willie said, pretending he hadn't noticed the lad was upset. 'I'll buy it. Where's this dragon?'

'On t'Moss.'

'Oh, aye. And what were *you* doin' on t'Moss on your own then, eh?'

'I weren't on me own, Uncle Willie. T'Chief were wi' me. An' 'e dint like it neither.'

The big dog flopped his mouth open, stuck his tongue out and looked inscrutable.

'Gerroff,' said Willie. 'That dog's scared of nowt. All right, lead the way. But if you're havin' me on, you little Arab, I'll . . .'

When the farmer had gone, Catherine came in with a mid-morning mug of tea for Hans, and he asked her, 'You hear any of that?'

'Bits.' His daughter sat on the piano stool. She was wearing a plain black jumper and baggy, striped trousers with turn-ups. 'Got the gist. What are you going to do about it, Pop?'

'Well,' said Hans, 'I don't really know. Obviously I don't like the sound of this baby business. And I'm not one to generalize about hysterical women. But still, I think if a child had gone missing virtually anywhere in the country we'd have heard about it, don't you?'

Cathy looked serious, as she often did these days, as if she'd suddenly decided it was time to shoulder the full responsibility of being an adult, as distinct from a student.

'No,' she said. 'Not necessarily.'

'What do you . . . ?' Hans looked puzzled. Then he said, 'Oh. That.'

'It's been exaggerated a lot, of course, but that doesn't mean it doesn't go on, Pop.'

'You're beginning to sound like Joel Beard.'

'Oh, I don't think so.'

'Well,' said Hans, 'if there really is a possibility of something of that nature, then he should tell the police, shouldn't he? But where's his evidence? His wife thought she heard a baby crying. As he said, it could have been any one of a dozen animals, or the wind or . . .'

Cathy said, 'A friend of mine at college did a study of so-called ritual child abuse. What it amounts to, in most of the cases which have been proved, is that the ritual bits – the devil-masks and the candles and so on – are there to support the abuse element. Simply to scare the children into submission. So in most cases we're not talking about actual Devil worship . . .'

'Just extreme evil,' Hans said. 'Where's the difference exactly?'

'I'm not an expert,' Cathy said, 'but I rather think there *is* a difference.' She grinned slyly. 'I think it's something Ma Wagstaff could explain to you if you caught her in the right mood.'

Cheeky little madam. Hans smiled. 'I'm the accredited holy man in these parts, in case you'd forgotten. Anyway, why didn't young Sam go to Ma Wagstaff for advice?'

'Because he hasn't lived around here very long. He doesn't know the way things operate yet.'

How they changed. There'd been a time, not so long ago, when Cathy had been dismissive, to say the least, of Ma Wagstaff and all she stood for.

'And you do, do you?' Hans said. 'You know how things operate.'

'I'm getting an inkling.'

'Perhaps we should discuss this sometime.'

'I don't think so,' Cathy said.

Hans frowned.

'I don't think words can really pin it down,' she said. 'Or that we should try to.'

She looked at him blandly. All open-faced and pain-free. Twenty-three years old, a light-haired, plain-faced girl – even Hans had to admit she was no great beauty. However, there was a knowingness about her that he hadn't been aware of before.

He felt old. Suddenly she was starting to look wiser than he felt. How they changed. Every time they came home from University they'd grown stronger and more alien. Catherine studying archaeology at Oxford and Barney, her twin (who he'd rather imagined would follow him into the Church) at the London School of Economics and now researching for a prominent Conservative MP – Barney, the one-time Young Socialist.

'Have you got a boyfriend, Cathy?' he asked suddenly.

'Why do you ask?'

'Because I'm your only surviving parent.'

Her nose twitched mischievously. 'And you'd got around to wondering if I was gay, I suppose.'

He felt his eyes widening. Was this indeed what he'd been wondering? One of those forbidding, shapeless lumps that lay in the mental silt.

Cathy swivelled suddenly on the piano stool, lifted up the wooden lid to expose the keys, and began to beat out the opening bars of 'Jerusalem'.

'I don't think I'm queer,' she said, addressing the keys. 'But some people find me a bit strange.'

*

142

The frosted peat was quite firm where he walked. Didn't even need his wellies today.

Fifty yards out, Willie stopped.

Bog oak, he told himself, that's all. Probably passed it hundreds of times, but they get turned around by the wind, bits break off.

The Moss looked like a dark sea sometimes. You came down from the village, across the road, and it was like clambering over the rocks to get to the bay. That was on a misty day, when the Moss stretched quickly to the horizon. But on a bright morning, like now, you could see how the bog actually sloped gently upwards, then more steeply towards the mountains, Kinder Scout in the distance.

On a beach there was driftwood. In a moss, bog oak, great chunks of blackened wood coughed up by the peat. Made good, strong furniture.

Benjie wouldn't cross the road to the Moss, but The Chief had followed Willie, reluctantly, big paws stepping delicately over the black pools at the edge, where it nearly met the tarmac.

Now, fifty yards into the Moss, The Chief stopped too and made a noise at the back of his throat that was half-growl and half-whine.

'Bog oak,' Willie said to the dog. 'You never seen bog oak before?'

Point was, though, he personally had never seen owt like this before. The size of it. The fact that it had suddenly appeared in a place where there were no trees, save a few tatty pines.

He walked up by the side of it, and its shape began to change, but it still didn't make you think of anything scarier than half an oak tree with its branches all crushed up and twisted.

But when he got around it, looking back through the branches towards the village, this was when his breath got jammed up in his throat, when he felt like he was swallowing half a brick.

Willie backed off to where the dog was crouching and

snarling, his black lips curled back over his teeth. 'All right, Chief,' Willie said hoarsely.

He looked back to where Benjie stood, forlorn in his red tracksuit.

'You're going t'ave to explain this,' Willie told himself, his right hand building up a rhythm on his hip pocket where there was a bunch of keys. 'Lad's countin' on you. Better come up wi' summat a bit quick.'

He straightened up.

'Bog oak.'

He'd stick to his story. The fact that he'd never seen bog oak like this before was *his* problem. Just had to make it sound convincing for the lad.

Willie marched boldly up to the thing, grabbed hold of the end of one of its branches to snap it off, about nine inches of it. 'Strewth!' It was like trying to snap a crowbar. It came though, all at once. 'Go on,' he said to The Chief. 'Fetch it.'

And he threw it as hard as he could, glad to get it out of his hand if truth were told. It felt cold and hard, just like iron or stone. But it was wood all right, nowt fossilized about it, too light – he'd hurled it into the wind and it landed barely ten feet away.

'Well, go on then!' Bloody hell, he'd thrown dozens of sticks for this dog over the years.

The Chief didn't move; the thick fur on the back of his neck was flattened, his eyes were dull and wary, his tail between his legs.

'You soft bugger,' Willie said.

What this was, the dog was close to Benjie, they'd grown up side by side. Only natural he'd picked up on the kid's fear. Aye, Willie thought, and it'd've put the shits up me too, at his age.

Then he thought, admitting it to himself, What do you mean, *at his age* . . . ?

He tried to look at the thing dispassionately. It was amazing, like a work of art, like bloody *sculpture*.

But it didn't make him think of a dragon. Dragons were from fairy tales. More than that, dragons were animals. All ight, they had wings and long scaly tails, but they were animals and there was nowt scary about animals.

Willie wanted to back off further, until he couldn't make out the details. He wanted to crouch down at a safe distance and growl at it like The Chief.

Basically he didn't want to see it any more, wished he'd never seen it at all because it was the kind of shape that came up in your dreams. This was stupid, but there was no getting round it.

The tangle of branches wrapped round, woven into each other like pipes and tubes, like a human being wearing its intestines on the outside.

And out of all this, the head rearing up on a twisted, scabby neck, and the head was as black as, as . . . as peat. It had holes for eyes, with the daylight shining through, and a jagged, widely grinning mouth, and on either side of the head were little knobbly horns.

And where one of the horns went into a knob, there was even the beginnings of another face, like one of them gargoyles on the guttering at St Bride's.

But what was worse than all this was the way the thing thrust out of the peat, twelve feet or more, two big branches sticking out either side of the neck-piece, like hunched shoulders, and then smaller branches like dangling arms and hands and misshapen fingers, like they had arthritis in them, like the Rector's fingers.

And when a gust of wind snatched at it, the whole thing would be shivering and shaking, its wooden arms waving about and rattling.

Dancing about.

Willie remembered something that used to scare the life out of him when he was little. The teacher, Ernie Dawber's uncle, telling them about Gibbet Hill where hanged men's skeletons used to dangle in chains, rattling in the wind.

'Oh, come on . . . !' Willie said scornfully. He was shivering himself now – cold morning, coldest this year, not expecting it, that's all there is to it, nowt else.

'Come on.'

Walked away from it across the Moss, towards the little lad and the village, wanting to run, imagining Benjie screaming, *Run, Uncle Willie, run! It's come out of t'bog and it's after you . . . ! Run!*

He kept on walking steadily, but the fingers of both hands were drumming away, going hard and steady at his thighs.

'Bog oak,' Willie made himself shout. 'Bog oak!'

PART FOUR

THE BURIAL

CHAPTER I

Across the border, heading south, Moira ignored all the big blue signs beckoning her towards the M6. Motorways in murky weather demanded one-track concentration; she had other roads to travel.

You should take a rest, Moira. The Duchess. *Unravel yourself.*

Well, sure, nothing like a long drive to a funeral for some serious reflection . . . for facing up to the fact that you were also journeying – and who knew how fast? – towards your own.

The countryside, getting rained on, glistening drably, looked like it also was into some heavy and morose self-contemplation. It was almost like she'd left Scotland and then doubled back: there were the mountains and there were the lochs. And there also was the mist, shrouding the slow, sulky rain which made you wet as hell, very quickly.

Cumbria. She stopped a while in a grey and sullen community sliding down either side of a hill. Wandered up the steep street and bought a sour, milky coffee in a snack-and-souvenir shop. A dismal joint, but there was a table where she could spread out the map, find out where she was heading.

Many places hereabouts had jagged, rocky names. Nordic-sounding, some of them. The Vikings had been here, after the Romans quit. And what remained of the Celts? Anything?

She looked out of the café window at a ragged line of stone cottages with chalet bungalows, Lego-style, on the hillside behind.

She watched a couple of elderly local residents stumbling arm-in-arm through the rain.

English people.

. . . this guy was telling us, at the conference this afternoon, how the English are the least significant people – culturally, that is – in these islands . . . mongrels . . . no basic ethnic tradition.

And what the hell, Moira wondered, were New Yorkers?

Mungo Macbeth, of the Manhattan Macbeths. Could you credit it?

Moira had another go at the coffee, made a face, pushed the plastic cup away.

She sighed. Poor Macbeth. Poor glamorous, superficial Macbeth. Who, back home, through the very nature of his occupation and his connections, would likely have whole queues of mini-series starlets outside his hotel room. Who, in New York, would have been chasing not her but his lawyer, wondering if a bonestorm was an Act of God or maybe worth half a million in compensation.

But who, because this was Scotland, the old ancestral muckheap, and because of the night – the crazy, surrealistic, Celtic night – had behaved like a man bewitched.

Moira took her plastic cup back to the counter, which was classic British stained-glass – stained with coffee, congealed fat, tomato ketchup.

'On your own?' the guy behind the counter said. He was lanky, late-twenties. He had a sneery kind of voice out of Essex or somewhere. Nowhere you went these days in Britain, did the people running the tourist joints ever seem to be locals.

She said, 'We're all of us alone, pal.' And, slinging her bag over her shoulder, headed for the door.

'You didn't finish your coffee,' he called after her. 'Something wrong with it?'

'It was truly fine.' Moira held up the back of a hand. 'Got all my nail varnish off, no problem.'

About half an hour later, she surrendered to the blue signs. On the motorway the rain was coming harder, or maybe she was just driving faster into it. At a service area somewhere around Lancaster, she found a phone, stood under its perspex umbrella, called her agent in Glasgow and explained where she was.

'Previous experience, Malcolm, told me not to call until I was well on the road, or you'd instantly come up with a good reason why I wasn't to cross the border.'

'Never mind that. I have been telephoned,' Malcolm said ponderously, the Old Testament voice, 'by the Earl's man.'

Oh, shit.

'Hoping you were fully recovered.'

'Right . . .' she said cautiously.

'And most apologetic about the abrupt termination of your performance the other night by the inexplicable precipitation from the walls of approximately a hundred stags' heads. Now, was that not an extraordinary thing to happen?'

'Bizarre.'

'Several people had to be treated for minor lacerations, and there were two broken arms.'

'Oh, dear.'

'So naturally the Earl wanted to reassure himself that you had not been damaged in any way.'

'I'm fine. Just fine.'

'Because you seemed to have disappeared. Along with one of his guests, a gentleman called, er, Macbeth.'

'Sorry,' Moira said. 'No more money.' She hung up and ran back into the rain, black hair streaming behind her, before he could say anything about witchy women.

The psychic thing.

A millstone, a fucking albatross.

She started the car, the eight-year-old BMW with a suitcase in the boot, the suitcase jammed up against the Ovation guitar sleeping in its black case like Dracula in his coffin – we only come out at night, me and that guitar, together. With sometimes devastating results.

The damned psychic thing.

If you really could control it, it would be fine. No, forget fine, try bearable. It would be *bearable*.

But going down that old, dark path towards the possibility of some kind of control. Well, you took an impulsive step down there, the once, and you found all these little side-paths beckoning, tiny coloured lanterns in the distance – follow *me*, I'm the one.

You dabbled. I said to you never to dabble.

The coloured lanterns, the insistent, whispering voices.

The comb has not forgiven you. You have some damage to repair.

Yes, Mammy.

She drove well, she thought, smoothly, with concentration. Down into England.

The way – many years ago, a loss of innocence ago – you travelled to the University in Manchester for all of four months before, one night, this local folk group, Matt Castle's Band played the student union.

Matt on the Pennine Pipes, an amazing noise. Growing up in Scotland, you tended to dismiss the pipes as ceremonial, militaristic.

Matt just blows your head away.

The Pennine Pipes are black and spidery, the bag itself with a dark sheen, like a huge insect's inflated abdomen. Matt plays seated, the bag in his lap, none of this wrestling with a tartan octopus routine.

'*Where d'you get these things?*'

'*Like a set, would you, luv?*'

'*I wouldn't have the nerve, Mr Castle. They look like they'd bite.*'

An hour and a couple of pints later he's admitting you can't buy them. There are no other Pennine Pipes. Perhaps there used to be, once, a long, long time ago. But now, just these, the ones he made himself.

How to describe the sound . . .

Sometimes like a lonely bird on the edge of the night. And then, in a lower register, not an external thing at all, but something calling from deep inside the body, the notes pulled through tube and bowel.

'*The Romans brought bagpipes with them. The Utriculus. Whether they were here before that, nobody knows. I like to think so, though, lass. It's important to me. I'm an English Celt.*'

Within a month you're singing with the band, trying to match the pipes . . . which you can't, of course, could anyone?

But the contest is productive: Matt Castle's Band, fifteen years semi-professional around the Greater Manchester folk clubs, is suddenly hot, the band offered its first nationwide tour – OK, just the small halls and the universities, but what it could lead to . . . maybe the chance – the only chance they'll ever get at their time of life – to turn full-time professional.

Only this tour, it has *got* to be with Moira Cairns, eighteen years old, first-year English Lit. student. Oh, the chemistry: three middle-aged guys and a teenage siren. No Moira and the deal's off.

Typically, the only pressure Matt applies is for you to take care of your own future, stick with your studies. *'Think about this, lass. If it all comes to nowt, where does that leave you . . . ?'*

And yet, how badly he needs you to be in the band.

'I can go back. I can be a mature student.'

'You won't, though. Think twenty years ahead when me and Willie and Eric are looking forward to our pensions and you're still peddling your guitar around and your looks are starting to fade off . . .'

Blunt, that's Matt.

About some things, anyway. There was always a lot going on underneath.

Moira shifted uncomfortably in her seat and caught sight of herself in the driving mirror. Were those deep gullies under her eyes entirely down to lack of sleep? She thought, Even five, six years ago I could be up all night and drinking with Kenny Savage and his mates and I'd still look OK.

More or less.

The further south she drove, the better the weather became. Down past Preston it wasn't raining any more and a cold sun hardened up the Pennines, the shelf of grey hills known as the backbone of England.

Some way to go yet. Fifty, sixty miles, maybe more. If she was halfway down the backbone of England, then Bridelow must be the arse-end, before the Pennines turned into the shapelier, more tourist-friendly Peak District.

Moira switched motorways, the traffic building up, lots of

heavy goods vehicles. Like driving down a greasy metal corridor. Then the Pennines were back in the windscreen, moorland in smudgy charcoal behind the slip-roads and the factories. Somewhere up there: the peat.

I have to do this, Matt had written. *It's as if my whole career's been leading up to it. It just knocked me sideways, the thought that this chap, the bogman, was around when they were perhaps playing the original Pennine pipes.*

Time swam. She was driving not in her car but in Matt's old minibus, her last night with the band. Matt talking tersely about piping to the Moss, how the experience *released* him.

And he'd written, *It was as if he'd heard me playing. I don't know how to put this, but as if I'd played the pipes and sort of charmed him out of the Moss. As if we'd responded to something inside us both. Now that's a bit bloody pretentious, isn't it, lass?*

And Moira could almost hear his cawing laugh.

She came off the motorway and ten minutes later, getting swept into naked countryside that was anything but green, she thought, Shit, what am I doing here? I don't belong here. I walked out on the guy fifteen years ago.

. . . traitorous cow . . .

Hadn't escaped her notice that one thing Lottie had not done was invite her to the funeral.

Always a space between her and Lottie. Never was quite the same after Moira found the nerve to get her on one side during her second pregnancy and warn her to take it easy, have plenty of rest – Lottie smiling at this solemn kid of nineteen, explaining how she'd carried on working until the week before Dic was born.

Never was quite the same with Lottie, after the termination and the hysterectomy.

The road began to climb steeply. It hadn't rained here, but it was cold, the tops of stone walls and fences sugared with frost.

Jesus, I am *nervous*.

It was gone 2 p.m., the funeral arranged for 4.30. Strange time. At this point in the year they'd be losing the light by then.

Her mouth was dry. She hadn't eaten, or drunk anything

since the two aborted sips of the filthy coffee in the Lake District, and no time now for a pub lunch.

The sky was a blank screen, the outlines of the hills now iron-hard against it.

Lottie was jealous back then, though she'd never let it show.

The countryside was in ragged layers of grey, the only colour a splash of royal blue on the side of some poor dead sheep decomposing by the roadside, tufts of its wool blown into a discarded coil of barbed wire. The sky harsh, blanched, without sympathy.

Unquintessential England. As hard and hostile as it could get. No water-meadows, thatched cottages or bluebell woods.

No reason for Lottie to be jealous. Was there? Well, nothing happened, did it? Matt was always the gentleman.

Was.

Can't get used to this. I *need* to see him buried.

In front of her, a reservoir, stone sides, a stone tower. Cold slate water. She followed the road across it, along the rim of the dam, slowing for a black flatbed lorry loaded with metal kegs, the only other vehicle she'd seen in three or four miles. Across the cab, in flowing white letters, it said,

BRIDELOW BEERS

The road narrowed, steepened. It was not such a good road, erosion on the edges, holes in the tarmac with coarse grass or stiff reeds shafting through. No houses in sight, no barns, not even many sheep.

And then suddenly she crested the hill, the horizon took a dive and the ground dipped and sagged in front of her, like dirty underfelt when you stripped away a carpet.

'Christ!' Moira hit the brakes.

The road had become a causeway. Either side of it – like a yawning estuary, sprawling mudflats – was something she could recognize: peatbog, hundreds of acres of it.

There was a crossroads and a four-way signpost, and the sign pointing straight ahead, straight at the bog, said BRIDE-LOW 2, but there was no need, she could see the place.

Dead ahead.

'Hey, Matt,' Moira breathed, a warm pressure behind her eyes. 'You were right. This is something.'

Like a rocky island down there, across the bog. But the rocks were stone cottages and at the high point they sheered up into the walls of a huge, blackened, glowering church with a tower and battlements.

Behind it, against a sky like taut, stretched linen, reared the ramparts of the moor.

Unconscious of what she was doing until it was done, her fingers found the cassette poking out of the mouth of the player.

She held her breath. There was an airbag wheeze, a trembling second of silence, and then the piping filled up the car.

Moira began to shiver uncontrollably, and it shook out all those tears long repressed.

She let the car find its way across the causeway.

On the other side was a shambling grey building with a cobbled forecourt. The pub. She took one look at it and turned away, eyes awash.

So she saw the village through tears. A cliff face resolved into a terraced row, with little front gardens, white doorsteps, houses divided by entries like narrow, miniature railway tunnels. Then there were small dim shops: a hardware kind of store, its window full of unglamorous one-time essentials like buckets and sponges and clothespegs, as if nobody had told the owner most of his customers would now have automatic washing machines; a fish and chip shop with some six-year-old's impression of a happy-looking halibut painted on a wooden screen inside the window; a post office with a stubborn red telephone box in front – British Telecom had now replaced most of them with shoddy, American-looking phone booths, but, thankfully, had forgotten about Bridelow.

The streetlamps were black and iron, old gaslamps. Maybe a man would come around at night with a pole to light them.

Well, it was conceivable. Much was conceivable here.

Moira saw an old woman in a doorway; she wore a fraying grey cardigan and a beret; she was as much a part of that doorway as the grey lintel stones.

156

Peat preserves, Matt had said.
Peat preserves.

From *Dawber's Book of Bridelow*:

RELIGION (ii)

Stone Circle
(upper moor)

E. Dawber
'78

THAT BRIDELOW WAS a place of pre-Christian worship is
beyond doubt. As has already been noted in this book, there
are a number of small stone circles dating back to Neolithic
times on the moor less than a mile from the village. The
original purpose of these monuments remains a matter for
conjecture, although there have been suggestions that some
are astronomically-oriented.

As for the village itself, the siting of the church on a
presumed prehistoric burial mound is not the only evidence
of earlier forms of worship. Indeed . . .

157

CHAPTER II

'Steady, Pop, just take it *ve* . . . ry steady.'

'No, leave me, please, I'll be fine, if I can just . . .'

'God, I never realized. How could you let it get to this and say nothing? How *could* you?'

Hans hissed, '*Shut up!*' with a savagery that shocked her. He pulled away and ducked into the church porch, and Cathy was left staring at Our Sheila who was grinning vacuously, both thumbs jammed into her gaping vagina.

Cathy turned away and saw why her father had been so abrupt: a large man was bearing down on them, weaving skilfully between the gravestones like a seasoned skier on a slalom.

'Catherine!' he roared. 'How wonderful!'

'Joel,' Cathy said wanly.

'So. You've come all this way for Matt Castle's burial. And you're looking well. You're looking . . . *terrific*. Now.' He stepped back, beamed. 'Did I spot your esteemed father . . . ?'

'In here, Joel.'

He was slumped on the oak bench inside the porch looking, Cathy thought, absolutely awful, the pain now permanently chiselled into his forehead. Joel Beard didn't appear to notice.

'Hans, I've been approached by two young chaps with guitars who apparently were among Matt Castle's many protégés in Manchester. They say they'd like to do an appropriate song during the service, a tribute. I didn't see any problem about that, but how would the relatives feel, do you think?'

Cathy's father looked up at his curate and managed to nod. 'I'll . . . Yes, we must consult Lottie, obviously. Perhaps, Cathy . . .'

Cathy said, 'Of course. I'll ring her now. And I'll come and tell you, Joel, OK?' Why couldn't the big nerk just clear off? But, no, he had to stand around in the porch like some sort of ecclesiastical bouncer, smiling in a useful sort of way, his head almost scraping the door-frame.

'Can we expect any Press, do you think? Television?'

Cathy said, 'With all respect to the dead, Joel, I don't think Matt Castle was as famous as all that. Folkies, no matter how distinguished, tend to be little known outside what they call Roots Music circles.'

'Ah.' Joel nodded. 'I see.' With those tight blond curls, Cathy thought, he resembled a kind of macho cherub.

'Staying the night, Catherine?'

'Probably. The roads are going to be quite nasty, I gather. Black ice forecast. In fact,' she added hopefully, 'I wouldn't hang around too long after the funeral if I were you.'

'Not a problem,' Joel said. 'I have accommodation.'

'Oh?' Damn. 'Where?'

'Why . . .' Joel Beard spread his long arms expansively. 'Here, of course.'

Hans sat up on the oak bench, eyes burning. 'Joel, I do wish you wouldn't. It's disused. It's filthy. It's . . . it's damp.'

'Won't be by tonight. I've asked the good Mr Beckett to supply me with an electric heater.'

'Hell,' Cathy said. 'Not the wine-cellar.' It was a small, square, stone room below the vestry where they stored the communion wine and a few of the church valuables. It was always kept locked.

'Ah, now, Catherine, this is a latter-day misnomer. The records show that it was specifically constructed as emergency overnight accommodation for priests. Did you know, for instance, that in 1835 the snow was so thick that the Bishop himself, on a pastoral visit, was stranded in Bridelow for over two weeks? When he was offered accommodation at the inn he insisted he should remain here because, he said, he might never have a better chance to be as close to God.'

'Sort of thing a bishop *would* say,' said Cathy.

'Ah, yes, but . . .'

'And then he'd lock himself in and get quietly pissed on the communion wine.'

Avoiding her father's pain-soaked eyes, but happy to stare blandly into Joel Beard's disapproving ones, Cathy thought, I really don't know why I say things like that. It must be you, Joel, God's yobbo; you bring out the sacrilegious in us all.

The digital wall-clock in the admin office at the Field Centre said 14.46.

'Er . . .' Alice murmured casually into the filing cabinet, 'as it's Friday and Dr Hall's not likely to be back from that funeral and there's not much happening, I thought I might . . .'

'No chance,' Chrissie snapped. 'Forget it.'

Alice's head rose ostrich-like from the files. 'Well . . . !' she said, deeply huffed.

Done it now, Chrissie thought. Well, bollocks, she's had it coming for a long time. 'I'm sorry, Alice,' she said formally, 'but I don't think, for security reasons, that I should be left alone here after dark.'

Alice sniffed. 'Never said that before.'

'All right, I *know* the college is only a hundred yards away and someone could probably hear me scream, but that's not really the point. There are important papers here and . . . and petty cash, too.'

She'd caught one of the research students in here when she returned from lunch. The youth had been messing about in one of the cupboards and was unpleasantly cocky when she informed him that he was supposed to have permission.

'Nothing to do with *him*, of course.' Alice smirked. 'Because you're not silly like that, are you?'

'I *beg* your pardon?'

'Him! In there. The one with no . . . personal bits.'

'Don't be ridiculous,' Chrissie mumbled, head down so that Alice would not see her blush. How stupid she'd been the other night, thinking . . .

'It was just a thought,' Alice said. She opened the bottom drawer of the smallest filing cabinet and brought out her make-up bag.

. . . when obviously it couldn't have been . . . what you thought. You were just more frightened than you cared to admit, going in there on your own . . .

'Going anywhere tonight?'

. . . it was just the way the thing was lying, and the projecting . . . item was just some sort of probe or peg to hold it together . . .

'What? Sorry, Alice . . .'

'I said, are you going anywhere tonight?'

'Oh, I thought I'd have a night in,' Chrissie said. 'Watch a bit of telly.'

She didn't move. She was still aching from last night. Roger had taken her to dinner at a small, dark restaurant she'd never noticed before, in Buxton. And then, because his wife was on nights, had accompanied her back to her bungalow.

Roger's eyes had been crinkly – and glittering.

His 'stress', as experienced at the motel, had obviously not been a long-term problem. Gosh, no . . .

'I wonder,' Alice said, 'if *Mrs* Hall will be with him at the funeral.'

'I think he likes to keep different areas of his life separate,' Chrissie said carefully.

Lottie said, shaking out her black gloves, 'To be quite honest, I wish he was being cremated.'

Dic didn't say anything. He'd been looking uncomfortable since the undertakers had arrived with Matt's coffin. For some reason, they'd turned up a clear hour and a quarter before the funeral.

'I don't like graves,' Lottie said, talking for the sake of talking. 'I don't like everybody standing around a hole in the ground, and you all walk away and they discreetly fill in the earth when you've gone. I'd rather close my eyes in a crematorium and when I open them again, it's vanished. And I don't like all the flowers lying out there until they shrivel up and die too or you take them away, and what do you *do* with them?'

Dic, black-suited, glaring moodily out of the window, his hands in his hip-pockets. Lottie just carried on talking, far too quickly.

'And also, you see, in a normal situation, what happens is the funeral cars arrive, and they all park outside the house,

161

with the hearse in front, and all the relatives pile in and the procession moves off to the church.'

'Would've been daft,' Dic said, 'when it's not even two minutes' walk.'

'Which means . . . I mean, in the normal way, it means the coffin doesn't leave the back of the hearse until it reaches the church door. Not like this . . . it's quite ridiculous in this day and age.'

The two of them standing alone in the pub's lofty back kitchen.

Alone except for Matt's coffin, dark pine, occupying the full length of the refectory table.

'But I mean, what on earth was I supposed to say to them?' Lottie said. 'You're early – go and drive him around the reservoirs for an hour?'

The relatives would be here soon, some from quite a distance, some with young children.

'I keep thinking,' Dic said, his voice all dried up, 'that I ought to have a last look at him. Pay my respects.'

'You had your chance,' Lottie said, more severely than she meant to. 'When he was in the funeral home. You didn't want to go.'

'I couldn't.'

Her voice softened. 'Well, now's not the time. Don't worry. That's not your dad, that poor shell of a thing in there. That's not how he'd want you to remember him.'

God, she thought, with a bitter smile, but I'm coping well with this.

Of course, half the Mothers' Union had been round, offering to help with the preparations and the tea and the buffet. And she'd said, very politely, No. No, thank you. It's very kind of you, but I can look after my own. And the old dears had shaken their heads. Well, what else could they expect of somebody who'd turn down Ma Wagstaff's patent herbal sedative . . .

Yes. She was coping.

Then Dic shattered everything. He said, 'Mum, I've got to know. What happened with that nurse?'

Lottie dropped a glove.

'At the hospital. The night he died.'

'Who told you about that?' Picking up the glove, pulling it on, and the other one.

'Oh, Mum, everybody knows about it.'

'No, they don't,' she snapped.

'They might not here, but it was all round the Infirmary. Jeff's girlfriend knew, who's on Admissions in Casualty.'

'They've got no damn right to gossip about that kind of thing!'

Dic squirmed.

'God, you choose your bloody times, my lad.'

'I'm sorry, Mum.'

'Not as if she was hurt. She had a shock, that was all. He didn't know where he was. He was drugged up to the eyeballs. She was a young nurse, too inexperienced to be on a ward like that, but you know the way hospitals are now.'

'They said he attacked her.'

'He *didn't* attack her. God almighty, a dying man, a man literally on his last legs . . . ?'

Dic said, unwilling to let it go, 'They said he called her, this nurse, they said he called her . . . Moira.'

Lottie put her gloved hands on the pine box, about where Matt's head would be, as if she could smooth his hair through the wood, say, Look, it's OK, really, I understand.

'Leave it, will you, Dic,' she said very quietly. 'Just leave it.'

'She's not coming today, is she? The Cairns woman.'

'No,' Lottie said. 'She's not.'

'Good,' said Dic.

Cautious as a fieldmouse, little Willie Wagstaff peeped around the door, sniffed the air and then tiptoed into the dimness of Ma's parlour.

The curtains were drawn for Matt, as were the curtains in nearly all the houses in Bridelow, but at Ma's this was more of a problem, the place all cluttered up as usual with jars and bottles and big cats called Bob and Jim.

He crept over to the table. In its centre was a large aspirin bottle, the contents a lot more intriguing and colourful than aspirins.

The principal colour was red. In the bottom of the bottle was a single red berry, most likely from the straggly mountain ash tree by the back gate. All the berries had vanished from that bugger weeks and weeks ago, but this one looked as bright and fresh as if it was early September.

Also in the bottle was about a yard of red cotton thread, all scrimped up. One end of the thread had been pulled out of the bottle and then a fat cork shoved in so that about half an inch of thread hung down the outside.

The bottle had been topped up with water that looked suspiciously yellowish, the tangle of red cotton soaked through.

'By the 'ell,' Wille said through his teeth. 'Nothin' left to chance, eh?'

'*You put that down! Now!*'

Willie nearly dropped it. Ma's eyes had appeared in the doorway, followed by Ma. Too dim to see her properly; she was in a very long coat and a hat that looked like a plate of black puddings.

'Bloody hell, Ma, scared the life out of me.'

'Coming in here wi'out knocking. Messing wi' things as don't concern you.'

'*Me* messing!' He gestured at the bottle. 'I bet that's not spring water, neither.'

'Used to be!' Ma glared indignantly at him. 'Been through me now. That strengthens it.'

'Oh, aye? I thought you were losing your touch.'

Ma stumped across to the table, snatched up the bottle and carried it over to the ramshackle dresser where her handbag lay, the size and shape of an old-fashioned doctor's bag. She was about to stow the bottle away then stopped. 'Who's carrying him, then?'

'Me. Eric. Frank Manifold Senior. Maybe young Dic. Why?'

'That Lottie,' Ma said. 'She's a fool to herself, that girl. If she'd let t'Mothers' Union give her a hand, we'd all be sleeping easier.'

'Eh?' He watched Ma passing the aspirin bottle from hand to hand, thoughtfully. 'Oh, now look, Ma . . . just forget it. I am not . . . Anyway, there'll be no chance, Lottie'll be watching us like a bloody hawk.'

'Aye, p'raps I'll not ask you,' Ma said, to his relief. The thought of opening Matt's coffin turned his guts to jelly.

'And anyway, why d'you need a thing like that? I thought it were all sorted out.'

'You *thought*.' Ma was contemptuous. 'Who're you to think, Willie Wagstaff?'

'Ma, I'm fifty-four years old!' Willie's fingers had started up a hornpipe on the coins in the hip pocket of his shiny black funeral pants.

'And never grown up,' Ma said.

'This is grown-up?'

Ma bent and put the bottle down on the edge of the hearth. The fire was just smoke, no red, all banked up with slack to keep it in until Ma returned after the funeral. She straightened up, wincing just a bit – not as sprightly as she was, but what could you expect – and faced him, hands clamped on the coat around where her bony old hips would be.

'It's like damp,' Ma snapped. 'Once you get an inch or two up your wall, you're in trouble. If your wall's a bit weak, or a bit rotted, it'll spread all the faster. It'll feed off . . . rot and corruption. And sickness too.'

'Ma . . .' Willie didn't want to know this. He never had, she knew that.

Ma picked up his thoughts, like they'd dropped neatly in front of her dustpan and brush. 'Comes a time, Willie Wagstaff, when things can't be avoided no longer. He were a good man, Matt Castle, but dint know what he were messing with. Or *who*.'

'Probably dint even know he were messing wi' owt.'

'And that wife of his, she were on guard day and night, nobody could get near. He were crying out for help, were Matt, by the end, and nobody could get near. Well . . .'

'Matt's dead, Ma,' Willie said warningly.

Ma picked up the aspirin bottle. 'And that,' she said, ramming the bottle deep into the bag, 'is why he needs protection. And not only him, obviously. This is *crucially* important, our Willie.'

'Oh, bloody hell,' said Willie. It had always been his way, with Ma, to pretend he didn't believe in any of this. Found it expedient, as a rule.

'A time ago, lad, not long after you left school, we had some trouble. D'you remember? Wi' a man?'

'I do and I don't,' Willie said evasively. Meaning he'd always found it best not to get involved in what the village traditionally regarded as woman's work, no matter how close to home.

Ma said, 'He were clever. I'll say that for him. Knew his stuff. Knew what he were *after*. But he were bad news. Wanted to use us. Had to be *repelled*.'

Willie *did* believe, though, at the bottom of him. Most of them did, despite all the jokes.

'What about him?'

Ma's lips tightened, then she said, 'They're allus looking for an opening, and this one stood out a bloody mile. And Matt Castle dint help, chipping away at it, making it bigger.'

'Eh?'

'This musical thing he were working on. T' Bogman.'

'Oh . . . aye . . .'

'Another way in, Willie. Weren't doing *that* on his own, were he?'

Willie went quiet. He knew Matt had been consulting with some writer, but the man never came to Bridelow, Matt always went to the man. Until the final few weeks when he couldn't drive himself any more.

He looked at his mother with her big, daft funeral hat and dared to feel compassion. She didn't need this, her time of life. 'Look, don't get me wrong, Ma . . .'

Ma Wagstaff's fearsome eyes flared, but they couldn't hold the fire for very long nowadays.

'. . . but you've bin at this for a fair few years now . . .'

'More than fifty,' Ma said wistfully.

'So, like . . . like I were saying to Milly . . . don't you ever get to, like . . . *retire*? I mean, is there nobody else can take over?'

Ma straightened her hat. 'There is one,' she said biblically, 'who will come after me.'

'But what 'asn't come yet, like,' Willie said, stepping carefully. You could push it just so far with Ma, and then . . .

The eyes switched from dipped to full-beam. 'Now, look, you cheeky little bugger! When I need your advice, that's when they'll be nailing me up an' all.'

Willie held up both hands, backed off towards the door.

'Which is not *yet*! Got that?'

'Oh, aye,' said Willie.

Outside in the hard, white daylight, he looked across at the church clock.

Half past three.

'On me way, Matt,' Willie said with a sniff and a sigh, rubbing his hands in the cold. 'I hope they've nailed *you* down, me old mate. Good and tight.'

CHAPTER III

GLASGOW

S hit, could this be the right place?

Realistically – no.

First off, there was no elevator. The stairway, when he managed to find it, was real narrow, the steps greasy. He didn't even like to think what that smell was, but if he was unfortunate enough to be accommodated in this block he'd surely be kicking somebody's ass to get the goddamn drains checked out.

Hardly seemed likely she'd trust her fortunes to a guy working out of a dump like this. But when he made the third landing, there was the sign on the door, and the gold lettering said,

THE M. W. KAUFMANN AGENCY.
PLEASE KNOCK AND ENTER.

Which he did, and inside it was actually a little better than he'd guessed it would be. Clean, anyhow, with a deep pink carpet and wall-to-wall file-cabinets. Also, one of those ancient knee-hole desks up against the window. And the knees in the hole were not, he noticed, in there because they needed to be concealed.

She was about eighteen, with ringlets and big eyes. She swivelled her chair around and looked at him the way, to his eternal gratitude, women always had.

'I . . . uh . . .' He stood in the doorway for a couple of seconds, trying to salvage some breath. This guy Kaufmann had to be pretty damn fit, working here.

'Mr Macbeth, is it?'

He nodded dumbly.

'Do excuse the stairs,' she said. 'Mr Kaufmann represents quite a number of singers.'

'Huh?' Doubtless there was some underlying logic here concerning singers and breath-control, but he was too bushed to figure it out. He hung around in the doorway while she went off to consult with M. W. Kaufmann in his inner sanctum.

Thinking, So you did this again, Macbeth. Put on a suit and tie this time, cancelled your lunch appointment, got busted for speeding by a cop with an accent so thick it sounded like he hadn't got around to swallowing his breakfast. You really did all of this. Over a woman. Again.

Maybe, he thought, as the kid beckoned him in, maybe this is what they call a mid-life crisis. Sure. Like all the other mid-life crises I been having since I turned twenty-nine.

'Mr Macbeth,' M. W. Kaufmann said. 'I am Malcolm Kaufmann.'

They shook hands, and, waving him to a chair, Kaufmann said, 'This all seems rather, er, irregular.'

'I'm an irregular kind of guy,' Macbeth said winningly.

Malcolm Kaufmann looked less than won. He was a small, foxy-eyed person with stiff hair the unnatural colour of light-tan shoes.

The secretary was hanging around, eyeing up Macbeth without visible embarrassment. 'Thank you, Fiona.' Kaufmann waved her out, eyeing up Macbeth himself but in a more discriminating fashion.

'So,' he said. 'You're in television, I understand.'

Macbeth confessed he was, planning to build up the image a little. Then he changed his mind and built it up a lot. How he was over here for the international Celtic conference, but also on account of his company was tossing around an idea for a major mini-series . . . piece of shlock about this American guy, doesn't know his ass from his sporran, comes over to Scotland to look up his Celtic roots and before he knows it he's besotted with this, uh, mysterious Scottish lady.

'I see,' Kaufmann said.

Yeah, I guess you do at that, Macbeth was thinking. Besotted with a beautiful, mysterious lady who sings like a fallen angel and has wild, black hair all down her back with just one single, long-established strand of grey. Under the spell of an enchantress who can make the earth move, *and* the walls and the ceiling, and after you meet her you don't sleep too good any more.

He said, 'Did Moira ever act?'

'Ah.' Kaufmann leaned back in his chair, tilting it against the wall, tapping his rather prominent front teeth with a ballpoint pen. 'Well, her first love, naturally, is her music, but I do believe . . .' Clearly searching his memory for the time she'd done a walk-on for some local soap.

Macbeth helped him out. 'Certainly has the charisma, don't you think?'

'Indeed, indeed. The same, er, quality, perhaps, as that apparent in . . . who shall I . . . ? Cher . . . ? Does that comparison do her justice, would you say?'

'Spoken like a good agent, Malcolm.'

Kaufmann's eyes narrowed. 'Don't be deceived by the surroundings, Mr Macbeth. I *am* a good agent. You say . . . that you encountered Moira at the Earl's recent Celtic gathering. That would be on the evening when her performance was unaccountably disrupted.'

'Right,' Macbeth said. 'Unaccountably disrupted.'

'By what appears to have been an earth tremor.'

'Which, when it happened, I don't recall having felt.'

'Really.'

'Maybe I'm insensitive that way,' Macbeth said.

'But you don't really think so.'

Macbeth shrugged. 'Like you say, she has charisma.'

They both nodded.

'Of course,' Macbeth said, 'this is early days. See, first off, what I'd really like is to meet with Moira over lunch before I leave here . . . discuss things informally.'

'And how long will you be here?'

'Two weeks, at the outside.'

'Well, I shall no doubt be in touch with her very shortly.' Kaufmann smoothed down his unconvincing hair. 'And I shall naturally inform her of your interest. Then perhaps the three of us might . . .'

'Yeah, that'd be, uh, that'd be just . . . She in town right now?'

'I fear not.'

'See, I thought if she was doing a gig someplace, I'd kind of like to be in the audience.'

Kaufmann smiled. 'This sudden interest in Moira . . . this is entirely professional, of course.'

'I'm a very professional kind of guy. However, I've long been a fan. Of the music. But also . . . Malcolm, this is kind of sensitive . . .'

'Which, as you pointed out to me a few moments ago, you are not.'

'Yeah, well, when I, uh, encountered the lady that night, I was a mite overwhelmed, I guess, by the essential, uh, Celtishness, if that's the word, of the occasion and, if I'm being honest, by the experience of Moira herself, and so . . . well, I believe I said a few things left her thinking – as you doubtless are thinking right now – what a Grade A dork this person is.'

'Oh, yes,' said Kaufmann. He paused. 'She can certainly be quite disconcerting.'

'Thank you for that. So I'd like to meet with her informally and maybe convince her that, in less-inhibiting circumstances . . .'

'I see. Well, sadly, Moira is *not* working tonight. Or in the city at present. She has a personal matter to attend to. And though, as her agent, I am obviously aware at all times of her whereabouts, no, I'm afraid I can't tell you where she is. That really *would* be irregular.'

'Ah . . . right,' Macbeth said.

'Perhaps you could leave a number with Fiona, where we can contact you.' The agent's face was blank.

'Right,' Macbeth said gloomily.

CHAPTER IV

Joel Beard had been standing there for a couple of minutes, over by the window in the Rector's study, his mouth slightly open.

'Hans,' he said urgently, as if the church was on fire, 'Hans, quickly, who on earth is that?'

The Rector couldn't manage anything quickly any more, but, yes, he too had seen the hooded figure. It had vanished now behind the church tower.

'I'm sorry, Joel?'

'Over there. Didn't you see it?'

'No. I mean . . . all kinds of women pass through that gate.'

Joel turned to him, a 'Got you' smile on his large, unlined face. 'I don't think I mentioned the gate, did I, Hans? And I don't think I mentioned a woman.'

'Well, obviously I assumed . . .' Hans grimaced and bent to his worse knee, feigning pain for once. *Bloody* man. Joel had spent three half-days with Hans, being shown around, shaking a few hands. Big, cheerful, amiable character, anxious to learn. But suddenly . . .

'I wouldn't be surprised,' Joel said in his flat, calm Yorkshire voice, 'if there weren't quite a lot of things you haven't noticed. Things that go on, hereabouts.'

'. . . the hell are you talking about?'

'Hell?' said Joel. 'Yes. I think I *am* talking about hell. For instance, Sam Davis, the young chap who was here this morning . . .'

Hans stared at him. 'How do you know about that?'

'When he came out, his Land Rover wouldn't start.' Joel flashed his teeth. 'I was around. I fixed it. We had a chat.'

'Mechanic too, eh?' the Rector said. 'You're obviously an endlessly useful man to have about the place.'

Joel, deaf to all sarcasm, said, 'I told Sam I'd go along to the farm, talk to his wife. And perhaps . . . perhaps do what I can to protect them.'

'Joel, if there's any protecting to be done in this parish . . .' God in heaven, this was the man's first full day in Bridelow, and he was taking over!

'Oh, I realized, of course, that you'd be along there yourself if it wasn't for your, er, leg. I explained all this to Sam, of course I did.'

'Made my excuses, did you?'

'Hans . . .' Joel Beard wore a hefty gold-plated crucifix on his chest. Joel, the avenging angel. For the first time, Hans was getting an inkling of how disruptive this man could turn out to be.

'Hans, I'm only trying to help,' Joel said, like a social worker addressing some uppity pensioner.

'The problem is, Hans, people sometimes don't realize the amount of sheer legwork involved in ministering to a rural parish. Admit it, now, you've needed help for quite some while, and been too proud to ask for it. Well, naturally, we all admire you for that, but there's a job of work to be done here, you know that.'

The Rector said coldly, 'I really don't know *what* you're talking about.'

'Perhaps,' Joel said gently, 'that's because you're too close to it. You know what I think? I think these filthy rites on the moors are only the tip of the iceberg.'

He glanced back out of the window to the place where the hooded woman had disappeared. *Stay away*, Hans pleaded inside his head. *Stay out of sight . . . for God's sake . . . whoever you are.*

'There's been talk, you know,' Joel said into the glass pane.

'I have to be frank, it's the only way I can be. And I think it's only fair you should know. A good deal of talk. At diocese level.'

Hans sat down suddenly, carelessly, in his armchair – and felt the pain might hurl him at the ceiling. 'Listen,' he gasped, gripping the chair arms, holding himself down. 'Has it ever occurred to you for one blessed moment that perhaps there are things *you* don't understand? I know you were at St Oswald's. I know the sort of bull-at-a-gate Christianity they go in for . . .'

'I only know what's in my heart.' Joel almost chanting, his eyes squeezed to slits, Joel the seer, Joel the prophet. 'I know that God is living in my heart, and therefore what I feel to be right and good must *be* right and good because it is His Word.'

God save us, Hans thought, from Born Again Christians cunning enough to get into the business proper. And God help me to restrain this man's excesses.

Leave him alone! Can't you see what you're doing to him?

Cathy, in the hall, ear to the study door. Dressed for the funeral, black jumper and skirt, coat over her arm.

Half an hour ago she'd sneaked down to the wine-cellar to discover that Joel had set up a camp bed on the stone flags and a card-table with candles, like a makeshift altar.

A bit eerie. A lot disturbing.

What the hell was this bloke trying to achieve, digging himself in, like a big mole, under the very heart of Bridelow?

'Talk,' Hans said. 'You say there's been talk. What kind of talk?'

Joel walked back to the centre of the room, stood in front of the piano, his hands behind his back, the polished cross flashing from the black of his cassock. Like a cheap medallion, Hans thought from the sour darkness of his pain.

'I'm not a humble man,' Joel said.

Hans, coughing, nearly choked.

'I know this,' Joel said. 'And I pray one day Almighty God will let me come to humility in my own way. But not . . . *yet*.'

His hands whipped round from behind his back. One was an open palm and the other a fist. They came together with a small explosion in the still, fusty air of the Rector's study.

'Not yet,' Joel Beard said softly, turning back to the window. Still, presumably, no sign of the woman in black. Whichever of them it was, Hans thought, she would do well to depart quickly and discreetly, the way they could when they wanted to.

'It's not the time, you see, for humility.' Joel standing behind Hans's chair now, blocking his light. 'The clergy's been humble and self-effacing for so long that it amounts to downright indolence. It's time, I believe, to remember the other Christ. The one who ejected the traders and the money lenders from the temple. There's worse than that here. Isn't there?'

'Look . . .'

Joel spat out, 'It's the Devil's lair!'

'It's . . .' Hans tried to get out of his chair, felt suddenly dizzy.

'That's what the talk's about.' Joel's eyes burning in the afternoon gloom. 'Satan walking openly in the street. Satan walking, bold as brass, to the very door of this church, where that filthy whore parades her . . . her parts.'

'No.' Hans felt old and ineffectual. 'It's not true.'

'Yes! There's a cult of Satan, making blood sacrifices on the moors, and this is where it's emanating from. God only knows how long it's flourished here.'

Cathy breathed in, hard.

Half an hour ago, Joel had caught her spying. Stood and watched her coming up the steps from the cellar, smiling at her from the vestry doorway. Cathy, red-faced, mumbling, 'Just seeing if there was anything I could do. To, er, to make you a bit more comfortable down there.'

Could have bitten her tongue off. She supposed lots of women would find him awfully attractive, with the tight golden curls, the wide smile – and that physique. Perhaps she really *was* gay.

Certainly she hated the man now. How could he say these things?

. . . that filthy whore parades her parts . . .

Our Sheila?

You're insane! She wanted to fling open the study door and scream it at him.

Joel said reasonably, 'We're not asking you to do anything yourself. Obviously, you've had to live with these people for a very long time. Big part of your life. And we all realize you're not well . . .'

'And who?' Hans asked wearily, as if he didn't know, 'are *we?*'

Joel, for once, was silent.

'The Bishop? Our newly appointed archdeacon? Perhaps he fancies you, Joel, have you thought about that?'

Joel Beard turned away in distaste. 'Christ says . . .'

'But . . . but *you're* not Christ, Joel,' Hans said, horrified at the hollow weakness of his own voice. He slumped back into the chair, into the endless cavern of his pain, his eyes closed.

The Rev. Joel Beard laughed agreeably. 'We'll crack this thing together, Rector. You and me and God.'

Hans heard him rubbing his hands. 'Well. Time's getting on. Funeral to conduct. Though I can't think *why* you left it until so late in the day.'

'Family request,' Hans mumbled, lying. 'Some relatives had . . . long way to travel.'

'Hmm. I see. Well, come on, old chap.' Joel's strong Christian hand on his shoulder. 'Soon be over.'

From behind the door, Cathy scurried away, pulling on her coat. He'd caught her once today. He'd never catch her again.

The two of them stood at the bottom end of the churchyard, not far from the lych-gate. There was a monument here on its own, stark and pointed, like an obelisk, one word indented on a dressed-stone plaque.

HORRIDGE.

'It was always pretty scary,' Shaw said, 'to think that one day I'd be under that too.'

Therese, in her ancient fox-fur coat, walked all round the monument. 'Is it a vault?'

'Something like that. I didn't take too much notice when they stuck my father in there. I'm sure that one of the reasons I was determined to unload the brewery was to avoid being buried here. I mean, I didn't think about it at the time, but it must have been at the back of my mind. To break the family ties with Bridelow, get the hell out of here. For good. I mean . . . not have to come to people's funerals who you hardly knew, because you're a Horridge. I reckon the old man would have sold out himself if he'd had half a chance.'

'Where would you *like* to be buried?'

'Somewhere warm. If it has to be in this country I'd prefer to be cremated.'

'I wouldn't mind.'

'Being cremated?'

'Being buried here,' Therese said. 'I like vaults.' She smiled, her eyes glinted. 'You can get out of them.'

Shaw shuddered, a feeling he was growing to enjoy. She looked very edible today, as ever. However, for the first time, he rather hoped she was *not* naked under that coat. It was so cold, though, that he didn't really imagine she could be. She'd attached a scarf-thing to it today, with the fox's head on the end. Shaw, who'd ridden to hounds two or three times whilst staying with friends, didn't find this offensive but suspected there were people in Bridelow who would; they appeared to have strong views about killing animals for pleasure.

She said, 'Have you ever seen him, your father?'

He knew her well enough by now to know exactly what she meant by that, but he pretended he didn't. 'Of course I've seen him. He didn't die until I was twenty-five. Come on, let's get a drink before the show starts.'

'It's your family vault, after all,' Therese said. 'You've got rights of access. Why don't we pop in and visit him one night?'

'For God's *sake*, Tess . . .' Not his bloody father, the sanctimonious old sod.

'I've told you before,' she said coldly. 'I don't like to be called Tess.' Then she turned her head and looked up into his face, and the fox's glass eyes were looking at him too. 'We could ask him, you see.'

He felt the chill wind raising his hairline even more, wished he'd worn his stylish new Homburg. She was playing with his mind again. Sometimes it was difficult to sleep.

'We could ask him if you were right. That he really did want to get out of Bridelow. That he would've had no objections at all to Gannons taking over the brewery. Give your mother something to think about.'

'I'd rather not, if you don't mind,' Shaw said. He was thinking about last summer, a warm day in August, when he'd found out about another side of Therese.

Over dinner one night in Manchester, he'd giggled nervously and said to her, 'You know, I'm beginning to think you must be some sort of vampire, only ever coming out at night.'

'Would you like that – if I was a vampire?'

'I don't know. What would it mean?'

'I could make you undead, couldn't I?'

'Er . . . haven't you got to be dead before you can be undead?'

She'd put down her glass and looked at him, red wine glistening on her lips, face still and golden in the moving candlelight, like a mask from some Egyptian tomb.

'And what,' she said, 'makes you think you aren't?' And he began to shake with desire, a new kind of desire which began at the bottom of his spine.

But he'd kept on at her in the car – it was a Range Rover this time, belonging, she said, to a friend – as she whizzed them down Deansgate around 1 a.m. What did she do at weekends, in the daytime? Social work, she said.

'*Social* work?'

And it was true; two days later they were out on the moors. He was following Therese in gloriously tight jeans and there were two friends called Rhona and Rob and a bunch of people Therese described loosely as 'offenders'.

Rhona, who was quite attractive, despite having a sort of crewcut, was apparently a professional social worker with the local authority. Rob, a lean, hard-looking man, was – amazingly – a policeman, a detective sergeant. You had to admire her cheek, being friends with a copper after all the cars and things she'd stolen.

They'd parked their vehicles in a long lay-by off the Sheffield road and after two hours of hard walking, Shaw's legs were starting to ache.

'Where are we going exactly?'

'Not far now,' Therese assured him. The six 'offenders', who were of both sexes and ranged in age from teens to about sixty, were fairly silent the whole way.

After a further few minutes, Therese stopped. They were on a kind of plateau, offering a magnificent view of miles of sunlit moorland and, more distantly, a huge expanse of darkness which he assumed was the Moss, with the hills behind it reaching up to Kinder Scout.

'Gosh, look,' Shaw said, 'there's the Bridelow road. We've come a hell of a long way round. If we'd just gone through the churchyard and carried on up the moor we'd have been up here in about half an hour.'

'It was better to come this way,' Therese said. 'Don't whinge, Shaw.'

There were stubby stones around where she was standing, arranged in a rough sort of circle, or maybe an egg-shape; it was hard to tell, they were so overgrown.

One of the older offenders was on his knees. He was probably exhausted. He had his arms around one of the bigger stones, a thing about two and a half feet high, and he seemed to be kissing it.

'What sort of offenders are they?' Shaw whispered.

'Just people who society considers maladjusted,' Therese said. 'It's stupid. They all have special qualities nobody seems to want to recognize.'

Rob said, 'We're helping to rehabilitate them.'

Therese had taken a few objects from Rob's backpack –

odd things, photographs in frames, a small pair of trainers, a large penknife – and arranged them around the circle, up against the stones.

They had a rough sort of picnic outside the circle of stones, with a whole cooked chicken, which everybody pulled bits off, and red wine. Afterwards, they all sat around in the springy yellow grass, not talking, the sun going down, Shaw starting to feel a little drunk, a little sleepy.

He was aware that Rob and Rhona had entered the circle and were murmuring to themselves in low voices. They seemed to have taken all their clothes off. They began to touch each other and then to have sex. Shaw was deeply shocked but kept quiet about it. It went on for some time. Until suddenly, dreamily, a plump, spotty, middle-aged woman called Andrea stood up and joined Rob and Rhona in the circle and began to behave as though there were some other people in there too.

'Hello, David,' she said joyfully, the first time she'd spoken all afternoon. 'All right, Kevin?'

She giggled. 'Yes,' she said. 'Me too. Do you like it here? It's nice, isn't it?'

At that stage Rhona and Rob left her and came out and sat with Therese and Shaw. Flies and midges buzzed around Andrea in the dusk. Shaw seemed to fall asleep. When he awoke he saw Andrea on her knees in the circle with her arms around what looked like two dusty shadows.

'Isn't it heartwarming?' Therese was whispering, as if they were watching a weepy from the back stalls. 'She's becoming reconciled to the loss of her brothers.'

'What happened to them?'

'They died,' Therese said. 'A long time ago. She killed them. With a penknife. They were only little. 'Course she was only a child herself. It was such a shame, they put her away for a long time.'

He didn't remember how they got back to the cars except that it was dark by then and it didn't seem to take nearly as long as it had taken them to get to the circle.

*

In the churchyard, Therese said, 'Is *she* here – your mother?'

'No, she . . . she thinks she's got that Taiwanese flu. I've tendered her apologies.'

'Funny, isn't it, the way she won't come into Bridelow.'

'She should leave. She's no connections here.'

'Why won't she leave?'

'I don't know,' Shaw said, but he did. His mother couldn't bear to be supplanted by Therese. His mother did not like Therese. This was understandable. Sometimes he wasn't sure that the word 'like' precisely conveyed his own feelings.

Her dark hair, swept back today, was mostly inside the collar of the fur coat. She wore a deep purple lipstick.

Nor, he thought, was 'love' appropriate. So *why* . . .

Therese nodded back towards the village. Shaw looked at his watch: three minutes to four, and the light was weakening.

. . . *why* . . .

Therese said, 'It's coming.' Meaning the funeral procession.

Shaw shuddered again, with a cold pleasure that made him afraid of her and of himself.

'You know,' Therese said, 'I think it's time you met *my* father. Properly.'

'Is he dead?' Shaw asked fearfully.

CHAPTER V

Everything that happened, the dreadful inevitability of it all, Ernie Dawber would remember in horribly exquisite detail. Like a series of grim cameos. Or the meticulously etched illustrations in the pre-war picture-book from which he used to tell stories to the youngest children on Friday afternoons, enjoying the measured resonance of his own headmasterly tones and then holding up the book to what was left of the light so they could all see the pictures.

Cosy, back then. Friday afternoons in mid-autumn, with Mr Dawber and The Brothers Grimm. Home to buttered toast for tea.

Now it was another Friday afternoon. But this time the text was being read to Ernie and *he* could see all the pictures, the pages turning over in a terrible, considered rhythm, until he wanted to leap up from his seat in the back row, crying out, *Stop . . . stop!*

He didn't leap up much any more. Sometimes, lately, he felt unsteady and disconnected in his head. But when he went to the doc's for some pills for it, the doc had made him have tests. Sorry he'd gone now.

No leaping up, anyroad. Nowt he could do except to witness it, for this was all he was now: the observer. The local historian, dry and factual. Not for him to comment or to judge.

Nothing that happened on this day would ever be recorded, anyway, in *The Book of Bridelow*. And so was best forgotten.

As if ever he could.

Cosy, too (the first picture) in the bar at The Man before the funeral, having a whisky for the cold, with his half of Black, his mind charting the changes from that warm evening when Matt Castle had brought them hope.

Although, unknown to him at the time, the Change must have begun on the bright March morning when the roadmen found the bog body.

Hand clenching on his glass of Black, now condemned as gnat's piss by them as knows. The only light in the bar is greenish-blue, from the old gas-mantle Matt Castle reinstated, childishly happy when he found it could still be made to work. Such small things seemed to delight Matt, painstakingly patching up frail memories of his childhood.

Unaware that he, too, was part of the Change.

Behind the bar, Stan Burrows in a black waistcoat, says passively, 'Tough about Gus Bibby, eh?'

'Why? What's up?'

'You not heard, Ernie? He's closing up the Stores.'

'No!'

'I could see it coming, me. Just not up to it no more. Bent double half the time. I went in for a bucket last week, had to climb up and get it meself. 'Sides which, he's selling nowt. What can you buy in Gus's you can't get in Macclesfield twenty per cent cheaper?'

'It's a matter of principle, Stan. We're glad enough to shop at Gus Bibby's when there's snow or floods and you can't get across the Moss. Anyway, what about his son?'

'How many days a year can't you get across t'Moss since they've built that road up? Nay, it's price of progress, int it?'

'*Progress*?' Ernie nearly choking on his so-so half of Black.

Stan saying, 'Nay, Bibby's'll shut and it'll stay shut. Who's going t'buy that place?'

'What about his son?'

'He'll not come back, will he? Got a good job wi' Gas Board in Stockport. Would you come back?'

'Aye,' said Ernie. 'I would.'

'How many's like you, though, Ernie? Any more. Be honest. How many?'

Second picture.

Halfway up the street, church behind him, looking down towards The Man. From up here, the pub looks as if it's built on the Moss itself.

A bitter wind has blown through Bridelow, snatching the leaves from the trees and bleaching the colour from the faces inside the front porches. The faces hovering, ghostly in the shadows, the bodies invisible in black.

The villagers start to step from their doorways; the coffin's coming.

A fair turn-out, thanks to Matt's folk-music friends from the Manchester circuit and outsiders with an interest in Bridelow like Dr Roger Hall. And the former brewery workers who failed to find employment in Buxton, Macclesfield, Glossop, or even Manchester and Sheffield; they're all here, except for the ones hunched over their fires with their Beecham's Powders and a bad case of Taiwanese flu, the like of which would never have got Across the Moss in the old days.

Ernie fancies he can hear wretched coughing from behind

the drawn curtains, as if the virus has spread to the stones themselves.

Turn the page, lad.

Up by the arched lych-gate now, watching people stepping down to the cobbles to join the ragged tail of the procession.

The blinds are down at the Post Office, soon to be the only shop remaining in Bridelow. Ernie hardly recognizes black-clad Milly Gill, who normally looks like a walking botanical garden. Is she in mourning just for Matt Castle, or for Bridelow itself?

The coffin's at a funny angle because of the respective heights of the men carrying it, from little Willie to gangling Frank. Are Willie and Milly Gill back together? Ernie hopes so; they need each other, time like this.

Lottie Castle follows immediately behind and, by 'eck, mourning becomes her, she's never looked as fine, the red hair swept back under a neat, black pillbox hat with a little veil, generous mouth set hard. With her, half a pace behind, is the lad, Dic, a leather case under his arm.

Go on, turn over, you've got to look . . .

The coffin on a wooden bier beneath the Autumn Cross, the Rector hunched stiffly before it, his strong hair slumped over his forehead, not quite hiding pearls of sweat, and the lines in his face like an engraving.

Behind the Rector bobs the new curate, curly-haired lad, built like a brick privy. Bit of a firebrand, by all accounts.

He'll be all right. He'll settle down. Won't he?

At the side, by the choir stalls, is Hans's lass, Catherine, who seems all of a sudden to have lost her youth. Anxiety on her firm, plain face; worried about her dad, and with good reason. Needs a long rest, that lad.

Two youngsters with guitars who Ernie doesn't recognize sing a wistful but forgettable ballad, stop and look around afterwards before realizing congregations aren't supposed to applaud, especially at a funeral.

Then the Rector gets down to it.

'Lord, we're here to thank you for the life of Matthew Castle, and to pray that his soul might . . .'

Ernie, in the centre of the rearmost pew, locates Ma Wagstaff without much difficulty – that's quite a hat Ma's got on, with those big black balls on it. Anyway, it's through Ma that he spots . . . *the mystery woman*. Otherwise he never would have noticed her, all in black like that and in the shadow of the pillar.

Ma turns around just once, with that famous penetrating stare. Thought at first the old girl was looking at *him*. And then he sees the black, hooded figure to his left, on the little seat wedged up against the stone pillar.

By 'eck. They're not usually as public as *this* about it, these women.

Pretty place, this church. Norman, was it, those huge arch-ways? And candles here and there, like in a Catholic church. Warm stained glass with Garden of Eden-type pictures full of flowers and fruit.

And the cross that hung above the carved wooden screen dividing the nave from whatever the altar area was called.

The cross was of green wood. Or at least wood that *had* been green last summer. Woven boughs, some with shrivelled, dead leaves still hanging from them. A cross from the woods and the hedgerows. Yeah, nice. And strange. One of several strange things in here – like the German Shepherd dog sitting stoically on a pew next to a small boy.

Well, why not?

But still just a wee bit weird.

Jesus, she'd be feeling at home here next. But she still kept the cloak about her; it was pretty damn cold in here and going to be a good deal colder outside, when the darkness came down.

Underneath the cloak, the jeans and jumper she'd travelled down in. No place to change. Wouldn't worry Matt how she looked, but jeans might not be viewed as entirely respectful at a funeral in these parts; keep them covered.

Also . . . *I don't want this place to know me. Don't want to be identified by Lottie or Willie or Eric or anybody who ever bought a Castle Band album.*

Not yet, OK?

Locking the car, she'd glanced up into the thickening sky, and thought, Before this burial's over, it's going to be fully dark. Matt Castle going out of the dark and into the last black hole, and the peaty soil heaped upon him under cover of the night.

But no bad thing, the dark.

I can't face anybody, she'd thought, standing alone in the muddy parking area behind the church, pulling up the deep hood until her face was lost, *traitorous cow*, I'll stay at the back, out of sight, I'll pay my respects in my own way. And then I'll get the hell out, and nobody'll be the wiser.

And yet . . .

She'd stared up at the church, at its dour, crenellated walls, at its Gothic stained-glass windows showing their dark sides to the sky, taking the light and giving out nothing. At all the pop-eyed stone gargoyles grinning foolishly down on her.

. . . somehow . . .

Followed the walls to the tower and the edge of the churchyard where the moor began in ochre tufts and gorse bushes, and in the distance there was a clump of rocks like a toad, and if you blinked the toad would be quivering, having leapt and landed five yards closer.

. . . *there's something here that knows me already*.

No people around at that time, only the sensation of them behind the drawn curtains. *Not* peering through the cracks at the stranger and the stranger's dusty BMW, nothing so obvious.

'This is a *knowing* place,' she'd found herself saying aloud.

Then, all too damn conscious of looking very like an extremely witchy woman, she'd passed through a wooden wicket gate under a steep, stone archway, to walk a while among Bridelow's dead.

There, at the top of the churchyard, was the hole awaiting Matt, the area immediately around it covered with bright emerald matting, luridly unconvincing artificial grass. She stood on it, on the very edge of the hole, staring down into the black, rooty soil. And saw again the smoke-choked mouth of the great fireplace at the Earl's castle, the clawing thing her mind had constructed there.

Mammy, how was he when he died, can you tell me that?

Backing away from the open grave, thinking, There are people here who can tell me that. And I can't ask.

Standing several yards from the church doorway now and feeling strongly that someone was watching out for her. But knowing from experience that this feeling of being watched wasn't necessarily a case of some*one* but some*thing*. That the watcher could be something in the air, something that existed purely to watch.

Spooking herself. Down here in England, where she had no heritage and there should be no reverberations.

'Aw, fuck this,' she'd said aloud, turning towards the church doorway, looking up . . . directly into the massively exaggerated, gaping pussy of the *Sheelagh na gig*.

'Shit,' Moira said. 'Was you, wasn't it?'

The *Sheelagh*. The exhibitionist. The stone effigy of a woman, compressed to the dimensions of a gargoyle. Thrusting out her privates and leering about it. A blatant fertility symbol (or something) almost always found in the stonework of churches, mostly in Ireland.

But rarely as prominent as this.

'Got yourself a prime spot, here, hen,' said Moira. She'd walked under the *Sheelagh na gig*, through the porch and into the church, feeling better now she knew who'd been watching her. This was OK, this was not the white-haired, white-faced man who'd tried to steal the comb and (maybe . . .) brought the bloody house down. This was something older, more benevolent (maybe . . .).

She'd been the first in church. She'd sat here alone inside her own dark shroud, concealed by a pillar, until . . .

Until Matt arrived.

'. . . we'll all of us remember the day Matt returned,' the Minister said. 'The gratitude felt by the whole village that its *second* most important institution was to be saved . . .'

He's not well, this minister, Moira thought. And he's

worried. A real sense of oppression coming off him. And there shouldn't be that in here. This is abnormal.

The old lady knows, the one in the really bizarre hat.

Hans leads them out into the churchyard, the pace all the more funereal because he can hardly walk.

As they near the doors, Ernie Dawber, standing up in his pew, sees the curate, Joel Beard, stride forward to take the Rector's arm. Then there's a rush of footsteps down the aisle and he sees Catherine squeeze past the coffin resting on the shoulders of Willie and Eric, Frank Senior and Young Frank and practically *throw* herself between the two clergymen, dashing the curate's hand aside and snatching her father's arm, clasping it.

By 'eck. No love lost there and she doesn't care who knows it.

The pews are emptying from front to back, which means Ernie will be the last out, except for the Mystery Woman. He glances behind just once, as he joins the end of the procession, but she's not there.

Sometimes they just disappear, these people.

The next picture is so black at first, because of the sky, that it's almost like a woodcut.

The graveyard packed like a dark fairground. But a circle of space at the top, where the moor looms above the rectangular hole in the soil, which, when the lamplight flares, is like the opening of a shaft.

Alfred Beckett, verger and organist, has lit a metal paraffin lantern which he holds up on a pole, hanging it over the grave as Hans completes the burial rite, his own version, some of it turned about, but all the old lines there.

'Man born of woman hath but a short time . . .'

As the phrases fade, like a curlew it begins.

The piping.

Ernie gasps, muffling his mouth with a leather-gloved hand, clutching a Victorian marble cross for support. A hush enclosing the churchyard as the cold and homeless notes roam the air.

He straightens up against the cross, brushing in relief at his overcoat. It's the lad. Dic. Matt's coffin on the ground at the edge of the grave and Dic standing by it, the Pennine Pipes under his arm and the wilderness music swirling up into the cold.

Only the lad. For just a few seconds . . .

Ernie moving closer. The lad plays well. His dad'd be proud. Tries to see Lottie's face, but her head's turned away. Someone weeping behind him.

Can't see the coffin any more. The four bearers lined up on either side of Dic, concealing the grave. Lamplight shows him the fingers of Willie Wagstaff's left hand starting to move against his thigh, a slow beat, in time with the piped lament.

Ernie finds he's standing next to the lamp-bearer, Alf Beckett, when somebody – likely a woman – whispers, 'Put it out, Alf.'

'Eh?'

'Put lamp out.'

Silently, Alf Beckett lowers the pole to the ground, unhooks the lantern, lays it on the grass at his feet, shuffling around to put himself in front of it so that no light is cast into the grave.

'That do?'

'Fine. Ta, lad.'

Oh, hell.

Quite soon, behind the pipes, there's a scraping and a scuffling on the ground, like mice or rats. Ernie tries to shut it out. He's not *supposed* to hear this. He looks up, away from it, and the only face he can see clearly is the Rector's, upturned to the sky, to what light remains.

The Rector also knows he is not supposed to hear or to see. He has his eyes tightly closed.

'*Get it over with,*' Ernie hisses. '*Get it bloody done!*'

Raises his eyes above the little graveside scrum but doesn't close them. Sees the black shapes of the sparse trees on the edge of the churchyard, where it meets the moor. The trees trembling. Has this withering, shrivelling sensation of something blowing towards them, off the moor, off the Moss. Irrational. His nerves. Like the night when he was scared the Moss would swallow the sun and it would never come up again. Come on, settle down, calm yourself, there's nowt you can do except keep your mouth shut and your eyes averted. Nowt here for the Book of Bridelow.

Dic keeps on piping, the same melancholy tune, over and over again, but erratic now, off-key; he's getting tired . . . but the noises behind him go on, the scuffling on the ground, and now a jarring creak and an intake of breath.

And then all hell . . .

'Stop! Let me through!'

Rough hands thrusting Ernie aside.

'Mr Beckett, where's the lamp? Stand back, will you. Stand *back*, I said, or somebody . . . will . . . get . . . hurt.'

The lantern snatched up, its gassy-white flame slanting, flaring in the furious eyes of the Rev. Joel Beard, smoke rolling from the funnel.

Hands grab at him to hold him back from the grave, but Joel, snarling, is big and fuelled-up with rage, the metal cross swinging as his cassocked chest swells and his elbows slam back.

The lamp flies up into the night and Joel catches it by its base as it falls, pushing Alf Beckett so that Alf spins sideways into Dic Castle and the Pennine Pipes make a squirming, ruptured noise, subsiding into empty, impotent blowing and wheezing.

The Rev. Joel Beard steps to where the coffin of Matt Castle lies at the grave's edge, and he lifts the lantern high.

CHAPTER VI

S he was not among those weeping when the Pennine Pipes began.

It got to her in other ways . . .

Hanging back behind the crowd, still as the headstones around her, Moira felt confused, puzzled . . . the pipes plucking at something inside her, starting this small, familiar tingle in her lower abdomen.

OK, she would have known anyway that it wasn't Matt she could hear, there wasn't the same lilting, light-as-air technique, the inimitable *agility*. Would have been no mistaking that.

And yet . . .

The Roman numerals on the church clock, lit-up, said 5.30. It *would* be dark at 5.30 this time of year. But the darkness had the icy, velvet quality of midnight, and whoever had organized this service had *known* it was going to end like this.

Why?

Sure as hell was the strangest funeral she'd ever been to, the minister and the principal mourners in a distant lamplit huddle, the freezing air over the entire churchyard somehow electric with this almost feverish, dreamlike tension, and the piping going on and on and *on*, like in a time-loop . . . so that you wound up mentally pinching yourself, asking, *is this real?*

Like, where am I? Did I drive across these unknown hills into some dream dimension?

Needing at last to break through, maybe talk to someone, hear the sound of her own voice, anybody's voice, she moved closer, symbolically tossing back the hood of her cloak . . . at the moment the lantern went down.

She saw the big shapes of the trees at the end of the churchyard. Below them, shadows intertwined. The amorphous tableau at the top of the small rise where Matt's grave was to be. From whence came the insistent, never-ending piping but no sounds of a funeral service, no suggestion of anyone leading the proceedings.

Only – under the pipes, as she drew close – a whispering, as if there was more than one person whispering but they weren't listening to each other, the voices rustling together like wind-dried leaves.

And she caught a passing perfume, a sick, sad smell.

Then, to her left, a small commotion. An expulsion of breath from a yard or so away, a dragging on her cloak and she was almost pulled down.

'*Stop!*' A man's voice, strong, authoritarian. '*Let me through.*' For just a second everything froze, and then there was this instinctive communal resistance, a tightening of the clutch of bodies around her. The whispering intensified, new urgency in it, the dead leaves really crackling now.

A scrabbling now, by her feet; some guy had been pushed over, rolled on to the cloak. He found his feet, she reclaimed the cloak. Somewhere nearby there was a struggle going on.

She didn't move. The lamp appeared again, bouncing wildly in the air, like some will-o'-the-wisp thing. In the spinning light she got a split-second picture of . . . must be Matt's boy, Dic Castle, playing the pipes, the bag trapped in an elbow, his face red with effort, and Willie Wagstaff next to Dic, Willie's eyes flitting anxiously, from side to side, and she could almost feel the rhythm of the little guy's famously impressionable fingers in her head, thud, thud . . .

Thud, thud. . . . And then the oil-lamp went up again, was held steady.

And Moira looked down, oh, Jesus, into Matt Castle's face framed in quilted white.

The smell. The perfume of the dead. The coffin lid off. His hair gone. Grave-dirt spilled on his closed eyes.

The way you never want to see them, the way you can't bear to remember them. And still you can't turn away your head; it won't move.

What have they *done* . . . ?

Moira began to shiver. She closed her eyes, and this was worse, like waking up in the fast lane, her senses lurching out of control, cracked images oscillating in the steamy half-light between perceived reality and illusion, the place where the whispers went.

. . . vaporous arms reaching from the smoky maw of a great fireplace . . .

. . . the splintering white of a skull-storm . . .

. . . dancing lights on the moor . . . a rock like an encroaching toad . . . pop-eyed gargoyles belching blood . . . an eruption of steaming intestine on stone . . .

All these reflecting one to another like in the shards of a

191

shattered mirror, while tiny, vicious, chattering voices gnawed at her eardrums and she felt something sucking around her shoes pulling her down, and she knew that if she didn't open her eyes she'd be screaming like a loony.

But when she did it was no better. She blinked in pain.

He lay there in his coffin. Matt Castle, not in a shroud but a plain, white T-shirt. And his grey-white hands, crossed over his chest, were fumbling at it.

Oh, God, oh, Jesus, his damned hands were . . .

'How dare you! How *dare* you!'

The man holding up the lantern, the big cleric she'd seen in the church earlier, this man's face bleached in the lamplight with rage and shock.

Below him, the old lady with the bizarre hat, sleeves pushed up and both arms in the coffin, pressing something into the dead hands of Matt Castle, crossed over his breast.

It was her hands moving, not his.

Moira saw a frightened, angry glazing in the eyes of the big man as he bent roughly down with the lamp; forced himself between the old woman and the body in the coffin.

She thought she heard him sob, or it might have been her.

The big minister guy had put his own hand in there . . . *Holy Christ, is this real* . . . ? . . . and brought it out, something clutched into a fist.

'Put that *back* . . .' The old woman's eyes flashing green-gold, like a cat's, in the lantern-light.

'This is . . . *unpardonable* . . .' Yeah, he *was* sobbing, the big man; sickened, shattered, furious at what he was doing.

'Joel . . .' The minister, the Rector, was there, on the other side of the grave, his face all twisted up, the fair-haired girl still holding on to his arm. 'Please. Put it back. I'll explain to you, I promise . . .'

'How . . . How *can* . . .'

'Turn away, Joel. Please. It isn't what you . . . Just *turn away.*'

The big clergyman lifted his left hand to the lamp. He was holding up a small bottle. Something moved in it, liquid. Moira glimpsed red.

'Joel . . . Give it to me . . . You don't know what . . .'

She saw that Joel was breathing rapidly now, a kind of wild, petulant hysteria there. She saw him rise to his full height, saw his arm pull back.

The Rector screamed, 'No!', shook out of the girl's grip, threw himself across the empty grave, one shoe reaching the phoney nylon grass mat on the other side, inches from the coffin . . .

. . . as Joel, breathing violently, hurled the bottle above all the heads towards the moor beyond the trees. Then he turned, put down the lamp and stumbled back into the crowd, his hands flailing.

Heard him clumping away, his outraged breathing. His sobs.

'Grab him, somebody, please . . .' The girl, and she meant the Rector. People pushing past Moira, reaching out for the minister as the false grass slid from under his shoe and he almost rolled into the open grave.

Several minutes later, the graveyard had quietly emptied, except for the group around the empty coffin. Mostly women and not whispering any more. At the centre was the one with the hat. She was the oldest of them. Two of the others replaced the coffin lid.

Moira had backed beyond the lamplight, was a short distance away, leaning up against this tall cross in the Celtic style. Trying to breathe.

Oh, God. Oh, Holy Jesus. What the fuck am I into here?

One of the women at the graveside was Lottie Castle.

Lottie's voice was very quiet, very controlled, carefully folded up tight. 'I can't believe . . . that any of this has happened.'

'Lottie . . .' It was Willie, coming up behind her.

'And *you* . . .'

'I know,' Willie said. 'I'm sorry.'

'I'll never forgive you, Willie. Or that . . . *her*.'

'She only wanted . . . Oh, Jesus Christ,' Willie wailed. 'This is awful. This is a right bloody mess. I can't tell you. Oh, God, Matt . . . Why'd it have to be Matt?'

'Willie,' the old girl in the hat demanded. 'Stop that skrikin' and fetch me that bottle back.'

'Ma, nobody's going to find that bloody bottle tonight. If ever.'

'Then we'll have t'do what we can.' She placed both hands on the coffin. 'Pass us me bag, Joyce, it's down behind that cross.' Moira tensed; at her feet was a thick vinyl shopping bag.

Lottie's leather boot slammed down hard on the coffin between the old woman's hands. 'You,' Lottie said, 'have done about enough for one day.'

The old woman's hat fell off. She looked startled. Like nobody ever spoke to her this way.

'You don't understand, girl.'

Moira sensed an even further drop in the temperature of the night air between them. 'No,' Lottie said. 'You're right. I don't understand any of this. I don't want to. Matt thought he did. He thought he *should*. Well, what good did it do him? Tell me that. I thought you'd try something. I told Willie to warn you off. It goes against everything I . . . everything I don't believe.'

'Please, lass,' the old woman coaxed. 'Let us get on with it, best we can. Let's try and put things straight before . . .'

'No. That's it. Finish. You've blown it, Mrs Wagstaff. You've turned the burial of my husband into a bloody circus. You even . . . involved my son in your pathetic, superstitious . . . Anyway, that's it. It ends here. Willie, you and Eric and the Franks are going to put that poor man in the ground.'

The old woman looked up at her. 'I beg of you, Mrs Castle . . .'

'Ha! The famous Ma Wagstaff begging? Don't make me laugh. Don't make it worse. Just get out of my way, you *silly* old bag.'

Lottie stood on the fake grass behind the coffin and raised a boot. 'Now. Have I got to push it in myself?'

She stopped. 'Where's Dic?'

Willie said, 'I told him to help them get Rector home. I thought it'd be best. Lad'd 'ad enough.'

One of the other women with Ma Wagstaff said hesitantly, 'Is he all right? Rector?'

'I don't know,' Willie said. 'Lottie, look . . . what Ma's on about . . . I know how bloody awful it seems. Hate it meself . . .'

'Then put my husband in the ground, Willie Wagstaff. And you . . .' Lottie stared contemptuously at Ma Wagstaff. 'If I ever see you near this grave again, I swear I'll wring your stringy old neck for you.'

She stood and folded her arms and waited. Moira knew she wouldn't move until the last shovelful was trampled down. When Ma Wagstaff looked at her she turned her back.

'Right, then.' Willie had a rope. He threw one end across the grave and another man caught it. 'OK, Frank. Where's t'other rope? Let's do this proper. I'm sorry, Ma, she's right. Nowt else you can do now. Let's get it filled in.'

Ma Wagstaff stood up, put on the hat with the black balls, dented now. She said, 'Well, that's it. It's started.'

'What has?'

'There were more of um here. At least one. I could tell. I could feel um. Like black damp.'

'Go home, Ma. Stoke thi' fire up, make a cuppa, eh? I'll be round later. See you're all right. Now, don't you look at me like that, I'm not a kid no more, I'm fifty-four . . . going on seventy, after today.'

'Black seed's sown,' Ma Wagstaff said ominously. 'Bury him tight and pray for us all.'

The old woman walked unsteadily away, her back bent. Like she'd been beaten, mugged, Moira thought. Several other women followed her silently down the cemetery path.

The church clock, shining bluish in the sky, said 5.42.

When the women reached the shadow of the cross where Moira stood, Ma Wagstaff stopped, stiffened, stared up at her. As Moira silently handed her the shopping bag, old embers kindled briefly in Ma's eyes. Neither spoke. Moira didn't know her.

And yet she did.

*

195

Hans lay stiffly on the old sofa in the Rectory sitting room. They'd put cushions under his knees, taken off his dog-collar. His eyes were wide open but Ernie Dawber could tell they wouldn't focus.

Hans kept trying to tell them something, but his mouth wasn't shaping the words.

'Can't fee . . . fee . . .'

'Pop, stay quiet. Let's put your overcoat over your legs. How's that? Mr Dawber, don't you think we should get the doctor to him?'

'I do. You go and make us some tea, Catherine. Dic, ring for an ambulance.'

When they'd gone, Ernie leaned over Hans. 'Don't try and talk, just nod, all right? Are you trying to say there's bits of you can't feel? Hey up, you don't have to nod that hard, just tilt your jaw slightly. Is it your arm? Your shoulder?'

Hans pushed an elbow back into the sofa, trying to raise himself. 'Chest. Shoulders.'

'Now, then . . .' Ernie raised a warning finger. 'Listen, lad, we've known each other a long time, me and thee. I'll be frank with you. I'm not a doctor, but my feeling is you've had a bit of a heart attack.'

The Rector squirmed in protest.

'Ah, ah! Don't get alarmed, now, I've seen this before. It's nowt to get panicked about. What you are is a classic case of a man who's been pushing himself too far for too long. I know this is not what you'd call an easy one, this parish, for a clergyman, and you've handled things with tremendous skill, Hans, and courage, over the years, anybody here'll agree with that . . .'

The Rector's eyes flashed frustration.

'Aye, I know. It's not the best of times to get poorly, what, with . . . one thing and another. And that Joel . . . by 'eck, he's a rum bugger, that lad. Impetuous? Well . . . But, Hans, be assured, they'll *cope*, the Mothers' Union. They *will* cope. They've had enough practice. Over the years.'

Wished he felt half as confident as he sounded. The trouble with Bridelow was so much had been left unsaid for so long that nobody even questioned the way the mechanisms operated any more. It was just how things were done, no fuss, no ceremony, until there was a crisis . . . and they found the stand-by machinery was all gunged up through lack of use.

When they heard the warble of the ambulance, Hans grabbed hold of Ernie's wrist and began to talk. 'I've buggered things, Ernie.'

'Don't be daft. Don't worry about Joel. This time next week he'll think it was all a bad dream.'

The Rector's dry face puckered.

'Don't think so? Oh, aye. Folk do, y'know. Things heal quick in Brid'lo. The thing about it . . . and I've been thinking about this a lot – and writing it down. Started a book – don't say owt about it, God's sake – Dawber's *secret Book of Bridelow*. Not for publication, like, Ma Wagstaff'd have a fit . . . just to bring all the strands together, reason it out for meself . . .'

'No, look . . .' Hans blinked hard.

'No, the thing about Bridelow . . . it's so *prosaic*. Know what I mean? Not sensational. No dressing up . . . or dressing down, for that matter. Nowt to make a picture spread in the *News of the World*. Joel? Nobody'd believe him, would they? You think about it.'

He patted the Rector's hand. 'No, better still, *don't* think about it. Get yourself a bit of a rest. *I'll* handle things. Brid'lo born, Brid'lo bred. Leave it to Uncle Ernie.'

This had been his forte as a headmaster. Getting the kids to trust him. Even when he hadn't the foggiest idea what he was doing.

As the ambulancemen crunched up the path, Hans said, 'Shurrup, you old fool and listen. It's Joel.'

'Like I said, we'll handle him.'

'No. You don't understand. Know where he's . . . where he's going to spend the night. Do you?'

'Back in Sheffield if he's got any sense.'

'No. He's . . . made up a bed. Little cellar under the church. Ernie . . . Don't let him. Not now. Not after this.'

'Oh,' said Ernie. 'By 'eck. You spent a night down there once, didn't you?'

'Only once,' said the Rector.

CHAPTER VII

GLASGOW

She told him that not only had she never eaten here, she'd never even been inside the joint before. And he, having stayed in better hotels most of his life, felt – as usual – like an overprivileged asshole.

She had the grouse, first time for that too. (Didn't Scots eat grouse on a regular basis, like Eskimos and sealmeat?) He joined her, a new experience for him also. The grouse wasn't so great, as well as which, it looked like a real bird, which made him feel guilty.

Afterwards, looking up from the sweet trolley, she said, 'I suppose you'll be wanting your pound of flesh, then.'

'Aw, come on, Fiona. I can buy a girl dinner without the question of flesh coming into it.'

'I should be so lucky.' She smiled enticingly. 'I was referring to Moira. You'll want to know about Moira.'

'Well,' he said, 'yeah. But only if this isn't gonna get you into any kind of, uh . . .'

'Shit?' said Fiona. 'I don't think so. I see all Mr Kaufmann's receipts, he never comes here. Anyway, it's nice to live dangerously for a change. I bet you live your whole life dangerously.'

'Me?' For one and a half years after leaving college he'd been a trainee assistant-director. The very next day he was an executive producer. Mom's company. 'Uh, well, not so's you'd notice.'

'You do *look* kind of dangerous, Mungo.'

'Looks can be deceptive.' Last thing he planned was to seduce this one.

'Irish,' she said. 'You look Irish, somehow.'

'So people keep telling me.'

'Mungo,' she said. 'Aw, hey, that's really incredible. Mungo Macbeth.'

'Of the Manhattan Macbeths. My Mom's real proud of that.' Giving her the condensed autobiography. 'From being a small kid, I learned how the actual King Macbeth was really a good guy whose name was unjustly blackened by this English hack playwright.'

'That's true, actually,' Fiona said. 'He wisny a bad guy.'

'I'm told they also used to play pipe-band records to me in my cradle,' Macbeth said, screwing up his nose. 'But that made me cry, so they hired this genuine Scottish nanny, used to sing me Gaelic lullabies. That part I remember. That was great. That was how I got into the music.'

'My dad used to sing me Tom Jones,' Fiona said glumly. '"The Green Green Grass of Home". *Not* so great.'

'*My* dad never got to sing me anything,' Macbeth said. 'He didn't last that long. He was kind of jettisoned by my mother's family before I was born. *They* are the Macbeths. My dad's name was Smith. I mean, Smith? Forget it. So, anyhow, this trip came up, she said, Go . . . go feel the true power of your Celtic heritage.'

'You feeling it?'

'I'm feeling a jerk is what I'm feeling. I won't say she was expecting a delegation from the clan Macbeth to turn out for me at the airport in full Highland costume, but you get the general picture.'

'Out of interest, have you actually seen anybody in a kilt since you got here? Apart from at the Earl's do?'

'Nope.'

'So what'll you tell her when you get home? Hey, would it be OK for me to have the profiteroles?'

'And just a coffee for me,' he said to the waiter. 'Make that two – I'll wait. What do I tell Mom? I'll say I had a peculiarly Celtic experience. I'll say it was too deep and personal to talk about.'

'Oh, wow,' Fiona said, rolling her big eyes. Problem was that tonight she didn't look eighteen any more. She was in a tight red dress – well, some of her was in it. Macbeth thought hard about Moira Cairns to take his mind off this comparatively minor but far from discountable temptation.

'I'll tell her I met a real witch,' he said. 'One of the weird sisters.'

'Aw, she's no' a witch,' Fiona said scornfully.

'No? What is she?'

'She's what my granny used to call *fey*. OK, maybe a bit more than that. Like, one day she was very annoyed with Mr Kaufmann . . . I mean she's usually *quite* annoyed with him but this was something . . . Anyway, here they are, raging away at each other, and she's about to storm out the door and then she just turns round, like she's gonny say something else, only she canny find the words. And *then* . . . one of the damn filing cabinets starts to shake and . . . I'm no' kidd'n' here . . . all four drawers come shoot'n' out at once. Really incredible. Awesome silence afterwards.'

'Coulda been an earth tremor.'

'That was what Mr Kaufmann said. But he still went all white, y'know? I mean, that filing cabinet was locked, I'm certain it was.'

'I can sympathize.' Macbeth shuddered, his mind making a white skull out of the tureen on an adjacent table. 'Listen, Fiona, I'm a little shaky on Moira's early career. She was at college in Manchester which is where she joined this local band, right?'

'Matt Castle's band. Matt Castle just died.'

'Oh, shit, really?' Remembering something mindlessly insulting he'd said about Matt Castle just after they met. What a shithead. A wonder she spoke to him at all after that.

The waiter brought Fiona's profiteroles. 'Hey, great,' Fiona said. 'So then she was approached about joining this rock band. Offered a lot of money, big money even for the time, to make two albums.'

'The Philosopher's Stone,' Macbeth said. 'But they only made one album.'

'Right. She split before they could get around to the second one. But, see, the word is that the reason they wanted her, apart from her voice, was that . . . You remember Max Goff, who owned Epidemic Records?'

'He was murdered, year or so ago. Some psychopath kid with a grudge.'

'Right,' Fiona said.

'I didn't know she was with his outfit. It was CBS put out the album in the States.'

'Well, the word *is*, Mungo . . .' Fiona leaned conspiratorially across the table, '. . . that the real reason Max Goff wanted her in the band was he'd heard she was psychic. He was very into all that. Like, he already had a couple of guys signed to Epidemic who were also psychics and he wanted to put them all together in a band, see what happened. Of course Moira didny know this, she thought the guy just liked the way she sang, right?'

'And what happened? I mean, that first album, that was terrific. I wore mine out.'

'Aye, but it all got very heavy, with drugs and stuff, and Moira broke her contract, came back to Scotland, went solo. Signed up with Mr Kaufmann, who's . . . well, he's no' exactly part of the rock scene.'

'I wondered about that.'

'The other singers on Mr Kaufmann's books are, like, mostly, y'know, nightclub or operatic or kind of Jimmy Shand type of outfits.'

'Who?'

Fiona dug into a profiterole; cream spurted. 'See, Moira made it clear she wisny gonny have anything to do with the rock scene ever again. And that's how it's been. She just does traditional folk concerts and selected cabaret-type dates. Really boring. Hell of a waste.'

'It's very intriguing. What do you think happened?'

Fiona shrugged. 'Most likely she just got in with a bad crowd. I used to think, well, maybe she was doing drugs in a big way. Heroin or something. And realized it was, like, a one-way street, y'know?'

'But you don't think that now?'

She shook her head. 'I know her better now. She's too strong. She widny touch drugs – not the kind that might get any kind of hold on her, anyway. I think it's more likely she just rejected the psychic stuff, the way they were fooling about, Max Goff and these guys. She knows what it can do, right? Like, if one person can shoot all the drawers out of a filing cabinet, what's gonny happen wi' four or five of them . . . ?'

'This is fascinating, Fiona.' The kid was smarter than he'd figured. 'You're saying maybe she came back to Scotland to, kind of, put herself in psychic quarantine. Maybe scared of what she could do.'

'I'm only guessing,' Fiona said, 'but how come she'll no play any of the old songs any more? I think she wants to put all that stuff behind her. But can you do that? Being psychic, I mean, it's no' like a jumper you can take back to Marks and Spencer. Drink your coffee, Mungo, 's gonny get cold.'

He drank his coffee, not tasting it. He'd been fooling himself that this thing about Moira was purely . . . well, more than physical . . . romantic, maybe. She was beautiful and intelligent, and he loved her music from way back. But maybe it went deeper. Maybe this was a woman who he'd instinctively known had been closer to . . . what? The meaning of things? Things that having money and influence and famous friends couldn't let you into?

Time of life, he thought, staring absently into Fiona's cleavage. Or maybe I really do have Celtic roots.

'Mungo,' she said. 'Can I ask you something?'

'Go ahead.' He could guess.

'All this stuff about a mini series . . .'

'Kaufmann told you about that?'

'I keep my ear to the ground.'

Or the door. He grinned. 'Yeah?'

'Was that on the level?'

'You mean, are we gonna go ahead with a film about, uh . . .'

'An American guy who comes over here to trace his roots and . . .'

'OK, OK . . .'

'. . . falls in love with this beautiful . . .'

'You're embarrassing me, Fiona.'

'Aw, hey,' she said. 'I think that's sweet.'
'So maybe you'll help me.'
'How?'
'Tell me where I find her.'
'I don't know,' Fiona said. 'Really.'

PART FIVE

OUR SHEILA

From *Dawber's* Secret *Book of Bridelow* (unpublished):

THE OLDEST WOMAN in Bridelow commands, as you would
expect, considerable respect, as well as a certain affection.

Ma Wagstaff? No, I am afraid I refer to Our Sheila who
displays her all above the church porch.

The so-called *Sheelagh na gig* (the spelling varies) is found
– inexplicably – in the fabric of ancient churches throughout
the British Isles: a survival of an older religion, some say, or
a warning against heathen excess. Usually it is lazily dismissed as 'some sort of fertility symbol'.

The shapes and sizes vary, but the image is the same: a
female shamelessly exposing her most private area. Pornography, I am glad to say, it isn't. The faces of these ancient
icons are normally grotesque in the extreme, their bodies
compressed and ludicrous.

Our Sheila, however, is a merry lass with an almost
discernible glint in her bulging stone eyes and a grin which is
more innocent than lewd.

Do not dismiss her as a mere 'fertility symbol'. She has
much to say about the true nature of Bridelow.

CHAPTER I

Round about 6.30, Chrissie had got a phone call from the police. Would she mind popping over to the Field Centre?

When she'd arrived the place was all lights. Police car and a van outside, an unmarked Rover pulling in behind her.

When the two CID men from the Rover walked across, they looked as if they'd been laughing. Now, facing her across her own desk, they were straight-faced by not exactly grim. 'I'm Detective Inspector Gary Ashton,' the tall one said. 'This is DS Hawkins' – waving a hand at the chubby one in the anorak. 'Now . . . Miss White.'

'Chrissie,' she said.

'Lovely.' He was a fit-looking bloke, short grey hair and a trenchcoat. Fancy that . . . even with policemen, fashion goes in circles.

'If you've been trying to get hold of Dr Hall,' she said helpfully, 'he went to a funeral, but it should be well over by now.'

'Thank you. We know,' Ashton said. 'He left early, apparently, and went home. He's on his way. Now, just to get our times right, when exactly did *you* go home?'

Oh, sugar, Chrissie thought. 'We finish at four forty-five,' she said.

Actually she'd left at 4.15. Just before four, Alice had fallen back on the irrefutable – claiming she had one of her migraines coming on. Chrissie had stuck it for fifteen minutes on her own and then thought, sod it, and gone to fetch her coat.

'Four forty-five,' Ashton said. 'Right.' They could tell when you were lying, couldn't they? If he could, he didn't seem too concerned.

'Now,' he said. 'You're responsible for locking up, are you?'

'I do it if there's nobody else. I wouldn't say I'm *responsible*. There's the caretaker, he comes on at five. And then a private security firm comes round a few times at night . . . that's just since *he's* been here. They were worried there might be a few, you know . . . weirdo types, wanting to have a look. Or something. What's happened, then? Has there been a break-in?'

'So when you left, everything was locked up. What d'you do with the keys?'

'The front and back door keys we drop off at the caretaker's office at the main college building. The keys to the bogman section . . . we keep those in here, I'm afraid. Is that bad? In one of the filing cabinets – but that's always locked at night, of course.'

If this chap's an inspector, she realized, it's got to be more than just a break-in.

'And the big doors at the back?'

'We never open them. Well, only when . . . when the bogman arrived in a van. They brought him straight in that way.'

'Do you go round and check those doors, Chrissie, before you leave? Round the outside, I mean.'

'Do I buggery,' said Chrissie. 'I'm an office manager, not a flaming night watchman. Look, come on, what's this all about? What's happened?'

Ashton smiled. 'So you didn't see or hear anything suspicious before you left?'

'No. Not tonight.' Oops.

'What d'you mean, not *tonight*?'

'Well . . . I thought I heard a noise in there, where . . . he is . . . a couple of nights ago, but it was nothing. Probably a bird on the roof.'

'You didn't raise the alarm?'

'What for? It was locked. I knew nobody could get in through those doors without making a hell of a racket, so there didn't seem . . .'

'Somebody got in tonight, Miss White.'

'Oh, hell,' said Chrissie. 'They didn't damage him, did they? Roger'll go hairless.'

*

She was cold. The BMW beckoned.

She could, after all, simply drive away from this.

Nobody invited you, girl.

Frost on the cobbles. No one else on the street. Curtains drawn, chimneys palely smoking.

Ah, the burden of guilt and regret. All he'd done for you, all he meant to you, and the thought that you'd never see him again.

Well, you saw him.

She shivered.

Problem with this place was there was nowhere you could even get a cup of coffee . . . except the pub.

She stood and stared at it from across the road. It was a large, shambling building set back from the street, with a field behind it and nothing behind that but peat. Dark sooty stone. Windows on three floors, none of the upper ones lit. Outside was a single light with an iron shade, a converted gaslamp, quite a feeble glow, just enough to light up the sign above the door: The Man I'th Moss. In black. No picture.

Didn't look like Lottie Castle's kind of place. Lottie was big sofas and art-nouveau prints.

Moira stepped lightly across the cobbles, peered through the doorway. Only a dozen or so people in the bar, Lottie not among them. Willie was there, with Eric Marsden. The big dollop of hair over Eric's forehead had gone grey but he looked no more mournful than he always had. Eric: the quiet one. In every band there was always a quiet one.

Go in then, shall I?

Why, it's Moira . . .

Come to help us re-form the band?

Just one problem. We had to bury Matt.

Never mind. Have a drink, lass.

She turned away, gathering her cloak about her. Moved quietly across the forecourt to the steeply sloping village street.

There was a guy leaning against the end wall of a stone terrace, smoking a cigarette. She kept her distance, walked down the middle of the street, along the cobbles.

Nothing for you here. Go back to what you know. The fancy

clubs and the small halls. You can play that scene until you're quite old, long as the voice holds out. Save up the pennies. In twenty years you can retire to a luxury caravan, like the Duchess. Sea views. All your albums collected under the coffee table.

As she came abreast of him, the guy against the wall turned and looked at her, muttered something. Sounded like 'Fucking hell'.

Then he tossed his cigarette into the road at her feet. 'And they tell me,' he said, 'that this used to be a respectable neighbourhood.'

'Who's that?' Too dark to make out his features.

'You don't know me.'

'But you know me, huh?'

'Yeah,' he said. 'But not nearly as well as my dad did.'

'Oh,' Moira said.

His voice had sounded different when she last heard it. Like high, pre-pubertal.

She sighed.

'Dic,' she said. 'You want to go somewhere and discuss all this?'

He laughed. A short laugh. Matt's laugh. A cawing.

'Well?' she said.

'I'm thinking,' he said from deep within his shadow.

''Cause I don't mind,' Moira said. 'I'm easy.'

'Yeah,' he said, 'we all knew that.'

Moira paused. 'That was your chance, Dic. I threw you that one. You gave the predictable, adolescent answer. So go fuck yourself, OK?'

She turned away, moved quickly up the street, clack, clack, clack on the cobbles. As good a way as any to do your exit. Grabbing the chance to go out angry; it helped. On either side of her were the gateposts of the stone cottages, a black cat on one, watching her like it knew her well. Lights behind curtains, lights from an electrified gaslamp projecting from an end wall, and over them all, like another moon, the illuminated church clock. Take it all in, you won't see it again. Bye-bye, Bridelow.

'All right!' It rang harshly from the cobbles like an iron bar thrown into the street.

It didn't stop her.

'Yeah, OK!' Running feet.

She carried on walking, turned towards the lych-gate, the corpse gate, but passed it by and entered the parking area behind the church, where it was very dark.

She was taking her keys out of her bag when he caught up with her.

'I'm sorry. All right?'

'Good. You'll be able to sleep.' Fitted the key in the car door. 'Night, Dic. Give my love to your mother.'

'Look . . .'

'Hey,' she said gently. 'I'm leaving, OK? You know your dad was screwing me, what can I say to that?'

'I want to talk about it.'

'Well, I'm no' talking here, it's cold and I'm no' going to the pub, so maybe you should just go away and *think* about it instead, huh? Call me sometime. Fix it up with my agent. I'm tired. I'm cold.'

'Where will you go?'

'And what the fuck does that have to do with you? I shall find a nice, anonymous hotel somewhere . . .'

'Look,' Dic said. 'There *is* somewhere we can talk. Somewhere warm.'

'Cosy.' Moira got into the car. 'Goodnight.'

'Moira . . .'

She started the engine, switched on the lights, wound down the window. 'By the way. Your playing, it was . . . Well, you're getting there.'

'I don't want to get there,' he said without emotion. 'I just wanted to please him.'

'Aye,' Moira said.

'It never did, though.'

'No,' she said.

A dumpy, elderly man walked through the headlamp beams. He wore a long raincoat and a trilby hat, like Donald's, only in better shape. 'Good evening,' he said politely, as he passed.

*

212

The lights were on in the church, ambering the pillars in the nave. A suitcase stood by the font.

Ernie Dawber watched the new curate manhandling a metal paraffin stove into the vestry.

'All right, lad?'

Joel Beard, alarmed, set down the stove with a clang.

'Ernie Dawber, lad. We met the other day, with Hans.'

'Ah, yes.' The curate recovered, stood up straight. He was wearing his cassock and the huge pectoral cross. 'Look, I'm sure you mean well, Mr Dawber, but I'd rather not discuss anything tonight, *if* you don't mind.'

'Beg your pardon?'

'The funeral, Mr Dawber. What happened at the funeral. You were about to tell me how innocuous it all was. I'm saying I'd rather not discuss it.'

'Well, I think we *should* discuss it, Mr Beard. Because it looks like you're in charge now.'

Joel Beard looked bewildered. He'd obviously rushed away from the graveside, dashed down to his little cell to recover and didn't yet know about Hans.

Ernie told him.

'Oh,' Joel said. 'Oh, my Lord.'

'Aye.'

'Is he going to be all right?'

'Happen,' said Ernie. 'If he gets some rest. If he doesn't spend all his time worrying what the bloody hell's going on back in Bridelow.'

Joel Beard gave him a hard look for swearing in church.

'Now look, lad,' Ernie said. 'Pull yourself together. You're not really going to kip down there?'

'I am.' Joel rested an arm on the edge of the font. 'It's quite clear to me that it's become even more important now for me to sleep in God's pocket. You were there today, I think, Mr Dawber. You saw what went on.'

'I saw a big, soft bugger making a bloody fool of himself,' said Ernie stoutly. 'Now, come on, it's getting cold. Pick up your suitcase; you can stay in my spare room for tonight, and we'll have a bit of a chat.'

Joel Beard made no reply. He stood very tall and very

still, the amber lights turning his tight curls into a golden crown.

'Good night, Mr Dawber,' he said.

The double doors crashed back. Roger Hall burst in, and he was white to the edges of his beard.

Chrissie was sitting at her desk, the senior detective, Ashton, casually propping his bum against it, hands deep into his trenchcoat pockets, the detective-sergeant playing with the zip on his anorak.

Roger just stood in the doorway breathing like a trainee asthmatic. He was wearing casual gear, the polo shirt and the golfing trousers. 'All right, what's happened?' Staring all round the room and finally noticing her. 'Chrissie . . . ?'

'Don't look at *me* like that, Dr Hall. I know less than you.' Obviously. Being the minion.

'How much *did* they tell you on the phone, Dr Hall?' Ashton asked, coming to his feet.

'Just . . . Just that . . . Is this on the level? It's not a joke?'

Ashton shook his head. 'Doesn't look like it, I'm afraid, sir.'

Roger glared across the office at the metal door. It was shut. 'It's unbelievable.' Shaking his head. 'What happened to the so-called security patrol?'

'We'll be talking to the company, sir, have no doubts. Meantime, we didn't like to touch anything until you got here, so if you'd be good enough to take us through . . .'

Roger nodded dumbly. Chrissie was almost feeling sorry for him. His face was like a crumpled flour bag. He looked like a parent who'd just learned his child had been found on a railway line. In fact, to him, if somebody had vandalized his beloved bogman, this was probably worse.

Which was why Chrissie didn't *quite* feel sorry for him.

The two detectives, Ashton and the chubby one in the anorak, waited while Roger went to unlock his personal high-security cabinet. He brought out both keys. The detectives followed him to the ante-room and then all three of them went through to the inner lab.

Chrissie stayed behind, both elbows on her desk, chin

propped in her hands, waiting for the eruption. She didn't
know whether to laugh or cry on his behalf.

'No . . . !' Roger's voice echoing back. 'Look . . . Inspector,
is it?'

'Gary Ashton, sir. Greater Manchester.'

'I'm . . . I just can't *believe* this has happened. What I . . .
Look, let me do some checks. It's possible . . . unlikely, but
possible . . . that there's a rational explanation. I've been away
for a few days this week. It's conceivable, I suppose, that
something was arranged and by some incredible oversight I
wasn't informed.'

'You mean whoever it was forgot to inform the caretaker
they'd be dropping in, sir? After dark?'

'No. You're right. Clutching at straws, I suppose. God
almighty, this is . . . How did they actually get in?'

'Quite professionally done, sir. The rear doors were forced,
both sets, but forced by somebody who knew how, if you see
what I mean.'

'It's . . . unbelievable.'

Chrissie heard a clang. Roger's fist hitting the metal table.

'If you wouldn't mind, sir . . . fingerprints.'

'Sorry. It's just . . . if anything, any one thing, had been
specifically calculated to fucking *ruin* me, this . . .'

'Ruin you, Dr Hall?'

'I . . . We had a lot riding on it. You don't get your hands
on one of these very often.'

'How valuable would you say? I mean, I realize you
can't . . .'

'*In*valuable. And yet not valuable at all to most people. You
could hardly stick it in your hall like a Rodin. It's beyond me,
the whole thing. And yet . . .'

Chrissie's head shot up out of her hands. *Never!*

'Well, sir, I expect you've got photographs. I'll also need to
know what kind of vehicle would be required, assuming it's
been removed from the immediate area.'

Bloody *hell*! Chrissie stood up. She found she was shaking.

'We'll obviously be searching the grounds pretty thor-
oughly. But if you wanted to get it away without damaging it
. . . would it need any special conditions? Refrigeration?'

'It's in peat, Inspector. Peat's a preservative. That's how he survived for two thousand years.'

'Of course. Sorry. Stupid of me. Anyway . . . We're clearly not looking for young tearaways here, so have you any idea, any notion at all, who in the wide world would go to so much trouble to . . .'

'Steal a two-thousand-year-old corpse.'

'Old as that? Well. Wouldn't be much use for medical research then? So what are we looking for? Bit of a nutter? A rich eccentric collector? I'll be honest, Dr Hall, I've not come across anything quite like this. It's a one-off.'

'It's unbelievable,' Roger said for about the fifteenth time, and Chrissie heard him pacing the echoing empty lab.

CHAPTER II

The girl who opened the Rectory door was sipping red soup off the top of an overflowing mug. She watched both of them cautiously over the rim.

'Sorry,' Dic said. 'It's an awkward time.'

She swallowed hot soup, winced. 'No problem. I'm on my own.'

'That's what I thought. We, er, we needed somewhere to talk . . . Sorry . . . your dad, is he . . . How is he?'

'They say it's a minor heart attack.' Tomato soup adhering to her lips. 'I'm not allowed to see him until tomorrow, he has to have rest. Ma Wagstaff says not to worry. He'll be OK.'

She sounded like this was supposed to be a reliable medical opinion. 'This is Moira Cairns,' Dic said.

'Hello,' Catherine Gruber said limply.

Moira sensed she was worried sick.

The porch light was a naked bulb. Above it, the gaping orifice, spread by stone thumbs, was deepened by the hard, unsubtle shadows it threw.

The *Sheelagh na gig*, lit for drama, grinning lasciviously at

Joel Beard. And he was appalled to think that everyone entering the church to worship God should have to pass beneath this obscenity.

Tradition, the antiquarians said. Our heritage. Olde Englande.

Joel Beard saw beyond all this, saw it only as symbolic of the legacy of evil he had been chosen to destroy.

A few minutes ago, he'd telephoned the Archdeacon from the kiosk in front of the Post Office, giving him a carefully edited summary of the evening's events in Bridelow. Not mentioning the appalling incident at the graveside with the bottle – which the Archdeacon might have judged to be, at this stage, an over-reaction on his part.

'Well, poor Hans,' the Archdeacon had said easily and insincerely. 'I think he should have a few months off, don't you? Perhaps some sort of semi-retirement. I shall speak to the Bishop. In fact I think I'll go and see him. Meanwhile you must take over, Joel. Do what you feel is necessary.'

'I have your support?'

'My support spiritually – and . . . and physically, I hope. I shall come to see you. Drop in on you. Very soon. Meanwhile, tread carefully, Joel. Will you live at the Rectory now?'

'The girl's still there, Simon. Hans's daughter. She'll have to go back to Oxford quite soon, I'd guess. But then there's Hans himself, when he leaves hospital.'

'Don't worry. We'll find him somewhere to convalesce. Meanwhile . . .'

'. . . I shall sleep in the church. In the priest's cell.'

'All alone down there? My God, Joel, you're a brave man.'

'It's God's House!' Joel had said, even he feeling, with a rare stab of embarrassment, that this was a naive response.

And *was* it God's House?

And which God?

As he entered the church of St Bride under the spread thighs of the leering Sheelagh, he experienced the unpleasant illusion of being sucked into . . .

No!!

*

'Long-haired girls,' Dic Castle said bitterly. 'Always the long, dark hair.'

Moira said, 'I can't believe this.'

'No?'

'*No*,' she said firmly.

The minister's daughter had left them alone in the Rectory sitting room. Dic had wanted her to stay, like he needed a chaperone with this Scottish whore, but she wouldn't. They could hear her banging at a piano somewhere, ragtime numbers, with a lot of bum notes. Letting them know she wasn't listening at the door.

'He never touched me sexually,' Moira said. 'He never came near. On stage, it was always him on one side, me on the other, Eric and Willie in between but a yard or two back. That was how it was on stage. That was how it was in the van. That was how it *was*.'

Somewhere, walls away, Catherine Gruber went into the 'Maple Leaf Rag', savaging the ivories, getting something out of her system.

'And you clearly don't believe me.' Moira was sitting on a cushion by the fireplace. Paper had been laid in it, a lattice of wood and a few pieces of coal.

Dic said, 'Followed him once. After a charity gig. She was waiting for him in the car park. About twenty-one, twenty-two. About my age. Long, dark hair.'

'When was this?'

'Fucking little groupies,' Dic said. He was semi-sprawled across a sofa, clutching a cushion. 'At his age. Er . . . 'bout a year ago, just before he . . . before it was diagnosed.'

Dic had a lean face, full lips like Matt. Dark red hair, like Lottie. Still had a few spots. 'And, yeah,' he said, 'I do know she wasn't the first.' Staring at Moira in her jeans and her fluffy white angora sweater, hands clasped around her knees, black hair down to her elbows.

'Because you still think the first was me. Sure. And you know something . . . Gimme a cigarette, will you?'

He tossed the cushion aside, got out a crumpled pack of Silk Cut and a book of matches. 'Didn't know you smoked.'

'Tonight,' she said, taking a cigarette, tearing off a match, 'I smoke.'

The minister's daughter was playing 'The Entertainer', sluggishly.

Moira said, 'Just answer me this. Earlier tonight, at your dad's funeral, at the graveside . . . I mean, how'd you feel about that?'

His face closed up, hard as stone. 'I just played the pipes. Badly. I didn't see anything.'

She nodded. 'OK.'

'So I don't know what you're talking about.'

'I understand. We'll forget that, then.'

He lit his own cigarette, said through the smoke, 'Mum said you wouldn't be coming anyway.'

'She didn't know.'

'You seen her?'

'No. And that's not because . . . Listen, I'm gonna say this. There was a time when I felt bad. Twenty, fifteen years ago. When I felt bad *because* I never came on to him, not even after a gig in some faraway city when we were pissed. And I felt bad that I was twenty years younger and I was taking off nationally, and he was maybe never going to.'

'I bet you did.' Dic sneered. 'I bet that really cut you up.'

She ignored it. 'I was thinking, if we'd slept together, just the once, to kind of get it over, bring down that final barrier . . . You got the vaguest idea what I'm saying?'

He just looked at her through the smoke.

'Anyway,' Moira said, 'we didn't. It never happened. Maybe that's another piece of guilt I'm carrying around. I don't know.'

The piano music stopped. Dic lay back on the sofa, hands clasped behind his head. Outside, the wind was getting up, spraying dead leaves at the windows.

There was a polite knock on the door and Cathy came in. 'I'm making some tea, if . . .'

'Oh, yeah, thanks.' Dic sitting up, looking sheepish.

'Be ten minutes,' Cathy said.

Moira said, as the door closed, 'Lottie. Your mother. She know about this?'

'We never discussed it.'

'But you think she knows, right?'

Dic shrugged.

'This girl. This so-called girl of Matt's. You know who she was?'

'No. I tried to find out from people at the folk club – The Bear, you remember the joint? Nobody seemed to know her.'

'So how do you know they were . . . ?'

'Because they went straight into this shop doorway. Would've taken a jack to prise them apart.'

'Right,' Moira said sadly. 'And she looked . . . like me?'

'Yeah. Superficially. Like you used to look.'

'Thanks a lot.'

Dic picked up the cushion and hurled it with all his strength at a bare wall. 'I didn't mean it like that, OK? I don't mean a fucking thing I say. I just like insulting people, yeah?'

'Sure,' Moira said. This wasn't getting either of them anywhere. She wished she'd stuck to her original plan and never agreed to come here with him. So he had problems. They'd made him stand there playing the pipes while they messed with his dad's body in its coffin. She could feel the confusion and the rage billowing out of him.

'Dic . . .' She was going to regret this.

'Yes?'

No, she wasn't. She wasn't going to say anything either of them might regret. She gathered up her cloak from the carpet. 'I'm away, all right?'

'Yeah.'

The hissing sound disturbed him. And the occasional popping. And the blue glow.

It came from the circular wick of the paraffin stove. Intense, slightly hellish, ice-blue needles pricking the dark, the close stone walls shimmering like the inside of a cave lit by a cold and alien sea-glare.

Joel turned the flame up fully until it was flaccid and yellow, and then he blew it out. The stove was having little or no effect anyway. His original plan had been to bring an electric heater down here, but there was no power point, and the nearest one in the church was too far away for Alfred Beckett's extension lead to reach.

Joel lit a candle.

With the stove out, the temperature must be plunging, but at least it didn't *look* as cold.

He sat on the side of the camp-bed, with the double duvet wound around him.

Cold he could live with, anyway, insulated by years of refereeing schoolboy rugby matches. Cold he could almost relish.

He'd taken off his boots but added an extra pair of rugby socks. When he lay down, his feet – projecting from the bottom of the bed – would touch the stone blocks of the far wall. That was how cramped this cell was.

But discomfort was good. It was a holy place. Above him the nave of St Bride's, around him its ancient foundations. Rock of Ages. A blessed place, a sanctuary where bishops – well, at least one bishop – had passed the dark, cold hours in sacred solitude.

If he hadn't been so bone-tired, so sated with righteous rage, Joel might have spent the night in holy vigil, on his knees on the stone floor, like some medieval knight. Praying for divine aid in the deliverance of Bridelow from its own dark dragon.

But his body and his mind were both demanding sleep . . . a state often at its most elusive when most needed. He was also rather appalled to find his loins apparently yearning for the comfort of a woman.

Before his conversion, Joel had exploited his God-given glamour at every opportunity – and there had been many. Now he did not deny himself the yearning, only its habitual, casual assuagement.

He told himself this unseemly erection in the House of God was merely a side-effect of the cold and the pressure of the duvet.

His watch told him it was not yet 10 p.m. But tomorrow, he felt, would be a long day. So he would allow his body sleep.

When he blew out the candle and lay back, the paraffin stench hung over him like a chloroform cloth. He must not sleep in this air. Clutching the duvet around him, he arose into the absolute darkness, followed his nose to the stinking heater and pulled it two yards to the oaken door. Bent almost double, he carried the appliance into the little tunnel which led to the stairway.

And then, leaving it out there, shuffled back to his cell. Locking the thick and ancient door of his sanctuary against the pagan night. Falling uncomfortably into the rickety bed.

Tread carefully, Joel.

What did the Archdeacon mean by that? Joel would tread with the courage and determination of the first Christians to walk these hills. Those who had driven the heathens from their place of worship and built upon it this church.

And whose holy task, because of the isolation of the place and the inbred superstition of the natives, had yet to be completed.

With God's help, Joel Beard would drive out the infidel. For ever.

Cathy was pouring boiling water out of a big white teapot, down the sink. 'Forgot to put the bloody tea in. I'm a bit impractical.'

'Well, don't bother for me,' Moira said. 'I have to go.'

'You're the singer, aren't you?' Cathy filled the kettle, plugged it into an old-fashioned fifteen-amp wall-socket. It was that kind of kitchen, thirty years out of date but would never be antique. Moira said wearily, yes, she was the singer.

Cathy said, 'Still, I bet you don't play the piano as good as me.'

Moira grinned. 'How long you known Dic?'

'Years. On and off. He'd come up to Bridelow with his father at weekends. I used to fancy him rotten at one time.'

'Used to?'

Cathy shrugged. 'That was when we were the same age,' she said elliptically.

Moira looked at her. A little overweight; pale, wispy hair

pulled back off a face that was too young, yet, to reflect Cathy's cute sense of irony.

'When we came in, you said you thought your father was knackered. You said it'd do him good to get out of this place for a while.'

'I said that, did I?'

Try again. 'You were born here?'

'So they tell me. I don't live here at present. I'm in Oxford.'

'Doing what?'

'Studying,' Cathy said. 'The principal occupation in Oxford, next to watching daytime telly and getting pissed.'

'What are you studying? Oh, hey, forget it. I'm tired of walking all around things. What I really want to know is what happened at Matt's funeral that fucked your dad up so bad. And who's the other minister, the big guy, and how come you don't like him. Also, who's the crone who fumbles in coffins, and why was your daddy letting it go on. That's for starters.'

Cathy straightened up at the sink. 'You can't do that.'

'Huh?'

'You can't just come into Bridelow and ask questions like that straight out.'

'Oh. Really. Well, I'll be leaving then.'

'OK,' Cathy said lightly.

The avalanche of liquid peat hit him like effluent in a flooded drain and then it was swirling around him and he was like a seabird trapped in an oil-slick, his wings glued to his body. If he struggled it would tear his wings from his shoulders and enter his body and choke him. He could taste it already in his throat and his nose.

But, even as it filled his dream, he knew that the tide of peat was only a metaphor for the long centuries of accumulated Godless filth in this village.

He knew also that he *did* have wings that could carry him far above it.

For he was an angel.

And if he remained still and held his light within him the noxious tide could never overwhelm him.

Joel dreamed on.

Although the stone room around him was cold, the black peat in the dream was warm. He remained still and the peat settled around him like cushions.

Inside his dreaming self, the light kept on burning. Its heat was intense and its flame, like the one inside the paraffin heater, became a tight, blue jet arising from a circle. It heated up the peat too.

In his dream he was naked and the peat was as warm and sensuous as woman-skin against him.

Moira waited for her by the Rectory gate.

It was bitterly cold. She imagined the walls of the village cottages tightening under the frost.

Cathy came round the side of the house, a coat around her shoulders. 'How'd you know I'd come after you?'

Moira shrugged.

'You're like old Ma Wagstaff, you are. You know that?'

'That's . . .'

'The crone, yes.'

'I hope not,' Moira said. Well, dammit . . . Willie's old mother? And he never said. All those years and he never said a word.

'I'm trying to understand it all,' Cathy said. 'Somebody has to work it all out before we lose it. Most people here don't bother any more. It's just history. I suppose that's been part of the problem.'

Moira realized she was just going to have to do some listening, see what came together. The church clock shone out blue-white and cold, as if it was the source of the frost.

'The old ways,' Moira said. 'Sometimes they don't seem exactly relevant. And people get scared for their kids. Yeh, you're right, they don't want to understand, most of them. But can you blame them?'

'It's not even as if it's particularly simple. Not like Buddhism or Jehovah's Witness-ism,' Cathy said. 'Not like you can hand out a pamphlet and say, "Here it is, it's all there." I mean, you can spend years and years prising up little stones all over the place trying to detect bits of patterns.'

Cathy fell silent, and Moira found she was listening to the night. The night was humming faintly – a tune she knew. People like me, she thought, we travel different roads, responding to the soundless songs and the invisible lights.

It's all too powerful . . . the heritage . . . maybe you should go away and when you get back your problems will be in perspective . . . go somewhere bland . . . St Moritz, Tunbridge Wells . . .

Bridelow?

Ah, Duchess, you old witch.

She said, 'So what *is* the history of this place? I mean, the relevant bits.'

'You need to talk to Mr Dawber. He's our local historian.'

'And what would he tell me?'

'Probably about the Celts driven out of the lowlands by the Romans first and then the Saxons.'

'The English Celts? From Cheshire and Lancashire?'

'And Shropshire and North Wales. It was all one in those days. They fled up here, and into the Peak District, and because the land was so crap nobody tried too hard to turn them out. And besides, they'd set up other defences.'

'Other defences?'

'Well . . . not like Hadrian's Wall or Offa's Dyke.'

'The kind of defences you can't see,' Moira said.

'The kind of defences *most* people can't see,' corrected Cathy. She looked up into the cold sky. Moira saw that all the clouds had flown, leaving a real planetarium of a night.

Cathy said, 'She'd kill me if she knew I was telling you all this.'

'Who?'

'Ma Wagstaff, of course.'

'And what makes you so sure she *doesn't* know?'

'Oh, *God*,' Cathy said. 'You *are* like her. I knew it as soon as I saw you at the door.'

'It's the green teeth and the pointy hat,' said Moira.

'I don't know what it is, but when you've lived around here for a good piece of your life you get so you can recognize it.'

'But your old man's the minister.'

'And a bloody good one,' Cathy snapped. 'The best.'

'Right,' Moira said. 'I'd like to meet him when he's feeling better.'

'We'll see.' Cathy walked past her, out of the Rectory gates, stood in the middle of the street looking up at the church. 'It's a sensitive business, being Rector of Bridelow. How to play it. And if it's working, if it's trundling along . . . I mean, things have always sorted themselves out in Bridelow. It's been a really liberal-minded, balanced sort of community. A lot of natural wisdom around, however you want to define wisdom.'

The moonlight glimmered in her fair hair, giving her a silvery distinction. Then Moira realized it wasn't the moonlight at all, the moon was negligible tonight, a wafer. It was the light from the illuminated church clock.

'They call it the Beacon of the Moss,' Cathy said.

'Huh?'

'The church clock. That's interesting, don't you think? It's not been there a century yet and already it's part of the legend. That's Bridelow for you.'

'You mean everything gets absorbed into the tradition?'

'Mmm. Now, Joel Beard . . . that's the big curate with the curly hair, the one and only Joel Beard, *Saint* Joel. Now, Joel's really thick. He thinks he's stumbled into the Devil's back yard. He thinks he's been called by God to fight Satan in Bridelow because this is where he can do it one-to-one. In the blue corner Saint Joel, in the red corner The Evil One, wearing a glittery robe washed and ironed by Ma Wagstaff and the twelve other members of the Mothers' Union.'

'The Mothers' Union?' Moira laughed in delight.

'Thirteen members,' Cathy said. 'There've always been thirteen members. I mean, they don't dance naked in the moonlight or anything – which, bearing in mind the average age of the Mothers, is a mercy for everyone.'

'Oh, Jesus,' said Moira, 'this is wonderful.'

'It *used* to be rather wonderful,' Cathy said. 'But it's all started to go wrong. Even Ma's not sure why. Hey, look, have you anywhere to stay tonight? I mean, you want to stay here? There's a spare room.'

This kid would never say she didn't want to be in the house alone.

'Thank you,' Moira said. 'I think I'd like that.'

Dic, who didn't drink much, had gone back to his father's pub and sunk four swift and joyless pints of Bridelow Black, sitting on his own at the back of the bar.

At one stage he became aware of Young Frank pulling out the stool on the other side of his table. 'Steady on, lad.' Tapping Dic's fifth pint with the side of a big thumb. 'It's not what it were, this stuff, but it'll still spoil your breakfast.'

Dic said, 'Fuck off, Frank.'

Frank got his darts out of his back pocket. 'Game of arrows?' Dic shook his head, making Frank's image sway and loom like something on a fairground ride.

'Come on, lad.' Frank's grating voice rising and fading out of the pub hubbub like a radio coming untuned. 'Life's gorra go on. You can't say you weren't expecting it. He were a good bloke, but he's better off dead than how he were, you got t'admit that.'

'Frank!' Dic clambered to his feet, sank the rest of his pint, most of it going into his shirtfront. 'Fucking leave it, will you?'

And then he was weaving and stumbling between the tables and out into the night.

He stood in the doorway a while, getting his breath together, then he strode across the forecourt and on to the street. The cobbles gleamed, frosty already, in the light of the big clock in the sky, shining like the earth from the moon in those old space pictures.

Dic began to moonwalk up the street, taking big strides, crashing into the phone box outside the post office, giggling like a daft sod. Coming up by the church, where he'd talked to Moira Cairns – there was her BMW, still parked there. Moira Cairns . . . Wouldn't mind poking that sometime, give her one for his old man. Maybe she owed him one, part of his inheritance.

He wished he had his pipes with him. Give them a fucking tune. Give them a *real* tune. Bastards. What were they at?

What were they fucking at down there? Hands in Dad's coffin, sick bastards.

Standing by the lych-gate with its cover like a picture-postcard well and a seat inside. Went in, sat down. Out of the blue light in here, anyroad. Right under the church but the sloping roof blocked it out. Dic nestled in the darkness, feeling warm. Closed his eyes and felt the bench slipping under him, like dropping down a platform lift into a velvet mineshaft. Dic threw his arms out, stretched his head back, accepting he was pissed but feeling relaxed for the first time since he didn't know . . .

He giggled. There was a hand on his thigh.

It moved delicately up to his groin like a big spider.

'Feels good,' Dic said, pretty sure he'd fallen asleep on the bench. Lips on the side of his neck and his nostrils were full of the most glorious soiled and sexy perfume.

The hand sliding his zip down, easing something out.

He pulled in his arms, hands coming together around the back of a head and soft hair. Hair so long that it was brushing the tip of his cock.

'Moira,' Dic whispered.

From *Dawber's* Secret *Book of Bridelow* (unpublished):

ALTHOUGH THERE HAS never been any excavation, it is presumed that the 'low' or mound on which St Bride's Church is built was a barrow or tumulus dating back to the Bronze Age and may later have been a place of Celtic worship.

Similar mounds have been found to enclose chambers, which some believe to have been used not so much for burial purposes as for solitary meditation or initiation into the religious mysteries. Some tribes of American Indians, I believe, fashioned underground chambers for similar purposes.

There has been speculation that the small cell-like room reached by a narrow stairway from the vestry occupies the space of this original chamber. The official explanation for this room is that it was constructed as overnight accommodation for itinerant priests who came to preach at St Bride's and were unable, because of adverse weather, to return that night across the Moss. However, there are few recorded instances of this being necessary, and when, in 1835, a visiting bishop announced his intention of spending the night there 'to be closer to God' he eventually had to be found a room at The Man I'th Moss after being discovered naked and distressed in the snow-covered churchyard at three o'clock in the morning!

CHAPTER III

The Moss was like a warm bath, and he left it with regret. Knowing, all the same, that he must. That there was nothing to be accomplished by wallowing.

So he strode out. And when he glanced behind him, what he saw took away his breath.

For it was no longer a black and steaming peat bog but a vast, sparkling lake, an ecstatic expanse of blue and silver reaching serenely to the far hills.

Its water was alive. Quiescent, undemanding, but surely a radiant, living element. No, not merely living . . . *undying. Immortal.*

And the water was a womanly element. Light and placid, recumbent. Generous, if she had a mind to be. If you pleased her.

He felt tufts of grass crisp and warm under his wet feet and was embarrassed, thinking he would surely besmirch it with filthy peat deposits from his bog-soiled body. But when he looked down at himself he saw that his skin was fresh and clean – not from the bog, but from the lake, of course.

And he was naked. Of course. Quite natural.

He stood at the tip of a peninsula. He thought at first it was a green island because the mound which rose, soft as a breast, from its centre was concealing the hills behind. But as he ascended the rise, new slopes purpled into being, and when he reached the summit the surrounding hills were an amphitheatre.

In the middle of which he stood.

Naked.

Appraised.

'*Shade the light! Shade it, damn you!*'

   '*What with?*'

'*Your hand, jacket, anything . . . You poor little sod, you're really frightened, aren't you . . . ?*'

'*No, it's just . . .*'

'*Don't be . . . Easier than you expected, surely, wasn't it? Soil's lovely and loose, obviously replaced in haste, everyone shit-scared, like you. Look, why don't you get the ropes? We can have this one out and into the Range Rover before we start on the other, OK?*'

'*All right. Now?*'

'*Got a firm grip, have we? You let it go and – I promise you, cock – we'll put you down there and bury you alive.*'

'*Yes, all right, yes, I've got it.*'

'*OK, now. Pull.*'

'*Oh . . . agh . . . Where shall I . . . ?*'

'*Just at the side will do. Right. Fine. Now, let's have the lid off.*'

'*What . . . ?*'

'*Have a little look at him, eh? Hah! See that . . . not even nailed down, they really were in a panic, weren't they? To think I was once almost in awe of these little people. How wrong can . . . Oh, now . . . Oh, look at that.*'

'*Oh!*'

'*Go on. Have a better look. Get closer. Put your fingers on his eyes.*'

'*I can't, I . . . Oh, God, how did I get into this?*'

'*No good asking Him, my friend, you've cut all your ties in that direction . . .*'

Ernie Dawber was soon aware of Something Happening in the churchyard.

A light sleeper, Ernie. Eyes and ears of the community, twenty-four hours a day. The headmaster's house overlooked the playground on the one side, and from the landing window there was no hiding-place at all for a pair of eight-year-olds sharing a packet of Embassy Gold.

Ernie's replacement as head teacher came from Glossop and had not been prepared for such dedication. In fact he'd said, more or less, that if they made him live over the shop, as it were, they could stick the job. He was a good lad, though, generally speaking, so the Education Authority had accepted his terms, allowed him to commute from Across the Moss . . . and sold the house to Ernie.

Who couldn't have had a better retirement present. He was always on hand – and more than pleased – to take groups of kids on nature rambles or do a spot of relief teaching in the classroom in an emergency.

And he could still watch the generations pass by. Through the landing window . . . the schoolyard. While through the back bedroom window, on the other side of the house . . . the graveyard. Full circle.

So all it took was the clink of a shovel, and Ernie Dawber was awake and up at the window.

They were being very quiet about it – as usual. He couldn't see much, just shadows criss-crossing through torchbeams, up at the top end, where the churchyard met the moor. Where Matt Castle had finally been planted and the earth piled at last on top of him.

Ernie watched for just over half an hour, and then the torches were extinguished.

'By 'eck,' he said, half-admiringly, hopping over the freezing oilcloth back to bed, 'tha's got a nerve, Ma.'

He remembered Joel Beard. What, really, could he have done? If their stupid curate was determined to spend the night in the little cellar under the church, how could he stop him?

Maybe the Rector's fears were unfounded. Maybe his experience and that of the Bishop all those years ago . . . Well, they were sensitive men. Not all clergymen were, by any means, and this lad certainly looked, well, not *dense* exactly, that wasn't quite the word. Dogmatic, set in his beliefs. Blind to other realities.

But at least, tucked up in his cell, he wouldn't be aware of what was happening up in the churchyard.

And that was a small mercy, Ernie thought, getting into bed. He felt a trifle dizzy but decided to disregard it.

*

He thought he recognized the naked woman on the hill. There was *something* about her, the way she looked at him, the way she smiled.

The way she seemed to say, *Are you man enough?*

He stood above her. Confident of his superior strength, his muscular limbs, his halo of golden curls. Their power over women. Oh, he was man enough.

For had he not fallen into the black peat and emerged from clear water, as clear as the Sea of Galilee? And had not the peat been washed from him?

Now the female lay in the grass before him, close to the summit of the green mound, her legs spread. He knew what she wanted.

Her wild hair was spread over the grass. Hair which reflected the light, changing like water. Hair which rippled like the lake.

He smiled his most superior smile. 'I know what you want.' Disdainful.

And if there was no disdain in the reaction of his body, this was another demonstration of his power. Proof that he certainly was man enough.

But, gently, she shook her head.

First, you must recognize me for what I am. And then worship me.

The lights were tiny, some distance away, a short procession of them. Torches, lanterns, Tilley lamps; whatever, people were carrying them, and they were carrying them openly across Sam Davis's farmland, and Sam gripped the bedroom window-ledge, bloody mad now.

'Right!'

'No!'

'I'm gettin' shotgun . . .'

'Sam, *no* . . . !'

'Shurrup,' he rasped. 'You'll wake kids.'

'I'm not letting you.' He heard her pull the cord to the light over the bed.

'Look . . .' Sam turned his back on the window. Esther, all white-faced and rabbit-eyed, sitting up in bed, blankets clutched to her chin. 'They're makin' a bloody fool o' me, yon buggers,' he whispered. 'Don't even hide their bloody lights no more.'

'We should never've come here.'

'Oh, don't bloody start wi' that again.'

'Why d'you think it were so cheap? It's a bad place, Sam.'

'It's the best *we'll* bloody get.'

'Nobody wanted it, and I don't just mean the land.'

'Aye,' he said. 'I know you don't mean the bloody land, rubbish as it is.'

'I'm scared,' she said, all small-voiced. 'It's an awful thing t'be scared of your own home, Sam.'

He snatched a glance out of the window; the lights had stopped moving, they'd be clustered up there in a circle of their own around what was left of the stone circle.

'Sam!'

'*Shurrup!*'

'Aren't *you* scared? Really. Aren't y—'

'Listen. What it does to me . . . it just makes me tampin' mad. Been goin' on weeks, months . . . and what have I done about it? Tell me that? Am I going t'stand here for ever, like an owd woman, frickened t'dearth?'

'You went to the vicar. That new feller's coming tomorrow. You said he were coming tomorrow.'

'Waste of bloody time. *And* the coppers. I keep telling yer. Couldn't even charge um wi' trespass 'cause it's got to be trespass wi' intent to do summat illegal, and worshipping the devil int even a criminal offence no more – sooner bloody nick you for a bald tyre. Bastards. Useless bastards. All of um.'

Kept saying it. Kept repeating it because he could hardly believe it, the things you could get away with. Was he supposed to sit around, with his finger up his arse, while them bastards up there were shagging each other front and back and sacrificing his beasts? No bloody *way*!

'You go out there,' Esther said, 'and I'm ringing the police, and I'll ring the bloody vicarage too and tell um where you are, I don't care what time of night it is.'

'Oh, shit!' Sam advanced on the bed, spreading his arms wide, cold by now in just his underpants. 'Bloody *hell*, woman. What do *you* suggest I do, then?'

'Come back to bed,' Esther said, trying her best to smile through the nerves that were making her face twitch. 'Please, Sam. Don't look. Just thank God they're up there and we're down here. Please. We'll talk about it tomorrow.'

'Well, thanks very much for your contribution.' Sam sighed. '"We'll talk about it tomorrow." Fucking Nora.'

He took one last glance.

The circle of light did not move.

'I've had it wi' talk,' Sam said.

First you must recognize me. For what I am.

'Recognize you?' He laughed. 'For what you are?'

He stood above her, looking down on her. The elongated shadow of his penis divided her lolling breasts like a sword.

'I *know* what you are,' he said. 'I know *precisely* what you are.'

He saw a blue calm in her eyes that was as deep as the lake, and for a moment it threatened to dilute his resolve.

Then he heard himself say, 'How *dare* you?'

She lay below him, placid, compliant.

'You're just a whore. How dare you seek my recognition? You're just a . . . a cunt.'

In an act of explicit contempt he lowered himself upon her, and her hands moved to her crotch, thumbs extended, to open herself for him.

He's . . . quite small, isn't he? I somehow expected him to be bigger. More impressive.'

'Quite manageable, really. Oh my, earth to earth, peat to peat . . . it would have been rather less easy to get at him in a week or two. Watch it now, be careful of his eyes. Mustn't be blasé.'

'I'm not. It's just I'm actually not as worried about, you know, touching this one. It doesn't seem like a real body, somehow. More like a fossil.'

'Lay him gently. You've done well so far. I'm proud of you. But lay him gently, he's ours now. And remember . . . never forget . . .'

'I know . . . I'll feel so much better afterwards.'

'Shut up. Join hands. In a circle. Around the body.'

It was not a rape; she was a whore, and a heathen whore. When he plunged into her, he found her as moist as black peat and packed just as tightly around him.

Light into darkness.

Not to be enjoyed. It was necessary.

'Whore,' he gasped with every breath. 'Whore . . . whore . . . whore . . .'

Lifting his head to seek out her eyes, looking for a reaction, searching for some pain in them.

'Whore.' Saw her mouth stretched into a static rictus of agony.

'Wh . . .' Tighter still around him.

And dry.

'. . . ore . . .'

Dry as stone.

No.

Too late; he thrust again. Into stone.

The pain was blinding. Immeasurable. The pain was a white-hot wire driven through the tip of his penis and up through his pelvis into his spine.

His back arched, his breath set solid in his throat. And he found her eyes.

Little grey pebbles. And her mouth, stretched and twisted not in agony but ancient derision, a forever grin.

'. . . in the midst of death we are alive . . .'

'. . . WE ARE ALIVE!'

(*'Go on . . . two handfuls . . . stop . . . not on his face . . . shine the light . . . there . . .'*)

'Behold, I shew you a mystery. We shall not sleep, but we shall

236

be changed. In a moment. In the twinkling of an eye. At the last trump – for the trumpet shall sound. And the dead shall be raised.'

'. . . AND THE DEAD SHALL BE RAISED!'

('OK, now fill in the grave . . . quickly, quickly, quickly . . .')

'Dust to dust, to ashes, to earth.

'DUST TO ASHES TO EARTH!'

('Now stamp it down, all of you. Together . . .')

'And the dead shall be raised corrupted . . . and we shall be changed.'

'. . . WE SHALL BE CHANGED.'

('Douse the lights. Douse them!')

CHAPTER IV

Another hard, white day, and she didn't like the look of it. It had no expression; there was a threat here most folk wouldn't see.

Not good weather, not bad weather. Nowt wrong with bad weather; you couldn't very well live in Bridelow if you couldn't put up wi' spot or two of rain every other day or a bit of wind to make your fire smoke and your eyes water. Or blizzards. Or thunder and lightning.

But this was no weather. Just cold air at night and a threat.

Everything black or white. Black night with white stars. White day with black trees, black moor, black moss.

Cold and still. Round about this time of year there should be some colour and movement in the sky, even if it was only clouds in dirty shades of yellow chasing each other round the chimney pots.

Shades. There should be shades.

Ma Wagstaff stood in her back kitchen, hands on woollen-skirted hips.

She was vexed with them cats too. She'd washed their bowl, first thing, and doled out a helping of the very latest variety of gourmet cat food Willie'd brought her from that posh super-market in Buxton – shrimp and mussel in oyster sauce. And the fickle little devils had sat there and stared at it, then stared at her. 'Well, that's it,' Ma growled. 'If you want owt else you can gerout and hunt for it.'

But the cats didn't want to go out. They mooched around, all moody, ignoring each other, looking up at Ma as if was her fault.

Bad air.

As Ma unbent, the cat food can in one hand, a fork in the other, her back suddenly creaked and then she couldn't stand up for the pain that started sawing down her spine like a bread knife.

Then the front door went, half a knock, somebody who couldn't reach the knocker. As Ma hobbled through the living room, the white light seemed to be laughing heartlessly at her, filling the front window and slashing at the jars and bottles.

The door was jammed and opened with a shudder that continued all the way up Ma's spine to the base of her skull.

'Now then,' Ma said.

On the doorstep was her youngest grandson with that big dog of his. Always went for a walk together before school.

Benjie said nowt, grinned up at her, gap-toothed, something clutched in one hand.

'Well, well,' said Ma, smiling through the agony. 'Where'd you find that?'

'Chief found it,' said Benjie proudly. 'Jus' this mornin', up by t'moor.'

'Ta.' Ma took the bottle and fetched the child in for a chocolate biscuit from the tin. The bottle wasn't broken, but the cork was half out and the glass was misted. The bit of red thread that hung outside for the spirit to grasp was soaked through and stuck to the bottle.

''Ey!' Benjie said suddenly. 'Guess what.'

'I'm too owd for guessin' games, lad.'

'Bogman's bin took!'

'Eh?'

'It were on radio. Bogman's bin stole.'

'Oh,' said Ma, vaguely, 'has he?'

The child looked disappointed. 'Are you not surprised?'

'Oh, I am,' Ma said. 'I'm right flabbergasted. Look, just get that stool and climb up theer and fetch us biscuit tin. Me owd back's playin' up a bit.'

Ma held up the bottle to the cruel light. Useless.

'Will it still work?' asked Benjie innocently, arms full of wooden stool. Ma had to smile; what did he know about witch-bottles?

'Would it *ever*'ve worked, lad?' She shook her head ruefully, wondering if she'd be able to stand up straight before teatime. 'That's what I keep askin' meself.'

Fine lot of use *she* was. She ought to be out there, finding out exactly what they were up against – even if it killed her – before two thousand and more years of care and watchfulness came to ruin.

Oh, she could feel it . . . mornings like this, everything still and exposed.

She looked down at young Benjie, chomping on his chocolate biscuit. It *will* kill me, she thought. I'm old and feeble and me back's giving way. I've let things slip all these years, pottered about the place curing sick babbies and cows, and not seeing the danger. And now there's only me with the strength inside. But I'm too old and buggered to go out and find um.

It'll come to *me*, though, one night, Ma thought, with uncustomary dread. When it's good and ready.

But will *I* be?

Joel Beard awoke screaming and sweating, coughing and choking on the paraffin air.

He sat on the edge of the camp bed, with the duvet wrapped around him, moaning and rocking backwards and forwards in the darkness for several minutes before his fingers were sufficiently steady to find the candle on its tray and the matches.

He lit the candle and, almost immediately, it went out. He lit it again and it flared briefly, with a curious shower of sparks, before the wick snapped, carrying the flame to the metal tray, where it lasted just long enough for Joel to grab his cross, his clothes and his boots and make it to the door.

On his way through the tunnel to the steps, he knocked over the paraffin heater, with a clatter and crash of tin and glass, and didn't stop to set it upright.

At the top of the steps he was almost dazzled by the white dawn, awakening the kneeling saints and prophets, the angelic hosts and the jewel-coloured Christs in the windows.

Deliverance.

He dressed in the vestry, where he found a mildewed cassock and put that on over his vest and underpants. But he did not feel fully dressed until his cross was heavy against his chest.

The air in the nave felt half-frozen; he could smell upon it the bitter stench of autumn, raw decay. But no paraffin. And the cold was negligible compared with the atmosphere in last night's dungeon.

He unbolted the church door, stood at the entrance to the porch breathing in the early morning air – seven o'clockish, couldn't be certain, left his watch in the dungeon, wasn't going back for it – and he did *not* look up, as he said, 'You're finished, you bitch.'

And then went quickly down, between the graves, to the gardener's shed, up against the perimeter wall.

The shed was locked, a padlock through the hasp. He had no key. He shook the door irritably and glared in through the shed's cobwebbed window. He could see what he wanted, a gleaming edge of the aluminium window-cleaning ladder, on its side, stretching the length of the shed. He also saw in the window the reflection of a face that was not his own.

Joel was jolted and, for a moment, could not turn round.

The face was a woman's. It had long, dark hair, steady, hard eyes and black whore's lips. The lips were stretched in a tight, shining grin which the eyes did not reflect.

Cold derision.

Remembered pain speared Joel's spine as he turned, half-hypnotized by the horror of it, turning as he would turn to stare full into the face of the Gorgon knowing it would turn him into stone, like the angels frozen to the graves.

He saw the still figure of a woman on the other side of the church wall, the village street below her. Her back was turned

to him. Slowly, she began to walk away, and because the wall
blocked her lower half she seemed at first to be floating. Her
long, black hair swayed as she moved, and in the hair he saw a
single thin, ice-white strand.

Joel felt a twisted revulsion. Twisted because there was
inside it a slender wafer of cold desire, like the seam of white
in the hair of the woman who walked away.

He watched her, not aware of breathing. She was wearing
something long and black. He watched her until she was no
more, and not once did she turn round.

Joel sobbed once, felt the savage strength of rage. He
bunched a fist and drove it through the shed window.

Ernie Dawber had heard about the bogman on the morning
news. So he wasn't exactly surprised when, round about
10.30, he heard a car pulling up irritably in the schoolhouse
drive.

Hadn't given much thought to how he was going to handle
this one. Too busy making notes for a daft book that would
never get published.

The page he was writing, an introduction, began:

*Bridelow might be said to operate on two levels. It has what
you might call an* underlife, *sometimes discernible at dusk when
all's still and the beacon is about to light up* . . .

He looked up from the paper and the room went rapidly in
and out of focus and swayed. Bugger. Not again. Damn.

He pushed his chair back, swept all the papers from his
desk into an open boxfile and went to let the man in.

'A raw day, Dr Hall.'

A word, Mr Dawber, if you're not . . . too *busy*.'

Innuendo. It was going to be all innuendo this time, he
could tell.

'I'm a retired man. I'm not supposed to be busy. Come in.
Sit down. Cup of tea? Or something a little . . .'

'No, thank you. Nothing.' Oh, very starchy. 'It's interesting that you don't seem at all surprised to see me, Mr Dawber.'

'I'm not daft,' Ernie said. 'That's how I got to be a
headmaster.'

Underneath Hall's open Barbour jacket was a suit and tie. An official visit.

'Well, at least shut the door,' Ernie said. 'It's the worst kind of cold out there.'

The archaeologist consented at last to come into the study. Ernie closed the boxfile and placed it carefully under his chair. 'Look around,' he said. 'You don't need a search warrant.'

'I haven't said anything to the police,' Hall said. 'Not yet. I'm giving you a chance either to bring it back or tell me where it is.'

Ernie didn't insult him by asking what he was talking about. 'Dr Hall, this is a very serious allegation.'

'Don't worry, I know enough about the libel laws not to make it in public. That's why I've come to see you. If we can keep it between the two of us and the, er . . . if it comes back undamaged, that'll probably be as far as it goes.'

'Now look, you don't really think . . . ?'

'Oh, I don't for one minute think you were personally involved. Besides, you were at the funeral, I saw you. Wouldn't have been time.'

'So I'm just the mastermind. The brains behind the heist. That it?'

'Something like that.'

'All right,' said Ernie Dawber. 'I'll be straight with you. Yes, I did come to you on behalf of the village and urge you to put that thing back in the bog. That was me, and I meant it. But – and I'll say this very slowly, Dr Hall – I do *not* know who stole the bogman from the Field Centre. I'll say it to you and I'll say it again before a court of law.'

And he truly didn't know. Nobody ever knew these things apart from those concerned.

Had his *suspicions*, who wouldn't have?

But nothing black and white. Ma Wagstaff was right. There was never anything in black and white in Bridelow, which was how it was that balance and harmony could always be gently adjusted, like the tone and contrast on a television set.

Shades of things.

Oh, aye, naturally, he had his suspicions. Nowt wrong with suspicions. Suspicions never hanged anyone.

Roger Hall had changed colour. His beard-rimmed lips gone tight and white. Dr Hall's tonal balance was way out.

'It's here, Dawber. I know it's here.'

'You're welcome to search . . .'

'I don't mean this house. I mean in Bridelow. Somebody has it . . .'

'Don't be daft.'

'That's if it hasn't already been put back in the bog. And if it has, we'll find it. I can have two coachloads of students down here before lunch. We'll comb that moss, inch by inch, and when we find the area that's been disturbed . . .'

'I wish I could help you, Dr Hall.'

'No, you don't.'

Ernie Dawber nodded. That was true enough. No, he didn't.

Joel lugged the ladder through the graveyard and into the church, dragging it along the nave, putting it up finally against a stone pillar next to the rood screen. He shook the ladder to steady it, then began, with a cold determination, to climb.

In his ankle-length black cassock, this was not easy. Close to the top, he hung on with one aching, bruised and blood-stained hand, the big, gilded cross swinging out from his chest, while he rummaged under the cassock for his Swiss Army knife, using his teeth to extract its longest, sharpest blade.

The topmost branches of the Autumn Cross were almost in his face. It was about six feet long, crudely woven of oak and ash with, mashed up inside for stuffing, thousands of dead leaves and twigs, part of a bird's nest, shrivelled berries and hard, brown acorns.

Disgusting thing.

Fashioned in public, he'd been told, on the field behind The Man I'th Moss, with great ceremony, and the children gathering foliage for its innards.

'Oh, Lord,' Joel roared into the rafters, 'help me rid your house for ever of this primeval slime!'

He leaned out from the ladder, one foot hanging in space, tiny shards of glass still gleaming amidst the still-bright blood on the hand gripping a rung. His fatigue fell away; he felt fit and supple and had the intoxicating sensation of grace in his movements.

Deliverance

Orange baling-twine bound the frame of the cross to a rusted hook sunk into a cross-beam. He swung his knife-arm in a great arc and slashed it through.

'Filth!' he screamed.

The Autumn Cross fell at once, and Joel watched it tumble and was glad.

A beginning.

The sapless, weightless artefact fell with a dry, slithering hiss. Like a serpent in the grass, he thought, satisfaction setting firm in the muscles of his stomach, his head filled with a wild light.

He did recoil slightly, throwing the lightweight ladder into a tilt, as the so-called cross burst apart on the stone flags, fragments of leaves and powdery dust rising all around until the belly of the church was filled up with a dry and brackish-smelling sepia mist.

Joel coughed and watched the filthy pagan detritus as it settled. A bigger job than usual for the women on the Mothers' Union cleaning rota.

He hoped the foul bitches would choke on the dust.

CHAPTER V

With a nod to Our Sheila, Moira slipped quietly into St Bride's church just before 10 a.m.

To be alone. To confront the spirit of Bridelow. Maybe find something of Matt Castle here.

Special place, Matt had said, a long, long time ago on a snowy night in Manchester. *It's got . . . part of what I've been trying to find in the music. That's where it is . . . where it was all along.*

Cathy Gruber had persuaded her to stay the night in the guest room. She'd slept surprisingly well, no awful dreams of

Matt in his coffin. And awoken with – all too rare these days –
a sense of direction: she would discover Matt, trace the source
of the inspiration. Which was the essence of the village.

Bridelow, last refuge of the English Celts.

*A more pure, undiluted strain than you'll find anywhere in
Western Europe.*

She stopped in the church porch.

Who said that? Who *said* that?

The American said it. Macbeth.

Macbeth?

Yeah, quoting somebody . . . some writer addressing the
Celtic conference. Stanhope, Stansfield, some name like that
. . . from the North of England.

Connections.

She felt like a small token in a board-game, manoeuvred
into place by the deft fingers of some huge, invisible, cunning
player.

And she knew that if she was to tap into Matt's imagination,
she was also going to have to confront his demons.

As she walked – cautious now – out of the porch, into the
body of the church, something whooshed down the aisle and
collided with her at chest-level.

'Hey!' Moira grinned in some relief, holding, at arm's
length, a small boy.

'Gerroff!' Kid was in tears.

'You OK? You hurt yourself?'

The child tore himself away from her, wailing, and hurled
himself through the door, an arm flung across his eyes, like
he'd been blown back by an explosion.

Moira's grin faded.

Something had changed.

The place looked bare and draughty. Even through the
stained-glass windows, the light seemed ashen and austere.
On a table near the entrance, next to the piles of hymn books,
all the lanterns and candlesticks had been carelessly stacked,
as if for spring cleaning. One of the slender, coloured candles
had rolled off the edge and lay snapped in two on the stone
flags.

She picked up the two halves, held one in each hand a

moment then placed them on the table and wandered up the central aisle of a church which seemed so much bigger than yesterday at Matt's funeral, so much less intimate, less friendly.

Something was crunched under her shoe. She looked down and saw curled-up leaves and broken twigs, shrivelled berries and bracken and acorns and all the rustic rubble of autumn scattered everywhere.

Like a savage wind had blown through the nave in the night. Looking up, she saw what was missing, what the mess around her ankles was.

Somebody smashed the Autumn Cross.

'No accident, this,' Moira said aloud. Shivered and wrapped her arms around her sweatered breasts. It was still cold, but after what she'd learned last night, she'd left the black cloak at the Rectory. This was obviously not a place in need of a spare witchy woman.

She stood by the rood screen and looked back down the naked church. She looked down at the mess all around her, on the stone floor and the scratched and homely pews. Saw, for a moment, a scattering of bleached white skulls. But she knew almost at once that it wasn't the same.

Or at least that *she* was not to blame this time.

This was a rape.

She experienced a moment of awe. *I walked into someone else's conflict.*

But it was not *quite* someone else's conflict. There was a connection, and the connection was Matt Castle.

Last night, she'd said to Cathy, just as abrupt as the girl had been, 'Why did they open Matt's coffin? What was in that bottle?'

'Ah.' Cathy's eyes cast down over the steaming mug of chocolate. 'You saw that.'

'Don't get me wrong, I'm not normally an intrusive person, but Matt meant a lot to me.'

'Dic obviously thinks so.'

'Oh. You heard that. I wondered if maybe you had one of those pianos that plays itself.'

'Those pianos don't play bum notes.' Cathy looked offended. 'No, I didn't have my ear to the door. Dic and I went for a drink the other night. I drove, he got a bit pissed. He said his father . . .'

'The boy's way off. There was nothing more complicated than friendship between me and Matt. He never . . .'

He never touched me.

Moira stumbled and fell into a dusty pew. Sat staring into the vaulted ceiling where the cross had been, but seeing nothing.

He never touched me.

That was true. Never a friendly kiss. Never a celebratory hug when a gig had gone down well or the first album had gone into profit. *Never touched me sexually. He never came near.*

But he looked.

Often she'd feel his moody gaze and turn and catch his eyes, and she'd smile and he wouldn't, and then he'd look away.

She bent painfully over the prayer-book shelf.

Clink. From outside, the sound of a chisel on stone.

I was thinking, if we'd slept together, just once, to kind of get it over, bring down that final barrier . . .

No. Wouldn't have got anything over. Would have started something bad. You knew that really, just as you really knew what was going on inside Matt Castle and chose to ignore it. Just a crush; he'll get over it. He didn't. He couldn't. He made you leave the band, before . . .

The clinking from outside was coming harder. Maybe they were demolishing the joint entirely.

Too choked to think about this any more, stomach tight and painful, Moira stood up, made her way slowly down the aisle to the doors. But when she grasped the ring-handles, the doors wouldn't open.

'Owd on! You'll have me off.' Sound of someone creaking his way down a wooden ladder up against the doors.

She leaned her back against the doors, took a few deep breaths, and called out after a few seconds, 'OK?'

'Aye.' The porch doors opened, and there was a smallish guy in his sixties, flat cap and a boiler-suit. Big, soft moustache, like a hearthbrush. 'Sorry, lass, dint know there were anybody in theer.'

He held a mallet and a masonry chisel. There were chips of grey stone and crumbly old concrete around the foot of the step-ladder.

'Storm damage?' Moira said.

'You what?'

'You repairing storm damage?'

'Summat like that.'

But then, looking up at the wall above the porch, she saw where the chippings had come from.

From the stones supporting the Exhibitionist. The *Sheelagh na gig*. Our Sheila.

'You're taking her down?'

'Aye.' He didn't sound too happy.

'Why?'

He gave her a level look. 'Alfred Beckett, verger, organist, dogsbody. Who are you?'

She grinned. Fuck it, she was here now, in the open, uncloaked. 'Moira. Moira Cairns. Used to work with . . . Matt Castle.'

The name felt different. A different, darker Matt Castle.

'Matt Castle, eh?' said Alfred Beckett. 'Right. 'Course.' He seemed to relax a little. 'How do.' He stuck out a stubby hand and Moira took it, stone dust and all. He had a firm grip; it pulled her back into what people took for the real world.

'So, Mr Beckett . . .' She glanced up at the ancient woman squashed into a stone plaque, fingers up her fanny. A few strokes of the chisel away from a serious loss of status.

'Aye,' Mr Beckett said, like a ragged sigh, and Moira saw he wasn't far from tears. He said he was following instructions. Didn't *want* to do it. *Hated* doing it. But he wasn't in an arguing position, was he? Vergers being a good way down the ecclesiastical hierarchy.

'And if I don't do it,' he said, '*he'll* do it hisself. And he won't be as careful as me.'

'Mr Beard,' Moira said.

'Aye. He'll smash her, like . . .'

'Like the Autumn Cross.'

'I'll see she's all right,' Alfred Beckett said. 'I'll keep her safe until such time as . . .'

He sighed, fished a packet of Arrowmint chewing gum out of the top pocket of his boiler-suit. Moira accepted a segment and they stood together chewing silently for a minute or so.

Then Mr Beckett said, 'Aye. It's a bugger.'

A scrap of cement fell from Our Sheila.

Moira said, 'But isn't she – excuse me, I'm no' an expert in these matters – isn't she protected in some way?'

'No, lass, she's . . .'

'I meant, isn't she a feature of a listed historic building?'

'Oh,' said Alfred Beckett. 'Aye. Happen. But Mr Beard reckons she's not safe and could fall on somebody's head. Same as she's not done for the past umpteen centuries.'

'Aye,' Moira said eventually. 'It's a bugger all right.'

'Now then. Why aren't you at school?'

Benjie threw his arms around Ma's waist and burrowed his head into her pinny. He started to sob.

She pulled him into the kitchen, shut the back door. 'Now, lad. What's matter? Tell owd Ma.'

Ma Wagstaff sat her grandson on the kitchen stool. Spine still giving her gyp, she reached up for a bottle of her special licorice toffees. Never been known not to work.

When it was out, Ma said, 'The bugger.'

Benjie with his swollen eyes and his wet cheeks bulging with toffee.

'The unfeeling, spiteful bugger,' Ma said.

Biggest thing that had ever happened to Benjie, Ernest Dawber putting him in charge of the Autumn Cross – a whole afternoon, inspecting the twigs and branches, acorns, bits of old birds' nests and stuff the other kids had brought, saying what was to go into the cross, what was right for it, what wasn't good enough. Standing proudly, top of the aisle, the day Alfred Beckett had come with his ladder, and the cross, all trimmed and finished, had been hoisted into place, and everybody cheering.

Biggest thing ever happened to the lad.

'Leave him to me,' Ma said. 'I'll sort that bugger out meself, just you see if I don't.'

Benjie stared at her, wildly shaking his head, couldn't speak for the toffee.

'Gone far enough,' Ma said. 'Got to be told a few things. For his own good, if nowt else.'

'No!' Benjie blurted. 'Don't go near it, Ma.'

Ma was taken aback. 'Eh?'

'. . .'s getting bigger, Ma. Every day, 's getting bigger.'

'What is, lad?'

'The dragon!' The little lad started crying again, scrambling down from the stool, clutching Ma round the waist again, wailing, 'You've not to . . . You've *not* to!'

Eh?

Mystified, but determined to get to the bottom of this, Ma detached his small hands from her pinny, squatted down, with much pain, to his height. 'Now then. Summat you've not told me. Eh? Come on.' She held his shoulders, straightening him up, feeding him some strength, not that she'd much to spare these days. 'Come on. Tell owd Ma all about it.'

He stared into her face, eyes all stretched with terror.

'Bigger, Ma . . . 's *bigger*.'

'He might look big to you, Benjie,' Ma said gently. 'But he's only a man.'

'No. 's a dragon!'

'Mr Beard?'

''s a *dragon*.'

So the new curate was in combat with the Forces of Evil.

As represented by Our Sheila and the Autumn Cross.

And whatever Willie's Ma was doing inside Matt Castle's coffin.

Last night – early this morning – as the dregs of hot chocolate were rinsed from the mugs, she'd at last got it out of Cathy, what it was all about – or as much of it as Cathy knew.

'So, the coffin's on the ground and the light's been lowered, and the lid is open . . .'

'I didn't see it!'

'And your friend, old Mrs Wagstaff has her hands inside . . .

250

and I'm wondering if maybe the old biddy has a passing interest in necrophilia . . .'

'That's a terrible thing to say!'

'I know . . . so tell me. What's going on, huh?'

'It was . . . I think it was . . . a witch bottle.'

'I thought you said she wasny a witch.'

'It's just a term. It's a very old precautionary thing. To trap an evil spirit . . . ?'

'Matt's spirit . . . ?'

'No . . . I don't know. Maybe if there was one around. In there with him.'

'In the coffin?'

'I don't know . . . it's no good asking me. You're going to have to talk to Ma. If she'll talk to you.'

And Lottie. Today it was important to talk to Lottie, because Lottie was not part of this place, had not been returning, like Matt, to the bosom of a tradition which was older than Christianity.

. . . a more pure, undiluted strain . . . than you'll find anywhere in Western Europe . . .

Moira had come through the lych-gate, was standing at the top of the cobbled street, the cottages like boulders either side under a blank, unyielding sky – a sky as hard as a whitewashed wall.

. . . this writer . . . Stanton, Stanhope . . .

. . . he's on his feet, and is he mad . . . this guy's face is . . .
this guy's face is . . .
this guy's face is . . .
White.

251

CHAPTER VI

The plump woman in the village Post Office looked like a chief Girl Guide, whatever they called them now. Also, although she wore no wedding ring, she struck Moira as a member of the Mothers' Union.

'I wonder, um, could you help me? I'm looking for Willie Wagstaff.' She'd forgotten to ask Cathy where Willie lived, and Cathy had set out to drive fifteen miles to the hospital to visit her dad.

'Willie? Have you been to his house?'

Moira smiled. 'Well, no, that's . . .'

'Sorry, luv, I'm not very bright this morning.' The postmistress rolled her eyes. 'Go across street, turn left and after about thirty yards you'll come to an entry. Go in there, and you'll see a cottage either side of you and it's the one on the left.'

Moira bought ten postage stamps and two packets of Arrowmint chewing gum in case she ran into Alfred Beckett again.

There was no answer at Willie's house, a narrow little cottage backing on to other people's yards. Moira wondered if he lived alone. She squashed her nose to the front window. There was a bowl of flowers in it, with ferns. A woman's touch. Females had always been drawn to Willie, born to be mothered. In the old days, it used to be said that otherwise worldly mature ladies would turn to blancmange when little Mr Wagstaff smiled coyly and let them put him to bed.

Moira was not that mature, yet. The reason she needed Willie was to talk about Matt, and also to meet his mother. She came out of the entry, unsure what to do next. There was no one else in the place she knew, except . . .

At the bottom of the village street, Moira found herself facing the pub, the last building, apart from a couple of wooden sheds, before the street widened into the causeway across the peatbog.

This was the difficult one.

Against the white morning, the pub looked hulking and sinister, like a gaol or a workhouse. Stonework so murky that in places it might have been stained by the peat. Outside on the forecourt, a man in an apron was cleaning windows.

A red-haired woman appeared in the porch, handed the man a steaming mug of tea or coffee, stopped and stared across the forecourt. Waited in the doorway, watching Moira.

You ready for this, hen?

'They're not Ancient Monuments, these circles. Ancient, possibly. Monuments . . . well, hardly.'

Joel Beard kicked at a stubby stone.

'No signs pointing um out, anyroad,' said Sam Davis. 'Not even proper tracks.'

'That's because they're not in the care of any Government or local authority department. Unlike, say, Stonehenge, where you have high-security fences and tunnel-access. Which is why these places are so open to abuse.'

The Reverend Beard, in his dark green Goretex jacket and his hiking boots, striding through the waist-high bracken. Action priest, Sam thought cynically.

'Lights, you say?'

Although they were less than a hundred yards from the first circle, it wasn't even visible yet. This was the most direct route from Sam's farmhouse, but he reckoned that mob last night must have come in from behind, over the hill.

'Cocky bastards,' Sam said, breathing harder, keeping pace with difficulty, due to shorter legs. 'Bold as brass. If wife hadn't kicked up, I'd've been up theer last night.'

Sam bunched his fingers into fists. 'I'd give um bloody devil worship.'

'I know how you feel,' the minister said, 'but you did the right thing in coming to me. This is my job. This is what I'm trained for.'

Sam Davis watched the big blond man flexing his lips, baring his teeth, steaming at the mouth in the cold air. It was all Esther's fault, this, making him drag the Church into it. 'Look, Mr Beard . . .'

253

'Joel . . .'

'Aye. Thing is, I don't want to turn this into some big bloody crusade. All I want is these buggers off me property. Know what I mean?'

The Reverend Beard stopped in his tracks. 'Sam, have you ever had foot-and-mouth disease on your land?'

'God. Be all I need.'

'Swine fever? Fowl pest? Sheep scab?'

'Give us a chance, I've only been farming two year.'

'The point I'm making,' Joel Beard said patiently, moving on, as the bracken came to an end and the ground levelled out, 'is that when a farmer's land is infected by a contagious disease, it's not simply a question of getting rid of the afflicted livestock. There are well-established procedures. For the purpose of, shall we say, decontamination.'

'Aye, but . . . let's get down to some basic facts, Joel. Who exactly are these fellers? Your mate, the Vicar . . . now he reckoned it's just kids, right?'

. . . could probably tuck a couple under each arm . . .

'Kids?' said Joel Beard.

'For kicks,' Sam said. 'Like drink. Drugs. Shoplifting. Kicks.'

'Hans Gruber said that?'

Sam shrugged. 'Summat like that. Right, this is it.'

'I beg your pardon . . .'

'The main circle. You're in t'middle of it, Joel. Told you it weren't much.'

Around them, sunk into tufts of dry, yellow grass, were these seven small stones, stained with mosses and lichens, none more than a couple of feet high, in a circle about fifteen feet diameter. Sam found it hard to credit them being here, in this formation, for about four thousand years.

'Don't know much about these things meself,' Sam said. 'Some folk reckon they was primitive astronomical observatories. You could stand in um and see where t'sun were risin'. Or summat.'

Personally, he didn't give a shit. By his left boot were two flat stone slabs, pushed together. The ground had clearly been disturbed. There were blackened twigs and ashes on the slabs.

'. . . but what that's got to do wi' bloody sacrifices is . . .'

'Sam!'

The Reverend Joel Beard shot up, like a charge of electricity had gone through him, and then, yelling 'Get back!', seized Sam Davis by the shoulders and shoved him out of the circle.

'What the . . . ?' Sam struggled out of Joel's grip, stumbled back into the bracken.

Joel was still in the circle, swaying like a drunk, swallowing big, hollow breaths through his mouth. His body bent into a fighting stance, hands clawed, eyes blinking.

Sam Davis stared at him. He was going to kill Esther for landing him with this big tosser.

'There's evil here,' Joel said.

Stupid sod looked ready for war. All that bothered Sam was how close the battlefield was to his kids. Down below, half a mile away, his farmhouse and its barns and buildings looked rickety and pathetic, like matchstick models he could kick over with the tip of his welly.

Joel Beard had closed his eyes. The sun, shuffling about behind weak clouds, had actually given him a faint halo.

For getting on ten minutes, Joel didn't move, except, at one point, to lift up both hands, on outstretched arms, as if he was waiting, Sam thought, for somebody to pass him a sack of coal. Then he spoke.

'I give you notice, Satan,' Joel said in a powerful voice, 'to depart from this place.' He'd unzipped his jacket to reveal a metal cross you could have used to shoe a horse.

Then he raised his hands so that they were parallel to his body and began to push at the air like this mime artist Sam had once seen on telly, pretending he was behind a pane of plate-glass.

'Bloody Nora,' Sam muttered to himself, crouching down among the ferns, unnerved by the whole thing but determined not to show it, even to himself. 'Got a right fuckin' nutter 'ere.'

Shaw Horridge watched them through binoculars from the Range Rover. It was parked on a moorland plateau about half a mile away. The binoculars, being Shaw's own, were very good ones.

The Range Rover belonged to a squat, greasy little man who lived in Sheffield and was unemployed. He called himself Asmodeus or something stupid out of *The Omen*.

'They're moving on, I think,' Shaw said.

Asmodeus had a beard so sparse you could count the hairs. He had the seat pushed back and his feet on the dashboard. 'Good,' he said, as if he didn't really care.

Shaw lowered his binoculars. 'What would you do if they came up here with spades and things?'

'I'd be very annoyed indeed,' Asmodeus said in his flat, drawly voice. 'I'd be absolutely furious. So would Therese, wouldn't you, darling?'

Therese was stretched out on the rear seat, painting her fingernails black. Shaw scowled. He didn't like Asmodeus calling her darling. He didn't at all like Asmodeus, who was unemployed and yet could afford a newish Range Rover.

And yet he was still in awe of him, having seen him by night, this little slob with putrid breath and a pot-belly, not yet out of his twenties and yet able to *change things*.

And he was excited.

'But what would you *do*?'

Asmodeus grinned at him through the open window. 'You're a little devil, aren't you, Shaw? What would *you* do?'

Shaw said, because Therese was there, 'Kill them.'

'Whaaay! You hear that, Therese? Shaw thinks he'd kill them.'

Therese lifted newly painted nails into the light. 'Well,' she said, 'we might need the priest, but I must say that little farmer's beginning to get on my nerves.'

Shaw tensed.

'Tell you what, Shaw,' Asmodeus said. 'We'll give you an easier one. How about that?'

They sat at one end of a refectory table, near an Aga-type kitchen stove, their reflections warped in the shiny sides of its hot-plate covers. Moira kind of jumpy inside, but Lottie pouring tea with steady hands, businesslike, in control.

And this was less than twenty-four hours after the set-to at Matt's graveside, Lottie laying into Willie and Willie's Ma and the other crones, while the minister was helped away into the vibrating night.

Over fifteen years since they'd been face to face. Lottie's hair was shorter. Her face was harder, more closed-up. Out on the forecourt, it had been, 'Hello, Moira', very nonchalant, like their meetings were still everyday events – no fuss, no tears, no embrace, no *surprise*.

No doubt Dic had told her Moira was around.

She sipped her tea and said Lottie was looking well, in spite of . . .

'You too,' Lottie said, flat-voiced. 'I always knew you'd become beautiful when you got past thirty. Listen . . . thanks.'

'For what?'

'For not coming when he wrote to you.'

'I was tied up.'

'Sure,' Lottie said. 'But thanks anyway. Things were complicated enough. Better this way.'

'This way?'

'His music,' Lottie said. 'His project. His beloved bogman. Now stolen, I believe.'

'Lottie, maybe I'm stupid, but I'm not with you.'

'It was on the radio this morning. Thieves broke into the University Field Centre out near Congleton and lifted the Man in the Moss. I find it quite amusing, but Matt would've been devastated. Like somebody kidnapping his father.'

'Somebody stole the bogman? Just like that?'

Lottie almost smiled. 'Hardly matters now, though, does it? Listen, I'll take you down in a bit, show you his music room. He left some stuff for you.'

'For me?'

'Tapes. Listen, I'm not pushing, Moira, but I think you should do it.'

'Do it?' She was starting to feel very foolish.

'Get together with Willie and Eric and Dic and record his

bogman music. I don't know if it's any good or not, I haven't heard much of it, but Matt saw it as his personal . . . summit? His big thing? Life's work?'

Moira looked hard at her, this austere, handsome woman, fifty-odd years old. Looked for the old indomitable spark in the eyes. Truth was, she was still indomitable, but the eyes . . . the eyes had died a little. This was not the old Lottie, this was a sad and bitter woman playing the part of the old Lottie.

'Then we'll do it,' Moira said. 'Whatever it's like.'

'Good. Thank you. But don't decide yet. You see – I'll be frank – if you'd come when he wrote to you . . . Well, he was quite ill by then, into the final furlong. He wasn't fit to record. Not properly. And then there was the other problem. And don't say, *what* other problem . . . let's not either of us insult the other's intelligence.'

'OK.' Moira leaned back and slowly sipped her tea. They sat there in silence, two women with little in common except perceived obligations to one man.

Mammy, how was he when he died? Can you tell me that?

This was the woman who could tell her. But Lottie had never had much patience with religion of any sort – organized or . . . well, as *dis*organized as whatever it was Ma Wagstaff was trying to do last night with her patent witch bottle.

'Lottie,' she said, 'I'm sorry. I didn't know. Well, maybe I knew inside of me, but I was young, too young to understand it. And nothing happened, Lottie, I swear it.'

Lottie shrugged. 'Better, maybe, if it had. Better for me, I can tell you, if he'd gone off with you. But after sticking with it, through all kinds of . . . Well, I wasn't prepared to have him spending his last days ignoring me, eaten up with old lust and regrets. So I'm glad you couldn't come.'

Lottie took her teacup to the sink, dropped it into a plastic bowl. The sink was a big, old-fashioned porcelain thing, pipes exposed underneath it with bits of rag tied around them. Not what Lottie's used to, Moira thought. Lottie is stainless-steel and waste-disposal.

'You've . . . had problems, then.' *Christ, everything I say to this woman is just so fucking facile . . .*

Lottie turned on the hot tap, held both hands under the

frenzied gush until the steam rose and her wrists turned lobster-red. 'You could say that.'

Eventually, turning off the water, wiping her hands on a blue teatowel, she said, 'I was married for twenty-eight years to a man who collected obsessions. The Pennine Pipes. The Mysteries of Bridelow. The Bogman . . .'

Moira said nothing. She was feeling faint. Her breath locked in her throat. She was getting a strong sense of Matt's presence in the room.

'. . . and you,' Lottie said.

In the lofty, rudimentary kitchen, Moira heard a roaring in her head, saw a flashing image of Matt in his coffin, white T-shirt, white quilted coffin-lining, before it was washed away by the black tide carrying images of a stone toad, dancing lights, the steam from writhing intestines liberated on to a flat stone . . .

'On the night he died . . .'

Moira swallowed tea, but the tea wasn't so hot any more and she was swallowing bile.

'On the night he died,' Lottie said, 'he sexually assaulted a nurse in the hospital.'

I'm not hearing this.

She started to look wildly around the kitchen. High ceiling with pipes along it . . . whitewashed walls with crumbling plaster showing through in places . . . stone-flagged floor like the church of St Bride . . . two narrow windows letting in light so white it was like a sheet taped across the glass.

And this awful sense of Matt.

'The nurse had long, dark hair,' Lottie said, almost wist-fully. 'He addressed her as Moira.'

The silence was waxen.

She felt scourged.

Lottie said, 'I wanted you to know all this . . .'

Matt was dodging about under the table, behind the pipes, vibrant, shock-haired Matt reduced to a pale, fidgeting thing, hunched in corners, flitting, agitated, from one to another, giving off fear, hurt, confusion.

'. . . before you made a firm decision about the music. You see? I'm being open about it. No secrets any more.'

Moira looked up into the furthest corner, near the back door, and a cobweb inexplicably detached itself from the junction of two pipes and hung there, impaled by a shaft of white light, heavy with glittering flies' corpses.

'Come with me.' Lottie rolled down the sleeves of her cardigan and strode across the kitchen to the back door, with its long, gaoler's key.

PART SIX

MOTHERS

From *Dawber's* Secret *Book of Bridelow* (unpublished):

THE MOST WIDESPREAD and powerful Celtic tribe in Northern Britain were the Brigantes, whose territory – known as Brigantia – included much of Yorkshire, Lancashire and Southern Scotland and had its southern boundary in the lower Pennines. The mother goddess of the Brigantes was Brigid, and it is believed that many churches dedicated to 'St Bride' were formerly sites of pagan Celtic worship . . .

CHAPTER I

The bloody media.

Over twenty cars parked outside the Field Centre, and men and women pacing the concrete forecourt, most of them turning round when Roger Hall's car pulled in – where the hell was he supposed to park with all these bastards clogging the place? Three cameramen, all swinging round, shooting his Volvo Estate as it manoeuvred about seeking space, as if he might have the bogman himself laid out in the back.

'No . . . no, I'm sorry . . .' Ramming his way through jabbing hands holding pocket tape recorders.

'Dr Hall, have you any idea yet . . . ?'

'Dr Hall, do you know when . . . ?'

'Can you just tell us, Dr Hall, how . . . ?'

'*No!*' He held up both hands. 'There'll be an official Press statement later.'

Bastards. Leeches. One of the double doors opened a few inches and he was hauled in. Chrissie and the other woman, Alice, got the door closed and bolted behind him.

Inspector Gary Ashton was sitting on Roger's desk. 'Any luck, sir?'

'Blank wall.' Roger was brushing at his jacket, as if the reporters had left bits of themselves on him. 'However . . .'

'I must say,' Ashton said, 'it seemed a bit of a long shot to me, that a bunch of villagers from Bridelow would go to all this trouble.' He smiled hesitantly. 'Look, I've had a thought. I hardly like to suggest this, sir, but I don't suppose there's a University rag week in the offing?'

'Don't be ridiculous,' Roger said.

'Well, I don't honestly think,' Ashton said tautly, 'that it's any more ridiculous than your idea about superstitious villagers. Which sounds a bit like one those old Ealing comedies, if I may say so, *sir.*'

Roger said, 'I think you should listen to me without prejudice. I think I know how they've done it.'

Liz Horridge stood frozen with terror at the edge of the pavement.

She was sweating hard; there seemed to be a film of it over her eyes, and a blur on the stone buildings around her turning the cottages into squat muscular beasts and the lych-gate into a predatory bird, its wings spread as if it were about to hop and scuttle down the street and overwhelm her, pinning her down and piercing her breast with its cold, stone beak.

She was leaning, panting, against the back of a van parked

on the corner where the main street joined the old brewery road.

Oh, and by the way, Mother, the Chairman's hoping to drop by tonight.

Who?

The Chairman, Gannons. Been planning to come for ages, apparently, but, you know, appointments, commitments . . .

Will he come here?

We'll receive him in the main office, show him around the brewery. Then, yes, I expect I'll bring him back for a drink. A proper drink. Ha!

Go. Get out. Got to.

She'd thought that when she got so far the fear would evaporate in the remembered warmth of the village, but the village was cold and empty, and a blind like a black eyelid was down in the window of Gus Bibby's general stores, which always kept long hours and would always be lit by paraffin lamps on gloomy days.

But it was Saturday afternoon. Gus Bibby did *not* close on a Saturday afternoon. Saturday had always been firewood day, and there'd be sacks of kindling outside. Always. Always on a Saturday.

Liz felt panic gushing into her breast. Maybe it wasn't Saturday. Maybe it wasn't afternoon. Maybe it was early morning. Maybe the whole place had closed down, been evacuated, and nobody had told her. Maybe the brewery itself had been shut down for weeks and the village had been abandoned.

. . . Chairman's hoping to drop by tonight . . .

No!

How could I not have seen it? How could I have sat there, pretending to examine Gannon's proposals and estimates and balance sheets, and not see his name?

Because it wasn't there . . . I swear . . .

Liz Horridge pumped panicky breath into the still, white air. Not far now. Not fifty yards. She could take it step by step, not looking at houses, not looking at windows.

Someone's door creaked, opened.

'Ta-ra then, luv, look after yourself . . . You what . . . ?'

Liz scuttled back into a short alleyway, squeezed herself into the wall. Mustn't let anyone see her.

'Yeh, don't worry, our Kenneth'll be up to see to it in t'morning. Yeh, you *do*. Ta-ra.'

Door closing.

Footsteps.

Liz clung to the wall. She wore an old waxed jacket and a headscarf over the matted moorgrass that used to be chestnut curls.

She emerged from the entry into the empty street, like a rabbit from a hole. Wanting. Needing. Aching.

To sit again at Ma Wagstaff's fireside, a warm, dry old hand on her sweating brow. *If he comes . . . scream. Don't matter what time.*

Can't turn back now. If you turn back now you'll surely die. Believe this.

'How are you, Pop?'

He was out of bed, that was a good sign, wasn't it? Cathy found him wearing a dull and worthy hospital dressing gown, sitting at his own bedside in a shabby, vinyl-backed hospital chair. He was in the bottom corner of a ward full of old men.

'Bit tired,' he said. 'They've had me walking about. Physiotherapy. Got to keep moving when you've had a coronary.'

Cathy clutched at the bed rails. 'They never told me that!'

'Had to drag it out of them myself. Soon as they get you in hospital you're officially labelled "moron".' His features subsided into that lugubrious boxer-dog expression.

'What's it mean, Pop?'

'Coronary thrombosis? Means a clot in the coronary artery. Means I was lucky not to christen Matt Castle's grave for him. Means I have to *rest*.' Putting on a pompous doctor-voice. '"We have to get ourselves together, as they say, Mr Gruber." Tell me about Joel. Please tell me he didn't sleep under the church.'

Cathy said carefully that she hadn't seen him today. Not a word of what she'd heard about him rampaging around the place in his post-funeral fury, ripping down anything that hinted of paganism. Just that she hadn't actually *seen* him. And that she didn't know where he'd slept.

'Storm gathering inside that chap,' Hans said. 'Hurricane Joel. Wanted to make sure he was somewhere else when it blew.'

'Don't you think about it, Pop. Get some rest. Let them do their tests, try and endure the hospital food and don't refuse the sleeping pill at night.'

'Cathy . . .'

'I know, but it's not *your* problem.'

Hans's head lolled back into the hard vinyl chair. 'I keep the peace. It's taken me years to strike the right balance.'

'Don't worry, they'll sort him out, Ma and the Union. They'll deal with him.'

'But . . .'

'They sorted you out, didn't they?'

Cathy smiled for him. Trying to look more optimistic than she felt.

Hans said bleakly, 'Cathy, Simon Fleming came to see me. They want me to go to the Poplars "for a few weeks' convalescence".'

'Where?'

'The Church's nursing home in Shropshire. Ghastly dump. Full of played-out parsons mumbling in the shrubbery. Nobody gets out alive.'

Cathy felt desperately sorry for him but couldn't help thinking it might be the best answer, for a while. Let the Mothers handle it. Whatever there was to be handled.

He didn't seem to have heard about the disappearance of the bog body, and she didn't tell him. He had enough to worry about already.

'Look, all you need,' Roger Hall said, 'is an exhumation order. That's not a problem, is it?'

Backs to the doors, the Press people assembled on the other side, Chrissie and Alice looked at each other. Roger playing detective. Didn't suit him. Chrissie wondered idly if Inspector

Garry Ashton was married or attached. She thought this business was rather showing up Roger for what he was: pompous, arrogant, humourless – despite the nice crinkles around his eyes.

Ashton said, a little impatiently, 'You were convinced earlier that the body was hidden in Bridelow.'

'Still am,' Roger said smugly.

'Go on,' Ashton said, no longer at all polite. 'Let's hear it.'

Chrissie liked his style. Also the set of his mouth and the way his hair was razor-cut at the sides.

Roger said, 'I attended a funeral in Bridelow yesterday. Matt Castle, the folk musician.'

'So I understand,' Ashton said. 'Mr Castle a friend of yours, was he?'

With a tingle of excitement, Chrissie suddenly knew what Ashton was wondering: did *Roger himself* have anything to do with the theft? The police must have spoken to the British Museum by now, learned all about Roger's battle to bring the bogman back up North. And why was he so keen to keep pointing the police in other directions?

Gosh, Chrissie thought . . . And Roger's obsessive attitude! The bogman intruding everywhere. And when the bogman was in a state of, er, emasculation, Roger himself was . . . unable to function. And complaining of clamminess and peat in the bed and everything. And then suddenly Roger *could* . . . with a vengeance! And the bog body had acquired what appeared to be an appendage of its own.

Chrissie felt a kind of hysteria welling up. *Stop it!* I'm going bloody bonkers. Or somebody is.

Suddenly she didn't want him touching her again.

'Castle?' Roger said. 'Not what you'd call a friend, no. But he was always very interested in the bog body, as many people were. Kept ringing me up, asking what we'd learned so far. And actually turned up here twice, wanting to see the body, which, of course, was *not* available for public viewing. Although I did allow it the second time.'

'Why'd you do that?'

'Because . . . because he was with someone I judged to be more reliable.'

He didn't elaborate; Ashton didn't push the point either. Chrissie thought of the writer, Stanage.

'So, anyway,' Roger said, 'it was Castle's funeral yesterday, and I thought I ought to show my face. I only went to the church service. Left before they actually put him into the ground. But I very much wish I'd stayed with it now, seen him buried.'

'I might be thick,' said Ashton, 'but I'm not following this.'

'All right, let's approach it from another angle. We've all been assuming that the break-in took place last night, right?'

'Have we, Dr Hall?'

'Ashton, look – can we stop this fencing? I know you're an experienced policeman and all that, but I've been doing *my* job for over twenty-five years too.' Angrily, Roger drew his chair from under the desk, scraping the Inspector's legs.

'Look. Because of the funeral and one or two other things, I didn't come in here at all yesterday. And you only found out about the burglary before me because our normally lazy caretaker just happened to try the doors for a change. Correct?'

Ashton came slowly down from the desk, stood looking down at Roger. Interested.

'But if he'd bothered,' Roger said, 'to check the doors the night before – and if he says he did he's probably lying, I know that man – he'd probably have found them forced then. My strong suspicion is the break-in happened the previous night. And that the body wasn't here at all yesterday.'

'And what does that say to you?'

'What it says to me, Inspector – and I might have to spend a bit of time explaining this to you – but what it says to me is that my bog body is buried in St Bride's churchyard.'

'I see,' Ashton said thoughtfully. 'Or do I?'

'The funeral!' Roger raised his hands. 'The grave – it's a *double* grave! What I'm saying is, dig up Castle's coffin, you'll find our body lying underneath. Trust me.'

. . . and there it was.

Oh, Lord. Oh, Mother.

Ma Wagstaff could see the thing from the top of the churchyard, the highest vantage-point in Bridelow.

It hadn't been there a week ago, had it? There was a time when she knew this Moss better than anybody. Couldn't claim that now. Getting owd now. Letting it slide.

Ma leaned on her stick and wondered if she could make it all the way out there without some help. She'd have been able to yesterday, but yesterday was a long time ago. Yesterday, though she hadn't realized it at the time, she still had some strength.

She'd thought that sooner or later it would come to her, but instead it had sent her an invitation. Brought by a little lad who for no good reason had decided the dragon – because the dragon was *there* – was responsible for breaking up his Autumn Cross.

And in a way he was right.

Right about that thing out there; Ma could feel its black challenge. And looking across at it, she could tell why he thought it was a dragon – those little knobbly horns you could make out even from this distance.

Only an owd dead tree, as sometimes came out of the Moss when there was storms and flooding.

Bog oak.

Except there hadn't been a storm.

So it was black growth, like the blackness that grew in Matt Castle, and she had to gauge its strength.

Ma hesitated.

Not one to hesitate, wasn't Ma, but if she went out there she'd be on her own. As well as which, somebody needed her help this side of the Moss; she'd known this for days. Well, aye, people was always needing owd Ma's help, but this was somebody as didn't want to ask, hadn't for some reason been able to overcome a barrier, and until this barrier was overcome there was nowt Ma could do. Now she could feel the struggle going on, and when the plea came she must be there to answer it.

Pulled this way and that, between the flames and the torrent. Oh, Lord. Oh, Mother, which way do I turn? Let it slide for so long, losing me grip.

I'll walk out then.

Walk out there following the river, staying near the water, gathering what power I can. Happen I can deal wi' this quick, nip it in t'bud. Stare it down, give it the hard eye, reshape it, turn it back into wood and only wood.

Leaning heavily on her stick, Ma Wagstaff followed the old, steep narrow path down from the churchyard, meeting the thin river at the bottom of the hill where it went under the path – a little bridge, no more than a culvert – and there was a scrubby field to cross before they reached the Moss.

I can make it. I can. Can I lean on you, Mother?

The last few steps were going to be the hardest, by far.

From two yards away, Ma Wagstaff's front door looked like the golden gates of heaven: unattainable.

Liz Horridge was aware of her mouth being wide open, gulping, a fish out of water, metabolism malfunctioning.

Agoraphobia.

Say it!

AGOR . . . A . . . PHOBIA!!! Common-enough condition, always so hard to imagine, until it came upon you in panic-attacks, convulsions, stomach-cramps.

Yet this . . . more like *claustro*phobia . . . not *enough* air . . . lungs bursting.

She'd tried to do it in planned stages, like an invalid learning to walk again. The first stage had been waiting for the postman, whom she hadn't seen face-to-face for months. When the van drew up, she'd be watching from the dining-room window, and if the postman was carrying a parcel she would run to open the front door, leaving it slightly ajar, and by the time he was tossing the parcel on to the mat, Liz had taken cover.

Yesterday, almost sick with apprehension, she'd waited for the post van down by the main gate, rehearsing how she'd handle it. Just taking a walk. Normally go the other way. Yes, it is cold. Bright, though. Bright, yes. Thank you. Good morning.

When the postman didn't come, she was so relieved. It had

been foolish. Trembling, she'd returned to the house to make Shaw's breakfast. But Shaw had gone. To be with *her*. Whenever he went out without saying even vaguely where he was going, it would always be to be with *her*.

Therese Beaufort had come into the house only once, had been polite but dismissive, had shown a vague interest in everything, except Liz, at whom she'd looked once, with a chilly smile before reappraising the drawing room, as if sizing it up for new furniture. Now she merely parked outside and waited, expressionless, not looking at the house (yes, I've *seen* your mother now, thank you).

And now there was . . .

Look, Liz, why don't we meet up?

And

Chairman's hoping to drop by tonight.

Fear. Despair. She'd walked away, down the drive, down the road, into terror, knowing she could not go home tonight. To the village, to Ma Wagstaff, to plead for sanctuary.

Liz Horridge fell down, tearing her skirt, feeling the small, jutting stones of Ma Wagstaff's front path gashing her knees. She began to crawl towards the door, feeling the emanations of the stone buildings heavy on her back as if they would crush her into the little pointed stones beneath her.

The whitened donkeystoned step gleamed like an altar.

Liz rose on her knees, tried to reach the knocker but managed only the letter-box which snapped at her fingers like a gin-trap.

'Mrs Wagstaff,' she managed to wail. '*Please, Mrs Wagstaff . . . let me in . . .*'

But nobody came to the door.

'I'm sorry! I couldn't stop it! It wasn't my fault about the brewery. Please . . . He's coming back. Please let me in.'

And then the stones came down on her. The weight of the village descended on her shoulders, taking all the breath from her and she couldn't even scream.

CHAPTER II

'*D*idn't know I was coming back to die . . . I mean, that's what people do, isn't it, and animals, go back home to die? But I wouldn't have. If I'd known. Last thing they need here's any deadwood.'

The voice frail, but determined. Going to get this out, if it . . .

Killed him. Yeah.

'*Just as well, really. That I didn't know.*'

All Moira could see through the windscreen was the Moss. The vast peatbog unrolling into the mist like the rotting lino in the hall of her old college lodgings in Manchester, half a life away.

The BMW was parked in the spot at the edge of the causeway where yesterday she'd sat and listened to the pipes on cassette. Now it was another cassette, the one from the brown envelope inscribed MOIRA.

'*Funny thing, lass . . . this is the first time I've found it easy to talk to you. Maybe 'cause you're not there. In the flesh. Heh. Did you realize that, how hard it was for me? Lottie knew. No hiding it from a woman like Lottie. Shit, I don't care who knows. I'm dead now.*'

Matt laughed. The cawing.

She'd followed Lottie into a yard untidy with beer kegs and crates. Beyond it was a solid, stone building the size of a two-car garage. It looked as old as the pub, had probably once been stables or a barn.

'Matt's music room,' Lottie said.

She'd been almost scared to peer over Lottie's shoulder, into the dimness, into the barnlike space with high-level slit windows and huge, rough beams. Dust floating like the beginnings of snow.

Lottie silent. Moira, hesitant. 'May I?' Lottie nodding.

Moira slipping past her, expecting echoes, but there was carpet and rugs underfoot and more carpet on the walls to

273

flatten the acoustics. She saw a table, papers and stuff strewn across it.

Shelves supported by cement-spattered bricks held books, vinyl records and tapes. Heavy old speaker cabinets squatted like tombstones and there was a big Teac reel-to-reel tape machine. Matt's scarred Martin guitar lay supine on an old settee with its stuffing thrusting out between the cushions.

Hanging over the sides of a stool was something which, from across the room, resembled a torn and gutted, old, black umbrella.

She'd walked hesitantly over and stared down at the Pennine Pipes in pity and horror, like you might contemplate a bird with smashed wings. It was as if he'd simply tossed the pipes on the stool and walked out, for ever, and the bag had maybe throbbed and pulsed a little, letting out the last of Matt's breath, and then the pipes had died.

Moira's throat was very dry. She was thinking about Matt's obsessions: the Pennine Pipes, the bogman and . . .

'*Can't help your feelings, can you? Like, if you're a married man, with a kid, and you meet somebody and you . . . and she takes over your life and you can't stop thinking about her. But that's not a sin, is it? Not if you don't . . . Anyway, I never realized that you . . . I never realized.*'

Matt's voice all around her now. Car stereos, so damned intimate.

Lottie had turned away, calling back over her shoulder, 'I'll be in the kitchen. Stay as long as you like. Lock up behind you and bring me the key. The parcel's on the table.'

And was gone, leaving Moira alone in the barn that was like a chapel, with the pipes left to die.

On the table, a thick, brown envelope which had once held a junk-mail catalogue for Honda cars. It had been resealed with Sellotape and

MOIRA

was scrawled across it.

Inside: the tapes, four of them, three of music. And this one, a BASF chrome, marked *personal*.

'Not a sin . . . if you don't do owt about it. But I always found it hard to talk to you. I mean . . . just to talk to you. Till it came time to tell you to get out of the band. That was easy. That was a fucking pushover, kid. I'm sorry the way that worked out, with The Philosopher's Stone. Sounded like a big opportunity. Like, for me too – chance to make the supreme sacrifice. But we can't tell, can we? We never can bloody tell, till it's too late.'

Rambling. He'd have been on some kind of medication, wouldn't he? Drugs.

'But when they told me I'd had me chips, I did regret it. Regretted it like hell. I thought most likely you'd just have told me to piss off, but there might have been a . . . Anyway, I'd have given anything for just one . . . just one time with you. Just one. Anything.'

Christ. Moira stared out of the side window to where half a tree had erupted from the Moss, like bone burst through skin.

'When you wrote back and you said you were too busy, I was shattered. I'd convinced meself you'd come. I just wanted to at least see you. Just one more time.'

Moira bit down on her lower lip.

'I'd tried to write a song. Couldn't do it. It was just a tune without words. Nothing. Best bloody tune I ever wrote, which isn't saying much – play it for you in a minute. Won't be much good, the playing, what d'you expect? Be the last tune I ever play. Gonna play it over and over again until I get it perfect, and then I'm gonna get Lottie to take me out and I'll play it to the fucking Moss. The Man in the Moss. That's what it's about. The Man in the Moss. That'll be me, too. Want to die with this tune in me head. This tune . . . and you.'

She felt a chill, like a low, whistling wind.

'It's called Lament for the Man. I want the Moss to take it. A gift. Lament for the Bridelow Bogman. Soon as I read about him, months ago, before it came out about the sacrifice element, I was inspired by him. Direct link with me own past. The Celts. The English Celts. Like he'd come out the Moss to make a statement about the English Celts. And I was the only one could interpret it – sounds arrogant, eh? But I believe it. Like this is what me whole life's been leading up to.'

275

Matt starting to cough. On and on, distorting because the recording level couldn't handle it. The car-speakers rattling, like there was phlegm inside.

'*Fuck it,*' Matt said. '*If I go back and scrub this I'll forget what I was gonna say. Sorry. Can you handle it? See, this was before they'd completed the tests on the bogman, before it was known about the sacrifice. Even then I was pretty much obsessed. I didn't care if we spent every penny we'd got. Lottie – she's a bloody good woman, Moira, I never deserved Lottie – she went along with it, although she loved that chintzy house in Wilmslow and she hated The Man I'th Moss, soon as she clapped eyes on it. But she went along with it. Sometimes I think, did she know? Did she know before me, that I was gonna snuff it? She says not. I believe her.*'

Across the Moss she could see the pub, a huge grey boathouse on the edge of a dark sea, its backyard a landing stage.

'*And then, soon after we came, the report came out about the bogman. About what he was. A sacrifice. To appease the gods so they'd keep the enemy at bay, make this community inviolate. Protect these Celts, these refugees from the fertile flatlands, the Cheshire Plain, Lancashire, the Welsh border. Invaders snatching their land, Romans, Saxons. And this, the old high place above the Moss – maybe it was a lake then. Bridelow.*'

Matt's voice cracked.

'*Bridelow. The last refuge. I cried. When I heard, I cried. He went willingly. Almost definitely that was what happened. Almost certain he was the son of the chief, everything to live for – had to be, see, to make a worthwhile sacrifice.*'

Voice gone to a whisper.

'*Gave himself up. Willingly. That's the point. Can you grasp that, Moira? He let them take him on the Moss and they smashed his head, strangled him and cut his throat, and he knew . . . he fucking knew what was gonna happen.*'

She stared through the windscreen at the Moss. Thick, low cloud lay tight to the peat, like a bandage on its putrefying, suppurating skin.

'*Hard to credit, isn't it? I mean, when you really think about it. When you try and picture it. He let the buggers do it to him. Young guy, fit, full of life and energy and he gives himself up in the*

*most complete sense. Can you understand that? Maybe it affects me
more because I've got no youth, no energy, and what life there's left
is dribbling away by the minute. But by God . . . I realized I
wanted a bit of that.'*

She thought about the bogman. The sacrifice. She thought
about Matt, inspired. Always so contagious, Matt's inspiration.
She thought, I can't bear this . . .

*'Can you get what I'm saying? Like, they took him away, these
fucking scientists, with never a second thought about what he meant
to Bridelow and what Bridelow, whatever it was called back then,
meant to him. So I wanted . . . I wanted in. To be part of that.
To go in the Moss, too. Lottie tell you that? Lottie thinks it's shit,
but it isn't. . . .'*

'No,' Moira whispered. 'It wouldn't be.'

*'. . . want some of me out there. With him. He's my hero, that
lad . . . I'm fifty-seven and I'm on me last legs – nay, not even that
any more, me legs won't carry me – and I've found a fucking hero
at last.'*

Matt starting to laugh and the laughter going into a choke
and the choking turning to weeping.

*'Me and Ma Wagstaff met one day. One stormy day. Ma
understands, the old bitch. Willie's Ma, you know? Says to me,
"We can help you help him. But you must purify yourself."'*

Out on the Moss, the dead tree like bone was moving. It
had a tangle of thin branches, as if it were still alive, and the
branches were waving, whipping against the tree.

'She says, You have to purify yourself.'

The tree was a bad tree, was about to take its place alongside
the encroaching stone toad on the moor, the eruption of guts
on an ancient, rough-hewn altar. Bad things forcing themselves
into Bridelow.

'And then you came to me . . .'

Moira's eyes widened.

*'I used to think she was . . . a substitute. Me own creation.
Like, creating you out of her, you know what I mean? An obsession
imposes itself on what's available. But I should've known.
Should've known you wouldn't leave me to die alone.'*

Her senses froze.

'So, as I go into the final round, as they say, I'm drawing

277

strength from the both of you. The bogman . . . and you, Moira.
Tomorrow's Sunday. I'll be going out on the Moss, to play. Last
time, I reckon. I'll need Lottie and Dic, poor lad, to get me there,
but I'll send them away, then there'll just be the three of us.'

'No,' she said. 'What *is* this?'

'*Me and thee and him.*'

Matt chuckled eerily.

Hard rain hit the Moss.

'No,' she said.

'*Thanks, lass. Thanks for getting me through this. Thanks for*
your spirit. And your body. It was your body, wasn't it?'

She wrapped her arms around herself, began to shake,
feeling soiled.

'*Ma said, You've got to purify yourself. But there's a kind of*
purity in intensity of feeling, isn't that right? Pure black light.'

'*I'll play now,*' Matt said, and she heard him lifting his
pipes onto his knees.

'*If you're listening to this, it means you're here in Bridelow. So*
find Willie, find Eric. And then find me. You'll do that, won't you?
Find me.'

The old familiar routine, the wheeze, the treble notes.

'*I won't be far away,*' Matt said.

And the lament began. At first hoarse and fragmented, but
resolving into a thing of piercing beauty and an awful, knowing
anticipation.

Out on the black Moss, as if hit by a fierce wind, the dead
tree lashed impatiently at its bones with its own sinuous
branches, like cords of gut.

Moira thought, There's no wind. No wind to speak of. The
Moss in the rain was dull and opaque, like a blotter. She didn't
want to look at the tree but a movement drew her eyes. Human
movement.

An old woman was hobbling across the peat; she had a
stick. A stringy shawl flapped around her head. She was
approaching the tree very deliberately, slow but surefooted.

She seemed to be wearing ordinary shoes, not boots or
wellingtons; she knew the peat, where to walk.

Cathy had said, *You're going to have to talk to Ma. If she'll*
talk to you.

It *is* her, isn't it?

The dead tree was about a hundred yards away. The old woman was walking around it now, poking experimentally at it with her stick and then backing away like a terrier.

A wavy branch lashed out, wrapped itself around the walking stick. Moira drew breath.

Another movement, quick and sudden, and the shawl was torn away from the woman's shoulders, thrown triumphantly up into the air on the tip of a wavy branch, like a captured enemy flag.

'Holy Christ!' Moira was out of the car, leaving the driver's door hanging open, stepping down from the causeway, hurrying into the Moss.

Where the sinewy, whipcord branches of the old, dead tree were writhing and striking individually at the old woman, Ma Wagstaff, pulsing like vipers. Moira running across the peat, through the rain, desperately trying to keep her footsteps light because she didn't know this Moss. There was no wind. The rain fell vertically. Behind her Matt's music on the car stereo was a dwindling whine.

'Mrs Wagstaff!' she screamed. '*Mrs Wagstaff, get away from it . . .*'

In the distance, over the far hills, behind the rain, the sun was a bulge in the white bandage of cloud and the flailing tree of guts and bones was rearing up against it; she was maybe sixty yards away now and the tree was tossing its head.

It had a head.

And its eyes were white; they were only holes in the wood, letting the sky through, but they burned white, and it was not a case of what you knew it to be, old and twisted wood, shrivelled, wind-blasted, contorted by nature into demonic, nightmare shapes – this was the old mistake, to waste time and energy rationalizing the irrational.

'Mrs Wagstaff, back off!'

What was the old biddy doing here alone? Where were the Mothers' Union, when she needed back-up?

'Mrs Wag . . . Don't . . . don't look . . .'

Moira stumbled.

'Don't look at it,' she said miserably, for Bridelow Moss had got her left foot. Swallowed it whole, closing around her ankle, like soft lips.

White eyes.

Black, horned head, white eyes.

'It's thee. It were always thee.'

Ma Wagstaff growled, stabbed at it one last time with her stick – the wood was so hard that the metal tip of the stick snapped off.

'Mrs Wag—'

Woman's voice screaming in the distance.

Nowt to do wi' her. Ma's job, this.

She moved away, like an old, experienced cat. Bait it. 'Come on, show thiself.' A dry, old rasp, not much to it, but she got it out. 'What's a tree? What's a bit of owd wood to me, eh? Show thi face. 'Cause this is as near as tha's ever going to get to Bridlo'. We seen to thee once . . . and it'll *stick*.'

Backing away from it, and all the muck coming off it in clouds. She was going to need some help, some strength. It'd take everything she'd got – and some more.

And not long. Not long for it.

All-Hallows soon. The dark curtain thin as muslin.

Dead tree out of the Moss, and made to live, made to thresh its boughs.

Him.

Taunt it.

'You're nowt.' Words coming out like a sick cough. 'You're nowt, Jack. You never was owt!'

Dead tree writhing and slashing itself at her, and though she was well out of range by now, she felt every poisoned sting.

Get it mad.

'Ah . . .' Ma turned away. 'Not worth it. Not worth me time. Bit of owd wood.'

But her heart was slamming and rocking like an old washing-machine.

Black horned head, white eyes.

Dead, but living in *him*.
White eyes.

CHAPTER III

There was a metallic snapping sound followed by a faint and desperate wailing.

'*Mrs Wagstaff . . .*'

The voice was familiar. But it didn't matter.

This was a funny little house, bottles and jars on every ledge, even on the edges of individual stairs. Sprigs of this and that hung from the ceilings and circulated musty smells.

The witch's den.

He sat in silence at the top of the stairs. Unperturbed.

'*Please, Mrs Wagstaff . . . let me in . . .*'

Then silence. He smiled. As children, they'd clustered by the church gate and whispered about the witch's house, not daring to go too close. *See the curtain move . . . ? It's her. She's coming . . . !*

It hadn't changed; only his perspective on it. The wicked witch. Perspectives changed. Now it was cool to be . . . wow, *wicked*! But Ma Wagstaff wasn't authentically wicked, never had been. Ma Wagstaff, let's face it, wasn't quite up to it and wouldn't be now. She'd conned them, generations of them.

Now *I'm* really rather wicked, he thought. If there's such a thing. Or at least I'm getting there.

He didn't move. His body didn't move.

The reason it didn't move was he didn't want it to. Suddenly, he had true self-control, and this amazed him. Or rather it amazed him to reflect on what a bag of dancing neuroses he used to be, so untogether he couldn't even regulate the sounds coming out of his own mouth.

Sher-sher-Shaw. Ster- ster-stuttering Shaw.

Amusing to imagine what he'd have been like if he'd been given this present task even a month ago, when he was still unconvinced. When he used to say, It's, you know . . . *bad*, though, isn't it? It might be fun, it might be exhilarating, but it's bad, essentially. Surely.

And were you good before, Shaw? Were you good when you were stuttering and dithering and letting your father dominate you? Is that your idea of what it means to be good? In which case, how does it feel to be bad?

Terminology. Nowadays Bad was cool, like Wicked. A step in the right direction.

How's it feel? Feels good. Alive. Quite simply that. I didn't know before what being alive *meant.* I said to her, *haven't you got to be dead to be undead?* And she said, *what makes you think you aren't?*

So I was dead and now I'm alive. I know that when I pull the handles, turn the switches, press the buttons . . . something will *happen.*

They'd told him he'd seen nothing yet. They'd told him there would be a sign. And now there was. And *what* a sign. Once again, Shaw couldn't resist it. He allowed his right hand to remove its leather glove and brush its palm across the top of his head.

A delicious prickly sensation.

The first time he'd felt it, he'd wanted to leap up and squeal with joy. But there was no need to do this any more. He could experience that joy deep inside himself, knowing how much more powerful and satisfying the feeling was if he *didn't* allow it to expend itself through his body, dissipating as he hopped about like a little kid, punching the air.

So Shaw Horridge's body remained seated quietly at the top of the stairs in Ma Wagstaff's house while Shaw Horridge's spirit was in a state of supreme exultation.

His hair was growing again! He was alive and he had made it happen.

Just a fuzz at first, then thicker than a fuzz – almost a stubble. He'd heard of men going to Ma Wagstaff for her patent hair-restorer, some claiming it worked. A bit. But not actually sure whether it had or not.

Not like this. No doubt about this. Where there'd been no hair, now there was hair.

All around him were Ma Wagstaff's bottles full of maybes.

Maybe if the wind's in the right direction. If the moon's full. If there's an R in the month. Quite sad, really. A grey little world of hopes and dreams. No certainties.

Hair-loss was natural in some people, his mother said. But it had taken Therese to prove to him that you didn't have to accept something just because it was supposed to be *natural*. Acceptance was just spiritual sloth.

Being truly alive was about changing things. Changing people, situations. Changing your state of mind. Changing the 'natural'.

Being alive was about breaking rules with impunity. Men's rules. Also the rules men claimed they'd had from God. 'Natural' rules. This was what she'd taught him. Learn how to break the rules – for no other reason than to break them – and you become free.

Thou shalt not kill. But why? We kill animals to eat, we kill people with abandon in wartime. We kill for the Queen, we kill for the oil industry? Where does the taboo begin?

He stretched his arms and yawned. Settled down to wait, aware of his breathing, fully relaxed. How could bad be bad when it felt as good as this.

Eventually, kneeling messily in the rain, Moira pulled her shoe out of the bog.

The shoe was full of water; she shook it out and put it on. By this time the old woman had hobbled to the edge of the Moss, where there was a gate leading into a field, beyond which was the pub and, further up, the hill on which the church sat.

The dead tree was still. It looked hard, heavy, almost stone-like. Too dense to move in the wind, even if there'd been one. But it moved for me, she thought, limping back to the car. And it moved for Ma Wagstaff.

Such things were almost invariably subjective. Like, how often did two people see a ghost, at the same time, together? Ghosts and related phenomena were one-to-one. You saw it and the person with you said, hey, what's wrong with you, what are you staring at, why've you gone so pale?

But the tree moved for Ma Wagstaff. And it moved, no question, for me.

She climbed behind the wheel and sank into the seat, drained. The cassette tape had ended. She flipped it out of the player.

Ma Wagstaff understands, the old bitch. She says to me, 'We can help you help him. But you must purify yourself.'

I am not getting this, Matt. What were you into, you and Ma?

And then

. . . whuppp.

Moira reeled back in the seat as something hit the windscreen. Like a big bird, covering the sky, darkening the car, it flapped there, wriggling and beating at the glass.

'Holy Jesus.'

It was snagged in the wipers, but it wasn't a bird . . . only a dark blue woolly shawl. Ma Wagstaff's shawl, snatched from her by the devil-tree. Blown across the Moss. Blown hard, directly at the car, like it had been aimed.

Moira began to pant, closing her eyes tight, squeezing on the steering-wheel until it creaked.

When she opened her eyes the shawl had gone, and the vertical rain showed there was still no wind.

OK. Move.

She switched on the engine; slammed the BMW into reverse, pulled it back on to the causeway, pointing it at Bridelow. The sky was dirty now, but she wondered if it would still be white through the eyeholes in the thing of wood on the Moss.

Ma said, You've got to purify yourself. But there's a kind of purity in intensity of feeling, isn't that right? Pure black light.

Right. Get off my back, Matt. You're sicker than I figured. Just get the *hell* off my back.

Moira drove erratically into the village street, bumping carelessly along the cobbles and over the kerb. Nobody about. No sign of the old woman. The cottages featureless and damp, a huddle.

Pure black light.

Black light? White light? What is this shit? Wished she could call the Duchess, but the Duchess wasn't on the phone. The Duchess wants to contact anybody, she doesn't mess with phones.

Moira sat in her car at the bottom of the street, ploughing her fingers through her hair. Exposed. And scared?

Oh, yes.

And maybe half-deranged. Couldn't properly express in words what she was doing here. Like she'd been sucked into the smoking fireplace that night at the Earl's castle and gone up the chimney and been spit out cold on Bridelow Moss.

Now everything was pointing at Ma Wagstaff, but Ma Wagstaff had run away.

She left the car in the street, squelched to the Post Office, peatwater oozing out of her shoes.

'Willie's not in,' she panted at the big, flowery Girl-Guide postmistress. 'Where would I find his mother's place?'

Weak as a kitten, Ma felt. Weak as a day-old kitten, its eyes not open yet. Weak and blind.

Help me, Mother.

Ma followed the river back, gratefully leaving the Moss behind. There was a crack starting in her walking stick where the black tree had snapped off the metal tip. Soon the stick wouldn't support even a skinny, spidery owd thing like her, and what would she do then?

It got her to the churchyard, God alone knew how, and she propped her old bones up against a stone cross. Looked up at the church porch, and it hit her like an elbow in the ribs.

Desecrated!

Oh, Mother. Oh, Jesus!

Over the door . . . a mess of crumbling old cement.

That *vandal*.

The Goths and the Vandals and the Angles and the Saxons and the Romans and the so-called Christians. All them raiders Bridelow had fought off over the long centuries. And the buggers still at the door with their battleaxes.

Inside the church, little Benjie's Autumn Cross all smashed. And the vile thing growing out on the Moss, waving Ma's torn shawl like a banner. And the seeping sickness within that saps health and takes jobs. And now Our Sheila smitten from the wall, thrown away like she was nowt more than one of them dirty magazines.

Grinding, in pain, the few teeth she'd got left to grind, Ma Wagstaff staggered through the graveyard, up to the top end, where Matt Castle lay, the earth still loose on him, covered by wreaths, already bashed about by the weather, petals everywhere.

The witch bottle lay in her coat pocket. Dead.

Moving like an owd crab on a pebble beach, Ma staggered by Matt's grave without stopping. The earth loose around him – not buried proper, not yet. Still airholes in the soil. Poor bugger might as well be lying stretched out on top.

The rain had stopped, but the clouds still bulged like cheeks full of spit. Ma stumbled out on to the moor, through the top wicket gate, between two tattered gorse bushes.

This was not the real moor; this was still Bridelow. Until you got over the rocks.

Below the rocks was the holy well, the spring, water bubbling bright as lemonade into a natural-hewn stone dish. The well they dressed with flowers in the springtime to honour the Mother and the water. Long before she reached it, Ma could hear it singing.

A rock leaned over the spring, like a mantelpiece over a hearth, above it the moor, which was not Bridelow.

Carved out of the stone, a hollow, with a little shelf.

On the shelf a statue.

'Mother,' Ma said breathlessly.

The statue was plaster. She wore a robe once painted blue, now chipped and faded. Her eyes were uplifted to the sky beyond the shelf of rock, her hands turned palms-down to bless the water trickling from the rock below her feet.

'Oh, Mother.' Ma dropped her stick. She'd made it home.

She fell down upon the stone, the edge of her woollen skirt in the rock pool; began to cry, words bubbling out of her like the water from the rock. 'I've brought thee nowt . . . Forgive me, Mother. Not properly dressed. Dint know I were coming, see.'

She sat up, crossed herself, closed her eyes, all hot and teary. Cupped her hands into the pool and brought the spring water to her eyes. And when they were touched by the water, she saw at last, through her eyelids, a warm, bright light.

Ma lifted up her hands into the light, and felt them touch the hem of the radiant blue robe of the Mother, the material that felt like a fine and silken rain.

She began to mumble, the old words dropping into place, words in English, words in Latin, words in an olden-day language that was neither Welsh nor Gaelic, words from the Bible, power-words and humble-words. Words to soak up the light and bring it into her blood. Come into me, Mother, give me light and give me strength, give me the holy power to face your enemies and to withstand . . .

The shadow fell across her.

The bright blue gauze dissolved. Ma's eyes opened into pain.

The curate stood astride the sacred spring. Big and stupid as a Victorian stone angel.

'So,' he said. 'This is it, is it?'

He kicked a pebble into the pool. 'It's even more tawdry than I expected, Mrs Wagstaff.'

'Go away,' Ma said quietly, looking down into the pool. 'What's it to do wi' you? Go on. Clear off. Come back when you're older.'

'*What's it to do with me?*' He stood there thick and hard as granite. 'You can ask that? Where did you get this?' With a hand like a spade, he plucked the Mother from her stone hollow. 'One of these Catholic shops, I suppose. Or was it taken from a church? Hmm?'

He held the statue at arm's length. 'Hardly a work of art, Mrs Wagstaff. But hardly deserving of this kind of grubby sacrilege.'

Ma was on her feet, blinding pain ripping through every sinew. 'You put that *back*! That's sacred, that is! Put it back *now*! Call yourself a minister of God? You're nobbut a thick bloody vandal wi' no more brains than pig shit!'

'And you,' he said, tucking the statue under an arm, 'are a poor, misguided old woman who ought to be in a Home, where you can be watched over until you die.'

Ma Wagstaff tried to stand with dignity and couldn't.

Joel Beard bent his face to hers. 'You're a throwback, Mrs Wagstaff. A remnant. My inclination as a human being is to feel very sorry for you, but my faith won't allow me to do that.'

Behind his eyes she saw a cold furnace.

'*Thou shalt not suffer a witch to live!*'

The statue hefted above his head like a club. Ma cowered.

'Oh, no . . .' He lowered the statue to chest-height. 'Don't cringe, Mrs Wagstaff. I wouldn't hurt you physically. I'm a servant of God. I merely remind you of the strong line the Bible takes on your particular . . . sub-species.'

Joel Beard put out a contemptuous hand to help her up. She looked at the hand and its fingers became a bundle of twisted twigs bound roughly together, and the connection was made with the thing on the Moss, two opposing terminals, the black and the white, each as dangerous and Ma stranded in the middle.

'Gerraway from me!' She shrank back, feeling that if she touched his hand she'd be burned alive.

'What are you afraid of, Mrs Wagstaff?'

'I'm afraid of denseness,' Ma said. 'Kind of denseness as rips down a child's offering, smashes it on t'stones . . .'

'But . . . but it was evil,' he said reasonably. 'Can't you people see that? Primitive. Heathen. It insulted the true Cross.'

Ma Wagstaff shook her head. 'Tha knows nowt. Tha's big and arrogant, and tha knows nowt. Tha's not fit to wipe Hans Gruber's arse.'

Joel Beard raised the statue of the Mother far above his head. His face severe. His golden curls tight as stone.

'All right, then,' he said. 'Be your own salvation, Mrs Wagstaff.'

Ma grabbed at the air, eyes widening in horror. She began to whimper. Joel smashed the Mother down on the rocks and her head broke easily, pounded to plaster-dust.

Ma Wagstaff cried out. The cry of the defeated, the gutted, the desolate.

Gone. Nowt left. Gone to dust.

Beating the plaster from his hands and his green hiking jacket, Joel Beard strode away across the dirty-yellow moorgrass. Fragments floated in the centre of the pool until the springwater scattered them, making widening circles over the Mother's headless body.

CHAPTER IV

For the first time since all this had begun, Lottie's hands began to shake, and she pressed them against the hotplate covers on the stove so that if the policeman had seen it he'd think she was simply cold.

It was a bad dream, switching from one dreadful scene to another until the horror was spinning about her like a merry-go-round of black shadow-horses, and whichever way she turned . . .

She turned back to the policeman, who, to give him his due, looked no happier about this than she felt. Steadying her voice, she said, 'You want to dig up my husband.'

'This is . . .' Inspector Ashton exhaled down his nose. 'Look, Mrs Castle, if there was any other way . . . It's not your husband we want to . . . see. It's the grave itself. Normally when there's an exhumation it's at the request of the coroner or the pathologist, to enable further examination of a body. In this case we don't want to touch the body, we don't even want to open the coffin. We . . . have reason to believe the grave may have been disturbed before your husband was placed in it.'

Lottie felt her face muscles harden. Somebody had blown the gaff on Ma Wagstaff and her primitive rituals. What the hell *else* had the old hag been up to?

'We have reason to believe,' Ashton said, 'that certain . . . stolen goods may be buried under your husband's coffin.'

'What goods?'

'I'd rather not say at the present time, if you don't mind, Mrs Castle.'

He'd turned up in the bar not long after Moira had left. On his own. Asked if he might have a word. All very casual and quiet.

Lottie thought about the implications. 'And what if I don't agree?'

Ashton sighed. 'It'll just take longer for us to get permission.'

'But you'll get it anyway.'

Ashton nodded. 'Between ourselves, what does bother me is that the person who's made the allegations about this . . . these stolen goods . . . has intimated that if we don't act on them quickly, he'll make his suspicions known to the media. I don't need to tell you what *that* would mean in terms of invasion of privacy, unwarranted intrusion into private grief, reporters all over your doorstep . . .'

'You mean,' said Lottie, 'that this man's blackmailing you?'

Ashton laughed. 'If only it was that simple. No, I was inclined to disbelieve him at first, but now I agree there's a strong basis for thinking something's down there as shouldn't be. And if we can handle our excavations discreetly, after dark, inconspicuous, no fuss . . .'

'Have you spoken to anyone else in the village?'

'No, I certainly haven't, and I'd be very much obliged if you'd keep this to yourself as well. Last thing we want is an audience. 'Course, we'll have to consult with the minister, but that won't be a problem, I shouldn't think.'

Lottie thought about Ma Wagstaff and her Old Ways and Matt's apparent acceptance of all this rubbish as part of the unique West Pennine tradition. Acknowledging, with much bitterness, Matt's part in all this.

'Right.' She pulled her hands from the stove. 'Go ahead. I'll sign whatever you want me to sign.'

'Thank you,' said Ashton. 'That's very brave of you, Mrs Castle.'

'Just one thing.'

He'd begun to button his trenchcoat; he stopped.

'Keep me out of it, Inspector. I don't want to know when you do it or what you find. I don't want to be involved.'

Ashton nodded, relieved. 'And you'll keep this to yourself?'

'Oh, I wouldn't want to alert anybody who might have cause to be . . . embarrassed.' Lottie smiled grimly. 'I certainly wouldn't.'

Suspicious, at first, as he came up the street. Fingers going on his thighs, nose twitching as if he had whiskers. Then he saw who it was, and she watched the sun come up in his cheeks and knew it was all right.

'Moira!'

More than ten years dissolved in the Pennine air.

'Willie, hey, I was looking for you the whole morning.'

'I were down me workshop. Doin' a bit o' bodgin' an' fettlin'.' He stepped back, put his hands on her shoulders like a dog on its hind legs. 'Eee, lass, I can't tell you . . . you're looking bloody grand.'

She thought he was going to lick her ears, but he backed off and they stood a couple of yards apart, inspecting each other. He hadn't changed at all: small and wary, brown hair down to his quick eyes. She didn't know what to say. So damn much to talk about, and none of it superficial.

It started to rain again. 'Once it starts,' Willie said, twitching his nose at the sky, 'it gets to be a bloody habit in Brid'lo.'

He smiled. 'Got time for a cup o' tea, lass?'

Did he think she was just passing through? 'Jesus, Willie,' Moira said, feeling close to collapse. 'I've got time for a whole damn pot.'

She would come in by the back door.

Same way he'd come in. It hadn't been locked, didn't even have a lock on it. He remembered how, as a child, he'd been dared to go in by other kids. Into the witch's den. He'd refused. He was afraid.

This time last year he'd still have been afraid. Even a couple of months ago he would.

He came to his feet and stood behind the balustrade, his hands around the wooden ball on top. It was sticky with layers of brown varnish. The paper on the walls was brown with age. There'd been flowers on it; they just looked like grease patches now.

Late afternoon dimness enclosing him. He'd have been afraid of that too, once. Afraid to open the bedroom doors, afraid of the ghosts within. Afraid of what he might disturb.

Afraid not to be afraid.

But not any more.

Willie had a teapot in a woollen tea-cosy made out of an outsize bobble hat.

'You make it yourself?'

'I have a friend,' Willie said, looking embarrassed about it, the way Willie had always looked embarrassed about women, although it never seemed to get in his way.

'You've a girlfriend here? In Bridelow?'

'More of an arrangement,' said Willie. 'Been on and off for years. What about you?'

'Oh. You know. Livin' alone, as the song says, is all I've ever done well.'

'Your song? Sorry, luv, I've not been keeping track.'

'Nanci Griffith. Found an echo. Sometimes other people take the songs right out of your head.'

'Aye,' Willie said. He took a long, assessing look at her as she sprawled in a fat easy-chair with a loud pattern of big yellow marigolds. 'You look good,' Willie said. 'But you look tired.'

'I don't know why. All I've done is wandered around and talked to people. Yeah, I'm knackered. Must be the air.'

'Air's not what it was,' said Willie. 'Fancy a biscuit? Cheese butty?'

'No, thanks.' She closed her eyes. 'It's nice in here. I could go to sleep in this chair.'

'Feel free.'

'No.' She forced her eyes open. 'You've got trouble here, Willie. Your ma. Like, I realize it's not my business, but I think she's got some private war on, you know?'

'Oh, aye. I know that all right. I . . .' He hesitated, refilling her teacup. 'How long you been here? I were looking out for you at Matt's funeral.'

'I was being low-profile,' Moira said. 'But I saw the business with the witch bottle, if that's . . .'

'Oh . . .' Willie sat down and crossed his legs, started up a staccato finger-rhythm on the side of a knee. 'I don't know. Sometimes I think we're living inside a bloody folk museum.'

'It's no' a museum,' Moira said. 'I just watched her out on the Moss. There's kind of a dead tree out there.'

'Bog oak,' Willie said. 'That's all it is.'

'Then why're your fingers drumming up a storm?'

'Shit,' Willie said. 'Shit, shit, shit.'

'Come on.' Moira dragged herself out of the chair. 'Let's go and talk to her.'

Moira's left foot was feeling cold and wet. She stamped it on the cobbles. 'Went out on the Moss with no wellies. Stupid, huh?'

Rainy afternoon in a small village, nobody else about, no distractions, and they were both on edge. The hush before the thunder.

It's in the air. A damp tension.

So quiet.

'Catch my death.' Moira smiled feebly.

Both of Willie's hands drumming. It happened to Willie through his fingers. People said it was nerves. But what were nerves for if not to respond to things you couldn't see?

'Hey, come on,' Moira said softly, 'what's wrong here, Willie?'

'I don't know.' He sounded confused. 'Nowt I can put me finger on.'

They'd hammered on Ma's door. Waited and waited. All dark inside.

Willie started blinking. The only noise in the street was the rapid rhythmic chinking of his fingers on the coins in one hip pocket and something else, maybe keys, in the other. It echoed from the cobbles and the stone walls of the cottages. Willie's fingers knew something Willie didn't.

'Willie, quick, come on, think, where would she be? Where would she go if she was scared?'

He looked swiftly from side to side, up and down the street. 'Willie . . . ?'

Hands wet with the once-holy spring water, white with powdered plaster. Wind blowing through her head. Mind a-crackle with shredded leaves and lashing boughs. No thoughts, only shifting sensations, everything shaken up like medicine gone sour in the bottle. Air full of evil sediment.

Sky white, trees black, church tower black.

Twisted legs and malformed feet crabbing it through the bracken and the heather.

Broken owd woman going back to her useless bottles.

'Let me help you, Mrs Wagstaff, for God's sake.' Long, striding legs, head in the clouds. Wanted to help for appearances' sake; wouldn't look good if he buggered off and owd Ma fell and broke a leg.

'*Gerroff me!*' she shrieked.

'You've got to turn away from all this! Make your peace with Almighty God. It's not too late . . .'

Screeching through the gale in her brain, 'What would you know? It's long too late!'

Wretched gargoyles screaming along with her from the church's blackened walls.

At the churchyard gate, relief for both of them, him going one way, to *his* church, not looking back; Ma the other, down towards the street. Sky like lead crushing her into the brown ground.

Top of the street, Ma stopped and squinted. Two people. Willie and a woman. The woman from the funeral, the woman from the Moss, the woman with the Gift.

Bugger!

Couldn't be doing with it. Questions. Concern. Sit down, Ma, have a cuppa, put thi' feet up, tell us all about it. Tell me how I can *help*.

Pah!

Ma turned back up the street, waited at the opening to the

brewery road till they'd gone past then took the path round the back of the cottages so nobody else would see the state of her.

'This?'

Water trickled dispiritedly from under the rock and plopped into the pool.

'Used to be a torrent,' Willie remembered.

'This is the holy well?'

The pool looked flat and sullen in the rain.

'There should be a statue,' Willie said.

'Of whom?'

'The . . . Mother. On that ledge. She had her hands out, blessing the spring. There's a ceremony, every May Day. Flowers everywhere. You can see it for miles. Then the lads'd come up from t'brewery, fill up a few dozen barrels, roll um down the hill. At one time, all the beer'd be made wi' this water, now it's shared out, so there's a few drops in each cask.'

Willie kicked a pebble into the pool. 'I'm saying "now". Gannons'll've stopped it.'

'Aye,' Moira said, 'there's no life here.' She bent down, dipped her hands in the pool. It felt stagnant. If Ma Wagstaff had come up here hoping for some kind of spiritual sustenance, she'd have gone away pretty damn depressed.

'Used to take it all wi' a pinch of salt,' Willie said. 'I mean . . . bit of nonsense, really. But we come up here. Every May Day we'd come up here, whole village at one time, all them as could walk. Then back to The Man, couple o' pints . . . bite to eat . . .'

Willie smiled. 'Good days, them, Moira. When you think back on it.'

'Hang on,' Moira said. 'There's something here.'

With both hands, she lifted it out, the spring water dripping from her palms. Dripping like tears from the eyes of the battered plaster head of the Mother of God.

'Oh, hell,' Willie said sorrowfully.

'The Mother?'

Willie nodded. 'There's three of um. Three statues. The young one, the Virgin, she's brought up on Candlemas – St

Bride's day, beginning of February. Then the Mother – this one – at Lammas. Then, at All-Hallows, they bring the winter one.'

'The Hag,' Moira said.

Willie nodded.

'The Threefold Goddess,' Moira said. 'Virgin, Mother, Hag.'

'Summat like that. Like I say . . . pinch of salt. Women's stuff.'

'Your ma . . . she'd never be taking it with a pinch of salt.'

'No,' said Willie.

'What about Matt?'

'He were different,' Willie said, 'when he come back. When we was lads it were just the way things *were*, you know? One of us'd be picked to collect stuff for t'seasonal crosses, collate it like, sort out what were what. We didn't reckon much on it. Bit of fun, like.'

'As it should be,' Moira said, pushing her sodden hair back to stop it dripping down her jacket. 'How else d'you get kids into it if it's no' fun?'

'Matt come back . . . wi' a mission. Know what I mean? Horridges had sold off brewery to Gannons and Gannons didn't want t'pub – it were doing nowt, were it? Local trade and a few ramblers of a Sunday. Perked up a bit when t'bogman were found, but not for long – nine day wonder sorta thing.'

'So Matt returns to buy the pub. Local hero.'

'*Exactly*. Spot on. Local hero, I tell thi, Moira . . . honest to God, he were me mate, but I wish he'd not come. You know what I mean?'

'I do now,' Moira said, hearing the tape in her head. 'He was an emotional man. An impressionable man. An obsessive man.'

Willie snorted. 'Can say that again.'

'But not a bad man,' Moira said.

'Oh no. I don't think so.'

'So somebody – or some*thing* was using him. He was a vessel. Willie, this bogman . . . ?'

'Oh, bugger.' Willie looked up into the sky, now putting down water with a good bit more enthusiasm than the Holy

296

Spring. The coins in his pocket chinked damply. 'I'm saying nowt. You've gorra talk to Ma.'

He heard her creaking into the hall below. 'Gerrout from under me feet, Bobbie.'

The cat.

Heard her feet on the bottom stairs and slid himself into a room which, as he'd ascertained earlier, was a box room full of rubbish, tea-chests, heaps of old curtaining, a treadle sewing-machine shrouded in dust.

Took her a long time and a lot of laboured breathing to reach the top of the stairs. Heard her in the bathroom, the dribble and the flush and the old metal cistern filling up behind her with a series of coughs and gasps.

He brought a hand to the crown of his head, felt his emergent, urgent bristles one last time, for luck. Luck? You made your own. He put his glove back on. For a moment, a while back, someone hammering on the front door had flung him back to that night last summer in the stolen car. The police! But then he'd concentrated – go *away* – and the knocking had stopped.

Flexing and clenching his powerful, leathered hands, he moved out onto the landing as the old woman sighed and braced herself to go downstairs.

Not much left of her. Old bones in a frayed cardigan. Hair as dry and neglected as tufts of last summer's sheepwool caught in a wire fence.

Some witch, he thought, rising up behind her.

Quite slowly – although he knew he'd made no sound – she turned around and looked up at him, at his fingers poised above her bony, brittle shoulders. Then at his face.

And he looked at hers.

They'd always said, in the village, how fierce her eyes were. How she could freeze you where you stood with those eyes, turn you to stone, pin you to the wall.

Shaw Horridge grinned. Come on, then.

Wanting her to do that to him. Focus her eyes like lasers. Wanting the challenge, the friction. Wanting something he could smash, like hurling someone else's Saab Turbo into a bus shelter.

Wanted to do it and *feel better*.

But her eyes surprised him. They were as soft and harmless as a puppy's.

For a moment, this froze him.

'Come on,' he said, suddenly agitated. 'Come on, witch.'

She stared calmly at him, heels on the very edge of the top stair. Wouldn't take much of a push. That was no good.

He said, 'Where's your magic, eh? Where's your fucking magic now?'

She bit her worn-down bottom lip, but otherwise didn't move. 'Don't you know me?' she said. 'Do you not know me?'

He shook his head. 'You're going to die,' he said. 'Don't you realize that?'

The withered old face crumpled into an apology for a smile. 'I'm dead already, lad,' Ma Wagstaff said, voice trickling away like sand through an egg-timer. 'Dead already. But it's nowt t'do wi' you. You'll be glad of that, one day.'

Her ancient face was as blank as unmarked parchment as she threw up her arms, hands wafting at the air. Her body seemed to rise up at him, making him lurch back into the landing wall, and then she flopped down the stairs, with barely a bounce, like an old, discarded mop.

CHAPTER V

The gypsy guy with the beat-up hat and the Dobermanns wasn't too sure about this. Still looked like he'd prefer to feed the stranger to the dogs.

'No,' Macbeth said. 'I don't even know her name.' Had to be easier getting to meet with the goddamn Queen. 'All I know is she isn't called Mrs Cairns.'

The guy's heavy eyebrows came down, suspicious. 'Who wis it told you where to come?'

'Uh, Moira's agent. In Glasgow. Listen, I'm not with the police. I'm not a reporter.'

'OK, well, you just stay here, pal,' the gypsy guy said, and to make sure Macbeth didn't move from the gates of the caravan site he left the two dogs behind. Macbeth liked to think he was good with dogs, but the Dobermanns declined to acknowledge this; when he put out a friendly hand, one growled and the other dribbled. Macbeth shrugged and waited.

The gypsy was gone several minutes, but when he returned he'd gotten himself a whole new attitude. Unbolting the gates, holding them back for the visitor. 'Wid ye come this way, sir . . .' Well, shit, next thing he'd be holding his hat to his chest and bowing. Even the Dobermanns had a deferential air. Macbeth grinned, figured maybe the old lady had sussed him psychically, checked out his emanations.

Whatever, in no time at all, here's Mungo Macbeth of the Manhattan Macbeths sitting in a caravan like some over-decorated seaside theme-bar, brass and china all over the walls.

'I'll leave ye then, Duchess . . . ?'

'Thank you, Donald.' Lifting a slender hand loaded up with gold bullion.

She was Cleopatra, aboard this huge, gold-braided Victorian-looking chaise longue. She had on an ankle-length robe, edged with silver. Had startling hair, as long as Moira's, only dazzling white.

'Well, uh . . .' This was bizarre. This was an essentially tacky situation. Awe was not called for. And yet this place was already answering questions about Moira that he hadn't even been able to frame.

She said, 'Call me Duchess. It's a trifle cheap, but one gets used to these indignities.'

Didn't look to be more than sixty. Younger by several centuries, he thought, than her eyes.

'And you'll come to the point, Mr Macbeth. Life is short.'

He blinked. 'OK.' Swallowed. Couldn't believe he'd come here, was doing this. 'Uh . . . fact of the matter is . . . I spent some time with your daughter, couple nights ago.'

'Really,' the Duchess said dryly.

'No, hey, nothing like . . . See, I . . .' This was his first meeting with Moira all over again. Couldn't string the words together. 'Can't get her off of my mind,' he said and couldn't say any more.

'You poor man.' The merest shade of a smile in the crease down one cheek. 'How can I help?'

Acutely aware how embarrassingly novelettish all this was sounding, how like some plastic character in one of his own crummy TV films, he said solemnly, 'See, this never happened to me before.'

The Duchess had a very long neck. Very slowly she bent it towards him, like a curious swan. 'Are you a wealthy man, Mr Macbeth?'

'One day, maybe,' he said. 'So they tell me.' Thinking, if she asks me to cross her fucking palm with silver, I'm out of here.

'The feeling I'm getting from you . . .' Those ancient, ancient eyes connecting with his, '. . . is that, despite your name, you've always been very much an American.'

'Is that the truth,' Macbeth confirmed with a sigh. 'All we got to do now is convince my mom.'

The Duchess smiled at last. 'I think I like you, Mr Macbeth,' she said. 'We'll have some tea.'

Later she picked up on the theme. 'You're really not what you appear, are you?'

'No?'

The Duchess shook her head. Tiny gold balls revolved in her earrings.

'This worries you. You feel you've been living a lie. You feel that all your life you've tried to be what people expect you to be. But different people want different things, and you feel obliged, perhaps, to live up to their expectation of you. You feel . . .' The Duchess scrutinized him, with renewed interest, over her gold-rimmed bone china teacup. 'You feel you are in your present fortunate position because of who you are rather than what you can do.'

Macbeth said nothing. He hadn't come here for this. Had he?

'Sorry to be so blunt,' the Duchess said.

'No problem,' Macbeth said hollowly.

'This is your job perhaps. People think you can open doors?'

'Do they just,' said Macbeth.

'Now you've woken up, and you're thinking, am I to spend my life . . . serving up the, er, goods . . . ? As a form of restitution? Paying back, even though I might be paying back to people who never gave me anything, or do I go out on my own, chance my arm . . . ?'

There were subtle alterations in her voice. Macbeth felt goose-bumps forming.

The Duchess said, 'Is there something more out there than piling up money? Even if that money's not all for me, even if it's helping the economy and therefore other people who might need the money more than me? Are there . . . more things in heaven and earth than you get to read about in the *New York Times*?'

Christ. He was listening to himself. By the time she sat back to sip more tea, he'd swear the Duchess had developed a significantly deeper voice and an accent not unlike his own.

Ah, this is just a sophisticated act. This is a classy stage routine.

'No it isn't,' the Duchess said crisply.

He almost dropped his cup. '*What* . . . ?' His hand shook.

'No, it isn't . . . going to rain,' the Duchess said sweetly. 'Although it was forecast. But then forecasts are seldom reliable, I've found.'

He guessed she'd never been to college. He guessed she hadn't always talked so refined. He guessed her life-story would make more than one mini-series.

Then he guessed he'd better start keeping a tighter hold on his thoughts until he was someplace else.

'I'm not a fortune-teller, you know,' she said, like some women would say, what do you think I am, *a hooker*?

'I, uh . . . Moira never said you were,' Macbeth said uncomfortably.

'I appear to be able to do it. Sometimes. But I don't make a practice of it.' She poured herself more tea. 'So why did I let you in here?'

Macbeth didn't know.

'Because I'm worried about the child,' she said. 'That's why.'

He said, 'I can understand that.'

'Can you?'

'I'm, uh, a Celt,' he said, and she started to laugh, a sound like the little teaspoon tinkling on the bone china.

'To be Celtic,' she said, 'is more an attitude than a racial thing. Like to be a gypsy is a way of life.'

'What about to be a psychic?'

Her face clouded. 'That,' she said, 'is a cross to bear. She'll tell you that herself. It's to accept there's a huge part of your life that will never be your own. It's to realize there are always going to be obligations to fulfil, directions you have to go in, even though you can't always see the sense of it.'

'That's what she's doing right now?'

The Duchess nodded. 'She has things to work out. Oh, I don't know what she's doing and I wouldn't dream of interfering, she's a mature person. But I am her mother, and mothers *are* always inclined to worry, so I'm told. I was only thinking – coincidence – just before you arrived, I wish she had someone who cared for her. But she's a loner. We all are, I fear. We learn our lesson. We don't like other people to get hurt.'

'You're saying you think Moira needs someone with her?'

The Duchess shrugged her elegant shoulders. 'Someone looking out for her, maybe. When Donald told me there was a man at the gate asking after Moira, I wondered if perhaps . . .'

Then she gave him the kind of smile that was like a consolatory pat on the arm. 'I don't really feel you're the one, Mr Macbeth.'

Sometimes, when he interviewed would-be film-directors, there was one nice, bright-eyed kid he could tell was never going to make it. And trying to let the kid down easy he'd always start out, 'I don't really feel . . .'

'Look, Duchess . . .' Macbeth felt like he was about to cry. This was absurd. He started to tell her about the night at the

Earl's castle, about Moira singing 'The Comb Song', and how it ended.

'Yes,' the Duchess said impatiently, 'I know about that.'

'So am I right in thinking Moira caused all that, the deer heads and stuff to come crashing down?'

The Duchess looked cross. 'The question is . . . pouff! Irrelevant! How can anyone ever really say, I did this, I caused this to happen? Perhaps you are a factor in its happening, perhaps not. I'll tell you something, Mr Macbeth . . . nobody who's merely human can ever be entirely sure of the ability to make *anything* happen. Say, if you're a great healer, sometimes it works . . . you're lucky, or you're so good and saintly that you get helped a lot. And sometimes it doesn't work at all. I once knew a woman called Jean Wendle . . . but that's another story . . .'

She lay back on the chaise and half-closed her eyes, looking at the wall behind him. 'Or, let us say, if you're a bad or a vengeful person, and you want to hurt somebody, you want to curse them . . . in the movies, it goes . . . *zap*, like one of those, what d'you call them . . . ray guns, lasers.'

He heard a small noise behind him, turned in time to see a plate, one of a row of five with pictures on them, sliding very slowly from the wall.

The plate fell to the floor and smashed. Macbeth nearly passed out.

From a long way away, he heard the Duchess saying, 'Doing damage, harming people is much easier but that's unpredictable too. Sometimes people dabble and create a big black cloud . . .' Throwing up her arms theatrically, '. . . and they can't control *where* it goes.'

Numbly, Macbeth bent to pick up the pieces of the plate. Maybe he'd dislodged it with the back of his head. The ones still on the wall had pictures of Balmoral Castle, where the Queen spent time, and Glamis Castle, Blair Atholl Castle and the Queen Mother's Castle of Mey.

He held two pieces of the broken plate together and saw, in one of those shattering, timeless moments, that they made up a rough watercolour sketch of the familiar Victorian Gothic façade of the Earl's place.

'Accidents happen,' the Duchess said. 'Leave it on the floor.'

Macbeth's fingers were trembling as he laid the pieces down. He needed a cigarette more urgently than at any time since he quit smoking six years ago.

'I never liked that one anyway,' the Duchess said.

Doubtless psyching out that Macbeth could use more hot tea, and fast, she filled up his cup and added two sugars.

He drank it all. She was offering him an easy way out. She was saying, what just happened – the plate – also, the skulls on the wall . . . this is kids' stuff . . . this is chickenshit compared to what a person could be letting himself in for if he pursues Moira Cairns.

Mungo Macbeth, maker of mini-series for the masses, thought maybe this was how King Arthur laid it on the line for any mad-assed knight of the Round Table figuring to go after the Holy Grail.

He'd often wondered about those less ambitious knights who listened to the horror stories and thought, Well, fuck this, what do I need with a Holy Grail? Maybe I should just stick around and lay me some more damsels, do a little Sunday jousting. How could those knights go on living with themselves, having passed up on the chance of the One Big Thing?

He said, 'Earlier, you said . . . about when a guy gets to wondering how much his life has really been worth and if there isn't more stuff in Heaven and Earth than he's reading about in the *New York Times* . . .'

The silent girl who'd brought the tea came back and took away the tray.

After she'd gone, he said, 'Duchess, why? I only met your daughter once, never even . . . Why? Can you tell me?'

Instead, the Duchess told him the story of a man who fell in love with the Queen of the Fairies and all the shit that put him into. Macbeth said he knew the songs. Tam Lin, Thomas The Rymer, all that stuff? But that wasn't the same thing, surely, Moira Cairns was a human being.

'That's quite true,' the Duchess said gravely. 'But remember this. Wherever she goes, that young woman . . . she's bound to be touched with madness. Now, who is the white man?'

'White man?'

'I thought perhaps you might be his emissary . . . White-skinned man? I don't think I mean race. Just a man *exuding* a whiteness?'

'Somebody *I* know?'

'You don't?'

'I don't know what you mean.'

'I believe you don't. All right. Never mind.'

Macbeth asked, 'Do you know where Moira is?'

'Oh . . . the little Jewish person, Kaufmann, tells me she's in the North of England.'

'Bastard wouldn't tell *me*.'

'You he doesn't trust. Strange, that – I find you quite transparent.'

'Thanks.'

'There was a man called . . . Matt?'

'Jesus, you intuited that?'

The Duchess sighed in exasperation. 'She told me.'

'Right,' Macbeth said, relieved. 'Matt, uh . . .'

'Castle. She thinks he was her mentor. I rather suspect she was his.'

'Right,' Macbeth said uncertainly.

'He's dead. She'll have gone to try and lay his spirit to rest.'

Macbeth squirmed a little. Was this precisely what was meant by things you couldn't find in the *New York Times*? Was this what Mom meant about uncovering his roots? He thought not.

The Duchess smiled kindly. 'You can leave now, if you wish, Mr Macbeth. I'll have Donald see you to the gate.'

'No, wait . . .' Two trains of thought were about to crash, buckling his usual A to B mental tracks. 'This, uh, white person . . .'

'A thin man with white hair and a very white complexion.'

The castle. The bones. White-faced man with a cut eye.

'Shit, I don't believe this . . . you got that outa my head. You pulled it clean outa my head.'

'Mr Macbeth, calm down. Two or three weeks ago, a man of this description came to consult me. As people do . . . occasionally. He didn't get in. Donald is my first line of defence, the dogs are the second, and Donald told me the dogs disliked this man quite *intensely*. On sight. Now . . . dogs can't *invariably* be trusted, they may react badly to – oh – psychic disturbance in a person, or mental instability. But when a man arrives in an expensive car and seems very confident and the dogs hate him on sight . . .'

Stanhope, Macbeth thought. Stansgate?

'And when Donald conveyed my message that I was unwell, he was apparently quite annoyed. He sent a message back that he had information about my daughter which he thought I would wish to know. I suggested Donald should let the dogs have him.'

'What happened?'

'He left.'

Stanley? Stanmore? 'Duchess, you think this guy meant her harm?'

'Two people arrive within a short period to talk to me about my daughter. One the dogs dislike. How did the dogs take to you, Mr Macbeth?'

'I wasn't invited to play rubber-bone, but I seem to be intact.'

The Duchess nodded. 'I don't know how you found me – no, don't explain, it's not important. I didn't mention the man to Moira, she has enough problems, I think. But if you wanted to help her, you might keep an eye open for him. If there was a problem and you were to deal with it, she need never know, need she?'

Macbeth started thinking about the knights and the Holy Grail.

And this guy . . . Stanton? Stansfield?

PART SEVEN

ANGELS

From *Dawber's* Secret *Book of Bridelow* (unpublished):

THE HISTORY OF BEER

BEER, OF COURSE, WAS brewed in Bridelow long before the seventeenth and eighteenth centuries. Ale was the original sacred drink, made from the water of the holy spring and the blessed barley and preserved with the richly-aromatic bog myrtle from the Moss.

Nigel Pennick writes, in his book *Practical Magic in the Northern Tradition*:

'Cakes or bread and ale are the sacrament of country tradition. The runic word for ale – *ALU* – is composed of the three runes *As*, *Lagu* and *Ur*. The first rune has the meaning of *the gods* or *divine power*; the second *water* and *flow*, and the third *primal strength*. The eating of bread and drinking of ale is the mystery of the transmutation of the energy in the grain into a form where it is reborn in our physical bodies.'

It follows, therefore, that, to some local people, the sale of the Bridelow brewery and the detachment of the beer-making process from its ancient origins, would seem to be a serious sapping of the village's inherent strength, perhaps even a symbolic draining away of its lifeblood.

CHAPTER I

'She's got to be in. I can hear the kettle boiling.'

And boiling and boiling. Whistling through the house. The kettle having hysterics.

'I've got a key,' Willie said, bringing out the whole bunch of them.

A dark, damp dread was settling around Moira. She took a step back on the short path leading to Ma Wagstaff's front door. Held on to a gatepost, biting a lip.

'What the f—' The door opening a few inches, then jamming and Willie putting his shoulder to it. 'Summat caught behind here . . .'

'Hey, stop, Willie . . . Jesus.'

Through the crack in the door, she'd seen a foot, black-shod and pointing upwards. She drew Willie gently back and showed him.

'Oh, Christ,' Willie said drably.

He didn't approach the door again. He said quietly, 'Moira, do us a favour. Nip across to t'Post Office. Fetch Milly.'

'What about a doctor?'

'She wouldn't thank you for a doctor. Just get Milly. Milly Gill.'

Moira didn't need to say a word. Milly Gill looked at her and lost her smile, shooed out two customers and shut up the post office. Ran ahead of Moira across the street, big floral bosom heaving.

When they got to the house, Willie had the front door wide open and tears of horror in his eyes. Milly Gill moved past him to where the old woman lay in a small, neat bundle at the bottom of the stairs, eyes like glass buttons, open mouth a breathless void, one leg crooked under her brown woollen skirt.

The body looked as weightless as a sparrow. Moira doubted she'd ever seen anything from which life was so conspicuously absent. A life which, obviously, had been so much more than the usual random mesh of electrical impulses. Even when it was moving, the little body had been the least of Ma Wagstaff.

This was a big death.

Willie Wagstaff stood in the front garden looking at his shoes, drawing long breaths. His hands hung by his sides, fingers motionless. The kettle's wild whistling ended with a gasp, and then Milly Gill came out and joined them. 'You'll need a doctor, Willie, luv.'

His head came up, eyes briefly bright, but the spark of hope fading in an instant.

'Death certificate,' Milly said softly. She took his arm. 'Come on. Post Office. I'll make us some tea.'

The street was silent, but doors were being opened, curtains tweaked aside. Shadowed faces; nobody came out – everybody sensing the death mood in the dusky air.

Moira thought bleakly, *They don't die like this, people like Ma Wagstaff. Not at a time of crisis. They don't have accidents and sudden heart attacks. They know when it's over, and they go quietly and usually in their own time.*

At the Post Office doorway, Milly Gill called out to the street at large, 'It's Ma Wagstaff. Nothing anybody can do.' She turned to Willie, 'No point in keeping it a secret, is there, luv?'

Moira heard Willie saying, 'I was only with her this morning.' The way people talked, facing the mindless robbery of a sudden death.

And I saw her less than an hour ago, and she was in some state, Willie . . . she was in some state.

'I'd guess it couldn't have been quicker,' Milly Gill said unconvincingly, leading them through the Post Office into a flowery little sitting room behind. 'She's still warm, poor old luv. Maybe she had a seizure or something, going upstairs. Sit yourselves down, I'll put kettle on and phone for t'doctor.'

'This is Moira Cairns,' said Willie.

'How d'you do. Plug that fire in, Willie, it's freezing.'

Scrabbling down by the hearth, Willie looked up at Moira through his mousy fringe, fishing out a weak smile that was almost apologetic.

'I should go,' Moira said. 'Last thing you need is me.'

Willie got to his feet, nervously straightening his pullover. 'I wouldn't say that. No.'

She thought, Poor Willie. Who's he got left? No mother, no Matt, no job maybe, no direction. Only fingers drumming at the air.

'Is there only you . . . No brothers, sisters . . . ?'

'Two sisters,' Willie said. 'There's always more girls. By tradition, like.'

Moira sat on the end of a settee with bright, floral loose-covers. The carpet had a bluebell design and there were paintings and sketches of wild flowers on the walls.

'Ah,' Willie said, 'she had to go sometime. She were eighty . . . I forget. Getting on, though. Least she dint suffer, that's the main thing.'

Oh, but she did, Willie . . . She couldn't look at him, her worried eyes following a single black beam across the ceiling. Two bunches of sage were hanging from it, the soft, musty scent flavouring the atmosphere. Homely.

'No hurry,' Milly Gill was saying in another room, on the phone to the doctor. 'If there's sick people in t'surgery, you see to them first. See to the living.'

When she came back into the sitting room, there were two cats around her ankles.

'Bob and Jim.' Willie's eyes were damp. 'Little buggers. Didn't see um come.'

Moira said, 'Your ma's cats?'

Willie smiled. 'Not any more. Cats'll always find a home. These buggers knew where to come. They'll not be the only ones.'

'This lady's with the Mothers' Union, right?'

Willie said, 'You know about that, eh?'

'I knew about this one when she first come in,' said Milly Gill. 'We'll have to have a talk sometime, luv.'

Her watchful, grey eyes said she also knew that women like Ma Wagstaff did not fall downstairs after having unexpected strokes or heart attacks. Willie's fingers had known that too, had felt it coming, whatever it was.

'Soon, huh?' Moira said.

Joel Beard said, 'Here? In my . . . in the churchyard?'

He and the policeman were standing in the church porch, the wet afternoon draining into an early dusk.

'It's a possibility, vicar,' Ashton said. 'It's something we have to check out, and the sooner we do it the less likely we are to attract attention. You haven't had any Press here, I take it?'

Joel Beard shook his curls. 'Why would they come here?'

'They would if they knew what we were proposing to do, sir, and these things have a habit of leaking out. So . . . I don't know if you've had experience of an exhumation before, but what it involves is screening off the immediate area and confining it to as few people as are absolutely necessary. You can be there yourself if you like, but I assure you we'll be very tidy. Now, the lights . . .'

'Lights? You mean you want to do it tonight? I thought these things took . . .'

'Not much more than a phone call involved these days, sir. We're under quite a lot of pressure to find this thing, as you can imagine.'

Joel said, 'It all seems so unlikely.'

It didn't, though. It connected all too plausibly. 'Inspector, how do you suppose that this was actually done? Without anything being seen?'

'This was what I was planning to ask you. Country churchyard, even at night somebody sees something, don't they? Perhaps they saw and they kept quiet, mmm? When was the grave dug?'

'I don't know,' Joel said. 'I imagine the day before. The Rector was in charge then, but he . . . he's in hospital. He's had a heart attack.'

'That's unfortunate,' Ashton said. 'No, you see, what's been suggested to us is that the grave was dug deeper than is normal and then the body was brought here and covered with earth and then the funeral went ahead as normal, with Mr Castle's coffin laid on top of the bog body.'

'That's preposterous,' Joel said.

It wasn't, though. Somehow there was a link here with the old woman and the bottle she'd been attempting to secrete into Castle's coffin.

'You see, our information is that there was a request from some people here for the body to be returned to the bog. And when it seemed unlikely that was going to happen, somebody decided to pinch it. Would you know anything about that, Mr Beard?'

'Good Lord,' Joel said. 'No, I certainly wouldn't. You

know, I think, on the whole, that I should like to be there when you . . . do it.'

'I thought you might,' said Ashton.

Moira felt weary and ineffectual, and she had a headache. Walking, head down, into the Rectory drive, she was speared by lights.

Cathy parked her father's VW Golf crookedly in front of the garage.

'How is he?'

'He's OK,' Cathy said quickly, unlocking the front door. 'I'm sorry, I didn't leave you a key, did I? I'm hopelessly inefficient.'

About her father – Moira saw she was playing this down.

Cathy unloaded plastic carrier bags and her long university scarf on to the kitchen worktops, all stark, white butcher's-shop tiling. 'I went into Manchester afterwards. Had to get away somewhere crowded, to think. Got loads of cold things from Marks and Sparks. You don't mind, do you? Pop sees to the cooking as a rule. I'm a disaster in the kitchen. Did you get to see Ma Wagstaff?'

'Yes,' said Moira.

'Did she talk to you?'

'No,' Moira said. 'I'm afraid not.'

Then Cathy discovered the sugar bowl was empty and went into the pantry, the little room under the stairs, for a new bag. 'Oh,' she said. 'The little scumbags.'

'Huh?'

Moira peered over her shoulder. Cathy was holding a brick. There was a small window in the pantry and the brick had clearly been used to smash it.

'Little bastards,' Cathy said. 'You know, this never used to happen. I know people say that all the time . . . "Oh, things were different when I was a kid and you could get in the cinema for sixpence. None of this vandalism in those days, kids had respect." But it's true. Even – what? – six months ago it was true in Bridelow. They *did* have respect.'

Cathy put the brick down on the floor. 'Now there's graffiti in the toilets at the parish hall. A week or two ago somebody had a . . . defecated on the seat inside the lych-gate. Can you believe that? In Bridelow?'

'You better check the house,' Moira said.

Cathy had a cursory look around the downstairs rooms. Everything seemed to be in order. 'Little sods. Everybody knows Pop's in hospital.' She looked at Moira. 'Oh. Yes. That's another thing. They're sending him to a convalescent home.'

'I thought it wasn't too serious.'

'Coronary,' Cathy said despondently. 'That's serious. They're sending him – committing him is how he sees it – to this Church nursing home down in Shropshire. At least a month. Which means Joel's got to move in here.'

'With you?'

'You're joking,' Cathy said. 'Even if I could bear to have him in the house, he's much too proper to countenance it. No, I'll go back to Oxford. Come up at weekends and see Pop. I mean, I expect you'll be wanting to be off, won't you?'

Moira said. 'Look, you got any hardboard in the garage or somewhere? We can block up this window.'

'Never mind, Alf Beckett'll fix it tomorrow.'

Moira said, 'Cathy . . . um . . . something bad's happened.'

Because of the Post Office's strict security regulations, Milly Gill's front door had two steel bolts and a fancy double lock, which she'd always thought was damn stupid in a place like Bridelow. Tonight, though, first time ever, Milly was glad to turn the key twice over and slide the big bolts. Even though she knew there were some things no locks could keep out.

The urgent banging on the door shook her. Willie Wagstaff never used the knocker. Willie would beat out his own personal tattoo with his fingers.

'Oh, Mother,' Milly Gill said, clutching her arms over her breast. 'I'm not going to be up to this.'

It was an hour since the doctor'd had Ma taken away, across the Moss. He'd said there might have to be a post-mortem, probably no more than a formality; it was most likely natural causes. But if there was reason to think she might have fallen accidentally, there'd have to be a public inquest.

Pity Bridelow didn't have a resident doctor any more; this was an Asian gentleman from Across the Moss who couldn't be expected to understand. Milly had pleaded with him not to let them cut Ma up if there was any way it could be avoided. It was important that all of Ma's bits should be returned to Bridelow for burial, not tissue and stuff left in some hospital wastebin.

More crashing at the front door.

'Who is it?' Milly shouted. Didn't recognize her own voice, it sounded that feeble.

'It's me. Alf.'

Milly tut-tutted at her cowardice. Why she should think there might be something abroad because something that happened to hundreds of pensioners every week had happened to Ma Wagstaff . . .

She undid the bolts and turned the key twice. 'I'm sorry, Alf. Not like me to be nervy.'

But, if anything, Alf Beckett looked worse than she felt. There was a streetlamp outside the door, a converted gaslamp with an ice-blue bulb. Its light made Alf look quite ill, eyes like keyholes.

'Milly,' he said. 'We're in t'shit.'

'Come in, luv,' Milly said. Her responsibility now, this sort of problem, keeping up community morale.

She sat Alf down on the floral settee. He was ashen.

'Now then, come on,' Milly said. 'It's all right. We'll get over this. We've had bad patches before.'

'No . . .' Alf shook his head. 'Listen . . .'

'It's my fault,' Milly said. 'We always left too much to poor old Ma. We thought she were immortal. Thought we could sit back, everybody getting on with their lives, foreign holidays, videos. Didn't seem to matter like it used to. And then when Ma started getting gloomy, we all thought it were just her age. Even me, daft cow. And now everything's happened at once, and it's shaken us. But we'll be all right, honest, luv.'

She got up to put the kettle on. 'I've sent Willie to t'Man

316

for a pint. Life's got to go on, Alf. Just means we'll have to have a bit of a get-together. Soon as possible. Sort this lad Joel Beard out for a start. Then we'll see what else we've got to tackle. Mrs Horridge, that's another thing . . .'

'Milly!' Alf Beckett's hearthbrush moustache looked bent and spiky. 'Police've come.'

'Eh? Because of Ma? Have they found summat?'

'No, no . . . Listen to me, woman, for Christ's sake.' Alf sat up on the couch, hands clasped so tightly together that his knuckles were whiter than his cheeks. 'It's t'grave. They're coming to dig Matt's grave up.'

In the narrow doorway to the back kitchen, Milly froze, filling it.

Alf said, 'Some bugger's told t'coppers as t'bogman's in theer.'

Milly felt sick. All churned up inside. Ma gone, the Rector in hospital. And her at the wrong time of life to cope with it all. She covered up her face with her hands and looked at him through her fingers.

'Lord,' she whispered. 'What've we done, Alf? What've we done in Brid'lo to deserve this?'

Cathy said to Moira, 'If Pop hears about this, he's going to do something stupid.'

She'd told Cathy only about Ma's death. Not about seeing the old woman out on the Moss fighting a dead tree.

She said, 'Like what?'

'Like discharge himself,' Cathy said glumly. 'Moira, I don't know what to do. They ran this place between them, Pop and Ma Wagstaff. They hardly ever met, but they had an understanding, you know?'

They were in the sitting room. Cathy had lit the fire. She was sitting on the sofa where Dic Castle had sprawled. She'd taken off her shoes and her thick woollen socks were planted on an old rag hearthrug dark with scorchmarks from stray coals.

'He doesn't talk much about it, but it was obviously really

317

tough for Pop when he first came here. He was pretty young –
younger than Joel. And a Southerner. With a funny German
name. Hell of a culture shock. Series of shocks, I suppose.'

'Like, when he finds out they're all heathens?'

'Is that what we are?'

Moira smiled. 'It's no' that simple, is it? I was up on the
moor with Willie Wagstaff earlier. We saw the holy well. Who's
that dedicated to? The goddess Brigid? St Bride? The Mother
Goddess? Or the Holy Mother of God?'

'Gets confusing, doesn't it?' Cathy said.

'And the cross that was in the church, made out of twigs
and stuff.'

'The Autumn Cross.'

'And there's a Winter Cross – yeh? – made of holly and
mistletoe and stuff, and then a Spring Cross, made of . . .'

'You've got it.'

Moira said, putting it all together finally, 'They can't make
up their minds *what* they are, can they?'

Cathy folded her legs on to the sofa. 'Like I said, you need
to talk to Mr Dawber, he can put it into an historical context.
But the first Church in Britain was the Celtic Church, and by
the time they came along I like to think Celtic paganism was
pretty refined, with this give-and-take attitude to nature and
animals and things.'

'In parts of Scotland,' said Moira, 'particularly some of the
Western Isles, it's not been so much a takeover as a merger.
Like, nobody could say the teachings of Christ were anything
less than a hell of a good framework for, say, human behaviour,
the way we treat each other. But . . .'

'. . . in isolated areas, there were aspects of life it didn't
quite cover,' said Cathy. 'Maybe still doesn't. And this area
was always very isolated. Cut off. Self-sufficient. Immune from
outside influences. We got electricity later than everybody else.
Piped water was a long time coming. Television signals are still
so lousy that most people haven't got one yet.'

'Yeh, but look . . .'

'. . . now it's a brick through your window and "Sheffield
United are shit" on the walls, and somebody has one on a
public seat – that's outside influences for you. Be a rape next.'

'Cathy, this bogman . . .'

'Oh, *he's* all right.'

'No, he's not. Matt Castle was besotted with him. The Man in the Moss. Matt was seeing him in Biblical terms – sacrificial saviour of the English Celts.'

'He died to save us all,' Cathy said. 'Gosh. Isn't that a terrible piece of blasphemy? Can you imagine the sleepless nights Pop had over this? The bogman: was he some sort of Pennine Jesus?'

'Or the anti-Christ, huh?'

Moira thought of the black, snaking branches of the tree on the Moss. Her head throbbed, as if the thing were lashing at her brain.

'OK,' she said hurriedly. 'Let's leave that be for a while. When they built the first Christian church here, they put it on the old sacred site and it's dedicated to Brigid, or Brigantia, now known as St Bride. And the ministers here have always had a kind of agreement with the priestess and her attendants who, in time, become known as the Mothers' Union, right?'

'All the Anglican Churches have Mothers' Unions. Young Wives' groups too.'

'Yeah, but most of them, presumably, don't recognize the symbolism: the mothers and the hags. The hags being the ones over the menopause.'

'When you're over the Change,' Cathy said, 'you go on to a new level of responsibility. Well . . . so I'm told. How do you know all this?'

'I read a lot of books. Now, OK, the bogman turns up again. The willing sacrifice. The pagan Jesus-figure who supposedly went to his death to save his people. That's one powerful symbol, Cathy. Regardless of what else it might be, it's a heavy symbol. It churns things up.'

'I've told you, he's all right.'

'What d'you mean he's all right? Somebody's *stolen* him. I'm telling you there are people around who will *do things* with a relic as powerful as that.'

'Look, it's OK, that's sorted out.'

'Sorted out?' She had to stand up, walk away from the fire, although she was shivering and it hurt when she swallowed.

'Moira, come on, sit down. I promise you, it's OK.'

'Why?' Moira demanded. 'Why is it OK, Cathy?'

'Because,' said Cathy simply, 'the bogman's had a full Christian burial.'

CHAPTER II

By now the sky was the colour of police trousers, Ashton thought prosaically, and damn near as thick. 'Tent would've been better,' he said as the rain started up again, steel needles in the arc lamp. 'Does it matter if he gets wet?'

'Depends what state he's in.' Roger Hall was struggling with his umbrella.

'Glad to see you're still sure he's down there.'

'Count on it,' Hall said.

Ashton's lads had erected a grey canvas screen, about seven feet high, around the grave; still just a mound of soil, no headstone yet, that saved a bit of hassle.

'Anyway, you've brought your own coffin, have you?'

'I wouldn't call it that,' Hall said. 'My assistant has it, over there.' Pointing at Chrissie White, shivering in fake fur, a plywood box at her feet.

'What's that white stuff inside then, Dr Hall?'

'Polystyrene chips. Shut that lid properly, Chrissie, we don't want them wet. We've also brought a few rolls of cling-film, Inspector. We wrap him in that first, so we don't lose anything.'

'Like a frozen turkey,' Ashton said. 'Anyway, it's good to see we haven't pulled a crowd. Yet. Let's just hope we can get this sorted before anybody knows we're here. Now, where's that gravedigger bloke?'

The big, curly-haired clergyman came over. Wearing his full funeral kit, Ashton noticed. Long cassock and a short cape like coppers used to have on point-duty in the good old days. He looked nervous. Might he know something?

'This is Mr Beckett, Inspector. Our verger.'

Little pensioner with a big, stainless-steel spade.

'You dig this grave first time around, Mr Beckett?'

'Aye, what about it?'

'Usual depth?'

'Six feet, give or take a few inches. No need to measure it, sithee, when tha's done t'job a few score times.'

'And when Mr Castle was buried, did you notice if the earth had been disturbed?'

'It were bloody dark by then,' said Mr Beckett uncompromisingly, patting his chest, as if he'd got indigestion.

But actually smoothing the bulge in his donkey jacket.

For, in its inside pocket, shrouded in household tissue, lay a little brown bottle.

Be his job, this time, to get the bloody bottle into Matt Castle's coffin, which they'd have to get out of the way before they could get at the bogman.

This was a new bottle. Alf had gone with Milly Gill to Ma Wagstaff's house, and he'd stood guard while Milly made it up, all of a dither, poor lass. 'I'm not doing it right, Alf, I'm sure I'm not doing it right.'

'It's thought as counts,' Alf had said, not knowing what the hell he was on about. 'Ma always said that.' Standing at the parlour door, watching Milly messing about with red thread and stuff by candlelight.

'Alf.'

'What?'

'Go in t'kitchen, fetch us a mixing bowl.'

'What sort?'

'*Any* sort. Big un, I'm nervous. Come on, hurry up.'

Alf handing her a white Pyrex bowl, standing around in the doorway as Milly put the bowl on the parlour floor, feeling about under her skirts. 'Well, don't just stand there, Alf. Bugger off.'

The door closed, only streetlight washing in through the landing window, ugly shadows thrown into the little hall, the bannisters dancing. Milly's muffled muttering. And then the unavoidable sound of her peeing into the Pyrex.

Alf, trying not to listen, standing where Ma's body must have landed. Looking up the stairs into a strange, forbidding coldness. Him, who'd patrolled the empty church on wild and windy nights and never felt other than welcome.

'Hurry up, lass. Giving me t'creeps.'

'This is Ma's house.' The sound slowing to a trickle. 'There's not a nicer atmosphere anywhere.'

Alf deliberately turning his back on the stairs.

'Aye. But that were when Ma were alive.'

This time Moira went off to make the tea. Gave her time to think.

She'd asked Cathy who was left in the Mothers' Union, apart from Milly Gill. Cathy had looked gloomy and said, don't ask.

Moira lifted the teapot lid and watched the leaves settle. Seemed the Mothers' Union wasn't what it used to be. Ma Wagstaff used to say they'd let things slide a bit, Cathy said.

Moira put the teapot on a tray with a couple of mugs. Some dead leaves hit the window. From the doorway behind her, Cathy said, 'Ma thought there was something out there trying to get in. She said the air was different.'

'How do you know all this, Cathy? Do you have to be a mother to be in the Mothers' Union?'

Cathy grinned. There were bags under her eyes and her hair looked dull in the hard kitchen light. 'They'll even take virgins these days.'

'Are you?'

'A virgin?'

'A mother.'

'Pop's an enlightened clergyman,' Cathy said, 'but not *that* enlightened.'

Two young coppers helped Alf with the spadework, which was a good bit easier – just when you didn't bloody need it – than he'd have expected under normal circumstances.

He was ashamed of this grave, the soil all piled in loose, big lumps, nothing tamped down. But he'd rushed the job, as rattled as anybody by that ugly scene between Ma Wagstaff and Joel Beard, and then Lottie Castle screaming at them to get her husband planted quick.

Three feet into the grave, getting there faster than he wanted to, he could see Joel peering down at them. Unlikely the lad'd know yet about Ma Wagstaff's death, nobody rushing to tell him after the way he'd been carrying on.

Thing was, Joel probably had no idea what he was up against. Just a bunch of cracked owd women.

Which, Alf conceded, wasn't a bad thing for him to think just now; at least he didn't suspect Alf, and he wouldn't be watching him too closely.

'The problem is,' Cathy said, 'that it's become more of a way of life than a religion.'

'Is that no' a good thing?'

'Well, yeah, it is for ordinary people, getting on with their lives. This sort of natural harmony, the feeling of belonging to something. It's great. Until things start to go wrong. And your brewery gets taken over and most of the workforce is fired. And your village shop shuts down. And your local celeb arrives to save your pub from almost certain closure and he's dead inside six months. And your placid, understanding Rector develops quite a rapid worsening of his arthritis, which Ma's always been able to keep in check. Except Ma's losing it, and she doesn't know why.'

Cathy looked at Moira's cigarettes on the chair-arm. 'How long's it take to learn to smoke?' She waved an exasperated hand. 'Forget it. Oh, this place is no fun any more. Atmosphere's not the same. People not as content. I've been home twice since the summer and it's struck me right away. Maybe that's the same all over Britain, with this Government and everything. But Bridelow was always . . .'

'Protected?'

'Yeah. And now it's not. I mean, somebody like Joel would never have got away with what he's done – ripping down that kid's cross. And Our Sheila . . . I mean, we've had these

323

religious firebrands before, maybe even my old man was a bit that way when he first arrived, but . . . something calms them down. Ma Wagstaff used to say it was in the air. Shades. Pastel shades. You know what I mean?'

'The old Celtic air,' Moira said. 'Everything misty and nebulous. No extremes. Everything blending in. You can sense it on some of the Scottish islands. Scotch mist. Parts of Ireland too. Maybe it was preserved here, like the bogman, in the peat.'

Cathy said, 'You're not going to rest until I tell you, are you?'

'And I do need to get to bed, Cathy. I feel terrible.'

Cathy sighed. 'OK. They stole the bogman back. They buried him in Matt Castle's grave before Matt went in.'

'Jesus,' said Moira. 'Who?'

'We're not supposed to know. But . . . everybody, I suppose. They're all in it. They've done it before. A few bits of bodies have turned up in the Moss over the years, and that's what they do with them. Save them up until somebody dies. And curiously, somebody always does – even if it's only an arm or a foot turns up – somebody conveniently snuffs it so the bits can have a Christian burial. Well . . . inasmuch as anything round here is one hundred per cent Christian. But this body . . . well, it's the first time there's been a whole one.'

'And the council discovered it, didn't they? So no way they could keep this one to themselves.'

'And then the scientific tests, revealing that this had been a very special sacrifice.'

'The triple death.'

'Mmm.'

'So Ma Wagstaff and Milly Gill and co. and . . . Willie? Is Willie in this?'

'Willie used to be a carpenter.'

'He did too.'

'And he's good with doors and locks. And then there's that mate of his, the other chap in the band . . .'

'Eric.'

'He works for a security firm now, in Manchester. The

same firm, as it happens, that was hired to keep an eye on the Field Centre.'

'Bloody hell.' Moira slumped back in her chair. 'It's beyond belief. It's like one of those old films, where everybody's conspiring. *Whisky Galore* or something. So the body's back home, in Bridelow soil.'

'It didn't go *completely* right. Milly says that right at the last minute Ma started getting funny feelings about it going in Matt Castle's grave.'

'I'm no' surprised.'

You've got to purify yourself. Of course.

'So she made up this witch bottle to go in Matt's coffin. It's got rowan berries in it, and red cotton and . . . the person making up the bottle has to pee in it.'

Moira said, '*Rowan tree, red thread / Holds the witches all in dread.*'

'What?'

'It's a song,' Moira said.

'Well, it's the wrong way round. Mostly it was the witches themselves who use the bottles, to keep bad spirits at bay. The spirits are supposed to go after the red berries or something and get entangled in the thread. It's all symbolic.'

'So she wanted to save Matt from evil spirits?'

Or maybe she wanted to save the bogman from something in Matt.

'I don't know,' Cathy said. 'I'm the Rector's daughter. I'm not supposed to know anything. We turn a blind eye.'

'But the bottle never got in the coffin, did it?'

'I don't know.'

'The supposed contaminant remains.'

'I don't *know*, Moira.'

He stood at the edge of the grave looking down. Forcing himself to look down.

Sometimes when he prayed he thought he heard a voice, and the voice said, You have a task, Joel. You must . . . not . . . turn . . . away.

Sometimes the voice called him Mr Beard, like the voice on

the telephone, a calm, knowing voice, obviously someone inside the village disgusted by what went on here.

One day, Joel hoped, he would meet his informant. When he encountered people in the street or in the Post Office, he would look into their eyes for a sign. But the women would smile kindly at him and the men would mumble something laconic, like 'All right, then, lad?' and continue on their way.

He stepped back in distaste as a shovelful of grave-soil was heaved out of the hole and over his shoes. Surely they had to be six feet down by now. He wondered whether, if they kept on digging, they would reach peat – the Moss slowly sliding in, underneath the village.

Insidious.

He looked over his shoulder and up, above the heads and umbrellas of the silent circle of watchers, at the frosty disc of the church clock, the Beacon of the Moss.

The false light. The devil's moon.

Perhaps that had to go too, like the pagan well and the cross and the monstrosity above the church door, before the village could be cleansed.

'More light, please.'

One of the policemen in the grave.

'You there yet?' The Inspector, Ashton. 'Swing that light round a bit, Ken, let's have a look.'

'Deeper than we expected, sir. Maybe it's sunk.'

'That likely, Mr Beckett?' The light swept across the verger's face.

'Aye. Happen that's what . . . happened.' Alfred Beckett's voice like crushed eggshell.

Ashton said, 'Right, let's have this one out, see what's underneath.'

Ernie Dawber had returned after dark from his weekly mission to the supermarket in Macclesfield, bringing back with him a copy of the *Manchester Evening News*, a paper that rarely made it Across the Moss until the following day.

The front-page lead headline said,

MASSIVE HUNT FOR BOGMAN

A major police hunt was underway today for the Bridelow bog body – snatched in a daring raid on a university lab. And a prominent archaeological trust has offered a £5000 reward for information leading to the safe recovery of The Man in the Moss.

'We are taking this very seriously indeed,' said . . .

'Oh, dear me,' Ernie Dawber said to himself, the paper spread out on the table where he was finishing his tea – toasted Lancashire cheese. 'What a tangled web, eh?'

Trying to keep his mind off what the doctor'd had to say. Well, what right had he to complain about *that*? Least he'd got a doctor of the old school who didn't bugger about – while there's life there's hope, medical science moving ahead at a tremendous rate; none of that old nonsense, thank the Lord.

Might just drop in and see Ma Wagstaff about it. Nowt lost in that, is there?

The doorbell rang.

Ernie didn't rush. He folded up the *Manchester Evening News* very neatly, preserving its crease. If it was Dr Hall, he didn't know what he'd say. As an historian he was glad the experts had got their hands on this particular body, been able, with their modern scientific tests, to clarify a few points. But equally Ma Wagstaff, with her instincts and her natural wisdom, had been right about putting the thing back.

Thank God, he thought, pulling at his front door, for instinct. All too aware that this was not something he himself possessed. Bit of psychological insight perhaps, now and then, but that wasn't the same thing.

So it had to be done, putting the bogman back in Bridelow earth. Commitment fulfilled.

All's well that ends well.

Except it hasn't, Ernie thought, getting the door open. It hasn't ended and it's not well. Lord knows why.

'By 'eck,' he said, surprised. 'And to what do I owe this honour?'

On his doorstep, in the rain, stood four women in dark clothing – old-fashioned, ankle-length, navy duffle coats with the hoods up or dark woollen shawls over their heads.

A posse from the Bridelow Mothers' Union, in full ritual dress. Could be quite disconcerting when you saw them trooping across the churchyard against a wintry sunset. But always a bit, well, comical, at close range.

'Can we talk to you, Mr Dawber?' Milly Gill said from somewhere inside whatever she had on.

Ernie identified the others in a second: Frank's wife, Ethel, Young Frank's wife, Susan. And Old Sarah Winstanley, with no teeth in. Probably the only remaining members of the Union fit enough to go out after dark this time of year.

He felt a warm wave of affection for the curious quartet.

'Now, then,' he said cheerfully. 'Where's Ma?'

No instinct, that was his problem.

'Thought you knew everything,' Milly Gill said in a voice as cold and dispiriting as the rain.

'I've been out,' Ernie said, on edge now.

Milly said quietly, 'Ma's died on us, and the churchyard's full of policemen digging up Matt's grave. Can we come in, Mr Dawber?'

Matt Castle's coffin came up hard.

It was like a big old decaying barge stuck in a sandbank; it didn't want to come, it wanted to stay in the dark and rot and feed the worms. They had to tear it out of the earth, with a slurping and a squelching of sodden soil and clay.

'Hell fire, you'd think it'd been in here years,' one of the coppers muttered, sliding a rope under one end, groping for one of the coffin handles.

Alf Beckett stayed on top, hands flat on the lid, knowing it hadn't been nailed down, knowing that if it slipped they could tip the corpse into the mud.

Thinking, *get it over, get it over . . . get the bloody thing found and have done with it.*

And wondering then if by any chance he was standing on the squashed brown face of the bog body. *Oh, what a mess, what a bloody mess.*

'All right,' the Inspector said as two men on the surface took the strain. 'Take it easy. Come out now, please, and keep to the sides.'

Alf scrambled out after the coffin. He was covered in mud.

'Lay it over there, please, don't damage it. Now, Roger . . . Dr Hall . . . time for you to take over, I reckon.'

'Right!' Dr Roger Hall strode into the lights, beads of water glinting in his beard. 'Now we'll see.'

Without ceremony, they dumped the coffin behind the piles of excavated earth, up against the canvas screen, well out of the light. Matt Castle: just something to be got out of the way, while everybody crowded round to gaze into the grave.

Except for Alf Beckett who shuffled behind the others, squatted down on the wet grass by the coffin, put a muddy hand inside his donkey jacket and brought out the witch bottle.

Whispering, 'Forgive this intrusion, lad,' as he felt along the muddy rim of the soil-slimy casket, hands moving up to its shoulders, thumbs prising at the lid, bracing himself for the stench, a sickening blast of gasses.

Some bloke barking, 'No . . . *no*. Not like that. Look, let *me* come down.'

Alf breathing hard, snatching at the lid as it suddenly sprang away. 'God help us.' Could he do this? Could he put his hands in there?

'Mind yourself, Dr Hall, bloody slippy down there.'

'. . .'s all right. Get that bloody lamp out of my eyes. Give me a light, give me a torch. Thanks.'

Alf thought it was worse that there was no light. He might not be able to see the body, but he'd have to touch it. Feel for the cold, rubbery hands . . . would they be rubbery or would they be slippery or flaking with decay? He didn't know, but he'd find out, prising the fingers apart to get them to hold the bottle.

Voice raised, muffled. Voice out of the grave.

'. . . Got to be . . . Chrissie, the trowel . . . pass me the trowel!'

'Take your time, Dr Hall, you won't get another chance.'

Hand inside, Alf could feel the quilted stuff and the stiff, lacy stuff, the lining. Felt more like nylon than silk.

Sweat bubbling up on his forehead to meet the rain, his moustache dripping.

The smell from inside the box was dank and rotten. Alf wrenched his head aside, looked away from the blackened hump of the coffin towards the people gathered round the open grave, Joel Beard singing out contemptuously, 'You see . . . *nothing*. Are you really surprised?'

Alf propping himself on his right arm, the hand splayed into the grass.

'Ashton, it *has* to be. I refuse to . . .'

It hit Alf Beckett, in a sudden burst of bewilderment. *The bogman. They can't find it . . . why can't they find it?*

And then his stomach lurched, hot vomit roared into his throat. His supporting arm collapsed, the nerves gone, and his mouth stretched into a scream so wide it seemed it'd rip his lips apart.

The scream was choked by the vomit.

His left hand, the one inside Matt Castle's coffin, had slipped, all five fingers dropping into a soft, cold and glutinous mess. A thin and viscid slithering thing was pulsing between them.

CHAPTER III

'This time,' Sam Davis said, 'you won't stop me.'

He'd already dressed by the time Esther awoke.

'Lights?' she said. 'Lights *again*?'

Sam nodded. Cradled in his arms was his dad's old twelve-bore shotgun.

'Get that out!' Esther shouted. 'I'll not have that thing in my bedroom.'

'Fair enough,' Sam said, patting the pockets of his old combat jacket.

'I *will* stop you,' Esther said, sitting up in bed, rubbing her eyes. 'If you go out with that gun I'll've called the police before you get to the end of the yard.'

'Please yourself.' Sam broke the gun. 'Man's got to look after his own.' He pulled a handful of cartridges from his jacket pocket and shoved a couple into the breech.

Esther started to cry. 'Don't waste um, luv,' Sam said. 'We tried your way. Big wanker. "Oh, Satan, get thee gone, I'm giving thee notice to quit."' Sam snorted. 'Now *I'm* giving um notice to quit. Wi' this. And they'll listen.'

'You're a bloody fool, Sam Davis,' Esther wept. 'You're a fool to yourself. Where will I be wi' you in jail for manslaughter? Where will your children be?'

'Shurrup, eh?' Sam said. 'You'll wake um. I'll be back in half an hour. Or less. Don't worry.'

'Don't *worry* . . . ?'

'I'll show it um. Happen I'll fire it over their heads. That's all it'll take.'

Sam Davis moved quietly out of the bedroom, and his wife followed him downstairs. 'I've warned you. I'll ring for t'police.'

'Aye.' Leaving the lights off, Sam undid the bolts on the back door. It was raining out, and cold enough for sleet.

When he'd gone, Esther, shivering in her nightie, said, 'Right,' and went to the phone.

The phone was dead. He'd ripped out the wire and pulled off the little plastic plug. Esther ran to the back door and screeched, 'Sam . . . *Sam!*' into the unresponsive night.

The nights were the worst times, but in a way they were the best because they hardened Lottie's intent to get out. By day – local customers drifting in around lunchtime, nice people – she got to thinking the pub was an important local service and there weren't many of those left in Bridelow and if she didn't keep it on, who would? And Matt. Matt would be so disappointed with her.

But at night, alone in the pine-framed bed which kept reminding her of her husband's coffin, enclosed by the still

strange, hard, whitewashed walls, she felt his stubborn obsess-
iveness in the air like a lingering, humid odour. And she knew
she'd paid back all she owed to Matt, long since.

If indeed he'd ever given her anything, apart from head-
aches and Dic.

She lay down the middle of the bed, head on a single white
pillow; for the first time entirely alone. Dic had gone off –
relieved, she knew – to his bedsit in Stockport; back on
Monday to the supply-teaching he was doing in lieu of a real
job. Dic looking perpetually bewildered all day, saying little,
mooching about rubbing his chin. Offering, in a half-hearted
way, to stay here until Sunday night, but Lottie briskly waving
him out – fed up with you under my feet, moping around, time
I had some space for myself.

To do what, though?

Well . . . to try and find a buyer for the pub, for a start.
That would be a picnic. Best she could hope for was to flog it
to some rich Cheshire businessman with romantic yearnings,
for conversion into a luxury home with an exclusive view of
peat, peat, peat.

Bloody peat. In the mornings she'd draw back the bedroom
curtains and the first thing she'd see would be black peat and
on to the scene her mind would superimpose Matt in his
wheelchair, sinking into the Moss and fighting it all the way,
and every bloody marsh-bird banking overhead would be
imitating the Pennine Pipes of blessed memory.

All I want is Bridelow Moss behind me. To be able to draw
back the curtains on to other people's gardens, parked cars, the
postman, the milkman, no hills in view over the tops of the
laburnums. (In other words, the view from the bedroom
window in Wilmslow which Matt had despised and which she
carried in her mind like a talisman of sanity.)

With the bedside light on, she gazed unblinking at the
ceiling, a single hefty black beam bisecting it diagonally so that
half the ceiling was light, half shadow.

'Ma . . .'

'. . . aye, gone.'

'. . . agstaff . . . dead . . . you didn't know?'

'. . . God, no . . .'

332

If walls could record voices and mood and atmosphere, The Man's ancient stones would have been crumbling tonight under the dead weight of suppressed emotion. The death of Ma Wagstaff: the underlying theme below all the trivial tap-room chat about Manchester United and the sodding Government, and the more meaningful analyses of working conditions under Gannons.

Lottie saying nothing, playing barmaid, pulling Bridelow Black for those committed to preserving the brewery and lager and draught Bass for those who'd been made redundant.

So Ma Wagstaff had gone.

Well, she was old, she was half-baked, she'd clung to her own loopy ideas of religion; let them be buried with her.

Not that anything stayed buried round here. The bogman rising again after who could say how many centuries, to cause torment and to haunt Matt's latter days. And now poor Matt himself rising again to help the police with their inquiries.

Which – jaw tightened, both hands clenching on the sheet for a moment – was none of her business, and none of Ma Wagstaff's any more. Just let it be all over. Just let them have found what they wanted and put Matt back in his grave and stamped down the soil.

What they wanted. She knew, of course, that it had to be the bogman. How honoured Matt would have been to know he'd be sharing his grave with his illustrious ancestor.

Most likely, she conceded, he *did* know. Matt always could keep a secret. Even from his wife.

Especially from his wife.

And that does it, Lottie thought. I'll talk to estate agents first thing Monday morning.

She put out the lamp and shut her eyes.

She was not lonely.

She was relieved at last of the horror and the pity of Matt and his illness and his all-consuming passions.

And relieved, too – now that Moira had been here, now that she'd received his taped begging letter – of the responsibility of overseeing the completion of Matt's magnum opus, his Bogman Suite. Moira's responsibility now. Poetic justice: one obsession taking care of another.

Not that Moira, presumably, had ever wanted to be Matt's obsession.

Lottie opened her eyes and stared searchingly into the darkness.

Or perhaps, obscurely, perversely, Moira *had*. She kept her ego under wraps, but it was there; it existed.

Maybe it *is* poetic justice.

You've been relieved. You're free to go.

The lino was as cold as flagstones under Ernie's bare feet, and although his bedroom slippers were under the bed, he didn't fetch them out; the cold was better.

I don't want comfort. I want the truth. An answer. What must I do? What is there left I can do?

Through the window, he could see the churchyard, gravestones wet with rain and blue under the Beacon of the Moss. Be one for me, happen, this time next year.

He couldn't, from here, see Matt Castle's grave, but he'd heard about all that from Alfred Beckett, who'd come pounding on his door while the dregs of the Mothers' Union sat dispiritedly drinking tea in his study. What can we do, Mr Dawber? Who's going to explain?

Me, he'd stated firmly. I'll explain, if necessary.

He'd never seen the Mothers in such a state and never imagined he would. Old Sarah Winstanley, with no teeth, just about said it all. No Ma. No teeth. No hope.

Not for me now, neither, with Ma gone.

'Everything's changing,' Millicent had said. 'Hardening. And now we've lost the Man, for good and all. They'll take him back to London this time, no question about that. Bad luck on this scale, Mr Dawber – it's not natural. Mary Lane died, did you hear? Pneumonia. Fifty-three, God forbid.'

Shades, Ma had said. *Them's what's kept this place the way it is*. They started talking about shades again, and it was not really his province. He'd promised Ma Wagstaff that he'd get the Man back, and now it was all falling through, and it was his responsibility. What was there *left*, in the time he had?

And then Milly had told them about Liz Horridge.

'I forgot all about it, wi' Ma being found not long after. I found her up Ma's front path. First time she's been seen in t'village for months. Well ... she were in a *shocking* state, banging her fists on Ma's door – "please, please", like this, whimpering, you know? I put me hand on her shoulder and she nearly had hysterics. "I want Ma, I want Ma." I says, "Ma's not here, luv. Come and have a cuppa tea," I says. She just looks at me like she doesn't know who I am, and then she pushes me aside and she's off like a rabbit. I rang the Hall to tell somebody, but Shaw's never there, is he?'

And Moira Cairns staying with young Cathy, in the Rectory, at the very heart of the village.

He looked down at the graves. Why had she come so secretly? And why hadn't she gone away again? He'd seen her walking down from the church this morning. Strikingly good-looking lass. Probably in her late thirties, looking it, because of that white strand in her hair, like the light through a crack in the door of a darkened room.

But what did they know about her?

'Nowt,' Ernie said aloud to the silent graves.

Should he say owt to the Mothers? He wasn't a stirrer, he wasn't a gossip, he'd always known more than he passed on, just as *Dawber's Book of Bridelow* was only ever a fraction of what the Dawbers knew about Bridelow.

Who'd take over the *Book* from him? No more Dawbers left in Bridelow. Happen it really was the end of an era. Happen the Bridelow to come wouldn't have the distinction that warranted a book of its own. Ernest Dawber, last of the village scribes. Chronicler of the Fall.

Alf Beckett's arrival had saved him. If Alf hadn't turned up, one of them, or all of them, would surely have sensed he had worries and sorrows of his own.

By 'eck, he'd been scared, had Alf Beckett. So scared, as he'd told them, that he could hardly keep his spade level when the time came to shovel the soil back on Matt Castle's coffin.

After finding no trace of the bogman.

'*They didn't find it?*' Milly Gill up on her feet in a flash, for all her weight. Alf shaking his head dumbly.

'What's it mean, Milly?' Frank's wife, Ethel, dazed.

'I don't know.' Milly's voice hoarse. 'I don't understand.'

'But it's good, isn't it?' the youngest of them, Susan, said. 'We dint want um to find it.'

'Of course it's not good,' Milly said. 'You don't suddenly get a miracle like that in the middle of a lot of bad. It's not the way of things. What frightens me: if he's not there, where in God's name is he?'

She broke off for a sip of tea. 'I'm sorry, Mr Dawber. I should've told you earlier. It were finding Ma. Knocked me back. Strange, though, isn't it? Everything's so terribly strange all of a sudden.'

When they'd gone, Ernie had telephoned the Hall himself. No answer. He'd go up there tomorrow, a visit long overdue.

'It must be deliberate, you know, all this,' Milly had said. 'An attack. Village is under attack.'

'Eh?'

'Like I said, things go in waves, Mr Dawber. Good times, bad times. We're used to that.'

'Aye . . .'

Ma had said, *What this is . . . it's a balancing act.*

'But this is an attack,' Milly said.

Ernie had been flummoxed for a minute. 'You mean the curate? Joel Beard?'

'Well, he's part of it. We let them disturb the Man in the Moss. We didn't do right by him. Now we've no protection. All sorts are coming in. Unsuitable people. Aye – people like him.'

'All my sources tell me,' Ernie said, 'that Joel's ambitions are being fuelled by the new Archdeacon, who fancies him summat rotten.'

'Joel Beard's gay?'

'Not as I know of, but the Archdeacon certainly is.' Ernie noticed old Sarah looking mystified. 'No, Joel Beard's incorruptible, I'm afraid. Whatever he's doing, he thinks he's doing it for the good of mankind.'

'They'll all be coming in soon,' Milly said despondently. 'Look at all them strangers at the brewery. Three of ours sacked, one of theirs brought in. Rationalization, they call it.

We don't see it till it's happened. Sometimes I think all we see is . . .'

'Shades of things. Aye.' Then Ernie had fallen silent, thinking of a woman in a black cloak at Matt's funeral. Moira Cairns, former singer with Matt Castle's Band.

Alf said, 'That bloke, Hall, he wouldn't accept it at first. Said he were convinced it were theer and if he had to dig all night he'd get it out.'

'Aye,' Milly said grimly. 'Happen somebody told him. Somebody wanted that grave dug up so *we'd* know there was nowt down there, apart from Matt. Oh, Christ. Oh, Mother, I don't like this.'

Alf sat down on the footstool Ernie would rest his feet on while thinking. 'This Hall, he even wanted to open Matt's coffin. Thought happen bogman were in theer.'

'God in heaven,' said Ernie.

'Joel Beard – he started kickin' up then. Wouldn't let um go near. Said they 'ad no permission except for t'take coffin out, like.'

'Quite right too,' Ernie said.

'Alf,' Milly said anxiously. 'The bottle. You did get the bottle in?'

'No.'

Milly Gill closed her eyes and clasped her hands together in anguish.

'Couldn't do it,' Alf said. 'Seemed no point.'

Milly said angrily, 'Did you even try?'

'Oh, aye.' Alf's hands had been dangling between his legs as he squatted on the stool. Ernie saw that both hands were shaking. 'I got lid off, no problem. Nobody were watching, thank Christ.'

They were all looking at him now. Alf Beckett, soaked to the skin, moustache gone limp, eyes so far back in his head that they weren't catching any light from Ernie's green-shaded desk lamp.

'Weren't theer!' Alf suddenly squealed. 'Matt weren't theer! Nowt in t'coffin but bloody soil!'

There'd been a silence you could've shovelled into buckets.

Ernie could still hear it now, as he stood looking over the graveyard, glittering with rain and the blue light of the Beacon of the Moss.

'And worms,' Alf had said finally, shaking on the little wooden footstool, staring at the floor. 'Handfuls of big, long worms.'

At the window, Ernie Dawber sighed very deeply.

Moira awoke with this awful sense of doom set around her like a block of ice.

She was hot and she was cold. She was sweating.

And she was whimpering, 'Mammy. Oh, mammy, please . . . don't let them.'

She'd dreamed a version of the truth. She was a little girl again, living with her daddy and her gran in the almost posh Glasgow suburb, catching the bus to school, Gran's warning shrilling in her ears, '. . . and you just be sure and keep away from the old railway, you hear?'

On account of the gypsies were back. The gypsies who still came every autumn to the old railway, caravans in a circle like covered wagons in a Western when the Indians were hostile.

Coming home from school, getting off the bus, the two darkskinned gypsy boys hanging round. 'Hey, you . . . Moira, is it? The Duchess wants tae see ye . . .'

'You leave me alone . . . Get lost, huh.'

'We're no gonny hurt ye . . .'

'You deaf? I said get lost.'

'Ye gonny come quietly, ye wee besom, or . . .'

Dissolve to interior. A treasure cave, with china and brass and gold. And the most beautiful, exotic woman you ever saw. 'My, you're quite a pretty child . . . Now, I have something . . . Think of it as a family heirloom . . . Tell no one until you're grown . . . Guard it with your life now!' This rich, glowing thing (which would be dull and grey to most people) heavy in your hand.

'You must remember this day, always. You *will* remember it, for you'll never be a wee girl again.'

And that night she had her first period.

Guard it with your life.

Moira sprang from her bed, snapped on the light. The guitar case stood where she'd left it, propped between a mahogany wardrobe and the wall. She dragged it out, lay it flat on the worn carpet, the strings making wild discordant protest as she threw back the lid, feeling for the felt-lined pocket, where might be stored such things as spare strings, plectrums, harmonicas.

And combs.

The door was tentatively opened, and Cathy appeared in rumpled pyjamas. 'What's wrong?'

Moira was shivering in a long T-shirt with Sylvester the Cat down the front.

'Moira, what's wrong?'

Moira's voice low and catarrhal, growly-rough, 'The broken window. Wasny just vandals.'

'You're cold.'

'Damn right I'm cold.'

'Come downstairs. I'll make some tea.'

Thrusting her hand again and again into the harmonica pocket. Nothing. She pulled out the guitar, laid it on the bed. Turned the case upside down. Picked up the guitar and shook it violently, and listened to nothing rattling inside.

When, slowly, she straightened up, her back was hurting. She felt arid, derelict. She felt old but inexperienced, incompetent. She felt like an old child.

Numbly, she reached behind the bedroom door for her cloak, to cover her thin, goosebumpy arms.

The cloak was not there. They'd taken that too.

Sam stumbled no more than twice. He knew his ground. Didn't need no light, although he had the powerful police torch wedged in his jacket pocket, case he needed to blind anybody.

It was pissing down. Sam wore his old fishing hat, pulled down, head into the rain.

Never been raining when these buggers'd been up here before. They wouldn't like that. Be an advantage for him, two years windblasted, rained on, snowed on.

There was a moon up there, somewhere buried in clouds, so the sky wasn't all that black. When his eyes had adjusted he could see the outline of the hill, and when he got halfway up it he could make out a couple of faint lights down on the edge of Bridelow.

But no lights above him now.

Moving round so he'd come to the circle from the bit of a hump behind it, he climbed higher, a lone blue-white disc floating into view, vague through the rain and mist. Beacon of the Moss.

Bloody church. Bugger all use they'd been, pair of um.

When he came to the bracken, Sam stopped, stayed very still, listening. Thought by now he'd have seen their lights, heard some of the chanting, whatever they did.

Sam went down on his haunches, the rain spattering the bracken. Quietly as he could, he snapped shut the breech of the gun, jammed the butt under his elbow and crouched there, waiting.

The rain coming down hard and cold, muffling the moor, seeping through his jacket. Might've brought his waterproof, except the thing would have squeaked when he moved. Have a hot bath when he got in, slug or two of whisky.

Sam hefted the twelve-bore. His mouth felt dry.

They were here. He could feel it. They were close.

Bastards. Stay aggressive. Aggression generated heat and aggression was better than fear.

Right. Sam moved in closer. He reckoned he was no more than twenty yards from the circle; couldn't see it yet. Just over this rise.

They were there; no question. But were they lying low, expecting him? Had they somehow heard him coming?

Sam pulled in a deep breath, drawing in rainwater and nearly choking. He stuck his finger under the trigger guard and went over the rise like a commando, stopping just the other side, legs splayed.

'All *right*, you fuckers!' he bawled. 'Nobody move!'

And nobody moved. Nothing. Not even a rabbit in the grass. Only the sound of the rain battering the bracken.

Holding the gun under his right arm, Sam fumbled for his

torch, clicked it on, swirled the beam around, finding one, two, three, four, five stubby stones, a circle of thumbs jabbing out of the moor.

'Where are you? Fucking come out! I'll give you your bloody Satan!'

Not frightened now. Bloody mad. *'Come on!'*

He thought about firing a shot into the bracken, case they were flattened out in there. But it wasn't likely, was it?

No, they'd gone. He switched off the torch, pushed it back in his pocket and did a 180-degree crouching turn, with the gun levelled.

Behind him, up on the moor, he glimpsed a fleeting white light. Didn't pause to think. Right. They're on the run. Move it.

Half-aware that he was departing from his own useless piece of moorland, Sam set off under a thickly clouded night sky with little light in it but an endless supply of black water; his jacket heavy with it and his faithful fishing hat, which once had been waterproof, now dripping round his ears like a mop rag.

He thought of his bed, and he thought of his kids and his wife, who he supposed he loved really, and he thought this was the stupidest bloody thing he'd do this year and maybe next, but . . .

. . . but them bastards were not going to get away with it, and that was that.

He tracked the light. Just one light, hazy, so probably a fair distance away. Heather under his boots now, waterlogged but better than the bracken, and the light was getting bigger; he was closing in, definitely, no question.

Two, three hundred yards distant, hard to be sure at night but the way the rain was coming down, crackling in the heather, there was no need to creep.

Sam strode vengefully onward.

Maybe it was due to forging on with his head down and his eyes slitted to keep the water out . . . maybe this was why Sam didn't realize for a few seconds that the light was actually coming, much more quickly, *towards him.*

A shapeless light. Bleary and steaming and coming at him through the rain . . . faster than a man could run.

'Hey . . . !' Sam stopped, gasping, then backed away, bewildered. His index finger tightened involuntarily and the gun went off, both barrels, and Sam stumbled, dropping it.

Something squelched and snagged around his ankle like a trap. He went down, caught hold of it – curved and hard – and realized, sickened, that he must have put his foot through the ribcage of a dead sheep.

Pulling at the foot, dragging the bones up with it, he saw the light was rising from the moor in front of him, misty and shimmering in the downpour.

And it seemed to him – soaked through, foot stuck in a sheep – that the light had a face, features forming and pulsing, a face veiled by a thin muslin curtain, the fabric sucked into a gaping mouth.

Sam's mouth was open too, now; he was screaming furiously into the rain, wrenching the torch from his pocket, thumbing numbly at its switch, until it spurted light, a brilliantly harsh directional beam making a white tunnel in the rain and mist, straight up into the face.

Where the tunnel of light ended suddenly. A beam designed to light up an object eighty yards away, and it shone as far as the rearing figure of light, a matter of four, five feet away.

Where it died. In the beam, the figure of light turned into a shadow, a figure of darkness and cold.

'No . . .' Sam Davis wanted chanting townies in robes and masks. He wanted sick, stupid people. Wanted to see them dancing, getting pissed wet through. Wanted to hear them praying to the fucking Devil, with their fire hissing and smouldering in the rain. Didn't want this. Didn't want it. No.

When the shadow stretched and the torch beam began to shrivel, as if all the light had been sucked out, leaving only a thinly shining disc at the end of the torch, Sam felt his bowels give way.

All the rage and aggression slithered out of him like the guts of a slaughtered pig, and the void they left behind was filled with a cold, immobilizing fear.

*

Lottie Castle came awake in swirling darkness.

Awakened by the cold air on her own body, exposed to the night, the sheets and blankets thrust away, her nightdress shed.

Her body was rolling about on the bed, drenched in sweat, arms and legs and stomach jerking and twitching with electricity, nipples rigid and hurting.

What's happening, what's *happening*?

She was ill. Her nervous system had finally rebelled against the months of agony and tension. She was sick, she was stricken. She needed help, she needed care. She should be taken away and cared for. She should not be alone like this, not here in this great shambling mausoleum.

Lottie began to pant with panic, feeling the twisted pillow sweat-soaked under her neck as it arched and swayed. She couldn't see anything, not her body, not the walls, nor even the outline of the window behind the thin curtains.

It couldn't be darker. But it wasn't silent.

And fright formed a layer of frost around Lottie's heart as she became aware that every muscle in her body was throbbing to the shrill, sick whinny of the Pennine Pipes, high on the night.

CHAPTER IV

At 8 a.m., the Sunday sky hung low and glistened like the underside of a huge aircraft.

It didn't menace Joel Beard, God's warrior, skimming across the causeway, hands warm in his gauntlets, deep and holy thoughts protected inside his helmet, his leathers unzipped to expose the cross.

Nourished by little more than three hours' sleep at Chris and Chantal's place in Sheffield, he felt . . . well, reborn. Talked and prayed and cried and agonized until 2 a.m. Old chums, Chris and Chantal. Born Again brethren, still with the Church of the Angels of the New Advent. Still strong in their faith.

'I sometimes wish I'd never left.' Joel reaching out for reassurance.

'Why? It was your great mission, Joel – we all knew that, it's terrific – to carry our *commitment*, all our *certainty*, into the straight Church.'

'But it's just so . . . lonely, Chantal. I didn't realize how . . . or how corrupt. That there were places where the Church allowed the evil to *remain* – real evil – for a *quiet life*. A quiet life – is that what it's come to? I mean, tonight, going back to the church, after this fiasco with the grave, it was there for anyone to see. The ghastly light from the clock that isn't really a clock, and all the sneering gargoyles and the place over the door where this revolting *Sheelagh na gig* thing used to be . . . And you realize . . . it's *everywhere*. How many country churches have these pagan carvings, the Green Man, all kinds of devil-figures? Demons. Twisted demon faces, everywhere, grinning at you – it's *our* Church!'

Yes . . . yes . . . yes . . . the pieces of so-called character clinging to old churches like barnacles to a wreck, the very aspects of ancient churches that tourists found so picturesque . . . 'Oh, yes, I've always been fond of old churches.' As if this was some sanctified form of tourism, when really they were soaking up the satanic.

'What it means is that the Church has been sheltering this filth, pressed to its own bosom, for centuries. What everyone finds so appealing about these old parish churches are the things that should not be there. *Am I the only one to see this?*'

They'd brought him food and coffee. Made up a bed for him in the sitting room. Sat up half the night with him. Prayed with him in his agony.

'I've had visions. Dreams. I've been tested. All the time I'm there I'm tested. It tries to twist me. How can I handle this? I'm only one man.'

'No. You're not only one man, Joel. We're here. We're in this together. Tens of thousands of us. Listen, you were our emissary. You've seen and you've come back. We hear you, Joel. We hear you!'

Yes.

He slowed for the cobbles, bumping up the street towards the church, its stonework black with age and evil.

'Say the word, Joel. Just say the word. We're with you.'

'I'm tired. I've only been there a couple of days, and I'm exhausted.'

'You'll sleep tonight, Joel. We'll cover you with our prayers. You'll sleep well.'

And he had. Even if it was only for a few hours. He'd awoken refreshed and ready for his first morning worship at St Bride's, no prepared sermon in his pocket, no script, no text. He would stride into that pagan place and cleanse it with the strength of his faith. His sermon would be unrehearsed; it would almost be like . . . speaking in tongues.

Cathy said, 'You look really awful.'

'Thanks.'

'I've been trying to understand it,' Cathy said.

'Don't. It won't do you any good.'

Cathy pushed the fingers of both hands through her hair. 'I mean, they broke in here, in this really obvious, unsubtle way and they didn't take the telly or the video, or even your guitar . . . just this comb. Does it *look* valuable?'

Moira broke the end off a piece of toast and tried to eat it. 'Looks like one of those metal combs you buy for grooming dogs, only not so expensive and kind of corroded. Like a lot of stuff over a thousand years old, it looks like junk.'

'Look,' Cathy said reasonably. 'Is it not possible it just sort of slipped out when you were bringing your stuff in? Should I search the garden?'

Moira shook her head, gave up on the toast.

'Should we call the police?'

'No . . . No, this is . . . Only guy I ever took the thing out for was . . . Matt Castle, and I never wanted to. Look, I'm sorry. Your father's had a coronary, you've got this Joel Beard moving into your house and I'm rambling on about a damn comb. What time are you leaving?'

'This afternoon – sooner if I can.' Cathy said she'd wait for the cleaner, to tell her to put Joel Beard in the room Moira had slept in and to get Alf Beckett to fix the pantry window. Then she'd pack a couple of suitcases for her father and drop them off at The Poplars, this home for clapped-out clergy. And then think about going back to Oxford.

'What are you studying at Oxford?'

'This and that,' Cathy said. 'Where will you go? Home?'

Moira didn't answer. Where was home anyway? Glasgow? The folk circuit? She felt motiveless. The white-tiled rectory kitchen looked scuffed but sterile, like a derelict operating theatre. Getting to her feet was an effort. The view from the window, of graves, was depressing. The sky was like a crumpled undersheet, slightly soiled.

'I don't know what to do,' Moira said, and the words tasted like chewed-out gum. 'When something dreadful's going down and you don't know what it is or how you connect . . .'

'Why do you have to connect? You just came to a friend's funeral. You can go home.'

'Can I?'

'Just take it easy, that's all. You can't drive all the way to Scotland without sleep, you'll have an accident. Why don't you book in somewhere for a night?'

'I look that bad?'

'You look like somebody walked off with your soul,' Cathy said with this shockingly accurate perception.

Holy Communion, by tradition, was at 9, but by 9.15 nobody had arrived.

Joel went to pick up a stray twig in the aisle, a piece of the Autumn Cross the cleaners had missed. He took it outside, through the churchyard, and dropped it on the cobbles outside the lych-gate. Depositing it safely on secular ground.

On his return he glanced above the doorway, where the *Sheelagh na gig* had hung, half afraid the thing would have left some murky impression of itself on the stonework beneath, but there was only dust. He'd sent the vile plaque to be locked away in the school cellars until such time as a museum might be persuaded to take it.

He waited, in full vestments, in the vestry doorway, looking over the backs of empty pews towards the altar. Yesterday evening he'd had Beckett bring the wine up from the cellar room and then had the room locked, and he'd taken the key and hurled it away across the Moss.

The church clock gave a single chime for 9.30. When nobody came to Holy Communion. It didn't really surprise him. How could anyone here kneel at the altar, accepting the blood and body of Christ – knowing what they knew?

Knowing that stipends and student grants added up to bugger-all, she tried to give Cathy some money for the two nights' accommodation.

Cathy laughed. 'After you were burgled?'

Moira didn't think she looked too convinced about the comb. Understandably, perhaps.

They were standing by the front gate of the Rectory. She felt weak and washed out and cold without her cloak. The raw air hurt her cheeks and made her eyes water.

Cathy said, 'You look like you're coming down with something. Hope it's not this Taiwanese flu.'

Moira looked down the hill towards The Man I'th Moss. Either side of the cobbled street, the cottages looked rough and random, like rocks left by a landslide. She said goodbye to Cathy, kissed her on the cheek. Cathy's cheek felt hot and flushed, Moira's lips felt cracked, like a hag's. She was remembering the day the Duchess had given her the comb. How she'd stood before her wardrobe mirror and the old comb had stroked fluidly through her short hair, like an oar from a boat sailing with the tide, and the hair had seemed suddenly so lustrous and longing to be liberated, and that was when it began, the five-year war with her gran, who thought children should be seen and not heard and not even seen without their hair was neatly trimmed.

'. . . if that's what you were thinking,' Cathy was saying in a low voice.

'Huh?'

'I said . . .' raising her voice, '. . . it wasn't Dic.'

'What wasn't?'

'Whoever broke in. You've been indicating it was a personal thing. I mean, how many people would know about that comb anyway?'

'I didn't say anything.'

'You didn't have to. You thought it was Dic. Well, he wouldn't do a thing like that and anyway he . . . he's away teaching.'

'Where's he teach?'

'I'm not telling you,' Cathy said. Her pale eyes were glassy with tears. 'Please, Moira, it wasn't him. It wasn't.'

Moira thought, What's happening to her? What's happening to me? When she picked up her fancy, lightweight suitcase and her guitar case they both felt like they were full of bricks, and her hair felt lank and heavy, suffocating, like an iron mask, as she made her way over the cobbles to the church car park.

In the room directly over the Post Office, Milly Gill brought Willie Wagstaff tea in bed.

'Shouldn't've bothered,' Willie grumbled.

Milly said, 'I'm your mother now.'

'Don't say that.'

Balancing her own cup and saucer in one hand – the Mothers were supposed to be good at balancing things – she got gracefully back into bed with him. She was wearing an ankle-length floral nightdress tied over the breasts with an enormous pink bow. She looked like a giant cuddly rabbit, Willie thought, never more grateful for her than he had been this past night.

'I'm everybody's mother now,' Milly said miserably. 'Who else is there? Old Sarah?'

'Shit,' said Willie. 'I don't want it to be you.'

Milly shrugged her big shoulders and still kept the cup balanced on the saucer. 'I've lived opposite Ma for twenty years. I've studied her ways, best I can. I've been . . . well . . . almost a daughter-in-law.'

'I was always led to believe,' Willie said, 'that Ma was

supposed to announce her successor. "There's one as'll come after me." And it weren't you, luv, I'm sure of that.'

'No,' said Milly. 'But Ma thought she'd be around for another ten years yet. I know that for a fact. Ma thought she'd see in the Millennium.'

'Who can say owt like that? Who the hell knows how long they've got?'

'Ma knew.'

'Aye. But she were bloody wrong, though, weren't she?'

Milly squeezed her lips tight.

'Makes you wonder,' Willie said bitterly, 'if it's not a load of old garbage, all of it, the whole caboodle. Makes you bloody wonder.'

'I'll not have that from you, Little Man,' Milly chided, 'even if you are in grief. That's part of the problem. That sort of talk's like decay.'

'Realism, more like,' Willie said, his fingers waking up, stretching themselves, then batting the side of his teacup in a soft chinking rhythm.

'Drink your tea. You're upset. We all are. I just wish I could get some insight about the Man.'

'Aye,' Willie said. 'And where's bloody Matt? Don't bear thinking about, this lot. Makes me think I'll happen have Ma cremated.'

'You never will!' Milly sat up so suddenly she actually spilled some tea.

'Nowt as goes in yon churchyard ever bloody stays down,' Willie protested. 'Aye, all right. I mean, no, I'll not have her cremated, settle down. Will you talk to Moira?'

'I don't know,' Milly said. 'Wasn't there talk of her getting into bad magic some while back?'

'Aye, and she got out again,' Willie said. 'You met her last night. How did she seem to you?'

'All right, I suppose,' Milly said grudgingly. 'But you can't tell. I should be able to tell, I know, but . . . Oh, Willie . . .' Her shoulders started to shake and she collapsed against him. 'I'm out of me depth. Why did she have to die like that? Why did she leave us?'

'Because she had no choice,' said Willie, almost managing to get his arm all the way around her. 'It's no good us keep getting worked up about it. What's done is done.'

But his fingers didn't accept it; they set up a wild, uncontrollable rhythm on Milly's arm, just below the shoulder. *Ma was killed . . . Ma was killed . . . Ma was. . . .*

'Stop it!' Milly sobbed. 'I know. I bloody *know*! But what can we do?'

'Talk to Moira,' Willie said.

The church clock chimed, for 10 a.m.

'Be late for church,' Willie said.

'Not going,' Milly said. 'Means nowt to me now, that place. He's destroyed it. In one day.'

'Aye,' Willie said. 'And the well.'

'You *what*?'

'Him or somebody. I never told you, did I? I forgot – what with Ma and everything. Me and Moira went up there looking for Ma, and the well had been wrecked. Statue smashed, right bloody mess.'

Milly rolled away from him, mashing her face into her pillow in anguish.

'I'm sorry, lass,' Willie said. 'I just forgot.'

Sunday morning and the whole village was unaccountably silent. Moira walked to the church car park and loaded everything into the BMW.

It was coming up to 10.45, which probably explained the silence. This would be the time of the Sunday morning worship.

She walked across to the public notice board next to the lych-gate.

SUNDAY:

> HOLY COMMUNION 9.0.
> MORNING SERVICE 10.30
> UNLESS OTHERWISE NOTIFIED

Life will go on. Unless otherwise notified.

She no longer felt observed. She wasn't worth it any more:

a thin, bewildered Scottish woman coming up to middle age and her hair turning white.

Everything was unreal. The clouds were like stone. Her head felt as if it was set in concrete. She needed to get away, to sleep and think and sleep.

And then, maybe, to find Dic, track the little shit down, deal with this thing.

She'd see Willie and then leave. She didn't feel like talking to him – or to anybody. But Willie was the other link; there were things Willie could tell her.

And he was a churchgoer, or always used to be. She was probably going to have to wait until they all came out.

She slipped through the lych-gate. It began to rain, quite powerfully. The gargoyles glared down at her. She moved quietly into the church porch, but there was no feeling of sanctuary here now. The sense of walking into the womb had gone with the *Sheelagh na gig*. It was merely shelter now, from the rain and nothing else.

Moira stopped, hearing a voice, a preacher's lilt, from the body of the church.

'. . . *Dearly beloved brethren, the Scripture moves us in sundry places to acknowledge and confess our manifold sins and wickedness, and that we should not dissemble nor cloak them before the face of Almighty God . . .*'

It was cold in the porch, colder than outside. She hugged herself.

And there was something wrong with that voice.

'. . . *Wherefore I pray and beseech you, as many as are here present, to accompany me with a pure heart and humble voice, unto the throne of the heavenly grace, saying after me . . .*'

The door to the church was closed. She would wait for a hymn and then go in.

'*Almighty and most merciful father, we have erred and strayed from thy ways like lost sheep . . .*

'*We have offended against thy holy laws . . .*

'. . . *and there is no health in us . . .*'

Cathy had been right. She was coming down with something, a cold, flu. Wasn't just shock. She was shivering again. Should go back to the car, turn up the heater.

And then it came to her, what was wrong.

There should be *responses*. All these lines the minister was intoning were supposed to be repeated by the congregation. He was leaving the spaces.

'*To the glory of thy holy name . . .*'

But nobody was filling them. Not one person in this congregation was participating.

'*Amen.*'

Nobody repeated amen. He might have been talking to himself.

Holy Jesus.

'*We shall sing . . . Hymn number six hundred and three. "Round The Sacred City Gather."*'

She waited for the organ or the harmonium or whatever. That sound they always made, like they were drawing breath for the first chord.

There was silence. Only that hollow gasping ambience these places had. And then the singing began.

> '*Round the sacred city gather*
> *Egypt, Edom, Babylon.*
> *All the warring hosts of error,*
> *Sworn against her, move as one.*'

A strong and strident tenor. One voice.

This guy was singing on his own.

And that was very seriously eerie. Moira began to feel scared.

> '*Get thee, watchman, to thy rampart,*
> *Gird thee, warrior, with thy sword . . .*'

Trembling, she pushed gently at the swing-door, opening it just an inch, just enough to peer in . . . and let out the voice, louder.

> '*Watch to prayer lest while ye slumber,*
> *Stealthy foemen enter in . . .*'

She almost screamed. Let go of the door, letting it swing back into place with an audible *thunk* that seemed to echo from the rafters.

I'm away. I'm out of here.

As she ran out of the porch, into the bleakly battering rain, she could still see him, fully robed, statuesque but crazy-eyed, arms flung out, balanced there on the steps before the altar place, singing to all those empty pews. All those completely empty pews.

She walked back along the cobbles, to where she could see down the street as far as The Man I'th Moss.

Not a soul.

But the silence was more sorrowful than sinister, hung down like her confidence, somewhere around the soles of her shoes.

She looked along the blank windows of the cottages. The only sign of presence was some chimney smoking cheerlessly. Maybe all this had something to do with the sudden death of Ma Wagstaff. A big death.

And the stealing of the *Sheelagh*, the removal of the candles, the toppling of the Autumn Cross. Like they didn't feel welcome in the church any more, these bewildered people who no longer knew where they stood in relation to their God or their Goddess.

She turned into the alley which led to Willie's house and she hammered on his door, her body flattened against it. Come on, Willie, come *on*.

Deserted. She tried, a little nervously, a couple of raps on the front door of the curtained cottage at the top of the street where Ma Wagstaff had lived and died. Finally, she found an old envelope in the car and wrote a careful note, walking back down the hill to push it into Willie's letter-box.

> Willie, I suppose we need to talk sometime about what we're going to do about Matt's music on the bog body. I don't suppose you feel any more like it than me at the moment, so I'll get in touch in a few weeks' time. I have to go home now . . .

Home. Where the hell was home?

Home is where the heart is, and I haven't got a heart, I haven't got a soul.

I have been burgled.

She stood in the street and looked from window to window, up and down, in search of life, and did not find it. But then, what the hell business was it of hers if the people of Bridelow wanted to lie low and boycott St Bride's and its unsympathetic new minister?

And turning on her heel, summoning energy from God knew where, she walked crisply, with determination, clop, clop, bloody clop on the cobbles, back up to the lych-gate and the car.

Almost falling into the arms of the Angel bloody Gabriel in white as he strode through the gate, his desperate solo service abandoned.

'I'm sorry,' he snapped. And then, with his hands still on her shoulders to separate their bodies, he began to stare at her. Seeing what she figured must be this sad, sluttish face; no make-up, hair awry, maybe a low and useless anger burning fitfully in the eyes.

His hands dropped away from her. His fists clenched. He began to tremble. He said, 'Who are you?' Golden curls tight to his head, Van Helsing-size cross looming out at her as his white linen chest swelled.

'*Who are you?*'

'Doesn't matter,' Moira said tonelessly. 'I'm leaving now.'

He blocked her path to the car, legs apart, this real big bastard in full Sunday vestments, humiliated in the sight of his God. Profile like Michelangelo's 'David' or something, a good head taller than she was and bellowing out, 'In the name of God . . . WHO ARE YOU, WOMAN?'

'Look, would you please get outa my way,' she said tiredly. Like she didn't have enough problems of her own.

'It's Sunday morning.' He was snarling now, through gritted teeth, rage choking him. 'And my church is empty. There is no congregation. No sidesmen. No organist.'

'Maybe it's just your sermons are crap,' Moira said. 'Look . . .'

He said, in a kind of wonder, backing off, his surplice billowing like a sail, 'You're *taunting* me.'

'Please . . .'

'I know who you are.' He was screaming it at the village. 'I know *what* you are!'

'Yeah, I'm sure you do, but would you please just get the hell out of my way?'

And knew, as she was saying it, that she shouldn't have used the word hell.

His face glowed red, bulging with blood.

She saw it coming but she didn't move. She took it from his massive open hand across the side of her face, from forehead to lower jaw. It would have hurt her less if she'd fallen, but she wouldn't do that. She stayed on her feet and she stared into his incandescent eyes.

Abruptly he spun away and strode back through the gate; she heard his footsteps crunching the gravel and then hitting the path. Finally she heard the church door crashing into place with an echo that didn't seem to fade but went on smashing from one side of her skull to the other as she moved unsteadily to her car.

CHAPTER V

Being Sunday, he could park in the street right outside and wait for some movement.

It was a dull, cold day in Glasgow, and a light gleamed out of the second floor of Kaufmann's scuffed tenement, which indicated Fiona had got it right. 'See, he often works on a Sunday, catching up with his VAT and stuff. But, Mungo, you tell him where you got this from I'm out the door; long as you realize that . . .'

Lucky he'd kept Fiona's home number. He owed the kid another dinner.

This Sunday morning convinced Macbeth that being a private investigator had to be about the most tedious occupation you could have outside of accountancy. The first hour, the car radio kept him amused with some bizarre soap-style drama about country folks in which nobody got killed, nobody seemed to be balling anyone else's spouse but two guys nearly came to blows in an argument about milk quotas. Only in Britain.

The second hour Macbeth fell to contemplating the futility of his life so far, the hopelessness of his quest, etc.

And then, just after 1 p.m., Malcolm Kaufmann came out of the building and spent some time locking the door behind him.

Kaufmann had on a long black overcoat over a pink polo shirt. Macbeth followed him to a crowded, chromium pub where Kaufmann ordered chicken sandwiches and, to Macbeth's dismay, sat down to eat them with two other guys he obviously knew.

Macbeth said shit a few times under his breath, ordered up a sandwich and a beer, sat as far away from Kaufmann as he could while still keeping him in view, and began to eat very slowly.

There were many women in the bar. Macbeth passed some time debating which one he'd make a move on if he hadn't been an investigator on a case. There was one in a dark blue velvet top who had to be wasted on the guy she was with; he was drinking too much and talking to other guys, she was on Diet Coke and probably only here to drive him home.

She had long, dark hair. Which, of course, was nothing at all to do with Macbeth picking her out, no way.

He was getting to thinking he *would* make a move, if only to make the woman's lunchtime more memorable, when Malcolm Kaufmann came swiftly to his feet, said a rapid goodbye to his pals and made an exit, weaving through the crowd with such practised agility that Macbeth almost lost him.

Couldn't be sure Kaufmann wouldn't get into a car or taxi and head off home, so he called after him in the street, and Kaufmann turned at the edge of the sidewalk and raised an eyebrow.

'Mr Macbeth. How very strange to see you.'

'We have to talk, Malcolm,' Macbeth said, trying to sound tough.

'Of course. We must arrange a time.'

'Like, now.'

'Oh, dear,' said Kaufmann. 'This sounds serious. What *can* the fair Moira have been up to?'

Macbeth walked right up to him. There was a cab idling not ten yards away, and he was taking no chances. 'We need to talk about a man,' he said, 'name of John Peveril Stanage.'

Ashton thought he should tell her himself, maybe test the water a bit. Also, he liked a pint around Sunday lunch when he got the time – unable, despite his divorce, to shake himself out of the feeling that Sunday lunchtime was special.

And he couldn't deny he was becoming quite fascinated by this place, a bit of old England only twenty miles from factories and warehouses, muck and grime and petty crime.

He drove across the Moss in his own vehicle, the Japanese sports car which was his first independent purchase with the bit of money left over after paying off his wife. A gesture. Ashton realized now that Gillian was probably right, it was bloody pathetic to buy a car like this at his age. Lump of flash tat, and he could never even remember what bloody make it was.

'Oh,' she said, looking up to serve him. 'It's you.'

No curiosity, he noticed. But then, if they *had* recovered anything from that grave, be all over the village, wouldn't it?

'Just thought I should officially inform you, Mrs Castle,' he said confidentially, across the bar, 'that we didn't find what we were looking for. I'm sorry we had to put you through this.'

There were no more than a dozen customers in The Man. None had looked up when he came in. Made a change; most pubs, they could smell a copper the same way he could scent illegal odours amidst tobacco smoke. Always somebody in a pub with something to hide, whether they'd been flogging nicked videos or their MOT was overdue.

'You have your job to do,' Lottie Castle said. She seemed weary, strained, nervy. Still looking good, though, he'd not been wrong about that. Tragedy suited some women. Something about recent widows, murder victims' wives especially;

stripped of all need for pretend-glamour, they acquired this harsh unadorned quality, the real woman showing through. Sometimes this excited him.

Must be getting warped, price of thirty years in the job.

'I had the feeling yesterday,' he said, 'that you thought we *might* have found something.'

She said, 'Wouldn't have surprised me either way. The bog body, wasn't it?'

'Somebody told you.' He wondered why she should make him think of murder victims' wives.

'Call it intuition,' Lottie said. 'What you having?'

'Pint of Black?'

'You'll be the only one,' she said.

When he raised an inquiring eyebrow she told him another bunch of jobs had gone, working men replaced by men in white coats brought in from Across the Moss. Rumours that Gannons might even close the brewery altogether, transferring all production of Bridelow Black to their new plant outside Matlock.

'Never,' said Ashton. 'How can you brew Bridelow Black in Matlock?'

'How can you brew German lager in Bradford?' said Lottie. 'People don't care any more. They've got the name, that's all that matters.'

'Thought the lads here were looking a bit cheesed.' Ashton nodded at the customers.

Lottie said, 'Gannons have apparently got tests showing the local spring water doesn't meet European standards of purity. Cost a substantial amount to decontaminate it. Added to which the equipment's antiquated. Where's the business sense in preserving some scruffy little dead-end village brewery on the wrong side of a bog?'

'Bloody tragic,' Ashton said, and meant it. 'Just about finish Bridelow, I reckon.'

'People've got to have work,' Lottie said. 'They'll move out. School'll shut. Church'll be operating every fourth Sunday. Still want this?'

'Better make it a bottle of Newcastle,' Ashton said. 'I wouldn't like to cause an incident.'

'The rot's already set in, I'm afraid,' Lottie said, pulling a bottle from under the bar. 'General store closed last week. Chip shop's on its last legs. How long the Post Office'll keep a sub-office here is anybody's guess.'

'Not good for you either. Dozen customers on a Sunday?'

'Be a few hikers in later,' Lottie said listlessly.

'I was told,' Ashton said smoothly, raising his voice a little, 'that some folk reckon all the bad luck that's befallen this village is due to that bogman being removed from the bog.'

Behind him, conversation slowed to a trickle.

'That's stupid,' Lottie said.

'You see, that's why we thought somebody might've had the idea of bringing it back to Bridelow. And where better to put it than at the bottom of an existing grave? Done it before, apparently, according to my source.'

'And who might that be?' asked Frank Manifold Snr from behind his half of draught Bass.

Ashton didn't turn round. 'Surprising as it may seem, Mrs Castle, I can understand it, the way people might be feeling. Problem is, we're talking about a prize specimen here. Experts from all over the world'd made plans to come and see it. It's almost unique. Invaluable. And so, you see, the police are under quite enormous pressure to get it back.'

There was no reaction from Lottie Castle. He was pretty sure now that she knew nothing.

'Well . . .' Ashton sucked some of the creamy froth from his Brown Ale. 'I suspect we're going to have to disrupt people's lives something terrible if we don't find it soon.'

By this time, the silence behind him sounded thick enough to sit on.

'Of course,' he said, 'if the bogman *was* in Bridelow or, say, back in the Moss . . . and somebody was to tell us, anony-mously, precisely *where* . . . Then, personally, I can't see us taking it any further.'

Ashton felt that if he fell off his stool the silence would probably support him.

'Now, another piece of information that's come my way, Mrs Castle,' he went on, 'is that a certain gentleman has agreed to provide sufficient money to create a permanent exhibition centre for the bogman. And that this centre might well be established here in Bridelow, thus ensuring that the bogman remains in his old home. And that the hundreds of tourists who come to see him will spend a few bob in the village and perhaps have a drink or two in this very pub. Perfect solution, you ask me. What's your own feeling, Mrs Castle?'

'My feeling?' Lottie began to breathe hard. She started to straighten glasses. To steady her hands he thought.

'Yes,' he said. '*Your* feeling.'

Lottie didn't look at Ashton, nor past him at the other customers, just at the glasses.

'I hope you never find it,' she said in a voice like cardboard.

He said nothing.

'Caused enough upset.' She started to set up a line of upturned glasses on the bar top.

'And, you know . . . I don't really think I care what happens to this village. I'll tell you . . . *Mr Ashton* . . . Anybody wants this pub, they can have it. For a song. You fancy a pub? Supplement your police pension? Bit of country air?'

He could see tears in her eyes, hard as contact lenses.

'Views?' she said. 'Lovely views?'

'Mrs Castle,' he said. 'Please. I'm sorry.'

'Peat?' she shrieked, slicing a hand through the line of glasses so that the last two instantly smashed against the beer-pumps. 'You want peat? Peat, peat and more fucking peat?'

Cassock wind-whipped around his ankles, Joel stood looking down the village street, his back to the church notice board, his face soaked by rain and by sweat. The sweat of rage and humiliation.

He shouldn't have struck her. It was unpremeditated, but it was wrong. And yet, because the woman was an incarnation of evil, it was also rather unsatisfactory.

. . . *shalt not suffer a witch to live*. Until the arrival of the sound-drenching rain and wind, he'd contemplated delivering his sermon from the middle of the street, denouncing the denizens of Bridelow to their own front doors.

What a damning indictment of Hans Gruber this was. Hans who packed the church at least twice on Sundays, a stranger who had been accepted by the villagers as one of their own.

One of their own!

Hans turning a blind eye to the lone, black-clad figure in the churchyard before the funeral – the hooded figure clearly exuding not respect, nor monastic piety, but a heathen arrogance.

And Gruber, the quisling, screaming at him, Joel, *'Put it back!'* as he snatched the bottle from the coffin.

Joel looked down the street towards Mrs Wagstaff's cottage. Its curtains were drawn, upstairs and down. This was another deliberate insult: *'I'll come to church for Hans Gruber's services, but I'll not even leave my bed for yours.'*

He began to shake with rage. Obviously, after the incident at the well, the harridan had poisoned his name in Bridelow.

The street was deserted. He strode to the telephone kiosk in front of the Post Office. The answer was clear. If, as a Christian, he had been rejected by the resident congregation, then he must summon his own.

'Just get me out of here, get me across those hills and you can break down,' she said. 'Or do what the fuck you like.'

She had this sore throat now.

Cathy had been talking about some kind of Taiwanese flu. Whatever the hell that was, it sounded like the BMW had it too.

'I get across these hills,' Moira told the car, 'I'm gonny book you into a garage and me into a hotel that looks sufficiently anonymous, and then I think I'm gonny die quietly.'

Out of the corner of an eye – the BMW making noises like Kenny Savage in the lavatory the morning after – she'd seen the dead tree on the Moss again. It didn't move but it didn't look so obviously dead any more, a white light shining like a gemstone in its dragon's eye.

She'd closed her own eye, the eye which was letting in the

image of the tree, and this hurt. It was the side of her face Joel Beard had slapped. Maybe the eye had gone black; she couldn't bring herself to look in the mirror.

I can't *believe* he got away with that. Normally I'd have torn the bastard's balls off.

The BMW retched, like it was about to throw up its oil or something.

'Maybe you didn't understand me.' She gripped the wheel, shaking it. 'Maybe you only understand German. In which case you'll never know that if you don't get me to that hotel . . . I'm gonny trade you in, pal . . .'

In the driving-mirror, through the rain coming down like sheet metal now, she could see the spikes of St Bride's Church, maybe two miles back across the Moss.

'. . . and you'll be bought at auction by some loony, tear-arse seventeen-year-old looking for something fast and sleek to smash up and get killed in, yeah?'

Yelling at the car because she didn't want to hear anything else coming at her through the rain and the engine noise. Didn't want to touch the radio-cassette machine on account of there was a tape inside with the late Matt Castle on it, Matt coming seriously unspooled.

Her head ached and her hair felt heavy and greasy, just awful. She pushed it away from her eyes. The Moss had gone from the mirror, it was all scrubby moorland with dark, unfinished drystone walls like slippery piles of giant sheep-shit.

She came to a signpost and hesitated, then pointed the car at the place that sounded biggest and closest.

Buxton. Some kind of inland resort. With hotels. Listen, hen, what you do is you book into the biggest, plushest hotel they have there – like the Buxton Hilton or whatever – and you take several aspirins and you get a night's sleep and then you do some hard thinking. You *can* still think, OK, you *can* still function. The comb is merely an artefact invested with symbol-ism by you and by your mammy and however many other gypsies have had it in their gold-encrusted fists – but to claim it holds part of your spirit, your essence, your living conscious-ness is just ridiculous sentiment. Right?

Sure.

The Buxton road doubled back round the Moss to the Bridelow moors in a steep, curving climb, with what seemed like a sheer cliff going up on one side and another sheer cliff going down on the other with just a low drystone wall between Ms Moira Cairns and a long, long drop into what, being largely invisible through this sheeting rain, might just possibly be Hell.

Come on, come . . . *on*.

The BMW was faltering, its engine straining, like the big rubber band that powered it was down to its last strand.

Sweating, she flung the damn thing into third gear and then to second, revving like crazy.

Except the engine didn't.

It stalled.

In the middle of a twisting, narrow road, barely halfway up a hill that looked about three times as steep now the BMW wasn't actually ascending it any more, this bastard stalled.

'Oh, shit' – hauling on the handbrake – 'I'm really screwed this time.' First time any car had broken down on her for maybe ten years.

Also, coincidentally, the first time she'd had flu or whatever the hell it was in maybe five. And worst of all . . .

Worst of all the handbrake couldn't hold it.

Now, *look* – treading hard on the footbrake – it isn't that the cable's snapped or somebody's been messing with it, it's just stretched too far. Garage'll have it fixed in ten minutes.

What you have to do now, assuming you get to the bottom of this hill OK, you have to shove this car into the nearest grass verge then get out and walk through the filthy rain – without, OK, the benefit of a mac or an umbrella -- until you come to a phone box or somebody's house.

Malcolm was always on at her to install a car phone. No way, she'd said. Malcolm said, When you want to be incommunicado you can just switch it off. She said, Incommunicado is my middle name, Malcolm, so where's the point in paying out fifty quid a month? But it's tax-deductible, Moira . . .

She wanted to scream with the terminal frustration of it: if she managed by some miracle piece of driving to deposit this magnificent piece of Kraut technology at the bottom of this bottomless hill, that was when her *real* problems would begin.

She didn't scream; her throat was hurting too much already.

Gently, oh, so bloody gently, she let out the brake and allowed the car to slip backwards down the hill, which now seemed almost fucking *vertical* . . . twisting her neck round over her shoulder to try and track the curves in the streaming wet road. Not much to see anyway but rain and more rain. She was no damn good at this; never been able to master that mirror-image coordination you needed for reversing.

Thing is to stay well into the left, hard against the sheer cliff – OK, steepish hill, that's all it is – the one going up.

And, God, if I can make it to the bottom in one piece I will walk through this filthy, blinding rain for ten miles, hear me?

This roaring in her ears, it had to be the blood, flushed up there by concentration and the flu.

Letting out the brake, going backwards in short bursts, then jamming on, feeling the wheels lock and slide on the rain-filmed road. OK . . . easy . . . you're OK . . .

Just as long as nothing's coming up behind you!

Then, alarmingly, she was going backwards in a sudden spurt, and when she jammed on the brakes it made hardly any difference, and the breath locked in her swollen throat.

Staring, helpless, as the car's rear end suddenly slid out into the middle of the narrow carriageway, skimming over the central white line, the tail end skidding off, aiming itself at the crumbling stones, no more than two feet high, set up between the road and Hell.

'Oh, my . . . *Christ*!'

Scared now . . . like *really* scared, Moira tried to jam both feet on to the footbrake, straightening her legs out hard, heaving her back into the seat until it creaked, the pressure forcing her head back and around until she was staring out of the front windscreen, the car slipping back all the while.

It was like going up the down escalator in one of those panicking nightmares, only with the thing on at triple speed and a wall on one side and an endless, open liftshaft on the other.

And the brakes were definitely full on . . . and gripping
. . . while the car was sliding backwards on the rain-slashed
road, and Moira's ears were full of this dark turbulence, turning
her vision black.

Black, black, black.

Black, it said.

BRIDELOW BLACK

. . . across the cab of the massive, dripping truck powering
down on the BMW like some roaring prehistoric beast.

Oh . . .

. . . Christ . . .

. . . Get it into first gear . . . !

She was starting to scream out loud, plunging the clutch
down, grinding the gearstick. But there was nowhere to go, the
windscreen full of black, the truck's engine bellowing then
scornfully clearing its throat as, with no great effort, it prodded
the little car and Moira Cairns through the disintegrating
drystone wall and the shimmering curtain of rain and over the
road's edge into the endless mist beyond.

CHAPTER VI

The old clergyman across the lounge was deeply asleep in
his chair, head back, mouth open.

'Lifetime of begging, you see,' Hans Gruber
explained to his daughter. 'He's turned into an offertory box.
You go over there, drop a pound coin in his trap and it'll
suddenly snap shut. Clack! Another quid for the steeple fund.'

Hans smiled.

Cathy said, 'You're feeling better, then.'

'Until I stand up. And a stroll to the loo is like the London
Marathon. But it's always better when you get out of hospital.
Even coming here.'

The Poplars was a Georgian house with a modern, single-
storey extension set amid flat, tidy, rain-daubed fields where
Cheshire turned imperceptibly into Shropshire. There were all

kinds of trees in the grounds except, Cathy had noted, actual poplars.

'Nearly as exciting as Leighton Buzzard,' Hans said. 'Makes me realize how much I love Bridelow. Its hardness, its drama.'

Cathy said nothing. Right now Bridelow had more drama than Beirut could handle.

Hans leaned forward in the chair, lowered his voice – even though, apart from the Rev. Offertory Box, they were alone in the lounge. 'I'm finished, aren't I, Cathy? I'm out.'

'Bollocks,' Cathy said, with less conviction than the choice of word implied.

Hans shook his head. 'Really wouldn't mind so much if it was going to be anybody but Joel. Thinks he's a New Christian, but he's actually more set in his ways than that poor old sod.'

Cathy squeezed his hand. 'You'll be back in no time.'

'No. I won't. Joel, you see . . . he's like one of those chaps in the old Westerns. Come to clean up Bridelow. Vocation. And Simon Fleming sees Joel as *his* vocation, and as long as he's archdeacon . . .'

'Joel might have bitten off more than he can chew, Pop. He put on his first Sunday service this morning, and nobody came.'

'You're not serious.' Cathy watched her father's mouth briefly wrestling with a most unChristian, spontaneous delight.

'Honest to God, Pop. A totally unorganized boycott. You know what Bridelow's like. Sort of communal consciousness. Apparently a few people started to drift along, got as far as the churchyard, realized the usual merry throng was not gathering as usual – and toddled off home. Does your heart good, doesn't it?'

'Certainly not,' said Hans, recovering his gravitas. 'It's actually quite stupid. Just get his back up, and then he'll do something silly. I don't mean go crying to Simon or the bishop or anyone, he's too arrogant. He'll want to sort it out himself. Damn.' Hans looked gloomy. 'That was really quite stupid of them. I can't believe Ma Wagstaff allowed it.'

'Ah.' Cathy lowered her eyes. Hans was wearing tartan bedroom slippers; somebody must have had a battle to get him into those.

'What's wrong?'

'I'm sorry, Pop,' Cathy swallowed. 'Something I haven't told you.'

Hans went very still.

The customers didn't stay long after Lottie had her flare-up. Led by tactful Frank Manifold Snr, they drank up smartish.

'What about you, pal?' Frank said to Inspector Ashton as he deposited his empty glass on the bar top. 'Haven't you got some traffic to direct or summat?'

Lottie said, 'It's OK, Frank. It's me. I'm overwrought.' She turned to Ashton. 'Have another. On the house.'

'No, this chap's right,' Ashton said. 'You've enough problems without me.'

'No,' Lottie said. 'I want your advice. I've had . . . intruders.'

When Joel arrived to take up residence at Bridelow Rectory, he found Alfred Beckett replacing a broken window in the pantry.

He stood over the little man. Perhaps, he ventured sarcastically, some explanation was due.

'Well.' Mr Beckett thumbed a line of putty into the window-frame. 'I *would* have been theer, like. Never missed a morning service in thirty year. Except in an emergency.'

Like this problem here. Which, as Mr Beard could see, he was at this moment putting right before it started raining again causing everything in the pantry to be soaked through and ruined.

'Mr Beckett,' Joel snarled. 'You are the *organist*.'

'Aye,' said Mr Beckett uncomfortably. 'That's true, like, but . . .'

'But nothing! You *knew* there would be no congregation. You knew no one would come.'

'Nay,' said Mr Beckett. 'Nobody come? Well, bugger me.'

Joel felt a red haze developing behind his eyes. He wondered briefly if the hypocritical little rat hadn't smashed the

367

Rectory window himself as a lame excuse for his non-appearance.

'Bloody vandals,' Mr Beckett said, expertly sliding in the new pane of glass. 'Never used to get no vandalism in this village, and that's a fact, Mr Beard.'

Joel stared at him.

You're nobbut a thick bloody vandal wi' no more brains than pig shit.

Joel snatched the ball of putty from the window-ledge and sent it with a splat to the pantry floor.

'Mrs Wagstaff,' he said icily. 'Mrs Wagstaff is behind all this.'

'Nay,' said Mr Beckett.

'Why can't *any* of you people tell the truth?' This devious little man was the only villager who derived a small income from the Church and doubtless could not afford to lose it. 'When I came past her cottage not half an hour ago, Mrs Wagstaff had not yet deigned to draw back her curtains. What, pray, is your interpretation of that?'

Mr Beckett scraped up his ball of putty.

''Cause she's bloody dead,' he said. 'Why d'you think?'

Feeling his holy rage congealing into a hideous mess, Joel walked numbly through the kitchen, down the hall and into Hans Gruber's study.

Had the old woman spoken to neighbours of her encounter yesterday by the pagan shrine? He remembered, with no pleasure now, the gratification he'd allowed himself to feel as he left her in the churchyard and watched her stumping angrily away. The feeling that he finally had her on the run.

Had she run hard enough to bring on a stroke? To give her a heart attack?

Was there a general feeling that he, Joel, was responsible for her death? And for Hans's collapse at the graveside? Was that what this was all about?

Joel sat bowed across Hans's desk, his fingers splayed over his eyes. Was this to be his reward for following his Christian instincts, reacting fiercely and publicly as God's blunt instrument?

Was it?

Joel lowered his hands and saw a tower of books before him on the desk. Amidst the acceptable, routine theology, he saw such inflammatory titles as *The Celtic Ray* . . . *The Virgin and the Goddess* . . . *Pagan Celtic Britain* . . . *The Celtic Creed* . . . *The Tenets of Witchcraft*. Evidence of Hans's attempts to rationalize this evil, the way one might seek to explain crime in terms of social deprivation.

When it came to basics, Joel had no great illusions about himself. He was not a scholarly man. His strength was . . . well, literally that. His strength.

He wasn't going to be able to work in this study. He'd lock the door on Hans's collection of pornography, just as he'd locked the dungeon door behind him. Ante-rooms to hell, both of them.

With a sweep of his arm which sent the books in the pile spinning to the four corners of the room, he experienced again the sublime grace of movement he'd felt as he leaned from the ladder and slashed the cord which bound the Autumn Cross.

Bound to be casualties. But he would go on. He must.

She led him out of the back door to an old barn of a place only a few yards from the main building. Unlocked the door.

'How did they get in?' Ashton asked.

'I don't know.'

'No windows forced?'

Lottie shook her head, bewildered.

'What's been taken?'

Lottie still shaking her head. 'Nothing. Nothing I can see.'

Ashton looked hard at her and let her see that he was looking. Was this a wind-up? Or was there a mental problem?

He didn't think so. She was standing in the middle of the barn, hands on hips, the sleeves of a bulky Scandinavian-type cardigan pushed up to the elbows.

She had firm, strong arms.

'Mrs Castle . . .'

'I know. You think I'm off my head.'

'I didn't say anything . . .'

'Well, me too, Mr Ashton. I think I must be cracking up.'

'Gary,' he said. 'And I'd like to help. If I can.'

'You not got better things to do? One of the lads was saying there's a big police hunt up on the moors.'

'That's South Yorkshire's,' Ashton said. 'Our manor finishes just this side of the Moss. We'll help if we're asked, but we've not been asked. I'm off-duty anyroad.'

'Who're they looking for?'

'Farmer. Don't ask me his name. Went off after some trespassers last night and didn't come back. Had his shotgun with him, that's the worry. Why? You think it might be the same hooligans broke in here?'

Lottie shook her head again. It wasn't so much a denial, Ashton thought, as an attempt to shake something out.

'But then,' he said gently, 'there wasn't a break-in here, was there, Mrs Castle?'

'There had to've been,' Lottie said, quietly insistent. 'There's no other explanation.'

Ashton sat down on the edge of a dusty old couch next to a black thing that made him think of a dead animal, all skin and bones. He saw Mrs Castle glance at it briefly and recoil slightly.

'What's this?' Ashton was curious. There was a flute bit sticking out of it, with airholes.

'That?' Lottie said. 'That's the Pennine Pipes, Mr Ashton. Primitive kind of bagpipe. My husband's instrument. Woke me . . .' She hesitated. 'Woke me up, Mr Ashton. About two o'clock this morning.'

'What did?'

'Them. The pipes. Somebody down here playing the pipes. You think I could mistake that noise after living with it twenty-odd years?'

Ashton experienced a sensation like the tip of a brittle fingernail stroking the nape of his neck.

He said, 'What did you do?'

'Well, I didn't go down,' said Lottie. 'That's for sure.'

'Perhaps somebody wanted to frighten you, Mrs Castle.'

She said, 'When you got Matt's coffin out, did you . . . ?'

'No,' Ashton said. 'We had no reason and no right to disturb your husband.'

She said, 'Do you mind if we go outside?'

'After you,' Ashton said. He pulled the wooden door into place behind them, quite thankful to be out of there himself. Place was like a mausoleum without a tomb.

Lottie Castle sniffed and one side of her mouth twitched in latent self-contempt. 'You know what it's like when you're alone. Or maybe you don't.'

'Yes,' he said. 'I do.'

'Things that would otherwise seem totally crazy go through your head.'

'True.'

'And with you lot digging up his grave, I thought . . . Well, it was as if he was . . .'

Lottie Castle thrust open the kitchen door. Ashton followed her in, quietly shut the door behind them and stood with his back to it.

'I didn't catch that,' he said. 'As if he was what?'

'As if you'd let him out,' Lottie Castle said in a parched monotone, looking down at the flags. 'And he'd come back. For his pipes.'

She turned her back on Gary Ashton and walked over to the stove.

'Listen,' Ashton said, wondering if he was cracking up. 'This piping. Was it, like – I'm sorry – any particular tune?'

'No,' she said. 'No particular tune.' She was silent a moment, then she said, 'When Matt used to get the pipes out, he'd flex the bag a bit, get the air circulating, make all these puffing, wheezing noises and then a few trills up and down the scale. Warming up, you know? Getting started.'

Lottie placed both palms on the hot-plate covers. 'Matt Castle getting warmed up,' she said. 'That was what I thought I heard.'

Hans moistened his lips with his tongue. Cathy got up. 'I'll fetch you a cup of tea.'

'No . . .' Her father moved in his chair, winced. 'No, it's all right. I . . .' He looked quietly down at his knees for a while. Then he said, 'They were talking about a plastic one. Back at the hospital, you know. I said to leave it a while. I said I was seeing a very experienced private therapist.'

Cathy smiled. 'Wasn't working though, was it?'

'No.' Hans sighed. 'She was talking, the last time I saw her, about something getting in and sapping her powers. Perhaps it was intimations of mortality. That was her way of expressing it – that she was coming to the end of her useful life. And maybe she could see the end, as well, of over a thousand years of tradition. And *I'm* wondering, too, if this is going to be the end of it.'

Cathy said nothing.

Hans said, 'Bit of a rag bag, the Mothers, aren't they? Now? Nobody to really take over. Nobody with Ma's authority. Milly Gill? I don't think so, do you? Nice woman, but too soft – in the nicest way, of course. And the rest of the village – well, modern times, modern attitudes. General loss of spirituality. I blame the eighties, Mrs Thatcher, all that greed, all that materialism. Some of it had to find its way across the Moss sooner or later.'

'It's still a good place, Pop, in essence.'

'Yes . . . as long as that essence remains. I'm very much afraid the essence has gone.'

Cathy thought they'd never come as close as this to discussing it. He'd always been too busy organizing things, fudging the issue. The issue being that the parish priest in Bridelow must become partially blind and partially deaf. This also was a tradition.

In the old days – which, in this instance, meant as recently as last year – it wasn't possible to get to Bridelow Brewery without passing the Hall.

The Hall was built on a slight incline, with heathery rock gardens. Ernie Dawber could remember when the old horse-drawn beer drays used to follow the semi-circular route which took them under the drawing-room window for the children to admire. The Horridges were always proud of their shire horses; the stable block had been a very fine building indeed, with a Victorian pagoda roof.

Now it was decaying amid twisted trees grown from hedges long untrimmed. No horses any more; it was heavy trucks and different entrances, no obvious link between the brewery and the Hall. Liz Horridge, Ernie thought, must be feeling a bit bereft. He shouldn't have left it so long. There was no excuse.

The Hall itself, to be honest, wasn't looking too good either. Big holes in the rendering, gardens a mess. Arthur Horridge would have a fit. Ernie was merely saddened at another symptom of the Change.

Gettin' a bit whimsy, Ernest?

Leave me alone, Ma. Give me a break, eh?

Fifty yards below the house, the drive went into a fork, the wider road leading to the brewery.

'By 'eck,' Ernie Dawber said, stopping to look.

For suddenly the brewery was more impressive than the Hall.

In the past it had always been discreet, concealed by big old trees. But now some of the biggest had been felled to give the Victorian industrial tower block more prominence.

Gannons's doing? Had they made out a case for the brewery as an historic building and got a Government grant to tart it up?

Bloody ironic, eh? They sack half the workforce, talk about shifting the operation to Matlock, but if there's any money going for restoration they'll have it. Happen turn it into a museum.

They'd even finished off repairing the old pulley system for the malt store, briefly abandoned last . . . May, was it? How soon we forget . . . when a rope had snapped and Andy Hodgson had fallen to his death. Accidental death – official coroner's verdict. No blame attached.

Don't want to put a damper on things, Ernest, but summat's not right.

Go away, Ma.

He had to stop this. Snatches of Ma Wagstaff had been bobbing up and down in his brain ever since he'd awakened,

373

like an old tune that'd come from nowhere but you couldn't get rid of it. Reminding him of his commitment. *Get him back.*

And if I don't? If I fail? What then?

He could only think of one answer to that. One he'd thought of before, and it had made him laugh, and now it didn't.

Well. Nagged from beyond the grave. You wouldn't credit it. Ernie straightened his hat, girded up his gaberdine, turned his back on the brewery, which suddenly offended him, and hurried up to the Hall.

He pressed the bell-push and heard the chimes echo, as if from room to room within the house.

Even as he pressed again, he knew there was nobody inside.

So she doesn't come down to the village any more . . . Well, she's always been a bit aloof. Not a local woman. Only to be expected with this bad feeling about the brewery. She supposed to subject herself to that when it wasn't her fault?

But you, Ernest . . . Nowt to stop you going to see her.

Ma . . .

. . . She were in a shocking state, banging her fists on Ma's door – 'please, please', like this . . .

'Please, Liz.' Ernie, sheltering under the overhanging porch as the rain came harder. 'Answer the door, eh?'

He remembered attending her wedding back in . . . 1957, would it be? This high-born, high-breasted Cheshire beauty, niece of Lord Benfold, on the arm of a grinning Arthur Horridge, boisterous with pride – free ale all round that night in The Man. 'Sturdy lass,' Ma Wagstaff had observed (they were already calling her Ma back in the 'fifties). 'Never pegged her own washing out, I'll bet.'

Ma talking then as if Eliza Horridge were nowt to do with her. As if there was no secret between them.

It was years before Ernie had put two and two together.

. . . put me hand on her shoulder and she nearly had hysterics. 'I want Ma, I want Ma . . .'

Oh, Lord, Liz. Answer the bloody door. Please.

*

Hans said, 'I realized a long time ago where the essence was. That a real centre of spirituality was what was important – that what *kind* of spirituality it was was, to a large extent, irrelevant.'

'You say you realized . . .' Cathy said slowly. 'Did that come in a blinding flash, or were you . . . tutored, perhaps?'

'Both. They started work on your mother to begin with. Through the well-dressing. She was always interested in flowers.' Hans laughed painfully. 'Can you imagine? Doing it through something as utterly innocuous as *flower arranging*? Millicent Gill it was taught her – only a kid at the time, but she'd been born into it. Flowers. Petal pictures. Pretty.'

'Yes,' Cathy said.

'Then flowers in the church. Nothing strange about that. But in this kind of quantity? Used to look like Kew Gardens in August.'

'I remember.'

'And the candles. Coloured candles. And the statues. I remembered commenting to the bishop – old Tom Warrender in those days, canny old devil – about the unexpected Anglo-Catholic flavour. "But they still turn up in force on a Sunday, do they, Hans?" he said. And then he patted me on the shoulder, as if to say, don't knock it when you're winning. Of course, even then I knew we weren't talking about Anglo-Catholicism – not in the normal sense, anyway. And then, when we'd been here a few years, your mother went into hospital to have you and Barney . . .'

'Which reminds me, Pop, Barney called from Brussels – he'll be over to see you before the end of the week.'

'No need. Tell him . . .'

'There's no telling him anything, you know that. Go on . . . When Mum was in hospital . . .'

'I was approached by Alf Beckett, Frank Manifold and Willie Wagstaff. They said the house was no place to bring babies into, far too dismal and shabby. Give them a couple of days and they and a few of the other lads would redecorate the place top to bottom. Be a nice surprise for your mother – welcome-home present from the village.'

'I didn't know about that.'

'Of course you didn't. Anyway, I said it was very good of them and everything, but the mess . . . Don't you worry about that, Vicar, they said. You won't even have to see it until it's done. We've arranged accommodation for you.'

'Ah,' said Cathy.

'They'd installed a bed in the little cellar under the church,' said Hans. 'The place had been aired. Chemical toilet in the passage. Washbowl, kettle, all mod cons. Of course, I knew I was being set up, but what could I do?'

Hans paused. 'I spent . . . two nights down there.'

'And?' Cathy discovered she was leaning forward, gripping the leatherette arms of her chair.

'And what? Don't expect me to tell you what happened. I came out, to put it mildly, a rather more thoughtful sort of chap than when I went in. Can't explain it. I think it was a test. I think I passed. I hope I passed.'

'But you didn't want Joel sleeping down there?'

'God, no. The difference being that I'd been there a few years by then – I was halfway to accepting certain aspects of Bridelow. They knew that. Somebody took a decision. That the vicar should be . . . presented. To Her. I think . . . I think if I hadn't been ready, if I hadn't been considered sufficiently . . . what? Tolerant, I suppose. Open-minded . . . then probably nothing would have happened. Probably nothing would have happened with Joel. But I didn't want him down there. I don't want to sound superior or anything, but that boy could spend fifty years in Bridelow and still not be ready.'

Cathy said, realizing this wasn't going to do much for her father's recovery, 'Suppose . . . suppose he *did* spend a night down there. And he was already worked up after that business at the funeral. And he stirred something up. Brought something on. Suppose he was tested – and failed?'

'Well,' Hans said. 'There's an old story Ernie Dawber once told me. About what really happened when that bishop spent a night down there in eighteen whenever. They say he went totally bloody bonkers.'

Hans patted Cathy's hand. 'But then,' he said, 'wouldn't have been much of a story at all if he hadn't, would it?'

There was a loud, urgent rapping on Willie's front door, which could only be Milly.

Who knew the door was hardly ever locked – certainly not when Willie was at home – but who'd knock anyway, for emphasis, when it was something important.

Willie had been re-reading Moira's note. It had been a relief at first; didn't think he could really apply himself to Matt's bogman music, not right now, not the way he was feeling.

But what did she mean, *I have to go home?* Why did she *have* to go so quickly she couldn't wait to say ta-ra?

'Aye,' he shouted. 'Come in, lass.'

'Willie.' She stood panting in the doorway, her flowery frock dark-spotted with rain.

'I were just going to make some toast for me tea. You want a slice?'

'Willie,' she said. 'Come and see this.'

''s up?'

'You've got to see it,' Milly gasped.

'It's pissing down. I'll need me mac.'

'Never mind that!' She pulled him out of the door, dragged him up the entry and into the street. 'Look.'

'It's a bus,' said Willie.

A big green single-decker was jammed into the top of the street outside the Post Office. Thin rivers of rain were running down the cobbles around its back wheels. On the back of the bus it said, *Hattersley's Travel, Sheffield.*

'Coach tour?' Willie said, puzzled. Coaches would come to Bridelow quite often in the old days. In summer, admittedly, not on a wet Sunday at the end of October.

'Look,' Milly said.

About forty people had alighted from the coach, mostly young people in jeans and bright anoraks. A small circle had gathered around the unmistakable, golden-topped figure of Joel

Beard. They stepped forward in turn, men and women, to hug him.

'Praise God!' Willie heard. As he and Milly moved further up the street, he heard the phrase repeated several times.

Willie looked at Milly through the lashing rain. 'What the bloody hell's this?'

Milly nodded towards two young men unwrapping a long, white banner. Gothic golden lettering explained everything – to Milly, anyway.

'Who the bloody hell,' said Willie, 'are the Angels of the New Advent?'

'They've got a church in Sheffield. Me cousin's daughter nearly became one about a year ago. They're fundamentalist Born Again Christians, Willie. They see the world as one big battleground, God versus Satan.'

'Like the World Cup?'

'It's not funny, Willie.'

'This is what you've dragged me out to see? A bloody Bible-punchers' outing?'

'You're not getting this, are you, Willie luv?' Milly's greying hair was streaming; her dress was soaked through. Willie noticed with a quick stirring of untimely excitement that she wasn't wearing a bra.

'What I'm saying, if you'll listen,' Milly hissed, 'is that they're God. *And we're Satan.*'

A short time later, Milly heard a small commotion and looked out of the Post Office window to see a group of people assembled in the centre of the street between the lych-gate and the Rectory.

One of them was Joel Beard. Someone held up the trumpet end of a loud-hailer and handed a plastic microphone to Joel.

'GOD IS HERE,' he blasted. 'GOD IS HERE IN BRIDE-LOW. YOU ARE ALL INVITED TO A SPECIAL SERVICE AT EIGHT P.M. TO REDEDICATE THE CHURCH IN HIS NAME.'

Milly felt a terrible trepidation. Obviously none of the villagers would turn up. But what effect was it going to have, all these no doubt well-meaning but dangerously misguided people stirring up the atmosphere?

'THIS IS AN OFFICIAL ANNOUNCEMENT. BRIDE-LOW HAS TONIGHT BEEN FORMALLY REPOSSESSED BY THE LORD.'

'Heathens out!' someone yelled.

'HEATHENS OUT!'

PART EIGHT

JOHN PEVERIL STANAGE

From *Dawber's* Secret *Book of Bridelow* (unpublished):

MEN

WHAT PART HAVE men really played in the history of Bridelow?

Not perhaps, if we are honest, a distinguished one, except for our late friend the Man in the Moss, who – we are told – gave his life for our community.

We have, I suppose, dealt with the more mundane elements: the business matters, employment, the sustenance of a measure of wealth – enough, anyway, to keep our heads above the Moss.

And we – that is, male members of the Dawber family – have acted as local chroniclers. Albeit discreet ones, for I am sure that if this present manuscript were ever to see the light of day our so-far hereditary function as the compilers of the dull but worthy Book of Bridelow would cease immediately to be a tolerated local tradition.

But as for the important things in life (and death), well, all that traditionally is the preserve of the women, and as far as most of the men have been concerned they are welcome to it. We are, in the modern parlance, a Goddess-orientated society, although the role of the Christian deity is more than politely acknowledged. (Thank You, Mother – and You too, Sir, is one of our phrases.)

However, men being men, there have been occasional attempts to disrupt the arrangement. And when a man is possessed of abilities beyond the normal and a craving for more, then, I am afraid, the repercussions may be tragic and long-lasting.

CHAPTER I

Macbeth pumped money into the coinbox, all the loose change he had.

A young female voice said, 'This is . . . hang on, I can't make it out . . . two four oh six, I think. I don't live here, I've just picked up the phone.'

Macbeth could hear a lot of people talking excitedly in the background. He said, 'Can I, uh, speak with Moira? Moira Cairns?'

'This is Bridelow Rectory.'

'Sure. I need to speak with Moira. Can you get her to the phone?'

'I'm sorry, I'm pretty sure we haven't got a Moira. We've got a Maureen. Would you like to speak to her?'

The glass of the phone booth was streaked with rain. It was going dark; all he could see were the lights of a fast-food joint over the road. Didn't even know which town this was. He'd just kept stopping at phones, ringing this number. First time anyone had answered.

The young female voice asked, 'Are you still there?'

'Yeah, yeah, I'm still here. Listen, ask around, willya? Moira Cairns, I . . . Chrissake, she *has* to be there.'

There was a long pause, then, 'I'm sorry,' the female voice said coldly. 'Your speech is profane. Goodbye.'

And hung up on him.

Hung up the fucking phone, just like that!

Macbeth raced out of the booth and across the street, bought a burger with a ten-pound note and got plenty of change. The burger was disgusting; after two bites he tossed it into a waste bin and took his change back to feed the phone.

He wasn't about to waste this number, all the time it had taken to obtain it. The call to the Earl, the waiting around for Malcolm Kaufmann, the blackmail.

'I called the Earl this morning, Malcolm. You remember the Earl? The man who asked if this Rory McBain, who was booked to entertain his guests, could perhaps be replaced by Moira Cairns? This coming back to you, Malcolm? The way the Earl was prepared to, uh, oil the wheels?'

This last item was a lucky guess, the Earl having denied any suggestion of making it worth Kaufmann's while.

None the less, it had gone in like a harpoon, spearing Malcolm to the back of his executive swivel chair.

'See, the longer it takes for me to find her, Malcolm, the more likely it seems I'm gonna have to reveal to Moira the extent of your co-operation in this, uh, small deception.'

At which Malcolm had pursed his lips and written upon his telephone memo pad a phone number. All he had. He swore it. Moira had phoned yesterday, left this emergency-only contact number, along with a message: no gigs until further notice.

'She done this kind of thing before?'

'All too often, Mr Macbeth.'

On top of the coinbox, Macbeth had three pounds and a couple of fifty-pence coins. He dialled again.

This time it was a different voice, male.

Macbeth said, 'Who's that?'

'This is Chris.'

'Chris,' Macbeth said. 'Right. Listen, Chris, I need to speak with Moira. Moira Cairns. You know her?'

'Oh,' said Chris. 'You rang a few minutes ago. You were abusive, apparently.'

'Je—!' Macbeth tightened his grip on the phone, calmed

himself. 'I'm . . . sorry. Just I was in a hurry. It's kind of urgent, Chris. Please?'

'Look,' Chris said. 'We're strangers here. Why don't you speak to Joel? Just hang on.'

Macbeth fed a fifty-pence coin into the phone. Presently a different guy came on. 'This is the Reverend Joel Beard. Who am I speaking to?'

'Uh, my name is Macbeth. I was told I could get Moira Cairns on this number, but nobody seems to know her, so maybe if I describe her. She's very beautiful, has this dark hair with . . .'

'With a vein of white,' the voice enunciated, slowly and heavily.

Macbeth breathed out. 'Well, thank Christ, I was beginning to think I'd been fed a bunch of . . . what?'

'I said, what did you say your name was?'

'Macbeth. That's M . . . A . . . C . . .'

'Ah. That's an assumed name, I suppose. I'd heard you people liked to give yourselves the names of famously evil characters as a way of investing yourselves with their – what shall we call it – "unholy glamour".'

'Huh . . . ? Listen, friend, I don't have time for a debate, but it's now widely recognized that the famously evil, as you call him, Macbeth was in fact seriously misrepresented by Shakespeare for political reasons and, uh, maybe to improve the storyline. He . . .' – shoving in a pound coin – 'Jeez, what am I doing? I don't want to get into this kind of shit. All I want is to talk with Moira Cairns, is that too much to ask? What the fuck kind of show you running there?'

A silence. Clearly the guy had won himself an attentive audience.

'The woman you're seeking' – the voice clipped and cold – 'has been driven away. As' – the voice rose – 'will be all of your kind. You can inform your disgusting friends that, as from this evening, the village of Bridelow, erstwhile seat of Satan, has been officially repossessed . . . by Almighty God!'

'YEEEESSSS!' The background swelled, the phone obviously held aloft to capture it, a whole bunch of people in unison. 'PRAISE GOD!'

And they hung up.

Macbeth stood in the rainwashed booth, cradling the phone in both hands.

'Jesus Christ,' he said.

Back in his hire-car, windows all steamed-up, he slumped against the head-rest.

Is this real?

I mean, *is* it?

The Duchess had indicated Moira had gone to this North of England village for the purpose of laying to rest the spirit of her old friend Matt Castle, whichever way you wanted to take that.

Whatever it meant, it had clearly left the local clergy profoundly offended.

But while Macbeth's knowledge of Northern English clerical procedure was admittedly limited, the manner of response from the guy calling himself The Reverend Joe-whoever and what sounded like his backing group was, to say the least, kind of bizarre.

Wherever she goes, that young woman, she's bound to be touched with madness.

Yeah, yeah, can't say I wasn't warned.

But there is a point at which you actually get to questioning yourself about how much is real. Or to what extent you are permitting yourself to be absorbed into someone else's fantasy.

But not unwillingly, surely?

Well, no. Not yet.

Truth is, it's kind of stimulating.

The time was 5.15. Macbeth left the car and returned to the diner across the street, on the basis that one sure way of restoring a sense of total reality would be another attempt to consume a greasy quarter-pound shitburger and double fries.

About an hour ago, before leaving Glasgow, he'd found a Sunday-opening bookshop where he bought a road atlas and a paperback.

He laid the paperback on his table next to the shitburger.

The cover showed a huge cavern full of stalactites and stalagmites. The angle of vision was roof-level, and way down in the left-hand corner was a small kid with a flashlight.

The book was called *Blue John's Way*. From inside the title page Macbeth learned it had been first published some thirty years ago, and this was apparently the seventeenth paperback impression.

On the inside cover, it said,

THE AUTHOR

John Peveril Stanage has emerged as one of the half-dozen best-loved children's writers of the twentieth century.

Basing his compelling stories on the history, myths and legends of the Peak District and the Southern Pennines, of which he has an unrivalled knowledge, he has ensnared the imagination of millions of young readers the world over.

Mr Stanage's work has been translated into more than fifteen languages and won him countless awards.

Not over-enlightening, and there was no picture. But then, Macbeth thought, the guy didn't exactly look like a favourite uncle; maybe the publishers figured he'd scare the readers.

But then again, that was obviously part of his intention, if *Blue John's Way* was typical.

A quote on the back from some literary asshole on the London *Guardian* said the book conveyed a powerful sense of adolescent alienation.

The bookseller had told Macbeth a growing number of adults were hooked on Stanage's stories for kids; apparently he was becoming a minor cult-figure, like C. S. Lewis.

'In America, I'm told,' the bookseller said, 'his books aren't even marketed as children's fiction any more.'

'That so?' Macbeth, whose reading rarely extended beyond possible mini-series material, had never previously heard of Stanage. 'He live down in – where is it? – the English Peak District?'

'He's publishing under false pretences if he isn't.'

'You got any idea precisely where?'

A shrug. Negative.

This morning, under pressure, the Earl had admitted to Macbeth that he personally had been unfamiliar with the work of Moira Cairns until a member of The Celtic Bond steering committee had drawn his attention to it. Yes, all right, *forcefully* drawn his attention . . .

'*So it was Stanage who was insistent Moira should be hired for this particular occasion?*'

'*He was keen, yes . . .*'

'*How keen?*'

'*He's a great admirer of her work.*'

'*Tell me, Earl, why is Mr Stanage on your steering committee?*'

'*Well . . . because he's a great authority on an aspect of Celtic studies – the English element – which is often neglected. And because he's . . . he's very influential.*'

And also rich, Macbeth thought. That above all. The crucial factor. The reason you're taking all this shit from me, Earl, the reason you deigned to accept this call at all.

Macbeth propped the paperback against a sauce bottle and re-read the blurb.

> John Clough is an unhappy boy growing up fatherless in a remote village in the Northern hills.
>
> He has never been able to get on with his mother or his sisters who live in a strange world of their own, from which John, as the only male, is excluded. At weekends, he spends most of his time alone in the spectacular limestone caverns near his home, where he forms a special bond with the Spirits of the Deep. With the Spirits' help, John discovers the dark secret his mother has been hiding – and sets out to find his true identity.

Macbeth went back to the counter, ordered up a black coffee and opened up the road-atlas.

'How long you figure it would take me to get to . . . uh . . . Manchester, England?'

'Never been, pal. Five hours? 'Pends how fast you drive.'

★

Last night Macbeth had called his secretary in New York to find out how seriously they were missing his creative flair and acumen. His secretary said he should think about coming home; his mom was working too hard. Which meant his mom was working *them* too hard and therefore enjoying him being out of the picture.

So no hassle.

Five hours? A short hop.

But they claimed Moira had been given an assisted passage out of town. *The woman you're seeking has been driven away.*

So she might no longer be in that area.

But she would not be the easiest person to get rid of if she still had unfinished business.

Macbeth was getting that Holy Grail feeling again. The One Big Thing.

What the fuck . . . He climbed back into the Metro, started up the motor.

CHAPTER II

'Right, let the dog see the rabbit. That the photo, Paul? Ta.'

'Got to be him, Sarge.'

'Not necessarily, lad, all sorts come out here purely to top umselves. I remember once . . .'

'It is, look . . .'

'Aye, well done, lad. Never've thought he'd have got this far in last night's conditions, no way. But where's the gun?'

The body lay face-up in the bottom of the quarry, both eyes wide as if seeking a reason from the darkening sky.

'Hell fire, look at state of his head. Must've bounced off that bloody rock on his way down. You all right, Desmond?'

'Just a bit bunged-up, Sarge. Reckon it's this flu.'

'Hot lemon. Wi' half a cup of whisky. That's what I always take. Least you can't smell what we can smell. Hope the poor bugger shit hisself *after* he landed.'

'What d'you reckon then?'

'Harry, if you can persuade your radio to work, get word back to Mr Blackburn as he can call off the troops, would you? And let's find that gun, shall we? I don't know; be a bloody sight simpler if we hadn't got his missus bleating on about him charging after Satanists.'

'Haw.'

'Ah now, don't knock it, Desmond. If you'd seen some of the things I've seen up these moors. All right, more likely poor sod'd been trying to find his way back home, *terrible* bloody conditions, gets hopelessly disorientated, wandering round for hours – what's he come, six miles, seven? – and just falls over the edge. But this business of intruders, somebody'll want it checked out, *whoever* they were, *whatever* they was up to . . .'

'Or if they even existed.'

'Or, as Paul says, if they even existed, except in the lad's imagination. I'd let it go, me, if we find that gun. Accidental, and you'd never prove otherwise, not in a million years. What we supposed to do, stake out the entire moor every night till they come back for another do?'

'Poor bugger.'

'Aye. Glad we found him before it got dark, or we'd be out here again, first light. Well, look at that, what d'you know, it's starting raining again, Desmond.'

'Yes Sarge.'

'Hot lemon, lad, my advice. Wi' a good dollop of whisky.'

'Oh Lord, we're asking you to intercede, to help us sanctify this place, drenched for centuries in sin and evil. Oh Lord, come down here tonight, give us some help. Come on down, Lord . . . shine your light, that's what we're asking . . . come on . . .'

'SHINE YOUR LIGHT.'

'Yes, and into every murky corner, come on . . .'

'SHINE YOUR LIGHT.'

'Through every dismal doorway . . .'

'SHINE YOUR LIGHT.'

'Into every fetid crevice . . .'

'SHINE YOUR LIGHT.'

391

And Willie shouted it too.

'SHINE YOUR LIGHT.'

It was easy. It was just pulled out of you, like a handkerchief from your top pocket. Nowt to it.

At first he'd felt right stupid. Felt bloody daft, in fact, as soon as he walked in, wearing his suit, the only suit in the place, so it was obvious from the start that he wasn't one of *them*.

Not that this had bothered them. They'd leapt on him – big, frightening smiles – and started hugging him.

'Welcome, brother, welcome!'

'Good to see someone's been brave enough to turn his back on it all. What's your name?'

'Willie.' Gerroff, he wanted to shout, this is no bloody way to behave in church. Or anywhere, for that matter, soft buggers.

'Willie, we're so very glad to have you with us. To see there is one out there who wants to save his soul. Praise God! And rest assured that, from this moment on, you'll have the full protection of the Lord, and there'll be no repercussions because you'll be wearing the armour of the Lord's light. Do you believe that? Is your faith strong enough, Willie, to accept that?'

'Oh, aye,' said Willie.

'No,' Milly Gill had said flatly and finally, when Mr Dawber wanted to go. 'It's got to be you, Willie. Mr Dawber looks too intelligent.'

'Thanks a bunch.'

'You know what I mean. You look harmless. It's always been your strength, Willie luv. You look *dead harmless*.'

'Like a little vole,' said Frank Manifold Snr's wife Ethel in a voice like cotton-wool, and Milly gave her a narrow look.

'Just watch and listen, Willie. Listen and watch.'

'What am I listening for?'

'You'll know, when you hear it.'

What he'd heard so far had left him quite startled. They sang hymns he'd never encountered before, with a rhythm and gusto he associated more with folk clubs. He felt his fingers begin to respond, tried to stop it but he couldn't. Felt an emotional fervour building around him, like in the days when he used to support Manchester City.

It had started with everybody – there'd be over fifty of them now – sitting quietly in the pews, as Joel Beard led them in prayer.

But when the hymns got under way they'd all come out and stand in the aisle, quite still – no dancing – and turn their faces towards the rafters and then lift up their hands, palms open as if they were waiting to receive something big and heavy.

When the hymn was over, some of the younger ones stayed in the aisle and sat there cross-legged, staring up at the pulpit, at their leader.

'Some of you,' Joel Beard said soberly, 'may already have realized the significance of tonight.'

Joel in full vestments, leaning out over the pulpit, the big cross around his neck swinging wide, burnished by the amber lights which turned his tight curls into a helmet of shining bronze.

A bit different from downbeat, comfortable old Hans with his creased-up features and his tired eyes.

But no Autumn Cross over Joel's head.

No candles on the altar. All statuary removed.

And despite all the people in their bright sweaters and jeans, with their fresh, scrubbed faces and clean hair . . .

. . . Despite the colourful congregation and despite the emotion, the church looked naked and cold, and gloomy as a cathedral crypt.

Joel said, 'Every few years, the realms of God and Satan collide. The most evil of all pagan festivals falls upon the Lord's day. Tonight, my friends, my brothers, my sisters, we pray for ourselves. For we are at war.'

Bloody hell, Willie remembered, it's . . .

'It is Sunday,' Joel said quietly. 'And it is All-Hallows Eve.'

New Year's Eve, Willie thought.

Time was when they'd have a bit of a do down The Man.

Except that always happened tomorrow, All Souls. Bit of a compromise, reached over the years with the Church. And a logical one in Willie's view. Imagine the reaction, in the days of the witchhunts, to a village which had a public festival at Hallowe'en. So they had it the following night, All Souls Night. Made sense.

Wouldn't be doing much this year, though. Bugger-all to celebrate.

'We have recaptured this church,' Joel Beard proclaimed, 'for the Lord.'

Sterilized it, more like, Willie thought, feeling a lot less daft, a lot more annoyed. Despiritualized it, if there's such a word.

'And it is left to us . . . to hold it through this night.'

'YES!'

Oh, bloody hell, they're never!

'PRAISE GOD!'

'We'll remain here until the dawn. We'll sing and pray and keep the light.'

'KEEP THE LIGHT!'

It's a waste of time, Willie wanted to shout. It's a joke. Apart from the Mothers doing whatever needs to be done – *in private* – Hallowe'en's a non-event in Bridelow. Just a preparation for the winter, a time of consolidation, like, a sharing of memories.

'I would stress to all of you that it's important to preserve a major presence here in the church.'

Nay, lad, give it up. Go home.

Joel said, 'If anyone needs to leave to use the toilet, the Rectory is open. But – hear me – go in pairs. Ignore all distractions. And hurry back. Take care. Make your path a straight one. Do not look to either side. Now . . . those who thirst will find bottles of spring water and plastic cups in the vestry. Do *not* drink any water you may find in the Rectory; it may have been taken from the local spring, which is polluted, both physically and spiritually.'

Willie was stunned. This was insane. This was *Bridelow* he was on about.

'And of course,' Joel said, 'we shall eat nothing until the morning.'

'PRAISE GOD!'

Willie slumped back into his pew next to a girl with big boobs under a pink sweatshirt with white and gold lettering spelling out, THANK GOD FOR JESUS!

'Have we been taken over, though?' Milly said. 'Have we lost our village? Gone? Under our noses?'

'Bit strong, that,' Ernie Dawber said with what he was very much afraid was a nervous laugh. 'Yet.'

They were in Milly Gill's flowery sitting room.

He'd set out for evensong, as was his custom; if there was a boycott it was nowt to do with him, damn silly way to react, anyroad.

She had caught up with him, suddenly appearing under his umbrella, telling him about the Angels of the New Advent. Time to talk about things, Milly said, steering him home, sitting him down with a mug of tea.

'You're the chronicler, Mr Dawber. You know it's not an exaggeration. You've watched the brewery go. You've seen people fall ill and just die like they never did before. You know as well as I do Ma didn't just fall downstairs and die of shock.'

'It's common enough,' Ernie said damply, 'among very old people.'

'But Ma Wagstaff?' Milly folded her arms, trying for a bit of Presence. 'All right? Who's taken the Man? Who's taken Matt Castle from his grave? Come off the fence, Mr Dawber. What do you really think?'

'You're asking me? You're in charge now, Millicent. I'm just an observer. With failing eyesight.'

'There you go again. Please, Mr Dawber, you've seen the state of us. We're just a not-very-picturesque tradition. What did I ever do except pick flowers and dress the well? And we meet for a bit of a healing – this is how it's been – and Susan says she can't stop long because of the child and it's Frank's darts night.'

'Young Frank needs a good talking to,' said Ernie.

'That's the least of it. They're all just going through the motions, and nothing seems to work out. It's like, we're going into the Quiet time – this is last midsummer – and Jessie

Marsden has to use her inhaler twice. We can't even beat our own hay fever any more. It'd be almost funny if it wasn't so tragic.'

The image speared Ernie again. Ma showing him the Shades of Things and making him promise to get the bog body back. And him failing her, in the end. But need this be the end?

'Happen you need some new blood,' he said finally.

'I don't think that's the answer, Mr Dawber. The strength is in the tradition. New blood's easy to get. Remember that girl who showed up a couple of years ago? Heard about Bridelow – God knows how – and wanted to "tap the source"? Place of immense power, how lucky we were, could she become a . . . a "neophyte", was that the word?'

Ernie Dawber smiled. 'From the Daughters of Isis, Rotherham, as I remember. Nice enough girl. Well-intentioned. You sent her away.'

'Well, Mr Dawber, what would you have done? We couldn't understand a word she was saying – all this about the Great Rite and the Cone of Power.'

'Come off it, Millicent. You knew exactly what she was saying.'

'Well . . . maybe it seemed silly, the way she talked. Made it all seem silly. It does, you know, when you give it names, like the Cone of Power. New blood's all right, in this sort of situation, when you're strong enough to absorb it. When you're weak it can just be like a conduit for infection.'

'That, actually,' Ernie said, 'was not quite what I meant by new blood. Let's try and look at this objectively. Everything was ticking over quite nicely – not brilliant, bit wackery round the joints – but basically all right, given the times we're in. Until this bog body turns up. The Man. It all comes back to the Man.'

'You think so, Mr Dawber? The Man himself, rather than what people have made of him?'

'It's all the same,' Ernie said. 'That's the whole point of a human sacrifice.'

Milly stood up and went to the window, opaque with night and rain. 'How long's it been raining now, Mr Dawber?'

'Over a day non-stop, has to be, and coming harder still.

Stream's been out over the church field since teatime, and the Moss . . . the Moss will rise. It does, you know. Absorbs it like a sponge. In 1794, according to the records, the Moss rose three feet in a thunderstorm.'

Ernie laughed.

'See, that's me. The chronicler, the great historian. Head full of the past, but we don't learn owt from it, really, do we? The past is our foundation, but we look back and say, nay, that was primitive, we're beyond that now, we've evolved. But we haven't, of course, not spiritually, not in a mere couple of thousand years. It's still our foundation, no matter how crude. And when the foundation's crumbled or vanished, we've got to patch it up best we can.'

Milly Gill didn't seem to be listening.

She said, 'I prayed to the Mother tonight. Sent Willy off to the church to learn what he could and then I went up to the Well with a lantern and knelt there in the rain at the poolside with the Mother's broken-off head in me hands, and I asked her what we'd done and what we could do.'

Milly fell silent. Ernie Dawber looked round the room, at the grasses and dried flowers, at Milly's paintings of flowers and gardens. At Milly herself, always so chubby and bonny.

For the first time, she looked not fat but bloated, as if the rain had swelled her up like the Moss.

'And what happened?' Ernie said after a while. He thought of himself as one of the dried-out roots hanging in bundles from the cross-beam. Shrivelled, easy to snap, but possessed of certain condensed pungency. Put him in the soup and he could still restore the flavour. He looked closely at Milly and saw she was weeping silently.

'Well?' he said softly.

'If she was telling me anything,' Milly said, 'I couldn't hear it. Couldn't hear for the rain.'

Shaw said, 'What have you got on under that cloak?'

'Not a thing.' Sitting at Shaw's mother's dressing table, Therese had rubbed some sort of foundation stuff into her face, to darken her complexion, and painted around her eyes. 'But it's not for you tonight. You can get excited though, if you like – make him jealous.'

Shaw touched her shoulder through the black wool.

She turned and looked at him, her eyes very dark. The look said, Get away from me.

Shaw winced.

He looked over at the bed, at his mother's well-worn dressing gown thrown across it. He was surprised she hadn't taken it with her.

'Therese,' he said, 'how was she really? When she left.'

'Your mother? Fine. She'll be enjoying the change.'

'I'm not *over*-happy about it. She's a dismal old cow, but . . .'

'Relax. Or rather, don't relax. Look, she didn't *want* to be here. She's really not very sociable these days, is she? Especially where the brewery's concerned.'

He watched Therese's eyes in the mirror. She could always, in any circumstances, make things happen. Yesterday, his mother had been almost hysterical when he said he'd be bringing the Gannons chairman over for drinks. This morning the old girl was missing but Therese – miraculously, shockingly – was in Shaw's bed, and Therese said, 'Oh, I popped in last night, and we had a terrific heart-to-heart, Liz and I. She's become far too insular, you know, losing all her confidence. Anyway, I persuaded her to go to the Palace in Buxton for a couple of days. Packed her case, ordered her a taxi before she could change her mind. Wasn't that clever of me?'

Yes, yes, he'd been so relieved. The old girl would have been suspicious as anything if he'd suggested it. He remembered the Malta idea. Hopeless. But trust Therese to win her confidence.

Trust Therese. Drifting around the house rearranging things; how the house had changed in just a few hours, a museum coming alive.

'What've you got there?'

She'd picked up a black cloth bag from the dressing table, tightened its drawstrings and set it down again.

'Hair.' She turned the word into a long, satisfied breath. 'Beautiful, long black hair.'

'Hair?'

'With a single gorgeous strand of white. I had to use a wig for so long. But there's no substitute for the real thing.'

'Can I look?'

'Of course not. Don't you learn *anything*? If it's taken out now, it loses half its energy. That was why it was important to leave her as long as possible. And it's nicely matted with blood, too, now, which is a bonus.'

'It's all moving too fast for me,' said Shaw. 'That comb . . . does that tie in?'

'Well, the comb was a problem at first, actually. It's had to be sort of reconsecrated. We're not touching that either until the moment comes.'

She stretched. Her slim arms – leanly, tautly muscular – emerging from the folds of the black cloak. 'Then I shall uncover the hair and run the comb through it. You know how combing your hair can generate electricity? If you comb it in the dark, looking into a mirror, you can sometimes see blue sparks. Ever done that?'

'With *my* hair?'

Therese laughed. 'Poor Shaw. One day, perhaps.'

Shaw said, 'I'm sure it must have grown another quarter of an inch since I . . . you know, since Ma Wagstaff.'

'There you are, you see. First you simply felt better. Now you even *look* better. And after tonight . . .'

Shaw said, 'I'm not sure I really want to be there. I'll be so scared, I'll probably screw up or something.'

'Nonsense.' Therese lifted the hood of the cloak. 'How do I look?'

Her voice had a husky, slightly Scottish edge.

Shaw shuddered.

CHAPTER III

Mungo Macbeth figured at first, irrationally, that he must have reached the coast.

Came over the hill through rain which was almost equatorial in its intensity, and there was this sensation of bulk water below and beyond his headlights. Too wide for a river – assuming Britain didn't have anything on the scale of the Mississippi in flood.

And there was a lighthouse across the bay. The light was a radiant blue-white and sent a shallow beam over black waves he couldn't see. Only, unlike a lighthouse, it wasn't rotating, which was strange.

Macbeth stopped the car and lit a cigarette. He'd pulled in for gas near Macclesfield, looked up into the hard rain and the lightless hills and abruptly decided, after six years, to take up smoking again. Thus far it was not a decision he'd had cause to repent.

He turned off the wipers and the headlights; the rain spread molecules of blue light all over the windshield.

The sign had said Bridelow, so this had to be it.

Or rather, *that* had to be it.

The road carried on straight ahead and from here it looked likely to vanish after a few yards under the black water. Which was no way to die.

Macbeth finished his cigarette, slid the car into gear – still not used to gears – and then set off very slowly, headlights full on, thinking of Moira, how mad she was going to be when he showed up. Wondering what her hair would look like in the rain.

Moira Cairns: the One Big Thing.

The later it got, the harder it rained, the more frightened Lottie became of the night and what it might hold.

Not that she was inclined to show this fear. Not to the customers and especially not to herself. Every time she caught sight of her face in the mirror behind the bar, she tightened her lips and pulled them into what was supposed to be a wry smile. In the ghostly light from Matt's lovingly reconstructed gas-mantle, it looked, to her, gaunt and dreadful, corpselike.

Lottie shivered, longed for the meagre comfort of the kitchen stove and its hot-plate covers.

'All right, luv?' Stan Burrows said. 'Want a rest? Want me to take over?'

Big, bluff Stan, who'd been the brewery foreman – first to lose his job under the Gannons regime. If she could afford it, it would be nice to keep the pub, install Stan as full-time manager.

And *then* clear off.

Lottie shook her head. He must have noticed her agitation. She thought of a rational explanation to satisfy him.

'Stan, it isn't . . . *dangerous*, is it? You know, with all this rain getting absorbed into the Moss. Doesn't flood or anything?'

'Well, I wouldn't go out theer for a midnight stroll.' Stan made a diving motion with stiffened fingers. 'Eight or nine foot deep in places. You might not drown but you'll get mucky. Still, I'm saying that – people *have* died out theer, but not for a long time. Don't think about it, best way.'

'Hard not to,' Lottie said. 'Living here.'

'Used to be folk,' said a retired farmer called Harold Halsall, 'as could take you across that Moss by night in any conditions. Follow the light, they used say. Beacon of the Moss. All dead now.'

'Fell in, most likely,' said Young Frank Manifold. 'Bloody place this is, eh? Moss on one side, moors on t'other, wi' owd quarries and such. Why do we bloody stay?'

Frank and his mates had spent the afternoon helping in the search for Sam Davis, found dead in a disused quarry just before dusk.

'Bad do, that, Frank.' Harold Halsall had picked up the reference. 'Used to be me brother's farm, that. Never did well out of it, our George – salesman now, cattle feed. Is it right that when they found yon lad's shotgun he'd loosed off both barrels?'

'Leave it, Harold,' said Stan Burrows, flicking a quick glance at Lottie. They'd spent nearly an hour discussing the Sam Davis incident before Harold had come in. Stan probably imagined that was adding to Lottie's nerves: the thought of being all alone here while whoever Sam had been chasing when he went over the quarry was still on the loose.

If it was only that . . . Lottie turned away.

'Tell you what.' Young Frank'd had a bit too much to drink again. More than one person had been saying it was time he went out and found himself another job. 'I wish I had a bloody shotgun. Fire a few off outside t'church, I would.'

Lottie groaned. Tonight's *other* topic of conversation.

'Soon bring that bastard out,' said Frank. 'Him and his children of God. Then I'd fill him in, good.'

'Don't think you would, Frank,' Stan Burrows said. 'He's a big lad, that curate. Once had trials for Castleford, somebody said. Nay, he'll quieten down. Let him get it out of his system. All he's doing's making what you might call a statement.'

'Twat,' said Frank.

'Don't rise to it,' Stan said. 'Best way. Mothers'll not . . .' Stan realized he'd uttered a word Lottie preferred not to hear in her bar. 'Aye,' he said. 'Well.'

It went quiet. Not sure what they were allowed to talk about. Be better for everyone, Lottie thought, when I've gone.

She heard running feet on the cobbles outside and the gaslight sputtered as the door was thrown open. The porch lamp showed up rain like six-inch nails.

All the lads looking up from their drinks.

'Jeez.'

He wore a sweater and jeans. He shook raindrops out of black, wavy hair. Lottie didn't recognize him.

'Wet enough for you?' she said. Nobody drove out for a casual pint at The Man I'th Moss on dark autumn nights, and he certainly wasn't dressed like a rambler.

'Wet enough for Jacques Cousteau,' he said and grinned,

brushing droplets from his sweater. It was, Lottie noticed, a very expensive soft-knit sweater. Cashmere, probably.

Lottie laughed. 'What would you like?'

'Scotch,' he said. 'Please. Any kind. No ice.'

'Oh,' she said, surprised. 'You're American. Sorry, I didn't mean to say it like that.'

'Bloody hell,' Young Frank Manifold called over. 'I know visibility's bad out there, mate, but I think tha's missed thi turn-off for Highway 61.'

It began just like any normal hymn – well, normal for them.

Sort of hymn Barry Manilow might have written, Willie thought. Slow and strong, with a rolling rhythm and a big, soaring chorus, undeniably catchy. One of the Angels of the New Advent was playing the organ, backed up by a portable drum machine with an amplifier set up under the lectern. Willie couldn't prevent his fingers going into action on his blue serge knees.

Didn't reckon much to the words. Modern language, but humourless. No style.

He glanced at the girl in the Jesus sweatshirt. Her eyes were glazed and unfocused. She had a certain look Willie had seen before, but usually on people who were on something.

High. She was high on God.

As he watched, slow tears rolled down her white cheeks.

The hymn soared on. Joel Beard stood in his pulpit, apparently soaring with it, eyes closed and palms upturned. Willie thought of his mother, now lying in a chapel of rest in Macclesfield. How was he supposed to make funeral arrangements when the service would have to be conducted by this pillock?

The drum machine stopped and then the organ trailed away, but the voices went on, and the words were no longer trite, no longer actually made any sense. Were, in fact, no longer what you might call words.

Willie listened to the girl.

'Holia . . . holia . . . amalalia . . . awalah . . . gloria . . . hailalalala . . .'

He was bewildered. All around him voices rose and fell and rose and swelled, ululating together in a strange, enveloping coda.

Everyone singing different words.

'*Ohyalala . . . holy . . . holy . . . malaya . . . amala . . .*'

He looked up at Joel, presiding Angel, and Joel was smiling, with his eyes closed.

For a while Willie closed his own eyes and was at once carried away on it, drifting, aware that his fingers were stretching, feeling as if they were coming directly out of his wrists, nerves extending. His fingers moved very lightly against his thigh, sometimes not quite touching it.

Something fluttering like a small bird in his own chest and rising into his throat.

'*Mayagalamala . . .*'

That was *me*.

Willie stopped, stood very still for a moment, opening his eyes and taking in the scene. All those upturned palms. All those eyes, closed or glazed.

He sighed and slid quietly out of the pew and down the aisle to the church door. It was bolted, but nobody heard him draw back the bolts and slip out into the teeming rain.

Standing in a spreading puddle at the edge of the porch, Willie looked up at where Our Sheila used to hold open her pussy. He closed his eyes against the cold dollops of rain.

'Speaking in tongues,' he muttered. 'Speaking, chanting, singing in tongues.'

Language of the angels. Open up your hearts to God and He'll fill your mouth with rubbish.

'It's a block,' he said to Milly Gill and Ernie Dawber. 'They're blocking everything out. They're surrounding umselves with sound and emotion. But it's like blanket emotion – you feel good, you feel you're being drawn into something. It's just like candyfloss. You know what I mean? Like . . . *psychic* candyfloss.'

Ernie couldn't remember when he'd heard such a long speech from Willie Wagstaff. Always such a shy lad, in and out of class. You kept forgetting he was Ma's son and therefore, even in a Goddess-oriented society, he must have picked up a few tips.

'It's stirring things up, though,' Milly said. 'And that's not good at All Hallows. You've got to be very careful at All Hallows.'

'We probably asked for it,' Willie said. 'Whole congregation going on strike like that.'

'He provoked it,' Milly said. 'He destroyed things dear to us. He provoked us. Were we supposed to sit there and listen to his pious ramblings after that?'

'Perhaps,' Ernie said reasonably, 'that was what he wanted to do. Provoke a confrontation. It's no great secret, if you know what you're looking for, that the religious practices in Bridelow are not as elsewhere. His brand of Christianity views it with very serious disapproval, not to say abject horror.'

'Hans could've said no to him,' Milly Gill said, 'Hans could've said he didn't want a curate.'

'Hans was a sick man, Millicent. He *did* need the help. And Bridelow does change people, you know. Straightened out, a lad like Beard could even be an asset. It's just everything happened so quickly. Left on his own in what he sees as an evil, pagan parish . . . The way he is now, everything's either black or white. Which is what Ma warned me about. Beware of black, she said, and beware of white.'

'Aye,' Willie said. 'But where's the black coming from?'

'Mr Beard thinks we're the black,' Milly said.

Ernie almost smiled. There she was in one of her endless wardrobe of floral dresses sitting on her flower-patterned sofa with her flower pictures on the walls, bundles of dried flowers and herbs dangling from the beams. She was life, she was colour. Flowers were all the children she'd never had.

Even if the flowers were wilting.

'You keep saying that,' Willie almost snapped. '"He's God, we're Satan". You're avoiding the bloody issue. There *is* bad here. Real bad. Ma saw it coming, and we all said, Ah, poor old woman's off her trolley. We ignored the signs. Look at that bloody tree as suddenly appears out on t'Moss. Did anybody really check that thing out?'

'I never go on the Moss,' Ernie admitted.

'No, you don't, Mr Dawber. You like t'rest of us – we can't turn it into allotments, so we ignore it. And when somebody like Matt comes back and he looks out there and he says, *That's where we're from* . . . Well, we pat him on the back; we know he'll settle down. That's the trouble, see, we've all bloody *settled down* . . . even the Mothers've settled down. This is not a place you can totally settle down, you've always got to keep an eye open and perhaps Ma was the last one who did.'

It's a balancing act, Ernie Dawber heard in his head, Ma nagging him again. Willie was right. Even this morning, going up to find Liz Horridge, he was telling her to go away, leave me alone, Ma, get off my back.

'I were out there,' Willie said, 't'other morning. Wi' t'dog. Young Benjie kept going on at me – "Oh, there's a dragon out there, Uncle Willie." "Nay," I said, "it's bog oak." But I went out t'ave a look, just to satisfy him, like. Dog come wi' me . . . and *he* knew what it were about. And what did I do? I buggered off sharpish. I dint listen to t'dog and I made fun of Ma. I made fun of Ma over Matt's coffin and the witch bottle – scared stiff she'd ask *me* to do it. I dint mind helping pinch t'bogman back, bit of a lark, that were. But opening Matt's coffin . . .'

Willie shuddered. 'Wimp,' he said. 'That's me.'

'She was right,' Milly said. 'Matt wasn't protected. We were putting him in as the Man's guardian. What use is a guardian without a sword?'

As usual, Ernie Dawber, schoolteacher, man of words, man of science, was floored by the exquisite logic of all this.

'Who . . . was it?' he asked delicately. 'Who dug them up?'

Milly's sigh was full of despair. 'I can't begin to guess, Mr Dawber. So many signs. We could see them, but we couldn't see a pattern. I've been praying to the Mother for a pattern. Can't seem to get through, even to meself. It's like all the wires are crossed. Or there's a fog.'

'There's a fog in the church,' Willie said. 'They're making one. White fog. You can't get through because it's like all your lines of communication've been pulled down. The holy well, the church. Ma. It's like the white and the black have joined forces to crush us.'

'And what are we supposed to do?' There was no colour in Milly's cheeks. 'What can we do when we're so weakened, and we don't know who we're fighting or why?'

Ernie Dawber thought, So many sad, bewildered, frightened people. An invisible enemy. An ancient culture feebly fighting for its soul.

He noticed that all of Willie's fingers lay motionless on his knees.

'You know what I think,' Ernie said calmly. 'I think we need another sacrifice.'

CHAPTER IV

Milly Gill shifted on the sofa. It creaked.

'Eh?'

Ernie Dawber smiled in a resigned sort of way. He was sitting on a straight-backed chair, still wearing his old gaberdine mac, his hat on his knees.

'I don't know the story of the Man in the Moss,' he said, 'any more than anybody does. Some say he came all the way from Wales, or even Ireland. That he was sent as a sacrifice. Well, that seems likely, but we don't really know for certain *why* he was sacrificed.'

Willie said, 'I thought . . .' Then he shut up.

'Some historians speculate it was to keep the Romans at bay,' said Mr Dawber. 'But we don't *know* that. And in the end the Romans weren't so bad. They were a relatively civilized people. Bit stiff and starchy, like Joel Beard, but nowt wrong with them really. They taught us how to build proper roads and walls and useful things like that, but I like to think we taught them a lot as well.'

'We?' said Willie.

'The Celts. The earliest real civilization in Europe. Cultured, spiritual. Knew how to fight when it was needed, but not military like the Romans. The Celts never sought to impose order, only to recognize the order that existed around them.

And the moods of nature and the atmosphere. "Shades of things," Ma said.'

'Aye,' said Willie, remembering. 'Shades of things.'

'Moderation,' said Mr Dawber. 'Equality. Respect for each other, nature, animals. For religions. A simple, logical philosophy and one I've tried to pass on to generations of schoolkids, just like my forefathers did. And do you know . . .'

'Aye,' Willie said. 'It worked. It always worked. Kids leave school, bugger off to the cities, rebel against their parents and their parents' values and that. But there's summat about Bridelow. What we learned here, we didn't reject. I suppose . . . 'cause it was so *different*. Radical, like, in its quiet way.'

'Little island, Willie. Sacred island of the Celts. Little island of moderation in an ocean of extremes. Takes some protecting that. A balancing act.'

Mr Dawber turned his hat round on his knees. He's nervous, Willie thought.

'I've written a new edition of *The Book of Bridelow*. What you might call the unexpurgated edition. Just for me own benefit really. Just to reason things out. You'll find it in a blue typing paper box on top of the big bookcase in my study.'

Willie said, 'Why're you telling us that?'

'Maybe it should be printed. Just one copy, to be kept in safekeeping, for posterity. As a reminder of how Bridelow was and *why* it was what it was. To look back on when everything's changed, when the outside world's absorbed us.'

Willie looked hard at the stately old chap, trying to remember what Mr Dawber had been like when he was young, when he'd taught him for four years. He couldn't.

He glanced at Milly, who was silent, pensive. 'Mr Dawber,' he said, 'why are you telling us now?'

'You see, that's the obvious explanation to me,' said Mr Dawber, looking down at his hat. 'That's what he died to save. Not to prevent anything as transient as another Roman invasion. He died to protect a way of life, a whole attitude. The Celtic way. Something worth dying for, don't you think?'

'Happen,' Willie said cautiously.

'I think I'd like to die for that,' said Mr Dawber.

Milly Gill leaned forward on the floral sofa and lifted one of his liver-spotted hands from his hat brim. 'What are you trying to say, Mr Dawber?'

The old chap said, 'Difficult times, lass. The outside's invading us. The White. The Black. Joel Beard. Gannons.'

'Yes,' Milly let go of his hand, 'it *is* an invasion. The worst kind. The kind you don't notice until it's on you.'

'You see, I don't quite know how it's done,' Mr Dawber said, matter-of-factly. 'I thought you might.'

'How what's done, Mr Dawber?'

'Why, the Triple Death, of course.'

'I don't like the way you're talking, Mr Dawber.'

'You see, I wouldn't like to cause any trouble for anybody. That is, I wouldn't like it to look like *murder*. So what I'll do is happen retire to the seaside. Health reasons. The owd chest's never been good. Got relatives in Bournemouth, you know.'

'Bournemouth,' Milly repeated.

'Aye, and nobody'll be interested enough to prove otherwise. I've packaged up the deeds and stuff, of the house, and I've left them with the manuscript, to go to Hans when he returns. With instructions that the house should be let, peppercorn rent, to somebody as needs one. Happen a new historian. Won't be called Dawber, but that wasn't much of a tradition, was it? Anyroad, I've tied things up very nicely, actually. I'll've gone. To the seaside.'

'Aye,' Willie said. 'You sound like you could use a holiday, Mr Dawber. Good long rest, eh?'

'I'll have that all right. In the Moss.'

Wearing a chilling half-smile, he carried on talking as if he couldn't see the pair of them staring at him, frozen.

'You know, when I first read the British Museum report it sounded quite horrific, but the more I thought about it . . . Well, the garrotting bit and the cutting of the throat – that was mostly symbolic. He wouldn't have felt any of that because they'd have tapped him on the head first, you see.'

'Mr Dawber . . .' Milly stood up. 'I can't believe what I'm hearing and I'll not have you talking like this in my house any more.'

'I'm an owd man, Millicent. I've done me bit, had some good times.'

'And you'll have some more.'

'No.' He shook his head. 'There'll be no more good times for any of us, unless we do summat drastic. They've taken the Man in the Moss. This is far worse than the University or the British Museum taking him. He's gone to the dark. And it's All-Hallows. The Celtic New Year's Eve.'

'I know what day it is,' Milly snapped. 'I'm supposed to be a bloody witch.'

'Time of change. Time to look back, store what's useful and important, discard the old stuff as isn't. Time when worlds overlap. Time to *act*. Sit down, Millicent.'

'Act?' Willie came aware of the power of the sheeting rain, could hear it smashing at the roof slates. A power surge brought a quiver to Milly's tulip-shaded standard lamp.

The lady bartender said, 'Stan, *would* you take over, I'm sorry,' and steered Mungo Macbeth into a back room, a big, chilly-looking kitchen.

'Who *are* you?' she demanded.

He told her his name again. He insisted he was a friend of Moira's. He repeated what he'd said in the bar, that he needed to talk to her. Urgently.

'She's not here. Why did you think she would be?'

The woman was good-looking with a strong face, but she also looked like she was carrying a lot of trouble, her eyes vibrant with anxiety. She crossed the flagged floor to a big iron stove and laid her hands on it.

Macbeth said, 'I didn't think she'd be *here*, specially. Not this inn. This was the first place I came to, is all. With lights on. After I crossed the bridge.'

'What bridge?'

'Over the water.'

'It's a bog,' she said. 'It's not water.'

'I'm a stranger. Never came this way before. I'm sorry if I seem ignorant, Mrs . . .'

'Castle,' she said.

'Oh, Jesus,' Macbeth said. 'I guess that means you're Matt Castle's . . .'

410

'Widow.'

'I'm sorry.'

'Why should you be?' she said sharply. 'You didn't know him, did you?'

All you could hear in the kitchen was the sound of rain splashing on the yard outside with the force of a broken fire-hydrant.

'No,' he said. 'I knew that Moira . . . thought a lot about him.' Shit. What'd I walk into here?

'Yes.' She bit her lip. 'Look, the last I heard, Moira was staying at the Rectory.'

'I called the Rectory. There were quite a few people there. They said she was, uh, no longer around.'

'The Born Agains, that would be. What would they know? How far've you come?'

'From Glasgow.'

'*Glasgow?* You drove all the way down from Glasgow? In this? Well, Mr . . . I'm sorry . . .'

'Macbeth.'

'Yes. Well, I suppose it isn't too surprising. Quite a few blokes have done crazy things for Moira Cairns.' A faint smile penetrated the anxiety. 'Look, we'll make some phone calls, shall we? See if we can find out where she is. There's a chap called Willie Wagstaff who might just know. It's funny he's not in tonight, actually. I'll give him a ring.'

'You're very kind. I'm sorry. I just had no idea who you were.'

'That's all right.'

'Is this your inn? What I mean is, you, uh . . .'

'Do you need somewhere to stay tonight, Mr Macbeth?'

She gave him a look that was almost a plea.

'I guess I do,' he said. 'You have a room?'

'Yes,' she said gratefully. 'I have a room.'

'I've spent the last couple of days studying and thinking,' Mr Dawber said. 'In the end, you see, I'm a man of logic.'

Christ, Willie thought, preserve us from logic.

'Bridelow's is a peculiar logic, but logic it is. But our grasp of it has been gradually weakened.'

'Can't build a wall,' Willie said. 'Can't keep the modern world out for ever.'

'We did have a wall,' Milly said despondently. 'But I don't think I was cut out to be a brickie.'

Willie longed to give her a cuddle. For his benefit as much as hers. Longed to build up the fire, with crackling logs to block out the rain. His kind of wall. He thought about Joel Beard and his born-again mob, exulting and singing in tongues in the dying church: *their* kind of wall.

Mr Dawber picked up Milly's chubby hand and held it. 'Tonight, lass. If this wall finally comes down, it'll most likely be tonight, because somebody has the Man and they'll use him for evil. And that'll finish it.'

Old bugger's spent more than a couple of days on this, Willie thought. Ma's been schooling him. *They're looking for openings. Looking for cracks in t'wall. Been gathering out there for years, hundreds of years.*

Mr Dawber looked steadily at Milly. 'You've got to replace the Man, my dear.'

'*Her?*' Willie spluttered. '*She* has?'

'Ma would have taken charge, but sadly, she's not here. Which puts you in the firing line, Millicent, I'm afraid, and you've got to be strong. You're a big girl, if you don't mind me saying so. Big enough to wield the knife.'

Milly screamed and dragged her hand away.

Mr Dawber said, 'I know it'll hurt you more than it hurts me, and I'm sorry, I really am, lass.'

He stood up and straightened out the skirts of his mac. 'When I said I didn't go out on the Moss any more, I wasn't being strictly truthful. I spent a lot of time out there last summer after the Man was found, working out where he lay in relation to the village and also in relation to the path marked out by the Beacon of the Moss. Result is, I know just the place to do it.'

'Nay,' Willie said. 'Moss'll have shifted. Besides, there were no beacon in them days.'

'You mean there was no church clock. The beacon was a

real beacon on the hill where the church now stands. And the Moss was more like a lake. Water to reflect the light.'

Willie stood up. 'Look, Mr Dawber, we'll forget you ever said all this if you will.'

Mr Dawber put on his hat. 'I'll leave you two for a bit. Perhaps you might summon the Mothers, what's left of them as are well enough to come out on a night like this, and have a chat about it.'

'Hey, come on,' Willie said. 'Get some sleep, Mr Dawber, eh? We'll see you tomorrow, have a proper chat. All right?'

'No, I'll not sleep. I've a few things to sort out. Few private things to burn. Letters and such.' He looked at his watch. 'It's ten to nine now. I'll be back for you soon after eleven.'

Milly shrank away from him. 'Mr Dawber, you don't seriously . . .'

'I *do*,' he said sternly. 'And it's got to be tonight. Tonight has the power. The word is Samhain, Millicent, although I realize the Mothers have gradually dropped the old terminology. And on a practical level, the Moss is swollen with rain; when it goes down, things will be absorbed again, taken in.'

'Mr Dawber,' Milly Gill whispered, 'don't do this to me. Please.'

'Perhaps, before I return, something'll have happened this night to make you see the sense of it. Ma dead? That young lad up on the moors? How many do you want? Where, for instance, is . . . ?' He pulled down his hat. 'Never mind.'

He turned round at the door, and a broad smile was channelled through the wrinkles, from the corners of his mouth to his eyes, and his face lit up like a Christmas tree.

'I'm not unhappy, tha knows. Be a lovely thing.'

Mr Dawber turned the key in the double lock and unbolted the front door to the fierce rain and the night.

CHAPTER V

'Y ou been there before? The house?'

'Mmmm.'

'I suppose,' Chrissie said, 'I should be flattered. It's possibly our first official date.'

'What did you say?' His eyes flicking over to her then back to the road, quick as the windscreen wipers.

'You haven't been listening to anything I've been saying, have you?'

'Of course I have.'

'Doesn't matter. You're obviously preoccupied.'

She hadn't wanted to come with him anyway, being actually in the process of trying to lose his attentions without losing her job. Even if he *had* been comparatively spectacular in bed of late.

'Did you say something about a date?'

'I said it was possibly our first official one. Where we're actually seen together without a collapsible coffin between us. I was being flippant, Roger.'

'You're here as my assistant,' he said coldly.

'Oh, thanks very much. You'll be paying me, then.'

Actually, there was no real need to be especially nice to him. No way he could get her fired, knowing what she knew about him and his dealings behind the scenes with the man they were going to meet.

'What a bloody awful night,' she said. Now they were up in the hills it was coming down so hard the wipers could hardly keep up. 'I wonder what witches do when it's pissing down.'

'What?' Almost a croak.

'Witches.'

'What about witches?'

'It's Hallowe'en. I was wondering what witches do when it's raining this hard. Whether they call it off. Or do it in the sitting room. Can't dance naked in this, can you? Well, I suppose you *could*. You're on a pretty short fuse tonight, Roger.'

'No, I'm not,' he snapped.

'Why don't you just tell me what's bothering you. Apart from the usual, of course.'

He didn't reply.

Sod this, Chrissie thought. 'Anyway, it was my understanding that your friend John Peveril Stanage lived in Buxton or somewhere. Why, pray tell, is he holding his Hallowe'en party in Bridelow?'

'Look.' It was too dark to see but she could tell his hands were throttling the steering-wheel. 'It's not a party. It's just a gathering. A few drinks and . . . a few drinks.'

'But not a party.' She was starting almost to enjoy this.

'And the reason it's in Bridelow . . . the Bridelow Brewery's been bought by Gannons Ales, right? And it now emerges that Stanage has been a major Gannons shareholder for some years and recently increased his holding, oh . . . substantially. Is now, in fact, about to become Chairman of the Board.'

'I suppose he's got to do something with all his book royalties and things. Apart from setting up bogman museums.'

Roger didn't rise to it, kept on looking at the road, what you could hope of see of it. 'Seems Shaw Horridge – that's the son of the original brewery family – is about to become engaged to Stanage's niece. They own Bridelow Hall. Which is where we're going.'

'I'll probably be underdressed,' Chrissie said, putting on a posh voice, 'for *Braidelow Hawl*.'

If it was *that* innocuous, why was Roger so nervy?

'Where's your wife tonight?'

'Working.'

'How are things generally?'

'So-so.'

'Everything all right in bed these days?'

'Chrissie, for Chr—' He hurled the car into low gear and raced up a dark, twisty hill.

'No clammy, peaty feelings any more?'

'What the hell's the *matter* with you tonight?'

'What's the matter with *you*?'

When they crested the hill she saw a strange blue moon. 'What on earth's that?'

'It's the Beacon of the Moss,' Roger said in a voice that was suddenly tired. 'Look, I'm sorry. Sorry I ever got committed to Stanage. I admit I'm in too deep, all right?'

She saw the bog below them. In the headlights it looked like very burned rice-pudding.

'It's as though he owns a piece of me,' Roger said. 'Bought me just as surely as he's bought Gannons Ales. I mean, last weekend, when I went to London . . . Chrissie, I didn't go to London. I was at Stanage's place.'

'In Buxton?'

'In Buxton, yes. That's where . . . Look, I'm a scholar, an academic, not religious, not impressionable. I'm basically a very sceptical person, you know that.'

Chrissie stifled it. 'Absolutely.' She allowed herself a deep, deep breath. 'But tell me this: who gave the bogman a penis?'

Roger slowed down for the causeway across the Moss. He seemed to slump on the wheel; she could have sworn she actually heard him gulp.

'I did.'

Ha!

'I used a piece of gut, what they thought was part of the duodenum.' He sounded relieved to be telling someone. 'Moulded with peat and something Stanage gave me . . . a . . . a stiffening agent.'

How ridiculously sleazy it sounded. Hadn't done much laughing, though, had she, when she saw the thing lying there projecting its bloody great menacing cock into the lights?

Actually, it was pretty sick.

They set off very slowly across the causeway. It seemed to be raining harder than ever here.

'Why?' she said. As if she really didn't know. Scholar. Academic. Sceptic. Not impressionable. Ha.

'He insisted it'd . . . you know . . . do the trick. Said I'd obviously become very close to the bogman, and the bogman had – this sounds very stupid – power. And I should use it.'

'And you didn't laugh in his face because you needed him. And his money.'

'No! I didn't laugh because . . . because he isn't a man you can laugh *at*. You'll know what I mean when you meet him. Look, do you really think I'd go discussing my private difficulties with . . . well, with anyone? I mean, my bloody wife's a *doctor*, and I couldn't talk to her about it. Of course, I did think things would be different with you.'

'Because I was a bit of a slag, I suppose. And not very bright in comparison with Doctor Mrs Hall. And because I was impressed with this big glamorous archaeologist who was on telly a lot, and flattered.'

'No, of course not, what do you think I . . . ?'

'Stick to honesty, Roger, you were doing very well. So you discussed your little . . . problem with Mr Stanage.'

'I didn't intend to. Well, obviously. He just seemed to know. He looked at me . . . *into* me, almost. Smiling faintly. As if he'd decided to find something out about me that I didn't want him to know. And then he said, "Try something for me, would you?" Sympathetic magic, he called it. I knew if I didn't give it a go, he'd know somehow. And if anyone saw it, I'd just blame the students. But then . . .'

'But then it started to work,' Chrissie said. Or something had. Probably the power of suggestion.

'As you know,' he said.

'You must have been half-dismissive and half-elated. And half-frightened, I suppose. I know that's three halves, but I'm not very bright, as we established. God almighty, Roger, what *have* you got yourself into?'

'He's . . . a strange man. His knowledge is very extensive indeed. But, yes, there *is* something I can't say I like.'

'Some of his books are very weird, Roger.'

'I haven't read his bloody books.'

'You should.'

'Just keep your mouth shut when we're there, that's all.'

'At the party?'

'*It's not* . . .'

'What is it, then?'

Roger drove up off the causeway, past the entrance to the big stone pub, The Man I'th Moss, and into the main village street. Halfway up the street, greasy light seeped out of a fish and chip shop, but it seemed to have no customers; not surprising in this weather. The blue moon turned out to be shining out of the church wall – must be a clock with a face each side of the steeple. But no hands, no numerals. How strange.

The clock lit up the inside of the car and Roger's bearded face. Chrissie began to feel uneasy.

'*Come on, then, Roger.*' As if the blue clock was lighting him up for interrogation. 'What else are you hiding?'

'Yes.' He turned right before the church, back into darkness. 'I'll tell you. Stanage says he can get the body back.'

'Oh, yes. Who from?'

'I don't know.'

'How?'

'I don't know.'

'What *do* you know?'

'He says we should all get together, those of us who've been close to him.'

'Him?'

'*Him.*'

Chrissie lit a cigarette. 'Turn round,' she said.

'What?'

'Turn the fucking car round, Roger, I'm not having anything to do with this.'

He stopped the car abruptly in the narrow road and it skidded into the kerb. The rain drummed violently on the roof and splashed the dark windows. It was savage and relentless, like a thrashing from God.

'Chrissie, please . . .'

She blew smoke in his face.

He choked back a cough. 'Chrissie, I don't want to go on my own.'

'Grow up, Roger.'

'Listen, I'm just a little bit scared too, can't help it. If only for my . . . for my reputation.'

'Well, naturally.'

'But *I* can't *not* go, can I? And say goodbye to everything.
And make him, you know . . .'

'Make him what?'

'Angry,' he said pathetically.

She couldn't see his face; she didn't want to. She gritted
her teeth. 'Turn it *round*, I said.'

'Lay off, eh, Frank?'

'I wanna know. Come on, he can't just fucking show up,
middle of the night, and not tell us why. Don't want no more
fucking mysteries in this place. Had it up to here with fucking
mysteries.'

'Go home, Frank, you've had too many.'

'Too many what? Listen, fart-face, you're not my fucking
foreman no more. Not your pub, neither. What's your name,
mate?'

Macbeth had had too many bad experiences of telling his
name to guys in bars. 'Kansas,' he said. 'Jim Kansas.'

'. . . kind of fucking name's that?'

'Frank, if you don't go home . . .'

'Aye? Go on. Finish sentence, Stan. What you goin' do if I
don't go?'

'I shall pick up that big bottle of Long John,' said Mrs
Lottie Castle, appearing in the doorway, 'and I'll use it to bash
out all of your front teeth, Frank Manifold. That's for starters.
Out!'

'It's raining,' Young Frank said.

And he giggled. But he went.

Macbeth started to breathe again.

'Sorry,' the barman Stan said to him. 'Everybody seems to
be on edge tonight.' The other guys in the bar were draining
their glasses, coming to their feet. 'We'll leave you to it, Lottie,
I think. Shut the place, I would. You'll get no more custom
tonight. Not in this.'

Now Stan looked meaningfully at Macbeth. Lottie said,
'He's staying.' Stan nodded dubiously and didn't move. 'He's
an old friend of Matt's,' Lottie said. 'Couldn't make it for the
funeral.'

'Right.' Stan accepted this and shrugged into his overcoat. ''Night then, Lottie. Good night, Mr Kansas.'

Macbeth was curious. This woman didn't know him from Bill Clinton and here she was letting her regular customers and the help go and him stay the night. Normal way of things, the woman being a widow, this would've been no big surprise, he had to admit. But she was a very *recent* widow. Also, she didn't seem to have even noticed what he looked like.

She looked tired. Drained. Eyes swollen. She dragged out a weary smile.

'Mr . . . Mungo. I've located Willie Wagstaff. He doesn't know where Moira is, but he says he doesn't mind talking to you if you don't keep him too long. He's at his girlfriend's – that's the Post Office. About a hundred yards up the street, same side.'

'Right. Uh, what did you . . . ?'

'I told him I thought you were all right. I hope you are.'

Macbeth said, 'Mrs Castle, what's going on here? Just why is everybody on edge? Who're all these people at the Rectory?'

'Ask Willie,' she said. 'And just so you know, he used to play the drums in Matt's band, so he's known Moira a long time. Do you want to borrow an umbrella?'

'Thanks, I have a slicker in back of the car. What if I'm late?'

'I'll still be up,' Lottie Castle said. 'Whatever time it is. Just hammer on the door.'

Lottie bolted the door behind him, top and bottom. Then she went through to the back door and secured that too.

She put on some coffee, partly to combat the rain noise with the warm pop-pop-pop of the percolator.

Earlier she'd pulled through a three-seater sofa from the living room that never got lived in. There was a duvet rolled up on the sofa.

Tonight's bed. Would have been, if she'd been alone in the pub. She'd put the American in Bedroom Three, the one Dic used when he was here. Soon as he'd left yesterday she'd changed the bedding, aired the room. It was just across the passage from her own.

Were bad dreams somehow stopped at source when you were no longer alone in the building?

That, of course, would depend on whether they *were* dreams.

On the refectory table was a local paper with the phone numbers of two estate agents ringed, the ones that specialized in commercial properties. Give that a try first, see if anyone was interested in a loss-making pub, before resorting to the domestic market.

Former village inn. Full of character. Dramatic rural location. Reduced for quick sale.

Well, did she have a choice? Was there any kind of alternative?

Lottie poured coffee, strong but with a little cream which she left unstirred, thin, white circles on the dark surface, because black coffee was apt to make her think of the Moss.

She left the cup steaming on the table, stood in the centre of the room for a moment with her sleeves pushed up and hands on her hips. 'Matt,' she said, 'you know I didn't want to come, but I didn't complain. I supported you. I gave up my lovely home.'

Strange, but all the time he was dying he never once allowed a discussion to develop about her future. But then, they never actually talked about him dying; just, occasionally, about him being ill. And yet he obviously wasn't afraid; he was just – amazing, when you thought about it – too preoccupied.

'You were always a selfish bastard, Matt,' she said.

Standing on the flags, hands on hips, giving him a lecture.

'Don't see why I should feel ashamed, do you?'

Feeling not so unhappy, because there was someone to wait up for.

She left on a wall-lamp in the kitchen, went through to the bar, leaving the door ajar. Switched the lights off one by one at the panel beside the mirror, leaving until last the disused brass gas-mantle which Matt had electrified.

The porch-light would stay on all night, gilding the rippling rain on the window. Lottie moved out into the darkened, stone-walled bar, collecting the ashtrays for emptying.

Wondering what Willie would make of the American with the silly name who'd driven down from Glasgow on the wettest Sunday of the year to find Moira Cairns.

Matt would have done that. Matt would have killed for Moira, and there was a time when she would have killed Moira because of it, but it didn't seem to matter any more.

When the gaslight came back on behind the bar, Lottie dropped all the ashtrays with a clatter of tin.

The gas-mantle was fitted with an electric bulb under the little gauzy knob thing and it looked fairly realistic. Or so she'd thought because she'd never seen the original gas.

Until now.

Oh, yes. This was gas, being softer, more diffused; she almost felt she could hear a hiss. Did they hiss? Or was that Matt?

Matt, whose face shone from the mirror behind the bar, enshrouded in gaslight.

Lottie stood with her back to the far stone wall. Her hands found her hips. Against which, untypically, they trembled.

She said, very quietly, 'Oh, no.'

Ernie Dawber knew that if he allowed himself to think about this, he would at once realize the fundamental insanity of the whole business.

He would see 'sense'.

But Bridelow folk had traditionally answered to laws unperceived elsewhere. Therefore it was not insane, and it required another kind of sense which could never be called 'common'.

So he simply didn't think about it at all, but did the usual things he would do at this time of night: cleaned his shoes, tidied his desk – leaving certain papers, however, in quite a prominent position.

Love letters, they were, from a woman magistrate in Glossop with whom Ernie had dallied a while during a bad patch in his marriage some thirty years ago. He'd decided not to burn them. After all, his wife had known and the woman was dead now; why not make one little bequest to the village gossips?

In the letter he was leaving for Hans, he'd written: 'Let the vultures in, why not? Let them pick over my bones – but discreetly. Let it be so that nothing of me exists except a name on the cover of *The Book of Bridelow*.'

Suddenly he felt absurdly happy. He was going on holiday.

He made himself a cup of tea and set out a plate of biscuits, wondering what archaeologists two thousand years hence might make of this.

. . . *the stomach yielded the digested remains of a compressed fruit not indigenous to the area but which may have constituted the filling for what nutritional documents of the period tell us were called 'fig rolls'.*

Ernie Dawber chuckled, ate two biscuits, drank his tea and sat back in his study chair, both feet on his footstool. He did not allow himself to contemplate the kind of knife which might be used to cut his throat or the type of cord employed for the garrotting or whether the blow to the back of his head would be delivered with a carpenter's mallet or a pickaxe handle.

But, feeling that he should at least be aware of what had happened on this particular day in the world he was leaving behind, he switched on the radio for the ten o'clock news.

Not such a bad time to be leaving. Chaos behind what used to be the Iron Curtain, more hatred between European nations than there'd been since the war. A psychopath killing little girls in the West Country.

But then, at the end of the national news, this:

Police who earlier today found the body of a man after a nine-hour search of the South Pennine moors say they've now discovered a woman's body, less than a mile away, in the burned-out wreckage of a car.

However, they say there appears to be no link between the two deaths. The first body, found in a quarry, has now

423

been formally identified as a 27-year-old farmer, Peter Samuel Davis.

The woman's body, not yet identified, was badly burned after the car, a BMW saloon, apparently left the road in wet conditions, plunged over a hundred feet into a valley bottom and burst into flames.

Ernie switched off the radio, his fingers numb, picked up his telephone and rang the Post Office.

Perhaps, before I return, something'll have happened this night to make you see the sense of it.

Sense, he thought, feeling cold all of a sudden. It's all gone beyond sense.

CHAPTER VI

Chrissie shrieked, 'Come on, come on, *come on!*' and beat with both fists on the door until it shook.

She was wearing a short mac said to be showerproof, but that depended what you meant by shower and she'd taken no more than two minutes to run like hell down the street and she was panting and absolutely bloody *soaked*.

When the door opened, Chrissie practically fell inside. 'God!' Shaking water out of her hair.

Expecting glasses chinking, laughter, maybe the clunk-ding of a one-armed bandit. Certainly not silence and dimness and a red-haired woman with lips drawn tautly back and pain-filled, frozen eyes.

'I'm sorry . . . I mean, this *is* a pub, isn't it? You're still open aren't you? I mean if you're not, I only want to use the phone. To call a taxi.'

'Box,' the woman said in a strangled whisper, as if she had a throat infection. 'Up the street.'

'Yes, I know, but I've no change, I . . . excuse me, but are you all right?'

'Really don't know. Better come in.'

'Thanks. God, what a night.'

'Car . . .' The woman cleared her throat. 'Excuse me. Your car broke down?'

'Actually, I had a row with my boss . . . boyfriend. Well, both. Although probably not either after tonight. I just got out of his car and walked off. Well, ran off, with this weather. I mean, isn't it awful? I'm making a puddle on your floor. Sorry.'

When she rubbed the rain out of her eyes, Chrissie saw she was indeed in what seemed to be a public bar. Nobody here, apart from her and the woman. 'Hey, I'm sorry. I really thought you were open and the door had just jammed or something and . . . You're really not well, are you?'

The woman had her back to the bar which was dark, only the shapes of bottles gleaming. 'Can you . . .' She gripped the edge of a table as if to steady her voice. 'Excuse me, but can you see a light-fitting, like an old gas-mantle, side of the bar?'

'Er . . . yes. Yes, I think so.'

'Is it on?'

'Well, no.' *Could she be blind?*

Then the woman just sort of folded in on herself as if afflicted by some awful stomach cramp or period pain, and Chrissie's brain dried out quickly. The Man I'the Moss. This was Matt Castle's wife. 'Hey,' she said, 'come on, sit yourself down. You on your own?'

Mrs Castle nodded and Chrissie led her to a corner seat opposite the bar and bent down to her. 'Make you a cuppa tea?'

She shook her head. 'I've got coffee. I'm OK. Honestly. Just a shock. I've had a shock.'

'Can I send for anybody? Relatives? A doctor?'

'Please,' Mrs Castle said. 'Just don't go, that's all. Come through. Phone's in the kitchen.' She got up and walked to the bar, and when she reached it a tremor seemed to pass through her and she pushed quickly through a door in the back wall.

Chrissie followed her into a big farmhouse-type kitchen, taking off her sodden mac and tossing it into a corner, useless thing. Underneath, she was wearing her navy-blue suit over a light blue silk blouse and pearls. Classy and understated for John Peveril Stanage's soirée, she thought with a sardonic shudder.

'Just go on talking,' Mrs Castle said. 'I'll be all right in a minute.' She was wearing a big, sloppy Icelandic-type sweater, but she still looked almost blue with cold and she hunched herself over the stove. Chrissie went and stood next to her and folded her arms.

'Well, this chap I was with, called Roger. Married, of course. I'm his bit on the side, except that's not as frivolous or irresponsible as it sounds, for either of us . . . well, it never is, is it, really?'

Mrs Castle was just looking into space. There was a full coffee cup on the table, but the coffee had gone cold, a whirl of cream almost solid on the top like piped icing.

'Roger's a prat,' Chrissie said. 'There's no getting around that. He's got a terrific opinion of himself and yet at the same time he's obviously a bit intimidated by his wife – she's a doctor. He wanted something else, less demanding. Which was me. One slightly shopsoiled divorcee off the bottom shelf – flattering, eh? High-powered wife, so he's looking for something cosy and undemanding and, worst of all, a bit cheap, you know what I mean?'

Mrs Castle nodded and struggled to smile, a little bit of colour in her cheeks. She was actually very attractive, good bones.

'I mean, you talk about undemanding, he didn't even have to go anywhere to pick me up. We work in the same office, I'm his secretary-cum-personal assistant – soon found out what *that* meant.'

Realizing she'd never talked to anybody about her and Roger before. Maybe this could turn out to be unexpectedly therapeutic.

'But at the end of the day,' Chrissie went on, 'his biggest love – I mean, listen to this – his biggest love, who's far more important to Roger than either me or his wife – is a squidgy little brown man who's been dead about two thousand years and came out of a bog. Now, can you . . . ? Ow!'

A kind of mad revulsion in her eyes, Mrs Castle had

suddenly swung round from the stove, grabbed hold of Chrissie's wrist and was digging her nails into it.

As if, Chrissie thought, pulling away, cold, to make sure I'm actually flesh and blood.

'I tell you what, Mrs Castle. I reckon you're the one who would benefit from talking about it.'

'Where are we going exactly?'

'Rog, mustn't be so *anxious*, m'friend! Mind holding the umbrella? Oops! Two hands, please, or you'll lose it.'

Huge golf umbrella; anything else would have been turned inside out by the sheer force of the downpour. Hard, vertical, brutal rain.

'There, that's stopped 'em from dithering.'

'I wasn't d—'

'Surrounded by *ditherers*! Don't worry, I like 'em. Shaw used to be a ditherer, didn't you, Shaw? Ditherer, stammerer, cowardly little bastard. Fixed it, though, didn't we? Fixed *everything*. Right, then, if we're all ready, in we go. Been here before, Rog?'

Darkness. Cold.

'Never. Pretty chilly, isn't it?'

'Chilly? This? Hear that, Tess? Poor Roger thinks it's chilly. This is Tess, my niece, aren't you, darling? And what shall we say about these others? What they are is a bunch of unfortunates befriended by the lass, she's *so . . . good . . . hearted.*'

'Uncle, please . . .'

'Apologies, my love. Yes, up the stairs is where we go. Onwards and upwards. Into the Attic of Death, do you like that?'

'Not really.'

'Relax, relax. Relax*ation*. The key to everything, Shaw knows that, don't you, m'boy? Up again. Ought to be a lift, be totally cream-crackered, time we get there. How you feeling now, Rog?'

'A touch light-headed, now, actually. How many drinks did I have, I can't . . .'

'Just the one, Roger, just the one. Famous for our cocktails, aren't we, Tess?'

'What's that smell?'

'New one on you, is it, Rog? What a terribly sheltered life you must have had, m'boy.'

'Oh, *dear God*.'

'Ah, now, let's not bring *that* chap into it, Roger.'

'I'm going to be sick.'

'No you're not, you're going to get used to it. No time at all. Now relax, the dead can't harm you.'

Don't look at it, don't look at it, don't . . . Oh, Lord, what's happening to my head?

'No, actually, I'm lying again. That's a common myth perpetuated by morticians. You're quite right, the dead can *indeed* harm you, in the most unexpected ways. The dead can harm you *horribly*.'

Laughter. Laughter all around.

By the time Macbeth walked into the room behind the Post Office the sense of there being something deeply wrong in this rain-beaten village – *everybody seems to be on edge tonight* – had become so real it was starting to affect the air; the atmosphere itself seemed thin and worn and stretched tight like plastic film, and faces were pressed up against it trying to breathe.

Two faces. One chubby and female that ought to have looked healthy and a small, male face under a brown fringe, a face out of *Wind in the Willows* or somesuch.

Both faces pressed up against the tight air of a small and crowded room full of flower pictures, flower fabrics and flowers.

Macbeth finding it hard to introduce himself. 'I, uh . . .' Harder still to explain what he was doing here. 'Mrs Castle – Lottie, right? – thought maybe you could tell me where I could find a . . . a friend of mine.'

'Aye,' the little guy said. 'Look, can I ask you, how close were you to Moira, lad?' A slow, kindly voice, but Macbeth felt the damp behind it.

'I guess I'd like to be closer,' he said frankly.

Rain from his black slicker dripping to the floral carpet.

Rain making deltas on the window and small pools on the sill.

Rain coming down the chimney and fizzing on the coalfire.

And yet all the flowers in the room – on the walls, in the pictures, on the woman's dress – contriving to look parched and dead.

The woman said bleakly, 'Since Willie spoke to Lottie we've had a phone call.'

'Moira?'

The woman's wise eyes were heavy with a controlled kind of sorrow.

A hammer inside Macbeth's brain beat out *no, no, no*.

'Sit down, lad,' the little mousy guy said, pulling a chair out from under a gate-legged mahogany dining table. On the table was a bottle of whisky, its seal newly broken; beside it, two glasses.

'Well, of course I don't believe in it, you see, Chrissie. I never have. All right, maybe it's not a question of not believing. I mean, is there a name for a person who just simply *doesn't want to know?*'

Chrissie warmed both hands around her coffee cup. 'For that matter, is there a name for a man who professes to be above all that superstitious nonsense but is more than happy to let it cure his impotence, and then he can go back to not believing in it again?'

'I think "bloody hypocrite" would be one way of putting it,' Lottie said. 'But . . .'

'But tonight . . . God, am I really saying this? Tonight you saw the ghost of your husband.' Chrissie shuddered; *it really did go all the way up your spine*. 'Wasn't going to use that word. Never liked it.'

'Ghost?'

'What does it mean, Lottie? Was he really there? I mean his . . . ?'

'Spirit? Was his spirit there?' Lottie's voice rose, discordant like a cracked bell. 'Yes. I think it was. And crushed. His spirit crushed.'

She thrust a fist to her mouth, swallowing a sob, chewing her knuckles.

'Let it come,' Chrissie said, and Lottie wept some hot, frightened tears. 'Yes, he *was* a man of spirit, always . . . endless enthusiasm for things, what first attracted me. But there's a negative side to enthusiasm, isn't there?'

'Ob . . . session?'

Lottie sniffed. 'First there was the woman. Moira. Not only beautiful, but young and – worst of all, worst of *all*, Chrissie – talented. The thing I couldn't give him. Support, yes. But inspiration . . . ?'

'You're beautiful too,' Chrissie said ineffectually.

'Thanks,' Lottie said. 'Was. Maybe. In the right light. Doesn't mean a lot on its own, though, does it? Don't get me wrong, it never . . . *flowered*, this thing over Moira. They never actually *did it*. I know that now. But I think that's worse in a way, don't you? I mean, the longing goes on, doesn't it? The wondering what it *might* have been. Maybe I should have let him work it out, but I gave him an ultimatum: her or me . . . and his son. Dic. He'd have lost Dic, too. It coincided, all this, you see, with an offer she got to join another band. He made her take it. It was "the right thing to do".'

'Martyrdom,' Chrissie said.

'He didn't get over her exactly. He just went in search of a new obsession and ended up reviving an old one. Which was coming back to Bridelow. Not my idea of heaven on earth.'

'Not tonight anyway,' Chrissie said, looking over to the window. It was like staring into a dark fishtank.

'Naturally, I encouraged him. Sent him up here at weekends with Dic and a picnic lunch. Safe enough – I just didn't think it would ever happen. Then they found that blasted bog body and he just went nuts over it. Kept going to see the damn thing, like visiting a relative in hospital or prison or somewhere. Next thing, he hears the brewery's been flogged off and this place is on the market, and I was just carried along, like a whirlwind picks you up and you come down somewhere else you never wanted to be.'

Lottie stopped, as if realizing there was little more to be said. 'And then he got ill and died.'

She nodded at the door to the bar. 'That gas-mantle. He worked for hours on it. Place was a tip, plastering needed doing, but all he was bothered about was his precious gas-mantle. Bit of atmosphere. Matt all over: tunnel vision.'

'I read once . . .' Chrissie hesitated. 'An article in some magazine at the dentist's. This chap said there were certain things they came back to. Gh . . . dead people . . . Christ, that sounds even worse. Anyway, things they'd been attracted to in life.'

'Aye. Makes sense he'd come back to his bloody gaslight, rather than me.'

'I didn't mean it that way. Sort of landmark for them to home in on. Like a light in the fog. You could always have it taken down.'

'He'd go daft. He'd hold it against me for ever.'

'What did he look like? His old self, or what?'

'He looked terrible.' Lottie started to cry again. Why can't you ever learn to button it, kid? Chrissie told herself.

'It was very misty,' Lottie said through a crumpled handkerchief. 'He kept fading and then . . . like a bad TV picture in the old days, remember? As if – I suppose your chap was right – as if he was trying to hold on to his old gas-mantle, for comfort, and something was trying to pull him back.'

'Back where?'

'Into the darkness behind the mirror. He couldn't see me, I'm sure he couldn't *see* me at all. Am I going mad, Chrissie?'

'No more than any of us. Do you want me to stay with you tonight? I've nowhere else to go.'

Lottie's hands clutched each other, began to vibrate. She's wringing her hands, Chrissie thought. I've never seen anybody actually wring their hands before.

'The truth is,' Lottie said, 'I hated him by the end. There was nothing *left* but the negative side. No enthusiasm, *only* obsession. He was, when it comes down to it, a very nasty man.'

Lottie stared into her empty coffee cup as if trying to read a message in the grains. 'But he was also dying, you see, and you aren't allowed to hate dying people, especially if the nastiness is to some extent out of character and therefore, you think, must be connected with the dying.'

Chrissie lit another cigarette. 'When my mother was dying, towards the end, I wanted it to be over. For her sake. But, if I'm honest, partly for my sake too.'

'I don't think we're talking about the same thing, luv. Christ almighty . . .' Lottie covered her ears – '. . . isn't this bloody rain *ever* going to stop?'

'Listen to me,' Chrissie said. 'When you thought . . . when you saw this . . . when he was in the mirror, tonight . . . did you hate him then?'

'No. I felt sorry for him. Don't get me wrong, I was very frightened, but at the bottom of that there was a pity. It was the gas-mantle. Putting that together, wiring it up, was about the only innocent, gentle thing he did here. I was irritated at the time, but when I look back . . . It's the only thing makes me want to cry for him.'

Chrissie stood up. 'I don't know why, but I think we should put it on. The light, I mean. The gas thing.'

'Why?'

'Because if that represents the nice, harmless side of him, perhaps you should show him you recognize that. I don't know, maybe it's stupid. But perhaps he wants your forgiveness, perhaps he wants to know you remember that side of him. The gentle side. So maybe, if you gave him a sign that you understood, then he . . . he'd be . . . you know . . . at peace. Isn't that what they say?'

'Who?'

Chrissie shrugged. 'Old wives, I suppose.'

'Old mothers in this village. OK.' Lottie came wearily to her feet. 'Let's try it.'

'Might make you feel better.'

'Might, at that.'

They went through to the darkened bar and Chrissie lifted the flap and went round to the customers' side, so they were standing either side of the brass mantle. In the arrow of light from the kitchen, she could see it was on a hinged base screwed into the wooden frame of the bar and projecting about eighteen inches. Behind it, on Lottie's side, was the mirror in a Victorian mahogany frame. Chrissie made herself gaze into the mirror and saw only her own dim reflection, looking rather pale and solemn.

'Perhaps we should say a prayer, Lottie.'

'No, thanks,' Lottie said.

'Well, at least think of him as you press the switch. Think of the good times.'

'My memory isn't what it was,' said Lottie. 'No, I'm sorry. You're doing your best. All right. Matt, listen, if you can hear me . . .'

At the end of the gas-mantle a feeble glow appeared.

'Switch it off a second, Lottie, let's get this right.'

'I didn't . . .' Lottie said, in a voice which rose in pitch until it cracked, '. . . switch it on.'

'Merciful God,' Chrissie pulled from somewhere in her past, 'please . . .'

The small light at once flared to a dazzling, magnesium white. Huge shadows reared. Lottie screamed once and backed off into the kitchen.

When the bulb exploded, with a crack like snapping bone, Chrissie found herself at the far end of the bar trying to hug the stone wall.

CHAPTER VII

'Listen,' Macbeth said, clutching Milly's plump arm, 'let me call the cops. Maybe it wasn't her car.'

'Don't make it worse, lad,' Willie Wagstaff said, his eyes hollowed out with grief. 'I've already been on to um. I said me wife were out in a BMW and I were worried sick after hearing the news. I didn't want to get involved in identification or owt, so in the end I said the wife's car were red and they said this one was grey – *had* been grey – and give me the registration, and I went off, sounding relieved. Relieved. Jesus.'

'I don't understand.' Macbeth stared desperately around the room. 'These things don't happen. I just don't fucking *understand*.'

'They do happen,' Willie said hopelessly.

'Especially here.' Milly was looking hard into the fire. 'Especially now.'

'Shurrup,' said Willie gruffly. 'How far you come, lad?'

'Glasgow.' The One Big Thing, he thought. God damn. And closed his eyes against the pain.

'She was special,' Willie said. 'We all knew that.'

'Yeah,' he whispered.

'Special like your mother,' Milly said. 'I think we knew that too. And now they're both dead.'

'Leave it, luv. It's coincidence.'

'Is it?'

Macbeth opened his eyes. Something badly wrong here, but did he care? And what could he do anyway? One week. Before that, Moira Cairns had been a face on an old album cover.

One week. A chance meeting, an inexplicable cascade of bones, a talk on the terrace in the aftermath.

There'd be another album now. The Best of Moira Cairns. In memoriam. Even if he'd never met her, he'd be grieving. In one week, she'd become the core of his existence – a woman whose last glance at him had said, fuck off.

'There was a guy,' he heard himself saying, 'who meant her harm.'

Donald told me the dogs disliked this man intensely. On sight.

Willie Wagstaff and his girlfriend were both staring at him.

'The Duchess wanted me to look out for her, you know? The Duchess said wherever she went she'd be . . . touched with madness.'

'Who's the Duchess?' Willie asked. Macbeth noticed that the fingers of Willie's left hand had struck up a rhythm on the side of his knee. He seemed unaware of it.

Macbeth said, 'Her mother.'

'The gypsy?'

Macbeth nodded. He looked out of the window. A big van with a blue beacon and an illuminated sign had stopped down the street. The sign said, Ambulance. 'Is this rain never gonna ease off? Is it normal?'

'No,' Milly said. 'It's not normal. Who was the man? You said there was a man. Who . . . meant her harm.'

Macbeth's mind slipped out of gear for a moment. He panicked, clutched at the air.

The air in the room, so dense. The rain bombarding the roof. The Duchess said, *If there was a problem and you were to deal with it, she need never know, need she?*

And how badly he'd wanted to deal with it and *wanted* her to know, and now it was too late to deal with it and, sure, she would never know.

'John Peveril Stanage,' he said.

And the other two people in the room slowly turned and looked at each other, and Willie blanched.

The fingers of both hands were slamming into his knees and this time he *was* aware of it but seemed unable to stop it.

When the ambulance arrived at the chip shop for Maurice Winstanley, both Maurice and his wife, Dee, were in a state bordering on hysteria.

'I knew summat like this'd happen. I never wanted to open, me,' Dee shrilled, a skinny little woman – how could you work in a chip shop and be that thin? It fascinated one of the ambulancemen for a couple of seconds until he saw how badly burned Maurice was.

They had to treat his arm best they could, but there wasn't a whole lot they could do on the spot, what with Maurice gawping around and then kind of giggling with pain, and his wife going on and on like a budgie on amphetamines.

'I says to him, Who's going to come out for chips, night like this? He says, What about all them young people up at t'church, they'll be starving before t'night's through. I says, All right, I says, you want to do it, you can do it on your own.'

The ambulanceman had fancied a bag of chips himself, specially after that drive over the hills and across the Moss: gruesome – he'd been driving and felt sure he could see the bloody peat rising and sucking; put one wheel in there you'd have had it.

'All right, Mr Winstanley, if we can get you out this way . . .'

'Where's your stretcher, then?'

'He can walk, can't he, Mrs Winstanley? I was going to say, we need to get him in as quick as we can. He might need to go to the burns unit.'

But chips would never be the same again. How gut-churning an appetizing smell like that could become when, on top of battered cod and mushy peas, there was the subtle essence of frazzled flesh, the result of Maurice Winstanley's right arm blistering and bubbling in the fryer.

'Lucky you haven't got a heart attack case, as well,' Dee said. 'He let out such a shriek.'

'I'm not surprised, luv. Any of us'd've gone through the roof.'

'Oh, this were *before* he stuck his arm in t'fat. I says, Now, what's up, I says. And he turns round, white as a sheet, I says, Whatever have you done? And *then* he does it. Thirty years frying and he shoves his arm in. I don't think he knew what he were doing at all.'

In the ambulance, racing back across the Moss, Maurice shivered and shook a lot, a red blanket round him, his arm in about half a mile of bandage. 'Never believe me, lad, she never will. I wouldn't believe me.'

'Don't matter how long you've been at it, Mr Winstanley, you can always have an accident.'

'No, not that.' Now Maurice *looked* like a chip shop proprietor. Maurice was a fat man. Maurice's big cheeks had that high-cholesterol glow about them and there were black, smoky rings around his eyes.

'She had to believe that, naturally,' Maurice said. 'She seen it happen. Fact it were only t'bloody agony of it brought me round, see, and I couldn't even feel that at first. I were looking at it a good two seconds. I thought, what's that pink thing in t'bloody fat?'

'Don't think about it, Mr Winstanley. We'll not be long now. What d'you reckon to United's chances, then?'

'I don't want to talk about *United*, lad! I hate bloody soccer. Listen, no, it weren't *that* she'll not believe, I've allus been a clumsy bugger. No, see, what it were as caused it in t'first place, I'd just seen summat as frickened life outer me. Froze me to t'spot, you know? Numb, I were. Numb.'

'Sounds like my mother-in-law.'

'Oh, Christ,' said Maurice Winstanley, subsiding into his pain. 'What's the bloody use?'

Even though Deirdre Winstanley opened all the windows into the rain, the smell of fried skin wouldn't go away; only seemed to get stronger.

When she opened the door, Susan Manifold, having seen the ambulance, ran across the street through the torrent, asking Dee what was wrong, could she help.

'His own fault,' Dee said. 'Silly bugger. Thirty years, I don't know.'

'Will he be all right?'

'Will any of us?'

'I'm sorry?' Susan Manifold stepped inside the chip shop, to escape the wet, wrinkling her nose at the smell.

'Well, look at it.' Dee gestured at the water, now level over the cobbles and the drains weren't taking it. She seemed more worried about that than Maurice's injury, or perhaps she was looking for something to take her mind off it.

'Will it flood?' Susan asked.

'Never has before, but there's always a first time. Look at them drains. Is there nowt you can do?'

'I'm not a plumber,' said Susan.

'No,' said Dee. 'But you're a Mother.'

'Oh, come on!' Susan flicked back her ash-blonde fringe. 'We can't alter the weather.'

'Could've, once. Not you, maybe, Susan. Happen before your time.'

'Old wives' tale,' Susan said carelessly, and the full horror of what she'd said came back at her like a slap in the mouth. She was betraying Milly Gill and the memory of Ma Wagstaff. But, God help her, *Mother* help her, she had no belief in it any more.

Upset, she walked back across the drowned cobbles. Frank

wasn't home yet from the pub. When he did arrive he'd be drunk and nasty. Another problem the Mothers were supposed to be able to deal with.

Dee Winstanley slammed the door. That was stupid, what she'd said. Stupid what Susan had replied. Stupid what Maurice had done. Stupid to have lived behind a stinking chip shop for thirty years.

Stupid, stupid, stupid.

And the smell wouldn't go away; the layer of fat, from fish and pies and peas and fried human skin, hung from the ceiling like a dirty curtain, and the fluorescent tubelight was a bar of grease.

Dee threw up the flap, stumbled behind the counter, slammed down the chromium lid on a frier full of flabby chips congealing together like a heap of discarded yellow rubber gloves.

Couldn't clean that tonight. Just couldn't.

'Cod and six pennorth o' chips. Please.'

The nerve of some people. 'We're closed,' Dee yelled into the thick air around the high counter.

'. . . and six pennorth o' chips.'

Dee sighed. Some people still thought it was funny to demand six pennorth o' chips, same as what they'd asked for in old money when they were kids.

'We've had to close early,' she explained patiently. 'Maurice's had an accident. Gone to hospital. All the chips are ruined.'

She peered through the shimmering grease at this persistent customer. Recognized the voice straight away, just couldn't put a name to it.

'. . . pennorth o' chips. Please.'

The customer clambered through the lardy light and she heard the clatter of coins on the glass counter.

'You deaf or summat, Matt? I can't serve you. It's Maurice . . . they've taken Maurice off in th'ambulance. He's had a . . .'

'. . . and six pennorth . . .'

*

At first there was no sound in the crowded, flowery sitting room, except for the endlessly percussive weather and Willie Wagstaff's fingers on his jeans picking up the same rapid rhythm.

'John Peveril Stanage,' Macbeth repeated in a stronger voice, because the name'd had the same effect as throwing three aces into a poker game.

Doing this for the Duchess.

Willie said, 'Never heard of him,' about a second too late to be convincing, and Macbeth, suddenly furious, was halfway out of his chair when there were four hollow knocks at the front door, all the more audible for being way out of synch with Willie's fingers and the rain.

'Mr Dawber,' Milly Gill said tonelessly, but made no move to answer the door.

CHAPTER VIII

Milly Gill half rose and then sat down again and looked at Willie and then at Mungo Macbeth.

'I'm sorry, Mr Macbeth. Sorry to've given you such awful news. But . . .' Spreading her hands: what else can I do?

Telling him to get the hell out in other words.

Macbeth stood up but made no move toward the door. 'I don't think so,' he said.

The hollow knocking came again, a little faster this time, a little closer to the tempo of Wagstaff's restless fingers.

'Why d'you do that?' Macbeth said, in no mood for tact. 'With your fingers.'

Willie looked non-plussed, like nobody ever asked him that before.

'He has a problem with his nerves,' Milly Gill said hastily. 'If you don't mind, Mr Macbeth, there's a gentleman come to see us.'

So they know who it is. Knocking comes at the door, latish, and they know what it's about before they open up.

439

'Sure,' Macbeth said. 'Thanks for your time.' Maybe he *should* go. Cancel his room at the inn, drive out of here, head back north. Maybe organize a flight home. And call on the Duchess? Could he ever face the Duchess again?

He nodded at Willie Wagstaff, followed Milly Gill to the door.

'Good luck,' he said, not sure why he said that.

And then something told him to turn around, and he found Willie on his feet, a whole series of expressions chasing each other across the little guy's face like videotape on fast-forward.

'Look.' Willie was clasping both hands between his legs like a man who badly needed to use the john. 'It's not nerves. It's . . .'

'Hey.' The big woman pulled back her hand from the door catch. 'A few minutes ago you were telling *me* to shut up.'

'I know, lass, but happen we've kept quiet too bloody long. This . . . Moira. Dead. Finished me, that has. Too many accidents. Going right back to that lad who fell off top of the brewery. Too much bad luck. And when I hear Jack's name . . . Hang on a minute, lad. Milly, let Ernie Dawber in.'

Milly said, 'If it's Jack – which I . . .' She swallowed. 'If it is, we've got to sort it out for ourselves.'

'Oh, aye. Like we've sorted everything else out. *Let him in.*'

This Ernie Dawber was a short, stout, dignified-looking elderly guy in a long raincoat and a hat. He didn't look pleased at being kept waiting in the rain. He looked even less pleased to see Macbeth.

'This bloke's a friend of Moira's,' Willie Wagstaff explained.

'Mungo Macbeth.'

Old guy's handshake was firm. Eyes pretty damn shrewd. 'My condolences,' he said. 'I'm sorry.'

'Mr Dawber,' Willie said, 'I'll not mess about. This lad – Mungo – reckons Moira . . .' He took a breath. 'He reckons there's a connection with Jack. With . . . John Peveril Stanage.'

Willie's voice was so thick with loathing that Macbeth had to step back.

'Not possible,' Ernie Dawber said. 'I know what you're saying, but it's not possible.'

'No?' said Willie.

'He was banished, Willie. In the fullest sense. Forty-odd years ago. In all that time he's never once tried to come back. And if your ma was here now she'd go mad at you for even saying his name.'

'Aye. But she's not. She's dead.' Willie's voice hardened. 'Suddenly. Under very questionable circumstances.'

Ernie Dawber shook his head. 'You're clutching at straws.'

Milly Gill said, 'Leave it, Willie. We've problems enough. Jack couldn't set foot in this village . . .'

'While Ma was alive!' Willie shouted.

'He's a rich man now, Willie, he's got everything he needs. And like Mr Dawber says, he's never once tried to get back in. Why should he?'

'Aye,' said Willie. 'Why should anybody want owt to do wi' Bridelow? Why's Bridelow suddenly important? Why's it on everybody's lips when things here've never been so depressed? Why? – Mr Dawber'll tell you, he's got the same disease.'

'Willie, stop it off!'

Willie brought a hand down on the gateleg table with a crack. 'Bogman fever! That little bastard's contagious. Look at Matt, he got too close for his own sanity. How close did you get, Mr Dawber, that you want to die for it as well? Did you ever think it'd got at *your* mind . . . staid, cautious old Ernie Dawber, man of letters?' He turned away. 'Ernie Dawber, human sacrifice. Don't make me laugh!'

'Stop it!' Milly Gill advanced on Willie like she was figuring to pull him apart. 'How dare you, little man? There's things we *never* can laugh at. Maybe something's turned *your* mind.'

'Jesus.' Macbeth stepped between them. 'Bogman fever? Human sacrifice? What kinda shit *is* this? Guy in the bar said everybody was on edge tonight, I figured he was making small-talk. Back off, huh?'

Removing his hat, Ernie Dawber stepped further into the room, leaving the door ajar behind him. No visible ease-up in the rain. 'Could I ask you, Mr . . .'

'Macbeth. Like the evil Scottish King, had all his buddies iced.'

'That's as maybe,' Ernie Dawber said. 'But could I ask you, sir, what precisely is your interest here?'

'I got nothing to hide.' Macbeth let his arms fall to his sides. 'I fell in love with a woman.'

The noise from outside was like Niagara.

'And now she's dead,' Macbeth said. 'Some bastard's keeping secrets about that, maybe it's time for me to research a few ancestral vices, yeah?'

He shifted uncomfortably. Starting to sound like some steep-jawed asshole out of one of his own TV shows.

'Perhaps,' said Ernie Dawber, 'we should all calm down and discuss this. And for what it's worth – history being my subject – despite the Bard's best efforts to convince us otherwise, Macbeth was actually quite a stable monarch.'

'Ernie . . .' Macbeth pulled out a chair. 'I wasn't so pissed about this whole thing, I could maybe get to like you.' He sat. 'Now. Somebody gonna tell me about John Peveril Stanage?'

Only Milly Gill still looked defiant. She folded her arms, pushed the door shut with her ass.

'Oh, hell, tell him, Willie,' Ernie Dawber said.

It had been novelty value, and now it was wearing off.

Chris wasn't stupid; he wasn't blind, being born-again to God didn't blind you to common sense.

Most of them were young. They sought, Chris conceded, a vibrancy and an excitement in religion which the Church had failed to give them. They found it at outdoor rallies, in marquees and packed rooms that were more like dancehalls. And now they were back where, for many of them, it had begun first time around in the stoneclad starkness of an old-fashioned church. To defend it, Joel had told them. Against evil. But an evil they could not see, nor comprehend.

And Chris, an elder of the Church of the Angels of the New Advent, was asking himself: is this man, this figure of almost prophet-like glamour, this embodiment of the biblically angelic, is this man *entirely sane*?

'Joel.' Chris shambled over to the lectern, a lean, bearded man in a lumberjack shirt. 'Er, how many hours has it been exactly?'

'Are you counting, Chris?'

'No, but . . . I know the heat's on in here, but it's still pretty cold. Bit of an ordeal for some of these kids.'

'You're saying their faith isn't strong enough?'

Like the PE teacher he used to be, Chris thought. Loftily disdainful of youngsters shivering on a wintry playing field.

'Of course not,' Chris said. 'But don't you think . . . don't you think this church is *clean* now?'

'This thing is deep-seated, Chris.' Joel clutched at the lectern for strength, the muscles tautening in his face. 'You think you can eradicate centuries of evil in a few hours?'

He looked down at the wooden pedestal lectern, as if seeing it for the first time, and then sprang back. 'Look! Look at this!'

The lectern was supporting a black-bound Bible, open across spread wings of carved oak.

'It's an eagle,' Chris said. 'Lots of them are eagles.'

'This is not an eagle.' Joel's hands retracted as if the lectern were coated with acid. 'Look.'

Chris didn't understand.

'An owl is a pagan bird,' Joel intoned calmly, like a bomb-disposal expert identifying a device. 'Step away from it. Go down and open the door.' He closed his eyes, breathed a brief, intense prayer for protection, gently detached the Bible, carried it to a choir stall.

And then hefted the lectern in both arms, as though uprooting a young tree.

'Door!' Joel gasped.

Feeling less than certain about this, Chris preceded him down the aisle. Hesitantly, he held open the church door and then the porch door until Joel had staggered out and, with an animal grunt, hurled the lectern far into the rainy tumult of the night.

They heard it crash against a tombstone.

'Filthy conditions.' Joel stumbled back into the church, slapping at his surplice, a strange, fixed look on his face. 'Is this natural, all this rain? Is it *natural*, Chris?'

'It's only rain, Joel.'

'You're not seeing this, Chris, are you? You're not seeing it at all.'

All heads were turned towards him as he walked back up the aisle. Chris sensed an element of uncertainty among their devotion. Perhaps Joel was slightly aware of it too, for he raised his eyes to the altar. 'Oh Lord, give them a sign. Give them proof!'

He stood where the lectern had been, his coronet of curls looking dull, as if tarnished by the rain. Chris found himself praying silently for deliverance from what was becoming a nightmare.

'It was . . .' Joel spread his big hands helplessly the width of the aisle, '. . . evil. Don't you see? It wasn't an eagle, it was an *owl*. A symbol of what *they* would call "ancient wisdom". It was a *satanic artefact*. Can't you understand? It had to be removed.'

'Praise God,' someone called out, but only once and rather feebly.

A man in a white T-shirt drifted up to Joel as if to congratulate him, shake him by the hand. When Joel opened his arms to embrace his brother, he felt a blast of cold air against his chest.

Puzzled, he looked down and saw that his pectoral cross was missing. Must have become hooked around the lectern, and he'd thrown it out of the door as well. He felt angry with himself. Now he had to *visualize* the cross. But he saw his brother Angel's open arms and he smiled.

His brother was smiling back. His brother's eyes were brown and swirling like beer-dregs in a glass.

'Thank you,' Joel said. 'Thank you for your support. Thank you for your faith.'

Couldn't recall the name. But he knew the face, although he'd seen it only once before.

'Joel,' Chris said, 'you OK?'

Seen the face by lamplight and edged with lace in a violated coffin.

Joel's eyes bulged. He felt his jaw tightening, his lips

shrinking back over his teeth, his throat expanding under pressure of a scream.

But he didn't scream. He would *not* scream. Instead, he stretched out his arms and grasped his terror to his bosom.

'Joel!' A voice behind him. Chris? But so far away, too far away, a dimension away from death's cold capsule in which Joel embraced a column of writhing darkness comprised of a thousand wriggling, frigid worms.

'Begone.' But it came out breathless, thin and whingeing, from between his clenched teeth.

He tried to project the missing pectoral cross in front of him, a cross of white fire.

Gasping, 'In the name . . . name of God.' As the cold worms began to glide inside his vestments and to feed upon him, to devour his faith. 'In God's name . . . *begone*!'

'Joel, stop it.' Hands either side of him, clutching at his arms.

The cross of fire had become a cross of ice.

Joel roared like a bull.

They were pinioning his arms while the cold worms sucked at his soul. His own brothers in God offering him as sustenance for the voracious dead.

'*Aaaaargh!*'

A boiling strength erupted in his chest.

In the centre of the silence, the black bag was brought to the woman.

From the bag, a thick, dark stole uncoiling. A slender vein of silver or white.

Winding it around her hands like flax and holding it up and showing it to the corpse, twisting it in the candlelight.

Hair. Human hair, two feet of it, three, bound together, with a strip of grey-white hair rippling through it.

The woman's hands moving inside the tent of hair with a certain rhythmical fluidity, as the pipes moaned, an aching lament. The watchers mumbling and, out of this, a single voice rising, a pale ribbon of a voice singing out, '*I conjure thee.*'

And winding back into the mumbling with the winding of the hair.

'He's coming.

He's coming and he's strong.'

Up against the vestry wall, four of the men around him so he couldn't break away, he wailed in despair, 'Whose side are you *on*?'

Blood in the aisle. One man sitting up on the flags, head in his hands, semi-concussed.

Chris pressing a tissue to a burst lip. 'Joel, it's all gone wrong. You're seriously scaring people. Some of the women want to leave, get out of here.'

'They can't. They can't go out there now. Not safe, do you not see?'

'Joel, I'm sorry, they're saying it's probably safer out there than it is here with . . . with you.'

'Lock and bar the doors. Go on. Do it now. LOCK AND BAR THE DOORS!'

'Joel, please, they're saying *you* . . . All that screaming and wrestling with . . .'

'With evil! The infested dead!'

'. . . with yourself, Joel! Oh, my God, this is awful. Somebody wipe his mouth.'

'Where *is* he?'

Joel flailed, but they held him.

'Where *is* he? The spirit. Was he expelled? *Tell* me.'

'Let's go back to the Rectory, shall we? Have a cup of coffee? Come back later. When we've all, you know, calmed down.'

'What's happened to your face?'

'You hit me, Joel.'

'No.'

'Yes! You were like a man poss . . . We couldn't hold you. Please, Joel. You've been under a lot of stress.'

'. . . fighting it . . . fighting for our souls. Stinking of the grave . . . filthy womancunt . . . let me . . .'

'Come on. You're scaring people. Let's get some air. Please.'

'Matt Castle. Spirit of Matt Castle. Soiled. *Soiled spirit.*'

'Joel, Matt Castle's dead . . .'

'And was *here!*'

'Look, Declan's hurt. I think he hit his head. He needs a doctor. Please.'

'Illusion. Temptation. They *want* you to open the doors and let them in. If you don't do it of your own free will, they'll get inside you, fill you up with worms, make you think things that aren't true. Let me go, I command you to let me go.'

'Let him go.'

'Chris?'

'Just let him go. We can't hold him all night.'

'Matt Castle. Its face was Matt Castle's. But I looked into its eyes and its eyes were the eyes of Satan.'

'Yes. Yes, but it's gone now, Joel. I swear to you it's gone. You . . . you defeated it. You were more powerful. You . . . you threw it to the ground and it . . . sort of disintegrated.'

'Ah.'

'Yes, we saw it. We did. Didn't we, Richard? So, Joel, come back to the Rectory, OK? You need a coffee. And a lie down. After your exertions. After your . . . Oh God, help me . . .'

'. . . was it wearing?'

'. . . your struggle.'

'What was it *wearing*?'

'I . . . Well, it wasn't . . . I mean, too clear. Not from where we were standing. A . . . a shroud, was it? And glowing. Sort of glowing?'

Joel felt his face explode. *'Liars!'*

His chest swelled, arms thrashed. One man was thrown across the vestry like a doll, spinning dizzily around until the stone wall slapped into his nose; they heard him squeak and a quick crack of bone, and then Joel's white surplice was blotting up bullets of blood.

'Come on! Let's get out now. Don't go near him.'

'What about Martin?'

'Pick him up, come *on*. Oh, my God. It's all right. It's all *right*! Somebody stop them *screaming*.'

Joel heard scrambling and scuffling, stifled shouts and squawks and screams, bolts being thrown, the soulless slashing of the rain and a shrilling from inside of him, something squealing to be free.

At first he wouldn't move, paralysed with dread. Then he began to laugh. It was only the mobile phone at the leather belt around his cassock.

He pulled it out and inspected it. A deep fissure ran from the earpiece to the push-buttons. He had difficulty dragging out the aerial because its housing was bent.

The phone went on bleeping at him.

He tried to push the 'send' button, but it wouldn't go in. Joel became irrationally enraged with the phone and began to beat it against the wall. Went on beating it when the bleeps stopped and a tinny little faraway voice was calling out, '*Mr Beard.*'

Would have continued until it smashed to pieces in his hand, had he not recognized the voice.

'*Mr Beard, can you hear me?*'

'Yes.'

'*Are you all right, Mr Beard?*'

'They've all gone.'

'*Who?*'

'The Angels.' He giggled. 'The Angels have flown.'

'*As angels are apt to do. You won't run away from this, will you?*'

'Never!'

'*Mr Beard, I told you once – do you remember? – about the Devil's light. How no one could cross the Moss at night except for those for whom the Devil lit the way.*'

'Yes. I remember. Isn't it time you told me who you were?'

'*I'll do better than that, Mr Beard. I'll meet you.*'

'When? Where?'

'*Tonight. Stay in the church. Be alone.*'

'No choice, have I? And yet I know . . .'

'*You could always run away from it.*' Teasing.

'I'll never do that. I'm not afraid, you know. I . . . tonight I've embraced evil and I know . . . I know that I am never totally alone.'

'*Well said, m'boy. Together we'll put out the Devil's light.*'

'Thank you,' Joel said. 'Nobody else believes in me. Thank you. Thank you for everything.'

He started to weep with the joy of the sure knowledge that he was not alone.

PART NINE

FEAST OF THE DEAD

From *Dawber's* Secret *Book of Bridelow* (unpublished):

SAMHAIN. (i)

IN BRIDELOW, NEW YEAR is celebrated twice. Once in late
February, at Candlemas, the feast of Brigid (and St Bride),
when we look forward to the first signs of Spring. And also,
of course, at Samhain – now sadly discredited as Hallowe'en
– the Feast of the Dead.

This remains the most mysterious of Celtic festivals, a
time when we remember the departed and the tradition
bequeathed to us. A time, also, when the dead may be
consulted, although such practices have been actively dis-
couraged because of the inherent danger to the health and
sanity of the living.

CHAPTER I

It was bad, what he learned about John Peveril Stanage. So bad it made Macbeth wonder how the hell the creep had ever gotten published as a writer for children without some kind of public outcry. And yet he felt there was something crucial they weren't telling him, something they were edging around.

'It was, I believe, an incident with the cats that was the first indication,' Ernie Dawber was saying. 'Because that was the first direct attack on Ma . . . not your ma, Willie, the old Ma.'

'Bob and Jim,' Willie said sadly. 'They was always called Bob and Jim.'

Very slowly Macbeth had been building up an image of this village as somewhere arguably more Celtic, in the ethnic and religious sense, than any known area of Scotland, Wales, Ireland or even upstate California.

And because he'd never seen the place, except at night and through equatorial rain, this image was clearer and more credible than it ought to have been.

He'd learned that Ma Wagstaff, some kind of matriarchal figure, had died under what the people of Bridelow, if not the medics, considered questionable circumstances.

He'd learned the significance of the Man in the Moss, about which he recollected reading a downpage item in the *New York Times* some months back.

Altogether, he'd learned more than it might normally have been considered wise for them to tell him, and he guessed they'd opened up to him for two basic reasons – A: because they saw what Moira's death had done to him. And B: because they and most other sentient beings in Bridelow had good reason to believe they were in some deep shit.

'What'd he do to the cats?' Macbeth asked, not sure he really wanted to know.

'More a question of what he *would* have done,' Willie said, 'if Old Ma hadn't caught him with his magical paraphernalia and his knife and the poor cat tied to a bread board. He'd be about twelve at the time.'

'Little swine,' Milly said. There were two cats on her knee, one black, one white.

'I can just about remember it,' Willie said. 'I were only a little kid. I remember Old Ma shut herself away for a long time – most of a day. Just her and the cats – one had white bandages on its front paws, thanks to Jack, but it was better than no head. And none of us was allowed to go near, except them as was summoned.'

'Always the practice at a time of crisis,' said Ernie Dawber. 'I remember, not long after I became a teacher at the school, Walter Boston, who was vicar then, he shuffled in one fine morning and called me out of class. I was to go and present myself to Old Ma at once. Well, I wasn't entirely sure in those days of Old Ma's role in the community, but I knew enough not to argue, so it was "class dismissed" and off I went.'

Ernie Dawber was sitting in a stiff-backed chair, his hat on his knees and a cup and saucer balanced on the crown of it.

'So, in I go, and there's Old Ma, sitting like you, Milly, cats on knees. And our Ma was there, too, still known as Iris in those days, although not for much longer. Anyroad, they said I was to go back and talk to each of the children in turn and find out if any of them had had . . . dealings . . . with Jack.'

Macbeth said, 'We talking about what I think we're talking about?'

'Depends,' Milly Gill said. 'Nowadays what they call ritual child-abuse is mostly just a cover for paedophile stuff. For Jack, the abuse was incidental, the ritual was the important bit.'

'Let's put this in context,' Ernie Dawber said. 'The Bridelow tradition is very much on the distaff side, and most of us accept this. It's a gentler, softer kind of, of . . .'

'Witchcraft?' Macbeth said.

Milly said, 'We don't like that word, Mungo. It implies you want to use it to *do* something. All we wanted was to keep a balance. It's more like, you know, conservation. That's why women have been best at it; not got that same kind of aggression, not so arrogant as men.'

'In general.' Ernie Dawber sniffed once. 'But what I wanted to say was that you don't get a tradition carried on this long unless there's a certain . . .'

'Power,' Milly said. 'Immense power.'

'. . . concentrated here,' said Mr Dawber.

'Power?' Macbeth was still sitting at the gateleg table. There was a small amount of whisky left in his glass. 'What kind of power we talking about?'

Milly rearranged the cats. 'Let's just say that if you wanted to *do* something you'd do it a lot better in Bridelow than you might elsewhere.'

Willie said, 'For most of the lads here it's no big deal. We used to say it were women's stuff – back in the days when you were allowed to talk like that. So it were a while before anybody realized that Jack . . . Stanage, I'll call him that, though that's just an invented name he writes under . . . that Jack Stanage had been, like . . . studying.'

'He always had a girl,' Ernie said. 'Any girl. Any girl – or woman – he wanted. This'd be from the age of about thirteen. Bit more precocious in those days than it might seem now.'

'Yes,' Milly said, and they all looked at her. Milly looked down at the cats and said no more.

'I didn't notice that so much,' said Willie hurriedly, 'him being a few years older than me. What I noticed was the money. He always had lots of money. He was generous with it too, if you went along with what he wanted you to do. He could show you a good time, could Jack.'

Milly didn't look up. 'Not when you're ten years old,' she said.

'Uh . . . yeah.' Macbeth reached over to his slicker, pulled out the paperback, *Blue John's Way*. Ernie Dawber picked it up with a thin smile.

'You read it?'

'Leafed through it. In light of what I just heard, I wondered if maybe . . .'

'Not so much an allegory, Mr Macbeth, as . . .'

456

'Mungo.'

'When I know you better, Mr Macbeth. Not so much allegory as a case of "only the names have been changed".'

'So let me get this right . . .' Macbeth was cautious. 'This is a guy who gravitates towards the, uh, arcane. A guy who might like to try and harness other people's powers, maybe.'

Willie looked up. 'What are you thinking about?'

Macbeth finished up his whisky. It made him feel no better. 'I'm thinking about Moira Cairns,' he said soberly. 'And I'm thinking about a comb.'

To Joel Beard, former teacher of physical education, the issue had always seemed such a simple one. If good was to triumph over evil then good required strength. Good needed to work out regularly and get into condition. Indeed, he found a direct correlation between the heavy pectoral cross and the powerful pectoral muscles needed to support it.

But he couldn't find the pectoral cross.

He'd found the wooden lectern, one of the owl's wooden wings missing, smashed up against the Horridge family tomb. Now he was down on his hands and knees in the sodden grass, the rain pummelling his back.

Not that he felt powerless without the cross, not that he felt like a warrior without his sword; he could stand naked and know that his spiritual strength came from within, but . . .

'Mr Beard . . . are you here?'

Joel stopped scrabbling in the grass, felt his back stiffen.

The fluid, tenor voice had curled with ease around the tumult of the night. It was, he realized suddenly, the voice of a man who might have been a priest.

It's all around you, Mr Beard . . . you'll see the signs everywhere . . . in the church . . .

Joel stood and was drawn towards the voice and the question which had tormented him for so many months.

'Who are you?'

They stood opposite each other at the porch door. Joel thought he was the taller, but only just. He couldn't see the man's face under his black umbrella.

457

The man stepped inside the porch and lowered the umbrella. 'You don't know me?'

'I've never seen you before,' Joel said, water cascading down his face. Sweet, refreshing rain? Rain out of darkness was not so sweet.

The man waited, languid, in the doorway under the porch lantern. He wore a loose, double-breasted suit of black or charcoal grey.

'It's many years since I was here, Mr Beard. It's changed, thankfully. Otherwise I simply wouldn't have been able to come in.'

Joel said, 'I took it upon myself to remove certain offensive artefacts.'

'Well done, m'boy.' The man's face split into a sudden grin, revealing large teeth, unexpectedly yellow in his candle-white face.

'Who are you?' Joel said. 'Why are you doing this?'

'My name,' said the man, extending a long, slender, white hand, 'is John. And I was born here.'

Joel took the hand firmly. He had developed a manly handshake which some recipients apparently found crushing. This hand, he found when his fingers closed on it, was not crushable; it was like high-tensile steel.

He recognized strength.

'May I come in?' he asked politely.

'M' dear boy . . .' The man called John stepped to one side. 'Interesting weather, have to say that. Washes away the murk of the past, perhaps.'

'Did you find it was . . . murky . . . when you lived here?'

'Mr Beard, it was layer upon layer. Tell me – small point – what are your views on the ordination of women?'

'I deplore it,' said Joel from the heart. 'I shall always deplore it.'

'Well said. Probably hasn't escaped your notice that the so-called spirituality of this place has been steered for generations by women.'

'They call *this* spirituality?' Joel gestured towards the space where the pagan abomination had spread her legs.

John lifted his hands. 'My point entirely. Expressed, in

various ways, many years ago. Before I was made to leave. Not much more than a boy at the time. Excluded. And then sent away. Do what they like, these close-knit communities.'

'Made to leave? Because you stood out against their witchery?'

John shrugged.

'It's barely credible,' said Joel.

'I'll be quite frank with you, Joel – may I call you Joel, I feel we've known each other so long now – I'll be quite honest, I promised myself that one day, I'd see them and their way of life destroyed. Can you understand that?'

'"Vengeance is mine sayeth the Lord." However, in certain circumstances, we're all tools, are we not? I've always seen myself as a tool.'

'Quite.' John pulled open the inner door into the church itself and stepped through into the amber-lit interior. He moved like a partially blind man, feeling his way. He kept touching things, placing his hands on the walls, the pillars, the pew-ends, as if surprised that he was not receiving electric shocks.

'It's been cleansed,' Joel said. 'But it's still vulnerable. Was Hans Gruber here in your time?'

'Who? Oh, the collaborating minister. No, I left many years before he arrived. Fellow called Boston in my day. But much the same, y' know. Much the same.'

'A quisling?'

'They're all tamed within a remarkably short space of time. Which is why I thought *you* should be alerted.'

'How did you know I'd come here?'

'Dear boy, could you have *resisted* it? Besides which, there *was* Archdeacon Flemming.'

'Oh.'

'Friends of friends, y' know.'

Joel was vaguely disappointed. He'd seen his mission to Bridelow in terms of divine orchestration rather than human machination. And yet, could not the two be interlinked?

'Gone mostly unchallenged for centuries y' know,' John said. 'And so when local papers were passed to me, relating your adventures in Sheffield, it was clear you were The Man for The Job, as it were. All the namby-pamby clerics around. All the airy-fairy, New Age nancy-boys. No. Anybody could rattle them, Joel, it was going to be you.'

John walked slowly up the nave. Even the amber lights failed to colour the pallor of his skin or the snow-white hair receding in ridges from his grey-freckled forehead.

'Used to have crosses here, made of twigs and things, dangling down. Kiddies would be sent out to collect the entrails.'

'Gone. I dealt with it. And their nasty little shrine at the edge of the moor.'

'But your friends have chickened out. Why was that?'

'There was . . .' Joel shook water from his curls, '. . . a manifestation of evil. Some of them couldn't . . . cope. John, I have to know . . . are you a priest?'

John's yellow teeth reappeared. 'Joel,' he said. 'I've told you as much as I can about me and more than I should.'

'I thought so,' said Joel. He paused. 'It isn't over, is it? If it were, you wouldn't be here.'

'Well deduced, Joel, m' boy. Have you ever been up to the lamp?'

Joel stared at him. He felt an almost chemical excitement in his stomach. 'The so-called Beacon?'

'I said we'd put it out, didn't I? I said between us we'd put out the Devil's Light. So. After you, m' boy.'

'Where?'

'To the stairs. Do you have a hammer?'

'I believe there's one in the shed, bottom of the churchyard.'

John looked at his watch. 'No time, old lad. Witching hour approaches. Have to make do with what we've got.'

He grinned, affable, relaxed and not quite like any priest Joel had ever encountered.

'Stanage fixed it,' Macbeth said, 'so Moira would be performing at the Celtic convention. He also requested that she play a certain song, called "The Comb Song", which was of, uh, personal significance to her.'

460

'I know.' Willie Wagstaff started to pour out more whisky, then changed his mind and capped the bottle. 'I was there, must be ten years ago, when that song was recorded. My contribution seems to have been chopped in the final mix, but she wanted friends around her during the session. She invited Matt and me, but Matt couldn't come, I think probably Lottie wouldn't let him.'

Macbeth was a mite dismayed. 'Said she hadn't told anyone the background to that song before.'

'She didn't, lad, far as I know. She just wanted us to be there. She never told us what it were about and I didn't ask.'

Macbeth felt a small pinprick of tears. Quickly, to cover up, he began to tell them about the deer-head incident.

'See, just before it happened, it grew real cold in that room and real tense, like a thunderstorm's on the way. Afterwards, this guy – who I now know to be Stanage – is close up to Moira, and he's bleeding from one eye. Probably got hit by a shaft of bone. Looking back, I get the feeling there was some kind of contest – that's too mild a word, some kind of struggle, battle of wills . . . and that's what caused it. I started thinking of two stags locking horns. But there was so much . . .'

'Energy.' Milly Gill was nodding. 'So much energy that it exploded in the atmosphere and brought down all these . . . things.'

'See, another thing, Moira felt pretty negative about the deer heads, the idea of guys like the Earl blasting off at defenceless animals for kicks and then hanging the heads on their walls. Not the old Celtic way, she said, to boast about, I dunno, the superiority of one species over another. Or maybe I read that someplace.'

Ernie Dawber chuckled. 'The Celts were more likely to display *human* heads. But even then, as you say, not gratuitously.'

'It does sound, doesn't it,' Milly said, 'if what you say about him bleeding is correct, that if there *was* a contest, then Moira won it.'

'He wouldn't like that,' Willy said. Macbeth sensed that beneath the table the little guy's fingers were beating bruises into his knees. He found his own fists were clenching.

'But why'd he target Moira, that's the question? What'd he want with her?'

Willie said, 'Well, it's no coincidence, is it?'

Ernie Dawber looked up at the wall-clock, hand-painted with spring flowers. 'I don't want to hurry you, but I'm not sure where this is getting us.'

Willie stood up suddenly. His nose twitched in disgust. 'Getting us a damn sight further than talk of sacrifice, Mr Dawber.'

Macbeth said, 'Sac . . . ?' and Ernie Dawber put a finger to his lips.

'Don't you think, for his own good, it would be better if Mr Macbeth were to leave us?'

'Bollocks to that.' Willie's eyes flashed and he thumped a hand down on the table.

Milly Gill said, 'Willie . . .'

'And bollocks to your daft ideas, Mr Dawber. We might have taken some bullshit off you when you was headmaster, but not any more. If Jack's behind this, least we know what we're up against.'

'And you think that makes it any better, Willie?' Ernie Dawber shook his head. 'No, this is a man who was a danger to us all at the age of sixteen. Now he's rich and powerful, he's had half a lifetime of indulgence in esoteric studies of what you might call the most dubious kind. He's got a hatred for Bridelow inside him that's been fermenting for about half a century. And you're saying we don't need drastic action to protect us?'

'If John Peveril Stanage is in some way responsible for the death of Moira Cairns,' Macbeth said grimly, 'please, just point me in the right direction and I will go bust this bastard's ass.'

Willie and his woman looked at each other, stark hopelessness in their eyes.

'I hope you're not trying to tell me,' said Ernie Dawber, with dignity, 'that our American friend is in some respect *less* irrational than I am?'

'I wouldn't try to tell you anything, Mr Dawber, you're the schoolmaster and I know my place.'

'Willie!'

'I've had it, lass. I've had enough of this crap. If you want to go out on the Moss and kill Mr Dawber, just do it.'

He stopped because the door had opened. Macbeth saw there was another woman in the room, standing quite still, watching them.

She was young, maybe mid-twenties. Rain sparkled in her thin, blonde hair and there were big globules of it like tiny winking lights against the dark blue of her duffel coat.

'You left the Post Office door unlocked again, Milly. You'll have armed robbers in.'

'Cathy.' Ernie Dawber stood up, his hat in one hand, the cup and saucer balanced on the other. 'I thought you'd gone back to college.'

'You really think I could leave at a time like this, Mr Dawber? Sit down. Please.'

The girl walked into the room, glanced at Macbeth and thought for a moment, then apparently decided to go ahead anyhow.

'Am I right in concluding, Mr Dawber, you've been offering yourself as a replacement for the Man in the Moss?'

Macbeth closed his eyes, wondering briefly what the prospects were of him awakening in his hotel bedroom in Glasgow with a real lulu of a hangover and Moira Cairns still alive someplace. When, with a sigh, he opened them again into the slightly tawdry light of Milly Gill's many-petalled parlour, Milly was saying, 'How long have you been on the other side of that door, Cathy?'

'Long enough.' The girl turned back to the old man. 'Mr Dawber, let's get one thing cleared up. The Man in the Moss was in what, in his day, would have been considered the prime of life. To us, he'd be a young lad.'

Ernie Dawber placed his cup and saucer on the table and took his hat in both hands.

'He was fresh meat, Mr Dawber,' said Cathy. 'Whereas you – and I trust you won't take offence – are dried-up, wizened and probably as tough as old boots. What I'm saying is, you wouldn't be much of a sacrifice, Mr Dawber.'

Ernie Dawber cleared his throat. 'In the last War, Catherine, when Hitler was planning an invasion of these shores from occupied France, the, er, pagans of southern England . . .'

'. . . held a ritual on the beach at Hastings or somewhere in cold weather, and an old man went naked and allowed himself to die of exposure, thus setting up a barrier against the Nazi hordes. I don't believe that old story either, Mr Dawber.'

Macbeth could tell by the way Ernie Dawber was turning his hat around in his hands that the poor old guy was close to tears.

Cathy said, 'I know you love Bridelow more than any man alive . . .'

'Any*one* alive, young lady.'

'Sorry. But throwing your life away isn't going to help anyone, least of all the poor devil who's got to do the deed. You won't accept this, I know you won't, but you're like a number of people who got too close to the Man in the Moss, you're drawn almost into another world. You contemplate things that under normal circumstances . . .'

'Cathy, lass, these are *not* normal circumstances.'

'Yes, but *why* are they not? Why's everything been allowed to go haywire? You've got to ask yourself when all this started and how. I've spent a long time talking to Pop, and . . .' Cathy pulled damp, pale hair out of an eye. 'Look, you know they've been seeing Matt Castle in the village.'

Willie Wagstaff jerked and stiffened and went white. Macbeth couldn't take any more. He got up, walked over to the window and listened hard to the rain until it turned the girl's steady voice into white noise, crazy disconnected phrases seeping out, like when you drove into a new state and your car radio was catching some stray police waveband.

'. . . and when she looked into the fryer, the fat had all congealed and gone black. Black. Like peat.'

Macbeth pushed his forehead up against the window, rolling it repeatedly on the cold, wet glass.

He was too tired for this but couldn't imagine how he'd ever sleep again.

From *Dawber's* Secret *Book of Bridelow* (unpublished):

THE TRIPLE DEATH

THREE WAS A SACRED number for the ancient Celts.

I don't know why. Nobody does, obviously.

But think of Christianity – the Holy Trinity. Now think of the Celtic triple goddess – maiden, matron, hag.

Think, if you like, of the Law of Three, as taught by the cosmologist Gurdjieff. '. . . One force or two forces can never produce a phenomenon,' writes his colleague, P. D. Ouspensky, going on to explain about (i) the positive force, (ii) the negative force and (iii) the neutralizing or motivating force.

I like to think of a three-pin plug, for the safe performance of which the third force, the Earth, is so essential, although I don't know if this is an adequate analogy.

Whatever the explanation, the Celtic gods appeared to have demanded a sacrifice in triplicate before the necessary energy might be released.

And sometimes the cycle of death seemed to operate according to some pre-set cosmic mechanism. For instance, the eminent Celtic scholar Dr Anne Ross has described the legendary demise of the sixth-century Irish king Diarmaid, whose triple death – by weapon, drowning and burning – was foretold by seers. Diarmaid poured scorn on this until his enemies struck at the Feast of Samhain, when the hall was set ablaze and Diarmaid run through with a spear. Seeking safety from the flames, the king plunged, fatally, into a vat of ale.

The Celts have always had a great sense of comic irony.

CHAPTER II

*D*eath. No peace in it.

You struggle towards the light and the light recedes, or maybe it's the bastard darkness has grabbed hold of your feet, hauling you back. Cloying, sweating darkness. Darkness like a black suit that's too small for you. Darkness like . . . black peat . . . the kind of dark you don't come out of until you're long, long dead and even then it's somebody's mistake.

Anything's better than this kind of darkness. Forget about Heaven, Hell would be better.

Joke.

So, OK, this guy, he goes to Hell, right, and it's not what he was expecting, no hot coals and stuff, just all these other guys standing around drinking cups of tea – up to their necks in liquid shit. And they pass him a cup and he's thinking, hey, you know, this could be a lot worse.

And then the Devil himself strolls in – horns, cloven hoofs, spiky tail, the whole getup, plus a big smile – and the guys' faces all drop.

And the first guy thinks, Hey, what's the problem, the Evil One seems affable enough? And then the Devil beams at them all and he says,

'OK, boys, teabreak over, back to your tunnelling . . .'

This could be the secret of the damned universe. Teabreak over, boys, back to the fucking tunnelling.

Oh, Jesus, help me. I'm cold and sweating and dead.

Timegap.

And you wake up into it again and there's the light in the middle distance, only this time the light doesn't back off, the light comes right at you, a big dazzling explosion of light and all you can think is, leave me alone, huh.

Just leave me alone, let me go back into the shit.

Into the black peat.

I'm not afraid of the dark. I'm crying, but I'm not afraid.

The minister's daughter, Cathy Gruber, pushed through the multitude of the Born Again, into the Rectory drawing room. Mungo Macbeth following, wondering how come she didn't throw all these jerks into the street.

A fire was blazing in the hearth, a sofa pushed close to the heat, a woman stretched across it; she had her eyes shut and she was breathing hard. Her long, dark hair hung damply over an arm of the sofa. A small group of people was clustered around. One guy was on his knees; he held an open prayer-book.

It looked as still, as solemn and as phoney as a Pre-Raphaelite death scene, Macbeth thought, as Cathy knelt down next to the guy with the prayer-book.

'How is she now?'

'In and out of sleep.'

'Has she spoken about it? She has to, you know, Chris. If she keeps all the details bottled up, it's going to cause a lot of trauma.'

Chris said, 'Who is this man?'

'I believe we talked on the phone.'

'Oh. The American. I passed you on to Joel, didn't I?'

467

'Some asshole zealot,' said Macbeth, and Cathy frowned at him.

'I'm sorry to say poor Joel's still in there,' Chris said. 'Still in the church.'

'Best place for him,' Cathy said. 'Let him cool his heels for a while. Chantal, can you hear me?'

The woman on the couch moved, eyelids twitching like captive moths. Cathy held one of her hands. 'This really is a wonderful lady,' Chris said to Macbeth. 'I don't know what we'd have done.'

'Cathy?'

'Makes you think you underestimated the benefits of an old-fashioned Anglican upbringing. She's not at all fazed by any of this.'

'Why I'm sticking close to the kid,' said Macbeth. 'I was fazed clean outa my tree some hours back.' He nodded at the sofa. 'This lady your wife?'

'We're united in God,' Chris said as Chantal's eyes opened and then shut again.

'What happened to her?'

'She was raped,' Chris said baldly.

Chantal moaned. Macbeth focused cynically on Chris, who looked to be about his own age and still had the remains of that bland, doped look you could guarantee to find on a proportion of fundamentalist Christians, Children of God, Mormons and sundry Followers of the Sublime Light.

Cathy stood up. 'Keep her warm. Call me if she wants to talk.' Maybe sensing the tension, she led Macbeth away.

The house seemed stuffed with men and women feeding their bland, doped faces with biscuits and potato-chips, and drinking coffee from paper cups. They were in small groups, many holding on to each other, and they weren't talking much, although a few were praying silently, heads bent and palms upturned against their thighs.

Macbeth decided this was probably better than mass hysteria.

'You want coffee?'

Cathy shook her head. He followed her into the hall; she

brought out keys, unlocked a door, led him into an unoccupied room with book cases and an upright piano.

Macbeth said, 'Cathy, reassure me. That woman really was *raped*? In addition to everything, we got a rapist on the loose?'

The girl pushed the door into place, stood with her back to it. 'She *thinks* she was raped. Seems she'd gone back alone to the church to plead with Joel to come out. Says she was thrown across a tomb and had sensations of . . . violation.'

Cathy looked him in the eyes, unsmiling. 'I'm afraid that what we have on the loose is something that used to be Matt Castle.'

The room was silent, apart from the rain on the window, which, by this time, Macbeth hardly registered.

'You believe that.' Already he knew better than to make it a question.

'It's a lot for you to swallow in one night,' Cathy said, 'but Bridelow used to pride itself on having a certain spiritual equilibrium. And now somebody's turned the place into a battlefield. Opposing forces. Black magic, as I understand it, doesn't work quite so well without there being something equally extreme to ignite it.'

'Like, opposites attract.'

Cathy nodded. 'My old man is an ordinary, old-fashioned country clergyman who's learned not to ask too many questions. Joel Beard's an extremist – same background as this bunch. Somebody engineered it that Joel should come to Bridelow with a mission to wipe out the remains of some very innocuous, downbeat paganism. We thought there was an understanding in the diocese that you don't put unstable fanatics into Bridelow, but I'd guess somebody was simply blackmailing the Archdeacon.'

'This is the boss-cleric.'

'As you say, the boss-cleric. Simon. Who's gay. And who's been more than a bit indiscreet in his time.'

'And the blackmailer? Stand up, John Peveril Stanage?'

'This is the one man whose name is never mentioned in Bridelow. The one writer whose books you will never see on the paperback rack in Milly's Post Office.'

'You were outside when I told them about that stuff with the bones in Scotland?'

Cathy went on nodding. She looked very young. Still had on her damp duffel coat and a college scarf wound under her chin. 'Mungo, I can't tell you how sorry I am about Moira. I sincerely blame myself. I should never have let her drive away in that state.'

He felt his eyes narrow. 'State?'

'I think I must have been the last person to see her alive. She was very down, I'm afraid. She'd picked up a bug of some kind. And she was upset over the burglary – someone broke in here and stole some things from her. Including this . . . famous comb. Which she kept in a secret pocket in her guitar case.'

'They stole the case?'

'Just the comb. Seemed silly. I'm afraid I didn't really believe her about that, at first.'

'Shit.' Macbeth clenched his fists. 'How would this sonofabitch know precisely where she kept the comb?'

'Mungo . . .' Cathy hesitated. 'She told me she'd only shown one person where she kept that comb.'

'Wasn't me.'

'No,' said Cathy. 'It was Matt Castle.'

'The ubiquitous Matt Castle. What was her relationship with this guy?'

'She was in his band. And that was all. She was always very insistent about him never touching her.'

'Yeah, but I bet he wanted to.'

'I *know* he wanted to. He was crazy about her. Men tended to . . . Oh, gosh, I'm sorry.'

'The irony of it,' said Macbeth, 'is I never got to touch her either.'

'But I doubt,' Cathy said, not without compassion, 'if you're of quite such an obsessive temperament.'

'Something hurts, is all. Maybe it's self-pity. I, uh, thought she was gonna change my life.'

'Maybe she has.'

'You mind if we get off this subject? Tell me about Castle.'

'Yes.' Cathy sat on the arm of what must have been her father's wing-backed fireside chair. 'Matt's son, Dic, reckons his father's lust . . . unrequited lust . . . for Moira, just got progressively worse with age. Eventually developing into almost a . . . perversion? About women with long, dark hair.'

Macbeth was seized, for the first time, by the reality of something more potentially soul-damaging than either grief or anger.

He said, 'That woman in the room across there . . .'

'Yes,' Cathy said calmly. 'I noticed that too.'

This was more like it. This was much more like Hell.

'Christ, I feel just awful.'

Pain in the head, behind the eyes. A growling pain. Put me back. Put me back into the nice, warm shit.

'You've got to come with me,' the Devil urges.

Hot coals roaring and crackling all around. The inside of a furnace, but without the pretty colours. A black furnace with one cold, flashing, piercing flame.

'Piss off, leave me alone.'

'Look, I haven't got much time.' Stabbing her through the eyes with his needle of light.

'You've got all the time there is, pal, all the time there ever was and all the time there's ever gonny be. That no' enough for you?'

'Please. For Christ's sake.'

'Listen, will you get rid of the damn light?'

'Sorry. I forgot you'd been in the pitch dark so long. I'll put it under my jacket, that any better?'

'Yeah. You're OK, Satan, you know that?'

'Try and sit up.'

'Get your fucking hands off me!'

'Listen to me, you have to get moving.'

'Who is this?'

'It's me. Dic. Dic Castle.'

Light on his face. Dark red hair, Matt's jawline, Matt's stubborn lips.

She coughed. It made her head ache. She said, all she could think of to say, 'Was it you? Was it you took my comb?'

'No,' he said. 'No I didn't. I know who *did*.'

'Who?' Her back hurt as she sat up. Like it mattered now.

'Bloke called Shaw Horridge. But that's not important right now.'

'No.' The name didn't seem to mean anything to her. 'Look, Dic, I don't want to seem stupid, but what are you doing here? What am I doing here? And where in Christ's name *is* here?'

Maybe they were *both* dead. Maybe he'd been sent to offer her a cup of tea.

'It's a storage building, back of the brewery.'

'Brewery?'

'Bridelow Brewery. You have to come now, Moira. Please. I'm supposed to have gone for a pee, that's all. They're going to start wondering where I've got to, and then we could be in a lot of trouble.'

She stood up. There was mist to struggle through, thick grey mist. A monster rose over her and opened its jaws.

Bridelow. Bridelow Black.

Her hands fiddled with her clothes. Sweater. Jeans. She seemed to be fully clothed. She felt naked and raw.

'Thought I was fucking dead. Dic, why am I no' dead?'

'They've had you on drugs.'

'Sure as hell wasn't speed, was it?'

'I don't know. I really don't know much about drugs.'

'Bridelow Brewery,' she said. 'Why's that scare me? Bridelow Brewery. Bridelow *Black*.'

On her feet now, panting, leaning against something, maybe a wall, maybe a door. He'd put out his light. They were just a couple of voices. 'Bridelow Black,' she breathed. 'Ran me off the road. Ran me over a damn precipice.'

'No precipice. There was a flat area over the wall next to the road. Then a slow drop after that. There was a lot of mist. They took you out . . .'

'Fat guy with a half-grown moustache.'

'Yeah. Name's Dean-something. Calls himself Asmodeus, after some biblical demon. Looks like a dickhead, but he isn't.'

'He hit me. Also, some big bastard in a dog-collar hit me. Everybody hits me.'

'Can you walk?'

'Three of them in the lorry. They were dragging me away. Who the hell are these people?'

'They all work at the brewery. Gannons fired the local men, brought in these people. Occult-followers from Sheffield and Manchester. Small-time, no-hope urban satanists. You can practically pick them up on street corners. Doesn't really care any more who he brings in, any low-life shit'll do.'

'Who's this?'

'Stanage.'

'Sorry, my head's, like, somewhere else. I'm not following this. Who's . . .'

'Can you walk?'

'Guess I can. Question is, do I want to?'

'Then walk out of here. Do it now. You walk out of here in a straight line until you get to the road. No, look, I'll come with you as far as the entrance, OK, then I've got to get back or I'm dead. I'll give you the lamp, but don't use it till you're out of sight of the brewery. Go to the Rectory. You remember where the Rectory is?'

'Rectory. Yeah. Near the church.'

'You remember Cath?'

'Dic,' she said, 'what's that noise? I was thinking it was the hot coals.'

'Coals?'

'Never mind.'

'It's just the rain, Moira. The rain on the roof. It's raining heavily, been like this for hours. You're going to get wet, can't be helped. OK, I'm opening the door. You see anybody . . . *anybody* . . . run the other way. Tell Cath . . . are you taking this in?'

'Doing ma best, Dic.'

'Tell her they're going to put out the light. In the church. The beacon.'

'Who's "they"?'

'Moira, listen, they've got my dad propped up in there. And his clothes. And the pipes. And me. And . . . you. Please, just go!'

'What did you just say?'

A shuddering creak and he pushed her out, and it was like

473

somebody had thrust her head down the toilet and flushed it. She gasped.

'Come on.' He took her arm. She could make out the shapes of trees and a sprinkling of small lights among the branches.

'Not that way.'

'What's that tower?'

'Part of the brewery. Can't you go any faster? I'm sorry. They catch you, I'm telling you, they'll kill you.'

She'd stopped. She was shaking. Somebody was pouring bucketfuls of water directly into her brain. She clapped her hands to her head.

She screamed.

'Christ's sake, shut up!'

'Dic. *My hair!*'

Voices. Lights.

'Moira, run! Take the lamp.' Thrusting it into her hands, heavy, wet metal. 'Don't use it till you're away from here.'

Running footsteps.

'My hair's gone!'

He pushed her hard in the back and then she heard him take off in the opposite direction, shoes skidding on the saturated ground.

'Dic?'

'Run!' He was almost howling. 'Just run! Don't lose that lamp!'

'Dic, what have they done to my hair? *Where have they taken my fucking hair?*'

CHAPTER III

S urprising how vulnerable you felt in a tomato-coloured Japanese sports car up here on a night like this. Ashton took it steady.

He wondered: how much water can a peat bog take before it turns into something the consistency of beef broth?

Not his manor, the natural world. The *un*natural world was

more like it. A number of the people with whom Ashton conversed at length – usually across a little grey room with a microphone in the wall – were creatures of the *un*natural world.

As for the *super*natural world . . .

I don't know why, Ashton told himself as he drove towards Bridelow Moss, but in a perverse sort of way this is almost invigorating. To be faced with something you can't arrest, matters which in no way can ever be taken down and used in evidence.

Completely out of your depth. He looked down at the Moss. There was an area of Manchester called Moss Side, in which the police also sometimes felt out of their depth, so choked was it with drugs and violent crime. Did the name imply that once, centuries ago, it had been on the edge of somewhere like *this*? And, if so, how much had changed?

Not the kind of thing policemen tended to think about.

Gary Ashton, facing retirement in a year or two, spent an increasing amount of time trying to think about things policemen did not tend to think about. Intent on not becoming just 'a retired copper' working as consultant to some flash security firm and regaling people who couldn't give a shit with his personal analysis of the criminal mind and endless stories about Collars I Have Felt.

Just lately, Ashton had been trying to talk to people as people, knowing that in a very short time he would be one of them.

A well-controlled tremor in her voice. *'Inspector Ashton, I'm extremely sorry to bother you at this time of night, but you did say if anything else disturbing occurred, I should let you know immediately.'*

Yes, yes, Mrs Castle, but I meant in the nature of a break-in. Unless a crime has been committed or is likely to be, I'm sorry but this is not really something the police can do anything about.

Except, he hadn't said any of that.

What he'd said was, 'Yes, I'll come, but as long as you understand I won't be coming as a policeman.'

Turning off the telly in his frugally furnished divorced

person's apartment, reacting to a peculiar note of unhysterical desperation in a woman's voice and getting into practice for doing things *not* as a policeman.

Surprising how vulnerable you felt not being a policeman on a very nasty night proceeding in an easterly direction across a waterlogged peatbog in a tomato-coloured Japanese sports car to see a woman about a ghost.

'Well,' Ernie Dawber said finally. 'I think it must be obvious to all of us where they are.'

Willie said, 'Macbeth wasn't fooled, you know. He knew we was keeping summat back.'

'Let's hope Catherine keeps him out of our way. Come on, Willie, there's nobody but us going to see to this.'

Milly Gill was hugging Bob and Jim and looking, Ernie thought, a bit like his mother had looked when she'd switched off the radio after the formal declaration of World War Two.

'What are you going to do?'

'Well, I know we're only men, Millicent, but we're going to have to stop this thing. Don't know how, mind. Have to see when we get there.'

Ernie put on his hat.

'Where?'

'The Hall. The brewery. By 'eck, I wish I'd listened to my feelings. So used to them coming to nowt, see, that's the problem. I remember examining the list of Gannons directors – last summer, this was, just after the takeover was mooted.'

'I know,' Willie said. 'J. S. Lucas. Occurred to me too, just momentarily, like, but I thought I were being paranoid.'

Milly looked blank.

'Lucas were t'name of Jack's father. Not many folk'd know that.'

Ernie watched Willie struggling into his old donkey jacket with the vinyl patch across the shoulders. Not seen that for some years. Lad had put on a few pounds in the meantime.

Milly Gill slid the cats from her knee. 'Well, all I can say is you seem determined, Mr Dawber, that one way or t'other, you'll not see tomorrow's sun.'

'Time comes, Millicent, when being an observer is no longer sufficient.'

'And what about you, Willie? Feller who liked to pride himself on his cowardice.'

'True,' Willie said. 'But this is family.'

'I'm just praying,' Ernie said, 'as they've not done owt to Liz Horridge.'

Willie grinned. 'Always had a bit of a thing for Liz, dint you, Mr Dawber?'

'She could've done no better than Arthur Horridge,' Ernie said generously.

'And might've done a good deal worse, eh?' Willie was over by the window. 'Not slackening off at all, bloody rain. Moss'll be treacherous for weeks.'

'We're not going to the Moss,' said Ernie. 'We're not going anywhere near the Moss.'

He was still thinking furiously about what young Catherine had said about obsession. That he himself had been trapped just as surely as Matt Castle and Dr Hall. That there was indeed something powerfully emotionally disruptive about the bogman.

Ernie glanced at Milly Gill, who was not, he reassured himself, in Ma's league. Not yet.

Determined that one way or t'other you'll not see tomorrow's sun.

Aye, well, Ernie Dawber thought, we'll have to see about that.

The tapping on the study door was firm but polite.

Cathy opened it. They were coming out anyway, though without much direction. At some point, Macbeth had suggested they simply call the cops, but Cathy said the cops must already be looking into Moira's death; how were they supposed credibly to plant the idea that the accident was in some way unnatural?

Chris stood in the doorway. 'We've come to a decision,' he said. 'Thank you for your hospitality, but we want to go back.'

'Back?' Cathy said.

'To the church.'

'Oh,' Cathy said. 'But you can't.'

Chris smoothed his beard. 'We're deeply ashamed, Cathy. We had no faith. We watched Joel struggling with the demon, and we thought he'd gone mad.'

'He has,' Cathy said tautly.

'And now this attack on Chantal. She was the only one of us whose belief in Joel was sustained when the chips were down. She went back and she was physically and spiritually attacked. Could have been killed. We let that happen.'

'Open up, did she?'

Chris stared at her in horror.

'I mean to you,' Cathy said irritably. 'Did she tell you exactly what happened to her?'

'Come on, Chris,' a woman's voice called from behind. 'It's only half an hour to midnight.'

'I'm sorry,' Chris said. 'God protect you. God protect you both.'

Cathy flung the door wide. There was a whole crowd of them gathered behind Chris.

'Let me spell it out for you. All of you. You've all been used. Joel was used. Somebody wanted to break down the church's defences – these are defences built up over centuries.'

'Yes,' said Chris. 'We were the last line of defence.' Not understanding, unlikely to be *capable* of understanding. 'And we were afraid. We lost faith in our brother, Joel. We deserted him when he most needed us, and it took the violation of our sister . . .'

'Sister?' Macbeth said. 'She's your goddamn wife!'

'And Joel was right too . . .' Chris backed away, 'about *this* man. Turn him out, Cathy. Turn him out and come with us.'

'Of course I'm not going to bloody turn him out! He's got good reason to be angry; a friend of his died tonight.'

Chris didn't blink.

'Come *on*, Chris. In God's name,' the woman behind him cried.

'I'm coming.'

Cathy grabbed his arm. 'What I'm saying to you, Chris, is that it's not safe for you to go back in that church. Any of you. You won't do yourselves any good and you'll probably do us all a lot of harm.'

Chris said pityingly, 'Our trust is in Almighty God. In whom, to our shame, we temporarily lost our faith. And for that we have much to make up. Whatever happens in there will be His will.'

'He gave you a brain, Chris. To think with, you know? Have you given up thinking for yourselves? Letting Him do all your thinking now, is it?'

Chris pulled his arm away, eyes full of drifting cloud. 'Pray for us, Cathy.'

'Yes,' said Cathy when they'd gone. 'But who am I supposed to pray *to*?'

Because he was used to making a recce before venturing in, Ashton drove once up the village street, turned around on the parking area by the church and drove slowly back towards the pub.

Just as well he was driving slowly. Twice, people hurried across the street, two men together and two women individually, flapping like chickens in the blinding rain.

There were lights in most front rooms, lights in the chip shop but a 'closed' sign on the door. Water gushed down the sides of the road, down the hill. Where did it all go? Into the Moss?

Ashton followed the water as far as the pub, where the only light was the hanging lantern over the front porch, illuminating the sign, *The Man I'th Moss*. No picture. What would it have shown? Why had they given the pub that name, possibly a couple of hundred years ago, when nobody could have guessed there was an ancient body in the bog?

Or could they?

Ashton pulled on to the forecourt and dashed for the door. Lottie Castle. He could spot a liar in seconds. He could also tell when people were deluded. And he could, of course, spot people who were daft or innocent enough to be led up the garden path.

But this Lottie Castle.

Now, here's a cool, intelligent woman who is definitely not

lying; a woman you could, with confidence, put in a witness box in front of George bloody Carman QC.

And here's a woman claiming to be haunted. You know why I half believe this? Ashton still quizzing himself as he huddled on the doorstep in his trench coat, ill-fitting slates in the porch letting water trickle down his collar.

Because this is a woman who sincerely *doesn't want* to believe it.

And is also, yes, an attractive widow. Well, what's wrong with that?

The woman who answered the door, however, was not Lottie Castle. But if Ashton the human being was disappointed, Ashton the copper was back on duty the second he identified her.

'Miss . . . er . . . Mrs White.'

'Chrissie.'

'Aye,' he said. 'Chrissie. And is Dr Hall here too?'

'Not exactly *here*, Gary . . . is it Gary tonight?'

'Hard to say,' Ashton said, stepping inside. 'Hard to say, now.'

Her own smooth, smoky voice taunting her as she struggled through the dripping wood, booming out from the old, disused recording studio in her head, the voice sneering,

> *Never let them cut your hair*
> *Or tell you where*
> *You've been, or where*
> *You're going to*
> *from here . . .*

Everything leaking out now from that slashed and razored head, raw thoughts exposed at birth to the cold and spitting night.

For a bad long time she'd stood alone among some trees and wept and sobbed and cursed and refused to believe it. *They can put it back, can't they? Christ's sake, they can sew people's arms back these days.*

480

First the horror, then the anguish. And then the horror and anguish and the rage, all shaken up, this wild, combustible cocktail.

'Who?' she screamed to the invisible sky. '*Who?*'

Them.

Dic had headed them off. They'd gone after Dic and she was alone in the filthy night, everything rushing back with nerve-searing intensity, the savage rain smashing it into her naked head along with the insistent bump, bump, bump of the taunting mental Walkman.

And the things Dic said.

Stanage.

Of course, yeah. The Celtic expert. The writer. John Peveril Stanage. Never read his books, too young for me, by the time I'd heard of him.

But I'm going to kill that man. That man is *dead*.

Memories.

On the plane to Dublin for a gig. Matt holding up a paperback, *The Bridestones.* '*Should read this. Tell you where I'm coming from.*' Moira politely looking up from Joseph Heller or somesuch. Mmm? Sure. Get around to it someday.

And then the American, Macbeth, at the Earl's Castle. '*This writer – Stanton, Stanhope? Is he* mad . . . *this guy's face is white.*'

John Peveril Stanage. The pale predator at the castle.

The comb-hunter.

The hair-surgeon.

Moira clung to a tree, its mesh of leafless branches keeping most of the rain off her. But when her head penetrated a jagged tracery of twigs, she could actually feel them graze her scalp.

She screamed in despair.

Last one, OK? Last scream. Last curse. Then you start to think. God, you drift through life listening to your conscience and your instincts and premonitions, all your airy-fairy feelings, and you never *think*.

Moira, listen, they've got my dad propped up in there.

Meaning an effigy? A dummy representing the spirit they wanted to conjure?

Necromancy. The black side of spiritualism. You collect, in the appropriately drawn and consecrated circle, the most intimate possessions of the dead person, those things . . .

. . . his clothes.

carrying his smell, his sweat. And those things . . .

. . . the pipes.

he would most hate to leave behind. And those . . .

. . . me. Dic.

people who were close to him. And . . .

And you.

the things after which he craved.

Moira moved deliberately out from under the tree, stared up into the sky until she was blinded by the rain, and then hung her head and let the night drench her.

They took the comb.

They cut off my hair.

They have me. They have my essence.

They have used these things to summon Matt Castle from the grave.

CHAPTER IV

How Young Frank Manifold had ended up at the brewery he didn't exactly remember.

What he did remember was his anger reaching gale-force as soon as the cold rain hit it. Slung out again! Slung out like a kid from the only pub in Bridelow.

Settle down, Frank.

Cool it, eh, Frank.

Don't you think you've had a couple too many, Frank?

Int it past your bedtime, Frank?

They'd say it once too often. In fact tonight they *had* said it once too often.

What Frank remembered first was bunching his fists on the pub forecourt and looking around for somebody to hit and seeing only rain and smeary lights in the windows of houses of folk as wouldn't come out in it merely for the pleasure of being filled in by Young Frank.

Another thing he'd thought about was hitting a wall, but he'd done that once before and his fist remembered and wouldn't go through with it.

The soft option would've been to go straight home and have a row with the wife. But if Susan didn't feel like a row she wouldn't let you have one, simple as that. Susan, who insisted that being in the Mothers' Union was just something you agreed to so as to keep the numbers up, but who could look at you through slitted eyes and take the anger out of you easy as letting tyres down.

Don't want that, he remembered thinking. Want to keep the anger.

Raging through the rain in just his jeans and his ordinary jacket, sopping wet-through in minutes.

Deciding at one stage, I know what I'll bloody do, I'll go up the church and duff over a few Born Again Christians.

Nowt against Christianity, *as such*. Nowt against Hans Gruber, a southerner but a straight-up bloke. Just that when it came to that big prat Joel Beard; when it came to T-shirts with JESUS SAVES on the front and grinning tossers stopping you in the street to asking how well you knew God; when it came to getting accosted by tasty women with PRAISE THE LORD across their tits . . .

When it came to it, truth was Frank didn't hate Born Again Christians anywhere near as much as he hated Gannons.

Which, he supposed, must be why he'd ended up pissing hard and high against the main door of the brewery, thinking maybe he could kick a couple of windows in before he sobered up.

Which was how come he saw the lights.

And how come he found the main door wasn't locked.

Well, this were a bit of a turn-up. Frank stood a while getting rained on and stared upwards. Summat weird about this. Light coming out the sides of the wooden boards on the topmost windows, the owd malt store as was.

From what Frank had heard from his ex-workmates and his

dad, that malt store hadn't been used in twenty years. When Gannons had the winching system repaired on the outside of the building there was no suggestion it had been for winching sacks all the way up to the top again, because the owd malt store'd been shut and boarded up. Make it look authentic for tourists, this was what everybody thought.

Frank wandered around to the side of the building, and there was the platform thing . . . right at the top.

Summat had been winched up there tonight. Obviously.

Fucking cowboy brewers. Happen the owd malt store'd been *refurbished*. Happen they was having a little cocktail party up there for the directors.

Right then. See about that.

Frank went in.

She knew, sure, how ill she was, soaked through and shivering, feverish, temperature racing up the thermometer, about to ring the little bell.

Knew also that she could never look into a mirror again. Not *ever*.

And yet her mind had never seemed so clear. A cold searchlight, ruthlessly spearing into dark and musty corners.

Felt weak as hell and sore, and she walked with difficulty through the leafless, waterlogged wood. But her mind was an athlete, leaping chasms of dark thoughts. Her mind was an engineer constructing complex bridges.

'What we're looking for,' Moira mumbled, stopping, moving closer to the stocky, blistered trunk of an oak, switching off the lamp, 'is something long-term.'

Like a long-term connection between Matt and Stanage.

This had happened before; Matt's enthusiasms were unstoppable. If Matt finds interesting echoes in a book, Matt goes in search of the author.

Take this as fact. Matt meets Stanage. Matt and Stanage find so much common ground that secrets are shared . . . at least on Matt's side.

Nobody other than Matt could have told Stanage about Moira Cairns and the comb. Say that by the time these two men meet, she's – stupidly – recorded 'The Comb Song' and both Matt and Stanage are scenting magic. And Stanage has stored all this away for future reference.

Moira sank down against the fat, scabby treetrunk, finding an almost sheltered spot between two huge protruding roots, enclosing her like legs. Sheets of rain on three sides; like crouching in a cavern behind a waterfall.

OK.

If Stanage has learned about the comb he's learned a whole lot more of Matt's secrets, maybe passing on a few tantalizing but useless bits of information of his own about the old Celts and the Pennine Pipes in return. Worth it, because he sees such terrific potential in Matt, the most wonderful raw material for his own research.

Because Matt, maybe like Stanage, is ruled by his compulsions. Only Stanage is cleverer.

She closed her eyes and she was back in the ballroom of the Earl's castle.

His face is an unhealthy white. He has light grey eyes and grey freckles on his expanse of forehead. There's a whiteness all about him, growing into arms like the branches of trees. Like antlers.

He is linked to the skulls on the walls. He is the horned god, the hunter of heads.

He has taken her hair.

And she sees it all with such brutal clarity, detached from her wonderful, magical comb-reared hair, her earliest, most important expression of individuality and free thought.

Hands to her head, couple of inches left, less in places. Aw, what the hell, you're alive, what d'you want, huh?

Revenge? She shivered with fever and fury.

Hands inside the guitar case. Stanage is feeling for the comb. He is feeling for your soul.

Two hundred miles away Matt Castle is lying in wait for death. Maybe Matt, in the last morphine minutes of his life, is also reaching out for you. Those arms of sick smoke coiling out of the baronial fireplace.

If Stanage gets access to your soul, to the core of Matt's craving . . .

485

. . . then Stanage will have a link with Matt that extends beyond death.

Stanage will have a hold on Matt's spirit.

With the comb and the cloak and the . . .

'Long-haired girls. Always the long, dark hair.'

Dic.

'After a charity gig. She was waiting for him in the car park. About twenty-one, twenty-two. About my age. Long, dark hair.'

The craving kept alive in the darkness of shop-doorways and the backs of vans.

And manipulated. And moulded and twisted.

Stanage has recreated me as spirit-bait for Matt. He's taken my soul and thrown away the husk.

But why, Moira wondered, so physically, achingly tired now, enclosed in the roots of a malformed oak tree, an electric lamp on her lap, *why can I think so well?* Why can I see all this so clearly, unless that's to be my final torture?

That and a dawning, unquenchable hatred for Matt Castle.

Frank made his way, quietly as his shoes would allow, up the narrow iron stairs, past the deep fermenting-tanks. Up another flight, past the coppers. It were bloody dark, but Frank had been up here that many thousand times it didn't matter. And the smell, the lovely, familiar smell. Better than sight, that smell. Better than women.

Halfway up the third flight leading to the mash tuns, Frank choked back what he thought was going to be a hiccup but turned out to be a sob. He stopped in a moment of despair. How was he going to live the rest of his life without this wondrous rich, stale, sour, soggy aroma? How was he going to survive?

He clambered to the top, staggered out on to the deck clutching for support at the thick copper pipe connecting the malt mill to the mash, the big tuns around him, his old mates. Get um out, a voice was rasping in his gut. Gannons. Get the bastards out. Get the brewery back for Bridelow.

He leaned, panting, over the side of one of the tuns and his breath echoed in its empty vastness.

One more flight. He went three-quarters way up to a door that'd always been kept locked for safety's sake for as long as he'd worked there.

Voices behind it.

'. . . not terribly subtle. What time is it?'

'Coming up to eleven-fifteen.'

'No time for that, then. Really, I' – a light laugh, half-exasperated – 'just can't get over what you've done. I really didn't think you were that clever. Now, look. You know, presumably, that we mustn't actually kill you. Not yet, anyway.'

'Don't care. Do what you want. You're just a slag. Couldn't give a . . .'

A crash. A moan. A rolling on floorboards.

'All right, come on, pick him up. Sit him next to his dear daddy. Let him have a good whiff. Bind his arms very firmly, palms up, OK? And at approximately ten minutes to twelve . . . are you listening? At ten minutes to twelve, you can open his wrists.'

Frank was in a fog. He heard it all but couldn't make sense of the words and some kept repeating on him.

Kill . . . whiff . . . palms up . . . open his wrists.

It was a woman's voice, not a local accent. More words tumbled down the steps, Frank's brain tripping over them. Sometimes he seemed to hear the key words before they joined actual sentences.

Trickle.

'Don't go mad. Just want a trickle at first. Steady plop, plop, plop. We'll be well into it by then. Once you get the trickle going, you come back and join us. Very quietly. You say nothing.'

Blood to blood.

'What if he screams?'

'He won't. If he does, you can cut another vein. Slow release is best. I mean, I was going to do this anyway; this way we get an instant connection, blood to blood.'

blood to . . .

'Oh, yeah? And who would it have been if this one hadn't suddenly become available?'

. . . blood?

'Oh. *Right.*'

Frank's hands were sticky on the iron stair-rail. Brain couldn't handle it. Past his bedtime. Turn back, go home, sleep it off, eh? But there was a voice he recognized, the voice that said it didn't care, the voice that called the female voice a slag. The voice of the owner of the wrists which would be opened at precisely ten to twelve, but just a trickle unless it screamed.

Frank screamed. Frank was screaming now.

As all the lights went on, Frank screamed, *'Dic!'* as a figure shimmered in the doorway at the top of the steps and a new smell mingled with the malted air, a smell just as warm, just as rich, just as moist, but . . .

The new smell went up Young Frank's nose and forced his mouth wide open like a bucket. He belched up half a gallon of beer and bile, which spouted up in a great brown arc and then slapped down on the metal steps.

'Manifold. You dirty, uncouth lout. Should have guessed.'

Frank looked up into supercilious, wrinkling nostrils.

He began dumbly to move up the steps, his shoes skidding on his own vomit, his hands trying to make fists, his chest locked tight with hatred, his drink-rubbery lips trying to shape a word which eventually came out like another gob of harsh sick.

'. . . *Horridge* . . .'

Gonna have you, said the rough voice in Frank's gut. This time gonna take you apart, you smarmy twat.

He slipped, and his hands splashed on the steps.

Shaw Horridge stood quite relaxed in the doorway, a shred of a smile on his lips. 'You are an absolute oaf, Manifold.'

Frank's fists turned into claws and he took what he imagined to be a great leap up the final three iron steps towards Horridge's throat.

Horridge didn't move at all until Frank's head was on a level with the top of the stairs, at which stage a foot went almost idly back. And then – momentarily – on top of the mellow aroma of malt, the sour stench of vomit and the sweet-rancid essence of rotting flesh, Frank experienced the absurdly pure tang of boot-polish as Shaw's shoe smashed through his teeth and was wedged for a second in his gullet.

Choked, retching, he threw up his arms to grab the foot, but the foot was . . . receding, just like the rest of Shaw Horridge.

Young Frank realized he was flying slowly and almost blissfully backwards.

It seemed a long time until he thought he heard a metallic *ching* as his head connected with something solid (metal everywhere in a brewery) and a dull, fractured *crump* somewhere inside his brains, wherever they might be splattered.

CHAPTER V

There was a rustling over the tumbling water noise; this was what awoke her (how could she have slept, how *could* she?) And half a second later there was a light in her eyes and people moving behind it.

Two of them.

Moira reared up, back to the tree, a spitting cat. 'Come on. Come on, then . . .'

Hands curling into claws. Pray that one is Stanage.

Because she would die before they'd take her back. She'd die raking his face.

One of them gasped.

The other said, 'By 'eck.'

He'd heard it before, so it was no big surprise. The hackneyed country and western, with chorus.

> *Leave your sor-row*
> *Come and join us*
> *Shed those sins,*
> *Find the joy within . . .*

One time, Macbeth had directed this made-for-TV picture about the crooked evangelist Boyd C. Beresford the Fourth. Spent a whole ten days cruising the Bible Belt, stuff like this churning out of the car-radio, out of hotel-room TV sets, out of mission halls and marquees – until even arid atheism began to look like a safe haven.

So he was not impressed. Not even when they started singing in tongues, because he knew how easy this stuff was to fake, even while you were convincing yourself you weren't faking it. And all the healing that lasted just long enough for the relatives to throw in a two-hundred-dollar donation. *You feeling better, sister? Or maybe your faith isn't yet strong enough for you to be healed?*

'Go away. Begone, heathen!'

This real big Born Again Christian on the church door. Stained jeans and a grungy parka. Tattoos on both wrists, one involving what looked like it used to be a swastika on fire before it got reprocessed into a bulky crucifix. Fascist punk finds God. It happened. Classic demonstration of what Cathy had said earlier about one extreme igniting another.

'Listen, I don't plan to cause any trouble,' Macbeth said wisely. 'All I want is to talk with Joel Beard. I would like for you to bring him out here. That too much of a problem?'

Cathy had said, 'Mungo, you have an open, honest face. You've got to get to Joel, talk some sense into him. Long as you go easy on the casual blasphemy, he has to listen to you – you're not from Bridelow and you're not a woman. Tell him what you like, but get him to evacuate that place. They think they're safe in there . . . they're just so naive, they're children . . .'

The big guy with the ex-swastika said, 'You got five seconds to get them filthy heathen feet the other side of this sacred threshold.'

Beat up on a pagan for the Lord. Jesus.

'Listen,' Macbeth said urgently. 'Go tell Joel that Pastor Mungo Macbeth of the, uh, East Side Evangelical Mission, would like to speak with him.'

'You're lying,' Swastika said, but with audibly less conviction than a moment ago.

'God will forgive you for that,' Macbeth said. 'Maybe.'

'He's not there,' Swastika blurted out.

'He is everywhere,' said Macbeth.

'No, Joel. I mean Joel. When we got here we couldn't find him. He's vanished.'

'What do you mean, vanished?'

'He's just gone.'

'Well, where'd he go, for Chr . . . Where might Reverend Beard have gone?'

Flash of fear in the guy's small eyes. 'Why d'you think we're praying so hard?'

'So your friends have returned.'

John stood bathed in blue light.

The blue was in the old glass around the enormous lantern. Round panes, set in the four exterior walls, were frosted white.

There wasn't much to it; Joel had expected more, perhaps the remains of a clock mechanism, but there was no sign of there ever having been one.

'I knew they would,' Joel said. 'I knew it was impossible for them to forsake their God for very long.'

John smiled, his teeth shining blue.

'Still,' Joel said, 'I won't say I'm not relieved. Shall I go down? Tell them what we're going to do?' He moved towards the top of the stone steps.

'Lord, no.' John's face grew solemn. 'They've fled once.'

'Yes,' Joel said. 'I'm sorry.'

The room was about nine feet square. In any other church it would be the belfry; here it was the lamphouse. The lantern hung from the pinnacle of the roof. It was perhaps five feet in diameter.

There was lead around the rims of the glass circles in the walls, but no remains of numerals; it had clearly never been a clock.

Inside the bluish milky glass set into an old iron frame, he could make out the incandescent shapes of three big electric bulbs.

John said, 'Used to be an oil lamp, you can tell. Big candles before that, probably. A lure for the spirits of the Moss.'

Joel remembered his nightmare in the cellar room, imagining the lantern laying an ice-blue beam over still water.

Channels of rain glistened like icicles on the glass. The light was quite ghastly, dehumanizing. John, with his pale, flat face, looked almost demonic. Joel glanced sharply away, afraid of the illusions this evil light could evoke. Though they'd been up here over half an hour, he became aware for the first time of a small door in the shadows to his left.

'What's in there, do you know?'

'Let's see, shall we?' John moved lightly across the boarded floor, pushed and twisted at a handle. 'No . . . 'fraid it's locked.'

Joel closed his eyes and listened to the singing. The hymn was trailing into a drone of tongues, male and female voices flowing into a bright river of praise. He tried to let it flow into him.

On all sides of them, up here in the tower, the night sky was roaring with rain.

'How long?'

'Little under ten minutes. Impatient, are we, Joel? Excited?'

'Why can't we just switch it off and go?'

'You see a switch anywhere, m' boy? Be on a circuit. Time-switch. Anyway, what good would that do? No. Have to smash it. Violence, I'm afraid. Strength. What you're about, isn't it Joel? Strength. Might. No room for namby-pamby, nancy-boy clerics on the Front Line, mmmm?'

'Yes,' Joel said. 'You're right. I'm ready for that. Midnight, then.'

Back at the Rectory, Macbeth said, 'What could happen to those people? Spell this thing out.'

Reaching the front door, he'd heard Cathy, on the hall phone extension, saying, 'I don't know, I'll call you back.' Putting down the phone to let him in.

Now, in the study, sitting on the edge of the piano stool, she said, 'How can I say what could happen? You're nowhere in this game until you accept that nobody can ever say for certain what's going to happen and anyone who thinks he can, or that he can manipulate it, is due for a hell of a shock one day.'

Macbeth said, 'What game?'

'Game?'

'You just said "in this game".'

Cathy shrugged. 'Life, I suppose.'

But he wasn't aiming to back off. 'OK, so what's the bottom line? What's the worst thing could happen? Before you answer, bear in mind what I saw in Scotland and that Moira is dead and that I don't believe I have a great deal I care about left to lose.'

Cathy said calmly, 'I've lived in Bridelow all my life. I've acquired knowledge of certain things, OK? And most of today I've been talking very seriously to my father who's had to deal with things most clergymen don't even read about.'

'Sure,' Macbeth said impatiently. 'What's your point?'

'Put it this way, if it was Pop in there, I'd be less worried.'

'So what you're saying is, in the great metaphysical ball-park, these guys are strictly little-league.'

'Let's say they're hardly ready for what they're up against. They create their own universe, you see, these people. In this little universe everything is down to the Will of God and all evil can be defeated fast as a prayer. When *real* evil shows its hand, it can be so traumatic they'll . . .'

'Flip?'

'Flip is right,' Cathy said. 'Flip is the least of it.'

'Real evil?'

'Stanage is the man no one here ever talks about. Stanage is evil beyond what ordinary people care to envisage.'

'OK,' Macbeth said. 'First thing, you can't stay here alone, case these people come back with some even more screwball ideas than they had when they left.'

She looked kind of suspicious. 'What's the alternative?'

'I reserved a room at the inn. You take that. I'll stay here.'

'Oh,' said Cathy. 'I see. The big macho bit. Mungo, how can I say this? You're the one who shouldn't be here on his own.'

'What you want me to do, drive outa here? Things didn't work out with Moira, let's draw a line under all of this? OK, we'll both stay here. I'll take the sofa. I'll call Mrs Castle.'

'Mungo, I'm not going to stay here. I'm going to Milly's. We have things to discuss and it's women only, I'm afraid. My advice is, take your room at The Man, get some sleep. You look all-in. If there's anything you can do, we'll ring you.'

'Oh,' Macbeth said.

'I promise.'

'Sure.'

This was Moira all over again. *Macbeth, just go away, huh?*

'I dint recognize you.' Willie was almost in tears. 'God help me, I didn't know who you were.'

'I think there was a similar problem,' Mr Dawber said drily, 'in the Garden of Gethsemane, on the Third Day.'

Willie could tell Mr Dawber was almost as pleased as he was, but there was a shadow across it.

Mr Dawber said, 'Seeing somebody you thought was dead, there's bound to be an element of shock. Take her home, Willie. Take her to Millicent.'

'Cathy,' Moira said, unsteadily on her feet, Willie's donkey jacket around her shoulders. Willie reckoned she also was in shock. 'Whatever you like,' he said. 'I can't believe this. I just can't believe it. It's a miracle. It were on t'news. They found your car, bottom of a bank.'

'I'll tell you about it,' Moira said.

'It *was* your car?'

'Oh, aye.'

Willie said, his voice rising, 'There were a body in it. Police found a woman's body!' He stared hard at her in the torchlight. He wondered if she knew where she was. He wondered if she knew what had happened to her beautiful hair.

He was glad that when he'd touched her, putting his jacket around her, she'd been stone-cold and damp, but solid.

Mr Dawber was silent. If he had any curiosity about the body in the BMW he was keeping it to himself.

'Let's not hang about,' Willie said. 'Mr Dawber?'

'You go,' the old man said quietly. 'I'll carry on.'

'You're never going up there on your own, Mr Dawber, no way.'

'I'll go if I want to,' Mr Dawber said, and there was a distance in his voice. 'Nobody tells the headmaster what to do. Remember?'

'Aye, and if I arrive back there without you, Milly'll kill me, you know that much, Mr Headmaster, sir.'

Mr Dawber said mildly, 'This lass'll be catching her death if you don't be on your way.'

'Please, Mr Dawber.'

'Dic.' Moira's body pulsed. 'Either of you seen Dic Castle?'

'Not since the funeral,' Willie said. 'Gone off teaching, Lottie said, in Stockport or somewhere. You seen him, Mr Dawber?'

There was no reply. Willie swung his torch round.

'Mr Dawber!'

Mr Dawber had gone.

Roger Hall asked, 'Is he mad?' The effects were wearing off; he didn't feel so elated, he did feel quite relaxed. He did *not* feel there was anything bizarre about this, why on earth should he?

Therese arched an eyebrow. She was not beautiful, but she was compelling. He wouldn't kick her out of bed.

'Well, of course he's mad,' she said. 'Didn't that occur to you?'

'He knows so much. How can you know so much, be so learned, and be insane?'

The candles around the circle were half burned down. The other people squatting cross-legged – the people Therese was 'helping', the people who did what they were told – gazed dull-eyed into the candle flames and never spoke.

'Look at it this way, Roger,' Therese said. 'You're quite a learned man yourself. Would you say *you* were insane?'

Matt Castle slumped in his chair. He wore a white T-shirt and was quite obviously and horribly dead, but he didn't offend Roger Hall any more.

Roger laughed. 'But Stanage . . . I mean, he does know what he's doing?'

Dic Castle, something as primitive as chloroform administered to him on a rag, was bound and taped into a metal-framed chair with his wrists upturned. This did not offend Roger either. Nor did the hypodermic on the table.

'He's done it before,' Therese said. 'Many years ago he dug up a corpse, dead no more than a week, to tap her knowledge. It is, as you've gathered yourself, all about knowledge. I thought that was just wonderful – he went into Bridelow churchyard at night and dug the old girl up with the sexton's spade. He was about nineteen at the time. He just, you know, has absolutely no fear. That's half the battle, when you think about it.'

'Yes.' She was right. Conquering fear was the vital first step. Fear of being caught out. Fear of the law. Fear of humiliation.

'Look at Shaw,' Therese said. 'Shaw was a fantastically good subject because he was so utterly screwed up, so socially backward to begin with. Six months ago, Shaw was scared to walk into a pub by himself; now he's killed two people and he's never been happier. He's out there now, and if anybody tries to disturb us, he'll . . . you know . . . without a second thought.'

'And you're telling me all this.' He wanted to pinch himself; he wanted to find the smell of Matt Castle nauseating. And he couldn't.

'You're one of *us*,' Therese said generously. 'You've been one of us for months. We'd never have got the Man out of the British Museum without your help, and you'd never have had the balls to get him out without ours. Come on, it's time. Have another drink.'

'I mustn't,' Roger said coyly, accepting a glass. 'One final question. Therese . . . what would have happened to Chrissie if she'd come to the house with me?'

'Who . . . ? Oh, the secretary. The divorced secretary with

no immediate family in the area. *That* Chrissie. Don't ask, Roger. Don't ask and you won't be told the truth.'

Therese poured them all a drink from an unlabelled brown wine bottle. 'Cheers,' said a dull, empty-looking woman called Andrea. Therese moved to a bench in the corner of the room opposite Matt and slipped a cassette into a black ghetto-blaster.

From the largest of several black bags, she withdrew the Pennine Pipes and laid them at Matt's feet.

From the portable ghetto-blaster seeped the weeping, far-away, opening notes of 'Lament for the Man'.

Dic squirmed.

From one of the bags, Therese took a pencil-slim plastic-handled craftsman's knife, which she handed to Owen, a weedy, expressionless man.

'I'll give you the signal,' Therese said. 'If it disturbs you, you may tape his mouth.'

CHAPTER VI

Refusing a whisky, Gary Ashton said, 'I'm not saying I don't believe this, ladies. I've seen too many weird things, put away too many weird people, we all do. Sometimes, you're face-to-face with real evil, and you're laughing it off. You laugh off criminals – blaggers, toe-rags. You don't think too hard about it, you're a copper. Not a shrink. Not a priest. You nick the buggers, put them away, that's where it ends.'

'Meaning you can't help us,' Lottie said.

'Far as the law's concerned, Mrs Castle, there's one crime been committed here. Somebody's pinched an archaeological relic.'

He'd sat there and he'd drunk coffee and he'd sympathized. He'd trusted them, too, both of them. They were frightened, more than if they'd been robbed. Although he knew bugger-all about wiring and such, he'd been and examined the electrified gas-mantle and fitted a new bulb, and, sure enough, it didn't come on. Fuse probably, he'd said. Where's the fuse-box?

And Lottie had said, never mind.

Truth was, the bloody thing had fused at the wrong time and put the shits up two women who were already mentally stressed.

Ghost in the mirror? Pipes in the night?

Strange atmosphere? Aye, there was. There was a strange atmosphere all over this whole village tonight, it hit you soon as you crossed the Moss. Too much rain, for a start, as if it was nature's attempt to cool something down, to put out a fire somebody was busy stoking under this place.

Put that in a bloody police report. Show that to the Superintendent. Strange atmosphere. *'There was a very strange atmosphere, boss.'*

And then Chrissie White said what he'd been faintly hoping she might.

'What if I knew who'd stolen the bogman?'

'Ah. Then I'd have a lot more leverage, wouldn't I, Chrissie?'

Chrissie said, 'Have you heard of a writer called John Peveril Stanage?'

'My kids used to read him avidly.' He glanced at Lottie. 'One grown up, now. The other still lives with his mother and her new feller. Aye, John Peveril Stanage. What about him?'

'He's got plans to fund a permanent museum for the bogman. As you know, Roger would run it. Stanage would have permanent access to the bogman.'

'So why would he nick it? I presume you are saying he nicked it. Or had it nicked.'

'I don't know,' Chrissie said. 'I just think he has.'

'Why?' Ashton began to feel less hopeful.

''Cause he's invited Roger to some sort of gathering at Bridelow Hall and he's told him he might be able to find out where it is.'

'That's not the same thing, Chrissie. Also, it's presumably only what Dr Hall's told you.'

'Well, that's right. I suspect there's a lot more to it than that. Can't you get some of your blokes and, raid it or something?'

'Oh, aye,' Ashton said. 'The police are always raiding

private parties at the homes of the rich and influential. Matter of course, Mrs White. Normal procedure. Happen the Chief Constable'll be one of the guests. Or the MP?'

'What if they're doing – I don't know what to call it – black magic, or something?'

'Well, it's not basically against the law, luv. Matter of religious preference, in the eyes of the British legal system. Unless it involves children or animals, of course. You think it does?'

Chrissie said, 'Roger's been messing about with the bogman.'

Ashton tried not to laugh. 'I really don't think that'd have them cancelling leave at the Vice Squad. Mrs White . . . Chrissie. And Mrs Castle . . . I sympathize, you know I do, or I wouldn't be here. If you want me to do anything as a policeman, I've got to have something hard, solid and preferably nothing at all to do with the supernatural.'

Lottie said angrily, 'You think I . . .'

Ashton held up a hand. 'No, I don't. That's why I came. You're a nice woman, and things are happening to you that you don't understand and don't particularly want to understand. I admire you, Mrs Castle.'

'But I'm wasting your time. All right, I'm sorry. You'd better get off home to your . . .'

'Flat,' said Ashton. 'What I said was, there was nothing I could do as a copper. As things stand. However, I also attempt to be a bit of a human being, on the side. Anything I can do in that capacity, I'll be happy to do it, just as long as it's not illegal and doesn't mean saying ta-ra to me pension. How's that?'

'Thanks,' Chrissie said despondently. 'But we're all of us semi-qualified human . . .' Breaking off at a hammering on the door. Lottie looked up sharply. Initial alarm, Ashton noted, soon subsiding into weariness.

'Oh, hell, I'd forgotten about him. I've not even made up his bed.'

'Who's this?'

'An American chap. Moira's boyfriend. Better let him in before he gets soaked.'

'I'll go,' Ashton said. 'Never know what else it might be this time of night, do you? Moira's your daughter, is she?'

Milly had given up on security. The Post Office door was on the latch. Cathy burst through it, throwing off her coat.

'Where is she?'

'I'm here. Just don't look at me.'

Milly had built up the fire with great cobs of coal. Moira was hunched over it, feet on the red-tiled hearth, a glass of Guinness between them. Her jeans and sweater hung from a wire line under the wooden mantelpiece. She wore a dressing gown of Milly's with a design of giant daisies. There was a pink towel around her head.

Cathy grinned helplessly.

Moira said, 'Take more than death to kill me, huh?'

Is that it? Ernie Dawber wondered. Determined not to see tomorrow's sun? And will anyone? Will we ever even see the sky again?

Getting a bit whimsy, Ernest?

Aye, I am that, Ma. Been whimsy all night. Offered meself as a sacrifice, Ma. Wanted to go out on the Moss and not come back. Bit pathetic, eh?'

He walked with a measured pace towards Bridelow Hall, shining his torch, making no attempt to conceal his approach.

Well, what would you have done, Ma? Doctor tells you it could be two years, could be six months. Or less. You start to think, where am I going to be when it happens? Where would I like to be more than Bridelow? Bridelow as it is now. With the shades of things and the balance. Where else could I go and actually be any bloody *use*?

His saturated hat was moulded to his head, the sodden brim as heavy as a loaded teatray.

Little problem in the brain, Ma. That's why I was thrown a bit when your Willie lost his rag and raised the issue of my mental state.

Ernie chuckled. I suppose you'd have seen the black glow on me too, eh, owd lass? And said nowt.

But did you see it around yourself?

Happen not.

Ernie became thoughtful.

He didn't need his torch lit when the Hall came into view. For the Hall was all lights, upstairs and down, and brought back, with a momentary thrill, a picture of the old days when Arthur and Liz held open house for the brewery workers and their relatives and friends. Which amounted to the whole village in those days. Liz in a glittery gown, Arthur permitting his stern eyes a twinkle behind those forbidding horn-rims.

And Shaw.

Shaw was never there on such occasions. Shaw, they said, was shy. Shaw could never say the headmaster's name. Mr Der-der . . .

'*Mr Dawber,*' Shaw said easily.

He stepped out from the brewery entrance gate, the stem of a stylish golf umbrella propped elegantly across his left shoulder. His dark suit was perfectly dry.

'Good evening, lad,' Ernie said heavily. 'I've come to see your mother.'

'Small problem there, Mr D. Mother's spending the weekend at a hotel in Buxton. Autumn break.'

'Brave of her, lad. Conquered the agoraphobia, then, has she?'

'She hasn't got agoraphobia, Mr Dawber. She's simply rather a retiring person. Shy, even.'

'As you were yourself, Shaw. Perhaps it's an hereditary problem. Dealt with yours, though, didn't you, lad?'

'One alters. As one gets older.'

Shaw Horridge, sheltered from the downpour, was smirking. It brought out the headmaster in Ernie.

'Perhaps heredity says it all.' Standing his ground, dripping. 'I'd like a chat, Shaw Horridge, and I'd like it now.'

He'd almost said, My Office. At once.

For a second, Shaw looked disconcerted.

Ernie pocketed his torch. 'I won't go away.'

'Won't you?' Shaw's smirk vanished and was replaced by an expression Ernie didn't recognize but which he found surprisingly menacing.

'Come up to the house, then,' Shaw said.

Two phone calls was all it took. One to Headquarters, one to the doctor's house. At least this was something Ashton could do – they'd given him a name in connection with an incident under investigation; he could check it out.

'Thanks very much, Doc,' Ashton said. 'Owe you one.'

Lottie was over by the stove again, deep lines in her face, the permanent frown. Years of Matt Castle in the making, Ashton reckoned, but not irreversible.

The American, Macbeth, was sitting at the kitchen table, watching him in silence, black hair stuck to his forehead, tension coming off him like vapour. Chrissie White was watching the American; what was coming off her wasn't quite seemly under the circumstances.

'Well, then,' Ashton said, putting down the phone. They were all staring at him now. 'Your Miss Cairns. I suppose I'm right in assuming she was nowhere near her middle-fifties?'

Macbeth breathed out in a rush. 'God damn.'

'Grey hair?' said Ashton. 'Somewhat overweight?'

'But . . .' Macbeth sat down next to Chrissie. 'But it was her car?'

'Clearly. With another woman's body in it. What's that say to you? Mrs Castle? Any other women missing?'

'God!' Macbeth had his head in his hands. His body sagged. Relief. No way you could fake that.

Chrissie smiled thinly. 'Well,' she said, *'that's* all right, then.'

Lottie said, 'What did she look like?'

'She was badly burned, apparently. As I say, mid-to-late fifties. Plumpish. Grey hair, quite short. So who is she? And what was she doing in Miss Cairns's car?'

Macbeth looked up. There were tears in his eyes.

Ashton let his gaze rest on the American. 'There is, of

course, another question. Two, perhaps. Where *is* Miss Cairns? And what does she know about this woman's death?'

'Hey,' Macbeth said. 'Come on . . .'

'Has to be asked, sir.' And other questions. Like, what's brought this American all the way from Glasgow in the worst driving conditions of the year so far, and what's he doing in this country anyway?

Macbeth said, 'How official is this?'

'Well, now,' Ashton said, 'that depends, doesn't it?'

Macbeth said nothing for nearly half a minute, then he spread his hands. 'OK. How much you know about a guy name of John Peveril Stanage?'

Chrissie gasped, and Ashton allowed himself a sigh of manifest satisfaction.

Moira was choking.

'Jesus, what the hell is this stuff?'

'Shurrup and get it down,' Milly said.

'Yeah, but what . . . ?'

'Ma Wagstaff's Crisis Mixture,' said Milly. 'Last bottle.'

'Tastes like something scraped off the floor at a foot clinic.'

Cathy said seriously, 'Drink it, Moira. We need you.'

She drank it. She drank it all, every last nauseating mushroom-coloured drop. All the time watching Cathy over the glass, the girl's narrow face taut with concentration.

'Dic.' Moira let Milly take the glass away. 'Thank you. Cathy, what are we going to do about Dic?'

'I told you, didn't I?' Cathy said. 'I said it wasn't Dic who took the comb.'

'Aye, you did. I'm sorry. But why's he with Stanage? How'd he get into this? And the girl. The woman.'

'Therese. Pure poison. Lady Strychnine.'

'But Dic was *helping* them.'

'Dic was helping *us*,' Cathy snapped.

'Us?'

'The Mothers.'

'You told me . . . Hang on, I'm confused, you said you weren't one. You said your father wouldn't . . .'

'I didn't know you well enough. I lied. It's OK to lie sometimes. Except to yourself.'

'Sure.' Moira sighed.

'Dic lied to himself a lot. He lied about his father. He lied about not hating his father.'

'I know. Maybe we all lied to ourselves about Matt.'

'Aye.' Willie Wagstaff was sitting on the arm of the sofa. 'I never wanted him to come back to Bridelow, me. He were too . . . disruptive, you know?' He paused. 'Like our Jack.'

'How it happened,' Cathy said, 'Dic read Stanage as a kid. His dad was all for it. Imaginative stuff, full of Celtic reverberations.' She looked up at Willie in appeal. 'They didn't *know*, you see. Matt had been away too long. He didn't know Stanage was Jack Lucas. Not at first.'

'Makes sense,' Willie said. 'It were a long time before any of us found out. Peveril. Stanage. Derbyshire place-names. Peveril of the Peak. Nothing too local. How *should* we know? He were never on telly, never give interviews to t'papers.'

'So, like a lot of kids,' Cathy said, 'Dic wrote him a fan letter. *Un*like a lot of kids, he got a reply inviting him to visit the great man. Beginning of a beautiful friendship. It was Stanage who persuaded Dic to learn the Pennine Pipes. Matt was delighted, as you'd imagine, Dic having always rejected traditional stuff.'

'Why would Stanage be so interested in Dic?' Moira asked.

'He wasn't. He was interested in Matt. They'd known each other as kids, obviously, and Stanage was looking for ways into Bridelow. That was *his* ruling obsession, to get back at them.'

'At . . . ?'

'At Bridelow. Specifically at the Mothers. The Bridelow establishment. The keepers of the Bridelow tradition. The keepers of . . . I don't know.'

'The balance,' Milly said. 'The keepers of the balance.'

'God knows,' said Willie, 'they tried to sort him out. They tried everything. He were just . . . just bloody *bad*, what can you say? And when he like . . . finally overstepped the mark, he had to go. He were halfway gone by then, anyroad, gone off to university, smartest lad ever come out of Bridelow. Can say that again.'

Moira said slowly, 'How do you mean, overstepped the mark?'

Willie looked at the others. Milly nodded. Willie said bitterly, 'He desecrated a grave.'

'Spell it out, little man,' Milly said softly.

'He dug up Owd Ma. That were me granny. Ma's ma. Been dead a week.'

'He had it all timed,' Milly said. 'The right day, the right hour, the right position of the moon, all this. He had to *know*, you see. He had to know what was being denied to him because he was a man.'

A gout of rain came down the chimney. On the fire, a red coal cracked in two with a chip-pan hiss.

Moira said, 'He did this? Necromancy? He tried to get information out of a dead woman?'

Willie reached for Milly's hand. She said, 'I was only a youngster. I only know what I was told later, by Ma. She said there were things he knew, things he threw in her face . . . that he couldn't possibly have learned from anyone else. So either Old Ma told him stuff on her deathbed, which is so unlikely as to be . . .'

Moira started to feel sick, and it wasn't Ma Wagstaff's Crisis Mixture. 'Willie, sooner or later Matt would know about this guy. What he was.'

'We never talked about it, lass. But, aye, sooner or later. But he'd be too far in, maybe, by then. To be charitable. In the end, though, it's two of a kind. Exiles wanting in.'

'Men,' said Milly. 'Men wanting knowledge.'

'And now he's doing it to Matt. What he did to your gran. Dic told me, he said, "He's got my dad." How can . . . ?'

'We know,' Milly said. 'Matt's coffin's full of soil.'

Cathy said, 'Listen, the night Dic brought you to the Rectory, afterwards he had a few drinks, got a bit . . . mixed up. He was approached. There was a sexual approach. He thought it was you.'

'What a compliment.'

Cathy frowned. 'Next day he told me about it. He's always told me things. He was in a hell of a state. He needed . . . calming down. You can tell how easily they get people.'

Moira nodded. She knew well enough.

'I said you were with me the whole time,' Cathy said, 'so it couldn't have been you.'

'Thank you.'

'And then we talked about it for ages. It was *our* only way in. For Dic to go along with it, see what happened. I think he saw it as a way of getting out of the influence of his dad and Stanage and the whole thing.'

Moira started shaking her head. Lamb to the slaughter.

'He's been through hell.' Cathy's eyes looking hot with sorrow. 'Yes, they've got Matt's body. Yes, they've been . . . arousing him.'

Moira covered her face with her hands.

'There's Stanage and this Therese. Calls herself Therese Beaufort. He claims, apparently, that she's his niece. That's crap. All kinds of people've been attracted to him over the years. He's, you know, he's . . . magnetic.'

'I know.' Moira rubbed her eyes. 'I know his kind. Who else?'

'Detritus. There's a Satanic-type cult based in Sheffield that's been holding rituals on the moors, in the old Bronze Age circles. Been going on for years. They move as close as they can to Bridelow – it's got a reputation in the occult world, as you can imagine. Place of power.'

Moira felt herself back in the churchyard, deformed stone across the moor, hopping like a toad, a quick splash of blood . . .

'Therese,' Cathy said. 'Tess – she's Tessa-something, Dic says, she came up from the Welsh border – Tess brings them along. They're revolting. That farmer – there was a farmer killed on the moor, Sam Davis – he came to see Pop last week. Lights in the night, rams killed. His wife reckoned they were even sacrificing babies.'

'It's not unknown,' Moira said. 'I believe some of these cults are actually breeding babies for sacrifice. How did this guy die?'

'Fell down a quarry at night. How do you know that, about the babies?'

'Read it in the *News of the World*,' Moira said quickly.

506

'Look, you say they get as close as they can to Bridelow. But they can't get *in*, right? You told me the other night there were defences. The kind you can't see.'

Milly said, 'Jack could let them in. Down in Cambridge, Jack was mixing with all kinds of people. Jack was learning all the time. We had to do something or else Bridelow'd be . . . just like everywhere else. Soiled. Only more so, because . . .'

'. . . because it was a place of power. Right?'

'We had to do something,' Milly said. 'Or Ma did. Ma was the only one could do it.'

'Why?' Moira hunched forward, hands clasped. 'I mean, what? What could Ma do?'

Milly looked down into her lap where Willie's hand lay.

'Come on, Milly,' Moira said almost angrily. 'What is it you're not telling me? Cathy, do *you* know?'

'Yes,' Cathy said. 'I think so.'

CHAPTER VII

Ernie had taken off his hat, placed it on the hallstand, where it was still dripping five minutes later when Shaw Horridge shouted, 'Get out. Get out, Mr Dawber. Get out before I kill you!'

Six months ago Ernie would have had a regretful laugh at that. Six months ago, Shaw wouldn't have been able to say it without a hell of a struggle. Now it was quite apparent that Shaw would indeed like to kill him and certainly could. And it wouldn't be his first time.

Feelings. Ernie had ignored his feelings, his whimsy. They were never specific enough, never quite *accurate*. He was a man and also a scholar in his own small way, and feelings, in Bridelow, were what women had.

And now, when it was probably too late, he was finding out what feelings were for.

He stood by the hallstand. Over his head hung a leaded lantern in a wrought-iron frame. Tasteful; one of Liz's earliest purchases.

'Your mother's no more in Buxton, lad, than we are now.'

'She *is*!' Shaw seemed about to stamp his foot. With his folded umbrella he prodded the air an inch or two from Ernie's eyes.

Ernie didn't move. 'Nearest she got to Buxton is a BMW motorcar at the bottom of a bank. She's in a police mortuary, lad. That's where your mother is.'

Known it as soon as he and Willie had found the Cairns lass. Known it, really, for most of the day. That she was dead.

'You're off your head, Mr Dawber.'

'Not yet, lad. Soon, happen. But not yet.'

'I've told you once to get out. I won't tell you again.' Shaw's eyes glittered like broken glass.

'Kill me, eh?'

'You think I won't?'

'No, I know you would.' Ernie picked up his wet hat, held it in front of his chest like a breast plate. Took a big, long breath. Saw before him the little lad in Class I of the infants. Fair-haired, fair-complexioned, tall but slightly built. Brought to school that first morning by stocky, swarthy Arthur Horridge, Arthur's dark brown hair already greying at the temples.

Ernie looked into Shaw's pale, malevolent eyes. 'Just like you killed your granny, eh, lad?'

Shaw drew back across the hall. His mouth twisted up and opened on one side, his face alternating between a sneer and a stare of more than slightly crazed, vacant incomprehension.

'What's this? What's this nonsense? What are you babbling about? You're an old fool, Mr Dawber.'

'Haven't they told you, Shaw? Hasn't your father told you?'

'My father's dead.'

'I only wish he were, lad.'

'I . . . You . . .'

'Your father's Jack Lucas. John Peveril Stanage.'

'That's . . . that's absolute crap.'

'You want to hear about this, Shaw?'

Shaw had backed up against the flock-papered far wall, his mouth twisting noiselessly from side to side, both hands over his head, hovering half an inch above his baldness.

'When I was a little lad' – Ernie leaned his back against the

508

hall stand, relaxed – 'there was a bit of a kerfuffle in Bridelow. Minor scandal, soon hushed up, years before I learned the details. Anyroad . . . Ma Wagstaff . . . Iris Morris in those days, young lass, bit of all right, too. But wild. Nowt anybody could tell her. Wasn't going to stay in little Bridelow, was she? Off to the city, our Iris, most weekends. Met a feller, as you'd expect. Educated smooth-talker, name of Lucas.'

Shaw Horridge was standing with his legs apart, panting a little.

'Came back pregnant. Wouldn't be the first one. Prospective father buggered off soon as he found out. The old story, and folks in Bridelow's always been liberal enough about that kind of thing. Except Iris was a bit special. Direct line, see. Presented to the Mother same week she was christened. Expected, somehow, to have a daughter.'

'This is nonsense,' Shaw said. 'I'm going to kill you.'

'Hear me out first, eh?'

'I killed someone else tonight. I killed Manifold. Young Frank. I killed him . . . just moments ago.'

'I don't think so,' Ernie said uncertainly. The idea of Shaw Horridge coping with Young Frank with a few drinks inside him was still a bit laughable. Wasn't it?

'I did. I'll show you.'

'Let me finish, lad, eh? Where was I? A daughter, yes. They expected she'd have a daughter first, that's the way it is usually. But no, it was a boy, and a most peculiar child. White. All over.'

'No!'

'Yes! Folks said, it's retribution. She sinned. Sinned not so much against God but against her heritage. And the child? A changeling, they said. Know what that is, Shaw? Child of another . . . species, shall we say. A cuckoo. That was the word they used, changeling's my word, as a folklorist – all nonsense, of course, happen just a genetic throwback. But "cuckoo" was what they said. Not out loud, of course. Whispered it, though, when Iris wasn't about. But then she got married to Len Wagstaff and had three more, and the family closed ranks a bit and the things John did later were covered up. At first. Until it wasn't possible to cover them up any more.'

'What things?'

'Pranks, at first. Not the worst you could say about them, but if you were being charitable you'd call them pranks. Cruel pranks.'

'Perhaps they made him feel better,' Shaw said.

'Eh?'

'You do something brave, you push yourself. And you start to feel better.'

'Do you?'

'Yes. You can do anything if you push yourself into places you wouldn't normally go.'

'Oh, aye?'

'Look at this, for instance. How do you think I got this?'

He was doing it again, letting his hands hover half an inch from the bald part of his head.

'I don't understand,' Ernie said.

'Can't you see?' Shaw leapt about flinging switches until the hall was blazing with lights. Wall lights, ceiling lights, lights over five mirrors reflecting his bounding figure. 'Look. *Look!* I was completely bald at the front. Even two weeks ago, I was bald.'

'Aye?'

'Well?' Shaw bent his head towards Ernie. It threw off light like a steel helmet. 'Well?'

'Well, what?' Ernie said.

Shaw straightened up. 'Know when it began to grow again? When I agreed to get rid of the old lady.'

'Your grandmother.'

'That's crap. You come here, you give me all this bullshit. How stupid do you really think I am, Mr Dawber?'

Ernie thought very carefully before he spoke.

'Stupid enough,' he said, stepping away from the hallstand, bracing himself, 'to think your hair is growing again.'

The fire hissed again. There was a visible bubbling among the coals.

'Have to get Alf Beckett to fit you a cowl on t'chimney,' Willie Wagstaff said prosaically to Milly.

Moira moved her legs closer to the fire, feeling she might never be truly warm again.

'Your brother? He's your brother?'

'Half-brother,' said Willie. 'But it counted for nowt. Once he'd gone he were never spoke of again. And after that, Ma never looked back.'

'And there was a new respect for Ma,' Milly Gill said. 'That she was able to do it.'

'Do what? What did she do?'

'Personal banishing rite,' Milly said. 'She walked around the village boundary three times within a day and a night. She walked barefoot, placing stones. Calling on . . . elements not usually invoked. But he was a strong presence, even then.'

'Be July of that year when he come back,' Willie recalled. 'End of his second year at Cambridge. Arrived in a fancy`sports car.'

'Wherever he went,' Milly said, 'he could make money or get people to give him things.'

'There's an owd tree,' Willie said, 'just this side of t'Moss, 'fore you get to t'pub. Jack piled his car into that. Broke both arms. Elsie Ball, as were landlady of The Man in them days, she dint recognize Jack at first. Went out to help him, but Jack wouldn't come out of his car, *couldn't* come out. Just sat there until the ambulance come. Ma were standing at top of street, she knew who it were. Too far apart to see each other's faces, but I remember Elsie saying clouds were coming down, hanging low, like a thunderstorm were about to burst.'

'And then Jack went away,' Milly said, 'and we never saw him again. He knew he'd never get back in, long as Ma were . . .'

'Alive,' said Willie, and Moira saw the fingers of his left hand beginning to crawl up the side of his knee.

'So,' Moira said, 'if he *wanted* to get back . . .'

'Why should he? He were rich. He were becoming famous. He had everything he could wish for.'

'Except his heritage,' Moira said.

'He tried to *destroy* his heritage,' Milly insisted.

'No. He tried to restructure it, surely. He tried to rebuild it around himself. It was a placid, earth-related, female religion, and he wanted to harden it into something he could use.'

Milly looked at her with suspicion.

'I've encountered it before,' Moira said. 'No. He was never going to walk away from that. All the time he'd be building up his armoury of contacts inside Bridelow. Matt and Dic we know about. There are probably others.'

'Shaw Horridge.' Willie's fingers were drumming hard. 'The brewery. He'd bought into Gannons. He must've done that purely to get hold of Bridelow Brewery.'

Who took the comb?

. . . bloke called Shaw Horridge, but that's not important right now . . .

'Yes,' Moira said.

Willie's fingers going like hell, both hands now. 'The bloody *scale* of the thing! Too big for us to see. Maybe we never wanted to see it. He'd gone. Right, Ma says, that's it. Never mention him again and you'll never see him again. And we never have.'

'Except,' said Milly, 'in Shaw.'

Willie looked at her. Moira watched his eyes widen.

'It was a Mothers' thing,' Milly said. 'Never talked about. I think Mr Dawber knew, but that's all. Probably not many people remember now, and I was just a child, but when Eliza McCarthy first arrived in Bridelow it was as Jack's girlfriend. All Jack's girlfriends were from wealthy backgrounds. Liz didn't last long, I don't suppose she was beautiful enough. It was probably just the family link with the Duke of Westminster that interested him.'

Milly pulled one of the cats on to her lap, began to stroke it from neck to tail. 'What happened, I believe, is that they had a row and Jack just drove away and left her in tears in the street. Which was where Ma found her. This was before the banishing.'

'Aye,' Willie said, something dawning. 'She spent the night with us. It were the year before me Dad died. He'd gone to The Man, he were in t'darts team, and I remember lying in bed and hearing Ma and this lass talking for hours.'

'Probably what you heard was Ma warning her off Jack. Next day, when Jack didn't come back, Ma introduced Liz to

Arthur Horridge and two months later they were engaged. Well . . . four days before the wedding, Liz is hammering on Ma's door in a terrible state. She's pregnant.'

Milly hauled the second cat on to her lap as if she needed reinforcement. 'Jack. Jack on the outside. He can't get into Bridelow but he can still get to his ex-fiancée.'

'Bastard.' Both of Willie's hands fell away from his knees.

Cathy shook her head in distaste. 'How could she?'

'You didn't know him,' Milly said. 'When I was nine years old, Jack took me and two other little girls for a walk on . . . Oh, you don't want to hear, it was nothing by comparison with what else he's done. But he could walk in and even if you didn't really like him he'd get what he came for. Liz – it wasn't rape, as such, you could learn to live with that. Anyway . . . Ma had a long chat with Arthur Horridge and Shaw was born, and he was Arthur's son and nothing more was ever said.'

'I can't believe all this,' Willie said. 'Can't believe we never *thought*. We didn't think of the bugger any more – better not to. Wrote his books under the name John Peveril Stanage, we knew that, so it was as if the Jack Lucas we knew had gone for good.'

'Pouring all his worst fantasies into his books, huh?' Moira said.

'Something like that. Takes that American lad to come in here and drop Jack's name in our laps before we put two and two together.'

'Oh,' said Cathy. 'Mungo! He still thinks . . .'

Moira spun so fast the towel unwound from her hair. Cathy's hand went to her mouth but failed to stifle a cry.

'They did that to you? They cut off all your . . . ?'

Moira let the towel fall.

'Oh, Moira!' Tears sprang into Cathy's eyes.

Deliberately calm, Moira said, 'They needed my hair to entangle Matt's spirit. They locked me in an outhouse in the dark. They couldn't kill me because that would have released *my* spirit, defeating the object. So they kept me in this sensory vacuum, sedated with mogadon or some shit that turns you into a comatose non-person so that your energy, your personality, your essence can be . . . stolen.'

Moira stood up, reached under the mantelpiece for her stiffening jeans. 'Cathy, I . . . You invoked the awful word "Mungo".' Disgusted to feel a tiny smile pulling on the muscles at the corners of her mouth.

'He still thinks you're dead,' Cathy said. 'He's over at The Man. I'd better call him.'

'Uh huh.' Moira shook her head. 'I don't know how Macbeth got here or why, and I don't have time to find out. I'm starting to see everything. Clear as hell.'

Her mind burning up with it.

They stood either side of the Beacon of the Moss, heads bowed.

Joel had asked, 'Shouldn't we pray?'

'We should meditate,' John had said.

Joel stood in the blueness of it and tried to concentrate his mind, to absorb the rise and fall of Tongues from beneath, to achieve a holy stillness. But his thoughts lumbered ape-like around the shadowed walls of the chamber. He could not see John's face, could only sense the man's awesome containment.

'It's time,' John said very quietly, raising his head.

Reaching up, beyond the top of the great lantern, he examined the chain by which it hung from the thick, long-ago-smoke-blackened beam. 'Come beneath it, Joel. Catch it when I release it.'

And while Joel crouched, arms full of light, John reached up and unhooked the chain.

The lamp was unexpectedly heavy. Joel stumbled but held it, pulling down several feet of electric flex which had been coiled between the beam and the wall. The lamp did not go out.

'Good,' John said. 'Now lower it to the floor.'

They both stood back. The pointed top of the lantern was on a level now with Joel's groin.

'Kick it in,' John urged.

Joel tried to see his face but saw only the bared blue teeth and blue steel ripples of hair.

He couldn't move.

'This is the pagan light. This is the lure. *Very few people dared cross the Moss, Mr Beard, except those for whom the Devil lit the way. Have you heard that legend? Have you heard it?'*

'Yes . . . !' Joel panicking. 'I heard it from you. You told me.'

'And do you believe it? Consider the evidence.'

'I believe,' Joel intoned, 'that this is a place of pagan worship. I have seen the signs. I have seen the woman with the spread cunt. I have *dreamed* of her. And I have seen the dead walk.'

'And you know that this night is Samhain, the Feast of the Dead, and that the light is shining out across the peat to welcome the dead to this place.'

'It shall not happen.'

Joel lifted his foot, aware as never before of its size and its weight, and he plunged it, with a shattering, through the glass of the lantern and watched the shower of shards, blue and then white, pierce the tumbling shadows.

'The bulbs, Joel. Now the bulbs!'

Joel felt his lips stretched tight as his foot went back again and again, lightbulbs exploding, all of them, whorls of jagged colour, and then there was the creak of a door opening, a rapid clumping of footsteps and his neck was wrenched back and the last thing he saw before the last bulb blew was John's luminescent teeth as the man held up a scimitar of white glass, nine inches long.

Joel bit rubber, and felt his knees buckle before he was even aware of the single dull, heavy blow on the back of his head.

For a long time there was only night, and then there was a lake and a naked woman on a hill, and the woman smiled with a sorrow deeper than the lake and Joel wanted to scream, *I recognize you. I recognize you now, for what you are . . .*

But the woman was gone and there was only a void of dark sorrow and John's voice, coming very quickly, words running together, some in an archaic and alien language, and a few that he could understand.

'. . . *that by the laying down of the blood . . .'*

Another, deeper male voice joining John's in fractured counterpoint.

'. . . *and shall be recompensed for that which we have borrowed* . . .'

Joel trying to speak, his arms pinned behind him, confusion and humiliation turning to a savage anger as his chest swelled and his elbows jerked and there was a grunt behind him and he spat out the rubber and jerked his head forward and inside him he let out a great roar of rage.

And only a liquid gurgle came out, and he felt his very soul was pouring out through his throat and something heavy thrust into the small of his back and there was a shattering explosion and Joel was out into the flooded sky and falling through the slipstream of his blood.

PART TEN

MOSS

CHAPTER I

Nobody in the house had been able to get to sleep anyway, because of the rain, and then The Chief started to howl, a terrified yelping sort of howl, sending Benjie hurtling down the stairs and his mam screaming from the landing, 'He'll go in a kennel, that dog, I'm warning you!' And The Chief carried on howling, even with Benjie's arms tight around his neck, and Benjie shouted back up, 'It's that dragon again, Mam!'

Heard his mam snort from the landing.

Mumbling into the dog's fur, '. . . same as killed me gran.'

And Benjie thought he should get dressed and take The Chief out into the street so his howling would wake up the whole village and everybody would be able to escape before the dragon came out of the Moss.

Moira was already dressed when they heard Alfred Beckett shouting in the Post Office, 'Shop! Shop!'

Milly brought him through and Alf stood there, getting his breath back, raindrops glittering in his moustache.

'They've put it out!' he gasped, holding on to the back of the sofa. 'Bastards've put out the light.'

Willie pushed past him and dashed through the office to the front door. 'He's right.'

'Beacon of the Moss,' Milly explained to Moira.

'What's that mean? That it's out?'

'It's happened before, obviously, power-failures and such, but with all the rest of it . . .'

'You're saying it's cumulative, right?'

'I'll go up,' Willie called back.

'No,' Moira snapped. 'There's been too much rushing in, far's I can see. Cathy, the Mothers – how many *are* there?'

'It's a ragbag,' Milly said.

'How d'you call a meeting?'

'The old days, used to be said we never needed to call them at all.'

'Well, how about we try the phone, huh?'

'They'll all be in bed.'

'Jesus wept! If I had any hair I'd be tearing it.'

Dic Castle knew that a common way of committing suicide was to cut your wrists while lying in a bath of warm water and that it was largely painless, letting life seep away.

He was not in a bath of warm water, but he supposed sedation had the same effect in that he was aware of *not* trying to scream through the sweating adhesive tape across his mouth but just sitting there, bound by string and wire to his chair, wondering how long before it was over.

His hands were painlessly numb, cloth tourniquets around both wrists so that the blood flow was regulated, like an egg-timer.

He wasn't even resentful any more. He'd got Moira out. He'd led them away from her and they didn't know she'd gone, the sound of the rain muffling her hysteria. Him? They thought he'd just chickened out and run away, and now they'd caught him, and maybe this was what they'd intended for him all along.

Blood to blood.

He watched their faces: Philip, the glum satanist; Owen, the ex-nurse who'd given him valium through a vein; Andrea, the care-in-the-community mental patient who'd killed but not exactly *murdered* two small boys many years ago; Therese, who thought she was already halfway to being a goddess; Dr Roger Hall, who just wanted to meet the Man in the Moss.

Real evil, Dic realized, was a bit bloody pathetic.

Outside, the apprentice at the gate, was feeble Shaw Horridge, probably more inadequate than any of them because he had had money and privileges on a scale incomprehensible to most of the others.

Over in the loft at the church, Dean – also known as Asmodeus – had been hiding for hours with Terence, the hulking occult bookseller from Salford, awaiting their mentor, the revered John. Slaveringly eager for whatever grotesque experience he'd prepared for them, the more perverse the more sensuously exciting.

Dic had ceased some while ago to be shocked. He'd already seen in his father the damage caused by the perversion of a Utopian dream. He was twenty-four. He'd seen Matt Castle's jolly, infectious pioneering spirit shrivel to a sour fanaticism. And then he'd died.

And now, because of his father, Dic would die too. Taped into a wooden chair with the blood draining slowly from his wrists.

Blood to blood.

Dic was staring across the circle, with a vaguely surprising sense of pity, into his father's eyes, when a movement made him turn his head. Therese had shuddered.

Therese was sitting cross-legged, although her legs were hidden in cloak and shadow. There were candles, ordinary white candles, in glass jars because of the draught, seven of them arranged around the circle, which had been painted on the wooden floor in white and was actually two concentric circles a yard apart. In the space between the circles they all sat, like shadowy partygoers gathered for charades.

Dregs.

But Therese had shuddered.

'Yes,' she breathed. 'He's done it. Can't you feel it?'

And as if she'd signalled to them, the inadequates started mumbling, some far back in their throats, making unintelligible noises as though trying to disengage their dentures.

Revolting bastards.

In time, the mumbling became more intense and seemed to encompass the figure sprawled, rotting and stinking, in the wooden armchair.

Dic could look at it now with little sense of shock and no sense of relationship. At the withering lips drawn back, the yellow of teeth, the stiff, spouting hair above eyes wide open but glazed like a cod's eyes on the slab.

His father.

*

Of course, if you'd suggested to Chris that it was a game, a recreation like golf or squash or amateur theatricals, Chris would have been most resentful and his reply would probably have been – as he would now admit – somewhat pompous and self-righteous.

Born in Hemel Hempstead, Chris was an accountant in Sheffield. He was thirty-seven, had had his own house, on what was now a minimal mortgage, since the age of nineteen. So that when he married Chantal four years ago life had not exactly been an uphill struggle, with foreign holidays and two cars from the beginning. And the fact that God had not yet seen fit to bestow upon them a child, well, perhaps that indicated God had other work for them.

Chris had always been a churchgoer. However, as he'd intimated in passing to the American, Macbeth, the Anglican faith had long since ceased to satisfy his intense need for a more dynamic relationship with his deity.

Baptism into the Church of the Angels of the New Advent, with its full-throated, high-octane worship and its promise of *real religious experience*, was the fulfilment of what Chris had been anticipating all his thinking life.

Within eighteen months, he'd become an elder of the Church, dealing with its finances, investing its reserves, getting the best deal for God.

It filled his life. *God*, therefore, filled his life.

And God was not a hobby.

The validity of the Church of the Angels of the New Advent had been confirmed by the acceptance at theological college of one of its founders, Brother Beard, who had been called by God to go out into the 'straight' Church and reform it from within.

God's reasoning had become all too clear to Chris when Joel had been called to Bridelow.

His appearance at their house last night in search of sanctuary had made Chris – and he was sure he could also speak for Chantal – feel very honoured and (he would have admitted this now) very excited.

When Joel had spoken of his discovery of the symbols of pagan devil-worship in the Lord's house, Chris had been, on the surface, appalled, and underneath (he might not yet have admitted this) thrilled.

And when Joel had telephoned them this morning with a dramatic plea which said, more or less, Bring in the troops, the war has begun, Chris's blood had begun to race.

It was not a recreation. It was not a hobby. It was not just an unusual and stimulating way of spending Sunday, hiring a coach and everyone piling in, prepared to fast through the night (bar the odd cup of coffee) to bring light where once was darkness.

It was a war.

When the initial joyous element had been rather dispelled through exhibitions of mental stress by, first, Joel and then (perhaps influenced by Joel's rather overheated display) Chantal, Chris, the Lord's accountant, had decided that a more precise and ordered approach was required if they were to avoid further humiliation.

When they'd returned, a little shamefaced, he'd taken it upon himself to bar the church doors and state that there was to be no more wandering in and out for coffee and anyone experiencing anything irregular should simply clasp the hand of his or her brother or sister and pray for it to pass.

And there had been hymns and prayers (without hand-clapping, since they had learned that some faiths considered there to be a demonic element in this), and the familiar flow of exhaltation had once more been attained.

Until Chris himself had heard a distant crash from somewhere above and foolishly disregarded it until the reality of their struggle became distressingly (at first) evident.

He heard and felt it begin.

It began with a cooling of the air and a creeping change in the tone of the chant.

Hoooolyamallaaagloriagloriamalalaglorytogodglorytogod

The girl next to him had been singing melodiously, her voice high and pure and sweet.

And then too sweet.

Cloying, in fact, with an acrid saccharine aftertaste, which he was actually beginning to taste in his own throat. And then becoming simpering and childish. Peevish and playground-rhythmical.

> *holygod holygod holyholyholygod*
> *goldyhod goldyhod golyhold holygold*
> *godlyhole godlyhole godlyhole . . .*

And then it happened very quickly . . . sort of *whooooosh*, like a small hurricane of bad breath. There was a wafting sugary smell which soon became sweetly putrid, like the bad orange at the bottom of the bowl, as the chant, the pure song of Tongues, suddenly was sounding raucous and guttural, women cackling hideously (enticingly) and men making grunting, retching, foul pig noises.

We're doing it, Chris thought, in a kind of euphoric dismay, as a slimy earth taste arose in his throat. *We are exorcizing the Evil*.

Just that nobody had told him it would be quite so unpleasant (and stimulating).

When Paul, their musician – who had, admittedly, never been all that proficient – began to force a vicious, grinding discordance through the organ pipes, Chris stepped out into the aisle and ran up the steps of the pulpit from where he observed that at least five Angels of the New Advent had begun hurriedly to divest themselves of their apparel.

He also saw three men, one a kind of albino with a cherub's mouth, emerge from the vestry and calmly let themselves out of the church by the main door.

They were laughing.

There was still no sign of Joel.

Joel?

Who *was* this Joel?

Chris saw no more, for he was attacked by one of his squealing sisters and his face clawed and he enjoyed it *immensely*.

Mungo Macbeth had specialized for over ten years in the downmarket kind of TV-movie in which people fell wildly in love and moved heaven and earth to find fulfilment in someone's arms.

Between times he'd done cop movies, about hard-bitten, cynical cops who, underneath it all, had feelings same as anyone else.

However, apart from the ones who'd given him parking and speeding tickets, Macbeth had never before met a cop who was not being played, at unreasonable expense, by some asshole with a beach house and security gates.

Love stories did not end, before they had even begun, with the death of the love object. And cop movies were never about cops who sat in your car in an endless monsoon, which, by the way, was becoming seriously frightening, and said, 'Well, I'm buggered if I know how to handle this, mate.'

They were parked up by the church in Macbeth's car on account of the grey-haired, weary-looking cop wasn't even sure his would stand up to the conditions.

Macbeth, also pretty tired, said, 'How about you just call up the precinct house and have a bunch of uniforms directed this way?'

Ashton said, 'How about you get sensible, pal?'

'I apologize.'

'Look,' Ashton said, 'it seems very likely a crime *has* been committed. But what scares the living shit out of me is that the possible criminal element in all this does not seem to be the worst aspect, if you get my meaning.'

'Yeah.'

'And if I were to contact my headquarters and somebody there did actually take me *seriously*, their first instruction – I know this much – would be: do nothing.'

Ashton scrubbed at the misted windshield. 'I'm not in the mood for some shiny-arsed politician telling me to do nowt. There's summat nasty here. I don't know how to react, but I *have* to. Right?'

'I dunno,' Macbeth said. 'It was different, somehow, when I thought Moira was dead.'

'How do you know she's not?' Ashton demanded, blunt as a sledgehammer.

'What are you saying?'

'Christ, I'm saying, *help me*. I'm saying I'm not playing this by the book because there's no book I know of covers it. I'm saying that normally, as a copper, I'd want nothing at all to do with you because I don't know you from Adam. But at least you look a bit too soft and innocent to be a villain, and if I'm not playing it as a copper I need some help and you're all I've bloody got.'

'OK,' Macbeth said reluctantly. 'First question: you equipped with a piece?'

'Eh?'

'Are you armed?'

'Are you thick?' Ashton said. 'Or just American?'

Macbeth shrugged and started up the car. 'OK,' he said. 'Let's crash the party.'

Hoping Moira would be there but not . . .

. . . not *involved*.

'OK, Lottie said fifty yards from the church, make a right, so if I reverse . . .'

He never got to do it. The hire-car was surrounded by people; they were banging on the windows and the roof.

Shortly after Shaw Horridge stopped screaming, Ernie Dawber tried to get past him to the front door, and this proved to be a bad mistake. His second bad mistake.

For a long time, Shaw had been tearing around the hall clutching at his head. He'd have been tearing his hair if there'd been enough to get a grip on.

It was a squarish hall with a high ceiling and these five mirrors, three of them full-length, put there by Liz to spread the light.

It had not been the place to break the spell.

How could the lad *ever* have convinced himself that his hair was growing again, when the opposite was true? Hadn't he looked in a mirror recently? And if he had, what had he seen?

Certainly not what all five mirrors had reflected tonight before Shaw's tenuous self-control had snapped and he'd picked up a chair of Victorian mahogany and swung it above his head around the walls, and his shining baldness was reflected a thousandfold in the hail of flying glass, as Ernie cowered on his knees by the hallstand, protecting his face with his hat.

When he made a dash for the door, Shaw was on him in one bound, his sharp, pale face aglitter with blood and glass bright as jewellery. 'How did you do it? How did you do it, old man?'

It was some minutes before Ernie came to understand that the poor, crazed boy was holding him responsible for the disappearance of his hair.

'Listen to me,' Ernie said gently. 'They lied to you, lad. They lied about everything. Your hair, the brewery, your poor mother. They . . .'

Bewitched him? Twisted his mind? Before Ernie could choose the least inflammatory words, Shaw's face convulsed. He snatched up the chair again and smashed it down on the hallstand an inch from Ernie's ear, snapping off two legs.

'Get it back!' Shaw shrieked. *'Get my hair back!'*

And if this was a dream it didn't matter. There'd be no awakening anyway. Dic thought about his mother, all she'd had to put up with from the bastard. She should have married a secondary-school head or a bank manager in Wilmslow, or an airline pilot working out of Ringway. All that grit gone to waste on a two-bit musical maverick committed to a primitive instrument you could barely get a proper tune out of.

Made him want to weep.

The candles were burning low. Either this or his vision was going.

. . . *blood to blood.*

He tried to catch the eyes of the bitch, Therese, as she cried, 'I conjure *thee*, Matthew! Empowered by the Highest Strength, I *conjure* thee!'

The candles guttered. The Pennine Pipes, lying like a dead cormorant in his father's rotting lap, began to throb and to squirm as though they were full of maggots.

527

'I *conjure* thee, Matthew, under penalty of being burned and tortured in the fires for ever and ever, I *conjure* thee to appear before me and to answer my questions . . .'

Air farting through the Pennine Pipes until they squeaked and heaved, in their wrapping of black hair with a single white streak.

'I *conjure* thee, Matthew, by the power of thine own base desires, to appear before me in a pleasant and human form and to present to me the spirit of thy father of the Moss . . .'

Slipping in and out of dream. Samhain, and they said the walls were thin as paper. He thought he saw a quiver on the yellow, peeling lips of his father's corpse.

'. . . I *conjure* thee.'

A man with a knife.

Nothing ornate or ceremonial. Just a cheap craftworker's knife with a red plastic handle.

One of the untouchables bending over Dic and huffing and panting.

'By the Highest Power and by the Angels of the Firmament . . .'

The numbing power of the drug fell away from Dic like an old raincoat, leaving him naked, all his nerves singing, his cheeks bulging like a trumpeter's with a vast scream taped into his face for ever.

'Mmmmmmm!' he screamed into the adhesive tape.

'. . . and by the Angels of the Deep and with the blood that was *thy* blood and shall be *again*, Matthew . . .'

The knife cut through the tourniquets at his wrists and Dic closed his eyes, feeling nothing in his numb, etiolated arms, and yet feeling the blood rise in fountains.

'I CONJURE THEE!'

CHAPTER II

'*Hey . . . stop this bloody car . . . come on.*'

Big, shambling guy Macbeth recognized as Stan, the bartender. But Stan wasn't interested in Macbeth.

'You're the copper, aren't you?'

'Happen,' Ashton said warily.

There was Stan and some of the other guys who'd been in the bar when Macbeth arrived, but not the kid who'd figured to punch him out. Also, there was Willie Wagstaff. Macbeth leapt out, grabbed the little guy by the arm.

'Willie, hey, listen up. The body in the car . . . this was not Moira.'

'Oh,' said Willie; his mind was clearly elsewhere; he kept glancing over his shoulder towards the church and around the street. Stan was bawling into the car window at Ashton.

'Bloody hooligans. Fanatics. You're the police, get um out!'

'Willie, that means she's not dead, you hear me?'

'I'm only one policeman, sir, and I'm off duty.'

'You knew, Willie. You *knew*, goddamn it.'

'They don't *know* you're on your own,' Stan said. 'Supposed to be flaming Christians, should've heard the language. Just knock on t'door and tell um t'sling their hooks. What's the problem? We're getting wet.'

Macbeth said, 'Goddamn it, you *know* . . . Willie, where is she?'

Gary Ashton, annoyed, was out of the car, slamming the door, holding both hands up. 'All right! Quieten down. What's so important?'

Macbeth backed out, looked around the small assembly. 'Cathy know about this?' Willie nodded urgently.

Eight or nine of them now, almost a mob. Macbeth said, 'Gary, there's a bunch of well-meaning but seriously misguided people in there. Take it from me, these guys aren't shitting you, they need to be got out.'

'And we need to get in,' Stan said soberly. 'Just don't want more trouble than we can handle.'

Ashton stood in the rain pulling on his jaw. 'OK,' he said eventually. 'If I can clear this church out for you, maybe you can do something for me afterwards, all right?'

Stan shrugged, causing his old-fashioned plastic raincoat to crackle. Willie said something about Mr Dawber, looking upset, his fingers compulsively chinking the coins in his pocket.

'And another thing,' Ashton said. 'I'm not a policeman. You've never *seen* a policeman here tonight. You got that?'

Moira pulled on the navy blue duffle coat. 'Jesus, haven't worn one of these in years. This makes me a Mother?'

'Mother, maiden, hag,' Cathy said. 'It's all the same in Bridelow.'

'Just as well,' Moira said. 'I don't qualify as any of the above. Where are we going?'

Milly led her out into the street. 'Not far. Mind you don't drown in the gutter.'

Not far turned out to be Ma Wagstaff's little stone terraced cottage, its step awash but still gleaming white in the beam of the lamp Dic had given to Moira.

'Listen, I'm getting worried about Dic,' she'd said a few minutes earlier to Cathy.

'Me too,' Cathy said. 'But they couldn't kill him, could they? For the same reason they couldn't kill you. Surely?'

'No,' Moira had said dubiously. 'But sometimes you can do more harm to someone than killing them'd be, you know?'

Milly unlocked the front door and put on lights. Moira took in a tiny and ancient parlour with more bottles than a pharmacy. Or maybe this *was* a pharmacy. There was a light glaze of sadness over the room.

'I don't know where to start,' Milly said.

'Well, we don't have much time. Where'd she keep her . . . you know, recipes and stuff?'

Milly smiled wryly. 'In her head.'

'Oh, shit.' Moira began to open cupboards in the sideboard

and found more bottles. There were a few dozen books; maybe there'd be papers stuffed inside one of them. 'What's upstairs?'

'Her bathroom. Her sewing room. Her bed.'

'Are we *sure* she copied it down?'

'I remember seeing a map, a plan, kind of. I know I did. Keeping Jack out, it wasn't something you went into lightly, you know.'

Moira felt a light breeze on one side of her face. It smelt vaguely of sage.

'Something that hadn't been done for centuries,' Milly said. 'And it had to be exact. I don't know what to say, maybe if . . .'

Moira turned very casually around and looked back through the doorway into the hall.

Where she saw a little woman in misty shades of grey and sepia, a little woman who might have been formed – had it been daylight, had there been sun – by the coalescence of dustmotes.

The little woman slowly shook her head.

And disappeared.

Moira turned back into the room. 'It's not here,' she said softly. 'Ma Wagstaff had no map.'

Chris picked up the pink T-shirt and held it up in front of him and started to laugh.

Across the front of the T-shirt was inscribed, THANK GOD FOR JESUS.

He looked at it for long seconds. It made no sense to him. No sense at all any more. It was gaudy. It was trite. It was meaningless. The girl, who was called Claudette, looked a whole lot better without it, curled up asleep under the pulpit wrapped in velvet curtains torn down from the vestry.

Nice tits, Chris remembered. Paused. Wasn't that a pretty bloody sinful thing to contemplate in the House of God?

Yeah, well . . .

She'd be pretty cold, though, Claudette, when she awoke. It was getting bitter in here. Those amber-tinted lights created a completely false impression of warmth, making the pillars seem mellow.

The communion wine had helped a bit. Gerry, the solicitor from Rotherham, had found two bottles in the vestry. Well, why not? It was a so-called pagan place, wasn't it? It wasn't a sin to drink heathen wine.

Sin. Chris shook his head. So trite.

Only problem was, after that wine, he wanted a pee.

'Forget it,' he'd decreed automatically about a quarter of an hour ago. 'Nobody goes out.' Although for the life of him he couldn't remember *why* nobody should go out. Except that while it might be cold in here it was extremely wet out there. Frankly, Chris reckoned he could probably use a piss, a pint and a bag of chips in that order.

Stupidest thing they'd done had been to let the bloody bus go. That was Joel again, silly sod. Burn your boats, he'd instructed them. Well, it was all right for him, he'd cleared off somewhere. Least he could have done was left his mobile phone around; they could have got Reg Hattersley out of bed and bribed him to fetch his coach back.

Chris surveyed his little band, all forty-seven of them, The Angels of the New Advent. High-flown name, eh, for an assorted bunch of misfits whose sole connecting factor was the conviction that their lives were one course short of a banquet. Only *one* course, note, they all had their own houses and decent cars and dishwashers, etc.

Some of them were wandering around, rubbing their heads. A couple had lit cigarettes. His watch told him it had gone midnight. This was getting ridiculous.

He remembered the singing breaking up into self-parody, and a few of them had torn clothes off, mostly the ones clad in propaganda clobber like this silly T-shirt. And then there'd been isolated outbursts of anger and resentment, mostly towards Joel Beard, who'd brought them to this dump and then abandoned them – but not before going berserk and assaulting Martin, who'd lost a tooth, and Declan, who was convinced he was suffering delayed concussion. And, of course, convincing Chantal she'd been raped by an evil spirit.

'I ask you . . .' Chris said scornfully, aloud.

When someone started banging on the door, he wandered across, suspicious.

'Whosat?'

'Who am I talking to?' An authoritative kind of voice.

'Yes?' Chris said, equally peremptory.

'This is the police,' the voice said levelly. 'I don't know who you are but I have to inform you that you have no legal right to occupy this building and I'm suggesting you vacate it immediately. If you unbolt this door and everyone comes out without any trouble, I can promise you that no further action is likely to be taken. If, however . . .'

'Yeah?' Chris said. This really *was* the police?

A distant voice berated him, his own voice within his chest. He heard it say, *Get thee hence, tempter*, what he might well have said out loud an hour ago. What a plonker he'd been.

'I do strongly advise you, sir, not to play silly-buggers. Open this door, please.'

Chris gazed at the oak door, probably six inches thick, at the iron bolts, four inches wide.

Where is your power? the inner voice bleated pathetically at the policeman. *Blow it down, why don't you, with your foul, satanic breath.*

Must've been nuts, Chris thought. All of us. Mass hysteria.

'Yeah, all right,' he said resignedly and drew back the bolts.

There were cheers of relief from the brothers and sisters sprawled among the pews.

Although glances were exchanged, Milly didn't ask her how she knew there was nothing in the house. There was silence, then Milly said, 'What are we going to do now?'

'Don't know about you,' Moira said. 'But I think I'm gonny cry.'

'Moira.' Willie was in the doorway, about a yard from where Ma's ghost had stood.

Milly shook her head. 'It's not here, little man.'

Willie nodded, unsurprised. 'She weren't much of a filer-away of stuff. 'Cept for foul-smelling gunge in the bottom of owd bottles.'

'Don't knock it,' Moira said. Less than half an hour after forcing down Ma's Crisis Mixture, she was, inexplicably, feeling stronger than she had in some while.

'Moira . . .' Willie glanced behind him to where the rain bounced off Ma's moon-white doorstep. 'Don't you think . . . ?'

'Yeah,' Moira said. 'I know. I know.' She sighed. 'OK. Come away in, Macbeth.'

Suddenly self-conscious, she found herself mindlessly reaching for the duffel-coat hood to cover the desolate ruins of her hair. 'Ach,' she said, and let her hands fall to her sides.

When he stumbled over the threshold, this Mungo Macbeth, of the Manhattan Macbeths, he was looking no more smooth and glamorous than the average drowned-rat hiker from the moor.

Willie had told her briefly how the guy had driven all the way from Glasgow with three crucial words: John, Peveril and Stanage.

'Mungo,' she said, her voice unexpectedly husky, 'I just don't know what I'm gonny do with you, and that's the truth.'

Macbeth smiled, a soft, stupid, wet-faced smile; she could tell he hadn't even noticed her hair.

'The one big thing,' he said, almost in a whisper, and it made no sense.

It fact it was all crazy, Moira thought. Horrifically crazy. He shouldn't be here. He didn't know what the hell he was into. He didn't have a chance.

And did any of them?

CHAPTER III

Eventually, Benjie had persuaded his mam to let him take The Chief to his bedroom, where the German Shepherd squeezed himself into the gap between the wardrobe and the wall, sat there with his ears down and panted a lot.

'Come on, lad,' Benjie whispered, sitting up in bed in his old ninja turtle pyjamas. But The Chief wouldn't move. He kept himself in this dark corner and there was pleading in his sad, brown eyes.

Above the noise of rain, Benjie could hear other village dogs howling in the distance. When he lay down and shut his eyes he realized that the way The Chief was panting meant he was *really* howling too, but The Chief was smart, the last thing he wanted was to have himself taken out to the shed.

When Benjie opened his eyes again, he saw light-beams flitting across the curtains, like car headlights.

Which would have been all right, only the back of the house overlooked the Moss and there were no cars on the Moss, except months ago when the lorries and JCBs had been out building up the road and they'd found the bogman.

Benjie scrambled to the end of his bed, leaned over and stuck his head through the gap in the curtains.

He gasped.

It were like Fireworks Night out there.

Lights all over the Moss, like smouldery bonfires. Lights shwooshing like rockets, through the rain, from one side to another, sometimes going across each other.

But no noise except for the howling dogs and the rain.

The lights lasted no more than ten seconds and then it was all gone and Benjie couldn't see anything apart from the water rolling down the glass.

But when he lay in bed, the light showed up in the space between his eyes and his closed eyelids. He saw the Moss lit up greenish now, all green and glowing, except for the Dragon Tree.

And that was *twice* as big now, its branches, all gnarled and knotted and black among whirling, spinning lights, two of them spiking up into the sky . . . arms like giant horns with groping claws on the end. And the whole thing was breathing, dragging up big, soggy lungfuls of peat, and soon it was going to burst and its arms would gather up the whole village.

Benjie felt a scream coming on and chewed the bedclothes instead, not wanting to be put out in the shed with The Chief and get gobbled up first.

★

Macbeth watched Chris and Chantal sink side by side into the sofa at the Rectory. They didn't seem like the same people. 'I really am tired,' Chris said. 'I'm shagged out.'

And then, clearly shocked at himself, he looked up at Cathy. 'I'm sorry. I don't know what I'm saying. Catherine, has something got inside me? Am I possessed?'

Cathy waved it away. 'Chris, you've got to tell me very quickly, no evasion. *What happened in there?*'

Chris tugged at his beard. 'I just don't know. First of all, it was fine, we felt . . . how we used to feel. Holy. Special. And then it all went wrong . . . *really* quickly. It went . . . dirty.'

'It was like baptism,' Chantal said, hugging herself with goosebumpy arms. 'Only in reverse. In our baptism . . . our *re*-baptism, we throw off some of our outer clothes – symbolically – and we're submerged in water. It could be a river, or we'll hire a public pool for an afternoon, and you come up cleansed and purified.'

'That's *it*,' Chris said, eyes full of agony. 'That's right. Only this was like being submerged and some of us threw off our Christian clothes and we came up not so much dirty . . . well, yes, dirty – but worse, really. Like it was *before*.'

'People smoking,' Chantal recalled. 'In church. But it didn't *feel* like church, it didn't feel like anywhere.'

'Yeah, and blaspheming in an everyday sort of throwaway fashion. And we drank . . . God forgive us, we drank the Holy Communion wine, like it was any old pop. It didn't matter. We were like the mass of godless people out there, we didn't need religion any more, we had no use for it. Catherine, I'm so confused. We'll burn in hell for this, I think we've already *started* to burn.'

'It's OK,' Cathy said soothingly. 'The fire's out, now.' She turned to Moira and Macbeth. 'It's obvious, isn't it? It was the final sterilization.'

'Well . . .' Moira said. 'You can't just drain the power of centuries out of stone, you can only take it out of people. So you let them absorb it through their mindless, passive rituals and then you snuff out the light, blow their shaky faith up in their faces and leave them empty and when they walk out, totally knackered like this guy here, they've drained out everything that was left in the church.'

'Forgive me,' Macbeth said, 'why'd they wanna do that?'

'Because the church is the sacred centre of the village,' Cathy said. 'It's got to be neutralized before you can . . .' She stopped for breath and couldn't go on.

'Replace it with something black and horrible,' Moira said.

'What . . . what can *we* do to help?' Chris asked, rather feebly.

Cathy rounded on him. 'You can keep your bums on that settee, call in all your friends and *don't move* until your coach comes for you. And then you can go away for ever.'

'Steady, Cathy.' Moira took her arm.

'Wants to know if he's possessed?' Cathy said with a sharp laugh. 'Well, of course he's possessed. Possessed of a very slow brain. Moira, look, there's a copper out there who wants to go up the Hall with Stan Burrows and a bunch of his mates and do some sorting out, as they put it.'

'So stop him,' Moira said.

'*You* try and stop him!'

'Look, they go up there mob-handed, God knows what could happen. It's pretty damned obvious – and we're looking at something planned months ago – that Stanage has shut down the church to deflect a lot of energy towards the second natural focus, the second-highest building in Bridelow. The brewery, right? And what's at the very top of the brewery building?'

'Th'owd malt-store,' Willie Wagstaff said impatiently. 'Disused. Moira, happen this is over me head, but why don't we go up there mob-handed and flush the buggers out?'

'Because you can't fight this thing with primitive violence. I swear to you, Willie, those guys go up there they'll wind up killing each other. It's like, how come you can put a bunch of ardent, Bible-punching born-again Christians in a *church* and they come drifting out an hour or so later with this amazing born-again *apathy*?'

'He's right, though, Moira,' Cathy said. 'We can't just stand around doing nothing. *Somebody* ought to go up there.'

'It's what I've been trying to *tell* you!' Willie cried, all eight fingers beating at his thighs. 'Somebody *has*. Mr *Dawber*'s up there. And Mr Dawber's been in a mind to do summat daft.'

'OK,' Moira said. 'Come on, Willie.'

'We'll go in my car,' Macbeth offered, moving to the door.

'Ah . . . not you, Mungo.'

'*What* . . . !' Macbeth counted three seconds of silence before he tore off his black slicker and slammed it to the Rectory lino with a noise like a gunshot. Willie jumped back. On the sofa Chris and Chantal gripped hands.

'Now listen up!' Macbeth snarled. 'Everybody just fucking *listen up*! I have *had* it. I have had it up to *here* with getting told to butt out. I am *sick to my gut* with being treated like some goddamn halfwit with a stupid name who had the misfortune to be born five generations too late to be part of any *viable heritage*. Either I'm in, or I start figuring a few things out for myself, and maybe I'll kick the wrong asses and maybe I won't, but that's your problem not mine.'

It all went quiet. Shit, Macbeth thought. Which reject script did that come out of? He picked up his slicker and put it on.

'OK,' said Moira carelessly. 'You drive, Mungo. Cathy, I don't know what to say, except *please* keep that cop off our backs for as long as you can. And maybe if you can get the Mothers together in one place, that might be best. Would everybody fit into Ma Wagstaff's parlour?'

Some of what happened next Macbeth did not follow. Several times he wished he'd never left Glasgow.

Once, he wished he'd never seen Moira Cairns.

Twice Ernie Dawber had said his throat was very dry and would it be possible to get a drink of water?

He was sprawled in a corner between the hallstand and the front door. There was broken glass all around him. He thought he'd sprained his ankle when he fell.

'When you ter-tell me.' Shaw Horridge was still standing, feet apart, amidst the wreckage of the mirrors. His mouth looked permanently twisted because of a cut which extended

his lower lip. There were stripes of blood down both cheeks.
Freckles of glass still glittered either side of his thin nose.

'What *can* I tell you?' Ernie croaked. 'He planted his seed
in Bridelow and that seed turned out to be you. Was Ma going
to have your mother turned away, same as they did with your
father, and leave Arthur Horridge humiliated three days from
the altar? 'Course she wasn't, she'd been in the same situation.'

'I cer-cer . . . I cer-cer-can't accept it, Mr Der-Der . . .
Aaagh!' With both fists, Shaw began to beat his own head.
Ernie felt his agony, the way he used to experience the lad's
frustration all those years ago, when Shaw was the best reader
in the class and couldn't prove it.

'They never told you, because not many outside the
Mothers' Union knew about it. Me, I put two and two together
after a bit, but I said nowt. It was none of my business. Ma
kept an eye on you but she'd never go too close. She never
wanted you to be *tempted* or to get too close to the shadow side.
For your own good. Please, lad . . . a cup of water?'

'If I ter-turn my ber-back on you, you'll be . . . out.'

'I don't think I can even walk, lad.'

'How der-der-do I know that? Ker-ker-keep talking.'

Ernie swallowed. 'I . . . remember once, Arthur came to
see me. Arthur knew, of course. Arthur was inclined to link
your stammer directly to the circumstances of your conception.
And he said, Ernie, he said, why doesn't she do something?
Ma? Why doesn't she cure the poor lad's stutter? Arthur, I
said, if you knew how much pain that causes Ma, her own
grandson . . .'

'Ger-grandson!' Angry tears joined the blood on Shaw's
cheeks. 'I used to stand outside wer-with the other ker-ker-
kids, der-daring each other to look into the wer-windows.
She'd cher-chase us all off. Wer-wer-witch. Owd witch!'

'She was frightened, Shaw. Frightened for you. Scared that
one day she might have to banish you as well because of what
might be in your blood. Didn't want you exposed to the shadow
side. That's why after your . . . after Arthur died, she'd never
come up to see your mother, even when Liz became agoropho-
bic and wouldn't come down to the village. She didn't want to

go near *you*. She didn't want you ever to know who you were or to become drawn to the shadow side.'

Which, in the end, he thought, you were. You were a sitting duck.

Wanted to ask, What happened to your mother? What happened after she forced herself to come down to the village and scream for sanctuary outside Ma's door? While you were inside, presumably. For who else would it be? Who else could destroy Ma's defences so surely? Who else would Ma allow to push her downstairs?

'I didn't ker-kill her, you know,' Shaw said suddenly. 'She said she was der-der-dead already. Dead already!'

And at that moment, directly above Ernie's head, the door chimes played their daft little tune and there was a banging on the glass panels and, 'Mr Dawber! Ernie!'

Shaw jerked from the waist, as if the electric doorbell had been connected to his testicles. 'Ger-go away!'

Ernie grabbed a breath and raised his voice. 'It's Willie Wagstaff, Shaw. Let him in, eh?'

'Mr Dawber!'

'Come on, Shaw!' Ernie shouted. 'You know Willie!'

Across the hall, the front door shuddered as a boot went into it, flat, under the lock. Shaw leapt across the hall and threw himself against the back of the door as the foot went in again, and then he sprang back, lurched towards Ernie, face full of blood and glass, terror, confusion and fury. He turned, tore open a white-panelled door on the other side of the hall and flung himself into the passage beyond as the front door heaved and splintered open.

Willie was alone. His eyes flickered under his mousy fringe in the bright lights. 'Ernie.'

'Give us a hand, Willie. Done me ankle, I think.'

'Where's the lad?'

'Let him go, eh? He's got a lot to think about. We need to get to the brewery, if it's not too late.'

'Never mind that.' Willie got a hand under Ernie's armpit. 'Can you . . . that's fine. That's excellent, Mr Dawber. Hang on to me. The brewery . . . Moira's seeing to that.'

'That lass? By 'eck, Willie, you're . . .'

'She's not just "that lass", Mr Dawber, take my word. Anyroad, Mungo's with her, the Yank. He give me his car keys; we need to get you back. You're our last hope, Mr Dawber. Come on. I'll tell you.'

The body was up against a huge metal tub. There was the smell of beer, the smell of vomit and a smell Macbeth would soon recognize again as the smell of blood.

'I don't know him,' Moira said. 'I've never seen him before.'

Macbeth covered his mouth with his hand. This was it. The final proof he'd half-imagined he was never going to get, that this affair was real, life and death. Bad death.

'This is crazy, Moira.' He grabbed hold of the iron railing, for the coldness of it. Only it was slick with something and he jerked his hand away. 'I never saw a stiff before. Never saw a dead relative. Never went to a funeral with an open coffin.'

Moira had nothing to say to this. She turned her lamp on the man's face. His whole head was a weird shape, like it had been remoulded. Violently. There was blood over the face and down from the rim of the big tank. Macbeth felt his gut lurch. He leaned over the side of the huge beer vat and he threw up, shamed by the way it echoed around the scrubbed metal.

He turned back to Moira, wiped his mouth. She was kind enough to direct the beam of her lamp away from him. Real macho stuff, huh? Either I'm in this with the rest of you or I'll go solo, start kicking asses.

Or maybe I'll just throw up the shitburger I had near Carlisle.

'I'm sorry,' he said. 'That was unavoidable. Thing is, I *do* recognize him. His name is Frank. He was in the pub earlier. He was pretty smashed.'

'He certainly looks pretty smashed now,' Moira said. Sounding harder than he liked to hear. He was shocked.

'He fell?' Looking up the steps, all slimy with something that stank.

'You could convince yourself of anything, Macbeth. OK, then – after you.'

'Up there?'

'Well, we're no' going back now.'

Oh, shit. Please. Get me outa here.

'OK. You stay down here, then. Wait for me.'

'No! Jesus. But, like, I mean, what if they're waiting for us?'

'There's nobody here, Macbeth.'

'How'd you know that?'

'I was . . . listening. And watching. And . . . you know.'

No, he didn't fucking know. But he wasn't going to make an issue of it. He went slowly up the metal steps. She stayed at the bottom, lighting his way, until he reached a blank wooden door.

He hesitated, looked back down the stairs at where the beam bounced off the white walls and cast a soft light on her. She looked smaller than he remembered inside this bulky duffel coat, too big for her by a couple of sizes. And yet she seemed strangely younger, without most of her hair.

Well, shit, of *course* he'd seen that, soon as he'd walked in out of the rain. It was the most awful mutilation, like slashing the *Mona Lisa*, taking the legs off of the *Venus de Milo*. It was a goddamn offence against civilization.

But was it *self*-mutilation? Was it like a novice nun cuts off all her hair to give herself to Christ?

And this was why he'd never even mentioned it. This was why, Willie being in the car too, all he'd said to her by way of explanation for him being here was, 'The Duchess asked me to look out for you.'

To which she'd made no reply.

Moira's face creased sympathetically now in the white light.

'Look, Mungo . . . fact is, if the sight of this poor guy made you chuck your lunch, you're not gonny find it too pleasant in there. There's no shame in that. Willie's pretty squeamish, too, which is why he was glad to go off in search of the old schoolmaster guy. So . . . if you . . . what I'm saying is, this isn't your problem. You really don't have to put yourself through this.'

'And you do?'

'Yeah,' she said. 'I'm afraid I do. Me more than anybody.'

He just stared down at her.

'Goes back nearly twenty years. This is the consequences of getting involved with Matt Castle.'

'He's dead.'

'Yeah,' Moira said.

Macbeth said, 'People here keep seeing his ghost. That's what they say. You believe that?'

'Yeah,' Moira said.

'What am I gonna find behind that door?'

'You don't ever have to know, Mungo. That's what I'm trying to tell you.'

'Aw, shit,' Macbeth said. 'The hell with this.' He scraped hair out of his eyes, opened them wide and pushed open the door with his right foot.

CHAPTER IV

Willie's youngest sister was in her dressing gown, making tea. 'Sleep through this weather? Not a chance. Our Benjie's messing about up there, too, with that dog. I've told him, I'll have um both in t'shed, he doesn't settle down.'

'Where's Martin?'

'Working up Bolton again. Takes what he can. Bloody Gannons.'

'Right,' Willie said. 'Well, if you can get dressed, our Sal. You've been re-co-opted onto t'Mothers.'

'Get lost, Willie. I told Ma years ago, I said I'll take a back seat from now on, if you don't mind, it's not my sort of thing.'

Aye, well, no arguing with that. Certainly *wasn't* her sort of thing these days. Sal's kitchen was half the downstairs now, knocked through from the dining room and a posh conservatory on the back. Antique pine units, hi-tech cooker, extractor fan. All from when Horridges had made Martin sales manager, about a year before Gannons sacked him.

'Anyroad,' Sal said. 'Can't leave our Benjie. God knows what he'd get up to, little monkey.'

'Well, actually,' Willie said, 'I wouldn't mind getting the lad in as well. We're going to need a new Autumn Cross, a bit sharpish.'

'Be realistic. How can a child of his age go out collecting bits of twigs and stuff on a night like this?'

'Aye, I can!' Benjie shouted, bursting into the kitchen, already half-dressed, dragging on his wellies. 'I *can*, Uncle Willie, honest.'

'Get back to bed, you little monkey, if I've told you once tonight, I've . . .'

'Lay off, eh, Sal. We need everybody we can get.'

'Is this serious, Willie? I mean, *really*?'

Willie said nothing.

'What's in that briefcase?'

'This and that.'

'Uncle Willie,' said Benjie, 'T'Chief's been howling.'

'They're all howling tonight, Benj.'

'And t'dragon. T'dragon growed, Uncle Willie. T'dragon's *growed*.'

When Milly caught Cathy's eye over the heads of the assembled Mothers they exchanged a look which said, this is hopeless.

Altogether there were seven of them squeezed into Ma's parlour, standing room only – although at least a couple were not too good on their pins and needed chairs.

'Susan!' Milly cried. 'Where's Susan?'

'Staying in with the little lad,' Ethel, Susan's mum, told her. 'Frank's not back. Likely on a bender. She won't leave the little lad on his own on a night like this.'

'Wonderful!' Cathy moaned. 'Hang on, what about Dee from the chippy? Needs must, Ethel.'

'She's had a shock, what with Maurice, she won't even answer the door.'

'Well, get somebody to bloody break it down. And if Susan's got to bring the kid along, do it, though I'd rather not. That'll be nine. Willie! How's it going? Any luck?'

'We found it, I think.' Willie came in clutching Mr Dawber's old briefcase. 'Here, make a bit of space on t'table.'

'How is he?'

'He's resting. Had a bit of a do wi' Shaw Horridge.' Willie was spreading out sheets of foolscap paper. 'Thank God for Mr Dawber, I say. Anything to do with Bridelow he collects. Whipped it off Ma 'fore she could put it back of t'fire.'

'Looks complicated.'

'It's not as bad as it looks. They're all numbered, see, and they join up, so we've got a complete map of t'village wi' all the key boundary points marked. Ma did um all barefoot. But that were summer. What you want is one woman at each, and each to take a new stone. Alf's got um ready for consecration, like, end of his yard.'

'How big are they, these stones?'

'Size of a brick, maybe half a brick. Some of um *are* bricks, come to think of it. Ma used a wheelbarrow.'

'We'll never do it,' Milly said in despair. 'Are you proposing to send old Sarah out to the top of Church Field with half a brick?'

'She could do one of the closer ones,' said Cathy. 'If you or I take the Holy Well . . .'

'We still haven't got enough.' Milly lowered her voice. 'And what kind of commitment we'll get out of half this lot I *don't* know. Ma was right. We've been hopelessly complacent. We let things slide. We haven't got a chance.'

'There's always a chance,' Cathy said, and even Willie thought her voice was starting to sound a bit frail. She was overtired, lumpy bags under her eyes, thin hair in rat's tails.

'What?' said Milly, approaching hysteria – and Willie had never seen *that* before. 'Against a feller who's spent half a lifetime stoking up his evil? Against that hideous girl? Against all them practising satanists?'

'They're idiots,' Cathy said. 'Any idiot can be a satanist.'

'Aye,' said Milly, 'and any idiot can make it work if they've got nowt to lose.'

'All *right*.' Cathy turned to Willie. 'How's Alf getting on?'

'Moaning,' Willie said. 'Reckons cement won't hang together wi' all the rain. Stan Burrows and them've fixed up a bit of a shelter for him. I told him, I says, you can do it again proper sometime, Alf, just make sure it sticks up tonight. I called in at Sal's, too, and young Benjie'll be along wi' a pile of stuff for a new cross. Reckon you can fettle it?'

'Aye,' said Milly. 'I suppose I can.'

'Don't you start losing heart, lass. Hey, our Sal's on her way too, what about that?'

'Never!' said Cathy. 'Ceramic hob on the blink, is it?'

'I'm persuasive, me, when I put me mind to it.'

'That'll make it ten, then,' Cathy said. 'Still, not enough. But we're getting there. Please, Milly, *please* don't go negative on me now.'

Macbeth closed the door behind him, as if to prove he wasn't really a wimp and could handle this alone, and he didn't come out for a long time, maybe half a minute, and there was no sound from him either. And Moira panicked. *I was wrong. They're all there. They're waiting for us.*

'Moira,' he called out, more than a wee bit hoarse, just at the point when she was about to start screaming. 'I think I need some help.'

At the foot of the final stairway, the air was really sour, full of beer and vomit, blood and death. She took a breath of it, anyway. She was – face it – more scared than he was, and whenever she was really scared, she went brittle and hard, surface-cynical. A shell no thicker than a ladybird's.

She wanted a cigarette. She wanted a drink.

She wanted *out* of here.

'Hold your nose,' Macbeth advised, opening the door. He sounded calm. Too calm. He was going to pass out on her any second.

And of course she didn't hold her damn nose, did she, and the stench of corrupted flesh nearly drove her back down the steps.

'I covered that one over,' Macbeth said. 'Couldn't face it.'

A circle within a circle. Candles burned down to stubs, not much more than the flames left, and all the rearing shadows they were throwing.

'Watch where you're walking,' Macbeth said.

The attic light was brown and bleary with sweat, grease, blood. Several chairs inside the circle. Two of them occupied.

One was a muffled hump beneath old sacking. 'All I could find,' Macbeth said. 'I don't think you should uncover it. I don't think *anybody* should. Not ever.'

A yellow hand poked out of the sacking.

She stared at it, trying to imagine the yellow fingers stopping up the airholes on the Pennine Pipes.

'It's this one,' Macbeth said behind her. 'Moira? Please?'

Moira turned and took a step forward and her foot squelched in it.

Congealing blood. Bucketsful.

'You don't have to do anything like that,' Cathy said. 'It's not as if I'm asking you to bare your breasts or have sex with anyone under a full moon or swear eternal allegiance to the Goddess.'

'Pity,' said the blonde one, trying, and failing, to hold her cigarette steady.

'All you have to do,' Cathy said, 'is believe in it. Just for as long as you're taking part.'

'I don't, though, luv,' Lottie Castle said. 'And I can't start now.'

However, Cathy noticed, she couldn't stop herself looking over their shoulders towards what was probably the gas-mantle protruding from the side of the bar.

Cathy had heard all about the gas-mantle, from the policeman, Ashton, who was standing by the door at this moment. Observing but keeping out of it because – as he'd pointed out – there was no evidence of the breaking of laws, except for natural ones.

'Yes, you do,' Chrissie said. 'You've always believed in it. That's been half the problem.'

'And how the hell would you know that?'

'Oh, come *on*. The last couple of hours I've probably learned more about you than anybody in this village. And you more about me than I'd like to have spread around.'

'Yes,' said Lottie. 'I suppose so. And how do you come into this, luv? Always struck me as an intelligent sort of girl, university education. Oxford, isn't it?'

'That's right, Mrs Castle, Oxford.'

'No polite names tonight. It's Lottie.'

'And I'm Chrissie,' said the blonde.

'You know about your husband,' Cathy said. 'You know what they've done.'

'Cathy luv, he ceased to be my husband the night he needed somebody else to close his eyes for him. Well, a fair time before that, if truth were known. I've had half a lifetime of Matt Castle, and that's more than *anybody* should have to put up with, and I can say that now, because I can say *anything* tonight, believe me.'

As soon as Cathy had walked in she'd spotted the two glasses, smelt the booze.

'All right,' she said. 'Forget your husband. Let's talk about your son.'

Lottie's face hardened immediately into something like a clay mask.

'Dic? What *about* Dic?'

'Just I don't think he's dead,' Macbeth said.

'Oh, Jesus. Jesus.' Moira put down her lamp in the blood, the light tilted up at Dic's face.

But they couldn't kill him, could they? For the same reason they couldn't kill you. Surely.

'Willie was right, Mungo. We should've been up here, mob-handed. Thought I was being clever. Being stupid. *Stupid!*'

But sometimes you can do more harm to someone than killing them'd be, you know?

'Tights,' Macbeth snapped. 'You wearing tights under there?'

'Huh . . . ? No. What's . . . ? Oh, Jesus . . . Dic . . . *please don't be dead.*'

'Shit,' said Macbeth. 'Handkerchief?'

'I dunno what's in these pockets, it's no' my coat . . . yeah, is this a handkerchief?'

'How big is it? OK, tear it in half. Fold 'em up. Make two tight wads.' Macbeth was peeling off the thick adhesive tape binding Dic's arms to the chair-arms. Both arms were upturned, palms of the hands exposed. Veins exposed. There was a welling pool of rich, dark blood at each wrist and it was dripping to the floor each side of the chair. There was a widening pond of blood, congealed around its blackened banks. Late-autumnal flies from the roofspace crawled around, drunk on blood.

'OK, now you hold his arm above his head. You're gonna get a lot of blood on you.'

'I got more blood on me than I can handle,' Moira muttered. 'You sure you know what you're doing, Mungo?'

'I never did it for real before, but . . . Ah, you don't need to hear this shit, just hold his arms. Right. Gimme one of the pads. See, we got to hold the . . . this is a pressure pad, right? So you push it up against the wound with both thumbs. Like *hard*. Idea is, we stop the blood with the pad, then I wind this goddamn tape round just about as . . . *tight* . . . as I can make it.'

'Is he breathing?'

'How the fuck should I know? Now the other arm. Hold it *up*, over his head . . . And, shit, get the tape off his mouth. Chrissakes, Moira, didn't we *do* that?'

The tape across Dic's mouth stretched from ear to ear. Moira tore it away, and Dic mumbled, 'Do you . . . have to be so rough?'

Moira jumped away in shock. Macbeth yelled, 'Keep hold of that fucking arm, willya?'

'Aw, Christ. You're no' dead.'

'I'm no' dead,' said Dic feebly, and he giggled.

'Don't talk,' said Moira. 'You're gonny be OK. Mungo?'

'He's lost a lot of blood.'

'Don't I know it. I'm paddling in it.'

'He needs to go to a hospital. This is strictly amateur hour. Can't say how long it's gonna hold. Far's I can see, they cut the vein. If they'd cut the artery this guy'd be long gone. They cut the vein, each wrist, taped his arms down. The blood goes on dripping, takes maybe a couple hours to drain the body. How long they had you like this, pal?'

'Not the faintest,' Dic said. 'I was on valium, I think. Intravenous. So I'd know what was happening but wouldn't care.'

'That's good. See, the dope slows down the metabolism and that goes for the blood flow too. This is weird stuff, Moira, this left me way behind a long time back.'

Moira said, 'Do you know why, Dic?'

Dic nodded at the hump under the sacks.

'Do me one favour,' Macbeth said. 'I saved your life, least you can do is let me keep that fucking thing under wraps.'

'That's Matt, isn't it, Dic?'

Dic nodded. He was lying back in his chair, both arms still flung over his head and black with dried and drying blood. Moira didn't recall ever seeing courage on this scale. Maybe the valium had helped, but it was more than that.

'Suppose you know,' Dic said, 'where they've gone.'

'We have to get you to a hospital.'

'When you're on valium and you're still terrified, you know it must be pretty awesome.'

'Looks pretty cruddy to me,' Macbeth said.

'We'll get you down the steps, OK? We'll get you out of here.'

'He's not sane, you know. I don't reckon he was all there to begin with, lived in his own fantasy world. Like Dad. And that guy Hall.' He closed his eyes. 'Bloody Cathy. The things you do for love, eh?'

'Mungo,' Moira said. 'How about you go downstairs to one of the offices, find a phone? Get us some transport for Dic.'

'You'll be OK?' Macbeth looked like he couldn't get out fast enough.

'Sure. Get hold of Cathy. You got the number?'

'Called it enough times from the phone-booth.' He hesitated in the doorway, Dic's blood on one cheek.

'Go,' Moira said.

When they were alone, she said, 'Dic, I need to ask you
. . . Matt . . .'

'I gave him blood,' Dic said. 'And you . . .' He nodded at
the thing in the other chair.

Moira sighed. Sooner or later she had to face this.

She hooked a finger under a corner of the sacking.

The dead couldn't harm you.

'You get used to him,' Dic said with a dried-up bitterness.
'You start to forget he ever looked any different.'

She pulled away the sacking. The smell was putrid. It was
the kind of smell that would never entirely leave you and some
nights would come back and hover over you like the flies that
were clustering around Matt's withered mouth, the lips already
falling from the teeth.

'I was afraid to look at him in his coffin,' Dic said. 'Mum
said there was no shame. No shame in that.'

'Dic,' Moira said. 'What's that in his lap?'

'The pipes.'

'That stuff wrapped *around* the pipes.'

'You know what it is.'

Moira reached out with distaste and snatched the bundle
from the lap of the corpse. Air erupted from the bag and the
pipes groaned like a living thing. Or a dying thing. She cried
out and dropped the pipes but held on to what had been around
the pipes, black hair drifting through her fingers in the
flickering candlelight. A glimmer of white.

'Which of them did it?' Her voice so calm she scared
herself. 'Which of them actually cut it off?'

Dic said, 'The woman, I'd guess. Therese. They wanted
him strong and . . . driven. You know?'

His eyes kept closing. Maybe he was about to pass out from
loss of blood. She didn't know what you did in these circumstances. Did you let him rest or did you try to keep him
conscious, keep him talking? He seemed to need to talk.

'I gave him blood,' he said. 'Blood feeds the spirit or
something like that. Blood's very powerful in magic. And
so . . .'

He winced, coughed, nodded at the hair.

'. . . so's desire.'

'And what,' Moira said, staring into Matt Castle's impenetrable, sightless eyes, stuffing the hair into a pocket of the duffel coat, 'did he get from the bog body?'

'Wrong question.' Dic's eyes closed and didn't open for several seconds. Moira was worried. Dic said, 'I think you should be asking . . . what it got from him.'

His eyes weren't focusing. 'Listen, I don't know whether they got what they were after. All kinds of noises were coming out of . . . that.'

Moira picked up the sacking, tossed it over Matt with a shudder.

'Hall was trying to talk to it. Had a few phrases in medieval Welsh. I don't think it made any sense. In the end he was screaming at it. Stanage was screaming at Therese. It didn't go how they hoped.'

'Does it ever.'

'I can't believe these people.'

'I can,' Moira said. 'What went wrong?'

'Couldn't find the comb was one thing. Stanage was furious.'

Moira bent over him. His eyes were slits. 'Dic, why couldn't they find the comb?'

'Because I'd . . . taken it. I think. Earlier on. I took it out of the bag. Knew they were saving it for the climax.'

'Where is it now?'

He tried to shake his head. 'I'm sorry,' Moira said. 'We'll get you out of here. Listen, if I leave you now . . . can you bear it? Mungo'll be back in a minute. Only I want to get away on my own. Dic, can you hear me?'

Dic's eyes were closed. He was half-lying in his chair, hands still thrown back behind his head. There seemed to be no more blood seeping under the tape.

Didn't they say that your blood stopped flowing when you died?

Dic's canvas-seated wooden armchair still stood in the pond of his blood, mostly congealed, like mud, like the surface of a peatbog.

'Dic?'

No reply. But he was still breathing, wasn't he? She touched his fingers; they felt cold, like marble.

'Dic, tell Mungo . . . tell him not to worry. Tell him . . . just tell him I've gone to meet the Man.'

CHAPTER V

There was a strange luminescence over the Moss, as though the rain itself was bringing down particles of light. She could see its humps and pools, and she knew there were people out there, could hear their voices, scattered by the rain. The Moss was swollen up like a massive pincushion and every heavy raindrop seemed to make a new dent.

She walked openly to the door of The Man I'th Moss and hammered on it, shouted 'Lottie!' a few times. All the lights were on, lights everywhere, in the bar, in all the rooms upstairs.

But nobody here.

OK.

She switched on her lamp and walked around the back to the yard where the stable block or barn place was, Matt's music room. Its door hung open, the hasp forced. They hadn't even bothered to disguise their visit when they came to borrow the Pennine Pipes.

Switching off her lamp, Moira went quietly in. She put on no lights. The air inside seemed to ripple with greens and browns, like sealight.

Mosslight.

The carpets on the wall tautened the air. Dead sound. No echoes.

She took off her coat, found the old settee, the one with its insides spraying out. Sat down, with the lamp at her feet, and thought peacefully of Matt and felt no hatred.

All gone.

Released.

*

It had taken her nearly ten minutes to get here. Ten minutes in which the rain had crashed down on her sparsely matted skull, and she'd yielded up her anger with a savagery even the night couldn't match.

Screamed a lot. Cursed him for what he'd done, all those years of lies and craving, abuse of Lottie, abuse of Dic, abuse of her from afar, divulging to the crazy Stanage the secret of the comb, letting Stanage set him up, set her up in Scotland.

Letting Stanage into his weaknesses. So that the long-haired girls appeared on cue. This Therese playing the part with an icy precision, drawing out of Matt the thin wire of desire by which they could anchor him.

I used to think she was . . . a substitute. Me own creation. Like, creating you out of her . . .

While he was no longer sure that this was not, in essence, Moira.

. . . I should've known. Should've known you wouldn't leave me to die alone. I'm drawing strength from the both of you. The bogman and you . . .

Had Stanage known that Matt was dying? Was Matt chosen *because* he was dying? So that his spirit, chained to Stanage and Therese, chained willingly to Bridelow by the old Celtic magic, could be controlled after his death?

So it could be used as a conduit.

To reach the Man, the spirit of the Moss, the guardian of the ancient Celtic community at the end of the causeway.

Moira walking quickly down from the brewery, finding her way quite easily this time back into the village. Avoiding the car racing with full headlights up the brewery road, probably in answer to Macbeth's summons. Avoiding any people she happened to see on the street – especially women.

This, God help me, is my task.

Go over it again. Get it right.

Here's what happened.

The villagers steal the Man to do with him what's been done so many times with bits of bodies found in the Moss: give him a good Christo-pagan burial at the next public funeral.

But this isn't just another bit of body. This is the complete perfectly preserved remains of the original sacrifice, laid down with due ceremony after undergoing the Triple Death.

This is powerful, this will reverberate.

And wise old Ma Wagstaff – realizing, presumably, just *how* powerful – mixes up her witch bottle with a view to protecting Matt's soul from any dark, peaty emanations.

Not realizing that it's the *Man in the Moss* who needs protection – against the tortured, corrupted, *manipulated* spirit of Matt Castle.

Got to get him back. Got to get him out of their control.

Got to lose all the hatred because that's *their* medium. Hatred. And lust. And obsession.

When Stan the bartender and Gary the cop came for Dic, Macbeth was pacing the room, trampling in the blood. Where is she, where the fuck *is* she? Almost ready to shake the poor guy, get some sense out of him.

'God almighty!' he heard from the bottom of the steps. 'It's Young Frank!'

'Don't touch him. You can't help him now.'

'He were three-parts drunk. Fighting drunk. Drunk most nights since he lost his job.'

'Maybe he fell, maybe he didn't. Either way, I'm having this place sealed off, so watch where you're treading, Stan.'

'Hey, come on willya,' Macbeth shouted. 'There's a guy up here *isn't* dead. Yet.'

'We're coming,' Gary the cop said. 'And I don't like that smell one bit.'

Thirty seconds later, he's pulling the sacking from the stiff – 'Fucking *Nora*!' – while Macbeth's demanding, 'Moira. You seen *Moira*? Lady with very, *very* short hair . . . Chrissakes!' And Stan's staring at all the blood, looking sick, and Dic's shifting very feebly in his chair.

'Right!' said Gary the cop. 'Who is *this*?'

Macbeth slumped against the wall. 'It's Matt Castle.'

'Thank you,' said Gary. 'At least we know *he's* not been murdered. Let's get an ambulance to this lad. And a statement later, I think.'

At which Dic came round sufficiently to start yelling, hoarsely, '*No!* I'm not going to hospital! I won't!'

'Hey, hey . . . All right, we'll not take you to hospital, but you can't stop here.'

'Take me to Cath,' Dic said, and Ashton looked at Macbeth. Macbeth nodded, and Stan got his arm behind Dic and helped him to his feet.

'Keep his arms over his head,' Macbeth said, 'else he's gonna start bleeding again.'

In back of Stan's ancient station wagon, Macbeth said quietly to Dic, 'Moira. Where's Moira go? Come on, kid, talk to me, I saved your goddamn life.'

'Said to tell you,' Dic mumbled, 'that . . . she'd gone to meet the Man.'

'Holy . . . *shit!*' Macbeth slammed his fist into the back of the seat.

'Yeah,' Dic said. 'I didn't like the sound of that either, but there wasn't much I could do.'

Drifting on an airbed of memories.

Hey, Matt, you remember the night the van broke down on the M1 and we put on a thank-you gig for the AA guys at three in the morning at the Newport Pagnell Services?

Blurry light coming off the Moss through the rain. They're out there, OK. And it's cold and it's wet and the Moss is filthy and swollen. No place to be, Matt. No place to commit yourself for all eternity.

Or until you might be summoned by those to whom you mortgaged your soul.

Hey, remember when you left the pipes in the hotel room in Penzance and Willie ran all the way back from the hall and I went on stage alone? And I only knew four solo numbers, and I'm into an encore of the first one before Willie dashes in with the pipes?

The slimy mosslight from the high windows awakening the

barn, finding the womanly curves of the old Martin guitar. This was your place, Matt, this was where you put it all together, this was your refuge.

. . . So I wanted . . . I wanted in. To be part of that. To go in the Moss too . . .

But you don't now. Do you?

It's warm in here. (Aw, hell, it's freezing; you just better wish it warm, hen, *wish* it warm until you can feel it.)

She picked up the lamp from the floor at her feet and took it across to a wooden table. She switched it on, directing its beam to the centre of the settee, picked up Matt's Martin guitar, went back and sat in the spot, with the light on her face.

She strummed the guitar. The strings were old and dull and it was long out of tune. One of the machine-heads had lost its knob, so she just tuned the other strings to that one.

It would do.

She sat back, closed her eyes against the lamp's beam, although the battery was running out and the light was yellowing. She imagined the Moss, black and cold and stagnant.

Now you're out there, you know the terrors the Moss holds, the deep, deep, age-old fear.

Death doesn't have to be like that, Matt.

Come on. Come on back. Come to the warm.

She pictured Matt as he'd been once. Stocky, muscular, vibrant with enthusiasm.

Come . . .

. . . come to . . .

to me.

And in a low and smoky voice, she began to sing to him.

The Mothers' Union was congregated in the high Norman nave of St Bride's Church.

Above the Mothers hung a ragged cross made of branches cut by Benjie from a rampant sycamore hedge at the bottom of the Rectory garden. The branches, still dripping, were bound with chicken wire and tangled up with hawthorn.

557

Cathy walked in, out of the rain, under the reassuringly gross, widened flange of the *Sheelagh na gig*, cement particles among the coils of her hair. Alf Beckett had also brought the statues out of the shed, and several long, coloured candles were lit.

He was up in the lamp room now, fixing up a high-powered floodlight supplied by Stan Burrows, who'd been in charge of the electrics for the Bridelow Wakes party which was usually held on the Church Field on May Day Eve. (Except for this year, when there was still too much media attention, due to the bogman.)

'*Twelve*,' Cathy said after a quick head-count. 'We're waiting for Moira.'

'She doesn't have to be here,' Milly said. 'If she's with us, she's with us.' Cathy was glad to see Milly had at last taken charge.

The assembly was not inspiring, including, as it did, women like Dee Winstanley, who'd declined to follow her mother into the Union on the grounds that they didn't get on, and two lesbians who ran a smallholding up by the moor and had never been allowed to become active members because their motives were suspect.

A pile of wet stones glistened on an old wooden funeral bier under the pulpit.

'All right!' Milly clapped her hands. 'Let's make a start, shall we? I want to begin by calling down a blessing on this church. If you'd all form a rough circle from where we've pushed the pews back.'

Milly wore a long, dark blue dress decorated by a single brooch in the shape of two intercurled holly leaves.

She closed her eyes.

'Our Father . . .' she began.

'And Our Mother . . .'

> . . . *sees herself in colours and*
> *she weighs her powers in her hand* . . .

'The Comb Song'. The song of night and invocation. In the singing of it, things happen.

And the comb, safe in its pocket in the guitar case, protects you from evil.

But this is not your guitar. This is Matt's guitar. Singing the song of invocation to the dead strings of Matt's guitar in Matt's music room, and *no* protection.

It was 1.30 in the morning.

The women filed silently out of the church, most of them muffled in dark coats, under scarves and hoods so Macbeth couldn't tell who was who.

There was a bulky one he figured was Milly. Two who were slightly built were walking together.

'Cathy?' he whispered. 'Cathy?'

Neither of the women replied.

Each clutched a stone.

They walked out of the church porch under a weird carving of a grotesque, deformed creature, all mouth and pussy. At this point they divided, some proceeding down the path toward the main gate, two moving up toward the graves, the others following a narrower path down into a field which disappeared into the peatbog.

'Moira? *Moira!*'

No answer. The rain continued.

'. . . the fuck am I gonna do?'

'Nowt,' said Willie Wagstaff. 'Nowt we can do. It's in the lap of the gods.'

Ernie Dawber was with him, leaning on a walking stick. They moved under the porch with Macbeth, gazing out toward the Moss. Nobody spoke for a while, then he said, 'Hallowe'en's over now, right?'

'Samhain, lad,' said Ernie. 'Let's not cheapen it. In Bridelow we used to celebrate Samhain on November first, so you could say our day is just beginning.'

'Or not,' said Willie. 'As the case may be.'

'Or not,' Ernie agreed.

Macbeth said, 'How deep is the, uh, Moss?'

'Normally,' Ernie said, 'no more than a few feet in most places. Tonight? I wouldn't like to guess. I don't think we've ever had rain this hard, so consistently, for so long, have we, Willie?'

'Could it flood?'

'Soaks it up,' said Ernie. 'Like a sponge. It's rivers that flood, not bogs.'

'There's a river running through it, isn't there?'

'Not much of one.'

'What are those women doing?'

'We never ask, lad,' said Ernie.

'Ever thought of becoming a local tour guide?'

Ernie shrugged.

Macbeth said, 'What are those lights?'

'I can't see any lights, lad.'

'It's gone. It lasted no time at all. It was, like, a white ball of light. It seemed to come out the bog. Then it vanished.'

'Didn't see it. Did you, Willie?'

'OK,' Macbeth said. He was getting a little pissed with this old man. 'Tonight, Mr Dawber, it's my belief you seriously offered your life for this place. I'm not gonna say that's extreme, I don't have enough of a picture to make judgements. What I would like to know is . . . that, uh, compulsion you had . . . has that . . . passed?'

Seemed at first like Ernie Dawber was going to ignore the question and Macbeth could hardly have blamed him for that. Willie Wagstaff didn't look at the old man. Rain apart, there was no sound; Willie was not performing his customary drum solo.

Then Ernie Dawber took off his hat.

'It seems silly to me now,' he said in his slow, precise way. 'Worse, it seems cowardly. I went to see the doctor t'other night. Been feeling a bit . . . unsteady for some weeks. They'd done a bit of a scan. Found what was described as an inoperable cyst.' Ernie tapped his forehead. 'In here.'

Willie's chin jerked up. 'Eh?'

'Could pop off anytime, apparently.'

'Aw, hell,' Macbeth said. 'Forget I spoke.'

'No, no, lad, it was a valid question. I've been writing a new history of Bridelow, one that'll never be published. Chances are I'll not even finish the bugger anyroad but it's about all those things I didn't dare put into the proper book. Maybe it's the *first* proper book, who can say?'

'I'd like to read that,' Macbeth said. 'One day.'

'Don't count on it, lad. Anyroad, I thought, well . . . it's given you a good life, this little place. You and a lot of other folk. And now it's in trouble. Is there *nowt* you can do? And when you're on borrowed time, lads, it's surprising how you focus in directions nobody in their right minds'd *ever* contemplate.'

He chuckled. 'Or maybe it's not our *right* minds that we're in most of the time. Maybe, just for a short space of time, I *entered* my right mind. Now there's a cosmic sort of conundrum for you . . . Mungo.'

'Thanks,' Macbeth said. He put out his hand; Ernie took it, they shook. 'Now, about those lights . . .'

'Aye, lad. I saw the lights. And that's another conundrum. The Moss is no man's land. No man has cultivated it. No man has walked across it in true safety. What we see in and on and around the Moss doesn't answer to our rules. I've not answered your other question yet, though, have I?'

Macbeth kept quiet. There was another ball of white light. It came and it went. In the semi-second it was there Macbeth saw a huge, awesome tree shape with branches that seemed to be reaching out for him. Involuntarily he shrank back into the porch.

'Is it past?' Ernie considered the question. 'No. If I thought it'd do any good, I'd be out there now offering my throat to the knife.'

He turned back toward the Moss. There was another lightball. Coming faster now.

'Quite frankly, lad,' said Ernie conversationally, 'I think it's too late.'

And in the chamber of the dead
forgotten voices fill your head . . .

It said, hoarsely, *Going to show me?*

Moira tried to stay calm but couldn't sing any more. She was desperately cold.

This famous comb.

This time she had no comb to show him.

But you never leave yourself open like that. You never confess weakness to them.

'What will you give me if I show you the comb?'

Six pennorth o' chips.

Laughter rippling from the corners of the room. The lamplight was very weak now in her face.

Behind the light, a shadow.

CHAPTER VI

They had told Chrissie to look out for a seat at the top of the church field. It wasn't hard. The church field was the piece of uncultivated spare land continuing down from the last of the graves to a kind of plateau above the Moss. Chrissie's torch found the seat on the very edge of the plateau.

What she hadn't expected was to find someone sitting on it.

Normally, this time of night, she'd have been scared to death of getting mugged. Somehow, holding this daft stone, that didn't seem a possibility.

She found herself sitting next to him on the wooden bench in the pouring rain. Someone had lent her a long, dark blue cagoule and she knew very little of her face would be visible.

It was like a dream. 'Hello, Roger,' she said.

He turned his head. His hair was flat and shiny, like tin. His beard dripped into the neck of his blackened Barbour.

He peered at her. He didn't seem to recognize her nose. 'Is it Chrissie?'

'It is indeed. Not a very nice night, Roger. One way and another.'

He was silent a long time. Then he said, 'I spoke to him.'

'Him?'

'*Him.*'

'That must have been nice for you both.'

'So it was worth it,' Roger said. 'In the end.'

'Was it? Was it really?'

'Oh, yes. I mean, it's knowledge, isn't it? Nothing is more valuable than knowledge.'

'What about love?' said Chrissie.

'I don't understand,' Roger said.

'No. I don't suppose you do. So what did he have to say to you?'

'Who?'

'*Him.*'

'Oh.' Roger stood up, drenched and shiny, and rubbed his knees as if they were stiff. 'Do you know, I can't really remember. I expect it'll come back to me.'

He didn't look at her and began, seeming oblivious to the rain, to stroll away along the path which led back from the plateau's edge and wound down towards the Moss.

Chrissie waited until he'd gone from sight and then gently placed her stone beneath the seat and stood very quietly and said the words they'd told her to say.

A curious thing.

Soon as Ernie Dawber admitted he too could see the balls of light, then they became clearer.

'It's a bit like ball-lightning,' Ernie said. 'There's been quite a lot of research, although the scientific establishment doesn't formally acknowledge it.'

Talking in his schoolmaster's voice, Macbeth thought, because it puts him on top of a situation he doesn't understand any more than the rest of us.

'They do seem to be a manifestation of energy anomalies within the earth's magnetic field. Often occur, I'm told, on fault-lines.'

'What's that mean?'

'And there's also a theory that they can interact with human consciousness. So that when we perceive them we actually bring them into existence, if that isn't back-to-front logic. What do you say, Willie?'

'I'm more worried about that tree-thing, Mr Dawber.

Young Benjie calls it a dragon. Bog oak, I thought it were. Come up out of t'Moss, all of a sudden like. Got a wicked kind of . . .'

Macbeth said, 'There are people out there, around the tree.'

'Daft buggers.' Ernie squinted through the rain.

Macbeth was watching a haze of light rising from the tree, as if someone had set fire to it. But the flames, instead of eating the wood, had risen through it, like one of those phoney log-effect gasfires.

The light had risen above the tree and its boughs looked to be clawing at it, as though to prevent it escaping, and the Moss itself seemed to rise in protest. Macbeth felt a thickening tension in his gut.

Mouth dry, he watched the haze of light spread out like a curtain and then hover over the Moss, maybe six or ten feet from its surface.

'This is . . . unearthly.'

The light was drifting towards the edge of the Moss, towards the hulk of a building near the peat's edge.

'All things are natural,' Ernie Dawber said with a tight-jawed determination. 'If some are . . . beyond our under-standing.'

'What's that place?' Thought he was hearing distant screams.

'Back of the pub,' Willie said. 'That's th'owd barn back of the pub, where we used to rehearse wi' Matt.'

'The light's over it. The light's hanging over the roof.'

Ernie Dawber said, 'I don't think I can see it any more.'

Moira Cairns put down the guitar and turned towards the door.

Two of them.

The mosslight on the two tombstone speaker cabinets either side of the door.

Both of them standing in the entrance with the cabinets either side of them.

John Peveril Stanage and the girl, Therese.

'So kill me,' Moira said simply.

'You know we can't,' Therese said. 'Not until you give him back.'

Moira reached to the table and turned the lamp on to them. Not much energy left in it now but enough to show her neither of these people was wet. Had they been inside the inn all the time? Had they been expecting her? Or was this merely the nearest vantage point for the Moss?

'Who are those people out on the Moss, then?' Moira asked. 'With the devil tree.'

'Do you know, m'dear,' he said, 'I can't actually recall any of their names.'

She remembered him so well now. The dapper figure, the white hair rushing back from his grey-freckled forehead like breakers on an outgoing tide. The cherub's lips. A man as white as the bones tumbling from the walls.

'I can't believe,' she said, 'all the trouble you've gone to. Getting to know Matt inside out, all his little compulsions. What are we looking at here? Years?'

'We don't have time for a discussion,' Stanage said. 'We want you to release him. You can't hold him for much longer, you simply don't have the energy.'

Moira said, 'Where's the Man? Made a big mistake, there, you know, John. You stole him away, you took responsibility for him. You took responsibility for the vacuum. The Moss'll no' wear that. Was an old guy in the village tonight, he'd figured out the way to square things with the Moss was another sacrifice. Maybe that was right.'

'It was *absolutely* right, m'dear,' Stanage said with a sudden smile. 'Saw to that on the *very stroke*, I believe, of midnight. When the Beacon of the Moss was extinguished, so was someone's life. A young, fit, active life . . . a *jolly good* replacement for the Man, if I say so myself.'

'Who?' Moira felt her face-muscles tightening, also her stomach.

'Why . . . just like the original sacrifice . . . a priest. The Triple Death – a blow, a slash – and a fall. And then gathered up and offered to the spirit of the Moss – *our* spirit. All square, m'dear. All square.'

565

'The Reverend Joel Beard? You killed the Reverend Joel Beard?'

'And consigned him to the Moss. Well, *hell*, sweetheart, don't sound so appalled. No friend of yours, was he? He struck you, word has it.'

'I suspect he mistook me for your friend,' Moira said. She let her gaze settle on Therese. Worryingly young. Black hair, perhaps dyed, sullen mouth. And the cloak. *Her* cloak.

'This is the wee slag, then, is it, John? Doesny look a lot like me. Did she wear a wig before she got hold of the real thing?'

'She's angry *enough*, Moira,' Stanage said less cordially. 'Don't make it worse.'

'*She's* angry? With *me*? Aw, Jesus, the poor wee thing, ma heart goes out. She's no' satisfied with ma hair now? Would she like to cut off ma leg? Would that make her happy, you think, John?'

Therese hissed and uncoiled like a snake and took a step towards Moira. Stanage laid a cautionary hand on her arm. Emerging from his dark sleeve the hand looked as white as an evening glove.

'This is futile,' Stanage said abruptly. 'Leave us, Tess. Would you mind awfully?'

'I çan take her,' Therese spat. 'She's old. Her sexuality's waning. She can't hold him. I can take him from her. Watch me.'

'Tess, *darling*, no one is questioning your lubricious charms, but I suspect this is not about sex. Leave us.' Steel thread in his voice. 'Please?'

Therese gathered up her cloak and left without another word. Stanage closed the door and barred it. Moira instinctively moved into a corner of the ruptured settee, clutching the electric lamp to her breast.

'Right. Bitch.' Obviously a man who could shed his charm like an overcoat that'd become too heavy. She became aware of a scar about an inch long under his right eye, a souvenir from Scotland.

And he was aware she was looking at it.

The barn seemed to shift on its foundations, and there was

a crunch and a series of flat bangs. She didn't let her eyes leave him; she knew what it was: books falling over as a shelf collapsed. The shelves were all makeshift, held up by bricks.

Neither of them had moved.

'Don't make *me* angry,' Stanage said.

'We seem to be a little short of bones in here,' Moira said. 'That affect your performance, does it? Books just don't respond so effectively. Maybe you just don't have that same affinity. I borrowed one of yours from ma wee nephew one time. Thought it was really crap, John. Lacked authenticity, you know?'

John Peveril Stanage was tightening up inside, she could tell that, could feel the contractions in the air. Mammy, help me. Mammy, wherever you are, I'm in really heavy shit here, you know?

'You want me to sing to you, John? Would that help your concentration?'

She began to sing, very softly.

> . . . *for the night is growing colder*
> *and you feel it at your shoulder* . . .

She could feel Matt Castle at her shoulder, a wedge of cold energy.

And more.

'*Shut up*,' Stanage said.

Could smell the peat in him now.

Pulling the blue plastic lamp between her breasts until it hurt. Feeling the shadow behind her, huge and dense and pungent with black peat. *Don't turn around. Don't look at him.*

But John Peveril Stanage was looking. Stanage was transfixed.

All at once there was complete quiet.

'The rain,' Macbeth said. 'The rain stopped.'

Damn futile observation; everybody here could tell the rain had stopped.

He found he was in the middle of a crowd under the smiling snatch people called Our Sheila; been so busy watching the weird lights on the Moss he hadn't noticed the Mothers returning. Without their stones.

One of them standing next to him, shaking out her hair. 'Where's Moira?' It was Milly.

'She's not with you?' Cold panic grabbed his gut. 'You're telling me you haven't *seen* her?'

'We couldn't wait for her. We had thirteen stones to put down. Cathy's had to take two.' Milly glanced around. 'Cathy not back yet?'

'Listen . . .' Macbeth grabbed her shoulders. 'Moira told Dic she'd gone to . . . meet the Man. I figured that meant she was part of your operation.'

Milly shook her head. 'I'd be *terrified* to meet the Man. I don't know, Mungo. I really don't know what she meant. I'm sorry.'

'You all right?' Willie demanded.

'Tired. Exhausted. We've done all we can. Willie. That's the most I can say. I doubt it'll be enough.'

'Oh.' Mr Dawber, looking out across the Moss. 'Oh, good God.'

In the centre of rainless stillness, there came a noise overhead like deep, bass thunder. Like the exploding of the night. Like the splitting of the sky.

And they all saw it.

The reason they all saw it was that Bridelow Moss was suddenly lit up like a football ground.

The Beacon of the Moss was back, not blue this time but ice-white and a thousand times more powerful.

'It's Alf's arc light,' some woman explained. 'Knew he'd have it fixed before long. What was that b . . . ? Oh, Mother. Oh, Mother, help us! What's *that*?'

At first, Macbeth was simply not able to believe it. There was no precedent. It was outside the sphere of his knowledge.

First thing he saw, snagged in the floodlight, was the malformed tree with branches like horns. The horns of a stag-beetle, he thought now. Because an insect was what the tree resembled.

Or a bunch of brittle twigs.

Insignificant compared with what was growing out of the Moss, beyond, behind and far, far above it.

It was happening on the edge of the light, at what was surely the highest point of the Moss. Macbeth thought of a mushroom cloud. He thought of Hiroshima. He thought of Nagasaki. He thought in images on cracked film in black and white.

He heard shrill screams from the Moss and he thought, *Shit, it's the end of the goddamn world*.

Mushroom was wrong. More like a dense bunch of flowers. Or a cauliflower. A gigantic, obscene black cauliflower burgeoning monstrously from the bog.

The silent air was dank with a smell like the grave.

And, up close, the sour smell of primitive, bowel-melting fear.

'What is it?' Milly screeched. 'What is it, Mr Dawber?'

'It can't be . . .'

'What? *What?*'

People clutching at one another.

Ernie Dawber said hollowly, 'It's burst.'

Macbeth just stood there watching the liquid vegetable form in a kind of slow motion.

'The bog's burst,' Ernie Dawber cried out, aghast. 'It's bloody *burst*! Everybody . . . into the church! *Fast!*'

'Where's Cathy?' Milly shrieked above the tumult of spreading panic. 'She went down to take the last stone.'

'Where? Where to?'

'To the pub. The back wall. Under the old foundation stone. It's the last one.'

As the air started to thicken, Macbeth began to run, down through the graveyard towards the street, and by the time his feet hit the cobbles, a wall of cold, black, liquid peat was thundering into the village like volcanic lava.

'What have you *done?*'

'I obviously have an affinity . . .' John Peveril Stanage grinned, '. . . with the Moss.'

'You are a fucking insane man.'

'What is sanity?' Stanage said, as the high windows blew out and the whole roof of the barn was smashed down by the blackest of nights.

From *Dawber's Book of Bridelow*:

THE BOG BURST

THE SCALE AND SEVERITY of the Bridelow Bog Burst has caused widespread shock and disbelief, although it was not without precedent.

Such phenomena have occurred infrequently within recorded history, usually after a period of inordinately heavy rainfall when the surface layer of vegetation becomes too weak to retain the liquefied mass of peat beneath.

Several minor bog-slides have been reported in recent decades. After a midsummer thunderstorm in 1963, a peat-slide affected a large area of Meldon Hill bog in the Northern Pennines, leaving two scars in the blanket peat about 230 metres long and 36 metres wide.

Many centuries earlier but closer to the site of our own disaster was the eruption of Chat Moss, near Manchester, which Leland, an historian in the reign of Henry VIII, records as having '*brast up and destroied much grounds and much fresche water fische therabowt and so carried stinking water into the Mersey and carried the roulling mosse to the shores of Wales, part to the Isle of Man and sum into Ireland.*'

One cannot but suspect a certain exaggeration in this account. But those of us who experienced the horror of that night, those who lost friends or loved ones or only their homes will carry with them to their own graves the smell, the texture and, for some, the very taste of the black and ancient vegetable matter we call peat.

From *Dawber's* Secret *Book of Bridelow* (unpublished):

Celtic comb
(iron?)
Beas.?

A TALL ORDER, owd lad.

To try and unearth the truth from the Black. To make sense out of what happened. To consider whether my beloved Bridelow has a future. And, if so, what kind.

I thought at first to put it off until after the official Government inquiry, from which there'll obviously be a report for public scrutiny. However, that's not likely to emerge for months, and when it does it's bound to be a dry Civil Service document full of scientific guff and a list of safety recommendations for communities which happen to be situated on the edge of large, unstable peatbogs.

'Ernie,' you said, 'you're the only man who can put all this into any sort of human and historical perspective. You must get it down while it's fresh. Before it becomes part of Bridelow Mythology.'

What you really meant was, While you're still with us, Ernie.

'And who'll read it, owd lad?'

'Let's hope,' you said sadly, 'that nobody outside of Bridelow will ever have to.'

So I'm writing this in your study at the Rectory while you're up at the church, conducting your first evensong since the Burst. Thanks to your charity, I've been sleeping (whenever the Lord permits it) in the little spare room at the top of the house.

Emergency accommodation. My own house, exposed up by the school, being one of the first destroyed.

Seemed, when it was happening, like Armageddon: most of what we knew and loved engulfed by a dreadful destructive force . . . perhaps the merciless anger of the Lord, which we had brought upon ourselves by clinging to our primitive Christian paganism while all those around us (them Across the Moss) had long since been converted and embraced the Light.

Embraced the light? Don't make me laugh. There's more black out there than you'll find in Bridelow even now, under its dark blanket of peat.

Peat preserves.

The Moss preserved the ancient dead and two millennia of fear, violence, sickness and dread. And other things of which we do not speak, of which we *cannot* speak. Of which Matt Castle, all those years ago, could not speak, only let it pour away, out of the pipes, as he wandered in his agony upon the Moss.

It has absorbed all our overflowing emotions, this Moss, like a gigantic psychic cesspit. It has preserved and it has neutralized. An archaic chemical cathartic.

Ignore me, Hans, I'm getting too deep. Or too whimsy, as Ma Wagstaff would sometimes rebuke me, poor owd lass.

Avoiding getting to the simple physical horror of it.

Thousands of tons of the filthy stuff. Liquefied peat. Stink? I don't think I'll ever get rid of it from the back of my throat. And certainly not from the back of my thoughts. Not as long as I breathe.

Cowering in the choir stalls, we could hear it descending all around the church, still hearing the echo of that cataclysmic thunderclap in aftershocks of rumbling and roaring, and we thought the church would implode, the walls collapse in upon us with a shattering shower of stained glass.

But the church held. The makeshift Autumn Cross swayed and rustled, the lights went out and came on again, bar the one above the door, but the church held.

More than my house did. Reason it went: it was on the wrong side of the street. The first explosion, the actual burst, sent the fountaining filth hundreds of feet into the air . . . why, bits of it were found on the moor, five or six miles away.

But when it settled into a mere tidal wave – a bit, they say, like the tip slide which killed all those poor kids in South Wales – it was the buildings on the west side of the street that took it: the Post Office, the chip shop, Bibby's General Stores (poor old Gus Bibby couldn't have known a thing; his flat over the shop was filled up in seconds with liquid peat as dark and evil-looking as the comfrey oil in one of Ma Wagstaff's jars).

Naturally, The Man I'th Moss, the most westerly building in the village, on the very edge of the bog, is now under a great morass of muck. Selling it won't be a problem for Lottie Castle now; just a question of collecting the insurance, more than enough for a semi in Wilmslow.

At least thirty people died in the village that night; how many were simply victims of the Bog Burst may never be established. Which is, you will agree, just as well.

Quite a few are believed to have perished instantly out on the Moss, although, again, an exact number will probably never be known. Perhaps, over hundreds of years, the bodies will be disinterred, perfectly preserved no doubt, like our Man. Museum pieces – although perhaps not, because the Burst will be part of *recorded* history, so people will understand.

Or will they? Do any of us, even now, know precisely what happened, or why?

Except for Dr Roger Hall, who was seen by his assistant, Mrs White, to be heading for the Moss a short time before

573

the Burst, most of those who died out there, in conditions which recall what I've read of the black horrors of the Somme, will remain unidentified. Many were likely to have been men and women long estranged from their families or disowned by their relatives because of the unacceptable practices in which they indulged themselves.

I know very little about so-called 'satanism', whether this is simply a convenient name we have given to those who seek personal power over others through supposedly supernatural means. Whether, as some say, they sacrificed newborn babies out on the moor in order to 'reconsecrate' the stone circle, I certainly don't know *that*. I do not *want* to know.

All I do know is that extremism of any kind has never taken root in Bridelow, where a practical paganism and a humble Christianity have comfortably linked hands for so long. Many of the dead, sadly, were members of the fundamentalist Christian group called, if I have this right, The Church of the Angels of the New Advent. A large number of them, including their leaders, Mr and Mrs Christopher Montcrieff, heard the mighty thunder-roar and – believing it to be the dawning of the Day of Judgment, as forecast in the Book of Revelations – rushed out of the Rectory into the street with arms and (I would like to think) hearts upraised.

And, in seconds, were buried alive.

Not that many would have remained alive for long under that glutinous mess, most being crushed or drowned or suffocated very rapidly, mouths and noses and lungs clogged for ever. Some of those who did survive had been trapped in pockets of air under beams or walls or other protective bullwarks – although just as many were killed by masonry which was crumbling like crisp toast under the weight of hundreds of tons of peat.

The first death, largely overshadowed by what was to come, remains officially unexplained.

The body in the BMW motor car did indeed prove to be that of my old friend Eliza Horridge. There will be an inquest, and it will probably record an Open Verdict, for Liz appears to have died not of injuries sustained in a car accident and the subsequent fire but some hours earlier and of hypothermia, due to exposure.

There is no question that Liz was suffering from an agoraphobia exacerbated by the fear that her presence was no longer welcome in Bridelow following the sale of the brewery to Gannons (I feel, therefore, that none of us who knew her is exempt from blame) and that, fearing the imminent reappearance of her old lover, John Lucas (whom I shall henceforth, to keep him at a distance, refer to by his adopted *nom-de-plume* of John Peveril Stanage) courageously overcame her illness to seek the aid of her one-time protector, Iris Wagstaff.

And when Ma – who then had herself but a short time left to live – failed to answer her door, Liz, feeling she dare not return home, became confused and wandered out on to the moor. I cannot bring myself to contemplate those cold, wet hours of mental agony and desperation before she succumbed to fatigue and lay down to the sad sleep from which she would never awaken.

I can only assume that her body was discovered on the moor by the sick, satanic brethren recruited by Stanage and his temptress and conveniently employed, most of them, by Gannons. And then (remember, we are not dealing here with wholly rational people) someone decided to put Liz's body into the car, from which they had removed Miss Moira Cairns, before destroying it. As the police could establish no link whatsoever between Liz and Miss Cairns, it was assumed the car had been stolen, but inquiries, I am told, are not yet complete.

As to the part played in this affair by the brewery . . . Well, as the economic heart of the village, it was obviously a target for someone with malice in mind.

I realize now that perhaps the very first death of what we might, quite justifiably, call Bridelow's War, was that of Andy Hodgson, the young worker who 'fell' to the ground during the reassembly of the rusted pulley-and-platform mechanism used originally for winching sacks to the highest level of the brewery . . . that old malt store which was to become the unholiest of temples.

It is my belief that Andy Hodgson was himself a foundation-sacrifice to consecrate the malt store, in one of several corruptions of Celtic ritual performed in an effort to crumble the edifice of our tradition. The platform was later used, there can be no doubt, to winch up the body of Matt Castle, stolen from its grave for despicable necromantic purposes.

It was early days, though, and Andy's death was clearly less elaborate than that of poor Joel Beard, for whom I shall always have a certain respect, whose body remains buried somewhere out on the Moss, and perhaps far more deeply now than was ever intended.

The brewery, in an eastern corner of the village, much shielded by trees, was unaffected by the Burst. When a certain police officer paid a discreet visit the following morning he did not find what he apparently had been expecting. The remains of Matt Castle and Young Frank Manifold had disappeared.

A mystery? Not, I suspect, much of one. I think, if I were to question a few former regulars of The Man I'th Moss, particularly the estimable Mr Stanley Burrows, I might discover that, in the aftermath of the Burst and all the panic and confusion, the number of bodies in the bog had been surreptitiously supplemented.

The aforementioned policeman, an untypically thoughtful and philosophical officer approaching retirement, wishes it to be recorded that he was *not* in Bridelow on the night of the disaster and is unlikely to return. Although, I am informed, this officer has been undertaking some private 'stress-counselling' with a certain widow, in his own time.

It was to be two days before the other bodies were discovered at the brewery. I shall come to this.

Those of us, including Benjie's dog and Ma's cats, who sought sanctuary in the church remained unharmed, although it was terrifying to feel the building almost rocking around us.

Surrounded by rescue-squads in the wan light of early dawn, we could see peat four or five feet deep in parts of the churchyard, like an obscene black parody of snowdrifts.

Most of the graves had disappeared, just the heads of crosses showing. Our Sheila remained in position, looking perhaps more disgruntled than usual with her most public parts gunged up with peat.

Although their yards and gardens were submerged, the houses on the right of the street, had been spared the worst, and these included Ma Wagstaff's cottage, wherein we came upon something inexplicably strange.

Dic Castle was sitting in Ma's old rocking-chair in an atmosphere of unexpected tranquillity. He had been brought to the house at his own request after Stan Burrows and a certain policeman had been unable to find Cathy Gruber. Curiously calm, Dic had insisted they leave him alone, and with so many horrors competing for their attention they didn't argue for long.

And so the lad sat himself down in the rocking chair and slept through all the roaring and the screaming, and he dreamed of an old lady rather irritably bandaging his wounds, continually assuring him that she had better things to do.

I myself have seen those wrists. Now, still within a week, the scars are scarcely visible.

I am a schoolteacher and an historian, a man of facts. I make no comments upon this.

The American, Mr Macbeth . . . Mungo, why not? . . . could so easily have followed the rest of us into the church and saved himself, but instead displayed exceptional and foolhardy courage.

I doubt if he himself knew whether it was Cathy or Miss Moira Cairns he thought he could save. But in his desperate race down the village street he must have felt himself to be close to the epicentre of an earthquake, drenched by the insidious black liquid, with cobs of semi-solid peat falling like bombs all around him and the crackling roar of collapsing buildings on the western side.

Eventually, the young man reached The Man I'th Moss, and must have been horrified by what he found.

For the pub began with the second storey, its ground

floor buried under a black avalanche, the lantern over the front door half submerged but still eerily alight.

Mungo knew the peat would be far too deep to enable him to reach the rear of the building in the normal way, so he waded out to the boundary wall – now no more than a foot above the surface – clambered on to it and moved perilously, like a tightrope walker, around the forecourt until he reached the yard at the rear, at the end of which was the remains of the barn which had been used by Matt Castle for his music.

An ante-room to hell.

. . . Oh, Jesus . . . the fuck am I gonna do? I can't handle this. There's nobody alive here. There . . . is . . . nobody . . . *alive*.

Clawing at his eyes, filling up with the black shit.

And what if I find her body? You expect me to deal with that, Duchess? You sent me down to here to bring her body back, that it? Well, fuck you, Duchess, f . . .

Hold it.

Voices. Close up.

Maybe these were echoes of voices from before the deluge, peat preserving the last blocked screams of the dying.

'Drop it. Darling . . . simply drop it. It'll pull you down. Drop the stone – listen to me, now – drop the stone and wade away because – believe this – another four or five paces and you'll be in over your head, and it won't matter. Drop the stone and back away now and save yourself. All you can do, m'dear.'

'Get *stuffed*!'

Cathy.

Macbeth saw that after the rain, after the blast, there was a lightness in the sky, still night but somehow drained of darkness. A phoney dawn, bringing things and people into visibility.

Cathy was waist-deep in the peat, her fine, fair hair gummed to her skull. She was looking up, but not at the rained-out sky.

Above her, balanced upon a fallen roof-spar, an apparition glowing white, or so it seemed, undamaged by the night or the storm of peat, was the writer, John Peveril Stanage.

Macbeth crouched on his wall.

It was clear that Stanage knew exactly why Cathy was holding, above the level of the peat, a single grey boulder, the kind from which these tough drystone walls had been constructed.

And it was clear also that he believed – part of the psychological mesh he'd helped weave, the mystical dynamic he'd set in motion long ago – that if this boulder should be put in place, in some *particular* place, he'd be able to proceed no further in the direction of Bridelow.

He *believed* this.

In the air, a glimmering, light on metal.

Stanage had hold of a length – five feet or so – of copper pipe.

This was not mystical.

Even as Macbeth struggled to his feet, the pipe began to swing.

'No!'

As he fell from the wall, the pipe smashed into Cathy.

Macbeth rolled into three feet of liquid crud and came up like a sheep out of the dip, found it hard to stand upright, the stuff up around his waist and it was so goddamn *heavy*, filling up the pockets of his slicker; he shrugged out of the slicker, stood there, breathing like a steam engine, black shit soaking into his fucking useless Bloomingdale menswear department cashmere sweater.

'Cathy . . . where the f . . . ?'

'Who are *you*?' said Stanage.

Macbeth scraped peat out of his eyes. 'It doesn't matter,' he said.

He heard Cathy spluttering beside him, glanced briefly at her – something oozing out the side of her head, something that wasn't peat. He pushed himself in front of her, slime slurping down the front of his pants; cold as hell.

'Cathy, just do as he says and get outa here, willya.'

Cathy's hands came out of the mire with a kind of sucking

sound and they were still clutching the grey stone. He saw her grinning, small white teeth in a small blackened face.

'Go!' Macbeth screamed. 'Get the fuck outa here!'

He heard the wafting of the copper pipe through the moist air and he threw himself forward and met it with his body, hard into the chest, and his skin was so cold and numb that if it cracked a rib, or maybe two, he didn't even feel it.

He wrenched hard on the pipe and heard a grunt and then Stanage was tumbling from the end of his roofspar and, breaking the surface of the Moss with a splat, and Macbeth went under. And when he came up, the peat felt a whole lot colder and he couldn't even cough it out of his lungs because of the long fingers like a wire garotte around his throat.

From *Dawber's* Secret *Book of Bridelow* (unpublished):

MUNGO MACBETH HAVING instructed her, in his distressingly restricted New York parlance, to remove herself, Cathy realized she had little choice but to do as he said. The girl cannot swim – even if anyone could in liquid of this consistency and temperature – and her only hope was to get help.

You must remember that Cathy was in a state of some bewilderment; she had not seen the bog burst, only heard the thunder roar, and, like most of us, could have had no concept of the scale of the devastation.

But the village must have looked very different, shockingly so, with the converted gaslamps on one side of the street protruding no more than a few feet from the murky surface of what had now become an extension of the Moss. And the poor girl must have been appalled by the sight of the collapsed cottages, the telephone box protruding from the peat like a buoy and the Post Office in ruins behind it.

She waded frantically back to the wall, placed the grey stone on top, hauled herself up after it and sat there a while, shattered by what she had seen and half-stunned by the blow from the pipe which had landed on her shoulder and rebounded on to the side of her head. She knew there was blood there, mingling with the rivulets of peatwater from her hair, but she did not touch the wound, preferring to remain ignorant of its extent and severity so long as she could function.

Cathy tells me – rather ashamed – that her mind at this point had simply blanked out Mungo Macbeth and what might be happening to him at the cold hands of John Peveril Stanage. She sat on the wall, with the grey stone on her knees. Beyond pain, beyond fear, beyond fatigue, beyond thought . . . even beyond prayer.

And when all feeling had gone, apart from a sense of failure and despair, something came to *her*.

Now . . .

Problems.

It is not my place to be credulous and speak of 'vision'. Nor would I wish to use the clinically dismissive term 'hallucination'.

Of course, I have read the stories, the 'eyewitness testimony', from Lourdes to Fatima to Knock and Walsingham, and occasionally I have been impressed and heartened but most times left cold and more than a little sceptical.

I have *heard* of similar eyewitness reports from the edge of bubbling streams in the Peak District of Derbyshire and – yes – from our own Holy Well above Bridelow. And these have not been chronicled at all, for, in the view of devout Roman Catholics, *Our* Lady is hardly considered to be the same figure as *Their* 'lady', although both have been 'seen' to shine with a silvery aureole, as of the moon rather than the sun.

Well. Cathy's Lady – you'll laugh, or perhaps you won't – wore a duffel coat.

She appeared to be sitting next to the lass on the wall. She was not beautiful, Cathy says, but her aura of feminine grace was so powerfully calming that the air became still and soft and moist, and even the rugged stones beneath her felt like cushions.

She remembers hanging her head, her chin upon her chest, and the lady stroking her hair. Or at least it *was* stroked.

*

About the duffel coat.

My researches tell me that the priests and priestesses of Ancient Britain – the shaman class, if you will – would usually be attired for ceremonial purposes in a loose, hooded garment of blue wool. Quite when the duffel coat, as we know it, reappeared I don't know; my knowledge of social history has never extended to fashion trends, but it has always struck me as curiously meaningful that, while most coats are fastened with plastic buttons or zips, the duffel is secured by pegs of wood. Or (even more interesting) of horn.

But I digress.

The next thing Cathy remembers is standing at a point halfway between the end of the pub forecourt and the first of the ruined cottages. The peat was up to her knees.

Our Lady of the Duffel Coat was gone.

And so was the stone.

Cathy says she felt nothing; neither relief nor the old despair. She was an empty vessel. It was not until later that she would recall the lady in any supernatural sense. She had been as real as the stone, which Cathy had no memory of depositing.

Now there was only the practical problem of avoiding death on the drowning side of the village.

The Beacon of the Moss was alight again, courtesy of Alf Beckett and his floodlight. It threw a strange glimmer on the black surface of a new river flowing between great banks of peat down the middle of the street. From out of a mound of peat, a stiffened arm protruded, the fingers curled and black.

From behind her, Cathy heard voices. She turned her back on the street and waded towards the sound, coming at last to the most southerly part of the village which ran down to the Moss near the causeway and where, she remembered, Lottie Castle was to have placed her stone.

It was here that Cathy became the last person to see Shaw Horridge and Therese Beaufort – later formally identified as one Tessa Byford – alive.

The effects of the Burst at this southern point were

somewhat less marked. Although the Moss had overflowed the causeway in places (which was to cause serious delays for the rescue service vehicles) it had not reached a life-threatening depth for an adult.

The man and woman were thigh-deep at the edge of the causeway, and Cathy was about to call out to them when she realized who they were. Lady Strychnine, as she'd referred to Therese, was hissing at Shaw to get back and leave her and attempting to disengage his hand from around her wrist. Shaw, it appeared, was trying to drag her back towards the village and laughing in a voice which Cathy has described to me as surprisingly coarse and cruel.

'Come on,' Shaw was shouting, almost gleefully. 'Come back. You can do it. You'll feel *so much better*.'

He kept repeating this phrase, hitting her with it, Cathy says, and pulling at her arm, and Therese was screaming shrilly and at one stage actually vomiting with fear.

'Lottie's stone, you see,' Cathy is telling me. 'Therese couldn't go past the stone. And it was then that I realized' – Cathy shakes her head in incomprehension – 'that it had worked. That we'd done it. That the Bridelow Mothers' Union was able to function.'

And knowing what she knew about the woman (not half of what we now know) Cathy felt no great pity when Shaw Horridge quickly let go of Therese's wrists and suddenly delivered an enormous blow to her face with his fist.

All this time Cathy had been backing away up the street towards the village centre, and she turned around just once to see Shaw Horridge walking very slowly and deliberately up the street with Therese's slender body hanging limply from his arms.

As I recorded earlier, it was two days before the corpses were found. This happened when an executive of Gannons accompanied the company's insurance assessor into the brewery to see what minor damage had occurred.

They would hardly have bothered to go into the malt loft even it had not been firmly locked and no keys apparent. As it was, they progressed no further than the second level where the 'coppers' stand.

These are the huge tanks in which the 'wort', as the initial preparation is known, is mixed with the hops (or bog myrtle in old Bridelow Brewery days) which preserve the beer and give it that all-important bitter quality.

It appeared that Shaw, quite methodically, had lit the oil-boiler and gone about the beer-making process on his own, something which, to my own knowledge, he had been able to do since the age of twelve under the paternal eye of Arthur Horridge.

The operation must have taken Shaw several hours, by which time the village was teeming with urgent life: fire and ambulance personnel, moorland rescue teams, television crews; at least two helicopters overhead. I wonder, what state was Therese in during this period? Was she conscious? Did she know what was to happen? Was she – already forcibly conveyed beyond a boundary which she had been psychologically incapable of crossing unassisted – in any state to object?

The copper, by the way, is also known as the 'brew kettle' because in it the hops are boiled into the wort preparatory to the addition of yeast.

They say the insurance assessor passed out after finding the bodies of Shaw and Therese, which must have boiled for nearly two hours before the boiler, reaching danger-level, had automatically cut out.

Was this, I wonder, another example – drowning, boiling and perhaps, in Therese's case, simultaneous strangulation – of that ancient mystery, the Celtic Triple Death?

What was Shaw's state of mind? Was he angry? Embittered? Remorseful? Or a dangerous brew of all three?

'Tell me,' I ask Cathy. 'When you heard them on the edge of the Moss, was Shaw stuttering, as he used to do? You know . . . *You'll fer-fer-feel ber-ber-better?*'

'No,' she says. 'I'm pretty sure he wasn't.'

'I'm glad,' I say.

*

Poor Mungo.

His larynx full of peat, his eyes staring up in terminal terror into the eyes of the madman Stanage, his mouth no doubt full of flip New York obscenities which he now knew he would never utter.

Poor lad.

The stranger in a strange land. Thrown upon the Scottish shore with the instruction, I am told, to discover his 'roots'.

By 'eck. How gullible some of these Americans are apt to be.

And the winds of fate . . . nay, the *typhoons* of fate, can sometimes pick you up and put you down precisely where you wanted to be. Only when you look around, do you realize it's the very *last* place you wanted to be.

He found his Celtic roots, all right. We might not wear kilts or speak a different language or owt like that, but I reckon we've been closer in Bridelow to the true Celtic way – *Shades of things, Ernest!* (Aye, thank you, Ma) – than you'll find in any lonely hamlet in Sutherland or Connemara.

And I think it will survive. I think the Mothers will watch over the rebuilding of a stronger Bridelow. I doubt they'll ever again 'let things slide'.

Cathy won't let them.

Did you know, Hans, by the way, that your daughter was coming to the end of her second and final year at a very reputable theological college outside Oxford? I bet you didn't. I bet she just kept telling you she was doing 'postgraduate research' or something of that order.

But Ma Wagstaff knew. Ma Wagstaff spoke more than once of the 'one who'll come after me' and everybody laughed because it sounded so quaintly biblical.

They have a fund, you know, the Mothers. A bank account in Glossop or Macclesfield or somewhere, to which unexpected windfalls and bequests are added from time to time, and there was sufficient money in that to put Cathy through theological college without anyone knowing.

If all goes well, it'll be The Reverend Cathy soon. And in

a few years, all things being equal, Bridelow will have its first woman minister. Oh, aye. You can count on it. You really think the Archdeacon won't give us his full backing in ensuring that the lass is appointed? By 'eck, lad, we've got enough dirt on that bugger to buy his soul off him, and we're not afraid to use it!

Makes you think though, doesn't it. Another giant step for mankind in little Bridelow: probably the first official Anglican clergyperson (as we'll have to say) equipped to serve both God and the Goddess.

By 'eck.

Could've given Macbeth twenty-five years at least, this bastard, his face white as a skull, white as the skulls that tumbled from the walls in the Earl's castle so long ago, in another time, another life.

But so goddamn strong. His hands so hard, so tight around Macbeth's throat that Macbeth figured one finger must have been driven, nail first, through the skin, through the flesh and up his windpipe where it had lodged and swollen to the size of a clenched fist.

He fought to breathe, but there was no air left, not anywhere in the world.

Stanage's eyes had receded into his skull as he thrust Macbeth's head down under the water once, twice. Second time he came up, Macbeth's eyes were popping too far out, probably, for eyelids to cover, and he was seeing nothing through the black water. Only his inner eyes saw everything, with a helpless clarity:

. . . *this is how it happens, this is how you drown.*

His lungs hard as concrete, his whole body filled up with peat.

. . . *gonna be preserved. For all time. For ever.*

'I remember you now,' he heard Stanage saying. 'Scotland, yes? An American. Followed the Cairns creature around like a bloody lamb.'

Stanage must have known the last question, the one Macbeth couldn't speak, the one which even his blacked-out eyes could no longer convey.

He said, almost gently, 'She died.'

And Macbeth stopped resisting, surrendered to the limitless night.

'Bloody unfortunate, really. Didn't want her dead at a crucial stage. But it'll be OK, I suppose; she won't be doing much yet. They're very bewildered, you see, m'boy. At first. It can take about three days – well, weeks, months, years in some cases. Oh, she was doubtless better prepared than most, but however developed they are, it's three days, minimum, 'fore they can do *damage.*'

Stanage wore a black jacket over a white shirt. The shirt was spotless; suddenly this was the worst thing, a spiritual travesty; Macbeth, dying, felt sick at the injustice of it.

'Caught her unawares, I think, when it came, m'boy. Even though she certainly did have a spirit. Damn well caught *me* unawares on one occasion, as you saw. Bitch. But the Scottish business, that was really . . .'

Forcing Macbeth under the dark water again; this time no struggle, get it over . . .

But Stanage brought him up again.

'. . . just a small clash of egos, in comparison. Small clash of egos. This, though . . . this is a splendid shake-up. Past and present, worlds colliding . . .'

Macbeth's eyes cleared a moment; he saw a big yellow grin.

'. . . roof coming in, I was expecting it, threw myself under a table. Central beam – oak beam – came down on her. If she'd had all her hair – ironic, really – I wouldn't have seen it happen. Not in quite such exquisite detail . . . crrrrrr*unch.* Like an eggshell.'

Eased his grip a fraction, so that a thin jet of air entered Macbeth's lungs. He used it.

'*Motherfucker.*'

Stanage laughed. 'What? Lord, no. You ever *see* my mother?'

Closed up Macbeth's throat.

'Fucked a sister or two. That was fun. For a while. Strengthens the old family ties. Goodnight, m'boy. Don't suppose *your* passing will cause much of a vibe on the ether.'

Last thing Macbeth saw, with gratitude, was some dark shit on Stanage's shirt.

Must've sprayed it out with 'motherfucker'.

From *Dawber's* Secret *Book of Bridelow* (unpublished):

THEY HAVEN'T FOUND his body and happen they never will.

Peat preserves.

Oh, aye, it does that. But how much of what peat preserves *should* be preserved?

It's not natural, that's the problem. Dust to dust. All things must pass. All things must rot. For in rotting there's change. That's the positive aspect of physical death. All things must *change*.

Nothing changes much in the peat; so peat, in my view, works against natural laws. Living on the edge of it, Bridelow folk have always been aware of the borderline between what is natural and what isn't.

This is not whimsy. But all the same, I've had a bellyful, so I've decided, on balance, that I won't die here. Happen my soul'll find its way back, who can say? But, the Lord – and Willie Wagstaff – decided one rainy night that the peat was not for me, so I'm taking the hint and I'll pop me clogs somewhere else, thank you very much.

Also, to be realistic, I think I need what time's left to me to do a bit of thinking, and I reckon Bridelow is too powerful a place right this minute to get things into any sort of perspective.

So.

I'm off to Bournemouth, owd lad.

Don't you dare say *owt*. And don't anybody panic either; when I say Bournemouth, I mean Bournemouth – I've a cousin runs a little guest house up towards Poole Harbour.

Your Cathy says she'll come and see me and bring Milly, and they'll try their hand at a spot of the old Bridelow healing. 'Doctors!' Cathy says. 'What do *they* know?'

Aye. What *do* the buggers know?

We'll see.

He could taste the peat on her face. Nothing ever tasted as good. He wanted to believe it. He didn't.

Wherever she goes, that young woman, she's bound to be touched with madness.

He thought, If we're *both* dead maybe I got a chance *this* side.

'I . . .'

'Don't talk. Not if it hurts.'

There was light in the sky; this time maybe the real thing: dawn.

All Souls Day.

His ass was wet. Everything was wet.

No.

The Duchess said, *Now, who is the white man?*

'No!' Macbeth screamed. 'Fuck you, Duchess!'

'She won't take too kindly to that.'

'No,' he said. 'Please. No tricks. No more tricks.'

He opened his eyes. Shut them tight again. 'Stanage, you motherf—'

'He's gone. Believe me. He's the other side. He can't get across. Whether he's alive or dead, he can't get across.'

Macbeth opened his eyes. Kept them open. Kept staring and staring.

'Eggshell,' he said. 'Said her head was smashed like an eggshell.'

'Whose head?'

'Yours? When the roof came in?'

'I hope not,' Moira said, putting a hand for the first time to the remains of her hair. She wrinkled her nose. 'But I sure as hell kept bloody still underneath that beam until he'd gone. Can you walk? I mean, can you stand up?'

Macbeth leaned his back against the wall and did some coughing. Coughed his guts up. Felt better. Not a whole *lot* better, and the way his goddamn heart was beating . . .

He got his eyes to focus on her.

'Are you real?'

'Do I no' look real?'

Her slashed hair was in spikes. Her face was streaked with black peat and blood. He couldn't tell what she was wearing except for peat.

'Uh . . . yeah,' he said. 'I guess you look real. 'And I . . . Did we come through this?'

'Come on,' Moira said. 'We need to move.'

Holding on to each other, Macbeth still feeling like he was dream-walking, they made it back across the forecourt to where the peat came no higher than their thighs.

And then Moira's plastic lamp went out, which seemed to bother her a lot. 'Just hang on, Mungo, thing's coming to pieces.'

'That's OK.' His brain felt like it was muffled. Mossy. 'We don't need a light any more. Sun's here. Someplace.'

Figured that even if she walked away from him at the top of the street, even if she walked away for ever, he had all the light he'd ever need.

'No,' Moira stopped. 'Been through a lot, me and this lamp. There's blood on it. Is it mine, or Stanage's?'

Macbeth panicked then. He spun around in the peat, saw the roof of The Man I'th Moss, the caved-in roof of the barn, spars and serrated masonry projecting jaggedly into the half-light.

'He's gone,' Moira said.

'You sure he's gone? How can you be *sure*? Someone like that, he can go that easy?'

He stared down into the peat, like a pair of hands might break and drag him down. Or even worse, if there were hands *down there, underneath* . . .

'Please God . . .' Macbeth breathed as a hand went around his arm.

'It's OK, Mungo.'

'Is it? Is it OK? Are you still real? Oh, Jesus . . .'

He started to weep.

'Mungo,' Moira said. 'Wasny that easy.'

Clawing at his hard, white face, at his nose, his teeth, going at him like a madwoman. Blood oozing, greasy, warm blood. And once I saw his eyes, never really seen his eyes before.

In his eyes is this, like, languorous amusement. The damage I'm doing is superficial, and he's laughing at me.

Behind him, there's a shadow on the moss. The shadow isn't moving.

Behind me . . .

This warm breath on my neck. I don't even have to turn around to know how putrid this breath is. Death-room breath.

But I do turn around. I turn my back on John Peveril Stanage, and Matt Castle is there.

Matt Castle is crouching on the Moss. He is very still, still as stone. Still as the bounding toadstone on the moor before it leaps.

His feet do not touch the peat. He's maybe five yards away but I can smell his breath. He is breath, all breath, a mist on the Moss. He's in his element is Matt Castle.

'I don't remember this,' Mungo said. 'I don't remember any of it.'

'These things sometimes happen out of time, you know?' Moira looked up at where the Beacon of the Moss shone down, not blue, somehow pale gold, like an early sun. 'In a twinkling.'

She looked down at the plastic lamp, its back piece hanging off where you put the batteries in. 'Dic gave me this when he rescued me from the outhouse. It's just a wee, cheap thing, made in Taiwan, where the flu comes from. It had gone out, and then it came on, and when it came on Matt's . . . essence, spirit . . . began to squirm, like Dic was sending him a message, you know? And I turned around and . . .'

. . . the light shines into the eyes of John Peveril Stanage and Stanage backs off, backs off too far. He's starting to scream — agony, bitter frustration, and somehow I'm hitting him with the

*light, the finest, brightest light ever came out of Taiwan . . . and
his eyes are this orangey colour floating further back, further
away, like the diminishing tail lights of a car disappearing into
the night . . .*

'Kept hitting him with the light, Mungo, but he'd gone over.
Gone out of the Bridelow circle. Maybe a couple of feet was all
it took. Like an electric fence, you know? Shock just hurled
him back. Maybe he drowned. Was no' my problem.'

She was still fiddling with the lamp, trying to put it back
together.

'And then there was just the two of us. You puking your
guts out, Mungo. I don't know what happened. Maybe we're
talking Providence, maybe . . . Here, hold on to this a wee
minute.'

She gave him the plastic base and two batteries fell out and
plopped into the peat. Then something else fell out after them
and she caught it.

What this was, Macbeth saw, was a little metal comb. Like
a dog comb with a whole bunch of teeth missing.

'Dic.' Moira stared at the comb. 'He stole it back. He told
me, but I . . .'

Moira Cairns started to laugh. Mungo Macbeth never heard
anyone sound quite so elated. Laughing fit to cause ripples in
the peat. Laughing enough to bring on another goddamn bog
blow-out.

She fell down in the swirling street with a filthy splash and
she dragged him down on top of her, both arms around his
neck, the comb in one hand, and she was kissing him hard on
the mouth and the peat on her lips tasted like maple syrup.

When eventually they came to their feet, she linked her arm
into his and started to lead him along the western side of the
street to where the Beacon of the Moss flashed a tired signal to
the sun. The black peat was quite deep around them, but it
was feeling cool, now, and good.

'Teabreak's over,' she said, turning towards him, the peat
around her hips. And she started to laugh again, in lovely big
peals. *'Teabreak's over, boys. Back to your tunnelling, yeah?'*

Mungo Macbeth said, 'Huh?'

From *Dawber's* Secret *Book of Bridelow* (unpublished):

HANS.

Before I go . . .

I can understand your feelings about the death of the young farmer, Sam Davis, but I don't think you should blame yourself; from what you've told me he was a headstrong lad and if he'd listened to you in the first place he'd have left well alone and might be alive today.

Easy for me to say, but it's what I believe.

And at least his stories of night activity among the circles on the moor were our pointer to the location of the bog body. It was obvious what they would do with him: switch him from the sanctity of the churchyard to the poisoned earth of a once-holy place which had systematically, over a long period, been reconsecrated in the name of evil.

Cold storage. Nowhere colder.

The policeman, I understand, expected to find him in the loft at the brewery, but his body was never taken there. I suspect that even Stanage knew that his ancient spirit would be impossible to confront unless it was diffused through Matt Castle. Matt Castle, who they thought they could command.

We are all so stupid, are we not, to believe that anything beyond the physical can ever truly be controlled by mankind?

So we all went up there, that's me and the Mothers and a few lads to do the labouring. Went by day, stroke of noon, with as much brightness in the sky as anyone has a right to expect this time of year.

You know, that place still reeks so much of evil that it could be an environmental and spiritual menace for centuries. I don't know what they'll be able to do about *that*.

Anyroad, Willie Wagstaff and Stan Burrows went in and dug up the bogman and dumped him in a wheelbarrow, and we brought him back to Bridelow.

Where he now lies in what I think you will agree is a place of ultimate safety.

R.I.P.

IRIS WAGSTAFF.
AND
FRIEND . . .

No witch bottle. We didn't want to insult her.

CLOSING CREDITS

CONCEPT: Carol Rickman. The Man in the Moss was formally unearthed when my wife, who'd just read a book on Lindow Man, said, 'I think you should do one about a bog body.' Cleverly, she said this in front of the right witnesses – my ever-helpful agent Andrew Hewson, and eagle-eyed editor at Pan-Mac, Bill Scott-Kerr – at one of those power lunches you hear about. She also kept a cool sub-editor's eye on the whole operation.

TECHNICAL ADVICE

(i) PEAT: Biologist Dr Fred Slater, curator of the University of Wales Llysdinam Field Centre at Newbridge on Wye, Powys, told me about bogs, bog-myrtle and bog oak, and, producing several key scientific reports, introduced the mind-boggling concept of a bog burst.

(ii) CELTIC LORE: Britain's premier Celtic authority, Dr Anne Ross, author of the seminal *Pagan Celtic Britain*, discussed some of her own experiences and referred me to Anthony Myers Ward, Celtic investigator and mysteriologist, who lives dangerously close to Bridelow and to whom I and the Mothers' Union owe a great deal. Paul Devereux put me on to David Clarke, author of the excellent *Ghosts and Legends of the Peak District* (Jarrold Books), who was good enough to make me a copy of a crucial videotape.

(iii) RELIGION: The Revds Ernie Rea, of the BBC, and John Guy, the vicar of Y Groes, got me out of a couple of potentially nasty ecclesiastical traps.

(iv) BEER: Jeremy Blundell showed Carol and me around the Three Tuns Brewery at Bishop's Castle in Shropshire, where quality real ales are produced with no evidence of supernatural intervention, and Iain Loe of CAMRA provided some useful background material.

(v) MEDICAL: Dr Viv Davies talked about heart conditions, Geraldine Richards and my dad, Arthur Rickman, about arthritis and Pamela

Baker, reflexologist and former nursing sister, explained (very colourfully) the drawbacks of wrist slitting.

My US agent Stuart Krichevsky (of the Madison Avenue Krichevskys) was good enough to vet certain aspects of Mungo Macbeth.

Nigel Pennick's *Practical Magic in the Northern Tradition* (Aquarian Books) helped to clarify certain important points, as did the British Museum's compendium report: *Lindow Man – the Body in the Bog*. Thanks also to Graham Nown, Kate Fenton, Rick Turner and Gordon Green's bog-snorkelling fraternity at Llanwrtyd Wells without whom I may never have appreciated just how unpleasant liquid peat can be.

Due to the demands of fiction, virtually none of the background information has gone unmolested, so remember, IT'S NOT THEIR FAULT.

CRYBBE

In memory of
JOACHIM 'LUPO' WOLF,
a genuine New Age healer,
who partly inspired this book

ACKNOWLEDGEMENTS

Crybbe is physically very similar to several towns along the middle section of the Welsh border. It's as close to Offa's Dyke as Knighton and, like Presteigne, it has its own curfew. However, neither of these towns shares Crybbe's basic problems and the people are rather friendlier . . . so don't be afraid to call in and spend some money.

It should also be noted that Crybbe Court was built around the same time – and to a similar design – as Monaughty, a former monastery grange now being very carefully restored by Douglas Blane, who was good enough to show us around.

An enormous number of people have been very helpful during the writing of this book.

They include, in alphabetical order: Dr Viv Davies, Mike Eatock, Alan Edwards, Dr Ashley Fraser, Nigel Fullerton, Tony Geraghty, John Hollis, Dave Howes, Canon Geraint Hughes, the Amazing Arthur Hyde, Alun Lenny, Ralph Parsons, Nicola Rolinson, Edna Williams and Robin Williamson.

Thanks particularly to Carol Rickman and Bill Scott-Kerr for deeply perceptive editing.

And to Anna and Colin Haycraft for . . . well, they know . . .

The spirit-path theory of ley-lines is explored extensively in *Symbolic Landscapes* by Paul Devereux (pub: Gothic Image), who was decent enough to discuss his conclusions with me, well ahead of the book's publication.

And finally, for anyone who suspects the amount of electricity failure experienced in Crybbe is a gross exaggeration, during the period of writing – just over a year – there were well over twenty power cuts in the otherwise-civilized area where we live, not thirty miles from the Border. This was quite normal. Thanks a lot, South Wales Electricity, you've been an inspiration.

PROLOGUE

'Beyond the fields we know.' That, according to the
Edwardian fantasist Lord Dunsany, was where we'd find
an enchanted country.
Dunsany was wrong. The magic is in those same fields.
And we don't know them at all.

J. M. Powys,
The Old Golden Land

IN Crybbe, night did not fall.

Night rose.

It welled out of the bitter brown earth caged in brambles in the neglected wood beyond the churchyard, swarming up the trees until they turned black and began to absorb the sky.

Collecting the shadows of graves, the night seeped out of the churchyard and across the vicarage lawn, where Murray Beech stood, knowing he was the wrong vicar for this parish but not knowing there couldn't be a right one.

Murray, with a certain distaste, was wondering how you went about an exorcism.

In the centre of the town, patches of night gathered like damp about the roots of timber-framed buildings. They'd been turned into shops now, and offices and flats, but they still shambled around the square like sad old drunks.

Puddles of night stained the boots of Jack Preece, plodding across the cobbles to toll the curfew bell from the parish church, as he did every night and would go on doing until – as, being a farmer, he expected – arthritis got him and young Jonathon took over.

When Jack went to ring the old bell, he walked alone. Nobody else on the streets, the town holding its breath, even the sagging old buildings seeming to tense their timbers.

Nobody went into the Cock; nobody came out. Same with the Lamb down the street.

Tradition.

There was a passageway a few yards from the steps of the Cock, the pub's upper storey bellying out above it. This was another of the places where the night was born, and the only place from which, in the minutes before the curfew, you could sometimes hear distinct sounds: moans and squeals and panting.

Silly young buggers. To prevent this kind of thing, there used to be an iron gate across the passageway, with a lock. But when they turned the building at the bottom of the passage into a radio studio, they took the gate off.

This was a matter of some concern to the town council, of which Jack Preece was a member (his father, Jimmy Preece, was the Mayor), and negotiations were in hand with Offa's Dyke Radio and the Marches Development Board to get the gate replaced.

Why?

Same reason as old Percy Weale had given, back in the sixteenth century, for the institution of the curfew: to safeguard the moral welfare of the town.

What other reason could there be?

Minnie Seagrove, sixty three, a widow, had no doubts at all where the night began.

It began in that thing they called the Tump.

She could see it from the big front window of her bungalow on the Ludlow road. Nobody else could see it better.

Not that she wanted to. Ugly great lumps like this were ten a penny in the North and the Midlands where Mrs Seagrove had lived. Only, in those areas, they were known as industrial spoil-heaps and were gradually removed in landscaping and reclamation schemes.

However, this thing, this Tump, wouldn't be going any-where. It was protected. It was an Ancient Monument – supposed to have been a prehistoric burial mound originally, and then, in the Middle Ages, there might have been a castle on top, although there were no stones there any more.

Mrs Seagrove didn't see the point in preserving just a big, unpleasant hump with a few trees on top. It was obviously not natural, and if it was left to her, the council would be hiring Gomer Parry with his bulldozers and his diggers to get rid of it.

Because that might also get rid of the black thing that ran down from the mound in the twilight and scared the life out of Minnie Seagrove.

All right, she'd say to herself, I know, I know . . . I could simply draw the curtains, switch on the telly and forget all about it. After all, I never noticed it – not once – when Frank was alive. But then, there didn't seem to be so many power cuts when Frank was alive.

How it came about, she was watching telly one night, coming up to *News at Ten*, and the power went off, and so she automatically went across to the window to see if the lights were on across the river, in the town.

And that was when she first saw it.

Horrible. Really horrible. It was . . . well, it was like the night itself bounding down from the Tump and rushing off, hungry, into the fields.

But why can't you just stop looking? Why can't you stay well away from that window when it's going dark?

I don't know.

That's the really frightening thing. I don't know.

Yes, I do.

It's because I can feel when it's there. No matter what I'm doing, what's on telly or the radio or what I'm reading, ever since I first dashed to the window during that power cut, I've always known when it's on its way down from the mound. Without even going to the window, I *know* when it's there.

And the reason I look – the reason I *have* to look, even though it scares me half to death – is that I have to know, I have to be sure *that it isn't coming this way*.

Crybbe: a small one-time market town within sight of Offa's Dyke, the earthwork raised in the Dark Ages to separate England from Wales.

A town like a dozen others on either side of the border; less distinctive than most.

Except that here, the night rose.

PART ONE

Some persons have super-normal powers not of a
magitien, but of a peculiar and scientific qualitie.

DR JOHN DEE,
Letter to Lord Burghley, 1574

CHAPTER I

SOMETIME – and please, God, make it soon – they were going to have to sell this place. And on evenings like this, when the sky sagged and the bricks of the houses across the street were the colour of dried blood, Fay would consider how they'd have to bait the trap.

On a fresh page of the spiral-bound notepad, she wrote:

FOR SALE
Bijou cottage in small, historic town amid spectacular Welsh border scenery. Close to all amenities, yet with lovely open views to rear, across pastoral countryside towards Offa's Dyke. Reasonably priced at . . .

. . . what? You couldn't make it too cheap or they'd be suspicious – and with good reason.

She'd suggest to her dad that they place the ad in the *Sunday Times* or the *Observer*, under 'rural property'. These were the columns guaranteed to penetrate the London suburbs, where the dreamers lived.

They probably wouldn't have heard of Crybbe. But it did sound appealing, didn't it? Cosy and tucked away. Or, alternatively, rather mysterious, if that was what you were looking for.

Fay found herself glancing at the bookshelves. Full of illusions. She saw the misty green spine of *Walking the Welsh Marches*. The enigmatic *Old Straight Track* by Alfred Watkins. And the worst offender: J. M. Powys's *The Old Golden Land*, which suggested that the border country was full of 'secret doorways', through which you could penetrate 'ancient mysteries'. And lots of pictures taken through lenses coated with Vaseline and wishful thinking.

She would really hate doing this to somebody, selling the house and perpetuating the myth. But not as much as she'd hate having to stay here. And you couldn't let your conscience run away with your life, could you?

9

Anyway, there were some people – like, say, the Newsomes – who rather deserved what this town was doing to them.

'Off to the pub,' the Canon called merrily from the hall. 'Fay, can you hear me? I said, I'm off to the boozer.'

'OK, Dad.'

'Spot of social intercourse.'

'You'll be lucky.' Fay watched him stride past the window towards the town square. The old devil still looked deceptively fit for someone who, ever so slowly, was going mad.

He would put on a wonderful performance for the prospective purchasers, always assuming they caught him on one of his better days. That Santa Claus beard and the matching twinkle. They'd love him. More importantly, they'd trust him, the poor sods.

But before she could unleash this ample bundle of ecclesiastical charm on the punters, there was just one minor difficulty to overcome.

The Canon didn't appear to want to leave Crybbe. Ever.

This was the central problem in Fay's life. This was what kept her awake at night.

Christ, how *could* he? He didn't tramp the hills, wasn't much interested in peregrine falcons or otters or bog-orchids. How, for God's sake, could he bear to go on living in this no-hope town now that the woman who'd brought him here had been dead for nearly a year?

Other recent settlers kept saying what a little haven it was. Convincing themselves. A handful of retired people – most of them rather younger than the Canon – drifted into the town every year. The kind who told themselves they needed to be closer to nature. But nature, for them, amounted to a nice view. They came here not to die, but to fade out. To sit amid soft greenery until they grew frail and lighter than air and the wind blew them away like dandelion seeds.

What happened in reality was that an ambulance eventually took them off, rattling along the narrow lanes to Hereford General, twenty-five miles away. Taking too long to get there because all the roads were B roads, clogged with tractors and trailer-loads of sheep, whose milky eyes showed that *they* had no illusions at all about fading into a green heaven.

'Don't do it, Dad,' Fay said, just to create a new sound – three minutes' walk from the so-called town centre and all you could hear was the clock on the mantelpiece and the wheezing of the fridge. 'Don't leave your mind in bloody Crybbe.'

The Canon seemed, perversely, to revel in the misery of the town, to relish the shifty, suspicious stares he encountered in the post office and all the drinks the locals didn't buy him in the pub.

His mind was congealing, like a fried egg on a cold morning. The specialists had confirmed it, and at first Fay had refused to believe them. Although once you knew, the signs were pretty obvious.

Decay was infectious. It spread like yellow fungus in a tree stump. Fay realized she herself had somehow passed that age when you could no longer fool yourself that you were looking younger than you felt.

Especially here. The city – well, that was like part of your make-up, it hid all the signs. Whereas the country spelled it out for you. Every year it withered. Only the country came up green again, and you didn't.

Fay took a deep breath. This was not like her at all.

On the table in front of her lay a small, flat, square box containing fifteen minutes' worth of tape she'd recorded that morning. On the box was written in pencil

Henry Kettle, dowser.

Later, Fay would create from the tape about six minutes of radio. To do this she would draw the curtains, switch on the Anglepoise lamp and the Revox editing machine and forget she was in Crybbe.

It was what kept her sane.

She wondered what kind of reaction she'd get if she told it like it was to the perusers of the property columns.

Fay picked up the pencil and wrote on the pad:

FOR SALE
Faded terraced house in godforsaken
backwater, somewhere in damp

11

no man's land long disowned by both
Wales and England.
Fully modernized – in 1960.
Depressingly close to bunch of run-down shops,
selling nothing in particular.
Backing on to infertile hill country,
full of dour farming types and pompous
retired bank managers from Luton.
No serious offer ignored.

In fact, she added, *we'd tear your bloody hand off . . .*

CHAPTER II

C LOSE UP, she was like a dark, crooked finger pushing
out of the earth, beckoning him into the brambles.

When he looked back from the entrance to the field,
she'd shrivelled into something more sinister: a bent and twisted
old woman. A crippled crone.

Or maybe just the broken stump of a fence post. Maybe
only that.

She hadn't been visible from here at all until, earlier that
day, Mr Kettle had put on his thick gloves and pulled away the
brambles, then pruned the hedge around her so that she stood
naked, not even a covering of moss.

Now he'd brought Goff to see his discovery, and he should
have felt a bit proud, but he didn't. All the time he'd been
cutting away the undergrowth something had been pulling at
him, saying, *Leave it be, Henry, you're doing no good here.*

But this was his job, and this stone was what showed he'd
earned his money. It made a nonsense of the whole business if
he didn't reveal the only real evidence that proved the line was
there, falling sure as a shadow across the field, dead straight,
between two youngish oak trees and . . .

'See that gate?'

'The metal gate?'

'Aye, but he's likely replaced generations of wooden ones,' Mr Kettle said, his voice rolling easy now, like the hills around them. Even without the final proof he'd have been confident of this one. Wonderful feeling it was, when you looked up and everything in the landscape – every hill and every tree, every hedge, every gateway – suddenly smiled at you and nodded and said you were right, you done it again, boy.

Like shaking hands with God.

Happening again, so suddenly like this, everything dovetailing, it had taken his mind off the doubts, and he'd been asking himself: how can there be anything wrong, when it all falls together so neatly.

He indicated the gate again. 'Prob'ly the cattle chose the spot, you following me?'

'Because they'd always go out that way! Out of the field, right?'

'You're learning.' Though it was still warmish, Mr Kettle wore a heavy tweed suit. He carried what once had been a medical bag of scuffed black leather, softened with age. The tools of the trade in there, the forked twigs and the wire rods and the pendulums. But the tools weren't important; they just made the clients feel better about paying good money to a walking old wives' tale like him.

Max Goff had a white suit, a Panama hat and the remains of an Aussie accent. For a long time Mr Kettle had found it hard to take him seriously, all the daft stuff he came out with about wells of sacred power and arteries of healing energy and such.

The New Age – he kept on about that. Mr Kettle had heard it all before. Twenty years ago they were knocking on his door in their Indian kaftans and head-bands, following him out to stone circles, like Mitchell's Fold up in Shropshire, where they'd sit smoking long, bendy cigarettes and having visions, in between pawing each other. Now it was a man in a white suit with a big, powerful motor car, but it was the same old thing.

Many, many times he'd explained to people that what he did was basically about *science*. Wonderful, yes – even after all

13

these years the thrill was there all right. But it was a natural thing. Nothing psychic about dowsing.

What sun there'd been had all but gone now, leaving a mournful old sky with clouds like a battle-flag torn into muddy, blood-stiffened strips. It hadn't been a good spring and it wouldn't be a good summer.

'Now look *up* from the gate,' said Mr Kettle.

'Yeah, that . . . church steeple, you mean?'

'No, no, before that. Side of that bit of a hedge.'

'Oh . . . that thing.'

The old girl was about a hundred yards down the field, separated from the hedge now, blackened against the light, no more than three feet tall. But she was there, that was the point. In the right place.

'Yes,' Mr Kettle said. *'That* thing.'

It was no good, he didn't like her. Even if she'd proved him right he didn't like the feeling coming off her, the smell that you could smell from a good distance, although not really.

'Is it a tree stump?' And then, 'Hey, you're kidding, it can't be!' The little eyes suddenly sparking. He'd be ruthless and probably devious in his business, this feller, but he had this enthusiastic innocence about him that you couldn't altogether dislike.

'Jeez,' Goff said. 'I thought they'd all gone!'

'Why don't you go over and have a look at 'er?' Mr Kettle put down his bag and sat on it under the hedge and patted the grass so that Arnold, his dog, would sit down, too. And they both sat and watched this bulky, bearded bloke making his ungainly way across the tufted meadow. Impatient, stumbling, because he'd thought they'd all gone, the old stones of Crybbe.

Mr Kettle, too, had believed they'd all gone, until this morning when they'd finally let him into the field for the first time and he'd located the line and walked slowly along it, letting it talk to him, a low murmur.

And then the tone had altered, strengthened, calling out to him, the way they did. 'I'm here, Henry, the only standing stone left standing within a mile of Crybbe.'

Or vibrations to that effect. As megaliths went, she wasn't impressive, but she hadn't lost her voice. Not a voice he liked, though; he felt it was high and keening and travelled on a thin, dry wind.

But it proved he hadn't lost his capacity to receive. The *faculty*.

'Still there, then, Arnold. Every time I goes out I reckon it isn't bound to work any more.' He scratched the dog's head. 'But it's still there, boy.'

The only conclusion Mr Kettle could reach about why this stone had survived was that there must've been a wood here and the thing had been buried in brambles. And if they'd noticed her at all, they, like Goff, might have thought it was just an old tree stump.

He could see the figure in the white suit bending over the stone and then walking all around, contemplating the thing from different angles, as if hoping she'd speak to him. Which, of course, she wouldn't because if Goff had possessed the *faculty* there'd have been no reason to send for Henry Kettle.

An odd customer, this Goff, and no mistake. Most of the people who consulted dowsers – that is, actually paid them – had good practical reasons. Usually farmers looking for a water supply for their stock. Or occasionally people who'd lost something. And now and then those afflicted by rheumatics, or worse, because they'd got a bad spring under the house.

'Why am I still thinking he's trouble then, Arnie?'

The dog considered the question, looked serious.

Well, hell, he didn't *want* to think that. Not at all, because this Goff was the first person who'd ever paid him to go ley-hunting.

'Mr Kettle,' he'd said, coming straight to the point, which Mr Kettle liked, 'I've been advised that this used to be quite a centre for prehistoric remains, and I wanna know, basically, what happened to them. Can you find out where they used to be? The old stones? The burial mounds? And I'm told you can kind of detect ley-lines, too, yeah?'

'Well,' Mr Kettle had said carefully, 'I know what you mean. It do sometimes seem they fall into straight lines, the old monuments.'

'No need to be coy with me, Mr Kettle. I'm not afraid to call a ley-line a ley-line.'

Now this had, at first, been a joy, taking the old chap back nigh on seventy years. He remembered – a memory like a faded sepia photo – being on a hazy hilltop with his father and other members of the Straight Track Club. Mr Watkins pointing out the little bump on the horizon and showing how the line progressed to it from mound, to stone, to steeple. The others nodding, impressed. The picture frozen there: Mr Watkins, arm outstretched, bit of a smile under his stiff beard.

Now, remarkably – and loath as Mr Kettle had been, at first, to admit it – this Goff had stumbled on something Mr Watkins would, no question, have given his right arm to know about.

So it had proved unexpectedly exciting, this survey, this ley-hunt. Bit of an eye-opener. To say the least.

Until . . .

One morning, knowing there had to have been a stone in a particular place in Big Meadow and then digging about and finding part of it buried near by, Mr Kettle had got a feeling that something about this was not regular. In most areas, old stones were lost gradually, over centuries, plucked out at random, when exasperation at the damage done to a plough or a harrow had finally overcome the farmer's inbred superstition.

But at Crybbe, he was sure, it had been systematic.

Like a purge.

Mr Kettle's excitement was dampened then by a bad feeling that just wouldn't go away. When he dug up the stone he thought he could smell it – something faintly putrid, as if he'd unearthed a dead sheep.

And, as a man who lived by his feelings, he wondered if he ought to say something. About the purge on the stones. About the history of the Court – John Dee, Black Michael and the hangings. And about the legends, which travelled parallel to history and sometimes, if you could decode them, told you far more about what had really happened than the fusty old documents in the county archives.

Mr Kettle, who kept his own records, was getting more and

more interested in Crybbe – wishing, though, that he didn't have to be. Wishing he could ignore it. Detecting a problem here, a serious long-term problem, and wishing he could turn his back on it.

But, as the problem was likely to remain long after he'd gone, he'd taken steps to pass on his fears. With a feller like this Max Goff blundering about the place, there should always be somebody who knew about these things – somebody trustworthy – to keep an eye open.

He supposed he ought to warn Goff, but the thought of 'something sinister' would probably only make the place more appealing.

'And, anyway, you can't tell these New Age types anything, can you, Arnold?' Mr Kettle was scratching the dog's head again. 'No, you can't, boy.'

Ten minutes later Goff was back, puffing, the flush in his cheeks making his close-mown beard seem even redder. Excitement coming off him like steam.

'Mr Kettle, let me get this right. According to your calculations, this is line B, right?'

'That's correct.'

'And by following this line, as you dowsed it, we suddenly come across what could be the only remaining stone in the alignment. Is it exactly where you figured it'd be?'

'Well . . .' Mr Kettle got to his feet and picked up his bag. Max Goff eyed it.

'Got the rods in there? Can we dowse the line some more, maybe find another stone?'

No, we bloody can't, Mr Kettle thought. You might as well ask, how about if we grabs hold of this electric cable to see if he's live?

He saw, to his dismay, that Goff was looking at him in some kind of awe; he'd found a new guru. It was not a role Mr Kettle fancied. 'Getting late,' he said. 'I ought to be away. Don't like driving in the dark these days.'

'When can you come again?'

'Look,' Mr Kettle said. 'I'm an old man. I likes my fireside and my books. And besides, you got it all now. You know where they all are. Or used to be.'

This Goff was a man whose success in business had convinced him that if you knew a source, knowledge and experience could be bought like . . . what would this feller buy? . . . cocaine? Mr Kettle, who still read two newspapers every day, knew a bit about Max Goff and the kind of world he came from.

'Maybe your role in this is only just beginning,' Goff said. 'How about I send a car for you next time?'

Money was no object for this bugger. Made his first million by the time he was twenty-seven, Mr Kettle had read, by starting his own record company. Epidemic, it was called. And it had spread like one. Now it was international magazines and book publishing.

'Well,' Mr Kettle said. 'Isn't much more as I can tell you, anyway. You've got the maps. Nothing more to be found, even if you excavates, I reckon.'

'Hmmm.' Goff was making a show of being unconvinced, as they followed what Mr Kettle now thought of, wrote of in his journal – but never spoke of – as the Dark Road, the Thoroughfare of the Dead. Returning at dusk, back into Crybbe, a town which had loitered since the Middle Ages, and probably before, in the area where England hardened into Wales.

On the very border.

CHAPTER III

I T WAS the seventh bell they always rang, for the curfew. Almost rang itself these days. Seventeen years Jack had been doing it. Didn't need to think much about it any more. Went regular as his own heartbeat.

The bell clanged above him.

Jack let the rope slide back through his hands.

Seventy-three.

His hands closed again around the rope.

Seventy-four.

He hadn't been counting. At any point during the ringing Jack could tell you what number he was on. His arms knew. His stomach knew.

One hundred times every night. Starting at ten o'clock. Newcomers to the town, they'd asked him, 'Don't you find it spooky, going up there, through that graveyard, up all those narrow stone steps, with the church all dark, and the bell-ropes just hanging there?'

'Don't think about it,' Jack would say. And it was true; he didn't.

There were eight bells in the tower, and that was reckoned to be a good peal for this part of the country.

For weddings, sometimes in the old days, they'd all be going. Even fairly recently – though not any more – it had been known for some snooty bride from Off to bring in a handful of bell-ringers from her own parish for the big day. This had only been permitted for weddings, sometimes. On Sundays, never. And not Christmas. Not even Easter.

And also, every few years some bearded clown in a sports jacket would pass through. And then the church or the town council would get a letter from the secretary of some group of nutters that travelled the country ringing other people's bells.

The town council would say no.

Occasionally – this was the worst problem – there'd be somebody like Colonel Croston who'd moved in from Hereford, where he was reckoned to have been in the SAS. He liked to keep fit. Jogged around the place.

And rang bells, as a hobby.

He'd been a pain in the neck at first, had Colonel Croston. 'No bell-ringers apart from you, Jack? That's appalling. Look, you leave this one to me.'

Jack Preece remembered the Colonel putting up posters inviting all able-bodied folk to come to the church one Friday night and learn the ropes. 'Give me six months. Guarantee I'll knock them into shape.'

Jack had gone along himself because he didn't like the thought of youngsters running up and down the stone steps and swinging on his ropes.

When the two of them had been waiting around for nearly an hour he let the despondent Colonel take him for a drink. 'Doesn't deserve these bells, Jack, this town.'

'Aye, aye,' Jack had said non-committally, and had permitted Colonel Croston to buy him a large brandy.

He hadn't bothered to tell the Colonel that even he only knew how to ring the curfew using the seventh bell. Well, no point in buggering with the others, see, was there? No point in making a show. They could have pulled the other bells down and flogged them off for scrap, far as Jack Preece was concerned.

Anyhow, what they'd done now, to save a lot of bother and pestering was to take down all the ropes. Except, of course the one that rang the seventh bell.

Some nights, Jack would be real knackered after a day's dipping, or shearing, or lambing. He'd stagger up them steps, hurting all over his body, dying for a pint and aching for his bed. Some nights he'd grab hold of that rope just to stop himself falling over.

Still the hundred would be done. And done on time.

And it was on nights like this that Jack felt sometimes he was helped. Felt the belfry was kind of aglow, and other hands were pulling on the rope beside his own.

Spooky?

Well, he didn't think about it. Where was the point in that?

They walked slowly into the town over a river bridge with old brick walls which badly need pointing, the river flat and sullen below. Past a pub, the Cock, with flaky paintwork and walls that had once been whitewashed but now looked grey and *un*washed.

A dark, smoky, secretive little town. There was still an afterglow on the fields, but the town was already embracing the night.

Mr Kettle had never been to Paris or New York. But if, tonight, he was to be flown into either of them, he suspected he wouldn't feel any more of a stranger than he did entering Crybbe – a town he'd lived within twenty miles of all his life.

This town, it wasn't remote exactly, not difficult to reach, yet it was isolated. Outsiders never had reason to pass through it on the way to anywhere. Because, no matter where you wanted to reach, there was always a better way to get there than via Crybbe. Three roads intersected here, but they were B roads, two starting in Wales – one leading eventually to Hereford, the other to Ludlow – and the other . . . well, buggered if he knew where that one went.

Max Goff, almost glowing in his white suit, was striding into the dimness of the town, like Dr Livingstone or somebody, with a pocketful of beads for the natives.

They'd take the beads, the people here. They wouldn't thank him, but they'd take the beads.

Henry Kettle didn't claim to understand the people of Crybbe. They weren't hostile and they weren't friendly. They kept their heads down, that was all you could say about them. A local historian had once told him this was how towns and villages on the border always used to be. If there was any cross-border conflict between the English and the Welsh they never took sides openly until it was clear which was going to win. Also, towns of no importance were less likely to be attacked and burned.

So keeping their heads down had got to be a way of life.

Tourists must turn up sometimes. By accident, probably. Mr Kettle reckoned most of them wouldn't even bother to park. Sure the buildings were ancient enough, but they weren't painted and polished up like the timber-frame villages on the Hereford black-and-white trail. Nothing here that said 'visit me' with any enthusiasm, because there was no sense of pride.

From the church tower, above the cobbled square, a lone bell was clanging dolefully into the musty dusk. It was the only sound there was.

'What's that?' Goff demanded.

'Only the curfew.'

Goff stopped on the cobbles, his smile a great gash. 'Hey, really . . . ? This is a real curfew, like in the old days?'

'No,' Mr Kettle said. 'Not really. That's to say, people are no longer required to be off the streets by nightfall. Just tradition nowadays. The Preece family, it is, performs the duty. One of 'em goes up the belfry, God knows how many steps, every night, summer and winter; nine-thirty, or is it ten?'

He looked up at the church clock but it was too dark to make out where its hands were pointing. He was sure there used to be a light on that clock. 'Hundred times it rings, anyway.'

'Might only be a tradition, but there's still nobody on the streets,' Max Goff observed. 'Is there?'

'That's 'cause they're all in the pubs,' said Mr Kettle. 'No, what it is, there's some old trust fund arranges for the bell to be rung. The Preeces get grazing rights on a few acres of land in return for keeping up the custom. Passed down, father to son, for four hundred-odd years. Being farmers, they always has plenty sons.'

They stood in the square until the ringing stopped.

'Crazy,' Goff said, shaking his big head in delight. 'Crayzee. This is the first night I've spent here, y'know? I've always stayed in Hereford. It's magic, Mr Kettle. Hey, we still on the line?'

'I suppose we must be. Aye, see the little marker by there?'

A stone no more than a foot high, not much more than a bump in the cobbles. Goff squatted next to it and held his palms over it, as though he expected it to be hot or to light up or something. The dog, Arnold, watched, his head on one side, as if puzzled by a human being who went down on all fours to sniff the places where dogs had pissed.

Two middle-aged women walked across the square talking in low voices. They stopped talking as they walked past Goff, but didn't look at him, nor Mr Kettle, nor each other.

Then they went rigid, because suddenly Arnold's head was back and he was howling.

'Jeez!' Goff sprang up. The two women turned, and Mr Kettle felt he was getting a very dark, warning look, the women's faces shadowed almost to black.

'Arnold!' With some difficulty – beginning to think he must have a bad spring under his own house, the way his rheumatism had been playing up lately – Mr Kettle got down on his knees and pulled the dog to him. 'Sorry, ladies.'

The women didn't speak, stood there a moment then turned and walked away quickly as the howling subsided because Mr Kettle had a hand clamped around Arnold's jaws. 'Daft bugger, Arnold.'

'Why'd it do that?' Goff asked, without much interest.

'I wish I knew, Mr Goff.'

Mr Kettle wanted some time to think about this. Because for a long time he'd thought it was just a drab little town, full of uninspired, interbred old families and misfits from Off. And now, he thought, it's more than that. More than inbreeding and apathy.

He unclamped the dog's jaws, and Arnold gave him a reproachful glance and then shook his head.

There were lights in some town houses now. They lit the rooms behind the curtains but not the square, not even a little. Folk in this town had never thrown their light around.

'OK?' Goff said, feet planted firmly on the cobbles, legs splayed, quite relaxed. Wasn't getting it, was he? Wasn't feeling the resistance? Didn't realize he was among the descendants of the people who'd pulled up the stones.

Mr Kettle was getting to his feet, one hand against the wall. Like his old bones, the brick seemed infirm. The people here, they cared nothing for their heritage.

And their ancestors had torn up the stones.

Goff was just a big white blob in the dim square. Mr Kettle walked to where their cars were parked in a little bay behind the church overhung with yew trees. His own car was a dusty VW Estate. Goff had a Ferrari.

'Come to dinner, OK?' Goff said. 'When I've moved into the Court.'

'You're going through with it, then?'

'Try and stop me.'

'Can I say something?' Henry Kettle had been thinking about this for the past fifteen minutes or so. He didn't much like Goff, but he was a kindly old chap, who wanted at least to put out a steadying hand.

'Of course.'

Mr Kettle stood uneasily in the semi-dark. 'These places . . .' he began, and sucked in his lips, trying to concentrate. Trying to get it right.

'I suppose what I'm trying to say is places like this, they – how can I put it? – they invites a kind of *obsession*.' He fell silent, watching the buildings in the square hunching together as the night took over.

A harsh laugh came out of Goff. 'Is that it?' he asked, rudely.

Mr Kettle unlocked his car door and opened it for Arnold. 'Yes,' he said, half-surprised because he'd thought he was going to say more. 'Yes, I suppose that *is* it.'

He couldn't see the dog anywhere. 'Arnie!' he called out sharply. He'd had this problem before, the dog slinking silently away, clearly not at ease, whimpering sometimes.

He hadn't gone far this time, though. Mr Kettle found him pressed into the churchyard wall, ears down flat, panting with anxiety. 'All right, Arn, we're leaving now,' Mr Kettle said, patting him – his coat felt lank and plastered down, as if he was the first dog ever to sweat. This was it with a dowser's dog; he'd pick up on the things his master was after and, being a dog and closer to these matters anyway, his response would be stronger.

Slipping his hand under Arnold's collar, Mr Kettle led him back to the car and saw Goff standing there quite still in his white suit and his Panama hat, like an out-of-season snowman.

'Mr Kettle,' Goff took a steep breath. 'Perhaps I oughta explain. This place . . . I mean, look around . . . it's remote, half-forgotten, run-down. For centuries its people lived from the land, right? But now agriculture's in decline, it doesn't provide extra jobs any more, and there's nothing here to replace it. This town's in deep shit, Mr Kettle.'

Mr Kettle couldn't argue with that; he didn't say anything. Watched Max Goff spread his hands, Messiah-style.

'And yet, in prehistory, this was obviously a sacred place,'

Goff said. 'We have this network of megalithic sites – a dozen or so standing stones, suggestions of a circle or a henge. And the Tump, of course. Strong indications that this was a major focus of the Earth Force. A centre of terrestrial energy, yeah? You see any signs of that energy now?'

'People pulled the stones out,' Mr Kettle said.

'Precisely. And what happened? They lost touch with it.'

'Lost touch with what?'

'With the life force, Mr Kettle! Listen, give me your opinion on this. Whaddaya think would happen if . . . ?'

Max Goff walked right up to Mr Kettle in the ill-lit square and looked down at him, lowering his voice as if he were about to offer him a tip for the stock market. Mr Kettle felt most uneasy. He was getting the dead-sheep smell.

'Whadda *you* think would happen,' Goff whispered, 'if we were to put the stones *back*?'

Well, Mr Kettle thought, that depends. Depends on the true nature of leys, about which we *know* nothing, only speculate endlessly. Depends whether they're forgotten arteries of what you New Age fellers like to call the Life Force. Or whether they're something else, like paths of the dead.

But all he said was, 'I don't know, Mr Goff. I wouldn't like to say.'

CHAPTER IV

HOW OLD was the box, then?

Warren Preece reckoned it was at least as old as the panelling in the farmhouse hall, which was estimated to be just about the oldest part of the house. So that made it sixteenth century or so.

He was into something here all right. And the great thing, the really fucking great thing about this was that no other bastard knew about it. Lived in this house all his life, but he'd never had cause to poke about in the chimney before – well, you wouldn't, would you? – until that morning, when his old man had shouted, 'Put that bloody guitar down, Warren, and get off your arse and hold this torch, boy.'

Piss off, Warren had spat under his breath, but he'd done it, knowing what a bastard the old man could be when a job wasn't going right.

Then, standing in the fireplace, shining the torch up the chimney – the old man on a step-ladder struggling to pull this crumbling brick out – a bloody great lump of old cement had fallen away and broken up and some of the dust had gone in Warren's eye.

'You clumsy bastard, Dad!' Warren fell back, dropping the torch, ramming a knuckle into his weeping eye, hearing masonry crumbling where he'd staggered and kicked out. If he made it to college without being registered disabled through living in this broken-down pile of historic crap, it'd be a real achievement.

'Come on, Warren, don't mess about! I need that light.'

'I'm f . . . Hang on, Dad, I can't flaming see.' Hunched in the fireplace, scraping at his gritty, watery eye.

And it was then, while picking up the torch – flashing it on and off to make sure the bulb hadn't broken when he'd dropped it – that Warren found this little tunnel.

It was no more than a deepish recess in the side wall of the fireplace, about eighteen inches off the ground. Which would have put it on a level with the top of the dog grate, when they'd had one. Must have been where he'd kicked back with his heel, hacking off a cob of sixteenth-century gunge.

Warren shone the light into the recess and saw what looked like carving. Put a hand inside, felt about.

Hey, this was . . .

'Warren! What you bloody doing down there, boy?'

Quickly he shoved bits of brick into the opening, ramming them tight with the heel of his trainer. Then shone the torch back up the chimney for the old man pretty damn fast.

In fact, for the rest of the day he'd been a very willing labourer – 'You stay there, Dad, I'll get it.' 'Want me to mix the cement down here and pass it up, Dad?' 'Cuppa tea, Dad?' Anything so the old man'd get the job done and bugger off out of the way.

The old man had been surprised and pleased, grinning through a faceful of soot, patting Warren on the shoulder. 'We done a good job there, boy. He won't set on fire again, that ole chimney. Fancy a pint?'

He'd never said that before. Well, not to Warren. Most nights, sometimes with Jonathon, he just went off to the Cock without a word.

So Warren, too, was surprised and almost pleased. But wasn't going for no pint with the old man tonight. No way.

'Told Tessa I'd be round, Dad. Sorry.'

The old man looked quite relieved. Warren had watched him tramping off up the track, eager to wash the dust out of his throat. So eager he hadn't bothered to clean up the mess in the hearth and so hadn't noticed anything he shouldn't.

Stupid git.

Warren got himself a can of Black Label from the fridge and went back to the fireplace to pull out them old bricks.

He'd got the box out, was squatting on the hearth, dusting it off, when he heard Jonathon's car. He'd tucked the box under his arm – bloody heavy, it was, too – and got it out through the back door and round the back of the barn, where he'd hidden it in the bottom of an old water-butt.

And gone up to his room and waited for Jonathon to piss off.

The way he saw it, you didn't seal up an oak box like this and stash it away in a secret compartment in the chimney unless there was something pretty damn valuable inside. And, as he'd discovered, just about anything a bit old was valuable these days.

Warren had a mate, a guy who got rid of stuff, no questions asked. He could be looking at big money here on the box alone. It was in good nick, this box, sealed up warm and dry for centuries. Warren looked at the box and saw a new amplifier for the band. He looked harder and saw this second-hand Stratocaster guitar. Felt the Strat hanging low round his hip, its neck slippy with sweat.

The curfew bell was tolling in the distance. His dad had

sunk a swift pint and plodded off up the tower to do his nightly duty, silly old bugger.

'Why do you keep on doing that, Dad? Don't pay, do it? And no bugger takes any notice 'part from setting their watches.'

'Tradition, boy. Your grandad did it for over thirty years. And when I gets too rheumaticky to climb them steps, Jonathon'll do it, right, son?'

Jonathon nodding. He was always 'son', whereas Warren was 'the boy'. Said something, that did.

What it said was that Jonathon, the eldest son, was going to get the farm. Well, OK, if Jonathon wanted to wallow in shit, shag sheep all his life, well, fair enough.

Warren didn't give a toss about going to college in Hereford either, except that was where the other guys in the band lived.

But Crybbe – he could hardly believe this – was where Max Goff was going to be.

Max Goff, of Epidemic Records.

He'd seen him. Been watching him for days. Somehow Max Goff had to hear the band. Because this band was real good, he could feel it. This band fucking *cooked*.

The box was in one of the sheds on the old workbench now. He'd rigged up an old lambing light to work by, realizing this was going to be a delicate operation. Didn't want to damage the box, see, because it could be worth a couple of hundred on its own.

Now. He had a few tools set out on the bench: hammer, screwdriver, chisel, Stanley knife. Precision stuff, this.

Warren grinned.

. OK, if it came to it, he *would* have to damage it, because he hadn't got all bloody night. But better to go in from underneath than cut the lid, which had a bit of a carving on it – nothing fancy, like, nothing clever, just some rough symbols. Looked like *they'd* been done with a Stanley knife. A sixteenth-century Stanley knife. Warren had to laugh.

Round about then, Crybbe had another power cut, although Warren Preece, working in the shed with a lambing light, wasn't affected at all.

*

But Fay Morrison was furious.

She'd always preferred to do her editing at night, especially on the days when she was producing complete programmes. There'd just be her and the tape-machine under a desk-lamp. And then, when the tape was cut together, she would switch off the lamp and sit back, perhaps with a coffee, and play it through in the cosy darkness. Only a red pilot-light and the soft green glow of the level-meters, the gentle swish of the leader tape gliding past the heads.

Magic.

This was what made radio so much more satisfying than television. The intimacy of moments like this. And the fact that you could do all the creative work on your own, only going into a studio for the final mix.

Fay really missed all that. Hadn't imagined she'd miss it *so much*.

Tonight, she'd waited until her father had wandered off to the pub for his nightly whisky and his bar-supper. And then she'd gone into her office, which used to be Grace Legge's sitting-room.

And still was, really, in the daytime. But at night you could switch off the G-plan furnishing and the fifties fireplace, and the front room of Number 8, Bell Street, Crybbe, became more tolerable, with only a second-hand Revox visible in the circle of light from the Anglepoise.

Fay had a package to edit for Offa's Dyke Radio. Only a six-minute piece to be slotted into somebody else's afternoon chat-and-disc show on what was arguably the worst local shoe-string station in the country.

But it was still radio, wasn't it? After a fashion.

And this morning, doing her contribution for a series on – yawn, yawn – 'people with unusual hobbies', Fay had actually got *interested* in something. For a start, he was ever such a nice old chap – most of the people around here, far from being quaint

29

rural characters, were about as appealing as dried parsnips.

And he'd actually been happy to talk to her, which was also a first. Until she'd come here, Fay had encountered very few people who didn't want to be on the radio: no cameras, no lights, and no need to change your shirt or have your hair done. But in this area, people would make excuses – 'Oh, I'm too busy, call again sometime.' Or simply refuse – 'I don't want to *be* on the wireless' – as if, by collecting their voices on tape, you were going to take their souls away.

Yes, it was *that* primitive sometimes.

Or so she felt.

But the water-diviner, or dowser, had been different and Fay had been fascinated to learn how it was done. Nothing, apparently, to do with the hazel twig, as such. Simply a faculty you developed through practice, nothing as airy-fairy as 'intuition'.

And it definitely was *not psychic*.

He kept emphasizing that, scrutinizing her a bit warily as she stood there, in her T-shirt and jeans, wishing she'd brought a sweater and a wind-muff for the microphone. It had been a bit breezy in that field, even if tomorrow was Midsummer Day.

'Do you think *I* could do it, Henry?' she'd asked, on tape. You always asked this question, sounding as if it had just occurred to you. There would then follow an amusing couple of minutes of your attempting to do whatever it was and, of course, failing dismally.

'You could have a try,' he'd said, playing along. And so she'd taken the forked twig in both hands. 'Hold it quite firmly, so it doesn't slip, but don't grip it too hard. And, above all, *relax* . . .'

'OK,' she'd heard herself say through the speaker. And that was when the power went off.

'Bloody *hell*!' Fay stormed to the window to see if the other houses in the street were off. Which they were.

It was the fourth power cut in a month.

'I don't believe it!'

OK, you could imagine that on some distant rock in the Hebrides, even today, there would be quite a few times when the power got waylaid on its way from the mainland.

But this was close to the epicentre of Britain. There were no high mountains. And they were not in the middle of an electric storm.

She couldn't remember if it was South Wales Electricity or Midlands Electricity. But neither could be up to much if they were unable to maintain supplies to a whole town – OK, a very *small* town – for longer than a fortnight without a break.

Hereward Newsome, who ran the art gallery in town, had complained to his MP and tried to get up a petition about it. But he'd given that up in disgust after collecting precisely fifteen signatures, all from newcomers, including Fay and her dad.

Of course, the Newsomes' problem did appear to be somewhat more serious. Not only were they having to suffer the power cuts but they were affected by other surges in supply which, Hereward swore, were almost doubling their electricity bills. He was getting into a terrible state about it.

Actually, Fay was a bit dubious about the huge bills being caused by a fault in the system. She grinned into the darkness. It was probably Jocasta's vibrator, on overdrive.

There was a bump and the sound of two empty spools clattering to the floor.

'Pushkin, is that you?'

Grace's cats got everywhere.

Fay decided she didn't like this room very much in the absolute dark.

She felt along the wall for the tape-recorder plug, removed it and went to bed.

Living in Crybbe would drive anybody to a vibrator.

Warren should have known.

Sixteenth-century lock. Not as if it was Chubb's finest, was it? Stanley knife into the groove, sliding it around a bit, that was all it took. Then the screwdriver pushed into the gap. Hit it just once with the palm of his hand.

It didn't exactly fly open, the box. Well, it wouldn't, would it? Being as how it had turned out to be lead-lined.

Fucking lead! No wonder it was so heavy. Good job he hadn't tried to cut into it through the bottom.

'Course that lead lining was a bit of a disappointment. Warren had been hoping the box weighed so much because it was full of gold coins or something of that order. Lead, even antique lead, was worth bugger all, he was pretty sure of that.

Funny smell.

Well, not that funny. Old, it smelled old and musty. He moved the lambing light closer, poked a finger in.

Cloth, it was. Some sort of old fabric, greyish. Better be a bit careful here, bloody old thing might disintegrate.

On the other hand, he couldn't afford to waste any time. His old man – who wasn't much of a drinker – might even now be on his way back from the church. He might, of course, have called back round the pub for one with Jonathon and his mates. (If Warren was in the pub with *his* mates and the old man came in, he'd turn his stool round, pretend he hadn't seen him, but Jonathon would call him over, buy him a pint; that was the kind of smarmy git Jonathon was.) But most likely he'd come home, getting a few early nights in before haymaking time and dipping and all that rural shit.

And as he came up the track he'd see the light in the shed.

Warren pulled the lamp down, away from the shed window. He couldn't see much through the glass, with its thick covering of cobwebs full of dust and dead insects, except that it was very nearly dark and there was a mist.

He was feeling cold now, wanting to get it over with and go back to the house. It was going to be no big deal, anyway. Old papers probably. Some long-dead bugger's last will and testament.

He prodded the cloth stuff with the end of the Stanley knife and then dug the blade in a bit and used the knife to pull the fabric out of the box in one lump.

What was underneath the cloth was whiteish and yellowish, like brittle old paper or parchment crumpled up.

He gave it a prod.

And the Stanley knife dropped out of Warren's fingers – fingers that had gone suddenly numb.

'Aaaa . . .'

Warren caught his breath, voice gone into a choke.

The knife fell into the box and made this horrible little chinking noise.

CHAPTER V

M R KETTLE raised a hand to Goff as he drove away. He was thinking, well, *somebody* had to buy the place. Better this rich, flash bugger – surely – than a family man with a cosy wife and perhaps a daughter or two, with horses for the stables and things to lose. Good things. Peace of mind. *Balance* of mind.

He left the town on the Ludlow road which would take him past the Court. It wouldn't be Goff's only home. Well, he'd move in and stride around for a while, barking orders to battalions of workmen, changing this and restoring that in the hope it would give the house some personality, a bit of atmosphere. And then he'd get tired of the struggle and go back to London, and the Court would become a weekend home, then an every-other-weekend home, then a holiday home, then just an investment.

Then he'd sell it.

And the process would begin all over again.

Dead ahead of him at this point, the Court crouched like an animal behind the Tump. The Tump was a mound which at some stage may or may not have had a castle on top. Trees sprouted from it now and brambles choked the slopes. The Tump was a field away from the road, about two hundred yards, and there was a wall around it.

Arnold whined once and crept into the back seat where he lay down.

Behind the wall, the Tump loomed black against the dull, smoky dregs of the dusk. All the more visible because there were no lights anywhere. Nothing. Had there been a power cut?

It had always been obvious to Mr Kettle that whether or not the Tump had once had a castle on it, before that – long, long before that – it had been a burial place of some importance.

33

He'd been up there but found no sign of it having been excavated. Which was not that unusual; mounds like this were ten a penny in the Marches.

The business of the stones. *That* was unusual.

What *would* happen if he put them back, the same stones where you could find them, substitutes where they'd vanished entirely? Well, probably nothing. Nothing would happen. That was what Mr Kettle told himself as he drove in the direction of the Tump along a road which vaguely followed the ley he'd marked on the Ordnance Survey map as 'line B'. The mound, of course, was on the line.

He was relieved when the road swung away from the ley and the shadow of the Tump moved over from the windscreen to the side window. Now, why was that? *Why* was he relieved?

He slowed for the final bend before the town sign and glanced in the mirror, seeing in the dimness the dog's intelligent eyes, wide, bright and anxious.

'He don't know really what he's takin' on, Arn,' Mr Kettle said, his voice softening as it always did when he and the dog were alone.

He put out his left hand to switch on the headlights. Towns ended very abruptly in these parts. Full streetlighting and then, in the blink of an eye, you were into the countryside, where different rules applied. But tonight there were no lights; it was all one.

People said sometimes that the Court must be haunted, whatever that meant. Atmospherics, usually. The couple of times he'd been in there it had been cold and gloomy and had this miserable, uncared for kind of feeling. In Mr Kettle's experience, so-called haunted houses were not normally like that – they could be quite bright and cheerful in the daytime, except for those cold bits. There were always cold bits.

But what was wrong with the Court was more fundamental. It was a dead spot. Nothing *psychic*, though, you understand? Just nothing thrived there. Indeed, he couldn't figure out why it hadn't been abandoned and left to rot centuries ago, long before it had become a 'listed' building, deemed to be of historic interest.

Arnold sprang up on the back seat and growled.

'And what's up with you now?'

The dog had his front paws on the back of Mr Kettle's seat, his furry head against his master's cheek, lips curled back, showing his teeth, white and feral in the gloom.

Mr Kettle tried to follow Arnie's gaze, thinking maybe the dog had caught sight of a badger ambling out of the hedge. But all he could see was the yellow of the headlights thrown back at him.

He rubbed at the windscreen. 'Bugger me, Arn, that mist's come down quick tonight, boy.'

But there was nothing moving in the mist. No noise, no lights, no badgers, not even tree shapes.

Only the Tump.

He was up in the highest field now, but at the bottom end by the wood, the lambing light at his feet, the grass wet and cold, the sweat on him mingling with the mist, the spade handle clammy with it. He didn't care; he'd never felt like this before.

Warren scraped the earth into the hole and pulled the turf back over it, slamming it down with the spade, jumping on it, getting it tight so nobody would know. Not that anybody came here; only the sheep, and the old man once or twice a year.

Beneath the turf and the soil and the clay was the old box, buried good and deep, with the Stanley knife still inside it. It seemed right, somehow, to leave the knife in the box.

Or it seemed *not* right to put his hand in the box and take the knife out.

Not with the other hand in there.

'Where did that come from?'

The dog snarled.

The Tump was off-centre in the mist. But it shouldn't have been there at all because he'd passed it, he must have, couple of minutes ago at least.

'Now just you sit down, you daft dog.' And then he looked

up at the Tump and said suddenly, softly, 'You're not right, are you?'

At that moment Arnold was thrown to the floor, as, without warning, the car lurched off to the right, the steering wheel spinning away so fiercely it burned the palms of Mr Kettle's hands when he tried to hold it.

'Oh no you don't, you bugger.' Addressing, through his teeth, neither the dog, nor the car, for he should have been half-expecting this, bloody old fool. Wrenching at the wheel, as the black mound rose up full in the windscreen.

From behind his seat, the dog's growl built to a yelp of terror.

'I know, I'm sorry!' Cursing the part of him which responded to nonsense like this; mad as hell at his bloody old, slowing body which no longer seemed to have the strength to loose it out.

Arnold cringed on the floor next to the back seat, shivering and panting. Then Mr Kettle felt the bumps and heard the clumps under the car, and knew what must have happened.

'We're in the bloody field!'

Common land. Unfenced. Flat and well-drained enough where it met the road to offer no obstacles to car wheels.

No obstacles at all, until you got to the humps and ridges. And then the wall.

They said the wall, which almost encircled the mound, had been built centuries ago of stones taken from the old castle foundations. It was not high – maybe five feet – but it was a very thick wall, and as strong and resistant as ever it'd been. He'd never thought about this before, but why would they build a wall around it?

Behind the wall, the Tump bulged and glowered and Mr Kettle's faculty started leaping and bounding the way his body hadn't managed to in thirty years.

The wild senses were rising up, leaving the body hobbling behind and the old car trundling across the field, going its own sweet way.

And something in Henry Kettle, something he used to be able to control, locking into the Tump's wavelength with a long, almost grateful shudder. As if it was going home.

Going back, rolling down.

'Silly young devil.' Mr Watkins chiding him when he rolled over and over, down from Clifford Castle, coming to rest at the feet of the stern old man. 'One day you'll learn respect for these places, boy.'

Mr Watkins, face in shadow under his hat.

One day you'll learn.

But he hadn't.

Hadn't been able to connect with it at all when he was up there with Goff, looking round, seeing where the Tump stood in relation to the stones.

Had it now, though, too bloody much of it, filling him up, like when they'd sent him to the hospital for the enema, colonic clean-out, whatever they'd called it, pumping this fluid through his backside and he could feel it going right up into his insides, terrible cold.

Something here that was cold and old and dark and . . .

. . . was no home to be going to.

'Oh Christ, Arnold,' said Mr Kettle. 'Oh Christ.'

Knowing it for the first time. Why they must have built a wall around it. Knowing a lot of things about the stones and the leys and why Mr Watkins had not . . .

Knowing all this as the car went over a ridge in the field – maybe one of the old ramparts when it had been a castle – and began to go downhill, and faster.

'I can deal with this, don't you worry!' 'Course he could.

Nothing *psychic* here. Understand *that*.

Stamping down on the brake – frantic now – but the car going even faster, ripping through the field like a tank. A muffled bump-clank, bump-clank, then the rending of metal and the car ploughing on like a wounded animal, roaring and farting.

In the windscreen, the trees on the Tump were crowding out of the mist, a tangle of black and writhing branches, spewing like entrails from a slashed gut, the centremost trees suddenly flung apart as if blown by a sudden gale, as if the wind was bursting out and over the mound like a fountain of air.

And he could see it. *He could see the wind* . . .

And as it rushed down, it took the form . . .

nothing psychic, nothing psychic, nothing . . .

of a huge black thing, a dog . . . hound . . . bounding down the mound and leaping at the car, an amber hunger smoking in eyes that outshone the headlights because . . .

'. . . you're bloody *evil* . . .'

Arnold screaming from behind. Not barking, not whimpering, but making the most piteously distressed and upsetting noise he'd ever been forced to hear.

All the time thinking – the words themselves forming in his head and echoing there – I've seen it. It was there. *I've seen Black Michael's Hound.*

And when the illusion of the wind and the thing it carried had gone he saw the headlight beams were full of stone.

Nothing to be done. Bloody old fool, he thought sadly, and suddenly it seemed he had all the time there was to ponder the situation and realize he hadn't touched the brake pedal, not once. The car having automatic transmission – only two pedals – what had happened was his foot had plunged down hard, time and time again, on the other one.

The accelerator.

Well, he did try to pull the stupid foot off, but his knee had locked and he saw through the windscreen that the thick, solid stone wall was being hurled at him by the night, and the night would not miss.

There was a hollow silence in the car and that seemed to last a *very* long time, and Mr Kettle could feel Arnold, his faithful dog somewhere close to him, quiet now. But his eyes'd be resigned, no light in them any more.

Mr Kettle put out a hand to pat Arnold but probably did not reach him before the impact killed both headlamps and there was no light anywhere and no sound except, from afar, the keening song of the old stone.

A few minutes later the electricity was restored. Bulbs flared briefly, stuttered, died and then came back to what passed, in Crybbe, for life.

Business had not been interrupted in either of the two bars

at the Cock, where, through past experience, a generator was always on hand. When the lights revived, closing-time had come and gone, and so had most of the customers.

Few people in the houses around the town realized the power was back, and the wavering ambience of oil lamps, Tilley lamps and candles could be seen behind curtained windows.

One electric light blinked back on and would remain needlessly on until morning.

This was the Anglepoise lamp on Fay Morrison's editing table. She'd unplugged the tape-machine before going to bed but forgotten about the lamp. All through the night it craned its neck over her desk-diary and a spiral-bound notepad, the one which often served, unintentionally, as a personal diary, especially when she was feeling angry and hopeless.

Across the page, in deeply indented frustration, the pencil lettering said,

. . . we'd tear your bloody hand off . . .

PART TWO

Although I have been able to divine water and do other
simple things of that kind for many years . . . I had not
thought that this faculty might be related to the formation
of ghosts.

T. C. LETHBRIDGE,
Ghost and Divining Rod (1963)

CHAPTER I

'No, no . . . don't hold him like that. Not so tightly. You're like a nervous kiddy riding a bike.'

'Oh, sorry. Like this?'

'Better. Don't think of him as an implement – he's an extension of your arms. Be comfortable.'

'I think I've got it. What do I do now?'

'Just walk across towards the tree – and don't be so nervous, girl.'

'Well, I've never done it before, Henry. I'm a virgin.'

She thought, shall I leave that?

Nah. Maria will only chop it. She'll think I'm trying to be clever. Too clever for Offa's Dyke Radio, God forbid.

Fay marked it up with a white Chinagraph pencil, sliced out just over a foot of tape with a razorblade cutter, spliced the ends, ran the tape again.

Crunch, crunch. Rustle, rustle.

'All right, now, Fay, ask yourself the question.'

'Huh? Oh, er . . . is . . . Is There Any Water Under Here? I feel a bit daft, to be honest, Henry. And there's . . . nothing . . . happening. Obviously haven't got your natural aptitude, if that's the word.'

' 'Course you have, girl. Anybody can do it as really wants to. It's not magic. Look, shall I help you?'

'Yes please.'

'Right, now, we'll do it again. Like this.'

'Oh, you're putting your hands . . .'

'Over yours, yes. Now relax, and we'll walk the same path and ask ourselves the same question.'

'OK. Here we go. Is there any . . . ? Fucking hell, Henry!'

Laughter.

'Caught you by surprise, did it?'

'You could say that.'

Pause.

'*Look, Henry, do you think we could do that bit again, so I can moderate my response?*'

Fay marked the tape. Fast forwarded until she heard herself say, 'OK, Take Two', made another white mark after that and picked up the razorblade.

Shame really. Never as good second time around. All the spontaneity gone. 'Whoops' had been the best she could manage the second time, when the forked hazel twig had flipped up dramatically, almost turning a somersault in her hands, nearly dislodging the microphone from under her arm.

'Whoops'. . . . not good enough. She started to splice the ends of the tape together, wondering if she had time to go into a field with the Uher and do a quick, 'Gosh, wow, good heavens, I never expected that,' and splice it in at the appropriate point.

The phone rang.

'Yes, what?' The damn roll of editing tape was stuck to her hands and now the receiver.

'Fay Morrison?'

'Yes, sorry, you caught me . . .'

'This is James Barlow in the newsroom.'

'*Which* newsroom?' Fay demanded, being awkward because the voice somehow reminded her of her ex-husband, who always called people by their full names.

'Offa's Dyke Radio, Fay.' No, not really like Guy. Too young. A cynical, world-weary twenty-two or thereabouts. James Barlow, she hadn't dealt with him before.

'Sorry, I was editing a piece. I've got tape stuck to my fingers.'

'Fay, Maria says she commissioned a package from you about Henry Kettle, the water-diviner chap.'

'Dowser, yes.'

'Pardon?'

'Water-diviner, James, is not an adequate term for what he does. He divines all kinds of things. Electric cables, foundations of old buildings, dead bodies . . .'

'Yeah, well, he obviously wasn't much good at divining stone walls. Have you done the piece?'

'That's what I'm . . .'

"Cause, if you could let us have it this morning . . .'

'It's not for News,' Fay explained. 'It's a soft piece for Maria. For Alan Thingy's show. Six and a half minutes of me learning how to dowse.' Fay ripped the tape from the receiver and threw the roll on the editing table. 'What did you mean about stone walls?'

'Tut-tut. Don't you have police contacts, down there, Fay? Henry Kettle drove into one last night. Splat.'

The room seemed to shift as if it was on trestles like the editing table. The table and the Revox suddenly looked so incongruous here – the room out of the 1960s, grey-tiled fire-place, G-plan chairs, lumpy settee with satin covers. Still Grace Legge's room, still in mourning.

'What?' Fay said.

'Must've been well pissed,' said James Barlow, with relish. 'Straight across a bloody field and into this massive wall. Splat. Actually they're speculating, did he have a heart attack? So we're putting together a little piece on him, and your stuff . . .'

'Excuse me, James, but is he . . . ?'

'. . . would go quite nicely. We'll stitch it together here, but you'll still get paid, obviously. Yes, he is. Oh, yes. Very much so, I'm told. Splat, you know?'

'Yes,' Fay said numbly.

'Can you send it from the Unattended, say by eleven?'

'Yes.'

'Send the lot, we'll chop out a suitable clip. Bye now.'

Fay switched the machine back on. Now it no longer mattered, Take Two didn't sound quite so naff.

'. . . whoops! Gosh, Henry, that's amazing, the twig's flipped right over. If your hands hadn't been there, I'd've . . .'

A dead man said, 'Dropped it, I reckon. Well, there you are then, Fay, you've found your first well. Can likely make yourself a bob or two now.'

'I don't think so, somehow. Tell me, what exactly was happening there? You must have given it some thought over the years.'

'Well . . . it's nothing to do with the rod, for a start. It's in you, *see. You're letting yourself connect with what's out there and all the things that have ever been out there. I don't know, sounds a bit cranky. You're, how can I say . . . you're reminding your body that it's just part of everything else that's going on, you following me? Never been very good at explaining it, I just does it . . . You can mess about with this, can't you, Fay, make it sound sensible? Feller from the BBC interviewed me once. He . . .'*

'Yes, don't worry, it'll be fine. Now, what I think you're saying is that, in this hi-tech age, man no longer feels the need to be in tune with his environment.'

'Well, aye, that's about it. Life don't depend on it any more, do he?'

'I suppose not. But look, Henry, what if . . . ?'

She stopped the tape, cut it off after 'Life don't depend on it any more.' Why give them the lot when they'd only use forty seconds?

Anyway, the next bit wasn't usable. She'd asked him about this job he was doing for Max Goff and he'd stepped smartly back, waving his arms, motioning at her to switch the tape off. Saying that it would all come out sooner or later. 'Don't press me, girl, all right?'

Later, he'd said, 'Not being funny, see. Only it's not turned out as simple as I thought it was going to be. Something I don't quite understand. Not yet, anyway.'

She hadn't pressed him. Very unprofessional of her. She had, after all, only approached Henry Kettle about doing six minutes for the 'people with unusual hobbies' spot because she'd heard Max Goff had brought him to Crybbe and it was her job to find out what Goff himself was doing here.

But she'd ended up liking Henry Kettle and actually liking somebody was sometimes incompatible with the job. So now nobody would know what he'd been doing for Goff unless Goff himself chose to disclose it.

Fay sat down, she and the room both in mourning now. He'd been a great character, had Henry, he'd leave a gap.

But if you had to go, maybe Splat wasn't a bad exit line at the age of – what was he, eighty-seven? Still driving his own car, too. Fay thought about her dad and the sports cars he'd had. He'd prefer Splat to arterial strangulation anytime.

Talking of the devil, she caught sight of him then through the window, strolling back towards the cottage with the *Guardian* under his arm, looking at ladies' legs and beaming through his big, snowy beard at people on either side – even though, in Crybbe, people never seemed to beam back.

The cottage fronted directly on to the street, no garden. Canon Alex Peters pushed straight into the office. He wasn't beaming now. He was clearly annoyed about something.

'Don't they just bloody love it?'

'Love what?' Fay joined some red leader to the end of the tape, deliberately not looking up, determined not to be a congregation.

'A tragedy. Death, failure – 'specially if it's one of the dreaded People from Off.'

'What are you on about, Dad?'

'That's what they say, "From Off. Oh, he's from Off." I've calculated that "Off" means anywhere more than forty miles away. Anywhere nearer, they say, "Oh, he's from Leominster" or "He's from Llandrindod Wells". Which are places not near enough to be local, but not far enough away to be "Off".'

'You're bonkers, Dad.' Fay spun back the finished tape.

'Anyway, this poor sod was apparently from Kington or somewhere, which is the middle category. Not local but not "Off". So they're quite content that he's dead but not as happy as they'd be if he was from, say, Kent.'

It clicked.

'You're talking about Henry Kettle.'

'Who?'

'Henry Kettle. The dowser I interviewed yesterday morning.'

'Oh God,' Canon Peters said. '*That's* who it was. I'm sorry, Fay, I didn't connect, I . . .'

'Never mind,' Fay said soothingly. Sometimes, on his good days, you were inclined to forget.

Her father, who'd been about to sit down, was instantly back on his feet. 'Now look . . . It's got nothing to with Dr Alphonse sodding Alzheimer.'

'Alois.'

'What?'

'Alois Alzheimer. Anyway, you haven't got Alzheimer's disease.'

The Canon waved a dismissive hand. 'Alzheimer is easier to say than arteriosclerotic dementia, when you're going gaga.' He took off his pink cotton jacket. 'Nothing to do with that, anyway. Always failed to make connections. Always putting my sodding foot in it.'

'Yes, Dad.'

'And stop being so bloody considerate.'

'All right then. Belt up, you old bugger, while I finish this tape.'

'That's better.' The Canon slung his jacket over the back of the armchair, slumped down, glared grimly at the *Guardian*. Fay labelled the tape and boxed it. She stood back and pulled down her T-shirt, pushed fingers through her tawny hair, asking him, 'Where was it, then? Where did it happen?'

Canon Peters lowered his paper. 'Behind the old Court. You know the tumulus round the back, you can see it from the Ludlow road? Got a wall round it? That's what he hit.'

'But – hang on – that wall's a bloody mile off the road.'

'Couple of hundred yards, actually.'

'But still . . . I mean, he'd have to drive across an entire field for Christ's sake.' When James Barlow had said something about Mr Kettle crossing a field she'd imagined some kind of extended grass-verge. 'Somebody said maybe he'd had a heart attack, so I was thinking he'd just gone out of control, hit a wall not far off the road. Not, you know, embarked on a cross-country endurance course.'

'Perhaps,' speculated the Canon, 'he topped himself.'

'Cobblers. I was with him yesterday morning, he was fine. Not the suicidal type, anyway. And if you're going to do yourself in, there have to be rather more foolproof ways than that.'

'Nine out of ten suicides, somebody says that. There's always an easier way. He was probably just confused. I can sympathize.'

'Any witnesses?' Above the tiled fireplace, opposite the

window, was a mirror in a Victorian-style gilt frame. Fay inspected her face in it and decided that, for a walk to the studio, it would get by.

Canon Peters said, 'Witnesses? In Crybbe?'

'Sorry, I wasn't thinking.'

'Wouldn't have known myself if I hadn't spotted all the police activity, so I grilled the newsagent. Apparently it must have happened last night, but he wasn't found until this morning.'

'Oh God, there's no chance he might have been still alive, lying there all night . . . ?'

'Shouldn't think so. Head took most of it, I gather, I didn't go to look. A local milkman, it was, who spotted the wreckage and presumably said to himself,"Well, well, what a mess," and then wondered if perhaps he ought not to call Wynford, the copper. No hurry, though, because . . .'

'He wasn't local,' said Fay.

'Precisely.'

Fay said it for the second time this week. 'Why don't you get the hell out of this town, Dad? You're never going to feel you belong.'

'I like it here.'

'It irritates the hell out of you!'

'I know, but it's rather interesting. In an anthropological sort of way.' His beard twitched. She knew she wasn't getting the whole story. What was he hiding, and why?

Fay frowned, wondering if he'd seen the spoof FOR SALE notice she'd scribbled out during a ten-minute burst of depression last night. She said tentatively, 'Grace wouldn't want you to stay. You know that.'

'Now look, young Fay,' Canon Peters leaned forward in the chair, a deceptive innocence in the wide blue eyes which had wowed widows in a dozen parishes. 'More to the point, there's absolutely no need for *you* to hang around. You know my methods. No problem at all to find some lonely old totty among the immigrant population to cater for my whims. In fact, you're probably cramping my style.'

He raised the *Guardian* high so that all she could see was

his fluffy white hair, like the bobble on an old-fashioned ski hat.

'Anyway,' he mumbled. 'Early stages yet. Could be months before I'm a dribbling old cabbage.'

'Dad, I'll . . . !' The phone rang. 'Yes, what . . . ? Oh. Mrs Seagrove.'

All she needed.

'Serves you right,' rumbled the Canon from the depths of the *Guardian*.

'I saw it again, Mrs Morrison. Last night. When the power was off.'

'Oh,' Fay said, as kindly as she could manage. 'Did you?'

'I can't bear it any more, Mrs Morrison.'

Fay didn't bother to ask her how she could see a huge coal-black beast when all the lights were out; she'd say she just *could*. She was one of the aforementioned lonely old Midland immigrant widows in a pretty cottage on the edge of town. One of the people who rang local reporters because they needed someone to make a cup of tea for.

'I'm at the end of my tether, Mrs Morrison. I'm going out of my mind. You wouldn't think anything as black as that could glow, would you? I'm shivering now, just remembering it.'

In other places they rang the police for help. But in Crybbe the police was Sergeant Wynford Wiley and nobody wanted to make a cup of tea for him.

'I've tried to explain, Mrs Seagrove. It's a fascinating . . .'

'It's not fascinating, my love, it's terrifying. It's no joke. It's frightening me out of my mind. I can't sleep.'

'But there's nothing I can do unless you're prepared to talk about it on tape. I only work for the radio, and unless we can hear your voice . . .'

'Why can't you just *say* someone's seen it without saying who I am or where I live?'

'Because . . . because that's not the way radio works. We have to hear a voice. Look,' Fay said, 'I really would like to do the story. Perhaps you could find someone else who's seen it and would be prepared to talk about it and have it recorded.'

Mrs Seagrove said bitterly, 'They all know about it. Mrs

Francis at the post office, Mr Preece. They won't admit it. They won't talk about it. I've tried telling the vicar, he just listens and he smiles, I don't think he even believes in God, that vicar. Perhaps if you came round this afternoon, we could . . .'

'I'm sorry,' Fay said, 'I've got several jobs on the go at the moment.'

'Ho, ho,' said the *Guardian*.

'Look,' Fay said. 'Think about it. It's quite easy and informal, you know. Just me and a portable recorder, and if you make any fluffs we can keep doing it again until you've got it right.'

'Well, perhaps if you came round we could . . .'

'*Not* unless you're prepared to talk about it on tape,' Fay said firmly.

'I'll think about it,' Mrs Seagrove said.

Fay put the phone down. Of course she felt sorry for the lady. And ghost stories always went down well with producers, even if the eye-witnesses were dismissed as loonies. Local radio *needed* loonies; how else, for instance, could you sustain phone-in programmes in an area like this?

But ghost stories where nobody would go on the record as having seen the apparition were non-starters. On that same basis, Fay thought ruefully, a lot of stories had been non-starters in Crybbe.

CHAPTER II

THE WINDSCREEN was in splinters. There was blood on some of them, dried now. And there were other bits, pink and glistening like mince on a butcher's tray, which Max Goff didn't want to know about.

'What are you saying here?' he demanded irritably. 'You're saying it's a fucking *omen*?'

He looked up at the hills shouldering their way out of the morning mist, the sun still offstage, just.

He turned and gazed at the Tump. A prosaic, lumpen word

for the mystic mound, the branches of the trees on its summit still entwined with tendrils of mist.

A thing so ancient, so haunted, yet so benign. Yeah, well, *he* believed in omens, but . . .

There was some kind of awful creaking, tearing sound as the breakdown truck hauled the car out of the wall. A heavy crump and a rattle as the VW's shattered front end came down on the turf, its radiator ripped off, car-intestines hanging out.

Max Goff winced. Beside him, Rachel Wade, his personal assistant, was saying in her deep voice, 'Don't be silly.' Spreading out her hands in that superior, pained, half-pitying way she had. 'All I'm saying is it's not exactly an *auspicious* start, is it?'

Goff stared coldly at Rachel in her shiny, new Barbour coat and a silk scarf. Knowing how much he'd depended on her judgement in the past, but knowing equally that this was an area where she was well out of her depth. A situation where the smooth bitch couldn't be relied upon to get it right. No way.

She didn't, of course, want him to go through with it. Nobody whose opinion was worth more than shit had been exactly encouraging, but Rachel was subtler than most of them. She hadn't said a word about the nylon sheets in their room at the Cock. Had made no comment about the coffee at breakfast being instant. Just sat there, languid and elegant and at ease, refusing everything they offered her with a professional smile. Yeah, OK, under normal circumstances Goff himself would have insisted on different sheets and ground coffee and some kind of muesli instead of Rice Krispies. But he might need the Cock again.

Actually, he might need to buy it.

He'd been pondering this possibility, deciding not to discuss it with Ms Wade just yet, when the local Plod had turned up, waiting respectfully in the lobby until he'd finished his Nescafé, then asking, 'Are you Mr Goff, sir? Mr *Max* Goff?' as if they didn't recognize him.

The body had been taken away by the time they got to the scene. Max Goff only hoped the poor old bastard had at least one surviving relative. He didn't really feel like identifying the Kettle corpse in some seedy white-tiled mortuary where the atmosphere was heavy with obnoxious smells and bodily gases.

If it came to that, Rachel could do it. She'd hired Kettle originally. And nothing ever fazed Rachel, just as nothing ever blew her mind – there was even something suspiciously nonchalant about her orgasms.

'Right, Tom,' somebody shouted, and the breakdown truck started across the field, the broken car on its back, a smashed coffin on an open hearse.

Then the truck stopped for some reason.

And, in that moment, the sun came out of the mist and the land was suddenly aglow and throbbing with life force.

And Goff remembered what day this was.

He turned towards the light, head back, eyes closing and the palms of his hands opening outwards to receive the burgeoning energy.

I am here. At the zenith of the year. I am in a state of total submission.

'It's the solstice,' he whispered. 'I'd forgotten.'

'Oh,' said the uncommitted Rachel Wade. 'Super.'

As if guided, Max Goff turned back to the open field, opened his eyes and saw . . .

. . . reflected, quite perfectly, in the rear window of Henry Kettle's smashed-up old Volkswagen on the back of the truck he saw the venerable mound, the Tump at Crybbe Court, and the sun above it like a holy lamp.

And the connection was formed.

Revelation.

The truck started up again, moved off towards the road.

Goff pointed urgently at the mound, talking rapidly, forefinger stabbing at the air between him and Rachel. 'Listen, when they built these things, the old Bronze Age guys, they'd, you know, consecrate them, according to their religion, right?'

Rachel Wade looked at him, expressionless.

'What they'd do is, they'd sacrifice somebody. I mean, the remains have been found, sacrifices, not burials – they have ways of telling the difference, right?'

Rachel freed a few strands of pale hair from the collar of her Barbour, flicked them back.

'And sometimes, right,' Goff surged on, 'at very important

sites, the high priest himself would be sacrificed. Without resistance. Willingly, yeah?'

Rachel said, 'How would they know that?'

'Know what?'

' "A", that he died willingly. And "b", that the fragments of bones or whatever belonged to a high priest?'

Goff was annoyed. 'Jeez, they *know*, OK? Doesn't matter how, I'm not a flaming archaeologist. But what it meant was, the sacrifice would put the seal on the sanctity of the place. The dead priest would live on as its guardian. For all time, right?'

A police sergeant came over, the same one who'd fetched them from the Cock. Big moon-faced guy, didn't strike Goff as being all that bright. 'We'd just like you to make a statement, if you would, sir.'

'Everything Max Goff does is a Statement,' Goff told him and grinned. 'Who was it wrote that?'

'*Time Out*,' said Rachel automatically and a little wearily. 'August 1990.'

The police sergeant didn't get it. 'You appear to have been the last person to see Mr Kettle alive, sir. You'll probably be called to give evidence to that effect at the inquest.'

'Shit,' Goff said. 'How . . . ? No, that's OK. That's fine. I'll join you back at the house. Ten minutes, right?'

'If you wouldn't mind, sir.'

'Point I was making,' Goff said, impatiently turning his back on the departing Plod, 'is that Henry Kettle was about as close as you could find to a kind of high priest these days. Guy in tune with the earth and its spirit, responding to its deeper impulses. Shamanic, yeah?' Closing his eyes, he felt the holy light of the solstice on his face. Carried on talking with his eyes squeezed tightly shut. Talking to himself really, letting his thoughts unravel, the connections forming.

'So Henry Kettle – how old was the guy? Eighty-five? How long did he have to go, anyway? So, OK, we have this old man, the shaman, homing in, a dead straight line across the field – straight at the mound, the Tump, right – and . . .'

Goff opened his eyes suddenly and fully, and was dazzled by radiant blobs of orange and blue spinning from the top of the mound.

'. . . and . . . whoomp!' He clapped his big hands violently together.

Smiling hugely at Rachel Wade. 'Listen, what I'm saying is, we're not looking at some bad omen here. It's a positive thing. Like the high priest going almost willingly to his death, like sacrificing himself all over again to put his life energy into my project. Whoomp!'

Rachel said, 'That's really sick, Max.' But Goff was looking up at the mound with a new pride, not listening.

'I bet if we mark out those tyre-tracks across that field we'll find they correspond exactly to line B.'

'Line B?'

'The fucking ley-line, Rachel.'

'Max, that's . . .'

Goff looked hard at Rachel. She shut up.

Jesus, she thought.

Whoomp.

CHAPTER III

'B IT for level, Fay.'

'OK, here we go . . .'

Mr Kettle said, '. . . *All right then, we know there's got to be water yereabouts* . . .'

'OK, that's fine, Fay . . . I'm rolling. Go in five.'

She wound back, set the tape running and took the cans off her ears, leaving them around her neck so she'd hear the engineer call out if he ran into problems.

Leaning back in the metal-framed typist's chair, she thought, God, I've been shunted into some seedy sidings in my time, but this . . .

. . . was the Crybbe Unattended Studio.

Ten feet long and six feet wide. Walls that closed in on you like the sides of a packing case. A tape-machine on a metal stand. A square mahogany table with a microphone next to a small console with buttons that lit up. And the chair. And no windows, just a central light and two little red lights – one above the door outside to warn people to keep away in case whoever was inside happened to be broadcasting live to the scattered homesteads of the Welsh Marches.

This studio used to be the gents' lavatories at the back of the Cock, before they'd built new ones inside the main building. Then some planning wizard at Offa's Dyke Radio had presumably stuck a plastic marker into the map and said without great enthusiasm: Crybbe – well, yeah, OK, not much of a place, but it's almost exactly halfway up the border and within a couple miles of the Dyke itself . . . about as central as we'll get.

Then they'd have contacted the Marches Development Board, who'd have told them: No problem, we can offer you a purpose-built broadcasting centre on our new Kington Road Industrial Estate at an annual rent of only . . .

At which point the planning wizard would have panicked and assured them that all that was required was a little room to accommodate reporters and interviewees (one at a time) and for sending tape down a land-line to Offa's Dyke main studios. All self-operated. No staff, no technicians. Very discreet. You walk in, you switch on, and a sound-engineer records your every word from fifty miles away.

Which was how they'd ended up with the former gents' at the Cock. A tired, brick building with a worn slate roof, at the end of a narrow passageway past the dustbins.

The original white tiles with worrying brown stains had gone now. Or at least were hidden behind the black acoustic screening which formed a little soundproof module inside the building.

But sometimes, especially early in the morning, Fay would swear she could smell . . .

'That's lovely, Fay, thanks very much.'

'Thanks, Barry,' Fay told the microphone on the desk. All engineers were called Barry.

'It's Elton, actually,' he said. 'Hang on, Gavin's here, he'd like a word.'

Elton. Jesus, nobody in this country who was called Elton could possibly be over twenty-one. Even the damned engineers at Offa's Dyke were fresh out of engineering school.

Gavin Ashpole came on the line, the station's news editor, an undeveloped rasp, unsure of whether it was supposed to sound thrusting or laid-back. He wanted to know if Fay was any closer to an interview with Max Goff about his plans for Crybbe Court. Or at least some sort of statement. 'I mean, is it going to be a recording studio, or what? We going to have famous rock stars helicoptering in? We need to know, and we need to know *before* we read about it in the bloody papers.'

'No, listen, I told you, his PA insists he doesn't want any publicity yet, but . . .'

Calm down, woman, don't rise to it.

'But when he's got things together,' Fay finished lamely, 'she says they'll tell me first. I . . . I've no reason to think she's bullshitting.'

'Why can't you doorstep him? Just turn up. Put the fucker on the spot.'

'Look, isn't it better to try and stay on the right side of the guy? There could be a lot of mileage in this one for us, in . . . in the future.' Hesitating because 'in the future' she wasn't going to be here, was she?

Absolutely no way she could tell him about the late Henry Kettle being hired by Goff to do some dowsing around the Court. Partly because she hadn't been able to persuade Mr Kettle to tell her what he was supposed to be looking for. And partly because loony Gavin Ashpole would start wondering how he could implicate the famous Goff in Henry's death.

'I don't know, Fay.' Ashpole switching to the Experienced News Editor's pensive drawl. 'I'm not into all this pussyfooting about. We're gonna lose out, here. Listen, try him again, yeah? If you don't get anywhere, we'll have to, you know, reconsider things.'

He meant if she didn't get him an interview soon they'd send in some flash kid from the newsroom to show her how it was done. Nasty little sod, Gavin Ashpole. All of twenty-four. Career to carve.

You've got to stop this, Fay warned herself, as the line went dead. You're becoming seriously obsessed with age. Good God, woman, you're not *old*.

Just older than almost everybody else connected with Offa's

Dyke Radio. Which, OK, was not exactly *old* old, but . . .

What it is, she thought, your whole life's been out of synch, that's the problem. Goes back to having a father who was already into his fifties when you were conceived. Discovering your dad is slightly older than most other kids' grandads.

And yet, when you are not yet in your teens, it emerges that your mother is threatening to divorce your aged father because of *his* infidelity.

Fay shook her head, playing with the buttons on the studio tape-machine. He'd given up the other woman, narrowly escaping public disgrace. Eight years later he was a widower.

Fast forward over that. Too painful.

Whizz on through another never-mind-how-many years and there you are, recovering from your own misguided marriage to a grade-A dickhead, pursuing your first serious career – as a radio producer, in London – and, yes, almost starting to enjoy yourself . . . when, out of the blue, your old father rings to invite you to his wedding in . . .

'Sorry, where did you say . . . ?'

'C-R-Y-B-B-E.'

'Where the hell is that, Dad? Also, more to the point, who the hell is Grace?'

And then – bloody hell! – before he can reply, you remember.

'Oh my God, Grace was the woman who'd have been cited in Mum's petition! Grace Legge. She must be . . .'

'Sixty-two. And not terribly well, I'm afraid, Fay. Money-wise, too, she's not in such a healthy position. So I'm doing the decent thing. Twenty years too late, you might say . . .'

'I might not say anything coherent for ages, Dad. I'm bloody speechless.'

'Anyway, I've sort of moved in with her. This little terraced cottage she's got in Crybbe, which is where she was born. You go to Hereford and then you sort of turn right and just, er, just carry on, as it were.'

'And what about your own house? Who's taking care of that?'

'Woodstock? Oh, I, er, I had to sell it. Didn't get a lot, actually, the way the market is, but . . .'

'Just a minute, Dad. Am I really hearing this? You sold that bloody wonderful house? Are you going senile?'

Not an enormously tactful question, with hindsight.

'No option, my dear. Had to have the readies for . . . for private treatment for Grace and, er, things. Which goes – I know, you don't have to tell me – goes against everything I've always stood for, so don't spread it around. But she's really not awfully well, and I feel sort of . . .'

'Sort of guilty as hell.'

'Yes, I suppose. Sort of. Fay, would you object awfully to drifting out here and giving me away, as it were? Very quiet, of course. Very discreet. No dog-collars.'

This is – when? – eleven months ago?

The wedding is not an entirely convivial occasion. At the time, Grace Legge, getting married in a wheelchair, has approximately four months to live, and she knows it.

When you return to a damp and leafless late-autumnal Crybbe for the funeral, you notice the changes in your dad. Changes which a brain-scan will reveal to be the onset of a form of dementia caused by hardening of the arteries. Sometimes insufficient blood is getting to his brain. The bottom line is that it's going to get worse.

The dementia is still intermittent, but he can hardly be left on his own. He won't come to London – 'Grace's cats and things, I promised.' And he won't have a housekeeper – 'Never had to pay a woman for washing my socks and I don't plan to start now. Wash my own.'

Fay sighed deeply. Cut to Controller's office, Christmas Eve. 'Fay, it's not rational. Why don't you take a week off and think about it? I know if it was *my* father he'd have to sell up and get himself a flat in town if he was expecting me to keep an eye on him.'

'This is just it, he *doesn't* expect me to. He's an independent old sod.'

'All right. Let's say you do go to this place. How are you supposed to make a living?'

'Well, I've done a bit of scouting around. This new outfit, Offa's Dyke Radio . . .'

'Local radio? *Independent* local radio? Here today and . . . Oh, Fay, come on, don't do this to yourself.'

'I thought maybe I could freelance for them on a bread-and-butter basis. They've got an unattended studio actually in Crybbe, which is a stroke of luck. And the local guy they had, he's moved on, and so they're on the look-out for a new contributor. I've had a chat with the editor there and he sounded quite enthusiastic.'

'I bet he did.'

'And maybe I could do the odd programme for you, if freelancing for a local independent as well doesn't break some ancient BBC law.'

'I'm sure that's not an insurmountable problem, but . . .'

'I know, I know. I'm far too young to be retiring to the country.'

'And far too good, actually.'

'You've never said before.'

'You might have asked for more money.'

Typical bloody BBC.

Fay spun back the Henry Kettle tape – why couldn't you rewind your life like that? – and let herself out, throwing the studio into darkness with the master switch by the door. But the spools were still spinning in her head.

She locked up and set off with a forced briskness up the alley, an ancient passageway, smoked brick walls with a skeleton of years-blackened beams. Sometimes cobwebs hung down and got in your hair. She wasn't overfond of this alley. There were always used condoms underfoot; sometimes the concrete flags were slippery with them. In winter they were frozen, like milky ice-pops.

She emerged into the centre of Crybbe as the clock in the church tower was chiming eleven. Getting to eleven sounded like a big effort for the mechanism; you could hear the strain.

There were lots of deep shadows, even though the sun was high, because the crooked brick and timbered buildings slouched together, like down-and-outs sharing a cigarette. Picturesque and moody in the evening, sometimes. In the daytime, run-down, shabby.

People were shopping in the square, mainly for essentials. The shops in Crybbe specialized in the items families ran out of in between weekly trips to the supermarkets in Hereford or Leominster. In Crybbe, prices were high and stocks low. These were long-established shops, run by local people: the grocer, the chemist, the hardware and farming suppliers.

Other long-established businesses had, like Henry Kettle, gone to the wall. And been replaced by a new type of store.

Like The Gallery, run by Hereward and Jocasta Newsome, from Surrey, specializing in the works of border landscape artists. In the window, Fay saw three linked watercolours of the Tump at different times of day, the ancient mound appearing to hover in the dawn mist, then solid in the sunlight and then stark and black against an orange sky. A buff card underneath said, in careful copperplate

THE TUMP – a triptych, by Darwyn Hall.
Price: £975.

Wow. A snip. Fay wondered how they kept the place open. She walked on, past a little, scruffy pub, the Lamb, past Middle Marches Crafts, which seemed to be a greetings-card shop this week. And then the Crybbe Pottery, which specialized in chunky earthenware Gothic houses that lit up when you plugged them in but didn't give out enough light by which to do anything except look at them and despair.

'Morning, Mr Preece,' she said to the Town Mayor, a small man with a face like a battered wallet, full of pouches and creases.

''Ow're you,' Mr Preece intoned and walked on without a second glance.

It had been a couple of months before Fay had realized that 'How are you' was not, in these parts, a question and therefore did not require a reply on the lines of, 'I'm fine, Mr Preece, how are *you*?' or, 'Quite honestly, Mr Preece, since you ask,

61

I'm becoming moderately pissed off with trying to communicate with the dead.'

Brain-dead, anyway, most of them in this town. Nobody ever seemed to get excited. Or to question anything. Nobody ever organized petitions to the council demanding children's playgrounds or leisure centres. Women never giggled together on street corners.

Fay stopped in the street, then, and had what amounted to a panic attack.

She saw the spools on the great tape-deck of life, and the one on the right was fat with tape and the one on the left was down to its last half inch. Another quarter of a century had wound past her eyes, and she saw a sprightly, red-faced little woman in sensible clothes returning from the Crybbe Unattended, another masterpiece gone down the line for the youngsters in the newsroom to chuckle over. *Poor old Fay, all those years looking after her dad, feeding him by hand, constantly washing his underpants . . . Think we'd better send young Jason over to check this one out?*

And the buildings in the town hunched a little deeper into their foundations and nodded their mottled roofs.

'Ow're you, they creaked. *'Ow're you.*

Fay came out of the passageway shivering in the sun, tingling with an electric depression, and she thought she was hearing howling, and she thought that was in her head, too, along with the insistent, urgent question: how am I going to persuade him to turn his back on this dismal, accepting little town, where Grace Legge has left him her cottage, her cats and a burden of guilt dating back twenty years? How can I reach him before he becomes impervious to rational argument?

Then she realized the howling was real. A dog, not too far away. A real snout-upturned, ears-back, baying-at-the-moon job.

Fay stopped. Even in the middle of a sunny morning it was a most unearthly sound.

She'd been about to turn away from the town centre into the huddle of streets where Grace's house was. Curious, she followed the howling instead and almost walked into the big blue back of Police Sergeant Wynford Wiley.

He was standing facing the police station and a woman. Who was hissing at him. Who was half his size, sharp-faced, red-faced, sixtyish, back arched like a cornered cat.

'What you want me to do?' Wynford was yelling, face like an Edam cheese. 'Shoot 'im, is it?'

'I don't care what you do,' the woman screeched. 'But I'm telling you this . . . *I don't like it.*' She looked wildly and irrationally distressed. She was vibrating. 'You'll get it stopped!'

The dog howled again, an eerie spiral. The woman seized the policeman's arm as if she wanted to tear it off. Fay had never seen anyone so close to hysteria in Crybbe, where emotions were private, like bank accounts.

'Whose dog is it?' Fay said.

They both turned and stared at her and she thought, Sure, I know, none of my business, I'm from Off.

The ululation came again, and the sky seemed to shimmer in sympathy.

'I said, whose dog is it?'

CHAPTER IV

FROM A wicker basket in the pantry Mrs Preece took the fattest onion she could find. She crumbled away its brittle outer layer until the onion was pale green and moist in the palm of her hand.

She sat the onion in a saucer.

'Stuff and nonsense,' commented Jimmy Preece, the Mayor of Crybbe. The sort of thing most of the local men would say in such situations.

With a certain ceremony, as if it were a steaming Christmas pudding, Mrs Preece carried the onion on its saucer into the parlour, Jimmy following her.

She placed it on top of the television set. She said nothing. 'A funny woman, you are,' Jimmy Preece said gruffly, but not without affection.

Mrs Preece made no reply, her mouth set in a thin line, white hair pulled back and coiled tight.

They both heard the click of the garden gate, and Jimmy went to the window and peered through the gap in his delphiniums.

Mrs Preece spoke. 'Is it *him*?'

Jimmy Preece nodded.

'I'm going to the shop,' Mrs Preece said. 'I'll go out the back way. Likely he'll have gone when I gets back.'

What she meant was she wouldn't come back until he was good and gone.

Jocasta Newsome, a spiky lady, said in a parched and bitter voice, 'It isn't working, is it? Even *you* have to admit that now?'

'I don't know what you mean.' Her husband was pretending he didn't care. He was making a picture-frame in pine, two ends carefully locked into a wood-vice to form a corner. The truth was he cared desperately, about lots of things.

'You,' Jocasta said. 'Me. It. Everything.' She was wearing a black woollen dress and a heavy golden shawl fastened with a Celtic brooch at her shoulder.

'Go away.' Hereward started flicking sawdust from his tidy beard. 'If all you can be is negative, go away.'

On the workbench between them lay the immediate cause of this particular confrontation: the electricity bill. He'd let sawdust go all over that deliberately. 'We'll query it,' Hereward had stated masterfully. 'Yes,' Jocasta had replied, 'but what if it's correct? How long can we go on paying bills like that?'

The worst of it was, they couldn't even rely on a constant supply. He'd never known so many power cuts. 'One of the problems of living in a rural area, I'm afraid,' the electricity official had told him smugly, when he complained. 'Strong winds bring down the power lines, thunder and lightning, cows rubbing themselves against the posts, birds flying into . . .'

'I'm trying to run a business here!'

'So are the farmers, Mr, ah, Newsome. But they've seen the problems at first hand, up on the hills. So *they*, you see, they realize what we're up against.'

Oh yes, very clever. What he was saying to Hereward,

recognizing his accent, was, You people, you come here expecting everything to be as smooth as Surrey. If you really want to be accepted in the countryside you'd better keep your head down and your mouth shut, got it?

Hereward growled and Jocasta, thinking he was growling at her, looked across at him in his new blue overalls, standing by his new wooden vice, and there was a glaze of contempt over her sulky eyes.

'The rural craftsman,' she observed acidly. 'At his bench. You're really rather pathetic.'

'I'm trying to rescue the situation,' Hereward snarled through clamped teeth, 'you stupid bitch.'

Jocasta looked away, walked out, slammed the studio door.

And in the vice, the newly constructed corner of Hereward's first frame fell symbolically apart.

Hereward sank to his knees.

Very deliberately, he picked up the two lengths of moulded wood and set about realigning them. He would not be beaten. He would not give up.

And he would not let her disdain get to him. If they couldn't sell enough original works of art they would, for a limited period, sell a number of selected prints at reasonable prices. And the prices would be kept reasonable because he would make the frames himself. Dammit, he *did* know what he was doing.

And he *had* recognized that there would be problems getting a new gallery accepted in a lesser known area. Obviously, places like Crybbe had fewer tourists – all right, *far* fewer. But those who came were the *right sort* of tourists. The intelligent, childless couples who didn't need beaches, and the cultured newly retired people with time to construct the quality of life they'd always promised themselves.

Slowly but emphatically, The Gallery would build a reputation among the discerning. They would travel from as far away as Shrewsbury and Cheltenham and even Oxford and London. The Gallery would expand, and then other specialist dealers would join them, and pretty soon it would be Crybbe for fine art, the way it was Hay-on-Wye for books.

'Of course, it took time,' he would say at dinner parties. 'Good Lord, I remember, in the early days, when, to save money, one actually made one's own frames . . .'

'Festival, is it?' Jimmy Preece's eyes were like screwheads countersunk into old mahogany. 'We never had no festival before.'

'Precisely the point, Mr Mayor.' Max Goff tried to smile sincerely and reassuringly, but he knew from hundreds of press photos that it always came out wide and flashy, like car radiators in the sixties.

'No.' Mr Preece shook his head slowly, as if they were discussing water-skiing or first-division football, things which, transparently, were not part of the Crybbe scene. 'Not round yere.'

Goff leaned forward. He'd given a lot of thought to how he'd sell this thing to the townsfolk. A festival. A celebration of natural potential. Except this festival would last all year round. This festival would absorb the whole town. It would recreate Crybbe.

'The point is, Mr Mayor . . . You got so much to be festive *about*.' Go on, ask me what the hell you got to be festive about.

The Mayor just nodded. Jeez.

'Let me explain, OK?' White-suited Goff was feeling well out of place in this cramped little parlour, where everything was brown and mottled and shrunken-looking, from the beams in the ceiling, to the carpet, to Jimmy Preece himself. But he had to crack this one; getting the Mayor on his side would save a hell of a lot of time.

'OK,' Goff said calmly. 'Let's start with the basics. How much you heard about me?'

Jimmy Preece smiled slyly down at his feet, encased in heavy, well-polished working boots with nearly as many ancient cracks as his face.

Goff flashed the teeth again. 'Never trust newspapers, Mr Mayor. The more money you make, the more the c . . . the more they're out to nail you. 'Specially if you've made it in a operation like mine. Which, as I'm sure you know, is the music business, the recording industry.'

'I've heard that.'

'Sex, drugs and rock and roll, eh?'

'I wouldn't know about those things.'

'Nor would I, Mr Mayor,' Goff lied. 'Only been on the business side. A business. Like any other. And I'm not denying it's been highly successful for me. I'm a rich man.'

Goff paused.

'And now I want to put something back. Into the world, if you like. But, more specifically . . . into Crybbe.'

Mr Preece didn't even blink.

'Because you have a very special town here, Mr Mayor. Only this town, it's forgotten just how special it is.'

Come on, you old bastard. As me *why* it's so flaming special.

Goff waited, keeping his cool. Very commendably, he thought, under the circumstances. Then, after a while, Jimmy Preece made his considered response.

'Well, well,' he said. And was silent again.

Max Goff felt his nails penetrate the brown vinyl chair-arms. 'I don't mean to be insulting here, Mr Mayor,' he said loudly, with a big, wide, shiny smile – a 1961 Cadillac of a smile. 'But you have to face the fact that this little town is in *deep shit*.'

He let the words – and the smile – shimmer in the room.

'Terminally depressed,' he said. 'Economically sterile.'

Still the Mayor said nothing. But his eyes shifted sideways like the eyes of a ventriloquist's doll, and Goff knew he was at last getting through.

'OK.' He pulled on to his knee a green canvas bag. 'I'm gonna lay it all down for you.'

Yeah, there it was. A hint of anxiety.

'Even a century ago,' Goff stared the old guy straight in the eyes, 'this town was home to over five thousand people. How many's it got now?'

Mr Preece looked into the fireplace. Breathed in as if about to answer, and then breathed out without a word.

'I'll tell you. At the last census, there were two thousand, nine hundred and sixty-four. This is in the town itself, I'm not including the outlying farms.'

From the canvas bag, Goff took a pad of recycled paper, opened it. Began to read the figures. 'Crybbe once had a grammar school and two primary schools. It's now down to a single primary and the older kids get bussed to a secondary school eight miles away, yeah?'

Mr Preece nodded slowly and then carried on nodding as if his head was working loose.

'Even as recently as 1968,' Goff said, 'there were four policemen in Crybbe. How many now?'

Mr Preece's lips started to shape a word and then went slack again as Goff zapped him with more statistics. 'Back in the fifties, there were three grocer's shops, two butcher's, couple of chemist's, and there was . . .'

Mr Preece almost yelled, 'Where you gettin' all this from?' But Goff was coming at him like a train now, and there was no stopping him.

'. . . a regular assize court earlier this century, and now what? Not even petty sessions any more. No justices, no magistrates. Used to be a self-sufficient local authority, covering a wide area from Crybbe and employing over seventy people. Now there's your town council. Not much more than a local advisory body that employs precisely one person part-time – that's Mrs Byford, the clerk who takes the notes at your meetings.'

'Look, what . . . what's all this about?' Jimmy Preece was shrinking back into his chair, Goff leaning further towards him with every point he made, but deciding it was time to cool things a little.

'Bottom line, Mr Mayor, is you got a slowly ageing population and nothing to offer the young to keep them here. Even the outsiders are mostly retired folk. Crybbe's already climbed into its own coffin and it's just about to pull down the lid.'

Goff sat back, putting away his papers, leaving Jimmy Preece, Mayor of Crybbe, looking as tired and wasted as his town. 'Mr Mayor, how about you call a public meeting? Crybbe and me, we need to talk.'

In the gallery itself – *her* place – Jocasta Newsome was starting to function. At last. God, she'd thought it was never going to

68

begin. She walked quickly across the quarry-tiled floor – tap, tap, tap of the high heels, echoing from wall to wall in the high-roofed former chapel, a smart brisk sound she loved.

'Look, let me show you this. It's something actually quite special.'

'No, really,' The customer raised a hand and a faint smile. '*This* is what I came for.'

'Oh, but . . .' Jocasta fell silent, realizing that a £1,000 sale was about to go through without recourse to the skills honed to a fine edge during her decade in International Marketing. She pulled herself together, smiled and patted the hinged frame of the triptych. 'It *is* rather super, though, isn't it?'

'Actually,' the customer said, turning her back on the triple image of the Tump, 'I think it's absolutely dreadful.'

'Oh.' Jocasta was genuinely thrown by this, because the customer was undoubtedly the *right kind*: Barbour, silk scarf and that offhand, isn't-life-tedious sort of poise she'd always rather envied.

The woman revived her faint smile. 'I'm sorry, I didn't mean to be rude. My boss thinks it's wonderful, and that's all that matters. I suppose it's the subject I'm not terribly taken with. It's only a large heap of soil, after all.'

Jocasta mentally adjusted the woman's standing; she had a boss. Dare she ask who he was? 'I'll pa . . . I'll have it packaged for you.'

'Oh, don't bother, I'll just toss it in the back of the jeep. Haven't far to go.'

How far exactly? Jocasta asked silently, directing a powerful ray of naked curiosity at the woman. It usually worked.

The door closed behind him. Max Goff stood a moment on the sunlit step, Crybbe laid out before him.

Jimmy Preece's retirement cottage was a fitting place for the Mayor to live, at the entrance to the narrow road off the little square, the one which led eventually to the Court – Jimmy Preece being the head of the family which had lived at Court Farm since sixteen-something at least.

It was fitting also for the Mayor because it was at the top of the town, with the church of St Michael on the right. And you could see the buildings – eighteenth, seventeenth century and earlier – staggering, gently inebriated, down the hill to the river, with its three-arched bridge.

From up here Goff could easily discern the medieval street-pattern – almost unchanged, he figured. The newer buildings – the school, the council housing and the small industrial estate – had been tacked on and could, no doubt, just as easily be flicked away.

It was bloody perfect.

Unspoiled.

And this was precisely *because* it was not a wealthy town, because it was down on its luck and had been for a long, long time. Because it was not linked to the trunk roads between Wales and the Midlands and was not convenient, never would be. No use at all for commuting to anywhere.

And yet, beneath this town, the dragon slumbered.

She was going to ring Darwyn Hall, the artist, immediately, but Hereward walked in, still wearing his artisan's outfit and carrying a mug of coffee. The mug was one of the misshapen brown things they'd felt obliged to buy from the Crybbe Pottery.

'Who was that?'

Jocasta was sitting at her desk in a corner of the gallery, putting the cheque away. It was a customized company cheque, the word *Epidemic* faded across it like a watermark. 'A sale, of course,' she said nonchalantly.

'Good God.' Hereward looked around to see which of the pictures had gone. 'Picking it up later, are they?'

'You should be looking in the window.' Jocasta just couldn't hold her cool any longer and an awful smirk of delight was spreading over her face like strawberry jam.

'You're joking,' Hereward said, stunned. He strode to the window and threw back the shutters. 'Good grief!' He turned back to Jocasta. 'Full price?'

'This is not a bloody discount store, darling.'

'Stone me,' said Hereward. 'The triptych. Just like that? I mean, who . . . ?'

Jocasta waited a second or two, adjusted the Celtic brooch at her shoulder and then casually hit him with the big one.

'Max Goff.'

'Gosh.' Hereward put down his cup. 'So it's true, then. He *has* bought the Court.'

'Sent his personal assistant to collect it,' Jocasta said. 'Rachel Wade.'

'This is far from bad news,' Hereward said slowly. 'In fact, this could be the turning point.'

Mrs Preece waited across the square with her shopping bag until she saw the large man in the white suit stride out past the delphiniums. He didn't, she noticed, close the garden gate behind him. She watched him get into his fancy black car and didn't go across to the house until she couldn't even hear its noise any more.

Jimmy was still sitting in the parlour staring at the wall.

Mrs Preece put down her shopping bag and reached over Jimmy to the top of the television set, where the onion was sitting in its saucer.

'You'll be late for your drink,' she said.

'I'm not going today. I 'ave to talk to the clerk before she goes back to the library.'

'What was he after?' demanded Mrs Preece, standing there holding the saucer with the onion on it.

'He wants us to call a public meeting.'

'Oh, he does, does he? And who's he to ask for a public meeting?'

'An interferer,' Jimmy Preece said. 'That's what he is.'

Mrs Preece said nothing.

'I don't like interferers,' Jimmy Preece said.

There was nothing his wife could say to that. She walked through to the kitchen, holding the saucer before her at arm's length as if what it had on it was not a peeled onion but a dead rat.

In the kitchen she got out a meat skewer, a big one, nearly

a foot long, and speared the onion, the sharp point slipping easily into its soft, moist, white flesh.

Then she took it across to the Rayburn and opened the door to the fire compartment. With a quick stab and a shiver – partly of revulsion, partly satisfaction – she thrust the onion into the flames and slammed the door, hard.

CHAPTER V

'THIS may seem an odd question,' the vicar of Crybbe said after a good deal of hesitation, 'but have you ever performed an exorcism?'

The question hung in the air for quite a while.

Sunk into his armchair in Grace's former sitting-room, Canon Alex Peters peered vaguely into the thick soup of his past. *Had* he done an exorcism? Buggered if he could remember.

The sun was so bright now – at least *suggestive* of warmth – that Alex had stripped down to his washed-out Kate Bush T-shirt, the letters in Bush stretched to twice the size of those in Kate by the considerable belly he'd put on since the doctor had ordered him to give up jogging. On his knees was a fiendish-looking black tomcat which Grace had named after some famous Russian. Chekhov? Dostoevsky? Buggered if he could remember that either.

'Ah, sorry, Murray. Yes, exorcism. Mmm.'

What should he say? East Anglia? Perhaps when he was in charge of one of those huge, terrifying, flint churches in Suffolk . . . Needed to be a bit careful here.

'Ah! I'll tell you what it was, Murray – going back a good many years this. Wasn't the full bell, book and candle routine, as I remember. More of a quickie, bless-this-house operation. Actually, I think I made it up as I went along.'

The Revd Murray Beech raised an eyebrow.

Alex said, 'Well, you know the sort of thing . . . "I have reason to believe there's an unquiet spirit on the premises, so, in the name of the Management, I suggest you leave these decent folk alone and push off back where you came from, there's a good chap." '

The Revd Murray Beech did not smile.

'Expect I dramatized it a bit,' Alex said. 'But that's what it boiled down to. Seemed to work, as I recall. Don't remember any come-backs, anyway. Why d'you ask?'

Although he wore the regulation-issue black shirt and clerical collar, rather than a Kate Bush T-shirt, young Murray Beech didn't seem like a real vicar to Álex. More like the ambitious deputy head of some inner-city comprehensive school. He was on the edge of one of Grace's G-plan dining chairs, looking vaguely unhappy about the can of lager Alex had put unceremoniously into his hand.

'You see, the way you put it then,' Murray said carefully, as though he were formulating a point at a conference, 'makes it seem as if . . . you knew at the time . . . that you were only going through the motions.'

'Well, that's probably true, old chap. But who knows what we do when we go through the motions?' A sunbeam stroked Alex's knees; the cat shifted a little to make the most of it. 'Do I understand, Murray, that someone has invited you to perform an exorcism?'

'This appears to be the general idea,' the vicar said uncomfortably. 'The central dilemma is, as you know, I'm not into sham. Too much of that in the church.'

'Absolutely, old chap.'

'You see, my problem is . . .'

'Oh, I think I know what your problem is.' Perhaps, Alex thought, it used to be my problem too, to an extent. How sure of our ground we are, when we're young ministers. 'For instance, Murray, if I were to ask you what you consider to be the biggest evils in the world today, you'd say . . . ?'

'Inequality. Racism. Destruction of the planet due to unassuageable . . . I'm not going to say capitalism, let's call it greed.' He eyed the *Guardian* on Alex's chair-arm. 'Surely you'd agree with that?'

''Course, dear boy. Spot on. Look, Tolstoy, would you

mind not sharpening your claws on my inner thigh, there's a good cat. So who wants you to do this exorcism?'

'Difficult.' Murray smiled without humour. 'Difficult situation. It's a teenager. Lives with the grandparents. Thinks there's some sort of' – his mouth pursed in distaste – 'disruptive etheric intrusion. In the house.'

'Poltergeist, eh? What have the grandparents got to say?'

'That's the difficulty. I'm not supposed to speak to them. This . . . person is rather embarrassed about the whole thing. Having read somewhere that so-called poltergeists are often caused by, or attracted to, a disturbed adolescent. You know that theory?'

'Rampant hormones overflowing. Smart boy. In my day, of course, the vicar would just have told him to stop wanking and the thing would go away.'

Murray said, 'It's a girl.'

'Oh.'

'She wants me to go along when her grandparents are out and deal with this alleged presence.'

'Oh dear.' Alex opened his can of Heineken with a snap. 'You're right, my boy, it *is* a difficult one. Erm . . .' He looked across at Murray, all cropped hair, tight mouth and steely efficiency. 'Do you suppose this youngster might have something of a . . . *crush* on you?' Well, it wasn't entirely beyond the bounds of possibility; there were some pretty warped kids around these days.

'Oh, I don't think it's that, Alex. That would be comparatively easy to deal with.'

'Glad you think so. What have you said to her, then?'

'We had a long discussion about the problems and insecurities of the post-pubescent period. Made more difficult in this case because she has no parents to go to – mother dead, father in the merchant navy. You see, I don't want to fail the kid. Because, you know, so few people in this town ever actually come to me for help. Especially with anything of a non-material nature – i.e. anything that doesn't involve opening jumble sales. It's obvious most of them find me an institutional irrelevance most of the time.'

'Wouldn't say that, old chap.'

'Wouldn't you? Oh, certainly, they're always there on Sunday. Well, enough of them anyway. So no congregation problems, as such, but . . .'

'That's what it's all about, old son. That's the core of it. Bums on pews.'

'Is it? Is that what you think?' The dining chair creaked as Murray hunched forward, chin thrusting. 'Have you ever looked out over *your* parishioners and seen all the animation, all the commitment, of a doctor's waiting room or a bus queue?'

Alex nodded. 'They're not *expressive* people in this town, I grant you. Perhaps a chap like you ought to be working in a more happening situation, as they say.'

Murray clearly thought so too. But Alex could see the difficulty. He'd been lucky to get a parish this size at his age, still in his twenties. Could be a key step on the way to the bishop's palace before he turned forty if he made the right impression.

They heard footsteps on the path, a key in the front door. 'Ah, here's Fay. Look, Murray, why don't we ask *her* about your problem? Used to be a teenage girl herself not awfully long ago.'

'No!' Murray Beech jerked on the edge of his dining chair. 'Not a word, if you don't mind, Alex. I don't want this turned into a joke on the radio.'

'Good God, Murray, I hardly think . . .'

'Please.'

'OK, if that's how you'd prefer it. I say, what's wrong with old Chekhov?'

The cat had leapt on to the chair-back next to Alex's shoulder, looking even less at ease than the vicar of Crybbe.

'Dad,' Fay called from the hall. 'You haven't got Rasputin in there, have you? If you have, just hold on to him.' There was a patter of paws. 'We may have a minor integration problem.'

The cat hissed in Alex's ear.

'I must go,' Murray Beech said, putting the unopened can of lager on top of Grace's little nest of tables.

The door opened and a dog came in, followed by Fay. The dog was straining on the end of a clothes-line. It was a rather bizarre dog. Black and white, the size of a sheepdog. But with a terrier's stance and enormous ears, like a donkey's.

The dog ignored Rasputin but sniffed suspiciously at Murray Beech, as the vicar came to his feet.

'Sorry about this, Dad,' Fay said. 'But you and Rasputin'll have to make allowances, show a little charity. Oh, hullo, Murray, I'm quite glad you're here.'

The dog ambled over to Alex. 'He's had a bereavement,' Fay said. 'Listen, Murray, do you know Mrs Byford?'

Halfway to the door, the vicar stiffened. 'The Old Police House?'

'That's the one, yes. Is she all right?'

'I'm sorry . . . What do you mean, "all right"?'

Alex, patting the dog, observed how inhibited Murray Beech became when Fay was around. Partly, he thought, because of what she did for a living and partly, no doubt, because he couldn't help fancying the arse off her. Open to that kind of thing now, too, since his engagement had gone down the toilet.

'This Mrs Byford,' Fay said, 'was throwing the most amazing wobbly. He' – looking at the dog – 'was howling in his cell at the nick, and Mrs Byford was reacting as if it was the four-minute warning or something. Really going for Wynford, the copper. "Get it stopped! I'm not having it! I don't like it!" Way over the top.'

'Perhaps she simply feels she has a right to peace and quiet,' Murray said tightly.

'Living next to the cop-shop? Drunks getting hauled in on a Saturday night? What the hell does she know about peace and quiet?'

Murray shrugged. 'I'm sorry, I have to go. I'll talk to you again, Alex.'

'Yes, call in any time, old chap.'

When the vicar had gone, Fay said, 'Creep.'

'No, just a duck out of water,' Alex said, stroking the rigid Rasputin. 'He'd be far more at home in Birmingham, preaching peaceful coexistence with Islam. Who's your extraordinary friend?'

'Um, yes. I'm sorry to spring him on you, but it all happened very quickly, what with this loopy woman – definitely something wrong with her.' Fay knelt down and detached the clothes-line from the dog's collar. 'He's called Arnold. He was Henry Kettle's dog. He seems to have been in the car when it crashed. Must have got out through a window afterwards. They found him this morning, sitting by the wreckage like the Greyfriars Bobby. Breaks your heart, doesn't it?'

Arnold rested his chin for just a moment on Alex's knee. There was a savage hiss from Rasputin. 'Poor old chap,' Alex said. He thought the dog had strangely kind eyes. 'But he can't stay here.'

Arnold glanced at Rasputin with disinterest then padded away. Fay said, 'I was afraid, to be honest, of what Wynford might have done to shut him up.'

'Oh, surely not.'

'I don't know, the police round here are . . . different. Wynford had him in this concrete coalshed kind of place. Hard floor, no windows, no basket or anything. A metal bucket to drink out of. Barbaric. So I thought, that's it, he's not staying here. Then Wynford and I had this terrific battle.'

'Oh dear,' Alex said. 'Poor chap.'

' "Oh, we has to let the RSPCA deal with it. We has to abide by the Procedures." "Bollocks," I said. "Send the RSPCA round to see me." '

'No contest,' Alex said.

'Listen, that guy is seriously weird. His features are too small for his head and they never alter. So I just opened the shed door and walked off, and the dog followed me. Wynford's left standing there, face getting redder and redder, like a pumpkin with a light inside on Hallowe'en.'

Arnold was pottering around the room, sniffing uncertainly, huge ears pricked.

'It's remarkable really, he doesn't seem to have been injured at all, though I don't suppose bruises would show up on a dog. Psychologically, though . . .'

'Yes, it's a damn shame. But Fay . . .'

'. . . psychologically, he could be in pieces.'

'But he can't stay here, Fay.' Alex sat up, trying to look

authoritative. 'Grace would have a fit. She wasn't at all fond of dogs. And neither's old Rasputin.'

'Dad' – Fay was wearing *that* expression – 'Grace is *bloody dead*. Anyway . . .' She squatted down beside Arnold, and cradled his black and white snout in her hands. Long black whiskers came out between her fingers. 'If he goes, I go too.'

Canon Alex Peters took a long swig of cold Heineken.

'Splendid,' he said.

CHAPTER VI

PEOPLE kept looking at her.

This was not usual. Normally, on these streets, even if you were greeted – 'Ow're you' – you were not looked at. You were observed, your presence was noted, but you were not directly examined.

Maybe, she thought, it was the dog. Maybe they recognized the late Henry Kettle's dog. Or maybe they'd never before seen a dog on the end of a thin, red, plastic-covered clothes-line that the person on the other end was now wishing she hadn't adapted because, every time the dog tugged at the makeshift lead, her right hand received what could turn out to be third-degree burns.

'Arnold, for Christ's sake . . .'

With Henry Kettle he'd appeared ultra-docile, really laid-back. Now he was like some loony puppy, pulling in all directions, wanting to go nowhere, needing to go anywhere. And fast.

You had to make allowances. He was disoriented. He'd had a bereavement. In fact, the worst thing that could happen to a one-man dog had happened to Arnold. So allowances definitely were called for. And one of the people who was going to have to make them was Canon Alex Peters. In Fay's experience all this cat-and-dog incompatibility business was grossly exaggerated. Even Rasputin would, in time, come around.

But another animal was another root in Crybbe. *And you don't want that, Fay, you don't want any roots in Crybbe.*

Bill Davies, the butcher, walked past with fresh blood on his apron, and he stared at them.

Fay was fed up with this. She stared back. Bill Davies looked away.

Maybe they were all afflicted with this obsession about dogs fouling pavements. She'd have to buy one of those poop-scoop things. On the other hand, did that kind of obsession really seem like Crybbe, where apathy ruled?

'For God's sake, Arnie, make up your mind.' They'd come to the square and he seemed to want to turn back. He circled miserably around, dragging the clothes-line and winding it round the legs of a woman bending over the tailgate of a Range Rover, shoving something in the back.

'Oh hell, I'm really sorry. Look, if you can stand still, I'll disentangle you. I'm very sorry.'

'No problem,' the woman said, looking quite amused. She was the first person who hadn't stared at them, which meant she must be from Off.

Of course she was – she was Max Goff's PA, Ms Coolly Efficient.

'We're not used to each other,' Fay explained. 'It's Henry Kettle's sheepdog, the poor chap who . . . I'm looking after him.'

'Oh, yes.' Rachel Wade stepped out of the loop of clothes-line. 'You're from the radio.'

'We all have a living to make,' Fay said and then, making the most of the encounter, 'Look, can I talk to you some time? I'm being hassled by my boss to find out what's happening to the Court.' That hurt, referring to Gavin Ashpole as a boss, which he wasn't and was never going to be.

'Sure,' Rachel said, surprising her.

'When?'

'Now if you like. We could go over to the Court, Max is out seeing people.'

'Great.'

'Hop in then,' Rachel said. But Arnold didn't want to. In the end Fay had to pick him up and dump him on the back seat, where he flattened himself into the leather and panted and trembled.

'Sorry about this.' Fay climbed into the passenger seat. 'He's – not surprisingly – more than a bit paranoid. He was in Henry's car when it . . . you know.'

'Oh dear, poor dog. I didn't know about that.' Rachel Wade started the engine. 'It's rather a mystery, isn't it. About old Kettle. Do you think he'd been drinking?'

'I didn't know him very well. I think a heart attack or a stroke or something seems more likely, don't you?'

'He was a nice old man.' Rachel swung the Range Rover off the square into the street that wriggled down past the church, the graveyard on the right, a few cottages on the left. The street narrowed and entered a wood, where the late afternoon sun was filtered away and the colours faded almost to grey. 'I don't believe all that dowsing stuff. But he was a nice old man.'

'Don't you? I thought . . .'

'Oh, *Max* does. Max believes it. Good God, yes. However, I don't get paid to share his wilder obsessions. Well, *he* thinks I do . . .' Rachel exhaled a short, throaty laugh.

They came out of the wood. A track to the left was barred by a gate with a metal sign. COURT FARM. Where the Preeces farmed. Jack, son of Jimmy, the Mayor, and Jack's two sons. She'd seen Jack once, slinking almost furtively out of the church, his nightly duty accomplished.

'And what exactly is Mr Goff's obsession with the Court?'

'I'll show you in a minute,' Rachel said affably.

This was too easy. Fay was suspicious. She watched Rachel Wade driving with a languid economy of movement, like people drove in films, only you knew they weren't in real, moving vehicles. This was the kind of woman who could change a wheel and make it look like a ballet. Made you despair.

Rachel said, 'Is that your father, the old clergyman? Or your grandfather or something?'

'Father. You've met him?'

'In the Cock. We got into conversation after my lighter fell off the bar and he picked it up.' Rachel smiled. 'In fact, if he'd been considerably younger, I'd almost have thought . . .'

Fay nodded wryly. 'The old knocking-the-lighter-off-the-bar routine. Then he carries out a detailed survey of your legs while he's picking it up. He's harmless. I think.'

'He's certainly a character.' Rachel pulled up in a walled courtyard amid heaps of sand and builders' rubble. Before them random grey-brown stones were settled around deepset mullioned windows and a dusty oak door was half-open.

Fay took a breath.

'Crybbe Court,' Rachel said. 'But don't get too excited.' She snapped on the handbrake. 'Leave the dog in the car, he won't like it. Nobody does, really, apart from historians, and even they get depressed at the state of it.'

She wondered what had made her think it was going to be mellow and warm-toned like a country house on a Christmas card.

'It's old,' she said.

'Elizabethan.'

She felt cold and folded her bare arms. Outside, it was a fairly pleasant midsummer's day; in here, stark and grim as dankest February.

Somehow, she'd imagined rich drapes and tapestries and polished panelling. Probably because the only homes of a similar period she'd visited had been stately homes or National Trust properties, everything exuding the dull sheen of age and wealth, divided from the plebs by brass railings and velvet ropes.

In Crybbe Court these days, it seemed, only the rats were rich.

The room was large, stone-floored and low-ceilinged, and apparently fortified against the sun. The only direct light was from three small, high-set windows, not much more than slits. Bare blue sky through crossed iron bars.

Fay said, 'I suppose it's logical when you think about it, the period and everything, but I didn't imagine it would be quite so . . .'

She became aware of a narrow, stone staircase spiralling into a vagueness of cold light hanging from above like a sheet draped over a banister.

'Ghastly,' Rachel said, 'is, I think, the word you're groping for. Let's go upstairs. It's possibly a little less oppressive.'

The spiral staircase opened into a large chamber with mullioned windows set in two walls. Bars of dusty sunshine fell short of meeting in the middle. It had originally been the main family living-room, Rachel explained. 'Also, I'm told, the place where the local high sheriff, a man named Wort, held out against the local populace who'd arrived to lynch him. Have you heard that story?'

'I've heard the name, but not the story.'

'Oh, well, he was a local tyrant back in the sixteenth century. Known as Black Michael. Hanged men for petty crimes after allowing their wives to appeal to his better nature, if you see what I mean. Also said to have experimented on people before they died, in much the same way as the Nazis did.'

'Charming.'

'In the end, the local people decided they'd had enough.'

'What? The townsfolk of Crybbe actually rebelled? What did they do, write "Wort Must Go" on the lavatory wall?'

'Probably, for the first ten years of atrocities. But in the end they really did come out to lynch him, all gathered out there in the courtyard, threatening to burn the place down with him in it if he didn't come out.'

'And did he?'

'No,' said Rachel. 'He went into the attic and hanged himself from the same rafters from which he'd hanged his offenders.'

'And naturally,' Fay said, 'he haunts the place.'

'Well, no,' Rachel said. 'He doesn't, actually. No stories to that effect anyway. And when Mr Kettle toured the house, he said it was completely dead. As in vacant. Un-presenced, or however you care to put it. Max was terribly disappointed. He had to console himself with the thought of the hound bounding across his path one night.'

'What?'

'Black Michael's Hound. Nobody ever sees Michael, but there is a legend about his dog. A big, black, Baskerville-type creature said to haunt the lanes on the edge of town. It comes down from the Tump.'

Fay thought at once of the old lady who kept telephoning her, Mrs Seagrove. 'I didn't know about that.'

Rachel looked at her, as if surprised anybody should *want* to know about it.

'When was it last seen?' Fay asked.

'Who knows. The book Max found the story in was published, I think, in the fifties. One of those "Legends of the Border" collections. The more recent ones don't seem to have bothered with it.'

Fay wondered if it would help Mrs Seagrove to know about the legend. Probably scare her even more. Or maybe Mrs Seagrove *did* know about it and had either invented or imagined her own sighting, which would explain everything. The problem with old ladies was you could never be quite sure of their state of mind, especially the ones who lived alone.

She asked bravely, 'Are we going up to the attic, then?'

'Certainly not,' Rachel said firmly. 'For one thing, it's not terribly safe. The floor's pretty badly rotted away up there and Max isn't insured against people breaking their necks. Unless they've been hanged.'

Fay shivered and smiled and looked around. 'Well,' she said. 'It could be wonderful, I suppose. If it was done up.'

'With a million pounds or so spent on it, perhaps.' Rachel prodded with a shoe and sent a piece of plaster skating across the dusty wooden floor. 'I can think of better things you could do with a million pounds.'

'Has it been like this since – you know – Tudor times?'

'Good God, no. At various times . . . I mean, in the past century alone, it's been a private school, a hotel . . . even an actual dwelling place again. If we had a torch you'd see bits of wiring and the ruins of bathrooms. But nothing's ever lasted long. It was built as an Elizabethan house, and that, in essence, is what it keeps reverting to.'

'And now?'

'No big secret. Max is a New Age billionaire with a Dream.'

'You don't sound very impressed.'

Rachel stood in the centre of the room and spread her hands. 'Oh God . . . He wants to be King Arthur. He wants to set up his Round Table with all kinds of dowsers and geomancers and spiritual healers and other ghastly cranks. He's been quietly infiltrating them into the town over the past year. And there'll be some kind of Max Goff Foundation, on a drip-feed from Epidemic, hopefully with the blessing of the Charity Commissioners. And people will get ludicrous grants to go off and search for their own pet Holy Grails.'

'Sounds quite exciting,' said Fay, but Rachel looked gloomy and rolled her eyes, her hands sunk deep into the pockets of her Barbour.

'Money down the drain,' she said.

'What's a . . . a geomancer?'

'It's some sort of spiritual chartered surveyor. Someone who works out where it's best to live to stay in harmony with the Earth Spirit, whatever that is, to protect yourself and your family against Evil Forces. Need I go on?'

There were passages leading off the big room and Fay took one and found herself in a dark little bedchamber. It was the first room she'd seen that was actually furnished. There was an old chest under the pathetically inadequate window and a very small four-poster bed.

'Like a four-poster cot, isn't it?' Rachel had drifted in after her. 'People were smaller in those days.'

It was no more than five feet high and not much longer, with very thick posts and an oak headboard with a recessed ledge. On the ledge was a pewter candle-holder with a candle stub in it. The drapes were some kind of cumbersome brocade, thick as tarpaulin and heavy with grease.

'It seems they'd leap into bed,' Rachel said, 'and draw all the curtains tight. And then blow out their candle. Having first read a passage from the Bible – you see there's space on the ledge for a Bible. Because they just *knew* that on the other side of the curtains, the evil spirits would be hovering *en masse*. Cosy, isn't it?'

'Claustrophobic.' Fay had never liked four-posters.

'However, if you want a *real* scare . . .' Rachel held out a box of matches, '. . . light the candle and look in the chest.'

She stood there holding the matchbox, not much more than another shadow in the dim, grimy bedchamber, only a crease in her Barbour at the elbow catching the light. The coat's dull waxen surface looked right for the period, and Fay had the alarming sensation that the dingy room was dragging them back into its own dark era. Was Rachel smiling? Fay couldn't see her face.

She found herself accepting the matchbox.

'Go on,' Rachel said. 'Light the candle.'

'OK.' She tried not to sound hesitant, asking herself, You aren't *nervous*, are you, Fay?

No, she decided. Just bloody cold. It might have occurred to me to wonder why she was wearing a Barbour on Midsummer Day. And she might have warned me about the temperature in this place.

She reached beyond the post at the bedhead and pulled the candle-holder from the recess. Struck a match. Saw the candle-tray was full of dead flies and bluebottles. Turned it upside down, but not all of them fell out.

Yuk. Fay lit the candle.

Shadows bounced.

'The chest under the window?'

She could see Rachel Wade's face now, in the candle-light, and it *wasn't* smiling. 'Look,' Rachel said, 'forget it. Come on. I was only joking.'

'No you weren't.' Fay smelled wax, from the candle and from Rachel's coat perhaps. 'I'd better open the blasted thing before this candle burns away.'

Rachel Wade shrugged. Fay crossed to the window which left only a smear of light across the top of the chest. Obviously not Elizabethan, this chest; it had black lettering stamped across its lid and was carelessly bound with green-painted metal strips.

Fay lifted the lid and lowered the candle.

She recoiled at once. 'Oh,' she said.

'Sorry.'

'What is it?'

Its eye-sockets were black and two upper teeth were thin

85

and curved. A small cobweb hung between them. The mouth was stretched wide in a fossilized shriek.

'It's a cat, isn't it? A mummified cat?'

'Tiddles. Max calls it Tiddles.'

'Cute,' Fay said and shuddered.

'Not very. It was found in the rafters. It may have been walled up there alive.'

'God.'

'Practical geomancy,' Rachel said. 'The spirit of the cat acts, apparently, as a guardian. They found half a horse behind the kitchen wall. Come on, let's go.'

CHAPTER VII

ASLEEP in his armchair, Canon Alex Peters dreamed he was asleep in his armchair. Tucked up in a soft blanket of sunbeams, he awoke in time to watch the wall dissolve.

It began with the fireplace. He was aware that Grace's dreadful see-through clock and the gilt-framed mirror were fading, while the black, sooty hole of the fireplace itself was getting bigger.

Gradually, the hole took over, becoming darker and wider and then spreading up through the mantelpiece, almost as far as the ceiling, until the whole chimney breast dissolved into a black passageway.

There formed a filigree of yellowish light, and then, dimly at first, Grace appeared in the passageway. Standing there, quite still.

'What happened to your wheelchair?' Alex asked. He was glad, of course, to see her back on her feet.

'No you're not,' Grace said. Her lips did not move when she spoke but her body became brighter, as if the spiderweb of lights was inside her, like glowing veins. 'You were glad when I died, and you'll be glad to know I'm still dead.'

'That's not true,' protested Alex. But you couldn't lie to the dead, and he knew it.

Grace turned her back on him and began to walk away along

the passage. Alex struggled to get up, desperate to explain. But the chair wouldn't let him. He shouted to the spindly, diminishing figure. 'Grace, look, don't go, give me a hand, would you?'

The chair held him in a leathery grip.

'Grace!' Alex screamed. 'Grace, don't go! I want to explain!'

Just once, Grace glanced back at him over her shoulder, and there was a pitying smile on her face, with perhaps a shadow of malice.

Max Goff did not, of course, have any immediate plans to live in Crybbe Court itself, Rachel Wade said. Good *God*, no.

Well, perhaps one day. When it was fully restored.

'You mean,' Fay said as they walked out into the sunlight, 'restored to what it would've been like if the Elizabethans had had full central heating and ten-speaker stereos.'

'You're getting the general picture,' Rachel confirmed, and showed her the place where Max actually would be living within the next week or so.

It was an L-shaped stone stable-block behind the house. It already had been gutted, plumbed and wired and a giant plate-glass window had been inserted into a solid stone wall to open up a new and spectacular view of the hills from what would be the living-room.

At least, the view *would* have been spectacular if it hadn't been semi-obscured by a green mound, like an inverted pudding basin or a giant helmet.

'His beloved Tump,' Rachel said. And there wasn't much affection there, Fay thought, either for the mound or for Max Goff.

'Is it a burial mound or a – what d'you call it – castle mound . . . motte?'

'Probably both. Either way it's pretty unsightly, like an overgrown spoil-heap. And decidedly creepy by moonlight. I mean, who wants to stare out at a grave? Whoever built this place had the right idea, I think, by putting a blank stable wall in front so it wouldn't frighten the horses.'

Fay realized the Court itself was built in a hollow, and the

Tump was on slightly higher ground, so that it seemed, from here, higher than it actually was. It loomed. The stone wall which surrounded it had partly fallen down on this side, revealing the mesh of dense bushes and brambles at the base of the mound.

'Poor Mr Kettle,' Fay said, reminded by the wall.

Rachel fingered a strand of pale hair, the nearest she'd come, in Fay's presence, to a nervous gesture. 'The bitter irony is that Max plans to move that wall. He calls it a nineteenth-century abomination. Some experts think it's older than that and should be preserved, but he'll get his way, of course, in the end.'

Rachel stepped on a piece of soft plaster and ground it into the newly boarded floor.

'He always does,' she said.

It was clear now to Fay that this was not the same Rachel Wade who, a week ago, had briskly swept her down the steps of the Cock with vague promises of an interview with Goff when his plans were in shape. Sure, on that occasion, she'd had a tape recorder over her shoulder. But even if she'd carried one today, she felt, Rachel's attitude would not have been markedly different.

Something had changed.

Fay said cautiously, 'So when is he going to talk to me? On tape.'

'Leave it with me,' Rachel said. 'I'll fix it.' She spread her arms to usher Fay back towards the wooden framework evidently destined to be a doorway.

'I hate having to ask this sort of question.' Fay stopped at the entrance. 'But he isn't going to be talking to anyone else, is he, first?'

'Not if I can help it. Listen, we've been walking around this place for the last forty-five minutes and I've forgotten your name.'

'Fay. Fay Morrison.'

'Would you like a job, Fay?'

'Huh?'

'Quite ludicrous salary. Seductively fast company car. Lots of foreign travel.'

Fay stared at her.

'Silly expenses,' Rachel said. 'Untold fringe benefits.' She'd turned her back on the big window. From the far end of the room, the hills had been squeezed out of the picture; the window was full of Tump.

'How long have you been doing this?' Fay asked. 'As Goff's PA.'

'Nearly four years now. I think I've done rather well on the whole. Although the physical demands are not too arduous. Max's bisexuality goes in alternating phases. During his DC periods he can leave you alone for months.'

The grey eyes were calm and candid.

'Jesus Christ,' Fay said.

'Oh, don't get me wrong – I don't mind *that*. I almost became an actress, anyway. And with Max, there's rarely anything terribly tiring. And never anything particularly *bizarre*. Well, except for the crystals, and he only ever tried that once. And anyway, one always has to weigh these things against the benefits. No, it's just . . .'

Rachel dug her fists deep into the pockets of her Barbour until Fay could see the knuckles outlined in the shiny, waxed fabric.

'. . . It's just I don't think I can go through with it *here*,' Rachel said. 'Do you know what I mean?'

Grace Legge came here to die, Dad came to go slowly loopy, and I came to watch.

'Yes,' Fay said bleakly, 'I know *exactly* what you mean. I'm beginning to realize how hard it is to get anything positive to take off here.'

She'd read somewhere that nobody could say for certain where the name Crybbe came from. It was obviously a corruption of the Welsh, and there were two possible derivations:

crib – the crest of a hill (which seemed topographically unlikely, because the town was in a valley).

or

crybachu – to wither.

89

'It appeals to him, you know,' Rachel said. 'The fact that failure is so deeply ingrained here. Brings out the crusader in him. He's going to free the place from centuries of bucolic apathy.'

'The first story Offa's Dyke got me to cover,' Fay remembered, 'was the opening of a new factory on the industrial estate. Quite a lively little set-up producing chunky coloured sandals – in fact I'm wearing a pair, see? They were providing eight local jobs and the Marches Development Board were predicting it'd be twenty before the end of the year.'

'Closed down, didn't it? Was it last week?'

'I'd have ordered another pair if I'd known,' Fay said.

They stared at each other, almost comically glum, then Rachel tossed back her ash-blonde hair and strode determinedly through to the room which would soon be a kitchen.

'Come on, let's get out of here, he'll be back soon.' She picked up two tumblers from the draining surface next to the new sink, and Fay followed her outside, where she dug a bottle of sparkling wine from the silt in the bottom of an old sheep trough – 'My private cellar.'

And then they collected a grateful Arnold from the Range Rover and wandered off across the field, down the valley to the river, where you could sit on the bank fifty yards from the three-arched bridge and probably not see the Court any more, nor even the Tump.

On the way down the field Fay looked over her shoulder to watch the Tump disappearing and saw a man among the trees on its summit. He was quite still, obviously watching them.

'Rachel, who's that?'

'Where?'

'On the Tump. I don't think it's Goff.'

Rachel turned round and made no pretence of not staring.

'It's Humble,' she said. 'Max's minder. He loves it here. He used to be a gamekeeper. He prowls the woods all the time, supposedly organizing security. I think he snares rabbits and things.'

'*Very* Green, I must say,' Fay said.

'Max's principles tend to get overlooked where Humble's

concerned. I think he sometimes serves the need that occasionally arises in Max for, er, rough boys.'

'I think I'm sorry I asked,' said Fay.

Alex awoke.

There was pressure on his chest. When he was able to open
his eyes just a little, with considerable difficulty, he looked into
blackness.

Oh Lord, he thought, I've actually entered the dark place.
I'm in there with Grace.

Yet he was still in the armchair. The chair was refusing to
let go of him. It had closed around him like an iron lung or
something. He was a prisoner in the chair and in the dark and
there was a pressure on his chest.

'Grace?' he said feebly. 'Grace?'

The darkness moved. The darkness was making a soft,
rhythmic noise, like a motor boat in the distance.

Alex opened his eyes fully and stared into luminous amber-
green, watchful eyes. He chuckled; the darkness was only a
big, black cat.

'Ras . . . Ras . . .' he whispered weakly, trying to think of
the creature's name.

The cat stood up on his chest.

'Rastus!' Alex said triumphantly. 'Hullo, Rastus. You
know, for a minute, I thought . . . Oh, never mind, you
wouldn't understand.'

He wondered if it was teatime yet. The clock said . . . what?
Couldn't make out if it was four o'clock or five. Around four,
Grace always liked a pot of tea and perhaps a small slice of
Dundee cake. She'd be most annoyed if he'd slept through
teatime.

Fay, on the other hand, preferred a late meal. Women were
so contrary. It generally saved a lot of argument if he ate with
them both.

Alex chuckled again. No wonder he was getting fat.

*

Rachel put the bottle in the river and took off her Barbour. 'I'll be thirty-six in January.'

'Happens to us all,' Fay said.

'I was . . . very much on top of the situation when I took the job. Nothing could touch me, you know? I was chief Press Officer at Virgin, and he head-hunted me. He said, name your price, so I doubled my salary and he said, OK, it's yours – can you believe that?'

She handed Fay the glasses, pulled the bottle out of the water and shot the cork at the bridge. It fell short and they watched it bobbing downstream. 'Does that count as pollution?' Rachel wondered.

'Why was Goff so attracted to Crybbe?'

Rachel poured wine until it fizzed to the brim of both tumblers. 'Magic.'

'Magic,' Fay repeated in a flat voice.

'Earth magic.'

'You mean ley-lines?'

'You know what all that's about? I mean, don't be ashamed, it's all speculation anyway.'

'Tell me what it means in the Crybbe context.'

'OK, well, presumably you know about Alfred Watkins who came up with the theory, back in the 1920s. Lived in Hereford, did most of his research in these hills. Had the notion, and set out to prove it, that prehistoric sacred monuments – standing stones, stone circles, burial mounds, all this – were arranged in straight lines. Just route markers, he thought originally, on straight roads.'

'I've got his book, *The Old Straight Track*.'

'Right. So you know that where four or five sites fell into a straight line, he'd call it a ley, apparently because a lot of the places where these configurations occurred had names ending in l-e-y, OK?'

'Like Crybbe?'

Rachel grinned. 'Well, he didn't know about Crybbe, or he'd probably have called them Crybbe-lines. You read through Watkins's book, you won't find a single mention of Crybbe.'

'I know. I looked. I was quite disappointed.'

'Because, apart from the Tump, there's nothing to see.

However, it seems there used to be bloody dozens of standing stones and things around here at one time, which disappeared over the centuries. Farmers used to rip them out because they got in the way of ploughing and whatever else farmers do.'

Rachel waved a dismissive hand to emphasize the general tedium of agriculture. 'Anyway, there are places in Britain where lots of ley-lines converge, ancient sacred sites shooting out in all directions. Which, obviously, suggests these places were of some great sacred significance, or places of power.'

'Stonehenge?'

'Sure. And Glastonbury Tor. And Avebury. St Michael's Mount in Cornwall. And other places you've probably never heard of.'

'But not Crybbe. You're really not going to tell me Crybbe was ever sacred to anybody.'

Rachel swallowed a mouthful of wine and wiped her mouth with a deliberately graceless gesture before topping up her glass. 'Down on your knees, woman, I'm afraid you're on holy ground.'

The bridge carried the main road into town and behind it Fay could see chimneys and the church tower. Wooded hills – a mixture of broadleaf and conifer – tumbled down on three sides. From anywhere at a distance, Crybbe looked quite picturesque. And that was all.

'So how come there aren't bus-loads of pilgrims clogging the roads, then? How come this is close to being Britain's ultimate backwater?'

'Because the inhabitants are a bunch of hicks who can't recognize a good tourist gimmick when they get one on a plate. I mean, they did rip out the bloody stones in the first place. That's why Max brought in Henry Kettle. He had to know where the stones used to be.'

'Henry divines the spots!'

'Sure. He pinpoints the location, then what you do is stick a pole in the ground at the exact spot. And if you're as rich and self-indulgent as Max Goff, what you do next is have lots of lovely new stones cut to size and planted out in the fields. Prehistoric landscape-gardening on a grand scale.'

'Gosh.' Fay was picturing a huge, wild rock-garden, with

daffodils growing around the standing stones in the spring, Crybbe suddenly a little town in a magic circle. 'I think that sounds rather a nice thing to do . . . don't you? I mean, bizarre, but nice, somehow.'

'Except it's not quite as easy as it sounds,' Rachel said. 'And it's going to cause trouble. Within a couple of weeks Kettle'd discovered the probable sites of nearly thirty prehistoric stones, couple of burial mounds, not to mention a holy well.'

'Wow.'

'And fewer than a quarter of the sites are on the eight and a half acres of land which Max bought with the Court, so if he's going to restore Stone Age Crybbe he's got to negotiate with a lot of farmers.'

'Ah. Mercenary devils, farmers.'

'And awkward sods, in many cases.'

'True. So how's he going to handle it?'

'He wants to hold a big public meeting to tell the people how he plans to revitalize their town. I mean, obviously you've got the considerable economic benefits of tourism – look how many foreign trippers flock to Avebury. But also – unwisely in my view – he's going to explain all the esoteric stuff. What ley-lines are really all about, and what they can do for the town.'

'Energy lines,' Fay said. 'I've also read that other book, *The Old Golden Land*.'

'By J. M. Powys, distant descendant of the great mystical writer, John Cowper Powys. Max loves that book. Coincidentally – or not, perhaps – he's just bought the company which published it. So he owns it now, and he likes to think he owns J. M. Powys . . . for whom He Has Plans.'

'He's coming here?'

'If he knows what's good for him. He'll have plenty of like-minded idiots for company. There are already nine New Age people living in the town in properties craftily acquired by Max over the past few months. Alternative healers, herbalists, astrologers.'

'Can't say I've noticed them,' Fay admitted.

'That's because some of them look quite normal. Only *they* know they are the human transmitters of the New Energy about to flow into Crybbe.'

'The idea being that ley-lines mark out some kind of force-field, channels of energy, which Bronze Age people knew how to tap into. Is that right?'

'The Great Life Force, Fay. And so, naturally, re-siting the stones will bring new life flowing back into Crybbe. Max reckons – well, he hasn't worked it out for himself, he's been told by lots of so-called experts – that Crybbe is only in the depressed state it is today because all the stones have gone. So if you put them back, it'll be like connecting the town for the first time to the national grid. The whole place will sort of light up.'

Fay thought about this. 'It sounds rather wonderful.'

'If you like that kind of fairy-tale.'

'Is it?'

'Oh, well, sure, what does it matter if it's true or not, it'll bring in the crowds, be an economic boost, a psychological panacea, create a few jobs. But you see, Fay, I *know* this guy.' Rachel held up the bottle, but Fay shook her head and Rachel poured what remained into her tumbler. 'I don't think I can stand to watch him being baronial at Crybbe Court, with his entourage of fringe scientists and magicians and minstrels and sundry jesters.'

'Is that the central point, at which all these ley-lines are supposed to meet. The Court. Or is it the church?'

'The Tump,' Rachel said. 'It's the Tump. It's not a centre, it's a sort of axis. The lines come off it in a fan shape. The Tump is like this great power station. Get the idea? I mean, really, isn't it just the biggest load of old rhubarb you ever heard?'

Rachel brought an arm from behind her head and lobbed the empty wine-bottle into the air. Arnold tensed, about to spring after it, until he saw where it was going.

There was a satisfying splash.

'Now surely,' Rachel said, 'that's *got* to be pollution.'

CHAPTER VIII

FAY walked back to the cottage, for Arnold's sake and to clear her head, although she hadn't drunk all that much wine – not compared to Rachel, anyway. Arnold, however, looked as if he'd been drinking heavily, veering from side to side on his tautened clothes-line. He was hopeless.

Goff had not returned when they arrived back at the Court. She'd left Rachel carrying the triptych into the stable-block, where it was to be double-locked into a store-room. Nearly a thousand quid's worth of less-than-fine art. Hereward and Jocasta Newsome would, for once, have good reason to appear appallingly smug.

'Whichever way you look at it, Arnie,' Fay said reflectively, 'our friend Goff is making waves in Crybbe.'

No bad thing, either.

Could she understand the guy's obsession? Well, yes, she could. A man who'd made his first million marketing anarchic punk-rock records in the mid-seventies. Waking up in the nineties to find himself sitting on a heap of money in a wilderness of his own creation. All the cars and yachts and super-toys he'd ever want and nothing to nurture the soul.

Not exactly a quantum leap, was it, from there to the New Age dream?

And, the more she thought about it, the proposed mystical liberation of an obscure Welsh border town from years of economic decay was a story that deserved a bigger audience than it was ever going to reach through Offa's Dyke Radio.

In fact, this could be the moment to approach her old chums at the BBC. How about a forty-five-minute radio documentary chronicling Goff's scheme to turn Crybbe into a New Age Camelot? She could hear a sequence in her head, lots of echoey footsteps and tinkly music, the moaning of men and machinery as massive megaliths were manoeuvred into position. It sounded good.

On the other hand, she had an arrangement with Offa's Dyke, and the little shit Ashpole would want first bite at every snippet that came out of the Goff camp.

. . . or we'll have to, you know, reconsider things . . .

Little turd.

And while Radio Four was the interesting option, a chance to prove she could still make national-quality programmes, Offa's Dyke was bread and butter. Of course, if there was a prospect of getting out of Crybbe and back to London or Manchester or Bristol in the foreseeable future, she could make the BBC programme and bollocks to O.D.

She passed the farm entrance and followed Arnold and the road into the wood, where the sudden darkness brought with it a wave of loneliness and resentment towards her dad. Why did the old bugger have to stay out here? All that cobblers about his having to sell the house in Woodstock to pay for Grace's treatment.

Somehow, Dad, Fay thought, all your money's gone down the pan. And tonight, the close of what appeared to have been one of his better days, seemed as good a time as any to make him tell her precisely how it had happened.

A bush moved.

It happened on the edge of her vision, just as she'd passed it, and she thought, it's the wind, then realized there was none.

Arnold growled.

Fay froze. 'Who's that?'

Bloody hell, the phantom flasher of Crybbe. Well, there had to be one. Fay laughed. Nervously.

There was also Black Michael's Hound.

You wouldn't think anything as black as that could glow, would you?

Thank you, Mrs Seagrove.

There was a snigger. An involuntary cry was snatched from Fay, and then he was off. She saw him vanish behind a tree then reappear, moving in a crouch, like a spider, up the field, in the direction of the farm, an unidentifiable shadow. Perhaps it was that man Humble, Goff's minder.

'Have a nice wank, did we?' Fay called after him. But it

wasn't funny, and that was why her voice cracked. She was discovering that back alleys in the city, full of chip-wrapping and broken glass, could sometimes be less scary than a placid sylvan lane at sunset.

Because there was the feeling, somehow, that if it *did* happen here, it would be worse.

Hereward Newsome couldn't wait to get home to tell his wife what he'd learned in the Cock.

Hereward went off to what he described to visitors as 'my local hostelry' perhaps two nights a week and stayed for maybe an hour. He considered a local hostelry was one of those things a man ought to have when he lived in the country, if he was to communicate with the locals on their own level.

'Why bother?' demanded Jocasta, who made a point of never going with him to the Cock. 'Why on earth should I learn about sheep and pigs? Why can't the locals learn about fine art and communicate with us on *our* level?'

'Because it's their town,' Hereward had reasoned. 'Pigs and sheep have been their way of life for centuries, and now the industry is in crisis and they feel their whole *raison d'être* is threatened. We should show them we understand.'

And he did his best. He'd started reading everything he could find in the *Guardian* about sheep subsidies and the Common Agricultural Policy so he could carry on a respectable discussion with the farmers in the public bar. He'd commiserate with them about the latest EC regulations and they'd say, 'Well, well,' or 'Sure t'be,' in their quiet, contemplative tones and permit him to buy them another couple of pints of Ansell's Bitter.

However, he was always happier if Colonel Croston was in there, or even old Canon Peters. He might not have much in common with either of them, but at least it would be a two-way conversation.

Tonight, however, he'd found common ground . . . in a big way.

Lights were coming on in the farmhouse as Hereward

parked the 2CV neatly at the edge of the slice of rough grass he called 'the paddock'. There was a Volvo Estate in the garage, but he never took that into town unless there were paintings to be shifted.

'It's me, darling.' Hereward hammered on the stable door at the side of the farmhouse. He kept telling her there was no need to lock it; that was the beauty of the countryside. But every other week she'd point out something in the paper about some woman getting raped in her cottage or a bank manager held to ransom in his rural retreat. 'But not in *this* area,' Hereward would say, looking pained.

Even though she'd have recognized his voice, Jocasta opened only the top half of the door so she could see his face and be sure he wasn't accompanied by some thug with a shotgun at his back.

'It *is* me,' Hereward said patiently, when his wife finally let him in. 'Listen, darling, what did I say about the turning point?'

'Coffee?' Jocasta said. Hereward frowned. When she was solicitous on his return from the pub it usually meant she'd just concluded an absurdly lengthy phone call to her sister in Normandy. Tonight, though, he'd let it pass.

'Sorry,' Jocasta said, plugging in the percolator. 'Turning point? You mean Goff?'

'You remember I told you about that guy Daniel Osborne, the homeopath? Who moved into a cottage in Bridge Street? With his wife, the acupuncturist? Now I learn that next door but one to him – this is quite extraordinary – there's a hypno-therapist who specializes in that . . . what d'you call it when they try to take people back into previous lives?'

'Regression.' Jocasta turned towards him. He thought she looked awfully alluring when her eyes were shining. He had her full attention.

'The fact is . . .' Hereward was smiling broadly. 'There're lots of them. And we didn't know it. All kinds of progressive, alternative practitioners and New Age experts. In Crybbe.'

'You're serious?'

'Look, I've just had this from Dan Osborne himself, they

can talk about it now. Seems Max Goff's been secretly buying property in town for months and either selling it at a very reasonable price or renting it to, you know, the *right* people. What we're getting here are the seeds of a truly progressive alternative community. That is, no . . . no . . .'

'Riff-raff,' Jocasta said crisply. 'Hippies.'

'If you must. In fact, it's the sort of set-up that . . . well . . . the Prince of Wales would support.'

'There's got to be a catch,' Jocasta said, ever cautious. 'It seems remarkable that we haven't heard about it before.'

'Darling, everybody's been ultra discreet. I mean, they don't look any different from your ordinary incomers, and there's always been a big population turnover in this area. Look, here's an example. You remember the grey-haired woman, very neat, very well-dressed, who was in The Gallery looking at paintings a couple of days ago. Who do you think that was?'

'Shirley Maclaine.'

'Jean Wendle,' said Hereward.

'Who?'

'The spiritual healer! She used to be a barrister or something and gave it up when she realized she had the gift.'

'Oh.' Jocasta digested this. 'Are you saying Crybbe's going to be known for this sort of thing? With lots of . . .'

'Tourists! Up-market *thinking* tourists! The kind that don't even like to be called tourists. It's going to be like Glastonbury here – only better. It'll be . . . *internationally famous.*'

'Well,' said Jocasta, 'if what you say is true, it's really quite annoying nobody told us. We might have sold up and moved out, not realizing. And it's still going to take time . . .'

'Darling,' Hereward said, 'if Goff can pull off something like this under our very noses, the man is a magician.'

The solemnity of the curfew bell lay over the shadowed square by the time Fay and Arnold came back into town, and she found herself counting the clangs, getting louder as they neared the church.

Fifty-seven, fifty-eight, fifty-nine . . .

There was something faintly eerie about the curfew. Was she imagining it, or did people make a practice of staying off the streets while it was actually being rung, even if they came out afterwards? She stood staring at the steps in front of the Cock, willing somebody to walk in or out to prove her wrong.

Nobody did. Nobody was walking on the street. There was no traffic. No children played. No dogs barked. Only the bell and the cawing of crows, like a distorted echo.

Seventy-three, seventy-four, seventy-five . . .

Every evening the curfew would begin at precisely ten o'clock. You could set your watch by it, and people often did.

How the custom had survived was not entirely inexplicable. There'd been a bequest by one Percy Weale, a local wool-merchant and do-gooder back in the sixteenth century. He'd left land and money to build Crybbe School and also a further twelve acres in trust to the Preece family and their descendants on condition that the curfew bell be rung nightly to safeguard 'the moral and spiritual welfare' of the townsfolk.

Should the Preece family die off or neglect the task, then the land must be rented out and the money used to pay a bell-ringer. But even in times of plague or war, it was said, the curfew bell had never been silenced.

Because hanging on to those twelve acres would be a matter of pride for the Preeces. Also economics. Fay was learning that farmers in these parts would do almost anything to hold what land they had and would lay in wait for neighbouring death or misfortune to grab more. When a farm was sold, the neighbours swooped like buzzards, snatching up acreage on every side, often leaving a lone farmhouse marooned in the middle, condemned either to dereliction or sumptuous restoration by city folk in search of a rural retreat. The Newsomes lived in one, with a quarter acre of their own surrounded on all sides by other people's property.

Ninety-eight, ninety-nine. One hundred. Although the sun's last lurid light was spread like orange marmalade across the hills, the town centre wore a sombre gown of deep shadows.

Fay noticed Arnold's clothes-line had gone slack.

He was sitting on the cracked cobbles, staring up at the

church tower, now overhung with florid cloud. As Fay watched him, his nose went up and, with a mournful intensity, he began to howl.

As the howl rose, pure as the curfew's final peal, with whose dwindling it mingled in the twilit air, Fay was aware of doors opening in the houses between the shops and the pubs on the little square.

No lights came on. Nobody came out. Arnold howled three times, then sat there, looking confusedly from side to side, as if unsure he'd been responsible for the disturbance.

Fay could feel the stares coming at her from inside the shadowed portals in the square, and the air seemed denser, as if focused hostility were some kind of thickening agent, clotting the atmosphere itself.

She felt she was being pressed backwards into the church wall by a powerful surge of heavy-duty disapproval.

Then someone, a female voice, screeched out, *'You'll get that dog out of yere!'*

And the doors began quietly to close, one by one, in muted clicks and snaps.

By which time Fay was down on her knees, clutching Arnold to her breast, squeezing his ridiculous ears, warming her bare arms in his fur.

Finding she was trembling.

Jack Preece came out of the church and walked away in the direction of the Cock, without looking at them.

CHAPTER IX

GRACE'S house was just an ordinary cottage in a terraced row which, for some reason, began in stone and ended in brick. Fay could pick it out easily because it was the only one in the row with a hanging basket over the front door. As hanging baskets went, this one wasn't subtle; she kept it bursting with large, vulgar blooms and watered them assiduously because this hanging basket was a symbol of something she was trying to say to Crybbe.

There was no light and no sound from inside, and she thought at first there must have been another blasted power cut. Then a light blinked on and off next door, and she heard a television from somewhere.

'He's gone to the pub,' she told Arnold. Most nights her dad would stroll over to the Cock for a couple of whiskies and one of their greasy bar-snacks.

She would wait up for him. Because tonight they were going to have this thing out. By the end of the week, no argument, there was going to be a 'For Sale' sign next to the hanging basket. And she would start work on the Goff documentary, which Radio Four were *definitely* going to commission. And Offa's Dyke Radio, the Voice of the Marches, could start looking for another stringer to justify the Crybbe Unattended.

But when Fay marched into the office, she found a note on her editing table informing her that Canon Alex Peters had escaped to bed.

> Not feeling terrifically well, to be honest. Having an early night, OK? So if you must have that dog in the house, keep the bugger quiet!

Fay smiled – she knew he'd come around – then frowned at the postscript.

> Oh yes, Guy rang. Wants you to ring him back.

Bloody Guy. Did she really need this on top of everything?

She turned the note over in case there was an addendum, *re* Guy. Eight years ago, her dad had been the only person with the perception to warn her off, everyone else having congratulated her, in some kind of awe, before they'd even met Guy in the flesh – one friend (you never forgot remarks like this) saying, '*You* . . . You and *Guy Morrison?*'

Never mind. All in the past. Especially Guy.

No regrets?

You had to be kidding.

Except he *would* keep phoning. As if she were just another

one of his contacts – *Oh, hey, listen, I'm going to be in your part of the world next week. Buy you a drink?*

Fay sat down at the editing table. Rachel had drunk most of the wine with no discernible effects, while Fay had consumed less than a third of the bottle and now the room was sliding about. In the light from the Anglepoise it still looked very Grace, this room: H-shaped tiled fireplace and, above it, an oval mirror in a thick gilt frame. On the mantelpiece was a clock with a glass case revealing a mechanism which looked like a pair of swinging testicles in brass.

This room – the whole house – was frozen in time, in a none-too-stylish era. Round about the time, in fact, when Fay's dad had split up with Grace and returned to her mother. It was as if Grace had given up after that – certainly she hadn't married until the Canon had come back into her life. She seemed to have lived quietly in Crybbe with her sister, until the sister died. Worked quietly in the library.

A quiet woman. A Crybbe woman. As Fay understood it, she'd been working in Hereford, for the diocese, when she'd had her fling with Alex.

'How could she come back here?' Fay said aloud, and picked up the phone to call Guy. Then put it back. She'd caught sight of Arnold, who was looking up at her in his unassuming way, one ear pricked, the other flopped over.

'Arnold, I'm sorry . . . What do you feel like for dinner?'

He may have wagged his tail, but she couldn't be sure, it was that kind of tail.

The kitchen had knotty-pine cupboards and pink-veined imitation-marble worktops, one of which bore her dad's beloved microwave. Arnold accepted stewed steak from a can, served on one of Grace's best china plates. When he'd finished, Fay let him out in the small back garden, where it was almost fully dark. There was no sign of Rasputin or Pushkin, his lieutenant. They'd be out hunting in the endless fields beyond the garden fence.

And in this pursuit they were obviously not alone. Somewhere out there a light-ball bobbed, possibly following the line of a hedge which was said to mark the old border between Wales and England. (Nobody in this town ever spoke of being

English or Welsh because, at various times in its undistinguished history, Crybbe had been in both countries.)

Fay watched the light for several minutes, listening. Illegal badger-digging was, she'd heard, one of the less-publicized local recreations. Nasty, vicious, cruel. But nobody had ever been prosecuted locally. She'd often wondered how Sergeant Wynford Wiley would react if she rang him up one night and directed him to a spot where it was actually taking place: spurts of squealing, scuffling and snuffling as the terriers were sent into the soil to rip the badgers from their set. There was a man who kept a pack of terriers on a farm two or three miles away, ostensibly for hunting foxes. Fay wished she could nail the swine.

But she suspected that, even if it was three o'clock in the morning when she rang, Wynford would claim a prior appointment.

The countryside. Where so many pastimes were sour and furtive. And tolerated.

Arnold trotted in from the garden.

Fay was very tired. She laid out a thick mat under her editing table and folded an old blanket on top it. 'I don't know what you're used to, Arnold, but the management will listen sympathetically to any complaints in the morning.'

Arnold sat quietly next to the mat. Apart from the episode in the square, he hadn't seemed a very demonstrative dog.

Fay brought him a bowl of water. 'I'm going to shut you in, Arnold. Because of the cats. OK?'

She scribbled a note to pin on the door, telling her father not to go into the office, if, as happened occasionally, he couldn't sleep and came down. *And don't let any CATS in there!*

Then she went to bed.

She never put on the bedroom light; the room looked squalid enough by daylight. It was almost as claustrophobic as the Crybbe Unattended Studio, and its wallpaper had faded to brown. Fay would have redecorated the place, but she wasn't staying, was she?

They weren't staying.

The bathroom had been modernized, with characteristic taste. A bath, shower and washbasin in livid pink and black.

Fay washed.

She looked in the mirror as she wiped the face people had been amazed at Guy Morrison falling for.

Guy used to say she should spell her name F-e-y, because she looked like a naughty elf. It had seemed like a kind of compliment at the time – she used to be naive like that. Especially where Guy was concerned.

And she wasn't going to waste any time speculating about what Guy might want, because the answer was no.

Snapping off the bathroom light, she found her way back to bed by the diffused rays of the midsummer moon – very nearly full, but trapped like a big silver pickled onion in a cloud sandwich.

She lay awake for a long time in her single divan, thinking about the curfew and the furtive figure in the hedge, about Henry Kettle and Arnold and the wall. Splat.

Horrible.

How did it happen? There'd be a post-mortem, forensic tests and an inquest, but only Arnold would ever really know, and he was only a dog.

' . . . *You'll get that dog out of yere* . . . '

Very sympathetic people in Crybbe. Very caring. Wonderful, warm-hearted country folk.

Miserable bastards.

Eventually, Fay fell asleep with the moon in her eyes – she awoke briefly and saw it, all the clouds gone, and she remembered that sleeping with direct moonlight on your face was supposed to send you mad. She giggled at that and went back to sleep and dreamed a midsummer night's dream in which she was lying in bed and Arnold was howling downstairs.

Oh *no*!

Fay flung the covers aside and sat up in bed.

Arnold's howling seemed to filter up from below, like slivers of light coming up through the cracks in the floorboards. It probably would be even louder from the Canon's bedroom, which was directly over the office.

She got out of bed and crept to the top of the stairs, hissing, 'Shut it, Arnold, for God's sake!'

Bare-footed, Fay moved downstairs. It was bloody chilly for a midsummer's night, especially when you were wearing nothing but a long T-shirt with several holes in it.

At the bottom of the stairs she stopped and turned back, picking up what she hoped was the sound of her dad's snoring. She ran a hand over the wall in search of the light switch, but when she found it and pressed, nothing happened. Everything Hereward Newsome had ever said about those cretins at the electricity company was dead right.

When she opened the office door, Arnold shot out and she caught him and he leapt into her arms and licked her face. 'Don't try and get round me,' she whispered. 'You are *not* sleeping on my bed.'

But when she carried him back into the office, he whimpered and jumped out of her arms and she went back and found him standing by the front door, ears down, tail down, quivering.

'Oh, Arnold . . .'

Did dogs have nightmares? Had he been reliving last night: an almighty crunch, an explosion of glass, his master's head in a shower of blood?

'I know, Arnold.' Patting him. 'I know.' His coat felt matted, almost damp. Did dogs sweat?

Christ, he couldn't be bleeding, could he? She picked him up and lugged him back into the office, automatically flipping the light switch by the door.

Damn! Damn! Damn!

'Arnold!' He'd squirmed out of her arms again and run away into the hall.

Fay clutched helplessly at the air. Torch . . . Candle . . . Anything. God, it was cold. Moonlight was sprinkled over the room, like frost. The light twinkled on the twisting testicular mechanism of the clock on the mantelpiece, fingered the mirror's ornate, gilt frame, quietly highlighting everything that was part of *then*, while the now things, the trestle editing table and the Revox were screened by shadow. As though in another dimension.

Everything was utterly still.

Get me, she thought, out of here. Out of this sad, forsaken house, out of this fossilized town.

Then a sudden, most unearthly sound uncurled from the fireplace. Like a baby's cry of joy, but also, she thought, startled and shivering, also like an owl descending delightedly on its prey.

It came again and it sang with an unholy pleasure and she saw Rasputin sitting massively in the hearth like an Egyptian temple cat on a sarcophagus.

Rasputin's emerald eyes suddenly flared, and he sprang.

Fay gasped and went backwards, clutching at the wall, involuntarily closing her eyes against imagined flashing claws.

But the huge cat was not coming at her.

When she looked again, he'd landed solidly in a beam of pallid moonlight on the varnished mahogany arm of the fireside chair, and he was purring.

In the chair Grace Legge sat rigidly, her brittle teeth bared in a dead smile and eyes as white and cold as the moon.

PART THREE

A car's steering wheel, like a dowsing rod, is designed to amplify small movements of the driver's hands; so a reflex twitch in someone who slips unconsciously into a dowsing mode would be enough to send a car travelling at a fair speed into an uncontrollable spin.

TOM GRAVES,
Needles of Stone

CHAPTER I

Memory is circling like a silent helicopter over these soft, green fields, strung together with laces of bright river. It's a warm day in June or July, a Friday – the day you heard they'd sold the paperback rights to The Old Golden Land.

Directly below, throwing a shadow like a giant sundial at three o'clock, is the Bottle Stone.

It's about five feet tall and four thousand years old. Nobody seems to know whether erosion or some damage long ago left it shaped like a beer-bottle, or whether it was always like that.

It seems now – looking down, looking back – to be as black as its shadow. But there's an amber haze – Memory may have created this, or maybe not – around the stone. Also around the people.

Six of them, mostly young, early twenties. They're sharing a very expensive picnic. You paid for it. You led them on a raid to this posh high-street deli, then the wine-shop. And then you all piled into a couple of cars – old Henry Kettle too, although he says he'd rather have a cheese sandwich than all these fancy bits and pieces – and you came out here because it was the nearest known ancient site, an obvious place to celebrate.

Memory hovers. It's trying to filter the conversation to find out who started it, who raised the question of the Bottle Stone Legend.

No good. The voices slip and fade like a radio between stations, and it's all too long ago. The first part you really remember is when Andy says . . . that there's a special chant, known to all the local children.

> *Johnny goes round the Bottle Stone,*
> *The Bottle Stone, the Bottle Stone,*
> *Johnny goes round the Bottle Stone,*
> *And he goes round ONCE.*

And the Big Mac went round and round the toilet bowl, and Joe Powys watched it and felt queasy.

He'd walked back to the Centre in a hurry and picked up the mail box. He hadn't looked at the mail, even though it seemed unusually profuse. Just ran into the shop and dumped it on the counter. Then he'd gone into the lavatory and thrown up.

The Big Mac had been everything they'd promised it would be. Well, big, anyway. Never having eaten – or even seen at close hand – a Big Mac before, he'd decided on impulse this morning that he should go out and grab one for breakfast. It would be one more meaningful gesture that said, Listen, I am an ordinary guy, OK?

Not a crank. Not a prophet. Not a hippy. No closer to the earth than any of you. See – I can actually eat bits of dead cow minced up and glued together.

But his stomach wasn't ready to process the message.

He washed his hands, stared gloomily at himself in the mirror. He actually looked quite cheerful, despite the prematurely grey hair. He had a vision of himself in this same mirror in ten years' time, when the grey would no longer be so premature. In fact, did it look so *obviously* premature now?

He flushed the lavatory again. Felt better. Went through to the kitchen and made himself a couple of slices of thick toast.

Fifteen minutes before he had to open the shop. He put the plate on the counter and ate, examining the mail.

There was a turquoise letter from America. It might have been his US agent announcing proposals for a new paperback reprint of *The Old Golden Land*.

It wasn't; maybe he was glad.

'Dear J.M.,' the letter began.

Laurel, from Connecticut, where she was newly married to this bloke who ran a chain of roadside wholefood diners. Laurel: his latest – and probably his last – earth-mysteries groupie, once lured spellbound to *The Old Golden Land*. Writing to ask for a copy of his latest book.

What latest book?

Then there was an unsolicited shrink-wrapped catalogue from a business-equipment firm. It dealt in computers, copiers, fax machines. The catalogue was addressed to

The Managing Director,
J. M. Powys Ltd.,
Watkins Street, Hereford.

In the head office of J. M. Powys Ltd., the managing director choked on a toast crumb. The head office was a three-room
flat in an eighteenth-century former-brewery, now shared by an
alternative health clinic and Trackways – the Alfred Watkins
Centre. The business equipment amounted to a twenty-five-
year-old Olivetti portable, with a backspace that didn't.

Powys didn't even open three catalogues from firms with
names like Crucible Crafts and Saturnalia Supplies, no doubt
offering special deals on bulk orders of joss-sticks, talismans,
tarot packs and cassette tapes of boring New Age music simulating the birth of the universe on two synthesizers and a drum
machine.

The New Age at the door again. Once, he'd had a letter
duplicated, a copy sent off to every loony New Age rip-off
supplier soliciting Trackways' patronage.

It said,

> This centre is dedicated to the memory and ideas of Alfred
> Watkins, of Hereford, who discovered the ley system –
> the way ancient people in Britain aligned their sacred
> places to fit into the landscape.

> Alfred Watkins was an archaeologist, antiquarian,
> photographer, inventor, miller and brewer. He doesn't
> appear, however, to have shown any marked interest in
> ritual magic, Zen, yoga, reincarnation, rebirthing, primal
> therapy, shiatsu or t'ai chi.

> So piss off.

He'd realized when he sent it that Alfred Watkins's work,
had he lived another fifty years, might have touched on several
of these subjects. Perhaps the old guy would have been at the
heart of the New Age movement and a member of the Green Party.
The recipients of the circular obviously realized this too and

113

kept on sending catalogues, knowing that sooner or later Joe Powys was going to give in and fill up Trackways with New Age giftware to join the solitary box of 'healing crystals' under the counter.

Because if he didn't, the way business was going, Trackways would be closing down within the year.

There were only two envelopes left now. One was made from what looked like high-quality vellum which he'd never have recognized as recycled paper if it hadn't said so on the back, prominently.

A single word was indented in the top left-hand corner of the envelope.

EPIDEMIC

Powys finished his toast, went to wash his hands, came back and turned the envelope over a couple of times before he opened it. It contained a letter which didn't mess around.

> Dear J. M. Powys,
> As you may have learned, Dolmen Books, publishers of The Old Golden Land, have now been acquired by the Epidemic Group.

Shit, Powys thought, I didn't know that.

> I am writing to you on behalf of the Group Chairman,

Max Goff, Powys thought, aghast. I've been acquired by Max bloody Goff.

> Mr Max Goff, who has long been an admirer of your work and would like to meet you to discuss a proposition.

. . . And from what I've heard of Max Goff's propositions to personable young blokes such as myself . . .

> We should therefore like to invite you to a small reception at the Cock Inn, Crybbe,

. . . I may have to invent a prior engagement . . .

*on Friday, 29 June at 12.30 p.m. I'm sorry it's such short
notice, but the acquisition of Dolmen was only confirmed this
week and I obtained your address only this morning.*
    Please contact me if you have any queries.
    Please contact me anyway.

      Yours sincerely,

      Rachel Wade,
      PA to Max Goff

Powys sat and looked around the shop for a while, thinking about this.

He could see on the shelves, among the dozens of earth-mysteries books by Alfred Watkins and his successors, the spine of the de-luxe hardback edition of *The Old Golden Land* and about half a dozen paperback copies, including the garish American edition with the Dayglo Stonehenge.

On the counter in front of Powys was a token display stand: dowsing rods and pendula. Mr Watkins might have been able to dowse, but he didn't have anything to say in his books about 'energy dowsing'. Or indeed about earth energies of any kind.

But all that was academic; the dowsing kits were selling well. Soon wouldn't be able to visit a stone circle without finding some studious duo slowly circumnavigating the site, dangling their pendulum and saying 'Wow' every so often.

Under the counter, because Powys hadn't had the nerve to put them on sale, was the box of 'healing' crystals which Annie – his new assistant with the Egyptian amulet – had persuaded him to buy. 'Got to embrace the New Age, Joe, and let the New Age embrace you. Mr Watkins wants you to let the New Age in, I can feel it. Sometimes I even think I can see him standing over there by the door. He's holding his hat and he's smiling.'

Wow!

Powys reached into the crystals box and helped himself to a handful of Sodalite (for emotional stability and the treatment of stress-related conditions).

Max Goff, he thought.
Max Goff!

Clutching the crystals, he discovered he was holding in his other hand a small, creased, white envelope, the last item of mail.

> Mr J. Powys,
> The Alfred Watkins Centre,
> Hereford.

Handwritten, not too steadily. Inside, a single sheet of lined blue notepaper.

> *Cwm Draenog,*
> *Titley,*
> *Kington*

Dear Mr Powys,
 If you have not already heard I am sorry to have to inform you of the death of my neighbour Mr H. Kettle.

What . . . ?

He was killed in a road accident in Crybbe where he was working and did not suffer.

Jesus Christ!

Mr Kettle left an envelope with me to be opened after his death in which he stated what he wanted to happen to his possessions as he did not trust solicitors. The house and all the contents is to be sold and the money sent to his daughter in Canada but he wants you to have his papers and his dowsing rods. If you would like to come to the house I am in most of the time and will let you into Mr Kettle's house.
> *Yours faithfully,*
> *Gwen Whitney (Mrs)*

J. M. Powys put down the letter. He ought to have opened the shop ten minutes ago.

The Sodalite crystals (emotional stability and the treatment of stress-related conditions) began to dribble through his fingers and roll across the wooden counter.

CHAPTER II

RACHEL noticed that Denzil George, licensee of the Cock, had several shaving cuts this morning. He'd obviously overslept, unused, no doubt, to rising early to prepare an 8 a.m. breakfast for his guests. What a torpid town this was.

'Parcel come for you,' the licensee said, placing a small package by Max's elbow.

'Thanks.' Max tossed it to Rachel.

'No stamp,' Rachel noticed. 'Obviously delivered by hand.'

'Better open it,' Max said, digging into some of the muesli he'd had delivered to the pub.

Rachel uncovered a tape cassette and a note. 'Who's Warren Preece?'

Max looked up.

'He's sent you a tape of his band.'

'Delivered by hand, huh?' Max put down his spoon thoughtfully. 'I dunno any Warren Preece, but the surname has a certain familiar ring. Maybe you should find out more, Rach.'

'Yes,' Rachel said, pushing back her chair. 'I'll ask the landlord.'

The Anglicans' *Book of Common Prayer* had nothing to say about exorcising spirits of the dead.

The Revd Murray Beech knew this and was grateful for it. But he was leafing through the prayer book anyway, seeking inspiration.

Murray was following the advice of Alex Peters and attempting to compile for himself a convincing prayer to deliver in an allegedly haunted house.

He came across the words,

'Peace be to this house and to all that dwell in it.'

This actually appeared under the order for The Visitation of the Sick, but Murray made a note of it anyway. Surely, with an alleged 'haunting' – Murray recoiled from the word in embarrassment – what you were supposedly dealing with was a sick property, contaminated by some form of so-called 'psychic' radiation, although, in *his* 'exorcism' – Oh, God – the prayers would be aimed at the troubled souls of the living. In his view, the health of a property could be affected only by the attitude and the state of mind of the current inhabitants, *not* by any residual guilt or distress from, ah, previous residents.

He looked around his own room. The neat bookshelves, the filing cabinets, the office desk with metal legs at which he sat, the clean, white walls – feeling a twinge of pain as he remembered the walls being painted by Kirsty exactly a fortnight before she'd said, 'I'm sorry, Murray. This isn't what I want.'

Murray looked quickly back at the prayer book, turned over a page, came upon the following entreaty:

'Oh Lord, look down from heaven, behold, visit and relieve this thy servant . . . defend him from the danger of the enemy.'

He breathed heavily down his nose. He abhorred words like 'enemy'. The duty of the Church was to teach not opposition, but understanding.

He was equally uncomfortable with the next and final part of the prayer book before the psalms began.

A COMMINATION
or
Denouncing of God's Anger and Judgements
against Sinners.

The first page ended on an uncompromising note.

'Cursed are the unmerciful, fornicators and adulterers,

covetous persons, idolaters, slanderers, drunkards and extortioners.'

'Not many of us left *un*cursed,' Murray muttered.

The curse of the modern minister's life, in his opinion, was the video-hire shop. Infinitely more alluring to teenagers than the church. And full of lurid epics in which members of the clergy in bloodied cassocks wielded metal crucifixes with which to combat scaly entities from Hell.

One result of this was that a few people seemed to think they should summon the vicar in the same way they'd call in Rentokil to deal with their dampness and their rats.

The telephone bleeped. 'I'll ring you when they're out,' she'd told him. He hadn't replied. At the time, he was considering going to her grandparents and explaining his dilemma. But he'd concluded this would not only be a cop-out, it would be wrong. Because she'd come to him in confidence and she was no longer a minor. She was eighteen and would be leaving school in two or three weeks.

Murray closed *The Book of Common Prayer* and picked up the phone. 'Vicarage.' '

'They're out,' Tessa said.

Barry, the overweight osteopath from upstairs, was between patients, eating a sandwich – herbal pâté on wholewheat.

'I've been taken over by Max Goff,' said Powys, disconsolate.

'Dolmen has, yeah, I read that. He can't do you any harm, though, can he? You're out of print, aren't you?'

'Between impressions,' Powys corrected him. 'Barry, are you really proposing to realign somebody's slipped disc with hands covered in soya margarine?'

'Beats olive oil. And cheaper. Hey, Mandy says she saw you coming out of McDonald's this morning.'

'Couldn't have been me.'

'That's what I thought,' Barry said dubiously.

'Anyway,' Powys said, 'Goff wants to see me. In Crybbe.'

'I thought you were going to say "in the nude" for a minute,' said Barry, wiping his hands on his smock. 'No, from what I hear he's surrounding himself with people sharing his own deep commitment to the New Age movement. If it's this lunch in Crybbe on Friday, several people I know have been invited and nobody's turning him down, because if he likes you, he invites you to join his Crybbe community, which means – listen to this – that you get offered a place to live, on very advantageous terms. And all kinds of fringe benefits.'

'Why aren't you there, then?'

'Bastard's already got an osteopath,' Barry said. 'Gerry Moffat. You believe that? He could have had me, but he went for Moffat. Moffat!'

'Who else?'

'Dan Osborne, the homeopath, he's moved in already. Superior bastard. Paula Stirling. Robin Holland. Oh, and that little French aromatherapist who was in Bromyard, remember her?'

'I can still smell her. Listen, do these people know what Max Goff *is*?'

'Used to be, Joe. Used to be. This is the new user-friendly, ozone-fresh Max Goff. Play your cards right and he'll let you feel his aura.'

'I wouldn't feel his aura with asbestos gloves,' said Powys.

'And he's got some pretty heavy mystical types as well,' said Barry. 'Jean Wendle, the spiritual healer, some guy who's reckoned to be Britain's biggest tarot hotshot and Andy Boulton-Trow. All converging on the New Age Mecca.'

'Andy?' Powys said. 'Andy's involved in this?'

'And there's a single kid,' says Andy, 'moving round the stone, very slowly at first, while all the other kids are sitting in a circle, clapping their hands, doing the chant. And by the time they finish the chant, he's back where he started. Got to be a "he", it doesn't work for girls.'

Andy Boulton-Trow, lean and languid, lying back in the grass, spearing a quail's egg from the jar beside him. His voice is deep and lazy, like a stroked cello.

'*And then he goes round again . . . only this time it's just ever-so-slightly faster . . .*'

> *Johnny goes round the Bottle Stone*
> *. . . and he goes round TWICE.*

'*And they keep on repeating it. And it gets faster and faster, building up the momentum, and the kid's got to move faster each time to maintain the pace.*'

> *Johnny goes round the Bottle Stone*
> *. . . and he goes round THRICE.*

> *. . . goes round FOUR times.*

> *. . . FIVE times.*

'*And how long do they keep it up?*' *Rose asks. She's looking radiantly happy today (this memory is agony).* '*How many times . . . ?*'

'*Oh.*' *There's a gleam in Andy's eye.* '*Thirteen. Thirteen times.*'

'*Must be jolly dizzy by then,*' *one of the others says – Ben Corby's girlfriend, Fiona Something.*

'*Ex-act-ly,*' *Andy drags out the word for emphasis.* '*The kid's completely confused. He's not thinking properly. And it's then that his mates all leap on him and, before he knows what's happening, they hustle him across to the fairy hill. Over there . . . see it?*'

'*Not much of a hill,*' *Rose observes.*

'*Fairies are not very big,*' *you tell her.* '*You could fit a couple of dozen on there.*'

Andy says, '*So they lie him face-down on the fairy hill . . . and that's when it happens . . .*'

'*What?*' *you ask.* '*What happens?*'

'*Whatever happens,*' *says Henry Kettle, searching in the cardboard picnic box for something uncomplicated and British,* '*it's all in the mind, and it don't do anybody any good, meddling with that old nonsense.*'

'Oh yeah,' Barry, the osteopath, said. 'Andy's right at the centre of things. As was old Henry Kettle. I suppose you heard about that.'

'Just now,' Powys said. He hadn't planned to mention Henry. 'I had a letter from his neighbour to say he was dead. I don't know what happened, do you?'

'Have to wait for the *Hereford Times* for the full story, but apparently it said on the local radio that his car went off the road and ploughed into a wall around Crybbe Tump. I don't know that area too well, but . . .'

'Crybbe Tump? He hit the wall around Crybbe Tump?'

'Killed instantly. Bloody shame, I liked old Henry. He helped you with the book, didn't he?'

Powys nodded.

'The buzz is,' said Barry, 'that Henry was doing some dowsing for Max Goff.'

'Dowsing what?'

Barry shrugged. 'Whatever he'd been doing, he was on his way home when it happened. There was a power cut at the time, don't know whether the streetlamps were off, that may have thrown him. Bloody shame.'

'A power cut,' said Powys.

'That significant?'

'Just a thought.' Powys shook his head, his mind whizzing off at a peculiar tangent, like a faulty firework.

CHAPTER III

FAY awoke late. She'd lain awake until dawn, eyes open to the bedroom ceiling, Arnold a lump of solid heat alongside her on the bed.

It was nearly nine before she came downstairs. Outside it was raining. The rain on the window was the only sound. There was no mail on the mat, no sign of the Canon.

The door to the office was closed, as she'd left it last night. The note to her father still pinned to it. *And don't let any CATS in there!*

122

Rasputin.

He must still be in the office.

She opened the door but did not go in.

'Rasputin,' she called. A morning croak in her voice – that was all it was. Really.

But she could not bring herself to go back into that room, not yet, though Arnold didn't seem worried. She left the door ajar, went through to the kitchen, let the dog out in the back garden.

When she turned back to the kitchen, Rasputin and Pushkin were both in the opposite corner, waiting by their bowls. Fay opened a can of Felix. The two cats looked plump and harmless. Perhaps it really *had* been just a horrific dream, conditioned by her own desperation.

She forked out a heap of cat food, straightened up.

'Right,' she said decisively and marched out of the kitchen and into the hall, where she tore the note off the office door and hit the door with the flat of her hand so that it was thrown wide.

She walked in, eyes sweeping the room like searchlights. She saw the Revox, two spools leaning against it. Her desk-diary open. Her father's note, about Guy's phone call. She raised her eyes to the H-shaped fireplace and the mantelpiece, to the see-through clock with the mechanism like a pair of balls still jerking obscenely from side to side.

The fireside chair was empty, its scatter cushions plumped out. If someone had been sitting in it the cushions would have been flattened.

Unless, of course, that person had tidily shaken them out and . . .

Oh, come on!

She made herself cross to the mirror and look into it at her own face.

The first shock was the incredible childlike fear she saw in her eyes.

The second was the other face. She whirled around in alarm.

The Canon was standing in the doorway. He wore pyjamas. His feet were bare. His hair was standing up in spikes, his beard sprayed out in all directions, like a snowstorm. His bewildered blue eyes were wide and unfocused.

He stared at Fay as if she were an intruder. Then the eyes relaxed into recognition.

'Morning, Grace,' he said.

While Max drove, Rachel took the cassette box from her shoulder bag.

'OK?'

'Go ahead,' Max said.

Rachel slipped the tape into the player and studied the plastic box. The band's name was typed in capitals across the plain label: FATAL ACCIDENT. She wrinkled her nose.

Drums and bass guitar blundered out of the speakers. Rachel lowered the volume a little. By the time the first track was over, they were parked at the back of the Court, next to the stable-block, where builders were busy.

Rain slashed the windscreen.

Max turned up the sound to compensate. He was smiling faintly. They sat in the Range Rover for two more tracks. The only words Rachel could make out on the last one were 'goin' down on me', repeated what seemed like a few dozen times. She consulted the inside of the label; the song was called 'Goin' Down on Me'.

'That's the lot,' she said neutrally. 'There're only three numbers.' Remembering where the Max Goff Story had begun, in the punk-rock era of the mid-seventies, she didn't add 'thankfully'.

Max began to laugh.

Rachel ejected the tape, saying nothing.

'Jeez,' Max said. 'Was that shit, or was that shit?'

Rachel breathed out. For a couple of minutes there, watching him smiling, she'd thought he might actually be enjoying it.

'You want me to post it down to Tommy, get him to send it back in a fortnight with the customary slip?'

'What . . . ?' Max twisted to face her. 'You want us to give the official piss-off to Mayor Preece's flaming grandson?'

124

'But if you tell him it's good you'll have to do something with it, won't you?'

Max shrugged. 'So be it. One single . . . not on Epidemic, of course. Coupla grand written off against tax . . .'

Then he thumped the top of the dashboard. 'No, hey, listen, I'll tell you what we do – you send this kid a letter saying we think the band has promise, we think it's a . . . an interesting sound, right? But we're not sure any of these three tracks is quite strong enough to release as a début single, so can we hear a few more? That'll buy some time – maybe the band'll split before they can get the material together. How's that sound to you?'

'It sounds devious,' Rachel said.

'Of course it does, Rach. Do it tonight. I mean, shit, don't get me wrong – they're no worse than say, The Damned, in '77. But it was fresh then, iconoclastic.'

'It was shit then, too.'

'Yeah, maybe,' Max conceded. 'But it was necessary. It blew away the sterile pretensions from when the seventies went bad. But now we're picking up from the sixties and we won't make the same mistakes.'

'No,' Rachel said, in neutral again.

A heavy tipper-lorry crunched in beside them. The rain had washed a layer of thick, grey dust from the door of the cab and Rachel could make out the words '. . . aendy Quarry, New Radnor.'

'Hey . . .' Max said slowly. 'If this is what I think it is . . .' He threw his door open, stepped down into the rain in his white suit and was back inside a minute, excited, raindrops twinkling in his beard.

'It *is*, Rach. The first stones have arrived. The Old Stones of Crybbe, Mark Two.'

'Oh,' said Rachel, pulling up the collar of her Barbour for the run to the stables. 'Good.'

But Goff, Panama hat jammed over his ears, made her watch while the stones were unloaded, pointing out things.

'Different sizes, right? Even where they'd vanished entirely, Kettle was able to figure out how tall they'd been.'

'Using his pendulum, I suppose.'

'Of course, what we're seeing here gives an exaggerated idea of what they'll look like *in situ*. Half of the length'll be under the soil. Maybe more than half. Like giant acupuncture needles in the earth.'

'Who's going to advise you about these things now Mr Kettle's dead?' Rachel wondered, as men in donkey jackets and orange slickers moved around, making preparations to get the grey and glistening monoliths down from the truck. One stone had to be at least fifteen feet long.

'And how do you know it's the right kind of stone?' Things were moving too fast for Rachel now. Max was an awesome phenomenon when he had the hots for something.

'Yeah, well, obviously, Kettle was good – and he knew the terrain. But Andy Boulton-Trow's been studying standing stones for nearly twenty years. Been working with a geologist these past few weeks, matching samples. They checked out maybe a dozen quarries before he was satisfied, and if he's satisfied, I'm satisfied.'

A clang came from the back of the truck, a gasp of hydraulics, somebody swore. Max called out sharply, 'Hey, listen, be careful, yeah? I want you guys to handle those stones like you're dealing with radioactive flaming isotopes.'

He said to Rachel, 'Andy's moving up here, end of the week. He's gonna supervise planting stones on our land. Then we'll bring the farmers up here, show 'em what it looks like and go into negotiations. Hey, you had a call from J. M. Powys yet?'

'He'll only have got my letter this morning, Max.'

'Give him until lunchtime then call him. I want Powys. I don't care what he costs.'

The customer was short and fat and bald. He wore denims, a shaggy beard and an ear-ring.

'You're J. M. Powys, right?'

Teacher, Powys thought. Or maybe the maverick in some local government planning department.

'You are, man. Don't deny it. I recognize you from the picture on the cover. You've gone grey, that's all.'

Powys spread his arms submissively.

'Hey listen, man, that was a hell of a book, *The Old Golden Land*.'

'Thanks,' Powys said.

'So what are you doing here, running a shop? Why aren't you writing more? Got to be ten years since *Golden Land*.'

'Even longer,' Powys said. 'More like twelve.'

You could count on at least one of these a week, more in summer. Sometimes they were women. Sometimes, in the early days of the Watkins Centre, friendships had developed from such encounters. *The Old Golden Land* had hit the market at the right time, the time of the great mass exodus from the cities, couples in their thirties in search of meaning and purpose.

People were very kind when they found out who he was. Usually they bought something from the shop, often a paperback of the book for him to sign. Most times he felt guilty. Guilty that he hadn't followed through; guilty that he'd written the thing in the first place and misled everybody.

'I did that one that takes a new look at Watkins's original leys,' he offered, a bit pathetically. *'Backtrack.'*

The bald, bearded guy waved it away. 'Disappointing, if you don't mind me saying so, J. M. No magic.'

'Wasn't really meant to be magical,' Powys said. 'The idea was just to walk the leys and see if they were as obvious now as when Watkins discovered them.'

'Yeah, and you found some of them to be distinctly dodgy. That's not what we want, is it?'

Powys laughed.

'Well, it's not, is it? People pouring scorn on the whole idea, your archaeologists and so on, and here's J. M. Powys defecting to the Establishment viewpoint.'

'Not exactly. What I feel is, we might have been a bit premature in explaining them as marking out channels of earth energy. Why not – because they connect so many burial mounds and funerary sites, even churchyards – why not simply paths of the dead . . . ?'

The customer stepped back from the dowsing display he'd been fingering. He looked shocked.

'Paths of the dead?' he said. 'Paths of the dead? What kind of negative stuff is that?'

Halfway through the door, he turned round. 'You *sure* you're J. M. Powys?'

'Fay?'

'Oh. Hullo, Guy.'

'You didn't return my call.'

'No, I didn't, did I? Well, Dad's having one of his difficult days.'

'He sounded fine last night.'

'Well, he isn't now,' Fay said testily. Maybe he thought she was making it all up about the Canon going batty. Maybe she ought to produce medical evidence.

'No. I'm sorry. It must be difficult for you.'

Oh, please, not the sympathy. 'What do you want, Guy?'

'I want to help you, Fay.'

No comment.

'I'd like to put some money in your purse.'

Fay began to smoulder. Purses were carried by little women.

'As you may know, I'm currently on attachment to BBC Wales as senior producer, features and docos.'

Guy had been an on-the-road TV reporter when she'd first known him. Then a regional anchorman. And then, when he'd realized there'd be rather less security in on-screen situations after he passed forty or so, he'd switched to the production side. Much safer; lots of corners to hide in at cut-back time.

'And I've got quite a nice little project on the go on your patch,' Guy said. 'Two fifty minute-ers for the Network.'

'Congratulations.' But suddenly Fay was thinking hard. It couldn't be . . .

Guy said, 'Max Goff? You know what Max Goff's setting up?'

Shit!

'He's developing a conscience in his middle years and putting millions into New Age research. Anyway, he's bought this wonderful Elizabethan pile not far from you, which he plans to restore.'

'And where did you hear about this, Guy?'

'Oh . . . contacts. As I say, we'll be doing two programmes. One showing how he goes about . . . what he's going to do. How the locals feel about him, this sort of thing. And the second one, a few months later, examining what he's achieved. Or not, as the case may be. Good, hmm?'

'Fascinating.' The *bastard*. How the hell had he pulled it off? 'And you've got it to yourself, have you?'

'Absolutely. It means Goff will have this one reliable outlet to get his ideas across in an intelligent way.'

Fay seethed.

No Radio Four documentary. Not even any exclusive insider stuff for Offa's Dyke. So much for Rachel Wade and her promises. All the time, they'd been negotiating with her ex-husband – obviously aware of the connection, keeping quiet, leading her along so she wouldn't blow the story too soon.

'So what I was thinking, Fay, is . . . Clearly we're not going to be around the whole time. We need somebody to keep an eye on developments locally and let us know if there's anything we should be looking at. I was thinking perhaps a little retainer for you – I can work it through the budget, we producers have full financial control now of a production, which means . . .'

Black mist came down. The smug, scheming, patronizing *bastard*.

When Fay started listening again, Guy was saying, '. . . would have offered you the official researcher's contract, but one of Max Goff's conditions is that we use the author of some trashy book which seems to have inspired him. Goff wants this chap to be the official chronicler of the Crybbe project and some sort of editorial adviser on the programmes. Of course, that's just a formality, I can soon lose him along the way . . .'

Fay put the phone down.

Screwed again.

The clock ticked. Arnold lay by her feet under the table. The chair where, in her mind, the smug, spectral Grace Legge had sat, was now piled high with box files. Nothing could sit in it now, even in her imagination.

Fay picked up the phone again and – deliberate, cold,

precise – punched out the number of the Offa's Dyke Radio news desk.

'Gavin Ashpole, please. Oh, it *is* you. It's Fay Morrison. Listen. I can put you down a voice-piece for the lunchtime news. Explaining exactly what Max Goff intends to do in Crybbe.'

She listened to Ashpole asking all the obvious questions.

'Oh yes,' she said. '*Impeccable* sources.'

Fay put down the phone, picked up the pad and began to write.

CHAPTER IV

THE police station was at the southern end of the town centre, just before the road sloped down to the three-arched river bridge. Attached to the station was the old police house. Murray Beech strode boldly to the front door and rapped loudly with the knocker, standing back and looking around for someone he might say hello to.

He very much wanted to be seen. Did not want anyone to think there was anything remotely surreptitious about this visit. Indeed, he'd been hoping Police Sergeant Wynford Wiley would be visible through the police-station window so he could wave to him. But he was not. Nobody was there.

As a last resort Murray had been round to Alex Peters's house, hoping to persuade the old man to come with him as adviser, witness and . . . well, chaperone. There'd been no sign of Alex or his daughter, no answer to his knocks.

But Murray didn't have to knock twice on the door of the old police house. She must have been waiting behind it.

'Good afternoon, Tessa,' he said loudly, putting on his most clergymanly voice.

Tessa Byford looked at him in silence. Eighteen. Dark-haired, dark-eyed, pale-faced. Often seen leather-jacketed on street corners with the likes of Warren Preece.

But not an unintelligent girl. A talented artist, he'd heard.

And more confident than most local girls. Born here, but brought up in Liverpool until her mother died and her father dumped her on his parents in Crybbe so he could go back to sea.

Murray could understand why she'd never forgiven her father for this.

He thought: sullen, resentful and eighteen. Prime poltergeist fodder . . . if you accept the tenets of parapsychology.

About which Murray, of course, kept an open mind.

He smiled. 'Well,' he said, 'I'm here.'

Tessa Byford did not smile back. Without a word, she led him into a small, dark sitting-room, entirely dominated by an oppressive Victorian sideboard, ornate as a pulpit, with many stages, canopies and overhangs.

Murray felt it was dominating him, too. He was immediately uncomfortable. The room seemed overcrowded, with the sideboard and the two of them standing there awkwardly, an unmarried clergyman and a teenage girl. It hit him then, the folly of what he was doing. He should never have come.

She looked down over his dark suit.

'You've not brought any holy water, have you?'

Murray managed a weak smile. 'Let's see how we get on, shall we?'

It occurred to him that, while she might be an adult now, this was not actually her house. He'd allowed himself to be lured into somebody else's house.

'You should've brought holy water,' she said sulkily.

Murray tried to relax. His plan was merely to talk to the girl, say a helpful prayer and then leave. He found a straight-backed dining chair and sat on it squarely – always felt foolish sinking into someone's soft fireside furniture, felt it diminished him.

'I still wish your grandparents were here.'

'Gone shopping,' she said, still standing. 'In Hereford. Won't be back until tonight. I only stayed to wait for you. I was going to give you another five minutes. Wouldn't stay here on me own. Not any more.'

Why did he think she was lying?

'I wish you'd felt able to discuss this with them.'

She shook her head firmly. 'Can't. You just can't.' Her thin lips went tight, her deep-set eyes stoney with the certainty of it.

'Have you tried?'

Tessa's lips twisted. 'Me gran . . . says people who are daft enough to think they've seen a ghost ought to keep it to themselves.'

'So you *have* tried to talk to her about it.'

Tessa, grimacing, went through the motions of wiping something nasty off her hands.

Murray tried to understand but couldn't. Neither Mrs Byford nor her husband appeared to him to be particularly religious. They came to church, if not every week. He'd watched them praying, as he did all his parishioners from time to time, but detected no great piety there. Just going through the motions, lip movements, like the rest of them. A ritual as meaningless as Sunday lunch, and rather less palatable.

There was no Bible on the shelf, no books of any kind, just white china above a small television set. No pictures of Christ on the wall, no framed religious texts.

And yet the room itself stank of repression, as if the people who lived here were the narrowest type of religious fundamentalists.

Tessa was standing there expressionless, watching him. The next move was his. Because he was trying so hard not to be, he was painfully aware of her breasts under what, in his own teenage days, had been known as a tank top.

'I know what you're thinking,' she said, and Murray sucked in a sharp breath.

'But I'm not,' she said. 'I'm not imagining any of it. You don't imagine things being thrown at you in the bathroom, even if . . .'

Her lips clamped and she looked down at her feet.

'If what?' Murray said.

'Show you,' Tessa mumbled.

Murray felt sweat under his white clerical collar. He stood up, feeling suddenly out of his depth, and followed Tessa Byford into the hall and up the narrow stairs.

*

'All right, Fay?'

'I don't know.'

She was going hot and cold. Maybe succumbing to one of those awful summer bugs.

All she needed.

'Give me a minute . . . Elton. I want to make a few adjustments to the script.'

'OK, no hurry. I've got a couple of pieces to top and tail. Come back to you in five minutes, OK?'

'Fine,' Fay said, 'fine.'

She took off the cans and leaned back in the studio chair, breathing in and out a couple of times. Outside it was still raining and not exactly warm; in here, she felt clammy, sticky. She pulled her T-shirt out of her jeans and flapped it about a bit.

The air in here was always stale. There should be air-conditioning. The Crybbe Unattended itself was probably a serious infringement of the Factories Act or whatever it was called these days.

And the walls of the studio seemed to be closer every time she came in.

That was psychological, of course. Hallucinatory, just like . . . She slammed a door in her mind on the icy Grace Legge smile, just as she'd slammed the office door last night before stumbling upstairs after the dog. She wondered how she was ever going to go into that room again after dark. She certainly wouldn't leave the dog in there again at night.

How primitive life had become.

'Fay!' A tinny voice rattling in the cans on the table. She put them on.

Ashpole.

'Fay, tell me again what he's doing . . .'

'Goff?'

She told him again about the New Age research centre, about the dowsers and the healers. She didn't mention the plan to reinstate the stones. She was going to hold that back – another day, another dollar.

'No rock stars, then.'

133

'What?'

'All a bit of a disappointment, isn't it, really,' Ashpole said.

'Is it?' Fay was gripping the edge of the table. Just let him start . . .

'Nutty stuff. New Age. Old hippies. Big yawn. Some people'll be interested, I suppose. When can we talk to the great man in person?'

'Goff? I'm working on it.'

That was a laugh. Some chance now. *I'll ask my ex-husband, he owns all the broadcasting rights.* God, God, God!

'Hmm,' Ashpole said, 'maybe we should . . .'

Without even a warning tremor, Fay erupted. 'Oh sure! Send a *real* reporter down to doorstep him! Why don't you do that? Get him to claim on tape that he's the son of God and he's going to save the fucking world!'

She tore off the cans and hurled them at the wall, stood up so violently she knocked the chair over. Stood with her back to the wall, panting, tears of outrage bubbling up.

What was happening to her?

'See that mirror?'

She was pointing at a cracked circular shaving mirror in a metal frame.

'It flew off the window-ledge,' Tessa Byford said. 'That's how it got the crack. 'Course, they accused me of knocking it off.'

'How can you be sure you didn't?'

It was a very cramped bathroom. Murray moved up against the lavatory trying not to brush against the girl.

Ludicrous. He felt completely and utterly ludicrous; he was suffocating with embarrassment.

'Look,' she said, oblivious of his agony, 'I just opened the door and it flew off at me. And other things. Shaving brush, toothpaste. But it was the mirror that started it. I had to look in the mirror.'

'It could have been a draught, Tessa.' Appalled at how strangled his voice sounded.

'It wasn't a bloody draught!'

'All right, calm down. Please.'

'And when I picked it up, the mirror, there was blood in the crack.'

'Your blood?'

'No!'

'Whose, then?'

'The old man's.'

'Your grandfather?'

'No, the old man! He used to live here. I saw him. I could see him in the mirror.'

'You're saying he's dead, this old man?'

'What do *you* think?' Tessa said, losing patience with him. Tension rising. The girl was disturbed. This was not what the Church should be doing. This was psychiatric country.

'And you think you saw his face in the mirror.'

'And other mirrors.' She sighed. 'Always in mirrors.'

'Tessa, listen to me. When you first told me all about this you said you thought it was a poltergeist and you thought it was happening because you were at that age when . . . when . . . But you're eighteen. You're not an adolescent any more.'

'No.'

He saw something moving in her dark eyes, and there was a little dab of perspiration above her top lip. Murray began to feel soiled and sordid. She said softly – and almost euphorically, he thought later – 'His throat was cut. When I saw him in the mirror, he'd cut his throat. Put his razor through the artery. That was where the blood . . .'

Murray swallowed. There was an overpowering smell of bleach.

'Would you mind,' he said, 'if we went back downstairs?'

When the studio phone rang it was Gavin Ashpole being soft-spoken and understanding. They all knew these days that if a woman flared up uncharacteristically it had to be a spot of premenstrual tension. Tact and consideration called for.

'So, when you're ready, love,' Ashpole said amiably, 'just give us the fifty-second voice-piece. And then you can play it by ear with Goff. I mean, don't *worry* about it – long as nobody gets him first, I'll be happy. Must go, the other phone, thanks, Fay.'

She shouldn't have exploded like that. Most unprofessional. Fay put on the cans, adjusted the mike on its stand.

'Ow!'

Bloody thing was hot.

Surely that wasn't possible with a microphone, even if there was an electrical fault. She didn't touch it again but looked round the back, following the flex to where it plugged into the console. Nothing amiss.

There was nothing to come unscrewed on this mike. It was a standard American-made Electro Voice, about six and a half inches long, gunmetal grey with a bulb bit enlarging the end, like . . .

Well, like a penis, actually.

Fay put out a finger, touched the tip, giggled.

Sex-starved cow. Pull yourself together.

'You ready now, Fay?'

'Oh yes, I'm ready, Elton. I really am.'

'Bit for level, then . . .'

She picked up the script, which would take up the story from the newsreader's link.

'It's widely known,' Fay enunciated clearly into the microphone, 'that Max Goff has been involved in setting up a charitable trust to . . .'

'Yeah, fine. Go in five.'

Fay composed herself. Not easy in this heat. The T-shirt was sticking to her again. Have to put in a complaint. Four, three, two . . .

'It's widely known that Max Goff has been involved in setting up a charitable trust to finance so-called "New Age" ventures – such as alternative healing techniques and the promotion of "Green" awareness.

'He's also interested in fringe science and the investigation of ley-lines, which are supposed to link standing stones, Bronze

Age burial mounds and other ancient sites across the landscape . . .'

Most times, when you were putting in a voice-piece – especially if, like this, it wasn't live – you weren't really aware of the sense of it any more. Only the pattern of the words, the balance, the cadence and the flow. It was conversational and yet completely artificial. Automatic-pilot stuff after a while. Easy to see how some radio continuity announcers simply fell in love with their own voices.

'The project will be based at sixteenth-century Crybbe Court, for which Mr Goff is believed to have paid in excess of half a million pounds.

'It's expected to be a major boost to the local economy, with . . .'

'Whoah, whoah,' Elton shouted in the cans. 'What are you doing, Fay?'

'What?'

'You're distorting.'

'Huh?'

'How close are you to the mike?'

'I . . .'

Fay tasted metal.

'Oh . . . !'

Her eyes widened, a movement went through her, like an earth tremor along a fault line. Her hands thrust the microphone away, revolted.

The mike fell out of its stand and over the end of the table where it dangled on its flex. Fay sat there wiping the back of a hand over her lips.

'What the hell . . . ?' said the voice in the cans. 'Fay? Fay, are you there?'

'Oh Lord, we humbly beseech you, look down upon us with compassion . . .'

Eyes tensely closed, Murray was trying to concentrate. He could still smell bleach from the bathroom, although they were downstairs again now, in the sitting-room that was full of repressed emotions, deep-frozen. In the shadow of the vast pulpit-sideboard.

Churchlike. More churchlike, anyway, than a bathroom.

But the Church was not a building. *He*, in this dark little parlour, at this moment, was the Church.

(Two feet away . . . an eighteen-year-old girl in holed jeans and a straining tank top. A girl he didn't think he liked very much any more. A girl with a glistening dab of sweat over her upper lip.)

And, because there was nothing to help him in *The Book of Common Prayer*, he must improvise.

'. . . look down with compassion, Lord, on our foolish fancies and fantasies. Lift from this house the burden of primitive superstition. Hold up your holy light and guide us away from the darkened recesses of our unconscious minds . . .'

His voice came back at him in a way he'd never experienced before in prayer. Not like in church, the words spinning away, over the congregation and up into the rafters. Or muted, behind bedside screens, against the chatter and rattle and bustle of a hospital ward.

Here, in a room too crowded with still, silent things for an echo, it all sounded as slick and as shallow as he rather suspected it was. He was stricken with isolation – feeling exposed and raw, as if his veneer of priestly strength was bubbling and melting like thin paint under a blowlamp.

Murray ran a damp finger around the inside of his clerical collar. He realized in horror that the only ghost under exorcism in this house was his own undefined, amorphous faith.

As if something was stealing that faith, feeding from it.

His collar felt like a shackle; he wanted to tear it off.

He knew he had to get out of here. Knowing this, while hearing his voice, intoning the meaningless litany.

'Bring us, Lord, safely from the captivity of our bodies and the more insidious snare of our baser thoughts. Lead us . . .'

Her voice sliced through his.

'I think it likes you, Vicar,' Tessa said sweetly.

His eyes opened to a white glare. The girl was holding the cracked shaving mirror at waist-level, like a spotlamp, and when she tilted the mirror, he saw in it the quivering, flickering image of a cowering man in a dark suit and a clerical collar – the man gazing down at his hands, clasping his rearing penis in helpless remorse, in a tortured parody of prayer.

Murray screamed and fled.

A few moments later, when he tumbled half-sobbing, half-retching into the street, he could hear her laughter. He stood with his back to a lamppost, sob-breathing through his mouth. He looked down and felt his fly; the zip was fully fastened.

He felt violated. Physically and spiritually naked and shamed.

A door slammed behind him, and he *still* thought he could hear her laughing. At intervals. As if whatever had got into her was sharing the fun.

CHAPTER V

'THE bitch doesn't get in here again. Not ever. Under any circumstances. You understand?'

Max was pulsing with rage. Rachel had seen it before, but not often.

Offa's Dyke Radio had run the item on its lunchtime bulletin – from which, Rachel had been told, the story had been picked up by a local freelance hack and relayed to the London papers. Several of which had now called Epidemic's press office to check it out.

And Goff's secretary in London had phoned Goff in time for him to catch the offending Offa's Dyke item on the five o'clock news.

'That report . . . from Fay Morrison, our reporter in Crybbe,' the newsreader had said unnecessarily at the end.

'Fay Morrison? Guy Morrison?' Goff said.

Rachel shook her head. 'Hardly likely.'

'Yeah,' Goff accepted. And then he spelled it out for her

139

again, just in case she hadn't absorbed his subtext. When he wanted the world to know about something, he released the information in his own good time. *He* released it.

'So from now on, you don't talk to *anybody*. You don't even *think* about the Project in public, you got that?'

'Maybe,' Rachel said, offhand, tempting fate, 'you should fire me.'

'Don't be fucking ridiculous,' Max snapped and stormed out of the stable-block to collect his bags from the Cock. He was driving back to London tonight, thank God, and wouldn't be returning until Friday morning, for the lunch party.

When she could no longer hear the Ferrari arrogantly clearing its throat for the open road, Rachel Wade rang Fay, feeling more than a little aggrieved.

They shouted at each other for several minutes before Rachel made a sudden connection and said slowly, 'You mean Guy Morrison is your *ex-husband*?'

'He didn't tell you? Well, of course, he wouldn't. Where's the kudos in having been married to me?'

Rachel said, thoughtlessly, 'He's really quite a hunk, isn't he?'

A small silence, then Fay said, 'Hunk of shit, actually.'

'Max was right,' Rachel said. 'You're being a bitch. You did the radio piece as a small act of vengeance because your ex had pushed your nose out.'

'Now look . . .'

'No, *you* look. Guy's programmes wouldn't have affected anything. You'd still have had the stories for Offa's Dyke Radio, *and* you'd have had them first. I do actually keep my promises.'

Fay sighed and told her that the truth was she was hoping to do a full programme. For Radio Four. However, with a TV documentary scheduled, that now looked like a non-starter.

'So I was cutting my losses, I suppose. I really didn't think it'd come back on you. Well . . . I suppose I didn't really think at all. I over-reacted. Keep over-reacting these days, I'm afraid. I'm sorry.'

'I'm sorry, too,' Rachel said, 'but I have to tell you you've burned your boats. Max has decreed that you should be banned from his estate for ever.'

'I see.'

'I can try and explain, but he isn't known for changing his mind about this kind of thing. Why should he? He *is* the deity in these parts.'

In the photograph over the counter, Alfred Watkins wore pince-nez and looked solemn. If there were any pictures of him smiling, Powys thought, they must be filed away in some family album; smiling was not a public act in those days for a leading local businessman and a magistrate. It was perhaps just as well – Alfred Watkins needed his dignity today more than ever.

'Don't forget,' Powys said, 'he'll be watching you. Any joss-sticks get lit, he'll be very unhappy.'

'No he won't,' Annie said. Annie with the Egyptian amulet, still living in 1971, before the husband and the four kids. 'He fancies me, I can tell by the way he smiles.'

'He never smiles.'

'He smiles at *me*,' Annie said. 'OK, no joss-sticks. If you're not back by tomorrow I'll open at nine, after I get rid of the kids.'

'I'm only going to Kington.'

'You're going back to the Old Golden Land,' Annie said, half-smiling. He'd shown her the letter from Henry's neighbour, Mrs Whitney. 'Admit it, you're going back.'

'What happens?' Andy says. 'Well, you go around the stone thirteen times and then you lie on the fairy hill and you get the vision. You see into the future, or maybe just into yourself. According to the legend, John Bottle went round the stone and when he lay on the mound he went down and down until he entered the great hall of the Fairy Queen with whom he naturally fell in love. It was so wonderful down there that he didn't want to leave. But they sent him back, and when he returned to the real world he became a great seer and prophet.

'Of course . . .' – Andy ate a black olive – '. . . he could never settle in the mundane world, and he knew that one day he'd have to go back . . .'

★

Powys drove his nine-year-old Mini out of the city, turning off before the Wye bridge.

In essence, Alfred Watkins had been right about the existence of leys. Powys felt this strongly. And Henry Kettle had been better than anybody at finding where the old tracks ran, by means of dowsing.

'After all these years,' he'd said once to Powys, 'I still don't know what they are. But I know they're there. And I know that sometimes, when you're standing on one, it can affect you. Affect your balance, like. Give you delusions sometimes, like as if you've had a few too many. Nothing *psychic*, mind, nothing like that. But they do *interfere* with you. Sometimes.'

They might interfere with you when you were walking along them, with or without your dowsing rods. Or when you were driving along a stretch of road which happened – as many did – to follow one of the old lines. Many accident blackspots had been found to be places where leys crossed.

Coincidence.

Of course. And you could go crazy avoiding stretches of road just because they happened to align with local churches and standing stones. Nobody really went that far.

Certainly not Henry. Who, you would have thought, was too experienced a dowser ever to be caught out that way.

But when an experienced dowser crashed into a wall around an ancient burial mound, it demanded the kind of investigation the police would never conduct.

He didn't expect to find anything. But Henry Kettle was his friend. He was touched and grateful that Henry had bequeathed to him his papers – perhaps the famous journal that nobody had ever seen. And the rods, of course, don't forget the rods. (Why should he leave his rods to a man who couldn't dowse?)

Powys left Hereford by King's Acre and headed towards the Welsh border, where the sun hung low in the sky. During his lunchbreak, he'd spent half an hour with the OS maps of Hereford and eastern Radnorshire. He'd drawn a circle around the blob on the edge of the town of Crybbe where it said:

The Tump
(mound)

He'd taken a twelve-inch Perspex ruler and put one end over the circle and then, holding the end down with one finger, moved the ruler in an arc, making little pencil marks as he went along, whenever he came upon an ancient site. When the ruler had covered three hundred and sixty degrees he took it away and examined all the marks, haphazard as circles and crosses on a football-pool coupon.

And stared into the map like a fortune-teller into a crystal ball or the bottom of a teacup. Waiting for a meaningful image or a pattern to form among the mesh of roads and paths and contour lines . . . mound, circle, stone, church, earthwork, moat, holy well . . .

But from a ley-hunter's point of view, it was all very disappointing.

There was a large number of old stones and mounds all along the Welsh border, but the Tump didn't seem to align with any of them. The nearest possible ancient site was Crybbe parish church, less than a mile away. He looked it up in Pevsner's *Buildings* and established that it was certainly pre-Reformation – always a strong indication that it had been built on a pre-Christian site. But when he drew a line from the Tump to the church and then continued it for several miles, he found it didn't cross any other mounds, churches or standing stones. Not even a crossroads or a hilltop cairn.

The ley system, which appeared to cover almost the whole of Britain and could be detected in many parts of the world, seemed to have avoided Crybbe.

'Bloody strange,' Powys had said aloud, giving up.

What the hell was there for Henry Kettle to dowse in Crybbe? Why had Max Goff chosen the place as a New Age centre?

Powys came into the straggling village of Pembridge, where the age-warped black-and-whites seemed to hang over the street instead of trees. Driving down towards Kington and the border, he felt a nervousness edging in, like a foreign station on the radio at night. He rarely came this way. Too many memories. Or maybe only one long memory, twisted with grief.

*

Fiona, Ben's girlfriend, laughing and burrowing in one of the bags for the bottle of champagne. 'Better open this now, warm shampoo's so yucky.'

Ben holding up a fresh-from-the-publisher copy of the book. On the cover, a symbolic golden pentagram is shining on a hillside. In the foreground, against a late-sunset sky, a few stars sprinkled in the corners, is the jagged silhouette of a single standing stone. Across the top, the title, The Old Golden Land. *Below the stone, in clean white lettering, the author's name, J. M. Powys.*

And below that it says, With photographs by Rose Hart.

Rose looks at you, and her eyes are bright enough to burn through the years, and now the pain almost dissolves the memory.

Ben saying, 'A toast, then . . .'

But Andy is raising a hand. 'There remains one small formality.'

Everybody looking at him.

'I think Joe ought to present himself to the Earth Spirit in the time-honoured fashion.'

Forget it, you think. No way.

'I mean go round the Bottle Stone. Thirteen times.'

Fiona clapping her hands. 'Oh, yes. Do go round the stone, Joe.'

CHAPTER VI

HENRY'S place was the end of a Welsh long-house, divided into three cottages. The other two had been knocked into one, and Mrs Gwen Whitney lived there with her husband.

Powys arrived around eight-thirty, driving through deep wells of shadow. Remembering Henry coming out to meet him one evening round about this time, his dog, Alf, dancing up to the car.

That night, twelve years ago, Powys pleading with Henry: 'Come on . . . it's as much your book as mine. *The Old Golden Land* by Henry Kettle and Joe Powys.'

'Don't be daft, boy. You writes, I dowses. That's the way

of it. Besides, there's all that funny stuff in there – I might not agree with some of that. You know me, *nothing psychic*. When I stop thinking of this as science . . . well, I don't know where I'll be.'

And an hour or so later: 'But, Henry, at the very least . . .'

'And don't you start offering me money! What do I want any more money for, with the wife gone and the daughter doing more than well for herself in Canada? You go ahead, boy. Just don't connect me with any of it, or I'll have to disown you, see.'

Silence now. The late sun turning the cottage windows to tinfoil. No dog leaping out at the car.

Mrs Whitney opened her door as he walked across.

'Mr Powys.' A heavy woman in a big, flowery frock. Smiling that sad, sympathetic smile which came easily to the faces of country women, always on nodding terms with death.

'You remember me?'

'Not changed, have you? Anyway, it's not so long.'

'Twelve years. And I've gone grey.'

'Is it so long? Good gracious. Would you like some tea?'

'Thank you. Not too late, am I?'

'Not for you, Mr Powys. I remember one night, must have been four in the morning when we finally heard your car go from here.'

'Sorry about that. We had a lot to talk about.'

'Oh, he could talk, Mr Kettle could. When he wanted to.' Mrs Whitney led him into her kitchen. 'I think it looks nice grey,' she said.

Later, they stood in Henry's cell-like living-room, insulated by thousands of books, many of them old and probably valuable, although you wouldn't have thought it from the way they were edged into the shelves, some upside down, some back to front. On a small cast-iron mantelshelf, over the Parkray, were a few deformed lumps of wood. Local sculpture, Henry called it. He'd keep them on the mantelpiece until he found more interesting ones in the hedgerows, then he'd use the old ones for the fire.

Mrs Whitney handed Powys a battered old medical bag. 'This was in the car with him. Police brought it back.'

A thought tumbled into Powys's head as he took the bag. 'What about Alf?'

'Oh, old Alf died a couple of years back. He got another dog – Arnold. Funny-looking thing. I says, "You're too old for another dog, Mr Kettle." "Give me a reason to keep on living," he says. Always said he couldn't work without a dog at his side. Arnold, he was in the car with Mr Kettle, too. He wasn't killed. A lady's looking after him in Crybbe. She'll have her hands full. Year or so with Mr Kettle, they forgot they was supposed to be dogs.'

Powys smiled.

'Daft about animals, Mr Kettle was. He's left half his money – I didn't put this in the letter – half his money's going to a dog's shelter over the other side of Hereford. Daughter won't like that.'

'Henry knew what he was doing,' Powys said. 'What's going to happen to the house?'

'She'll sell it. She won't come back, that one. She'll sell it and it'll go to some folks from Off, who'll put a new kitchen in and one of them fancy conservatories. They'll likely stop a couple of years, and then there'll be some more folks from Off. I don't mind them, myself, they never does no harm, in general.'

Powys opened the medical bag. The contents were in compartments, like valuable scientific equipment. Two remodelled wire coat-hangers with rubber grips.

Mrs Whitney said, 'There's a what-d'you-call-it, pendulum thing in a pocket in the lid.'

'I know,' Powys said. 'I remember.'

'Mr Kettle had his old dowsing records in . . . you know, them office things.'

'Box files.'

'Aye, box files. Must be half a dozen of them. And there's this I found by his bed.'

It was a huge old black-bound business ledger, thick as a Bible. He opened it at random.

. . . and in the middle meadow I detected the foundations

*of an old house from about the fifteenth century. I got so
engrossed in this I forgot all about finding the well . . .*

He could hear Henry chuckling as he wrote in black ink
with his old fountain pen, edge to edge, ignoring the red and
black rules and margins.

He turned to the beginning and saw the first entry had been
made nearly twenty years earlier. Out of four or five hundred
pages, there were barely ten left unfilled. End of an era.

Powys closed the ledger and held it, with reverence, in both
hands.

'His journal. I doubt if anybody else has ever seen it.'

'Well, you take it away,' said Mrs Whitney. 'Sometimes I
had the feeling some of them things Mr Kettle was doing were
– how shall I say? – not quite Christian.'

'Science, Mrs Whitney. He was always very particular about
that.'

'Funny sort of science,' Mrs Whitney said. 'There's a letter,
too, only gave it to me last week.'

A pale-blue envelope, 'J. M. Powys' handwritten in black
ink.

'Oh, he was a nice old chap,' Mrs Whitney said. 'But, with
all respect for the departed, he'd have been the first to admit
as he was more'n a bit cracked.'

For Fay, there would be no secret pleasure any more in editing
tape in the office at night, within the circle of Anglepoise light,
a soft glow from the Revox level-meters, and all the rest in
shadow.

For none of what dwelt beyond the light could now be
assumed to be simply shadow. Once these things had started
happening to your mind, you couldn't trust anything any more.

That evening, she and the Canon watched television in what
used to be Grace's dining-room at the rear of the house and
was now their own sitting-room. Two bars of the electric fire
were on – never guess it was summer, would you?

Arnold lay next to Alex on Grace's enormous chintzy sofa.

The dog did not howl, not once, although Fay saw him stiffen with the distant roll of the curfew. He'd be sleeping upstairs again tonight.

She watched Alex watching TV and sent him mind-messages. We have to talk, Dad. We can't go on here. There's nothing left. There never was anything, you ought to realize that now.

Alex carried on placidly watching some dismal old black and white weepie on Channel Four.

Fay said, at one point, 'Dad?'

'Mmmm?'

Alex kept his eyes on the screen, where Stewart Granger was at a crucial point in his wooing of Jean Simmons.

'Dad, would you . . .' Fay gave up, 'care for some tea? Or cocoa?'

'Cocoa. Wonderful. You know, at one time, people used to say I had more than a passing resemblance to old Granger.'

'Really?' Fay couldn't see it herself.

'Came in quite useful once or twice.'

'I bet it did.'

Fay got up to make the cocoa, feeling more pale and wan than Jean Simmons looked in black and white. In one day she'd hung up on Guy, betrayed Rachel, demolished relations with Goff before she'd even met him. And caught herself about to give a blow job to a microphone in the privacy of the Crybbe Unattended Studio.

What I need, she thought, is to plug myself into a ley-line, and she smiled to herself – a despairing kind of smile – at the absurdity of it all.

The box files wouldn't all fit in the boot of the Mini. Three had to be wedged on the back seat, with the doctor's bag.

But the ledger, the dowsing journal of Henry Kettle, was on the passenger seat where Powys could see it, Henry's letter on top.

Just past the Kington roundabout he gave in, pulled into the side of the road and, in the thinning light, he opened the letter.

Dear Joe,

I'm doing this now, while I feel the way I do. If it all sorts itself out you'll probably never read this letter. None of it will make much sense to you at first and if it never does make any sense it means my fears will be groundless.

What it comes down to is I've been working out at Crybbe for a chap called Max Goff who's bought Crybbe Court.

The nature of the job is dowsing some old alignments where the stones and such have all gone years ago, and it's been giving me the shivers, quite honestly, that whole place. Don't get me wrong, there's nothing psychic or any of that old rubbish, but it's not right and as far as I can work out it's a long-term kind of thing. I intend to keep an eye on the situation in the weeks and months and, God willing, the years ahead and keep on revising my notes, but I'm not getting any younger and you could go any time at my age and I feel as how I ought to inform somebody. You have had some daft ideas in your time but you're a good boy basically and the only person I can think of who I can trust not to dismiss this out of hand as an old fool's ramblings.

God knows, I'm not infallible and I could be wrong and I don't even know as yet the nature of what's up in Crybbe, only I get the feeling it's long-term, and I'd like to think there was somebody who could keep an eye on what that Goff's up to.

Now my daughter, we've grown apart, no kidding myself any more. She's out in Canada and she's VERY WELL OFF. So I've written to my solicitor in Hereford informing him that as well as all the papers my house is to be left to you. Consider it as a token of my confidence.

Yours sincerely,

H. Kettle
(Henry)

'God almighty,' Powys said.

He could see lights coming on in Kington, through the trees. On the other side of the road, darkening hills. Somewhere, on the other side of the hills, Crybbe.

Leaving him the house was ridiculous. He'd probably changed his mind by now, anyway.

But the letter was dated 19 June.

Only two days before Henry's death.

Powys opened the ledger at the last completed page. It also was dated 19 June.

> *Quite a successful day. Located three more old stones. One of them would be eleven feet above the ground, which would make it quite rare for the Crybbe area, the nearest one as high as that being down near Crickhowell. I have been over this twice to make sure. It is very peculiar that there should have been so many big stones in such a small area. I tried to date this big one, but all I could come up with was 1593 when it was destroyed. It seemed certain to me that this was done quite deliberately, the whole thing taken out and broken up. This was all quite systematic, like the burning down of monasteries during the Reformation.*
>
> *What intrigues me is how this Goff could have obtained the information about there having been stones here when even I had never heard of them. Sometimes I feel quite excited by all this, it is undoubtedly the most remarkable discovery of prehistoric remains in this country for many years, even if the archaeologists will never accept it. At other times, however, I do get quite a bad feeling that something here is not right, although I cannot put my finger on it. I have always disliked the Tump for some reason. Some places are naturally negative, although perhaps 'natural' is not the word I want. The Welsh border is a very funny place, but I am sure there is a good scientific explanation.*

The last entry. Neatly dated and a line drawn under it. Two days later Henry Kettle was lying dead in his car under Crybbe Tump.

It was dark when Powys got back to Hereford. He lugged the box files up the stairs to his little flat above Trackways and left them in the middle of the floor, unopened. It would take months to explore that lot.

But he was committed now.

He went down to the shop and put on the lights. From his photograph, Alfred Watkins frowned down on the counter. Powys could see why: Annie had put the box of 'healing' crystals on display.

He wrote out a note and left it wedged under the crystals box.

> Dear Annie,
>   Please hold fort until whenever. I'll call you. Don't light too many joss-sticks.

Feeling a need to explain, he added,

> Gone to Crybbe.
> P.S. Don't get the wrong idea. It might be old, but it's not golden.

When he put out the lights in the shop, he noticed the answering machine winking red.

A woman's low, resonant voice.

'J. M. Powys, this is Rachel Wade at Crybbe Court. I wanted to remind you about Friday. I'd be grateful if you could call back on Crybbe 689, which is the Cock Hotel or 563, our new office at Crybbe Court. Leave a message if I'm not around. Things are a little chaotic at present, but we'd very much like to hear from you. If you can't make it on Friday, we could arrange another day. Just please call me.'

'I'll be there,' Powys said to the machine. 'OK?'

He went upstairs to bed and couldn't sleep. He'd seen Henry barely half a dozen times in the past ten years. If the old guy really had left him his house to underline his feelings about Crybbe then they had to be more than passing fears.

'What have you dumped on me, Henry?' he kept asking the ceiling. And when he fell asleep he dreamt about the Bottle Stone.

CHAPTER VII

THE following day was overcast, the sky straining with rain that never seemed to fall. After breakfast, Jimmy Preece, gnarled old Mayor of Crybbe, went to see his son.

He found Jack tinkering with the tractor in the farmyard, his eldest grandson, Jonathon, looking on, shaking his head.

'Always the same,' Jack grunted. 'Just when you need it. Mornin', Father.'

'I been telling him,' Jonathon said. 'Get a new one. False economy. This thing gets us through haymaking, I'll be very surprised indeed.'

Jimmy Preece shook his head, then he nodded, so that neither of them would be sure which one he was agreeing with.

'Got to take an overview,' said Jonathon, this year's chairman of the Crybbe and District Young Farmers' Club. 'Going from day to day don't work any more.'

'Break off a minute, will you?' Jimmy said. 'Come in the 'ouse. I want a bit of advice.'

He knew that'd get them. Jack straightened up, tossed his spanner into the metal toolbox and walked off without a word, across the farmyard to the back door. 'Warren!' he roared. 'Put that bloody guitar down and make some tea.'

In the kitchen, waiting for the kettle to boil, Warren whipped the letter out of his back pocket and read it through again. He'd thought at first it might have been Peter, the drummer, pulling his pisser again. But where would Peter have got hold of Epidemic headed notepaper?

> Dear Mr Preece,
>   Thank you for sending us the cassette of *FATAL ACCIDENT*, which I return.

*Max Goff has listened with interest to your songs and
believes there could be considerable potential here . . .*

It was signed by this Rachel Wade, the snooty tart Warren
had seen driving Max Goff around. It had to be genuine.

Well, fuck, what had he got to be surprised about? Max
Goff hadn't got where he was today without he could spot a
good band when he heard one.

Have to get working, then. Have to get a few more numbers
together. Get on the phone to the boys, soon as the old man
and bloody Jonathon were out the way.

Warren took their tea. They were sprawled around the big
living-room, grandad getting his knackered old pipe out.
Looked like the start of a long session, and the phone was
in the same room. Warren was nearly grinding his teeth in
frustration.

Stuff this, he'd walk into town and use the phone box by
the post office. He left the tray of mugs on a stool and cleared
out quick, before the old man could come up with some filthy
old job for him.

Out in the hallway, though, he stopped, having second
thoughts. Warren liked to know about things. He tramped
loudly to the main door, kicked it shut, then crept quietly back
and stood by the living-room door, listening.

And soon he was bloody glad he had.

Fay had decided that what she must do, for a start, was get her
dad out of the town for a few hours so she could talk to him.
Really talk.

It seemed ridiculous that she couldn't do this in the house,
but that was how it was. Often, in Crybbe, you simply couldn't
seem to approach things directly. There were whole periods
when everything you tried to do or say was somehow deflected.

In the same way, she felt the place smothered your natural
curiosity, made the urge to find out – the act of wanting to
know – seem just too much trouble.

It wasn't that the air was in any way soporific, she thought, unlocking the Fiesta. Not like the famous country air was supposed to be, or the dreamy blue ozone at the seaside that sent you drifting off at night on waves of healthy contentment.

Here, it was as if the atmosphere itself was feeding off you, quietly extracting your vital juices, sapping your mental energy, so that you crawled into bed and lay there like a dried-out husk.

Had the air done this to the people? Or had the people done it to the air?

Or was it just her, living with an old man whose mind was seizing up.

Fay gave him a blast on the horn. Come on, Dad, you're not changing your mind now.

In the local paper she'd found a story about people in a village fifteen miles away receiving some kind of conservation award for adopting their local railway station, planting flowers on the embankments, that kind of thing. Ashpole had agreed it would probably make a nice little soft package. End of the programme stuff, keep it down to four minutes max.

From the back seat, Arnold barked. It was a gruff, throaty bark, and his jaws clamped down on it as soon as it was out. It was the first one Fay had ever heard him produce. He must be settling in. She leaned over and ruffled his big ears, pleased.

Alex emerged by the front door at last. It had been far from easy persuading him to come with her, even though he did seem much better today, more aware.

He sat with his hands on his lap as she drove them out of town, on the Welsh side. 'Hope you know a decent pub over there, my child.'

'We'll find one.'

The sky was brightening as she drove into the hills, the border roads unravelling through featureless forestry, then open fields with sheep, a few cows, sparse sprinklings of cottages, farm buildings and bungalows.

The little railway station was on the single-track Heart of Wales line, which went on to Shrewsbury. It wasn't much more than a halt, with a wooden bench and a waiting room the size of a bus-shelter.

Fay had arranged to meet the Secretary of this enthusiastic committee which existed to defend the unprofitable line against what seemed to be a constant threat of imminent closure by British Rail. He turned out to be a genial guy and a good talker, and he'd brought along a couple of villagers who spent their weekends sprucing up the station surrounds, cutting back verges, planting bulbs. They were friendly and self-deprecating.

In Crybbe it would have to have been the newcomers who took the job on. But Crybbe didn't have a station, anyway. Only B-roads.

Interviews done, she stood for a moment at the edge of the line, looking out towards the hills and thinking what a quiet, serene place this actually was. Untampered with. All the old patterns still apparent.

A buzzard glided overhead, then banked off like a World War II fighter, flashing the white blotches under its wings.

She thought, it's me. All this is wonderful. It isn't mean and tight and stifling at all. I'm just a sour bitch who thinks she's had a raw deal, and I'm blaming the poor bloody border country.

Alex was in the car, white beard brushing his *Guardian* as he read, still managing without glasses at pushing ninety. He was wearing a baggy cardigan over his Kate Bush T-shirt. Fay thought suddenly, I wish I knew him better.

'. . . and Mrs Wozencraft's cottage – old Jessie Wozencraft – that's his as well, he's bought that.'

'Good luck to him,' Jonathon said. 'Old place is near enough falling down.'

'That's not the point, Jonathon,' said Jack Preece. 'point your grandad's makin' is . . .'

'Oh, I know what he's sayin' – and he's dead right. What bloody use is an acupuncturist in Crybbe?'

'What do they do, anyway?'

'They sticks needles in you, to cure things.'

'Wouldn't stick any in me, boy, I hates them injections.'

'It don't matter what they does!' Warren heard his grandad

thumping the chair-arm. 'It's the principle. Retired folk I don't mind so much, give 'em a bit of bird watchin' and a library book and they don't bother nobody, and they always dies after a few years anyway. What *I* object to is these clever-arsed fellers as wants to *change* things to what they thinks they should be, if you know what I'm sayin'. Everything pretty-pretty and no huntin' the little furry animals. And no jobs either, 'cause factories spoils the view.'

'Market forces, Grandad. You can't do nothin' about market forces.'

'Nine properties, 'e's had so far, I counted. Nine! Everything for sale within a mile of town, he's bought it.'

'Many as that, eh?'

Warren didn't like the way this conversation was going. He fingered the crisp Epidemic notepaper in his pocket.

Jonathon said, 'Well, nobody else'd've bought 'em, would they? Not with interest rates the way they are. All right, it's speculation . . .'

'It's not just speculation, Jonathon. There's a purpose to it, and it's not right. You heard that woman on the wireless. New Age and psychic powers. I don't know nothin' about any of it and I don't want to, and I don't want *him* doin' it yere.'

'Woken a lot of people up to it, that bit on the radio,' Jack said. 'Everybody talkin' about it in the Cock last night, the post office this morning. Lot of people's worried it's going to bring the hippies in.'

'What are any of 'em but hippies? Quack healers, fortune-tellers . . .'

'Who is she, Father? Somebody said it was that girl who lives with 'er dad, the old feller with the beard.'

'Fay Morrison,' Grandad said. 'Nice enough girl. Comes to council meetings.'

'Tidy piece,' Jonathon said.

Warren knew who they meant. Seen her the other night, coming back from the Court with that dog. Followed her behind the hedge. Spying, most likely, she was, nosy cow.

'I admit I never wanted 'em to put that radio studio in,' his grandad said. 'But if it 'adn't been for this girl nobody'd've believed it. They years it on the wireless, it brings it 'ome to 'em, isn't it?' Warren heard the old feller sucking on his pipe. 'Ah, but he's a crafty bugger, that Goff. Comes to my door tryin' to get round me, all the things he's goin' to do for the town. Get the Mayor on his side, first – tactics, see.'

'Well, we can't stop him. Can't block market forces, Grandad.'

'We can stop him takin' our town off us to serve his whims!'

'And how're we supposed to do that?'

'He wants a public meeting, we'll give him one.'

'What are you sayin' here, Father? Give him a rough time? Let him know he isn't wanted?'

Behind the door, Warren began to seethe. This was fucking typical. Here was Max Goff, biggest bloody independent record producer in the country, on the verge of signing Fatal Accident to Epidemic. And these stick-in-the-mud bastards were scheming to get rid of him.

Jonathon was saying, 'See them stones he had delivered? Bloody great stones, dozens of 'em.'

'Building stone?'

'No, just great big stones. Huge buggers. Like Stonehenge, that kind.'

Things went quiet, then Warren heard his grandad say, 'He's oversteppin' the mark. He's got to be stopped.'

Warren wanted to strangle the old git. He wanted to strangle all three of them. Also that fucking radio woman who'd let it all out and stirred things up. The one who shouted after him through the hedge that night, called him a wanker.

Every pub they'd tried had stopped serving lunch at two o'clock – so much for all-day opening – and so they'd wound up at this Little Chef, which didn't please him. 'Bloody cooking by numbers. Two onion rings, thirty-seven chips. All this and alcohol-free lager too. And these bloody girls invariably saying, "Was it all right for you?" as if they're just putting their knickers back on.'

'At least they're there when you want them,' Fay said,

getting back on the A49. 'Would you like to see Ludlow?'

'Like to go home, actually.'

'God almighty! What is it about that place?'

'Left my pills there.'

'I know you did. But luckily, *I* brought them. What's your next excuse?'

Alex growled. 'Wish I'd had a son.'

'Instead of me, huh?'

'Sons don't try to manage you.'

'Dad, I want to talk to you.'

'Oh God.'

'Was that the first time Guy rang, the other night?'

'Hard to say, my dear. Once I put the phone down I tend to forget all about him. He may have rung earlier. Does it really matter?'

'I don't mean just that night. Has he rung any other time when I've been out?'

'Can't remember. Suppose he could have done. I didn't think you cared.'

'I don't. It's just Guy's coming down to make a documentary about Max Goff, and I was wondering how he found out there was something interesting going on. I know you tend to absorb local gossip like a sponge and then somebody squeezes you a bit and it all comes out, and then you forget it was ever there.'

'You think I told him?'

'Did you?'

'Did I? God knows. Say anything to get rid of him. Does it matter?'

Fay glanced in her wing mirror then trod on the brakes and pulled in violently to the side of the road. 'Of course it bloody matters!'

'I think you're overwrought, my child. You're young. You need a bit of excitement. Bit of stimulation. Country life doesn't suit you.'

'*Crybbe* doesn't suit me.'

'So why not simply . . . ?'

She said carefully, 'Dad. You may be right. There may be nothing at all wrong with Crybbe. But, yes, I think it's time I left. And I think it's time *you* left. You've no reason to stay. You've no roots there, no real friends there.'

He said sadly, 'Oh, I have.'

He wasn't looking at her. He was looking straight out at the A49, lorries chugging past.

'Who? Murray Beech? He'll be off, first chance of a bigger parish. He's got nothing to thank Crybbe for – his fiancée didn't hang around, did she?'

'No,' Alex said. 'Not Murray.'

'Who then?'

He didn't reply.

Fay fiddled with the keys in the ignition. Alex talked to everybody, old vicars never changed. A friend to everyone, essence of the job. But how many did he really know?

'What are you saying, Dad?'

'Grace,' he whispered, and Fay saw the beginning of tears in his old blue eyes.

She put a hand on his arm. 'Dad?'

'Don't ask me about this, Fay,' Alex said. 'Please. Just take me home.'

CHAPTER VIII

O N top of the Tump it all came clear.

You could see over the roofs of the stables and Crybbe Court itself, which was sunk into a shallow dip. And there, only just showing above the trees, was the church tower. But then the trees hadn't always been so high – or even there at all.

The church was at the high point of the town, the main street sloping down to the river. From here you couldn't see the street or the river – but you *could* see the fields on the opposite bank, rising into hills thickened now with forestry. And at one time, before the introduction of the voracious Sitka Spruce from Alaska, that might have been bare hillside, and there would have been other markers to pick up the line.

Joe Powys looked all around him and saw how clearly the Tump had been positioned to dominate the town, even the church, and draw in the landscape like the corners of a hand-kerchief.

That old feeling again, of being inside an ancient mechanism. At the centre of the wheel.

Identifying the line took an act of imagination because there were no markers any more. But Henry Kettle had discovered where upright stones had once been aligned to guide the eye from the Tump to the distant horizons.

But there was something about it that Henry Kettle didn't like.

Powys moved away from the highest point and stood next to a twisted hawthorn tree. The sky was a tense, luminous grey, swollen like a great water-filled balloon, and he felt that if it came down low enough to be pricked by the tree's topmost thorns, he'd be drowned.

It was his own fault. Places like this could ensnare your mind, and your thoughts became tangled up with the most primitive instincts, old fears lying hidden in the undergrowth like trailing brambles.

As quickly as he could, but still very carefully, Powys came down from the Tump, climbed over the wall and didn't look back until he was well into the field, heading towards the road, where he'd left the Mini. Halfway across the field, there was a bumpy rise, and it was here that he found the hub-cap.

He sat on a hummock with the disc on his knee. It was muddy and badly rusted, but he could still make out the symbol in the centre – two letters: VW.

'Still the same car, then, Henry. How old is it now? Twenty-two, twenty-three?'

Holding Henry's hub-cap, Powys looked back at the Tump.

I have always disliked the Tump for some reason. Some places are naturally negative.

Powys thought, Sinister bloody thing that must once have appeared as alien as a gasworks or a nuclear reactor. He looked down at the wall, realizing that the section he'd climbed over was just a few yards from the part where the stonework was so obviously scraped, but hadn't collapsed because it was too hard for that. Harder than the rusting heap of twenty-year-old tin Henry Kettle drove.

From the foot of the wall, shards of broken glass glimmered like dew in the trodden-down grass.

Christ, Henry, how could this happen?

Henry, can you hear me?

Although perhaps 'natural' is not the word I want . . . But I am sure there is a good scientific explanation.

You misled us, Henry. Nothing psychic, you kept saying. We should have realized it was just a dirty word to you, a word for phoney mediums and fortune-tellers at the end of the pier. Ancient science was your term, because it didn't sound cranky.

He could see the tracks now, grass flattened, lumps of turf wrenched out. The field was unfenced and the car must have cut across it diagonally, ploughing straight on instead of following a sharpish left-hand bend in the road.

Powys left the metal disc on the hummock and scrambled up to the road, collecting a hard look from a man driving a Land Rover pulling a trailer.

Now, if Henry was driving out of town, he'd be pointing straight at the Tump, then the road curved away, then it was directed towards the Tump again, very briefly, then came the left-hand bend and you were away into the hills.

But Henry never made the left-hand bend. The car left the road, taking him into the field. He might not have noticed what he'd done at first, if it was dark. And then the field went quite suddenly into this slope, and . . . crunch.

Not so far-fetched at all, really. There'd be an accidental-death verdict and nobody would delve any deeper. All the rest was folklore.

He went back into the field, walked down towards the Tump, skirting its walled-in base, not knowing what he was hoping for any more.

Come on, Henry. Give us a sign.

It began to rain. He ran to a clump of trees to shelter and to watch the Tump, massive, ancient, glowering through the downpour, as magnificently mysterious as the Great Pyramid.

Powys turned away and wandered among the trees, emerging on the other side into a clearing beside a building of grey-brown stone.

Crybbe Court?

No, not the Court itself, the stable-block – now seriously renovated, he saw. There was an enormous oblong of glass set in the wall – a huge picture-window, facing the Tump.

Behind the building he could see the corner of a forecourt, where two men stood in the rain looking down on four long, grey, jagged stones.

Powys stiffened.

One of the men was dark and thin and was talking to the other man in a voice which, had he been able to hear it, would probably have reminded him of a stroked cello.

'Least you can do, mate,' Andy tells you. 'Look at all the money the book's going to make. Think of it as a kind of appeasement of the Earth Spirit.'

Fiona claps her hands. 'Oh, go on, Joe. We'll all sit here and chant and clap.'

'Bastards.' You look at Rose, who smiles sympathetically. Reluctantly you stand up, and everybody cheers.

Well, everybody except Henry. 'Don't wanna play about with these old things.' Quaint old Herefordshire countryman.

Andy leaning on an elbow. 'I thought you weren't superstitious, Henry. Ancient science and all that. Nothing psychic.'

'Aye, well, electricity's science too, but you wouldn't wanna go sticking your fingers up a plug socket.'

Thankful for his advice, you make as if to sit down.

'Not got the bottle for it, Joe?'

Ben starts clapping very slowly, and the others – except Henry – pick up the rhythm. 'Joey goes round the Bottle Stone, the Bottle Stone, the Bottle Stone . . .'

Crybbe was forty-five minutes away. Minor roads all the way once they'd left the A49. Neither of them spoke; Fay was thinking hard, bringing something into focus. Something utterly repellent that she hadn't, up to now, allowed herself to contemplate for longer than a few seconds.

A woman in a cold miasma, frigid, rigid, utterly still. Not breathing. *Past* breathing . . . long past.

She looked in the driving mirror, and there was Arnold, the dog, sitting upright on the back seat; their eyes met in the mirror.

You saw her, Arnold. You saw *something*. But did *I*?

Did I see the ghost of Grace Legge?

Ghost. Spirit of the dead. And yet that image, the Grace thing, surely was without spirit. Static. Frozen. And the white eyes and that horrible smile with those little, thin fish-teeth.

That was her. Her teeth. Tiny little teeth, and lots of them, discoloured, brittle. The memory you always carried away, of Grace's fixed smile, with all those little teeth.

She'd been nothing to Fay, just Dad's Other Woman. No, not exactly nothing. Twenty years ago, she'd been something on the negative side of nothing. Somebody Fay had blamed – to herself, for she'd never spoken of it, not to anyone – for her mother's death. And she'd blamed her father, too. Perhaps this was why, even now, she could not quite love him – terrible admission.

She had, naturally, tried hard for both of them when she came down for the wedding. Water under the bridge. An old man's fumbling attempts to make amends and a very sick woman who deserved what bit of happiness remained for her.

Perhaps her dad thought he'd killed them both. Both his wives.

Compassion rising, Fay glanced sideways at Alex, sitting there with his old green cardigan unbuttoned and ATE USH in fading lettering across his chest.

What this was about – *had* to be – was that he, too, had seen something in the night.

And what must that be like for an old man who could no longer trust his own mind or even his memories? If she wasn't sure what she'd seen – or even if she'd seen anything – what must it be like for him?

Fay clutched the steering wheel tightly, and goose pimples rippled up both arms.

That's why you can't leave, Dad. You've seen something that none of your clerical experience could ever prepare you for. You're afraid that somehow she's still there, in the house you shared.

And you're not going to walk out on her again.

Henry Kettle had written,

It is very peculiar that there should have been so many big stones in such a small area.

Long after Andy and the other man had walked away, Powys still stood silently under the dripping trees, staring in fascination at the recumbent stones in the corner of the courtyard.

Megaliths.

And Andy Boulton-Trow, whom Powys hadn't seen for twelve years. Designer of the cover of *The Old Golden Land.* Painter of stones, sculptor of stones, collector of stone-lore.

The stones lay there, gleaming with fresh rain. Old stones, or new stones? Did it matter; one stone was as old as another.

Stones didn't speak to him the way they spoke to Henry Kettle, but he was getting the idea. Max Goff, presumably, intended to place new stones in the spots identified by Henry.

And the obvious man to select and shape the stones – an act of love – was Andy Boulton-Trow, who knew more about the nature of megaliths than anyone in Europe. Powys had met Andy at art college, to which Andy had come *after* university to learn about painting and sculpture . . . with specific regard to stone.

From beyond the courtyard, he heard an engine start, a vehicle moving away.

Then all was quiet, even the rain had ceased.

Powys slid from the trees and made his way around the side of the stone stable-building to the corner of the courtyard where the stones lay.

*

Fay drove into Crybbe from the Ludlow road. The windscreen wipers squeaked as the rain eased off.

She thought, We're never going to be able to talk about this, are we, Dad? Not for as long as you live.

She stopped in front of the house to let him out. 'Thank you,' he said, not looking at her. 'It's been . . . a pleasant day, hasn't it?'

'I'll put the car away. You stay here, Arnold.'

She backed the car into the entry, a little tunnel affair in the terrace, parking too close to the wall; there was only just room to squeeze out. 'Come on, Arnold.'

Alex was waiting for them at the back door. His face was grave but his blue eyes were flecked – as they often were now – with a flickering confusion.

'Got the tea on, Dad?'

'Fay . . . I . . .'

He turned and walked into the kitchen. The kettle was not even plugged in.

'Fay . . .'

'Dad?'

He walked through the kitchen, into the hall, Fay following, Arnold trotting behind. At the door of the office, Grace's sitting-room, he stood to one side to let her pass.

'I'm so sorry,' he said.

At first she couldn't see what he meant. The clock was still clicking away on the mantelpiece, the fireside chair still piled high with box files.

'The back door was open,' Alex said. 'Forced.'

She saw.

They must have used a sledgehammer or a heavy axe because it was a tough machine, with a metal top.

'Why?' Fay felt ravaged. Cold and hollow and hurting like a rape victim. 'For God's sake, *why?*'

Her beloved Revox – night-time comfort with its swishing spools and soft-glowing level-meters – had been smashed to pieces, disembowelled.

A few hundred yards of tape had been unspooled and mixed up with the innards, and the detritus was splattered over the floor like a mound of spaghetti.

CHAPTER IX

THE women who had, in recent years, been powerfully attracted to Joe Powys had tended to wear long, hand-dyed skirts and shapeless woollies. Sometimes they had frizzy hair and sometimes long, tangled hair. Sometimes they were big-breasted earth-mother types and sometimes small-boned and delicate like Arthur Rackham fairies.

Sometimes, when Powys fantasized – which was worryingly rarely, these days – he imagined having, as he put it to himself, a bit of smooth. Someone scented. Someone who shaved her armpits. Someone who would actually refuse to trek across three miles of moorland to find some tiny, ruined stone circle you practically had to dig out of the heather. Someone you could never imagine standing in the middle of this half-submerged circle and breathing, 'Oh, I mean, gosh, can't you feel it . . . can't you feel that primal force?'

The woman facing him now, he could tell, was the kind who'd rather see Stonehenge itself as a blur in the window of a fast car heading towards a costly dinner in Salisbury.

But even if she'd been wearing a home-made ankle-length skirt with a hemline of mud, clumpy sandals and big wooden ear-rings, he would, at this moment, have been more than grateful to see her.

She said, 'I think you could let him go now, Humble. He really doesn't look very dangerous.'

'Find out who he is first,' said the hard-faced bastard with a grip like a monkey-wrench, the guy he'd first seen frowning at him through the window of a Land Rover when he was checking out the Tump.

He made Powys bend over the vehicle's high bonnet, which tossed another pain-ball into his stomach.

This man had punched him in the guts with a considered precision and such penetration that he was seriously worried about internal bleeding.

'Ta very much.' Deftly removing Powys's wallet from the

inside pocket of his muddied jacket. Not a local accent; this was London.

'If this is a mugging,' Powys said awkwardly, face squashed into the bonnet, 'you could be . . .'

'Fucking shut it.' His nose crunched into the metal, Powys felt blood come.

'Don't even twitch, pal, OK?'

'Mmmph.'

'Right, then, I'm going to have a little butcher's through here, see what you got by way of ID, all right?'

'Humble, if you don't let him go I'm going to call the police.'

'Rachel, you do your job, I do mine. Our friend here don't want that. Ask him. Ask him what he was doing on private property. Ain't a poacher. Ain't got the bottle.'

He cringed, expecting Humble to tap him in the guts again to prove his point. But the pressure eased and he was allowed to stand. His nose felt wet, but he didn't think it was broken. He looked at the woman, who must be close to his own age, had light, mid-length hair and calm eyes. 'I'm sorry,' she said. 'Humble's used to dealing with the more urban type of trespasser.'

'Trespasser?' Powys wiped off some blood with the back of a hand. 'Now, look . . . You tell this bloody psycho . . .' He stopped. What could she tell him? He wondered where Andy Boulton-Trow had vanished to.

'All right now, are we?' Dipping into Powys's wallet, Humble smiled with the lower half of a face which had all the personality of a mousetrap. He pulled out a plastic-covered driving licence and handed it to the woman. She took it from him reluctantly. Opened it out. Gave a little gasp.

'Oh dear,' she said.

'Yeah, don't tell me. One of Max's bits of fluff.' Humble smirked. 'In which case, no problems, he'll have been enjoying himself.'

Rachel closed the licence and held out her hand for the wallet. Very carefully she put the licence back, then she handed the wallet to Powys.

'Not entirely accurate, Humble,' she said. 'And when he

hears about this, Max, I suspect, is going to have you strung up by the balls.'

Police Sergeant Wynford Wiley was shaking his great turnip head. 'Mindless.'

'Mindless?' said Fay. 'You think it's *mindless*?'

'We always prided ourselves,' Wynford said, thick blue legs astride the wreckage. 'Never suffered from no vandalism in this town. Not to any great extent, anyhow.'

Only vandalism by neglect, Fay thought dully. She wondered why she'd bothered to call the police now. Wynford was just so *sinister* – like one of those mean-eyed, redneck police chiefs you saw in moody American movies set in semi-derelict, one-street, wooden towns in the Midwest.

'Think somebody would've seen 'em, though.' The gap narrowed between Wynford's little round eyes. ''Course, Mrs Lloyd next door, deaf as a post, see. Knock on the door, she don't answer. You got to put your face up to the window.'

Fay imagined Wynford's face, flattened by glass. Give the poor old girl a heart attack.

He said, 'Scene-of-crime boy'll be over later, with his box of tricks. I'll knock on a few doors along the street, see what I can turn up.'

He paused in the doorway, looked back at the wreckage.

'Mindless,' he said.

Fay turned to her dad for support, but Alex, gazing down his beard at the Revox ruins, had nothing to say.

'Doesn't it strike you as odd,' Fay said clinically, 'that this tornado of savagery appears somehow to have focused itself on one single item? I'm no criminologist, but I've witnessed my share of antisocial behaviour, and this, Sergeant, is *not* what I'd call mindless. Psychopathic, perhaps, but mindless in the sense of randomly destructive, no.'

Wynford's big, round face was changing colour. Nobody, she thought, contradicts Chief Wiley on his own manor.

'What you sayin' 'ere, then? Somebody wants to stop you broadcastin'? That it?'

'It's possible. Isn't it?'

'And *is* it gonner stop you broadcastin'?'

'Well, no, as it happens. I . . . I've got a portable tape recorder I do all my interviews on, and I can edit down at the studio in town, there's a machine there. But would they know that?'

'Listen.' Wynford was now wearing an expression which might have been intended to convey kindness. Fay shuddered. 'He – they – just came in and smashed up the most expensive thing they could find. Then, could be as 'e was disturbed – or, *thought* 'e was gonna be disturbed, maybe 'e yers somebody walkin' past . . .'

'Maybe he wasn't disturbed at all,' Fay said. 'Maybe he just left because he'd achieved what he set out to do.'

'I think you're watchin' too much telly.'

'Can't very well watch too much TV in Crybbe. The power's never on for longer than three hours at a stretch.'

Wynford turned his back on her, opened the office door. Arnold walked in, saw Wynford and growled.

'See you've still got that dog. Didn't leave *'im* in the 'ouse, then, when you went out?'

'What? Oh. No, he came with us,' Fay said. 'What happened with the RSPCA, by the way? Does anybody want to claim him?'

'No. I reckon 'e's yours now. If 'e stays.'

'How do you mean?'

'Well. If 'e don't take off, like.'

He was wearing such a weird smile that Fay pursued him to the front door. 'I don't understand.'

Wynford shrugged awkwardly. 'Well, you might wake up one day, see, and . . .'e'll be . . . well, 'e won't be around any more.'

Fay felt menaced. 'Meaning what? Come on . . . what are you saying?'

Wynford's face went blank. 'I'll go and talk to some neighbours,' he said, and he went.

'Dad,' Fay said, 'I've said this before, but there's something very wrong with that guy.'

'Sorry, my dear?' Alex looked up. His eyes were like floss.

'Sit down, Dad, you've had a shock.'

'I'm fine,' Alex said. 'Fine. If there's nothing I can do here, I'll probably have an early night.'

Fay watched the policeman walk past the window, imagined him peering through it with his face squashed against the glass, like a robber in a stocking mask.

She recoiled, stared at the gutted hulk of the Revox, a bizarre idea growing in her head like a strange hybrid plant.

She turned to Arnold, who was standing placidly in the doorway gazing up, for some reason, at Alex, his tail well down.

'Christ,' Fay said.

Something had occurred to her that was so shatteringly preposterous that . . .

'Dad, I have to go out.'

'OK,' Alex said.

. . . if she didn't satisfy herself that it was completely crazy, she wasn't going to get any sleep tonight.

'You go and walk off your anger,' Alex said. 'You'll feel better.'

'Something . . .' Fay looked around for Arnold's plastic clothes-line. 'Dad, I've just got to check this out. I mean, it's so . . .' Fay shook her head helplessly. 'I'll be back, OK?'

She took J. M. Powys to her room at the Cock. The big room on the first floor that she shared with Max. But Max was in London.

The licensee, Denzil, watched them go up. J. M. Powys looked, to say the least, dishevelled, but Denzil made no comment. Rachel suspected that if she organized an orgy for thirty participants, Denzil would have no complaints as long as they all bought drinks in the bar to take up with them.

Rachel closed the bedroom door. The room was laden with dark beams and evening shadows. She switched a light on.

So this was J. M. Powys. Not what she'd imagined, not at all.

'Don't take this wrong, but I thought you'd be older.'

'I think I *am* older.' He tried to smile; it came out lop-sided. There was drying blood around his mouth. His curly hair was entirely grey.

'Er, is there a bathroom?'

'Across the passage,' Rachel said. 'The *en-suite* revolution hasn't happened in Crybbe yet. Possibly next century. Here, let me look . . . Take your jacket off.'

It was certainly an old jacket. The once-white T-shirt underneath it was stiff with mud and blood.

Gently, Rachel prised the T-shirt out of his jeans. The colours of his stomach were like a sky with a storm coming on. 'Nasty. That man is a liability.'

'I've never . . .' Powys winced, 'been beaten up by a New Age thug before. It doesn't feel a lot different, actually.'

Rachel said, 'Humble has his uses in London and New York, but . . . Just move over to the light, would you . . . I really don't like the way he's going native, I caught him laying snares the other day. Look, Mr Powys, I don't know what I can do for bruising, apart from apologize profusely and buy you dinner. Not that you'll thank me for that, unless you're into cholesterol in the basket.'

'I don't mind that. I had a Big Mac the other day.'

He sounded almost proud. Perhaps J. M. Powys was as loony as his book, after all.

Addressing the fireplace, Alex said, 'Why? You've always been so houseproud. Why do this?'

He mustn't touch anything. Fingerprints. Couldn't even tidy the place up a bit until they'd looked for fingerprints. Waste of time, all that. They wouldn't have Grace on their files.

Alex started to cry.

'Why can't you two get on together?'

A tangled ball of black, unspooled tape rustled as he caught it with his shoe. Like the tape, the thoughts in his head were in hopeless, flimsy coils and, like the tape, could never be rewound.

All the way up the High Street, Fay kept her eyes on the gutter.

She saw half a dozen cigarette-ends. A crumpled crisp

packet and a sweet-wrapper. Two ring-pulls from beer cans. And a bus ticket issued by Marches Motors, the only firm which ran through Crybbe – twice a week, if you were lucky.

But neither in the gutter nor up against the walls did she find what she was looking for.

When Arnold stopped to cock his leg up against a lamppost, Fay stopped, too, and examined the bottom of the post for old splash-marks.

There were none that she could see, and Arnold didn't hang around. He was off in a hurry, straining on the clothes-line as he always did on the street. She'd have to get him a lead tomorrow.

Now *there* was a point. Fay steered Arnold past Middle Marches Crafts and the worn sign of the Crybbe Pottery, which her dad said was about to close down. There was a hardware shop round the corner.

Hereward Newsome was emerging from The Gallery. 'Oh, hi, Fay. Out on a story?'

'You're working late.'

'We're rearranging the main gallery. Making more picture space. Time to expand, I think, now the town's taking off.'

'Is it?'

'God, yes, you must have noticed that. Lots of new faces about. Whatever you think of Max Goff, he's going to put this place on the map at last. I've been talking to the marketing director of the Marches Development Board – they're terribly excited. I should have a word with him sometime, they're very keen to talk about it.'·

'I will. Thanks. Hereward, look, you haven't got a dog, have you?'

'Mmm? No. Jocasta had it in mind to buy a Rottweiler once – she gets a little nervous at night. Be good deal more nervous with a Rottweiler around, I said. Hah. Managed to talk her out of that one, thank God.'

'Do you know anybody who *has* got one?'

'A Rottweiler?'

'No, any sort of dog.'

'Er . . . God, is that the time? No, it's not something I tend to notice, who has what kind of dog. Look, pop in sometime; there's a chap – artist – called Emmanuel Walters. Going to be very fashionable. You might like to do an interview with him about the exhibition we're planning. Couple of days before we open, would that be possible? Give you a ring, OK?'

She nodded and smiled wanly, and Hereward Newsome walked rapidly away along the shadowed street, long strides, shoulders back, confident.

Fay dragged Arnold round the corner to the hardware shop. Like all the other shops in Crybbe, there was never a light left on at night, but at least it had two big windows – through which, in turn, she peered, looking for one of those circular stands you always saw in shops like this, a carousel of dog leads, chains and collars.

There wasn't one.

No, of course there wasn't. Wouldn't be, would there? Nor would there be cans of dog food or bags of Bonios.

The streets were empty and silent. As they would be, coming up to curfew time, everybody paying lip-service to a tradition which had been meaningless for centuries. She was starting to work it out, why there was this artificial kind of tension in the air: nobody came out of anywhere for about three minutes either side of the curfew.

Except for the newcomers.

'Fay. Excuse me.'

Like Murray Beech.

Walking across the road from the church, one hand raised, collar gleaming in the dusk.

'Could I have a word?'

When he reached her, she was quite shocked at how gaunt he appeared. The normally neatly chiselled face looked suddenly jagged, the eyes seemed to glare. Maybe it was the light.

Fay reined Arnold in. There was a sense of unreality, of her and the dog and the vicar in a glass case in the town centre, public exhibits. And all the curtains parting behind the darkened windows.

Sod this. *Sod it!*

173

'Murray,' she said quite loudly, very deliberately, 'just answer me one question.'

He looked apprehensive. (In Crybbe, every question was a threat.)

Fay said, 'Do you know anybody with a dog?' The words resounded around the square.

The vicar stared at her and his head jerked back, as if she'd got him penned up in a corner with her microphone at his throat.

'Anybody,' Fay persisted. 'Any kind of dog. Anybody in Crybbe?'

'Look, it was about that I . . .'

'Because I've been scouring the gutters for dog turds and I can't find any.'

'You . . . ?'

'Not one. Not a single bloody dog turd. Surprise you that, does it? No dog turds in the streets of Crybbe?'

Fay became aware that she was coiling and uncoiling the clothes-line around her fingers, entwining them until the plastic flex bit into the skin. She must look as mad as Murray did. She felt her face was aflame and her hair standing on end. She felt she was burning up in the centre of Crybbe, spontaneous emotional combustion in the tense minutes before the curfew's clang.

'No dog turds, Murray. No dog leads in the shops. No . . .' The sensation of going publicly insane brought tears to her eyes. 'No rubber bones . . .'

Murray pulled himself together. Or perhaps, Fay thought, in comparison with me it just looks as though he's together.

'Go home, Fay,' he said.

'Yes,' Fay said, 'I will.'

With Arnold tight to her legs, she turned away and began to walk back in the direction she'd come along the silent street. It was nearly dark now, but there were no lights in any of the houses.

Because people would be watching at the windows. The woman, the vicar and the dog. A tableau. A little public drama.

She turned back. 'It's true, though, isn't it? Apart from Arnold here, there aren't any dogs in Crybbe.'

'I don't know,' Murray said. It was obvious the idea had never occurred to him. 'But . . . well, it's hardly likely, is it?' She couldn't see his face any more, only his white collar, luminous like a cyclist's armband.

'Oh yes,' Fay said, 'it's likely. Anything's likely in this town.'

'Yes, well . . . I'll just . . . I'll just say what I've been asked to say before . . . before you go.'

There came a heavy metallic creak from the church tower. The bell swinging back.

and . . . *Clangggg!*

It had never sounded so loud. The peal hit the street like a flash of hard, yellow light.

Arnold sat down in the road and his head went back.

Fay saw him and fell on her knees with both hands around his snout.

As the first peal died, Murray Beech said, 'I've been asked . . . to tell you to keep the dog off the streets.'

'What?'

'Especially at . . . curfew time. People don't . . . they don't like it.'

Rage rippled through Fay. She looked up into the vicar's angular, desperate face.

'*What?*'

Her hands unclasped. She came slowly to her feet.

She watched as Arnold swallowed, shook his head once and then quivered with the vibration from the tower as the great bell swung back.

Clangggg!

Arnold's first howl seemed to rise and meet the peal in the air above the square with an awful chemistry.

'Who?' Fay said quietly.

'Go home!' the vicar hissed urgently. 'Take the thing away.'

'Who told you to tell me?'

There was a shiver in the night, the creak of the bell hauled back.

Fay shrieked, '*Who told you, you bastard?*'

The bell pealed again, like sheet-lightning. Arnold howled. The old buildings seemed to clutch each other in the shadows.

And she was hearing the muffled clatter of his footsteps before she was aware that Murray Beech was running away across the square, as if Hell was about to be let loose in Crybbe.

CHAPTER X

'YOU really didn't have to go to all this trouble,' J. M. Powys said. 'Chicken in the basket would have been fine.'

Rachel said, 'Care to send down for some?'

'Forget it.' He was remembering how she'd massaged the bruises on his stomach with her lips. What happened? How did this come about?

The room, overlooking the cobbled square, bulged from the Cock's aged frame above an entryway. Once, they'd heard footsteps on the stones directly underneath.

Lights shone blearily from town houses, and the room's leaded windows dropped a faint trellis on the sheets.

They lay in complete silence for a long time before he turned to her and said, 'Er . . . well . . .'

'Don't look at *me*,' Rachel said. 'I certainly didn't intend it to happen. I know I'm hardly the person to claim she isn't a whore, but we didn't even know each other until a couple of hours ago. And I'm not actually promiscuous. Most of the time these days I can take it or leave it.'

It had been the curfew which had seemed to shatter the idyll. They'd fallen apart, Powys feeling bewildered, Rachel looking almost perturbed.

He didn't even remember getting into bed. They hadn't drunk anything, or smoked anything and it was not yet ten-thirty. He'd quite fancied her, certainly, but there'd been other things on his mind. Like serious pain.

He thought she was smiling. It *felt* like she was smiling. In her deep and opulent voice, she said, 'Perhaps we should think of it as one of those whirlwind passions.'

'Well, I'm glad you're not annoyed,' said Powys. He

couldn't remember much until the curfew, crashing in like an alarm clock hauling him out of a hot dream. 'That curfew,' he said. 'Kind of eerie, don't you think? Did you hear a dog howling at the same time, at one point? Or was that me?'

'No, it was a dog all right. Really rather spooky, J.M.'

'Why do people keep calling me J.M.?'

'It sounds classier than Joseph Miles.'

He remembered the circumstances in which she'd seen his driving licence. Suddenly his stomach was hurting again.

'Tell me,' she said. 'Are you really a descendant of John Cowper Powys?'

'I wouldn't entirely rule it out.' To take his mind off the pain, he flicked aside a few strands of fine, fair hair to admire the curve of her long neck. 'Hey, look, what would Max Goff say if he found out I'd been in his bed with his . . . ?'

His . . . what, exactly?

'Don't worry about that, he'd be honoured. I'm only a minion; you're his inspiration. But he isn't going to find out.' Rachel turned her face towards him. 'I won't even tell him you were trespassing on his property.'

'I wasn't trespassing. It was what you might call an exploratory tour.'

'Quite,' said Rachel. 'You were snooping.'

'Well, probably. Look, I really am sorry about . . .'

'J.M., I'm not a virgin. The unwritten part of my job description includes ensuring that the boss goes to sleep fully relaxed.'

'What?' He was shocked.

'Routine,' Rachel said dismissively. 'Like winding up an alarm clock.'

'Stone me.' He found this impressively cool and candid. And rather sad. He felt a faintly surprising tenderness coming on.

'I must say,' Rachel said, 'I was genuinely surprised to find out who you were. I was rather expecting J. M. Powys to be a vague, if benevolent old cove in a woolly hat and half-moon glasses. By the way, I think your book's a dreadful sham. Do you mind?'

'*Golden Land*?' He started to smile. He'd been right about Rachel. Nothing Arthur Rackham about this woman. 'Why do you think that? No, I don't mind at all. I don't bruise as easily as a cursory examination might suggest.'

'Well, let's not talk about that now.'

'No, go on. Talk about it.'

'Really?' Rachel faced him across the bed, not touching. 'OK. Well, the central premise, if I have this right, is that there's a hidden link between us and the earth, a link known to our remote ancestors, but which we've forgotten about.'

'The psychic umbilicus.' As time went on, Powys had grown less and less convinced he'd written this crap.

'And, by going to the various ancient shrines, stone circles, holy wells, places like that, we can unblock the doorways and find our way back, as it were, into the Old Golden Land. Which seems to be your metaphor, or whatever, for this kind of harmony with the environment, feeling a part of one's surroundings. Us and the earth feeding each other?'

Powys nodded. 'What's wrong with it so far?'

'Nothing at all,' Rachel said. 'Perfectly commendable. Except it's translated itself into all these old hippies staggering about with their dowsing rods and holding up their hands and feeling the Earth Spirit. I mean – let's be realistic about this – if these are the people with the keys to the cosmos, then God help us.'

Powys was impressed. 'I think you could be my ideal woman.'

'Jesus,' said Rachel. 'You really *are* mixed up.'

After a minute or two, he said, 'I got a lot of it wildly wrong. It was nearly thirteen years ago, that book. I was too young to write it. I'd like to do it again. Or better still, I'd like not to have done it in the first place.'

'It's a bit late for that,' Rachel said. 'You do realize you're largely responsible for Max's very costly fantasies?'

'What does that mean?'

'It means he's going to be the first king of the Old Golden Land, and he wants you to be the Royal Scribe and tell the world about it.'

'Oh, my God. You think I should disappear?'

Rachel pulled his left hand to her breast. 'Not just yet. If you really have found the flaws in your own arguments, I can't help wondering if you might not be the one person who can bring him to his senses.'

Jocasta Newsome didn't know which was worse: spending a night in with Hereward or being alone.

She thought about lighting a fire, but, like most aspects of country life, it had lost its magic.

Could she ever have imagined there'd come a time when a log-fire in an open fireplace would not only fail to induce a small romantic thrill but would actually have become a drag? In the end, she'd been forced to admit that logs were messy, time-consuming and not even very warm. The only one who got overheated was Hereward, chopping away and coming in covered with sweat – nearly as damp as most of his logs, which were so full of sap that when you threw them on the fire they just sat there for hours and hissed at you.

And the Aga, of course. Very attractive, very prestigious for dinner parties. But it wasn't made to run all the radiators one needed for a barn like this. If they wanted proper oil-fired central heating, they'd have to install a boiler – electric heating was, of course, out of the question with all the power cuts and Hereward turning white when the quarterly bill arrived.

It had now become Jocasta's ambition to make sufficient money out of The Gallery to sell it and acquire premises somewhere civilized. With or without Hereward, but preferably without.

This morning Rachel Wade had phoned to say Max Goff had been terribly pleased with the Tump triptych. And would they please look out for more pictures of ancient sites. Or any local landscapes by local artists.

Local artists! There were none. Even Darwyn Hall was Birmingham-born.

This afternoon, just before closing time – after school, presumably – another 'local' artist had called in. A girl of seventeen or eighteen. An odd, dark, solemn girl. Would they like to put on an exhibition of her drawings?

Well, God forbid it should ever come to that. Children's drawings!

The girl's portfolio was now propped against the antique pine dresser in the kitchen – 'Yes, of course we'll *look* at them, my dear, but our artists do tend to be experienced professionals, you know.'

She'd let Hereward examine them when he returned from his weekly attempt to become accepted in the public bar of the Cock by proving he could be as boring as the natives. If they only knew how far ahead of them in the boredom stakes he really was, he'd never have to buy his own drinks again.

Jocasta stretched like a leopard on the sofa.

She herself was bored out of her mind. Farmers were said to shag sheep in these hills. Maybe she should go out and find a ram.

'Sex magic.' Rachel was telling Powys the sordid story of her life as Goff's overpaid PA. 'That was the other thing that almost pushed me over the edge.'

'Isn't all sex magic?' Thinking, particularly, of tonight.

'Certainly not,' said Rachel.

'Yeah, I know. I do know what you're talking about. Aleister Crowley, all that stuff?'

Rachel said, 'Fortunately, it didn't last. Though Crowley was about the same build as Max, Max couldn't summon Crowley's stamina. Not too pleasant while it lasted, though. Lots of dressing up and ritual undressing. The idea appeared to be to build up the power and then direct it at the moment of orgasm. He was the Great Beast, I was . . .'

'The Scarlet Woman?' Powys vaguely remembered Crowley's autobiography, remembered not finishing it.

'Terribly tawdry,' Rachel said. 'Needless to say, it didn't work – or I presume it didn't. Point is, Max isn't a wicked man, it's just a case of what you might call Bored Billionaire Syndrome. You've got all the money you'll ever want, all the women and all the boys. But you're not . . . quite . . . God.'

'What can one do about this minor shortfall?'

Rachel said, 'He's doing it.'

And Powys nodded, resigned, as she told him about Goff's plans to restore the prehistoric legacy of Crybbe. 'Crybbe's Max's psychic doorway. His entrance to your Old Golden Land.'

'As identified by Henry Kettle.'

'And how reliable was *he*? Is dowsing for real?'

'It was in Henry's case. Henry was red hot.'

'The modern equivalent of the Stone Age shaman.'

'Who said that?'

'Max.'

'Figures,' Powys said. He sighed. 'Last night I went round to Henry's house to pick up his papers, his journal. Apparently he wanted me to have them. Anyway, it was pretty clear Henry had a few misgivings about what Goff was asking him to do – well, not so much that as what he was finding. He didn't like the Tump.'   •

'*I* don't like the Tump,' Rachel said.

'And leys – we don't really know anything about leys. All this energy-lines stuff is what people *want* to believe. Henry was quite impatient with the New Agers and their designer dowsing rods. He used to say we shouldn't mess with it until we knew exactly what we were messing *with*.'

Powys watched the lattice of light on the bedspread. 'A more plausible theory says leys are spiritual paths to holy shrines, along which the spirits of the ancestors could also travel. Evidence shows a lot of psychic activity at places where leys cross, as well as mental disturbance, imbalance.'

'Obviously the place to bring out the best in Max,' Rachel said drily. 'Excuse me, J.M., I need a pee.'

In the end, Jocasta had gone ahead and lit a fire, for what it was worth. The logs fizzed, the flames were pale yellow and the smoke seeped feebly between them, as she lay on the sheepskin rug enjoying, in a desultory way, a favourite fantasy involving the Prince of Wales in his polo outfit.

There was a crack from the logs and something stung her

leg. Jocasta screamed and leapt up. A smell of burning – flesh probably – made her beat her hands against her thigh in a panic.

She switched on a table-lamp with a green and yellow Tiffany shade and stood next to it, examining her leg.

Nothing visible, except a tiny smudge, Jocasta licked a finger and wiped it away, pulled down her skirt and was swamped by a sudden mud-tide of self-disgust.

From the living-room window she could see the lights of the town through the trees at the end of the paddock. The paddock itself was like a black pond. She fetched from the kitchen the portfolio of drawings brought in by the girl. If the kid was any good at all, she might sell them very cheaply. Not in the gallery itself, of course, but in the small gift section they were setting up in a little room at the side.

Jocasta sat on the sofa and opened the portfolio by the light of the Tiffany lamp.

At first she was simply surprised. She'd expected landscapes and she'd expected an immature hesitancy of touch.

So the things that surprised her were the strength and vigour of the drawing in Indian ink, spatters and blotches used for effect, boldly controlled in the manner of Gerald Scarfe and Ralph Steadman.

And the fact that they were not landscapes, but interiors with figures.

An old man shaving.

The eyes, wide open, magnified in a shaving mirror to alarming effect. The chin tilted, the throat uplifted to the razor.

A tumbler on a window-ledge collecting the blood.

At first she was simply surprised.

Then the shock set in. The realization, with a rush of bile to the throat, of what was depicted in the drawing. She tore her gaze away, covering the drawing, in horror, with her hands.

Then the lights went out.

Through the window, she saw that the lights of the whole town had gone out, too.

Jocasta didn't move. She was sitting there on the sofa staring into the sputtering half-dead logs in the grate, but seeing, swimming in her mind, the image of the thing on her knee, still covered by her hands, an old man cutting his own throat with a razor.

She thought she was sweating at first.

Under her hands the paper felt wet and sticky and, like the sap oozing from the green logs on the open fire, something warm seemed to be fizzing and bubbling between her fingers.

Jocasta let the portfolio fall to the floor and shrivelled back into the sofa, almost sick with revulsion.

J. M. Powys stood by the window, bare feet on bare boards. Looking down on the street, at a few customers emerging from the main entrance of the Cock directly below. The last he saw before all the lights went out was a couple of men stumbling on the steps and clutching at each other, obviously drunk but not conspicuously merry.

He'd been here several times, but never at night. Never heard the curfew before. And now, as if the curfew had been a warning that the town would close down in precisely one hour, somebody had switched off the lights.

Such coincidences were not uncommon on the border.

He remembered manufacturing the phrase The Celtic Twilight Zone as the title for Chapter Six of *Golden Land*.

The border country – any border country – has a special quality. Two cultures merging, two types of landscape, an atmosphere of change and uncertainty. In such places, it used to be said, the veil between this world and others is especially thin. Border country: a transition zone . . . a psychic departure lounge . . .

Rachel returned, slipped out of the robe, joined him at the window, naked. The moon was out now, and her slender body was like a silver statuette.

'You get used to it,' Rachel said, 'living in Crybbe.'

'The electricity?'

'It seems we're on the end of a power line, or something. So whenever there's a problem elsewhere it trips a switch and the whole valley goes off. Something like that. It'll be back on in a few minutes, probably.'

Powys put out a hand to her then held back and put the hand on the cool window-ledge. Things to sort out first, before he allowed himself to forget.

'Henry Kettle,' he said. 'His car went out of control and crashed into the wall around the Tump. Freak accident. What did Goff have to say about that?'

Rachel said, 'You don't want to hear that. Come back to bed, J.M.'

They did go back to bed. But she told him anyway.

'The nearest thing to a Stone Age shaman. I mentioned that.'

She lay in the crook of his arm, his hand cupped under a breast.

Powys said, 'Nobody knows a thing about Stone Age shamans or what they did.'

'Maybe it was Bronze Age.'

'Know bugger all about them either.'

'Max said they would sometimes sacrifice themselves or allow themselves to be sacrificed to honour the Earth Spirit or some such nonsense.'

'Theory,' Powys said.

'He said it must have been like that with Henry Kettle. Getting old. Knew he was on borrowed time. So he . . . consciously or subconsciously, he decided to end it all and put his life energy into Max's project. Max was standing there looking at the wreckage of Kettle's car. "Whoomp!" he kept saying. "Whoomp!" And clapping his hands.'

'OK, you've convinced me,' Powys said. 'This guy's wanking in the dark, and he has to be stopped before it goes all over everybody.'

Arnold whimpered. Fay awoke, feeling the dog trembling against her leg.

Although the bedroom light was out, she knew somehow that *all* the lights were out.

Knew also that in the office below, the little front room that had been Grace Legge's sitting-room, *she* was in residence.

Pottering about, dusting the china and the clock. The empty grin, eye-sockets of pale light.

And would she see, through those resentful, dead sockets, the hulk of the wrecked Revox and the fragments of its innards sprayed across the room?

Or was that not a part of her twilit existence?

Oh, please . . . Fay clutched Arnold.

Probably there was nothing down there.

Nothing.

Probably.

PART FOUR

Most of the natives once stood in superstitious awe of the ancient standing stones which are dotted up and down Radnorshire. Even today there are farmers who prefer to leave the hay uncut which grows round such stones, and some people avoid them at night as they would a graveyard.

W. H. HOWSE,
History of Radnorshire

CHAPTER I

AROUND mid-morning, Fay picked up the phone and sat there for several minutes, holding it to her ear, staring across the office, at nothing. The scene-of-crime man had just left, a young detective with a metal case. Lots of prints on the Revox and the desk, but they'd probably turn out to be her own and her father's, the SOCO had said cheerfully, fingerprinting them both. Everybody was a bit of a pro these days. He blamed television.

Fay held the phone at arm's length as it started making the continuous whine that told you you'd knocked it off its rest. She looked into the mouthpiece. The SOCO had fingerprinted that as well.

She tapped the button to get the dialling tone back. Could she really make this call?

. . . And what's the story, Fay?

It's very bizarre, Gavin. The fact is, I've discovered there are no dogs in Crybbe.

No dogs in Crybbe.

None at all. That is, except one.

Just the one.

Yes, mine. That's how I found out.

I see. And how come there are no dogs in Crybbe, Fay?

Because they howl at the curfew bell, Gavin. People don't like that.

That figures. But if there are no dogs in Crybbe, how do you know they howl at the curfew?

Well, I don't. I'm assuming that's the case, because Arnold howls at it. That's Arnold, my dog. Least, I think he's my dog.

Yes, well, thank you very much, Fay. Look, this illness your old man's got. This dementia. Anything hereditary there, by any chance?

'Oh *God!*'

Fay crashed the phone down.

Arnold lay at her feet, an ungainly black and white thing with monster ears and big, expressive eyes.

The only dog in Crybbe.

This morning, Fay had gone out soon after dawn into an intermittent drizzle. She'd followed a milkman, at whom no dogs had barked no matter how carelessly he clanked his bottles. She'd followed a postman, whose trousers were unfrayed and who whistled as he walked up garden paths to drop letters through letter-boxes and on to doormats, where they lay unmolested by dogs.

She'd walked down by the river, where there was a small stretch of parkland with swings for the children and no signs warning dog owners not to allow their non-existent pets to foul the play area.

Finally, at around 8.15, she'd approached a group of teenagers waiting for the bus to take them to the secondary school nine miles away.

'Does any of you have a dog?'

The kids looked at each other. Some of them grinned, some shrugged and some just looked stupid.

'You know me, I'm a reporter. I work for Offa's Dyke Radio. I need to borrow a dog for an item I'm doing. Can any of you help me?'

'What kind of dog you want?'

'Any kind of dog. Dobermann . . . Chihuahua . . . Giant, wire-haired poodle.'

'My sister, she had a dog once.'

'What happened to it?'

'Ran away, I think.'

'We 'ad a dog, we did.'

'Where's it now?'

'Ran off.'

'I was your dog, *I'd* run off,' another kid said and the first kid punched him on the shoulder.

'Listen, what about farm dogs? Mr Preece, has he got a sheepdog?'

'Got one o' them Bobcats.'

'What?'

'Like a little go-kart thing with four-wheel drive. Goes over hills. You got one o' them, you don't need no sheepdog, see.'

'Yes,' Fay had said. 'I think I see.'

She didn't see at all.

Powys left Crybbe before seven and was back before ten, a changed man.

He wore a suit which was relatively uncreased. His shoes were polished, his hair brushed. He was freshly shaven.

He parked his nine-year-old Mini well out of sight, in the old cattle market behind the square, and walked across to the Cock, carrying a plausible-looking black folder under his arm.

Taking Rachel's advice.

'Don't let him see you like that. You have to meet his image of J. M. Powys, so if you can't look older, at least look smarter. Don't let him see the car, he mustn't think you need the money – he's always suspicious of people who aren't rich. And you don't know anything about his plans.'

'Isn't Humble, the New Age minder, going to tell him he caught me nosing around?'

'I think not.'

He entered the low-ceilinged lobby of the Cock, where all the furniture was varnished so thickly that you could hardly tell one piece from another. It was like sitting in a tray of dark chocolates left on a radiator. Powys wedged himself into what he assumed to be an oak settle, to wait for Rachel.

Guy Morrison would be here, she'd told him, starting work on a documentary. He'd once worked with Guy on a series of three-minute silly-season items on Ancient Mysteries of the West for a Bristol-based regional magazine programme – J. M. Powys hired as the regular 'expert interviewee'. His clearest memory was of the day he'd suggested they look beyond the obvious. Taking Guy down to Dartmoor to see a newly discovered stone row believed to be orientated to the rising moon. He remembered the TV reporter looking down with disdain at the ragged line of stones, none more than eighteen inches high, barely below the level of his hand-stitched hiking boots. 'Let's move on,' Guy had said, affronted. 'I'm not doing a piece-to-camera in front of *that*.'

Presently, the Cock's taciturn licensee, Denzil George, emerged from some sanctum and glanced across. He displayed no sign of recognition. Still been in bed, presumably, when Powys was sliding out of a side door into the alley just after six-thirty this morning.

'. . . do for you?' Denzil said heavily. Powys thought of some shambling medieval innkeeper, black-jowled, scowling, lumpen-browed.

'Nothing at all, thanks, mate. I'm waiting for . . . ah, this lady, I think.'

Rachel had appeared on the stairs, sleek in a dark-blue business suit. 'Mr Powys?'

'Good morning. Am I too early?'

'Only a little. We're terribly glad you were able to make it. Mr George, I'm taking Mr Powys along to the Court, so if Mr Goff calls in, tell him we've gone on ahead, will you? And lunch as arranged, OK?'

Rachel tossed a brilliant smile at the licensee, and Denzil stumped back into his lair, where Powys imagined him breakfasting on a whole loaf of bread without slicing it.

'Very svelte,' said Rachel, surveying Powys on the steps outside.

'You're surprised, aren't you? You thought I probably hadn't worn a suit since the seventies. You thought it was going to be the wide lapels and the kipper tie.'

'Had a momentary fear of flares, then decided you were too young,' Rachel said flatteringly. 'Come along, J.M.'

A few minutes later he was admiring her thighs pistoning in and out of the dark skirt, as she drove the Range Rover, impatiently pumping the clutch, long fingers carelessly crooked around the wheel.

'We're going to the Court?'

'Couple of hours before they all arrive. I thought you'd like to see the set-up, or lack of one.'

She drove directly across the square and then thrust the

vehicle into a narrow fork beside the church. Powys remembered coming out of this lane last night in the same seat, nursing his nose, feeling foolish.

The nose still hurt. But this morning, he thought, with a kind of wonder, he was feeling more . . . well, more focused than he had in years.

And he wanted to know more about Rachel.

She swung the Range Rover between stone gateposts, briefing him about today's lunch. 'Informal gathering of the people at the core of the venture. New Age luminaries. A few supportive locals – newcomers, mostly. And Max's advisers.'

'Andy Boulton-Trow?'

Rachel parked in the courtyard. 'Of course, you know him.'

'All earth-mysteries people know each other. Andy – we were at art college together, which is where *The Old Golden Land* started. Both got into mystical landscapes. Auras around stone circles, Samuel Palmer moons over burial mounds on the Downs. Andy was a mature student, he'd already been to university.'

'He seems a very deep guy. Laid-back.'

'I suppose so,' said Powys.

Rachel parked outside the stable-block. 'Max says Boulton-Trow's knowledge of stones and prehistoric shamanic rituals is second to none.'

'Yeah, possibly.'

'But you wrote the book,' Rachel said.

Powys smiled. 'Andy professes to despise commercial books on earth mysteries. Comes from not needing the money.'

'Private income?'

'Inherited wealth. Something like that. Never discussed it.'

Rachel said, 'And who's Rose Hart?'

'She took the pictures for the book,' Powys said quietly.

Rachel made no move to get out of the vehicle.

'There were four of us,' Powys said, looking straight through the windscreen. 'Sometimes five. Andy and me and Rose, who was studying photography, and Ben Corby, who thought of the title – comes from an old Incredible String Band song – and flogged the idea to a publisher.'

He paused. 'Rose was my girlfriend. She's dead.'

'Don't talk about it if you don't want to,' Rachel said. 'Come and look at the crumbling pile before the others arrive.'

Rachel had keys to the Court. One was so big it made her bag bulge. 'Watch where you're stepping when we go in. It's dark.'

Not too dark to find Rachel's lips.

'Thanks,' he said quietly.

Rachel didn't move. The house was silent around them.

Back from the town, around mid-morning, Fay came in quietly through the kitchen door; Arnold didn't bark. He was shut in the kitchen with Rasputin, who was glaring at him from a chair. Arnold seemed glad to see her; he wagged his tail and planted his front paws on her sweater.

'Good boy,' Fay said.

Then she heard the wailing. A sound which clutched at her like pleading fingers.

Dad?

'Stay there,' she hissed. 'Stay.'

Wailing. The only word for it. Not the sound of a man in physical pain, not illness, not injury.

She moved quietly into the hallway. The office door, two yards away, was ajar. Little was visible through the gap; the curtains were drawn, as they might be, she thought, in a room where a corpse is laid out.

Her movements stiff with dread, Fay removed her shoes, padded to the door, and peeped in.

In the office, in the dead woman's sitting-room, the drawn curtains screening him from the street, Canon Alex Peters was sobbing his old heart out.

He was on his knees, bent over the slender wooden arm of the fireside chair in which Grace Legge had seemed to material-ize. His head was bowed in his arms and his ample shoulders trembled like a clifftop before an avalanche.

Fay just stood there. She ought to know what to do, how to react, but she didn't. She'd never known her dad cry before. When he'd displayed emotions, they were always healthy, masculine emotions. Bluff, strong, kindly stuff.

In fact, not emotions at all really. Because, most of the time Alex, like many clergymen, was an actor in a lot of little one-man playlets put on for the sick, the bereaved and the hopeless.

He'd be mortified if he thought she'd seen him like this. Fay crept back across the hall. It was so unbearably sad. So sad and so crazy.

So unhealthy.

So desperately wrong.

She moved silently back into the kitchen and attached Arnold's clothes-line to his collar. 'Let's go for a walk,' she whispered. 'Come back in an hour and make a lot of noise.'

As she slowly turned the back-door handle, a trailing moan echoed from the office.

'I will,' Alex sobbed. 'I'll get rid of her. I'll make her go.'

His quavering voice rose and swelled and seemed to fill the whole house. A voice that, if heard in church, would freeze a congregation to its pews, cried out, 'Just – please – don't hurt her!'

Fay walked away from this, quickly.

CHAPTER II

THERE really was a rope dangling from the steepest part of the roof. Powys could just about reach its frayed end. 'Careful,' Rachel warned. 'You'll fall into the pit.'

The rope felt dry and stiff. 'This is a touch of black humour?'

'Well, it's obviously not the original rope, J.M. Somebody probably put it there to hold on to, while doing repairs or something. Creepy up here, though, isn't it?'

The attic was vast. There were small stabs of blinding daylight here and there, signifying holes in the roof or missing slates. Underfoot, jagged gaps through which you could see the boarded floor of the room beneath.

'I don't know why I brought you up here, really,' Rachel said. 'I usually avoid this bit – *not* that I'm superstitious.'

She was spotlit by two thin beams from roof-gaps. He remembered her standing next to him, naked, in the window last night, pale, slim, silvery. She'd brought a small flashlight, and he shone it to the upper extremity of the rope, where it was tied around a beam.

'How many poor bastards did the Hanging Sheriff dispose of up here?'

'Hard to say, he was only sheriff for a year. But you could be hanged for most things in those days. Stealing cattle or sheep, picking your nose in church . . .'

'That's how Wort got his rocks off, do you think? Watching people dangle?'

Rachel wrinkled her nose in distaste. 'They say he was obsessed with what you might call the mechanics of mortality, what happens the moment the spirit leaves the body. Him and his friend, John Dee.'

'Not *the* John Dee?'

'The guy who was Elizabeth I's astrologer. His old family home's along the valley.'

'Of course it is,' said Powys, remembering. 'It's a farm now. I went over there when I was doing *Golden Land*. Somebody told me Dee had been into ancient sites and dowsing.'

'Well, he must have been into hanging, too,' Rachel said. 'If he was a mate of Michael Wort's.'

A jet of wind flew across the attic with a thin whine like a distant baby crying. The rope started to sway, very slowly.

Powys said, 'He was certainly into magic, but back in the sixteenth century magic and science were filed in the same drawer.'

He put out a hand to stop the rope swinging. He didn't like this rope with its dangling strands – somehow more disturbing than if there'd been an actual noose on the end. A sense of something recently severed.

'Anyway,' said Rachel, 'the last hanging up here was Wort's

own. There was some sort of peasants' revolt in the town, and one night they all gathered outside wielding flaming torches and threatening to burn the place down unless he came out.'

'We know you're in there . . .' Powys said flippantly, still holding the rope, not feeling at all flippant.

'So he shuffled up here and topped himself. That's one story. Another says there was a secret tunnel linking this place with Crybbe church and he escaped.'

'Where was he buried?'

'I don't know,' Rachel said. 'I never really thought about it. Probably at some crossroads with a stake through his heart, wouldn't you think? Naturally, they say he haunts the place – or rather his dog does.'

'This place?'

'The town. The outskirts. The quiet lanes at sunset. Over the years, according to Max, people have claimed to come face to face with this big black dog with glowing eyes. And then they die, of course. Like in *The Hound of the Baskervilles*.'

Powys took his hand away from the rope, and it began to swing again, very gently.

'Rachel, luv,' he said, 'can you hear voices?'

'Shit.' Rachel moved to the stairs. 'Nobody was supposed to be here for another hour.'

She went swiftly down the steps, Powys following, not wanting to be left alone up here, where Rachel believed the only danger was the unstable floor. Blessed are the sceptics. For they shall be oblivious of the numinous layers, largely unaffected by the dreary density of places, unbowed by the dead-weight of ancient horror.

While people like me, he thought, would no more come up here alone than pop into a working abattoir to shelter from the rain.

Only a short way down the stairs, Rachel disappeared.

Powys shone the torch down the twisting stone steps. The beam just reached to the great oak door at the bottom.

'Rachel!' He felt panic in his throat, like sandpaper. There was a creak to his left; he spun round and the beam found a shadowed alcove he hadn't noticed on the way up here.

Suddenly, white light blasted him and he hid his eyes behind an arm.

'This,' Rachel said, from somewhere, 'is the only part of the house I really like.'

'What's known as a prospect chamber.'

The window directly facing them, almost floor to ceiling, was without glass. In fact, it wasn't really a window, simply a gap between two ivy-matted gables. A rusting iron bar was cemented into the gap at chest-height.

The prospect chamber was tiny, too small for any furniture. But it had a view.

Powys's eyes widened.

He saw they were directly above the cobbled forecourt. Then there were the two gateposts and then the straight road through the wood. Over the tops of the trees he could see the weathercock on the church tower.

Without the wood, the town would be at his feet.

And everything – the gateway, the road, the church – was in a dead straight line.

He'd seen this view before.

In fact, if he turned and looked over his shoulder . . .

He *did* turn and looked only into blackness.

But if he could see through the walls of the house, what he would see behind him, following the same dead straight line . . . would be the Tump.

'Is this opening as old as the house?'

'I presume so,' Rachel said. 'Spectacular, isn't it?'

'Which means Wort had it built. Maybe *this* is why John Dee came here, nothing to do with the bloody hangings. Rachel, have you ever actually *seen* a ley-line?'

'This?'

'It's textbook. In fact . . .' He leaned across the iron bar, not pushing it because it didn't look too steady. 'This is the strongest evidence I've seen that the ley system was recognized in Elizabethan times. We know that John Dee occasionally came back to his old home and during those times he studied dowsing and investigated old churches and castle sites. He called it, in his records and his letters, treasure hunting. But what kind of treasure, Rachel? You know, what I think . . .'

He stopped. There were the voices again.

'Humble,' Rachel said. 'And somebody else.'

Powys's stomach contracted painfully.

'I don't think Humble actually got round to apologizing to you, did he?' said Rachel.

'I owe him one.'

'Don't even contemplate it. He's a very nasty person. Ah, they were waiting for Max.'

The black Ferrari hit the gravel with an emphatic crunch. Humble stepped out and opened the driver's door. Andy Boulton-Trow was with him.

'I don't like the company he keeps either,' Powys said.

'Humble? Or Boulton-Trow?'

'Either.'

Rachel said, 'Is there something I don't know about you and Boulton-Trow?'

> *Joey goes round the Bottle Stone,*
> *The Bottle Stone, the Bottle Stone,*
> *Joey goes round the Bottle Stone,*
> *And he goes round . . .*

'Hold it!'

They all look at Andy.

'It's widdershins,' he says.

'What?' says Ben.

'Widdershins. Anticlockwise. You're going round the wrong way, Joe.'

'Why?'

'Because that's what you have to do. I was watching a bunch of kids. It's traditional. Widdershins, OK?'

You shrug, but you aren't entirely happy about this. Old Henry Kettle gets up, turns his back and walks off, down towards the river.

'OK,' Ben says. 'Start again.'

Sod it. Only a game. You start to tramp slowly around the stone. There's a smile on your face because what you're thinking about is how much you love Rose and how glad you are that they managed to get her name on the cover.

And he goes round . . . ONCE.

When Guy came to the door, Fay simply pretended there was nobody in, knowing it had to be her ex-husband calling in on the way to his lunch date with Max Goff and his cohorts.

Knowing, also, that if Guy was in the mood he was arrogant enough to have lined her up as today's emergency standby leg-over. *Fay, hi! (Long time, no bonk!)*

Behind the bathroom door she clenched her fists.

There was a second ring.

Fay sat on the lavatory with the lid down. The lid was still topped by one of Grace's dinky little light-green candlewick loo-mats.

Grace. Her dad thought that Grace Legge, dead, had smashed the Revox. Somehow. It was insane. And there was no way they could talk about it.

There was no third ring.

Arnold sat at Fay's feet and wagged his tail. He never reacted to the doorbell.

Only the curfew bell.

'Arnold,' Fay said, 'do you want to talk about this?'

Arnold looked at her with sorrowful eyes. Even when his tail was wagging his eyes were sorrowful.

She held his muzzle between her hands. She couldn't remember ever feeling so confused, so helpless. So completely wiped out.

The phone rang in the office. Fay drifted down to answer it, not in any hurry. She wished she'd put on the answering machine, but the thing had been disabled so many times by power cuts that she'd almost abandoned it.

'Hello.'

There was a hollow silence at the other end.

'Yes. Hello.'

'Mrs Morrison?' A local accent. Male.

'Yes. Who's that?'

'Mrs Morrison, you been told.'

'Have I? Told what?'

'So this is your last warning, Mrs Morrison. You 'ave till weekend.'

'To do what?'

But, of course, she knew.

'And what if I don't?' Fay said grimly. 'What if I say I have no intention of even considering getting rid of the dog? Especially as nobody seems prepared to explain what the hell all this is about?'

'You been told,' the voice said. 'And that's it.'

CHAPTER III

GOMER Parry did plant hire.

He operated from an old wartime aircraft hangar up the valley, outside the village where he lived. In this hangar he had two lorries, the heaviest tractor in the county, a big JCB, a small JCB and these two bulldozers.

You didn't hire the equipment; what you hired was Gomer Parry, a tough little bloke with mad, grey hair and wire-rimmed glasses.

Been a farmer for nearly twenty years before the magic of plant hire had changed his life. Sold most of his land to buy the old hangar and the machinery. Gomer Parry: sixty-four now, and he never looked back.

Gomer could knock buildings down and make new roads through the forestry. He could dig you a septic tank and a soakaway that soaked away even in Radnorshire clay. And during bad winters, the highways authority always hired him as a snow-plough.

This was the only time other people recognized the truly

heroic nature of his job. They'd pour out of their homes, dozens of them, as he busted through the last snowdrift to liberate some remote hamlet that'd been cut off for a fortnight. Big cheers. Mug of tea. Glass of Scotch. Good old Gomer.

But last winter had been a mild winter. Bugger-all snow anywhere. And only Gomer saw the heroic side of the other things he did.

A few months ago he'd done this broadcast about the perils of digging drainage ditches and such. Explaining it to that little girl from the local radio. How, for him, it was like a military exercise – although not modern military; more like in these epic films where the knight gets into his armour, which is so heavy he has to be winched on to his horse. It was in these terms that Gomer Parry spoke on the radio of his life at the controls of the JCB.

Probably gave the listeners a good laugh. Certainly didn't bring him any more work. He couldn't remember a worse year, the local farmers – his regular clients – tighter than ever. Constipated buggers sitting there waiting for a laxative from Brussels. Farmers wouldn't fart these days unless they got an EC grant for it.

So Gomer Parry, feeling the pinch, had been very near excited when he had a phone call from Edgar Humble.

He'd played darts with Edgar Humble in the public bar at the Lamb in Crybbe. Edgar didn't say much, which was unusual for a Londoner; he just kept beating you at darts. But Gomer knew who employed him, and that was why he was very near excited when he got the call, because from what he'd heard here was a bloke who was going to need plenty plant hire.

'Knock walls down, can you?' Edgar Humble asked.

'What kind of walls?'

'Stone wall. Victorian, I'd say. Thick, solid. Five, six feet high. Couple of feet thick in places. Too much for yer?'

Gomer had almost laughed down the phone. 'Put it this way,' he said. 'If I'd been in business round Jericho way, all those years ago, they wouldn't have needed no bloody trumpets.'

*

'Max,' Rachel said, 'this is J. M. Powys.'

Max Goff put on his Panama hat. Bizarre, Powys thought. Eccentric. But not crazy. Those are not crazy eyes.

Goff looked at Powys for a good while. He had a beard like red Velcro. 'How long you been here?'

'Since last night,' Powys said steadily. 'I stayed at the Cock.'

'Yeah? Shit hole, huh? I hope you put it on my tab.' Goff grinned at last and stuck out a stubby hand. 'Hi, J. M. Welcome to Crybbe. Welcome to the Old Golden Land.'

Powys took the hand. Goff's grip was flaccid. Powys said, 'You think this is the Old Golden Land?'

The countryside was colourless. Mist was still draped around the Court like grimy lace curtains.

'Not yet,' Goff said. 'But it will be. Listen, if I'd known you were here I'd've driven back last night.'

'That's OK. Ms Wade was looking after me.'

Rachel was standing behind Goff in the courtyard. Powys deliberately didn't look at her. Neither, he noticed, did her boss, the man who overpaid her for little extras.

Goff jerked his Velcro chin at the two men at his side. 'This is Edgar Humble, my head of security.'

'Mr Humble,' Powys said tightly.

'And Andy Boulton-Trow, who of course you know, yeah?'

Andy wore a white shirt and black jeans. Close up, he looked even thinner than he'd been twelve years ago. You could see the bones flexing in his face as he smiled. It was a quick, wide smile.

It made Powys feel cold.

'Joe.'

'Andy,' he said quietly.

'Long time, my friend.' Andy's hair, once shoulder-length, was shaven right to the skull, and he was growing a beard. It would be black.

They hadn't met since Rose's funeral.

Goff said, 'Now Henry Kettle's gone, Andy's my chief adviser in the Crybbe project. Andy knows stones.'

Chief adviser. Jesus.

There was a big difference between Andy Boulton-Trow and Henry Kettle. What it came down to was: Henry would have said, don't mess with electricity until you know what you're doing. Andy would say, sure, just hold these two wires and then bring them together when I give you the nod, OK?

'So you lost Henry,' Powys said.

Andy dropped the smile.

'Tragic,' Goff said. 'There's gonna be a Henry Kettle memorial.'

A memorial. Well, that was all right, then. That made up for everything.

'We haven't decided yet where it's gonna go.'

'But somewhere prominent,' Andy said.

Powys didn't say a thing.

'J.M.,' Goff said, 'we need to talk, you and I. At length. I have a proposition. Hell, we all know each other, I'll spell out the basics. I want you to write me a sequel to *Golden Land* for Dolmen. I want it to be the Crybbe story. The – hey, what about this? – The *New* Golden Land.'

Goff beamed and looked round, Powys thought, for applause.

'What I'm talking here, J. M., is a substantial advance and the quality republication in under a year's time of the original *Golden Land*, to pave the way. Revise it if you like. New pictures. In colour. Whatever.'

Sure. Scrap Rose's pictures, Powys thought dully. Get better ones.

'And there's a place for you here.'

'A place?'

'A place to live. A beautiful house with a view of the river. Part of the deal. Rachel will take you there after we eat.'

'Mr Goff . . .' He wondered why people kept giving him houses.

'Max.'

'I have a place already. I run a little shop in Hereford called Trackways, which . . .'

'I know,' said Goff.

'. . . which is more than a shop. Which is a kind of museum to Alfred Watkins as well, the only one of its kind in Hereford, which . . .'

'But it doesn't *need* to be in Hereford,' Goff said. 'And it doesn't have to be a little shop. Come over here.'

He led Powys to a corner of the courtyard and pointed across the field behind the stables, about a hundred yards from the Tump, where the trees began to thicken into the wood.

'As befits the stature of the man, the Watkins Centre needs to be a major development in, let's say, an eighteenth-century barn.'

On the edge of the wood was a massive, tumbledown barn complex, beams and spars poking out of it like components of a badly assembled dinosaur skeleton.

'Place needs to be big enough to house a huge collection of Watkins's photographs and ley-maps, and scores of original paintings of ancient sites. And it needs to be here. In Crybbe.'

Powys felt like a cartoon character who'd been flattened by a steam-roller and become a one-dimensional mat.

Lowering his voice, Goff said, 'I know your situation, J.M. I know you put all the money from *Golden Land* into Trackways, and I know how difficult it must be keeping Trackways afloat.'

He clapped Powys on the back. 'Think about it, yeah?'

Goff strolled back to the silent group of three standing next to the Ferrari. 'Rach, there's been a slight change of plan. We have lunch at two, we spend the afternoon in discussion groups then we assemble, early evening, at the Tump.'

Powys saw part of a cobweb from the attic floating free from a padded shoulder of Rachel's blue business suit.

'The Tump?'

'A ceremony,' Goff said. 'To launch the project. We're gonna knock down the wall around the Tump. Maybe that's where Mr Kettle's memorial should be. We're gonna finish what he began. We're gonna liberate the Tump.'

Andy Boulton-Trow nodded.

Goff grinned massively. 'It's the beginning,' he said. 'Come on, let's get back to the Cock, see who shows up.'

★

From the top of the farmyard there was a fine view of the river and the Welsh hills behind. But Jimmy Preece and his son Jack were looking, for once, the other way, up towards the Court. This was a view Jack had been conditioned, over the years, to avoid – as if, when he emerged from the farmyard gates, he was to wear an imaginary patch over his right eye.

This afternoon a great black cloud hung over the Tump.

Below it, the bulldozer was bright yellow.

'Gomer Parry's,' Jack said.

'Sure t'be,' Jimmy said. 'And only one reason 'e's down there.'

'So what you gonner do, Father?'

'No choice, Jack. I shall 'ave to 'ave a word with 'im when 'e gets back.'

The two men stood in silence for over a minute.

Then Jack mumbled, almost to himself. 'Sometimes . . . sometimes I wonders, well, so what? What if 'e *do* come down, that ole wall? An' the ole bell . . . what if 'e *don't* get rung some nights?'

Jimmy Preece was too certain of his son even to reply. Jack was like him. Jonathon was like Jack. And Warren – well, Warren was only a second son, so it didn't matter, anyway, about Warren.

The Mayor was about to walk away, back into town, when he heard Jack saying, '. . . And the ole box. If the ole box is gone, do it matter?'

Jimmy Preece stopped and turned and walked back very slowly to where Jack stood, a bigger man than Jimmy, habitually in dark-green overalls.

'The ole box?'

'I don't know, Father, 'e's gone. Maybe. Might've gone. Hard to say, isn't it, without pulling the whole wall out?'

Jimmy Preece said, 'Can't 'ave gone, Jack. Sometimes them ole bricks subside. I told you, anyway, leave 'im alone, that old box. Keep 'im walled up. Tell Jonathon when 'e's thirty and married. Never tell Warren.'

'Found some bits of plaster and stuff in the fireplace,' Jack said. 'Poked about a bit and the bricks fell out the cavity.'

'Put 'em back, block 'em up.'

'That's what I was doin'. Cavity, though, see, cavity was empty, Father.'

'That case, you got a job to do, Jack. You get in there and find where the box's fallen to, then you put 'im back on the ledge and you seals the bugger up proper. And another thing, Jack, you get that dog seen to. Last night . . .'

'I know. Yeard 'im from the belfry even. I phoned 'er up. I give 'er till weekend.'

'This is the weekend,' said Jimmy Preece. 'Get Jonathon to do it.'

Jack Preece looked down at his boots. 'Gets to me sometimes, Father, that's all. Why us?'

He walked off without saying goodbye, because none of the Preeces ever said goodbye to each other; only ''Ow're you' on Christmas morning.

CHAPTER IV

THE one time Rachel had seen Guy Morrison, at a preliminary meeting with Max in London, he'd been wearing a lightweight suit with sun-glasses in the breast pocket and carrying a briefcase and a mobile phone.

Today, Guy was in director mode. He wore denims and a leather pouch, like a holster, on his belt. He had blond hair and craggy features. A TV man from central casting, Rachel thought. At his shoulder stood a dumpy, stern-faced girl with straight black hair and a waterproof clipboard.

Hustling J.M. off to the Cock, Goff had told Rachel over his shoulder, 'Morrison wants to do a few exterior shots of the Court with nobody about. Stick around till he shows, Rach, keep an eye on him.'

'Who is this, Catrin?' Guy Morrison asked the black-haired girl in Rachel's hearing. 'Remind me.'

'Guy, this is Rachel Wade, Max's PA.' Catrin's accent had a clipped sibilance Rachel identified as north-west Wales.

'Of course, yes.'

Rachel offered him a languid hand. 'We've spoken on the phone.'

Guy Morrison took the hand and held it limply for an extra moment, looking steadily, unsmiling, into her eyes. 'You're almost everything your voice implied, Rachel Wade.'

'Good,' said Rachel, with a tight, tired smile.

Guy Morrison dropped Rachel's hand, stepped back, looked around the courtyard then up into the sky again, where clouds and mist still formed a damp canopy.

He frowned. 'I wanted some GVs today. Establishing shots. But this weather's not conducive. At all. So I've told the crew, Rachel Wade, to set up in that stable-place. Acceptable to you, yes?'

'Fine.'

'Because what I thought I'd do after lunch is bang off a brief opening interview with Max Goff. Background of sawing and rubble everywhere. Traces of sawdust on the white suit, emphasizing the hands-on approach. May not use it, but I'm not happy unless there's something in the can on Day One.'

'You'd better see how he feels about that.'

Guy Morrison nodded and turned away. She watched him pace the courtyard, looking up at the hills fading into mist and at the Court itself, grey and spectral in its small hollow, like an old galleon half-sunk into a mud-flat.

When they arrived back at the Cock, close to 1 p.m., a car was being parked on the square, close to the steps: a silver-grey Ford Escort with an Offa's Dyke Radio sticker on its windscreen.

The driver got out and came over.

'Rachel, is it? Could I just have a word?'

Guy Morrison, peering at the car-sticker and registering it was only local radio, went ahead, up the steps, with his assistant.

'I'm from Offa's Dyke Radio. We carried a report yesterday without checking the details with you.'

Rachel had never seen this person before. He was a shortish, muscular man, about twenty-five, with a half-grown moustache.

'Word reached me you weren't happy about what went out, and I just want you to know I've looked into it. Gavin Ashpole. News Editor. You'll be seeing more of me.'

'Good,' said Rachel dismissively. 'Now if . . .'

'Problem is, we've been using a freelance, Fay Morrison, in Crybbe, but it hasn't been working out.'

'Apart from this one instance,' Rachel said, 'I don't think . . .'

'So, from now on, any *major* stories in this area, we're going to handle direct. What Mr Goff's doing amounts to a major story, naturally, so if there's anything you want to say, anything you want to get out on Offa's Dyke Radio, you call me direct. Here's my card.'

'Thank you.'

'In fact – this is off the record – we're considering putting a staff reporter into Crybbe. Especially if your thing takes off and the population starts to expand.'

'Really.'

'In which case' – Ashpole spread his hands, palms down in a flat, cutting movement – 'we'd simply stop using Morrison altogether.'

'I see,' Rachel said.

What an appalling little creep, she thought.

Over a bland buffet lunch – carnivores catered for, but strictly no smoking – Max Goff explained his plan to publish, in perhaps two years' time, *The Book of Crybbe*.

'Gonna be an illustrated record of the project,' said Goff. He paused and looked into his audience. 'And a blueprint for the Third Millennium.'

Warm applause. They'd needed extra tables in the dining-room at the Cock.

Goff said, 'I've asked J. M. Powys to write the book. Because his work remains, to my mind, the most inspiring evocation of a country still able to make contact with its inner self.'

Powys smiled modestly. The magical, mystical J. M. Powys. Too old, he thought miserably, to become someone else. Too young not to want to.

About forty people were there, some from London and elsewhere, to hear about the project and consider getting involved. Thin, earnest men in clean jeans and trainers and women in long skirts and symbolic New Age jewellery. Powys didn't know most of them. But he felt, dispirited, that he'd met them all before.

There was a delicate-looking tarot-reader called Ivory with a wife old enough to be his mother and big enough to be his minder. A feminist astrologer called Oona Jopson, in whose charts, apparently, Virgo was a man. She had cropped hair and a small ring through her nose.

After Goff sat down, Powys listened idly to the chat. He heard an experimental hypnotist talking about regression. 'I've got an absolute queue of clients, mostly, you know, from London, but what I'd really like is to get more of the *local* people on the couch . . .'

Apart from Andy Boulton-Trow, the only person he'd actually encountered before was the spiritual healer, Jean Wendle, from Edinburgh, who was older than the rest, grey-haired with penetrating eyes.

'This really your scene, Jean?'

'This? Heaven forbid. Crybbe, though . . . Crybbe's interesting.'

'You reckon?'

'Well, goodness, Joe, you said it. If you hadn't revealed what a psychically charged area this was, none of us would be here at all, would we?'

'You're very cruel.'

She narrowed her eyes. 'Come round one night. We can discuss it. Anyway. . . .' She smiled at him. 'How are things now?'

He looked around the room for Rachel, couldn't see her.

'I think things are finally looking up,' he said.

Later, Goff took him into a corner of the dining-room and lowered his voice.

'Confidentially,' he said, 'I need somebody who understands these matters to make sure this arsehole Morrison doesn't screw up. Part of the deal, he uses you as script consultant. No J. M. Powys, no documentary. J. M. Powys disagrees with anything, it doesn't go out.'

'That'll be fun.'

Goff put a hand on Powys's arm. 'Hey, you know when I first knew I had to have you write the book?'

Powys smiled vacantly, beyond embarrassment.

'See, when I first came to Crybbe, the very first day I was here, I look around and suddenly I can see this about the border country being a spiritual departure lounge. I'm standing down by the river, looking over the town to the hills of England on one side and the hills of Wales on the other. And that other phrase of yours, about the Celtic Twilight Zone, I'm hearing that, and I'm thinking, yeah, this is it. The departure lounge. It just needs a refuel, right? You know what I'm getting at here? You can feel it in this room right now. All these people, all reaching out.'

'Maybe they're reaching out for different things.'

'Ah shit, J.M., it's all one thing. *You* know that. Down to generating energy and throwing it out. What you put out you get back, threefold. Jeez, pretty soon, this town is gonna *glow*.'

'Seems to me there are things you need to work out, Joe,' Andy Boulton-Trow said. 'Maybe this is the place to do it.'

Those lazy, knowing, dark-brown eyes gazing into your head again, after all these years. I can see your inner self, and it's a mess, man.

Andy was probably Goff's role-model New Ager. He had the glow. Like he'd slowed his metabolism to the point where he was simply too laid-back to be affected by the ageing process.

'Let's talk,' Andy said, and they took their wine glasses into the small, shabby residents' lounge just off the dining-room.

Andy lounged back on a moth-eaten sofa, both feet on a battered coffee-table. Somehow, he made it look like the lotus position.

He said, 'Never got over it, did you?'

Powys rolled his wine-glass between his hands, looking down into it.

'I mean Rose,' Andy said.

'It was a long time ago. You get over everything in time.'

Andy shook his head. 'You're still full of shit, Joe, you know that?'

'Look,' Powys said reasonably, trying to be as cool as Andy. 'We both know I should never have gone round the Bottle Stone. And certainly not backwards.'

'Bottle Stone?' Andy said.

'And certainly not backwards. I should have told you to piss off.'

'I'm not getting you,' Andy said.

'What I saw was . . .' Powys felt pain like powdered glass behind his eyes. 'What I saw was happening to *me*, not Rose.'

'You had some kind of premonition? About Rose?'

'I told you about it.'

Andy shrugged. 'You had a premonition about Rose. But you didn't act on it, huh?'

'It was *me*.'

'You failed to interpret. That's a shame, Joe. You had a warning, you didn't react, and that's what's eating you up. Perhaps you've come here to find some manner of redemption.'

Andy shook his head with a kind of laid-back compassion.

If it was a big job, Gomer Parry worked with his nephew, Nev. Today Nev had just followed him up in the van and they'd got the smaller bulldozer down from the lorry, and then Nev had pushed off.

No need for a second man. Piece of piss, this one.

Unless, of course, they wanted him to take out the whole bloody mound.

Gomer chuckled. He could do that too, if it came to it.

He was sitting in the cab of the lorry, listening to Glen Miller on his Walkman. The bulldozer was in the field, fuelled up, waiting. Not far away was a van with a couple of loudspeakers on its roof, such as you saw on the street at election time. Funny job this. Had to be on site at one o'clock to receive his precise instructions. Seemed some middle bit had to come out first. Make a big thing of it, Edgar Humble had said. A spectacle. No complaints there; Gomer liked a bit of spectacle.

With the Walkman on, he didn't hear any banging on the cab door. It was the vibrations told him somebody was trying to attract his attention.

He took off the lightweight headphones, half-turned and saw an old checked cap with a square patch on the crown, where a tear had been mended. Gomer, who was a connoisseur of caps, recognized it at once and opened his door.

'Jim.'

'What you doin' yere, Gomer?' the Mayor, Jimmy Preece, asked him bluntly.

'I been hired by that Goff,' Gomer said proudly. 'He wants that bloody wall takin' out, he does.'

'Does he. Does he indeed.'

'Some'ing wrong with that, Jim? You puttin' a bid in for the stone? Want me to go careful, is it?'

Jimmy Preece took off his cap and scratched his head. Even though it was still drizzling, he didn't put the cap back on but rolled it up tighter and tighter with both hands.

'I don't want you doin' it at all, Gomer,' he said. 'I want that wall left up.'

'Oh aye?' Gomer said sarcastically. 'Belongs to you, that wall, is it?'

The Mayor's eyes were watery as raw eggs. 'You're not allowed, take it from me, Gomer, that's a fact. Been there for centuries, that wall. He'll have a protection order on 'im, sure to.'

'Balls,' said Gomer. 'I was told he was Victorian, no older'n that.'

'Well, you was told wrong, Gomer. See, I don't want no argument about this. No bad feeling. Just want you to know that we, that is me and Jack and several other prominent citizens of this area, includin' several farmers and civic leaders, would prefer it if the wall stayed up.'

Gomer couldn't believe it.

'Just 'ang on, Jim, so's I gets this right. You're sayin' if I falls that thing, then . . .'

Jimmy Preece tightened his old lips until his mouth looked like a complicated railway junction.

'You bloody well knowed why I was yere, di'n't you?' said Gomer. 'You knowed exac'ly.'

'I been invited,' the Mayor said sadly. 'That Goff, 'e phone me up and invited me to watch. Silly bugger.'

'So what you're sayin', if I brings him down, that wall, you'll . . .'

'I'm not sayin' nothin',' the Mayor said firmly. 'I got no authority to order you about, and I don't intend . . .'

'Oh no, Jim, you're only bloody threatenin' me! You're sayin' if I starts workin' for Goff, then I don't get no work nowhere else around yere. Right.'

Gomer levelled a grimy forefinger at the Mayor. 'You bloody stay there! Don't you bloody move! I'll get a witness, an' you can say it again in front of 'im.'

The Mayor said calmly, 'You won't find no witnesses in this town as'll say I threatened you, Gomer, 'cause I 'aven't. You can do what the hell you likes for Mr Goff.'

''Cept pull that wall down, eh?'

''Cept pull that wall down,' the Mayor agreed.

CHAPTER V

WHAT have you got to lose?' Rachel had asked him, and he wondered about this.

The cottage was on a little grassy ridge, overlooking the river. Rachel told him Max had been so taken with the little place he'd thought of spending nights here himself until work on the stable-block was finished. But, with extra builders, overtime, bonuses, it looked as if the stables would be habitable within the next few days. And Max had to spend a long weekend in London, anyway.

'So it's yours,' Rachel said. 'If you want it.'

It had only four rooms. Kitchen, bathroom, bedroom and this small, square living-room, with a panoramic, double-glazed view downstream.

'A writer's dream,' Rachel said non-committally.

'Furnished, too,' Powys said.

'It was a second home. The first thing Max's agent did was to acquire a list of local holiday homes and write to the owners offering disproportionate sums for a complete deal, basic furniture included. Just over a third of them said yes within two days – boredom setting in, wouldn't it be nice to have one in Cornwall instead? Then, out of the blue, here's Fairy Godfather Goff with a sack of cash.'

'And you say he's in London for the weekend?'

'That's the plan,' Rachel said. 'But – you may be glad to hear, or not – I'm staying.'

Powys kissed her.

'Mmm. I'm staying because there's a public meeting to organize for next week. The people of Crybbe come face to face with their saviour for the first time and learn what the New Age has to offer *them*.'

'Should be illuminating. You think any of them know what New Age means?'

'J.M., even *I* don't know what it means. Do you?'

'All I was thinking, if it involves having big stones planted in their gardens, country folk can be a tiny bit superstitious. Especially stones their ancestors already got rid of once.'

Rachel perched on the edge of a little Jotul wood-burning stove. She licked a forefinger and made the motions of counting out paper money. 'Rarely fails,' she said. 'And if they're really superstitious, they can always move out and sell Max the farm for . . .'

'A suitably disproportionate sum,' said Powys. 'It's another world, isn't it? So, er, you'll be on your own this weekend.'

Rachel moved a hip. She was wearing tight wine-coloured jeans and a white blouse. 'Max suggests I move out of the Cock and into the stables.'

'But nobody'll be there to know one way or the other, will they?' Powys had been quite taken with the reproduction brass bed upstairs.

'There's Humble, in his caravan. He doesn't like me.'

'Does he like anybody?'

'Debatable,' said Rachel.

'I'm sure we can work something out. What's the rent on this place, by the way?'

'I think it's part of the advance against royalties. There'll be an agreement for you to sign. This gives you a small – small to Max, but not necessarily to you – lump sum as well. If you don't finish *The Book of Crybbe* he gets the cottage back. He also reserves the right to install standing stones or other ritual artefacts on your lawn.'

'Rachel, luv, help me. What do I do?'

'My advice? Take it, but ask for a bigger lump sum. He won't double-cross you. He's a very determined man. This town does *not* know what's hit it. Not yet. I'd feel better if you were here as some sort of fifth column. He'll listen to you.'

Powys shook his head, bemused.

Perhaps you've come here to find some manner of redemption.
Perhaps.

All he had to do was make one phone call and Annie would dive on the chance of taking over Trackways for an unspecified period. Just her and Alfred Watkins and an ever-broadening selection of New Age trivia. It might even start making a reasonable profit.

Rachel said, 'One more thing. If you'd like a word processor, please specify the make and model, to match your existing software.'

Powys thought about this, chin in hands, patched elbow on the pine dining-table. 'New ribbon for the Olivetti?'

When they reached the Tump, they split up, for the sake of appearances. It was 7 p.m. The rain was holding off, but the evening was very still and close, the sky hanging low, looking for trouble.

Rachel looked around and saw quite a big semi-circle of people, many more than had been at the lunch.

Word had got around that something was going to happen. Word very soon got around in this town, she'd found.

'What's going on, Ms Wade?' Jocasta Newsome was posing dramatically against the lowering sky in a glistening new ankle-length Barbour, conspicuously more expensive than Rachel's.

'Max is going to get rid of the wall around the Tump.'

'Oh,' said Jocasta, disappointed. 'That's all?'

'It's a major symbolic gesture,' Rachel said patiently.

'Is that a television camera?'

'They're making a documentary about Max.'

'Oh.' Jocasta brightened. 'That's . . . er . . . oh, Guy Morrison, isn't it? I think he's rather good, don't you?'

'Yes, excellent,' Rachel said absently. 'Excuse me.'

She'd seen Fay on the edge of the field, with the dog still on the end of a clothes-line. Fay looked forlorn in a royal-blue cagoule that was too long for her. She wore no make-up and her hair was damp and flattened.

'I know,' she said. 'Don't tell me. He's here.'

'Do you mean Guy? Or the Offa's Dyke man?'

Fay raised both eyebrows. 'Surrounded, am I?'

'I'm sorry about this, Fay, I really am.'

'They rang me,' Fay said. 'Offa's Dyke rang and said, don't bother with it, we're covered. I think they're trying to edge me out.'

'Ashpole's a tedious little man.'

'Poisonous,' Fay said.

'Fay, look, perhaps there's something . . .' If she could somehow turn Max round, fix it so he'd only talk to Fay. Most unlikely.

'Not your problem, Rachel, if I can't function here. Tempted to blame it on the town, but that's the easy answer, isn't it?' Fay grinned. 'If you really want to do something, I suppose you could suggest Ashpole might get some terrific actuality of the wall coming down if he stood directly beneath it . . .'

She wound the end of the clothes-line more firmly around her hand. 'Come on, Arnold, we'll go down by the river.'

*

Max Goff was on the summit of the Tump. He had a microphone on a long lead. The dripping trees were gathered around him.

Crouched under a bush, Guy Morrison's cameraman was shooting Goff from a low angle. It would look very dramatic, this apparition in white against the deep-grey sky and the black trees. On his knees next to Goff, as if in worship, Guy's soundman held a two-foot boom mike encased in a windshield like a giant furry caterpillar.

There were two big speakers on the roof of a van at the foot of the mound.

'This has been a dramatic and tragic week,' said Goff.

'Yeah, not too bad for level,' the soundman said.

'It fucking better be, pal,' the assembly heard. 'I'm not saying it again.'

Behind the speaker van, Powys smiled.

Guy Morrison said, 'I'm not pleased with him, Joe. He dropped this on me without any warning at all. A spontaneous idea, he said. He's got to learn that if he wants spontaneity we have *got* to know about it in advance.'

I have always disliked the Tump for some reason.

Powys thought, What does the wall mean, Henry? Why is there a wall around it?

He scrambled across the field, away from the crowd, unable to shake the feeling that perhaps getting rid of the wall was not the best thing to do – but wondering whether this feeling had been conditioned by Henry's misgivings about the mound.

Halfway across the field he saw the hub-cap from Henry's Volkswagen, glinting in a bed of thistles. It reminded him that his own car was still parked in a layby alongside the road at the end of this field.

Henry's journal was in the car.

Bloody stupid thing to do. Anybody could have nicked the car, gone off with the journal.

Behind him Goff's voice boomed out of the speakers. 'I'm glad-ad that-at so many of you were able to come today-ay.'

Powys moved swiftly through wet grass towards the road.

He reached it at a point about fifty yards from the layby. The white Mini was there; it looked OK.

'Is that your car?'

A lone bungalow of flesh-coloured bricks squatted next to the layby, and at the end of its short drive stood a stocky, elderly woman in a twinset and a tartan skirt, an ensemble which spelled out: incomer.

'Yes, it is,' Powys said, taking out his keys to prove it; unlocking the boot.

'You arrived just in time, dear, I was about to report it to the police.'

'Yes, I'm sorry, I got delayed.'

Actually, I was beaten up and then went to bed with a woman I'd never seen before but whose voice I'd heard on my answering machine, but you don't want to hear about all that.

Henry Kettle's journal lay where he'd left it, on top of the spare tyre.

'What's going on over there?' She had a Midlands accent.

'They're pulling down the wall around the mound.'

'Why are they doing that?'

Did she really want to know this? 'Well, because it's a bit ugly. And out of period with the Tump. That's what they say.'

'I'll tell you one thing, dear, that wall's never as ugly as the thing in the middle. I don't like that thing, I don't at all. My husband, he used to say, when he was alive, he used to say he'd seen prettier spoil-heaps.'

'He had a point,' Powys said, opening the driver's door.

'I'm on me own now, dear. It frightens me, the things that go on. I'd leave tomorrow, but I wouldn't anywhere near get our money back on this place, not the way the market is. It wouldn't buy me a maisonette in Dudley.'

Powys closed the car door and walked over.

'What did you mean, it frightens you?'

'You from the local paper, dear?'

'No, I'm . . .'

A shopkeeper.

'I'm a writer. My name's Joe Powys.'

'I've never heard of you, my love, but don't take it to heart.

219

Mrs Seagrove, Minnie Seagrove. Would you like a cup of tea? I'm always making tea for people in that layby. Lorry drivers, all sorts.'

'I won't put you to that kind of trouble,' said Powys. 'But I *would* like to know what, specifically, frightens you about that mound?'

Mrs Seagrove smiled coyly. 'You'll think I'm daft. That girl from the local radio thinks I'm daft. I ring her sometimes, when it gets on top of me, the things that go on.'

'What things are those? I'll tell you honestly, Mrs Seagrove, I'm the last person who's going to think you're daft.'

Following the river, Fay walked Arnold down the field, towards the bridge, close to where she and Rachel had gone with the bottle of wine on a sunny afternoon that seemed like weeks and weeks ago.

It was one of Fay's 'thinking' walks. She wanted, as someone once said, to be alone.

Before leaving, she'd pored over some of the books in her small 'local' collection – Howse's *History of Radnorshire*, Ella Mary Leather's *The Folklore of Herefordshire*, Jacqueline Simpson's *The Folklore of the Welsh Border*. Not quite sure what she was looking for.

Anything to do with dogs, really. Dogs and bells.

There'd been separate entries on both. Two books referred to the Crybbe curfew, one of only a handful still sounded in British towns – purely tradition – with two of them along the Welsh border. There was all the usual stuff about the bequest of Percy Weale, wealthy sixteenth-century wool merchant, to safeguard the moral welfare of the town. One book briefly mentioned the Preece family as custodian of the tradition.

Fay untied Arnold's clothes-line. He snuffled around on the riverbank, going quite close to the water but never getting his paws wet. Interested in something. Perhaps there were otters. The river looked fat, well-fed by rain.

Not raining now, but it probably would before nightfall, the clouds moving in together like a street gang, heavy with menace.

It was only since coming to Crybbe that Fay had begun to regard intangibles like the sky, the atmosphere, climatic changes as . . . what? Manifestations of the earth's mood?

Or something more personal. Like when a mist seemed to cling to you, throwing out nebulous tentacles, as if you and it . . . as if it *knew* you.

And the atmosphere hereabouts – threatening or blandly indifferent – was not an expression of the earth's mood so much as . . . She stopped and stared across the darkening river at the huddle of Crybbe.

Not the earth's mood, but . . . the *town's* mood.

This thought came at the same moment as the shot.

Fay whirled.

The riverside field was empty, the clouds united overhead, thick and solid as a gravestone. There were no more shots and no echo, as if the atmosphere had absorbed the shock, like a cushion.

Everything still, the field unruffled, except for a patch of black and white – and now red – that pulsed and throbbed maybe twenty yards from Fay.

'Arnold?' she said faintly. 'Arnold?'

CHAPTER VI

FROM where Rachel was standing, Max Goff, arms folded, resembled an enormous white mushroom on the Tump.

In tones which, roughed by the speakers, didn't sound as reverent as they were perhaps intended to, Goff paid a brief tribute to Henry Kettle, said to be among the three finest dowsers in the country, killed when his car crashed into the obscene Victorian wall built around this very mound.

'No way we can know what went through Mr Kettle's head in those final moments. But I guess there was a kind of tragic poetry to his death.'

Rachel closed her eyes in anguish.

'And his death . . . began a minor but significant preliminary task which I intend to complete today.'

Max paused, looked down at his feet, looked up again. The cameraman could be seen zooming in tight on his face.

'The Victorians had scant respect for their heritage. They regarded our most ancient burial mounds as unsightly heaps which could be plundered at will in search of treasure. And to emphasize what they believed to be their dominance over the landscape and over history itself, they liked to build walls around things. Maybe they had a sense of the awesome terrestrial energy accumulating here. Maybe they felt threatened. Maybe they wanted to contain it.'

Or maybe they didn't fool themselves it even existed, Rachel thought cynically.

'But whatever their intention.' Goff began to raise his voice. 'This wall remains a denial. A denial of the Earth Spirit.'

He lifted an arm, fist clenched.

'And this wall has to come down as a first symbolic act in the regeneration of Crybbe.'

People clapped. That is, Rachel noticed, members of the New Age community clapped, raggedly.

'Only it won't be coming down today,' Humble said.

Rachel's eyes snapped open.

'We got a problem, Rachel. This is Mr Parry. The bulldozer man.'

A little man in wire-rimmed glasses stuck out a speckled brown hand. 'Gomer Parry Plant Hire.'

'How do you do,' said Rachel suspiciously. 'Shouldn't you be down there with your machinery?'

'Ah, well. Bit of a miscalculation, see,' said Gomer Parry. 'What it needs is a bigger bulldozer. See, even if I hits him high as I can reach, that wall, he'll crash back on me, sure to. Dangerous, see.'

'Dangerous,' Rachel repeated, unbelieving.

'Oh hell, aye.'

'OK. So if it needs a bigger bulldozer,' Rachel said carefully, 'then get a bigger bulldozer.'

'That,' said Gomer Parry, 'is, I'm afraid, the biggest one I got. Other thing is I got no insurance to cover all these people watchin'.'

Rachel said, very slowly, 'Oh . . . shit.'

'Well, nobody said it was goin' to be a bloody circus,' said Gomer Parry.

Goff stood there, on the top of the Tump, still and white; monarch of the Old Golden Land.

He was waiting.

He came across the field in loose, easy strides, the twelve-bore under his arm, barrel pointing down. He wore a brown waterproof jacket and green wellingtons.

It was darker now. Still a while from sundown, but the sun hadn't figured much around here in a long time.

'Sorry, miss.' Cursory as a traffic warden who'd just handed you a ticket. 'Shouldn't 'ave let 'im chase sheep, should you?'

'*What?*'

It was only afterwards she realized what he'd said. Fay, on her knees, blood on her jeans, from Arnold.

The dog lay in the grass, bleeding. He whined and twitched and throbbed.

'Move back, miss. Please.'

And she did. Thinking it had all been a horrible mistake and he was going to help her.

But when she shuffled back in the grass, almost overbalancing, he strolled across and stood over the dog, casually levelling his gun at the pulsating heap.

Fay gasped and threw herself forward, on top of Arnold, feeling herself trembling violently, like in a fever, and the dog hot, wet and sticky under her breasts.

'Now don't be silly, miss. 'E's done for, see. Move away, let me finish 'im off.'

'Go *away*!' Fay screamed. 'Fuck off!' Eyes squeezed closed, lying over Arnold. The dog gave a little cry and a wheeze, like a balloon going down.

'Oh no,' Fay sobbed. 'No, please . . .'

Lying across the dog, face in the grass, blind anger – *hatred* – rising.

*

They both saw the dog fall, not far from the river, a blur of blood. The woman running, collapsing to her knees. Then the man wandering casually across the field.

'The bastard. Who is he?'

'Jonathon Preece,' Mrs Seagrove said, white-faced, clinging to her gate. 'From Court Farm.'

'What the hell's he think he's doing?'

'I wish I could run,' Mrs Seagrove said, her voice quaking with rage and shock. 'I'd have that gun off him. Look . . .' She clutched his arm. 'What's he doing now, Joe? He's going to shoot her, he's going to shot the girl as well!'

Incredibly, it did look like it. She'd thrown herself over the dog. The man was standing over them, the gun pointing downwards.

'Do you know her?'

'Too far away to tell, Joe.' Mrs Seagrove began to wring her hands. 'Oh, I hate them. I hate them. They're primitive. They're a law unto themselves.'

'Right.' Powys was moving towards the field. Common land, he was thinking, common land.

'Shall I call the police?'

'Only if I don't come back,' Powys said, shocked at how this sounded. For real. Jesus.

He slipped and scrambled to his feet with yellow mud on his grey suit. 'Shit.' Called back, 'What did you say his name was?'

'For God's sake, be careful. Preece, Jonathon Preece.'

'Right. You stay there, Mrs Seagrove. Get ready to phone.' Jesus, he thought, realizing he was trembling, what kind of place *is* this?

Guy Morrison was about to tear his hair. This was a two-camera job and he only had one. How was he supposed to shoot Goff *and* the destruction of the wall with one camera?

What this needed was a shot of the bulldozer crashing through, with a shower of stone, and a cut-back to Goff's triumphant face as he savoured the moment from his eyrie on the Tump. It would be a meaningful sequence, close to the top of the first programme, maybe even under the titles.

But how was he supposed to get that with one crew? If he'd known about this beforehand, he'd have hired a local news cameraman as back-up – Griggs, for instance. But he *didn't* know about it in advance because this arrogant, fat bastard was playing his cards too close to his chest.

At least the delay was a breathing space.

'Which you want to go for, then?' the cameraman, Larry Ember, asked him, pulling his tripod out of the mud close to the summit of the mound.

Guy pushed angry, stiffened fingers through his blond hair. 'Whichever we go for, it'll be wrong,' he said uncharacteristically. 'Look, if we set up next to Goff, how much of the bulldozer stuff do you reckon you can shoot from here?'

'Useless,' Larry Ember said. 'You're shooting a wall collapsing, you got to be under the thing, like it's tumbling towards you. Even then, with one camera, you're not going to get much.'

'Maybe we can fake it afterwards. Get the chap to knock down another section of wall round the back or something. We've got no choice, I need to get his reactions.'

'Could always ask *him* to fake it afterwards.'

'Perhaps not,' said Guy.

'Fucking cold up here,' Larry said. 'What kind of summer is this?'

A swirling breeze – well, more than a breeze – had set the trees rattling around them.

'Going to rain, too, in a minute.' Larry Ember looked up at a sky like the inside of a rotten potato. 'We should have had lights up here. I told you we needed a sparks, as well. You can't cut costs on a job like this.'

'I didn't *know* it was going to happen,' Guy hissed. 'Did I? I thought it was going to be a couple of talking heads and a few GVs.'

Goff lurched over, white jacket flapping in the wind. 'Some flaming cock-up here. Switch that damn thing off for now, Guy, will you?'

'You the producer, or is he?' the cameraman wondered provocatively.

'Go along with him. For now.' Guy had gone red. His dumpy, serious-faced assistant, Catrin Jones, squeezed his arm encouragingly. Guy knew she'd been in love with him for some time.

Below them, the speakers on the van began to crackle. Goff's voice came out fractured. '. . . et . . . chel Wade . . . up here. Get Rach . . . ade . . . up here NOW.'

Catrin zipped up her fleecy body-warmer. 'It's a funny thing . . .'

'Nothing,' snapped Guy, 'about this is funny.'

'No, I mean it's so cold and windy up here and down there . . . nothing.' She waved a hand towards the crowd below – some people drifting away now. 'No wind at all, nobody's hair is blowing or anything.'

'OK.' Guy prodded Larry Ember's left shoulder, bellowed down his ear. 'Executive decision. Let's get down there. Take a chance, shoot it from below.'

'. . . ucking sticks gonna blow over.' Larry clutched his camera as the wind buffeted the tripod. The wind seemed to be coming from *underneath*. Catrin's clipboard was suddenly snatched from her hands and wafted upwards with a wild scattering of white paper, like a bird disturbed.

She squealed. 'Oh *no*!' Clawing frantically at the air.

'Leave it!' Guy said.

'It's the shot-list!'

'Just let it go!'

Five yards away, Goff was shrieking into the microphone, to no effect. The sound had gone completely.

'. . . king weird, this set-up.' Larry's words snatched into the swirling wind.

'One more shot!' Guy screaming down the cameraman's ear again. 'Get Goff. Get him *now*!'

Goff's arms were flailing, the wide lapels of his white jacket whipped across his chin, the trees roaring around him, the sky black. He was out of control.

Guy wanted this.

Powys edged round the field, concealed – he hoped – by gorse-bushes and broom, then crossed it diagonally, approaching the man, Jonathon Preece, from behind, as quietly as he could. Feeling himself quivering: outrage and apprehension. He could see the woman lying not quite flat, spread across the dog, looking up now at Preece.

Heard her harsh whisper. '. . . done, you bastard?'

'I'm allowed,' Preece said with, Powys thought, surprising belligerence, the shotgun under his arm, barrel unbroken. 'If a dog's threatening sheep . . .'

'There *are* no bloody sheep!'

'There is in that next field,' he insisted. 'Up there, 'e was. I seen 'im before. We 'ad four lambs killed up there t'other week.'

'You're lying! This dog wasn't even here last week.'

'If a farmer got reason to think . . .' Waving his arms for emphasis, the gun moving about under one.

'You going to shoot *me* now?'

Jonathon Preece looked down at the gun under his arm and stepped back a pace or two. Powys froze, only three or four yards behind him now. Preece bent down, watching the woman all the time, and laid the shotgun on the grass to one side.

'See. I put 'im down now, the ole gun. You go 'ome. Nothing you can do.' A bit defensive now. 'I'm within my legal rights, you ask Wynford Wiley. Can't be 'elped. No place for dogs, sheep country.'

The woman didn't move. Powys saw a tumble of tawny hair over a blue nylon cagoule.

A curious thing happened then. Although it was way past 9 p.m. and the sky was deep grey – no trace of sunlight for hours – a shadow fell across the field like an iron bar.

And down it, like a gust of breath through a blowpipe, came a harsh wind.

'What's he doing? What *is* he doing?'

Rachel couldn't believe it. Max was jumping up and down on the summit of the mound, his white jacket swirling around him, his white trousers flapping, as if he was trying to keep his balance, struggling to stay on his feet.

227

'Looks like 'e's been caught in a hurricane,' Gomer Parry observed.

But there was no wind. The trees behind Goff on the Tump appeared quite motionless, while Goff himself was dancing like a marionette with a hyperactive child wielding the strings.

He's just angry, Rachel thought. Out of his mind with rage because the wall isn't collapsing and the PA system's broken down. Teach him to hire local firms for a job like this.

She was aware, on the edge of her vision, of Andy Boulton-Trow in his white shirt and his tight, black jeans looking up at the dancing bear on the mound. Andy's beard-shadowed face was solemn and watchful, then it split into a grin and he started shaking his head.

He saw Jonathon Preece look up in sudden alarm as the shaft of wind made a channel of black water across the river, from bank to bank.

There was a strangled yelp from the woman or the dog or both, but he couldn't hear either of them clearly because of the wind.

It came like a hard gasp of breath.

Bad breath.

The wind smelled foul. And as Powys, choking, reeled away from it, his senses rebelled and the whole scene seemed to go into negative for a moment, so that the sky was white and the grass was red and the river gleamed a nauseous yellow.

He stumbled, eyes streaming, a roaring in his ears.

And when the noise faded and the halitosis wind died and his vision began to clear, Joe Powys found he was holding the twelve-bore shotgun.

It was heavier than he expected, and he stumbled, almost dropping it. He gripped it firmly in both hands, straightened up.

Jonathon Preece roared, 'Who the 'ell . . . ?' Powys saw his face for the first time – raw pink cheeks. Age maybe twenty-two or three.

'Steady, pal.'

228

'You give me that gun, Mister!'

'Advise me, Jonathon.' Powys pointed the shotgun in the general direction of Jonathon Preece's groin. 'I've never used one of these before. Do I have to pull the two triggers to blow both your balls off, or is one enough?'

He was gratified to see fear flit, fast as an insect, across Jonathon Preece's eyes. 'I don't know who you are, mister, but this is none of your business.'

Powys felt himself grinning. In his right hand, the barrel of the twelve-bore was comfortably warm, like radiator pipes. The stock fitted into his armpit, firm as a crutch.

'You watch it, Mister. Ole thing'll go off.'

'Yes,' Powys said.

He raised the barrel, so that it was pointing into Jonathon's chest.

'You put 'im down. Be sensible!'

His finger under the trigger-guard, so firm. He thought, this man deserves what's coming to him. This man needs to die. He felt a hard thud of certainty in his chest. An acute satisfaction, the flexing of an unknown muscle.

He drank in the dusk like rough ale, closed his eyes and squeezed.

'Nnnn . . . oooo.'

Saw, in slow-motion, the chest of Jonathon Preece exploding, the air bright with blood, a butcher's shop cascade.

A tiny, feeble noise. He turned. The woman in the blue cagoule was up on her knees now, breathing hard. The tiny, feeble noise came out of the lump of sodden fur exposed on the grass.

'Arnie!' She looked up at Powys; he saw tear-stained, blood-blotched cheeks, clear green eyes and a lot of mud. 'Oh God, he's hanging on. Can you help me?'

Powys's mouth was so dry he couldn't speak.

Jonathon Preece screamed. 'You got no bloody sense? Gimme that gun!'

'I . . .'

'Please,' the woman begged.

'Gimme it!' The farmer took a step forward.

From out of the town's serrated silhouette came the first sonorous stroke of the curfew.

Powys looked down in horror at the gun. It felt suddenly very cold in his hands.

'Gimme . . .'

'Get it yourself,' Powys said, backing away, far enough away for Jonathon Preece, in this light, to remain unsure of what was happening until he heard the splash.

When the gun hit the water, Powys saw Mrs Seagrove hurrying down the bank towards them and then he saw Jonathon Preece's purpling face and became aware, for the first time, as the farmer advanced on him with bunched fists, that Jonathon Preece was bigger than he was. As well as being younger and fitter and, at this point, far angrier.

'You fuckin' done it now, Mister. Antique, that gun is. Three generations of my family 'ad that gun.'

Powys shrugged, palms up, backing off. He felt loose, very tired suddenly. 'Yeah, well . . . not too deep just there . . . Jonathon. Be OK. When it dries out.'

Preece's head swivelled – Mrs Seagrove coming quickly towards them, red-faced, out of breath – and he stopped, uncertain.

Mrs Seagrove stood there in her twinset and her plaid skirt, breathing hard, eventually managing to gasp, 'Did you see it? *Did you* . . . ?'

Powys looked at her, then at Jonathon Preece who'd turned to the river, was glaring out. The river looked stagnant. Preece hesitated, stared savagely into the drab water, started to say something and then didn't.

'Please,' the woman said from the grass.

It began to rain, big drops you could see individually against the hard sky.

Powys pulled off his jacket and knelt down. The dog's eyes were wide open, flanks pulsating. Powys didn't know what to do.

The dog squirmed, blood oozed.

Powys laid the jacket down. 'Put him on this.' He slid both hands beneath the dog. 'Gently. We'll get him to a vet. You . . . you never know your luck.'

In the river now, almost up to the tops of his wellingtons, Jonathon Preece bellowed, 'I know your face, Mister. I'll 'ave you!'

'Oh, piss off,' Powys said, weary of him. He heard Mrs Seagrove wailing, 'You must've seen it. It was coming right at you. It went *through* you.'

CHAPTER VII

JEAN Wendle was living in a narrow town house on the square. Inside, it was already quite dark. She put on a reading lamp. Its parchment shade made the room mellow.

Gold lettering on the book spines, the warm brass of a coal-scuttle in the hearth. It reminded Alex of his first curate's house in Oxfordshire, before he'd been promoted into an endless series of vast, unheatable vicarages and rectories. She'd certainly brought the warmth of her personality into the place.

Jean Wendle made him sit in a smoker's bow chair, his back to the fireplace, with its Chinese screen, facing a plain, whitewashed wall.

'Some days,' Alex said, 'it seems fine. I mean there might be nothing wrong. Or perhaps that, in itself, is an illusion. Perhaps I think I'm all right and everybody else sees me as stark, staring . . .'

'Shush.' Touch of Scottish in her voice, he liked that. 'Don't tell me. Don't tell me anything about it. Let me find out for myself.'

Yes, he really rather fancied her. Sixtyish. Short, grey hair. Still quite a neat little body – pliable, no visible stiffening. Sort of retired gym-mistress look about her. And nice mobile lips.

Cool fingers on his forehead. Moving from side to side, finding the right spot. Then quite still.

Quite sexy. Would he have let himself in for this if he hadn't fancied her a bit?

Not a chance.

'Don't talk,' she said.

231

'I wasn't talking.'

'Well, don't think so loudly. Not for a moment or two. Just relax.'

Taken him a few days to arrive into the cool hands of Jean Wendle. Well, a few nights – tentative approaches in the pub. Not a word to Fay. Definitely not a word to Grace.

And why shouldn't he? What was there to lose? The GP in Crybbe was a miserable beggar – hadn't been much to poor old Grace, had he? Drugs. Always drugs. Drugs that made you sleepy, drugs that made you sick. And at the end of the day . . .

Gradually, he and reality would go their separate ways. Rather appealing in one sense – what did reality have to commend it these days? But not exactly a picnic for anyone looking after him. Alex knew what happened to people who lost their minds. It sometimes seemed that half his parishioners had been geriatrics. They remembered having a wash this morning, when it was really days ago. They peed in the wardrobe, by mistake.

Fay, now – that child was suffering a severe case of misplaced loyalty. If he couldn't get rid of her, it was his solid intention to pop himself off while he could still count on getting the procedure right. She'd thank him for it one day. Better all round, though, if he could make it look like an accident. Fall off the bridge or something.

Would have been a pity though, with all these alternative healing characters swanning around, not to give it a try first. What was there to lose?

The first chap he'd been to, Osborne, had not been all that encouraging. Almost as depressing as the doc. Alex got the feeling old age was not what the New Age was about.

And all this 'like cures like' stuff. A drop of this, a drop of that. Little phials of colourless liquid, touch of the medieval apothecary.

'How long before it starts to work?'

'You mustn't expect dramatic results, Alex,' Osborne told him. 'You see, holistic medicine, by definition, is about improving the health of the whole person. Everything is interconnected. Obviously, the older one is, the more set in its ways the body is, therefore the longer . . .' He must have seen the expression in Alex's eyes. 'Look, my wife's an acupuncturist, perhaps that might be more what you . . .'

'All those bloody needles. No thanks.'

'It isn't painful, Alex.'

'Pain? I don't mind pain!'

Just the image of himself lying there, an overstuffed pincushion.

This kind of healing was a good deal more dignified, if you concentrated on those cool hands and didn't think too hard about what was supposedly going on in the spirit world.

He'd grilled her, naturally.

'Dr Chi? Dr bloody Chi? You don't *look* like a nutter, Wendy. How can you seriously believe you're working under the supervision of some long-dead Chinky quack?'

'My name's Jean,' she'd corrected him softly.

'Dr Chi!' Alex draining his Scotch. 'God save us.'

'Do you really want to know about this, Alex, or are you just going to be superior, narrow-minded, chauvinistic and insulting?'

'Was I? Hmmph. Sorry. Old age. Senile dementia.'

'Are you really old enough to be senile, Alex? What are you, seventy?'

'I'm certainly way past flattery, Wendy. Way past eighty, too. Go on, tell me about this Peking pox-doctor from the Ming dynasty.'

He'd forced himself to listen patiently while she told him about Dr Chi, who, she said, she'd once actually seen – as a white, glowing, egg-shaped thing.

'The name is significant. Dr Chi. Chi is the oriental life force. Perhaps that's the name I've subconsciously given him. I don't know if I'm dealing with a doctor from the Ming dynasty, the T'ang dynasty or whenever. He doesn't speak to me all sing-song, like a waiter serving chicken chow mein. All I know is there's a healing force and I call him Dr Chi. Perhaps he never was a human doctor at all or perhaps he's something that last worked through a Chinese physician. I'm not clever enough to understand these things. I'm content to be a channel.

Good gracious, don't you believe in miracles, Alex? Isn't that the orthodox Anglican way any more?'

Regarding the Anglican Church, he wasn't entirely sure what he believed any more.

Powys found the page, ran his finger down the column headed Veterinary Surgeons. 'OK, D. L. Harris. Crybbe three-nine-four.'

Mrs Seagrove dialled the number and handed him the phone.

The woman in the bloodstained blue cagoule sat in the hall. The dog lay on Powys's jacket on the woman's knee, panting.

'Have a cup of tea while you're waiting,' Mrs Seagrove said.

She shook her head. 'No. Thank you. We may have to take him somewhere.'

The number rang for nearly half a minute before a woman answered.

'Yes.'

'Mr Harris there, please?'

'What's it about?' Local accent.

'We've got a very badly injured dog. Could you tell me where to bring it?'

A silence.

'Dog, you say?' Shrill. As if he'd said giraffe or something.

'He's been shot.'

'I'm sorry,' the woman said flat-voiced. 'But Mr Harris is out.'

'Will he be long? Is there another vet?'

'Sorry.' Cool, terse. 'We can't help you.'

A crackle, the line broke.

'I don't believe it,' Powys said. 'She said the vet was out, I asked when he'd be back or was there anyone else, and she said she couldn't help me. Can you believe that? This was a vet's, for God's sake.'

'Wrong,' Fay Morrison said bitterly. 'This was a *Crybbe* vet's.'

*

'What the fuck was happening up there?' Max Goff lay on his bed in his room at the Cock.

'You tell me,' said Andy Boulton-Trow.

'I never felt so high. Like, at first I was really angry, really furious at the inefficiency. Why weren't they bringing the flaming wall down, why was nothing happening, why was the sound failing?'

'And then?'

'Then I felt the power. The energy. I never felt anything so heavy before. It took off the top of my skull. That ever happen to you?'

'Once or twice,' Andy said.

'Come to London with me,' Goff said. 'Stay at my place.'

'I have things to do here.'

'Then I'll stay here. We'll stay in this room. You got things to teach me, I realize this now. We'll stay here. I'll get rid of Ms Wade. I'll send *her* back to London.'

Andy placed a hand on Max's knee.

'You go back to London, Max. There's such a thing as too much too soon. You'll get there. You'll make it.'

Andy didn't move his hand. Max shivered.

'Took off the top of my skull. And then the curfew started.'

'Yes,' Andy said. 'The curfew.'

'I don't think I like that curfew,' Jean Wendle said, pouring Earl Grey, after the treatment. 'I don't know whether it's the bell or what it represents. I don't like restrictions.'

'Oh, quite,' Alex said. 'Couldn't stand it if it was a *real* curfew. But as a bit of picturesque traditional nonsense, it's all right, isn't it?'

'I think it is a real curfew, in some way,' Jean said. 'I don't know why I think that. Well, yes, I do – people *do* stay off the streets while it's being rung, have you noticed that? But I think there's something else. A hundred times a night is an awfully big tradition.'

'I suppose so.'

Alex would give her the benefit of the doubt on anything tonight. He didn't remember when he'd last felt so relaxed, so much at peace. And him a priest. Best not to go into the implications of all this.

'It's a very odd little town,' Jean said. She drew gold-dusted velvet curtains over a deep Georgian window.

'Aren't they all.'

'No, they aren't. This is. There are – how can I put it? – pockets of strange energy in this town. All over the place. People see things, too, although few will ever admit it.'

'See things?' Alex was wary.

'Manifestations. Light effects. Ghosts.'

'Hmm,' said Alex. 'Good cup of tea.'

'Being on the border is a lot to do with it. When we make a frontier . . . when we split something physically asunder in the landscape, especially when we build something like Offa's Dyke to emphasize it, we create an area of psychic disturbance that doesn't go away.'

Alex stirred his tea, wishing she'd talk about something else.

Jean said, 'Do you think they've taken on more than they can handle? Max Goff and the New Age people?'

'I thought you were one of them.'

'I like to keep a certain distance,' Jean said. 'I like to watch. Can they control it, I wonder? Or is it too volatile for them?'

'Oh, we can't control anything,' Alex said. 'That's something everybody learns sooner or later. Least of all control ourselves.'

It was well after midnight by the time they came out of the vet's.

Without Arnold.

'I couldn't stand the way he was looking at me,' Fay said. 'It's not been his week, has it? He's in a car crash, sees his master die. Saved from the clutches of the Crybbe constabulary, finds he's become a kind of pariah in the town. Then he gets shot.'

The Mini had been parked for over two hours on a double yellow line outside the vet's surgery in Leominster, fifteen miles from Crybbe. The nearest one from which they'd managed to get a response. The vet handling night-calls had been understanding but had made no comments either way about the wisdom of farmers shooting dogs alleged to be worrying sheep.

The vet had said Arnold would probably live. 'Just don't expect him to be as good as new with all that lead inside him.'

One of the back legs had taken most of it. Bones had been broken. The vet had seemed a bit despondent about that leg. Fay had spent half an hour holding Arnold at different angles while the vet examined what he could, removing shotgun pellets. He might have to operate, he said, and got Fay to sign a paper relating to responsibility if Arnold died under anaesthetic.

Now Fay and Powys were standing on the pavement, unwinding. It was very quiet in Leominster, the other side of midnight. No menace here, Fay thought.

J. M. Powys was shaking out his jacket. It was scarcely identifiable as a jacket any more. It looked as if someone had faced a firing squad in it.

'Oh God,' Fay said. 'I'm so sorry.'

J. M. Powys dangled the jacket from an index finger and looked quite amused. J. M. Powys. Bloody hell. 'It's hard to believe you're J. M. Powys. I thought you'd be . . .'

'Dead.'

'Well, not quite.'

'That lady, Mrs Seagrove. She called you Mrs Morrison. You're not Guy's wife, are you?'

'No,' Fay said. 'Not any more.'

She explained, leaning on an elderly Mini in a quiet street in Leominster, lights going out around them. Explained quite a few things. Talking too much, the way you did when you'd been through something traumatic. Only realizing she was shooting her mouth off, when she heard herself saying, 'I've got to get out of that place, or I'm going to implode. Or maybe I'll just kill somebody.'

She pulled both palms down her cheeks. Shook her hair, like a dog. 'What am I going on about? Not your problem. Thanks for everything you've done. I shall buy you a new jacket.'

'I don't want a new jacket.' Powys opened the car door. 'I like them full of patches and sewn-up bits.'

He drove carefully out of the town, dipping the headlights politely when they met another vehicle. They didn't meet many. The lights sometimes flashed briefly into the eyes of rabbits sitting in the hedgerows. Once, J. M. Powys had to brake for a badger scampering – that was really the word, she'd have expected badgers to lumber – across the road and into a wood.

Fay realized she hadn't phoned her dad. He'd be worried. Or he wouldn't, depending on his state of mind tonight. Too late now.

'Arnold!' Powys said suddenly, breaking five minutes of slightly sleepy silence.

'What?'

'Arnold. Not Henry Kettle's dog? You aren't the person who's looking after Henry's dog?'

'And not making an awfully good job of it, so far.'

'Stone me,' said Powys. 'Sometimes coincidence just seems to crowd you into corners.'

'Especially in Crybbe,' Fay said. She wished she was travelling through the night to somewhere else. Virtually anywhere else, actually.

The bones were very white in the torchlight. There were also some parchment-coloured bits, skin or sinew, gristle.

'Ah,' Tessa said, less than awed. 'I know what that is.'

Warren was miffed. How the fuck could she know anything about it?

'Yeah,' Warren said. 'It's a hand.'

'It's a Hand of Glory.'

'What you on about?'

'A dead man's hand.'

'Well, that's bloody obvious, isn't it?'

'A hanged man's hand,' Tessa said.

Warren squatted down next to her. The spade lay on the grass, next to a neat pile of earth and the square of turf, set carefully to one side so it could be replaced.

'Which means it's got magic powers,' Tessa said. 'Where'd you find it?'

'Around.'

'All right, *don't* tell me! What's that Stanley knife doing in there?'

'Well, I . . .' Buggered if he was going to tell her he'd been scared to put his hand in and take the knife out. 'I'm seeing what effect it 'as on it. You know, like you puts an old razor-blade under a cardboard pyramid and it comes out sharp again. New Age, that.' Warren cackled. 'I'm learnin' all about this New Age, now, see. 'Ow'd you know that?'

'Know what?'

''Bout it being a hanged man's hand.'

'I think I'd like to draw it,' Tessa said. 'Maybe I'll come up here again.'

'No.' It was *his* hand. 'Keep diggin' it up, the ground'll get messed up and somebody else might find it.'

'They won't. Do you know why you brought it here, Warren?'

'Good a place as any.'

Tessa smiled.

'What you done with them other drawings, the old feller?'

'Got fed up with him,' Tessa said. 'Passed him on.'

'Who to?'

'Dunno where he might end up,' Tessa said mysteriously. 'Part of the fun.' She smiled and fitted a forefinger down the front of Warren's jeans and drew him towards her, across the old box.

'Let's do it here . . . do *it* . . . by the box. Leave it open, see what happens.'

'Prob'ly come crawlin' out an' pinch your bum,' Warren said slyly. 'Anyway, it's too late now, for that.'

Tessa took her finger out of Warren's jeans. 'I wait᾽ᴊ for you.'

'Had a job to do.'

'What was so important?'

'You'll find out,' Warren said.

Tessa reached out and touched a white knuckle-bone.

'Cold,' she said. 'It's nice and cold.'

'It was cold in the river, too,' Warren said.

Rachel lay in the brass bed. When he slid in gratefully beside her, she awoke.

'J.M.?'

'I couldn't put a light on. The power's off again.'

He'd lit up Bell Street with the headlights, watching the small figure in bloodstained blue nylon walking to her door. When she was safely inside, he drove back into the lightless main street, where all the windows were blind eyes. Then down the hill and over the bridge. A tight right turn, and there was the perfect little riverside cottage. He'd almost expected it not to be there, like a dream cottage.

The presence of Rachel in the bed reinforced a sense of home. Before she could ask, he told her where he'd been, poured it all out, the whole bizarre episode.

'Arnold?' Rachel sat up in the darkness. 'Jonathon Preece shot Arnold?'

He told her about the shotgun, how he'd come to pick it up from the grass.

'I really wanted to kill him. I thought I *had* killed him at one point. I could feel myself pulling the triggers, both triggers, and then his chest . . . It was as if time had skipped a beat, and I'd already shot him.'

'You're overtired,' Rachel said.

'Then the dog – Arnold – whimpered, and I was back in the second before I did it. Arnold was Henry Kettle's dog.'

'I know.'

'You don't know how badly I wanted to kill that guy.'

'This doesn't seem like you, J.M.'

'No,' Powys said. 'It didn't.'

There was a window opposite the bed. Across the river, he saw a few sparse lights coming on, like candles on a cake.

'Power's back.'

'And you're a hero, J.M.,' Rachel said, moulding her body into his. 'Although you'll be a marked man in Crybbe if anyone finds out.'

PART FIVE

You won't need to worry and you won't have to cry
Over in the old golden land.

ROBIN WILLIAMSON
From the album
'Wee Tam and the Big Huge'

CHAPTER I

'No, don't move 'im yet, Gomer.'

Jack Preece ambled across the field to where Gomer Parry and his nephew, Nev, were preparing to get the bulldozer back on the lorry.

'Don't speak to me, Jack.' Gomer didn't turn round. 'Embarrassed? Humiliated, more like!'

'Aye, well, I'm sorry, Gomer.'

'Sorry? You bloody should be sorry, Jack Preece. Never before have Gomer Parry Plant Hire failed to carry out a contract. Never! I should 'ave told your dad where 'e could stick 'is . . .'

'Only, see, the district council's 'avin' a bit o' trouble on the new landfill site over Brynglas,' Jack Preece said. 'Need of an extra bulldozer, quickish, like. Three days' work, sure t'be.'

Gomer Parry turned shrewd eyes on Jack Preece, standing in the damp old field, between downpours, his back to the Tump and the famous wall – still intact, except for the bits of masonry dislodged when old Kettle had his crash.

'Reckon you can do it, Gomer?'

Gomer shot him a penetrating look through his wire-rimmed glasses. 'Something goin' on yere, Jack. Don't know what it is, but there's something.'

'Aye, well,' Jack Preece said, eyes averted. 'No need to worry about your reputation, Gomer, anyway. You'll be all right. We looks after our own, isn't it.'

He started to walk away then turned back. 'You seen Jonathon about?'

'Not lately,' Gomer said.

'Boy didn't come 'ome last night.'

'Likely 'avin' 'is end away somewhere,' said Gomer. 'Only young once, Jack.'

'Aye,' said Jack. 'Sure t'be.'

*

243

Powys drove back to Hereford, loaded up a couple of suitcases, a box of books, his Olivetti and two reams of A4.

'Aha,' said Barry, the osteopath from upstairs. 'Ensnared! He's got you. I knew he would. What was the deciding factor, Powys. The money?'

Powys shook his head.

'The women?'

Powys said, 'Just hold that door open for me, would you?'

'I knew it! It's the Summer of Love in Crybbe. You always were a sucker for a cheesecloth cleavage.'

'Barry,' said Powys, 'don't you have somebody's spine to trample on?'

'Good luck, Joe,' Annie said wistfully.

'What d'you mean "good luck"?' He'd noticed the crystals had been joined on the counter by a small display of astrological amulets in copper. Where the hell had she found those?

'You're going back,' Annie said.

'I am not "going back".'

Annie and Barry smiled knowingly to each other.

During the return drive it rained. It rained harder the nearer he got to Crybbe. Powys did some thinking, images wafting across his mind with the rhythm of the windscreen wipers.

Seriously unseasonal rain was throwing the river over the banks like rumpled bedclothes. He saw an image of a shotgun getting slowly pushed downstream, its barrels clogged with corrosive silt. Unless Jonathon had managed to retrieve it. Would he ever find out? And would Jonathon report him to the police?

Unlikely. He hoped. Well, it was a question of image: the farmer who let a townie in a suit pinch his gun and toss it in the river. They'd love that in the saloon bar of the Cock, it would go down in the folk history of the town.

Rachel was spending the morning at the Court, organizing workmen putting finishing touches to the stable-block. He thought of going to see Mrs Seagrove.

He carried his suitcases into the cottage. It was a good cottage, a better home than his flat. It had wonderful views over the river – slopping and frothing feverishly, after hours of heavy rain.

He couldn't stay here for long though. Not on false pretences. There was no way he was going to write the New Age Gospel According to Goff.

And the sequence by the river last night kept replaying itself. The feeling of the warm gun, the knowledge that he was not only capable of killing but *wanted* to kill. The bar of shadow across the grass and the river, all the way from the Tump, where Henry Kettle died.

And Arnold, Henry Kettle's dog. A dowser's dog, Henry used to say, isn't like other dogs.

It wasn't raining any more. Through the large window in the living-room, he saw the clouds had shifted like furniture pushed to the corners of the room, leaving a square of light. Fifty yards away, the river, denied its conquest of the meadow, slurped sulkily at its banks. On the other side of the river, in a semi-distant field – probably Goff's land – Powys saw two tiny figures, one holding a couple of tall poles.

He thought, The dodmen. Alfred Watkins's term for the prehistoric surveyors who had planned out the leys, erecting standing stones and earthworks at strategic points. The surveyors would, Watkins imagined, have held up poles to find out where tall stones would be visible as waymarkers. Now modern dodmen were at work, recreating prehistoric Crybbe in precisely the way it was presumed to have been done four thousand or so years ago.

From here, Powys couldn't even make out whether they were dodmen or dodwomen. But he was prepared to bet one of them would be Andy Boulton-Trow.

Calm, laid-back, ominiscient old Andy.

I think Joe ought to present himself to the Earth Spirit in the time-honoured fashion . . .

. . . the very least you can do, mate . . .

. . . think of it as a kind of appeasement.

Now Andy was personally supervising the operation to open up the town of Crybbe to the Earth Spirit.

On past experience of this irresponsible bastard, did that sound like good news?

*

245

'I think,' Hereward Newsome said, almost shaking with triumph, 'that I've cracked it.'

'You saw him?'

'He's gone back to London. I saw Rachel Wade. She said, go ahead.'

Hereward took off his jacket, hung it over the back of the antique-pine rocking-chair by the Aga, sat down and began to roll up his shirt-sleeves. 'But we need to move fast.'

'Why?' If Jocasta wasn't as ecstatic as she might have been, this was because Hereward's news had eclipsed her own small coup.

'I mean a buying trip. To the West Country, I'd suggest, and pronto. There's Ernest Wilding at Street, Devereux in Penzance, Sally Gold in Totnes, Melanie Dufort in . . . where is it now, some place near Frome? All specializing in megalith paintings – or they were. And there have to be more. What happened to the Ruralists? Where's Inshaw these days?'

'Not far from here, I heard.'

'Oh.' He stood up. 'Anyway, I'm going to make some calls now. Strike while Goff's hot. If we go down there this weekend, fetch a few back to put in front of him on Tuesday when he comes back.'

Hereward paced the kitchen. Any second now, Jocasta thought, he'll start rubbing his hands. Still, it *was* good news.

'You ought to see his proposed exhibition hall. Rachel showed me this huge barn he's going to rebuild. It'll be a sort of interpretive centre for prehistoric Crybbe and the whole earth mysteries thing. He's looking for maybe seventy paintings. *Seventy!* Darling, if we can provide *half* of those we're talking . . . let's be vulgar, if we can get the kind of stuff he wants, we're talking megabucks.'

'Why can't we go *next* weekend?'

'Look . . . so we close the gallery for a day. What have we got to lose, with Goff out of town? And the way things have been, can we afford to delay?'

'Hereward!' God, he was so irritating. 'What about Emmanuel Walters?'

'Oh.' Hereward sat down. 'It's Sunday, isn't it?'

'Ye-es,' Jocasta said, exasperated, 'it is. And it's a bloody good job one of us is efficient.' Adding nonchalantly, 'I've even arranged a celebrity to open the exhibition.'

'Oh yes?'

Jocasta's lips cemented into a hard line. Even if it was a member of the Royal Family it wouldn't impress Hereward at the moment, still on his Max Goff high.

'It's Guy Morrison.'

'Oh. Er, super. Didn't he used to be . . . ?'

'He's producing and presenting the documentary the BBC are doing on Max Goff and Crybbe. He seems very pleasant. He agreed at once. I think he's at rather a loose end. He's spending the weekend here, getting to know the town. Getting to know the people who count.'

'Not much use coming to The Gallery, then.' Hereward guffawed insensitively.

Jocasta scowled. That was *it*. 'I know,' she said, 'why don't you go to the West Country on your own? I'll stay behind and handle the private view.'

'Yes, I suppose it makes sense.'

Jocasta knew it made no sense at all. Good old Hereward, always anxious to be accepted by artists as a friend, someone who understood the creative process, would spend hundreds of pounds more than she would. But at least she'd get rid of him for a couple of days. Increasingly, Jocasta had been thinking back with nostalgia to the days when they'd had separate jobs and only met for a couple of hours in the evening.

Hereward said – a formality, she thought – 'Will you be all right on your own?'

Just for a minute she thought about last night and those drawings and the sticky feeling on her hands which had proved, when the lights came on, to be no more than perspiration.

'I shall be fine,' she said.

Mrs Seagrove brought him tea in one of her best china cups – as distinct, she pointed out, from the mugs she took out to the lorry drivers in the layby.

'I thought I'd seen the last of you, Joe. How's the doggie?'

'We think he's going to be OK.'

'That's good.' She was wearing today a plaid skirt of a different tartan. 'I'm not Scottish,' she said. 'Frank and I used to go up there every autumn, and we'd visit these woollen mills.'

There was a picture of Frank on the sideboard. He was beaming and holding up a fish which might have been a trout.

'He was thrilled when we got this place, so near the river. He joined the angling club. It was a shame. Turned out to be not a very good river for fishing. And the problem was, Joe, Frank could see the river, but I could only see *that*.'

She sat with her back to the big, horizontal window with its panoramic view across the river to the woods and, of course, the Tump.

'About that . . .' Powys said.

'I thought you'd come about that.' Mrs Seagrove held her teacup on her kilted knees, flat and steady as a good coffee-table. 'Well, I'm glad somebody's interested. Mrs Morrison's always too busy. Unless I want to talk about it on the radio, she says. Well, I said, would you make a spectacle of yourself on the wireless?'

'Last night, you said something was coming at us. From the Tump?'

'People are fascinated by these things. I'm not. Are you, Joe?'

'Well, I used to be. Still am, in a way, but they worry me now.'

'Quite right. I'm not interested, I've never been interested.'

'It nearly always happens to people who are not interested,' said Powys.

'I think I know when it comes now, what time, so I draw the curtains and turn the telly up, but some nights I just have to go and look, just to get it out of the way. I'm scared to death, Joe, but I look, just to get it out of the way.'

'And what time is it?'

'Usually after nine o'clock and before they ring that bell in the church. Not always. It's early sometimes, almost full daylight – although it goes dark all of a sudden, kind of thing, like as if it's bringing its own darkness, do you know what I mean? And just once – it was that night the poor man crashed his car – just once, it was later, about half-tennish. Just that once.'

Powys said, 'It's a dog, isn't it? A big, black dog.'

'Yes, dear,' said Mrs Seagrove very quietly. 'Yes, it is.'

'How often have you . . . ?'

'Seven or eight times, I've seen it. It always goes the same way. Coming from the . . . the mound thing.'

'Down from the mound, or out of the mound?'

'I couldn't honestly say, dear. One second it's not there, the next it is, kind of thing. I'm psychic, I suppose. I never wanted to be psychic, not like this.'

'Is it – I'm sorry to ask all these questions – but is it obviously a dog? It couldn't be anything else?'

'You ask as many questions as you like, dear. I've been finding out about you, I rang a friend of mine at the library in Dudley. No, that's an interesting point you make there – is it really a dog? Well, I like dogs. I wouldn't be frightened of a dog, would I? Even a ghost dog. Naturally, it'd be a shock, the first time you saw it, kind of thing, but no, I don't think I'd be frightened. Oh dear, I wish you *hadn't* asked me that now, it's disturbed me, that has, Joe.'

'I'm sorry.'

'I don't want to stay here. I'd be off tomorrow, but how much would I get for this, even if I managed to sell it?'

'If you really wanted to go quickly,' Powys said, 'I think I could find you a buyer. You'd get a good price, too.'

'Not you?'

'Good God, no, not me. I couldn't afford it, even if . . . Look, leave it with me for a day or two.'

'I don't know what to say, dear.' Mrs Seagrove's eyes were shining. 'In a way, I'd feel bad about somebody having this place. But they might not be psychic, mightn't they?'

'Or they might be quite interested.'

'Oh no,' she said. 'Nobody's interested in evil, are they?'

CHAPTER II

GUY dropped by.

She opened the back door, thinking it was the milk-man come for his money, as was usual on a Saturday.

'Fay. Hi.'

'Oh, my God.'

She wouldn't have chosen to say that, but Guy seemed pleased at the reaction. Perhaps he saw it as an urgent suppression of instinctive desire.

'Thought I'd drop by, as I had some time on my hands.' Incandescent smile. 'Spending the weekend here, getting acclimatized.'

New crowns, Fay spotted. Good ones, of course.

'Crew's gone back, but I've been invited to open some shitty art exhibition tomorrow night. Must be a bit short on celebrities in these parts if they want *me*.' Guy laughed.

Still a master of double-edged false modesty, Fay thought, wishing she'd changed, combed her hair, applied some rudimentary make-up.

And then despising herself utterly for wishing all that.

'Come in, Guy. Dad's gone for a walk; he'll be devastated to have missed you.'

'How is he?' Guy stepped into the hall and looked closely at everything, simulating enormous interest in the chipped cream paintwork, the wallpaper with its faded autumn leaves, the nylon carpet beneath his hand-stitched, buffed, brown shoes.

He wore a short, olive, leather jacket, soft as a very expensive wallet.

'We used to have some fascinating chats, your father and I, when I was in Religious Programmes.'

'I expect he learned quite a lot,' Fay said, going through to the kitchen.

'That was how I swung the Crybbe thing, you know. It cut plenty of ice with Max Goff, me being an ex-religious-affairs producer. Indicated a certain sensitivity of touch and an essentially serious outlook. Nothing crude, no juvenile piss-taking.'

'Tea or coffee?' Fay said. 'Why did you leave Religious Programmes, anyway? Seemed like a good, safe earner to me. Just about the only situation where you can work in television and still get to heaven.'

'Well, you know, Fay, there came a time when it was clear that Guy Morrison had said all he needed to say about religion. Is it ground coffee or instant?'

'Would I offer you instant coffee, Guy?'

'I don't like to make presumptions about people's financial positions,' Guy said sensitively.

'We're fine.'

'I did tell you, didn't I, that I'd probably have brought you in as researcher, except for this J. M. Powys problem?'

'Thanks, but I doubt I'd've had time, anyway. Pretty busy, really.' The handle came off the cup she was holding – that'd teach her to lie twice.

'He was foisted on me, Fay. Nothing I could do.'

'I met him last night. Seemed a nice bloke.'

Just before lunch, J. M. Powys had phoned to ask how Arnold was. Comfortable, Fay had said, having been on the phone to the vet as early as was reasonable. Stable. As well as can be expected.

Guy crinkled his mouth. 'One-book wonder, J. M. Powys. A spent force.'

Must be a nice bloke if Guy despises him, Fay thought. She began to filter the coffee in silence.

Eventually, Guy, sitting at the kitchen table, said, 'Long time since we met face to face, Fay. Three years? Four?'

'At least.' Physically, he'd hardly changed at all. Perhaps the odd characterful crease, like the superb-quality leather of his jacket. Pretty soon, she thought in dismay, he'll be looking too comparatively young ever to have been married to me.

Guy said, 'You're looking . . . er, good, Fay.'

What a bastard. She made a point of not replying in kind.

Guy said, 'Quite often, you know – increasingly, in fact – I find myself wondering why we ever split up.'

'Didn't it have something to do with you screwing your production assistant?'

Guy dismissed it. 'Trivial, trivial stuff. I was young, she threw herself at me. You know that. I'm essentially a pretty faithful sort of person. No, what we had . . .' He pushed Grace's G-plan dining chair away from the table and leaned back, throwing his left ankle over his right knee and catching it deftly with his right hand. He obviously couldn't quite remember what they'd had.

'I often wish we'd had children, Fay.'

Oh hell.

Guy's intermittent live-in girlfriend had apparently proved to be barren. Fay remembered him moaning about this to her one night on the phone. She remembered thinking at the time that infertility was a very useful attribute for an intermittent live-in girlfriend to have. But Guy was at the age when he wanted there to be little Morrisons.

'I'm at the Cock.'

'What?'

'The Cock Hotel,' Guy said. 'It's an appalling place.'

'Dreadful,' Fay said, pouring his coffee.

'I think I'm going to have to make other arrangements when we start shooting in earnest.'

'I should.'

'Can you think of anywhere?'

'Hasn't Goff offered you accommodation?'

'Nothing suitable, apparently. He says. Though we do have special requirements – meals at all hours.'

Sore point, obviously.

'Still,' Fay said cheerfully. 'I've heard he's going to buy the Cock, turn it into a New Age Holiday Inn or something.'

She brought her coffee and sat down opposite him. If anything, he was even more handsome these days. It had once been terribly flattering to be courted by Guy Morrison. And unexpectedly painless to become divorced from him.

'I've changed, you know, Fay.'

'Hardly at all, I'd've said.'

'Oh, looks . . . that's not what it's all about. Never was, was it?'

Of course not, she thought. However, in your case, what else is there to get excited about?

'And you're obviously just as arrogant,' she said brightly.

'Confidence, Fay,' he said patiently. 'Not arrogance. If you don't continually display confidence in this business, people think you're . . .'

'A spent force? Like J. M. Powys?'

'Something like that. I should have held on to you,' he said softly, a frond of blond hair falling appealingly to an eyebrow. 'You kept me balanced. I was terribly insecure, you know, that's why . . .'

'Oh, for God's sake, Guy, you were never insecure in your life. This is *me* you're giving all this bullshit to. Let's drop this subject, shall we?'

He looked hurt. But not *very* hurt.

'How did you get on yesterday?' Fay asked him, to change direction. 'They never managed to pull the wall down, did they?'

'Don't ask,' Guy said, meaning 'ask'.

'All went wrong, then?' This was probably the reason Guy was here. He was in urgent need of consolation.

'I've just been looking at the rushes.'

'What, you've been back to Cardiff?'

'No, no, I sent Larry to a video shop in Leominster last night to transfer the stuff to VHS so I could whizz through it at the Cock. When he came back, he said, "You're not going to like this," and cleared off quick. I've just found out why. Good grief, Fay, talk about a wasted exercise. First, there's bloody Goff – plans a stunt like that and doesn't tell me until it's too late to hire a second crew and then . . .'

'But it didn't happen, anyway. The wall's still there.'

'I know, but we had what ought to have been terrific footage of Goff going apeshit on top of the Tump, when the sound system packed in and the bulldozer chap said he couldn't do it. But the light must've been worse than I thought or Larry hadn't done a white-balance or something – he denies that, of course, but he would, wouldn't he?'

'What, it didn't come out?' Fay, who'd never worked in television, knew next to nothing about the technicalities of it. 'I thought this Betacam stuff didn't need much light.'

'Probably something wrong with the camera, Larry claims. First this big black thing shoots across the frame, and then all the colour's haywire. By God, if there's any human error to blame in Cardiff, somebody's job could be on the line over this.'

'But not yours, of course,' said Fay. 'Hold on a minute, Guy.' She was listening to a vague scraping noise. 'It's Dad. He can't get his key in the door.'

Fay dashed into the hall, closing the kitchen door behind her and opening the front door. The Canon almost fell over the threshold, poking his key at her eye.

'Thank God.' Fay caught his arm, whispered in his ear, 'Come and rescue me, Dad. Guy's here, and he's in a very maudlin mood.'

'Who?' He was out of breath.

'Guy, you remember Guy. We used to be married once. I've got this awful feeling he's working up to asking me to have his baby.'

A blurred film had set across the Canon's eyes. He shook his head, stood still a moment, breathing hard, then straightened up. 'Yes,' he said. 'Fay. Something you need to know.'

'Take your time.'

'Tape recorder. Get your tape recorder.' His eyes cleared, focused. 'There's been an accident. A death. Everybody's talking about it. I'll tell you where to go.'

'There'll be no delay,' the dodman said. 'We start tonight.'

'Don't you need planning permission?' Powys asked.

The dodman only smiled.

As expected, he'd turned out to be Andy Boulton-Trow with a mobile phone and a map in a transparent plastic folder.

'There are six we can put in immediately. Either on Max's land around the Court or on bits of ground he's been able to buy. Not a bad start. You're getting one, did you know that?'

'Thanks a bunch.'

'The top of your little acre, where it meets the road. See?' Andy held out his plastic-covered photocopy of Henry's map. 'Right there.'

It was a large-scale OS blow-up. The former location of each stone was marked by a dot inside a circle and the pencilled initials, H. K.

They were standing in Crybbe's main street, just above the police station, looking down towards the bridge. Two of Andy's dodmen were making their way across, carrying white sighting-poles. Powys asked him how long it had been going on, all this planning and surveying and buying up of land.

'Months. Nearly a year, all told. But it's all come to a head very rapidly. In some curious way, I think Henry's death fired Max into orbit. Henry's done the leg-work, now it was down to Max to pull it all together. There are more than fifty workmen on the project now. Stables'll be finished by Monday, ready for a start on the Court itself next week. First half-dozen stones in place by tomorrow night. That's moving, Joe.'

'No, he doesn't piss about, does he?'

'All that remains is to persuade the remaining few die-hards either to sell their land or accept a stone on it. Hence Tuesday's public meeting. A formality, I'd guess. He'll have bought them off by then. Agent's out there now, negotiating. Farmers will do anything these days to stay afloat. Caravan sites, wind-farms, you name it. They take what comes. Most of them have no choice.'

Powys wondered if you could stop people planting a standing stone close to where you lived, perhaps diverting some kind of energy through your house? How would a court make a ruling on something which had never been proved to exist?

'It seems amazing,' he said, 'that there were so many stones around here and every single one of them's been ripped out.'

'Except for one Henry found. Little bent old stone under a hedge.'

'Do you think they destroyed them because they were superstitious?'

Andy shrugged.

'Because you'd think, if they were superstitious, they'd have been *scared* to pull them out, wouldn't you?'

'People in these parts,' Andy said, 'who knows how their minds work?'

Powys looked up the street towards the church tower.

'There's a major ley, isn't there, coming from the Tump, through the Court, then the church, right through the town to the hills?'

'Line one.' Andy held out the plan.

'I was up in the prospect chamber at the Court. It might have been constructed to sight along that ley.'

'Might have been?'

'You think it was?'

'Yes. I think so.' Andy's black beard was making rapid progress, concealing the bones of his face. You couldn't tell what he was thinking any more.

'John Dee,' Powys said. 'John Dee was a friend of Michael Wort's, right? Or, at least, he seems to have known him. We know John Dee was investigating earth mysteries in the 1580s, or thereabouts. Is it possible Dee was educating Wort and that they built the prospect chamber as a sort of observatory?'

'To observe what?'

'I don't know. Whatever they believed happened along that ley.'

Two cars came out of the square at speed, one a police car. Obviously together, they passed over the bridge and turned right not far beyond Powys's cottage.

'Took their time,' Andy observed.

'What's happening?'

'Body found in the river,' Andy said with disinterest. 'That's why we had to stop work down there. They get very excited. Not many floaters in Crybbe. Yes, I think you could be close to it. But perhaps it was Wort who initiated Dee into the secret, have you considered that? He was a remarkable man, you know.'

But suddenly Powys was not too concerned about which of them had initiated the other.

It was quiet again in the street. The cars had vanished down a track leading to the riverbank.

Fay's fingers were weak and fumbling. For the first time, she had difficulty working the Uher's simple piano-key controls.

Nobody had even covered him up.

She'd expected screens of some kind, a police cordon like there always were in cities. She'd never seen a drowned man before, in all his sodden glory.

Nobody had even thrown a coat over him, or a blanket. They'd simply tossed him on the bank, limp and leaking. Skin blue – crimped, corrugated. Eyes wide open – dead as a cod on a slab. Livid tongue poking out of the froth around his lips and nostrils.

Tossed on the bank. Like somebody's catch.

Gomer's catch, in this case.

Gomer Parry, who'd found the body, was only too happy to give her what he described as an exclusive interview. He told her how he'd come to check on his bulldozer, which was over there in Jack Preece's field, awaiting its removal to the council's Brynglas landfill site on Monday, when he'd spotted this thing caught up in branches not far from the bank.

''E'd not been in long,' Gomer said knowledgeably. 'Several reasons I got for sayin' that. Number one – no bloatin'. Takes . . . oh, maybe a week for the ole gases to build up inside, and then out 'e comes, all blown up like a life-jacket. Also, see – point number two – if 'e'd been in there long . . . fishes woulder been at 'im.'

Gomer made obscene little pincer movements with clawed fingers and thumb and then pointed into the river, no longer in flood, but still brown and churning, bearing broken branches downstream.

They'd been frozen to the fringe of a silent group of local people on the wet riverbank. They were half a mile from the bridge, on the bend before the river moved across the Crybbe Court land, flowing within two hundred yards of the Tump.

'Current brings 'em in to the side yere, right on the bend, see,' Gomer said. 'Then they gets entangled in them ole branches and the floodwater goes down, and there 'e is, high an' dry. They've 'ad quite a few yere, over the years. Always the same spot.'

Gomer sat down on a damp tree stump, his back to the

body, got out a battered square tin and began to roll himself a cigarette. 'Nibbled to the bone, some of 'em are,' he said, with unseemly relish. 'So I reckon, if I was to put a time on it, I'd say 'e's been in there less than a day.'

Fay thought she knew exactly how long he'd been in there. Approximately twenty hours. Oh God, this was dreadful. This was indescribably awful. Her fingers went rapidly up and down with the zip of her blue cagoule.

'Now, you notice that wrinkling on 'is face,' Gomer said. 'Well, see, that's what you calls the "washerwoman's 'ands" effect.'

'Gomer!' The colour of Sergeant Wynford Wiley's face was approaching magenta as he loomed over the little man in wire-framed glasses.

'When your wealth of forensic knowledge is required,' Wynford said, 'we shall send for you. Meanwhile, all this is totally *sub joodicee* until after the inquest. And *you* should know that,' he snapped at Fay.

'Look, Wynford,' Fay snapped back, to beat the tremor out of her voice. '*Sub judice* applies to court cases, not inquests. Nobody's on trial at an inquest.'

Really know how to make friends, don't I? she thought as Wynford bent his face to hers. He didn't speak until he was sure he had her full attention. Then, very slowly and explicitly, he said, 'We don't like *clever people* round yere, Mrs Morrison.'

Then he straightened up, turned his back on her and walked away.

'Fat bastard.' Gomer bit on his skinny, hand-crafted cigarette. 'You got all that, what I said?'

'Yes,' Fay said. 'But he's right. I won't be able to use most of it, not because it's *sub judice*, but because we don't go to town on the gruesome stuff. Especially when relatives might be listening.'

Christ, how could she go through the motions of reporting this story, knowing what she knew? Knowing, if not exactly how, then at least why it had happened.

There was a little crowd around the body, including its father, Jack Preece, and its younger brother, Warren Preece.

Jack Preece's face was as grey as the clouds. He looked up from the corpse very steadily, as if he knew what he would see next and the significance of it.

And what he saw next was Fay. His tired, hopeless, brown eyes met hers and held them. It was harder to face than a curse.

She thought, *He knows everything*. And she dragged her gaze away and looked wildly around her, but there was nobody to run to for comfort and nowhere to hide from Jonathon Preece's dead eyes and the eyes of his father, which held the weight of a sorrow she knew she could only partly comprehend.

CHAPTER III

NOT one person had appeared to recognize Guy Morrison. Twice today he'd circuited this dreary town, and nobody had done more than glance at him with, he was forced to admit, a barely cursory interest.

Guy liked to be recognized. He needed to be recognized. He was insecure, he readily admitted this. Everyone he knew in television was insecure; it was a deeply neurotic business. And it was a visual medium – so if people started to pass you in the street without a second, sidelong glance, without nudging their companions, then it wouldn't be too long before the Programme Controller failed to recognize you in the lift.

Altogether, a legitimate cause for anxiety.

And Fay had depressed him. Living like a spinster, watching her father coming unravelled, in the kind of conditions Guy remembered from his childhood – remembered only in black and white, like grainy old 405-line television. He couldn't understand why Fay had failed to throw herself at him, sobbing, 'Take me away from all this', instead of bustling off with her Uher over her shoulder in pursuit of a local news item that would be unlikely to make even a filler-paragraph in tomorrow's Sunday papers.

Guy, rather than attempt to construct a conversation with the Canon, had claimed to be overdue for another appointment, and thus had ended up making his second despondent tour of the town centre.

Country towns were not supposed to be like this. Country towns were supposed to have teashops and flower stalls and Saturday markets from which fat, friendly Women's Institute ladies sold jars of home-made jam and chutney sealed by grease-proof paper and rubber bands.

Without a crew, without Catrin and her clipboard and without even a hint of recognition from the public, Guy felt a sudden sense of acute isolation. He'd never been anywhere quite like this before, a town which seemed to have had all the life sucked out of it, bloodless people walking past, sagging like puppets whose strings had been snipped.

He was almost inclined to cancel his room at the Cock and race back home to Cardiff.

Instead, in the gloomy late-afternoon, as it began to rain again, he found himself strolling incuriously into The Gallery, where he and Jocasta Newsome would soon recognize a mutual need.

Outside, Powys had found some logs for the Jotul stove. They were damp, but he managed to get the stove going and stacked a couple of dozen logs on each side of it to dry out.

He couldn't remember bleaker weather at the end of June.

His cases stood unpacked by the window. On the ledge, a blank sheet of A4 paper was wound into the Olivetti.

Life itself seemed very temporary tonight.

Just before seven, a grim-faced Rachel arrived, Barbour awash. She tossed the dripping coat on the floor.

'Coffee, J.M. I need coffee. With something in it.' She collapsed on to the hard, orange sofa, flung her head back, closing her eyes. 'I suppose you've heard?'

Powys said, 'They found a body in the river.'

Rachel said. 'What are you going to do, J.M.?'

'Do they know what happened?'

'I don't think so. They haven't questioned anyone except the father and Gomer Parry.'

Powys went into the little kitchen to look for coffee and called back, 'Have they found the gun?'

'Not so far as I know,' Rachel said. 'Perhaps Jonathon Preece didn't find it either. Perhaps the place where you threw it was deeper than you thought. Humble, who seems to know what he's talking about, says there are all kinds of unexpected pot-holes in the riverbed. He says nobody in their right mind would attempt to wade across, even in a dry summer, when the water level's low.'

'Humble?' Powys's voice had an edge of panic.

'He volunteered the information. In passing. I wasn't stupid enough to ask him. I feigned disinterest.'

Not a difficult act, he accepted, for Rachel.

He returned with two mugs and a bottle of Bell's whisky. 'I can't find any coffee, but I found this in a cupboard.' He poured whisky into a mug and handed it to Rachel. 'Can't find any glasses either.'

Rachel drank deeply and didn't cough or choke.

Powys said, 'What do you think I ought to do?'

Rachel held the mug in both hands and stretched out her long legs to the stove in a vain quest for heat. 'I think we should wait for Fay. She's going to come here after she's filed her scrupulously objective story about the drowning tragedy at Crybbe.'

'That won't be easy. What's she going to say?'

'It seems,' said Rachel, 'that minor flooding at Crybbe has claimed its first victim.'

She looked tired. There were dark smudges on her narrow face. 'Just hope they don't find the gun. I don't know what water does to fingerprints, do you?'

As the second stroke of the curfew hit the reverberation of the first, clean and hard, Warren Preece tossed his used Durex, well-filled, into the alley and zipped up his jeans.

'Close,' he said. 'But I reckon I can improve on it if I puts my mind to it.'

Tessa Byford was leaning back against the brick wall of

the Crybbe Unattended Studio, still panting a little. 'You're confident tonight.'

'Yeah.' The trick, he'd learned (he'd learned it from Tessa, but he'd allowed himself to forget this), was to time it so you came in the split second before the bell crashed. Tonight he'd lost his load a good five seconds before the first bong. Still near as buggery took the top of his head off, though – always did here – but it could be better.

Warren got a special kick out of thinking of his old man up the tower, waiting to pull on the rope while he, Warren, was down here bonking his brains out. Dead on time again tonight: nothing would come between Jack Preece and that bell, not even his favourite son drying out in some police morgue.

'Ask not,' Warren intoned, 'for whom the ole bell tolls. It tolls tonight, ladies and gen'lemen, for Jonathon Preece, of Court Farm, Crybbe.'

He giggled.

There was a snap of white – Tessa pulling up her knickers.

Warren said, 'I been feelin' – just lately, like – as if I'm the only guy in this town, the only one who's really alive sorter thing. The only walkin' corpse in the graveyard. Bleeargh!'

Warren wiggled his hands and rolled his eyes.

Written two new songs, he had, in the past couple of days. Red-hot stuff, too. Didn't know he had it in him – how *much* he had in him. He reckoned Max Goff's tape would be ready in a couple of weeks. Goff was going to be real blown away by this next one.

'What would you have done, Warren, if that woman hadn't come out of the studio before we got started? Or if she'd come out in the middle?'

'Woulda made no difference. Or I coulda saved some for 'er, couldn't I? Takin' a chance, she is, comin' yere this time o' night. An' she wouldn't say a word, see, 'cause I seen what 'appened by the river, 'ow they killed poor Jonathon. Poor Jonathon!'

Warren started to grin. 'Oh, you should've seen 'im, Tess. Lyin' there with 'is tongue out. Just about as wet and slimy as what 'e was when 'e was alive. I couldn't 'ardly keep a straight face. And – you got to laugh, see – fucking Young Farmers' . . .'

Warren *did* laugh. He placed both hands flat on the brick wall and almost beat his head into it with laughing.

'. . . fuckin' Young Farmers' needs a new chairman now, isn't it? Oh, shit, what a bloody crisis!'

'You going to volunteer, Warren?'

'No.' Warren wiped his streaming eyes with the back of a hand. 'I'm goin' into the Plant Hire business.' He went into another cackle. 'I'm gonna hot-wire me a bulldozer.'

She was the kind of woman who, in normal circumstances, he would have taken care to avoid, like sunstroke. She was vain, pretentious, snobbish and too bony in the places where one needed it least.

But these were not normal circumstances. On a wet Saturday evening in Crybbe, Jocasta Newsome was almost exotic.

Guy had her on the hearthrug, where damp logs spat the occasional spark into his buttocks.

She was tasty.

And grateful. Guy loved people to be grateful for him. She was voracious in a carefree sort of way, as if all kinds of pent-up emotions were being expelled. She laughed a lot; he made her laugh, even with comments and questions that were not intended to be funny.

Like, 'And your husband – is he an artist?'

Jocasta squealed in delight and ground a pelvic bone painfully into his stomach.

Guy said, just checking, 'You're sure there's no chance he'll be back tonight?'

'Tonight,' said Jocasta, 'Hereward will be in one of those awful restaurants where the candles on the tables are stuck in wine-bottles and some unshaven student is hunched up in the corner fumbling with a guitar. He'll be holding forth at length to a bunch of artists about the beauty of Crybbe and how well in he is with the local yokels. He'll be telling them all about his close friend Max Goff and the wonderful experiment in which he, Hereward, is playing a pivotal role. The artists will drink bottle after bottle of disgusting plonk paid for, of course, by Hereward and they'll think, "What a sucker, what an absolutely God-sent wally." And they'll be mentally doubling their prices.'

Jocasta propped herself up on one arm, her nipples rather redder than the feebly smouldering logs in the grate.

'Oh yes,' she assured him. 'We are utterly alone and likely to remain so for two whole, wonderful days. How long have *you* got, Guy? Inches and inches, if I'm any judge. Oh my God, what am I saying, I must be demob happy.'

The thought of *two whole days* of Jocasta Newsome didn't lift Guy to quite the same heights. He reached for his trousers.

Dismay disfigured her. 'What are you doing? I didn't mean . . .'

'Just going to the loo, if you could direct me. Guy Morrison never goes anywhere without trousers. Not the kind of risk one takes.'

'Oh.' Jocasta relaxed. 'Yes. We're having a downstairs cloakroom made, but it isn't quite . . . Up the stairs, turn left and there's a bathroom directly facing you at the end of the passage. Don't be long, will you?'

Thankfully, she didn't qualify the final entreaty with another dreadful *double entendre*.

Guy slithered into his trousers and set off barefoot up the stairs, slightly worried now. Happily married women were fine. *Un*happily married women were worse than unattached women. They clutched you as if you were a lifebelt. They were seldom afraid of word getting out about you and them. And while it might be all right for pop stars, scandal was rarely helpful to the careers of responsible producer-presenters in Features and Documentaries.

Bare-chested on the stairs, he shivered. The walls had been stripped to the stonework. Too rugged for Guy Morrison. He probably wouldn't come here again. He decided he'd open the exhibition tomorrow night and slide quietly away. A one-night stand was OK, but a two-night stand carried just a hint of commitment.

The lights went out.

'Oh, blast!' he heard from the drawing-room.

'What's happened?'

'Power cut,' Jocasta shouted. 'Happens all the time. Take it slowly and you'll be OK. When you get to the bathroom you'll find a torch on top of the cabinet.'

Guy stubbed his toe on the top banister-post and tried not to cry out.

But he found his way to the bathroom quite easily because of a certain greasy phosphorescence oozing out of the crack between the door and its frame.

'Funny sort of power cut,' he said, not thinking at all.

'Police say there are no suspicious circumstances, but they still can't explain how Mr Preece, whose family has been farming in the area for over four hundred years, came to be in the river.'

'That report,' the Offa's Dyke newsreader said, *'from Fay Morrison in Crybbe. Now sport, and for Hereford United . . .'*

Fay switched off Powys's radio.

It was thirty-three minutes past ten and almost totally dark.

'Must've been awkward for you.' J. M. Powys rammed a freshly dried log into the Jotul and slammed the iron door on it.

Fay, in a black sweat-suit, was cross-legged on the hearth, by the stove.

'Not really,' she said. 'In cases like this you're not expected to probe too hard. If it'd been a child, I'd be spending most of the night talking to worried mothers about why the council needed to fence off the river. Then tomorrow, this being Crybbe, I'd have to explain to Ashpole why the worried mothers were refusing to be interviewed on tape. But in a case like this, it's just assumed he killed himself. Be an open verdict. Unless . . .'

'Unless they find the gun.' Powys switched on a green-shaded table-lamp. Rachel drew the curtains against the night and the rain and the river.

Fay said, 'If anybody had any suspicions, we'd have heard from the police by now. All the same, Jack Preece . . .'

'His father,' Powys said.

'Yes. Jack Preece knows. I could see it in his eyes when we were down by the river, with the body.'

'Knows what?'

'I think he knows Jonathon had gone out to shoot Arnold.'

Rachel sat down on the sofa. 'What makes you . . . ?'

'Just a minute. Hang on.' Powys stood up. 'You say Jonathon *had gone out to shoot Arnold*. You're saying he'd deliberately targeted Arnold?'

Fay nodded.

'Do I get the feeling there's a history to this?'

Fay swallowed. 'If I tell you this, you're going to switch to small talk for a few minutes and then look for an excuse to get rid of me. It's so weird.'

'Fay.' Powys spread his arms. 'I'm the bloke who wrote *The Old Golden Land*. Nothing's too weird.'

There was a longish silence. Then the green-shaded table-lamp went out.

'Bugger,' Rachel said.

'OK,' Fay said slowly. 'You can't see my face now, and I won't be able to see the incredulity on yours.'

She took a long breath. She told them about dogs in Crybbe.

'How long have you known this?' Powys asked.

'Only a day or so. I should be doing a story on it, shouldn't I? A town with no dogs? Jesus, it's not common, is it? But life here is so much like a bad dream, I'm sure if I sold it to the papers, when all the reporters arrived to check it out, there'd be dogs everywhere, shelves full of Chum at the grocer's, poop-scoops at the ironmonger's, posters for the Crybbe and District Annual Dog Show . . .'

She was glad they couldn't see the helpless tears in her eyes.

'I can't *trust* myself here,' Fay said, fighting to keep the tears out of her voice. 'I can't trust myself to perceive anything correctly. Too much has happened.'

'Have you thought about why it could be?' Powys asked, a soft, accepting voice in the darkness. 'Why no dogs?'

'Sure I've thought about it – in between thinking about my dad going bonkers, about holding on to my job, about somebody breaking in and smashing up my tape-machine, about being arrested for manslaughter, about living with a gho . . .'

about lots of things. I'm sorry, I'm not very rational tonight.'

'So what you're saying is' – Rachel's *very* rational voice – 'that, because you wouldn't get rid of Arnold, Jonathon Preece deliberately set out to shoot him?'

'I had a phone call. An anonymous call. Get rid of him by this weekend, or . . .'

'Or he'd be shot?'

'There was no specified threat. Just a warning. I think Jack Preece was the caller. Therefore it seems likely he sent Jonathon out with the gun.'

She heard Powys fumbling with the stove and its iron door was flung wide, letting a stuttering red and yellow firelight into the room.

His face looked much younger in the firelight. 'If this is right about no dogs – I'm sorry, Fay, if you say there are no dogs, I believe you – we could be looking at the key to something here.'

'You're the expert,' Fay said.

'There aren't any experts. This is the one area in which nobody's an expert.'

'If all dogs howl at the curfew,' Rachel said logically, 'why don't they just get rid of the curfew? It's not as if it's a major tourist attraction. Not as if they even draw attention to it. It just happens, it's just continued, without much being said. OK, there's this story about the legacy of land to the Preeces, but is anybody really going to take that away if the curfew stops?'

'I don't think for one minute,' said Powys, 'that that's the real reason for the curfew.'

Fay sat up, interested. 'So what *is* the real reason?'

'If we knew that we'd know the secret of Crybbe.'

'You think there's something to know? You think there's a good reason why the place is as miserable as sin?'

'There's something. Fay, how did you come to get Henry's dog. I mean, did you know him well?'

'Hardly at all. I'd done an interview with him on the day he died.'

'That's interesting. What sort of an interview? What was it about?'

'Er . . . dowsing. I wanted to know what he was doing in

Crybbe, but it was obvious he didn't want to talk about that, so . . . Anyway, it was never used.'

'Have you still got the tape?'

'I imagine so. If you want to hear it, come down to the studio sometime. Up the covered alley behind the Cock.'

'Tomorrow morning?'

'Nine o'clock?'

'Fine.'

'And about Arnold, I got him from the police because it was obvious nobody else was going to. He was howling away in full daylight, and I'm pretty sure now that if I hadn't taken him, he'd have been dead. They'd have killed him. Before nightfall. Before the curfew.'

The torchlight shone in Jocasta's eyes.

'It's me,' Guy said. 'Look . . .'

'Yes, I know. Come here, I'm cold.'

'I haven't been,' said Guy. 'I couldn't go.'

'I don't understand – you've got the torch.'

'Jocasta,' Guy hissed urgently, closing the drawing-room door quietly behind him. 'For Christ's sake, why didn't you tell me we weren't alone?'

Jocasta felt *very* cold. She began to tremble, crawled to the sofa and scrabbled for her dress.

'Who is he?' Guy demanded. She couldn't see him, only the torch. 'Is he your father?'

Jocasta tried to speak and couldn't. She tried to stand up, tried to step into her dress, got her legs tangled, fell back on the rug.

'I waited,' Guy said. 'But he didn't come out.'

Jocasta, squatting on the rug in the torch circle, struggled vainly to zip up her dress. No eager fingers to help her now.

'What the hell's going on, Jocasta?'

She found her voice, but didn't recognize it. 'My father,' she said slowly, 'is in Chiswick. My husband, Hereward, is somewhere in Somerset. There is nobody here. Nobody here but us, Guy.'

A log shifted in the grate, sending up a yellow spark-shower, like a cheap firework.

'Then who the fuck was that old man in the bathroom? Having a shave, for crying out loud, with a . . . with a . . .' His voice faltered. 'With a cut-throat razor.'

The improbability of the scenario seemed to occur to him at last.

'How could I see him? How could I see him when all the lights . . . ?'

Guy's voice went quiet. 'He was a strange kind of yellow,' he said unsteadily. 'A very feeble shade of yellow.'

The torchlight wavered as he advanced on the sofa. 'Where are my clothes? I'm getting out of here.'

'*No!*' Jocasta leapt at him, clutching the arm which held the torch. He dropped it. It lay on the floor, its beam directed into the fireplace. The logs looked dead and grey in the strong, white light.

'Don't go,' Jocasta implored. 'You can't go. You can't leave me. For God's sake, don't leave me here with . . . with . . .'

CHAPTER IV

THE following morning, Sunday, just before 9 a.m., there was a sudden burst of sunlight, a splash of dripping yellow in a washed-out, watercolour sky.

The light looked to be directly over the Tump, the trees on its sides and summit massing menacingly around the watery orb. It was, Rachel thought, as if a green-gloved hand had reached out from the foliage, snatched the emergent sun and crunched it like an egg.

'I think we should call the police,' she said.

'Why?' said Humble. 'Whoever done it saved us a job.'

The Tump squatted under the sun, fat and smug. You could almost think the Tump was the culprit – as if the great mound had taken a deep breath, pulled in its girth and then let go, bellying out and crumbling the wall before it.

Then Rachel had seen the bulldozer, still wedged in the rubble.

'And there's Gomer Parry,' she said. 'What's he going to say?'

'Proves him wrong, dunnit? He reckoned the machine wouldn't go frew the wall.'

'Without the wall collapsing on it. Which it has.'

A chunk of wall about fifteen feet wide had been smashed in or wrenched out and then the bulldozer plunged in again. Clearly an amateur job, but the spot had been well-chosen. It would leave a jagged gap directly under the huge picture-window in the stable-block.

'All we do about Gomer, we just pay him off,' Humble said. He was unshaven. He wore a black motorcycle jacket. Half an hour ago he'd rung J. M. Powys's riverside cottage. 'Put Rachel on.' She'd been quite shocked, didn't see how he could possibly have known about her and J.M.

It meant Max would know by now. Max would not be particularly annoyed that she was with J. M. Powys, but she'd done it without clearing it with him first – *that* was the serious offence.

Time to move on, Rachel decided abruptly. The façade's crumbling. Time to negotiate a settlement.

'I think the bulldozer's damaged,' she said. 'Look at the way the blade-thing is twisted.'

'Couple of thou' should see Gomer right. See, Rachel, you bring in the Old Bill, you're causing unnecessary hassle. Somebody might get the idea we paid him to do it. Max would not like that.'

'Him? You sound as if you know who did it.'

'Yeah, well, I got my suspicions.'

'Would you like to share them?'

'I keep my eyes open,' Humble said.

'Not much you don't know, is there, Humble?'

Humble smirked. 'Not much, Rachel. Not much.'

The metal plate on the door said, *When red light is showing, do not attempt to enter.*

The red light was on.

Not sure what to do, Powys walked around the dull, brick building which had once been a lavatory. When he arrived back at the door he was holding up a foot.

'Oh shit, what's this?'

Making a face, Powys scraped off the used condom against a corner of the wall.

She was watching him in some amusement from the studio door, open now, the red light still on.

'Sorry, should have warned you. You'll never pick up a dog turd in this town, but French letters . . . an all-too-common hazard. Especially just here.'

Powys looked around and counted five of the things, shrivelling into the gravel. 'Favourite place,' Fay said. 'The grunts and squeals can be quite disconcerting when you arrive here in the dark.'

'Maybe it's the red light gets them going.' Powys looked up at the sign. ' "Do not attempt to enter." Obviously nobody takes much notice of that.'

'Come in,' said Fay.

He followed her into the little building and looked around. 'Incredible. A radio studio in Crybbe.'

'Geographically convenient.' Fay was unpacking two reels of quarter-inch tape. 'It's certainly not a reflection of the importance of the town.'

She set the tape rolling. 'I won't waste time. This is one bit. Henry Kettle's dowsing masterclass.'

'*OK. Here we go. Is there any . . . ? Fucking hell, Henry!*'

'*Caught you by surprise, did it?*'

Powys grinned. 'Bit like sex, isn't it. The first time. Did the earth move for you?'

'Certainly did when he put his hands over mine. The rod just sort of flipped over. I did wonder afterwards if he was *making* it happen. Just to get it over with, get me off his back. He was obviously very busy. But I can be quite persistent, I suppose.'

He thought she probably could. She looked very nice this morning, in a dark skirt and a glittery kind of top.

She noticed him studying the ensemble. 'I'm going to

church afterwards.' Pushing the buttons on the tape-machine and flipping the controls on the console. 'Then I've got to go and pick up Arnold from the vet's.'

'He's OK?'

'Actually the vet said on the phone that I might get a bit of a shock when I saw him, but there was nothing to worry about. Have you ever been inside the church?'

He shook his head. 'But you're a regular churchgoer, I suppose. With your dad in the business.'

'Oh hell, nothing to do with that. And I'm not, actually. What it is, Dad tells me Murray – that's the vicar – is doing his sermon on the New Age Phenomenon In Our Midst. I'll probably get a story out of it. Murray's a very mixed-up person. The town's damaged him, I think.'

'You think this town damages people?'

'It's damaged me,' said Fay. 'Listen, this is the bit. Obviously, what I was really interested in was what Henry Kettle was doing for Goff, and at one point I asked him, straight out.'

'. . . So, tell me, Henry, you're obviously in the middle of a major dowsing operation here in Crybbe. What exactly does that involve?'

'Oh, I . . . Oh dear. Look, switch that thing off a minute, will you?'

'He was waving his arms about, the way people do when you ask them a question they can't answer.'

'And did you switch off?'

'I did, I'm afraid,' Fay said. 'Sometimes you flip the pause button a couple of times to make it look as if you have and then record the lot, but I was starting to like him. "Don't press me, girl," he kept saying.'

'Did he say anything to indicate he was bothered, or upset by what he was finding?'

'I think he did, and it must be on the other tape.' Fay spun all the way back and pulled the reel off the deck. 'Hold this a minute, would you, er . . . sorry, I don't actually know what the J. M. stands for.'

'Joe.'

'Joe Powys. Mmm. It's a whole different person. Now, Joe

Powys, some answers.' She had her fists on her hips, the second reel clutched in one. 'Who killed Henry Kettle?'

'Ah,' he said.

'You don't think it was an accident at all, do you?'

'Well,' he said, 'I don't think it's who killed him so much as *what* killed him. I'm sure nobody tampered with his brakes or anything.'

'So you think it might be something, shall we say . . . supernatural? And *don't* say it depends what I mean by supernatural.'

'How about you put the tape on, then we'll talk about it?'

'And you went to see Mrs Seagrove again, didn't you?'

'We loonies have to stick together.'

'So you *did* go to talk about the black dog . . . OK, OK, I'll put the tape on.'

She dragged the yellow leader tape past the heads, set it running on fast forward, stopped it. 'Somewhere around here, I think. I'd caught up with Henry in the wood between the Court and the church. I'd come straight from another job and I still had about half a tape left, so I just ran it off, walking along with Henry. When you're putting a package together you need lots of spare atmos and stuff.'

'Atmos?'

'Ambient sounds. Birdsong, wind in the trees. Also, I needed bits of him trudging along doing his dowsing bit. Radio's nearly as much of a fake as telly, you reshape it afterwards, rearrange sentences, manufacture pauses for effect – using spare ambience. So here's Henry in the wood. I hope.'

'*That's curious. That* is *curious.*'

'That's it. Hang on a minute, Joe, I'll find the start. OK, here we go . . .'

' . . . *keep you a minute, Fay, just something I need to look at. Bear with me.*'

'*That's OK, Mr Kettle. Can I call you Henry during the interview? Makes it more informal.*'

'*You please yourself, girl. Call me a daft old bugger if you like.*'

Powys felt almost tearful. Every time someone like Henry died, the world faded a shade further into neutral.

'*Well, bugger – don't mind me, Fay, talking to myself. That's curious. That is curious. If I didn't know better, I'd almost be inclined to think it wasn't an old stone at all. Funny old business . . . Just when you think you've come across everything, you find something that don't . . . quite . . . add up. Come on then, Fay, let's do your bit of radio, only we'll go somewhere else if you don't mind . . .'*

Powys said, 'Can you just play that bit again.'

'*. . . almost be inclined to think it wasn't an old stone at all . . .*'

'That's the bit.' There was a parallel here, something from Henry's journal. 'Fay, where was this, can you show me? Have you time before church?'

'We'll have to be a bit quick, Joe,' Fay said, rewinding.

Murray Beech watched his sermon rolling out of the printer with barely an hour to go before the service. Normally he worked at least three weeks in advance, storing the sermons on computer disk. This one had been completed only last night, at great personal risk – Murray had twice lost entire scripts due to power cuts.

But the electricity rarely failed in the morning, and the printer whizzed it out without interruption.

Certain claims have already been made for the effects of this so-called New Awakening . . .

Why am I doing this? he asked himself.

Because it's what they want to hear, he answered shamefully. Never imagined it would come to this. What harm were they causing, these innocent cranks with their ley-lines and their healing rays?

Ironically, Murray had come to Crybbe aware of the need for tolerance with country folk, their local customs, their herbal remedies. But it had proved to be a myth. Country people, *real* country people weren't like this, not in Crybbe anyway, where he'd never been offered a herbal remedy or even a pot of home-made jam. And where the only custom was the curfew, an unsmiling ritual, performed without comment.

On a metal bookshelf sat the three-volume set of Kilvert's diary, given to him by Kirsty when he told her he was leaving Brighton to become a vicar in the border country.

'Just like Kilvert!' She'd been thrilled. He'd never heard of Kilvert, so she'd bought him the collected diaries, the record (expressively written, if you liked that sort of thing) of a young Victorian clergyman's life, mainly in the village of Clyro, about twenty miles from Crybbe. Kilvert had found rich colours in nature and in the people around him. He'd also found warmth and friends, even if he did have a rather disturbing predilection for young girls.

Murray's stomach tightened; he was thinking of dark-eyed Tessa, a sweat dab over her lips.

Loneliness.

Loneliness had brought him to this.

I've no friends here.

Kirsty had spent a week in Crybbe, long enough to convince her this was not the border country beloved of Francis Kilvert.

'*You once said you'd follow me anywhere my calling took me. Africa . . . South America . . .*'

'*But not Crybbe, Murray. I'd die. I'd wither.*'

She'd given him Kilvert's diary for his birthday two years ago.

Exactly two years ago. Today was his birthday.

'Is there *no* chance of your finding a living down here, Murray?' his mother had asked this morning, on the phone.

They'd been proud, of course, as he had, when he'd been given Crybbe – such a large parish, such a young man.

Nobody else wanted it.

No home-made jam. No Women's Institute. No welcome at the primary school. No harvest-supper. No bell-ringers. No friends. No wife.

He could, of course, have betrayed the inert, moribund villagers by siding openly with the New Age community, who at least sought some kind of spirituality, albeit misguided. He would, perhaps, have made friends, of a sort, amongst them.

But he knew his role as priest was to support his parishioners, even if they did not support him, apart from token mute appearance at his services. Even if they did not deserve him.

Murray was disgusted with himself for thinking that.

Loneliness. Loneliness had brought him to this.

The only way either of them knew into the wood was through the Court grounds. When they arrived there in Fay's Fiesta, Rachel was outside the stables with one of the interior designers, a small, completely bald man she introduced as Simon.

'What this place is about,' Simon was saying, 'is drama. Drama and spectacle.'

Powys didn't even have to go inside to see what he meant. The original stable doors had been replaced with huge portals of plate-glass, through which you could look down into a kind of theatre, the kitchen and dining-room walled off from a single cavernous room, the length of the building, ending in a wide, wooden desk, its back to the huge picture-window.

And the Tump.

When Max was sitting at his desk, he would be directly under the mound'. From the top of the room it would look as if the great tumulus with its wavy trees was growing out of his head.

Especially now that . . .

'What happened to the wall?'

Rachel grimaced. 'Person or persons unknown came in the night to do Max a big favour, using Gomer Parry's bulldozer. I'm sure Humble knows who it was, he tends to be out there in the small hours, killing things. But Humble isn't saying.'

The attack on the wall, the opening up of the stable-block, with glass at either end . . . the formation of a conduit between the Tump and Crybbe.

Powys looked at it through Goff's eyes: a stream of healing energy – deep blue – surging through the stables, through the Court itself, through the wood to the church and then into the town.

Equally, though, you could see the Tump as a huge malignant tumour, assisted at last to spread its black cells and bring

secondary cancers to Crybbe, a town already old and mouldering.

'Natural drama,' Simon, the designer, said. 'Great.'

In the centre of the wood was a huge hole, newly dug, around
five feet deep.

'Must be destined for a big one,' Powys said. 'And they're
making sure it's going to be visible.'

Fay looked around in horror. 'There was a bit of a clearing
when I was here with Henry, but nothing . . . nothing like
this.'

The immediate area was strewn with chainsaw carnage.
Stumps of slaughtered trees, heaps of wet ash where branches
had been burned.

Looking back the way they'd come, Powys could see the
roof of the Court. 'I reckon most of this wood's going to disappear. They want to open up the view from the prospect
chamber, reconnect the town with the Court – and the Tump.'

'But you can't just chop down a whole wood!' Fay glared
at Rachel, who backed off, holding up both hands.

'Listen, I know nothing about this. This is Boulton-Trow's
province.'

'Aren't trees like this protected?'

'I should imagine so,' said Rachel. 'But it's hardly an
imprisonable offence. You can take out injunctions to prevent
people chopping down individual trees, but once they're gone,
they're gone, and if you do it quietly, well . . .'

'Like starting from the middle and working outwards,'
Powys said. 'I don't know how old this wood is, but the indication from the prospect chamber is that at the end of the
sixteenth century it wasn't here at all. I reckon it was planted
not to give the Court more privacy but so the townsfolk couldn't
see the Court. So they could pretend it wasn't there. Just as
the stable-block was put in to block the Court off from the
Tump. They were scared of something.'

He was balancing on the edge of the hole, looking down.
'So, Fay, this is where Henry discovered there'd been a stone.'

'I think so. Must be.'

'And yet he had the feeling the stone that stood here wasn't an *old* stone.'

'That's what he seemed to be saying.' Fay was more concerned about the wholesale destruction of the wood. 'And these are supposed to be bloody *New Age* people!' She peered through what remained of the trees. 'Can I get to the church this way?'

'Sure,' Rachel said. 'Five minutes' walk. There's a footpath, newly widened. Goes past a redbrick heap called Keeper's Cottage, which is where Boulton-Trow's living.'

'He lives here?' Powys said, surprised. 'In the wood?'

'Yes, and rather him than me. Go past it, anyway, Fay, and you're in the churchyard in no time.'

'Thanks.' Fay pulled a bunch of keys from her bag. 'Do me a favour, Joe, I've got to catch Murray's blasted sermon. Could you bring my car round to the church when you've finished here. It's got the Uher in the back. I'll need to interview him afterwards.'

She vanished into the bushes. Like an elf, he thought.

'I came to a decision this morning,' Rachel said.

She sat down on a tree stump. 'I'm going to quit.'

'Good. I mean, that's terrific. You're wasted on that fat plonker.'

'I'm becoming peripheral anyway. Max doesn't listen to me any more. He's getting so fanatical I don't think there's anything you or I can do to stop him. Also, he's entering one of his DC phases. He's besotted with Boulton-Trow.'

'Andy? Is it reciprocated?'

'You know the guy better than me, J.M.'

'He's an opportunist.'

'There you are, then.'

He watched her, pale and graceful in this arboreal charnel house. She brushed a stray hair out of one eye.

He said, 'When will you tell him?'

'Probably after his public meeting on Tuesday.'

'That's marvellous, Rachel. You won't regret it. Coming to church?'

Rachel stood up. 'Oh gosh, far too busy. Least I can do is

make sure his stable-block's ready for him. Besides, I'm not a churchy person. I'm one of those who thinks it's a waste of Sunday – what do you call that, an atheist or an agnostic?'

He put an arm around her waist. 'You call it a smug bitch.'

He grinned, happy for her.

CHAPTER V

'A ND let's pray now,' Murray Beech said, head bowed, 'for the soul of our brother Jonathon Preece . . .'

Kneeling in a back pew, Fay tensed.

'. . . taken so suddenly from the heart of the agricultural community he served so energetically. Those of us who knew Jonathon – and can there be any here who did not? – will always remember his tireless commitment to the Young Farmers' movement and, through this, to the revival of an industry in which his family has laboured for over four hundred years.'

Powys slid the Uher into the empty pew next to Fay and slipped in after it. Fay kept on looking directly ahead, over the prayer-book ledge, seeing, near the front of the church, the heads of Jack Preece and Jimmy Preece. One of the few places you ever saw these heads uncapped.

'And we pray, too,' Murray intoned passionlessly, 'for the Preece family in its time of sorrow and loss . . .'

Fay saw young Warren Preece, head nodding rhythmically now and then, as if connected to some invisible Walkman.

Saw Mrs Preece, Jimmy's wife, hands clasped in prayer. Expecting to see a damp tissue crumpled in her palm. But Mrs Preece, seen side-on, looked as dry-eyed and stern as her husband. They seemed to have their eyes open as they prayed – if indeed they *were* praying.

Looking around, Fay found that everyone's were open, everyone she could see.

Crybbe: a place where emotions were buried as deep as the dead.

Wisely, perhaps, Murray didn't make a big deal of it. He

went into the Lord's Prayer and didn't mention Jonathon Preece again.

Fay relaxed.

What had she expected? A denunciation from the pulpit? All heads turned in mute accusation?

Whatever, she breathed again. And became aware of the significance of something she must surely have noticed already: the presence of her father, on the end of a pew two rows in front of her and Powys.

The Canon went to church every Sunday, sometimes attending both the morning and evening services. He sat near the front and sang loudly – 'Bit of moral support for young Murray; boy needs all the back-up he can get.'

So what was he doing further back, a couple of rows behind the nearest fully occupied pew? Could it be something to do with there being only one other person on Alex's pew and this person being at the same end of the pew as Alex? And being a woman?

'Bloody hell,' said Fay to herself. 'He's found a totty.'

Guy Morrison woke up into the greyness of . . . 5.a.m., 5.30?

He found his watch on the bedside table.

It told him the time was 11.15.

For crying out loud! He turned over and found he was alone in a king-size bed of antique pine, in a pink-washed room with large beams in the ceiling and a view, through small square panes, of misty hills. He'd never seen this view before.

Guy lay down again, regulating his breathing.

He saw a door then, and a glimpse of mauve tiles told him it led to an *en suite* bathroom, which put him in mind of another bathroom, full of seeping yellow.

With a momentary clenching of stomach muscles, *everything* came back.

He remembered peeing on his shoes in the dark paddock because she wouldn't let him return to that bathroom – not that he needed much persuading.

He remembered them staying in the kitchen for a long time, drinking coffee – him not talking much and not listening much either, after she'd been gushing like a broken fire-hydrant for an hour or so – until it was nearly light and she'd decided it was safe to go to bed. This bed. He remembered waking up periodically to find her hanging on to him in her fitful, unquiet sleep and wondering how he could ever have found her so attractive.

Guy pushed back the duvet to find he was naked, and he couldn't see his clothes anywhere. If he went downstairs like this it would be just his luck to find the vicar and the entire bloody Women's Institute having morning coffee in the drawing-room.

He went into the *en suite* bathroom, looked at himself in the mirror and was horrified at the state of his hair and the growth of his beard, detecting a distressing amount of grey and white stubble. He looked around for something to shave with – normally, he used a state-of-the-art rechargeable twice a day – and could find only a primitive kind of safety razor.

Remembering, at this point, the old man with the cut-throat razor in the other bathroom. And hours later in the well-lit kitchen, thrusting aside his fourth cup of coffee, asking her directly, 'Are you telling me it was a *ghost*?'

He'd once done a documentary about ghosts. They were, the programme had suggested, nature's holograms. Something like that. You might get images of the dead; you could just as easily have images of the living. When the phenomenon was eventually understood it would be no more frightening than a mirage.

This one was frightening, he supposed, only briefly, in retrospect. What had he really felt when he saw the glow around the door and then walked into the bathroom and the old man had looked up and met his eyes? Fear, or a kind of fascination?

Did this old man have eyes? He must have had. Guy couldn't recall his features. Only a figure bent over the washbasin, shaving. The image, perhaps, of a man who had lived in this house for many years and perhaps shaved thousands of times in that very basin – well, perhaps not that actual basin, but certainly in the room. And this mundane, everyday ritual had imprinted itself on the atmosphere.

The apparition was frightening, Guy decided, because it

happened at night during a power cut. Also, because he was feeling a few misgivings about what he'd got himself into and was perhaps a little jittery anyway.

Guy shaved with the razor, his first wet-shave in years, and cut himself twice, quite noticeably – no pieces-to-camera for *him* for a couple of days. Perhaps this chap didn't have an electric shaver because he couldn't rely on one with all the power cuts they apparently had. Jocasta had gone on and on last night about the power cuts and the exorbitant electricity bills. How living in the country wasn't a simple life at all and certainly not cheap. How she couldn't get out of here fast enough. How her poor husband was weak and naive beyond comprehension.

Guy didn't like the sound of that bit at all, much preferred screwing happily married women whose only need was a touch of glamour in their lives.

The true horror of the night, now he thought about it, had been the hours he'd spent with a furrowed-faced Jocasta in the kitchen afterwards, listening to her whingeing on and on.

'Guy, where are you?'

He looked around the bathroom door and saw her standing by the bed. She wore a floor-length Japanese silk dressing-gown and fresh make-up. Façade fully restored. She must have spent an hour or so in here before he was awake.

'Good morning, Jocasta.' Guy stepped naked and smiling into the bedroom, forgetting about the two cuts on his face, staunched by small pieces of soft toilet tissue. Perhaps . . . Perhaps he could afford to give her just one more . . .

But she didn't look at him in any meaningful way. 'Please get dressed,' Jocasta said crisply. 'I want to show you something.'

Guy's smile vanished.

'Your clothes are in Bedroom Two, across the passage. Coffee and croissants in ten minutes.'

And Jocasta swished away, leaving him most offended. Women did not turn their backs and swish away from Guy Morrison.

When he arrived in the kitchen nearly twenty minutes later,

he was fully dressed, right up to his olive leather jacket, and fully aware again of who he was. He accepted coffee but declined a croissant. He must, he said, be off. Perhaps she could give him a time for the exhibition opening, keeping it as tight as possible because he had quite a few people to see.

Jocasta pushed a large folder towards him across the kitchen table. 'I'd be glad,' she said, 'if you could take a look at these.'

'Look, I *am* rather pushed . . .'

'It won't take a minute.' She was very composed this morning, probably embarrassed as hell about last night's tearful sequence. He opened the folder in a deliberately cursory fashion. What the hell was all this about? Was he expected to *buy* something?

The drawing was pen-and-ink. The face was inspecting itself in a mirror. Every wrinkle on the face – and there were many – was deeply etched. The eyes were sunken, the cheeks hollow, the nose bulbous.

Guy inhaled sharply. He looked up at Jocasta in her Japanese dressing-gown, could tell she was working hard to hide her feelings, holding a mask over her anticipation. Anticipation and something else. Something altogether less healthy.

He looked down at the drawing again. He felt a deep suspicion and a growing alarm.

'Is this some sort of joke?'

'Is it him?' Jocasta asked.

'I don't know what you mean. Who did these?'

'Is it *him*?'

Of course it was him. It was either him or Guy was going mad. His deep suspicion was suddenly drenched in cold confusion and a bitter, acrid dread.

'Look at the next one.'

All the sensation had left his fingers. He watched them, as if they were someone else's fingers, lifting the first drawing, laying it to one side, face-down on the table.

He didn't understand.

A moment earlier, he saw, the old man had slashed his throat. The open razor had fallen from one spasmed hand – it was drawn in mid-air, floating a fraction of an inch below a finger and thumb – while the fingers of the other hand were pushing into the opened throat itself, as if trying to hold the slit tubes together, to block the tunnels of blood.

The blood was black ink, blotch upon blotch, spread joyously, as if the pen nib was a substitute for the cut-throat razor.

Guy thrust the drawing aside, came raggedly to his feet. He stumbled to the sink and threw up what seemed like half a gallon of sour coffee.

It was not the drawing, he thought as he retched. It was the knowledge of what, if he'd stayed a moment longer in the bathroom last night, he would have seen.

He wiped his mouth with the back of a hand, saw Jocasta watching him in distaste, knew exactly what she was thinking: that perhaps all men were as pathetic as her husband.

'I'm sorry,' Guy said. He washed his hands and his face, snatched a handful of kitchen towel to wipe them. No, dammit, he wasn't sorry at all.

'I think you owe me an explanation,' he said coldly.

Murray Beech leaned out of his pulpit, hands gripping its edges, as if he were sitting up in the bath.

'And what,' he demanded, '*is* this so-called New Age? Can there be any true meaning in a concept quite so vague?'

He paused.

'The New Age,' he said heavily.

He glared out into the church – late-medieval and not much altered. 'Some of you may remember a popular song, "This is the Dawning of the Age of Aquarius".'

'He's going to knock it, then,' Powys whispered to Fay.

'Well, of course he's going to knock it,' Fay said, out of the side of her mouth. 'That's why I'm here.'

The Uher sat on the pew at her side, its spools turning, the microphone wedged between two prayer books on the ledge. She was recording the sermon for her own reference. She wouldn't get anything of broadcast quality at this range and she hadn't got permission anyway. She'd talk to him on tape afterwards, throw his own words back at him and see how he reacted.

' "Harmony and Understanding",' Murray quoted, ' "Sympathy and Trust Abounding".'

Alien concepts in Crybbe, Fay thought cynically. The vicar's words must be settling on this comatose congregation with all the weight of ash-flakes from a distant bonfire.

Caught in white light from a small Gothic window set high in the nave, Murray Beech – light-brown hair slicked flat, metallic features firmly set – was looking about fifteen years older than his age. A man with problems.

Fay's dad shuffled and coughed. He didn't know she was here.

Who was this woman, then? Slim and small-boned, she wore a wide-brimmed brown felt hat which concealed her hair and neck.

The Vicar announced there would be a public meeting in Crybbe on Tuesday night, when the members of this congregation would be asked to consider the merits of the New Age movement and decide to what extent they would allow it to infiltrate their lives.

Now, he had no wish to condemn the obviously sincere people who offered what appeared to be rather scenic short-cuts to their own idea of heaven. Indeed, it might be argued that any kind of spirituality was better than none at all.

The Canon coughed again; the woman next to him was very still. Almost . . . almost *too* still.

'We have a choice,' said Murray. 'We can pray for the strength and the will to confront the reality of a world defiled by starvation, injustice and inequality – a world crying out for basic Christian charity.

'Or,' he said, with the smallest twist of his lips, 'we can sidestep reality and amuse ourselves in what we might call the Cosmic Fairground.'

Everyone alive moved a little, Fay thought, watching the woman. Even sleeping people moved.

No. Not here. You can't follow him here. Not into church.

Murray hauled himself further up in his pulpit, raised his voice.

'How appealing! How appealing it must seem to live in a little world where, if we're sick, we can pass off the health services and the medical advances of the past hundred years as irrelevant and call instead upon the power of . . . healing crystals.'

Powys smiled.

But Fay had stiffened, feeling the tiny hairs rising on her bare arms. Her father's face was turned towards the pulpit. He had never glanced at the woman by his side. Fay thought, I can see her, *but can he?*

'. . . a little world, where, if we feel we are suffering a certain starvation of the soul, we need not give up our Sunday mornings to come to church. Because all we need to do is to go for a stroll along the nearest ley-line and expose ourselves to these famous cosmic rays.'

Fay heard him as if from afar. She was looking at her father. And at the woman. *Neat, small-boned, wide-brimmed hat concealing her hair and neck. And unnaturally still.*

The church was darkening around Fay. The muted colours had drained out of the congregation. Everything was black and white and grey. Nobody moved. Murray Beech, flickering like an ancient movie, black and white in his surplice, was gesturing in the pulpit, but she couldn't hear him any more.

She stared hard, projecting her fear and – surprised at its strength – her uncontrollable resentment. Until she felt herself lifting from the pew, aware of a sudden concern in the eyes of Joe Powys, his hand reaching out for her from a long, long way away, but not touching. Fay rising on a malign wave while, at the same time, very slowly, the woman sitting next to her father began, for the first time, to move.

Began, very slowly, to turn her head.

And Fay was suddenly up on her feet in the silent church, shrieking aloud, 'How dare you? Get out! How dare you come in here!'

Gripping the prayer-book shelf so hard that it creaked.

'Why?' Fay screamed. 'Why can't you just get on with your death and leave him alone?'

Then everybody was turning round, but Fay was out of the church door, and running.

CHAPTER VI

WHEN the Mercedes estate carrying Simon and his three young assistants had vanished into the lane, Rachel watched Andy Boulton-Trow, stripped to the waist, supervising the loading of three long stones into the back of a truck. There was a small digger in the back, too, one of those you could hire to landscape your own garden.

'Last ones,' Andy said, jabbing a thumb at the stones. He'd acquired, very rapidly, an impressive black beard, somehow hardening his narrow jaw.

Rachel said, 'The others are in?'

'The ones that are safe to put in, without arousing complaints from the landowners. We've got a nice one here for your friend Joe.'

He didn't, she noticed, put any kind of stress on the words 'your friend'.

'And then I'm pushing off for a day or two,' Andy said, stretching.

'Is Max aware of this?'

'I really don't know, Rachel.'

She wondered if perhaps he was pushing off somewhere *with* Max. 'A very heavy guy,' Max had said once. 'He knows all the options.'

Whereas J.M. had implied that while Andy knew as much about earth mysteries as anybody could reasonably be expected to, it was unwise to trust him too far. 'He takes risks, especially when the potential fall-guy is someone else.'

The implication being that he, J. M. Powys, had once been the fall-guy. One day, away from here, he would tell her about this.

'What's going on over there?' Rachel had seen a cluster of men emerging from the rear entrance of the Court. Two of them carried a rotting plank which they hurled on a heap of rubbish in a corner of the courtyard.

'Big clean-out,' Andy said. 'Before the renovation proper begins. All the junk from upstairs – the detritus of the various attempts to modernize the Court, anything not in period – has to go. Didn't Max tell you?'

'I think he mentioned something,' Rachel said uncomfortably. He hadn't, of course. Increasingly, things had been happening around her without any kind of consultation.

Like the appropriation of Gomer Parry's bulldozer in the night?

Max liked to live dangerously; she didn't. She was deeply glad to be leaving his employ.

'Make a good bonfire,' Andy Boulton-Trow said, nodding at the pile of rubbish. 'Maybe we should organize one for Lammas or something. A cleansing.'

He stretched his lithe body into the truck. 'Have fun,' he said.

Powys raced out of the church, clutching the Uher by its strap. She'd left it there, on the pew, still recording, with a motor-hum and a hiss of turning spools.

He scanned the churchyard, but she was gone. He ran to the gate, looked both ways, thought he could hear running footsteps, but there was nobody in sight. He glanced over his shoulder and saw a white-bearded, dog-collared old man in the church entrance, also looking from side to side.

Her father. Both of them looking for Fay.

Powys stabbed vaguely at the Uher's piano-key controls until the hum and hiss ceased with a final whirr. Then he slung the machine over his shoulder, stuck the microphone in his pocket and set off towards Bell Street. Or would she have gone to the studio?

Making an outburst in church was a clear sign of instability. People who made outbursts in church were usually basket-cases.

Except in Crybbe. Leaping up and screaming, Powys thought, was surely a perfectly natural reaction to the miasma of almost-anaesthetized disinterest emanating from that congregation.

Bloody weird, though, what she'd said.

Why can't you just get on with your death and leave him alone?
Bloody weird.

As he came to the corner of Bell Street, he almost lost a
foot to a familiar red Ford Fiesta, shrieking round the corner
in low gear, crunching over the kerb.

The driver saw him, and the Fiesta squeaked and stalled.
The passenger door flew open and bumped the Uher, and the
driver called out, 'Get in!'

Powys climbed in and sat with the Uher on his knee. 'You
left this in the church,' he said.

'Thanks.' Fay started the engine and the car spurted into
the square.

'Your father . . .'

'Fuck my father,' she snapped, and she didn't speak again
until they passed the town boundary and there were open hills
all around and a rush of cold air through the side windows, the
glass on both sides wound down to its limits.

Fay breathed out hard and thrust her small body back into
the seat, the Fiesta going like a rocket down a lane originally
created for horses.

'Got to be something awry,' she said remotely, 'when the
most newsworthy item on the tape is the reporter having hysterics.'

Powys said, 'When's visiting time at the vet's, then?'

She turned towards him. 'You want to come?'

'I've got a choice? Watch the road, for Christ's sake!'

She said, 'You want me to talk about it, I suppose.'

'Up to you.'

'Well,' she said, 'I suppose if I can talk about it to anybody,
I can talk about it to you. Don't suppose I'll be telling you
anything you haven't heard before.'

'That's right,' Powys said. 'I'm an accredited crank. And
I'll be a dead crank if you don't . . .'

'Yet so cynical.' Fay slowed down. 'You didn't used to be
cynical. Unless that wide-eyed, wow-man-what-a-mind-blower
feel to *The Old Golden Land* was a put-on.'

'Well,' he said, 'the light-hearted element kind of dissipated.' He closed his eyes and the past tumbled down to him, like a rock slide.

> *Joey goes round the Bottle Stone*
> *And he goes round ONCE.*

What's happening is you're developing a link with the stone, in an umbilical kind of way. You're feeling every step you take, bare feet connecting sensuously with the warm, grassy skin of the earth. And all the while the terrestrial magnetism – let's imagine it exists – is seeping up through the soles of your feet . . .

> *And he goes round TWICE.*

Stop it.

He rubbed his eyes. 'That *was* your dad, was it, with the white beard? Rachel told me about him. She said he was, er, something of a fun guy for his age.'

'He was always fun,' Fay said. 'That was the problem. Clergymen aren't supposed to have that much fun.'

Powys watched her drive, *not* like Rachel. She bumped the gears, rode the clutch and went too fast round blind bends.

He tried to watch the landscape. 'Nothing like this where I grew up. Love at first sight, when I came down here.'

'Where was that? Where you came from.'

'Up north. Very industrialized part. A long bus-ride to the nearest cow. Every square yard, for as far as you could see, built on for about the fourth time. Where we lived they'd eradicated grass like a disease. It's quite nice now, if you like Georgian-style semis with concrete barbecue-pits.'

Fay said, 'I grew up in old vicarages and rectories, in little villages with thatched houses. And Oxford for a time.'

'Deprived childhood, huh?'

'There's more than one kind,' Fay said. 'Not many ley-lines where you came from, I suppose.'

'You just had to work harder to find them,' Powys said, stiffening as Fay clipped the hedge to avoid an oncoming lorry.

'Bloody loony.'

Could she, he wondered, really be referring to the innocent lorry driver?

'How long has he known Jean Wendle?'

'Who?'

'Your dad. He was sitting next to Jean Wendle. In church.'

After a moment, Fay trod on the brakes. The Fiesta was almost in the middle of the road. The driver of a BMW behind them blasted his horn and revved in righteous rage.

'What?'

She didn't seem to notice the middle-aged, suit-and-tie-clad BMW driver thrusting up two furious fingers as he roared past.

'Jean Wendle,' Powys said. 'The healer.'

Fay gripped the wheel tightly with both hands, threw her head back and moaned.

'Oh God, Joe. That was Jean Wendle?'

'It was.'

Fay unclipped her seat-belt.

'Would you mind taking over, before I kill us both? I think I've made the most awful fool of myself.'

Alex had given Murray Beech the usual can of Heineken, and this time Murray had snapped it open and drunk silently and gratefully.

'You heard my sermon,' Murray said. They were in the living-room at the back of the house in Bell Street. The vicar was slumped in an armchair. He looked worn out.

'And you heard my daughter, I suppose,' Alex said.

'What was the matter with her?'

'You tell me, old boy.' Alex had once been chaplain to a rehabilitation centre for drug addicts; Murray reminded him of the new arrivals, lank-haired, grey-skinned, eyes like mud.

'What did you think of my sermon?'

'Good try,' Alex said. 'Full marks for effort. Couple of Brownie points, perhaps, from the town council. Then again, perhaps not. What d'you want me to say? You and I both know that this fellow Goff's congregation's going to be a bloody sight more dedicated than yours.'

'Sour grapes, eh?'

'You said it, old chap.'

'I don't know what to do,' Murray said, desolate.

Alex sighed.

'I could be good at this job,' Murray said. 'Anywhere else, I could be really good. I'm a good organizer, a good administrator. I *like* organizing things, running the parish affairs, setting up discussion groups, counselling sessions. I've got ideas. I can get things done.'

'Archdeacon material, if ever I saw it.'

'Don't laugh at me, Alex.'

'Sorry.'

'You see, I did what I thought was right in the context of my position in Crybbe. The sermon, I mean. I expected people to come up to me outside. You know . . . Well said, Vicar, all this. I thought I was echoing their own thoughts. I know they don't like what's happening at the Court.'

'How d'you know that?'

'Not from listening to them talk, that's for certain. They don't even seem to talk to each other. No chit-chit, no street-corner gossip. Do you think that's natural? Nobody said a word to me today. I was standing there holding out a hand, thanks for coming, nice to see you, hope you're feeling better now, the usual patter. And some of them were taking my hand limply, as if I was offering them a sandwich at the fête. Then they'd nod and trudge off without a word. No reaction in church either except for Fay's outburst and the boy, Warren Preece, who was staring at me with the most astonishing malevolence in his eyes.'

'Which boy's that?'

'Warren Preece? The Mayor's grandson, the younger brother of the chap who drowned in the river. Looking at me as if he blamed me for his brother's death.'

'Doesn't make much sense, Murray.'

'Didn't to me, either. I tried to ignore it. Perhaps it was nothing to do with his brother. He's a friend of the girl, Tessa Byford. You remember I asked you about exorcism.'

'Oh. Yes. How did that go?'

'You haven't heard anything, then?'

'Nothing at all, old chap. Didn't it go well?'

'You're sure you haven't heard anything? You wouldn't lie, to save my feelings?'

'Sod off, Murray, I'm a Christian.'

Murray said, 'That girl's seriously disturbed. Tessa Byford. The Old Police House. I think I'm talking about evil, Alex. I think I was in the presence of evil. I think she invited me in to flourish something in my face. As if to say, this is what you're up against, now what are you going to do?'

'And what did you do?'

'I ran away,' Murray said starkly. 'I got the hell out of there, and I haven't been back, and I'm scared stiff of meeting her in the street or a shop because I think I'd run away again.'

'Oh dear,' Alex said.

Murray leaned his head back into the chair and closed and opened his eyes twice, flexing his jaw.

Alex said, 'I seem to remember asking you what you thought were the world's greatest evils.'

'I expect I said inequality, the Tory government or something. Now I'd have to say I've seen real evil and it was in the eyes of a schoolgirl. And now, I don't know, in a boy of eighteen or nineteen. What does that say about *me*?'

'Perhaps it says you've grown up,' Alex said. 'Or that you've been watching those X-rated videos again. I don't know either. I've been fudging the bloody issue for years, and now I'm too old and clapped out to do anything about it. Perhaps, you know, this is one of those places where we meet it head-on.'

'Crybbe?'

'Just thinking of something Wendy said. May look like a haemorrhoid in the arsehole of the world, but the quiet places are often the real battlegrounds. Some of these New Age johnnies are actually not so far off-beam when you talk to them. You come across Wendy?'

Murray looked blank.

'Strict Presbyterian upbringing,' Alex said. 'No nonsense. Yet she apparently cures people of cancer and shingles and things with the help of an egg-shaped oriental blob called Dr Chi. Now, I ask you . . . But it's all terminology, isn't it. Dr

Chi, Jesus Christ, Allah, ET . . . There's a positive and a negative and whatever all this energy is, well, perhaps we can colour it with our hearts. Pass me another beer, Murray, I don't think I'm helping you at all.'

'I thought you weren't supposed to drink.'

'Sod that,' said Alex. 'Look at me. Do I seem sick? Do I seem irrational?'

'Far from it. In fact, if you don't mind my saying, I've never known you so lucid.'

'Well, there you are, you see. Dr Chi. Little Chink's a bloody wonder. And there's you trying to drive his intermediary out of town. We think we're so smart, Murray, but we're just pupils in a spiritual kindergarten.'

'I think I'm cracking up,' Murray said.

'Perhaps you need to consult old Dr Chi as well. I can arrange an appointment.'

Murray stood up very quickly and headed for the door. 'Don't joke about this, Alex. Just don't joke.'

'Was I?' Alex asked him innocently. 'Was I joking do you think?'

CHAPTER VII

'**B**UT . . .'

Well, she couldn't say she hadn't been warned.

The vet, an elderly, stooping man in a cardigan, said there'd been quite a concentration of shotgun pellets in the dog's rear end.

'Fairly close range, you see. Must have been. If he'd moved a bit faster, the shot would have missed him altogether. I got some of them out, and some will work to the surface in time. But he'll always be carrying a few around. Like an old soldier.'

Arnold was lying on a folded blanket, his huge ears fully extended. His tail bobbed when Fay and Joe appeared. His left haunch had been shaved to the base of the tail. The skin was vivid pink, the stitching bright blue.

'But he's only got three legs,' Fay said.

'I did try to save it, Mrs Morrison, but so much bone was smashed it would have been enormously complicated and left him in a lot of pain, probably for life. It's quite unusual for the damage to be so concentrated. But then, dogs that are shot are usually killed.'

'He's a survivor,' Fay said.

Arnold was not feeling sorry for himself, this was clear. He thumped his tail against his folded brown blanket and tried to get up. Fell down again, but he tried. Fay rushed to pat him to stop him trying again.

'Never discourage him from standing up,' the vet said. 'He'll be walking soon, after a fashion. Managed a few steps in the garden this morning. Falls over a lot, but he gets up again. He's young enough to handle it with aplomb, I think. Be cocking his stump against lampposts in no time. Need a lot of attention and careful supervision when he's outside, for a while. But he'll be fine. Some people can't cope with it, you know. They have the dog put down. It's kinder, they say. Kinder to them, they mean.'

With a stab of shame, Fay found herself thinking then about her father.

'And there's one thing,' the vet said. 'He won't be considered much of a danger to sheep now. I can't see this particular farmer coming after him again.'

'Most unlikely,' Powys agreed.

There must have been twenty or thirty people around the Court this afternoon, pulling things down, turning out buildings like drawers. And this was a Sunday; every one of them, no doubt, on double-time. Money no object.

The Crybbe project seemed to have taken on a life of its own. Everything was happening unbelievably quickly, three or four months' work done inside a week. As if Max knew he had to seize the place, stage a *coup* before bureaucracy could be cranked into action against him.

And it was happening all around Rachel, as if she wasn't

there. Had Max ordered her to stay behind here just to make this point?

Max's own energy seemed to be pumped entirely into his project, as if he didn't have an empire to run. Even from London, directing people and money to Crybbe.

Because, unknown to its hundreds of employees, this was now the spiritual centre of the Epidemic Group. Crybbe. The Court.

The Tump.

She'd caught sight of a specimen of his proposed new logo: a big green mound with trees on it. In Max's vision, all the power of Epidemic – the recording companies, the publishing houses, the high-street shops – would emanate from the Tump.

On a wall in the stable there was a map of the town with every building marked. The ones owned by Epidemic and now inhabited – or soon to be – by alternative people had been shaded red. She'd counted them; there were thirty-five properties, far more than Max was publicly admitting. Far more than even she had known about.

She tried to imagine the town as the alternative capital of Britain, with thousands of people flooding in to take part in seminars, follow the ley-lines with picnic lunches, consult mystics and healers. People in search of a spiritual recharge or a miracle cure.

A kind of New Age Lourdes.

Crybbe?

Rachel shook her head and wandered across the courtyard, head down, hands deep in the pockets of her Barbour. Couldn't wait to get rid of this greasy bloody Barbour for good.

She arrived at the burgeoning rubbish pile, which would soon consist of the entire non-Tudor contents of the Court. Leftovers from four centuries. Reminders of the times when the Court's other incarnations had been a private school (failed), a hotel (failed), even a billet, she'd been told, for American servicemen during World War II.

It was a shame; a lot of the stuff they were throwing out would be quite useful to some people and some of it valuable. A darkwood table, scratched but serviceable. A wardrobe which was probably Victorian and would sell, cleaned up, for several hundred quid in any antique shop. Peanuts to Max.

Money to burn. Hardly New Age. What happened to recycling?

The pile was over twelve feet high. Filthy carpets which, unrolled, would probably turn out to be Indian. A rocking-chair. A couple of chests, one thick with varnish, the other newer, bound with green-painted metal strips, black lettering across its lid; you couldn't make out what it said.

Rachel looked hard at the second chest. Where had she seen it before?

Good Lord! She ran to the chest and pulled up its lid. They couldn't do this . . .

But they had.

Exposed to full daylight, Tiddles, the mummified cat, looked forlorn, a wisp of a thing, his eye-sockets full of dust, one of his sabre-teeth broken, probably in transit to the heap.

Tiddles, the guardian. Evicted.

She looked up at the Court, its lower windows mainly boarded up, the upper ones too small to give any indication of what was going on inside.

One thing she knew. Tiddles might not be Tudor – seventeenth century, somebody had suggested – but he was part of that place. He would have to go back.

Goes round FOUR times.

The earth force (assume it exists) rising up through the soles of your feet, a kind of liquid light. Up into your legs and then, into the body itself, the solar plexus, the first major energy centre. Feel it forming into a pulsing ball of warm, white light, while the chant goes on, the rhythmic clapping . . .

And he goes round FIVE times.

'Powys, I need to tell you . . .'

'Sorry?'

'Are you OK, Powys?'

'Yes, sorry, I was . . .'

Powys driving Fay's Fiesta through a delirium of damp trees, their foliage burgeoning over the road. Fay sitting in the passenger seat with Arnold on the blanket on her knee, fondling the dog's disproportionately large ears.

'Powys, I need to tell you why I went berserk in church.'

He said nothing. She seemed a good deal more relaxed now; something had obviously resolved itself.

'Have you ever seen a ghost?'

He shook his head. 'Terrible admission, isn't it? My belief in ghosts is founded entirely on hearsay.'

'Who exactly is Jean Wendle?'

'She's a spiritual healer. One of the more convincing ones. Nice woman. Used to be a lawyer. Barrister. Or an advocate, as they say in Scotland. Very high-octane. Then she found she could heal people, so she gave up the law to devote her life to it. They were about to make her a judge at the time. It caused . . . uproar in legal circles.'

'Oh!'

'You remember now?'

'Yes. It was in the papers, wasn't it? How long's she been in Crybbe?'

'As I understand it,' he said, 'she was one of the first of Goff's big-name signings. Rachel says Max wanted to put her into this old rectory he's bought, a couple of miles outside town. But she insisted on being at the heart of things, so she's living in a town house on the square.'

'I didn't know she knew my father.'

'Jean gets to know everybody. Unobtrusively.'

'She was sitting so still,' Fay said. 'In church. So very still.'

'She slows her breathing sometimes. She's a bit uncanny. She . . . intuits things. Absorbs atmospheres and interprets what's really going on. I'm impressed by Jean. Scares me a bit too, I must admit.'

'Scared me,' Fay said, 'in church. I thought I was seeing Dad's late wife.' She paused. 'Again,' she said.

They were coming into Crybbe. Powys slowed for the 30-m.p.h. speed limit.

'You said . . . *late* wife?'

'She was called Grace Legge. The house we live in was hers. She died last year. I saw her last week.'

'Bloody hell, Fay.'

'I'd never seen one before. You know how it is – you've read about ghosts, you've seen the films, you've interviewed people who swear they've seen one. But you don't . . . quite . . . believe they exist.'

'Except in people's minds,' he said.

'Yes.' Fay ran her fingers deep into Arnold's warm fur. 'I don't recommend the experience. You know what they say about the flesh creeping? The spine feeling chilled? Grace was ghastly, dead. What's the time?'

'Ten past five.'

'We haven't eaten,' Fay remembered. 'No wonder I'm shooting my mouth off. Light-headed. You coming in for something, Powys? Omelette? Sandwich? I'm afraid Dad'll be there, so forget everything I said about Grace.'

'Thanks, but I ought to find Rachel.'

Powys pulled up at the bottom of Bell Street, took out the keys and passed them to Fay.

Arnold tried to stand up on Fay's knee. 'Hang on,' Powys said. He went round to open Fay's door and she handed Arnold to him while she got out and shook off the dog hairs.

As Powys handed Arnold back, as gently as he could, Fay looked him hard in the eyes. Serious, almost severe.

'If you've got any sense, Joe Powys,' she said, 'you'll piss off out of Crybbe pronto and take Rachel with you. She's gold. She's the only person I know around here who's got her act together. Come on, Arnie, I'm afraid we're home.'

'What about you? Strikes me you need to get out more urgently than any of us.'

'Why? Because I'm losing my marbles like Dad?'

And like me? he wondered, walking down the street towards the river.

And immediately twelve years fell away and he was going around the stone again.

Round and round. Mesmeric. Tribal.
Widdershins, widdershins . . . against the sun, against nature . . .

. . . And he goes round SEVEN times . . .

Powys stood on the bridge and threw up his hands, warding it off, wiping it away, but the atmosphere was thick with it. He could feel Memory's helicopter beating the air above his head with great sweeping, buffeting strokes. It had never been so powerful. He was standing upright on the bridge, but his mind was ducking and crouching, cowering. He looked around for somewhere to run to, but it was all around him.

. . . EIGHT times . . .

Fluidity of movement, breathing changing rhythm. Something else breathing for you, running beside you . . . widdershins, widdershins . . . and doing your breathing.

. . . NINE . . .

Can't stop. Can't stop.
Out of your hands now.
Widdershins, widdershins.

. . . TEN . . .

Below you, the tiny figure running around the stone.
Widdershins . . . all wrong.
Below. The stone and the running figure.
Widdershins.
All wrong.

. . . ELEVEN . . .

And the ball of light rising up hard, bright, glowing, pulsing . . . into the chest.

Widdershins.

Engulfing your heart, but it's no longer warm, and it's bursting, with a shocking rush into your head, where it's . . .

WIDDERSHINS!

He was inside the running figure now, pounding across the bridge and into the short gravel drive of the little black and white riverside cottage.

Powys flung himself on to the long-unmown lawn, soft and damp and full of buttercups and dandelions.

He lay on his stomach with his face into the grass, his eyes closed and the cool vegetation pressed into the sockets. Kept rubbing it in until it was a green mush and not so cool any more.

'You're going back,' Annie had said.

Back to the Old Golden Land. Back – he'd told himself – to find out what had happened to Henry Kettle. Back – they said behind his back – to find redemption.

The cold in his stomach told him he was back, but that there was no redemption to be found here.

He opened his eyes and blinked and then the screaming started to come out of him like aural vomit, for at the top edge of the little ridge on which the cottage stood, something black and alien thrust out of the grass.

The stone was only five feet tall but looked taller because of the prominence of its position.

Its base was fat and solidly planted in the earth. It maintained its girth until, three feet above the ground, it tapered into a neck, presenting the illusion of a large black beer-bottle.

CHAPTER VIII

PREVIOUSLY, the cardboard box had contained a new kind of foot-massaging sandal from Germany which Max was trying out on the advice of his reflexologist. As a coffin it was not entirely satisfactory.

She'd found the box in Max's bedroom, which was built into the eaves over the far end of the long room where his desk stood. The four-poster bed, facing the mound, had deep-grey drapes. Max had not spent a single night here yet, but it seemed to Rachel that the atmosphere in the room was already foetid with tension and a lingering sense of suffocated longing. Rachel thought of the nights of the Great Beast and the Scarlet Woman and was sickened and ashamed. She'd snatched the shoe-box and fled.

The box was necessary. There was no way she could carry Tiddles's chest up to the attic on her own. As she knelt in the yard by the rubbish pile, she was worried the mummified cat would come apart or disintegrate while being transferred from the chest. He felt as light as wads of dust under an old sofa.

'Poor little devil,' Rachel said. 'You certainly haven't much energy left to put into Max's project.'

Returning Tiddles to his sentry post in the Court would, she decided, be her last meaningful task in Crybbe.

And she didn't want witnesses.

For over an hour Tiddles lay in his box on the kitchen table in the stables while Rachel waited for the workmen to finish clearing the Court. It was gone 7 p.m.; still she could hear them inside, while a van waited in the courtyard.

At nearly 8 p.m., she threw on her Barbour, picked up the shoe-box, marched purposefully across to the Court's main entrance and hauled open the dusty oak door.

There was a clang from above. A thump. The sound of a large piece of furniture being hurled to the floor.

What were they *doing* up there? And who exactly were they?

Not – judging by the quality of the stuff they'd tossed out – a knowledgeable antique dealer among them. Rachel decided it was time to throw *them* out.

Or time, at least, to establish the identity of the smart-arse who was deciding so arbitrarily which items of furniture to discard.

With the shoe-box under her arm, she went in.

'Hello . . . Excuse me!'

Her voice seemed to go nowhere, as if she was shouting into a wind-tunnel.

The Court was so full of noise. Ceiling-shaking bangs and crashes, as if the entire building was being torn apart. Yet no one had come out of here in at least a couple of hours and the rubbish pile was no higher than it had been when she'd found the cat's wooden chest.

'HELLO!'

She looked around. Half-light floated feebly through the high-level slits and barely reached the stone floor.

Rachel followed the sounds and stormed up the spiral stone staircase.

'Excuse me.' Calling out as she neared the first floor. 'I need to lock this place up for the night, so if you could give me some idea how long you're going to be . . .'

She stepped out into the main chamber, where families had lived and where the Hanging Sheriff, Sir Michael Wort, had held out against the rebel hordes.

'Oh,' Rachel said.

She was alone.

The weak evening light washed through two mullioned windows, but the shadows were taking over now.

Well, she certainly wasn't going to play hide-and-seek with a bunch of silly buggers getting paid well over the odds to clean the place out before morning. She had half a mind to lock them in. Except the keys were in her bag, in the stables.

There was a double crash from above and the sound of glass shattering.

'What the hell . . . ?'

Rachel bounded angrily up the next spiral. Didn't they

303

know how easily they could kill themselves up there, or bring half the ceiling down? Had nobody warned them about the state of the floor?

The heavy door to the attics was ajar. They'd been given keys, then. That bastard Max must have had another set made without even telling her. She thrust through the arched doorway, past the alcove concealing the entrance to the prospect chamber. Up towards the attics.

It was only when she was halfway up the steps that it occurred to her that among the bangs and the crashes there'd been no laughter, none of the usual banter of men working together, no shouted directions, no oaths, no . . .

No voices at all.

And now she was standing here, on the last stairway, far above her blades of light through broken slates, and it was absolutely silent.

'What,' Rachel demanded, 'is going on?'

What was more disquieting than this sudden inexplicable cessation of bangs and crashes was the hairline crack she detected in her own voice. She cleared her throat and gave it more vehemence.

'Come on, I haven't got all night. Where are you?'

Rachel did not remember ever being superstitious. She did not believe in good luck, bad luck, heaven, hell, psychic forces or the secret power of ley-lines. She found the whole New Age concept not only essentially unsound but, for the most part, very tedious indeed.

Yet – and for the first time – she found the place not just gloomy in a sad, uncared-for kind of way, but in the sense of being oppressive. And yes, OK, eerie. She admitted to herself that she didn't want to go so far into the attic that she might see the rope hanging from the ceiling, even though she knew it could not be a very old rope.

But this was a side issue. Something to be acknowledged and perhaps examined later with a raising of eyebrows and a glass of whisky beside the Jotul stove in J. M. Powys's riverside retreat.

For here and for now, there was only one serious, legitimate fear: a fear of the kind of men who, on hearing a woman calling out to them and coming up the stairs, would stop what they were doing, slide into the shadows and keep very, very quiet.

Until this woman appeared at the top of the steps, with nothing to defend her except a dead cat in a shoe-box.

So no way was she going all the way to the top.

Rachel steadied her breathing, set her lips in a firm line, tossed back her hair and began to descend the spiral stairway. If the men in the attic were unaware of the instability of the floor and the danger to themselves, that was their business. They were presumably well-insured.

If they fell, they fell. She hadn't been hired as caretaker of Britain's least-stately home, and she wasn't prepared to tolerate being pissed around any longer. Tomorrow – perhaps even tonight – she would phone Max in London and inform him that she had quit. As of now.

As she descended the twisted stairway it began to grow darker. When she reached the bottom, she found out why. The door sealing off the prospect chamber and the attics must have swung closed behind her, cutting off the light from the first-floor living-hall.

She pushed it with the flat of her hand.

It didn't move.

She put the shoe-box on the stairs and pushed hard with both hands.

It was an oak door, four inches thick and it did not move.

Well, it might have jammed.

'Look, would somebody mind helping me with this door?'

No response.

Or – oh, God, can I really credit this? – the bastards might have locked her in.

It was important to hold on to her anger.

'When I get out of here,' Rachel said suddenly, icily, without thinking, 'you can consider yourselves officially fired.'

Which, on reflection, was a pretty stupid thing to say. They'd never let her out. She tried again.

'Now look, don't be stupid. It's very dangerous up here. The floor's full of holes, you know that. And I haven't got a torch.'

She threw her weight against the door, half-expecting somebody to have quietly unlocked it so that it opened suddenly and she went tumbling down the stairs. Such was the mentality of people like this.

But all that happened was she hurt her shoulder.

'Look, would you mind letting me out?'

She stopped suddenly and leaned back against a wall, breathing hard, an awful thought occurring to her.

What if Humble was behind this?

Suppose, as she would normally have expected, the workmen had actually cleared off hours ago. Who, after all, really worked until 8 p.m. on a Sunday evening? Certainly not the kind of unskilled vandals who'd been let loose in here.

What, then, if it had been Humble who had come up here and made a lot of noise to lure her inside? He'd never liked her, and he knew she didn't like him. He might think she was putting the knife in for him with Max. Maybe Max had found out what Humble had done to J.M. that night. Maybe Humble's job was on the line, and he thought she was responsible.

But if Humble was behind this he would have needed an accomplice. One of them up here to make all the racket, one to lock the door after she'd gone through.

Which still meant that someone was up here with her now, on this side of the locked door. Keeping very, very quiet.

Rachel spun round.

It was so dark with the door closed that she could hardly see as far as the twist in the staircase which took it to the attic. Anything could be around that bend, not six feet away.

'Humble!'

Not much authority left in her voice, nor much anger. She was a woman alone in the darkness of a decaying old house, with a man who intended her harm.

'Humble, listen . . . whichever side of the door you are . . . I don't know why you're doing this. I wish you'd tell me, so we can have it out. But if it's anything to do with what happened the other night with J. M. Powys, I want you to know that I haven't said anything to Max and I don't intend to. A mistake is a mistake. Humble, can you hear me?'

The door didn't have a handle, only a lock. She bent down

and tried to look into the keyhole, to see if there was a key in the other side.

She couldn't tell one way or the other; it was too dark. Her own keys were in her bag, on the kitchen table.

'Humble, look, if you've heard what I said, just unlock the door and I'll give you time to get out of the building. I don't want any unpleasantness because . . .'

Oh, what the hell did it matter now?

'. . . because I'm handing in my notice tomorrow. I've got another job. In London. You won't have to deal with me again. Did you hear that? Do you understand what I'm saying? Humble!'

Rachel beat her fists on the oak door until she felt the skin break.

She had grown cold. She wrapped her Barbour around her and sat down on a stone stair next to the cardboard coffin and listened hard.

Nothing. She couldn't even hear the birds singing outside, where there was light.

But from the attic, clearly not far beyond the top of the spiral stairway, came a single, sharp, triumphant bump.

CHAPTER IX

HE remembered . . . TWELVE . . . spiralling down out of the sky, seeing the stone thickening and quivering and throbbing, the haze around it like a dense, toxic cloud. At which point Memory went into negative, the fields turned purple, the river black. Everything went black.

He didn't remember the scramble of feet, all four of them rushing the new author, J. M. Powys, picking him up, carrying him to the so-called fairy mound and dumping him face-down on its grassy flank with shrieks of laughter.

He was only able to construct this scene from what Ben Corby had told him years later.

From Ben's story, he'd tried to form an image of Rose, but

he couldn't be sure whether she was laughing too or whether she'd stopped short, her face clouding, feeling premonition like a small tap on the shoulder from a cold, stiff hand.

Every time he pushed himself into replaying the scene in his head, he forced Rose to be laughing when they dumped him on the mound. He always put the laugh on freeze-frame and then pulled the plug. So that he could climb out of it without breaking down.

Powys stood in the neutrality of a sunless summer evening and put both hands on the Bottle Stone – at its shoulders, where it began to taper into the neck – and pushed hard.

It was solid. A proper job, as Henry Kettle would have said. Probably several feet of the thing underground, the earth compressed around it, a few rocks in there maybe. Turfs of long grass embedded at the base. It might have been here for four thousand years. You could dig for three hours and it would still be erect.

It needed a JCB to get it out.

But first he had to force himself to touch it, to walk all round it (only not widdershins, *never* widdershins). This stone, a cunningly hewn replica of something which had speared his dreams for twelve years.

He also reserves the right, Rachel had said, *to install standing stones or other ritual artefacts on your lawn.*

All down to Andy Boulton-Trow. He could imagine Andy's unholy delight at finding, among Goff's collection of newly quarried megaliths, one roughly (not roughly, *exactly*) the size and shape of the Bottle Stone.

Or maybe, knowing that Powys was coming to Crybbe, he'd actually had one cut to shape and then planted it in a spot that would emphasize the correlation of the stone and the river, recreating the fateful scene of twelve years ago.

Rough therapy? Or another of Andy's little experiments?

Fifty yards away, the brown river churned like a turbulence of worms towards the bridge.

The Canon was angry.

'And you didn't tell me. You didn't even *tell* me.'

They'd taken one of the big cushions from the sofa in what was now their living-room, at the rear of the house, and put it on the rug in front of the fire, and then put the three-legged dog on the cushion.

Arnold didn't object to this at all, but something in Alex had clearly snapped.

'It's got to stop, Fay. It isn't helping. In fact, it's making things a good deal worse.'

'I'm sorry. I didn't want to get you all worked up.'

'Well I *am* worked up. Even though it was young Preece and he's dead. Divine retribution, if you ask me.'

'That's not a very Christian thing to say, Dad.'

'Listen, my child.' Alex, kneeling on the rug, waved a menacing forefinger. 'Don't you ever presume to tell *me* what's Christian.'

He went down on his hands, face to face with Arnold. 'Poor little perisher. Shouldn't be allowed out with you, Fay, the way you get up people's noses.'

'Oh, I get up people's noses, do I?'

'If you got up noses for a living, you couldn't do a better job. Coming here with your superior Radio Four attitude – "Oh dear, have to work for the little local radio station, never mind, at least there's no need to take it seriously . . ."'

'Now just a minute, Dad . . .'

' " . . . Oh, God, how am I expected to do any decent interviews with people who're too thick to string three coherent sentences together?" '

The Canon clambered awkwardly to his feet and then dumped himself into an armchair he'd battered into shape over several months. He swung round, as if the chair was a gun-turret, training on her a hard, blue glare. A once-familiar glare under which she used to crumble.

'You,' he said, 'were never going to adapt to their way of life, because it was the *wrong* way to do things, because they keep their heads down and don't parade in front of the council offices with placards if they don't get their bins emptied.'

'Dad, I'm supposed to be a reporter . . .'

'And when this fat fellow – what's his name? . . . Goff –

when this meddling lunatic arrives with his monumentally crazy scheme to turn the place on its head . . . Well, guess who can't get along with him *either*. Why, it's Miss Sophisticated Fay Peters, late of Radio Four! And she won't get back to London where she belongs . . .'

'Dad, you know bloody well . . .'

'. . . because she has this astonishing notion that her dilapidated old dad won't be able to manage without her! Jesus *Christ!*'

Alex slumped into silence.

Fay couldn't speak either. If this was Jean Wendle's doing, it was remarkable. Lucid, cogent, powerful, clear-eyed. He might have been ten years younger and in total control of himself.

She was shaken. He was right, of course, even if there was a lot he didn't know.

Or maybe there were things he did know.

When she did finally manage to utter something, it wasn't what she'd had it in mind to come out with at all.

'Dad,' she heard this pathetic little-girl voice saying, close to tears. 'Dad, why is Grace haunting us?'

Warren never even saw his grandad until the old bugger was on him.

He was out by the Tump, thinking how much bigger it looked now from the side where the wall had been ripped out. Old thing could breathe now.

Big, fat mound. Like a giant tit.

Gomer'd carted his bulldozer away, moaning it'd cost over two thousand quid to repair it; Warren thought that was a load of old crap, Gomer trying it on. Who gave a shit, anyway? Standing here, Warren felt again the raw, wild power he'd first experienced the night he buried the old box. He would've been in town, up the alley, shagging the arse off Tessa, except she'd wanted to go to this poncy art exhibition, could you believe that?

He'd left the old man at home, drinking. Never used to

310

drink at home. Gone to pieces since Jonathon drowned, the elder son, the heir.

Warren was the heir now. They'd have to give the bloody old farm to him. You had to laugh, sometimes.

Jonathon was being planted on Wednesday. An inquest would be opened tomorrow. Warren had wanted to go along with the old man, who had to give evidence that the stiff really was Jonathon Preece. But they said after he'd done that, it'd be adjourned for a few weeks, so they'd have a long wait before they heard all the interesting stuff from the pathologist who'd cut Jonathon up on the slab.

After the inquest had been opened, the body'd be released for burial, but the old man said they wouldn't be having it back at the house. Another disappointment for Warren, who'd planned to come down in the night and look under the shroud at all the stitches where the pathologist had put Jonathon's guts back.

From behind, the hand came down on Warren's shoulder like a bird's claw.

'What you doin' yere, boy?'

Warren would've turned round and nutted him, if he hadn't recognized the voice.

'Ow're you, Grandad?'

'I said, what you doin' yere?'

'I come for a walk, like. Free country, innit?'

'Come with me, boy, I want a word with you.'

'Sorry, Grandad, got no time, see. Got to meet somebody down the town.'

The old git looked real weird tonight. Skeletal. Skin hanging loose over his bones. Powerful grip he had, though, and he used it now on Warren's arm, above the elbow, digging into the muscle.

'Ow! Bloody gedoff, you old . . . Where we goin'?'

Jimmy Preece pulled him all the way to the edge of the field, well away from the Tump and the hole where the wall had been – pointing at this gap now, saying in a hard, rough voice,

'You know anythin' about that, boy?'

'What you on about?'

'You know what I'm on about.' The old bugger's eyes were twin glow-worms, burrowed deep in his frazzled face. 'The feller as nicked Gomer's bulldozer and rammed it through that wall. You know him, boy?'

'I never . . . I swear to God!'

Next thing Warren knew, he was on his back in the grass, half-stunned. The old git'd knocked him clean off his feet with one massive swipe across the face.

'Never use the name of God in sight of that thing again, you understand me, boy?'

Warren lay there, felt like his face was afire and his brains were loose. 'You mad ole . . . you got no right . . .'

His grandad put out a hand and helped him to his feet.

'Sorry, boy. Nerves is all shot, see, what with Jonathon and now this.'

Warren backed off. Stood with a hand over his blazing cheek.

'Warren, you and me got to talk.'

'That's what you calls it, is it?'

His grandad took his cap off, scratched his head, replaced the cap.

'Jonathon dyin', see, that changes things. With Jonathon around, didn't matter if you went through your life without knowin' nothin'. Your dad, 'e's the first Preece 'ad less than three children. Weren't 'is fault your mam left 'im, but that's besides the point. I only 'ad two sisters, but if anythin'd 'appened to me, they'd have done it, no arguments.'

'What you on about?'

'The bell, Warren.'

'Oh, that ole thing. Stuff that.'

'You what, boy?'

'Stuff it. I done some thinkin' about that. You can all get bloody stuffed, you think I'm ever gonna take over that bell from Dad. Jonathon might've been mug enough, but I couldn't give a fucking shit, you wanna know the truth, Grandad. My future's not round yere, see. I'm a musician.'

'Music?' The old feller spat hard, once. Gobbed right there on the grass. 'Music? Pah!'

Warren backed off, felt his face contorting. His finger was out and pointing at the old bastard's sucked-in face.

'You know *nothin*',' Warren snarled. 'You wanner know about my music, you ask Max Goff. 'E's gonner sign me, see. 'E's gonner sign the band. So you can do what you like. You can fuckin' disinherit me . . . you can keep your run-down farm. And you can take your bell and you can shove it, Grandad. I couldn't care less.'

His grandad went quiet, standing there, face as grey as the stone.

'I shouldn't worry,' Warren sneered. 'One o' them new-comers'll take it on. That Colonel Croston, 'e's keen on bells.'

'No! The Preeces done it through plague and droughts and wartime when ringing bells was an offence. But we done it, boy, 'cause it's got to be done, see. Got to be.'

The old feller near desperation. Touch of the pleading there now. Stuff him.

'I don't wanner talk to you no more, Grandad. You're not all bloody there, you ask me.'

'Warren, there's things . . .'

'Oh yeah, there's things I don't know! Always, ever since I was so 'igh, people been tellin' me there's things I don't know. Maybe I don't wanner know, maybe . . . What's up with you now?'

His grandad was looking past him at something that caused his mouth to open a crack, bit of dribble out the side, false teeth jiggling about. Disgusting.

He turned and began to walk back towards the road, towards the town, Warren slinking half a dozen paces behind. When the gap between them was wide enough, Warren turned and saw what looked like the sunset reflected in one of the top windows of the old house, just below the roof-line.

Except there wasn't any sun, so it couldn't be a sunset.

Warren shrugged.

CHAPTER X

THE smell happened first.

It happened quite suddenly, as if in the cracking of a rotten egg. The smell and with it the light. Elements of the same change.

The smell was filthy. Sulphur, and something cess-pit putrid.

The light came in oily yellows, the yellow of candles made of animal fat and the yellow of pus from a wound gone bad. The light came from no particular direction but glistened on the stone walls like lard.

Rachel shrank from the walls, but she couldn't get away from the stairs. Where she crouched, it was no longer dry and dusty but wet, warm and slick, like phlegm. She touched a stone step just once, and something unpleasant came off on her fingers. She tried to wipe them on the oak door, but that also was coated with a thick, cheesy grease, gritty here and there with what felt like fly corpses.

Rachel pulled the hand away in disgust, wiped it on her Barbour, knowing she could no longer bring herself to beat on this door. Her fists were sore and peeling, anyway, and if there was anyone out there they weren't going to help her. Perhaps they were waiting for the cool, superior, professional woman to break down, to shriek and sob and plead.

'I can't stand this,' she said aloud. 'I shall be sick.'

Which couldn't make the atmosphere any more foetid.

But if I was a woman with any imagination, she thought, I would be very, very frightened.

For the Court, always so drab and dusty and derelict – gloomy, but no more menacing than an empty warehouse – had swollen into a basic sort of life.

Ludicrous. A grotesque self-delusion. But that was what it felt like. Flickerings of things. Presences in the shadows. The smell itself was like the house's own foul breath.

She began to breathe hard herself. Broke out in a coughing fit. Then tried to breathe slowly and selectively, keeping her mouth closed, because the air was so rancid that when she took it in, there gathered at the back of her throat a richly cloying, raw-meat taste like sweating, sweet salami. Rachel – suffocating, closing her mouth, closing her eyes, trying to close down all her senses; trying, above all, not to hear – thought, I need air. I need light. I need to walk up these few steps.

I need the prospect chamber.

Soft, fresh evening air. Gentle evening light.

The prospect chamber. Eight, ten steps away.   -

But I can't move from here. I can't move because of . . .

. . . those taunting sounds from the darkness above.

Sometimes soft, rustling like satin. Sometimes loud as a foundry overhead. And then stopping for a period of tense, ominous quiet – until it begins again, louder and closer. Then distant again. I am here, I am there, I can be anywhere I choose in an instant because I'm not hu . . .

Shut up! Shut up!

It's what he *wants* you to think.

Creaks. Thrustings. What might have been hollow footsteps on wood, flat footsteps on stone. On stone steps.

He's coming down!

Stopping just before the bend, not six feet away from where she crouched, holding her arms around herself, beginning to shiver.

Pull yourself together. Someone is trying to terrify you. It's only another person. You can handle people; you always could. You are cool and controlled; you can be remote, haughty, offhand, intimidating. You are flexible. You can be dominant, or compliant, at will.

All you have to do is stride up there and face whoever it is.

Yes, but *that's* what he wants.

And what if you go up there and there's . . .

Nothing.

Nothing but the dark.

'Help me!' Rachel was screaming out seconds later, her voice, always so calm and deep, now parched and bitter with anger and despair. 'Hum . . . ble! Andy! Anybody! Please!'

Then, in a soft and aching whisper, she said, 'J.M.?'

And her eyes filled uncontrollably with tears. *When I get out of here, I'm going to get us both away. Tonight. That's a promise.*

If I get out of here. If I ever get to breathe the sweet night air.

God help me, Rachel thought, but I'm not going to scream any more. When she'd screamed, the scream had come up from her stomach, like bile.

When she looked down at herself she saw that her Barbour's waxy surface gleamed sickly yellow like the walls. She wanted to take it off, but she didn't like the cold. She'd never liked the cold.

She wanted to remove her shoes, so as to move more quietly up the stairs towards the prospect chamber, but the thought of that ooze between her toes . . .

She closed her eyes. Closed her eyes and opened them, and rose, picking up the cardboard box containing the dead cat, the guardian.

'Come on, Tiddles,' Rachel said, wiping the tears away.

She wished the appalling sounds would begin again, if only to muffle her footsteps.

They did not. Silence woven as thick as a tapestry hung over the stairs, which were visible only because of the phosphorescence which seemed to move with her, not so much lighting the way as holding her close, in a thick and stifling miasma.

When she looked back there was merely an oily blackness behind her, in the place near the door where she had crouched.

Rachel couldn't remember a nightmare this bad. She was sweating in the clammy Barbour which seemed to have become part of this place, as if the yellow light steaming from the walls was re-vaporizing on the wax of the coat in clusters of tiny bubbles.

She came to the bend in the stairs.

All she had to do was follow the spiral.

To her left would be the alcove concealing the door to the prospect chamber. Above her – how far above her she couldn't tell because there was no light and she could not remember – would be the attic.

Better not to think about the attic. Shut it out.

I don't go into the attics. I'm not superstitious, I just don't go into the attics . . .

Two steps.

Two steps to the alcove and the prospect chamber and light and air. She could stand in the opening and shout and scream and *somebody* would have to hear her.

Oh, please. Please don't let the door be locked.

Rachel made it to the second step and was about to fall into the alcove, throw herself at the door to the prospect chamber . . .

This is the only part of the house I like.

. . . when – to a shattering chorus of harsh clangs and grinding, strangled creaks, a malfunctioning clock-mechanism amplified a thousand times – the greasy darkness shredded before her like a rotting curtain, revealing the attic all lit up in bilious yellow, except for the quivering shadow of the rope hanging from the apex of the roof, turning slowly, stretched taut.

By something palely shining, the source of all the light, noosed and squirming.

It was not far off 10 p.m., the night sidling in, when Powys drove the Mini between the gateposts of the Court and became instantly aware of the Tump behind the house.

He could not see the Tump, but he saw for the first time that the trees towering over the Court from behind were the trees growing out of its summit.

Once you knew this you could almost see the shadow of the great mound outlined in the Elizabethan stonework of the Court itself; the Tump and house fused into a single . . .

. . . entity.

Even as he had that thought, something flared in the house,

and then went out, like a light-bulb which explodes the second it's switched on. He saw a momentary afterglow in one of the small windows immediately below the eaves.

Maybe Andy's in there. Maybe I can wait behind the door until he comes out. And then I'll start hitting him.

Powys accelerated, drove around the house to the courtyard, parked in front of the stable-block, next to the Range Rover – felt a pang of gratitude when he spotted that, longing to see Rachel again.

The stable door was unlocked; he went in.

'Rachel?'

The place was dim; although it probably faced west, there was little light left in the sky. From here, at the top of the long room, now sectionalized, you looked down towards the big picture-window and the grey and smoky Tump.

'Rachel, luv, you in there?'

Maybe the light, way up in the house, had been her, with a torch. *I don't like that. It may not frighten her up there, but it scares the crap out of me.*

And why had the torch gone out?

'Rachel!'

He looked around for light switches, found a panel of them behind the door, pressed everything. Concealed lighting came on everywhere without a blink.

On the kitchen table was a scattering of magazines. New Age stuff. And a black leather bag, open. Rachel's bag.

He went outside again, anxiety setting in with the dusk. He looked across at the Court. Soon the sky and the stone would meld and the house would be an amorphous thing balanced on the edge of the night.

Powys moved to the rear entrance, trying not to crunch gravel. He pushed the door, but it didn't give. Locked.

He didn't waste time with it, but followed the walls of the house around to the front and almost cried out when something big and black reared up in his path.

It didn't move. It was a massive rubbish pile, except many of the items on it didn't look like rubbish to Powys, even in this light. Near the top of the heap was an enormous double wardrobe, Victorian Gothic, its top corner projecting sharply out of the pile, as if in protest.

This time Powys tried the front door, and found that it too was locked.

He looked back along the dead straight drive into the wood, listening to the silence. No birds left to sing.

Directly above him, he knew, would be the prospect chamber, set into the highest eaves, the house's only orifice when the doors were locked and barred.

Powys stepped back from the door and shouted as loud as he could up in the direction of the chamber's hidden maw.

'Rachel!'

A moment in a void.

Then he saw

a glowing filament of sporadic pale-yellow zig-zagging the length of the eaves, like very feeble lightning.

He heard

a scream so high and wild it might have been an animal on the brink of violent death in the woods.

And then a chasm opened under all his senses.

You land with a breathtaking thump on the fairy mound, not hearing the laughter, only aware of the pit beneath you, an endless lift shaft. You're falling, down and down and down, faster and faster, a tiny point of white light far below you . . . a point of light, which gets no larger the further you fall because what it is . . . is the light reflecting from a spearhead, dirty and speckled with rust, as you can see quite clearly in the long moments before you feel the tearing agony, watching the spear's shaft disappearing into your stomach in an explosion of blood.

'Noooooooooo!'

He staggered frantically but uselessly about, trying to position himself below her, as she plummeted from the prospect chamber like a shot bird, the Barbour billowing out, waxy wings against the leaden sky.

319

But she crashed down in the only place he could not hope to throw himself in her path, and he actually heard her neck break as it connected with the projecting corner of a Victorian Gothic wardrobe of old, dark wood.

Something came after her – a small, grey-brown wisp of a thing.

PART SIX

. . . In many such cases it has been suspected that there was an unconscious human medium, commonly an emotionally disturbed adolescent, at the root of the manifestations. If these effects can be produced unconsciously, it is reasonable to suppose that people can learn to produce them by will. Indeed, in traditional societies young people who have evident talents for promoting outbreaks of psychical phenomena are marked out as future shamans . . .

JOHN MICHELL,
The New View Over Atlantis

CHAPTER I

MONDAY morning and, over the dregs of an early breakfast, Fay finally found out the truth about her father, Grace and the house. And wound up wishing, in a way, that she'd remained ignorant, for in ignorance there was always hope.

It was not unknown for Alex to be up for an early breakfast – on one best-forgotten occasion five or six weeks ago he'd been clanking around in the kitchen at 5 a.m. and, when his swollen-eyed daughter had appeared in the doorway, had admonished her for going out and not leaving him any supper.

No, it hadn't made any sense, except in terms of the quantity of blood reaching her dad's brain, and Fay was resigned to it. With a cold, damp apprehension, she'd accepted there would come a time when it might be necessary to change the locks on the front door and deprive him of a key so he wouldn't go out wandering the streets in the early hours in search of a chip-shop or a woman or something.

However, there were still times – like last night – when it might almost be in remission.

But last night – *Dad, why is Grace haunting us?* – they'd parted uncomfortably, Alex mumbling, 'Talk about it in the morning.' The prospect of him remembering had seemed so remote that even Fay had expunged it from her memory.

Then this morning, she'd come down just before eight, and there was her dad fishing a slice of bread out of the toaster with a bent fork and making unflattering observations about the quality of Taiwanese workmanship.

'Been remiss,' he'd mumbled. 'Shouldn't have tried to cover up.'

'So you burnt the toast again,' Fay said. 'No big deal, Dad.'

'No – *Grace*, you stupid child. I'm trying to say I should have told you about Grace.'

'Oh.'

323

And out it all came, for the first time, as if the blood supply to his brain had suddenly tripled, making him more cogent, more aware of his own defects than she could ever remember. This Wendle woman . . . was it conceivable she'd pulled off some astonishing medical *coup* here?

'Grace . . .' Alex said. 'This lady with whom I'd had a small dalliance over twenty years earlier, she rather more serious about it than I. I mean, she really wasn't my type at all, not like your mother. Grace was a very proper sort of woman, prissy some might say.'

'I never liked to say it myself, Dad.'

'Such a sheltered life, you see, here in Crybbe. And then the secretarial job with the diocese. I think – God help me – I think she really believed that having an affair with a clergyman was somewhat less sinful than having a less . . . er, less physical relationship with a layman.'

'Nearer my God to thee,' Fay said wryly.

'Quite. She was quite *unbearably* understanding when . . . when your mother found out and threatened to get us all, via the divorce courts, into the *News of the World*. Tricky period. Things were quite hairy for a while. But, there we are, it ended surprisingly amicably. Quite touching, really, at the time.'

Fay said, 'You mean she accepted her martyrdom gracefully, as it were, to save your precious career.'

Alex lowered his eyebrows. 'Quite,' he said gruffly. 'Of course I felt sorry for Grace and we kept in contact – in an entirely platonic way – for many years.'

'Even when Mum was alive?'

'Platonically, Fay, platonically. Came back to Crybbe to live with her sister, as you know, then she died, and Grace was alone, a very aloof, proper little spinster in a tidy little house. Terribly sad. Do you think I might have another . . . ?'

'I'll pour it.'

'Thank you. And then, of course, I had the letter from young Duncan Christie at the cathedral, just happening to mention Grace was in a pretty depressed state. Not too well, sister recently dead. Feeling pretty sorry for herself, and with reason. Never been quite the same since . . . you know. Well . . .'

'You've told me this bit. A chance for you to make amends.'

'Nemesis, you see. I *had* ruined the poor woman's life, after all.'

'That might be questionable.'

Alex shook his head, in a rare hair-shirt mood. 'And, well, I just happen to turn up there one day, just passing through, you know. And I just happened to stay. So, after all these years, Miss Legge finally becomes Mrs Peters – or, as she liked to put it, Mrs *Canon* Peters. And Alex resigns himself to a year or two of ministering to this rather severe elderly lady, incurably ill and incurably set in her ways – odd, really, she seemed much older than me, although she was twenty-odd years younger.'

'Yes, but . . .'

'I know. I'm coming to it. Woodstock. Why didn't I sell this place when Grace died and go back to Woodstock?'

'The very question I've been trying to ask you for months, Dad.'

'Er . . . Yes.' Alex slurped milk into his coffee. Fay looked up as hard rainspots hit the window. The dried-blood bricks of the houses across the street gleamed drably.

'You see, there are things you don't know about Woodstock. Like the fact that it, er . . . well, it wasn't mine to sell, actually.'

Fay closed her eyes.

'Still belonged to Charlie Wharton. I may have conveyed the impression I'd bought it off him. Fact is, I was only sort of keeping it warm for his retirement, and I was surviving rather longer than either of us had envisaged. And they were about to boot him out of the bishop's palace, you see, so he was pretty anxious to have the place back. In fact, I, er, well, I might have been facing a spot of legal action to remove me if I hadn't cleared off when I did. To be honest.'

Might have guessed, Fay thought. Might have bloody guessed.

'So what it comes down to,' she said, smiling icily, 'is that you were rather more anxious to move in with Grace than she was to have you.'

'Well. Until I, er, raised the possibility of marriage.'

Fay nodded, still smiling.

'Problem is, as you know, money and I have never got along terribly well together. Ladies, horses, unwise investments . . .'

Alex stirred his coffee. The rain came down harder. Fay noticed a damp patch near the kitchen ceiling. It was getting bigger.

'Dad,' she said, 'you are a total, unmitigated shit.'

Alex went on stirring his coffee and didn't deny it.

Fay went to wash the breakfast dishes, digesting the information and its significance: that her father was not a wealthy man, that his total assets amounted to little more than a very small terraced cottage in a back street in Crybbe. A cottage which, even if sold to, say, Max Goff, would hardly pay a year's rent on a basement room in Battersea.

She wondered what kind of pension he'd got. And if he had debts she knew nothing about.

So much to think about that it seemed silly even to raise the issue. However . . .

'You've seen her, haven't you? Since she died, you've been seeing her.'

'Oh, Fay.' Alex rubbed his eyes. 'This part's so difficult. The past few months – such a blur. I don't know what I've done, what I've seen. These past couple of days . . . It's as though I'm waking up. Wendy perhaps, I don't know.'

'You know what I'm talking about, though. Let's not piss about here, Dad. Grace's ghost.'

She shivered, just saying the words, Grace's empty fish-smile in her mind.

'I . . . This really is hard. Especially for me, as a priest. All my life . . . so many anomalies. So many things one can't encompass within the scriptural parameters. That business in Y Groes a year or two ago. And now young Murray and his evil children.'

'You haven't told me about *that*.'

'Sworn to silence, child. And, you see, there's always a rational explanation, always a psychological answer. Murray pushing ahead with his career in the blissful certainty that a clergyman can operate more effectively if he *doesn't* believe.'

'Sod Murray, Dad . . . Grace.'

'You don't have to bring me back to the bloody point. I'm not rambling.'

'Sorry.'

'All right. So I'm guilty of whatever crime it might be to smooth things out for two elderly folk in a bit of a mess. The problem is, when Grace popped her clogs rather sooner than expected, my overwhelming reaction, I'm sorry to say, was one of relief. There we are. Truth out. I'd got a roof over my head and she wasn't under it any more. How's that for a Christian attitude?'

'Not so deplorable.'

'It may not seem deplorable to you, wretched child, but I wanted to suffer. I *needed* to suffer. I'd been getting away with things all my life and here I was again landing on my feet.'

Fay thought, Christ, what's he saying? Is he saying that, in his dislocated mental condition, he *created* Grace's ghost, a resentful avenging presence to remind him of his sins?

'And you,' Alex said. 'Why the devil did *you* have to come back and look after me? I didn't want to inflict myself on you. Prissy little Grace didn't want you in her house.'

The crux of it. He might be able to project Grace, like a gruesome magic-lantern slide on his own dusty mental screen.

But you can't make me see her, Dad. You can't do that.

How could she tell him what she'd seen? (Did I really see it? *Did* I see it?) What would *that* do for his remission?

'OK, Dad,' she said. 'Drink your coffee. I understand. Look, I've missed the news now.'

Fay switched on the Panasonic radio on the kitchen window-ledge. She had indeed missed the news and had to listen to a couple of minutes of sport before the headlines were repeated.

'*And to recap on today's main story: in Crybbe, police are investigating the death of a personal assistant to billionaire business-man Max Goff. The dead woman, thirty-five-year-old Rachel Wade, appeared to have fallen from a high window in historic Crybbe Court. This is Offa's Dyke Radio News. Next bulletin: ten o'clock.*'

For long, long seconds, Fay didn't move at all. Stood frozen at the sink, a damp dishcloth hanging from one hand.

The kitchen clock, two minutes fast, said 9.17.

Alex, sliding his chair back, getting to his feet, said, 'How come you didn't pick that one up, Fay?'

'I normally make the police calls before you get up,' Fay said numbly. 'We had breakfast instead. Offa's Dyke have an early duty reporter, in at half past five.'

'Ah.' Alex brought his coffee cup to the sink. 'Expect you'll be off to find out what happened.' He looked up, his beard pure white in the dull morning. 'You all right, Fay? How well did you know this woman?'

'Fine, Dad,' said Fay. 'No, I . . . I didn't know her *very* well. Excuse me.'

Arnold struggled to his feet to follow her out of the room, fell over again. Fay picked him up and carried him into the office, her face buried in his fur.

As she put him down on the fireside chair, she caught a glimpse of her own face in the gilt-framed mirror, a face as pale as dead Grace.

Fay picked up the phone, called the Information Room at Divisional HQ.

'Not much we can tell you, I'm afraid.'

'It was an accident, though?'

'All I can say is, investigations are proceeding.'

'You mean, it might *not* have been an accident?'

'Hang on a minute,' the police voice said, then she heard, 'Yes, sir, it's Fay Morrison from Offa's Dyke. Sure, just a sec. Mrs Morrison, the duty inspector would like a word.'

'Good morning, Mrs Morrison, Inspector Waring here. I wonder if you'd be good enough to pop into the police station at Crybbe, see the Chief Inspector.'

'Why?'

'Just a few things you might be able to clear up for us.'

'Like what?'

'I think I'd rather the chief told you that, if you don't mind.'

'Oh, come on,' said Fay. 'Off the record.'

A moment's hesitation, then, 'All right, off the record, we've a chap helping with inquiries, Joseph Miles Powys. Says he was with you yesterday.'

'What?'

'Would you mind, Mrs Morrison, just popping into the station? They won't keep you long.'

'I'm . . . I'm on my way,' Fay said.

CHAPTER II

IN his room at the Cock, Guy awoke at nine-thirty.

He'd come back here for a good night's sleep, but it hadn't been one, and he awoke realizing why.

He blinked warily at the overcast, off-white morning. At his suitcase on the floor by the dressing-table. At the wardrobe door agape, exposing his leather jacket on a hanger.

And, finally, at the portfolio against the wall next to the door. Especially at that.

He should never have slept with those drawings in the room. In the practical light of morning, Guy knew he should have left the portfolio in his car. Or, better still, dumped them back at The Gallery after his abortive attempt to quiz the girl.

On his way to the bathroom, he picked up the portfolio and left it propped up in the passage, hoping somebody would nick the thing. It was still there when he returned after a pee and a very quick wash – he didn't like spending too long in bathrooms any more, even by daylight.

Back in his room, Guy burrowed in his suitcase for his rechargeable shaver. He shaved, bending down to the dressing-table mirror, wondering about Jocasta, what kind of night she'd had.

Well, yes, he'd felt bad about Jocasta, in a way, especially when she'd clutched at his arm, pleading, 'One more night – just one night. Hereward'll be back tomorrow. Guy, I can't . . . I *can't* spend a night there alone.'

'Look,' he'd argued reasonably. 'Why not lock yourself in your, er, suite? You don't have to go near that bathroom, do you? I promise you, I'll find out about this, I'll tackle the girl again tomorrow.'

'You won't,' Jocasta had wailed. 'Your crew'll be back and you'll spend all day filming and you'll forget all about me. I've been very stupid, I know . . . but please, can't you just . . . ?'

'No!'

Jocasta had sniffed and wandered back into The Gallery, leaving him alone on the street with the stiff-backed portfolio under his arm.

Dammit, he'd done what he could. Opened her poxy exhibition, been charming to the invited guests, none of whom – it seemed to Guy – could get away fast enough.

And he'd tried to get at the girl, the damned girl in black with the cruel, dark eyes.

'There she is!' Jocasta grabbing his arm in front of everybody, hissing at him and writhing like an anaconda.

'Where? Who?'

'The one who brought those drawings in.'

'You invited her?'

'Of course I didn't. She's just turned up. Guy, we've got to make her tell us what it's all about.'

'*We? We* have?'

The girl had spoken to nobody, just wandered around inspecting paintings, wearing a faintly superior, supercilious expression – as well she might, he'd conceded, given the standard of work on show: the artist, Emmanuel somebody or other apparently specializing in brownish *pointilliste* studies of derelict farmyards.

To Guy, the girl looked far too mature and aware to be still at school.

Jocasta pushing the portfolio at him – 'Please . . . talk to her. She'll be impressed by you. She won't dare lie.'

But the girl didn't seem even to have heard of Guy Morrison, which didn't make her any more endearing. Add to this the dark-eyed unfriendly face – and the attitude.

'I was very interested,' Guy began smoothly, 'in the drawings you gave Mrs Newsome. The ones in this folder.'

'I don't know anything about them.'

'That's interesting. She tells me you asked her to try and sell them for you.'

'Don't know what you're on about. She's a nutter, that woman. You know she's on Valium and stuff, don't you?'

'Are you saying you didn't do these drawings? In which case, who did?'

'Why don't you get lost, blondie,' Tessa Byford said loudly, sweet as lemon, 'you're really not my type.'

She turned away from Guy Morrison and melted into the 'crowd' – a dozen or so people looking uncomfortable, feeding each other canapés and surface-chat. Except for one very thin woman with stretched, yellow-white skin, standing alone and smiling vacuously at Guy, with small needle-teeth.

Guy smiled back, but she didn't acknowledge him, and he went outside with the portfolio under his arm, to be followed by the faintly tipsy, hysterical Jocasta.

'No!' he'd said firmly. 'Do you understand? No!'

Which was how he'd come to walk away still holding the portfolio, feeling angry and confused. Needing a good night's sleep so he could think this thing out. The girl had obviously known about the ghost of the old man haunting the Newsomes' house. Had given Jocasta the drawings in a calculated attempt to terrify her.

But why? What had the girl got against Jocasta? Was there something Guy didn't know?

In the privacy of his room he'd thought of examining the drawings in some detail, but he found he didn't want to take them out of their folder. The whole business seemed less frightening now than distasteful.

Not the sort of thing Guy Morrison needed while shooting an important documentary.

He didn't need the dreams either.

Last night Guy had dreamed he was back on the rug in front of the fire, where Jocasta straddled him, swinging her hips tantalizingly above his straining loins.

'Yes, yes . . .' Guy urged in the dream, but she held herself just a fraction of an inch away so he could feel the heat of her but not the touch of her skin.

'Please,' he moaned. 'Please come down.'

Her face was above his; she seemed to be floating, both

hands in the air. He felt her pubic hair brush the tip of his . . .

'Come . . . down . . . on me.'

'No!' Jocasta said calmly.

'Oh please! Please . . . I can't, I can't . . . *I can't hold on!*'

He tried to put his arms around her neck to pull her down on him, but his arms went right through her, as though she had no substance.

He dreamt then – the way you did sometimes – that he woke up, still feeling alarmingly excited. He was in his room at the Cock and he could still feel her presence above him, her bodily musk in his nostrils. He moaned and breathed in deeply.

And almost choked.

She smelt foul.

A decaying, rancid smell that filled up his throat and turned the sweat on his body to frost, and when he opened his eyes he stared into the whitened, skeletal face of the woman from The Gallery with the little needle-teeth.

He really woke up then, in a genuine cold sweat.

No more nights alone in the Cock, Guy Morrison decided. Tonight . . . well, tonight would have to be a very special night for his adoring production assistant, Catrin Jones.

The lesser of several evils.

Chief inspectors were getting younger. This one was a kind of Murray Beech in blue; steely eyed, freshly shaven although he may have been up most of the night.

'Yes,' she said. 'We'd been to pick up my dog from the vet's. I . . . I needed somebody to drive the car so I could keep the dog on my knee.'

'No,' she said. 'No I haven't known him long. Just a couple of days in fact. In this job you get to know people quite well quite quickly.'

Don't ask what was wrong with the dog, she pleaded silently. *It has nothing whatsoever to do with this. Nothing.*

'We got back . . . I suppose it would have been shortly before seven. Yes, he drove back. The last I saw of him, he was walking home . . . to the cottage he was living in. Max

Goff had commissioned him to write a book about Crybbe.'

'Miss Wade?' she said, 'Yes, I . . . got on very well with her. I suppose we had similar backgrounds.'

'Rose?' she said later. 'Rose who . . . ?'

'Rose Hart,' replied Chief Inspector William Hughes, a high flier from Off. 'Have you heard of her?'

'No . . . Oh, wait a minute. Photographs by Rose Hart. On the cover of *The Old Golden Land*, it said "Photographs by Rose Hart". Is that who you mean?'

'You don't know anything about her? You never met?'

'No . . . What's the connection here?'

'Mrs Morrison, I have to be intrusive. What's your relationship with Joseph Miles Powys?'

'What?'

'Were you sleeping with him?'

'What . . . ?'

'I'm sorry, I have to ask this.'

'Of course I wasn't bloody sleeping with him. I'd only known the bloke a couple of days.'

'And how long had he known Miss Wade?'

'Oh.' Fay leaned back in the metal chair in the bare little room. There was a table and two other metal chairs; the Chief Inspector in one, Wynford Wiley in the other. Fat, florid, red-necked Wynford Wiley, with a suggestion of a smile on his tiny lips.

'I see what you mean,' Fay conceded quietly.

'Two days? Three days? Four perhaps?'

'Yes, OK. It was what you might call a whirlwind romance.'

'Quite normal for some people, Mrs Morrison.'

'Yes, but Rachel wasn't . . .'

'No?'

'No. Listen. Perhaps relationships do form quickly when . . . when you aren't happy.'

'Miss Wade wasn't happy?'

'She . . . She wasn't happy working for Max Goff, no. She wasn't happy about what he was doing in Crybbe. She thought he was pouring money down the drain. The thing is . . . it wasn't too easy to quit, she was being paid an awful lot of money as Goff's PA.'

The way you babbled under interrogation, no matter how smooth you thought you were at handling people.

'How unhappy would you say she was?'

'Look,' Fay said, rallying. 'I think it's time you made it clear what kind of investigation this is. What do you suspect? Suicide? Or what?'

'Or what?' repeated the Chief Inspector.

'Or murder, I suppose,' Fay said.

'What do *you* think it was?'

'I don't know the circumstances. Are you trying to say – I mean, is this the bottom line? Powys pushed poor Rachel out of the window because she found out he was having it off with me? I mean, bloody hell, come *on* . . .'

'It wasn't a window, Mrs Morrison. It was something called the prospect chamber. Do you know it?'

'No. That is . . . I've heard of it.'

'Did you go out again last night, after Mr Powys had brought you home?'

'No.'

'Is there anybody who can . . . ?'

'My father.'

'I understand he's not been very well, Mrs Morrison. I believe he gets a bit confused.'

'Oh God, Hughes, do you get a kick out of this?'

'It's my job, Mrs Morrison.'

'Still, what have I got to complain about? It'll sound interesting on the radio tonight, won't it?'.

Wynford Wiley grinned, which wasn't pleasant. 'Which radio you gonner 'ave it on, Mrs Morrison?'

He looked down at his big hands. Hands like inflated rubber gloves, twirling a pen.

'Only I yeard Offa's Dyke Radio wasn't too happy with you lately, see. Just what I yeard, like.'

Hughes said, 'Mrs Morrison, do you know what happened to Rose Hart?'

Fay shook her head slowly.

The Chief Inspector consulted a file on the table in front of him.

'Twelve years ago,' he said, 'Rose Hart and Joe Powys were sharing a flat in Bristol. It was a Victorian building in a not very pleasant area of town, and Mr Powys told the inquest they were hoping to move somewhere else.'

'Inquest?' Fay said faintly.

'At the rear of the house was an overgrown area which couldn't really be called a garden. One afternoon Joe Powys went up to London to see his publisher – this is what he told the inquest. When he got back he couldn't find Rose anywhere, but a window was wide open in the flat – this is the fourth floor.'

'Oh no,' Fay said.

'Joe told the coroner he dashed downstairs and out the back, and there she was. Rose Hart.'

Fay brought a hand to her mouth. There *was* such a thing as coincidence. Wasn't there?

'The verdict was accidental death. Nobody quite believed that, everybody thought she'd killed herself, but coroners tend to be kind. When there's room for doubt, when there isn't a note . . .'

'That's very sad,' Fay said.

'It certainly was, Mrs Morrison. Half-buried in this overgrown patch at the back of this building in Bristol, where they lived, there were these old railings.'

'Jesus,' Fay whispered.

'They had spikes, rusty iron spikes. Three of them went through Miss Hart. One deeply into the abdominal area where she was carrying what was thought to be Mr Powys's baby.'

Fay said nothing.

'Very messy,' Hughes said.

CHAPTER III

PEOPLE were flinging themselves out of windows to the ground, and the grey masonry was cracking up around them.

The single bolt of lightning had caused a great jagged cleft in the tower. Fire and smoke spewed out.

'What's this one mean?' Guy Morrison asked.

Adam Ivory didn't look up. His wife whispered, 'This card is simply called The Tower. Or sometimes The Tower Struck by Lightning. It signifies a cataclysm.'

'Is that good or bad?' Guy was not greatly inspired by the tarot. What he'd really been after was a crystal-ball type of clairvoyant. One could do things with crystal balls televisually. He supposed it might be possible to match up some of these images with local scenes, but it would be a bit contrived.

'What I mean is, are we talking about something cataclysmically wonderful, or what?'

'It can be either way,' Hilary Ivory said. She was older and bigger than her husband; her hair was startlingly white. 'Good or evil. A catharsis or simply a disaster, with everything in ruins. It depends on the spread.'

The cameraman, Larry Ember, looked up from his viewfinder, the Sony still rolling. His expression said, How long you want me to hold this bloody shot?

Guy made small circles with a forefinger to signify Larry should keep it running. Initially this was to have been no more than wallpaper – images of New Age folk doing what they did. But then he'd persuaded Adam Ivory, who called himself a tarotist, to try and read the future of the Crybbe project.

Guy had managed to convince him that this was being shot with Goff's full approval and would in no way threaten the Ivorys' tenure of this comfortable little town-centre apartment. It occurred to him that the opportunity of relocating to form part of a like-minded community in Crybbe had been something of a godsend for Adam and Hilary; the tarot trade couldn't have been very lucrative in Mold.

Ivory had agreed to be recorded on VT while doing his reading but had stipulated there was to be no moving around, no setting up different angles, no zooming in or out, or anything which might affect his concentration.

Larry had done a bit of snorting and face-pulling at this. Cameramen weren't over-concerned about public relations and it was evident to Guy that this cameraman thought this interviewee was a snotty little twerp.

Guy Morrison would not have disagreed completely, but in the absence of a crystal-ball person, this might be the best he'd get in the general area of divination.

The camera had been rolling for nearly seven minutes, and for the last four the shot had been entirely static: Adam Ivory – who wore a suit and looked more like a dapper, trainee accountant than a clairvoyant – intent on the spread of nine cards, the last of which was The Tower.

Little gaily dressed puppet-figures hurling themselves to the ground.

Guy thought of Rachel Wade. An unfortunate incident. It would bring regional news crews into Crybbe, if they weren't here already. Trespassers on his property.

'Adam, are you going to tell us what the cards are indicating?' Guy asked softly.

Silence.

Larry Ember, who'd been a working cameraman when Guy was still at public school, stepped back from his tripod, the camera still running.

He looked straight at his director, the way cameramen did, conveying the message, You're supposed to be in charge, mate, what are you going to do about this fucking prat?

Then, turning away from Guy, Larry lit a cigarette.

Hilary Ivory was on him in seconds, furiously pointing at her husband and shaking her hair into a blizzard. Guy tensed, just praying she didn't snatch the cigarette out of Larry's fingers; he'd once known a film-unit cameraman who'd hit a woman in the face for less than that.

Adam Ivory himself rescued the situation. He moved. Larry bent over his camera again.

Ivory's movement amounted to taking off his glasses, cleaning the lenses on the edge of the black tablecloth and putting the glasses back on again.

He resumed his study of the cards and Larry's shoulders slumped in disgust.

Time, Guy realized, was getting on. Goff was coming back, he'd heard, in the wake of this Rachel Wade business.

His eyes were drawn back to The Tower. It would be inexcusably tasteless to cut from shots of policemen and the upstairs window at the Court to these little puppet-figures tumbling from a greystone tower struck by a bolt of lightning. Pity.

Adam Ivory looked up suddenly, eyes large and watery behind the rimless glasses.

The soundman's boom-mike came up between Ivory's legs, fortunately out of sight.

'Forget it,' Ivory croaked. 'Scrap it.'

'Scrap it?' Guy said. '*Scrap it?*'

He didn't believe this.

'I'm sorry,' Ivory said. 'It isn't working. I don't think it's . . . It's not reliable. The cards obviously don't like this situation. I should never have agreed to do a reading in front of a TV camera. As well as . . .'

He fell silent, staring hard at the cards, as if hoping they'd rearranged themselves.

'As what?' Guy said, trying to control his temper. 'As well as what?'

'Other negative influences.' Ivory glanced nervously at the glowering cameraman and glanced quickly away. 'The balance is so easily affected.'

Guy said carefully, 'Mr Ivory, are you trying to say the cards were . . . the prediction was unfavourable?'

The camera was still running. Guy very deliberately walked around to Ivory's side of the table and peered over his shoulder at the cards. He saw Death. He saw The Devil.

'I am not . . .'

Ivory swept the nine cards together in a heap. Guy noticed his fingertips were white.

338

'. . . trying to say . . .'

He snatched his hands away, as if the cards were tainted.

'. . . anything.'

And pushed both hands underneath his thighs on the chair, looking like a scared but peevish schoolboy.

Larry Ember shot half a minute of this then switched off and slid the camera from its tripod. 'Fucking tosser,' he muttered.

Hilary Ivory went to her husband, looking concerned in a motherly way.

A single tarot card fell over the edge of the table. Guy picked it up. It was The Hanged Man.

He put it carefully on the table, face-up in front of Ivory.

'What's this one mean?'

'It's very complicated,' Hilary said. 'The little man's hanging upside down by his foot, so it's got nothing to do with hanging, as such.'

'Look, would you please leave?' the tarotist almost shrieked, his face sweating like shrink-wrapped cheese under the TV lights. 'I . . . I don't feel well.'

Larry Ember lit another cigarette.

'No,' Mr Preece said, 'I won't.'

He and his wife had not been inhospitable. Catrin Jones, Guy's production assistant, had been given the second-best chair and a cup of milky instant coffee.

'But you see . . .' She didn't know where to begin. The blanket refusal was not at all what she'd expected, even though she conceded it had been a difficult week for Mr Preece, with the drowning of his grandson and everything.

'Biscuit?' offered the Mayor.

'Oh no, thank you.'

Catrin wondered why there was an onion in a saucer on top of the television.

'Because what we were thinking,' she said rapidly, 'is that it would be far better to talk to you in advance of tomorrow night's public meeting rather than afterwards at this stage, because . . .'

'You *are* talkin' to me,' said the Mayor simply.

'On camera, Mr Preece,' Catrin said. 'On camera.'

'I'm not going to change my mind. I'm keeping my powder dry.'

'Oh, but, you see, you won't be giving anything away because it won't be screened for months!' Catrin's voice growing shrill and wildly querulous. 'And it's not a great ordeal any more being on television, we could shoot you outside the house so there wouldn't be any need for lights, and as well as being terrifically gifted, Guy Morrison is well-known for being a very understanding, *caring* sort of producer.'

'That's as maybe,' Mr Preece said. 'All I'm sayin' is I don't 'ave to be on telly if I don't want to be, and I *don't*.'

'But, you will be during tomorrow night's meeting. What's the difference?'

'I doubt that very much.'

'Mr Preece, you are supposed to be chairing the meeting.'

'Aye, but as *you* won't be allowed in with that equipment, it makes no odds, do it?'

Catrin, outraged, sat straight up in her chair. 'But it's a *public* meeting! Anybody can go in. It's all arranged with Max Goff!'

'Max Goff?' Mr Preece's leathery jowls wobbled angrily. 'Max Goff isn't running this town *yet*, young woman. And if I says there's no telly, there's no telly. Police Sergeant Wynford Wiley will be in attendance, and any attempts to smuggle cameras in there will be dealt with very severely.'

'But . . .' Catrin was close to tears. She had never before encountered anyone less than delighted and slightly awed at the possibility of being interviewed by Guy Morrison.

''Ave another cup of coffee,' said the Mayor.

What he kept seeing was not Rachel plunging out of the sky. Not the willowy, silvery body broken on the rubbish pile.

He would not think of that – not here, in this grim Victorian police station. If he thought of that he'd weep; he wasn't going to indulge in that kind of luxury, not here.

No, what he kept seeing was the grey-brown thing, falling like smoke.

He'd seen it again as he waited for the police. It lay where it had landed, three or four yards from the pile, light as the fluff which collected in a vacuum cleaner.

I've seen them before, Powys thought now. In museums, in glass cases, labelled: *remains of a mummified cat found in the rafters, believed to have been a charm against evil.*

The cat had fallen to the ground *after* Rachel.

He hadn't told them that.

'And you heard her scream, did you?'

'She cried out. Before she fell.'

'She wasn't screaming as she fell?'

'I don't think so. I mean, no, she wasn't . . .'

'Didn't that strike you as odd?'

'Nothing struck me at the time, except the sheer bloody horror of it.'

Telling it four times at least. How he'd attacked the rubbish heap, frantically hurling things aside to reach her.

Lifting her head. Staring into her face, eyes open so wide that you could almost believe . . . until you felt the dead weight, saw – last desperate hopes corroding in your hands – the angle of the head to the shoulders.

Staring stricken into her face, and the curfew bell began to toll, a distant death knell.

'. . . can we return to this point about the door, Mr Powys. You say you tried the rear door to the courtyard and found it locked. You couldn't budge it.'

'No. It was locked. I put my full weight against it.'

'Then how do you explain why, when we arrived, this door was not only unlocked but was, in fact, ajar?'

'I can't explain that. Unless there was someone else in there with Rachel.'

'Someone other than you . . .'

'Look, I've told you, I . . .'

They'd gone over his statement several times last night and then said OK, thank you very much, you can go home now, Mr Powys, but we'll undoubtedly want to talk to you again.

But he knew, as he tried to sleep back at the cottage, that they were out there, watching the place, making sure he didn't go anywhere.

And it was no real surprise when the knock came on the door at 8 a.m., and the car was waiting – a car, to take him less than a quarter of a mile across the bridge to the police station.

'*You didn't tell us, Mr Powys, that this wasn't exactly a new experience for you. You didn't tell us about Rose.*'

So who had?

Somebody had.

He sat on the metal chair, alone in the interview room, wishing he still smoked. He could hear them conversing in the passage outside, but not what they were saying.

'*So you went to Leominster with Fay Morrison?*'

'*Yes.*'

'*Attractive woman, Mrs Morrison.*'

'*Yes.*'

'*What was wrong with the dog?*'

'*He had a badly injured leg.*'

This could lead back to Jonathon Preece in no time at all. Holistic police-work. Everything inter-connected.

Joseph Miles Powys, I am arresting you on suspicion of the murders of Jonathon Preece, Rachel Wade and Rose Hart. You don't have to say anything, but anything you do say . . .

Perhaps I *should* confess, he thought, looking up to the single, small, high window and seeing a hesitant sun in the white sky, wobbling nervously like the yolk of a lightly poached egg.

Maybe I did it. Maybe I killed her, as surely as if I'd been standing behind her in the prospect chamber, with both hands outstretched.

He thought, If I start believing that, we're all finished. So he went back to thinking about the cat.

CHAPTER IV

THE sun was out for the first time in ages, but hanging around unsurely like a new kid in the school doorway.

Fay walked aimlessly up the hill from the police station towards the town square and the Cock, pausing by the railings alongside the few steps to its door. Even a weak sun was not kind to this building; its bricks needed pointing, its timbers looked like old railway sleepers.

The Cock didn't even have a sign, as you might have imagined, with a bright painting of a proud rooster crowing joyfully from the hen-house roof. But, knowing Crybbe, would you *really* imagine a sign like that?

And anyway, whoever said the name referred to that kind of cock? A far more appropriate emblem for this town, Fay thought, would be a decidedly limp penis.

Crybbe. *Crybachu* (to wither).

Fay looked down the alley towards the brick building housing the Crybbe Unattended Studio and wondered if she'd ever go in there again. They were obviously handling the Rachel Wade story themselves; nobody had even attempted to contact her.

I need the money, Fay realized suddenly. I need an income. I need a job. Why are they doing this to me?

She thought of Joe Powys – I think *I've* got problems – helping the police with their inquiries. Quite legitimately, by the sound of it.

Rachel Wade . . . the dead woman, Rachel Wade.

He couldn't have . . . surely. She liked Joe. He seemed so normal, for the author of a seminal New Age treatise.

Well, comparatively normal.

Oh God, what was happening?

She didn't notice the door open quietly in a narrow town house to the left of the Cock, didn't hear the footsteps. When she turned her head, the woman was standing next to her, looking across the square to the church.

343

'Good morning, Fay.'

Fay was too startled, momentarily, to reply. She'd never seen this woman before, a woman nearly as small as she was, perhaps a quarter of a century older.

Well, never seen the *face* before.

'Jean Wendle?' Fay said.

'I am.'

Last seen in a hat, sitting very still, impersonating the ghost of Grace Legge.

'May I perhaps offer you a coffee?' Jean Wendle said.

Catrin Jones knew Guy would be furious about the Mayor's ban on cameras at tomorrow's public meeting.

She also knew from experience that when bad news was brought to him Guy had a tendency to take it out on the messenger.

The need to salvage something from the morning had brought her to this subdued, secluded house opposite the church, at the entrance to the shaded lane leading down to Crybbe Court.

'I'd be delighted to help you, any way I can,' said Graham Jarrett, hypnotherapist, small, silvery haired, late-fifties.

'I was thinking perhaps this, what is it, recession . . . ?'

'Regression.'

It was very quiet and peaceful in the house, with many heavy velvet curtains. Catrin could imagine people here falling easily into hypnosis.

'Yes. Regression,' she said. 'This is . . . past lives?'

'Well, we don't like to talk necessarily in terms of past lives,' Graham Jarrett said, matter-of-fact, like a customer-friendly bank manager. 'But sometimes, when taken back under hypnosis to an area of time prior to their birth, people do seem to acquire different personalities and memories of events they couldn't be expected to have detailed knowledge of.'

'Fantastic,' Catrin said.

'I certainly wouldn't be averse to having you film a session, if the client was in agreement.'

'That would be excellent,' Catrin said.

'But I have to warn you that many of them do prefer it to be private.'

'Oh, listen, my producer – Guy Morrison – is a wonderfully reassuring man. They would have nothing to worry about with Guy.'

'Perhaps he would like to be regressed himself?' said Graham Jarrett with a meaningful smile.

'Oh. Well . . .'

'Or you, perhaps?'

'Me?'

'Think about it,' Graham Jarrett said lightly.

Fay sat in the wooden bow-chair. Jean Wendle was on the edge of a huge, floppy sofa with both hands around a mug of coffee. She wore a white cashmere sweater and pink canvas trousers.

'I heard it on the news,' she said. 'About poor Rachel Wade.'

'Yes,' Fay said, wondering if she'd also heard about Powys helping with inquiries.

'It's a crumbling old place, the Court. What was she doing there at that time of night?'

'I don't know. I've only heard the news, too. I'll expect I'll be finding out. All I know is . . .'

Oh, what the hell, the woman was supposed to have been a lawyer, wasn't she? Maybe she could help.

'All I know is, the police aren't convinced it was an accident. Joe Powys apparently saw her fall and called the police. They're kind of holding him on suspicion.'

A sunbeam licked one gilt handle of a big Chinese vase with an umbrella in it then crept across the carpet to the tip of Jean Wendle's moccasins.

'Oh dear,' Jean said.

Fay told her how things had been between Joe and Rachel, in case she wasn't aware of that. She described her own interrogation by the police. What they'd told her about Rose.

'Can they hold him, do you think?'

'It doesn't sound as if they have any evidence to speak of,' Jean said. 'They can't convict on a coincidence. They also have to ask themselves why this man should engineer the death of his lover in the same way that a previous girlfriend died and then immediately report it as an accident – knowing that the police would sooner or later learn about the earlier misfortune. I wonder how they found out about that so quickly. Did Joe tell them himself, I wonder? Do you mind if I smoke?'

Fay shook her head. Jean went across to the Georgian table, put down her coffee mug, lifted the lid on an antique writing-box, found a thin cigar and a cheap, disposable lighter. She picked up a small, silver ashtray and brought everything back to the sofa.

'It could be, of course, that the police are looking at possible psychiatric angles.'

Fay was thrown.

Yes, I'm an accredited crank, Joe had said. Had said several times, variations on the same self-deprecating theme.

'You're saying they think he's possibly a psychopath who's into pushing women out of upstairs windows. And – I don't know – subconsciously he's seeking help and that's why he called the police after he'd done it?'

Jean shrugged. 'Who knows how the police around here think? Perhaps they'll do some checks with Bristol police to find out if he really was in London the afternoon Rose died. If they arrest him he'll need a solicitor. Until they decide what they're going to do, I don't think there's anything *we* can do. Meanwhile . . .'

Jean Wendle turned serious, quizzical eyes on Fay.

'Tell me about yesterday. In the church. Tell me what that was all about.'

Fay sighed. It seemed so long ago. And, in retrospect, so foolish. Also, it said too much about her state of mind that even when Jean had turned in the pew to look at her, she was still seeing somebody else.

'It's very silly,' she said. 'I thought you were Grace Legge – that's my father's late wife.'

Jean Wendle nodded, showed no surprise at all. 'You've been seeing this woman?'

346

'Once. I think. I mean, how can anyone say for sure? They don't really exist do they, only in our minds.'

'That depends.'

'On what we mean by existing, I suppose. Well, all I can say is that, whatever it was, I'm not anxious to see it again.'

Jean smiled. She was, Fay thought, the sort of woman – sharp, poised – you wouldn't mind being like when you were older. That is, you wouldn't mind so much being older if you were this relaxed.

'I don't quite know what came over me. You were just so completely still that the thought occurred to me that there was nobody at all sitting next to Dad, but *I* was seeing Grace.'

Jean said, 'The time you really did see her – when you saw whatever it was you saw – where was this?'

'In the house. In the office, which used to be her "best" room. The room that, when she was alive, I suppose she thought of as her sacred place – so neat and perfect because nobody really used it. Maybe she thought this room had been violated by my desk and the equipment and everything. Or maybe I *thought* she'd be angry and so I conjured up this fantasy . . .'

'You don't think that for one minute,' Jean said.

'No,' Fay admitted. 'All right, I don't think that.'

'Then please, only tell me what you *do* think. And stop looking at me as though you're wondering what I might change you into.'

'Miss Wendle . . .'

'Jean.'

'Jean. Look, I'm sorry, but it gets you like this after a while, Crybbe. I've been here nearly a year, and it gets to you.'

'You mean you can't relate to the people here. You don't understand what makes them tick.'

'Do you?'

'Well, I think . . .' Jean lit the cigar at last. 'People talk a lot about energy. Energy lines, ley-lines. Trying to explain it scientifically. Makes them seem less like cranks if they're talking about earth energies and life forces.'

She inhaled deeply, blew out a lot of blue smoke.

'The pronouncements of New Age folk are wrapped up in so much glossy jargon. Concealing massive ignorance.'

'What are you doing in Crybbe, then, if you think it's all bullshit?'

'Oh, it isn't *all* bullshit, not by any means. And at least they're searching. Trying to reach out, as it were. Which itself generates energy. In fascinating contrast to the natives, who appear to be consciously trying not to expend any at all. And perhaps to the electricity company, who can't seem to summon sufficient to see us through an entire day.'

'I'm sorry. What are you saying?'

'I'm saying that perhaps the people of this town are as they are because they've known for generations what a psychically unstable area this is, and most people – sadly, in my view – are afraid to confront the supernatural and all it implies. For instance, I should be very surprised if you were the only person who was seeing the shades of the dead in this town.'

Fay shivered slightly at that. *The shades of the dead* . . . It sounded almost beautiful. But Grace wasn't.

'I try to avoid letting anything get touched by the dead hand of science or indeed pseudo-science,' Jean said. 'But let's suppose that in certain places certain forms of energy collect. Our friend Joe Powys says in his book that the border country is . . . Have you read it?'

'The psychic departure lounge.'

'Yes, and poor Henry Kettle, the dowser, couldn't abide such terminology because he was really awfully superstitious and terrified of admitting it.'

'Nothing psychic.'

Jean waved her cigar. 'A terrible old humbug, may he rest in light. Henry, of course, was just about as psychic as anyone can get. Anyway, your ghost. Grace. Did she speak?'

'Not a word.'

'And she didn't move?'

'No.'

'Harmless, then.'

'I'm so glad,' Fay said sceptically.

'Can I explain?'

'Please do.'

'OK, if we stick to our scientific terminology, then pockets of energy can accumulate in certain volatile areas, and in such areas, the spirits of the dead, usually in a most rudimentary form, may appear. Like a flash of static electricity. And they go out just as quickly. Or you'll get sounds. Or smells.'

'The scent of fresh-cut lilies or something.'

'Or fresh shit,' Jean said harshly. 'It depends.'

'I'm sorry. I wasn't flippant when it was happening to me.'

'I doubt you were,' Jean said. 'All right, sights or sounds or smells – or tastes even. Rarely anything simultaneous, because there's rarely sufficient energy to support it. If there was a massive accumulation of it then one might have a complete sensory experience.'

'I only saw her. And it was cold. It went cold.'

'Energy loss,' Jean said. 'Quite normal. So, if I may give you some advice, if you should see your Grace again, blink a couple of times . . . and she'll be gone. She can't talk to you, she can't see you; there's no brain activity there. Entirely harmless.'

'Not pleasant, though,' Fay said, reluctant to admit feeling better about the idea of Grace as a mindless hologram.

'No,' Jean said, 'the image of a dead person is rarely pleasant, but it's not as much of a problem as these damned power cuts.'

'You really think that's connected?'

'Oh, it has to be. Psychic activity causes all kinds of electrical anomalies. Voltage overloads, or whatever they call them. Sometimes people will find they have terrific electricity bills they can't explain, and the electricity people will come along and check the meters and the feeds, and they'll say, "We're awfully sorry, madam, but you must have consumed it, our equipment cannot lie." The truth is the householders may not have used it, but *something* has.'

Fay remembered poor Hereward Newsome and his astronomical bills.

'But your wee ghost,' Jean said, 'is the least of your problems here. Sporadic psychic activity on that level isn't enough to cause power fluctuations on the Crybbe scale. Whatever's happening, there's much more that needs to be explained before you can get close to it.'

'You've been very reassuring,' Fay said. 'Thank you. I'm

also very impressed with what you're doing for Dad. He's almost his old self again. I mean, do you really think there's any hope of . . . ?'

'I never discuss my patients,' Jean said severely.

By the time Fay left Jean Wendle's house, the sun had vanished behind an enormous black raincloud and she hurried down the street to make it home before the rain began again.

She saw Guy across the square, followed by his cameraman with the camera clamped to his shoulder and a tripod under his arm. Guy made as if to cross the road towards her, but Fay raised a hand in passing greeting and hurried on. She couldn't face Guy this morning.

'Fay,' someone said quietly.

She turned her head and then stopped.

Blink a couple of times, Jean Wendle had advised, but this apparition didn't disappear.

'Joe,' she said.

He looked terrible, bags under hopeless eyes, hair like cigarette ash.

'They had to let me go,' he said. 'Insufficient evidence.'

Fay said nothing.

'Can we talk?'

'Maybe it's not a good time,' Fay heard herself say. 'I don't think you killed Rachel, let's just leave it at that for now.'

Which was the last thing she wanted to do. She bit her upper lip.

'They had you in, presumably,' he said.

'Yes.'

'And they told you about Rose.'

'Yes.'

'And that's why you don't want to talk about it.'

'Look,' Fay said. 'I've lost the only real friend I had in this town, I *desperately* want to talk about it, I just . . .'

'It wasn't an accident,' Powys said.

'What?'

'It wasn't an accident. After she fell, something else came out.'

'What are you saying?'

'A cat.'

Fay looked at him. There was something seriously abnormal about all this. About Joe Powys, too.

'I don't mean a live cat. This one's been dead for centuries.'

'Tiddles,' Fay said faintly, getting a picture of black eye-sockets and long sabre-teeth.

And her. *She* was becoming abnormal. She had to get out of here.

'Cats that've been dead for hundreds of years don't hurl themselves three storeys to the ground while somebody puts on a light-show under the eaves.'

'Hallucination,' Fay said.

'No.'

Fay thought about Jean Wendle and the energy anomalies, about Grace, about the curfew and the howling and the town with no dogs.

Joe said, 'Can you spare the rest of the day?'

No! she wanted to shriek, and then to push past him and run away down the street and keep running.

'I might have a job. I have to go home and talk to my father and check the answering machine.'

'If it turns out you're free, can I pick you up? Say, twenty minutes?'

'I . . .'

Would that be entirely safe? she wanted to ask. Am I going to be all right as long as I stay away from open windows?

'All right,' she said.

CHAPTER V

'THEY said, Don't leave town. Or words to that effect.'
Joe Powys floored the accelerator.
'Fuck them,' he said.

Fay tried to smile.

They'd left Crybbe on a road she wasn't too familiar with, the road into Wales by way of Radnor Forest, which didn't seem to be a forest at all but a range of hills.

He hadn't said where they were going.

She didn't care. She felt apart from it all, in a listless kind of dream state. She was watching a movie about a woman who was out for a drive with a murderer. But in films like this, the woman had no reason to suspect the man was a murderer, only the viewers knew that; they'd seen him kill, she hadn't.

The woman in this particular movie had a black and white three-legged dog on her knee. Must be one of those experimental, surrealist epics.

The car moved out of an avenue of trees into a spread of open, sheep-strewn hills with steep, wooded sides and hardly any houses.

Before they left she'd written a note for her dad, fed the cats and listened to the answering machine, which said, '*Hi, Fay, this is James Barlow from Offa's Dyke. Just to say we understand Max Goff's coming back to Crybbe and he'll probably be holding a press conference around four this afternoon, following this Rachel Wade business. But don't worry about it, Gavin says to tell you he'll be going over there himself . . .*'

So I'm free, Fay thought bitterly. Free as a bloody bird.

As if he were watching the same movie, Powys said, 'If I killed her, why would I report it?'

'Why did you?'

'Had to get an ambulance. There might have been a chance.'

'Did she . . . ? Oh God, did she die instantly?'

'I heard it, you know, snap. Her neck.'

She thought his voice was going to snap too and tried not to react. 'What were you doing there, anyway? How come you happened to be under the window when she fell?'

'Still don't know how much of that was coincidence. Don't know if she saw me. If she was trying to attract my attention and fell against the bar. But she didn't call out to me. She just screamed. As if she was screaming at something inside the house.'

'And couldn't she get out? The house was locked up with her in it?'

'It was locked when I tried the doors. It wasn't when the police got there. So they say. Work that one out.'

'So she was killed by somebody in the house . . . *If* she was killed. Humble?'

'Well, they didn't like each other. But that doesn't explain the light. Doesn't really explain the cat either.'

'Maybe Rachel was holding the cat, for some reason, and it took longer to reach the ground because there was no weight left in it. Joe, I have to ask you this . . . What exactly were you doing at the Court?'

'Told the cops I was looking for Rachel. I think I was really looking for Andy. Oh God . . .' He sighed. 'What happened was he'd planted a stone outside the cottage, an exact replica of a thing that's been hanging over me for years.'

'A stone?'

'The Bottle Stone. Do you want to know this? It'll be the first time I've talked about it to anybody. Apart from the people there.'

'Do you want to tell me?'

'I don't know . . . OK. Yeah.'

He fell silent.

'What do you want?' Fay said. 'A drum roll?'

'Sorry. OK. It goes back over twelve years. To the Moot.'

'The Moot,' Fay said solemnly.

'It's organized every year by *The Ley-Hunter* magazine. It's a gathering of earth-mysteries freaks from all over the place. We meet every year in a different town to discuss the latest theories and walk the local leys.'

'I bet you all have dowsing rods and woolly hats.'

'You've been to one?'

Fay laughed. It sounded very strange, laughter, today.

'This particular year,' Powys said, 'it was in Hereford. Birthplace of Alfred Watkins. Everybody was amazed there wasn't a statue – nothing at all in the town to commemorate him, which is how I came to establish Trackways a couple of years later. But, anyway, all the big names in earth mysteries were there. And we were all there too. Rose and me. Andy. Ben Corby, who was at college with us, bit of a wheeler-dealer, the guy who actually managed to sell *Golden Land* to a publisher. And Henry Kettle, of course. We knew there was a deal coming through, and on the Monday morning after the Moot, before we all set off for home, Ben rang the publishers and learned they'd flogged the paperback rights for ten thousand quid.'

Powys smiled. 'Bloody fortune. Well, it was a nice day, so we decided, Rose and I, to invite the others – the people who'd been in on the book from the beginning – to come out for a celebratory picnic. We wondered where we could go within reach of Hereford. Then Andy said, "Listen," he said, "I know this place . . ." '

She looked out through the side window of the Mini. She didn't recognize the country. One hill made a kind of plateau. She counted along the top – like tiny ornaments on a green baize mantelpiece – three mounds, little tumps. A thin river was woven into the wide valley bottom.

Powys was dizzily swivelling his head. 'Somewhere here . . .'

The third mound had a cleft in it, like an upturned vulva.

'Yes,' he said. 'Yes.' He hit the brakes, pulled into the side of the road. 'It was down there.'

'The Bottle Stone?'

Powys nodded.

'Let me get this right,' Fay said. 'This . . . legend, whatever it was . . .'

'It's a common enough ritual, I've found out since. It can be a stone or a statue or even a tree – yew trees are favourites for it. You walk around it, usually anticlockwise, a specific number of times – thirteen isn't uncommon. And then you have an experience, a vision or whatever. There's a church in south Herefordshire where, if you do it, you're supposed to see the Devil.'

'But you didn't see anything like that?'

'No, just this sensation of plunging into a pit and becoming . . . impaled. And there was nothing ethereal about it, I can feel it now, ripping through the tissue, blood spurting out . . .'

'Yes, thank you, I get the picture.'

'But it happened to *me*. That was the point. No indication of any danger to Rose.'

'Was she unhappy?'

'Not at all. That day at the Bottle Stone, she was *very* happy. That's what's so agonizing. I've had twelve years to get over it . . . I can't. If I could make sense of it . . . but I can't.'

'And it was . . . how long, before . . . she fell?'

'Not quite two weeks. OK, thirteen days.'

'Hmm.' Fay's fingers were entwined in the fur around Arnold's ears. 'Was . . . was she unhappy at all afterwards? I mean, pregnant women . . .'

'It was at a very early stage. I don't even know if it had been officially confirmed.'

'She hadn't told you?'

Powys shook his head. 'The post mortem report – that was the first I knew about it.'

'So this experience you had on the so-called fairy mound . . . What are your feelings about that? Do you feel you were being given a warning, that there was something you should have realized?'

Powys said, 'You're interviewing me, aren't you? I can spot the inflection.'

'Oh God, I'm sorry, Joe. Force of habit. How about if I try and make the questions less articulate?'

'No, carry on. At least it's more civilized than the cops. No, it didn't make any sense. Any more than the average nightmare.'

'And you told Rose?'

'No.'

'Why not?'

'Because it had been such a nice day up to then. Because the future looked so bright. Because I didn't want to cast a pall. I just said when they dumped me on the mound I must have fainted. I said I was very dizzy. I did tell Andy about it after . . . after Rose died.'

'And what did he say?'

'He said I should have told Rose.'

'That was tactful of him.'

'And what do *you* think, Fay? What do you think I should have done?'

'What about Henry Kettle. What did *he* say?'

'He wanted nothing to do with it. He used to say this kind of thing was like putting your fingers in a plug socket.'

Fay glanced at him quickly, uneasily, over Arnold's ears. Was it possible that Joe Powys was indeed insane? Or, worse perhaps, was it possible he was *sane*?

He was hunched over the steering wheel. 'Oh, Fay, how could I have killed Rachel?'

He looked at her. 'I'm not saying I was in love with her. We'd only known each other a couple of days, but . . .'

She looked up into the hills, all the little tumps laid out neatly.

He said, 'Think Arnold can manage a walk?'

Arnold struggled to his feet on Fay's knee.

'He obviously thinks so,' Fay said. 'Come on, then. Let's go and find the Bottle Stone.'

Max began to breathe hard.

It was astonishing.

'Take me over again, Mel,' Max said. 'Then maybe we'll get Guy Morrison and his crew to come up with you. We have to have pictures of this. For the record.'

He leaned forward, thoughts of Rachel's death blown away by all this magic.

Melvyn, his helicopter pilot, took them over the town again

356

making a wide sweep of the valley. Max counted six standing stones – first time round he'd missed the one by J. M. Powys's cottage near the river.

He couldn't believe it. A week ago Crybbe was scattered . . . random, like somebody'd crapped it out and walked away. Now it had form and subtle harmonies, like a crystal. It had been earthed.

He could spot, clear as if it had been blasted in with a giant aerosol paint-spray, the main line coming off the Tump. It cut through the Court, cleaved a path through the woods until it came to a small clearing, and in the centre of this clearing, surrounded by tree stumps and chain-sawed branches, there was a tall stone, thin and sharp as a nail from up here.

Lucky he owned the wood. Lucky, also, that nobody in Crybbe seemed to give a shit about tree conservation.

Nice work, Andy.

Andy. Such a plain and simple user-friendly name. But the thought of Andy made him shiver, and he liked to shiver.

The line eased out of the wood, across the graveyard and sliced into the church, clean down the centre of the tower. Then it ploughed across the square and hit this building.

Which building?

'Go in a bit, Mel.'

The helicopter banked, and Max looked back. Shit, it was the Cock, he'd never realized the line cut through the pub . . . the pub he'd known intuitively he had to buy. Maybe, sleeping there in that crummy room, he'd picked up the flow. These things happened when you were keyed into the system.

His thoughts came back to Rachel. Who, for once, had not been keyed in. Who hadn't known how to handle country people. Who hadn't believed in the Crybbe project, hadn't believed in much.

Should he feel any kind of guilt here? Leaving her to handle things while he was in London, knowing she was out of sympathy with the whole deal?

'OK, Max?'

'Yeah, sure, Mel. Take us in.'

Thrown out on the fucking rubbish heap – like the Court

itself didn't want anybody in there hostile to the project. Rough justice. Jeez.

Was this fanciful, or what?

What he'd do, he'd have some kind of memorial to Rachel fashioned in stone. A plaque on a gate or a stile along the ley-walk, well away from the Court. Couldn't have people staring up at the prospect chamber – 'Yeah, this was where that woman took a dive, just here.'

But accidents were bad news. First thing, he'd need to have that cross-bar replaced, arrange things so the whole room was sealed off until it was fully safe.

They cleared the river and headed back over the town towards the Court. The other leys were not so obvious as the big one down the middle; this was because fewer than half the new stones were in place, several farmers refusing to give permission until after the public meeting. Or, more likely, they were holding out to see how keen he was, how much he was prepared to pay. Yeah, he could relate to that.

Cars in the courtyard. People waiting for him. Press conference scheduled for 5 p.m.

He looked at his Rolex. It was 11.15. Time to find out precisely what had happened. Talk to the police before he faced the newsmen and the TV crews, whose main question would be this:

Mr Goff, this is obviously a terrible thing to happen. It must surely have overshadowed your project here?

The press were just so flaming predictable.

Arnold was in fact moving remarkably well. 'He doesn't think he's disabled,' Fay said. 'He just thinks he's unique.'

They climbed over a stile. Arnold managed to get under it without too much difficulty. She picked him up for a while, carried on walking across the field with the dog in her arms. The few sheep ignored them.

The sky was full of veined clouds, yellow at the edges, like wedges of ancient Stilton cheese.

Powys had watched Fay wander down the field and at one

point Memory, vibrating on its helipad, turned her into Rose in a long white frock and a wide straw hat, very French Impressionist.

He blinked and Rose was Fay again, in light-blue jeans and a Greenpeace T-shirt.

She put Arnold down. He fell over and got up again.

Fay stopped and turned to him.

'Where is it, then?'

He said faintly, 'It isn't here.'

'I thought perhaps there was something wrong with my eyes,' Fay said.

'I don't understand it. This was the field. There's the river, see. The hills are right. There's the farmhouse, just through those trees.'

Fay didn't say a word.

'You think I'm bonkers, don't you?'

'Scheduled ancient monuments don't just disappear,' she said. 'Do they?'

CHAPTER VI

ONE of the women who cleaned the church was paid to come into the vicarage on weekdays to prepare Murray's lunch. He rarely saw her do it, especially in summer; it would just be there on a couple of dishes, under clingfilm. Variations on a cold-meat salad and a piece of fruit pie with whipped cream. She never asked if he enjoyed it or if there was something he would prefer.

He lifted up a corner of the clingfilm, saw a whitish, glistening smudge of something.

Mayonnaise. He knew it could only be mayonnaise.

But still Murray retched and pushed the plate away. This had been happening increasingly, of late – he'd scraped the lunch untouched into the dustbin. He never seemed to miss it afterwards, rarely felt hunger, although he knew he was losing weight and even he could see his face was gaunt and full of long shadows. Pretty soon, he thought sourly, there would be rumours going around that he had Aids.

Next week he might let it be known that he was interested in a move. He would see how he felt.

Today was not the day to do anything hasty.

Today he'd left the vicarage as usual, before eight, and walked the fifty yards to the church. Where he'd found what he'd found.

The church door had not been damaged because it was never locked. Nothing had been torn or overturned. Only the cupboard in the vestry, where the communion wine and the chalice were kept, had been forced.

Murray had heard of cases where centuries-old stained glass had been smashed or, in the case of Catholic churches, plaster statues pounded to fragments. Swastikas spray-painted on the altar-cloth. Defecation in the aisle.

Nothing so unsubtle here.

What was missing was that element of frenzy, of uncontrolled savagery. This was what had unnerved him, made him look over his shoulder down the silent nave.

Candles – his own Christmas candles – had been left burning on the altar, two of them, one so far gone that it was no more than a wick in a tiny pool of liquid wax. Between the candles stood the communion chalice, not empty.

What was in the bottom of the cup was not mayonnaise.

Murray had looked inside once, then turned away with a short, whispered, outraged prayer – it might have been a prayer or it might have been a curse; either way it was out of character. His reserve had been cracked.

With distaste, he'd placed the chalice on the stone floor, remembering too late about fingerprints but knowing even then that he would not be calling in the police, because that was all they'd done.

And it was enough.

It was inherently worse than any orgy of spray-paint and destruction. The single small, symbolic act, profoundly personal, almost tidy. Appalling in its implication, but nothing in itself, simply not worth reporting to the police and thus alerting the newspapers and Fay Morrison.

'They always ask you,' he remembered a colleague with an urban parish complaining once, 'if you suspect Satanism. What are you supposed to say? It's certainly more than anti-social behaviour, but do you really want some spotty little vandal strutting around thinking he's the Prince of Darkness?'

But this, he thought – staring down at his cling-wrapped lunch, suddenly nauseous and unsteady – this is another gesture to *me*. It's saying, come out. Come out, 'priest', come out and fight.

However, as he'd thought while rinsing out the chalice this morning, *this* can hardly be down to Tessa Byford, can it?

Murray had thrown away the candles, performed a small, lonely service of reconsecration over the chalice and decided to keep the outrage to himself. By the time the Monday cleaner came in at ten, there had been no sign of intrusion.

As for the small cupboard in the vestry – he would unscrew it from the wall himself and take it to an ironmonger's in Leominster, explaining how he'd had to force the lock after being stupid enough to lose the key. Silly me. Ha ha.

Impractical souls, vicars. Absent-minded, too.

Just *how* absent-minded he was becoming was brought dramatically home to him when the doorbell rang just before two o'clock and he parted the lace curtains to see a hearse parked in front of the house with a coffin in the back.

It had slipped his mind completely. But, even so, wasn't it at least a day too early?

'Ah, Mr Beech,' the undertaker said cheerfully. 'Got Jonathon Preece for you.'

'Yes, of course.'

'Funeral's Wednesday afternoon, so it's just the two nights in the church, is it?'

'Yes, I . . . I wasn't expecting him so soon. I thought, with the post mortem . . .'

'Aye, we took him for that first thing this morning and collected him afterwards.'

'Oh. But didn't you have things to, er . . . ?'

'No, we cleaned him up beforehand, Mr Beech. If there's no embalming involved, it's a quick turnover. Right then, top of the aisle, is it? Bottom of the steps before the altar, that's where we usually . . .'

'Yes, fine. I'll . . .'

'Now you just leave it to us, Mr Beech. We know our way around. We'll make him comfortable.'

'In that case,' Jean Wendle said firmly, 'do you mind if I come in and wait? If that wouldn't be disturbing you.'

A refusal would be impossible. This was a deliberate, uncompromising foot-in-the-door situation, it having occurred to Jean that if she took it easy, she might actually get more out of the wife.

Mrs Preece took half a step back. With no pretence of not being reluctant, she held the cottage door open just wide enough for Jean to slide inside. There were roses around the door, which was nice, which showed somebody cared. Or *had* cared.

'Thank you.'

The first thing Jean noticed in the parlour was a fresh onion on a saucer on top of the television.

She was fascinated. She hadn't seen this in years.

Mrs Preece actually had hair like an onion, coiled into a tight, white bun, and everything else about her was closed up just as tight.

She looked unlikely to offer her guest a cup of tea.

'I do realize things must be very difficult for you at present,' Jean said. 'If there is anything I can do . . .'

Mrs Preece snorted.

Jean smiled at her. 'The reason I'm here, the public meeting will be upon us tomorrow evening and I felt there were one or two things I should like to know in advance.'

'If you're yere as a spy for Mr Max Goff,' Mrs Preece said bluntly, 'then there's no need to dress it up.'

Jean was not unpleasantly surprised.

'Do you know, Mrs Preece,' she said, being equally blunt, 'this is the first experience I've ever had of an indigenous Crybbe person coming right out with something, instead of first skirting furtively around the issue.'

'Maybe you been talking to the wrong people,' said Mrs Preece.

'And who, would you say, are the "wrong" people? By the way, I wouldn't waste that nice onion on me.'

'I *beg* your pardon.'

'Just don't tell me,' Jean said levelly, 'that the onion on the saucer is there to absorb paint smells or germs. You put it there to attract any unwelcome emanations from people you don't want in your house. And when they've gone you quietly dispose of the onion. Will you be getting rid of it when I leave, Mrs Preece?'

Mrs Preece, face reddening, looked down at her clumpy brown shoes.

'Or am I flattering myself?' Jean said.

'I don't know what you're talking about.'

'Och, away with you, Mrs Preece. I'm no' one of your London innocents.'

'You're none of you innocent,' Mrs Preece cried. 'You're all as guilty as, as . . .' Her voice dropped. 'As guilty as sin.'

'Of what?' Jean asked gently.

Mrs Preece shook her head. 'You're not getting me going, I'm not stupid. You must know as you're doing no good for this town.'

'And why is that, Mrs Preece? Do you mind if I sit down?'

And before Mrs Preece could argue, Jean had slipped into the Mayor's fireside chair.

'Because it seems to me, you see, that all the new people love Crybbe just exactly the way it is, Mrs Preece. They would hate anything to happen to the local traditions. In fact that's why I'm here. I was hoping your husband could tell me a wee bit about the curfew.'

Mrs Preece turned away.

'I'm also compiling a small history of the town and its folklore,' Jean said.

'Nothing to tell,' Mrs Preece said eventually. 'Nothing that's not written down already.'

'I don't think so. I think there is a remarkable amount to tell which has never been written down.'

Mrs Preece stood over Jean. She wore a large, striped apron, like a butcher's. Discernible anxiety in her eyes now.

'Tell *me* about it, Mrs Preece. Tell me about the ritual which your husband's family has maintained so selflessly for so many centuries.'

'Just a bequest,' the Mayor's wife said. 'That's all. A bequest of land a long time ago in the sixteenth century. Depending on the bell to be rung every night.'

'This is codswallop,' Jean Wendle said. 'This is a smoke-screen.'

'Well, we 'ave the documents to prove it!' Mrs Preece was getting angry. 'That's how much it's codswallop!'

'Oh, I'm sure you do. But the real reason for the curfew, is it not, is to protect the town from . . . well, let's call it the Black Dog.'

Mrs Preece's face froze like a stopped clock.

Into the silence came lazy footsteps on the path.

'Be my husband back.' Very visibly relieved.

Damnation, Jean almost said aloud. So close.

But it wasn't the Mayor. A thin, streaky haired youth with an ear-ring shambled in without knocking.

'All right, Gran? I come to tell you . . .'

'You stay outside with them boots, Warren!'

'Too late, Gran.' The youth was in the living-room now, giving Jean Wendle the once-over with his narrow eyes.

Ah, she thought. The surviving grandson. Interesting.

'Hello,' Jean said. 'So you're Warren.'

''s right, yeah.' From his ear-ring hung a tiny silvery death's head.

'I was very sorry to hear about your brother.'

Warren blew out his mouth and nodded. 'Aye, well, one o' them things, isn't it. Anyway, Gran, message from the old . . . from Dad. All it is – they brought Jonathon back and 'e's in the church.'

'I see,' said Mrs Preece quietly. 'Thank you, Warren.'

'In 'is coffin,' said Warren.

Jean observed that the boy was somewhat less than grief-stricken.

'Lid's on, like,' Warren said.

Jean thought he sounded disappointed.

'But 'e's not screwed down, see, so if you wanna go'n 'ave a quick look at 'im, there's no problem.'

'No, I don't think I shall,' his grandmother said, 'thank you, Warren.' Tiny tears were sparkling in her eyes.

'If you're worried the ole lid might be a bit 'eavy for you, Gran,' Warren said considerately, 'I don't mind goin' along with you. I got half an hour or so to spare before I got to leave.' He turned to Jean. 'I got this band, see. We practises most Monday and Wednesday nights.'

Mrs Preece said, her voice high and tight, 'No, *thank you*, Warren.'

Warren watched his grandmother's reaction with his head on one side. This boy, Jean registered with considerable interest, is trying not to laugh.

'See, it's no problem, Gran,' Warren said slowly and slyly. ''Cause I've already 'ad 'im off once, see, that ole lid.'

He stood with his hands on narrow hips encased in tight, leather trousers, and his lips were just the merest twist away from a smirk.

Jean had been listening to the tension in the air in the small, brown living-room, humming and then singing. dangerously off-key, sending out invisible wires that quickly tautened and then, finally, snapped.

'Get out!' Mrs Preece's big face suddenly buckled. 'GET OUT!'

She turned to Jean, breathing rapidly. 'And you as well, if you please.'

Jean stood up and moved quietly to the door. 'I'm really very sorry, Mrs Preece.'

'Things is not right,' Mrs Preece said, sniffing hard. 'Things is far from right. And no you're not. None of you's sorry.'

They'd stopped for coffee but hadn't eaten, couldn't face it.

Fay still felt a bit sick and more than a bit alone. She badly needed someone she could rely on and Joe Powys no longer seemed like the one. But while she felt slightly betrayed, she was also sorry for him. He looked even more lost than she felt.

'All I can think of,' he said, driving listlessly back to Crybbe, 'is that the stone near the cottage is the actual one – the Bottle Stone.'

'You mean he had it dug up under cover of darkness and . . .'

'Sounds crazy, doesn't it?'

'I'm afraid it does, Joe. Why would Boulton-Trow want to do that, anyway?'

'Well, he knows that was the worst thing that ever happened to me, and . . .'

'And he wanted to bring it all back by confronting you with the stone again? That would make him . . . well, you know . . . quite evil. I can't imagine . . .'

'I'm sorry. I'm asking too much of you. Maybe I ought to stay out of your way for a while.'

Fay looked at him hopelessly. 'Maybe we'll take some time and think about things. See what we can come up with.'

She decided she'd go, after all, to Goff's press conference, in a private capacity, just to listen. See what questions other people raised and how they were answered.

'I don't think we *have* much time,' Joe Powys said. 'I really don't.'

'Why? I mean . . . before what?'

'I don't know,' he said.

He looked broken.

Alone again, Mrs Preece shut herself in the living-room, fell into her husband's sunken old chair and began to cry bitterly, her white hair spooling free of its bun, strands getting glued by the tears to her mottled cheeks.

When the telephone rang, she ignored it and it stopped.

After some minutes Mrs Preece got up from the chair, went to the mirror and tried to piece together her bun without looking at her face.

Out of the corner of her right eye she saw the onion in its saucer on top of the television set.

Then Mrs Preece let out a scream so harsh and ragged it felt as though the skin was being scoured from the back of her throat.

The onion, fresh this morning, was as black as burnt cork.

CHAPTER VII

GOFF said, 'As you say, Gavin, it's been a hell of blow, obviously cast a pall over things here. Rachel'd been with me nearly four years. She was the best PA I ever had. But you ask if it's gonna dampen my enthusiasm for what we're doing here . . . I have to say no, of course it isn't. What we have here is too important for Crybbe . . . and for the human race.'

Gavin Ashpole, of Offa's Dyke Radio, nodded sympathetically.

At the back, behind everybody, Fay groaned. Nobody noticed her, not even Guy.

There were about a dozen reporters and two TV crews in the stable-block, everybody asking what Fay thought were excruciatingly banal questions.

But, OK, what else *could* they ask? What did they have to build on? If it hadn't involved Max Goff, all this sad little episode would have been worth was a couple of paragraphs in the local paper and an Offa's Dyke one-day wonder. A small, insignificant, accidental death.

OK, Goff didn't want the residue of anything negative hanging on him or the Crybbe project. But if Rachel had been here, she'd have talked him out of this mini-circus; it wasn't worth a press conference, which would only draw the wrong kind of attention.

But then, if Rachel had been here . . . Fay felt the clutch of sorrow in her breast and something else less definable but close to anxiety.

Joe had said, 'Got to sort this out. I'm going to find him.'

'Boulton-Trow? Is that wise?'

'I want to take a look at this place he's got, in the wood.'

'I saw it. Yesterday, when I took the short-cut to church. It might be better inside, but it looks like a hovel.'

'We'll find out.'

'I didn't like it. I didn't like the feel of the place.'

Joe had shrugged. She'd felt torn. On one hand, yes, he really ought to sort this thing out, even it meant facing up to his own delusions. On the other hand, well, OK, she was scared for him.

'You go to your press conference,' he'd said, touched her arm hesitantly and then walked away, head down, across the square towards the churchyard.

So here she was, sitting a few yards behind Guy's stocky, aggressive-looking cameraman, Guy standing next to him, occasionally whispering instructions. The chairs had been laid out in three rows in the middle tier of the stable-block, so that the assembled hacks were slightly higher than Goff.

And yet, somehow, he appeared to be looking down on them.

Goff was at his desk, his back to the window and the Tump, as if this was his personal power-source.

'Max,' one of the hacks said, 'Barry Speake, *Evening News.* Can I ask you what kind of feedback you're getting from the local community here? I mean, what's the local response to your plans to introduce what must seem to a lot of ordinary people to be rather bizarre ideas, all this ley-lines and astrology and stuff?'

Goff gave him both rows of teeth. 'Think it's bizarre, do you, Barry?'

'I'm not saying *I* think it's bizarre, Max, but . . .'

'But you think simple country folk are too unsophisticated to grasp the concept. Isn't that a little patronizing, Gary?'

There was a little buzz of laughter.

'No, but hold on.' Goff raised a hand. 'There's a serious point to be made here. We call this New Age, and, sure, it's new to us. But folks here in Crybbe have an instinctive understanding of what it's about because this place has important traditions, what you might call a direct line to the source . . . Something I'd ask the author, J. M. Powys, to elaborate on, if he were here . . . Yeah, lady at the back.'

Fay stood up. 'Mr Goff, you're obviously spending a lot of money here in Crybbe . . .'

'Yeah, just don't ask me for the figures.'

Muted laughter.

Fay said, 'As my colleague tried to suggest, it *is* what many people would consider a slightly bizarre idea, attempting to rebuild the town's prehistoric heritage, putting back all these stones, for instance. What I'd like to know is . . . *why Crybbe*? Who told you about this place? Who told you about the stones? Who said it would be the right place for what you had in mind?'

Goff's little eyes narrowed. He was wearing, unusually, a dark suit today. Out of respect for the dead Rachel? Or his image.

'Who exactly are you?' he said. 'Which paper you from?'

'Fay Morrison.' Adding, 'Freelance,' with a defiant glance as Ashpole.

'Yeah, I thought so.'

He'd never actually seen her before. He was certainly making up for that now, little eyes never wavering.

'I'm not sure how relevant your question is today,' Goff said. 'But, yeah, on the issue of how we came to be doing what we're doing here, well, we've been kicking this idea around for a year or two. I've had advisers and people looking . . .'

'What kind of advisers? Who exactly?' The questions were coming out without forethought, she was firing blind. In fact, what the hell was she doing? She hadn't planned to say a word, just sit there and listen.

Goff looked pained. 'Ms Morrison, I don't see . . . Yeah, OK . . . I have many friends and associates in what's become known as the New Age movement – let me say, I don't like that term, it's been devalued, trivialized, right? But, yeah, it was suggested to me that if I was looking for a location which was not only geophysically and archaeologically suited to research into forgotten landscape patterns and configurations but was also suited – shall we say atmospherically – to research into human spiritual potential, then Crybbe fitted the bill.'

He produced a modest, philanthropic sort of smile. 'And it was also clearly a little down on its luck. In need of the economic boost our centre could give it. So I came along and looked around, and I . . . Well, that answer your question?'

'Was it the late Henry Kettle? Did he suggest you came here?'

'No, I sought advice from Henry Kettle, in a very small way, at a later stage. We were already committed to Crybbe by then. What are you getting at here?'

Goff leaned back in his leather rock-and-swivel chair. He was alone at the desk, although Humble and a couple of people she didn't recognize were seated a few yards away. Fay didn't think Andy Boulton-Trow was among them.

'Well,' she said, still on her feet, 'Henry Kettle was, of course, the *first* person to die in an accident here, wasn't he?'

'Aw now, hey,' Goff said.

Several reporters turned their heads to look at Fay. Maybe some of them hadn't heard about Henry. He was hardly a national figure, except in earth-mysteries circles. His death had been a minor local story; his connection with Goff had not been general knowledge, still wasn't, outside Crybbe.

It occurred to her that what she'd inadvertently done here was set the more lurid papers up with a possible Curse of Crybbe story. She imagined Rachel Wade looking down on the scene from wherever she was, rolling her eyes and passing a hand across her brow in pained disbelief.

Fay started to feel just a little foolish. Gavin Ashpole, sitting well away from her, was smirking discreetly into his lap.

She knew Goff had to make a move here.

He did. He gave the hacks a confidential smile.

'Yeah, take a good look,' he said, extending a hand towards Fay. 'This is Ms Fay Morrison.'

More heads turned. Guy's, not surprisingly, was one of the few which didn't.

'Ms Morrison,' drawled Goff, 'is a small-time freelance reporter who earns a crust here in town by stirring up stories nobody else can quite see.'

Some bastard laughed.

'Unfair,' Fay said, starting to sweat, 'Henry Kettle . . .'

'Henry Kettle' – Goff changed effortlessly to a higher gear – 'was a very elderly man who died when his car went out of control, probably due to a stroke or a heart attack. We'll no doubt find out what happened when the inquest is held. Meantime, I – and any right-thinking, rational person – would certainly take a dim view of any sensation-mongering attempt to make something out of the fact that my company had paid him a few pounds to do a few odd jobs. I think suggesting any link between the death of Henry Kettle in a car accident and Rachel Wade in a fall is in extremely poor taste, indicating a lamentable lack of professionalism – and a certain desperation perhaps – in any self-styled journalist who raised it.'

Goff relaxed, knowing how good he was at this. Fay, who'd never been much of an orator, lapsed, red-faced, into a very lonely silence.

'Now,' Goff said, not looking at her, 'if there are no further questions, I have ten minutes to do any TV and radio interviews outside.'

The heads had turned away from Fay. She'd lost it.

'You don't do yourself any favours, do you, Fay?' Ashpole said drily, out of the side of his mouth, passing her on the way out, not even looking at her.

'I suppose,' Guy Morrison said, 'you'd know about all the suicides around here, wouldn't you?'

Seven p.m. The only other customer in the public bar at the Cock was this large man, the local police sergeant, Wynford somebody. He was leaning on the bar with a pint, obviously relieved at unloading the two Divisional CID men who'd spent the day in town in connection with this Rachel Wade business.

Guy was feeling relieved, too. His heart had dropped when Max Goff had approached him immediately after the conclusion of the appalling press conference – Guy expecting to be held responsible for his wayward ex-wife and, at the very least, warned to keep her out of Goff's way in future.

But all Goff wanted was for the crew to get some aerial pictures of Crybbe from his helicopter, so that was OK. Guy had sent Catrin Jones up with Larry and escaped to the pub. Sooner or later he'd be forced to have a discreet word with Goff and explain where things stood between him and Fay – i.e. that she was an insane bitch and he'd had a lucky escape.

Meanwhile, there was this business of the suicide and the haunting. This was upsetting him. He wouldn't be able to concentrate fully until it was out of the way because Guy Morrison didn't like things he didn't understand.

He waited for Wynford's reaction. He'd got into suicides by suggesting that perhaps Rachel Wade had killed herself. Would they ever really know?

Guy Morrison was an expert at manipulating conversation, but Wynford didn't react at all.

As if he hadn't noticed the silence, Guy said, 'Doesn't do a place's reputation any good, I suppose, being connected with a suicide. I was talking to that woman who runs The Gallery. It seems her house is allegedly haunted by a chap who topped himself.'

Wynford didn't look up from his beer, but he spoke at last. 'You been misinformed, my friend.'

'I don't mean anything recent,' Guy said. 'This probably goes back a good while. Talking about the same place, are we? Heavily renovated stone farmhouse, about half a mile out of town on the Hereford road?'

'Yes, yes,' Wynford said. 'The ole Thomas farm.'

'Well, as I said, it could be going back quite a while. I mean, any time this century, I suppose, maybe earlier.'

How long had there been cut-throat razors anyway, he wondered. Hundreds of years, probably.

'Bit of a romancer, that woman, you ask me,' Wynford said. 'From Off, see.'

Meaning a newcomer, Guy supposed. It was an interesting fact that he personally was never regarded as a stranger in areas where he was recognized from television. If they'd seen you on the box, you'd been in their living-rooms, so you weren't an intruder.

Except, perhaps, here in Crybbe.

'No, look,' Guy said, 'this happened in the bathroom. Oldish chap. Cut his own throat with one of those old-fashioned open razors.'

Wynford licked his cherub's lips, his eyes frosted with suspicion.

'What's wrong?' Guy asked.

'Somebody tell you to ask me about this, did they?'

'No,' Guy said. 'Of course not.'

'You sure?'

'Look, Sergeant, what's the problem here?'

Wynford had a drink of beer. 'No problem, sir.'

'No, you *do* . . .' Guy was about to accuse him of knowing something about this but keeping it to himself.

He looked into the little inscrutable features in the middle of the big melon face and knew he'd be wasting his time.

Wynford swallowed a lot of beer, wiped his mouth. His face was very red. He's on the defensive, Guy thought, and he doesn't like that.

He was right. Wynford looked at him for the first time. 'Somebody said you was married to that Fay? Or is it you just got the same name?'

'No, it's true, I'm afraid. We were married for . . . what? Nearly three years, I suppose.'

Wynford smiled conspiratorially, a sinister sight. 'Bit of a goer, was she?'

What an appalling person. Guy, who didn't like people asking *him* questions unless they were about his television work, looked at his watch and claimed he was late for a shoot. And, actually, they had got something arranged for later; Catrin had set up one of those regressive hypnotist chaps and agreed to be the subject.

Should be entertaining. Perhaps in some past life she'd actually been someone interesting. He wondered, as he strolled into the square, what crime she could have committed to get landed with the persona of Catrin Jones.

In the Crybbe Unattended Studio Gavin Ashpole sniffed.

He knew the place used to be a toilet, but that wasn't what he could smell.

This was a musky, perfumed smell, and the odd thing was

that Gavin wasn't sure he could actually smell it at all. It was just *there*.

Probably because Fay Morrison used this studio for an hour or so every day.

There were a few of her scripts on the spike in the outer room. All hand-written, big and bold in turquoise ink.

Gavin picked up the phone and sniffed the mouthpiece. Sweating comfortably, cooling in his shell-suit. Gavin was a fitness freak, kept a hold-all in the back of his car with his jogging gear and his trainers inside. Any spare half hour or so he'd get changed, go for a run. Tuned your body, tuned your mind, and other people could sense it, too. You were projecting creative energy, dynamism.

He'd got an hour's running in tonight. Been up into the hills. Felt good. In control of himself and his destiny. Within a year he'd either be managing editor of Offa's Dyke or he'd have moved on.

Unlike Fay Morrison, who was over the hill and going down the other side fast. Left to him, the station would never have agreed to use her stuff. She was unreliable, awkward to deal with. And obviously unbalanced.

Bloody sexy, though.

The thought hit him surprisingly hard, a muscular pulse, where you noticed it.

He hadn't really considered her on this level before. She was older than he was. She'd had a lot more experience on radio, and although she never mentioned that, it was always there in the background, making her sound superior.

And she was a nutter. Not rational. Not objective as a reporter.

He'd see the boss tomorrow and explain precisely what had happened at Goff's press conference. She's doing us a lot of damage, he'd say. If she's put Max Goff's back up, who else is she antagonizing? No need to say anything to her or put anything in writing, just fade her out. Use less and less of her material until she stops bothering to send any. Then we'll put somebody else in.

Gavin attached a length of red-leader to the end of his tape.

It hadn't taken much editing, just a forty-second clip for the morning.

He rang the newsroom to tell them he was ready to send, put on the cans, waited for the news studio to come through on the line.

He felt Fay in the cans. She'd worn them over that dark-blonde hair.

Sexy bitch.

He stretched his legs under the desk, feeling the calf muscles tighten and relax, imagining her in here with him, in this tiny little studio, not big enough for two, you'd be touching one another all the time.

Projecting forward to tomorrow night. He was back in Crybbe covering the public meeting, the big confrontation between Goff and the town councillors. Fay had followed him in here, apologizing for her behaviour, saying she'd been worrying about her father, letting it take her mind off her work, couldn't handle things any more, couldn't he see that?

He could see *her* now, kneeling down by the side of his chair, looking up at him.

Got to help me, Gavin.

Why should I help you?

I like muscular men, Gavin. Hard men. Fit men. *That's* how you can help me, Gavin.

He put his hands out, one each side of her head, gripped her roughly by the hair.

Her lips parted.

'Gavin!'

'Huh?'

'We've been calling out for five minutes.'

'You couldn't have been,' Gavin rasped into the micro-phone. He was sweating like a bloody pig.

'We could certainly hear you panting, mate. What were you doing exactly?'

'Very funny, Elton. I've been for a run. Six miles. You going to take some level or not?'

'Go ahead, I'm rolling. Hope you're going to clean up in there afterwards, Gavin.'

Angrily, Gavin snapped the switch, set his tape turning. This was another little clever dick who'd be looking for a new job when he was managing editor.

He took his hand out of his shell-suit trousers, put it on the desk below the mike and watched it shaking as if it wasn't his hand at all.

CHAPTER VIII

O N reflection, maybe chopping holes in this particular wood wasn't such a crime. It was not a pleasant wood. Something Powys hadn't consciously taken in when they were here yesterday and Fay had been so incensed about the slaughter of the trees, and Rachel had . . .

No. He didn't like the wood.

And it was uncared for. Too many trees, overcrowded. Trees which had died left to rot, strangled by ivy and creepers, their white limbs sticking out like the crow-picked bones of sheep, while sickly saplings fought for the soil in between the corpses.

The wood was a buffer zone between the Tump and the town, and some of what would otherwise have reached the town had been absorbed by the wood, which was why it had such a bad feel and why people probably kept out.

And perhaps why Andy Boulton-Trow had chosen to live here.

Until you reached the clearing, the path was the only sign that anyone had been in this wood for years. It was too narrow for vehicles; a horse could make it, just about. But nobody with a car would want Keeper's Cottage.

It was redbrick, probably 1920s, small and mean with little square windows, looked as if it had only one bedroom upstairs. It was in a part of the wood where conifers – Alaskan Spruce or something – had choked out all the hardwoods, crowding in like giant weeds, blinding Keeper's Cottage to the daylight.

A sterile place. No birds, no visible wildlife. Hardly the

pick of Goff's properties. Hardly the type of dwelling for a Boulton-Trow. Even the gardeners which he assumed certain Boulton-Trows would employ wouldn't be reduced to this.

The door had been painted green. Once. A long time ago.

Powys knocked.

No answer. Unsurprising. Nobody in his right mind would want to spend too much time in Keeper's Cottage.

OK, either he isn't here or he is, and keeping quiet.

Powys felt old sorrow and new sorrow fermenting into fury. He called out, 'Andy!'

No answer.

'Andy, I want to talk.'

Not even an echo.

Powys walked around the cottage. It had no garden, no outbuildings, only a rough brick-built shelter for logs. The shelter was coming to pieces, most of the bricks were loose and crumbling.

So he helped himself to one. A brick. And he went to the back of the house, away from the path, and he hefted the brick, thoughtfully, from hand to hand for a moment or two before hurling it at one of the back windows.

A whole pane vanished.

Powys slipped a hand inside and opened the window.

Dementia, Alex thought, was an insidiously cunning ailment. It crept up on you with the style of a pickpocket, striking while your attention was diverted.

One didn't wake up in the morning and think, hello, I'm feeling a bit demented today, better put the trousers on back to front and spray shaving foam on the toothbrush. No, the attitude of the intelligent man – saying, Look, it's been diagnosed, it's there, so I'm going to have to watch myself jolly carefully – was less effective than one might expect.

And the problem with this type of dementia – furred arteries not always letting the lift go all the way to the penthouse, as it were – was that the condition could be at its most insidiously dangerous when you were feeling fine.

Today he'd felt fine, but he wasn't going to be fooled.

'Keep calm, at all times,' Jean Wendle had said. 'Learn how to observe yourself and your actions. Be detached, watch yourself without involvement. I'll show you how to do this, don't worry. But for now, just keep calm.'

Which wasn't easy when you lived with someone like Fay, who'd made a career out of putting people on the spot.

She'd come in just after six and put together rather a nice salad with prawns and other items she obviously hadn't bought in Crybbe. Bottle of white wine, too.

And then, over coffee . . .

'Dad, we didn't get a chance to finish our conversation this morning.'

'Didn't we?'

'You're feeling OK, aren't you?'

'Not too bad.'

'Because I want to get something sorted out.'

God preserve me from this child, Alex thought. Always has to get everything sorted out.

'The business of the Revox. You remember? The vandalism?'

'Of course I remember. The tape recorder, yes.'

'Well, they haven't actually pulled anybody in for it yet.'

'Haven't they?'

'And perhaps you don't think they ever will.'

'Well, with that fat fellow in charge of the investigation, I must say, I'm not over-optimistic.'

'No, no. Regardless of Wynford, you don't really think . . .'

'Fay,' Alex said, 'how do you know what I think or what I don't think? And what gives you . . . ?'

'Because I heard you talking to Grace.'

'Oh,' said Alex. He had been about to take a sip of coffee; he didn't.

Fay was waiting.

'Well, you know,' Alex said, switching to auto-pilot, 'I've often had parishioners – old people – who talked to their dead husbands and wives all the time. Nothing unusual about it, Fay. It brought them comfort, they didn't feel so alone any more. Perfectly natural kind of therapy.'

'Dad?'

'Yes?'

'Has Grace brought *you* comfort?'

Alex glared with resentment into his daughter's green eyes.

'Why did you think it was Grace who smashed up the Revox?'

He started to laugh, uneasily. 'She's dead.'

'That's right.'

Alex said, 'Look, time's getting on. I've a treatment booked for eight.'

'With Jean? What's she charging you, out of interest?'

'Nothing at all. So far, that is. I, er, gave her a basic outline of the financial position and she suggested I should leave her the fee in my will.'

'*Very* accommodating. Perhaps you could make a similar arrangement regarding your tab at the Cock. Now, to return to my question . . .'

Alex stood up. 'Let me think about this one, would you, Fay?'

How could he tell her his real fears about this? Well, of *course* dead people couldn't destroy property on that scale. Even poltergeists only tossed a few books around. Even if dead people felt a great antipathy to someone in their house, it was only living people who were capable of an act of such gross violence.

But perhaps dead people were capable of making living people do their dirty work.

Did I? he asked himself as he walked up Bell Street. Was it *me*?

Alex felt terribly hot and confused. Just wanted to feel the cool hands again.

The microphone was in the way. Jarrett had it on a bracket-thing attached to the ceiling so that it craned over the couch like an old-fashioned dentist's drill.

Guy said, rather impatiently, 'What do we need that thing for, anyway, if we're recording the whole session on VT?'

'I understand that, Guy,' Jarrett said, 'but *I* need it. I keep a record of everything. Also, it acts as a focus for the subject.

I'm using the microphone in the same way as hypnotists used to swing their watches on a chain.'

'OK,' Guy said, 'I'll go with that. We'll do some shots of the mike, make it swim before our eyes. OK, Larry?'

'No problem, I'll do it afterwards, come in over Catrin's shoulder. We OK with the lights?'

Guy looked at Graham Jarrett, small and tidy in a maroon cardigan, silvery haired and just a tiny bit camp. Graham Jarrett said, 'One light may actually assist us if it isn't directly in her eyes, because we'll all be thrown into shadow and Catrin will be in her own little world. Can you make do with one, say that big one?'

'I don't see why not,' Guy said, gratified, remembering the hassle he'd had with Adam Ivory. Nice to know some New Age people could live with television.

Jarrett arranged a tartan travelling rug over the couch and patted a cushion. 'OK then, Catrin, lie down and make yourself comfortable. I want you to be fully relaxed, so have a good wriggle about . . . Where's your favourite beach . . . somewhere on the Med? West Indies?'

'Porth Dinllaen,' Catrin said patriotically. 'On the Lleyn, in north Wales.'

Guy turned away, concealing a snigger.

Jarrett adjusted the mike, switched on a cassette machine on a metal table on wheels, like a drinks trolley. 'OK, can we try it with the lights?'

Guy signalled to the lighting man, and Catrin's face was suddenly lit up, he thought, like a fat Madonna on a Christmas card. There was a tiny, black, personal microphone clipped into a fold of her navy-blue jumper.

'Right, Catrin,' Jarrett said softly. 'It's a soft, warm afternoon. You're on the beach . . .'

'Hang on,' Tom, the soundman, said. 'Let's have some level. Say something, Catrin. Tell us what you had for lunch.'

It was another twenty minutes or so before everyone was satisfied. Guy watched Jarrett taking off Catrin's shoes and draping another travelling rug over her stumpy legs, just below the knees. No bad thing; Catrin's legs wouldn't add a great deal to the picture. Only wished he'd known about this far enough in advance to have set up someone more photogenic. He thought, with some amazement, back to this morning, when the night-terrors had persuaded him that he ought to invite Catrin to share his room tonight. He shuddered. Thank heaven he hadn't said anything to her.

'OK,' said Jarrett. 'It's very warm, not too hot, just pleasant. Perhaps you can hear the sea lapping at the sand in the distance. And if you look up, why there's the sun . . .'

The big light shone steadily down.

'Happy, Catrin?'

Catrin nodded, her lips plumped up into a little smile.

'But I don't want you to look at the sun, Catrin, I'd like you to look at the microphone. You must be quite comfortable with microphones, working for the BBC . . .'

Guy, watching her intently, didn't notice her go under, or slide into a hypnotic trance or whatever they did. Nothing about her seemed to change, as Jarrett took her back to previous holidays when she was a child. He almost thought she was putting it on when she began to burble in a little-girl sort of voice, about her parents and her sister and paddling in the sea and seeing a big jellyfish – lapsing into Welsh at one point, her first language.

She would fake it, he knew; she wouldn't want to let him down.

But then Catrin started coming out with stuff that nobody in their right mind would fake.

Hard against the streaming evening light, Jack Preece took the tractor into the top meadow and he could tell the old thing was going to fail him, that poor Jonathon had been right when he said it was a false economy.

Nobody had open tractors like this any more. Tractors had changed. Tractors nowadays were like Gomer Parry's plant-hire equipment, big shiny things.

Jack had sworn this old thing was going to see them through the haymaking, which would mean he could put off the investment until next year, maybe check out what was available secondhand.

But Jonathon had been right. False economy. Especially if it failed him in the middle of the haymaking and he had to hire one from Gomer to finish off.

Jonathon had been right, and he'd tell him so tonight, least he could do.

Jack hadn't been in yet to see his son's coffin; couldn't face it. Couldn't face people seeing him walking into the church, the bloody vicar there, with his bank-manager face and his phoney words of comfort. The bloody vicar who didn't know the score, couldn't know the way things were, couldn't be any help whatever.

But that was how vicars had to be in this town, Father said. Don't want no holy-roller types in Crybbe. Just go through the motions, do the baptisms and the burials, keep their noses out and *don't change nothing . . . don't break the routine.*

And Jack wouldn't break *his* routine. He'd go into the church as usual tonight to ring the old bell, and he'd go just a bit earlier – but not so much earlier as anybody'd notice – so he could spend five minutes alone in there, in the near-dark, with his dead son.

Jack urged the tractor up the long pitch, and the engine farted and spluttered like an old drunk. If it couldn't handle the pitch on its own any more then it was going to be bugger-all use pulling a trailer for the haymaking and he'd be going to Gomer for help – at a price.

He'd be going to Warren too, for help with the haymaking this time, and the price there was a good deal heavier. All these years, watching Warren growing up and growing away, watching him slinking away from the farm like a fox. Jack thinking it didn't matter so much, only one son could inherit – only enough income from this farm to support one – and if the other one moved away, found something else, well, that could only help the situation. But now Jack needed Warren and Warren knew that, and that was bad because there was a streak of something in Warren that Jack didn't like, always been there but never so clear as it was now.

'Come on, then.' Jack talking to the tractor like she was an old horse. Be better off with an old horse, when you thought about it.

'Come on!'

Could be tricky if she stalled near the top of the pitch and rolled back. Jack was ready for this happening, always a cautious man, never had a tractor turn over on him yet, nor even close to it.

'*Go on!*'

Bad times for the Preeces.

Not that there'd ever been good times, but you didn't expect that. You held on; if you could hold on, you were all right. Farming wasn't about good times.

He'd be fifty-five next birthday, of an age to start taking it a bit easy. No chance of that now.

He saw himself going into the church to ring the bell in less than two hours' time, and Jonathon lying there in his box. What could he say?

You was right, son, was all he'd mumble. You was right about the ole tractor.

When what he really wanted to say – to scream – was, *You stupid bugger, boy . . . all you had to do was shoot the bloody dog and you winds up . . . bloody drowned!*

Father always said, You gotter keep a 'old on your feelin's, Jack, that's the main thing. You let your feelin's go, you're out of control, see, and it's not for a Preece to lose control, we aren't *privileged* to lose control.

Bugger you, Father! Is that all there is? Is that all there'll ever be? We stands there in our fields of rock and clay, in the endless drizzle with our caps pulled down so we don't see to the horizon, so we don't look at the ole Tump, so we never asks, *why us?*

Tears exploded into Jack's eyes just as he neared the top of the pitch and through the blur he saw a great big shadow, size of a man, rising up sheer in front of him. He didn't think; he trod hard on the brake, the engine stalled and then he was staring into the peeling grey-green paint on the radiator as the tractor's nose was jerked up hard like the head of a ringed bull.

The old thing, the tractor, gave a helpless, heart-tearing

moan, like a stricken old woman in a geriatric ward, and the great wheels locked and Jack was thrown into the air.

He heard a faraway earth-shaking bump, like a blast at a quarry miles away, and he figured this must be him landing somewhere. Not long after that, he heard a grinding and a rending of metal and when he looked down he couldn't see his legs, and when he looked up he could only see the big black shadow.

It was very much like a *hand*, this shadow, a big clawing black hand coming out of the field, out of the stiff, ripe grass, on a curling wrist of smoke.

As he stared at it, not wanting to believe in it, it began to fade away at the edges, just like everything else.

CHAPTER IX

ALTHOUGH her eyes were fully open, she wasn't looking at anything in the room, not even at the microphone suspended six inches above her lips. There was a sheen on her face, which might have been caused by the heat from the single TV light. The only other light in the draped and velvety room was a very dinky, Tiffany-shaded table-lamp in the corner behind Guy Morrison and the camera crew.

GRAHAM JARRETT: 'Can you describe your surroundings? Can you tell me where you are?'
CATRIN JONES: 'I am in my bedchamber. In my bed.'

They understood she was called Jane. She only giggled when they asked for her second name. But strangely, after a few minutes, Guy Morrison had no difficulty in believing in her. She spoke, of course, with Catrin's voice, although the accent had softened as if a different accent was trying to impose itself, and the inflection was altered. This was not Catrin, not any Catrin he knew.

JARRETT: 'Is it night?'
CATRIN: 'It is dark.'

JARRETT: 'So why aren't you asleep?'

CATRIN: 'I ache too much.'

JARRETT: 'Are you not well?'

CATRIN: 'I'm aching inside.'

JARRETT: 'You mean you're unhappy about something?'

CATRIN (*sounding distressed*): 'I'm aching inside . . . *inside*. (*Long pause and a mixture of wriggles, half-smiles and soft moans.*) 'My sheriff's been to take his pleasure.'

Strewth. This really was not shrill, plump, chapel-raised Catrin, from Bangor.

Also, Guy realized, watching Catrin licking her lips suggestively, it was suddenly not useable footage.

CATRIN: '*He* watches me. Sometimes he comes in the night and I can see him and he watches me. I awake. The room . . . so cold . . . He is here . . . uurgh . . . he's . . . His eyes. His eyes in the darkness. Only his . . . eyes . . . aglow.'

Catrin was rolling from side to side, breathing in snorts. The tartan rug slipped from her legs. She dragged her skirt up to her waist and spread her legs.

CATRIN (*screaming*): 'Is that what you've come to see?'

'Wonderful,' Alex murmured. 'I think this is the only thing I live for these days.'

The cool hands.

'You,' Jean Wendle said, 'are an old humbug.'

'That's Dr Chi's diagnosis, is it?'

'Shush.'

'Hmmph.'

After the treatment, Jean made coffee but refused to let Alex have any whisky in his. 'Time you took yourself in hand,' she said.

'No chance of *you* taking me in hand, I suppose?'

Jean smiled.

'This dementia of yours,' she said, sitting next to him on the sofa. 'When I said the other night that you should relax and observe yourself, I think I was teaching my grandmother to suck eggs. I think you almost constantly observe yourself. I think you have a level of self-knowledge far beyond most of the so-called mystics in this town.'

'Oh, I'm just a bumbling old cleric,' Alex said modestly.

'This . . . condition. Unlike, say, Alzheimer's, it's far from a constant condition. Sometimes the blood flow to the brain is close to normal, is that right? I mean, like now, at this particular moment, there is no apparent problem.'

'I don't know about that,' Alex said. 'Some people would say consulting someone who communes with a long-dead Chinese quack is a sure sign of advancing senility. Oh hell . . . I'm sorry, Wendy, I've sheltered so long behind not taking anything seriously.'

'It's Jean.'

'Yes, of course. I . . . I want to say you've made a profound difference to me. I haven't felt so well in a long time. I feel I'm part of things again. That make sense?'

'When precisely did you first suspect there was something wrong with your general health?'

'Oh . . . I suppose it would be not long after poor old Grace died. Feeling a bit sorry for myself. I'd had a spot of angina, nothing life-threatening, as they say, but my morale . . .'

'Because Grace had died?'

Alex sat back, said, 'You scare me, Wendy. Bit too perceptive for comfort. Yes, I was low because of the guilt I was feeling at being initially really rather relieved that she'd popped off.'

He paused for a reaction but didn't get one.

Jean stood up, went away and returned, looking resigned, with a bottle of Bell's whisky. 'Perhaps you can start taking yourself in hand tomorrow.'

'God bless you, my dear.' Alex diluted his coffee with a good half-inch of Scotch.

A silence. Alex thought he could hear a distant siren sound, like a police car or an ambulance.

'I gather you've been talking to my daughter.'

Jean rested a hand lightly on his thigh. 'I don't think she knows quite what to make of you.'

Alex looked at Jean's hand, not daring to hope. 'And what about you, Wendy? Do you . . . ?'

The siren grew louder. Jean stood up and went across to the deep Georgian window.

She looked back at him over a shoulder, her little bum tight in pale-blue satin trousers. Coquettish? Dare he describe that look as *coquettish*?

'Oh, I think I can make something of you,' Jean said.

'Fire Service.'

'Hello, it's Fay Morrison from, er . . . from Offa's Dyke Radio. Can you tell me what's happening in Crybbe? Where's the fire?'

'You've been very quick, my girl. I don't think they've even got there yet. It isn't a fire. It's a tractor accident. Tractor turned over, one person trapped. The location is Top Meadow, Court Farm. One machine. No more details yet I'm afraid.'

'Court Farm? Bloody hell!' Fay reached for the Uher. 'Thanks a lot.' She put the phone down. 'What do you want to do, Arnie? You coming, or are you going to wait here for Dad?'

Thinking, what if he's here on his own when the curfew starts? Who's going to keep him quiet?

Arnold was lying under what used to be an editing table before somebody smashed the Revox. He was obviously finding it easier to lie down than sit. He wagged his tail.

'OK, then, you can come. Need any help?'

Arnold stood up very carefully, shook himself and fell over. Stood up again, seemed to be grinning, like he often did.

Before leaving the office she forced herself, as she always did now, to look back from the doorway to the fireplace, the mantelpiece with its testicular clock, the armchair where the ghost of Grace Legge had materialized.

She tried to avoid this room now, after dark.

She wished she could talk to Joe Powys.

Preferably on the ground? Away from any windows?

Don't be stupid.

She looked at the clock and saw it was nearly nine and realized she was worried about Joe and had been for over an hour; that was why she was sitting over the phone.

She'd never once worried about Guy. Guy was always OK. In any difficult situation Guy would either find a way out or simply walk away from it as if it had never happened to him. Whereas Joe was vulnerable because, as anybody who'd read his book could deduce, he was a professional believer. Present him with a crackpot theory and he'd make it sound sensible – which was what made him so useful to Max Goff.

She hadn't heard from him since he'd told her he was going to look for Andy Boulton-Trow.

Joe was like a child in a dark bedroom where there's a monster in the wardrobe and a dwarf behind the dressing-table and the lampshade is a human head on a string and every deep shadow is alive, and he was out there now in a town full of deep, deep shadows.

JARRETT: 'Do you live in a house?'

CATRIN: 'At the inn. We all live at the inn. Me and my sisters and my father. My father is the . . .'

JARRETT: 'The licensee? The landlord?'

CATRIN (*contemptuously*): '*He'll* never be a lord.'

JARRETT: 'And what's the name of the inn?'

CATRIN: 'The Bull. There's another inn called the Lamb, where Robert lived.'

JARRETT: 'Robert? Who is Robert?'

CATRIN: 'My man. He's hanged now. The Sheriff hanged him.'

JARRETT: 'Jane, can I ask you this? The Sheriff had your . . . Robert . . . hanged. And now he sleeps with you? Is that what you're saying?'

CATRIN (*laughing, tears on her face*): 'He doesn't sleep much!'

Guy was transfixed. Something astonishing was happening

here. No way had Catrin the imagination to conjure stuff like this.

Unless Jarrett had broken through the inhibitions to a deeper layer of the girl . . . perhaps this was the *real* Catrin.

But what about all the Crybbe references? Was it even conceivable that his production assistant was the reincarnation of a woman who had lived in this same town in the reign of Elizabeth I?

Guy didn't understand; he was at a disadvantage; he hated that.

Approximately fifteen minutes later he began to hate the situation even more. Jarrett had brought the character, Jane, several years forward in an attempt to discover how long the Sheriff's exploitation of her had continued, and the responses were becoming garbled.

> CATRIN: 'But I am the best of us all, he says, and he will never leave me, never . . . never. I'm stroking his beard, his hard, black beard. Never leave me . . . never, never, NEVER!'
> JARRETT: 'Jane, please listen . . .'
> CATRIN: 'I'll come down . . . I'll come down on you.'

Catrin began to giggle and to roll her head again. She started to ignore Jarrett's questions. He looked vaguely puzzled by this and left her alone to squirm about for a few minutes. Larry Ember took the opportunity to change the tape and his camera battery.

Then Catrin blinked, as if trying to focus on something, the giggling slowly drying up.

And her lips went into a pout.

> CATRIN (*with a new authority*): 'Come here. I'm cold.'

Her voice had changed again. It was affected, now, and petulant. And very English.

> CATRIN: 'Come on! For Christ's sake, Guy!'

Guy froze. Larry looked up from his viewfinder, the camera still rolling.

CATRIN: 'We are utterly alone and likely to remain so for two whole, wonderful days. How long have *you* got? Inches and inches, if I'm any judge.'

A profound chill spread through Guy.

CATRIN: 'There's a bathroom directly facing you at the end of the passage.'

Catrin smiled. Guy thought he was going to scream.

CATRIN: 'Don't be long, will you?'

Guy Morrison strode erratically into shot, dragging a wire, nearly bringing the light down.

'Fucking hell, Guy,' Larry Ember yelled.

Guy ignored him, shook his shoe out of the lamp wire, clutched at Graham Jarrett's cardigan. 'Wake her up. For Christ's sake, man, wake her up!'

CHAPTER X

I T was cold in the wood.

Still, he waited.

The words in his pocket, scribbled in the pages of a pocket diary, kept appearing in his mind, as though the lines were rippling across a computer screen.

'*Alle the nyte came strange noyses and lytes and the dogges howled in the yarde and when he vysyted me in myne chamber he apered lyke a clowde and a yellow cullor in the aire.*'

By nine-thirty, the air was singing with tension, as if great pylons were carrying buzzing, sizzling power cables across the darkening sky.

Joe Powys was standing by the new stone in the clearing, around the centre of the wood, a hundred yards or so from Keeper's Cottage.

This stone, narrow, like a sharpened bone, would be on the line from the Tump, through the Court to the church.

At either end of the clearing, undergrowth had been hacked away to form the beginning of a track. Or to reinstate an old one. He knew all about this track now. This was the legendary secret passage between the Court and Crybbe church, along which Sir Michael Wort was said to have escaped.

Like most legends, it was a literal interpretation of something more complex.

Something suggested by the notes he'd found in Keeper's Cottage, which had turned out to be a primitive kind of schoolhouse.

Primitive in that there was no electricity, only candles, and it was not very clean. It smelled of candles and mould . . . and paint.

There was a mattress and a duvet. Andy (or someone) had slept here. Like a monk might sleep in a little whitewashed cell with no worldly possessions. Or a rich philanthropist might feel the need to live like a squatter for a while to restructure his consciousness.

Or a modern man might have a need, somehow, to shed centuries . . .

> '. . . tolde me he woulde come at nyte in hys spyryte, by the olde roade.'

These were Andy's own notes, hand-written; Powys had discovered them in the only modern luxury item to be found in Keeper's Cottage – absurdly, a black leather Filofax.

The Filofax had been kept in what once might have been a bread-oven inside the stone open fireplace, which suggested this hovel was rather older than it appeared from the outside.

Upstairs, Powys had found a single room with a skylight,

which appeared to be used as an artist's studio. There was a table with brushes and palettes on it and coloured inks and a large assortment of paints, oil and acrylic.

There was turpentine and linseed oil and other dilutants in tightly corked medicine bottles. He uncorked one and sniffed incautiously.

It was urine.

Another one looked like blood.

Eye of newt, he thought, toe of frog.

Christ.

This room, with its skylight, was the only well-lit area of the house; all the windows in the sides of the building were screened by dense conifers.

There was a work in progress on an easel – a canvas underpainted in black and yellow-ochre. Shapes of buildings and a figure.

He decided not to sniff the painting.

There were two chairs up here, just as there were two downstairs. Andy and a lover.

Or a pupil.

He didn't know quite why he thought that. Maybe it was because someone else had been doing what he himself was doing – copying out pages of material from the Filofax. In the bread-oven had been a small pile of loose-leaf pages with writing on them in a different hand – bold, big letters. A schoolboy hand. Or a schoolgirl. There was also a paperback book on Elizabethan magic, with pages marked. He'd read one – and immediately put the book into his pocket, to study later.

The Filofax had contained about thirty loose-leaf pages of closely written notes, together with hand-drawn plans and maps. Powys had sat down at the table with the artist's materials on it, a rough-hewn item of rustic garden furniture. He'd copied everything out as carefully as he could, including the maps and plans, some of which made sense, some of which didn't.

He could have stolen the Filofax; that would have been simpler.

But he suspected that what he held here was something like what the old magicians called a *grimoire*, a book of magical secrets, a Book of Shadows. It belonged only to one person. To anyone else – if you believed in all this, which he was rather afraid he did – it could be as insidiously dangerous as a radio-active isotope.

So what you did, you copied it out.

He stopped copying at one stage, his wrist aching, a distant siren sounding in his head like the beginning of a migraine.

'What the hell am I doing?'

I mean, am I out of my mind?

He'd crossed again into the Old Golden Land, where every-thing answered to its own peculiar and archaic logic.

So, by candlelight, he'd gone on copying material from the Filofax into the blank pages of a slim blue book of his own with photographs of stones and mounds in it and maps of Britain networked with irregular thin black lines. Indented gold letters on the cover spelled out, *The Ley-Hunter's Diary 1993.* They sent him one every year; he carried it around, the way you did, but this was the first time he'd ever actually written in one.

It took him a long time.

And if Andy had come back, caught him at it?

So what? The bastard had more explaining to do than he did.

He was scared, though. You couldn't not be, in this environ-ment. Not if you were inclined to believe it worked.

As he wrote, he started to understand. Not all of it, but enough. Enough to convince him that the original source of some of these notes was probably Dr John Dee, astrologer to Elizabeth I. That Dee, who lived along the valley, who was not psychic but studied people who were, had been the recipient of the visit from the man who came 'at nyte in hys spyryte'.

And that the visitor was Michael Wort, High Sheriff of Radnorshire.

And you can prove that?

Of course not. What does that matter? *I* believe it.

But you're not rational, Powys. You're a certifiable crank.

He'd put the Filofax back into the bread-oven, wishing there was somewhere to wash his hands, and climbed out through the window again, walking away into the dusk, the wood a gloomy, treacherous place now, spiked with fallen branches and bramble tentacles.

The night coming on, and he didn't feel so certain of his ability to deal with this, this . . .

diabolical sorcerie.

This phrase appeared several times in the text.

Standing, now, by the stone, feeling the tension like an impending thunderstorm, only denser. And the feeling that when the storm broke and the rain crashed down, the rain would be black and afterwards the earth would not be cleansed and purified but in some way poisoned.

Acid rain of the soul.

He moved a few feet away from the stone, stood behind a thick old oak tree bound with vines and creepers. The logic of the Old Golden Land told him that right next to the stone was not the place to be when the storm broke.

It also told him that the ringing of the curfew every night was some kind of climax and if he wanted to get a feel of what was going on, he ought to stay near that stone for . . . what?

He stretched his arm towards the sky to see his watch.

For less than half an hour.

He was frightened, though, and really wanted to creep back through the wood to the nearest lights.

So he thought about Henry Kettle and he thought about Rachel. And found himself thinking about Fay too.

She sped through the shadowed streets, Arnold on the passenger seat.

Not the other son – what was his name? . . . Warren – not him, surely.

She could hear her own voice-piece. *The accident came only a week after Warren's brother, Jonathon, was tragically drowned in the swollen river near his home . . .*

The usual reporter's moral conflict taking place in her head.

Better for the Preece family if it was someone else. Better for the media if it was another Preece – Double Disaster for Tragic Farm Family.

Better for her, in truth, if she was away from Offa's Dyke Radio, which was clearly in the process of ditching her anyway. And away from Crybbe also, which went without saying.

Headlights on, she dropped into the lane beside the church. Nothing like other people's troubles to take your mind off your own.

Other, brighter headlights met hers just before the turning to Court Farm, and she swung into the verge as the ambulance rocketed out and its siren warbled into life.

Still alive, anyway. But that could mean anything.

Fay drove into the track. She'd never been to Court Farm before.

Firemen were standing around the yard, and there was a policeman, one of Wynford's three constables. Fay ignored him; she'd always found it easier to get information out of firemen.

'Didn't take you long,' one said, teeth flashing in the dusk. 'You wanner interview me? Which way's the camera?'

'No need to comb your hair,' Fay said. 'It's radio.'

'Oh, in that case you better talk to the chief officer. Ron!'

Firemen were always affable after it was over. 'Bugger of a job getting to him,' Ron said. 'Right up the top, this bloody field, and the ground was all churned up after all this rain. Still, we done it. Bloody mess, though. Knackered old thing it was, that tractor. Thirty-odd years old.'

'It just turned over?'

'Ah, it's not all that uncommon,' said Ron. 'I reckon we gets called to at least two tractor accidents every year. Usually young lads, not calculated the gradients. Never have imagined it happening to Jack Preece, though.'

'*Jack* Preece?'

'Hey, now, listen, don't go putting that out till the police confirms the name, will you? No, see, I can't figure how it could've happened, Jack muster been over there coupla thousand times. Just shows, dunnit. Dangerous job, farming.'

'How is he? Off the record.'

'He'll live,' Ron said, changing his boots. 'Gets everywhere this bloody mud. His left leg's badly smashed. I don't know . . . Still, they can work miracles these days, so I'm told.'

Fay got him to say some of it again, on tape. It was 9.40, nearly dark, because of all the cloud, as she pulled out of the farmyard.

She was halfway down the track when a figure appeared in the headlights urgently waving both arms, semaphoring her to stop.

Arnold sat up on the seat and growled.

Fay wound her window down.

'Give me a lift into town, will you?'

It was too dark to see his face under the cap, but she recognized his voice at once from meetings of the town council and the occasional ''Ow're you' in the street.

'Mr Preece!'

Oh, Christ.

'Get in the back, Arnold,' Fay hissed. As she pushed the dog into the back seat, something shocking wrenched at her mind, but she hadn't time to develop the thought before the passenger door was pulled open and the Mayor collapsed into the seat next to her, gasping.

'In a hurry. Hell of a hurry.'

The old man breathing heavily and apparently painfully as they crunched down the track. As she turned into the lane, Mr Preece said, 'Oh. It's you.' Most unhappy about this, she could tell. 'I didn't know it was you.'

'I'm terribly sorry,' Fay said, 'about Jack. It must be . . .'

'Aye . . .' Mr Preece broke off, turned his head, recoiled. 'Mighter known! You got that . . . damn *thing* in yere!'

'The dog?'

The shocking thought of a couple of minutes ago completed itself with an ugly click. As she was pushing Arnold into the back seat she'd felt the stump of his rear, left leg and heard Ron, the leading fireman, in her head, saying, *left leg's badly smashed*.

'Mr Preece,' Fay said carefully, 'I'd like to come and see you. I know it's a bad time – a terrible time – but I have to know what all this is about.'

He said nothing.

Fay said, 'I have to know – not for the radio, for myself – why nobody keeps a dog in Crybbe.'

The Mayor just breathed his painful soggy breaths, never looked behind him at what crouched in the back seat, said not a word until they moved up alongside the churchyard and entered the square.

'I'll get out yere.'

'Mr Preece . . .'

The old man scrambled out. Started to walk stiffly away. Then turned and tried to shout, voice cracking up like old brown parchment.

'You leave it alone, see . . .' He started to cough. 'Leave it *alone*, you . . .'

Mr Preece hawked and spat into the gutter.

'. . . stupid bitch,' he said roughly, biting off the words as if he was trying to choke back more phlegm and a different emotion. And then, leaving the passenger door for her to close, he was off across the cobbles, limping and stumbling towards the church.

He's going to ring the curfew, Fay thought suddenly.

His son's just been mangled within an inch of his life in a terrible accident and all he can think about is ringing the curfew.

Jonathon had been saying for months – years even – that it was time they got rid of that old tractor.

Probably this wasn't what he'd had in mind, Warren thought, standing in Top Meadow, alone with the wreckage of the thing that had crippled his Old Man, all the coppers and the firemen gone now.

The Old Man had been working on that tractor all day, giving himself something to concentrate on, take his mind off Jonathon and his problem of having nobody to hand over the farm to when he was too old and clapped out. Then he'd mumbled something about testing the bugger and lumbered off in it, up the top field, silly old bastard.

Testing it. Bloody tested it all right.

Warren had to laugh.

With the last of the light, he could more or less see what had happened, the tractor climbing towards the highest point and not making it, sliding back in the mud, out of control, tipping over, the Old Man going down with it, disappearing underneath as the bloody old antique came apart.

But Warren still couldn't figure how he'd let it happen, all the times he'd been up here on that bloody old tractor.

At least, he couldn't see *rationally*, like, how it had happened.

It was the *un*rational answer, the weird option, glittering in his head like cold stars, that wouldn't let him go home.

He followed the big tracks through the mud by the field gate, up the pitch to the point where the tractor had started rolling back prior to keeling over. He followed the tracks to the very top of the rise, to where the tractor had been headed, glancing behind him and seeing the trees moving on top of the old Tump half a mile away.

By the time he was on top of the pitch, he was near burning up with excitement. It hadn't seemed like the right part of the field at all, but that was because he'd come in by a different gate, looking at it from a different angle.

Warren hesitated a moment and then dashed back down to the tractor. Somebody had left behind a shovel they'd been using to shift the mud so the firemen could get their cutting gear to the Old Man. He snatched up the shovel, carried it back up the pitch, prised away the top sod – knowing instinctively *exactly* where to dig – threw off a few shovelfuls of earth, and there it was, the old box.

The jagged thrill that went through him was like white-hot electric wire. 'Oh, fuck, oh fuck.' Blinded by his power. 'I done it. Me.'

His fingers were rigid with excitement as he opened the box, just to make sure, and he almost cried out with the euphoria of the moment.

He couldn't see proper, but it was like the hand of bones, the Hand of Glory in the box had bent over and become a fist.

It was curled around the Stanley knife, gripping it, and the blade was out.

Warren shivered violently in horror and pleasure – the combination making him feel so alive it was like he was a knife himself, sharp and savage, steely and invulnerable.

The only indestructible Preece.

CHAPTER XI

A T first, the figure was dressed in dark clothes so that when it filtered through the twilit trees only the soft footsteps and the rustlings told Powys anyone was coming.

He moved behind his oak tree, sure it was going to be Andy. Holding himself still, packing away the anger and the grief – an unstable mixture – because, for once, he intended to have the advantage.

What he had to do was break this guy's habitual cool. To raise the vibration rate until the bass-cello voice distorted and the lotus position collapsed in a muscular spasm.

He'd never seen Andy anything but laid-back. This, he realized, was the most impenetrable of all screens. Laid-back people were not evil. Laid-back people were wise. Evil people ranted like Hitler.

They weren't people you'd known half your life. And they were never called Andy.

But then, Powys thought, watching the figure enter the clearing and move towards the stone, the stench from a rotten egg was only apparent when the perfectly rounded, smooth, white shell was cracked.

The stone gleamed pearly grey, collecting what light remained, a ghostly obelisk. Powys watched and tried to slow his breathing. Not yet time; to get a stake into Dracula, you had to wait for daylight.

Or, in this case, until the curfew was over. The curfew was central to the Crybbe experience. The curfew was pivotal. Whatever had been building up – tension, fear, excitement – climaxed and then died with the curfew.

He'd experienced it twice, in radically different ways. The first night with Rachel, when they'd wound up in bed at the

Cock so fast they hadn't even been aware of the chemicals interacting until the chemicals had fully interacted. And then by the river, when he'd found the shotgun in his hands and come within a twitch of blowing Jonathon Preece in half.

He lifted the sleeve of his sweatshirt to expose his watch; it was too dark to be certain, but he was sure it must be ten o'clock.

Ten o'clock and no curfew?

Staggering into the church, Jimmy Preece was faced with its silent, solitary occupant, a wooden arrow pointing at the altar rails.

He stood gasping in the doorway, and there was Jonathon's smooth, mahogany coffin shining like a taunt, a pale gleam of polish in the dimness.

Mr Preece couldn't find his breath, his legs felt like wet straw, and the urge to pray had never been as strong.

Please, God, protect us, he wanted to cry out until the words leapt into every corner of the rafters and came back at him with the illusion of strength.

And illusion was all it would be. He remembered the trouble there'd been when the old vicar was ill and the diocese had sent a replacement who'd turned out to be one of these Charismatics, some new movement in the church, this chap spouting about something he called Dynamic Prayer, shouting and quivering and making them all sing like darkies and hug each other.

No end of disturbance, until a phone call to the bishop had got rid of him. Not the border way, they told him. Not the *Crybbe* way.

Oh, Jonathon, Jonathon . . . Mr Preece felt his chest quake in agony, and he turned away, groping for the narrow, wooden door to the belfry.

The old routine, making his painful way to the steps. But, for the first time, the routine resisted him and his foot failed to find the bottom step. Twenty-seven years he'd done it, without a break, until Jack started to take over, and now Jimmy Preece had come back and he couldn't find the blessed step.

Mr Preece squeezed his eyes shut, dug his nails into his cheeks, raised his other foot and felt the step's worn edge slide under his shoe.

What time was it? Was he late?

His chest pumping weakly like these old brass fire-bellows his wife still kept, although the leather was holed and withered. His foot slipped on the edge of the second step.

Come on, come on, you hopeless old bugger.

He set off up the narrow stone steps, some no more than two foot wide.

Used to be . . . when he was ringing the old bell every night . . . that . . . these steps was . . . never a problem . . . even when he'd been working . . . solid on the lambing or the haymaking and was . . . bone tired . . . because . . .

Mr Preece paused to catch a breath, six steps up.

Because sometimes, in the old days, he'd just, like, *floated* to the top, like as if there were hands in the small of his back pushing him up the steps, and then the same hands would join his on the rope, because it was meant.

But tonight there were different hands, pressing down from above, pressing into his chest: *go back, you poor, tired old bugger, you don't wanner do this no more.*

A son in the hospital. A grandson in his coffin.

What if you dies on the steps?

One Preece in the hospital. One in his coffin. One in a heap on the flagstones. And Warren.

Best not to think about Warren.

And a silence in the belfry.

No!

In a rage, Mr Preece snatched out his dentures, thrust them down into a pocket of his old tweed jacket, forced some air into his broken bellows of a chest and made it up two more steps.

He'd do it. He'd be late but he'd do it. Never been so important that he should do it.

He saw the light above him and the ropes. Never more important, now the wall around the Tump had been breached and something was in the Court.

As had been shown by the death of that woman.

But it had never been in the church. It couldn't get into the church.

No, it couldn't.

But it wasn't Andy Boulton-Trow, waiting by the stone.

It was a woman. Well, a girl.

And naked now.

She stood with her back to the stone, as if sculpted from it, her eyes closed and her mouth open, and the night sang around her.

Jesus God, Powys whispered, the voyeur behind the oak tree, stunned into immobility.

The pupil!

It was one of those nights when the thoughts were so deep you couldn't remember getting home or putting the car away. Some small thing brought you back into your body – like the tiny grind of metal in metal as your Yale key penetrated the front-door lock.

Fay could just about read her watch in what remained of the light and the glow from neighbouring windows; she couldn't believe how rapidly the days had been shortening since Mid-summer Day.

Mr Preece was already a couple of minutes late with the curfew. She imagined him toiling up all those steps to the belfry, poor old sod.

Obsessive behaviour. Did he really think the family might lose Percy Weale's sixteenth-century bequest if the curfew remained unrung for a single night because of a dire family crisis? Had to be more than that. Joe Powys would find out.

Oh, God, Powys, where are you?

One thing was sure: Jack Preece wouldn't be ringing the curfew for a long, long time – if ever again.

What does it mean, Joe?

She ought to have gone with him, even if this was something

crazy between him and Boulton-Trow, something that went back twelve years or more.

It was so easy at night to believe in the other side of things, that there *was* an other side. That Rachel – and Rose – had died because of a magic with its roots four centuries deep . . . or perhaps deeper, perhaps as old as the stones.

With Arnold tucked, not without some effort, under her arm, Fay went into the house. It was far too late now to send the tape for the morning news. The late-duty engineer at Offa's Dyke would be long gone. She'd have to go into the studio early in the morning again, having rung Hereford General to find out Jack's condition.

She lowered the dog to the doormat.

'I wish I could trust you, Arnold,' Fay said, not quite knowing what she meant. His tail was well down; he looked no happier than she was. Jonathon Preece had set out to kill him and had died in the river. Arnold had lost a leg, so might Jack Preece by now . . .

If this was the seventeenth century she'd have been hanged as a witch, Arnold stoned to death as her familiar.

Stop it, you stupid bitch.

She clenched her fists and felt her nails piercing the palms of her hands. Everyone around her seemed to be carrying a burden of possibly misplaced guilt. Powys for Rose and Rachel. Her dad for Grace and for her mother. She herself . . .

Fay went down on her knees in the hall, the front door open to the street behind her. She buried her head in Arnold's fur. Arnold who looked no more evil than . . . than Joe Powys. As she began quietly to sob, all the lights went out in the neighbouring homes.

Bloody electricity company. How *could* this keep happening?

Fay choked a sob in bitter anger and punched at the wall until her knuckles hurt. Oh God, God, God, God, God.

She stood up shakily.

'Dad?'

There was no response.

She closed the front door behind her. He'd either gone to bed or he was still over at Jean Wendle's having his treatment.

Or his end away if he'd got lucky. Fay sniffed and smiled. She'd once asked the local doctor what the Canon's condition meant libido-wise. 'He'll be less inhibited,' the doctor had said. 'By which I mean he'll *talk* about it more often.'

The Canon wasn't back.

But – Arnold whimpering – somebody was.

As Fay stiffened in the darkness of the hallway, she saw a vague yellowish light under the door of the office.

Very slowly the office door began to open.

Fay caught her breath.

It did not creak; she only knew it was opening because the wedge of yellow light was widening, and it was not the soft and welcoming, mellow yellow of a warm parlour at suppertime.

This was the yellow of congealing fat, the yellow of illness.

The hallway was very cold. It was a cold she remembered.

'Grace?' Fay heard herself say in a voice she didn't recognize, a voice that seemed to come from someone else.

She felt her lips stretch tight with fear. She kicked the office door open.

'*Did she speak?*' Jean Wendle had asked.

'*Not a word.*'

Grace Legge wore a nightdress. Or a shroud. Was this what shrouds looked like?

'*And she didn't move?*'

'*No.*'

Grace was standing by the window, very straight, a hand on a hip, half-turned towards Fay. She was haloed in yellow light. The yellow of diseased flesh. The yellow of embalming fluid.

She was hovering six inches off the floor.

'*Harmless, then.*'

'Grace,' Fay said slowly. 'Go away, Grace.'

But Grace did not go away. She began to move towards Fay, not walking because her feet were bound in the shroud, which faded into vapour.

Fay backed away into the hall.

Dead eyes that were fixed, burning like small, still lamps. Burning like phosphorous.

'*She can't talk to you, she can't see you; there's no brain activity there . . . Blink a couple of times . . . and she'll be gone.*'

Fay shut her eyes, screwed them tight. Stood frozen in the doorway with her eyes squeezed tight. Stood praying. Praying to her father's God for deliverance. Please make it go away, please, please, please . . .

She smelled an intimate smell, sickly, soiled perfume, and felt cold breath on her face. She opened her eyes because she was more afraid not to, opened them into a fish-teethed snarl and yellow orbs alight with malice, and spindly, hooked fingers – the whole thing swirling and shimmering and coming for her, rancid and vengeful, filling the room with a rotting, spitting, incandescent yellow hatred.

Fay began to scream.

CHAPTER XII

IT was fear that drew Minnie Seagrove to the window of her lounge. Fear that if she didn't look for it, it would come looking for her.

For a short while, there was a large, early moon. It wasn't a full moon, not one of those werewolf moons by any stretch, but it was lurid and bright yellow. It appeared from behind the Tump. Before it became visible, rays had projected through the trees on the top of the mound like the beams you saw seconds before the actual headlights of an oncoming car. The trees on the Tump were waving in the breeze· even though the air all around Minnie's bungalow was quite still.

She'd come to associate this breeze with an appearance of the Hound.

Afterwards, Mrs Seagrove sat with her back to the window in Frank's old Parker Knoll wing chair, feeling its arms around her and hugging a glass of whisky, the remains of Frank's last bottle of Chivas Regal malt.

Oh Lord, how she wished she hadn't looked tonight.

'I'm that cold, dear,' she said, pretending she was talking

to young Joe Powys or anybody who'd believe her. 'I can't keep a limb still. I don't think I'll ever get warm again.'

Powys knew it was on its way when the naked girl at the stone began to moan and shiver.

When the moon rose, he saw that the girl was certainly no more than twenty and might even be significantly younger, which made him uncomfortable. He wondered for a time if she was real and not some kind of vision. What kind of a girl would come alone at night into this appalling place and take off all her clothes?

Powys was not at all turned on by this.

He was afraid. Afraid, he rationalized, not only for her but *of* her.

Afraid because he suspected she knew what was coming, while he could have no conception, except of ludicrous phosphorous fur, fiery eyes and gnashing fangs, and Basil Rathbone in his deerstalker, with his pistol.

He found his fingers were tightly entwined into some creeper on the trunk of the oak tree. He squeezed it until it hurt.

The silence in the neglected wood was absolute. No night birds, no small mammals scurrying and scrabbling. If there was any sound, any indication of movement, of change, it would be the damp chatter of decay.

Max could not move. His eyes were wide open. He took his breath in savage gulps.

He lay in awe, couldn't even think.

He could smell the candles.

As if in anticipation of a power failure, the room had been ringed with them – Max half-afraid they'd be black. But no, these were ordinary yellow-white candles, of beeswax or tallow, whatever tallow was. They didn't smell too good at first, kind of a rich, fatty smell.

Now the smell was as intoxicating as the sour red wine.

The mattress was laid out on the third level of the stable-block, so he could lie in the dusk, and take in the Tump filling the window, stealing the evening light, surrounded with candles, like a great altar.

Max lay under the black duvet, feeling like a virgin, the Great Beast/Scarlet Woman sessions with Rachel a faint and farcical memory.

For the first time in his adult life, Max was terrified.

And then, when the dark figure rose over him in the yellow, waxy glow, even more frightened – and shocked rigid, at first – by the intensity of his longing.

Warren looked up into the sky, at the night billowing in, and he *loved* the night and the black clouds and the thin wind hissing in the grass, his insides churning, his mind clotted with a rich confusion.

But the curfew was coming and the box was screaming at him to close the lid.

He slammed it down.

Then, bewildered, he started to claw at the earth with his hands, set the box down in the hole.

Heard a rattling noise inside, the hand battering the side of the box.

It don't wanner go back in the ground.

It's done what it came for.

Now it wants to go back in the chimney.

And, sure enough, when Warren picked up the box the rattling stopped, and so he ran, holding it out in front of him like a precious gift, down from field to field until he reached the farm, where nobody else lived now, except for him and the Hand of Glory.

In the end, the curfew did come, a strained and hesitant clatter at first, and then the bell was pounding the wood like a huge, shiny axe, slicing up the night, and the girl was gone.

Joe Powys wandered blindly through the undergrowth, repeatedly smashing a fist into an open palm.

The night shimmered with images.

The bell pealed and Rose, in a pure white nightdress, threw herself from a third-floor window, fluttering hopelessly in the air like a moth with its wings stuck together, falling in slow motion, and he was falling after her, reaching out for her.

In the spiny dampness of the wood, Powys cried out, just once, and the curfew bell released, at last, his agony.

He staggered among the stricken, twisted trees and wept uncontrollably. He didn't *want* to control it. He wanted the tears to flow for ever. He wanted the curfew bell to peal for ever, each clang comet-bright in the shivering night.

The bell pealed on, and with that high, wild cry Rachel tumbled into the air, and then Rose and Rachel were falling together, intertwined.

A needle of light, like the filament of a low-wattage electric bulb zig-zagged across the eaves.

Silently, in slow-motion, the rusty spike pierced the white nightdress and a geyser of hot blood sprayed into his weeping eyes.

CHAPTER XIII

MAX awoke to find himself alone, damp and smouldering, like a bonfire in the rain.

The cold deluge had been the curfew. When the curfew was gone, he realized at last, the town would be free.

He got up and shambled to the big window, wrapped in the black duvet. It was too dark to see the Tump; it didn't matter, he could *feel* the Tump. It was like the stables and maybe even the Court itself had been absorbed by the mound, so that he was, in essence, *inside* it.

No going back now, Max.

Feeling very nearly crazy, his face and hands slashed by boughs and bushes, Powys followed a dead straight line back into Crybbe.

As if the path was lit up for him. Which perhaps it was – the bell strokes landing at his feet like bars of light. All he did was lurch towards the bell, each stroke laid on the landscape heavy as a gold ingot. And when he emerged from the wood into the churchyard, scratched and bleeding from many cuts, he just collapsed on the first grave he came to.

Its stone was of new black marble, with white lettering, and when he saw whose grave it was he started to laugh, slightly hysterically.

GRACE PETERS
1928–1992
Beloved wife of
Canon A. L. Peters

And that was all.

Powys scrambled to his feet; from what he knew of Grace she would take a dim view of somebody's dirty, battered body sprawled over her nice, clean grave.

He walked stiffly through the graveyard, out of the lychgate, into the deserted square, his plodding footsteps marking sluggish time between peals of the curfew.

The power was off. Hardly a surprise. In four or five townhouse windows he could see the sallow light of paraffin lamps. Then, with a noise like a lawnmower puttering across the square, a generator cranked into action, bringing a pale-blue fluorescent flickering into the grimy windows of the old pub, the Cock.

Yes, Powys thought. I could use a drink. Quite badly.

It occurred to him he hadn't eaten since pushing down a polystyrene sandwich in this very pub before setting off to find his old mate, Andy Boulton-Trow. He didn't feel hungry, though. A drink was all he wanted, that illusory warmth in the gut. And then he'd decide where to go, whose night to spoil next, whose peace of mind to perforate.

He clambered up the steps and pushed open the single, scuffed swing-door to the public bar.

It was full. Faces swam out of the smoke haze, palid in the stuttering fluorescence. The air was weighed down, it seemed to Powys, with leaden, dull dialogue and no merriment. He felt removed from it all, as though he'd fallen asleep when he walked in, and being here was a dream.

'Brandy, please,' he told Denzil, the Neanderthal landlord. 'A single.'

Denzil didn't react at all to whatever kind of mess the wood had made of Powys's face. He didn't smile.

So where was the smile coming from? He knew somebody was smiling at him; you could feel a smile, especially when it wasn't meant to be friendly.

'Thanks,' he said, and paid.

He saw the smile through the bottom of his glass. It was a small smile in a big face. It might have been chiselled neatly into the centre of a whole round cheese.

Police Sergeant Wynford Wiley had sat there wearing this same tiny smile last night and early this morning while his colleagues from CID had been trying to persuade J. M. Powys to confess to the murder of his girlfriend.

'Been in a fight, is it, Mr Powys?'

Wiley looked more than half-drunk. He was sitting in a group of middle-aged men in faded tweeds or sleeveless, quilted body-warmers. Summer casual wear, Crybbe-style.

'You want the truth?' Powys swallowed some brandy but still didn't feel any warmth.

'All I ever wants is the truth, Mr Powys.' Wynford was wearing an old blue police shirt over what looked like police trousers.

'Amateur dramatics,' Powys said wearily. 'I've been auditioning for the Crybbe Amateur Dramatic Society. Banquo's Ghost. What do you think of the make-up?'

Wynford Wiley stopped smiling. He stood up at once, rather unsteadily. Planted himself between Powys and the door. And came out with that famous indictment of intruders from Off, those few words which Powys suddenly found so evocative of the quintessential Crybbe.

'We don't *like* clever people.' Wynford stifled a burp. 'Round yere.'

There was that thrilled hush which the first spark of confrontation always brings to rural pubs.

Powys said, 'Maybe that's why this town's dead on its feet.' He finished his brandy. 'Now' – placing his glass carefully on the bar-top – 'why don't you piss off and stop bothering me, you fat bastard.'

He listened to himself saying this, as if from afar. Listened with what ought to have been a certain horrified awe. He'd done it now. Thrown down a direct public challenge to the authority of the senior representative for what passed for the law in this town. In order to retain his authority and his public credibility, Sergeant Wiley would be obliged to take prompt and decisive action.

And Sergeant Wiley was drunk.

And Powys didn't care because tonight he'd seen the appalling thing that was known locally as Black Michael's Hound and witnessed the dark conflagration of its union with a young woman, and in terms of total black menace, Wynford Wiley just didn't figure.

'Let's slip outside, shall we, Mr Powys?'

Wynford held open the door. To get out of here, Powys would have to step under his arm, and as soon as he was outside the door the arm would descend. He was likely to wind up in a cell. If he resisted he would wind up hurt in a cell. If he ran away the town would soon be teeming with coppers. Anyway, he was too knackered to run anywhere, even if there'd been anywhere to run.

'Don't make a fuss, Mr Powys. I only wanner know 'ow you got that face.'

Powys couldn't think of a way out. He stepped under Wynford's arm and the arm, predictably, came down.

Somebody held open the door for Wynford and the big policeman followed him out, hand gripping his elbow. At that moment, as if to make things easier for the forces of the law, the power came back on, or so it seemed, and Wynford's face shone like a full moon.

Powys froze in the brightness, momentarily blinded. Wynford reeled back.

There was a figure behind the light, maybe two. The light was blasting from something attached like a miner's lamp to the top of a big video camera carried on the shoulder of a stocky man with a Beatles hairstyle (circa Hamburg '62) and an aggressive mouth.

Whom Powys recognized at once as Guy Morrison's cameraman, Larry Ember.

'You carry on, Sarge.' Larry Ember moved to a lower step and crouched, the light still full on Wynford. 'Just pretend we ain't here.'

Wynford was squinting, mouth agape. 'You switch that bloody thing off, you 'ear me? When did you 'ave permission to film yere?'

'Don't need no permission, Sarge. Public place, innit? We were just knocking off a few routine night-shots. You go ahead and arrest this geezer, don't mind us, this is nice.'

Wynford blocked the camera lens with a big hand and backed into the pub door, pushing it open with his shoulders. He glared at Larry Ember over the hot lamp. 'I can 'ave you for obstruction. Man walks into a pub, face covered with cuts and bruises, it's my job to find out why.'

'Yeah, yeah. Well, there was a very nasty accident happened up at a place called Court Farm tonight while some of us, Sergeant, were safely in the pub getting well pissed-up. As I understand it, this gentleman was up to his neck in shit and oil helping to drag some poor bleeder out from under his tractor. Fact is, he'll probably be in line for an award from the Humane Society.'

Powys kept quiet, wondering what the hell Larry Ember was on about.

'Well . . .' Wynford backed off. 'That case, why didn't 'e speak up, 'stead of being clever?'

'He's a very modest man, Sarge.'

Wynford Wiley backed awkwardly into the pub, stabbing a defiant forefinger into the night. 'All the same, you been told, Powys. Don't you leave this town.'

'Dickhead,' said Larry Ember, when the door closed. 'Shit, I enjoyed that. Best shots I've had since we came to this dump. You all right, squire?'

'Well, not as bad as the guy under the tractor. Was that on the level?'

'Sure. We didn't go, on account of our leader was otherwise engaged, shafting his assistant.'

'Well, thanks for what you did,' Powys said. 'I owe you one.'

'Yeah, well, I was getting bored.' Larry swung the camera off his shoulder, switched the lamp off. 'And I figured he'd never arrest you in his state, more likely take you up that alley and beat seven shades out of you.'

The cameraman, who'd obviously had a few pints himself, grabbed Powys's arm and started grinning. 'Hey, listen, *you* know Morrison, don't you? Bleedin' hell, should've seen him. We shot this hypnotist geezer, taking young Catrin back through her past lives, you know this, what d'you call it . . . ?'

'Regression?'

'Right. And in one life, so-called, she's this floozy back in the sixteenth century, having it away with the local sheriff, right?'

Powys stiffened. 'In Crybbe?'

'That's what she said. Anyway, in real life, Catrin's this prim little Welshie piece, butter wouldn't melt. But, stone me, under the 'fluence, she's drooling at the mouth, pulling her skirt up round her waist, and Morrison – well, he can't bleedin' believe it. Soon as we get back, he says, in his most pompous voice, he says, "Catrin and I . . . Catrin and *I*, Laurence, have a few programme details to iron out." Then he shoves her straight upstairs. Blimey, I'm not kidding, poor bleeder could hardly walk . . .'

'What time was this?'

'*Ages* ago. Well over an hour. And they ain't been seen since. Amazing, eh?'

'Not really,' Powys said sadly.

The few oil lamps in the houses had gone out and so had the moon. The town, what could be seen of it, was like a period film-set after hours. An old man with a torch crossed his path at one point; nothing else happened. Powys supposed he was going back to the riverside cottage to sleep alone, just him and the Bottle Stone.

He couldn't face being alone, even if it was now the right side of the curfew and the psychic departure lounge was probably closed for the night.

What was he going to do? He had an idea of what was happening in Crybbe and how it touched on what had happened to him twelve years ago. But to whom did you take such ideas? Certainly not the police. And if what remained of the Church was any good at this kind of thing, it wouldn't have been allowed to fester.

He could, of course, go and see Goff and lay it all down for him, explain in some detail why the Crybbe project should be abandoned forthwith. But he wasn't sure he could manage the detail or put together a coherent case that would convince someone who might be a New Age freak but was also a very astute businessman.

What it needed was a Henry Kettle.

Or a Dr John Dee, come to that.

What *he* needed was to talk to Fay Morrison, but it was unlikely she'd want to talk to him.

He passed the house he thought was Jean Wendle's. Jean might know what to do. But that was all in darkness. Faced with a power cut, many people just made it an early night.

As he slumped downhill towards the police station and the river bridge, something brushed, with some intent, against his ankles. It didn't startle him. It was probably a cat, there being no dogs in Crybbe.

It whimpered.

Powys went down on his knees. 'Arnold?'

It nuzzled him; he couldn't see it. He moved his hands down, counted three legs.

'Christ, Arnold, what are you doing out on your own. Where's Fay?'

He looked up and saw he'd reached the corner of Bell Street. Sudden dread made his still-bruised stomach contract.

Not again. Please. No.

No!

He picked Arnold up and carried him down the street. If the dog had made it all the way from home, he'd done well, so soon after losing a leg. Arnold squirmed to get down and vanished through an open doorway. Powys could hear him limping and skidding on linoleum, and then the lights came back on.

Powys went in.

He couldn't take it in at first, as the shapes of things shivered and swam in the sudden brilliance. Then he saw that Arnold had nosed open the kitchen door and was skating on the blood.

PART SEVEN

. . . but we could not bring him to human form. He was
seen like a great black dog and troubled the folk in the
house much and feared them.

Elizabethan manuscript, 1558

CHAPTER I

MAX Goff said, 'I came as soon as I heard.'

Indeed he had. It was not yet 8 a.m. Jimmy Preece was surprised that someone like Goff should be up and about at this hour. Unhappy, too, at seeing the large man getting out of his car, waddling across the farmyard like a hungry crow.

Mr Preece remembered the last time Goff had been to visit him alone.

This morning he'd been up since five and over at Court Farm before six to milk the few cows. He couldn't rely on Warren to do it – he hadn't even seen Warren yet. Mr Preece was back on the farm, which he still owned but was supposed to have retired from eight years ago to make way for future generations.

Becoming a farmer again was the best way of taking his mind off what had happened to the future generations.

Everything changing too fast, too brutally. Even this Goff looked different. His suit was dark and he wore no hat. He didn't look as if he'd had much sleep. He looked serious. He looked like he cared.

But what was it he cared *about*? Was it the sudden, tragic death of Jonathon, followed by the grievous injury to Jonathon's father?

Or was it what he, Goff, might get out of all this?

Like the farm.

Mr Preece thought of the crow again, the scavenger. He hated crows.

'Humble said you'd be here.' Goff walked past him into the old, bare living-room, where all that remained of Jack was a waistcoat thrown over a chair back. No photos, not even the old gun propped up in the corner any more.

Goff said, 'Reason I came so early is the meeting. It's the public meeting tonight. What I wanted to say – there's time to call it off, Mr Mayor.'

'Call 'im off?' Jimmy Preece shook his head. No, it would be an ordeal, this meeting, but it couldn't be put off. The meeting would be his best opportunity to make it clear to this Goff that he wasn't wanted in Crybbe, that this town had no sympathy with him or his ideas.

There would, however, be a great deal of sympathy – *overwhelming* sympathy – for old Jim Preece, who'd lost his grandson and whose son was now lying maimed for life in Hereford Hospital.

Goff would have realized this. Cunning devil.

No way Mr Preece wanted that meeting calling off.

'Too late now. People coming yere from all over. Never get word out in time.'

'If we start now, Mr Mayor, spread the word in town, get it out on Offa's Dyke Radio . . .'

'No, no. Very kind of you to offer, but the town council sticks to their arrangements, come fire, flood. And personal tragedy, like.'

He'd be making time today to pay a final visit to each of the farmers with land around Crybbe, make sure they all understood about the need to keep the stones away. He thought they were still with him, but money could turn a farmer's head faster than a runaway bull.

'Thought I should at least make the offer, Mr Mayor. And tell you how sorry I was.'

'Aye.'

There was a long silence. Mr Preece noticed circles like bruises around Goff's eyes and his beard not as well manicured as usual.

'Well,' Mr Preece said. He might as well say it now, make it clear where they stood. 'I expect you'll be wonderin' 'bout the future of this place. What's gonna happen if Jack's crippled and with Jonathon gone, like.'

'It's a problem, Mr Mayor. If there's any way I can help . . . We're neighbours, right?'

'No,' Jimmy Preece said. 'There's no way you can 'elp. And no I won't be sellin' the farm.'

Goff spread his legs apart and rocked a bit. He didn't laugh, but he looked as if he wanted to.

'Aw, jeez, I realize you got to be in an emotional and anxious state, Mr Mayor, but if you're thinking maybe I'm here because I'm angling to buy the place, let me say that was about the last thing . . . I'm not a fucking property shark, Mr Preece.'

'No,' Jimmy Preece said, and it might have been a question.

'This family's been here four, five centuries, yeah? Isn't there another son, young, er . . . ?'

'Warren,' said Mr Preece.

'Yeah, Warren.'

'Who don't want anything to do with farming, as you well know, Mr Goff.'

'Huh?'

' 'E's gonner be a star, isn't that right?'

'I don't . . .'

'Pop guitarist, isn't it? You're gonner make the boy a millionaire. Sign 'im up, turn 'im into a big star so he 'e can get his lazy arse out of Crybbe and don't need to 'ave nothing to do with us ever again . . . You ask me if there's anything you can do, Mr Goff, I reckon you done enough.'

For the first time, Murray Beech had locked the church for the night. He'd waited until the curfew was over and then walked over with the keys, surprised to find Jimmy Preece and not his son emerging from the belfry.

In an arid voice, from which all emotion had been drained, Jimmy Preece had explained why he was here, leaving Murray horrified. He'd remembered hearing the ambulance, wondering who it was for. How could lightning strike twice, so cruelly, at a single family? How could any kind of God . . . ?

Murray often wondered just how many of his colleagues in the church seriously believed any more in a Fount of Heavenly Wisdom. Perhaps there should be a confidential survey, some sort of secret ballot within the Organization. No one could fault the basic Christian ethic but Murray couldn't help wondering if it wasn't in the best interests of sustaining a credible, relevant, functioning clergy to have this anachronism known as God quietly phased out. God was a millstone. Three times as many people would seek clerical help with their personal problems if they didn't have to cope with God.

And without God the question of sacrilege would not arise, and nobody, he thought now, standing by the altar rail, would have to cope with . . . *this*.

The church door had not been forced last night. A window had simply been smashed in the vestry.

This morning Jonathon Preece lay apparently undisturbed, a silent sentinel, still, presumably – and Murray was not inclined to check – in his coffin, still safely supported on its bier, a slim metal trolley, only slightly more ornate than those used in hospitals. The coffin was still pointing at the altar with its white and gold cloth.

Neither the coffin nor the bier had been disturbed. Only the altar itself. In the centre of the cloth, a silver dish had been heaped high with something brown and pungent.

Murray approached with trepidation and distaste to find the substance in the dish was not what he'd feared.

Next to the dish was the tin from which the brown gunge had been scraped.

It was dog food.

Murray was almost relieved.

And so puzzled by this that he failed to carry out a more detailed inspection of the church and therefore did not find out what else had been done.

Goff raised a faint smile and both hands. 'I'm starting to understand, Mr Preece. I see where you're coming from. The boy sent me a tape, right?'

'You tell me, sir, you tell me.'

'Sure I'll tell you. This kid . . .'

'Warren.'

'Warren, yeah. Mr Mayor, you know how many tapes we get sent to us? Jeez, I don't even know myself – a thousand, two thousand a year. How many we do anything with? In a good year – two. Young . . .'

'Warren.'

'Sure. Well, the reason he got further than ninety-nine point nine per cent of the others was he sent it to the Cock and I listened to it myself. The normal thing is I pay guys to pay other guys to listen to the tapes on the slushpile, saves me a lotta grief, right? But I didn't wanna appear snobbish, big London record chief sneering at local hopefuls. So I listened to the tape and I had a letter sent back, and what it said was, this stuff isn't basically up to it, but we aren't closing the door. When you feel you've improved, try us again, we're always prepared to listen. You know what that means? You'd like me to give you a frank and honest translation, Mr Mayor?'

Jimmy Preece swallowed. 'Yes,' he said. 'I'd like you to be quite frank.'

'I'm always frank, Mr Mayor, 'cept when it's gonna destroy somebody, like in the case of this tape. You ever hear your grandson's band, Mr Preece?'

'Used to practise in the barn, till Jack turned 'em out. Hens wouldn't lay.'

'Yeah, that sounds like them,' said Goff, smiling now. 'Crude, lyrically moronic and musically inept. They might improve, but I wouldn't take any bets. My advice, don't let the kid give up sheep-shearing classes.'

It went quiet in the living-room at Court Farm. In the whole house.

'Thank you,' Jimmy Preece said dully.

'No worries, Mr Preece. Believe me. The boy'll make a farmer yet.'

Behind the door, at the foot of the stairs, Warren Preece straightened up.

His face entirely without expression.

CHAPTER II

JEAN'S narrow town house had three floors and five bedrooms, only three of them with beds. In one, Alex awoke.

To his amazement he knew at once exactly who he was, where he was and how he came to be there.

Separating his thoughts had once been like untangling single strands of spaghetti from a bolognese.

Could Jean Wendle be right? Could it be that his periods of absent-mindedness, of the mental mush – of wondering what day it was, even what time of his life it was – were the results not so much of a physical condition but of a reaction to his surroundings? Through living in a house disturbed by unearthly energy. A house on a ley-line.

No ley-lines passed through *this* house. Something Jean said she'd been very careful to establish before accepting the tenancy.

Why not try an experiment, Jean had suggested. Why not spend a night here? An invitation he'd entirely misunderstood at first. Wondering whether, in spite of all his talk, he'd be quite up to it.

Jean had left a message on Fay's answering machine to say Alex wouldn't be coming home tonight.

She'd shown him to this very pleasant room with a large but indisputedly single bed and said good night. He might notice, she said, a difference in the morning.

And, by God, she was right.

The sun shone through a small square window over the bed and Alex lay there relishing his freedom.

For that was what it was.

And all thanks to Jean Wendle. How could he ever make it up to her?

Well, he knew how he'd *like* to make it up to her . . . Yes, this morning he certainly felt up to it.

Alex pushed back the bedclothes and swung his feet on to

a floor which felt satisfyingly firm under his bare feet. He flexed his toes, stood, walked quite steadily to the door. Clad only in the Bermuda shorts he'd worn as underpants since the days when they used to give ladies a laugh, thus putting them at their ease. Under the clerical costume, a pair of orange Bermuda shorts. 'I shall have them in purple, when I'm a bishop.' Half the battle, Alex had found, over the years, was giving ladies a laugh.

There was the sound of a radio from downstairs.

'. . . *local news at nine o'clock from Offa's Dyke Radio, the Voice of the Marches. Here's Tim Benfield.*

'*Good morning. A farmer is critically ill in hospital after his tractor overturned on a hillside at Crybbe. The accident happened only days after the tragic drowning of his son in the river nearby. James Barlow has the details . . .*'

Barlow? Should have been Fay, Alex thought. Why wasn't it Fay?

Alex found a robe hanging behind the door and put it on. Bit tight, but at least it wasn't frilly. In the bathroom, he splashed invigorating cold water on his face, walked briskly down the stairs, smoothing down his hair and his beard.

He found her in the kitchen, a sunny, high-ceilinged room with a refectory table and a kettle burbling on the Rayburn.

'Good morning, Alex.' Standing by the window with a slim cigar in her fingers, fresh and athletic-looking in a light-green tracksuit.

'You know,' Alex said, 'I really think it bloody well is a good morning. All thanks to you, Jean.'

Jean. It struck him that he'd persisted in calling her Wendy simply because it was something like her surname which he could never remember.

He went to the window, which had a limited view into a side-street off the square. He saw a milkman. A postman. A grocer hopefully pulling out his sunblind.

Normality.

Harmless normality.

He thought about Grace. Perhaps if he left the house then what remained of Grace would fade away. Fay had been right;

there was no reason to stay here. Everything was clear from here, a different house, not two hundred yards away – but not on a spirit path.

Spirit paths. New Age nonsense.

But he couldn't remember the last time he'd felt so happy.

Hereward Newsome was seriously impressed by the painting's tonal responses, the way the diffused light was handled – shades of Rembrandt.

'How long have you been painting?'

'I've always painted,' she said.

'Just that I haven't seen any of your work around.'

'You will,' she said.

He wanted to say, Did you really do this yourself? But that might sound insulting, might screw up the deal. And this painting was now very important, after the less-than-satisfactory buying trip to the West Country. An item to unveil to Goff with pride.

Hereward had returned the previous afternoon, terrified of facing Jocasta, with two hotel bills, a substantial drinks tab and a mere three paintings, including a study of Silbury Hill which was little more than a miniature and had cost him in excess of twelve hundred pounds.

To his surprise, his wife had appeared almost touchingly pleased to have him home.

She'd looked tired, there were brown crescents under her eyes and her skin seemed coarser. She'd told him of the terrible incident at the Court in which Rachel Wade had died. Hereward, who didn't think Jocasta had known Rachel Wade all that well, had been more concerned at the effect on his wife, who looked . . . well, she looked her age. For the first time in years, Hereward felt protective towards Jocasta, and, in an odd way, stimulated.

He'd shown her his miserable collection of earth-mystery paintings.

'Never mind,' she'd said, astonishingly.

He'd trimmed his beard and made a tentative advance, but Jocasta felt there was a migraine hovering.

This morning they'd awoken early because of the strength of the light – the first truly sunny morning in a week. Jocasta had gone off before half past eight to open The Gallery, and Hereward had stayed at home to chop logs. On a day like this, it was good to be a countryman.

Then the young woman had telephoned about the painting and insisted on bringing it to the house, saying she didn't want to carry it through town.

He thought he'd seen her before, but not in Crybbe, surely. Dark hair, dark-eyed. Darkly glamorous and confident in an offhand way. Arrived in a blue Land Rover.

She wore a lot of make-up. Black lipstick. But she couldn't be older than early-twenties, which made her mature talent quite frightening.

If indeed she'd done this herself; he didn't dare challenge her.

It was a large canvas – five feet by four. When he leaned it against the dresser it took over the room immediately. What it did was to draw the room into the scene, reducing the kitchen furniture to shadows, even in the brightness of this cheerfully sunny morning.

The painting, Hereward thought, stole the sunlight away.

He identified the front entrance of Crybbe Court, the building looking as romantically decrepit as it had last week when he'd strolled over there out of curiosity, to see how things were progressing. Broken cobbles in the yard. Weeds. A dull grey sky falling towards evening.

The main door was open, and a tall, black-bearded man, half-shadowed, stood inside. Behind the figure and around his head was a strange nimbus, a halo of yellowish, powdery vapour. The man had a still and beckoning air about him. Hereward was reminded in a curious way, of Holman Hunt's *The Light of the World*, except there was no light about this figure, only a sort of glowing darkness.

'It's very interesting,' Hereward said. 'How much?'

'Three hundred pounds.'

Hereward was pleased. It was, in its way, a major work, lustrous like a large icon. This girl was a significant discovery. He wanted to snatch his wallet out before she could change her mind, but caution prevailed. He kept his face impassive.

'Where do you work?'

'Here. In Crybbe.'

'You're . . . a full-time, professional painter?'

'I am now,' she said. 'Would you like to see the preliminary sketches?'

'Very much,' Hereward said.

She fetched the portfolio from the Land Rover. The sketches were in Indian ink and smudged charcoal – studies of the bearded face – and some colour-mix experiments in acrylic on paper.

He wondered who the model was, didn't like to ask; this artist had a formidable air. Watched him, unsmiling.

And she was so *young*.

'Does it have a title?'

'It speaks for itself.'

'I see,' Hereward said. He didn't. 'Look,' he said, 'I'll take a chance. I'll buy it.'

She'd watched him the whole time, studying his reaction. She hadn't looked once at the painting. Most unusual for an artist; normally they couldn't keep their eyes off their own work.

'Could I buy the sketches, too?'

'You can have them,' she said. 'Keep them in your attic or somewhere.'

'I certainly won't! I shall have them on my walls.'

The girl smiled.

'One thing.' She had a trace of accent. Not local. 'I might be doing more. Even if it's sold, I'd like the painting in the window of your gallery for a couple of days. No card, no identification, just the picture.'

'Well . . . certainly. Of course. But you really don't want your name on a card under the picture?'

Shook her head. 'You don't know my name, anyway.'

'Aren't you going to tell me?'

She left.

It was not yet ten o'clock.

*

The Mayor of Crybbe was seeing his youngest grandson for the first time as a man.

An unpleasant man.

He'd patrolled the farm, checking everything was all right, collected a few eggs. Then noticed that something, apart from the tractor, was missing from the vehicle shed.

When he got back to the house, he saw Warren landing hard on the settee, like he'd been doing something else, heard his grandad and flung himself down in a hurry.

'Where's the Land Rover, Warren?'

'Lent it to a friend.'

'You . . . *what?*' Mr Preece took off his cap and began to squeeze it.

'Don't get excited, Grandad. She'll bring it back.'

'*She?*'

'My friend,' said Warren, not looking at him. He hadn't even shaved yet.

When Mr Preece looked at Warren, he saw just how alone he was now.

'Come on, Warren, we got things to do. Jonathon's funeral tomorrow and your dad in hospital. Your gran rung yet?'

'Dunno. Has she?'

'She was gonner phone the hospital, see what kind of night Jack 'ad, see when we can visit 'im.'

'I hate hospitals,' said Warren.

'You're not gonner go?'

'Can't see me goin' today,' said Warren, like they were talking about a football match. 'I'll be busy.'

Jimmy Preece began to shake. Sprawled across the settee was a hard, thin man with a head shaved close until you got right to the top when it came out like a stiff shaving brush. A sneering man with an ear-ring which had a little metal skull hanging from it. A man with flat, lizard's eyes.

Before, it had been an irritation, the way Warren was, but it didn't matter much. You looked the other way and you saw Jonathon, you saw the chairman of the Young Farmers' Club. You saw Jimmy Preece fifty years ago.

Now this . . . his only surviving grandson.

He tried. 'Warren, we never talked much . . . before.'

Warren's laughter was like spit. 'Wasn't no reason to talk, was there? Not when there was Dad, and there was good old, reliable old Jonathon.'

'Don't you talk like that about . . .'

'And now you wanner talk, is it? What a fuckin' surprise this is. Fair knocks me over with the shock, that does.'

Jimmy Preece squeezed his cap so tightly he felt the fabric start to rip.

This . . . *this* was the only surviving Preece, apart from himself, with two good legs to climb the stairs to the belfry.

'Now you listen to me, boy,' Jimmy said. 'There's things you don't know about . . .'

'Correction, Grandad.' Warren uncoiled from the couch, stood up. 'There's things I don't *care* about. Big difference there, see.'

Jimmy Preece wanted to hit him again. But this time, Warren would be ready for it, he could tell by the way he was standing, legs apart, hands dangling loose by his sides. Wouldn't worry him one bit, beating an old man.

Jimmy Preece saw the future.

He saw himself prising Mrs Preece out of her retirement cottage, dragging her back to this old place. He saw himself running the farm again, such as it was these days, and ringing the old bell every night until Jack was out of hospital, and then Mrs Preece caring for her crippled son, and what meagre profits they made going on hired help as he, Jimmy Preece, got older and feebler.

He knew, from last night's ordeal, how hard it was going to get, ringing that bell. Jack must've sensed it, but he hadn't said a word. That was Jack, though, keep on, grit your teeth, do your duty. You don't have to like it but you got to do it.

Going to be hard. Going to be a trial.

While this . . . this *thing* slinks around the place grinning and sneering.

Going to be no fall-back. A feeble old man, and no fall-back.

'Why don't you just let it go, Grandad,' Warren said, with a shocking hint of glee. 'What's it worth? Think about the winter, them cold nights when you're all stiff and the old steps is wet and slippery. Could do yourself a mischief, isn't it.'

Jimmy Preece seeing his youngest grandson for the first time as a man.

A bad man.

He wanted to take what Goff had told him this morning and hurl it in Warren's thin, snidey face.

Instead, he turned his back on his sole remaining grandson and walked out of the house, across the yard.

Warren went back into the fireplace and lifted out the old box.

He set the box on the hearth and opened the lid.

The hand of bones looked to be lying palm up this morning, the Stanley knife across it, the fingers no longer closed around the knife.

Like the hand was offering the Stanley knife to Warren.

So Warren took it.

CHAPTER III

. . . an did bringe out hys bodie and shewde hym to the crowde with the rope about hys necke . . .

Joe Powys lay on the floor still wearing last night's sweatshirt, flecked with mud and stuff from the woods and some blood from later. He was alone; she'd slipped quietly away a few minutes ago.

The hanged man was obviously the High Sheriff, Sir Michael Wort, displayed by his frightened servants to the angry townsfolk to prove that he really was dead. So if they'd seen his body, how did the legend arise that Wort had perhaps escaped down some secret tunnel?

Only one possible answer to that.

It had been in his head almost as soon as he woke, half-remembering copying out the material and half-thinking, it was part of some long, tortured dream. But *The Ley-Hunter's Diary*

1993 was there, in his jacket on the floor by his pillow, and it was still throwing out answers. Not very credible answers.

The door was prodded open and Arnold peered round. Powys beckoned him, plunged his hands into the black and white fur. It felt warm and real. Not much else felt real.

Arnold licked his hand.

Powys looked around the room, at the dark-stained dressing-table, the wardrobe like an upturned coffin, the milk-chocolate wallpaper. Not the least depressing room he'd ever slept in.

'Don't blame me for the décor.'

She stood in the doorway.

She was in a red towelling bathrobe, arms by her sides, hands invisible because the sleeves were too long.

'It's certainly very Crybbe,' he said.

Fay nodded. 'And I'm never going to sleep here again, that's for sure.'

He'd awoken several times during the night on his makeshift bed of sofa cushions laid end to end.

Once it was Arnold licking his forehead. And once with an agonizing image arising in his mind: an exquisitely defined, twilit image of Rachel's broken body, both eyes wide open in a head that lolled off-centre, the perfect, pale, Pre-Raphaelite corpse, Ophelia, 'The Lady of Shalott' . . .

Lady cast out upon a Rubbish Heap.

He'd stood up, hearing Fay moaning in the bed. 'Oh God.' Twisting her head on the pillow. 'It hurts. It really hurts. It was just numb for a while, now it really hurts.'

'Let me take you to a hospital.'

'I'm not leaving this room.'

'And I thought Arnold looked a mess,' she said. 'What's the time? There's only one reliable clock in this house and I couldn't bear to look at it.'

Powys consulted their two watches on the bedside cupboard. 'Half nine. Ten. Mine's probably right, yours is cracked. So it's ten.'

'Even my watch has a cracked face.' Fay smiled feebly. 'I was lying there, thinking, you know, it can't be as bad as it feels, it really can't. Then I staggered to the bathroom mirror . . . And it was. It really bloody was.'

The cut ran from just below the hairline to the top of the left cheek. The left eye was black, blue, orange and half-closed.

'The bitch has scarred me for life.'

He remembered all the blood on the linoleum and thought she actually looked a good deal better than the quaking thing he'd found curled up on the kitchen floor, incapable, for a long time, of coherent speech.

'It's *never* going to heal,' Fay said bleakly.

'It will.' But she was probably right. There'd be a long-term scar. This town was good at leaving scars. He swung his legs out of bed; quite decent, still wearing his boxer shorts, but he doubted she'd have noticed if he'd been naked.

'She's back now, all right. It's her house again.'

'Grace?'

'She's repossessed it.' Fay shivered and held her robe together at the throat. 'It's like . . . When she was alive, there was this thin veneer . . . of gentility, OK? Of politeness. Now she's dead there's no need to keep up appearances, it's all stripped away, and there's just this . . . this rotting core . . . Resentment. Hate. Just don't let anybody tell me the dead can't feel hatred.'

'Maybe they can just project it. Maybe we're not even talking about the dead, as such.'

Fay's right profile was all white. She turned her head with a lurid, rainbow blur and her mouth tightened with the pain.

'And don't let *anybody* tell me again that they're harmless. Joe, she flew at me. She was hovering near the floor – everywhere this icy stillness – and then she sprang. There was a perfumy smell, but it was a kind of mortuary perfume, to cover up the rotting, the decay, you know?'

Powys said helplessly, 'I've never seen a ghost.'

Then what did you see last night? What in Christ's name was that? The raging black horror in the wood. He was sure the girl at the stone would be killed or die of fright, but the bitch knew what she was doing.

'So I'm backing out of the office,' Fay said. 'Thinking, She can only exist in there. Jean Wendle said I should blink a couple of times, close my eyes and when I opened them she'd be gone, she's only a light effect, no more real than voices on quarter-inch, fragments of magnetic dust, and I hit the pause button and the voice cuts out in mid-sentence. So I took the advice. I closed my eyes – and I got out of the room fast because she can't exist outside there, can she? That's *her* place, right?'

Fay's fingers were white and stiff around the collar of the red robe.

'And I'm in the hall. I've closed the door behind me. I've slammed the door. In its . . . in Grace's face. And suddenly, just as I'm . . . She's there too. She's right up against me again, *in my face*. Grace has . . . had . . . *has* these awful little teeth, like fish-bones. And, you know, the kitchen door's opposite the office door, and so I just *threw* myself across the hall and into the kitchen, and I . . . that's all I remember.'

'You hit your head on a sharp corner of the kitchen table.'

She's right, he thought. She can't stay here tonight. Any more than I can spend it with the Bottle Stone. 'It was too dark to see much. I thought you were . . .'

'Thanks.'

'What would *you* think . . . ?'

'No, I mean . . . thanks. You keep rescuing me. That's not the way it's supposed to be any more.'

'Arnold waylaid me at the top of the street and dragged me down here with his teeth.'

The dog wagged his tail, staggered to the edge of the bed and looked down dubiously.

'Good old Arnie,' said Fay. 'I'd just virtually accused him of exacting some awful psychic revenge on the Preece family for trying to shoot him. Come on, I'll make some breakfast. We have to eat.'

Neither of them had mentioned the Bottle Stone. He wished he could prove to her it had all happened, but he couldn't. He couldn't prove anything – yet.

'I wanted to call a doctor last night,' he told her. 'But you started screaming at me.'

'I hate doctors.'

'You ought to see one, all the same.'

'Sod off. Sorry, I don't mean to be churlish, but nothing seems to be fractured. Cuts and bruises. Anyway, look at the state of *you*.'

Powys picked Arnold up to carry him downstairs.

Fay said, 'I wonder what he sees.'

He thought, I think I've seen what he sees. He said, 'The other time you saw this Grace thing, what time was it?'

'After midnight.'

'What was it like on that occasion?'

'She didn't move. Very pale. Very still. Like a lantern slide.'

At the foot of the stairs, the office door remained closed.

'Figures,' Powys said. 'She wouldn't be up to much after midnight. Or, more correctly, after ten – after the curfew. It probably took all her energy just to manifest. But last night, it was just minutes *before* the curfew. That's when it's strongest. That's when the whole town's really charged up. Before the curfew shatters it.'

'What are you on about?' Fay shook her head, looked at the kitchen floor. 'God, what a mess. Who'd have thought I had so much blood in me?'

'I think . . .'

'You mention doctors or hospitals again, Joe, I'll never sleep with you again.'

Fay grinned, which was the wrong thing to do because it pulled on the skin around her bruised eye.

She had to go back into the office to answer the phone. It looked, as it always did in the mornings, far too boring to be haunted.

The call was from her father, sounding wonderfully bright and happy. Last night, while she was sitting by the sink, Joe trying to bathe her eye, the phone had rung and Jean's message, amplified by the answering machine, had been relayed across the hall.

'I can't believe it,' Alex said now. 'I feel tremendous. I feel about . . . oh, sixty-five. Do you think I'm too old to become a New Age person?'

'You going to stay at Jean's for a while, Dad?'

'I'll probably drift back in the course of the day. Don't want to lose touch with old Doc Chi at this stage.'

'Dad's shed a quarter of a century overnight,' Fay told Powys. 'No woman is safe.'

'Well, keep him away from the Cock.'

'Why?'

'It seems to have aphrodisiac properties. It turns people on.'

'I don't follow you.'

He told her, at last, about getting beaten up by Humble, and Rachel taking him to hers and Goff's room. What had happened then, the sudden inevitability of it. 'It was the right time, coming up to curfew time. I mean, Rachel was not . . . promiscuous. Nor me, come to that. I mean, lonely, sex-starved, but not . . . Anyway, I just don't think we'd ever have got together . . . if it hadn't been for the time. And the place.'

'I don't understand.'

'All right, think about the condoms. All those used condoms in the alley, up by the studio. In a town surrounded by open fields, doesn't it strike you as odd that so many couples should want to do it standing up in an alley?'

'I never really thought about it. Not that way.'

'And last night, again at the Cock, again in the hour before the curfew, your ex-husband was suddenly overwhelmed with lust for his production assistant and whisked her upstairs.'

'Catrin? Guy and Catrin?'

Powys nodded. 'Why do they call it the Cock?' He was buttering more toast; it was, she reckoned, his fifth slice. How long since he last ate? 'Is that what it's really called?'

'Certainly hasn't got a sign to that effect,' Fay said.

'What do you know about Denzil, the landlord? Got many kids, for instance?'

'I don't know. He isn't married, I don't think. Somebody once told me he put it about a bit, but I mean . . . You're getting carried away, Joe.'

'I'm a loony. I'm allowed.' He spread the toast with about

436

half a pot of thick-cut marmalade. 'Sorry, look, I haven't got this worked out yet. Whatever I say's going to make you think I'm even more of a loony.'

'No – hang on – Joe, I . . .' Fay clasped her hands together tightly, squeezing them. 'I'm sorry about yesterday. I had no right to dispute your story. Town full of ghosts, no dogs . . . I mean, Christ . . . I'm sorry.'

He put a hand over both of hers. Sighed.

'Tell me,' Fay said.

So he told her. He told her about the cottage and the magical Filofax and the art studio.

'Blood?' Fay touched her temple, winced. 'Urine? What does it mean?'

'I don't really know. But I wouldn't have one of those paintings on *my* wall.'

And then he told her about the girl at the stone, and the apparition.

'You saw it? You saw Black Michael's Hound?'

'I don't know what it was. Maybe the hound is something it suggests. Whatever it is, it's feeding off the energy which starts to build up in this town, probably at dusk. And it comes in a straight line, from the Tump, through the Court and on towards the church. It's evil, it's . . . cold as the grave.'

Fay shivered inside her robe. 'And this girl was . . . getting off on it?'

'Something like that. When the curfew began, she'd gone. She'd done this before, knew the score.'

'What does that tell us about the curfew?'

'That the curfew was established to ward something off. I think we're talking about Black Michael. Look . . .' He took from his jacket a slim black paperback, *Elizabethan Magic* by Robert Turner. 'I found this in the bread-oven with the Filofax. I nicked it. There's a couple of chapters on Dee, but what I was really interested in was this. The page was marked.'

He opened the book at a chapter headed 'Simon Foreman, Physician, Astrologer and Necromancer (1552–1611)'. There was a picture of Foreman, who had a dense beard and piercing eyes.

'The book talks of a manuscript in Foreman's handwriting, evidently something he copied out, much as Andy did in his Filofax. It's the record of an attempt to summon a spirit, and . . . look . . . this bit.'

> *He cast out much fire and kept up a wonderful ado; but we could not bring him to human form: he was seen like a great black dog and troubled the folk in the house much and feared them.*

'So what it's suggesting,' Powys said, 'is that the black dog image is some kind of intermediary state in the manifestation of an evil spirit. In this case, the spirit's furious at not being able to get any further, so he's coming on with the whole poltergeist bit. There's a famous legend in Herefordshire where a dozen vicars get together to bind this spirit and all that's appeared since is a big black dog.'

'So when we talk about Black Michael's Hound . . .'

'We're probably talking about the ghost of Michael himself. We know from these notes of Andy's – which I'm attributing to John Dee, for want of a more suitable candidate – that Michael Wort, while alive, appeared to have taught himself to leave his body and manifest elsewhere . . . travelling by the "olde road", which is presumably a reference to ley-lines. Spirit paths. And then there's this legend about him escaping by some secret passage when the peasantry arrived to lynch him. Dee, or whoever, records that Wort's body was brought out after he hanged himself, to prove he was indeed dead. So maybe he escaped *out of his body* . . . along the "olde road", maybe his ghost was seen – bringing a lot of black energy with it – and they managed to contain it . . . to reduce it to the black dog stage . . . by some ritual which has at its heart the curfew.'

'How does that stop it?'

'Well, making a lot of noise – banging things, bells, tin-cans, whatever – was popularly supposed to be a way of frightening spirits off. Maybe by altering the vibration rate; I'm not really qualified to say.'

'This is . . .' Fay held on to his hand, 'seriously eerie. I mean, you're the expert, you've been here before, but Christ, it scares the hell out of me.'

'No, I'm not,' he said. 'I'm not any kind of expert. I wrote a daft, speculative book. I'm not as qualified as most of these New Age luminaries. All I know is that Andy Boulton-Trow, with or without Goff's knowledge, is experimenting with what we have to call dark forces. He's probably been doing it for years . . . since . . . Well, never mind. Now we know why Henry Kettle was getting the bad vibes.'

'Boulton-Trow put Goff on to this place?'

'Probably. Something else occurred to me, too. I don't know how much to make of it, but . . . try spelling Trow backwards.'

'Tr . . . ?' Her eyes widened. 'Jesus.'

'I mean, it could be pure coincidence.'

'There are too many coincidences in Crybbe,' Fay said. She stood up. 'OK, what are we going to do about this?'

'I think . . . we need to get everything we can, and quickly, on Michael Wort. Any local historians you know?'

Fay smiled. 'In Crybbe, Joe, an historian is somebody who can remember what it said in last week's paper.'

'What about the local-authority archives? Where, for instance, would we find the transactions of the Radnorshire Society?'

'County Library, I suppose. But that's in Llandrindod Wells.'

'How far?'

'Twenty-five, thirty miles.'

'Let's get over there.' He started to get up. 'Oh God.' Sat down again. 'I can't. I have to go to Hereford Crematorium. It's Henry Kettle's funeral.'

'You can't not go to Henry's funeral,' Fay said. 'Look, *I'll* go to the library. Tell me what we're looking for.'

'You can't drive with that eye.'

'Of course I can. And they're only country roads. What am I looking for?'

'Anything about Wort – his experiments, his hangings, his death. And the Wort family. If they're still around, if we can get hold of any of them. And John Dee. Can we establish a connection? But, I mean, don't make a big deal of it. If we meet back here at . . . what? Four o'clock?'

'OK. Joe, look . . . is there *nobody* we can go to for help?'

'What about Jean Wendle?'

'Ha.' Fay put a hand up to her rainbow eye. 'Her assessment of Grace wasn't up to much, was it? Harmless, eh?'

'We're on our own, then,' Powys said.

CHAPTER IV

CRYBBE town hall was in a short street of its own, behind the square. An absurdly grandiose relic of better days, Colonel Colin 'Col' Croston thought, strolling around the back to the small door through which members of the town council sneaked, as though ashamed of their democratic role.

Tonight, the huge Gothic double doors at the front would be thrown open for the first time in twenty years. Suspecting problems, Col Croston had brought with him this morning a small can of Three-in-One Penetrating Oil to apply to the lock and the hinges.

Col Croston let himself in and strode directly into the council chamber. The cleaner would not be here until this afternoon, and so Col made his way to the top of the room where the high-backed chairman's chair stood on its platform.

He sat down in the chair. There was a pristine green blotter on the table in front of him, and on the blotter lay a wooden gavel, unused – like the chair – since local government reorganization in 1974.

Before reorganization, the rural district authority had been based here. But 'progress' had removed the seat of power to a new headquarters in a town thirty miles away. Now there was only Crybbe town council, a cursory nod to local democracy, with ten members and no staff apart from its part-time clerk, Mrs Byford, who dealt with the correspondence and took down the minutes of its brief and largely inconsequential meetings.

The council chamber itself had even been considered too

big for the old RDC, and meetings of the town council were self-conscious affairs, with eleven people hunched in a corner of the room trying to be inconspicuous. Although their meetings were public, few townsfolk were ever moved to attend.

Tonight, however, it seemed likely the chamber would actually be too small for the numbers in attendance, and the chairman would be occupying, for the first time in nearly twenty years, the official chairman's chair.

The chairman tonight would be Col Croston.

Mrs Byford, the clerk, had telephoned him at home to pass on the Mayor's apologies and request that he steer the public meeting.

'Why, surely,' Col said briskly. 'Can hardly expect old Jim to be there after what's happened.'

'Oh, he'll be there, Colonel,' Mrs Byford said, 'but he'll have to leave soon after nine-thirty to see to the bell, isn't it.'

'Shouldn't have to mess about with that either at his age. All he's got to do is say the word and I'll organize a bunch of chaps and we'll have that curfew handled on a rota system. Makes a lot of sense, Mrs Byford.'

The clerk's tone cooled at once. 'That bell is a *Preece* function, Colonel.'

Oh dear, foot in it again, never mind. 'All got to rally round at a time like this, Mrs Byford. Besides, it could be the first step to getting a proper team of bell-ringers on the job. Crying shame, the way those bells are neglected.'

'It's a Preece function,' Mrs Byford said from somewhere well within the Arctic Circle. 'The meeting starts at eight o'clock.'

Minefield of ancient protocol, this town. Col Croston often felt Goose Green had been somewhat safer.

Col was deputy mayor this year. Long army career (never mentioned the SAS but everybody seemed to know). Recommended for a VC after the Falklands (respectfully suggested it be redirected). But still regarded becoming deputy mayor of Crybbe as his most significant single *coup*, on the grounds of being the only incomer to serve on the town council long enough to achieve the honour – which virtually guaranteed that next year he'd become the first outsider to wear the chain of office.

His wife considered he was out of his mind snuggling deeper into this hotbed of small-minded prejudice and bigotry. But Col thought he was more than halfway to being accepted. And when he made mayor he was going to effect a few tiny but democratically meaningful changes to the way this little council operated – as well as altering the rather furtive atmosphere in which it conducted its affairs.

He often felt that, although it gave a half-hearted welcome to new industry, anything providing local jobs, this council appeared to consider its foremost role was to protect the town against happiness.

Indeed, until being asked to chair it, he'd been rather worried about how tonight's meeting would be handled. He'd been finding out as much as he could about Max Goff's plans and had to say that the New Age people he'd met so far hadn't invariably been the sort of head-in-the-clouds wallies one had feared. If it pulled in a few tourists at last, it could be a real economic shot in the arm for this town.

So Col Croston was delighted to be directing operations.

With a mischievous little smile he lifted the gavel and gave a smart double rap.

'Silence! Silence at the back there!'

Whereupon, to his horror, Mrs Byford materialized in the doorway with a face like a starched pinny.

'I hope, Colonel, that you're banging that thing on the blotter and not on the table.'

'Oh, yes, of course, Mrs Byford. See . . .' He gave it another rap, this time on the blotter. It sounded about half as loud. 'Ha ha. Well, ah . . . your morning for the correspondence, is it?'

Mrs Byford stalked pointedly to the corner table used for town council meetings and placed upon it the official town council attaché case.

'Glad you came in, actually,' Col Croston said. 'I think we ought to send an official letter of condolence to the relatives of that poor girl who had the accident at the Court.'

'I see no necessity for that.' Mrs Byford began to unpack her case.

442

'There's no *necessity*, Mrs B. Just think it'd be a sympathetic thing to do, don't you?'

'Not my place to give an opinion, Colonel. I should think twice, though, if I were you, about making unauthorized use of council notepaper.'

Col Croston, who'd once made a disastrous attempt to form a Crybbe cricket club, estimated that if he bowled the gavel at the back of Mrs Byford's head, there'd be a fair chance of laying the old boot out.

Just a thought.

It was Bill Davies, the butcher, who rang Jimmy Preece to complain about the picture. 'I'm sorry to 'ave to bother you at a time like this, Jim, but I think you should go and see it for yourself. I know you know more about these things than any of us, but I don't like the look of it. Several customers mentioned it, see. How *is* Jack now?'

'Jack's not good,' Jimmy Preece said, and put the phone down.

He could see trouble coming, been seeing it all the morning, in the calm of the fields and the weight of the clouds.

In the cold, gleeful eyes of his surviving grandson.

Ten minutes after talking to Bill Davies, the Mayor was walking across the square towards The Gallery, traders and passers-by nodding to him sorrowfully. Nobody said, ''Ow're you'. They all knew where he was going.

Even in today's profoundly pessimistic mood, he was not prepared for the picture in the window of The Gallery. He had to turn away and get some control of himself.

Then, face like parchment, he pushed through the pine-panelled door with its panes of bull's-eye glass.

The woman with too much make-up and a too-tight blouse opened her red lips at him. 'Oh. Mr Preece, isn't it? I'm so terribly, terribly . . .'

'Madam!' Mr Preece, his heart wrapped in ice, had seen in the gloating eyes of the yellow-haloed man in the picture that the accident to Jack and the drowning of Jonathon were only the start of it. This was what *they*'d done with their meddling and their New Age rubbish.

'That picture in the window. Where'd 'e come from?'

'My husband brought it back from Devon. Why, is there . . . ?'

'Did 'e,' Mr Preece said heavily. 'Brought it back from Devon, is it?'

Couldn't stop himself.

'Devon . . . ? Devon . . . ?'

Saw the woman's lips make a colossal great 'O' as he raised a hand and brought it down with an almighty bang on the thick, smoked-glass counter.

The cremation was at twelve, and Powys was late. He felt bad about this because there was barely a dozen people there. He spotted Henry's neighbour, Mrs Whitney. He noted the slight, unassuming figure of another distinguished elder statesman of dowsing. And there was his old mate Ben Corby, now publishing director of Dolmen, newly acquired by Max Goff.

'Bloody minister never even mentioned dowsing,' Ben said.

It had been a swift, efficient service. No sermon. Nothing too religious, *nothing psychic*.

Powys said, 'I don't think Henry would have wanted to be wheeled in under an arch of hazel twigs, do you?'

'Too modest, Joe. All the bloody same, these dowsers. Look at old Bill over there – he wouldn't do me a book either.'

Powys smiled. 'Henry left me his papers.'

'In that case, *you* can do the book. *The Strange Life of Henry Kettle*, an official biography by his literary executor. How's that? Come and have a drink, my train back to Paddington's at ten past two.'

Ben Corby. Plump and balding Yorkshireman, the original New Age hussler. They went to a pub called the Restoration and sat at a window-table overlooking a traffic island with an old stone cross on it.

'Golden Land Two,' said Ben. 'How long? A year?'

Not the time, Powys thought, to tell him there wasn't going to be a book.

'Seen Andy lately?' he asked.

'Great guy, Max,' Ben said. 'Best thing that could've happened to Dolmen. Been burdened for years with the wispy beard brigade, wimps who reckon you can't be enlightened *and* make money. Give me the white suit and the chequebook any day. The New Age movement's got to seize the world by the balls.'

'Andy,' Powys said patiently. 'You seen him recently?'

'Andy? Pain in the arse. He wouldn't write me a book either. He's always been an élitist twat. Hates the New Age movement, thinks earth mysteries are not for the masses . . . But, there you go, he knows his stuff; I gather he's giving Max good advice.'

'Maybe he's just using Max.'

'Everybody uses everybody, Joe. It's a holistic society.'

'How did Andy get involved?'

Ben shrugged. 'I know he was teaching art at one of the local secondary schools. Had a house in the area for years, apparently.'

That made sense. Had he really thought Andy was living in a run-down woodland cottage with no sanitation?

But why teaching? Teaching what?

'Andy's hardly short of cash.'

'Maybe he hit on hard times,' said Ben. 'Maybe he felt he had a duty to nurture young minds.'

Young minds. Powys thought of the girl at the stone. And then a man leaned over and tapped him on the shoulder.

'Excuse me, Mr Powys, could I have a word? Peter Jarman, Mr Kettle's solicitor.'

Peter Jarman looked about twenty-five; without his glasses he'd have looked about seventeen. He steered Powys into a corner. 'Uncle Henry,' he said. 'We all called him Uncle Henry. My grandfather was his solicitor for about half a century. Did you get my letter?'

Powys shook his head. 'I've been away.'

'No problem. I can expand on it a little now. Uncle Henry's daughter, as you may have noticed, hasn't come back from Canada for his funeral. He didn't really expect her to, which, I suspect, is why he's left his house to you.'

'Bloody hell. He really did that?'

'Seems she's done quite well for herself, the daughter, over in Canada. And communicated all too rarely with Uncle Henry. He seems to have thought you might value the house more than she would. This is all rather informal, but there *are* formalities, so if you *could* make an appointment to come to the office.'

'Yes,' Powys said faintly. 'Sure.'

'In the meantime,' said young Mr Jarman, 'if you want to get into the cottage at any time, Mrs Whitney next door is authorized to let you in. Uncle Henry was very specific that you should have access to any of his books or papers at any time.'

'You told me,' Jocasta Newsome said, suppressing her emotions, but not very well, 'that you hadn't managed to buy much in the West Country, and you proceeded to prove it with that mediocre miniature by Dufort.'

Hereward nervously fingered his beard. Now that it was almost entirely grey, he'd been considering shaving the thing off. As a statement, it was no longer sufficiently emphatic.

The black beard of the dark-eyed figure in the picture seemed to mock him.

'Where did it come from, Hereward?'

'All right,' he snapped, 'it wasn't from the West. A local artist sold it to me.'

Jocasta planted her hands on her hips. 'Girl?'

'Well . . . young woman.'

'Get rid of it,' Jocasta said, not a request, not a suggestion.

'Don't be ridiculous.'

'Take it back. Now.'

'What the hell's the matter with you? It's a bloody good painting! Worth eight or nine hundred of anybody's money, and that's what Max Goff's going to pay!'

'So if Goff's going to pay the money, what's it doing in our window upsetting everybody?'

'One man!' He couldn't believe this.

'The Mayor of this town, Hereward. Who was so distressed he nearly cracked my counter.'

'But . . .' Hereward clutched his head, 'he's the *Mayor*! Not a bloody cultural arbiter! Not some official civic censor! He's just a tin-pot, small-town . . . I mean, how *dare* the old fuck come in here, complaining about a picture which isn't even . . . an erotic nude or . . . or something. What's his problem?'

'He calmed down after slapping the counter,' Jocasta admitted. 'He apologized. He then appealed to me very sincerely – for the future well-being of the town, he said – not to flaunt a picture which appeared to be heralding the return of someone called Black Michael, who was apparently the man who built Crybbe Court and was very unpopular in his day.'

'He actually said that? In the year nineteen hundred and ninety-three, the first citizen of this town – the most senior *elected* member of the town council – seriously said *that*?'

'Words to that effect. And I agreed. I told him it would be removed immediately from the window and off these premises by tonight. I apologized and told him my husband obviously didn't realize when he purchased it – "in the West Country" – that it might cause offence.'

For a moment, Hereward was speechless. When his voice returned, it was hoarse with outraged incredulity.

'How dare you? How bloody *dare* you? Black bloody Michael? What is this . . . bilge? I tell you, if this gallery is to have any artistic integrity . . .'

'Hereward, it's going,' Jocasta said, bored with him. 'I don't like that girl, she's a troublemaker. I don't like her weird paintings, *and I want this one out.*'

'Well, I can't help you there,' Hereward said flatly. 'I promised it would stay in the window until tomorrow.'

Jocasta regarded him as she would something she'd scraped from her shoe. It occurred to him seriously, for the first time, that perhaps he *was* something she'd like to scrape from her shoe. In which case, the issue of his failed trip to the West, his attempt to recover ground by buying this painting on the artist's eccentric terms, all this would be used to humiliate him again and again.

She turned her back on him and as she stalked away, Hereward saw her hook the tip of one shoe behind the leg of the wooden easel on which sat the big, dark picture.

He tried to save it. As he lunged towards the toppling easel, Jocasta half-turned and, seeing his hands clawing out, must have thought they were clawing at her. So she struck first. Hereward felt the nails pierce his cheek, just under his right eye.

It was instinctive. His left hand came back and he hit her so hard with his open palm that she was thrown off her feet and into a corner of the window, where she lay with her nose bleeding, snorting blood splashes on to her cream silk blouse.

There was silence.

A bunch of teenage boys just off the school bus, home early after end-of-term exams, gathered outside the window and grinned in at Jocasta.

The picture of the unsmiling man with the yellow halo in the doorway of Crybbe Court had fallen neatly and squarely in the centre of the floor and was undamaged. Its darkness flooded the gallery and Hereward Newsome knew his marriage and his plans for a successful and fashionable outlet in Crybbe were both as good as over.

Assessing his emotions, much later, he would decide he'd been not so much sad as angry and bitter at the way a seedy little town could turn a civilized man into a savage.

Jocasta didn't get up. She took a tissue from a pocket in the front of her summery skirt and dabbed carefully at her nose.

Hereward knew there was blood also on his torn cheek. He didn't touch it.

Outside, the schoolkids began to drift away. Jocasta had her back against the window, unaware of them.

Still she made no attempt to get up, only said calmly, voice nasally blocked, as if she had a cold, 'I accepted some drawings from that girl a few days ago. Sale or return. Do you remember them?'

'I didn't make the connection,' Hereward said quietly.

'They were drawings of an old man.'

'I didn't see them.'

'He was cutting his own throat.'

'Yes,' Hereward said dully. '. . . *What*?'

'The reason I don't want this painting here is that the other night, while you were away, the figure, the likeness of this old man, the old man in the drawings, was seen in our bathroom.'

Hereward said nothing.

'Not by me, of course,' his wife assured him. 'But the man I was sleeping with swears it was there.'

Everything was completely still in The Gallery. Hereward Newsome stunned, aware of a droplet of blood about to fall from his chin. Jocasta Newsome lying quietly in the window, red splashes like rose petals on her cream silk blouse.

CHAPTER V

FAY had a whole pile of books and just two short names. She was alone in the reading room of the County Library in Llandrindod Wells, nearly thirty rural miles from Crybbe and another world: bright, spacy streets, a spa town.

Two names: Wort and Dee.

Fortunately there was an index to the dozens of volumes of transactions of the Radnorshire Society, a huge collection of many decades of articles by mainly amateur scholars, exploring aspects of the social, political and natural history of the most sparsely populated county in southern Britain.

There were also books on Tudor history and three biographies of John Dee (1527–1608) whose family came from Radnorshire.

She read of a farmhouse, Nant-y-groes, once the Dee family home, at Pilleth, six miles from Crybbe. But it had, apparently, been demolished and rebuilt and was now unrecognizable as Elizabethan.

Dee himself had been born in the south-east of England but had always been fascinated by his Welsh border ancestry. The name Dee, it seemed, had probably developed from the Welsh *Du* meaning black.

History, Fay discovered, had not been over-generous to this

mathematician, astronomer and expert on navigation – perhaps because of his principle role as astrologer to the court of Elizabeth I and his lifelong obsession with magic and spiritualism. Most schoolchildren learned about Walter Raleigh and Francis Bacon, but John Dee hardly figured on the syllabus, despite having carried out major intelligence operations in Europe, on behalf of the Queen, during periods of Spanish hostility.

Two hours' superficial reading convinced Fay that John Dee was basically sound. He studied 'natural magic' – a search for an intelligence behind nature. But there was no serious evidence, despite many contemporary and subsequent attempts to smear him, of any involvement in black magic.

Dee wanted to know eternal secrets, the ones he believed no human intelligence could pass on. He sought communion with spirits and 'angels', for which a medium was required.

Fay read of several professed psychics, who sometimes turned out to be less well-intentioned than he was. People like the very dubious Sir Edward Kelley, who once claimed the spirits had suggested that, in order to realize their full human potential, he and Dee should swap wives.

Now *that*, Fay thought, was the kind of scam Guy might try to pull.

But there was no mention of Dee working with Sir Michael Wort in Radnorshire.

She skipped over all the weird, impenetrable stuff about Dee's so-called Angelic Conversations and went back to the Radnorshire transactions.

It emerged that while Dee himself might not have been a medium he clearly was, like Henry Kettle, an expert dowser.

In 1574, he wrote to Elizabeth's Lord Treasurer, Lord Burghley, requesting permission to seek 'hidden treasure' using a method that was scientific rather than magical (nothing psychic, Fay smiled) involving a particular type of rod.

He was also most interested in folklore and local customs, druidic lore and landscape patterns.

OK. Speculation time.

If there were such things as ley-lines, the mounds and stones which defined them must have been far more in evidence in Dee's time.

If ley-lines had psychic properties, Dee's interest in the remains would have been of a more than antiquarian nature.

If he'd been in the area in the 1570s he could hardly have failed to run into Wort.

If Dee felt that Wort had knowledge or psychic abilities he lacked, he might have been inclined to overlook the sheriff's less savoury practices.

Fay looked up Wort and found only passing references. No mention of hangings. His name was in a chronological list of high sheriffs, and that was all.

She looked up Trow and found nothing. She looked in the local telephone directories, found several Worts and several Trows, noted down numbers.

Then she simply looked up Crybbe and found surprisingly little, apart from references to the curfew, with the usual stuff about the legacy of Percy Weale, a mention of the town hall as one of the finest in the area.

Had Crybbe received so little attention because, for much of its history, it had been in England? Or was it, as she'd intimated to Powys, because local historians weren't too thick on the ground.

It was almost as though nobody *wanted* the place to have a history.

And so Fay emerged from the library with only one significant piece of information.

It came from a brief mention of Crybbe Court in an article dated 1962 about the few surviving manor houses of Radnorshire. Crybbe Court, which the writer said was in dire need of extensive restoration, had been built in the 1570s by a local landowner, Sir Michael Wort, who later served as High Sheriff of the county and who lived there *until his death in the summer of 1593*.

It was precisely four centuries since the hanging of Black Michael.

'Oh, what the hell,' Colonel Col Croston said. 'Don't see why not.'

'I'm really very grateful,' Guy told him.

It was the first piece of genuine co-operation to come his way. Well, from the locals, anyway. Whether you could call this chap a local was highly debatable, but he *was* the deputy mayor.

As soon as Guy had found out that the public meeting wasn't, after all, going to be chaired by old Preece, he'd driven off by himself to the deputy's home, a partly renovated Welsh long-house across the river, about a mile out of town on the Ludlow road.

Col Croston had turned out to be an affable, pale-eyed, sparse-haired, athletic-looking chap in his fifties. He lived quite untidily with a couple of labradors, who rather resembled him, and a tough-looking little wife who didn't. There was a mechanical digger working on a trench fifty yards or so from the house. 'Try and ignore the smell,' the Colonel had greeted him breezily. 'Spot of bother with the old septic tank.'

What the deputy mayor had just agreed was to let Guy shoot a few minutes of videotape in the meeting before it actually started, so there would at least be some pictures of an assembly of townsfolk and councillors. Guy would milk this opportunity for character close-ups of the taciturn, grizzled faces of Old Crybbe.

His heart lurched. He wished he hadn't thought of grizzled old faces. With bulbous noses and bulging eyes and blood fountains from severed arteries.

'And . . . er . . . Colonel,' he said hurriedly. 'What I'd also like, if you have no objections, is a little interview with you, possibly before and after, outlining the issues – the town's attitudes to becoming a major New Age centre.'

'Well, I'll do my best, Guy. But I must say, one of the things I was hoping to learn in there tonight is what exactly New Age *is*. Drink?'

'Thanks, just a small one. You like it here, Colonel?'

'Col. Name's Colin. Well, you know, got to settle somewhere. No, it's not a bad place. Once one gets used to their little peculiarities. Like the dogs – used to take these chaps into town of a morning, pick up the paper, that kind of thing. Always well-behaved, never chase anything. But a word or two was said and now I walk them in the other direction. Compromise, you see. Secret of survival in the sticks. I don't mind.'

'So if I were to ask you how people here feel about Max Goff and . . .'

'Ho!' said Mrs Croston, passing through, wearing a stained boiler suit.

'Ruth's not terribly impressed with Mr Goff,' Col said. 'My own feeling is it's no bad thing at all, long as it doesn't get out of hand. You've got to have an economy, and this place has ignored the possibilities of tourism and that kind of business for too long. Agriculture's going down the chute so, on the whole, I think we're quite fortunate to have him.'

'Will you say that on camera?'

'Oh . . . why not? Long as it's clear I'm speaking personally, not on behalf of the council.'

'Super,' Guy said. 'Now what about all these prehistoric stones Goff's sticking in the ground?'

'Ah well, there've been rumblings there, I have to say. Fine by me, but country folk are incredibly superstitious. Who, after all, got rid of the original stones? Money, however – money does tend to overcome quite a lot, doesn't it? But I wouldn't be at all surprised if some of them started disappearing again.'

'Interesting,' Guy said. 'So you think there'll be fireworks in there tonight.'

Col laughed. 'Will there be disagreement? Oh yes. Will there be suspicion, resentment, resistance? Definitely. Fireworks? Well, they'll listen very patiently to what Goff has to say, then they'll ask one or two very polite questions before drifting quietly away into the night. And then, just as quietly, they'll do their best to shaft the blighter. That's how things are done in Crybbe. If they don't like you, best to keep the removal van on standby with the engine running.'

'Doesn't sound as if it would have made very good telly, in that case, even if we got in.'

'Excruciatingly boring telly,' Col confirmed. 'Unless you've got some sort of infra-red equipment capable of filming undercurrents. 'Nother one?'

'No . . . no thanks.' Guy covered his glass with a hand.

'Sounds like you have this place pretty well weighed up, Col.'

'Good Lord, no. Only been here a few years. That's just about long enough to realize one needs to've been established here a good six generations to even get close to it. Annoy the hell out of me, these newcomers who profess to be like that' – Col hooked two fingers together – 'with the locals after a month or two. I know where I stand, and I don't mind. We've got an interesting home with about fourteen acres I'm still trying to decide what to do with. And I'm the token outsider on the council, which is just about as close as anyone can aspire to get. When I'm Mr Mayor I'll try to effect a few minor structural changes on the council which will doubtless disappear when the next chap takes over. Mrs Byford will see to that – she's the clerk. Mayors come and go, Mrs B doesn't.'

'Is that Tessa Byford's mother?' Guy watched the Colonel's eyes.

'Grandmother.' No specific reaction. 'The girl, Tessa, lives with them. What they call in Crybbe a problem child. Shows a lot of promise as an artist, apparently – that's not a very Crybbe thing to be, as you'll have realized. She'll leave, go to college and never come back. They all do.'

'All?'

'Anybody who doesn't want to be a farmer or a shopkeeper or some such. Sad, but that's the way it tends to be.'

'Ah,' said Guy, 'but will she move away *now* – now there's a place for artistic types? Now Crybbe looks set to become a little melting pot for ideas and creativity?'

'Look, Guy, creativity and ideas have always been frowned upon in Crybbe – and, before you ask, no, I certainly won't say any of *that* on camera. 'Nother drink, did I ask you?'

Graham Jarrett was just too smooth, too confident. Powys didn't trust him. He'd wander down to your subconscious like he owned the fishing rights.

'I assure you,' Jarrett insisted, 'that this is on the level. I've checked dates, I've checked what facts I can and . . . Now, here's something . . . The Bull. The girl said she lived at the

Bull, and as you know there's no such pub in Crybbe any more.
But I've discovered the Bull was actually the original name of
the Cock. And that's not a cock-and-bull story . . .' Graham
Jarrett straightened his cardigan. 'I have it on very reliable
authority.'

He'd given Powys a transcript of the Catrin tape without
argument, because Graham Jarrett wanted to be in The Book,
didn't he?

'OK, how many other cases have you encountered where
the subject is regressed to the very same town where the
regression is taking place?'

'It's been known. Very often they specifically return to a
town because they feel they've been there before.'

'But she didn't. She came here to work.'

Jarrett opened his hands. 'Stranger things . . .'

'Yeah, OK. But you've got a situation here where one personality is fading and another just forces its way in over the
top, right?'

Graham Jarrett shrank back into the dark-green drapery of
his consulting room. Powys was sure there must be more on
the tape than there was on the transcript. Jarrett claimed he'd
given the cassette to Guy, but he wouldn't have done that before
making a copy.

'I know what you're going to suggest, Joe.'

'Well?'

'Don't. Don't even use that word "possession" in here.'

There was a bonus for Guy in his visit to Col Croston's
house. He'd raised the matter of the suicide, the old man
and the razor, less inhibited about it now and less intimidated
by it as time went on. There'd been no disturbance in his
room at the Cock last night, unless one included Catrin's shrill
moments of ecstasy. Catrin had been quite amazing. With the
light out.

'No,' Col Croston said. 'Can't say I have.' But he'd referred
the question to his wife, neither of them, fortunately, seeming
over-curious about Guy's interest in local suicides.

'I know,' Mrs Croston had said. 'Why not ask Gomer? Gomer knows everything.'

The little man working on the soakaway to the Crostons' septic tank had been only too happy to come out of his trench for a chat. There was a disgustingly ripe smell in the vicinity of the trench and Guy found that he and Gomer Parry were very soon left alone.

'Good chap, the Colonel,' Gomer said. "Ad this other job lined up, over to Brynglas, see, and it was postponed, last minute. Straightaway, the Colonel says, you stick around, boy, do my soakaway. Fills in two days perfect. Very considerate man, the Colonel.'

It didn't take him long to get a reaction on the suicide. Unlike most people in this area, Gomer appeared to have a healthy appetite for the unpleasant.

'Handel Roberts.' Gomer beamed. 'Sure to be.'

And who precisely was Handel Roberts?

'Copper,' said Gomer. 'While back now. I wasn't so old, but I remember Handel Roberts all right. Didn't Wynford tell you about this? No, I s'pose 'e wouldn't. Coppers, see. They don't gossip about their own.'

Gomer broke off to wipe something revolting from his glasses with an oily rag.

He blinked at Guy. 'That's better. Aye, Handel Roberts. He was station sergeant, see, like Wynford. Only there was twice as many police in them days, before there was any crime to speak of – there's logic, isn't it? Well, this was the time they'd built the new police 'ouses as part of the council estate. And it comes to Handel retiring and the County Police lets him carry on living in the old police 'ouse, peppercorn rent, sort of thing, everybody happy. Until – I forget the details – but some new police authority takes over and they decides the old police 'ouse is worth a bob or two so they'll sell it.'

Guy could see where this was going. Old Handel Roberts, unable to afford the place, no savings, nowhere to go.

Nowhere but the bathroom.

'Ear to ear,' Gomer said with a big grin. 'Blood everywhere. But 'e 'ad the last laugh, the old boy did. They couldn't sell the police 'ouse after that, not for a long time. And then it was a cheap job, see. Billy Byford 'ad it for peanuts. Newly wed at the time – Nettie played 'ell, wouldn't move in till Billy stripped that bathroom back to the bare brick, put in new basin, bath, lavvy.'

Guy said delicately, 'And he still, er, that is Handel Roberts, was believed to haunt the place, I gather.'

'Well, you're better informed than what I am,' Gomer said. 'Anything funny going on there, Nettie'd've been off like a rabbit. Oh hell, aye. Want me to tell you all this for the telly cameras? No problem, just gimme time to get cleaned up, like.'

'No, no . . . just something I needed to check.'

'Anything else you wanner know, you'll find me around most of the week. 'Ad this job lined up with the council, but it's been put back, so I'm available, see, any time.'

'That's very kind of you indeed, Gomer. I won't hesitate. Oh, there is one final thing . . . Handel Roberts, what did he look like?'

Gomer indulged in a long sniff. He seemed immune to the appalling stench from the soakaway.

'Big nose is all I remember, see. Hell of a big nose.'

Powys drove to Fay's house, but there was no one in. He didn't know where else to go, so he sat there in the Mini, in Bell Street. It was two-thirty. He'd bought some chips for lunch and ended up dumping most of them in a litter bin, feeling sick.

He'd learned from Graham Jarrett that Rachel's body had been sent for burial to her parents' home – somewhere in Essex, Jarrett thought. He ought to find out, send flowers, with a message.

Saying what? *I think I know why you died, Rachel. You died because of a cat. A cat placed in the rafters to ward off evil spirits. You died because a four-hundred-year-old dead cat can't hurl itself from the building. Because somebody has to be holding it and, unfortunately for you, nobody else was around at the time.*

The Bottle Stone was no more than a sick coincidence, albeit the kind that questioned the whole nature of coincidence.

But the cat had been part of the ritual procedure to prevent something returning. Before the spirit could regain its occupancy, the cat had to go.

Just a little formality.

Powys took a tight hold of the steering wheel.

I am not a crank.

CHAPTER VI

Powys waited half an hour for Fay. She didn't show. He couldn't blame her if she'd just taken off somewhere for the night or possibly for ever, she and Arnold, battle-scarred refugees from the Old Golden Land.

Leaving him to convince Goff that the Crybbe project was a blueprint for a small-scale Armageddon.

On impulse, he started the car and drove slowly through the town towards the Court.

The afternoon was dull and humid. The buildings bulged, as though the timber frames were contracting, squeezing the bricks into dust. And the people on the streets looked drained and zombified, as if debilitated by some organic power failure affecting the central nervous system or the blood supply.

Which made Powys think of Fay's dad, the old Canon, whose blood supply had been impeded but who now was fast becoming a symbol of the efficacy of New Age spiritual healing.

Maybe everybody here could use a prescription from Jean Wendle's Dr Chi. Maybe, in fact, Jean, the acceptable, self-questioning face of the New Age, was the person he ought to be talking to this afternoon.

But first he would find Goff and, with any luck, Andy too. Sooner or later Andy had to resurface. It seemed very unlikely, for instance, that he wouldn't be at tonight's public meeting.

Rachel had said Goff was 'besotted with Boulton-Trow'. If

here was indeed a sexual element, that would mean complications. But Goff wasn't stupid.

However, even as he drove into the lane beside the church he was getting cold feet about making a direct approach to Goff, and when he arrived at the Court he saw why it was useless.

Something had changed. Something with its beginnings, perhaps, in an effluvial flickering in the eaves two nights ago.

Powys drove out of the wood, between the gateposts and, when the court came into view, he had to stop the car.

You didn't have to be psychic to experience it.

Where, before, it had worn this air of dereliction, of crumbling neglect, of seeping decay – the atmosphere which had caused Henry Kettle to record in his journal,

> . . . *the Court is a dead place, no more than a shell. I can't get anything from the Court.*

– it was now a distinct and awesome presence, as if its ancient foundations had been reinforced, its Elizabethan stonework strengthened. As if it was rising triumphantly from its hollow, the old galleon finally floating free from the mud-flats.

He knew that, structurally, nothing at all had altered, that he was still looking at the building he'd first seen less than a week ago as a shambling pile of neglect.

It had simply been restored to life.

Its power supply reconnected.

Occupancy regained.

There was a glare from the rear-view mirror. The Mini was stopped in the middle of the narrow drive, blocking the path of a big, black sports car. Goff's Ferrari, headlights flashing. As Powys released the handbrake, prepared to get out of the way, the Ferrari's driver's door opened and Goff squeezed out, raising a hand.

Powys switched the engine off.

'J.M.! Where ya been?'

Goff, untypically, was in a dark double-breasted suit over a white open-necked shirt. He looked strong and, for a man of his girth, buoyantly fit.

'You're a very elusive guy, J.M. I've been calling you on the phone, putting out messages. Listen, that problem with the cops . . . that's sorted out now?'

'I'd like to think so, Max.'

'Fucking arsehole cops can't see further than the end of their own truncheons. They got so little real crime to amuse them in these parts, they can't accept a tragic accident for what it is.'

Powys said nothing. He was pretty sure Goff must have known about him and Rachel.

'Listen,' Goff said, 'the reason I've been trying to track you down – I need you at the meeting tonight. I don't anticipate problems, I think the majority of people in Crybbe are only too glad to see the place get a new buzz. But . . . *but* I'm the first to recognize they might find me a little – how can I put this? – overwhelming? Larger than life? Larger than *their* lives, anyhow. You, on the other hand . . . you're a downbeat kind of guy, J.M. Nobody's gonna call you flash, nobody's gonna call you weird.'

'That a compliment, Max?'

Goff laughed delightedly and clapped Powys on the shoulder. 'Just be there, J.M. I might need you.'

Powys nodded compliantly, then said casually, 'Where's Andy these days, Max?'

Goff's little eyes went watchful. 'He's around.'

'Just for the record . . . this whole idea, the idea of coming to Crybbe. That was Andy's, wasn't it?'

'It was mine,' Goff said coldly.

'But you did know about Andy's ancestral links with the Court?'

Dangerous ground, Powys. Watch his eyes.

Goff said, 'You got a problem with that?'

'I was just intrigued that nobody talks about it.'

'Maybe that's not yet something you advertise.' Goff went quiet, obviously thinking something over. Then he put a hand on Powys's shoulder.

'J.M., come over here.' He steered Powys into the centre of the drive, to where the Court opened out before them like

460

an enormous pop-up book. 'Will you look at that? I mean really look.'

Powys did, and felt, uncomfortably, that the house was looking back at him.

'J.M., this was once the finest house in the county. Not that it had much competition – this part of the border's never been a wealthy area – but it was something to be envied. You can imagine what it musta been like. This introverted, taciturn region where, by tradition, survival means keeping your head down. And this guy builds a flaming *palace*. Well, jeez – to these people, they're looking at a Tower of Babel situation. Here's a guy who takes a pride in the place he lives, who loves this countryside, who wants to make a statement about that. They couldn't get a handle on any of it, these working farmers, these . . . *peasants*.'

Powys said, to get the name out, 'Sir Michael Wort.'

'Listen, this guy has been seriously maligned.'

'He hanged people.'

'Goddamn it, J.M., *all* high sheriffs hanged people.'

'In the attic?'

'Arguably more humane than public execution. But, yeah, OK, that was the other thing about him they couldn't handle. He was a scientist. And a philosopher. He wanted to know where he came from and where he was going to. He wanted to find – what's that phrase? – the active force . . .'

'The force above human reason which is the active principle in nature.'

'Yeah.'

'Definition of natural magic. John Dee.'

'Yeah. I got this Oxford professor who's so eminent I don't get to name him till he comes through with it, but this guy's doing a definitive paper on the collaboration between John Dee and Wort. Has access to a whole pile of hitherto unknown correspondence.'

'From the Wort side?' Powys thought of Andy's Filofax, wondered whether the professor had been given *all* the correspondence.

'Maybe. Yeah. Maybe, also, some of Dee's papers that came

into Wort's possession, all authenticated material. This is heavy stuff, J.M. Point is, you can imagine how the people hereabouts reacted to it back in the sixteenth century?'

'Pretty much the way some of them are reacting to your ideas now, I should have thought.' Powys wondering how Dee's private notes – if that was what they were – had fallen into Wort's hands. Unless Wort had taken steps to acquire them in order to remove any proof of the collaboration.

'They drove Wort to suicide, the people around here. A witch hunt by ignorant damn peasants, threatening to burn down the Court.' Goff stood up straight, his back to his domain. 'Tell you one thing, J.M. No fucker's gonna threaten to burn *me* out.'

'You do have this one small advantage. You haven't hanged anybody. Yet.'

Goff laughed. 'You really wanna know about this hanging stuff, doncha? Listen, how many people get the opportunity to study precisely what happens when life is extinguished? When the spirit leaves the body?'

'Doctors do. Priests do.'

Goff shook his head. 'They got other things on their minds. The doctor's trying to save the dying person, the priest's trying to comfort him or whatever else priests do, last rites kinda stuff.'

Powys saw Goff's eyes go curiously opaque.

'Only the watcher at the execution can be entirely dispassionate,' Goff said. Powys could tell he was echoing someone else. 'Only he can truly observe.'

CHAPTER VII

O N a helter-skelter hill road, a mile and a half out of Crybbe, there was a spot where you could park near a wicket gate with a public-footpath sign. The path, quite short, linked up with the Offa's Dyke long-distance footpath and was itself a famous viewpoint. From just the other side of the gate, you could look across about half the town. You could see the church tower and the edge of the square, with one corner of the Cock. You could see the slow, silvery river.

From up here, under a sporadic sprinkling of sunlight from a deeply textured sky, Crybbe looked venerable, self-contained and almost dignified.

It was nearly 5 p.m.

They'd come out here because there were secrets to exchange which neither felt could be exchanged in Crybbe; there was always a feeling that the town itself would eavesdrop.

When Powys had returned to Bell Street, Fay had been in her car outside, with Arnold. 'Dad's not back yet. Tried to steel myself to go in. Couldn't do it alone. Feeble woman chickens out.'

'Well, if you've left anything in there that you want *me* to fetch,' he said, 'forget it.'

'I suspect you're being indirectly patronizing there, Powys, but I'll let it go.'

Her eye actually looked worse, the rainbow effect quite spectacular. Part of the healing process, no doubt. He was surprised how glad he was to see her again.

Although there must be no involvement. Not this time.

Up here the air was fresher, and a gust of wind carrying a few drops of rain, hit them like a sneeze. It was unexpected and blew Arnold over; he got up again, looking disgruntled.

'I'm beginning to feel I'm part of Andy's game,' Joe Powys said. 'Suppose he left all that stuff in the bread-oven for me to find, to give me a chance to figure it all out – while knowing there was nothing I could do about it.'

'And *have* you figured it out?'

'Black Andy,' Powys said. 'I mean . . . Black Andy? How can anyone called Andy possibly be evil? Andy Hitler, Andy Capone. Andy the Hun, Andy the Ripper.'

'So you're convinced now. It's Andy Wort?'

'Families often change their name if something's brought it into disrepute. Why shouldn't they simply reverse it?'

'I made some enquiries. That's why I was late. There are no Worts left in Crybbe. What remained of the family seemed to have sold up everything – well, *nearly* everything, and moved down to the West Country. As for the Bottle Stone . . .'

'Please,' Powys said. 'Let's not . . . I think that whole episode was Andy trying out his emergent skills, weaving a fantasy around a stone, creating a black magic ritual, seeing what happened.'

'Yes, but . . .'

'Look down there,' Powys said. 'Goff's prehistoric theme park. The old stones back in place.'

They could see a sizeable megalith at a point where the river curved like a sickle.

'On that bit of tape you played me, Henry was puzzled by a standing stone he'd located because it didn't seem to be an *old* stone. He recorded the same problem in his journal. Experienced dowsers can date a stone with the pendulum, asking it questions – too complicated to explain, but it seems to work. Anyway, Henry noted that he couldn't date this particular stone back beyond 1593 . . . *when it was destroyed.*'

'After Wort's death. The townsfolk destroyed the stones after his death.'

'Perhaps they were advised to . . . to stop him coming back along the spirit paths. But the point is . . . perhaps Henry couldn't date the thing earlier than 1593 *because that was also when it was erected.*'

There was another gust of wind and the blue cagoule Fay carried under her arm billowed behind her like a wind-sock.

'*Wort* erected the old stones of Crybbe. They weren't prehistoric at all. He was marking out his own spirit paths, along which he believed he could travel outside of his body.'

'Are we saying here that Wort – perhaps in collaboration with John Dee – had created his own ley-lines . . . ?'

'Look,' Powys said. 'There's this growing perception of leys as ghost roads . . . paths reserved for the spirits . . . therefore, places where you could contact spirits. Sacred arteries linking two worlds – or two states of consciousness. New Agers say they're energy lines – in their eternal quest for something uplifting, they're discarding the obvious: leys tend to link up a number of burial sites – tumps, barrows, cemeteries, this kind of thing.'

'No healing rays?'

Powys shrugged. 'Whether this rules out the energy-line theory I don't know – we might just be talking about a different kind of energy. There's certainly a lot of evidence of psychic phenomena along leys or at points where they cross. And ghosts need energy to manifest, so we're told.'

'And Crybbe, for some reason, has all these curious pockets of energy, fluctuations causing power cuts, all this . . .'

'I'd be interested to know how many people in Crybbe have seen a ghost or experienced something unnatural. Hundreds I'd guess. Especially along the main line, which comes down from the Tump, through the Court, the church, the square . . . and along the passage leading to your studio. I'm surprised nothing strange has happened to you in there, with this kind of hermetically sealed broadcasting area.'

'Maybe it has.'

'Oh?'

'I don't think I want to talk about it,' Fay said, tasting Electrovoice microphone. 'Look . . .' She spread out the cagoule on the damp grass at the edge of a small escarpment overlooking the town. She patted it. They both sat down.

'Let's not mess about any more,' Fay said. 'We're not kids. We've both had some distinctly unpleasant experiences in this town. Let's not be clever, or pseudo-scientific about this. Let's not talk about light effects or atmospheric anomalies. I've had it with all that bullshit. So. In simple, colloquial English, what's actually happening here?'

She looked down on Crybbe. The sky had run out of sunlight, and it was once again a mean, cramped little town surrounded by pleasant, rolling countryside, to which the inhabitants seemed entirely oblivious. Almost as if they were deliberately turning their backs on it all, living simple, functional lives on the lowest practical level, without joy, without beauty, without humour, without any particular faith, without . . .

'I've had a thought about the Crybbe mentality,' Fay said. 'But you're the expert, you go first.'

'OK,' Powys said. 'This is what I think. I reckon Andy's got hold of a collection of family papers – may have had them years for all I know – relating to Wort's experiments. Some of them seem to have been written by an outsider, perhaps John Dee, relating how Wort came to visit him – *in spirit* – using what he calls the "old road".'

'Wort was haunting him?'

'No, I think Wort was alive then. I'd guess he'd found a way . . . You said you wanted this straight . . . ?'

'Yes, yes, go on.'

'OK. A way to project his spirit – that's his astral body – along the leys, in much the same way as it's suggested the old shamans used to do it, or at least *believed* they could do it.'

'The psychic departure lounge,' said Fay.

'Glib, but it wasn't far out. And I've seen a transcript of the so-called regression of Catrin Jones. The character assumed by Catrin seems to be suggesting that not only was the sheriff bonking her – and quite a few other women – on a fairly regular basis in his physical body, but that he was also able to observe them while not actually there in the flesh.'

'Quite a bastard.'

Powys nodded. 'And in conclusion she says something on the lines of, "He swears he'll never leave me . . . never." Which suggests to me that Wort believed he would still be able to use these spirit paths, these astral thoroughfares, *after his death*. Except there's something stopping him, so he can only actually manifest as a . . . black dog or whatever.'

'The curfew.'

'Every night at ten o'clock somebody goes up the church tower and rings the curfew bell one hundred times, and when the bell sounds, the energy which has been gathering along the leys is released and dissipated. We know this happens, we've both experienced it.'

Fay stood up, held out a hand. 'Come on. I'll tell you my theory about the Crybbe mentality.'

She led him a few paces along the footpath, Arnold hobbling along between them, until the town square came into view, the buildings so firmly defined under the mouldering sky that she felt she could reach out and pinch slates from the roofs. They stood on the ridge and watched a school bus stop in the square. A Land Rover pulling a trailer carrying two sheep had to wait behind the bus. Traffic chaos hits Crybbe.

Fay extended an arm, like a music-hall compère on the edge of a stage.

'Miserable little closed-in town, right? Sad, decrepit, morose.'

'Right,' said Powys, cautiously.

'The border mentality,' Fay shouted into the wind. 'Play your cards close to your chest. Don't take sides until you know who's going to win. Here in Crybbe the whole attitude's intensified, and it operates on every level. Particularly spiritual.'

A big crow landed on the wicket gate and watched them.

Powys said, thoughtfully, 'But there isn't any noticeable spirituality in Crybbe.'

'*Precisely.* You've seen them in church, sitting there like dummies. Drives Murray mad. But they're just keeping their heads down. *Never take sides until you know who's winning.* Doesn't matter who the sides are. The Welsh or the English. Good or evil.'

Fay's cagoule rose up from the ground in the wind, and the crow flew off the gate, cawing. Fay went back and scooped up the cagoule.

Powys said, 'Strength in apathy?'

'Joe, look . . . being a vicar's daughter isn't all about keeping your frock clean and not pinching the cream cakes at the fête. You learn a few things. Confrontation between good and evil is high-octane stuff. The risks are high, so most people stay on the sidelines. Even vicars . . . What am I saying? . . . *Especially* vicars. But maybe it's harder to do that in Crybbe because the psychic pressure is so much greater, so they have to keep their heads even lower down.'

'Neither good nor evil can thrive in a place without a soul. Who was it said that?'

'Probably you. More to the point, "We don't like clever people round yere." Who said *that*?'

'Wynford Wiley. The copper.'

'Well, there you are. We don't like clever people. Says it all, doesn't it.'

'Does it?'

'Yes . . . because, for centuries, Crybbe's been avoiding making waves, disturbing the psychic ether or whatever you call it. If anybody happens to see a ghost, they keep very quiet about it until it goes away. Don't do anything to encourage them, don't give them any . . . energy to play with. If they see the black dog, they try and ignore it, they don't want it to get ideas above its station. How am I doing so far?'

'Go on.'

'Traditionally, dogs react to spirits, don't they? Dogs howl, right? Dogs howl when someone dies because they can see the spirit drifting away. So, in Crybbe, dogs simply get phased out. Maybe they've even forgotten *why* they don't like them, but traditions soon solidify in a place like this. The dogs, the curfew, there may be others we don't know anything about. But, anyway, suddenly . . .'

'The town's flooded with clever people. Max Goff and his New Agers.'

'Absolutely the worst kind of clever people,' said Fay. 'Dabblers in this and that.'

The rain came in on the breeze. Pulling on the blue cagoule, Fay looked down into the town and saw that the air appeared motionless down there; it was probably still quite humid in the shadow of the buildings.

'It's hard to believe,' Powys said, 'that Andy didn't know about all this when he planted on Goff the idea of establishing a New Age centre in Crybbe. Especially if he's a descendant of Michael Wort. He'd know it could generate a psychic explosion down there, and maybe . . . Christ . . .'

He took Fay's hand and squeezed it. The hand felt cold.

'. . . maybe generate enough negative energy to invoke

468

Michael Wort in a more meaningful form. Get him beyond the black dog stage. Of course he bloody knew.'

'In just over three hours' time,' Fay said, 'the public meeting begins. Crybbe versus the New Age. Lots of *very* negative energy there.'

PART EIGHT

Let us forget about evil. This does not exist. What does exist is imbalance, and when you are severely imbalanced, particularly in the negative direction, you can behave in very extreme and unpleasant ways.

DAVID ICKE,
Love Changes Everything

CHAPTER I

EVEN for Crybbe the night was rising early.

It rose from within the shadowed places. In the covered alleyway behind the Cock. Beneath the three arches of the river bridge. In the soured, spiny woodland which started where the churchyard ended with a black marble gravestone identifying the place where Grace Legge, beloved wife of Canon A. L. Peters was presumed to rest.

It filtered from the dank cellars of the buildings hunched around the square like old, morose drinking companions.

It was nurtured in the bushes at the base of the Tump.

It began to spread like a slow stain across the limp, white canopy of the sky, tinting it a deep and sorrowful grey.

And not yet seven-thirty.

'Give us a white-balance,' Larry Ember said, and Catrin Jones stood in the middle of the street and held up her clipboard for him to focus on.

Guy Morrison looked at the sky. 'Shoot everything you can get. I can't see it brightening up again. I think this is it.'

'Wasn't forecast,' Larry said. 'No thunderstorms.'

'And I can't see there being one in there,' Guy said, glancing at the town hall. 'This is probably a wasted exercise.'

'What you want me to do then, boss?'

'We've got permission to go in and grab some shots of the assembly before it starts, so shoot absolutely everything you can, plenty of tight shots of faces, expressions – I'll point out a few. Then just hang on in there till they actually ask you to leave, and then . . . well, stay outside, close to the door, and Catrin I will try and haul out a few punters with opinions. Though I'll be very surprised if these yokels manage to muster a single opinion between them.'

The Victorian façade of the town hall reared over the shallow street like a gloomy Gothic temple, its double doors spread wide to expose a great cave-mouth, through which the younger townsfolk wandered like tourists. Many had probably never been inside before; there weren't many public gatherings in Crybbe.

Guy ordered shots of their faces, shots of their feet. The feet are probably saying more than the faces, he thought in frustration. At least they're moving.

For the first time he began to wonder how he was going to avoid making a stupefyingly boring documentary. He'd been determined to keep the voice-over down to a minimum, letting events tell their own story. But to get away with that, one needed a pithy commentary on these events from a collection of outspoken locals. So far, the only outspoken local he'd encountered had been Gomer Parry, who lived at least three miles outside the town.

'What are we going to do?' he whispered despairingly to Catrin – showing weakness to an assistant, he *never* did that.

Catrin gave his thigh a reassuring squeeze. 'It'll be fine.'

'. . . God's sake, Catrin, not in public!'

Catrin. How *could* he have?

This place was destroying him.

Parking his Escort XR3 in the old cattle market behind the square, Gavin Ashpole had no fears at all about *his* story being boring.

This was the beauty of radio. The place might *look* like a disused cemetery, but you could make it *sound* like bloody Beirut. Whatever happened here tonight, Gavin was going to put down a hard-hitting voice-piece for the ten o'clock news describing the uproar, as beleaguered billionaire Max Goff faced a verbal onslaught by hundreds of angry townsfolk fearing an invasion by hippy convoys lured to the New Age Mecca.

Somebody had suggested to Gavin that perhaps he could try out the new radio-car on this one. Park right outside the meeting, send in some live on-the-spot stuff for the nine-thirty news.

Gavin thought not; the station's only unattended studio was not three minutes' walk from the town hall.

And he hadn't been able to drag his mind away from last night's interrupted fantasy in that same studio. Somehow, he had to get little Ms Morrison in there.

Ms Morrison who'd really screwed any chance she had of holding down the Offa's Dyke contract. Who'd failed to provide a report on last night's tractor accident. Who hadn't even been reachable on the phone all day.

'I'll go in live at nine-thirty,' he'd told the night-shift sub, James Barlow. 'And I want a full two minutes. I don't care what else happens.'

He was thinking about this as he parked his car in the old livestock market. Unusually dark this evening; even the sky looked in the mood for a set-to.

Humid, though. Gavin took off his jacket, locked it in the boot and slung his Uher over his shoulder.

Two cars and a Land Rover followed him into the market. Half a dozen men got out. Tweed suits, caps, no chat, no smiles. Farmers, in town for the meeting, meaning business.

I like it, Gavin told himself. Everybody who was anybody in the district was going to be here tonight to listen, with varying degrees of enthusiasm or hostility to Goff's crazy, hippy schemes. There was a small danger that if the opposition was too heavy, Goff might have second thoughts and decide to take his New Age centre somewhere else – like out of Offa's Dyke's patch, which would be no use at all. But this was highly unlikely; Goff wasn't a quitter and he'd probably already invested more than Gavin could expect to earn in the next ten years, even if he did become managing editor. No, Goff had gone too far to pull out. Too many people relying on him. Danger of too much bad publicity on a national scale if he let them down.

He crossed the square and followed everybody else into the side-street leading to the town hall.

Gavin quickened his pace and walked up between a couple – skinny guy with a ratty beard and a rather sultry wife. Gavin *had* to walk between the man and woman because they were so far apart, not talking to each other. Obviously had a row.

That was what he liked to see. Acrimony and tension were

the core of all the best news stories. It was building in the air.

Gavin mentally rubbed his hands.

Alex and Jean were taking tea in the drawing-room.

The Canon, wearing his faded Kate Bush T-shirt, was standing in front of the Chinese firescreen, legs comfortably apart, cup and saucer effortlessly balanced in hands perfectly steady.

Earlier, he'd spotted himself in a mirror and it had been like looking at an old photograph. Hair all fluffed up, the famous twinkle terrifyingly potent again. Old boy's a walking advert for the Dr Chi New Age Clinic.

He was aware that Jean Wendle had been looking at him too, with a certain pride, and several times today they had exchanged little smiles.

'So.' Jean was on the sofa, hands linked behind her head. Jolly pert little body for her age. 'Shall we go? Or shall we stay in?'

Several times today she'd looked at him like that. Just a quick glance. One really was rather too old to jump to conclusions; however . . .

'Which do you think would be most, er, stimulating?'

'Och, that depends,' Jean said, 'on what turns you on. Perhaps your poor old brain is ready at last for the intellectual stimulus of public debate, as Max strives to present himself, gift-wrapped, to the stoical burgers of Crybbe.'

'Give me strength,' said Alex.

'Fay'll be there, no doubt.'

'Won't want *me* in her hair.'

'Or there's Grace. All alone in Bell Street. Will she be worried, perhaps, that you haven't been home for a couple of nights?'

'I thought you said she didn't exist as anything more than a light form.'

'She didn't. Unfortunately, she's become a monster.'

'Uh?' Alex lost his twinkle.

'Tell me,' Jean said. 'Have you ever performed an exorcism?'

*

The Cock was no brighter than a Victorian funeral parlour, Denzil, the licensee, no more expressive than a resident corpse. Half past eight and only two customers – all his regulars over at the town hall.

J. M. Powys stared despairingly into his orange juice, back in his habitual state of confusion. Everything had seemed so clear on the hillside overlooking the town, when Fay was aglow with insight.

Arnold lay silently under the table. Possibly the first dog in several centuries to set foot – all three of them – in the public bar of the Cock. 'We can't,' Fay had warned. 'Sod it,' Powys had replied, following the dog up the steps. 'I've had enough of this. Who's going to notice? Who's going to care?'

And, indeed, now they were inside there was nobody except Denzil to care, and Denzil didn't notice, not for a while.

Powys glanced up at Fay across the table. 'It could all be crap,' he said.

'There.' Fay was drinking tomato juice; it was a night for clear heads. 'You see . . .'

'What?'

'You're back in Crybbe. You're doubting yourself. You're thinking, what the hell, why bother? It's easy to see, isn't it, why, after four centuries, the apathy's become so ingrained.'

'Except that it could though, couldn't it? It could all be crap.'

'And we're just two weirdoes from Off trying to make a big deal out of something because we don't fit in.'

'And if it's not – not crap – what can we do about it?'

'Excuse me, sir.' Denzil was standing by their table, low-browed, heavy-jowled. He picked up their empty glasses.

'Thanks,' Powys said. 'We'll have a couple more of the same.' Glanced at Fay. 'OK?'

Fay nodded glumly.

'No you won't,' Denzil said. 'Not with that dog in yere you won't.'

'I'm sorry?'

'Don't allow no dogs in yere.'

Powys said mildly, 'Where does it say that?'

'You what, sir?'

'Where does it say, "no dogs"?'

'We never 'ad no sign, sir, because . . .'

'Because you never had no dogs before. Now, this is interesting.' Powys tried to catch his eye; impossible. 'We're the only customers. There's nobody else to serve. So perhaps you could spell out – in detail – what this town has against the canine species. Take your time. Give us a considered answer. We've got hours and hours.'

Powys sat back and contemplated the licensee, who looked away. The bar smelled of polish and the curdled essence of last night's beer.

'No hurry,' Powys said. 'We've got all night.'

Denzil turned to him at last and Powys thought, Yes he does . . . He really does look like a malignant troll.

'Mr Powys,' Denzil said slowly. 'You're a clever man . . .'

'And we . . .' said Fay, '. . . we don't like clever people round yere.' And collapsed helplessly into giggles.

Denzil's expression didn't change. 'No more drinks,' he said. 'Get out.'

It was getting so dark so early that Mrs Seagrove decided it would be as well to draw the curtains to block out that nasty old mound. Ugly as a slag-heap, Frank used to say it was.

The curtains were dark-blue Dralon. Behind curtains like this, you could pretend you were living somewhere nice.

'There,' she said. 'That's better, isn't it, Frank?'

Frank didn't reply, just nodded as usual. He'd never had much to say, hadn't Frank. Just sat there in his favourite easy-chair, his own arms stretched along the chair arms. Great capacity for stillness, Frank had.

'I feel so much safer with you here,' Mrs Seagrove said to her late husband.

CHAPTER II

L IKE an old castle, the church was, when the light was going, with the tower and the battlements all black.

Something to *really* break into. Not like a garage or a school or a newsagent's. Magic, this was, when you got in, standing there in the great echoey space, shouting out 'fuck' and 'piss'.

When you broke into a church, there was like an edge to it.

Sacrilege. What did it mean? What did it really mean? Religion was about being bored. They used to make him come here when he was a kid. Just you sit there, Warren, and keep it shut until they gives you a hymn to sing . . . and don't sing so bloody loud next time, you tryin' to show us up?

So when he stood here and shouted 'fuck' and 'piss', who was he shouting it at? His family, or the short-tempered ole God they didn't like to disturb by singing too loud?

Tonight he didn't have to break in; nobody'd bothered to lock the place after he'd done the window in the vestry, when he'd been up the belfry and then doled out this plate of dog food on the altar.

Still couldn't figure why he'd done that. Tessa's idea, she'd given him the can. Next time she'd have to explain. He was taking no more orders, not from anybody.

Warren ground his teeth and brought his foot back and slammed it into the side door, wanting to kick it in, anyway. Because it was a rotten old door that'd needed replacing years ago. Because he wanted to hear the latch splintering off its screws.

Because he wanted Jonathon to know he was coming.

Me again, Jonathon. You don't get no peace, bro, till you're in the ground.

There was a real rage in him tonight that just went on growing and growing, the more he thought about that bastard

Goff and the way he'd tricked him. Warren could see right through the layers of blubber to the core of this fat phoney. The *real* reason he'd had a nice letter sent back to Warren with the tape was he didn't know how Warren's grandad stood on the question of Warren being a professional musician – for all Goff knew the old git could've been 'supportive', as they said. And the old git was the Mayor, and Goff couldn't afford to offend *him*.

Warren got out his Stanley knife, *the* Stanley knife, and swaggered up the aisle to the coffin, saw its whitish gleam from this window over the altar that used to be stained glass, only the bloody ole stained bits blew out, once, in a gale, on account the lead was mostly gone, and they filled it up with plain, frosted glass like you got in the windows of public lavs – typical, that, of the cheapo bastards who ran the Church.

Anyway, what was left of the white light shone down on reliable, steady, trustworthy ole Jonathon.

Saint Jonathon now.

He flicked out the blade, felt his lips curling back into a tight snarl as he sucked in a hissing breath and dug the point into the polished lid, dagger-style, and then wrenched it back, getting two hands to it, one over the other.

Sssccccreeeeagh!!!!!

Remember me, Jonathon?

I'm your brother. I was there when you died. Maybe you don't remember that. Wasn't a chance I could very well miss, though, was it? Not when that feller sets it up for me so nice, chucking the old gun in the drink – couldn't go back without that, could you bro? Couldn't face the ole man . . . steady, reliable, ole Jonathon lost the bloody family heirloom shooter.

Didn't see me, did you? Didn't see me lying under the hedge, the other side of the bank? Well, people don't, see. I'm good at that, even if I don't know nothing about farming and I'm a crap guitarist.

Always been good at not being seen and watching and listening. And you gets better at that when you know they don't give a shit for you, not any of the buggers. You learn to watch out for yourself, see.

Anyway, so there you are, wading across the river, getting closer

*and closer to my side. Hey, listen . . . how many times did the ole
man tell us when we were kids: never get tempted to cross the river,
that ole river bed's not stable, see, full of these gullies.*

*See, you might not remember this next bit, being you were in a
bit of trouble at the time, like, bit of a panic, churning up the water
something cruel. And, like, if you did see me, well, you might still
be thinking I was trying to rescue you, brotherly love, all that shit.*

*Might've thought I was trying to hold your head above the
water. Well, fair play, that's an easy mistake to make when you're
floundering about doing your best not to get yourself drowned.*

Anyway, you failed, Jonathon.

*Gotter admit, it's not often a bloke gets the chance like that to
drown his goodie-goodie, smart-arse, chairman of the Young
Farmers' brother, is it?*

Worth getting your ole trainers soaked for any day, you ask me.

Gotter laugh, though, Jonathon. Gotter laugh.

It was quite impressive inside. Late nineteenth century perhaps.
High-ceilinged, white-walled. And a white elephant, now, Guy
thought, with no proper council any more.

He was watching from the entrance at the back of the hall,
while Larry Ember was doing a shot from the stage at the front.
People were pointing at Larry, whispering, shuffling in their
seats. Real fly-on-the-wall stuff *this* was going to be, with half
the punters staring straight into the lens, looking hostile.

'Make it quick, Guy, will you,' Col Croston said behind a
hand. 'I've been approached about six times already by people
objecting to your presence.'

Catrin said, 'Do they know who he *is*?'

'Stay out of this, Catrin,' said Guy. 'Col, we'll have the
camera out within a couple of minutes. But as it's a public
meeting, I trust nobody will try to get *me* out.'

'I should sit at the back, all the same,' Col said without
opening his mouth.

'Look!' Larry Ember suddenly bawled out at the audience,
leaping up from his camera, standing on the makeshift wooden
stage, exasperated, hands on his hips. 'Stop bleedin' looking at

me! Stop pointing at me! You never seen a telly camera before? Stone me, it's worse than little kids screaming "Hello, Mum". Pretend I'm not here, can't yer?'

'Maybe you *shouldn't* be yere, then,' a man shouted back.

'Sorry about this,' Guy said to Col Croston. 'Larry's not terribly good at public relations.'

'Better get him out,' Col said. 'I'm sorry, Guy.'

'I suspect we're all going to be sorry before the night's out,' Guy said, unknowingly blessed, for the first time in his life, with the gift of prophecy.

A hush hit the hall, and Guy saw Larry swing his arms, and his camera, in a smooth arc as though he'd spotted trouble at the back of the room.

The hush came from the front left of the hall, occupied by members of the New Age community and – further back – other comparative newcomers to the town. The other side of the hall, where the Crybbe people sat, was already as quiet as a funeral.

The hush was a response to the arrival of Max Goff. Only the trumpet fanfare, Guy thought, was missing. Goff was accompanied. An entourage.

First came Hilary Ivory, wife of the tarotist, carrying her snowy hair wound up on top, like a blazing white torch. Her bony, nervy husband, Adam, was way back, behind Goff, even behind Graham Jarrett in his pale-green safari suit. There were some other people Guy recognized from last Friday's lunch party, including the noted feminist astrologer with the ring through her nose and a willowy redhead specializing in dance-therapy. There were also some accountant-looking men in John Major-style summerweight grey suits.

Max Goff, in the familiar white double-breasted and a velvet bow-tie, looked to Guy like a superior and faintly nasty teddy bear, the kind that wealthy American ladies kept on their beds with a pistol inside.

Would you turn *your* town over to this man?

Guy watched Goff and his people filling the front two rows on the left, the chamber divided by its central aisle into two distinct factions, Old Crybbe and New Age, tweeds against talismans.

He felt almost sorry for Goff; this was going to be an historic fiasco. But he felt more sorry for himself because they weren't being allowed to film it.

Alex drained his cup in a hurry and bumped it back on its saucer, hand trembling slightly.

Exorcism. Oh God.

'Well, obviously, I was supposed to *know* about things like that. Been a practising clergyman for damn near three-quarters of my life. But . . . Sometimes she was . . . in my bedroom. I'd wake up, she'd be sitting by the bed wearing this perfectly ghastly smile. Couple of seconds, that was all, then she'd be gone. Happened once, twice a week, I don't know. Fay came down to stay one weekend. I was in turmoil. Looked awful, felt awful. What did she want with me? Hadn't I done enough?'

Jean put on her knowing look.

'Yes,' Alex said, 'guilt again, you see. A most destructive emotion. Was she a product of my obsessive guilt – a lifetime of guilt, perhaps?'

Jean nodded.

'Poor old Fay. I think she thought I'd finally slipped into alcoholism. Anyway, she sent me to the doctor's, he sent me for tests and they discovered the artery problem. Everything explained. Poor old buffer's going off his nut. Can't be left alone. And that was how Fay and I got saddled with each other.'

'And do you feel you need her now?'

'Well, I . . . No, I'm not sure I do. Wendy, this . . . this Dr Chi business . . . Look, I don't mean to be offensive . . .'

'Of course not,' said Jean solemnly.

'But this renewed, er, sprightliness of mind . . . It's just that I don't honestly feel I'm the most worthy candidate for a miracle cure.'

Jean stood up, went over to the window and drew the curtains on the premature dusk, bent over to put on the lamp with the parchment shade, showing him her neat little gym-mistressy bum. Came back and sat down next to him on the settee, close enough for him to discover she was wearing perfume.

'There are no miracles, Alex, surely you know that by now.'

She didn't move an inch, but he felt her coming closer to him and smelled the intimacy of her perfume. He felt old stirrings he'd expected never to feel again. And yet it was somehow joyless.

'Dr Chi and I have done almost all we can for you, Alex. You've been here more than a day. Intensive treatment.'

'It seems longer.'

Jean nodded. 'You feel well now?'

Alex cleared his throat. 'Never better,' he said carefully.

'So why don't you go home?'

'Ah,' said Alex.

Jean looked steadily at him in the lamplight, unsmiling.

He said, 'What time is it?'

'Approaching eight. She'll be there soon, Alex.'

'Will she?'

'Only one way to find out,' Jean said gently. 'Isn't there?'

'Oh now, Wendy, look . . .'

'Perhaps . . .' She stood up and went to lean against the mantelpiece, watching him. 'Perhaps it worries you that once you leave this house, your mind will begin to deteriorate again. And when you face her once more, the guilt will return.'

He squirmed a little.

'You might not be responsible for actually bringing her spirit back.' Her eyes narrowed. 'I think we can blame Crybbe for that. But you do seem to have made her rather more powerful in death than she was in life. You've projected upon her not only the portion of guilt to which she may or may not have been due, but all the guilt due to your wife and, no doubt, many other ladies and husbands and whatnot . . . and, bearing in mind your rather poor choice of profession, perhaps your God himself. Is that not so, Alex?'

'I . . .'

'You've been feeding her energy, Alex. The way I've been feeding you. A kind of psychic saline drip. So I'm afraid it's your responsibility to deal with her.'

Alex began to feel small and old and hollow.

'When you leave here . . .' Jean said regretfully. 'This

house, I mean. When you do leave, there's a chance you'll lapse quite soon into the old confusion, and you'll have that to contend with, too. I'm sorry.'

Alex stared at her, feeling himself withering.

'No Dr Chi?'

Jean smiled sadly. 'I never did like scientific terms.'

'I'm on my own, then.'

'I'm afraid you let her get out of hand. Now she's become quite dangerous. She won't harm you – you're her source of energy, you feed her your guilt and she lights up. But . . .' Jean hesitated. 'She doesn't like Fay one bit, does she?'

'Stop it,' Alex said sharply.

'You've known that for quite a while, haven't you? You would even plead with Grace not to hurt her. It didn't work, Alex. She appeared last night to your daughter in a rather grisly fashion, and Fay fell and cut her head and almost put out an eye.'

Alex jerked as though electrocuted, opened his mouth, trying to shape a question with a quivering jaw.

'She's all right. No serious damage.' Jean came back and sat next to him again and put a hand on his shoulder. 'Don't worry, Alex, it's OK. You don't have to do anything. I won't send you away.'

Alex began quietly to cry, shoulders shaking.

'Come on,' said Jean, taking her hand away. 'Let's go to bed. That's what you want, isn't it? Come along, Alex.'

Jean Wendle's expressionless face swam in his tears. She was offering him sex, the old refuge, when all he wanted was the cool hands.

But the cool hands were casually clasped in her lap and he knew he was never going to feel them again.

He came slowly to his feet. He backed away from her. She didn't move. He tried to hold her eyes; she looked down into her lap, where the cool hands lay.

Alex couldn't speak. Slowly he backed out of the lamplight and, with very little hope, into the darkness.

CHAPTER III

THE Crybbe dusk settled around them like sediment in the bottom of an old medicine bottle.

'Thank you, Denzil,' Powys said to the closed door of the Cock. 'That was just what we needed. Of course it's not crap. Can't you feel it?'

He started to grin ruefully, thinking of New Age ladies in ankle-length, hand-dyed, cheesecloth dresses. *Can't you feel that energy?*

Not energy. Not life energy, anyway.

'Fay, where can we go? Quickly?'

He was aware of a picture forming in his head. Glowing oil colours on top of the drab turpentine strokes of rough sketching and underpainting. Everything starting to fit together. Coming together by design – someone else's design.

'Studio,' Fay said, opening her bag, searching for the keys. 'Right.'

He didn't need the gavel. Didn't need even to call for silence. In fact, he rather wished he could call for noise – few murmurs, coughs, bit of shifting about in seats.

Nothing. Not a shuffle, not even a passing 'Ow're you' between neighbours. Put him in mind of a remembrance service for the dead, the only difference being that when you cast an eye over this lot you could believe the dead themselves had been brought out for the occasion.

Been like this since Goff and his people had come in and the cameraman had left: bloody quiet. Sergeant Wynford Wiley, in uniform, on guard by the door as if he was expecting trouble.

No such luck, Col Croston thought. Not the Crybbe way. No wonder the cunning old devil had stuck this one on him. Thanks a lot, Mr Mayor.

*

Gavin Ashpole's Uher tape recorder and its microphone lay at the front of the room, half under the chairman's table and a good sixty feet from where Gavin himself sat at the rear of the hall. The stupid, paranoid yokels had refused to accept that if he kept the machine at his feet he would not surreptitiously switch it on and record their meeting.

He saw a man from the *Hereford Times* and that snooty bastard Guy Morrison. Nobody else he recognized, and Gavin knew all the national paper reporters who covered this area.

There was no sign of Fay Morrison.

Bitch.

The Newsomes sat side by side, but there might have been a brick wall between them, with broken glass along the top.

Hereward had planned to come alone to the meeting, but Jocasta had got into the car with him without a word. The inference was that she did not want to remain alone in the house after this alleged experience (about which Hereward was more than slightly dubious). But he suspected the real reason she'd come was that she hoped to see her lover.

With this in mind, Hereward had subjected each man entering the hall to unobtrusive scrutiny and was also watching for reactions from his wife. The appalling thought occurred to him that he might be the only person in the hall who did *not* know the identity of the Other Man.

He could be a laughing stock. Or she a liar.

Col looked at the wall-clock which the caretaker had obligingly plugged in for the occasion. Five minutes past eight. Off we go then.

'Well,' he said. 'Thank you all for coming. I, er . . . I don't think . . . that we can underestimate the importance of tonight.'

Why did he say that? Wasn't what he'd *meant* to say. The idea was to be essentially informal, take any heat out of the situation.

'Let me say, straight off, that no decisions will be made tonight. That's not what this meeting's about. It's simply an attempt to remove some of the mystery – and some of the myths, too – about developments here in Crybbe. Developments which are transpiring with what might seem to some of us to be rather, er, rather bewildering speed.'

Bloody bewildering speed, by Crybbe standards.

'And let me say, first of all, that, apart from minor planning matters, the changes, the developments, introduced to Crybbe by Mr Max Goff, are, for the most part, outside the remit of local government and require no special permission whatsoever.'

'What we doin' yere, then?' a lone voice demanded. A man's voice, but so high-pitched that it was like a sudden owl hoot in a silent barn.

Nobody turned to look whose it was. Obviously the voice spoke for all of Crybbe.

Col looked up and saw Hereward Newsome staring at him. He smiled. Hereward did not.

'Can I say, from the outset,' Col said, 'that from here on in, only questions directed through the chair will be dealt with. However – what are we doing here? This – as it happens – was a point I was about to move on to. What *are* we doing here?'

Col tried to look at everyone in the room; only those in the New Age quarter, to his right, looked back.

'We're here tonight . . . at the instigation of Mr Max Goff himself. We're here because Mr Goff is aware that aspects of his project may appear somewhat curious – even disturbing – to a number of people. What's he *doing* erecting large stones in fields, even if they do happen to be his own fields? Why is he so keen to purchase property for sale in the locality?'

Col paused.

'What *is* this New Age business really all about?'

On a single page of *The Ley-Hunter's Diary 1993*, with a fibre-tipped pen in a none-too-steady hand, Powys had drawn the rough outline of a man with his arms spread.

Fay thought it looked like one of those chalk-marks homicide cops drew around corpses in American films.

'The Cock,' Powys said breathlessly. 'Why do they call it the Cock? It's self-explanatory.'

'This is going to be rather tasteless, isn't it?'

'Look.' Powys turned the diary around on the studio desk to face her. He marked a cross on the head of the man. 'This is the Tump.'

He made another cross in the centre of the man's throat. 'Crybbe Court.'

He traced a straight line downwards and put in a third cross. 'The Church.' It was in the middle of the chest.

'And finally . . .'

Where the man's legs joined he drew in a final cross.

'The Cock,' he said. 'Or more precisely, I'd *guess*, the alleyway and perhaps this studio.'

She looked at him uncertainly, his face soft focus in the diffused studio lighting. 'I don't understand.'

'The Cock, which used to be called the Bull, occurs precisely on the genitalia. If we want to get down to details, this studio would cover the testicles, and the erect . . . er, organ would project into the square very much as the pub itself leans. I remember when I spent the night there with Rachel I was thinking the upper storey hung over the square like a beer gut. Close, but . . . Anyway, we were in the room which is directly over the passage, the alley, and we're on that same line now.'

'Joe, this is ridiculous.'

'Not really. You ever do yoga, anything like that?'

'Never had the time.'

'OK, well, Eastern mysticism – and Western magic – suggests there are various points in the human body where physical and spiritual energy gathers, and from where it can be transmitted. The chakras.'

'I've heard of them. I think.'

'So what we *could* be looking at here are some of the key chakras – the centre of the forehead – mental power; the throat, controlling nervous impulses; the centre of the breast, affecting emotions. And the sex glands, responding more or less to what you'd expect.'

Fay leaned back against the tape-machine. 'I'm still not

getting this, Joe, you're going to have to spell it out. Like, simply.'

'The town . . . is the man. Is the town.'

'Oh shit . . . *What* man?'

'Wort. Black Michael. In essence he's never gone away. He's fused his energy system, his spirit, with the town. I'm not putting this very well.'

'No, you're not.'

'This girl Jane – the character assumed by Catrin Jones – speaks of the sheriff promising he'll never leave her. He hasn't. He's left the sexual part of him here. His cock.'

Fay looked down at the Electrovoice microphone, eight inches long with a bulb-like head. 'Jesus . . .'

'It might even be – I don't know – *buried* somewhere . . .'

'Powys, I don't want to hear this. This is very seriously creepy.'

'So anybody making love – having sex, love doesn't come into it – is getting some added . . . impetus, buzz, whatever, from a four-hundred-year-old . . .'

Fay never wanted to do another voice-piece with that microphone. 'Come on,' she said, between her teeth, 'let's get out of here before – if what you say is correct – we start ripping each other's clothes off.'

Ironically – given the ragged quality of local communal singing, the absence of a trained choir or the will to form one – the church was widely known for its excellent acoustics.

And so the Revd Murray Beech heard it all.

Standing, appalled, behind the curtain separating the side entrance from the nave, he heard everything.

The astounding confession, and then the bumps and crashes.

It was not long after eight, although dark enough to be close to ten, the churchyard outside reduced to neutral shades, the birdsong stilled, the small, swift bats gliding through the insect layer.

When Murray had first picked up the noises he'd been on

his way to the public meeting at which, he rather hoped, he would be able to assume the role of mediator, while at the same time putting a few pertinent theological questions to the self-styled heralds of the New Age.

He was wearing a new sports jacket over his black shirt and clerical collar. He'd felt more relaxed than for quite some time. Had, in fact, been looking forward to tonight; it would be his opportunity to articulate the fears of townsfolk who were . . . well, unpractised, let us say, in the finer techniques of oratory.

At least, he *had* been relaxed until he'd heard from within the church what sounded like a wild whoop of joy. In this situation it might, in fact, be wise to summon the police.

Or it might not. He'd look rather foolish if it turned out to be a cry of pain from someone quite legitimately in the church who'd, say, tripped over a hassock.

Also he hadn't reported the minor (by lay standards) acts of vandalism of the past two nights. And if this intruder did turn out to be the perpetrator of those sordid expressions of contempt, a quiet chat would be more in order. This was a person with serious emotional problems.

So Murray had hesitated before going in quietly by the side door, noting that its latch had been torn away and was hanging loose, which rather ruled out the well-meaning but clumsy parishioner theory.

No, sadly, this was the sick person.

'*Well, well,*' he heard now. '*Don't* you *look cheesed-off?*'

As, behind the floor-length curtain, he could not be seen from anywhere in the church, the remark could not have been aimed at him.

Which meant Warren Preece was addressing his dead brother. His – if this crazed boy was to be believed – murdered brother.

The confession had emerged in a strange intermittent fashion, incomplete sentences punctuated by laughter, as if it was a continuous monologue but some of it was being spoken only in Warren's head.

It was deranged and eerie, and Murray remembered the malevolence of Warren's face in the congregation on Sunday, the way the hate had spurted out in shocking contrast to the unchanging stoical expressions of his father and his grand-parents.

Murray was in no doubt that this boy at least *believed* he'd drowned Jonathon. The hard-working, conscientious, older brother slain by the youthful wastrel. Almost like Cain and Abel in reverse.

He ought, he supposed, to make a quiet exit, summon the police and let them deal with it. And yet there was, in this situation, a certain social challenge of a kind not hitherto appar-ent in Crybbe. The inner cities were full of disturbed youths like Warren Preece – always a valid project for the Church, although some ministers shied away.

If Warren Preece was a murderer, Murray could hardly protect him. But if there was an element of self-delusion brought about by guilt, causing a strange inversion of grief, he could perhaps help the boy reason it out.

He heard footsteps but could not be sure from which direc-tion they came or in which direction they were moving, for these acclaimed acoustics could, he'd found, sometimes be confusing.

With three sharp clicks, the lights came on, and Murray clutched at the curtain in alarm.

'*Very nice,*' he heard. '*Very nice indeed.*'

And the perverse laughter again, invoking an image in his head of the communion chalice on the altar and what it had contained.

A sudden, white-hot sense of outrage overrode his prin-ciples, his need to understand the social and psychological back-ground to this, and he swept the curtain angrily aside.

'All right!'

Murray entered the nave in a single great stride, surprised at his own courage but aware also of the danger of bravado, his eyes sweeping over the body of the church, the stonework lamplit pale amber and sepia, the stained-glass windows rend-ered blind and opaque.

And in the space between the front pews and the altar rail, the aluminium bier empty and askew like an abandoned supermarket trolley.

'Stay where you are!' Murray roared.

And then realized, in a crystal moment of shimmering horror, how inappropriate this sounded. Because the only Preece in view had no choice.

The vicar wanted to be sick, and the bile was behind his voice as it rose, choking, to the rafters lost in their shadows.

'Come out! Come out at once, you . . . you *filth* . . .!'

Another slack, liquid chuckle . . . '*eeeheheh* . . .' trailing like spittle.

Murray could not move, stood there staring compulsively into the closed, yellowed eyes of Jonathan Preece.

The open coffin propped up against the pulpit like a show-case, the body sunk back like a drunk asleep in the bath, the shroud now slashed up the middle to reveal the livid line of the post-mortem scar, where the organs had been put back and the torso sewn up like a potato sack.

Jonathon's corpse splayed in its coffin like a pig in the back of a butcher's van, and Murray Beech could not move.

His nose twitched in acute, involuntary distaste as the smell reached him. Otherwise, he was so stiff with shock that he didn't react at first to the swift movement, as a shadow fell across him and he heard a very small, neat, crisp sound, like a paper bag being torn along a crease.

When he looked down and saw that his clerical shirt had come apart – a deep, vertical split down the chest and upper abdomen, so that he could see his white vest underneath turning pink then bright red – he couldn't at first work out precisely what this meant.

CHAPTER IV

THE square was absolutely empty. Flat, dead quiet under a sky that was too dark, too early.

Powys looked up at the church tower hanging behind the serrated roofs of buildings which included the town hall. Behind him, leaning towards him, was the Cock.

They stood in the centre of the square, which was where the navel would be.

'We're on the solar plexus,' Powys said. 'The solar plexus, I *think*, is the most significant chakra, more so than the head. It's like the centre of the nervous system – I *think* – where energy can be stored and transmitted.'

Fay hung on to his arm, wanting warmth, although the night was humid.

'You see, I've never gone into this too deeply. It's just things you pick up in passing. We may not even be looking at chakras at all.'

Fay began to shiver. She began to see the town as something covered by a huge black shadow, man-shaped. She knew nothing about chakras, almost nothing about ley-lines, energy lines, paths of the dead . . .

'It's happening tonight,' she said. 'Isn't it? Black Michael's coming back.'

'Yeah.' Powys nodded. 'I think it's possible.'

It was working. From the rear of the hall – packed out, way beyond the limits of the fire regulations – Guy Morrison saw it all as though through the rectangle of a TV screen, and, incredibly, it was working.

In spite of his evangelical white suit, Goff was starting to convey this heavy, sober sincerity, beside which even the authoritative Col Croston looked lightweight. Col in his ornate Gothic chairman's chair, Max Goff standing next to him at the table, having vacated a far humbler seat, but oozing Presence.

Goff standing with his hands loosely clasped below waist-level.

Goff, looking down at first, saying, not too loudly, 'I want you to forget everything you ever heard or read about the New Age movement. I'm gonna give you the Crybbe version. I'm gonna tell you how it might relate to this town. I'm gonna make it simple, no bull.'

Then slowly raising his eyes. 'And the moment I cease to make sense to any one of you, I wanna know about it.'

Smiling a little now, an accessible kind of smile, if not exactly warm. 'I want you to stand up and stop me. Say, "Hey, we aren't following this, Max." Or "Max, we don't believe you. We think you're trying to pull the wool." '

It could have sounded patronizing. It didn't. Guy could see only the backs of the heads of the two distinct factions – New Age, Old Crybbe. No heads moved on either side. They'd been expecting a showman in a white suit, but Goff had changed. Even his small eyes were compelling. Not a showman but a shaman.

'You see, what I don't want is any of you people just sitting there thinking, "Who is this lunatic? Why are we listening to this garbage? Who's he think he's kidding?" because . . .'

Bringing his gaze down very slowly from the back rows to the front rows, taking in everybody.

'. . . Because I'm *not* kidding. I *never* kid.'

'I look at this town,' Fay said, 'and I don't see streets and buildings any more, I only see shadows.'

Powys didn't say anything. He'd been seeing shadows everywhere, for years.

'When there's a gust of wind,' Fay said, 'I look over my shoulder.'

Maybe it's me, he thought. Maybe I've contaminated her.

'And when the lights go out . . .'

'Look,' Powys said quickly, 'he's always been there. Bits of him.' He kept snatching breath, trying to keep his mind afloat. 'Just like, behind us, along the passage there's a pool of sexual energy that fills up in the hours approaching the curfew. Accumulates in the place where the studio is. No doubt other forms of energy gather elsewhere. But it all dissipates when the curfew bell starts to ring. Each night, the ringing of the curfew frustrates the spirit's attempts to collect enough energy to activate all the power centres simultaneously.'

'All right,' Fay said. 'So, one hundred strong, evenly spaced tolls of the bell sends the black energy back to the Tump with its tail between its legs. Why do real dogs howl?'

She looked down at Arnold, lying on the bottom step in front of the Cock, panting slightly.

'I'm guessing,' Powys said. 'OK?'

'It's all guesswork, isn't it? Go on. This is the big one, Joe. Why – precisely – do dogs howl at the curfew?'

'Right.' He sat down on the second step, and Arnold laid his chin on his shoe. 'I've been thinking about this a lot. The curfew's a very powerful thing. It's like – an act of violence. It hits the half-formed spirit like a truck. And the spirit wants to scream out in rage and frustration. Now. There are two possibilities. Either, because it's at this black dog stage, it communicates its agony to anything else in the town on the canine wavelength. Or it simply emits some kind of ultrasonic scream, like one of those dog whistles people can't hear. How's that?'

'Well,' Fay conceded, 'it does have a certain arcane logic.'

She looked up at the church tower.

Powys pushed at his forehead with the tips of his fingers. 'Somebody – let's continue to call him John Dee – saw what was happening, what Michael Wort had left behind – in essence an opening for him to return, to . . . possess Crybbe, literally, from beyond the grave. And he recommended certain steps – get rid of the stones, build a wall around the Tump, ring the curfew every night, one hundred times. Avoid any kind of psychic of spiritual activity which will be amplified in an area like this anyway and could open up another doorway. And so the rituals are absorbed into the fabric of local life and Crybbe becomes what it is today.'

'Morose,' Fay said. 'Apathetic. Resistant to any kind of change. Every night the curfew leaves the place literally limp.'

Guy Morrison was clenching his fists in frustration. This would have been terrific television. He looked around for the Mayor of Crybbe – the man who, more than anybody else in the entire world, he now wanted to strangle.

Jimmy Preece was, in fact, not six yards away, on the end of a row close to the back – presumably so that he could slip away to ring his precious curfew. Guy moved forward a little to see how the Mayor was taking this and discovered that, for a change, Mr Preece's face was not without expression.

He looked very nervous. His Adam's apple bobbed in his chicken's neck and his eyes kept blinking as though the lids were attached by strings to his forehead, where new wrinkles were forming like worm-casts in sand.

The poor old reactionary's worried Max is going to win them over, Guy thought. He's afraid that, by the end of the night, this will be Max Goff's town and not his any more.

And why not?

For Goff, indirectly, was promising them the earth. But somebody had told him about the way business was done in this locality and about the border mentality, and he was handling it accordingly. What he was telling them, in an oblique kind of way, was, I can help you – I can recreate this town, make it soar – if you co-operate with me. But I don't need you. I don't need anybody.

Goff was talking now about his dreams of expanding the sum of human knowledge and enlightenment. Speaking of the great shrines of the world, subtly mentioning Lourdes and all the thousands of good, hopeful, faithful people it attracted all year round.

Mentioning – in passing – the amount of money it made out of the good, hopeful, faithful thousands.

'But tourism's not what I'm about,' Goff said. 'What I'm concerned with is promoting serious research into subjects rejected by universities in Britain as . . . well, let's say as . . . insufficiently intellectual. The growth of basic human happiness, for instance, has never been something which has tended to absorb our more distinguished scholars. *Far* too simple. Life and death? The afterlife? The *before*life? The human soul? Why should university scientists and philosophers waste time pondering the imponderable? Why not simply study the psychology of the foolish people who believe in all this nonsense?'

Goff paused, with another disarming smile. 'You shoulda stopped me. Tourism is an option this town can explore at its leisure. You want tourists, they can be here – tens of thousands of them. You don't want tourists, you say to me, "Max, this is a quiet town and that's the way we like it." And I retire behind the walls of Crybbe Court and I become so low profile everybody soon forgets I was ever here.'

Guy conceded to himself that, had he been the kind of person who admired others, he might at this moment have admired Goff. This was *very* smart – Goff saying, Of course nobody's *forcing* this town to be exceedingly wealthy.

Laying it on the line for them: I have nothing to lose, you have everything to gain.

Not even the faintest hint of threat.

How could they resist him?

'*They'll listen very patiently to what Goff has to say, then they'll ask one or two very polite questions before drifting quietly away into the night. And then, just as quietly, they'll do their best to shaft the blighter . . .*'

But why should Col Croston think they'd want to? This man was offering them the earth.

'Limp. Stagnant.' Powys lowered his voice, although they were alone in the square. Afraid perhaps, Fay thought, that the town itself would take offence, as if that mattered now.

Over the roofs of shops, she could see the Victorian-Italian-ate pinnacle of the town-hall roof, the stonework blooming for the first time in the glow from its windows. There were probably more people in there tonight than at any other time since it was built. All the people who might be on the streets, in the pubs, scattered around town.

'And then Goff arrives,' Powys said. 'Unwitting front man for Andy Trow, last of the Worts, a practising magician. The heir. Crybbe is his legacy from Michael.'

Fay sat next to him on the step, Arnold between them. Apart from them, the town might have been evacuated. Nobody emerged from the street leading to the town hall, nobody went in.

'OK,' she said. 'He's put the stones back – as many as he can. He's knocked a hole in the wall around the Tump, so that whatever it is can get into the Court – the next point on the line, right?'

'I saw its light in the eaves. I watched it spit . . . Rachel out. Along with the cat. Not much of a guardian any more, but it was there, it had to go. The next point on the line is the church, supposedly the spiritual and emotional heart of the town, from where the curfew's rung. Jack Preece rings the curfew, Jonathon, his son, was to inherit the job. Something's weeding out Preeces.'

'No wonder old Jimmy was so desperate to get to the church after Jack had his accident.'

'He's a bit doddery, isn't he, the old chap?'

'Stronger than he looks, I'd guess. But, sure, at that age he could go anytime. Joe, can nobody else ring it? What about you? What about me? What about – what's his name – Warren?'

'I don't see why not. But it was a task allotted to the Preeces and perhaps only they know how vital it is. The big family secret. The Mayor's probably training this Warren to take over. He's got to, hasn't he?'

Fay was still trying to imagine taciturn, wizened old Jimmy Preece in the role of Guardian of the Gate to Hell. No more bizarre, she supposed, than the idea of Crybbe Court being looked after by a mummified cat.

'What happens,' she said, 'if the curfew doesn't get rung?'

Powys stood up. 'Then it comes roaring and spitting out of the Tump, through the Court, through the new stone in the wood and straight into the church – *through* the church, gathering enormous energy . . . until it reaches . . .'

He began to walk across the cobbles, his footsteps hollow in the dark and the silence.

'. . . here.'

He stood in the centre of the square. The centre of Crybbe.

'My guess is there used to be a stone or a cross on this spot, but it was taken down with all the stones. I bet if you examine Goff's plans, you'll find proposals for some kind of monument. Wouldn't matter what it was. Could be a statue of Jimmy Preece.'

'The Preece Memorial,' Fay said.

'Wouldn't *that* be appropriate?'

Fay was silent, aware of the seconds ticking away towards ten o'clock. Sure she could feel something swelling in the air

499

and a rumbling in the cobbles where Arnold lay quietly, not panting now.

'So what do we do?'

'If we've got any sense,' Powys said, 'we pile into one of the cars and drive like hell across the border to the nearest place with lots of lights. Then we get drunk.'

'And forget.'

'Yeah. Forget.'

Fay said, 'My father's here. And Jean.'

'And Mrs Seagrove. And a few hundred other innocent people.'

The rumbling grew louder. Fay was sure she could feel the cobbles quaking.

'We can't leave.'

Powys said, 'And Andy's here somewhere, Andy Wort. I don't even like to imagine what he's doing.'

'It's too quiet.'

'Much too quiet.'

Except for the rumbling, and two big, white, blazing eyes on the edge of the square.

Powys said, 'What the hell's that?'

The eyes went out, and now the thing was almost luminous in the dimness. A large yellow tractor with a mechanical digger on the front.

'I'm gonner park 'im yere.' They saw the glow of a cigarette and two tiny points of light from small, round spectacles. 'Nobody gonner mind for a few minutes.'

'It's Gomer Parry,' Fay said.

'Ah . . . Miss Morris, is it?'

'Hello, Gomer. Where are you off to?'

'Gonner grab me a swift pint, Miss. Just finished off down the Colonel's, got a throat like a clogged-up toilet. Flush 'im out, see?'

They watched Gomer ascending the steps to the Cock, a jaunty figure, entirely oblivious of whatever was accumulating.

The commotion of the digger's arrival had, for just a short time, pushed back the dark.

Powys said, 'Fay, look, we've got to start making our own

500

waves. It'll be feeble, it probably won't do anything, but we can't drive away and we can't just stand here and watch.'

'Sure,' Fay said, more calmly than she felt.

'We need to try and break up that meeting well before ten. Because if they all start pouring out of the town hall and there's something . . . I don't know, something in the square . . . I don't know what might happen. We're going to have to break it up, set off the fire alarm or something.'

'I doubt if they've got one, but I'll think of something.'

'I didn't necessarily mean you.'

'I'm the best person to do it. I've got nothing to lose. I have no credibility left. What *you* need to do – because you know all the fancy terminology – is go and see Jean, see if she's got any ideas. And make sure Dad lies low. Can you take Arnold?'

'Sure.'

He looked down at her. He couldn't see her very well. She looked like an elf, if paler than the archetype. A plaster elf that fell off the production line at the painting stage, so all the colours had run into one corner of its face.

He put his arms around her and lightly kissed her lips. The lips were very dry, but they yielded. He felt her fear and hugged her.

Fay smiled up at him, or tried to. 'Watch it, Joe,' she said. 'Remember where you are.'

CHAPTER V

*H*ave you ever performed an exorcism?

Sitting in the near-dark in Grace's parlour. Sitting awkwardly, with his elbows on the table where Fay used to keep her editing machine until . . . until somebody broke it.

And the only voices he could hear were Jean's and Murray's alternately repeating the same strange question.

Exorcism.

Well, have I?

Canon Alex Peters remembered the sunny afternoon when Murray was here – only about a week ago – the very last sunny afternoon he could remember.

Remembered exploring his memory with all the expectation of a truffle-hunter in Milton Keynes . . . finally dredging up the Suffolk business. *'Wasn't the full bell, book and candle routine . . . more of a quickie, bless-this-house operation.*

'Actually I think I made it up as I went along.'

Grace's chair waited in front of Grace's fireplace. The brass balls twisted in the see-through base of Grace's clock, catching the last of the light, pulsing with the final death-throes of the day.

And now, when you really need the full bell, book and candle routine, you haven't got the right book and the only bell in town is the bloody curfew which we don't talk about.

Candles, though. Oh yes, plenty of bloody candles. Everybody in power-starved Crybbe has a houseful of bloody candles.

Alex dipped his head into his hands and moaned.

What are you doing to me, Wendy? I can't handle this, you know I can't.

He looked at the clock. He could see the twisting balls but not the time. But it must be getting on for nine.

Nine o'clock and Alex sitting waiting for his dead wife, and frightened.

Oh yes. Coming closer to the end didn't take away the fear.

'Dear Lord,' said Alex hopelessly. 'Take unto Thee Thy servant, Grace. Make her welcome in Thine Heavenly Kingdom, that she should no longer dwell in the half-light of limbo. Let her not remain in this place of suffering but ascend for ever into Thy holy light.'

Alex paused and looked across at the mantelpiece as though it were an altar.

'Amen,' he said, and lowered his chin to his chest.

He had no holy water, no vestments, no Bible, no prayer book.

An old man in faded Kate Bush T-shirt, tracksuit trousers and an ancient, peeling pair of gymshoes, standing, head bowed in the centre of the room, making it up as he went along.

What else could he do?

Certainly not this strident stuff about commanding unquiet spirits to begone. Not to Grace, a prim little lady who never even went to the newsagent's without a hat and gloves.

'Forgive me, Grace,' Alex said.

He sat down in the fireside chair, which had been hers, on those special occasions when the sitting-room was in use.

'Forgive me,' he said.

And fell asleep.

Fay slipped into the hall unprepared for the density of the crowd.

How could so many be so silent?

Every seat was taken and there were even more people standing, lining every spare foot of wall, two or three deep in some places.

Wynford Wiley, guardian of the main portal, turned his sweating cheese of a head as she came in, rasping at her. 'Not got that tape recorder, 'ave you?'

Fay held up both hands to show she hadn't, and Wynford still looked suspicious, as if he thought she might be wired up, with a hidden microphone in her hair. For Christ's sake, what did it matter?

She stood just inside the doors and saw the impossibility of her task. There must be over three hundred people in here. Joe Powys hadn't been entirely serious, but he'd been right: the best thing they could have done was pile into the car and make a dash for civilization. And she'd been so glib: *I'll think of something*.

Fay looked among the multitude, at individual faces, each one set as firm as a cardboard mask. Except in the New Age ghetto, towards the front of the hall, to her left, where there was a variety of expressions. A permanent half-smile on the nodding features of a small man in a safari suit. A woman with an explosion of white hair wearing a beatific expression, face upturned to the great god Goff.

Max was being politely cross-examined on behalf of the

townsfolk by the chairman, craggy Colonel Croston, who Fay knew from council meetings – the only councillor who'd ever spoken to her before the meetings.

'I think one thing that many people would like me to ask you, Mr Goff, is about the stones. Why is it necessary to install what I suppose many people would regard as crude symbols of pagan worship?'

Goff seemed entirely at ease with the question.

'Well, you know . . .' Leaning back confidently in his chair. 'I think all that pagan stuff is a concept which would raise many an eyebrow in most parts of Wales, where nearly every year a new stone circle is erected as part of the national eisteddfod. I realize the eisteddfodic tradition is not so strong here on the border any more – if it ever was – but if you were to place these stones in the ground in Aberystwyth, or Caernarfon, or Fishguard, I doubt anyone would even notice. The point is, Mr Chairman . . . all this is largely symbolic. It symbolizes a realization that this town was once important enough to be a place of pilgrimage – like Lourdes, perhaps. And that *it can be again.*'

Spontaneous sycophantic applause burst from the New Age quarter.

Is he blatantly lying, Fay wondered. Or does he seriously believe this bullshit?

Or are we, Joe Powys and I, grossly, insultingly, libellously wrong about everything?

But almost as soon as she thought this, she began to feel very strongly that they were not wrong.

It was ten minutes past nine, the chamber lit by wrought-iron electric chandeliers, and she just *knew* there was going to be a power cut within the next half hour.

'Come in, Joe,' Jean Wendle said. 'I fear we shall be losing our electricity supply before too long.'

'How do you know that?'

Carrying Arnold, he followed her down the hall and into her living-room, where a pleasant Victorian lamp with a pale-blue shade burned expensive aromatic oil.

'There's a sequence,' Jean said, perching birdlike on a chair-arm. 'Tea?'

'No time, thanks. What's the sequence?'

'Well, temperature fluctuation, to begin with. Either a drop or a raising of the temperature. Coupled with a kind of tightening of the air pressure that you come to recognize. Y'see, these new trip mechanisms or whatever they use do seem to be rather more vulnerable to it than the old system. Or so it seems to me.'

Jean crossed her legs neatly. She was wearing purple velour trousers and white moccasins. 'No time, eh? My.'

He put Arnold down. 'When you say "it" . . . ?'

'It? Oh, we could be talking about anything, from the geological formation – did you know there's a fault line running up through mid Wales and right along the border here, there've been several minor but significant earthquakes in recent years. So there's the geology, to start with . . .'

'Jean,' Powys said, 'we're in a lot of trouble.'

'Aye,' Jean Wendle said, 'I know.'

'So let's not talk about temperature fluctuations or rock strata, let's talk about Michael Wort.'

'What about him?'

Powys sat down, gathered his thoughts and then spent three minutes telling her, in as flat and factual a way as he could manage, his and Fay's conclusions. Ending with the shadow of Black Michael falling over Crybbe, whatever remained of his bodily power centres fused with the town's, the exchange of dark energy.

He felt Arnold pushing against his legs in the way he'd done last night in Bell Street, before leading him to the blood and the semi-conscious Fay. Powys reached down a hand and patted him, and Arnold began to pant. He's aware of the urgency, too, Powys thought. But then, he's a dowser's dog.

'It'll try and take the church tonight,' he said. 'And then . . . God knows . . .'

Jean sat and listened. When he finished she was silent for over a minute. Powys looked at his watch and then bit on a knuckle.

'That's very interesting,' Jean said. 'You may be right.'

Arnold whined.

'Shush.' Powys laid a hand on the dog's side. Arnold was breathing rapidly.

'We haven't any time to waste, Jean. I think . . . it seems to me I need to get over to the church and ensure that . . . well, that old Preece makes it to the belfry. I can't think what else I can do that's halfway meaningful, can you?'

Jean thought for a moment and then shook her head.

'What I think is . . . in fact I know . . . that you ought to go for the source.'

Her eyes were very calm and sure.

Powys said, 'I don't know what you mean.'

'The source, Joe. Where it begins.'

He thought of the great dark mound with its swaying trees and the blood of Henry Kettle on its flank.

'That's right,' Jean said. 'The Tump.'

'I . . .' It was forbidding enough by daylight.

'Don't think you can handle that?'

'I don't see the point. I'm not a magician. I'm not a shaman. I'm just a bloody writer. Not even that any more.'

No, he might just as well have said, I don't think I *can* handle it. This was Jean Wendle he was talking to. Jean Wendle the psychic. Also Jean Wendle the barrister. The human lie-detector.

'Oh, Joe, Joe . . . You're like Alex. You won't face up to the way it is. To what has to be done. You lost the wee girl, Rose, you lost Rachel Wade.'

'No.' He shook his head. He didn't understand. He hadn't understood when it happened – either time – and he didn't understand now.

What am I *missing*? Suddenly he was in a mental frenzy. Why did she have to say that? Why did she have to slap him across the face with the incomprehensible horror of Rose and Rachel? And was he *missing* something?

'Don't let yourself lose this one,' Jean said.

Fay?

Please . . . What can't I *see*?

'And when I get to the Tump,' he asked weakly. 'What am I supposed to do then?'

'You're looking for Boulton-Trow, aren't you?'

He stared at her, Arnold throbbing against his ankle.

'If Boulton-Trow has orchestrated all this, then he has to stand somewhere, has he not, with his wee conductor's baton. He has to have a podium, from which – if you really want to end all this – you must dislodge him. I'm sorry, Joe, it's never easy. You know that really, don't you? You could indeed lend Mr Preece a supporting arm as he climbs the steps to the belfry, but are you going to be there again tomorrow night, and the night after?'

Powys stood up. His legs felt very weak. He was afraid. He gathered the trembling Arnold awkwardly into his arms, looked vaguely around. 'Where's the Canon?'

Jean saw him to the door. 'Don't worry about Alex. He's coming to grips with his past, too.' She gave his arm a sympathetic squeeze. 'It's the night for it.'

Col Croston was pleased and yet disappointed, too. It was going smoothly, Max Goff was making his points very cogently and even impressing *him*, as the strictly neutral chairman. And, no, he hadn't expected fireworks.

But wasn't this just a little bit *too* tame?

Hadn't once had to bang his gavel or call for silence. Just that spot of aggression towards the cameraman – minor pre-meeting nerves. And that single, reedy interruption during his introduction. All of this before he'd even called on Goff to address the meeting.

And now the fellow had been given a more than fair hearing.

'Right,' Col said. 'Well, I think I've put all *my* questions, but what about all of *you*? What's the general feeling? I think we at least owe it to Mr Goff for him to be able to walk away from here tonight with some idea of how the townsfolk of Crybbe are reacting to his ideas.'

Wasn't awfully surprised to get a lot of blank looks.

'Well, come on, don't be shy. This is a public meeting and you are, in fact, the public.'

When he did get a response it came, unsurprisingly, from the wrong side of the room.

The large, middle-aged woman with the white hair was on her feet.

'Yes,' said Col. 'Mrs Ivory, isn't it? Go ahead.'

'Mr Chairman,' Mrs Ivory said sweetly, 'I'm sure we must seem a pretty strange lot to the local people.'

She paused. If she was waiting to be contradicted, Col thought, she'd be on her feet for the rest of the night.

'Well . . .' Mrs Ivory blushed. 'I suppose we all have adjustments to make, don't we. I know I got some *very* odd looks when I went into a sweetshop and said I preferred carob to chocolate, actually, and didn't mind paying the extra for a non-dairy alternative.'

Good grief, Col thought, is this the best you can do?

'What I mean is, Mr Chairman, I suppose we *have* got what seem like some funny ideas, but, well, we're *harmless*, and I don't mind people thinking I'm an eccentric, as long as they accept me as a *harmless* eccentric. That's the point I want to make. We don't want to take over or impose some weird new regime. We're not like the Jehovah's Witnesses – we won't be knocking on doors or handing out pamphlets saying, "Come and join the New Age movement." We're gentle people, and we're not going to intrude and . . . well, that's all I have to say really. Thank you.'

'Thank *you*, Mrs Ivory,' said Col. 'Well, there you are, I think that was very, er . . . a valuable point. So. What about some local reaction? Mr Mayor, you're down there on the floor of the meeting tonight, somewhat of a new experience for you, but what it *does* mean is you *are* entitled to speak your mind. Give us the benefit of your, er . . .'

He was going to make a little New Age sort of joke then, about the Mayor's 'ancient wisdom', but decided perhaps not.

'. . . years of experience.'

He watched Jimmy Preece rising skeletally to his feet.

'Not expecting a sermon. Just a *few* words, Mr Mayor.'

'Well, I . . .' Jimmy Preece looked down at his boots, and then he said prosaically, 'On behalf of the town, I'd like to thank Mr Goff for coming along tonight and telling us about his plans. Very civil of 'im. I'm sure we'll all bear in mind what 'e's 'ad to say.'

And the Mayor sat down.

Col looked helplessly at Max Goff.

At the back of the room Fay Morrison looked at her watch, saw it was coming up to twenty minutes past nine and was very much relieved. Within a couple of minutes the meeting would be wound up and all these people would go their separate ways. They'd be off the line, away from what she was slowly and less incredulously coming to think of as the death path.

'Thank you, Mr Mayor,' Goff said, rising to his feet. 'Thank you, Mr Chairman. But this is only the start of things . . .'

What?

Goff said, 'I'd like you to meet at this point some of the people you'll be seeing around town. For those who wanna know more about the heritage of the area, the distinguished author J. M. Powys will be, er, with us presently. But I'd like to acquaint you, first of all, with some of the very skilled practitioners who, for an introductory period, will be making their services available entirely free of charge to anyone in Crybbe who'd like to know more about alternative health. As Hilary said a few moments ago, there'll be no proselytizing, they'll simply be around if required, so first of all I'd like you to meet . . .'

He stopped. The chairman had put a hand on his arm.

'One moment, Mr Goff, I think we appear to have another question . . . Think I saw a hand going up at the back. Oh.'

Col had recognized Fay Morrison, the radio reporter. This was a public meeting, not a media event; however, in the absence of any worthwhile response from the floor, he supposed it would be all right to let her have her say.

'Yes,' he said. 'Mrs Morrison.'

Goff's head spun round. 'This is not a press conference, Mr Chairman.'

'Yes, I'm aware of that, Mr Goff, but Mrs Morrison *is* a resident of Crybbe.'

'Yeah, sure, but . . .'

509

'And I *am* the chairman,' Col said less affably.

Goff shut up, but he wasn't happy.

Col was. This was more like it.

'Go ahead, Mrs Morrison.'

'I'd like to know if Mr Goff is going to introduce us to his chief adviser, Mr Boulton-Trow.'

'I'm afraid,' Goff said coldly, 'that Mr Boulton-Trow is not able to be with us tonight.'

'Why not?'

Goff dropped his voice. 'Look, Mr Chair, I've had dealings with this woman before. She's a load of trouble. She makes a practice of stirring things up. She's been fired by the local radio station for inaccuracy, she's . . .'

'Mr Goff . . .' Thin steel in Col's voice. 'This is a public meeting, and I'm the chairman. Go ahead, Mrs Morrison, but I hope this is relevant. I don't want a slanging match.'

'Thank you, Mr Chairman,' Fay said. 'I've certainly no intention of being at all argumentative.'

Oh God, *go for it, woman.*

'I'd simply like to ask Mr Goff what contribution he expects will be made to the general well-being of Crybbe by employing a descendant of perhaps . . . perhaps the most hated man in the history of the town.'

She paused. People were turning to look at her, especially from the Crybbe side of the room.

Goff was on his feet. 'This is ridiculous . . .'

The chairman slammed down his gavel. 'Please!'

'I'm referring,' Fay said, raising her voice, 'to the sixteenth-century sheriff known popularly, since his death, as Black Michael, and widely known at the time for unjustly hanging . . .'

'Mrs Morrison,' said the chairman. 'With the best will in the world, I don't honestly think . . .'

'Andy Trow has, of course, reversed his real surname. He's Andy Wort, isn't he, Mr Goff?'

There was a silence.

Oh fuck it, Fay thought. Take it all the way.
'He's also, I understand, your lover.'
And the lights went out.

CHAPTER VI

Please. Take my arm.

Better?

Good.

Do you remember when I used to offer you my arm in the street and you absolutely refused to accept it. 'Not until we're married,' you would say, even though you were quite poorly. Worried about your reputation, I suppose. Bit late for that.

And then, of course, when we were married it was quite impossible, with you in a wheelchair and me pushing the damn thing.

All right now, though, isn't it?

Yes. All right now.

Which way shall we go? No, you choose. Down to the river? No?

To the church! Yes, of course. Bring back some memories. Young Murray did rather well, I thought. Yes, I agree about the amendments to the vows; saved any embarrassment, didn't it? Indeed it did.

It is dark, isn't it? Careful now. Mind you don't trip over the kerb or the end of your shroud.

Do tell me, won't you, if you're feeling tired.

Jolly good.

As Joe Powys drove, on full headlights, into the lane that slipped down beside the church, he formed an image of Crybbe as an old and poorly built house riddled with damp. Periodically new people would move in and redecorate the rooms: bright new paint, new wallpaper, new furniture. But the wet always came through and turned the walls black and rotted the furniture.

And eventually people stopped throwing money at it and just tried to insulate themselves and their families as best they could. It wasn't much fun to live in, and the people who stayed there were the ones with few prospects and nowhere else to go.

And that was the basic socio-economic viewpoint.

Trying to explain the supernatural aspects in terms of rising damp was more complicated.

If only he could speak to the shadowy figure who, in the late 1500s, had attempted to install, just above ground-level, an effective damp-proof course.

Let's assume this man was John Dee, astrologer at the court of Queen Elizabeth I.

Powys braked hard as a baby rabbit shot from the hedgerow into the centre of the road and then stopped, turning pale, terrified eyes into the headlights.

He switched off the lights, and the rabbit scampered away.

Just for a moment, Powys smiled.

There's a portrait. John Dee in middle age. A thin-faced man with high cheekbones. Watchful, but kindly eyes. He wears a black cap, suggesting baldness, and has a luxuriant white beard, like an ice-cream cone.

In Andy's notes, Dee (if it is he) gives only graphic descriptions of experiences, like the visit of the spirit (Wort) in the night.

Perhaps somewhere Dee has documented the action he took to contain the rampant spirit after Wort's death.

Dee never seems to have been very wealthy. Towards the end of his life he was virtually exiled to the north, as warden of Christ's College, Manchester. With Elizabeth dead and James on the throne – James who was in constant fear of Satanic plots and clamped down accordingly on all forms of occultism – the elderly Dee was forced to defend himself and his reputation as a scholar against various accusations that he practised witchcraft. Ill-founded accusations, no doubt, but these were dangerous, paranoid times.

So what would the penurious Dee do if contacted by old friends or relatives in Crybbe with tales of hauntings and oppression by dark forces invoked by the late Sir Michael Wort?

He drove past the turning to Court Farm and could see no lights between the trees. No lights anywhere. He might, out here, be twenty miles from the nearest town. It was like driving back in time, or into another dimension

> To Percival Weale,
> Merchant of Crybbe
> My Dear Mr Weale,
>   It was with much sorrow that I received your letter
> informing me that our mutual associate, Sheriff Wort
> continues to torment the town from a place beyond this life.
> It has long been apparent to me that the etheric layer is so
> dense upon the atmosphere along the border of Wales and
> England that it may not always be so comfortable a place of
> habitation . . .

And did Dee, old, impecunious and in constant fear of arrest, appeal to Percy Weale to make financial provision for the curfew to be rung (so that the most dangerous hours of darkness might remain peaceful) and to assign some long-established local family to the task?

And being unable to travel to Crybbe himself, did he vaguely suggest that if the malignant spirit were to be controlled it was essential for the stones to be removed, the Tump walled in and the spiritual energy level to remain low.

> And you must warn the townspeople to continue with their
> lives but not to expand the town to any great extent and,
> above all, to offer no challenge to the spirit. And, as for the
> hand and any other of his limbs or organs that should come
> to light, no purpose will be served in their destruction. You
> must take these and enclose them in separate and confined
> places – I would suggest within a chimney or fireplace or
> beneath a good stone floor – where they may never be exposed
> to the light or the air. This is far from satisfactory, but my
> knowledge does not extend to more. Forgive me.

Powys drove between the gateposts of Crybbe Court and

felt the house before he saw it, a dark and hungry maw.

He thought, *Hand? What hand? I don't know anything about a hand.*

Get your act together, Powys.

He thought about Fay and started to worry, so he thought about Rachel instead, and he looked up towards the house and felt bitterly angry.

Better keep to the path, I think, my dear. Somewhat safer, in the dark.

Not that they take much care of this path, or indeed the church itself, never much in the way of civic pride in Crybbe. Poor old Murray's got his hands full.

Ah. Now. I know where we're going.

We're going to your grave, aren't we?

Now, look, before you say anything, I'm sorry it had to be down at this end – not exactly central, I realize that, another few yards, in fact, and you'd be in the wood. But it's surely shady on a warm day, and you never did like too much sun, did you? I suppose you spent most of your life in the shade, really, and . . . well, you know, I always had the impression that was how you wanted it to be.

I know, I know . . . the flowers. I keep forgetting, memory isn't what it was, as you know. You bring a few flowers with the best of intentions, and then you forget all about them and the next time you come they're all dead and forlorn and there are stalks and seed-pods everywhere, all a terrible mess, and I do understand the way you feel about that, of course I do.

Hello, who's this?

Oh, Grace, look, it's young Murray.

No, don't get up, old chap.

Well, er . . . it's a lovely night, isn't it?

Yes. Indeed.

What's that?

Cain and Abel?

I'm sorry . . . I'm not quite getting your drift. What you're saying is, Abel killed Cain?

Well, not in my version, old son, but I suppose you modernists have your own ideas.

Abel killed Cain, eh?
Well, if you say so, Murray, if you say so.

Arnold was not at all happy about being left in the Mini. Joe Powys had pushed back the slide-opening driver's window several inches to give him plenty of air, and he stood up on the seat and pressed his head through the gap and whined frantically.

'I can't take you,' Powys said. 'Please, Arnold.'

He'd left the dog a saucer of water on the back shelf. Poured from a bottle he kept in the boot because the radiator had been known to boil dry.

Knowing full well that he was doing all this just in case, for some unknowable reason, he didn't get back.

'Good boy,' he said. 'Good boy.'

He locked the car and moved quickly, uncomfortably away. He didn't want to be here. He *felt* he was in the wrong place, but he didn't trust his own feelings. He trusted Jean Wendle's feelings because Jean was an experienced psychic and a Wise Woman, and he was just a writer; and when it came to dealing with real life, writers didn't know shit.

The Mini was tightly parked in a semi-concealed position behind the stable-block. Powys carried a hand-lamp with a beam projecting a good fifty yards in front of him. It was probably a mistake; he should be more surreptitious. What was he going to do – stand amid the ruins of the wall, pinning Andy in the powerful beam as he cavorted naked in the maelstrom of black energy?

'It all sounds,' he said aloud into the night, 'so bloody stupid.'

Earth mysteries.

Book your seats for a magical, mind-expanding excursion to the Old Golden Land.

A fun-filled New Age afternoon. A book of half-baked pseudo-mystical musings on your knee as you picnic by a sacred standing stone, around it a glowing aura of fascinating legend.

As he moved uncertainly across the field towards the Tump, it struck him that it was past ten o'clock and there'd been no curfew. Well, it was late last night, too. Took old Preece longer to make it to the belfry.

But he still thought, That's where I should be. Or with Fay. Not here.

Or am I just trying to put it off again, the confrontation, afraid my reasoning's all to cock and this man, with his precise, laid-back logic and his superior knowledge of the arcane, is going to hold up another dark mirror.

As was usual with these things, he didn't notice it was happening until it had been happening for quite some time.

Climbing easily over the ruins of the wall, where somebody had taken a bulldozer for a midnight joy-ride, the rhythm of his breath began to change so that it was a separate thing from what he was doing, which was labouring up the side of the mound. Normally, to do this, he would be jerking the breaths in like a fireman on a steam train shovelling more and more coal on, breath as fuel. But he was conscious, in an unconcerned, dreamlike way, of the climb being quite effortless and the breathing fuelling something else, some inner mechanism.

Each breath was a marathon breath, long, long, long, but not at all painful. When you discovered that you, after all, possessed a vast inner strength, it was a deeply pleasurable thing.

He followed what he thought was the beam from the lamp, until he realized the lamp had gone out but the beam had not, as though he was throwing a shadow, a negative shadow, which made it a shadow of light.

Out of the tufted grass and into the bushes, moving with ease, watching his legs doing the work, as legs were meant to do, tearing through the undergrowth in their eagerness to take him to the summit of the mound.

The source.

Each breath seeming to take minutes, breathing in not only air, but colours, all the colours of the night, which were colours not normally visible to undeveloped human sight.

Moving up the side of the Tump, between bushes and tree trunks and moving effortlessly. Effortlessly as the last time.

goes round . . . thrice . . .

goes round . . .

CHAPTER VII

NOBODY panicked.

Well, they wouldn't, would they? Not in Crybbe. They'd be quite used to this by now. Part of everyday life. Every*night* life, anyway.

So there were no screams, no scrambles for the door. Guy Morrison knew this because he was standing only yards from the exit where the fat policeman, Wiley, was doubtless still at his post.

'Only a matter of time, wasn't it?' Col Croston called out. 'Don't worry, it often happens during council meetings. Mrs Byford's gone to switch on the generator.'

It was a bloody mercy, in Guy's opinion.

The woman was completely and utterly *insane*!

For the first time, Guy was profoundly thankful he and Fay had never had children.

He hoped that by the time the lights came on she'd have had the decency to make herself scarce. The sheer *embarrassment* of it!

'Guy?'

Somebody snuggled against his chest.

'Just as well it *is* me,' he whispered, and she giggled and kissed his neck.

A worrying thought struck him.

'You're not wearing lipstick, are you, Catrin?'

'Not any more,' Catrin Jones said, and Guy plunged a hand into his jacket pocket, searching frantically for a handkerchief.

'No, I'm not,' Catrin said. 'Honest. I'm sorry.'

'Shut up then,' he hissed, conscious of the fact that nobody else appeared to be talking.

'Won't be long now,' Col Croston shouted cheerfully. At least, Guy thought, it would be an opportunity for him to pretend the five minutes before the power cut had never happened.

He became aware that somebody had drawn back the curtains at the windows, and what little light remained in the sky showed him a scene like the old black and white photographs he'd seen of the insides of air-raid shelters in the blitz, only even more overcrowded. All it needed was someone with rampant claustrophobia to start floundering about and there'd be total chaos.

But nobody moved and nobody spoke and it was quite uncanny. He felt Catrin's hand moving like a mouse in one of his hip pockets. When they got back to Cardiff he'd suggest she should be transferred. Something she couldn't very well refuse – six months' attachment as an assistant trainee radio producer, or anything else that sounded vaguely like promotion.

As his eyes adjusted, Guy was able to make out individual faces. A fat farmer who hadn't taken off his cap. That cocky little radio chap trying vainly to see his watch. Jocasta Newsome and her husband – strange that she wasn't talking; perhaps they'd had a row.

The radio bloke – at least this outfit had had the good sense not to have Fay covering the meeting – was on his feet and moving to the door.

'Just a minute,' Guy heard Wiley say officiously. 'Where you think you're goin'?'

'Look, I've got an urgent news report to go down. Gavin Ashpole, Offa's Dyke Radio.'

'Well, you can 'ang on yere. Studio won't be workin' if there's no power, is it?'

'Then I'll do it by phone. Do you mind?'

'I'm not bein' offensive, sir, but you might 'ave lifted somebody's wallet in there and be makin' off with the proceeds.'

'Oh, for . . . Look, pal, I've got an expensive tape recorder on the floor under the chairman's table. You can hold it to ransom if I don't come back. Now, *please*.'

'Lucky I recognizes your voice, Mr Ashpole,' Wynford Wiley said genially, and Guy heard a bolt go back.

'Thanks.'

Guy heard the door grinding open, but he didn't hear it close again. He didn't hear anything.

Had he been looking through the viewfinder of a camera, it would have seemed at first like a smear on the lens.

Then it took shape, like a sculpture in smoke, and a figure was standing in the central aisle between the two blocks of chairs. It looked lost. It moved in short steps, almost shuffling, like a Chaplinesque tramp in an old film, but in slow-motion. There was a yellowish tinge to its ill-defined features. It was a man.

His nose was large and bulbous, his eyes were pure white and he was moving down the aisle towards Guy Morrison.

Even without his razor, Guy would have known him anywhere.

Guy screamed.

'*No! Get away! Get back.*'

Catrin gasped and moved sharply away from him.

But ex – *very*-ex – Police Sergeant Handel Roberts continued to shuffle onwards as if the room were not illegally overcrowded but empty apart from Guy Morrison and himself.

'Jocasta!' Guy screamed. 'Look! It's him. It's *him*!'

Closing his eyes, throwing an arm across his face, he plunged forward like someone making a desperate dash through flames to the door of a blazing room.

There was a ghastly, tingling moment of damp and penetrating cold, and then he was on his knees, his head in her lap, his hands clawing at her dress, mumbling incoherently into her thighs. He began to sob. 'Oh God, Jocasta, it *is* . . .'

Jocasta Newsome didn't move. When he opened his eyes he saw there were lights in the room, but different lights, fluorescent bars high on the walls. He blinked up at her face and found it harsh and grainy in the new light and frozen into an expression of ultimate disdain.

'You filthy bastard,' the thin, bearded man next to her said.

Moving like a train through the night, the track unrolling before you, a ribbon of light, straight as a torchbeam. There are deep-green hills on either side – deep green because they are dense with trees – and the silver snaking river, all of this quite clearly visible, for they do not depend on sunlight or moonlight but have their own inner luminescence.

There are no buildings in this landscape, no farms or

cottages or barns or stables or sheep-sheds, no cars, no tractors, no gates, no fences, no hedges. In some places, the trees give way, diminishing themselves, become not separate, defined, organic entities but a green wash, a watercolourist's view of trees. Then they fade into fields, but with the spirit of the old woodland still colouring their aura.

It is a strange land at first, but then not so strange, for what you see is the true essence of the countryside you know. This is a country unviolated by Man.

This is the spirit landscape.

What you once presumed to call the Old Golden Land.

And the unfurling ribbon of light is what, over half a century earlier, your mentor Alfred Watkins had presumed to call the Old Straight Track.

Alf. Alf Watkins, isn't it? You here too?

No answer. He isn't here. You're alone. Lying between two tall trees on top of the Tump in the heat, and moving like a fast train in the night.

Until, with no warning, the track buckles in front of you, and the night shatters into a thousand shards of black glass.

'Remember me?'

A whisper. Tumult in the hall. Nobody else heard the whisper, dry as ash.

'Who's that?'

'Oh . . . don't reckernize the voice, then, is it? Yeard it before, though, you 'ave.'

'Huh?'

'Crude.'

'What?'

'Lyrically . . . mor . . . onic.'

'What the . . . ?'

'An' musically . . . musically *inept*.'

'Jeez, you must be . . .'

'Can't even remember my fuckin' name, can you?'

'Listen, I'll talk to you later. Tomorrow. Make an appointment.'

'You're a bloody old bag of shit, you are.'

'Listen, I can understand . . .'

'Don't let the kid give up sheep-shearing classes. That's what you said.'

'Yeah, but . . .'

'I knows 'ow to shear sheep, already, though, see. What you do is . . .'

Gavin Ashpole was discovering that there was virtually nowhere quite as dark as a tiny, windowless, unattended radio studio during a power cut.

Belonging as it did to Offa's Dyke Radio, the Crybbe Unattended, unlike the town hall, did not have a generator. The emergency lighting amounted to an old bicycle lamp which Fay Morrison left on the table in the outer office. It took several minutes and a lot of explicit cursing for Gavin Ashpole to find it.

He knew time must be getting on as he sat down at the desk to transcribe his notes and scramble together a voice-piece. A phone call confirmed it.

'Gavin! Where've you been, man? You're on air in two minutes!'

'Huh?' Gavin aimed the bicycle lamp at his watch. It said 9.28. Shit, shit, shit.

'Much of a story, is it, Gav? We've left you a full two minutes, as instructed.'

'Sod all,' he said tersely. 'And you're getting it down the phone – the fucking power's off. Listen, James, cut me back to one and shove it back down the bulletin. Bring me in around 9.35, OK?'

'Not sure we've got . . .'

'Just do it, eh? Take down the link now, I'll keep it tight. OK, ready? There's been a hostile reception tonight for billionaire businessman Max Goff at a packed public meeting to discuss his plans for a so-called New Age mystical healing centre in the border town of Crybbe . . . from where Gavin Ashpole now reports. Got that?'

Gavin hung up.

He had enough for one minute with what he'd already written. He pulled off his tie, stretched out his legs, switched off the lamp and waited for the studio to ring.

Sodding power cut. Maybe he should have brought the radio car after all. He could have done an exclusive interview with the famous Fay Morrison.

Stupid slag. She deserved everything she was going to get. Everybody knew Max Goff was pretty well-established in shirt-lifting circles, but, unless you were seriously suicidal, you didn't bring up this issue before about three hundred witnesses including a couple of suits who looked like outriders from the Epidemic legal department.

He should sue the pants off the bitch.

pants off the bitch.

Aaaah!

Went through him like a red-hot wire. He nearly took off.

Sssssstrewth!

He wanted her.

In truth, he wanted anybody, but superbitch Fay Morrison was the one whose image was projected naked into his lap with its legs wrapped around him in the dark.

Hot.

Stifling in here, warm air jetting at him like a fan-heater.

Too fucking hot.

And who was there to notice, anyway, if he took off his trousers?

The phone rang. 'Gavin, news studio, can you hear this OK?'

Plugged into the news. '. . . *Major row erupted in the Commons tonight when Welsh Nationalist MP Guto Evans challenged the Government's* . . .' Then faded down, and James Barlow's voice in the earpiece. 'Gavin, we'll be coming to you in about a minute and a half, and you've got fifty seconds, OK?'

'Yeah,' Gavin croaked. 'Yeah.'

The fluorescent bars were only secondary lighting, linked to what must have been a small generator. The room was still only half-lit, and the light from the walls was blue and frigid.

Fay, unmoving at the rear of the hall, knew that something had changed and the light was part of it; it altered the whole ambience of the room and better reflected the feeling of the night.

In that it was a cold, unnatural light.

She couldn't understand, for a moment, why so few people were taking in the ludicrous spectacle of her ex-husband, the sometimes almost-famous TV personality, making such an incredible prat of himself all over the appalling Jocasta Newsome.

Then she heard the silence. Silence spreading like a stain down the hall, from the people at the front who'd seen it first.

Fay looked and didn't believe, her eyes hurrying back to stupid Guy – standing in the aisle now, dusting off his trousers, mumbling, 'Sorry, sorry, must have tripped.'

Col Croston, up on the platform next to Max Goff, didn't see it either, at first; Goff's back was turned to him. 'Ah,' Col Croston saying. 'Here we are. Lights. We can continue. Splendid. Well, I think, if there are no more questions, we'll . . . Sorry?'

Max Goff's hand on his arm.

'You want to say something? Sure. Fine. Go ahead.'

Fay was not aware that Goff had actually asked the Colonel anything, but now the bulky man was coming slowly, quite lazily, to his feet and opening his mouth as if to say something monumentally significant. But there was no sign of the large, even, white teeth which normally shone out when the smooth mat of red beard divided. A black hole in the beard, Goff trying to shape a word but managing only:

'Aw . . .'

And then out it all came.

He's being sick, said the sensible part of Fay's mind. He's been eating tomato chutney and thick, rich strawberry jam full of whole, ripe strawberries.

'Awk . . .'

A gob of it landed – *thoppp!* – on the blotter in front of Max Goff.

In the front row, Hilary Ivory exploded into hysterics and

struggled to get out of her seat, something crimson and warm having landed in her soft, white hair.

Fay saw that Max Goff had two mouths, and one was in his neck.

He threw back his head with an eruption of spouting blood, raised both white-suited arms far above his head – like a last, proud act of worship. And then, overturning the table, he plunged massively into the well of screams.

CHAPTER VIII

HIS own light was in his eyes.

'You know, Mr Powys,' Humble said, 'Mr Trow was dead right about you.'

The hand-lamp was tucked into the cleft between two tree roots. Humble was sitting in the grass a few feet away from the lamp.

He couldn't see Humble very well, but he could see what Humble was holding. It was a crossbow: very modern, plenty of black metal. It had a heavy-looking rifle-type butt, which was obviously what Humble had hit him with. Back of the neck, maybe between the shoulder-blades. Either way, he didn't want to move.

'What he said was,' Humble explained, 'his actual words: "Joe Powys is *very* obedient." He always does what he's told. Somebody tells him to go to the Tump, he goes to the Tump.'

Powys's senses were numbed.

'Well, that's how I prefer it,' Humble said. '*Making* people do fings is very time-consuming. I much prefer obedience.'

'Where's Andy?' Powys was surprised to discover he could still talk.

'Well, he ain't here, is he? Somebody indicate he might be?'

Humble lifted his crossbow to his shoulder, squinted at Powys. He was about ten feet away. There was a steel bolt in the crossbow.

Powys cringed.

'Pheeeeeeew,' Humble said. 'Straight frew your left eyeball, Mr Powys.'

Powys didn't move. You live in fear of the unknown and the unseen and, when you're facing death, death turns out to be a yobbo with a mousetrap mouth and a lethal weapon favoured by the lower type of country-sport enthusiast.

'But it won't come to that,' Humble said. 'Seeing as obedience is one of your virtues. I won't say that's not a pity – I never done a human being with one of these – but if I got to postpone the experience, I got to postpone it. On your feet, please, Mr P.'

'I don't think I can. I think you broke my collar-bone.'

'Oh, that's where you keep your collar-bone these days, is it? Don't fuck with me please, get up.'

And Powys did, accepting without question that this guy would kill him if he didn't. Humble stood up, too. He was wearing a black gilet, his arms bare. Humble was a timeless figure, the hunter. He killed.

'Now, we're going to go down off the Tump, Mr Powys, on account you can't always trust your reactions up here, as you surely know. We're going to go down, back over that wall, OK?'

'Where's Andy?' Powys said.

'I'm empowered to answer just one of your questions, and that wasn't it, I'm sorry.'

Powys tripped over a root and grabbed at a bush. 'Aaah.' Thorns.

'Keep going, please. Don't turn round.'

Powys froze. *He's going to kill me. He's going to shoot me from behind.*

Something slammed into his back and he cried out and lost his footing and crashed through the thorn bush and rolled over and over.

'. . . did tell you to keep going.'

As he lay in a tangle at the foot of the mound, Humble slipped down beside him, just inside the wall.

'I'll tell you the answer, shall I? Then you can work out the question at your leisure. The answer is – you ready? – the answer is . . . *his mother*. Now get on your feet, over the wall and across to the old house.'

The night has gathered around Warren, and he's loving it. Earned himself a piece of it now – a piece of night to carry round with him and nibble on whenever he's hungry.

And he's still hungry, his appetite growing all the time.

He's off out of the back door of the town hall and across the square, into the alley by the Cock, the Stanley knife hot in his right hand. Only it's not *his* hand any more; this is the Hand of Glory.

The ole box is just a box now, and what's in the box is just bones. His is the hand and his will be the glory.

Felt like doing a few more while he was in there. That Colonel Croston, of the SAS. That'd have been a laugh.

Incredible, the way he just walked in the back way and the lights had gone, dead on cue, like wherever he goes he brings the night in with him.

He has this brilliant night vision now. Just like daylight. *Better* than daylight 'cause *he* can see and no bugger else can.

Standing behind this fat phoney, big man on a squidgy little chair, glaring white suit – you'd have to be blind *not* to see him – and all the time in the world to choose where to put it in.

Didn't need to choose. The Hand of Glory knew.

Brilliant. Thought he'd be squealing like a pig, but he never made more than a gurgle.

Brilliant.

There's someone behind Tessa in the alley. Tall guy.

'Who's this?'

Tessa laughing. 'My teacher.'

'How's it going, Warren?' the teacher saying. 'How are you feeling?'

Warren grinning, savouring the night in his mouth, and his eyes are like lights. Headlights, yeah.

'Good lad,' says the teacher.

*

Minnie Seagrove was not too happy with the Bourbon creams.

It was long after nine when she placed a small china plate of the long brown biscuits on one of the occasional tables and set it down by the side of Frank's chair at just the right height. Putting the camping light on the table next to the plate, still dubiously pursing up her lips. 'I do hope they're all right, Frank. They're nearly a month over the sell-by date. I remember I bought them the day they took you into the General. They'd just opened that new Safeways near the station, and I thought I'd go down there from the hospital, 'cause it's not far to walk, take me mind off it, sort of thing.'

Tears came into Mrs Seagrove's eyes at the memory. 'I bought a whole rainbow trout, too. I thought, he's never managed to catch one, least I can do is serve him one up for his first dinner when he comes out.'

She turned away and grabbed a Scottie from the box to dab her eyes. They were Kleenex really, but Mrs Seagrove called all tissues Scotties because it sounded more homely.

'Had to throw it in the bin, that trout. Well past its sell-by. Still, you *did* come back from the General, after all, didn't you, Frank?'

Looking at him through the tears, Mrs Seagrove had to keep blinking and on every other blink, Frank seemed to disappear. She applied the Scottie to her eyes again and sat down opposite him. He didn't look well, she had to admit.

'Eat your Bourbons, Frank,' she said. 'There'll be nothing left of you if you go on like this. I know, I'll put the wireless on – you can listen to the local news.'

Mrs Seagrove kept the wireless on the sideboard. To tell the truth, it wasn't her kind of wireless at all. Justin had bought it for them last Christmas but one. It was a long black thing with dozens of switches and you could see all these speakers through the plastic grilles, big ones and little ones, all jumbled up. Why they couldn't make them with just one speaker and cover it up neatly like they used to, she'd never know.

Being that changing stations was so complicated, she had it permanently tuned to Offa's Dyke Radio. She'd have preferred

Radio Two herself, that young Chris Stuart had ever such a comforting voice, but Frank said if you were living in a new place you ought to keep up with what was happening around you, even if it wasn't very interesting. Mrs Seagrove certainly found most of it quite boring – too much about councils and sheep prices – so she put it on quite low tonight (Frank had good ears, better than hers) and she only turned it up when she heard that Max Goff mentioned.

'. . . *at a packed public meeting to discuss his plans for a so-called New Age mystical healing centre in the border town of Crybbe . . . from where Gavin Ashpole now reports.*'

Gavin who? What had happened to Fay Morrison? She might have been a bit awkward about the . . . thing. But she did seem quite a nice girl when you actually met her.

'. . . *Townsfolk listened in hostile silence as Max Goff explained his plans to turn Crybbe into a kind of New Age Lourdes, bringing in thousands of tourists from all over the world and providing a massive boost for the local economy. However, he said, it would be up to the town whether it* . . . *Oh* . . . *Oh, you bitch* . . . *oh, you* . . . *oh, please* . . .'

Mrs Seagrove recoiled from the wireless as if a wasp had flown out of one of the speakers.

'Frank, did you hear that?'

'*Oh* . . . *oh* . . . *please* . . . *yes* . . . *yes, do it* . . . *! CHEW IT OFF!!*'

There was a long silence and then the voice of the newsreader came back.

'*I'm sorry, I* . . . *I'm not sure what happened there. We'll try and return to that report* . . . *er, other news now* . . .'

'Frank,' said Minnie Seagrove. 'Did you hear that, Frank? That's your precious Offa's Dyke Radio for you. Chris Stuart never goes to pieces like that. Did you hear . . . Frank?'

Frank's chair was empty.

All the Bourbon biscuits were still on the plate, six of them, arranged in a little semi-circle.

'Frank? Frank, where are you?'

Breathing faster, Mrs Seagrove turned and switched off the wireless and turned back to the chair and rubbed her eyes with the screwed-up tissue, but Frank was gone and the door was closed.

She started to feel very confused.

Get a grip, Minnie, get a grip.

Nothing was right. *Nothing* was right. Mrs Seagrove went to the window and flung back the curtains. 'It's you, isn't it? It's *you*.'

Great, ugly slag-heap thing. She'd probably be able to see the church if it wasn't for that; always liked to see a church in the distance, even if she didn't go.

She could see the mound quite clearly tonight, even though there was no moon. It was a bit like the mound was lit up from inside, not *very* lit up, sort of a yellowish glow like a lemon jelly.

She thought she could see a shadow moving across the field. 'Is that you, Frank?' She banged on the window. 'You're not going out in that wet grass this time of night!'

He was stupid sometimes, Frank, like a little boy. He'd walk down to that river and just stare at it, wondering why he never caught that many fish.

She pulled her walking shoes from under the sideboard. You come back here, Frank Seagrove. It's not safe out there!'

CHAPTER IX

FAY was still seeing it like a bad home video: fuzzy, ill-lit, full of camera-shake and over-reaction. Women screaming, people staring at each other in shock, trying to speak, faces hard and grainy in the blue, deep-freeze light. Stricken Max Goff convulsing on the floor. Col Croston bending over him.

'Get a doctor!'

Portly man from Off shouldering his way to the front. Fay recognized him as the local GP.

Wynford Wiley – probably the last to react – moving like a sleepwalker, Fay following in his considerable wake, u) the central aisle, pushing past Guy. Hilary Ivory stumbling towards them, face in a permanent contortion like that painting of Munch's – *The Scream* – etched in similar stark, nervy colours because of the stammering lights.

Hilary's hands squeezing her hair and then the hands coming out like crimson rubber-gloves and Hilary's shrieks almost shredding Col's crisp command,

'Nobody move! Nobody leaves the hall!'

And then, turning to the doctor, 'Bloody obvious, man. Had his throat slashed.'

At which point, spangled brightness burst out of the wrought-iron chandeliers – an electrical blip – and Fay saw the Mayor, Councillor James Oswald Preece, standing on the edge of the raised area, holding his arms as though, with his frail frame, he could conceal the carnage.

'Silence!'

Even Wynford Wiley stopped, so suddenly that Fay almost bumped into his big blue back. The big lights stuttered out again, leaving the Mayor with a momentary jagged aura of yellow and black.

'Listen to me!'

'Is he dying?' a woman demanded from the New Age quarter.

One of the men in suits said, 'Look, I'm his legal adviser, and this is . . .'

'Is Max *dead*?'

'. . . I insist you call an ambulance.'

'*Is he . . . ?*'

'Will . . . you . . . be . . . *quiet*, madam!'

A new and significant Jimmy Preece, Fay saw. No longer the husk of a farmer, flat-capped, monosyllabic – 'ow're you, 'ow're you . . . Authority there now. Resonance.

'Now,' Jimmy Preece said. 'I'm not going to elaborate on this. Isn't the time. So don't none of you ask me. I'm speaking to you as your First Citizen, but I'm also speaking as a Preece, and most of you'll know what I'm saying yere.'

The Mayor's eyes flickered to one side. 'For all the new-comers, I'd ask you to accept my word that . . . that we are all in . . . well . . .'

He stopped. His jaw quivered.

'. . . in *serious, mortal danger* . . . '

He let this sink in. Fay looked around to see how they were all taking it. Some of the Crybbe people looked at each other with anxiety and varying amounts of understanding.

'Serious. Mortal. Danger,' Jimmy Preece intoned again, almost to himself, looking down at his boots.

The lawyer said, 'Oh, for heaven's sake, man . . .'

'And it's more than us what's in danger. And it's more than our children and . . . and their children.'

The doctor stood up, flecks of blood on his glasses.

'No!' somebody shouted. 'Oh God, no!' And the New Age quarter erupted.

Jimmy Preece held up a hand. 'I . . .' His voice slumped. 'I'm sorry he's dead.'

'. . . through the oesophagus, I'd imagine,' the doctor told Col Croston quietly, but not quietly enough.

'I mean it,' the Mayor said. 'I wished 'im no harm, I only wished 'im . . . gone from yere.'

Fay glanced at Guy. His face sagged. His blond hair, disarranged, revealed a hitherto secret bald patch. Catrin Jones was several yards away, looking past him to where Larry Ember was walking up the aisle, camera on his shoulder.

'Who let you in?' Jimmy Preece said wearily, 'Switch that thing off, sir, or it'll be taken from you.' Guy turned, tapped Larry's arm and shook his head.

To the side of Guy, the Newsomes mutely held hands.

'I'm going now,' Jimmy Preece said, 'to see to the bell. I urge you all – and this is *vital* – to stay absolutely calm.'

'. . . come with you, Jim,' somebody said.

'No you won't. You'll stay yere. You'll *all* stay yere.'

'Ah, look . . .' Col Croston said, 'Mr Mayor, there's been a murder here. It's not a normal situation.'

'No, Colonel, it's not normal, and that's why nobody goes from yere till I sees to the bell. I don't say this lightly. Nobody is to leave, see. Nobody.'

'Who's to say,' Col came close to the Mayor, 'whoever did this isn't still in the room?'

'No. 'E isn't yere, Colin, you can . . .'

Wynford Wiley pleaded, 'Let me radio for assistance, Jim. Least let me do that.'

'Leave it, Wynford. You're a local man, near enough. This is not a police matter.'

'But it's a murder,' Col Croston protested.

'It's a *Crybbe* matter, sir!'

'Jim,' Wynford whined, 'it's more than my . . .'

'Your *job*?' A blue vein throbbed in the Mayor's forehead. 'Your piffling little *job*! You'll take out your radio, Wynford Wiley, and you'll put 'im on that table.'

Wynford stood for a moment, his small features seeming to chase each other around his Edam cheese of a face. 'I can't.' He hung his head, turned away and trudged back towards the main door.

But when he reached it, he found his way barred by four large, quiet men of an unmistakably agricultural demeanour.

'Don't be a bigger fool than you look, Wynford,' said the Mayor, walking slowly down the aisle. 'Just give me that radio.'

Wynford sighed, took out the pocket radio in the black rubber case with the short rubber aerial and placed it in Jimmy Preece's bony, outstretched hand.

'It's for the best, Wynford. Now.' The Mayor turned and looked around him. 'Where's Mrs Morrison?'

Oh Christ.

'I'm here, Mr Preece.'

His deeply scored lips shambled into something that might have become a smile. 'You're not very big, Mrs Morrison, but you been stirring up a lot o' trouble, isn't it?'

'What's that supposed to mean?'

One of the men opened a door for him. Another handed him a lamp, a farmer's lambing light.

'Means I don't want you left in yere,' said Jimmy Preece. 'Christ alone knows what ole rubbish you'd be spoutin'.'

He pushed her out of the door in front of him.

Outside, it was fully dark.

It was only 9.40.

*

532

'*Oh my God, my God . . . Oh . . .* '

'It's only a dead body,' Mr Preece said. 'It can't hurt you. Any more than that Goff can hurt anyone now.'

'It's horrible,' Fay said.'It's . . . perverse. You knew it was here, didn't you, like . . . like this?'

She was shaking. She couldn't help it.

'No,' said the Mayor. 'I didn't think it was gonner be like this. But it don't surprise me.'

'But, Mr Preece, it's your own grandson. How can you bear it?'

'I can bear it, 'cause I got no choice,' said Mr Preece simply. He turned the light away from the coffin and pulled her back, but she could still see the image of Jonathon showcased like a big, grotesque Christmas doll.

Glad the power was off. Only wished somebody would disconnect the atmosphere.

Was she imagining this, or was it Jonathon she could smell, sweet corruption, bacteria stimulated by exposure to the dense, churchy air?

'Would you mind if I waited outside?'

'You'll stay yere.'

'It's . . . I'm sorry, Mr Preece, it's the smell.'

'Aye. We should lay him flat and put the lid back on.'

Don't ask me to help. Please don't ask me to help.

'Gonner give me a hand, then?'

No . . . ! But he was taking her arm. 'We 'ave time. Ten minutes yet, see.' Guiding her into the body of the church. She held fingers over her nose.

'Mr Preece . . .'

'What?'

She took her hand away from her face. 'Why me? Why'd you really bring me along?'

The question resounded from invisible walls and rafters.

'Just hold that.' Giving her the lambing light.

Fay stayed where she was, well back, and shone the light on the coffin, looking away.

'Closer, girl. Shine it closer.'

She felt him watching her. She moved a little closer. The

smell was appalling. She imagined bloated, white maggots at work inside Jonathon Preece, although she knew that was ludicrous. Wasn't it?

Fay pushed knuckles into her mouth to stifle the rising panic.

Mr Preece was on his knees beneath the coffin, its top end propped against the pulpit. 'Never get 'im back on that trolley. Lay 'im . . . flat . . . on the ground. All we can do.' He pushed at the coffin until it was almost upright and the body began to sag and belly out, like a drunk in a shop doorway.

'Jesus, Mr Preece, he's slipping! He's going to fall out! He's going to fall on me!'

'Push him back in, girl! Put the light down.'

'*I can't!*'

'Do it, woman!'

She did. She touched him. She pushed his chest, felt the ruched line of the post-mortem scar. He was cold, but far from stiff now, and she remembered him on the riverbank, soaked and leaking, tongue out and the froth and his skin all crimped.

She closed her eyes and pretended the stink was coming from elsewhere, until the coffin, with its sickening cargo, was flat on the stones and Jimmy Preece was fitting the lid on. Then she was bending over a pew, retching, nothing coming up but bile, like sour, liquid terror.

'Dead, poor boy,' Jimmy Preece said.

She stood up. Wiped her mouth on her sleeve. The smell was still in the air, sweetly putrid. Would she ever get away from that smell?

Heard herself saying, 'Who was it, Mr Preece? Who did this? Who made a sideshow out of him?'

'Dead,' he said. 'Can't hurt you now, can 'e?' He came close. 'Won't hurt that dog, neither, will 'e?'

Oh no. Something had been whispering to her that it was going to be this, but she'd kept pushing it back.

'That's why you brought me, isn't it? That's why you made me touch him.'

He stood there, recovering from the exertion, his breathing like coins rattling in a biscuit tin. Max Goff stabbed to death, something unspeakably vile seeping into Crybbe, but it was the death by drowning of one Jonathon Preece, young farmer of this parish . . .

'Family thing,' he said, voice as dry as wood ash. 'Something I 'ave to know before I die. Jack sent Jonathon out to make away with that animal of yours.'

'And why?' she said, but he didn't answer that.

'And he never came back.'

'OK, I'll tell you,' Fay said, in a rush. 'I'll tell you what happened. OK?'

His words of a moment long ago lurched back at her . . . *Before I die? Have to know before I die.*

She didn't even want to think what he meant by this, so she told him everything. Everything except for the feelings Joe Powys had said he'd experienced on the riverbank with the gun in his hands and the urge to kill.

Mr Preece went on breathing like a dying man. When she'd finished, he said, 'There's more to it than that.'

'No, there isn't, I swear.'

'Jonathon was a strong boy and a good swimmer. 'E also – unlike that brother of 'is – 'e had a bit o' common sense.'

'I'm sorry,' Fay said. 'I can't tell you what happened when we'd gone. Perhaps . . . I mean, with hindsight, we should have stayed. With hindsight, we should never have thrown the gun in the river in the first place. I'm sorry. I really am desperately sorry. Mr Preece . . .' She was aware of her voice becoming very small and a bit pathetic.

He was moving away towards the entrance, pulling out a pocket watch the size of a travel alarm-clock. It had big luminous hands.

'Right,' he said. 'You can wait in the porch, by yere, but you don't go out. You don't open that door until the bell's finished, you understand?'

'I want to come up with you.'

'We goes up alone,' he snapped. 'Now you remember what I said, you keep that door *shut*. Understand?'

'Yes. Look . . . Mr Preece . . .'

'Make it quick, Miss, make it very quick.'

She was remembering how controlled he'd been in the town hall, how sure that the killer had left the building.

'You know who did this . . . to Jonathon, don't you? And you know who killed Max Goff when the lights were out.'

He turned his back on her and mounted the first step.

'*Don't you?*'

He didn't look back, and a turn in the spiral staircase took the light away.

'Is *that* a Crybbe matter, as well?' she yelled. 'Or is it . . . ?'

God, she thought, as the darkness in the church became, for a while, absolute, I can still smell it. Still smell Jonathon.

And she put her hands over her face.

Is it a family matter? was what she'd almost said.

Because it ought to be Warren he was bringing up here tonight. *It ought to be Warren.*

She heard the Mayor stumble on the steps.

'Are you all right, Mr Preece?'

She heard another footstep, and his ratchet breathing starting up again, like a very old lawn-mower.

Quietly, she began to ascend the steps, until she could see his wavering torchbeam reflecting from the curved stonework. And then the beam was no longer visible and she climbed two or three steps until the stairway curved round and she could see the weakening glimmer once more.

The footsteps above her stopped. There was a long silence, and then,

'Get *back*, you . . .'

He began to cough, and she could hear the fluid gathering in his lungs and throat, like thick oil slurping in the bottom of a rusty old can.

'All right, I'm sorry, I'm going back . . . all right.'

Clattering back to the foot of the stairway, thinking, if anything happens to him now, am I going to have the guts to go up there, drag him out of the way or climb over him and pull on the rope a hundred times?

Have I the strength to pull a bell-rope a hundred times? (There's a kind of recoil, isn't there, like a gun, and the rope shoots back up and sometimes pulls large men off their feet.)

God almighty, will I have the strength to pull it *once*?

Leave him. He knows what he's doing. He won't stumble and break his ankle. He won't have a stroke. He won't have a heart attack. He's a Preece.

Like Jack, mangled by his own tractor, under intensive care in Hereford.

Like Jonathon, putrefying in his coffin just a few yards away.

But was there, at the heart of the Preece family, something even more putrid?

She stood at the bottom of the steps, waiting for the blessed first peal which only a few nights ago, walking Arnold in the sad streets of this crippled town, she'd dreaded.

Presently, she saw the light hazing the stones again and heard his footsteps.

Don't understand.

He's coming down.

She heard his rattling breath, then there was a clatter and the light was all over the place and she heard the lamp rolling down from step to step.

It went out as she caught it.

'Mr Preece . . . are you?'

He stood before her breathing roughly, breathing as though he didn't care if each breath *was* his last.

Fay flicked frantically at the switch and beat the lamp against the palm of her left hand until it hurt. It relit and she shone it on him and reeled back, almost dropping the thing in her shock, and the beam splashed across the nave.

She held the lambing light with both hands to stop it shaking and shone it at the wall to the side of Mr Preece so it wouldn't blind him and terrify her with the obscenity of it.

It was wrapped around him like a thick snake.

'What is it?' Fay whispered, and as the whisper dried in her throat she knew.

Perhaps it was winding itself around his neck, choking out of him what little life remained.

Mr Preece let it fall to the stone floor.

He said hoarsely, 'It's the bell-rope, girl. Somebody cut the bell-rope.'

And even Jonathon, with his putrid perfume and his post-mortem scar, hadn't scared her half so much as the stricken face of his grandfather, an electric puzzle of pulsing blood vessels, veins and furrows.

CHAPTER X

GRACE PETERS
1928–1992
Beloved wife of
Canon A. L. Peters

White letters.

Cold, black marble.

Pressing his forehead against it, he thought, A. L. Peters. That's me, isn't it? But it isn't my grave. Not yet, anyway. Only one of us is dead, Grace.

What am I doing here?

He remembered now, walking in a dignified fashion through the darkened streets, arm in a crook parallel to his chest. In his best suit, of course, with his dog-collar; she would not be seen out with him if he were attired in anything less.

Certainly not a faded T-shirt with the flaking remains of Kate Bush across his chest.

Peered down at it. Too dark to read the words, not white and gleaming like the letters on the grave. But he remembered the name, Kate Bush. Who the hell *was* Kate Bush, anyway?

Ought to know that.

Or maybe not. He could hear somebody, a woman, saying;
'There's a chance you'll lapse quite soon into the old confusion, and you'll have that to contend with, too. I'm sorry.'

Sorry. Well, aren't we all? Hmmph.

Cold black marble.

Cool hands.

What was all that about?

Alex shook his head.

Well, here I am, sitting on Grace's grave at the less-fashionable end of Crybbe churchyard at God knows what time of night. Haven't the faintest idea how the bloody hell I got here. Not exactly a cold night, but this is no place to spend it.

Wonder if I simply got pissed? And a bit maudlin, the way you do. Stagger along to pay your respects to the little woman. Sorry if I dislodged some of these dinky chippings that your will was so insistent we should use to make this end of the churchyard look like a bloody crazy-golf course. No wonder old Murray had you shoved out here – probably hoping the wood would overgrow the thing. And the sooner the better. Stupid cow, no taste at all, God knows how I ever got entangled with you.

Guilty? Me? Bloody hell, you *ensnared* me, you conniving creature.

Alex clambered to his feet. Chuckled. Don't take any notice of me, old girl, I'm rambling again. *Must* have been on the sauce, I could certainly do with a pee.

He stumbled into the wood and relieved himself with much enjoyment. There were times, he thought, when a good pee could be more satisfying than sex.

Consideration for the finer feelings of his late wife, who – let's get this in proportion once and for all – *did not deserve it*, had taken him deeper into the wood than he'd intended, and it took him a while to find his way back to the blasted churchyard.

Emerging, in fact, several yards away from Grace's grave, catching a foot on something, stumbling, feeling himself going into a nosedive.

'Damn.' Alex threw out both hands to break his fall. Bad news at his age, a fall, brittle bones, etc. – and, worst of all, a geriatric ward.

Something unexpectedly soft broke his fall. One hand felt cloth, a jacket perhaps.

'Oh gosh, terribly sorry.' Thinking at first he must have tripped over some old tramp trying to get an early night. This was before he felt all the wet patches.

'Oh dear. Oh hell.' It was all very sticky indeed, and his hands felt as if they were covered in it already. Tweedy sort of jacket. Shirt. And blood; no question of what the sticky stuff was.

'Hello. Are you all right?'

Bloody fool. Of course the chap wasn't all right. Wished he had a flashlight; couldn't see a damn thing.

Tentatively, he put out a hand and found a face. It, too, was very wet, horribly sticky and unpleasantly cold. Poor beggar must be slashed to ribbons. He lowered his head, listening for breathing. None at all.

There wasn't a clergyman in the world who didn't recognize the presence of death.

'Oh hell.'

Alex's sticky fingers moved shakily down over the blood-caked lips, over the chin, down to the neck where he felt . . .

Oh God. Oh Jesus.

I've . . .

I've stumbled over my own body!

I was wrong. I *am* dead. I think I've been murdered. Grace, you stupid bitch, why didn't you tell me? Is this how it is? Is this what happens? Oh Lord, somebody get me away from here. Beam me up God, for Christ's sake.

For the body wore a stiff, clerical collar.

Crybbe Court in view again.

'Uh!'

Humble had prodded him in the small of the back, presumably with the butt of the crossbow.

They were on the edge of the Tump field, facing the courtyard. As Powys looked up at the black house, its ancient frame seemed to tense against the pressure of the night. There was a small sparkling under the eaves, like the friction of flints, and the air was faintly tainted with sulphur.

Powys felt his anger rekindle.

In the moment of the sparks, he'd seen the hole in the eaves that was the prospect chamber. Below it, slivers of light had figured the edge of a piece of furniture halfway up the pile of rubbish which had broken Rachel Wade's fall and her neck.

'We're going in,' Humble said, picking up the lamp from the grass.

'You might be going in,' said Powys. 'It's too spooky for me, quite honestly.'

Humble laughed.

'You must think I'm fucking stupid,' Powys said. 'You want me to go up to the prospect chamber and kind of lose my balance, right?'

It would, he knew, make perfect sense to the police.

'Since you ask,' Humble said, 'that would be quite tidy, yeah, and it would save me a bit of trouble. But if you say no, I get to use this fing on you, which'll be a giggle anyway, so you can please yourself, mate, I ain't fussy.'

'How would you get rid of the body?'

'Not a problem. Really. Trust me.'

'None of this scares you?'

'None of what?'

'Like, we just saw a light flaring under the roof. It wasn't what you'd call natural . . .'

'Did we? I didn't.'

Humble stood with his back to the broken wall around the Tump, a hard, skinny, sinewy, ageless man. Powys could run away and Humble would run faster. He could go for Humble, maybe try and kick him in the balls, and Humble would damage him quickly and efficiently before his shoe could connect. He could sit down and refuse to move and Humble would put a crossbow bolt into his brain.

Powys said, 'You don't feel a tension in the air? A gathering in the atmosphere? I thought you were supposed to be a countryman.'

Humble snorted, leaning on the butt of his crossbow.

'There are countrymen,' he said, 'and there are hippies. I'm fit, I've got good hearing and ace eyesight. I'm not a bad shot. I can snare rabbits and skin 'em, and I can work at night and I ain't scared. Ghosts, evil spirits, magic stones, it's all shit. If the people who employ me wanna believe in it, that's fine, no skin off my nose.'

Blessed are the sceptics, Powys thought.

Rachel was a sceptic.

'And I get paid *very* well. See, I can go in that house any time of the day or night, I don't give a shit. I can piss up the side of a standing stone in the full moon. So what? Countrymen ain't hippies, Mr Powys.'

He was telling Powys indirectly who it was who'd locked the door when Rachel was in the Court. And, maybe, who'd pushed her out.

He got paid very well.

'Andy pays you,' Powys realized.

Humble said, 'I'm in the employ of the Epidemic Group as security consultant.'

'And Andy's been paying you as well.'

Humble lifted his crossbow. 'Let's go.'

'Where's Andy?'

'I said, let's *move!*'

'No.'

'Fair enough,' Humble said. 'Fair enough.'

He moved backwards a few paces into the field until he was almost invisible against the night.

'OK, you made your decision. I got to get this over wiv in a couple of minutes, so you got a choice. You can run. Or you can turn around and walk away. Just keep walking, fast or slow as you like, and you'll never know. Some people like to run.'

Oh Jesus, Powys thought. For the past twelve years he hadn't really cared too much about life and how long it would last.

'I thought you'd never shot anybody.'

'Not wiv a crossbow. On the two other occasions,' said Humble, 'I used a gun.'

Fay, he thought obliquely. Caught an image of the elf with the rainbow eye. I'm going to lose Fay.

'Or, of course,' said Humble reasonably, 'you can just stand there and watch.'

He brought up the crossbow. Powys instinctively ducked, went down on his knees, his arms around his head.

Through his arms, he heard a familiar lop-sided semi-scampering.

'No!' he screamed. 'No, Arnold! Get back! Get away!'

He saw the black and white dog limping towards him from the darkness and, out of the corner of his eye, watched the crossbow swivel a couple of inches to the right.

'Beautiful,' Humble said, and fired.

*

She ran at the door and snatched at the bolts, throwing one of them back before Mr Preece grabbed her from behind and pulled her away.

She struggled frantically and vainly. He might look like a stretcher case, but his arms were like bands of iron.

She felt her feet leave the floor, and he hauled her back from the porch and set her down under the stone font. The lambing light was in her eyes, but it didn't blind her because it was losing strength, going dimmer.

'What the *fuck* are you doing, Mr Preece? What bloody use is *this* place as protection?'

All she could hear from behind the dying light was his dreadful breathing, something out of intensive care at the chest clinic.

'There's no spirituality here any more. All there was was the bell and now you can't reach that, there's no way you can resist . . . him . . . in this place. A church is only a church because the stones are steeped in centuries of worship . . . human hopes and dreams, all that stuff. All you've got here is a bloody *warehouse*.'

'Stay quiet,' Jimmy Preece hissed. 'Keep calm. Keep . . .'

'Oh, sure, keep your head down! It's what this piss-poor place is all about. Don't make waves, don't take sides, we don't want no *clever people*. Oh!' She bent her head into her arms and sobbed with anger and frustration.

Needing the rage and the bitterness, because, if you could keep them stoked, keep the heat high, it would burn out the fear.

She looked into the light – not white any more, but yellow, her least-favourite colour, the yellow of disease, of embalming fluid. The yellow of Grace Legge.

How would he come?

Would he come like Grace, flailing and writhing with white-eyed malevolence?

How would he come?

'What's going to happen, Mr Preece?' she said. It was the small voice, and she was ashamed.

'I don't know, girl.' There was a wheezing under it that she hadn't heard before. 'God help me, I don't know.'

She thought about her dad. At least he'd be safe. He was with Jean, and Jean was smart. Jean knew about these things.

'She can't talk to you, she can't see you, there's no brain activity there . . . Entirely harmless.'

No she doesn't. She isn't smart at all. A little knowledge, a little intuition – nothing more dangerous. Jean only *thinks* she's smart.

And now Powys had gone to Jean, saying, help us, O Wise One, get us out of this, save Crybbe, save us all.

Oh, Powys, whatever happened to the Old Golden Land?

It began with a rustling up at the front of the church near the coffin, and then the sound of something rolling on stone.

'What's that?'

But Mr Preece just breathed at her.

She clutched at the side of the font, all the hot, healthy anger and the frustration and bitterness drenched in cold, stagnant fear. She couldn't move. She imagined Jonathon Preece stirring in his coffin, cracking his knuckles as his hands opened out.

Washerwoman's hands.

Fay felt a pain in her chest.

'Oh, God.' The nearest she could produce to a prayer. Not too wonderful, for a clergyman's daughter.

And then came the smell of burning and little flames, a row of little, yellow, smoky flames, burning in the air, four or five feet from the floor.

Fay watched, transfixed, still sitting under the font, as if both her legs were broken.

'Heeeeeeeee!' she heard. High-pitched – a *yellow* noise, flecked with insanity.

Jimmy Preece moved. He picked up the light and walked into the nave and shone what remained of the light up the aisle.

'Aye,' he said, and his breathing was so loud and his voice so hoarse that they were inseparable now.

Down the aisle, into the lambing light, a feeble beam, a figure walked.

Fay saw cadaverous arms hanging from sawn-off sleeves. Eyes that were as yellow-white as the eyes of a ghost, but still – just – human eyes.

The arms hanging loosely. Something in one hand, something stubby, blue-white metal still gleaming through the red-brown stains.

Behind him the yellow flames rose higher.

A foot kicked idly at something on the stone floor and it rolled towards Fay. It was a small tin tube with a red nozzle. Lighter fuel.

Warren had opened up the Bible on its lectern and set light to the pages.

'Ow're you, Grandad,' Warren said.

CHAPTER XI

THERE were too many people in here.

'Don't touch him, please,' Col said. There was quite a wide semi-circle around Goff's body into which nobody, apart from this girl, had been inclined to intrude. There'd be sufficient explanations to make after tonight as it was, and Col was determined nobody was going to disturb or cover up the evidence, however unpleasant it became, whatever obnoxious substances it happened to discharge.

The girl peered down, trying to see Goff's face.

'I paint,' she explained casually. 'I like to remember these things.'

'Oh. It's Tessa, isn't it. Tessa Byford.'

Col watched her with a kind of appalled admiration. So cool, so controlled. How young women had changed. He couldn't remember seeing her earlier. But then there were a few hundred people here tonight – and right now, he rather wished there hadn't been such a commendable turn-out.

He was angry with himself. That he should allow someone to creep in under cover of darkness and slash the throat of the guest of honour. Obviously – OK – the last thing one would expect in a place like Crybbe. And yet rural areas were no longer immune from sudden explosions of savage violence – think of the Hungerford massacre. He should – knowing of the underlying trepidation about Goff's plans – have been ready to react to the kind of situation for which he'd been training half his life. He remembered, not too happily, telling Guy Morrison how the Crybbe audience would ask Goff a couple of polite questions before drifting quietly away.

And then, just as quietly, they'll shaft the blighter.

Shafted him all right.

Whoever it was had come and gone through the small, back door, the one the town councillors used. It had been unlocked throughout. That had been a mistake, too.

Couldn't get away from it – he'd been bloody lax. And now he was blindly following the orders of a possibly crazy old man who'd decreed that nobody was permitted to depart – which, if the police were on their way, would have been perfectly sensible, but under the circumstances . . .

He didn't even *know* the circumstances.

All he knew was that Jimmy Preece had the blind support of an appreciable number of large, uncompromising, tough-looking men and, if anybody made an attempt to leave, the situation was likely to turn ugly.

Not – looking at Max Goff sprawled in his own blood – that it was particularly attractive as things stood.

Every so often, people would wander over to Col, some angry, others quite sheepish.

'It doesn't make a lot of sense, now does it, Colonel?' Graham Jarrett argued, sweat-patches appearing under the arms of his safari suit. 'A man's been murdered, and all we're doing is giving his murderer time to get clean away.'

'Not if he's in this room we aren't,' said Col very quickly.

Jarrett's eyes widened. 'That's not likely, is it?'

'Who knows, Mr Jarrett, who knows?'

Graham Jarrett looked around nervously, as if wondering which of the two or three hundred people it might be safest to stand close to. The main exit was still guarded by large, uncommunicative farmers.

'Can't be long now, anyway,' Col said. 'I'd guess the Mayor's already been in touch with the police.'

No chance. This is a *Crybbe matter*.

Madness. It didn't even have the logic of a street riot. And Col Croston, who'd served six terms in Belfast, was beginning to detect signs of something worryingly akin to sectarianism.

New Age versus Old Crybbe.

The Crybbe people scarcely moved. If they went to the toilets they went silently and returned to their seats. They did not converse among themselves. They seemed to know what this was about. Or, at least, they appeared satisfied that Jimmy Preece knew what it was about and there seemed to be this unspoken understanding that they should remain calm, restrain their emotions.

Bloody eerie. Just as they behaved in church. Admirable self-control or mindless apathy? Beggared belief, either way, and Col Croston knew he couldn't allow the situation to continue much longer. He was under pressure from the New Age delegates who, while in a minority of about twenty to one, were making virtually all the noise. So much for relaxation techniques and meditative calm. Struck him there was a lot they might learn from the indigenous population.

A man in a suit, one of the Epidemic lawyers, said, 'Look – let us out of here now and we'll say no more about it. But if this goes on, I'm warning you, you're all going to be in very serious trouble. Impeding the course of justice'll be the very least of it.'

'I've found,' Col told him, very clipped, 'that in a situation like this, telling people what serious trouble they're going to be in is the fastest way to inflame what could be a highly combustible situation. I estimate there are more than three hundred adults in this room and the fact that one of them happens to be dead could just turn out to be the very least of our worries. Now please sit down.'

Aware of a sudden commotion by the main doors, he yelled into the New Age quarter, 'Will somebody please restrain that lady!'

The feminist astrologer was threatening to damage the

genitals of one of the farmers if he didn't get out of her way. It was Catrin Jones, physically stronger than the astrologer and also a woman, who was finally able to lead her back to her seat.

'They're not real, these people.' The astrologer shook her spiky head. 'They're bloody zombies. Everything's freaky.'

The Cock being empty and Denzil looking at a bit of a loose end, Gomer Parry thought it was only reasonable to have *two* pints, aware this could conceivably put him over the limit. But what kind of copper stopped a digger driver trundling along a country lane at 30 m.p.h.?

It was after ten when he drove out of the square in the yellow tractor with the big shovel raised up out of the way. The roads were about as quiet as you could get.

Fact everywhere was a bit on the quiet side. This Goff was obviously a big attraction. Not a soul on the streets and with all the lights out, Crybbe looked like one of them film-sets when everybody'd gone home.

Pulling out on to the Ludlow road, something else struck Gomer: he hadn't heard the bell. They *never* didn't ring that bell. Used to be said that old Jimmy Preece – well, young Jimmy Preece as he'd have been then – had even rung the curfew the day he got married. A hundred bongs on his wedding night; Mrs Preece wouldn't be that lucky.

Poor old devil back on the night-shift now, then. Talk about bad luck . . . you wouldn't credit it. Even if Jack pulled through with both legs still attached, didn't seem likely he'd be in any state to make it up them old steps for a good long while. Have to be putting the arm on that young tearaway, Warren.

Gomer was never sorry to leave Crybbe – miserable old place: miserable buildings, miserable folk – but he was never that happy about going home neither, not since his old lady had handed in her mop and bucket. He'd work every hour of daylight to put off that terrible moment when he had to get his own keys out instead of seeing the door opening as he tramped across· the yard and hearing the old kettle whistling on the Rayburn.

When midsummer was past and the working days started getting shorter, Gomer's spirits started to droop, and tonight had been a freak foretaste of autumn, black clouds crowding in for a storm that never came, and dark by nine.

Now there was mist as well. That came down bloody quick. Gomer snapped on the full beams, only to discover his left headlight bulb had gone.

Bollocks. No copper'd be able to resist pulling him in to point this out, and then he'd get a good whiff of Gomer's breath . . . Mind just blowing in this yere nozzle, sir . . . Oh, dear, afraid I'll have to ask you to accompany me to the station. Well, Gomer could already see the smile cracking up the fat features of that bastard Wynford Wiley, and he couldn't stick that.

What he'd have to do then was switch off the headlights and try and get through the mist on the itsy-bitsy sidelights which were bugger-all use on these roads on the best of nights.

So he flicked off the heads and slowed down to about twenty, and it was still like skin-diving in a cesspit and he had to drop down to second gear.

Bloody Crybbe.

Didn't know why he said that, you couldn't blame *everything* on Crybbe.

Well, you *could* . . .

Gomer hit the brakes. 'What the 'ell's that?'

Bloody hell fire, it's the old Tump. Where'd he come from?

Hang on a bit, boy, you done something a bit wrong yere. Isn't usual to see that thing straight up ahead, looming out of the mist so sudden like that, enough to scare the life out of you.

Hello . . . not on the road now, are we?

We surely are not!

Bloody teach you to go over the limit. Thought you could handle a couple of pints, no problem, but the thing is, you're getting older, boy, your reactions isn't what they was, see.

And now, look what you done, you gone clean off the road, over the verge and you're on the bloody common now and if you keep on like this you'll be knocking down that Goff's wall for him after all and buggering up your digger like they done the bulldozer.

Gomer was about to pull up sharp when the front end took a dip and he realized that if he didn't go with it he was likely to turn this thing over. And he thought about Jack Preece . . . talk about lightning striking twice. Well, he didn't like this, not one bit.

'I can't stand it!' Hilary Ivory shrieked suddenly. 'This room's so black and negative. It's oppressing me, I've got to have air. And I can't stand to look at *him* any more!'

'Well, I'm sorry, but I'm not going to cover him up,' Col told her. 'Really daren't risk disturbing anything, isn't that right, Sergeant?' Wynford Wiley nodded vaguely, his cheese face sliced clean of expression; he'd given up – *he* should be directing this situation and look at him . . . jacket off, tie around his ear, glazed-eyed and sweating like a pig.

'All I can suggest is you look the other way, Mrs Ivory, I'm sorry.'

'It's *your* fault,' Hilary turned furiously on her husband. 'You knew it was coming. You should have warned him. What use is a seer who sees and doesn't tell?'

'Me?' Hitherto gloomily silent, Adam Ivory was stunned into speech. 'You didn't want me to say a word, you bloody hypocritical cow!' Halfway out of his seat, gripping his knees. 'You didn't want to throw a shadow over things. You didn't want to lose your cosy little flat in your cosy little town in . . . in . . .'

'Just a minute.' Col Croston jumped down from the platform and strode over to where the couple were sitting amidst Jarrett, a bunch of healers, the Newsomes and Larry Ember standing up, smoking a cigarette, his camera held between his ankles.

'What's this about? What are you saying?'

Guy Morrison said wearily, 'Adam reads tarot cards. He saw disaster looming.'

'Oh,' said Col, disappointed. 'I see.'

'No, you don't,' said Guy. 'Don't knock it, Col. This is a

very weird set-up. Guy Morrison used to think he knew everything there was to know about the supernatural, i.e. that the whole thing was a lame excuse for not milking real life for everything one could get.'

Guy made a steeple out of the fingers of both hands and pushed them together, hard. 'But for once,' he said, 'Guy Morrison was wrong.'

'What d'you mean exactly?' Col looked for somewhere to sit down. There wasn't a spare chair, so he squatted, hands on thighs. 'What's the score here, as you see it, Guy? I mean, Christ, I've been around. Been in some pretty odd places, among some pretty primitive people, but, well, we don't notice things under our noses, sometimes. We think it's what you might call . . . what? Rural eccentricity, I suppose.'

'No. Look . . .' Guy had taken off his expensive olive leather jacket. He didn't seem to notice it was lying on the floor now, entangled in dusty shoes. 'Which is Mrs Byford? Ask her if she knows her granddaughter's some kind of witch . . . that girl, the artist. Ask her about the ex-policeman who cut his throat in her bathroom. Go on. Ask her.'

Oh hell, Col Croston thought. Bit barmy. He decided not to tell Guy the girl was here, displaying an anatomical interest in the corpse.

'You think I'm crazy, don't you? Ask her!'

'Shut up,' Jocasta Newsome hissed. 'Just shut up, Guy. Just for once.'

Guy whirled on her, eyes alight. '*You* know I'm not crazy, you of all people. You showed me the drawings. You sent me to talk to the bloody girl. You . . . uuurh.'

Hereward Newsome's thin, sensitive, artistic hands were around his throat. 'You . . . smooth . . . self-opinionated . . . bastard!'

Col Croston leapt up as Guy's chair crashed over into the aisle, the chair's and Guy's legs both in the air, Hereward, teeth clenched, trying to smash Guy's head into the boarded floor. 'No wonder . . . she wanted you to . . . open the fucking . . . exhibition.' Col Croston gripping Hereward's shoulder, wrenching him off, as Catrin Jones – 'Guy!' – fell down heavily beside her producer. 'Are you all right?' Lifting his head into her lap. 'Guy?' Staring up, appalled, at the madman with the thinning hair and the greying, goatee beard, held back by his collar like a snarling dog, hands clawing at the air.

'He's only been screwing my wife,' the madman spat, and Catrin froze – maybe he was not so mad, after all – allowing Guy's head to fall to the floor with an audible thump.

Larry Ember was cradling his camera, ostensibly to save it from being kicked, the lens pointed casually at the scene below him. 'One for the Christmas tape,' he murmured to Tom, his soundman. 'Got to keep the old spirits up, ain'tcha?' On the same tape were the pictures he'd surreptitiously shot of Max Goff's body, while carrying the camera under his arm at waist level.

'You'll put that thing away!' Sharp-featured Mrs Byford, the council clerk, was on her feet, back arched.

'Wasn't aware it was out, darlin'.' Larry inspecting his trousers.

'Colonel!'

'Come on, old boy, please. Leave the thing under the table, hmm?'

'I don't think so, squire.' Larry raising the camera to his shoulder, aiming it at Col, adjusting the focus.

'Guy, would you mind exerting your . . . ?'

But Guy, still sprawled half-stunned in the aisle, was staring over the Colonel's shoulder, eyes widening. 'She . . . *she*'s there . . . Jocasta . . . *tell them . . .*'

The girl stood on the edge of the platform. She wore black jeans and a black top. Even her lipstick was black. Her skin, in the blue fluorescence, was like a grim, cloudy day.

A small, grey-faced man, perhaps the husband, snatched ineffectually at Mrs Byford's arm as she stepped out, screeching, 'Tessa! What you doing in yere . . . ? Get out . . . No, I . . .'

'Nobody gets out,' Tessa said sweetly.

Guy was up, staggering, one hand massaging the back of his head, the other groping for the cameraman's arm. 'The girl. Shoot her. I want the girl.'

As Larry advanced slowly towards the girl, camera on his shoulder, eye hard to the projecting viewfinder, Mrs Byford launched herself at him from behind, pummelling his back, clawing at his neck.

'Nettie!' the grey-faced man shouted. 'No! Don't cause no . . .'

Col pulled her off with one hand, getting his face scratched. 'Mrs Byford! Guy, can't you stop this stupid bastard before . . .'

'So . . .' Guy was panting, 'this is Mrs Byford, is it? Perhaps she can tell us all about Handel Roberts, who topped himself in her bathroom . . . *and yet was in this room tonight!*'

'Now listen, Mr Clever TV Man . . .' Guy turned slowly and painfully and looked into tiny, round eyes and a small, fleshy mouth set into a face too big for them.

'Handel Roberts is *dead*,' said Wynford Wiley.

'*Exactly*,' said Guy.

Col's feelings about newcomers who tried to take over, assuming a more elevated intellect and an understanding of the rural psyche, were warning him to take it easy. But there was an ice-ball forming in the pit of his stomach.

'Stop it!' Jocasta Newsome, rising like a Fury. 'Stop it, stop it, stop it! What are you all trying to do?'

'Aye,' a man's voice said. 'Can't you, none of you, control yourselves?'

'At least we're not brain dead!' – the feminist astrologer with the ring through her nose – 'Look at you all . . . you're fucking pathetic. Somebody tells you to sit there and don't move again until they tell you you can stand up and leave. A man's been brutally murdered . . . You don't even react! What kind of fucking morons . . .'

A girl in her twenties, built like Catrin Jones, only more muscular, stamped across the room, 'You'll shut your mouth, lady, or I'm gonner shut it for you.'

'Oh yeah, we'll all shut our mouths and turn a blind eye and ask no questions. And where has that got *you* all these years? Max Goff was the only promising thing that ever happened to this shithole, and what do you do? . . . you kill him, like . . .'

like the bloody savages did to the missionaries. Except the
weren't savages really, at least they had this ethnic . . .'

'Sit down, the pair of you!' Mrs Byford's husband wa
quaking. 'Can't you see, this is what it wants . . . Jimmy Preec
said, be calm. He knows . . . it's what it *wants* . . . rowin
and . . . and conflict, everybody all worked up, like.'

'Mr Byford is absolutely right,' Col said, wondering wha
the hell Mr Byford was on about. '*I'm* going to go out and fin
the Mayor, call the police and get this . . .'

'No you're not, Colonel . . .'

'Look . . .'

And then there was a crash from the front of the hall. Larr
Ember hadn't exactly *dropped* his camera – which Col suspecte
no self-respecting TV cameraman *ever* did, even if he'd bee
shot – but he'd certainly put it down quite heavily, and he wa
stumbling back along the centre aisle, moaning in some distress
both hands over his face.

Col Croston looked up at the platform; there was no sign c
Tessa Byford. 'What's wrong, man, you OK?'

Guy grabbed Larry's arm; Larry shook him off, the way a chil
does, in a kind of frenzy. He'd abandoned the camera in th
middle of the floor – unheard of in Guy's experience – and wa
threshing towards the entrance.

'Sorry, pal.' A tweeded arm in his way.

Larry took his hands away from his face. 'Oh Lord!' th
man said, and Larry's knee went up into a corduroy crotch.

'Right,' the cameraman shouted, 'I'm out of here.' Hittin
the doors with his shoulder, and they burst open and the nigh
came in, and Guy strove for the exit, followed by the Ivory
and the men in suits, and Catrin Jones was dragged along too
'Stop them!' somebody screamed. 'Shut them doors!'

For just a moment, Larry Ember turned around in th
doorway. Hilary Ivory screamed, and Guy nearly fell back int
the room.

Larry's right eye, his viewfinder eye . . .

'Just get me away from that girl.'

554

'I think it's a blood vessel,' Guy said nervously.

'I'm going in tight on her,' Larry recalled, voice unsteady. ..nd her eyes . . . are actually fucking *zooming back*. Giving ..e daggers, Guy. And then she's in the bleed'n' camera. Dag-..rs, Guy, know what I mean?'

Larry's eye looked like a squashed tomato.

'Maybe . . . maybe several blood vessels,' Guy said. 'I don't ..ow . . . Look, you get some air, I'll get Catrin to fetch your ..mera.'

'Leave it!' Larry screamed. 'I don't wanna see the bleed'n' ..pe, all right? I wan' it destroyed . . .'

Two of the farmers on the doors were struggling to close ..em again, but now there was a wild crush of people fighting .. get out. Larry and Guy were pushed out into the square. ..et them go!' Col shouted. 'Or somebody's going to get hurt.'

There was hysterical laughter from behind him. 'They'll be ..urt, all right, Colonel,' shrilled Mrs Byford.

And Col Croston heard what seemed at first to be a very ..ncouraging noise; the curfew bell was ringing, the familiar, ..eady clangs.

'It's the Mayor!' he called back into the room. 'Panic over. ..e said it'd be OK to leave when the curfew began. Everybody ..st sit down for a moment and we'll file out in an orderly ..shion.'

'You fool,' somebody said quietly.

Few among the Crybbe people had even moved.

And he knew why, quite soon, as a second bell began a ..ollow, discordant counterpoint, and then a third came in, and .. fourth, and then they were all going.

Col stood and looked at the rows of stricken, frightened ..ces.

'What's going on?'

Never, in this town, had he seen such obvious reaction on .. many faces.

He wanted to cover his eyes, his ears. It was like being ..iolently awoken in the dead of night by the sudden, shattering ..langour of a roomful of alarm-clocks.

Only louder. The loudest noise there'd ever been in Crybbe,

a blitz of bells, hard and blindingly bright, bells to break windows, and loosen teeth and the foundations of ancient buildings, bells to burst the sky and burn up the air.

For the first time in his life, Col Croston, the only qualified bell-ringer in the town, was stilled by a most basic primitive terror, like a cold, thin wire winding around his spinal cord.

Because there was no way it could be happening. With one single exception, all the bell-ropes had been taken down years and years ago.

Tonight, in some unholy celebration, the bells of Crybbe were ringing themselves.

CHAPTER XII

THE first bell had begun at the moment Warren Preece cut his grandfather.

'You,' Mr Preece had said, dead-voiced, as the Bible burned. No surprise there, Fay noticed. No horror at the reptilian thing prancing, white-eyed in the firelight – the thing for which Fay had at first felt only revulsion, becoming aware soon afterwards that revulsion was actually one of the *lower* forms of fear.

Mr Preece said, 'I 'oped to 'eaven it wouldn't be, but at the heart of me I always knew it was.'

Tipped up his brother in the coffin, slashed the shroud. Not much left in Warren Preece, Fay concluded numbly, that you could call human.

'You don't even know it all yet, Grandad.' Warren grinned meaningfully. 'Got a bit to learn yet, see.'

''Ow long you been in yere, Warren?'

'Long time, Grandad.' Warren put on a whining, old-man voice. ' "Oh, 'e was a strong boy, Jonathon. Good swimmer." '

Shadows leapt with the flames from the blazing Bible. Scorched scraps of pages flew into the air; billowing, black snowflakes.

'Smart boy, Jonathon,' Warren said. 'Bit o' sense. Not like that brother of 'is, see.'

'Oh, Warren,' the old man said sorrowfully. 'You never once tried to . . .'

Warren smiled slyly. ''E wasn't that good a swimmer, though, Grandad.'

The Bible began to crackle.

'Not with somebody sittin' on 'is head, anyway.'

Fay wanted to reach out to Mr Preece and hold him back, but she couldn't get her body to shift, and, God knew, the poor old bloke was moving slowly enough, fragmented motion, like a battered clockwork toy winding down.

'Mr Preece . . . don't do anything . . .' The old man was advertizing his uncontainable anger as clearly as if it were written on sandwich-boards and lunging for his grandson as awkwardly as he would if he were wearing them.

'Come on then, Grandad.' Warren lounged against the carved wooden side of a back pew. 'Let's get this over. Owed you one for a couple o' days. Since you knocked me down, like. Shouldn't 'ave done that, Grandad. Bad move . . . see.'

Mr Preece lurched ineffectually forward as Warren's right hand described a lazy arc. And then he stopped, unsure what had happened.

Fay's hand went to her mouth. There was another fine line on the contour map of the Mayor's face, five inches long, neatly dividing the withered left cheek into two.

Then Warren was jumping back, the silver skull bouncing from his ear, the hand which held the knife leaping and twirling as though given life by the touch of fresh blood.

Oh Christ . . . Fay was barely aware of backing off. Her mind was distancing itself too, not wanting to cope with this.

'Heeee!'

You wouldn't expect, Fay thought remotely, almost callously, as the curfew bell began to toll, that Mr Preece would bleed so normally, in such quantity, through skin like wornout, dried-up leather.

As she watched him bleed, a question rolled into her head and lay there innocuously for a few seconds before starting to sizzle like a hot coal.

'Listen . . .' Warren Preece hissed in excitement.

Who was ringing the curfew?

'Yeah!' Warren leapt on to a pew, looking up to the rafters, both fists clenched, one around the knife, and shaking.

A droplet of Jimmy Preece's blood fell from the blade and landed on a prayer book.

And then the other bells began, and Fay clapped her hands to her ears, although it was not so loud in here – nothing to what it would be in the streets.

It just . . . *could not be happening.*

The Mayor of Crybbe stood very still. He did not raise a hand to his cheek and the blood poured down his face, copious as bitter tears.

By his feet, the lambing light expired.

But the fire from the Bible was enough to show her the crazed Warren dancing on a pew to the discordance of bells, blood glistening on the knuckles of the fist that held the knife.

The smoke made her cough, and Warren seemed to notice for the first time that he and his grandfather were not alone. He leapt – seemed to float in the smoky air – over the back of the pew, and put himself between Fay and the porch, bouncing on the balls of his feet, grinning at her, slack-jawed, vacant.

Jimmy Preece sagged against the font, unmoving. She couldn't even hear his breathing any more.

'Who . . . who's ringing the bells?' That could *not* be her speaking. Nobody sounding like that could ever have passed a BBC voice-test.

'Well, can't be me,' Warren said conversationally. 'An' it can't be Grandad, can it, Grandad?'

Mr Preece, Fay thought bleakly, might have died. Heart failure. Blood pressure – a stroke. Respiratory congestion.

''E sez, no,' Warren said. 'Sez it's not 'im neither. An' I been in yere ages, an' nobody come in with me, see. Wonder what *that* means?'

Is that what Crybbe does? Is this the kind of 'rebel' produced by a sick old town from which all unfurtive, abandoned pleasure has been bled?

'Maybe ole Jonathon . . .' Warren suggested. 'Maybe 'e's come crawlin' out of 'is coffin. Bleeeaagh!'

He hunched his shoulders. Tossed the knife from the right hand to the left and then back again. 'Tell you what . . . why'n't you go up an' 'ave a look, lady? Go on . . .'

When she didn't move he suddenly lurched at her, the knife creating whingeing sounds as he made criss-cross slashes in the yellow, smoky air. 'Hey, it's *you* . . .'

Fay began to back away, coughing, in the opposite direction, up the nave until she could feel the heat from the petrol-soaked Bible on her back.

Warren produced a high-pitched trumpeting noise. 'This is Offa's Dyke Radio!'

He slashed the air again, twice.

'Voice of the Marches!' he said. 'Yeah!'

'That's right,' Fay said, cheerfully hysterical. 'Voice of the Marches. That's me.'

Warren stopped. Reflected a moment. 'We done a good job on your ole tape recorder, didn't we?'

Oh my . . . *God*.

'Yes,' she said weakly. 'Very impressive.'

His face went cold. Should have kept her mouth shut.

He opened the hand which held the Stanley knife, looked down at it, the hand and the knife's long, metal handle both splattered with criss-cross layers of blood, bright fresh blood on brown dried blood.

'Hand of Glory,' Warren said. And the fingers clenched again.

As he advanced on her, up the aisle, she saw – almost hypnotized – that his eyes were altering.

She'd never seen Warren Preece close-up before (only – Oh my God – his spidery shape scurrying across a field at sunset) and she was sure that she wasn't seeing him now.

Something in the eyes. The eyes were no longer vacant. Someone in residence.

'Aaah.' The heat at her back was acutely painful. She couldn't go any further: fire behind her, the knife coming at her. She went rigid, looked back towards the door, saw Jimmy Preece had slipped to the floor by the font.

'Black Michael,' she said, as the savage heat at her back

became too much to bear and she was sure her clothing was about to catch fire. 'You're Black Michael.'

Warren Preece obviously took this as a huge compliment. He grinned lavishly, and the bloodstained Stanley knife trembled in his hand as he closed in.

'Say hello,' he said, 'to the Hand of Glory.' And lunged.

Fay threw herself sideways, landing hard on the stone. Crawled, coughing wretchedly, to the top of the altar steps, where the firelight was reflected in Jonathon Preece's closed coffin. A storm of shrivelled scraps of burning paper wafted from the Bible; she saw an orange core of fire eating through to the spine and the varnish bubbling on the wooden lectern as she rolled over, drew back her foot and stabbed out once, sharply.

The lectern shook. It was made of carved oak, caked in layer upon layer of badly applied varnish, which dripped and blistered and popped. It moved when she hit it with her foot, but not enough, and she fell on her back beside the coffin, her face stinging from the heat and sparks, as Warren Preece sprang up the steps and the short, reddened blade of the Stanley knife came down at her, clasped in a fist gloved in smoke.

She curled up, and the bells clanged like wild, drunken laughter.

The bells, he thought, the bells of hell. Ringing to welcome old Alex.

He stood in the graveyard, looked up at the church tower, saw the window-slits outlined in light, glowing a feeble yellow at first and then intensifying to pure white as the clangour grew louder until it seemed the walls would crumble and there would only be these bright bells hanging in the night.

Welcome to hell.

No one more welcome in hell than a unfrocked priest, except . . . *except* . . . a priest who ought to have been unfrocked and escaped the dishonour through devious means.

Oh Lord, yes. *No* one more welcome in hell.

The bells rang randomly, as one might expect, a mocking parody of the joyful Sunday peal.

The bells of hell hurt his ears as they were meant to do and would continue to do, he assumed, for ever and ever.

He brushed against the Bible and it set light to the black vest he was wearing; little flames swarmed up his chest.

He seemed absolutely delighted. Looking proudly down at himself, dropping down a couple of steps, grinning hugely, as the petrol-soaked spine of the heavy old Bible collapsed into red-hot ash and the two halves toppled from the lectern.

Fay rammed both feet into the wooden stem.

Very slowly it began to fall towards him, and Warren didn't move.

He opened his arms wide, as the lectern fell like a tree, and he embraced it, hugging the blistering stem to his chest.

'Yeah!'

Roaring and blazing.

Fay didn't move, watched in hypnotized awe until she felt and smelt something burning, very, very close, and found a single charring page wrapped around her arm.

Book of David, she read, the page curling sepia, reminding her of the opening credits of some dreadful old American Civil War movie, and she found that her lungs were full of smoke.

CHAPTER XIII

HIS body jerked in the grass, a convulsion. The crashing bells he accepted as the death vibrations of a brain cleaved by a steel bolt.

'Mr Powys.'

Oh Christ, he thought at once, it wasn't me, it was Arnold; he wants me to see what he's done to Arnold before he puts me into me.

He'd flung himself at the dog, just as Fay had done in the field by the river when Jonathon Preece had been strolling nonchalantly across with his gun. But Powys had missed. Arnold had kept on running, towards Humble and his crossbow, leaving Powys sprawled helplessly, arms spread, waiting for the end. The way you did.

'Mr Powys.'

He rolled very slowly on to his back, pain prodding whatever was between his shoulder-blades, the place where Humble had hit him with the butt of the crossbow.

'It is you, isn't it? Joe?'

He focused on a face in the middle of a pale-coloured head-scarf. He saw a woolly jumper. Below that some kind of kilt. Campbell tartan, Memory told him ridiculously.

'Mmmm . . .' Couldn't get the name out.

'It's Minnie Seagrove,' she said clearly. 'I want you to speak to me, please. Say something. I'm ever so confused tonight. I've been seeing Frank, and now it's bells. Bells everywhere.'

Powys came slowly to his feet. He didn't know about seeing Frank, but they couldn't both be hallucinating bells.

Mrs Seagrove gazed anxiously up at him, although she looked rather calmer than he felt. Behind her the Tump swelled like a tumour that grew by night. From out of the town came the wild pealing.

Powys was disoriented. He looked rapidly from side to side and then behind him. 'Where's . . . ?'

'That's another thing, I'm afraid,' Minnie Seagrove said. 'I think I've killed the man with the . . . what do you call it?'

'What . . . ?'

'Thank God. It's your voice. Here . . .' She pushed some-thing into his hand – his lamp. 'I can't switch it on, it's got a funny switch on it.'

Powys switched it on, and the first thing it showed him on the ground was the crossbow. And then an outstretched, naked arm.

'Now just don't ask me how I got here,' Mrs Seagrove said, 'because I don't know. It's been a very funny night, all told. But there you were, on the ground and this man with the thingy

– crossbow – pointing it down at you – he had the lamp on – taking aim, like. I thought, Oh God, what can I do? And I came up behind him when the bells started, and it put him off, sort of thing, the bells starting up like that, so sudden. Put him off – just for a second. And I *still* wasn't sure any of it was really happening, do you understand? I thought, well, if it's a dream, no harm done, sort of thing, so I hit him. Is he dead, Joe? Can you tell?' ·

'I shouldn't think so, Minnie.' Powys kicked the crossbow out of the way and bent over Humble with the lamp, nervous of getting too close, ready to smash the lamp down in Humble's face if he moved.

He stood up, finally. 'Er . . . what exactly was it you hit him with?'

'He's dead, isn't he, Joe? Come on now, I don't want any flim-flam.'

'Well, yes. He is actually.'

The back of Humble's head was like soft Turkish Delight.

'Bring the light over here, please, Joe. It was like an iron bar. Only hollow. Like a pipe. I threw it down somewhere . . . Here . . .'

Powys crouched down. It was indeed a piece of pipe, with jagged rust at one end and blood at the other. He didn't touch it. It seemed likely that Humble, for all his strength and his spectacular night vision, was one of those people with a particularly thin skull.

'It isn't a dream, is it, Joe?'

'Well, not in the accepted sense, no. But really, I mean . . . don't worry about it.' He put his hands on her shoulders. 'You did save my life. He wasn't exactly what anybody would call a nice man. In fact, offhand, I can only think of one person who's actually nastier. No, maybe two, now.'

He thought of something else and played the beam over the weapon again. Experienced a moment of pure, liquid euphoria; wanted to laugh aloud.

It looked like the tip of Henry Kettle's exhaust pipe.

He kept quiet about it, all the same. Don't tie this thing down too hard to reality. She's keeping herself together because she isn't yet fully convinced it's not part of the dream, like Frank. 'Look, Minnie, you didn't see a dog, did you? He . . . he might have been hit, I don't know.'

'He ran off,' said Mrs Seagrove. 'He was off like the clappers, over that way.'

She pointed at the gap where the stone wall had been broken down.

'The one I mean is a black and white dog,' Powys said gently. 'Escaped from my car. Left the window open too wide. But he couldn't have been going like the clappers, he's only got three legs now. You remember, he was shot.'

'Yes, it was the same dog. Fay Morrison's dog. Joe, what's going on? What's up with the bells?'

'God knows. Be nice to think it was a few of the townsfolk up in the tower, ringing every bell they've got as a sign they've finally woken up to something after a few centuries.'

He looked over his shoulder towards Crybbe Court, remembered the sparking under the eaves, like flints. Could see nothing now.

Which didn't mean a thing.

'Joe.'

'Mmm?'

'What's that?'

There was a ray of light playing among the trees on the Tump, flickering erratically.

And then a dog began to bark.

'Stay here,' Powys said.

'With *him*? Not likely.'

The dog was barking fiercely.

Powys watched the light moving among the trees.

'Who is it, Joe?'

'I think it's one of those other people I mentioned who are even nastier than Humble.'

Mrs Seagrove said, 'You're frightened, aren't you, Joe?'

Alex had remembered who Kate Bush was now.

Dark hair and sort of slinky. Seen her on the box once, a

few years ago, at young Fay's flat. Made the usual comments –
if I was forty years younger, etc. – and the next day Fay had
presented him with this T-shirt as a bit of a joke, and he'd
become quite attached to the garment, made him feel youthful,
having Kate Bush next to the skin.

Even tried to listen to the music.

Going up that hill . . . make a deal with God.

Alex was going down the hill, towards the river.

He stood on the bridge and stared down at the dark water.

'Rather funny, really,' he mused aloud to the river. 'I
thought I was dead. Can you believe that?'

Always been able to talk to rivers. Sometimes they even
burbled back. Not this one, this being a Crybbe river.

'Must have gone out for a breath of air, wound up in the
sodding boneyard, mooning over old Grace's plot. Went for a
Jimmy in the woods, came back and could've sworn I found
my own body. No – honest to God – I remember tripping over
something, about to fall flat on my face and it broke the fall.
It wore a dog-collar. And there was blood. Got it on my hands.
Felt awfully sticky.

'Jolly convincing, really.'

Alex rubbed his hands together and they felt strangely stiff.
He held them out and couldn't see them at all.

You're an old humbug, Alex. Who was it said that? Not
Grace, not Fay, not . . .

Wendy!

How could he have forgotten Wendy so soon. Only left her
house . . . when? Was it tonight? Or was it last night? Or was
it last week?

She said something like, Go back out there and you might
start losing your marbles again. But you've got to do it, Alex.
Got to go back.

Why? *Why* had he got to go back?

Because Wendy knows best, Wendy has cool hands.

Actually, he thought suddenly, for the first time, they're
quite *cold* hands. And they all think they know best, don't
they? The doctors, your relatives.

Suddenly Alex felt quite angry.

You start to lose your mind and everybody wants a bit. Even if you could get it back, it wouldn't be worth having. Shop-soiled. Messed about.

He said a civil goodnight to the river and began to walk back up the hill towards the square.

Deal with God. Why, after sixty years looking after His best interests, doesn't the bugger ever want to talk business with *me*?

The street had been quiet when he was walking down to the river; now he could hear people moving about, up over the brow of the hill, around the square.

Alex came to a house with a paraffin lamp burning in the window. He stopped and held up his hands.

They were covered with dried blood.

'Oh Lord,' Alex said, and it didn't start out as a prayer.

Frightened?

Well, how could you not be? But it was no bad thing, most of the time. The worst thing was a belief that you were in some way protected if you did what somebody else said was right. Like walking into the Humble situation because Jean Wendle had told him he needed to go back to the source.

But he always did what he was told. Max Goff: *There's a place for you here – think about it.*

Andy Boulton-Trow: *I think Joe ought to present himself to the Earth Spirit in the time-honoured fashion.*

I mean go round the Bottle Stone. Thirteen times.

Even dear old Henry Kettle: *My house is to be left to you. Consider it as a token of my confidence.*

Sod them all. But then he thought about Fay, with her rainbow eye.

'No,' he told Minnie Seagrove. 'I'm not frightened.'

And it's too dark to see me shaking.

He was scared, for instance, to set foot on the Tump; even Humble had said you couldn't always trust your reactions up there.

So they'd stay on the ground and, where possible, outside the wall.

He'd briefly considered taking Humble's crossbow. But he didn't know how to work it, and this was no time to learn.

That was another problem: what was he going to do about Humble? There was no way this one could be suicide or an accident. And while the police would never suspect Minnie Seagrove, they'd be hauling Joe Powys in within half an hour of the body being found. Minnie would, of course, explain the circumstances, but circumstances like these would sound more than a little suspect in court.

They began to walk around the perimeter of the Tump towards the light.

'Quietly,' Powys said. 'And slowly.'

The dog wasn't barking any more. If Andy had done anything to Arnold, he'd kill him.

OK, I'm full of shit, but I'm not going to obey instructions any more, not from you, not from Goff. And especially not from Jean.

Jean, of course – it made appalling sense – was not protecting him, she was protecting *Andy*, and Andy, typically, had wanted him to know that before he died.

Humble had said, *I'm empowered to answer just one of your questions . . . I'll tell you the answer, shall I? Then you can work out the question at your leisure. The answer is – you ready? – the answer is . . . HIS MOTHER.*

He would trace the Wort family tree later, if he ever got out of this. Meanwhile, it had a dispiriting logic, and it cleared up a few questions about Jean that he'd never even thought to ask. The idea of an experienced barrister giving it all up to act as the unpaid, earthly intermediary for Dr Chi had never sounded too likely. Jean's professional life had been built on ambition, power and manipulation: dark magic.

But she's *cured* people. That can't be dark magic. What about Fay's dad?

Oh, Jesus.

'What's wrong?' Mrs Seagrove whispered.

Fay had started pulling at Jimmy Preece's clothing and slapping at his face and screaming at him through the smoke. 'Please, Mr Preece, please, you *can't be . . .* '

Just a sign of life, anything, a blink, a twitch. Where did you keep a pulse in a neck like an old, worn-out concertina? 'Mr Preece!'

She pulled him down from the font and he collapsed on her, dead-weight, and she had to let him slide to the floor, managing to get both hands under his head before it hit the stone. But she could do no more because the appallingly blackened, smoke-shrouded scarecrow thing was dancing down the aisle, its clothes smouldering and its eyes all too alight. Her own eyes weeping with the smoke, with pity for Jimmy Preece and with fear for herself, she ran through the porch and began to wrestle with the bolts, throwing herself, coughing and sobbing, against the doors.

When she was out, she didn't look back, but she carried inside her head the image of the blackened monster and the scorched smell of him, knowing that if she stopped to breathe he would be on her.

She ran gasping through the churchyard and out of the lychgate, her lungs feeling like burst balloons, the bells crashing around her like bombs. She could hear voices in the square and she ran towards them, eyes straining, looking for lights.

But the nearer she got to the square and the louder the voices became, the darker it got, as if there was not only night to contend with, but fog. She thought at first it was her eyes, damaged by the smoke, but quite soon the bells stopped and Fay began to realize there was something about the square that was unaccountably wrong.

CHAPTER XIV

'FIRST off, anybody got a torch? Yes? No?'

The bells had stopped, and the silence ought to have glistened, Col Croston thought, but it didn't. The silence after the bells was the ominous silence you could hear when the phone rang and you picked it up and there was apparently nobody on the other end but you knew there *was*.

It was too dark to see who was with him on the square, but he could guess. Or rather, he could guess who was *not* on the square i.e. anybody born and bred within the precincts of the ancient town of Crybbe.

Graham Jarrett said, 'A torch is not normally considered essential for a public meeting, even in Crybbe. Besides, even when the power's off it's not usually as dark as this.'

'No. Quite.'

The town-hall doors had been slammed and barred behind the last of them and then, minutes later, Col had watched as they were opened again, just briefly, and a bloated figure had emerged, stood grotesquely silhouetted between two men and then tumbled without a word down the six steps to the pavement.

The late Max Goff had rejoined his New Age community. Col let him lie where he fell; somebody would have to explain this to the police and he didn't see why it had to be him.

Around the square, tiny jewels of light appeared, people striking matches. But almost as soon as a match was struck it seemed to go out, as if there was a fierce wind. Which there wasn't. Not any kind of wind.

There weren't even any lamps alight in the windows of the town houses tonight.

'OK, listen,' Col shouted. 'We need some lights. Anybody with a house near here, would they please go home and bring us whatever torches or lamps or even candles they can find. I also need a telephone. Who lives closest?'

'We have a flat,' Hilary Ivory said. 'Over the Crybbe Pottery.'

Hereward Newsome said, 'There's a phone in the gallery, that'd probably be quickest.'

'Good. I'll come with you. Stay where you are and keep on talking, so I can find you. Mrs Ivory, if you could find your way to your flat and bring out any torches et cetera.'

'I don't think we have torches, as such. When the electricity goes out we use this rather interesting reproduction Etruscan oil lamp. Would that do?'

'I'm sure it looks most attractive, but one of those heavy-duty motoring lanterns with a light each end might be a little more practical.'

'We haven't got a car.'

Col whistled tunelessly through his teeth.

'Colin, I'm over here.'

'Yes, OK, got you, Hereward. Now listen everybody, I don't know any more than you do what the hell's going on here tonight. What I do know is that none of us should attempt to leave the scene until after the police arrive. I'm going with Hereward to his gallery to ring headquarters and acquaint them fully with the situation. Any questions?'

'Oh lots,' Graham Jarrett said dreamily. 'And I may spend the rest of my life trying to find the answers.'

'Just hurry it up,' a woman said. 'There's an awful smell.'

'I can't smell anything.'

Actually he could, but didn't want to draw attention to it. It rather smelled as if a couple of people had lost control of their bowels, and, frankly, that wouldn't be too surprising under the circumstances.

'God, yes. It's vile.' Sounded like the woman who ran the craft shop, Magenta-something.

'Well, obnoxious as it might be, try not to move too far away. Lead on, Hereward. Keep talking.'

'Strange,' Hereward said, 'how when anyone asks you to keep talking you can never think of anything to say . . . Good grief, Colin, she was right about that smell. It's dreadful.'

In certain periods of his SAS career, Col had been exposed

for long hours to various deeply unpleasant bodily odours, but he had to admit – if only to himself – this was the most sickening. It was more than simply faeces, though there was certainly that. There was also a dustbin kind of pungency and all manner of meaty smells – newly killed to faintly putrid.

'No power, and now the drains are blocked. You'll probably turn on the tap, when you get home, Hereward, and find the bloody water's off, too. I really do think it's about time I put a bomb under my esteemed colleagues on the council. Not that they can actually *do* anything except talk about it.'

'You can certainly count on *my* support. For as long as I'm here, anyway. Look, I'm sorry about what happened in there. I overreacted, I suppose.'

'Wouldn't any of us, old chap? Some of these TV types do tend to think they have a kind of *droit de seigneur* wherever they happen to be hanging up their . . . Is it far, Hereward?'

'No, that is . . . I'm sorry, one gets disoriented in the dark, especially as dark as this. I've never known it this dark, I . . . it really should be about here, Colin. Can you feel the wall?'

'I can feel some kind of surface. Is there a timber-framed bit next to your place?'

'Actually, there is, and it goes straight from that to the large window, but . . .'

'Maybe we're on the wrong side of the square. Pretty easy to do, even when you're on what you think of as familiar ground.'

'No, I don't think . . . Oh hell, I seem to be way out.'

'Isn't there a pavement in front of your gallery? Because we're still on the cobbles, you know.'

'I thought there was a pavement all around the square, actually. Shows how you . . .'

A few yards away Col heard a woman scream. 'It's gone. It's gone, I tell you, Hilary, the whole bloody front . . . All I can feel is this . . . urrrgh, it's filthy.'

'Colonel Croston, can you help us, please. It sounds terribly stupid, but Celia's lost her Pottery.'

'Look.' Col took a step back. 'Let's calm down and get this in proportion. Funny, how you live in a place for years but never quite notice what order the shops are in. Right . . . Between the Crybbe Pottery and The Gallery we've got the Lamb, OK, and that . . . what's it called?'

'Middle Marches Crafts,' Hereward said.

'Right. And then, after the Pottery, the road starts sloping down to the bridge and across from there, we've got the Cock. Hereward . . .' He paused, confused. 'The Cock's got its own generator, hasn't it?'

'Yes, it has.'

'So why isn't it on?'

'Colin . . .' A brittle panic crumbling from Hereward's voice. 'Something's horribly wrong, don't you feel that?'

'It's *all* wrong . . .' Hilary's companion wailed. 'Nothing's the same.'

'If we only had light,' Col said. 'I know – cars. If somebody has a car parked on the square, they can open it up and switch on the headlights, then we can see where we're at.'

'Look . . .' Hereward breathing rapidly. 'I don't want to start a panic, but there were cars parked on three sides of this square when I went into the meeting. We haven't bumped into a single one, have we?'

'Well, they can't all have been nicked. Just spread the word. We're looking for anybody with a car parked on the square. Just . . . do it, Hereward, please.'

Col walked to the side of the building, felt wood and some type of chalky plaster. And the cobbles, under his feet.

Knowing full well that the pavement around the square had been replaced two years ago, and there'd already been one there for years before that. And now there were cobbles. Again.

He steadied his breathing.

Face facts. It was true; everything was different. Road surface, buildings . . . even the atmosphere itself. What would it look like . . . *What would it look like if they could actually see any of it?*

Mass hallucination, Col decided logically. Some kind of gas, perhaps. Why had the townsfolk refused to come out of the town hall and, indeed, locked themselves in? Because they knew what was happening, they knew it was too dangerous to go into the square.

Were the bells some form of alarm? Had somebody actually rehung all the ropes for this occasion?

And why didn't the locals warn everybody else? Because they only suspected what it might be and were afraid of being laughed at?

Or because they *wanted* the newcomers to be exposed to it?

It was insane. Any way you looked at it, it was all utterly insane.

Concentrate. Col dug the nails of his left hand into the back of his right. Just for a few moments there, completely forgot this was not, so far, the night's most appalling development. Max Goff savagely killed in front of all of them, and *that* was no hallucination.

Something touched his arm and, such was the state of his nerves, he almost swung round and struck out with the side of his hand.

'Colonel Croston.'

'Who's that?'

'It's Fay Morrison. Keep your voice down.'

'Mrs Morrison!'

'Christ, Colonel . . .'

'I'm sorry,' he whispered. 'Where the hell's Jim? You left with him, the Mayor . . .'

'He's . . . he's in the church. Listen . . . I've been following you around for the last ten minutes. I couldn't approach you until you knew. At least . . .'

'I don't know anything, Mrs Morrison. I've never been more in the dark. Excuse the humour. It isn't felt.'

'But you know everything's changed. I heard you talking to Hereward. You realize this is not, in any sense, the Crybbe we know and love.'

'Oh, now, look . . . !'

'I'm trying to keep calm, Colonel.'

'I'm sorry. This is beyond me. Some kind of gas, I suspect.'

'Colonel . . .'

'Col.'

'Col. Forget about gas. Please listen. First of all, I think Mr Preece is dead. Stroke, heart attack maybe, I don't know about these things. But I do know Max Goff was killed by *Warren* Preece, you know who I mean?'

'The grandson. Punkish type. Where is he?'

'He's hurt. He's badly burned. There was a fire. In the church.'

'Are you serious?'

'Yes, I know, you can't see any flames. But you can't see anything else either, can you?'

Col gripped her arm. He wanted to feel she was real.

'Please don't,' she said. 'I've got a burn.'

'I'm sorry, but this . . . Jesus.'

'Just listen. If you think this is mad, don't say anything. Just walk away and keep it to yourself.'

He tried to see her eyes, but all he could make out was the white of her face. 'OK,' he said.

'On this night,' Fay Morrison said. 'And I mean *this* night, this actual night, exactly four hundred years ago, a large number of people gathered in the square, where we are now, trying to decide what to do about the High Sheriff, who'd taken to hanging men and compelling their wives to have sex with him. And there were various other alleged examples of antisocial behaviour even by sixteenth-century standards that I won't go into now. But the bottom line is the people of this town decided they'd taken enough.'

He would have stopped her, he was in no mood for a local history lecture, but he supposed he'd given his word he'd listen to what she had to say.

'You can imagine the scene,' she said. 'A bit of a rabble, not exactly organized. Not much imagination, but angry and scared, too. Only finding courage in numbers, you know the kind of thing. So they march on Crybbe Court, flaming torches, the full bit. And there are a lot of them, and it really wasn't something this Sheriff would have expected. Not the border way. Keep your heads down, right? Don't make waves. But they did – for once. They made waves. They surrounded the Court and they said to the servants, men-at-arms, whatever,

"You send this bastard out or we're going to burn this place down." Maybe they set light to a barn or something to reinforce the threat, but, anyway, it was pretty clear to the Sheriff by now that he was in deep shit.'

From somewhere close to what he imagined was the centre of the square, Col could hear Graham Jarrett, the hypnotist guy, shouting, 'You're taking absolutely the wrong attitude, you know.'

'He seems to have gone into the attic,' Fay said, 'and topped himself.'

'Hear him out, will you?' a woman bawled. Sounded like that astrologer Oona Jopson, shorn head, ring through nose, who'd threatened to emasculate the doormen.

Fay said, 'What you have to remember about this particular Sheriff is that he was skilled in what I'm afraid we have to call the Black Arts. Except he thought it was science.' She paused. 'Do you want me to stop?'

'I'm not laughing,' Col said. 'Am I?'

'I'll carry on then. Before he hanged himself. Or while he was hanging himself – I mean, don't think I'm an expert on this stuff, I'm not – but, anyway, he left something of himself behind. It's called a haunting, Col. Still with me?'

'Open mind,' Col said. 'Go on.'

'It wasn't a spur-of-the-moment job. He'd been planning this for a long time. Dropped hints to his women. Expect more of the same when I'm gone.'

'Look,' Graham Jarrett was shouting, 'if you'll all just quieten down a minute, we'll do a bit of reasoning out. But I think we've been selected as participants in a wonderful, shared experience that's really at the core of what most of us have been striving for over many years.'

'And here we are . . . panicking!' the Jopson woman piped up. 'Well, I'm not panicking, I've never been so excited.'

Guy Morrison shouted, 'What about poor bloody Goff? He didn't look too excited. He looked a bit bloody dead to me.'

'Yeah, but *was* he?' Jopson. '*Is* he? I mean, how much of that was for real? How much of what we perceive is actual reality?'

Col Croston said, 'Jesus Christ.'

'It smells so awful,' the woman from the crafts shop, which now sold mainly greetings cards, said.

'It smells awful to *us*, that's all. Or only to you, maybe. To me, it's a wonderful smell. It smells of reality, not as it is to us these days, with our dull senses and our tired taste-buds and our generally limited perception of everything. What we're feeling right now is the *essence* of this place. I mean, shit, this is . . . this is *higher consciousness*.'

'And is she right?' Col asked Fay Morrison in a low voice.

'What do you think?'

'I think she's nuts.'

Guy said, 'Has anybody tried just walking away from here in any direction, just carrying on walking until they find an open door or somebody with a torch or a lamp?'

'My . . .' There was the sound of some struggling. 'Give me some *space*.' It was Jocasta Newsome. 'My husband . . . he said he was going to get help. He's . . . I can't find him.'

'Don't worry,' Graham Jarrett said. 'He'll be around. I don't think he can go anywhere, you see, I don't think anyone can. I don't think there's any light to be found.'

'I think there is, Graham,' a new voice said. A cool, dark voice. Lazy.

'Who's that? Is that Andy?'

Col Croston heard Fay Morrison inhale very sharply, through her mouth.

'I think,' the dark voice said, 'that we should consider how we can find our own light.'

'Who's that?' Col whispered.

'Boulton-Trow.'

'I don't think I know him.'

'I mentioned him during the meeting. You haven't forgotten that, have you?'

'Oh,' said Col. 'That.'

Her outburst. It occurred to Col that there was something personal at the back of this. That Fay Morrison had some old, probably sexual score to settle with Boulton-Trow. Anyway, it was all rather too much for a practical man to take. He had to reassemble his wits and get to a phone.

'Well, thank you, Mrs Morrison,' Col said. 'You've given me a lot of food for thought.'

'Col, it has to be food for action, or something unbelievably awful's going to happen.'

'Look,' Col said. 'I'll come back to you, OK?'

'No, don't go . . .'

But he'd gone.

'Oh, please . . .' Fay Morrison breathed into the foul-smelling dark. 'Please . . .'

CHAPTER XV

THE dog was in a pool of light on the side of the Tump where the grass looked almost white, and the dog was barking non-stop.

'Wait,' Joe Powys whispered to Minnie Seagrove. 'Don't go any closer. Stay out of the light.'

He moved quietly around the base of the Tump to see what was happening, who it was. *Don't look at me, Arnold. I'm not here. Ignore me.*

There was a single spotlight directed at the mound from the field, on the side facing the road, the side from which Henry Kettle had come on his last ride in his clapped-out old Volkswagen Variant.

The light went out. The dog stopped barking.

Powys waited.

He heard a vehicle door slam. Moved closer. Saw a match flare and then the red glow on the end of a cigarette.

'Well,' a voice said, 'you buggered yourself yere all right, boy.'

'Gomer!' Mrs Seagrove had appeared at Powys's side. 'It's Gomer Parry!'

'Oh Christ!' they heard, and an orange firefly crash-landed in the field.

'Gomer, it's Minnie Seagrove. You replaced my drains.'

'Flaming hell, woman, what you tryin' to do, scare the life out of me? Bloody dog was bad enough. Hang on a second.'

Two small lights appeared in the front of what proved to be a tractor with an unwieldy digger contraption overhanging the cab. Powys had last seen it parked in the square.

He whispered, 'Ask him if he's alone.'

'Course I'm bloody alone. Who you got there with you, Mrs Seagrove?'

'It's a friend of mine.'

'Choose some places to bring your boyfriends, all I can say.'

'You mind your manners, Gomer Parry. We're coming down.'

He was scrabbling in the grass when they reached him. 'Dropped my ciggy somewhere.' The digger's sidelights were reflected in his glasses. 'Sod it, won't set afire, grass is too bloody wet.' He peered at Powys. 'I seen you before, isn't it? You was with that radio lady, Mrs Morris, hour or so ago. Put yourself about, don't you, boy?'

'Gomer!' Mrs Seagrove snapped.

'Aye, all right. Nice lady, that Mrs Morris. Very nice indeed.'

'Pardon me for asking, Mr Parry,' Powys said, deadpan, 'but somebody wouldn't by any chance be paying you to take out the rest of the wall?'

'Now just a minute! You wanner watch what you're sayin', my friend.'

'Only it's, er, kind of outside normal working hours.'

'Aye, well,' said Gomer Parry. 'Bit of an accident, like. Got a bit confused, what with the ole power bein' off, no streetlights, and I come clean off the road. Dunno what come over me, never done nothin' like that before, see, never.'

'Don't worry about it,' Powys said. 'Not as if you're the first.'

'What's that?' said Gomer, suspicious. 'Oh, bugger me . . . 'Enry Kettle! Is this where 'Enry Kettle . . . ?'

'You knew Henry?'

'Course I knew 'im. 'Enry Kettle, oh hell, aye. Wells, see. Wells. 'E'd find 'em, I'd dig 'em. Talk about a tragic loss. Friend o' yours too, was 'e?'

He nodded and put out his hand. 'Joe Powys.'

Gomer shook it. 'Gomer Parry Plant Hire.'

Powys did some rapid thinking. Gomer had gone off the road, probably at the same spot as Henry. And yet Gomer had survived.

'What happened? When you came off the road?'

'Bloody strange,' Gomer said. 'Thought I muster been pissed, like – sorry Mrs S – but I'd only 'ad a couple, see. Anyway, it was just like I'd blacked out and come round in the bloody field . . . only I never did. And then it was like . . . well, it was like goin' downhill with a hell of a strong wind up your arse – sorry, Mrs . . .'

'You see anything?'

'Oh, er . . .' Gomer scratched his face. 'Got in a bit of a panic, like, tell the truth. See all sortser things, isn't it? Thought I seen a feller one second, up there, top o' the Tump, 'mong the ole trees, like, but nat'rally I was more bothered 'bout not turnin' the ole digger over, see. Best one I got this. Customized. Fixed 'im myself, big David Brown tractor an' half of this ole JCB I got off my mate over Llandod way. Bloody cracker, this ole thing. Managed to stop 'im 'fore I reached the ole wall, if 'e 'ad gone into it, I'd've been pretty bloody sore about it, I can tell you.'

'Word has it,' said Powys, 'that you were pretty bloody sore when somebody borrowed your bulldozer.'

'Don't you talk to me 'bout that!' said Gomer in disgust. 'Bloody vandals.'

'You were warned off, weren't you? You could've had this wall down no problem, but they warned you off.'

''Ow'd you know that?' demanded Gomer.

'Made sense.'

'Oh aye? You know anythin' else makes sense?'

'Going back to this figure on the top of the Tump. Where exactly were you when you saw him?'

'You're askin' a lot o' questions, Mister. You with the radio, too?' Although he didn't sound as if he'd mind if this were the case. 'No, see, I said I *thought* I seen 'im. 'E was prob'ly another tree with the light catchin' 'im funny, like.'

'Your headlights are that powerful, that you could see a

man standing on top of the Tump when you're coming downhill and the lights are pointing down?'

'Light. Only got one 'eadlight workin', Joe.'

'So when you said a tree caught in the light . . .'

'Aye,' Gomer said thoughtfully. 'You're right. Not possible, is it? See, I'll tell you what it was like. You know kids when they gets a torch and they wants to frighten other kids and they flashes it under their chin and their face lights up really weird, on account of half it's in shadow. Well, it was like that, see, only it was like his whole body was lit up that way. Scary. Only I'm strugglin' with the wheel, I thinks, get off, it's only an ole tree.'

Minnie Seagrove looked at Powys. 'I used to think things like that when I first saw the Hound. You do. You look for explanations, sort of thing.'

'The hound?' said Gomer.

Arnold began to bark.

'Right,' said Gomer, opening the door of the cab. 'If there's anybody else up there I'm gonner bloody find out this time.'

The single headlight spotlit the Tump again, and Powys watched as Arnold ran into the white circle.

Ran. Arnold *ran* into the light.

He'd lost a leg just a few days ago, and he was *running*.

Was this Arnold?

'Arnold!' Powys shouted. 'Come on!'

The dog trotted down to the foot of the mound and ambled across. Powys bent down and the dog snuffled up at him and licked his hands. Gently, Powys slid one hand underneath. He could actually feel the stitching.

Arnold squirmed free and made off, back across the field towards the Tump, looking back at Powys every few yards and barking.

'He's found something,' Minnie Seagrove said. 'He wants to show you something.'

I can't believe this, Powys thought. This is seriously weird. He isn't even limping.

Arnold's tail started to wave when he saw Powys was following him. He ran a few yards up the side of the Tump and then sat down.

He *sat* down.

The dog with only one back leg *sat down*.

Arnold barked. He turned around and put his nose into the side of the Tump and snuffled about. Then he turned round again and started to bark at Powys.

Powys thought – the words springing into his mind in Henry Kettle's voice – *he's a dowser's dog.*

He wandered back to the digger, rubbing his forehead. 'Gomer, what are the chances of you doing a spot of excavation?'

'What?' Gomer said. 'In there?'

'Be a public service,' Powys said. 'That Tump's a liability. If it wasn't for that Tump, Henry Kettle would be alive today and locating wells.'

'Protected Ancient Monument, though, isn't it?' Gomer said. 'That's an offence, unauthorized excavation of a Protected Ancient Monument.'

'Certainly is,' said Powys.

'That's all right, then,' said Gomer, glasses twinkling. 'Where you want the 'ole?'

CHAPTER XVI

THE acoustic in the square was tight and intimate, like a studio, and the voice was deep and resonant: strong and melancholy music. Wonderful broadcasting voice, Fay thought, trying to be cynical. Radio Three, FM.

'When you think about it,' the voice said, 'any town centre's an intensely powerful place; it's where energy gathers from all directions, thoughts and feelings pouring in. It's where we go to tap into a town, to feel its life rhythm.'

Pure radio, Fay thought. The purest radio of all, because we can't see anything. No distractions. He can design his own pictures in our minds.

'The town centre is where the centuries are stored,' Andy said. 'Smell them. Smell the centuries.'

All I can smell, Fay thought, is shit. Four hundred years of shit. And all I can hear is bullshit. Had to keep telling herself that. This was Andy Boulton-Trow, of Bottle Stone fame. Descendant of Sheriff Wort, scourge of Crybbe, black magician, the most hated man in . . .

'What you can smell,' Andy Boulton-Trow said (and she felt, most uncomfortably, that he was speaking directly to *her*), 'is many centuries of human life. There haven't always been sewerage systems and hot water and fresh vegetables. This town lived on the border of two often hostile countries, and it had to live within itself. It ground its own flour, killed its own meat and kept its own counsel.'

He paused. 'And its secrets. It kept its secrets.'

Fay thought, drab secrets densely woven into a faded, dirty old tapestry.

Boulton-Trow's voice was the only sound in the square. The only sound in the world – for this square *was* the world. None of them could leave it, except – perhaps – by dying.

Should have been a terrifying thought. Wasn't.

She couldn't remember, for the moment, quite what he looked like, this Boulton-Trow. Only that he was tall and dark and bearded. Like Christ; that was how people saw Him.

But she couldn't see Boulton-Trow. She couldn't see anybody. You'd have thought your eyes would have adjusted by now, so that you'd be able to make out at least the shapes of men and women. But unless they were very close to you, you could see nothing. This darkness was unnatural.

Not, however, to Andy. She could feel that. He knew his way around the darkness. If anybody could lead them out of here it would be him, and that would be comforting to these people.

Perhaps it was comforting to her.

But there was no immediate comfort in Andy's message.

'And now you come here, and you want Crybbe to give up its secrets to you. To lay open its soul to you. You want to feel its spirit inside you. Isn't that right?'

'We want to help it rediscover its own spirit,' someone said. 'Surely that's what this is about, this experiment.'

'This experiment.' Andy laughed. 'And who's the subject of this experiment? Is it Crybbe? Or is it us? Maybe we're here to let the town experiment on us. It's an interesting idea, isn't it? Maybe Crybbe can work its own alchemy if you're prepared to put yourselves into the crucible. Perhaps what you're experiencing now is a taster. Can you handle this? Are you strong enough?'

Talk about a captive audience, Fay thought. It was an uneasy thought. She was a captive, too. Would she not also go along with anything this man suggested if he could lead her out of here, back into where there were lights.

'Sense of place,' Andy said. 'You want to feel that sense of place that finds an echo in your own hearts. You want to belong. You want to lay yourself down in a field on a summer's evening and you want the mysteries to come to you, whispered in your ears, drifting on the air and smelling of honeysuckle.'

'Yes,' a woman said faintly. 'Yes.'

Andy paused and the night held its breath.

'That's not how it works,' he said. 'You know that really, don't you? *This* is how it works. *This* is Sense of Place. Feel it. Smell it. Secrets come out like babies, writhing and covered in blood and slime. And all of us genteel New Age people, we turn up our noses and we start to scream. Let me out of here! I can't bear it! Give me my picturesque half-timbered cottage and my chintzy sofa and my books. Give me my incense and my crystals and my immersion tank. Give me my illusions back. Yeah?'

Nobody spoke.

'I can't give you your illusions back,' Andy said gently.

The silence was total..

Radio, Fay thought desperately. It's only radio. You know the techniques, you know the tricks. He's standing there at the mixing desk, the Presenter and also the Engineer, playing with the effects, adjusting the atmos.

'But if you trust me,' Andy said, 'I can give you the true secrets of Crybbe. Think about this. I'll be back.'

And the voice was gone.

'Andy!' Jarrett shouted into the pungent night. 'Don't go!'

'He can't go,' Oona Jopson said. 'Can he?'

'Stop!' Powys shouted.

The mechanical digger groaned.

Arnold barked.

'Take it slowly, OK. We could be coming to something.'

Gomer's customized digger had an extra spotlight, mounted on the cab. It wasn't as strong as the single headlight, but at least you could focus it on the target.

Powys had been worried the wall would be a problem, but Gomer had done some skilled manoeuvring, putting on a show, riding the digger like a trick-cyclist, plant-hire choreography, tapping the wall with the edge of the shovel in exactly the right places, until the stones crumbled apart like breezeblocks. Powys asking him, 'Out of interest, how long would it have taken you to take this wall apart with the bulldozer?'

Gomer had leaned out of his cab, his cigarette pointing upwards from his mouth so the red end was reflected in his glasses. 'You what, Joe? This ole wall? Gimme hour or so, you'd never know there'd been a wall yere. Tell you what – bloody hurt me, that did, havin' to say I couldn't 'andle 'im without a bigger 'dozer.'

Afterwards, it had just been a question of removing enough rubble to get the digger to the Tump. And after that . . .

'Piece o' piss,' Gomer said. 'Sorry, Minnie.'

Mrs Seagrove sat on a broken section of the wall, dust all over her kilt, Arnold lying across her knees, watchful, both of them watching the action.

'Isn't he good, though, Joe?' she said as Gomer went into the Tump like a surgeon. 'Isn't he a marvel?'

Powys smiled. She was loving it. He wondered if she remembered killing Edgar Humble, or if she still half-thought that was all a dream, no more real now than Frank, her dead husband.

'Hold it a minute, Gomer, we've got . . .'

Gomer backed up, raised the shovel. Powys slid under it, lumps of earth falling on him from its great metal teeth.

'Minnie, can you pass me the hand-lamp?'

It looked like an opening. No more than five feet in, and they could be into some kind of tunnel. He shone the light inside and he could see a roof of solid stone, like the capstone of a dolmen.

'Gomer, we've cracked it.'

'Course we 'ave, boy. Want me to widen the 'ole?'

'OK.'

He stepped back and the shovel adjusted itself then went in again.

He couldn't believe this. They'd gone in at precisely the spot where Arnold had been sitting (*sitting* – a leg short and he was sitting) and after no more than twenty minutes they were into the heart of this thing.

Powys looked up towards the sky, black and starless.

'Henry?' he said. 'Is this you, you old bugger?'

Fay moved among them, listening, but speaking to no one.

It was obvious by now that Col Croston was not coming back to her. Perhaps, like Hereward, he'd gone to try and find a way out of the square.

'We're not in a different time zone,' Graham Jarrett was saying. 'It's not as simplistic as that. We're in what you might call a timeless zone. A place where the past and present exist in the same continuum.'

'What he was saying, about the town centre,' Adam Ivory said. 'I think that's literally central to this experience. The town centre's this kind of energy vortex . . .'

Fay moved on. They were creating a dream within a dream, the way New Age people tended to do, moving around scattering meaningless jargon, making themselves comfortable inside the experience.

But Jean Wendle, the most experienced of them all, was not here.

Or was she?

Fay moved around in the darkness, almost floating, coming to sense the nearness of other bodies and the emotions emanating from them: fear and exhilaration in equal quantities now. But she doubted there was one of them who would not prefer this experience in retrospect, returning to the square by daylight:

Yes, this was where it happened, just about here, yes, you can still feel the essence of it, yes, it'll never be the same again for me, this place, always be special, yes, it was like an initiation, becoming a part of this town. And now I feel I can tap into it whenever I want to, and I can really work here effectively now because I belong, because I've felt the Spirit of Crybbe.

Fay moved on. Through the radio world.

And now he was inside the Tump.

He'd been inside them before – burial chambers, passage graves. It was suggested that many of the stone dolmens or cromlechs around the country had once been covered over, like this, with earth.

The passageway was perhaps three and a half feet wide, and was low, and he had to walk painfully bent over. He directed the beam at the walls and the ceiling; the structure appeared to be a series of cromlechs joined up, like vertebrae, wide slabs of grey-brown stone overhead, a floor of close-packed earth.

He turned around, with difficulty, and he couldn't see the entrance any more. He wasn't naturally claustrophobic, but he shuddered briefly at the thought of the opening being sealed behind him, great bucket-loads of earth dumped back and rubble from the wall heaped across so that nobody would ever know there was a passageway, so that he slowly suffocated in here and became one more well-preserved pile of bones in a forgotten Bronze Age burial chamber.

He stopped.

His chest tightened.

Gomer. Could he really trust Gomer Parry?

So many old allegiances, never spoken of, in Crybbe. And new ones, too. Could you ever know exactly who belonged to whom?

Maybe he should have asked Gomer to come with him, but he couldn't leave Mrs Seagrove outside on her own.

Look, don't think about it, OK. Too much at stake to go back now. Concentrate on where you are, what it can tell you.

Keep going . . .

It would probably be an actual Bronze Age grave, although he doubted he was the first person since then to enter this mound. You couldn't excavate a prehistoric burial chamber in under an hour.

But was he the first to get inside since Michael Wort?

Abruptly it ended.

Out of the passage and into the chamber itself, wider, maybe eight feet in diameter, but not quite circular any more. It was cold in here; the air smelled old and rank.

In the centre of the chamber was a single flat stone.

On the stone was a wooden box.

Powys stopped at the entrance to the chamber, put the lamp on the ground, stood blocking the entrance, head bowed.

They didn't have boxes in the Bronze Age, not carved oak boxes anyway, with iron bands and locks.

He stood staring at the box in the lamp's beam, and his breathing tightened. The box was about twelve inches deep and eighteen inches square. It sang to him, and it sang of ancient evil.

Oh, come *on* . . .

He walked across the chamber to the box, and found he couldn't touch it.

There is no evil, only degrees of negativity.

Powys started to laugh, and then, quite deliberately, he bent down and switched off the lamp.

What is this about?

Well, he couldn't see the box any more, or the inside of the stone chamber; he could be anywhere, no visual images, no impressions coming in now.

Just me. And it. This is a *real* fairy hill, and I'm in the middle of it, and I've come here of my own free will and there's no Andy and no Jean and I'm scared. I've put out the light to induce a state of fear, and the nerve-ends are bristling with it, and I'm ready.

I'm ready.

'Hereward?'

'Yes.'

'Thank God.'

'Why? Why are you thanking God?'

'Because I thought . . . I thought you weren't going to come back. Hereward, I'm so desperately sorry. I was only trying to get away. All I've ever wanted is to get away from here.'

'And you thought Guy Morrison would take you away?'

'No . . . yes . . . Oh God, I don't know what I thought. I was just so lonely and messed up. He – Guy – was passing through, he wasn't part of Crybbe, he was going somewhere, and I was stuck fast. I was like someone just dashing outside and thumbing a lift. And he stopped. I'm sorry, that's all mixed up, I'm not very clear tonight, not very articulate.'

'Don't cry.'

'I'm sorry. I'm sorry about the picture, too, but you don't know what pictures can do.'

'Oh, I do.'

'I'm not talking about aesthetics.'

'I know.'

'Do you?'

'Pictures are doorways.'

'Yes.'

'Artists put elements of themselves into pictures, and also elements of other things. The man in that picture of Tessa's, he's her teacher, you know. He has a studio in the woods, and she's been going down there and he's been teaching her how to paint. And what to paint. How to make a picture into a doorway.'

'How do you know that?'

'Because, in the picture, he's standing in a doorway, like The Light of the World, in reverse, because he's so dark. But darkness and light, it's all the same when you can't see, isn't it?'

'I don't . . .'

'I'm going through the doorway, Jocasta.'

'Hereward?'

'It really is the only way out of here, through the doorway. The only way out for me, anyway.'

'Hereward, I'm getting very scared.'

'There's no need to be scared. Come here, darling. There.'

'No. No, please.'

588

'There . . . there . . .'
'Aaaugh.'
'There.'

Hereward felt the woman go limp, and his hands fell away from her throat. He felt himself smiling into the dark as he walked away.

The lamp was alight, and the door was ajar. When he pushed, it swung open at once, and Hereward found himself in the comfortingly familiar setting of his own workshop next to The Gallery.

A candle glowed on the workbench, where he'd made frames. *Do you know, in the early days, we used actually to make our own frames . . .*

Fragments of frames were scattered over the bench and the floor; a corner section was still wedged in the wood-vice. He wouldn't need to make frames any more; that phase was over. Perhaps he'd employ someone to do it.

'Don't suppose you'd be interested in a job, would you?' he said to the shadow sitting on the bench, next to the candle.

The shadow stopped whittling at a piece of framing-wood with its Stanley knife and slipped to the floor.

Hereward saw it wasn't really a shadow; it was just black.

CHAPTER XVII

LAUGHTER in the dark.
Laughter like ice-crystals forming in the air.
'Andy.'
Who did you think it was going to be, Joe? Did you think you were finally about to meet Sir Michael himself?

Andy, but he wasn't here.

He was mainly grey, shimmering to nearly white at his fingertips, the extremities of him.

Andy, but he wasn't there.

Powys heard the voice in his head. He spoke aloud, but he heard the replies in his head.

He wasn't thinking about this too hard, analysis was useless. Couldn't play new games by old rules.

Don't touch him. He can't harm you.

BUT DON'T TOUCH HIM.

'The box. What's in the box, Andy?'

Why don't you open it, Joe? The lock's no big deal. Ornamental, as much as anything. Also it's very old. Pick up a stone. Break the lock.

'I don't think so.'

No? You're still very much full of shit, Joe, you know that? You go to all this trouble to get into here, and you won't face up to the final challenge. What's the problem? Not got the guts, Joe? Not got the bottle? Think about this . . . think hard . . . what's it all been worth, if you don't open it?

'Maybe I will,' Powys said.

You'll find a couple of stones behind you, near where you left your lamp. One's narrow and thin, it used to be a spearhead. The other's chunky, like a hammer. You can slide the spearhead into the crack below the lid.

'But not here.'

The eyes were white, though. The eyes were alight, incandescent.

Andy, but he wasn't here.

'I'm not going to open it here. You can piss off, mate. I'm going to pick up the box, and I'm going to take it away.'

You don't want to do that, Joe. You might awaken the Guardian. You don't want that.

'No. *You* don't want that. But you can piss off.'

Powys felt a trickle of euphoria, bright and slippery as mercury and, very quickly, he covered it up. Smothered it with fear. Stay frightened. At all costs, stay frightened.

A rapid pattering on the close-packed earthern floor, and something warm against his leg.

'Arnie.'

Stay frightened. It might not be.

He bent down.

And the growling began.

He felt Arnold's fur stiffen and harden under his hand, and the growling went on, a hollow and penetrating sound that came from far back in the dog's throat, maybe further back than that. Maybe much further back. The growl was continuous and seemed to alter the vibration of the night.

'You're not growling at *me*, are you, Arnie?'

The grey thing hung in the air like an old raincoat, but he was fairly sure that Andy was not there any more.

Powys switched on the lamp and the grey thing vanished.

He walked over to the stone in the centre of the chamber and he picked up the wooden box.

Warm. Cosy. Just as before. The deep, Georgian windows, the Chinese firescreen, the Victorian lamp with the pale-blue shade burning perfumed oil.

'I wondered,' she said, 'if you would come back.'

'Hullo, Wendy,' Alex said.

She was dressed for bed.

And how.

Black nightdress, sort of shift-thing, filigree type of pattern, so you could see through it in all the right places. Alex couldn't take his eyes off her.

'Sit down,' Jean said.

'Wendy, there's something awfully funny happening out there, did you know?'

'Funny?'

'Well, I'd been down to the river and came back up the hill and when I got to near the top, just at the entrance to the square, it all went very dark. I mean, I know it's obviously dark without the electricity supply, but this really was extra dark, as if there was a thick fog. Lots of people about the square, I could hear them talking, but I couldn't *see* any of them.'

'Oh my.'

'And . . . hard to explain this, but it was as if there was a sort of screen between all these people and me. Now, I know what you're going to say – the only reason there's a screen between me and the rest of the world is because I've erected it myself – but it wasn't like that. Not at all. This was really, well, physical, but not . . . How do you explain it?

'I think you should come and sit down Alex and not let yourself get too worked up about this.'

'That's what you think, is it?'

'I think you need to calm down.'

Alex slumped into the sofa and she came down next to him, light as a bird, perching on the edge of the cushion, and the shift-thing riding up her legs. Pretty remarkable legs, had to admit that.

'And I heard Fay,' Alex said. 'I'd walked back – couldn't seem to make progress, you see, kept on walking and wasn't getting anywhere. You know that feeling? Happens in dreams sometimes. Anyway, I'm coming up the hill again, and this time it's Fay I can hear, talking to some chap. Telling him about how all the people had gathered in this very square, exactly four hundred years ago to the night, to get up a posse to go along and lynch old whatsisname . . . Sheriff Wort.'

'I see,' Jean said. She leaned over and picked up his left hand. One of her nipples was poking through the black filigree stuff.

Alex swallowed. 'Then this chap she was talking to, he must have drifted away. I said, "Listen, Fay," I said, "why don't you tell me – tell *me* – what all this is about . . . ?" But she couldn't hear me. Why couldn't she hear me, Wendy?'

Jean said, 'What's this on your hands?'

'Blood,' he said quickly. 'It's Murray Beech. He's been stabbed to death. Only realized as I was walking up the hill.'

'Stabbed to death,' Jean said neutrally. 'I see.'

'Don't you believe me?'

'Alex, I believe *you* believe that Murray Beech has been stabbed to death. And what about Grace?'

'She took me to her grave. We walked together. I think we came to an agreement.'

'I see.'

'But you don't really believe any of this, do you, Wendy?'

Jean smiled.

'Or do you?'

'Alex,' said Jean, 'would you like to sleep with me?'

Alex's throat went dry.

'Well?' she said gently.

'Oh gosh,' Alex said. 'Do you think I could manage it?'

Jean smiled. 'Perhaps we should find out.'

'That's what you think, is it?'

The answer burned quietly, like a kind of incense, in her eyes.

Alex stood up. He felt very calm. Calmer than ever he could remember feeling before. He did not know the meaning of the word 'dementia'. His heart was strong. His eyes, he knew, were twinkling quite dramatically.

The aromatic oil from the lamp was exquisite.

Jean unwound from the sofa and he took her in his arms. His breathing rate quickened at once. She tilted her face to kiss him, but he ran a hand into her soft, short hair and pressed her face to his chest, bent his head and whispered into her ear.

'You cunning bitch.'

Her body went rigid, and he let her go.

What a waste, he thought. What a tragic bloody waste.

When Jean Wendle faced him from across the room, her eyes were in deep shadow, her lips were drawn back and the inside of her mouth looked so black that she seemed, momentarily, to have no teeth at all.

The aromatic oil from the lamp smelt like the floor of a urinal.

'Oh my. You've blown it, now, Alex,' Jean whispered, voice like tinder.

Alex shook his head.

'You'd had it. You were finished. You were going very rapidly into the final decline. A bed in the bottom corner of the geriatric ward, to where the naughty boys are consigned, the nurses treating you like a difficult child when you try to pinch their bottoms. Poor old man, he used to be a priest.'

'Nothing more welcome in hell than an unfrocked priest,' Alex mused. 'Except perhaps a priest who ought to have been unfrocked but never was, because he was too damned plausible – all his life, so plausible, right up to the end, shafting old ladies.'

'I brought you back,' Jean said. 'I fed you energy.'

'But what kind of energy?'

'Ach.' Jean turned away with a dismissive wave of the hand. 'You blew it.'

'I don't think so,' Alex said. 'I made a deal. I went up the hill and I made a deal.'

He smiled. His heart was strong and his eyes still twinkled.

Jean Wendle turned her head and peered at him, curious. He saw in her face a pinched look, ravages, and not the ravages of years.

'Made a deal,' Alex said. 'After a period of protracted and considered negotiation, the Management and I formulated the basis of an agreement, nothing binding, either party retaining the right to pull out at any given time if the Second Party should happen to lose his bottle.'

Alex walked out of the room. 'Good night, Wendy.'

Bloody waste, he thought sadly.

Joe Powys came out of the passage into the night, into a blinding light and the face of Edgar Humble.

He didn't have to force the fear.

'Hold it. Don't move.'

Powys half out of the hole in the side of the Tump, the wooden box in his arms, Arnold at his ankles.

Humble's eyes were fully open, his lips apart.

'You're dead,' Powys said from a throat full of hairline cracks.

'Course he's fucking dead,' Gomer Parry said, leaning out of his cab. 'Sorry, Minnie.'

Humble lay across the jaw of the digger, quite stiff now, one arm still flung out and his crossbow on his chest. The big shovel was almost blocking the entrance to the passage.

Minnie Seagrove wasn't looking.

Gomer said, 'What you got there, then, Joe?'

'Buried Treasure,' said Powys. 'Is that thing safe?'

'Gimme a second.' Gomer raised the shovel so Powys could climb out from underneath it.

'Right, then.' The little man climbed out of his cab, rubbing his hands on his overalls. 'We got a bit o' talkin' to do yere, Joe. First off, you finished in there? Got what you want?'

'I think so.'

'Safe to block 'im up again, then.'

'Don't see why not.'

'Good. Mind out, then.'

He climbed back into his cab, cigarette end waggling, lowered the shovel, started to tip Humble's body over the entrance of the hole.

'What the hell are you doing, Gomer?'

Minnie Seagrove turned away as Humble's remains tumbled into the soil and rock.

'Nicked that box, did you?' Gomer shouted.

'What?'

'Treasure trove, that, boy. I won't say nothin' if you don't.'

'I had to tell him, Joe,' Minnie Seagrove said. 'I said, I'll go to the police and admit everything. And you'll speak up for me, won't you, Joe? You're a famous writer, that'll count for quite a lot. But he wouldn't hear of it.'

'Bollocks,' said Gomer. 'Could be centuries before they finds 'im, if ever. And if they does turn 'im up, 'ow could it possibly have anythin' at all to do with a sweet little old lady? Sorry, Minnie, I didn't mean old . . .'

The more Powys thought about it, the less difficult it became to fault.

'You can't leave him near the entrance.'

'I shall drag 'im in just as far as 'e'll go, then I'll fill this 'ole up and pack 'im tight, see, and pile up them stones, so it looks like the wall collapsed on it, like.'

'I can't stop to help you, Gomer, I'm sorry. I've got to go somewhere and I don't think there's much time.'

'No problem. I'll take Minnie 'ome.'

'And could you do me another favour – take Arnold, too.'

'I'll take him,' Mrs Seagrove said.

'I'll come back for him.'

I hope.

Or Fay will.

'Thanks, Arnie,' said Powys, putting the box down and sinking his hands into Arnold's fur, rubbing his face against the dog's encouragingly cold nose.

Arnold licked him once.

'And thank Henry for me,' Powys said, 'if you see him around.'

He picked up the box. It was quite heavy but not too unwieldy. He balanced the lamp on top. 'You're *sure* this is going to be all right? I have the awful feeling it'll look like an excavation site.'

'Joe,' said Gomer patiently, 'this yere is Gomer Parry Plant Hire you're dealin' with. I already got the reputation of havin' fucked up once on this site – sorry, Minnie – and I'm not gonner risk 'avin' myself pulled in by that Wiley if I can 'elp it, am I?'

Gomer lit another cigarette, lowered his voice. 'Wynford Wiley,' he said. 'Wouldn't give 'im the satisfaction. Fat bastard.'

Powys nodded. 'Minnie. I . . .'

'She never did nothin',' Gomer Parry said gruffly. 'So you got nothin' to thank 'er for, is it? Bugger off. Good luck.'

CHAPTER XVIII

IF anything, it was stronger now. She thought she'd get used to it, like when you were staying on a farm during the manure-spreading season, but this wasn't manure and it was getting stronger.

In it there was human waste and animal waste, raw meat, blood perhaps, body odours, rancid fats . . . and now smoke.

Woodsmoke? Maybe.

Or was it the church? Could she smell the fire in the church because the church was on the line linking the centre of the square with the Court and the Tump?

Joe Powys would know. Or he wouldn't. Either way, it would be good to have him here. Not such a world-class crank after all, not when you listened to this bunch.

Fay walked among them, the night still alive with natural radio.

'He'll come back.' Graham Jarrett.

'What if he doesn't?' Hilary Ivory.

'I tried walking.' One of the lawyers, in tones of defeat. 'I kept on walking, looking for a light. I kept walking, and I just felt like I was fading out . . . fading away. Losing my physical resistance to the air, becoming absorbed in the atmosphere. I mean, it was very soporific, in a way. I think it'd be good to die like that. But not yet. I got scared. I thought, I've got to go back. And when I thought that, I *was* back. Like I hadn't been anywhere.'

'There's nowhere to go.' Oona Jopson. 'Accept it. Relish it. It's not likely to happen to you again.'

'Good.'

'Or maybe it will. Maybe we're being opened up to a permanent kind of cosmic consciousness, you know?'

She wondered what was happening outside the square. Was the church alight? Was Jimmy Preece alive? And what about Warren? Were the Crybbe people attending the meeting still inside the town hall? And what of their relatives in the town – had they any idea what was happening? Perhaps it had happened before, the town square sealing itself off in the past – a past which was always close to the surface of this town.

Not for the first time tonight, Fay genuinely wondered if this was some long and tortured dream. And, if it was not a dream, whether, when (if) it was over, it would have no more significance than if it had been.

Somebody was coughing very weakly, a thin scraping sound.

'Where's Colonel Croston?'

'I'm here. Who's that.'

'It's Dan Osborne, Colonel, I'm a homeopathic practitioner, but I have a medical qualification. There's a woman here in a bad way. Over here, just come towards my voice. I'm bending across her, you won't walk into her.'

'OK, I'm on my way. Do you know who she is?'

'She's wearing what feels like a silk blouse and . . . a fairly tight skirt. She's got . . . thick hair, quite long I suppose.'

Guy said, 'Is she wearing a thickish sort of necklet thing?'

'A torque, I think. Dear God, what's this . . . ?'

'Jocasta! What's happened? Where are you?'

'She's . . . The bloody torque's been twisted into her neck. Please, Christ, just hold still . . .'

'OK, Mr Osborne, I'm here. Is she OK?'

'I don't know. She didn't bloody well do this to herself, did she? Somebody's tried to garrotte her with her own . . .'

'OH GOD! GET ME OUT OF THIS!' The woman from the crafts shop hurling herself about the Crybbe vacuum, bouncing off people. Somebody had to crack up, sooner or later.

Have one for me, Fay thought.

Col Croston sat down on the cobbles, cross-legged, and looked hard at the darkness. Held his own hand up in front of his face from six inches. He could see it. Just. Could tell it was a hand, or was that because he knew it was a hand?

The woman would live. Her throat would be a mess, but she'd be OK. She'd tried to speak. 'Who did this?' he asked, but if she'd identified her attacker he hadn't been able to make out the name. Wouldn't be much use anyway; how could you go after anyone without light?

I am here, Col said silently, letting his eyes half-close. I can sense myself. I can sense my toes (flexing them and then letting them relax), my calves (trying to tighten the muscles in his legs and letting them relax), my thighs . . . my stomach . . .

An exercise.

As a soldier (all his family were soldiers), Col had gravitated to the SAS not because of a need for action and physical stress, but because he wanted to *feel* life and for that, he'd decided, one needed to be out on the edge of something, always within sight of the abyss.

Rather thought he'd got over that stage now.

. . . chest (tighten, breath in, hold it . . . relax . . .), shoulders . . .

Mind control. Expansion of the senses. Spent two weeks with a meditation expert learning techniques for dominating the body in tight spots. Optional course for officers; some of the chaps thought it was all crap. Not Col. He'd actually taken it further, after the course.

. . . neck . . . face (tensing the muscles in his cheeks and jaw, letting the tension go).

At the end of this exercise – he'd done it many times over the past twenty or thirty years – there should be a moment of pure awareness. Awareness of oneself and one's situation. And sometimes . . .

. . . back of the head . . .

. . . one emerged from it and everything looked clearer. And one knew precisely what to do next. Probably elements of yoga and meditation in there, so it was never wise to tell some of the chaps one was indulging in this sort of thing, or they'd be putting it round the Colonel talked to plants and things. Not a word to these New Age characters either, or they'd be recruiting him as an emblem.

Gradually, his breathing slowed and the voices around him in the void began to fade.

'Warm night, isn't it?'

'Hmm?'

'Stuffy. Humid.'

'Yes, it is really.'

Old chap in a T-shirt sitting in a doorway a few yards away.

'Colonel Croston, isn't it?'

'Col. Hey, just a minute . . .'

He could *see* this chap. It was still dark, but he could see him, could see his white beard and what it said on the front of his T-shirt. Didn't make any sense, half-faded, but he could . . .

'It's Canon Peters, isn't it? Seen you in the Cock.'

'Alex.'

Col turned around to look at the square. He could see the shapes of buildings, very dimly; he could hear the sound of people talking and possibly screaming although there was nothing immediate about this, no involvement; more like the sound of someone's TV set from a distance.

'Heard you talking to my daughter,' the old man said. 'Young Fay.'

'Fay Morrison. Yes. I was. But you weren't . . . with us, were you? You weren't in . . . in . . . Look, Canon, can you help me to understand this? When you heard us talking, could you, you know, *see* us?'

'No.'

Col sighed. 'Thought not. Started out thinking it was some sort of gas. Some leakage from somewhere. Or an MOD experiment, just the kind of place they'd choose. And now I'm inclined to think it's something psychological coming out. Some mass-psychosis thing. I can't begin to . . . I mean, what your daughter had to say was interesting in a purely academic sense, but not . . . Frankly, I'm lost, Canon. Where does one start . . . ?'

'Question I've been asking most of my life. Kept putting off having to answer it.'

Keep cool, Col instructed himself. Keep your head. And for God's sake, don't go back in there. (In *where*? And how did I get out?)

'Canon . . .'

'Alex.'

'Do you know what's happening?'

'Only the vaguest notion, old chap. But I believe I'm getting there.'

'It *is* something . . . psychological, isn't it? Damned if I'm going to use that other word.'

'Good Lord, no, old boy, never say that.'

'Well.' Col levered himself to his feet. He could actually see lamps in some of the houses on this side of the square. 'You know a man's been murdered?'

'Oh yes. Murray Beech, the vicar.'

'The *vicar*?'

'Stabbed to death. Lying in the churchyard. And the church is on fire. Look . . .'

Col looked up from the blackness of the square and the vague shapes of roofs, and saw the sky blooming red and orange.

'And you know the strangest thing?' said Alex. 'Nobody's come out to watch.'

'You've rung the fire brigade I take it.'

'No.'

'Good God, man, it might burn down.'

'It might. But if the fire brigade come, they'll have to go in through the square, won't they, and they might just mow down a lot of innocent people who didn't appear to see them coming. Or not be able to get through. I don't know. Don't know *what* would happen. But I think, on balance, that it's safest to let it burn, don't you? Only a bloody church.'

The old chap looked gloomy, but, Col noted, entirely in command of his faculties. The word around town had been that Canon Peters was losing his marbles.

'I think,' the Canon said, 'that we're in the middle of what used to be known technically as A Crybbe Matter. However, on this occasion, there's been outside interference and the locals are seriously out of their depth. That's my feeling.'

'Can we help?'

'That's a very interesting question,' Alex Peters said.

Silly children's game, Fay thought, Hilary Ivory on one side of her, the cameraman, Larry Ember on the other. Or perhaps only their voices. Their voices and their hands.

Silly children's game, New Age nonsense, where's the harm? No harm.

'We're all going to pool our energy,' Andy's voice making soft chords in the night air. 'We're going to bring down the light.'

Silly children's game. No harm in it. Make a circle, everybody hold hands, dance gaily, stop, hold out hands to the sky as if in welcome. Wasn't there something like this at the end of *Close Encounters*? And something else. Wasn't it in something else?

Very silly.

'Got him?'

'Just about. Bit stiff. Bit of rigor.'

Col heaved the corpse across his shoulder, fireman's lift job.

Behind him, flames were coming through the church roof.

He followed Alex, the body over his shoulder. I am here. I'm walking through a churchyard with a dead vicar over my shoulder and the church is on fire.

This is not like Belfast, after a bomb blast. There are no spectators, no fire brigade, no police, no Army. Only the hungry flames chewing up the night.

'I trust,' Alex said, 'that when we get to the town hall, you'll have no difficulty getting us in.'

'Count on it,' Col Croston said through gritted teeth.

The box became unaccountably heavy and Joe Powys had to put it down in the courtyard.

Open it?

The Mini was still parked up by the stable-block. It had been his intention to load the box into the boot and then drive it out of Crybbe, but there was some uncertainty. What did you do with these things?

Open it.

You could take in into a church – a real, functioning church, outside of Crybbe, and place it on the altar. But you never knew, with churches in the border country, what other forces might be at work, what damage you might be inflicting on some other quiet and vulnerable community while the people slept.

Or open it.

Or you could throw it into a deep lake. This had been done in numerous legends to calm an excitable spirit, in a ceremony normally involving about twelve priests.

He didn't have twelve priests to hand. Also this was not the whole unquiet spirit.

Not the whole thing. But unquiet, yes. Walking back to the Court, holding the box with both hands, the lamp balanced on top, he'd had the illusion of something moving inside.

Open it . . .

Psychological trickery. Mind games. I'm not listening.

OPEN IT!

CHAPTER XIX

SOMEHOW they had formed a circle in the dark. When you moved around in this formation, you couldn't, of course, see the individual people comprising the circle, but soon you began to see the collective thing, the movement, the circle itself.

'A ring of pure golden light,' Hilary Ivory breathed. 'Isn't it beautiful? And we've made it ourselves. *We've* made it.'

Yes, Fay thought remotely, it *is* rather beautiful. But it's not quite golden. More a darkish yellow. The yellow of . . . of what?

Hilary held her right hand, Larry Ember her left. Hilary breathed and sighed, as if she was making love, while Larry chuckled to himself, not in a cynical or ironic way, but a chuckle of pleasure. Pleasure in self-discovery.

Round and round they went in a slow circle, mindlessly, innocently round and round, like children in the schoolyard.

The air was still pungent, but the pungency was fortifying and compelling now. Tobacco could seem noxious and nauseous the first time you inhaled it, but when you were accustomed to it, it was deeply satisfying.

So it was with the scent of shit and blood and rotting vegetables, as the human circle revolved, quite slowly at first, anticlockwise, in the opposite direction to the sun, which was OK, Fay reasoned dreamily, because there was no sun, anyway, at night.

Every face was blue-lit, anxious and staring bleakly at Alex without enmity but without any hope either. A quarantine situation: nobody was to go outside, nobody from outside was to come in because of what else might enter.

But Col Croston had got them into the hall, without too much difficulty. He knew both men on the rear door – Paul

Gwatkin, one of the three Gwatkin brothers who, between them, farmed Upper Cwm and Lower Cwm, and Bill Davies, the butcher. Decent chaps, both of them.

'Paul,' Col had said, very reasonably, 'it's essential that my friend the Canon and I come in, and I have to tell you that if you don't get out of the way I may hurt you quite badly. Problem is, I was never trained to hurt people only slightly. You see my problem.'

'And I hope, Colonel,' said Bill Davies, standing aside, 'that you might be startin' to see ours.'

Col had laid a sympathetic hand on the butcher's shoulder. 'We're here to help, Bill.'

'Wastin' your time, I'm afraid, Colonel, it's . . .'

'I know,' Col said. 'A Crybbe matter.'

Now, standing on the platform with its table and two empty chairs, Alex addressed the assembly, quite cordially.

'Good evening. Some of you know me, some of you don't, some of you might have seen me around. Peters, my name. For what it's worth, I appear to be the only living priest in town. And you, I take it, are what one might call the backbone of Crybbe.'

He looked carefully at his audience, perhaps three hundred of them, men outnumbering women by about two to one, the majority of them older people, over fifty anyway – such was the age-ratio in Crybbe. The scene reminded him of the works of some painter. Was it Stanley Spencer, those air-raid shelter scenes, people like half-wrapped mummies?

'Strange sort of evening,' Alex said. 'I expect you've noticed that, otherwise what are you all doing penned up like sheep left overnight in the market? Hmm?'

No response. Nobody did anything to dispel the general ambience of the stock-room at a mortuary. The blue-faced refrigerated dead.

What would it take to move these people? And, more to the point, had he got it?

As Alex stood there and watched them, he saw himself as they must be seeing him. Bumbling old cleric. Woolly haired, woolly headed; mind known to be increasingly on the blink.

But he'd made a Deal, if only with his inner self. He thought about the possible implications of the Deal, and a suitably dramatic quote occurred to him, from the Book of Revelations.

His head and his hairs were white like wool, as white as snow; and his eyes were as a flame of fire.

'Right,' Alex said, stoking the fire, summoning it into his eyes. 'If that's the way you want it. Colonel, would you ask Murray to step inside?'

'Huh?' Col Croston glanced sharply at Alex, who merely nodded. 'Oh,' Col said and walked out.

Alex said bluntly, 'I understand Max Goff was slaughtered like a pig in here tonight.'

Some of the women looked away. Nobody spoke. Alex let the silence simmer for over a minute, observing finally, 'You seem to have thrown the body out. Out of sight out of mind, I suppose. Didn't know the chap myself. However, I did know *this* poor boy.'

Col Croston had returned with his arms full. Paul Gwatkin and Bill Davies didn't try to stop him, but neither seemed anxious to help him with his bloody burden.

'He's sorry he was late,' Alex said. 'He was obliged to stop on the way, to get murdered.'

Col carried the corpse around the table, where the blotter was brown with dried blood, and curling.

Alex said, 'You remember Murray? Young Murray Beech?'

Col dropped the body like a sack of coal, and it rolled over once, on to its back, a stiff, bloody hand coming to rest against the knee of a woman on the front row, Mrs Byford, clerk to Crybbe town council. She did not move, except to shrink back in her chair, as if retracting the essential Mrs Byford so that the dead hand was only touching her shell.

'That's right,' Alex said. 'Pretend he's not there. But then, you never noticed he *was* here, did you? He was only another vicar from Off. And now he's dead. But I'll tell you one thing . . . he isn't as bloody dead as any of *you*.'

He saw Murray Beech's body, in the light, for the first time. The front of his black clerical shirt had been slashed neatly from neck to navel. The shirt was soaked and stiff.

Mrs Byford delicately removed the hand from her knee, her mouth beginning to quiver. Murray's own mouth was widened from one corner, like a clown's. It continued almost to an ear. Or what remained of an ear.

Alex lowered himself into the chair where another body had slumped. It was sticky. He looked down into a blotter thick with blood and lumps and clots. 'Talk to me,' he said. 'Tell me about what happened four hundred years ago when your ancestors went out to lynch this chap Wort. What had *they* got in the way of incentive that you haven't, hmm?'

He noticed the Police Sergeant, Wiley, near the back, in full, if disarranged, uniform. Not exactly rushing to open an investigation into the killing of Murray Beech.

Col Croston, back in the chairman's chair, next to Alex, called out, 'No need for inhibition. Consider the issue thrown open to the floor.'

'Well, come on,' said Alex, in exasperation. 'Who's the old bat in the front row trying to avoid Murray, what about *you*? Mrs Byford, isn't it?'

Mrs Byford spoke with brittle clarity, like an icicle cracking. 'Tell this rude old gentleman, Colonel, that we have no intention of moving from yere nor of entering into any discussion on the subject.'

Alex said, 'Did you have much to do with Murray, Mrs Byford? Your granddaughter did. She sought his assistance. As a priest. She wanted him to exorcise a ghost from your house.'

'No!' Mrs Byford pushed her chair back into the pair of knees behind her and stood up. Murray's hand appeared to reach for her ankle and she gave a shrill cry. 'It's lies!'

'Poor old Murray was quite thrown at first,' Alex said. 'Not every day you're recruited to cast out a malevolent spirit. Anyhow, he came to me for advice, and I said, go along and play it by ear, old boy. Nothing lost. So off he goes to the Old Police House. Don't suppose you were around at the time, were you?'

Alex could see a number of people beginning to look worried, not least Wynford Wiley, the copper.

'And where do you think he found the evil spirit, Mrs Byford?'

606

''E wasn't evil!' Wynford spluttered out. ''E was . . .'

'Where do you think he found this malignant entity?'

Her back arched. 'Stop this, you go no right to . . .'

'You know, don't you?'

'Keep calm, woman,' an old man said from behind. 'You got to keep calm, isn't it.'

Alex stood up. 'He found the evil, Mrs Byford . . . He found it in her eyes. Ironic, isn't it?'

Mrs Byford's hands, half-clawed, began to tremble. She stumbled into the aisle and stood there, shaking.

'Now . . .' Alex sat down. 'No, please, Mrs Byford, I'm not trying to bully you. Look, sit in one of the empty chairs on the other side. Thank you. Right, now, did that gentleman mention the necessity of keeping calm? Keeping the low profile? Avoiding direct confrontation? Let's discuss this – but very quickly, please, time's running out. Ah. Mr Davies.'

'What can we do?' The butcher, Bill Davies, had left his post by the door and was approaching the platform, a big man with a sparse sprinkling of grey curls. 'We got to live yere, isn't it.'

'The Mayor,' said Paul Gwatkin. 'Where's the Mayor?'

'He's probably dead,' Col Croston said flatly.

'You don't know that,' said Wynford Wiley.

'And the church is on fire,' Col said. 'Don't suppose you know *that*.'

'Aye, we know that,' the clerk's husband, little Billy Byford said tiredly, and sighed. His wife gave him a glance like a harpoon.

'These yere hippy-types,' said Bill Davies. 'This Goff. If they 'adn't arrived, with their experimentin' and their meddlin' . . . They think it's a wonderful game, see. They think the countryside's a great big adventure playground. Do what you like, long as you shuts the odd gate. They wouldn't think of strollin' across their motorways, climbin' all over their power stations. Oh no, you 'andles all that with care and if you don't know nothin' about it you stays out of it.'

'Sit down, Mr Davies,' said Mrs Byford. 'There's nothing to explain.'

'I'm gonna say this, Nettie. City-type dangers is something

they takes for granted – never questions it. But they never thinks there might be risks in the country, too, as they don't understand. Well, we don't understand 'em properly neither, but at least . . . *at least we knows there's risks.*'

'The inference being,' said Col, 'that Crybbe is an area with a particularly high risk-factor.'

'You live yere,' said Bill Davies, 'you learn there's things you can do and things you can't do. Maybe some people's more careful than others, maybe some people takes it more serious, like. But that's same as with a lot o' things, anywhere you goes, isn't it?'

'Mr Davies, we don't have to explain nothing,' Mrs Byford said.

Bill Davies ignored her. 'And it's not like you can get 'elp, neither. Can't write to your MP about it, can you? You 'as to live with it, just like your parents and your grandparents, and you accepts the constraints, like.'

The butcher sat down two seats away from Mrs Byford, on the left of the central aisle and crossed his legs defiantly.

'Thank you,' said Col. 'I'm very grateful to you, Bill. Canon?'

'Yes, indeed. I think Mr Davies has put his finger on it. I can understand entirely that there are certain prevailing phenomena in this particular town which the residents have long felt unable to discuss with outsiders. Problems which, I suspect, first, er, materialized during the reign of James I, when anyone found displaying an interest in matters of a . . . a shall we say, supernormal nature . . . was in serious danger of being strung up for witchcraft.'

He looked down at the blood-spattered blotter, saw that nothing at all had changed. Outside, the church was burning, and a gullible crowd was suspended in the thrall of something even the devil-fearing James I would have been hard-pressed to envisage.

'And one can see,' said Alex, 'how this quite-understandable reticence would, given the comparative remoteness of the town, become, in time, more or less endemic. Yes, I can understand why it's been allowed to fester.

'But, by God . . .' Alex stood up, his hands either side of the bloodstained blotter, summoning the flames, 'if you don't take some action tonight you'll regret it for the rest of your dismal little lives.'

CHAPTER XX

THE box was making a strange noise, a rolling, creaking sound, suggesting that the item inside had been dislodged from whatever secured it.

OPEN IT!

'Not a chance,' Joe Powys said aloud, attempting to sound confident, in control. But for whose benefit?

The box lay in the centre of the courtyard, the lamp on top of it, its beam directed at the Court, no more the derelict warehouse, the disused factory without echoes of laughter or the residue of sorrow.

Periodically, Powys would look up towards the eaves, but there were no flickerings any more, no ignition sparks. The Court was fully alive now and crackling and hissing at him.

OPEN IT!

The appalling temptation, of course, was to break open the box to confirm that it did in fact contain what he suspected. Which was the mummified head of Sir Michael Wort, or at least *a* head.

But Powys was scared to look into the eyes of Black Michael, even if only the sockets remained. There was too much heavy magic here; Andy, the shaman, the heir, was projecting himself at will along the spirit path, able to manifest a disembodied presence in the Tump and probably elsewhere, while his physical body was . . . *where?*

The old ley-line, which progressed from the Tump to the square and beyond had been reopened, a dark artery to the heart of Crybbe. Reopened for the ancestor, Black Michael.

Whose head now lay in an oak box at Powys's feet. The head was a crucial part of the process and as long as he had

609

the head he was part of it, too, until the pressure became unbearable.

So what am I going to do with it?

He thought, as he'd thought so many times, I could walk out of this situation, I could leave the box lying on the ground, leap into the car and accelerate back into what passes for the Real World. I could simply stop *believing* in all of this. Because if you don't invite it into your life it simply doesn't occur.

Blessed are the sceptics.

For they shall . . .

they shall . . .

die with a broken neck on a convenient rubbish heap.

Powys closed his eyes to ambush renegade tears. You daft bastard, this is Crybbe, where normal rules don't apply. Where, once you're in the game, you have to go on playing.

Because Fay is down there in that sick little town with Jean Wendle and probably Andy Trow, and the twisted essence of something four centuries old at the door, and Fay could go – snap! – like Rachel, like Rose. But you wouldn't die, Powys, you'd go on living with the knowledge of what you failed to prevent – even though you were fully aware, at last, of what was happening – because you were scared and because you thought it expedient, at this stage of the game, to take the sceptic's way out.

All right, *all right*. I'll play. Deal me in.

He tried to envisage the layout. The Tump was the head, the church was the centre of the breast, the town square was the solar plexus and the Cock was the genitalia.

He realized he must be standing on Black Michael's throat (the throat chakra, influencing the nervous system, controlling stress, anxiety).

There came another noise from the box, like the head rolling from side to side, and his eyes were wrenched open, the breath catching in his chest like a stone.

I've got to get rid of it.

He snatched the lamp, bent down and examined the box. It was bound not with iron as he'd imagined but with strips of lead. It occurred to him that it was probably not locked at all and all he had to do was raise the lid and . . .

No . . .

He sprang to his feet and backed away.

God help me . . . I've got the four-hundred-odd-year-old head of Michael Wort in a box, and I don't know what the hell to do with it.

The Court wanted it, he could tell that. The Court squatted in its hollow with the vengeful, violated Tump hunched over it, glowering. The Court throbbed with an ancient need, and Powys knew that it wanted him inside it so that it could digest his spirit and spit him out like poor Rachel, like Tiddles the mummified cat which had been stuck for centuries, a tiny, constricting hairball in its throat.

The throat had been blocked. The Court had coughed and the blockage had come out of the mouth.

The open mouth was the prospect chamber.

What he had to do – the clear, bright certainty of it – went through him like a fork of cold and jagged lightning.

'I can't,' he told the night. 'I don't have the strength. I don't have the courage.

'I can't.'

It still made no sense, of course, according to what was accepted as normal, but it answered to the logic of the place. It extended the rules of the game to put him in with a chance.

What he had to do was enter the Court and carry the box up the stone stairs to the prospect chamber. And then he had to stand in the opening, lift the box above his head and cast it out into the night so that it fell on to the rubbish heap and smashed, symbolically, to pieces.

A ritualistic, shamanistic act which would sever the connection between Black Michael and the Court, leave a meaningful crater, a great pothole in the middle of the spirit path.

And, well . . . he knew that the ritual would be more perfect, more complete, if *he* went out of the prospect chamber, too, his arms wrapped around the box.

Sacrifice. Always more energy with a sacrifice. Perhaps also, because he was hijacking Andy's ritual, he'd be releasing and recycling the energy created by Rose's fall and Rachel's.

He stood with one foot on the box and thought about this.

It was a complete load of New Age crap.

But if he believed in it, it might work. If he was prepared to give up his life he'd be creating so much energy that . . .

'Christ!'

He kicked the box along the cobbles. God save us from New Age philosophy. Energy. The life force. Mother-sodding-earth.

Not got the bottle for it, Joe?

Powys gave the Court a baleful glare.

'Yeah, OK, you can play it that way, if you want,' he told the house. 'You can spit me out, like Rachel and Tiddles the cat.'

'But when I go . . . *he* goes.'

He picked up the box, put the lamp on top and followed the beam towards the main door. It would, he knew, be open.

Alex simply walked out of the town hall, down the steps and the few yards to the end of the street leading to the square. He glanced behind him once at the blue light from a high window, listened to the noise of the generator from the basement, looked above the buildings to the orange glow in the sky from the church. Reality, or as much of it as a bumbling old cleric might perceive.

He thought about the Deal.

If he walked into the square, he doubted he'd get out of it so easily, if at all.

This would be it.

It was like one of those experiments you did at school in your very first physics lesson. Fay couldn't recall the technicalities of it, but it was all to do with making your own electricity and you did something like turning a handle – really couldn't remember the details, never any good at science – and this little bulb lit up, just faintly at first, but the faster you did whatever it was you did, the brighter the bulb became, the more sustained was the light.

There they all were, moving round in the circle – backwards, anticlockwise – the thin golden ring (or not gold, it was yellow, the yellow of . . . of . . .).

And there it was, in the centre of the circle. New Age schoolchildren dancing around a lamppost and making the lamp light up, like the bulb in the physics lesson, through the power they were helping to generate.

'Faster, please,' the Teacher saying in that wonderfully smooth voice, like an old cello, and they were able, without much effort, to move faster, Fay beginning to tingle with the excitement of what they were doing – making light.

An incandescent blob in the air, yellow and fuzzed at the edges, but filaments of hard white light forming at the centre, extending out like branches or veins, blood-vessels – light vessels – the whole thing pulsing with it. Hilary Ivory beginning to quiver and moan, as if reaching orgasm. Larry Ember, on the other side, giggling wildly. Never heard a cameraman giggle before, dour bastards in general, this must really be something coming.

'All my life!' she heard a woman (probably that loopy Jopson woman) cry in ecstasy. 'All my life I've waited for *you* . . .'

'Michael,' a man – the Teacher – said. Simply that, nothing more.

And a woman said, 'Yes, Michael. The Archangel Michael, slayer of dragons.'

No, Fay thought, confused, not him . . . that's wrong . . .

But what did it matter?

Couldn't very well contradict them, could she, not all of them, everybody shouting in unison now, a great chant.

'Michael . . . *Michael* . . . MICHAEL . . . *MICHAEL!*'

The Being of Light was responding to the summons, the filaments forming into a complexity of vibrating muscles, pipes and organs, rippling into arms and legs, and between the legs – bloody hell, Fay thought . . .

Realizing she was chanting, too.

'*Michael . . . Michael . . .*'

The bells erupted again, a huge joyful clangour, cracking the night into splinters.

*

The sound of bells in a blazing church.

The rational explanation, Col Croston thought, was that flames had been funnelled into the tower, creating a huge gas-jet which exploded into the belfry.

He stood in the town-hall doorway and peered into the street. Above him the night sky was frying. If Jimmy Preece was indeed dead, this made him the First Citizen of Crybbe. An auspicious start to his year of office; at this rate he'd be mayor of a burned-out ghost-town before morning.

He looked for Alex, but the end of the street still dropped off the edge of the world, and Alex was gone and Col's sorrowful feeling was that he would never see the old man again.

CHAPTER XXI

BEFORE, the last and only time he'd been inside Crybbe Court, it had been very much Henry's *dead place*; now it was repellently alive.

It had been cold and dry; now it was warm and moist, and going into it was disturbingly, perversely sexual. The Court was a very old woman, grotesquely aroused, and she wanted him.

The main door had not been locked. He ventured quietly in, the box under his arm. Stone floor, low ceiling and slits of windows set high in the walls. And the walls leaked.

Joe Powys ran a cautious finger along the stone and found it warm and slimy. Under the light, he saw dead insects on the walls, all of them quite recently dead, not husks. Moths, flies and bluebottles trapped in a layer of . . . fat, it smelled like fat.

Or tallow maybe, grease from candles made of animal fat.

Crybbe Court was alive and sweating.

He moved towards the stone stairs, thinking, inevitably, of Rachel. What had it taken to make her so hot and feverish and desperate to get out of here that . . . ?

But you don't know what happened, you don't *know*.

Though you'll soon find out, as you retrace her steps up these stone steps, butcher's shop slippery now, like the walls.

Coming to the first floor – the big family living-room and the bedchambers off. In one of these, Fay had told him, Tiddles the mummified cat had slept, most recently, in a chest that was not very old. Tiddles had come down from the rafters, but had never left the house, presumably, until she and Rachel had been hurled out of the prospect chamber.

Fay.

Picturing her standing in the field overlooking Crybbe, the blue cagoule streaming from under her arm, her rainbow eye watering in the wind.

It made him so sad, this image, that he had a wild urge to dump the box and race out of the Court – filthy, clammy, raddled old hag – and run back to Crybbe to find Fay and hold her, even if they only had a few minutes before . . .

Before whatever was to happen happened.

He wore his sense of foreboding like the black bag over a condemned man's head. Yet he was still half-amazed at what he was planning to do: black comedy, a bizarre piece of alternative theatre. Verdict: took his own life while the balance of mind was disturbed.

The voice of the police inspector, Hughes, landed in his head. *Are you sure he didn't say anything to you, Mrs Morrison, by way of a suicide note, so to speak? Or did he assume, do you think, that his method of taking his own life would be self-explanatory?*

Well, he *was* a crank, wasn't he? You only had to read his book.

He wondered if the day would ever come when an inquest would concede that the balance of mind might be affected by prevailing psychic conditions.

Bloody New Age crap.

There was a stench of rancid fat. He felt sick.

It would be good, in a way, to be out in the fresh air.

As Col turned the corner of the back street linking the town hall with the churchyard, there was an enormous splintering roar and a belch that shook the ground. And then – as if massive furnace doors had been flung wide – huge, muscular arms of flame reached out for the heavens.

'Go easy,' Col said. 'I think the church roof's collapsed.'

There were about twenty men with him, the youngest and strongest of them. Bill Davies, the butcher, was there, and all three burly Gwatkin brothers.

'God preserve us,' one of them said and then turned away, embarrassed, his face already reddened in the glare from the church.

'It's down to you now,' Col said. He hoped to God the stone walls of the church would contain the fire so that it wouldn't spread into the town, but the heat was unbelievable; anything could happen. Crackling splinters – in fact, great burning brands – were being thrown off, and every so often there'd be chaotic clanging of the bells.

'What we're going to do . . .' Col said. 'All over the church-yard, you'll see pieces of wood ablaze. I want six of you to get the ones you can handle at one end and bring them out. This is bloody dangerous, so be *damned* careful, but we've got to have light where we're going.'

'Why can't we just go 'ome and get torches?' a young lad, seventeen or eighteen, said.

'Do as he says, boy,' Bill Davies grunted. 'Nobody goes out of this street. You step into that square, you'll wish you'd stayed and burned.'

As a handful of men climbed over the churchyard wall, Bill Davies took Col aside. 'I'm not wrong, am I, Colonel?'

'Look, be a good chap . . .'

'Tell me, Colonel. I 'ave to know, see. Is it . . . in that square . . . Oh hell, is it the year 1593 over there, or is it an illusion? Is this town living an illusion, do *you* know?'

Joe Powys went up the stairs, past a small landing with an oak door four inches thick, which was open, revealing the stairs to the attic.

Walking up the steps, towards the death-chamber of Michael Wort with what he believed to be the head of Michael Wort in a wooden box under his arm.

People like me would no more come up here alone, he remembered thinking, than pop into a working abattoir to shelter from the rain.

But you *aren't* alone, are you?

The box was heavy.

Trying to avoid touching the walls because the stone was slick with something that felt like mucus. Suspecting that if he switched off the lamp, it would glow on the stones, luminous.

And so he came, at last, to the alcove leading to the prospect chamber.

When he put down the box to open the door, he felt Rachel was standing at his side. Remembering being here with her. How two wafers of light from holes in the roof had crossed just above her head and he'd recalled her standing by the window of the room at the Cock, naked and pale and ethereal.

Now he could almost see her calm, silvery shade; they'd go hand in hand into the prospect chamber.

This . . . is the only part of the house I really like.

And together they'd take the head of Michael Wort back into the night.

He turned the metal handle and put his shoulder to the old, oak door.

New Age Heaven.

Blissful, blissful, blissful.

'I want to touch him,' the woman next to her cried. 'I want to bathe in him.'

Michael, *Michael*, MICHAEL, *MICHAEL!*

The Being of Light lifted his head and spread his arms to embrace his town. Bright people were gathering around him, both sexes, shimmering, all shapes and sizes, from the large, smiling man in the incandescent white suit to the tiny little lady, mouth opening in delight to reveal small, sharp white teeth, like a fish's, like . . . like . . .

Couldn't remember.

But she didn't want to remember. She'd never felt so warm and yet so free. She saw herself soaring above Crybbe, and the town was decked out in ribbons of soft, coloured light anchored by ice-bright, luminescent standing stones. Floating over the square, she saw the old buildings in a lambent Christmas-card glow. But some of them were not so old, their timbers looked sturdy and neatly dovetailed, especially the inn, which had a simple strength and a sign with a large, rough beast upon it; and indeed, there were farm animals in the square around a cart with wooden wheels and sacks of grain on it. There was a cow, three horses, a pig. And a dog! Black and white like . . . like . . .

Couldn't remember.

'Fay.'

Who was Fay?

'Listen to me.'

'Yes,' she sang. 'Yes, yes, yes, I'm listening.'

But she had no intention of listening; this was the wrong voice. It didn't sound like a cello, it sounded old and frail, an ancient banjo, cracked and out of tune.

She laughed.

Everyone was laughing.

New Age Heaven.

'Fay,' Alex said into her ear. 'Listen to me, please.'

'Yes, yes, yes,' she sang. 'But you'll have to come with me. Can you float? Can you float like me?'

She wasn't floating. She was part of a' group of thirty or forty people, hands linked, slowly and gloomily moving around in an untidy, irregular circle.

Alex could see most of them now, in the spluttering amber of the blazing church.

In the centre of the square, where, in many towns, there was a cross, a man stood. A tall man, stripped to the waist. He had dark, close-shaven hair and a black beard. His eyes were closed. He was sweating. His arms hung by his side but slightly apart from his body, the palms of his hands upturned. The ragged circle of people moved around him, anticlockwise.

The old buildings seemed to be leaning out of their foundations and into the firelight, like starved tramps at a brazier.

The buildings had never looked more decrepit or as close to collapse.

Similarly, the people. Alex followed Fay around, walking behind her, peering into the faces of the men and women in the circle, horrified at how weak and drained they looked, some of them obviously ill. On one side of his daughter was a stocky man with a sagging belly and one eye badly bloodshot. He was moaning faintly and saliva dribbled down his chin. Fay's other hand lay limply in a flabby hand full of rings, obviously not very expensive ones, for they looked tarnished now and the joints of the fingers were swollen around them. The woman's hair was in wild, white corkscrews; her lips were drawn back into a frozen rictus; she was breathing in spurts through clenched teeth.

Diametrically opposite this woman, Alex saw Fay's ex-husband Guy Morrison, his blond hair matt-flat, exposing a large, white bald patch; his mouth down-turned, forming pouches of slack skin from his cheek to his once-proud jawline. Next to him a fat girl was sobbing inconsolably to herself as she moved sluggishly over the cobbles. On the other side of this girl, a thin woman with shorn hair was breathing with difficulty, in snorts, blood sparkling on her upper lip and around her nose, from which a small ring hung messily from a torn flap of skin, and every time she took a breath part of the ring disappeared into a nostril. She didn't seem aware of her physical distress; nor did any of the others.

'Fay,' Alex whispered.

Fay's skin was taut and pallid, her green eyes frozen open, her lips stretched in anguish, which made the words issuing from them all the more pathetic.

'Flying away, high, into the light. Can't keep up with me, can you?'

He didn't even try. He stood in the shadows and watched her drift away.

He'd had to stop himself from pulling her out of the circle. He had the awful feeling that he would simply detach her body, that her mind would remain in the ring and she would never get it back, would be a vegetable.

Which was the very worst thing of all; Alex knew this.

He stood and watched her for two more circuits of the town square. A lurid flaring of amber from the dying church picked out that woman from The Gallery, ugly blue bruises around her throat, dried vomit on her chin, coughing weakly; couldn't see her husband.

Very gently he separated Fay's fingers from those of the woman next to her and slipped her small, cold right hand into his left. With his right hand he found the damp, fleshy fingers of the white-haired woman.

And so Alex slipped into the circle and began to move slowly round.

He realized at once that he'd made a terrible, terrible mistake.

His legs began to feel heavy and cumbersome. At first he felt as if he'd stepped into a pair of wellingtons several sizes too big and was wading in them through thick, muddy water, and then the weight spread up to his thighs – he was in the middle of a river in cumbersome waders – and finally it was as though both legs had been set in concrete; how he managed to move he didn't know, but he kept on, at funeral pace, his arms feeling limp as though the blood were draining away into the other hands, his life energy passed along the chain.

Progressive torpor. This was how it happened. Initiation ceremony. They were always saying, the newcomers, how much they wanted to fit in, become part of the community.

Now here they were, all these bright, clever, New Age folk, achieving overnight what some people waited years to attain.

All moving at last to the rhythm of Crybbe.

PART NINE

In actuality, of course, dowsing as an activity is no more
spiritual than riding a bicycle: spirituality is in the
person . . . Compared to this rich matrix of mystery the
New Age 'energy' ideas are conceptually bankrupt.

PAUL DEVEREUX
Earth Memory – the Holistic
Earth Mysteries Approach to
Decoding Ancient Sacred Sites

CHAPTER I

THE digger was crunching through the wood like a rhino on heat, Gomer Parry at the wheel, grinning like a maniac, dead cigarette, burned to the filter, clenched between his teeth. Minnie Seagrove holding on to the makeshift passenger seat, which didn't have a working safety-belt, a three-legged black and white dog balancing, just about, on her knee and glaring out of the window, barking away.

This had all come about after they arrived back at Minnie's bungalow and Gomer, spotting the flames coming out of the town, reckoning it had to be the church, raced to Minnie's phone to summon the fire brigade and found the bloody old phone lines were down or something.

Anyway, the phone was off and so was the one in the kiosk by the layby.

'Something bloody funny yere.'

They'd climbed back into the digger, Gomer heading back towards the town, foot down, headlight blasting at the night and then – 'Oh my God, Gomer, look out!'

Bloody great wall of metal, Minnie's hands over her eyes, the dog going berserk and Gomer flattening the brakes and damn near wrenching the ole wheel out of its socket.

Flaming great articulated lorry had jack-knifed across the road at – *precisely* – the spot Gomer himself went adrift earlier on. Was this a coincidence? Like hell it was.

No sign of the driver, no blood in the cab, couldn't have been hurt, must've buggered off for help. So Gomer did this dynamite three-point turn and they were thundering off again. 'Gonna find out what the bloody 'ell's afoot, 'ang on to your knickers – sorry, Minnie, but I've 'ad enough o' this mystery. You can push Gomer Parry *just so far*, see.'

'Where are we going, Gomer?'

'Back way into Crybbe. Tradesman's entrance. Never done it all the way on four wheels before.'

And Gomer lit up a ciggy one-handed and spun the digger off the road and into the field, keeping well away from the Tump this time, although he could tell it'd taken a hammering tonight, that ole thing, not got the power it had, see, just a massive great lump of ole horseshit now, sorry Minnie.

So it was round the back of the Tump, back to the Court and into the wood.

'Ole bridle path, see.'

'But we can't get through here, Gomer.' Minnie no doubt wondering, by this time, why he didn't drop her off home. But it wasn't safe for a woman alone tonight. Besides, he liked an audience, did Gomer Parry. Not been the same since the wife snuffed it.

'If a 'orse can make it up here,' he told Minnie, 'Gomer Parry can do it in the best one-off, customized digger ever built.'

So now the digger was flattening bushes either side and ripping off branches. 'Five minutes gets us out the back, bottom end of the churchyard, and we can see what the score is . . .

'Fuckin' Nora, what the 'ell's this?'

For the second time in ten minutes, Gomer was on top of the brakes and Minnie was pulling her nails off on the lumpy vinyl passenger seat.

The headlight'd found a bloody great stone right in the middle of the flaming road.

'Who the . . . put that thing there?' Gomer was out of his cab sizing up the stone, seven or eight feet tall but not too thick. Arnold, out of the cab, too, standing next to Gomer, barking at the stone, looking up at Gomer, barking at the stone again.

'What you reckon to this then, boy?'

Woof, Arnold went. Smart dog.

'Dead right, boy,' said Gomer, looking up at the bright orange sky, like an early dawn 'cept for the sparks. 'Dead right.'

Back in the cab, Gomer lit up another ciggy, grinned like a potentially violent mental-patient and started to lower the big shovel.

★

And Fay, soaring above the town, far above the opalescent stones and the soft, pastel ribbons, felt a momentary lurch of nausea as the tallest, the brightest of the stones shivered, its radiance shaken, its magnesium-white core dying back to a feebly palpitating yellow.

The yellow of . . .

'. . . *Fay* . . .'

The yellow of . . .

'*Please, F . . .*'

The yellow of disease.

The yellow of embalming fluid.

The yellow of pus from an infected wound.

The yellow of Grace Legge.

'. . . Fay?'

'Dad?'

She turned and saw his face, and his skin looked as white as his hair and his beard. She saw him against what looked like the flames of hell, and his old blue eyes were full of so much mute pleading that they were almost shouting down this sick, dreadful chant.

Michael . . .

Michael . . .

MICHAEL . . .

MICHAEL!!!

screamed the poor, stricken, gullible bastards in the circle, and she could see them now. She could *see* them. She was gripping her dad's hand, and she could see them all in the light of Hell, and hell was what they looked like.

Hell also was what Fay *felt* like.

Her lips were like parchment and when she tried to wet them she found her tongue was a lump of asbestos.

Michael, she wanted to say. It's Michael *Wort*.

But she couldn't even make it to a croak.

Her eyes found the centre of the square, where the Being of Light was formed, pulsing with vibrant, liquid life energy, platinum-white.

Pulsing with energy, all right – *their* energy – but it was the very darkest thing she had ever seen in all of her life.

Andy Boulton-Trow, a tall, bearded man, just an ordinary man – *once* – had been fitted for a black halo; it shimmered around him like the sun in a monochrome photo negative.

The halo was the shadow of Black Michael. There were pinpoints of it in Trow's eyes which had flicked open and were looking steadily, curiously into hers.

She put all the strength she had into squeezing her dad's hand. It felt as cold as her own.

Trow did not move, his gaze like black velvet. Playing with her.

Who are you? the eyes were asking. Have we met?

The complete, charismatic, black evangelist.

Somehow, Fay had milked a little strength from her poor father, enough to observe and to make simple deductions.

You've had us all going around your Bottle Stone, haven't you. Children of the New Age. Follow anybody, won't they? Look at them now. Look at the Jopson woman, led by the ring in her nose and then – gentle tweak – you tear through her flesh, and she doesn't know or care. Look at bloody Guy – show him his own reflection in a mirror shaped like a TV screen and watch him slash his wrists. Look at Graham Jarrett, away in the ultimate hypnotic trance, lost his toupee and his nose needs wiping. Look at them. Look at what you've done.

Arteriosclerotic dementia.

You have good days. Sometimes you have two or three good days together and you realize what a hopeless old bugger you were the other day when the lift failed to make it to the penthouse.

And then, one night, along comes a very cunning lady with an amorphous Chinese blob on a lead (which, as you thought, does not exist, but why else would she be trailing a lead?) And all the time you're with her, you're fine, you're wonderful, you're on top of the situation.

Until it becomes apparent that the lady is a prominent member of the Opposition, planning a startling little *coup* in this dead-end backwater where surely nothing that happens can be of any significance in the Great Scheme of Things.

But old habits die hard. Once a priest . . .

Yes, all *right*, Guv, I confess, I've never exactly been up there with Mother Theresa and Pope John the Twenty-third. I've cut a few corners. I've coveted my neighbour's wife. OK, several wives of several neighbours, and it wouldn't be half so bad if it had only stopped at the coveting stage. I was weak. I used to think it was OK, as long as you left the choirboys alone, but I was never attracted to choirboys, anyway, obnoxious little sods.

Here, Boss, scrap of prayer for you, this'll bring back a few memories.

Oh God, merciful Father, that despisest not the sighing of a contrite heart . . .

Got the message? I'm *sorry* . . . I really am sorry.

Listen, I know about the Sins of the Fathers. I know *all* about that.

But not Fay, please – look at her; what has she ever done to you?

Thing is – look, don't take this the wrong way, but no God of mine ever took it out on the kids. That's more *his* god's style. Can you see him there? He represents everything you're supposed to abhor. And he's winning, damn it, the bastard's winning!

OK, here's another bit, how much do you want, for Christ's sake? Listen, this . . . this is the essence of it.

Lighten our darkness, we beseech Thee, O Lord, and by Thy great mercy defend us from all perils and dangers of this night . . .

Lighten our darkness, geddit?

Come on, Guv'nor . . . we had a *deal* . . .

The stone actually broke. Cracked in two.

Split off a couple of feet from the base just as Gomer was getting underneath. Raised the shovel to ground level to have another go and gave it a bit of a clonk, accidental-like, and off it came like a thumb in a bacon-slicer.

Gomer backed up, smartish, but luckily the big bugger fell the other way, straight flat across the road. Whump!

'Teach me to rush the job, Minnie. 'Ang on to your, er . . . hat.'

Slipping down to low gear he drove right over the thing. Bit of a bump, but not much worse than one of them ramps they call a sleeping policeman.

'A big fat sleeping policeman.' Gomer burst out laughing. 'Call it Wynford Wiley.'

There were big, fat tyre-marks across the middle of the stone. Gomer accelerated past Keeper's Cottage with one disparaging sideways glance. That could do with knocking down, too.

There was the merest tremor in Trow's gaze; enough for Fay to pull her eyes away. Turned to her father and found that Hilary Ivory, on the other side, had also turned her face, in faint confusion, towards the old man in the Kate Bush T-shirt.

Alex tried to smile. He couldn't speak.

Hilary looked at Fay, her eyes troubled. She didn't understand. The first step to recovery – the moment when, quite suddenly, you don't understand.

But Alex's hands were warm.

Dad?

A deep warmth seeped into Fay's right hand and rippled up her arm and into her breast. She could feel her heart drumming. Alex's eyes were vibrantly blue. They made the fire in the sky look cheap and lurid. He turned his head towards Hilary Ivory, and she started to smile, like people smile when they're coming out of anaesthetic.

Alex's hand tightened around Fay's.

Fay grinned.

'You old bugger,' she said, quite easily.

On the other side, Larry Ember, recipient of the warmth from her own left hand, demanded gruffly, 'What the bleed'n hell's this?'

Alex's lips were white. Almost as white as the beard around them. First they tried to smile, then they were trying to shape a word.

'C . . .'

His hands hot now, but his lips were white. ˎ

'Dad?'

Fay squeezed his hand, almost too hot to hold.

She felt strong enough to risk a glance to the centre of the square where Trow was no longer still, but moving within his own darkness. Squirming.

Trow screamed once,

'*Michael!*'

The cello grotesquely off-key.

Alex found his word.

'Colonel?' he said mildly, and the piercing blue faded from his eyes; clouds were in them now. He dropped Hilary's hand, held on to Fay's for an extra moment and then let that go too.

There was a gap now between Fay and her dad, a clear gap in the circle, and the backcloth, the screen of false reality, was torn away and the flames in the sky were no longer phantasmal but a source of savage heat and acrid fumes.

'Now.' Col Croston's crisp voice, and the Crybbe hordes poured through the gap, bearing their flaming torches, farmers in tweed trousers and sleeveless body-warmers over their vests, Bill Davies, incongruously clad in his butcher's apron, Wynford Wiley ludicrously wielding his truncheon. Faces she'd seen on the streets – ''Ow're you, 'ow're you' – now hard with determination below the blazing brands. The circle in disarray. Lights appearing in windows. From somewhere in the innards of the Cock, the sound of a generator starting up.

Col Croston, bringing up the rear, scanning the square.

'Over there! That's the man. The Sheriff! Don't let him . . .'

The Sheriff?

'Right!' Fay was screaming. 'The Sheriff! He's in the cen . . .'

But she couldn't, in fact, see the man they were looking for. Andy Boulton-Trow had gone from the square.

He's taken his darkness back into the night.

'Larry! Camera!'

Guy was in a mess. He'd lost his jacket, lost his cool, lost his hair. 'Larry, we have to get this . . .'

'Piss off, Guy,' Larry Ember shouted happily, from somewhere.

Fay found she was giggling. Hysterics. Absurd.

'Dad?'

Alex managed a smile.

'Dad . . . We did it! *You* did it.'

Alex touched her arm, stumbled. Sat down quietly on the cobbles. Fay went down beside him, taking his hand.

Which was not so hot any more, not very hot at all. The blue in his eyes had drifted away. Far away. Gently and discreetly, Alex slid over on to his side. He was breathing. Just.

Hilary Ivory crouched down next to Fay. 'Is he OK? I used to be a . . . a nurse . . . Well, sort of alternative nurse, really.'

Fay didn't reply. She pulled off her cotton top, rolled it into a ball, slid it between Alex's head and the cobbles.

'Dad?' Softly.

Fairly sure he couldn't hear her.

She picked up his hand; very little warmth remained. Alex's lips moved and she put an ear to his mouth. One word came out intact.

'Deal,' he said.

Alex's breathing ended almost imperceptibly.

Fay sat for a long time on the cobbles holding her father's cooling hand under the hot red sky.

CHAPTER II

A SINGLE candle burned in the attic at Crybbe Court. It was two inches thick and sat in a blackened pewter candle-holder with a tray, laid on the topmost stone step. It was a tallow candle and it stank; it filled the roofspace with a pungent organic stench; it reeked, somehow, of death.

Or perhaps this was because of the wan and waxy aura it gave to the rope.

The old, frayed rope which had hung from the central joist in the attic was gone. Its replacement was probably just as old, but was oily and strong. An inch thick, it dangled four feet from the apex of the roof, and at the end was a noose, a very traditional hangman's noose secured with ten rings of rope.

It was into this noose that Andy Boulton-Trow fitted his head.

He had, it would emerge, studied hanging.

The original short-drop method, with the rope only a few feet long and the condemned person's feet almost touching the ground, resulted in a rather prolonged death by slow strangulation. Whereas the long-drop system, introduced in Britain in the late nineteenth century, by which the subject fell about ten feet, perhaps through a trapdoor, brought about a swifter and more merciful death by fracturing neck vertebrae. In the sixteenth century, it appeared, Sir Michael Wort had experimented with both techniques and others besides.

A trapdoor had been constructed in the attic floor, originally to dispose of bodies after execution by dropping them into a narrow, windowless, well-like chamber directly underneath.

In later years, more squeamish owners of the house had boarded over the trapdoor space, but the floor remained weak at this point, the boards had rotted, there were cracks. When Andy Boulton-Trow stood on the beam, nearly two feet thick, from which the executees – and Sir Michael himself – had taken a final step, he could see a few jagged black holes below his feet.

First, he had taken off his shoes and his trousers, so that he stood naked now in the candlelight with the noose loosely around his neck.

For the purposes of magical projection, a modification of the short-drop method was the most appropriate. That it had worked, to a significant extent, for Michael had been amply demonstrated to Andy tonight. Andy, who had spent twice as many years as Michael in study and preparation, was warm after his sprint through the wood, still angry at the damage to the stone and the débâcle in the square. But the night was churning with chaos, and out of chaos . . .

There was little time to waste. He was hot inside, with excitement and anticipation.

To make sure everything was still in working order, he and Humble had once hanged a fisherman Humble had chanced upon, casting alone into the upper reaches of the river. It had not really been necessary, but Humble had enjoyed it.

Just as Humble would enjoy watching Andy hang. So why wasn't he here?

Perhaps he was. Humble could be quite discreet.

Andy put both hands behind his head and tightened and adjusted the noose under his chin. It was so easy to make a mistake.

He stood on the floor-joist in the candlelight and began to visualize, to bring himself to the necessary state of arousal.

He visualized the woman who'd looked at him across the square, telling him with her eyes that she was slipping out of the enchantment. Andy smiled; he would return for her one night, quite soon perhaps.

A small wind drifted through the holes in the slates; there was no wind tonight.

'Good evening, Michael,' Andy said. 'Again.'

He closed his eyes, and Michael was within him once more, a now-familiar sensation. In his solar plexus he felt a stillness which was also a stirring, and there was the familiar small tug at the base of his spine.

In time, the walls of the Court evaporated, and he saw the town at his feet. He held back, and the vapours rose within him. He felt the blazing chaos that was Crybbe, the dissolution of barriers, the merging of the layers, one with another, the lower levels open to the higher levels, the atmosphere awash with spirit.

He felt his destination.

And when the time was right, he stepped lightly from the beam.

There was a bright light, a widening carpet of light, and something rolling along it, towards him.

This was the first thing he was really aware of after he stepped into space and the noose tightened above his Adam's apple.

There was no pain, only darkness and then the carpet of light and the thing that was rolling.

Rolling very slowly at first, but its momentum was increasing. And then he was staring into the face of Michael Wort.

The eyes had gone. The lips had gone. There was some hair, but not much; most of the beard had disappeared. There were gaps in the ghastly brown and yellow grin; few people in Michael's day had kept their teeth beyond middle age.

'Michael,' he said eventually.

The noose was still around his neck but it was slack. There was no pain in speech.

Behind the lamp, he saw a pair of sneakers and legs in muddy jeans.

'He came with me,' Joe Powys said. 'He couldn't manage the steps on his own.'

Andy had smashed through the floor, spinning and twisting. He'd screamed once, but it had sounded more like triumph than terror, suggesting he was unaware of anything having gone wrong.

Well, you wouldn't be, if this was the first time you'd hanged yourself.

The way he was lying in the centre of the windowless, stone chamber was bent, unnatural. Powys said, with little concern, 'Can you move?'

'I don't know,' Andy said, his feelings sheathed. 'What did you do?'

'I saved your life.'

'Thanks,' Andy said. 'You fucker.'

Powys said nothing. He was shaking.

'Humble,' Andy said, after a while. 'He was supposed to have killed you.'

'Yeah?'

'He will.'

'Can't see it,' Powys said, 'somehow.'

He had the feeling both of them were in shock. He put a hand out to the wall; it was dry again, and dusty. The Court was a dead place again. The room was narrow enough for there to be an enforced intimacy, and yet there was a distance, too, because the Court was dead.

'I nearly killed *myself*, though,' he said, still appalled enough at what might have happened to want to hear himself talking about it. 'Seems absolutely bloody insane when I look back, but I had this idea that the only way I could straighten things out was to take the head up to the prospect chamber and hurl us both out. I couldn't have been thinking straight. Well, obviously. But you don't, do you, in these situations?'

'And what stopped you,' Andy asked him, 'from killing yourself?'

Powys smiled weakly. 'Couldn't get in. The door in the alcove was locked, and there was a sign that said: Danger. Keep Out.'

The final bitter irony. Rachel had saved his life. He'd stood outside the door, on the greasy stairs, and felt her there again, cool and silvery. *You really can do better than this, J.M.*

'So then I saw the light in the attic. Thought maybe you were up there, but there was only one rope. Hate nooses. Went back outside and broke into the stable-block, through a window, with a brick. I pinched a bread knife. Brought it up to the attic and sawed through most of the rope until it was just hanging together by a few threads. Where I'd cut it, I covered it up with the coils of the noose.'

He saw that Andy was thinking very hard, the muscles in his face working.

'I figured it out,' Powys said. 'It came clear. When I saw the noose. You were going to do' – he pointed a foot at the head – 'what he did. On the four-hundredth anniversary of his death. I couldn't believe it at first. I can't understand that level of obsession.'

'Of course you can't.' Andy glanced up at him, eyes heavy with contempt. 'You puny little cunt.'

'We're talking sex magic, aren't we? I was once at a signing session for *Golden Land*. Some regional book fair, and one of the other writers there was this retired pathologist. He said, apropos of something, that a remarkable number of hangings which look like suicide are actually accidents. Blokes – or teenage kids in a lot of cases – trying for this uniquely mind-blowing sexual buzz you're supposed to get from hanging by the neck. Like, when the rope jerks, you jerk off down there, too. That it?'

Andy said nothing. Powys could see him trying surreptitiously to move different muscles.

'And with sex magic, you use the build up of sexual tension to harden and focus your will. And then, at the moment of orgasm . . . whoosh. Max Goff used to play about with it. Who taught him? You?'

Andy was stretching his neck, easing it from side to side.

'Sex and death. Hell of a powerful combination. This was how Black Michael pro . . .'

'Don't call him that,' Andy snapped.

'This was how Sir Michael Wort . . . Bloody hell, Joe Powys always does what he's told . . . ! This was how *Black fucking Michael* projected himself into Crybbe, fused his spirit with the spirit of the town so that the town is the man is the town is the . . .'

Andy stopped trying to flex muscles and stared at Powys in the electric lamplight, and his eyes were so strange that Powys wasn't sure any more which of them he was talking to, Andy or Michael. But, clearly, the stage Andy had been striving to reach was something that went beyond personalities.

'What did it really mean, though?' Powys said. 'Was it simply a quest for eternal power? Some kind of semi-physical immortality?'

You have to fracture the cool, he remembered telling himself. To damage this guy, you have to tip his balance, dislodge him from his mental lotus position. Even lying there, with unknown injuries, he can, maybe, still take you unawares.

'Or is it,' Powys said casually, 'just the ultimate ego-trip? Getting your end away from beyond the grave?'

He had to look away. The blackness from Andy's eyes came out like iron spikes.

Iron spikes. Images of Rose cruelly speared his own cool, and he stared back into the eyes of the thing that had so dispassionately manipulated their fate.

'I can't move,' Andy said suddenly, the first sign of human panic. 'I can't fucking move, Joe. I can't move my arms or my legs. I'm fucking paralysed.'

'What I think . . .' Powys remembered conversations with Barry the osteopath, his neighbour in the Trackways building. '. . . is your back was broken in the fall. You can obviously move your neck. What about your shoulders? Try shrugging your shoulders.'

Andy's shoulders convulsed. There was a sudden sheen of sweat on his body.

'How's your breathing?'

'I can breathe.'

'In that case,' Powys said slowly and callously, 'you'll probably be what's known as a tetraplegic. It won't be much fun, but no doubt a lot of innocent people'll be saved a lot of grief by your confinement in Stoke Mandeville or wherever you wind up.'

'You're a worthless piece of shit, Joe.'

'Me? *I'm* shit?'

'You couldn't even kill me.'

'You're safer like this. Dead, you could be a problem.'

Andy turned his head and looked into the eye-sockets of Black Michael. As an exercise in mummification, Powys thought, Michael had turned out to be rather less impressive than Tiddles.

He said, 'Where are the other bits buried?'

'Why should I tell you that?'

'The head, naturally, was in the Tump. Did you ever go into the Tump? Physically, I mean.'

'No.'

'And the genitals are under the Cock. Walled up somewhere in the cellars. I'd guess, somewhere directly beneath that passageway leading to the studio. The heart under the church – is there a crypt?'

Andy didn't reply.

'And who would have buried your bits, Andy, after the hanging? Humble?'

'Where is Humble?' Occurring to Andy, perhaps, that there might be more wrong than he knew.

Powys said, 'What's happening down in the town? What's on fire?'

'Not my problem,' Andy said.

'You're beyond me.' He was getting impatient. And nervous. He was face to face with the man who'd smashed his life and all he wanted to do was get out of here. Call an ambulance, anonymously. Man with a broken back. Tried to hang himself. Take him away.

Yet there were things he had to know.

'Look . . . I mean . . . For Christ's sake, *why*? Is your mother behind this?'

'What?'

'Jean Wendle.'

Andy laughed. It wasn't a very strong laugh, suggesting his breathing was not, after all, unaffected. 'There's no blood link between Jean and me. She's my spiritual mother, if you like. It's a concept you wouldn't understand.'

'Which of you is the descendant, then?'

'Listen . . . Jean had been studying Wort for years, right? There's almost . . . this kind of Michael Wort Society. Very exclusive, Joe. Not for the New Age morons. Not for the wankers. Not for the . . . authors of popular trash books. Not for the . . . the fucking *popularizers*. For the Few. And now . . .'

Andy began to cough.

'I can't feel that,' he said. 'I can't feel it in my guts, you know?'

'And now . . . what?'

'The New Age.' He gave a short, wheeze of a laugh. 'Suddenly this . . . worldwide movement dedicated to throwing esoteric knowledge at the masses. Max Goff – millions of pounds to . . .'

'So you hijacked Goff.'

'Well put. Yeah, I hijacked Goff. He loved me. In all kinds of ways.'

'To provide the money and the psychic energy you needed to condition Crybbe for the Second Coming of Black Michael.'

Andy grimaced. 'Let's get this right, there was no Second Coming. We were just completing Michael's plan. I've had access to all his papers since I was sixteen, and to the people who could explain what it all meant. And then it got to the stage where I knew more than any of them. We were completing the plan. Patching up the damage John Dee did. Also, removing the Preece problem and altering the psychic climate.'

'Stirring things up. Emotional conflict. Anger, bitterness, confusion.'

'We awoke the place,' Andy said, 'from centuries of sleep. An unhealthy, drugged sort of sleep. Psychic Mogadon, self-administered. I've been planting little time bombs, like . . . OK, I took a job for a few months, teaching art at the local high school. I wanted a girl. I wanted to take a girl living in Crybbe and *turn* her. There was a perfect one – I mean, this happens, Joe, there's always somebody there who fits, and she was entirely perfect. I worked with this kid over a year. I taught her to paint, I mean *really* paint . . .'

'In your studio. In the wood.'

'Sure. I taught her the arts. The real arts. You give them a little at that age, they become quite insatiable. She was a natural. She can make paintings that become doorways . . . But that's something else. Also, I used her . . . to penetrate the Preece clan. And in the heart of the Crybbe household, I – well, Michael and I – we created *the most wonderful* little monster, a creature entirely without heart, dedicated to destruction. In the heart of the Preece household. Again, ripe for it. Warren Preece. Maybe you'll meet him. Everybody ought to meet Warren.'

'You're a scumbag, Andy,' Powys said.

'So kill me,' Andy said quietly.

There was silence in the little well-like cell, its ceiling jaggedly open to the attic.

'You still got that bread knife? Kill me. Cut my throat. It's easy. Even Warren managed to cut Max Goff's throat tonight, with a Stanley knife.'

'*What?*'

'You didn't know about Max? He was killed in the public meeting during a power cut. It was quite beautiful. And perhaps the most beautiful thing of all is that when this is all over, who's going to get the blame for this orgy of destruction? The New Age movement. You've got to laugh. Warren says that. Got to laugh.'

Powys said coldly, 'You're insane. Your brains have turned to shit. I'll get you an ambulance.'

'No, you'll kill me, Joe.'

'Like I said, I wouldn't trust you dead.'

'You'll kill me. Look, you're squeamish about knives, use the rope. Strangle me. No hassle. I'm weak, I'll go easy. It'll just look like I hanged myself and the rope broke.'

He'd almost forgotten the noose still hanging loosely around Andy's neck. Hesitantly, he walked across, began to remove the rope, trying not to touch Andy's skin. 'Just in case you're lying about not being able to move your arms. Hate you to try and do it yourself.'

Andy grinned, white teeth exploding through the beard.

'Do it!'

'No.'

'OK, something you didn't know. Rose, right? Poor spiked little Rosie. And the baby was spiked too, yeah? Your baby, Joe?'

Powys shook his head. 'I've got past that. I don't want to kill you for that. I'm happy you're going to be a paraplegic or a tetraplegic. I hope your breathing degenerates, you'll be even safer in an iron lung.'

'It wasn't your baby, Joe.'

His hands froze on the rope.

'I'd been fucking Rose quite intensively for several months. I've always found I can get any woman, any man . . . I want. Part of the Wort legacy, if you will. Also, it was my understanding that, come bedtime, the great visionary writer's creative imagination would tend to go into abeyance, and so . . .'

Powys wrenched down the noose, jerked Andy's head back, slammed the knot tight into the back of the neck. Andy grinned up at him; even the whites of his eyes were almost black.

Abruptly, Joe Powys let the rope go slack and pulled the noose over Andy's head.

'I'll get you an ambulance,' he said.

CHAPTER III

GOMER couldn't get near the church, least not within thirty yards. Not much he could have done, though, anyway. Be a long time before that ole place saw another service. If ever. Roof mostly gone, windows long gone. Still some flames – plenty wood in the nave, pews and stuff, to keep them well-nourished for some hours yet – but the worst was over. The stone walls would stay up, and so would the tower, even it wasn't much more than a thick chimney by now.

'Bugger-all use fetchin' the fire brigade,' Gomer concluded. 'Burned 'imself out, see.' He turned to his companion; no way of hedging round any of this. 'Pardon me askin' this, but your Jonathon – was 'e gonner be cremated anyway, like? 'Cause, if 'e 'ad to . . .'

'Gonner be buried. And he still will be, whatever's left.'

They'd come upon Jimmy Preece sitting on the low part of the churchyard wall watching the fire. The digger had crunched out of the wood and there the old feller was, hunched up, knotted and frazzled like a rotting tree stump, sounding like it was gonner take Dyno-Rod to clear his lungs. And it was clear straight off to Gomer that nothing happening tonight would have been a mystery to Jimmy Preece.

'Who done this, Jim?' he asked bluntly. 'And don't give me no bull.'

Arnold the dog limped over to Jimmy Preece and stood there, watchful. Jimmy Preece leaned down, hesitated for several seconds and then patted him. Arnold wagged his tail, only twice and just as hesitant, and then plodded off. Gomer had the feeling this was a very strange thing, momentous-like and patting a dog was only part of what it was about.

'I'm glad,' the Mayor said, to nobody in particularly. 'Wish I was dead, but I'm glad. Couldn't go on, see.'

'What couldn't?'

'You're not a Crybbe man, Gomer, is the problem.'

'Well, hell, Jim, I'm only a few miles up the valley, born an' bred.'

'Not a Crybbe man,' Jimmy Preece said firmly. Gomer was near fuming.

'Who done it, Jim? Too late for all that ole crap. Just bloody spit it out.'

Something gave. Jim's grimy face wobbled and what had looked like a smear of thick oil down one side of it gleamed in the firelight and didn't look like oil any more. When he opened his mouth the words oozed out in a steady stream.

'Same one as run your bulldozer in the wall, same one as slashed my face, same one as left me to suffocate, same one as . . . as done for Jonathon.'

The Mayor looked away. 'Pretended I was dead, see – didn't take a lot o' pretendin'. Wanted to close the ole door to the tower, keep the fire out, last duty, see. Then I was gonner lie down. Next to Jonathon.'

Gomer saw Minnie Seagrove trying to climb out of the digger and held up a hand to tell her to stay where she was.

'Couldn't do it,' Jimmy Preece said, studying his boots now. 'Not got the guts. Fire too hot. Ole body sayin', get me out o' yere. Ole body allus wins.'

'Where is 'e, Jim?' Gomer had no doubts who they were talking about any more. 'Where is 'e? Dead?'

'That's all I got left to hope for,' said Jimmy Preece. 'But I reckon we've long ago given up all rights to hope. In Crybbe.'

'Jim . . .' Gomer feeling sorry for him now, town falling apart, family collapsing round his ears. 'I'd like to 'elp.'

The Mayor stared for a long time into the ruined church before he replied.

'You really wanner do some'ing, Gomer?'

'What I said.'

'Then get rid of all these bloody stones for me. Do it before morning, while every bugger's otherwise engaged, like. Whip 'em out. Make it like so's they was never yere, know what I'm askin'?'

'Tall order,' said Gomer. 'Still . . . Only I don't know where they all are. Seen a couple around, like.'

'I'll tell you where they are. Every one of 'em.'

'Might mean goin' on people's property, though, isn't it? Trespassin'.'

'Depends on what you thinks of as other people's property, isn't it?'

'Course, if it was an official council contract, like . . .'

'Consider it an official council contract,' said Jimmy Preece, wearily.

They carried Alex into The Gallery, Joe Powys and the capable-looking guy who'd introduced himself as Col Croston.

He was quite a weight.

'Obviously too much for his heart,' Col said. 'And it was a hell of a big heart. How old was he?'

'Old,' Fay said distantly. 'Pushing ninety.' She sniffed. 'Pushed too hard.'

Alex had still been lying on the cobbles when Powys had stumbled uncertainly into the square, seemingly bringing the lights with him – the power was back. He'd walked past Wynford Wiley and Wiley had hardly glanced at him. Guy Morrison had nodded and said nothing. He'd gone directly to where Fay sat, close to the steps of the Cock, guarding her father's body like a mute terrier. 'I thought you were going to be dead, too,' was all she'd said, and then had laughed – unnaturally, he thought, and he wasn't entirely surprised.

They put Alex on the only flat, raised surface in The Gallery, the display window, under mini-spotlights. He looked peaceful, laid out with pictures. 'He'd hate that,' Fay mumbled. 'Looking peaceful.'

'Don't suppose,' Col Croston said, 'that there's much I can say, is there? The awful thing is, nobody will ever know what he achieved in the last few minutes of his life. Even I can't begin to explain it, and I was there. And I know . . .' He broke off, looking uncharacteristically lost. 'I don't know *what* I know, really. I'm sorry.'

'He won't mind,' Fay said. 'It was quick, and he never became a vegetable, did he? That was all he was scared of. The geriatric ward. He might have done something silly. Like half a bottle of malt whisky and some pills, or a last train to Soho or somewhere, with a view to departing in the arms of some . . . ageing harlot.'

She's rambling, Powys thought. She's blocking it out. Her body's producing natural Valium. Everybody has a breaking point.

From behind them, a small, raw cry.

After letting them in, the woman who ran The Gallery, Mrs Newsome, had remained silently in the doorway, leaving Powys wondering about the weals and bruising on her throat.

Now she was pointing at a door to the left of the glass counter. It was a white door, but there were marks and smears all over it now, in red.

Col saw the blood, flung out an arm to hold everyone back, snapped, 'What's behind there?'

'He . . .' It wasn't easy for her to talk and her voice, when it emerged, was like a crow's. 'Hereward's workroom.'

'Anybody in there,' Col called out harshly, 'will get back against the wall and keep very still. Understood?'

The marks on the door included smeared fingerprints and one whole palmprint.

'Mrs Newsome, have you any idea . . . ?'

The act of shaking her head looked as painful as talking.

Col shrugged and nodded. 'Everybody keep back then,' he said and hit the door with a hard, flat foot, directly under the handle. Powys wondered why he didn't simply open it. Shock value, he supposed, as the door splintered open and Col jumped back and went into a crouch.

'Oh, Christ.' Powys stared into the shadowed face of the man he'd left fifteen minutes earlier lying crippled in the centre of a little stone chamber.

Remembered thinking as he'd run out of the Court that Andy might not be so badly injured as he appeared. That someone practised in yoga and similar disciplines might be able to contort his body sufficiently to simulate a broken spine.

But Powys hadn't gone back. He'd kept on running all the way to the car and then driven to the phone box on the edge of town. Which worked, thank God. 'Ambulance, yes. And . . . police, I suppose. And the fire brigade. In fact, send the lot. Jesus. In force.'

'God in heaven,' Col Croston was saying. 'Don't come in, Mrs Newsome.'

The face, Powys saw with short-lived relief, was only in a very large painting – Andy dressed in the kind of sombre clothing Michael Wort might have worn, standing by a door meaningfully ajar. Powys remembered Andy talking about a girl, the artist, who could 'create doorways'. With that in mind, he didn't look at it again. But what was beneath it was worse.

The unframed canvas was hanging on the wall above a wooden workbench with sections of frames strewn across it and, fastened to the side, a large wood-vice with a metal handle and wooden jaws.

The vice would hold a piece of soft timber firmly, without damaging it, unless you really leaned on the handle, in which case it would probably squash anything softer than iron.

Powys nearly choked. He didn't go in. Blood was still dripping to the sawdusted floor and there were deltas down the walls made by high-pressure crimson jets.

The dead man was on his knees, the jaws of the vice clamped like the hands of a faith-healer either side of this giant red pepper, his head, once.

Powys's stomach lurched like a car doing an emergency stop.

Col Croston emerged expressionless, pulling the door closed behind him. 'Mrs Newsome . . . Let's get some air, shall we?'

Her face began to warp. Col Croston took her arm and steered her into the square. Powys quickly closed the door behind them and stood with his back to it; he didn't want to hear this.

'What's in there?' Fay said from far away.

'A body.'

'Is it Hereward? Hereward Newsome?'

'Hard to say, he's been . . . damaged. And I don't know

him. And if I did, it wouldn't help. Look, Fay, can we . . . ?'

'Warren Preece,' Fay said, as if this explained everything. 'I expect Warren Preece did it.'

She took a last disbelieving look at her dad and watched Powys flick off the lights. She didn't move. He took her hand and towed her into the street. She went with him easily, like one of those toy dogs on wheels. From down the hill, across the river, blue emergency beacons were strobing towards the town with a warble of sirens.

Powys pulled Fay into a side-street. 'It'd be a bit daft to leave town, but I'd rather not be the first in line to make a police statement, would you?'

'Where shall we go?'

'My cottage?' They were in a street of narrow terraces and no lights. 'Or your house?'

'I suppose it is my house now,' Fay said, still sounding completely disconnected. 'Unless Dad's left it to some mysterious totty. I mean . . . I don't want it. I'll take the cats, but I'm not having Grace. Can you give a house to charity?'

He took hold of her upper arms, gently. 'Fay, please.'

She looked at him in mild enquiry, her green eyes calm as rock pools at low tide.

'I need you,' Powys said, and he hadn't meant to say that.

Fay said, 'Do you?' from several miles away.

He nodded. They seemed to have been through years of experience together in about two days.

He'd tried to explain briefly what had happened. About the Tump, the head in the box. About Andy. Not about Jean Wendle; it wasn't the time.

What he wanted to tell her now was that something had been resolved. He wanted to say reassuring things about her dad.

But as he reached out for her he felt his body breaking up into awful, seismic shivers. It's not over – the words squeezed into his brain like the fragmented skull of the man in the vice – *it's not over*.

CHAPTER IV

JOE had left the candle behind.

Taken the lamp but brought the candle down from the attic and left it on the floor in the open doorway, well out of the reach of Andy Boulton-Trow.

The candlelight would guide the paramedics with their stretcher to the room where Andy lay, feeling no pain, only a frigid fury which he knew he had to contain if he were to preserve the legacy.

Andy fancied he could hear distant sirens; didn't have much time. He picked up the head of Michael Wort and held it above him – oh, yes, he could use his arms, he'd lied about that. But not his legs; he couldn't feel his legs or his lower body, only the bubbling acid of rage which he would have to control and channel.

'Michael,' he hissed, and his lungs felt very small and also oddly detached, as though they were part of some ancillary organism.

The head of Michael Wort had no eyes, its remaining teeth were bare, its skin reduced to pickled brown flakes. But the skull was hard.

Andy looked deep into the dark sockets and summoned the spirit of the man who, four hundred years ago this night, had dared to seize the Infinite.

'*Dewch*,' he whispered, '*Tyrd i lawr*, Michael.' He lay back and – balancing the head on his solar plexus – closed his eyes, slowed his breathing, began to visualize with an intensity he'd never known. '*Tyrd i lawr*.'

The first police car arrived as they approached the bridge. Joe didn't want to cross at first, in case they were stopped. Joe was a worrier. Fay didn't see any problem.

And the car didn't stop.

As the police car warbled away, she remembered something. 'Where's Arnold?'

'Mrs Seagrove's looking after him. He's . . . Well, I'll tell you. Some time.'

Some time? Fay looked at him curiously. Then said to herself, *My father's dead*. Every time she thought of something else, she was going to make herself repeat this, with emphasis. What she wanted was to be suddenly overcome with immeasurable grief, to sob bitterly, throw a wobbly in the street.

No parents at all any more. No barrier. In the firing line now. Stand up, Fay Morrison. Bang.

Bang.

Bang!

Fay stopped. *MY DAD'S DEAD*.

Yes. But that wasn't the whole point. This was Crybbe. In Crybbe, death wasn't necessarily the worst thing that could happen to you. He'd looked peaceful under the gallery spotlights, with the paintings. But *was* he at peace, or was he going to hang around, like Grace, as some kind of psychic detritus? Was this the destiny of the dead of Crybbe, to moulder on, like the town?

'Psychic pollution,' she said suddenly. 'What can you do about psychic pollution?'

She peered over the bridge parapet, down to where the dark water loitered indolently around the stone buttresses.

'Nuclear waste you can just about bury,' she said. 'Hundreds of feet underground in immovable granite. And, maybe, after four hundred years . . .' She straightened up. 'You know, I really underestimated the . . . the *toxicity* of this town.'

Joe was staring at her. *I need you*, he'd said, the words sounding strange. Probably because nobody had actually said that to her before. Not her dad, not Offa's Dyke Radio, not even her old boss at Radio Four. Certainly not Guy. (We could be good for each other, Fay.) No. Nobody.

She looked at Joe in the light of the streetlamp at the end of the bridge. She thought he was a nice guy. She could, in better circumstances, be quite seriously attracted to him.

He still looked sort of wary, though.

'Maybe they were right,' he was saying, 'with their curfew and their Crybbe mentality. Maybe it was the best they could do. Maybe they just hadn't got the knowledge or the resources to handle it.'

'Handle what exactly, Joe?'

'I don't know. I don't suppose we'll ever know. Whatever . . . properties it has. To amplify things. The Old Golden Land. Where psychic doorways are easy to open.'

'And pretty near impossible to close.'

'John Dee knew it,' Joe said. 'Wort knew it. Just goes a lot deeper than either of them probably imagined. When you think about it, the great Michael Wort was probably just another loony. Like Andy. He didn't know what the fuck he was doing either.'

They were approaching the cottage which overlooked the river.

Fay said, without thinking about it, 'Is that the Bottle Stone I can hear?'

'*What?*'

'Thin drone, like the hum from a pylon.'

'I can't hear anything.'

'Probably nothing.'

'Probably,' he said uncertainly. 'Funny, isn't it? We build up this big theory about Black Michael, and because he was four hundred years ago we think he's some kind of god. But he was just another . . . just another pollutant.'

Out of the night came a slow clapping of hands. Ironic, essentially mocking applause.

'Persuasively argued, Joe,' Jean Wendle said.

Joe Powys froze.

Jean Wendle was leaning against the cottage wall. She was wearing a pink velour tracksuit. She looked elegant and relaxed.

Two police cars went rapidly past, followed by a fire-engine.

Joe froze, and Fay sensed it wasn't because of the police cars, not this time.

648

'But quite wrong,' said Jean. 'And you know it.'

He didn't say anything.

'Michael Wort,' said Jean, 'had one of the finest of the Renaissance minds. Scientist, philosopher . . . these terms simply cannot encompass Michael's abilities. We no longer like to use words like magus, but that's what he was, and the reason he isn't as famous as Francis Bacon and Giordano Bruno and even – God forbid – John Dee . . . is that he realized the futility of books and so never wrote any. And also, of course, he lived not in Florence or Rome, or even London. But in Crybbe.'

Fay could see Joe trying to say something, trying to frame words.

'If he never wrote anything,' she said, 'how do you know he was so great?'

'Because,' said Jean, 'like all great teachers, he passed on his knowledge through training and through experience.'

Another police car went past, followed by another fire-engine.

'There's a Michael Wort tradition,' Jean said. 'It began with his own family, and then was passed to selected scholars.'

'What kind of tradition?'

'Fascinating stuff,' Jean said. 'All to do with the spirit landscape, and the interpenetration of planes. Knowledge we are only now beginning to approach.'

'They called him Black Michael,' Fay said.

'As they would. In Crybbe.'

'He hanged people.'

'He studied death, and he utilized his period as high sheriff to pursue that study. That was all.'

How bizarre, Fay thought. All hell breaking loose up in the town and here we are, three uncommitted observers from Off, calmly discussing the background as if it's a piece of theatre.

'Knowledge,' said Jean, 'isn't evil.'

'And what about what happened on the square? What about the killing of Max Goff? What about . . . ?'

'You know, as I do, my dear, that there are some very misguided and unbalanced people in Crybbe, and there always have been. People Michael was trying to help.'

649

'I didn't know,' Fay said, 'that you knew so much about Michael Wort.'

'You didn't ask,' said Jean. Her short grey hair shone like a helmet in the street light.

'Fay . . .' Joe said.

'Joe's trying to tell you to come away,' Jean said. *'He doesn't want to end what he began.'*

'Which is?'

'The Bottle Stone,' Jean said gently. 'Come and see the Bottle Stone.'

'No!' Joe backed away.

'He blames it for everything,' Jean said. 'For all his problems, all his failed relationships. The deaths of his women.'

'Fay.' Joe sounded suddenly alarmed. 'I don't know what she's doing, but don't fall for it. I meant to tell you. Jean and Andy are in this together. She sent me up to the Tump tonight, she set me up for Humble . . .'

'Did he tell you,' said Jean, 'how the Bottle Stone followed him here?'

'Yes,' Fay said, her throat suddenly quite dry. 'He told me that.'

'Come and see the Bottle Stone, Fay. Come on.'

'Fay.'

'Come along,' said Jean.

She rose from the wall and picked her way carefully to the gate of the cottage. 'Come *on!*'

Fay glanced at Joe. 'Don't,' he said quietly. 'Please.'

I meant to tell you.

She turned and followed Jean Wendle.

They went around the side of the cottage and across the damp lawn to the piece of land at the rear. Jean had produced a small torch and they followed its thin beam. Fay could hear the river idly fumbling at its banks.

Jean stopped. She directed the beam a short way across the grass until it found the thick, grey base of a standing stone. Then Jean casually flipped the torch up so that they could see the top of the stone.

'It doesnae look awfully like a bottle, does it?' Jean said.

The stone appeared no more than three and half feet tall. It was fairly wide, but slim, like a blade.

Fay said, 'It doesn't look *anything* like a bottle.'

Andy Boulton-Trow lay on his back, holding the head above him with both hands. The hands didn't ache now.

'Michael,' he said, 'forgive me. It was a shambles. I was using weak, stupid people. I failed you.'

In the doorway, the candle was burning very low. He'd thought he could hear sirens a while back. He couldn't hear anything now.

Joe Powys hadn't rung for an ambulance.

Joe Powys had lied.

CHAPTER V

'ONE more, I make it,' Gomer said, a short trail of recumbent stones in his destructive wake. 'Then that's the lot.'

'You know, Gomer,' Minnie Seagrove said, sitting quite placidly next to him in the cab, the three-legged dog on her lap. 'You've surprised me tonight.'

'Surprised myself,' Gomer said gruffly. 'I'll be very surprised if I collect a penny for all this.'

'No, what I mean is . . . Well, I'd come to the conclusion – and I'm sorry if this sounds insulting – I'd come to the conclusion that there weren't any really decent men in Crybbe. Like, men we used to say would do *anything* for you. Nothing too much trouble, sort of thing . . . if it was the *right* thing.'

'Done a few bloody wrong things tonight, Minnie, my love,' Gomer said, plunging the digger halfway down the riverbank. 'That's for certain.'

'No they weren't. They weren't wrong things at all. You've saved me from being arrested for murder, you're working overtime at a minute's notice to help that poor old chap who looks like he's on his last legs. And you've been no end of help to young Joe . . .'

Gomer ploughed through an unstable-looking fence and up into the field that served as a narrow flood-plain for the river.

'I got no regrets about gettin' you out of a bit o' bother,' he said. 'An' I'd stand up in court an' say so. But that Joe – well, I'd like to think that young feller'll keep 'is mouth shut, see, that's all. You know much about 'im?'

'Not a lot,' said Minnie. 'But I'm sure he's all right.'

'It's rather sad, really,' Jean said. 'They're all bottle stones to Joe.'

Fay started to feel faint. To pull herself together, she said – screamed it out inside her head, like biting on something hard, to fight extreme pain,

MY FATHER IS DEAD.

And wondered if Jean knew about that yet. Jean who'd given him a new lease of life. Which he'd expended in what appeared at this moment to be a distressingly futile way.

Fay felt sick.

'I don't know precisely what happened,' Jean was saying. 'Over this girl of Joe's, Rose, I mean. Whether it was an accident, or suicide, or . . .'

'Or what?'

Jean put a hand on Fay's arm. 'Look, my dear, it's over. It's all in the past. Whatever happened, there's nothing we can change now. Nobody we can bring back to life.'

'No,' Fay said numbly.

Something white in places caught her eye, over to the right of the Bottle Stone. Joe Powys's muddy T-shirt. He was standing on the other side of the perimeter wall, watching them silently, like an abandoned scarecrow.

'About Andy,' Jean said. 'Andy's not a bad boy. A little wild, perhaps, in his younger days, a little headstrong. His lineage is not a direct one to Michael, but he developed a very strong interest in the Tradition from his early teens. And, give him his due, he didn't deviate in his resolve to discover things for himself.'

'And the Bottle Stone ritual?'

'Exists not at all,' said Jean sadly, 'outside the head of J. M. Powys.'

'He showed me the field,' Fay said. 'Where it happened.'

'And was there a Bottle Stone there? And a fairy mound? With a fairy on it?'

'What about Henry Kettle? He was there too. There was nothing wrong with Henry Kettle.'

'Oh? Henry told you, did he? He said he was there?'

A police car howled a long way away.

'No,' Fay said bleakly.

'Oh, my dear . . .'

Fay was bent over, gripping her thighs with both hands. She felt a stabbing stomach-cramp coming on.

'Oh God,' she breathed. 'Oh God.'

And as Andy's breathing, shallow as it was, began to regulate, he looked into the dark sockets and saw within them pinpricks of distant light.

He watched the lights as they came closer – or, rather, as he moved closer to *them*, his consciousness was focused and drawn into the sockets, now as wide as caverns.

He felt the familiar tug at the base of his spine, and never before had it felt so good, so strong, so positive, so indicative of freedom. For, while imprisoned within his twisted body, Andy could no longer feel anything at all at the base of his spine.

When it happened – and he'd been far from certain that it would under such conditions – there was an enormous burst of raw energy (O Michael! O Mother!) and he was out of his body and soaring towards the lights.

'It's a shame about Crybbe,' Jean said. 'But it's no different in any of these places. You ask the ordinary man in the street in Glastonbury how he feels about the Holy Grail. How many miracles he's seen. They're not the least bit interested and indeed often quite antagonistic.'

Looking beyond the stone, Fay could not longer see Joe. Perhaps he'd crept away.

'So you can imagine how they reacted in Crybbe,' Jean went on. 'A place so remote and yet so conducive to psychic activity. Can one blame the peasantry? I don't know. The knowledge has always been for the Few. Not everyone has the spiritual metabolism to absorb it. Not everyone has the will to see through the dark barriers to the light.'

All at once, as if to illustrate Jean's point, the stone which bore no resemblance at all to a bottle was lit up from its grassy base to its sharp, fanglike tip.

'Goodness,' Jean said. 'Whatever's that?'

Beyond the stone, there was a kind of parapet overlooking the river and to one side, dropping down to the flood-plain, a narrow, muddy track, its entire width now taken up by a crawling, grunting monster with it single bright eye focused on the stone.

Fay saw a wiry figure leap from the creature and advance upon the stone. Jean flashed her torch at it and the light was reflected in a pair of old-fashioned wire-rimmed National Health glasses.

'Evening, ladies. Gomer Parry Plant Hire. I realize it's a bit late, like, but I got official instructions to remove that stone, see.'

Jean stiffened. 'I *do* beg your pardon.'

'Official council operation.'

'Now why is it,' Jean asked smoothly, 'that I rather doubt that?'

'Madam, I got special authorization yere from the Town Mayor 'isself.'

'Oh, Gomer,' Fay blurted out. 'The Mayor's dead.'

'Miss Morris?'

'Isn't it sad?' said Jean. 'Isn't it primitive? There was once a notorious farmer, you know, in Wiltshire, known as Stone-breaker Robinson, who devoted his energies to eradicating megalithic remains from the face of the countryside. It's been popularly thought that such Philistine ignorance was dead.'

She turned to Gomer Parry. 'Do yourself a big favour, little man. Go home to bed.'

'Do *me* a favour.' Joe Powys scrambled down from the perimeter wall. 'Flatten the bloody thing.' He stood next to Gomer.

Jean switched off her torch. Now both Gomer and Powys existed only as wavy silhouettes in the headlight's blast.

But the stone was fully illuminated.

'What are you afraid of, Joe? Afraid of what you'll do to Fay?'

He didn't say anything. He seemed to be shaking his head.

'I shouldn't worry, my dear,' Jean said to Fay. 'You can stay at my house tonight.'

'Flatten it,' Powys said.

'Lay one finger on that stone, little man,' said Jean, 'and, I promise you, you'll regret it for what passes for the rest of your life.'

'It's not an old stone, Gomer,' Powys said. 'If it was a genuine prehistoric monument, *I* wouldn't let you touch it.'

There was a flurrying then in the track of the headlight. It was so fast that Fay thought at first it was an owl until it veered out of the light. At which point it ought to have disappeared, but it didn't. It carried its own luminescence, something of the will-o'-the-wisp.

'Oh my G . . .' Fay gasped as, with a small, delighted whimper, it landed on her feet.

'Arnold!'

The dog jumped up at her; she felt his tongue on her legs.

'Oh God, Arnold.' She pushed her hands deep into his fur. Felt him stiffen.

The air above the standing stone seemed to contract, and to draw into it the headlight beam. The headlamp itself grew dim, fading to a bleary yellow.

The yellow of . . .

Fay felt Arnold's hackles rise under her hands. He growled from so far back in his throat that it seemed to come not from him at all but from somewhere behind him.

'Bloody battery!' Gomer Parry ran for his cab.

. . . of disease

embalming fluid

Grace Legge.

The stone glowed feebly at its base, rising in intensity until its tip was lit with a magnesium radiance, and Fay felt an intense cold emanating from it, a cold that you could almost see, like steam from a deep-freeze.

The yellow, and the cold. And the aura of steam around the stone formed into an unmistakable shape of a beer-bottle.

But it was the one word that did it.

'Yesssss.' Drawn from Jean Wendle's throat like a pale ribbon of gauze.

And Fay flew at her.

She smashed her open palm so hard into Jean's face that Jean, caught unawares, was thrown back, off her feet, and Fay heard a small crack and felt wetness in her hand and pain too, as if it had been broken. Heard Joe Powys crying, '*Gomer . . . Go for it . . . Now . . .* ' Saw the lights in the stone shiver and shrink and the digger's lone headlight brighten and the metal beast heaving about, its shovel raised high like a wrecking hammer.

For several icy-white, agonizing seconds, Andy Boulton-Trow once again experienced his whole body . . . a savage, searing sensation, a long, physical scream.

The experience came as the lights exploded and he was tossed contemptuously back into his body like a roll of old carpet.

He was still staring, from a place beyond the boundaries of despair, into the sockets in the head of Michael Wort. The sockets were just as black but no longer empty. The eyes of Michael Wort swirled like oil. The smile made by the exposed, chipped, brown teeth was malign.

The head felt heavy.

Gomer was not proud of what happened. There was no control, no precision . . . no *finesse*.

With a wild, hydraulic wrench, the cast-iron shovel came

down several feet too quickly and simply smashed in the top of the stone.

He leaned out of his cab and heard the uppity Scotch woman shrieking.

There was a sudden, unnatural strength in Andy's arms.

He raised the head. He brought it down.

The skull smashed into his own.

Michael.

He felt his nose shatter in a cloud of blood.

Michael.

He felt his teeth splinter into fragments.

He raised the head again, his fingers splayed around shrivelled skin and wisps of hair.

Michael

     Michael

       Michael . . .

The blows continued, with a vengeful intensity, long after Andy was dead.

From the doorway, Warren Preece looked on, fascinated by the head clutched in the two hands, the arms moving ferociously up and down until the other head on the floor was red pulp.

The ole candle was near burnt to nothing when Warren picked it up.

But then, so was Warren. Stripped to the waist, and his chest was black, like charcoal. He could smell his own scorched skin. He figured his lips had been burnt away, too, so that his teeth were stuck in this permanent grin, like the head that was now rolling across the dusty, boarded floor towards him.

'Got to laugh.'

He didn't have to tell the head. The ole head was laughing already at what it'd done.

Warren picked it up and stuck it under his arm, like one of them ghosts.

Two heads are better than one.

Got to laugh.

With his other hand he picked up the candle, just melted wax now, but he picked it up, squeezed it tight, so the boiling hot wax bubbled up between his fingers, feeling painful as hell. Feeling good.

He held up his hand, and there was wax dripping down the clenched fist, so it was like the hand had become the candle, the wick sticking up through his knuckles with a little white flame on the end.

Hand of Glory.

He went over to the Teacher, brought his hand down to get some light on the face. The face looked good, all smashed, one eye hanging out. Wished he could take this head too, bung it under his other arm, but cutting off a head with a Stanley knife would take too long. Thought about it with the other feller, before deciding on the vice.

Never mind.

Warren walked out of the room, by the light of his own hand. He felt really full of power now, like he'd just done a one-man gig in front of thousands of his fans.

With the head under his arm, he walked down the ole steps in a sprightly kind of way. Felt like he owned the place. Probably did. Least, he owned the farm now, with every bugger else dead or crippled, like.

Strolled through the ole baronial hall-type place straight to the front door, his hand held out before him. He could smell the skin smouldering now. Pretty soon it'd all start frizzling off and there'd be nothing left but wax and bones.

The real thing. The authentic Hand of Glory.

The front door of Crybbe Court was open wide, and Warren Preece walked out into the spotlights.

Just like he'd always known it'd be, one day.

The courtyard was lined with people, silent, awestruck like. Warren recognized a few of them, local farmers and shop-keepers and such. But also there were two ambulances and . . . FIVE cop cars. All the headlights trained on the door he'd just come out of.

'All right?' Warren yelled.

Didn't seem much point to the candle, with all these spot-lights, so he squashed it out between his legs. Then he held up the head with both hands, way up over his own head, like the FA cup.

'Yeah!' Warren screeched.

About half a dozen coppers were coming towards him in a semi-circle. Warren stuck the head under his arm and fished out his Stanley knife.

'Come on, son,' one of the coppers said. 'Let's not do this the hard way.'

Warren flicked out the blade and grinned.

''Ow're you, Wynford,' he said.

CHAPTER VI

'I ALWAYS imagined,' said Fay, 'leaving Crybbe for the last time and driving off into the sunset.'

There was a peach-coloured glow in the eastern sky, over the English side of Offa's Dyke.

'But it must be better,' she said, 'driving into the dawn.'

Powys drove. They were in his Mini.

All of them. Arnold half-asleep on her knee. Two resentful black cats with Russian names in a laundry basket on the back seat.

Fay would probably have brought her dad as well, if the body would've fitted in the boot. But she'd get him out. He wasn't going to be buried in Crybbe.

Once they'd crossed the town boundary, past the signpost at the top of the hill, Joe stopped the car. He took her hand – the other one, not the one that was nearly broken rupturing Jean Wendle's nose – and led her out to the famous viewpoint, near the stile.

Below them, Crybbe was a sombre, smoky little town which had sometimes been in Wales and sometimes in England but had never belonged to either.

The real owners of Crybbe were hidden in its own shadows

and weren't apparent at dawn, for Crybbe's time, as Fay had long ago realized, was dusk.

She could see smoke still rising from the ruins of the church. The nave had collapsed, but the bell-tower remained, Col Croston had told her a few minutes ago. And one bell still hung – the seventh bell.

'Which I intend to ring myself,' Col said. 'Every night, in the ruins. These picturesque old traditions,' he said with a tight smile, 'shouldn't be allowed to lapse.'

When the stone was down they hadn't even looked for Jean Wendle. What could they do about her anyway? She'd committed no crimes.

Nobody had seen her since.

'I didn't believe her, of course,' Fay said now.

'You bloody did,' said Joe.

'She had me going for a while,' Fay said. 'However – as I *did* try to tell you at one point yesterday – I checked out the Bottle Stone. It *was* in that field in Radnor Forest and it *was* shaped like a bottle and he *did* take it away.'

Powys reeled.

'I'm a reporter,' Fay said. 'I came back that way from the library and went to the nearest farm. Took a while – you know what farmers are – but I got it out of them. That land – about eighteen acres – still belongs to the Trows. It was funny, the farmer actually called them Worts, sort of contemptuously. He rents the grazing, but they wouldn't sell the land.'

'Andy?'

'Andy showed up there – about ten years ago, the guy said, but it was probably twelve – with a stone on the back of a lorry, and he had the stone planted in the middle of the field, which annoyed the farmer, but he couldn't do anything about it. Andy promised to come back and take it away, and he did – last week.'

'Why didn't you . . . ?'

'You kept saying you didn't want to talk about the Bottle Stone, and anyway . . .'

'And there was I, thinking you had faith in me.'

'Oh, I did, Joe. That's the point – I didn't need to have the Bottle Stone bit confirmed. It was . . . a formality.'

Powys said, 'Your eye looks better.'

'Let's not start lying to each other at this stage,' Fay said.

'Of course . . .' Chief Inspector Hughes, hands in pockets, was pacing the square. 'There are still things we *don't* understand.'

'Really?' Col Croston was trying to sound surprised. A slow, dawn drizzle glazed the square. There was the acrid, dispiriting smell of fire and water.

'Oh, I've got *most* of it,' Hughes said quickly. 'And I think I grasp the social pressures which caused it.'

Col had forgotten that Hughes was one of the 'new' policemen with a degree in something appropriate.

'You look at the background,' Hughes said. 'The kid's stifled by it. Rural decline, brought up in this crumbling farm. And let's face it, this town's a good half-century behind everywhere else.'

'At least,' said Col.

'So young Preece listens to rock music and he dreams . . . without much hope. And then along comes Salvation with a capital S, in the shape of our late friend Mr Goff. He sends Goff a tape of his band, and Goff, no doubt conscious of the politics of the situation, responds favourably.'

'How do you know this?'

'Letter from Epidemic in Warren's pocket. Charred, but readable. We can only assume he made another approach to Goff and Goff told him to clear off. I'm telling you all this, Colonel, in the hope you can throw a bit of light . . .'

'All new to me, Chief Inspector.'

'So we're assuming this is what pushed Warren over the edge. Given all the other pressures – losing his only brother and then his father's tractor accident. The boy seems to be of limited intellect – must have thought the whole world was against him.'

'Psychiatrists will have a field day,' said Col. 'Where is he now?'

'Hospital. I'd like to think he was going to be fit to plead one day, but I wouldn't put money on it. He took most of

Wiley's nose off with that Stanley knife before we disarmed him.'

'Lovable little chap. I'm furious with myself. I was just yards away when he killed Goff.'

'Who would have expected it?'

'I was *trained* to expect the unexpected, for God's sake. Do you know how many he's killed? I make it four – Goff, the vicar, poor old Hereward Newsome . . . and of course that chap Trow.'

'Tie things up nicely if he put his hand up to the Rachel Wade business, too – her signature was on the letter suggesting Warren's music wasn't half bad. But what I was going to ask you, Colonel . . . the Trow killing's somewhat different in style. I can't go into details, but Warren seems to have finished him off by bludgeoning him with this other skull. We thought we had another murder when he came out of the old house with that thing, but it's obviously of some age. So where did it come from? Have any graves been disturbed locally?'

Col thought this over. 'Well, he was obviously in the church, and there are a couple of tombs in there. Might be worth sifting through the ruins.'

'Oh, we'll do that, all right. Obviously, it's not a major issue, but it's something we have to clear up.'

'Well, I have to congratulate you, Chief Inspector. You seem to be putting it all together very nicely.'

Hughes nodded. 'Open and shut, really,' he said.

Fay said, 'I could be making a fortune at this very moment. There'll be a hundred reporters here before breakfast, like a flock of pigeons scrabbling for crumbs. Even poor bloody Ashpole seems to have missed it all.'

'And what are they all going to say?'

'Hard to say precisely *how* they'll work it, but I can guarantee that, by tonight, Warren Preece will be very famous.'

'And Michael Wort?'

'Who's Michael Wort?' said Fay.

More to the point, Joe Powys thought, *where* is Michael

Wort? Back – hopefully – in his own carefully constructed limbo. He was still unsure what had happened over the Bottle Stone – whether it had been installed at the riverside cottage and then replaced with another stone, or whether the power of suggestion had made him *see* the Bottle Stone in the tense, burgeoning atmosphere before Rachel's death. In that case, where was the original Bottle Stone now?

Powys looked over his shoulder, half-expecting to see the thing sprouting from the earth behind him.

Fay said, 'I have to say it didn't occur to me for quite a while that what she . . . what Jean was doing at the stone was trying to generate – in *me* – enough negative energy for him – Andy, Wort, whatever – to make some kind of final leap. To save himself . . . itself.'

'It occurred to me,' Powys said.

'Well, it would, wouldn't it. You're a clever person. And you know what we thinks about clever people yereabouts.'

Arnold limped towards them and fell over. He stood again and shook himself, exasperated.

Fay Morrison and Joe Powys looked at each other. Eyebrows were raised.

Neither of them had said a word about Arnold's remarkable turns of speed at critical moments. One day, Fay thought, she'd dare to mention that strange, glowing, phantom *fourth leg*. But not yet.

'He's a dowser's dog,' Joe said laconically.

As she bent down to pick up the dog, a disturbing thought struck her. 'What about the girl . . . Tessa?'

'She should really be taken away,' Joe said, 'and put through some kind of psychic readjustment programme. Except they probably don't exist, so she'll go on causing minor havoc, until she grows up and turns into something even nastier. Like Jean.'

'Is there nothing anyone can do?'

'World's full of them,' Powys said. 'Crybbe'll always attract them, and sometimes it'll manufacture its own.'

'We can't just leave it.'

'We bloody can.'

'Yes,' Fay said. 'I suppose we can.'

And she turned her back on the town, albeit with an uncomfortable feeling that one day they might feel they had to come back.

They got into the car. They were going to Titley, to Henry Kettle's cottage, which Joe had said was the best sanctuary he could think of. For a few weeks at least, he said, there'd be a danger of residual nasties from Crybbe clinging to them. Grace-type things.

Fay said, 'Can we handle that?'

'Count on it,' Joe Powys said grimly.

From the back seat, Rasputin the cat mewed in protest at his confinement in the laundry basket.

Fay said, 'When you said you, er, needed me . . . what did you mean exactly?'

'I don't know. It just came out. Heat of the moment.'

He turned on the engine.

'However . . .' Joe said, looking straight ahead through the windscreen. 'I know what I'd mean if I were to say it now.'

Fay smiled. 'What did the police say to you?'

'They said, "Don't leave town." '

Joe Powys grinned and floored the accelerator.